THEATRE
AND
STAGE

Frontispiece *Angus McBean*

SIR BARRY JACKSON

Director of the Shakespeare Memorial Theatre, Stratford-upon-Avon, and Governing Director of the Birmingham Repertory Theatre.

THEATRE AND STAGE

AN ENCYCLOPÆDIC GUIDE TO THE PERFORMANCE OF ALL AMATEUR DRAMATIC, OPERATIC, AND THEATRICAL WORK

Edited by

HAROLD DOWNS

Assisted by well-known Authorities and Celebrities in the Theatrical World

Foreword by

SIR BARRY JACKSON

IN TWO VOLUMES:
VOLUME I

GREENWOOD PRESS, PUBLISHERS
WESTPORT, CONNECTICUT

Library of Congress Cataloging in Publication Data

Downs, Harold, 1890- ed.
Theatre and stage.

Reprint of the ed. published by New Era Pub. Co., London.
1. Theater--Dictionaries. 2. Amateur theatricals.
I. Title.
[PN2035.D6 1978] 792'.03 77-28803
ISBN 0-313-20222-2

ISBN 0-313-20222-2 SET
ISBN 0-313-20223-0 VOL. 1
ISBN 0-313-20224-9 VOL. 2

Published by permission of Pitman Publishing Limited,
39 Parker Street, London WC2B 5PB

Reprinted in 1978 by Greenwood Press, Inc.,
51 Riverside Avenue, Westport, CT. 06880

Printed in the United States of America

10 9 8 7 6 5 4 3 2 1

FOREWORD

By Sir Barry Jackson

MOST people are born into the world with a definite urge to express themselves in some particular direction, such as that of art, science, literature, sport, politics—and so on. We need not fall back upon the comfortable doctrine of predestination in considering how far each person succeeds ultimately in following his or her own special bent; the Parable of the Talents is more fitting to the case. For environment, both physical and mental, comes quickly into play, and it is usually by sheer determination rather than by unguided chance that natural aims and abilities survive the thwarting of unfriendly circumstance.

Certain powers are latent in all of us—at first—to a remarkable degree, though for lack of cultivation they quickly atrophy. Children, for example, often show an astonishing aptitude for drawing; and if the draughtsmanship of these young artists were in any way comparable with their imagination, surprising results would frequently ensue. But from want of encouragement and training such early efforts in most cases run to waste, so that both vision and technique soon die together. I well remember the description once given me, by a country vicar, of the drawings made by a lad in his village school; yet that boy afterwards became a farm labourer, and in all probability never touched pencil and paper again. He was, unfortunately, no Giotto, with a Cimabue to find him sketching in the fields and bear him off to Florence.

Perhaps the strongest and most nearly universal of all early human tendencies is that which leads the mind to express itself in terms of drama. Classically defined as "Representative Action," drama reveals itself as a mainspring in all the original, unorganized games devised by children—games of make-believe and "Let's Pretend." Those who in later years choose the Drama as their walk in life begin—if the weaker among them do not always end—by feeling a passion for their work equal to that of all great artists. The quality of final greatness lies in the survival of this feeling, still pure and undiluted, in face of material conditions.

I recall, in this connexion, the owner of a London theatre who appeared to have no real interest in the Drama, and whom, therefore, I once asked why he was concerned in stage affairs. He replied that as a youth he had been wildly enthusiastic—even to the extent of saving money carefully, when a poor man, to join a dramatic society for the sake of a chance to act. Obstacles and other claims, however, had gradually killed this love, until now he found that possession of bricks and mortar gave him sole satisfaction. In other words, his urge to create had been entirely supplanted by desire to control—an example, I suppose, of what psychologists call sublimation, and an instance of what is always happening to the artists in the world.

But fortunately the Drama has innumerable devotees, and the army of its faithful servants is great indeed. Hence comes the enormous growth of the Amateur

Dramatic Movement, which does far more than merely keep pace with the decline of the professional stage. The causes of that decline need no repetition, nor can one serve any good purpose by enlarging on them. But what is so amazing is the way in which the amateur has leapt into the breach, and by so doing not only saved the Drama in this country from virtual extinction, but breathed literally new life into it. In prosperous days, the world was too much with the Theatre; getting and spending, it laid waste its powers, and if true to a certain public, it was often not true to itself. Compelled to it by his necessities, but none the less both learning and teaching a great lesson in the process, the amateur proclaims the old truth that the play's the thing, to which scenery, costumes, properties, and the company itself, are but accessories.

Apart from its value to the community as a whole, the Amateur Dramatic Movement, by the outlet that it offers to creative work, can enrich the lives of countless individuals. It stands for independence and for progress simultaneously, and in it the will to survive is matched by the courage to experiment. Its strength is great because, as was said above, the dramatic is of all secondary instincts the most nearly universal, as it is also, perhaps, the most educative when adequately used. Recognizing this, the leading amateur societies have not contented themselves with easy imitation, but have sought out and worked hard to develop all kinds of new plays and fresh ideas. Young authors especially are indebted to them; never before, certainly, has the budding playwright had such allies or such opportunities. Discoveries will be many as the work of the amateur societies continues to extend still further throughout the country.

Side by side with the encouragement of new writers must be placed the resuscitation of old ones—a branch formerly all too neglected. The simplicity of our early English plays not only renders them peculiarly adapted to performance on small stages with few adventitious aids—it is something actually refreshing in itself, and possessing an unexpected delight and appeal for audiences somewhat sated by modern sophistication. Indeed, I rank the revival of old authors as equal in value to the support of new ones—for a living Drama can only draw sustenance from its roots. That the old authors demand no fee is, of course, a further advantage to societies of limited resources.

Altogether, it is difficult to resist the conclusion that some potent force is at work in all this dramatic activity—the Spirit of the Theatre, perhaps, refusing to accept defeat. Cheerfully the amateur has shouldered a heavy burden, but the labour being one of love, its weight is scarcely felt in all the excitement of advance and exploration. The Amateur Dramatic Movement is, in fact, typical of England, which has always achieved more through the efforts of her private citizens, working independently towards a common end, than through governmental action. Consequently, there is no doubt whatever that the Drama will not only live, but will increase in stature through the coming years, and—observing what they have already done—I look to the amateur societies to win for it nothing less than a complete renascence.

LIST OF CONTRIBUTIONS IN THE VOLUMES

CONTRIBUTORS

William Armstrong
Robert Atkins
Clifford Bax
Frederick Bentham
Edward W. Betts
John Bourne
Ivor Brown
E. Martin Browne
Clive Carey
Andre Charlot
D. Graham Davis
F. E. Doran
Harold Downs
Edward Dunn
Darrell Fancourt
Elsie Fogerty
James R. Gregson
Sir Cedric Hardwicke
Alfred Hartop
Arnold L. Haskell
H. P. Hollingdrake
Isabel Jeans
Mary Kelly
Gertrude Lawrence
S. R. Littlewood
Ralph Lynn
Joseph Macleod
Michael MacOwan
Norman Marshall
Robert Nesbitt
Robert G. Newton
Hermon Ould
Dudley S. Page
L. du Garde Peach
A. E. Peterson
M. Gertrude Pickersgill
J. B. Priestley
C. B. Purdom
Madame Marie Rambert
Reginald A. Rawlings
Philip J. S. Richardson
Sir Ralph Richardson
Arnold Ridley
D. Kilham Roberts
Flora Robson
H. Samuels
Hugh Arthur Scott
A. H. Sexton
Hal D. Stewart
Dame Sybil Thorndike
Gwynneth Thurburn
Nevil Truman
Horace Annesley Vachell
Dumayne Warne
H. W. Whanslaw
Edwin C. White
Geoffrey Whitworth
Harcourt Williams
T. G. Williams
Angus Wilson

CONTENTS OF VOLUME ONE

CONTENTS

A

ACTING IN COMEDY

ACTING IN FARCE

ACTING IN NATURALISTIC DRAMA

ACTING IN ROMANTIC DRAMA

ACTING IN SHAKESPEARE'S PLAYS

ACTING IN TRAGEDY

AMATEUR MOVEMENT, PAST AND FUTURE, THE

AMATEURS, PLAYWRIGHTS AND PRODUCTIONS

Maurice Seymour, Chicago

GERTRUDE LAWRENCE

ACTING IN COMEDY

GERTRUDE LAWRENCE, Actress. Has played lead in comedy at most London theatres and in New York; Author of "A Star Danced"

IN the modern theatre there is an interplay of forces which, inevitably, influences the style of acting that is popular, or desirable, or essential during any era of fashion.

Theatrical fashions, as ladies' fads, change from era to era. What is popular in West-End theatres this year, or during any year, is certain to undergo modification before more than a decade or so has passed. What director or producer, or financial backer, or commercial manager, considers actors and actresses must contribute to theatrical performance through production will assuredly change with the new mood of the sentient moment for exploitation in the business theatre.

Concurrently, revolutionary experiments in narrow, though not necessarily insignificant, circles, are undertaken by pioneers at work with the underlying idea of forcing upon the influential men and women in the theatre ideas, technique, and methods which they have convinced themselves are superior to, or more appropriate than, the familiar methods that have their reflection in ordinary theatre-going spheres.

Nevertheless, the certainty is that what is presented for entertainment will, in some measure, be conditioned by what those who are responsible for the provision of theatrical fare consider to be desirable, and in this connexion the responsible persons are unlikely to be actors or actresses.

It is true that some plays are "put on" because they have parts for which particular "stars," actors or actresses whose names are box-office magnets, are exceptionally suited; but it is equally true that players are made to fit parts, and that the appeal of personalities weakens or strengthens with the changing moods of the theatre-going public.

What the essential qualities are at any given moment can be stated confidently only in conformity and harmony with the spirit of the times. The theatre-going public is as unpredictable as Woman—or politicians. Similarly, the factors that influence the material that is filtered through the theatre are inconstant.

During war, lightness and brightness, colour and spectacle are wanted; are even necessary. Industrial depression adversely affects not only the economics of play production and performance, but also the style and quality of public entertainment.

The March of Time both turns history's pages and makes the fashionable of To-day the demoded and unwanted of To-morrow.

I would like to consider more closely these generalizations and to deduce from them first principles of production and acting in relation to aesthetically satisfactory public performances, but, instead, must be satisfied to generalize further about Comedy and acting in it.

Searching for an interesting rather than a perfect definition of Comedy, I unearthed the following: "A comedy is a humorous play in which the actors dominate the action. . . . Pure comedy is the rarest of all types of drama; because characters strong enough to determine and control a humorous plot almost always insist on fighting out their struggle to a serious issue, and thereby lift the action above the comic level. On the other hand, unless the characters thus stiffen in their purposes, they usually allow the play to lapse into farce. Pure comedies, however, have now and then been fashioned, without admixture either of farce or of serious drama . . . to compose a true comedy is a very serious task; for in comedy the action must be not only possible and plausible, but also a necessary result of the nature of the characters." Stimulated by this quotation from Clayton Hamilton's *The Theory of the Theatre*, I began to think of what is required for acting in comedy.

The late Sir Seymour Hicks, one of the last of the brilliant comedy actors of his particular era ("they made their reputations in plays different in texture and technique from those that meet popular demands to-day") dealing with the selection of plays for production, especially by amateurs, asked: "Why not work up from Tom Robertson, who was one of the moulders, if not the makers, of modern comedy, to the giants of yesterday, to-day, and to-morrow—Jones, Pinero, Carton, Grundy, Wilde, Barrie, Lonsdale, Shaw, Maugham, and others?"

Then he asked another question and answered it in his own book entitled *Acting*: "*Good* acting should be *definite* acting, where sentences are started and finished, not slid into and shuffled out of. To be indefinite has become so very fashionable, I presume, because to show any emotion to-day is not good form. But the sooner the actor realizes that to lead his audiences, and not to be led by them, the better for his art and the listeners themselves."

His enumeration of the writers of comedies could now be elaborated to include names such as J. B. Priestley, Noel Coward, St. John Ervine, Sean O'Casey, T. S. Eliot, R. C. Sherriff, Terence Rattigan, and, alas, not many others.

The theatre in Britain, as elsewhere, has altered since the nineteenth century ended.

Playgoers who are approaching the conclusion of the allotted three score years and ten recall "the good old days" in the theatre and have in mind "musicals" or "straight" plays quite different from those which, for example, were produced between the two world wars, and the young generation of to-day, more readily drawn to "the pictures" and familiar with screen technique, are, consequently, not so enthusiastic about "the legitimate stage," with its basically different requirements. Their interest in theatrical fare, which a quarter of a century ago was sometimes assumed to be revolutionizing both Drama and the Theatre, has become dull-edged.

Just as plays that reflect the spirit of the times in which they are written quickly "date," so the acting that is deemed to be suitable for the interpretation of types of plays at any given time undergoes metamorphosis. Such change delights some, but not all.

Even in this second post-world-war era there are suggestions that it would be well to discard some of the new methods and to revert to some of the old, thus bringing back vigour and virility to what is sometimes alleged to be the jaded theatre.

Illustratively, when the fashion for "throwing away lines" becomes annoyingly obtrusive pleas are heard for the re-introduction of "ham" acting; when lighting is manipulated in the interests of artistic presentation but with resultant disappointment to those who want to see as well as to hear and to feel in the theatre, there is a renewed demand that plays should be "lit up."

These are reminders of change more than evidence of the maintenance of effectiveness.

Certainly the subject is many-sided, and it is not surprising that we write or speak of the art of acting, the technique of acting, the purpose of acting, the significance of acting—and even the mystery of acting.

Good acting in comedy calls for a delicate blend of aptitude, ability, artistry, and aestheticism. I would humbly add patience, perseverance, and long apprenticeship. These must be in the equipment of the player who wishes to act in any of the three main forms of Comedy—the Comedy of Poetry, think of Shakespeare's plays; the Comedy of Manners, Congreve will furnish illustrations; the Comedy of Intelligence, draw upon Molière for examples. And, perhaps, I ought to add to these four A's, Aptitude, Ability, Artistry, and Aestheticism, three I's—Intuition, Insight, and Intelligence.

It is often said that to write a comedy is more difficult than to write a tragedy. There is truth in the contention just as, I think, there is when I contend that for acting in comedy, if it is to be technically adequate and artistically effective, all the principles of interpretation through acting must be applied selectively and successfully.

There should be laughter without tears, and tears through laughter. There may be slickness and smartness, but there must be sense and sincerity; control without constriction, awareness without angularity; firmness without rigidity.

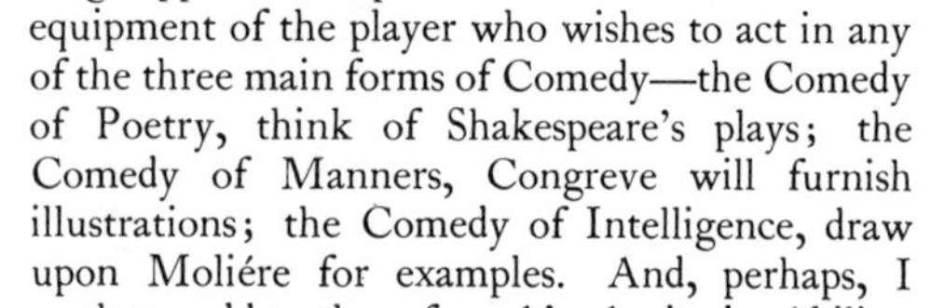

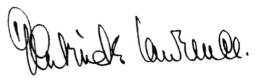

Stage Photo Co.

RALPH LYNN

ACTING IN FARCE

RALPH LYNN, Actor. Among his most brilliant interpretations of farce are his performances in "Tons of Money" and "It Pays to Advertise"

TO be a success in farce is not as easy as it appears to be to the average theatre-goer. It has been said that anybody who can write can turn out the first act of a play, and it has often been thought that any actor who can act can be successful in farce. Well, just as there are many writers of plays who find the second and the third acts, especially the third, too difficult for them, so there are many actors and actresses who find it impossible to leap the hurdles that they are bound to come across when playing in farce.

I remember the well-known dramatic critic, Mr. James Agate, once wrote something about the art of farce writing that struck me as being very much to the point. One has always been given to understand, he pointed out, that the actors of the old Italian *commedia dell'Arte* made the play up as they went along. The author contributed a sketchy plot, a book of words to be used or discarded at will, a few conventional types of character, and left the rest to the taste, wit, fancy, and invention of the actors, who then introduced gags, business, or any other matter of amusement.

Probably I remember that because there are so many who think that it is simplicity itself for an actor in farce to make up his lines as he goes along, to gag as the resourceful music-hall comedian in a revue does upon occasions necessary or unnecessary.

Well, work in farce, like any other kind of skilled work, is simple when the requisite technique has been learned. This applies to workers who have nothing to do with the theatre. It applies also to games and sports. The golfer cannot play a good game until he knows how to use his clubs—and he has to know much more than that—the swimmer splashes about rather than swims until he is a master of strokes, and we all —or some of us—know the surprises of skating until we can control our feet!

Technique is a word that has been overworked by the highbrows—but it stands for something very real and necessary. It may be more natural to think of the art of acting in tragedy or in romantic comedy than it is to talk about the technique of acting in farce—yet in my opinion acting in farce is more difficult acting than any other type of acting, and English-made farce is better for English audiences than French or any other kind of farce.

The Era years ago summed up the situation to a nicety: "Beginning with Aristophanes upward, the miracle and morality plays—where the comic element was purely farcical—from Molière, who raised farce to purest comedy, passing *The Comedy of Errors* and *The Taming of the Shrew*, up the centuries to Foote, Buckstone, Burnand, and Pinero, it is clear that farce has held a firm place in the affections of the playgoer. The English farce, the home-made article, has generally been worthy of its place, and whether inclining to burlesque and extravaganza, or encroaching on the domains of comedy itself, has appealed strongly to the English people, who, prone enough to 'take their pleasures seriously,' have rather preferred genuine and hearty farce to the social satire of the French stage and the stodgy philosophy of the German. . . . English farce, while relying also on situation, depends largely on character-drawing, and makes sterner demands upon the ability of the players. And, where French and American farce, by its very nature, tends to become *risqué*, the English leans more towards burlesque. . . . To weave a complete tangle, and, finally, to draw out every thread and present a perfect, if fantastic, pattern, should be the aim of every craftsman in the art of farce."

To think in this way about farce-making helps actors—and, of course, actresses—to understand what is wanted for acting in farce.

A farce is not a thing that just happens; it is a piece of writing that has to be skilfully made. There must be an idea in it. The characters may be "away" from human nature, they may be, no doubt will be, exaggerated, but they must not be too remote from it, and it is the task of the actor to endow the character he portrays with some semblance of human nature.

The "machinery" of the farce "works" the characters; the actor must make them.

An actor without humour will never make a successful actor of farce. Although he must be a master of technique, he must also be—and this is most important—a farcical actor by aptitude and inclination. It is true to say that the farcical actor, like the poet, is born—and that both farcical actor and poet must also make themselves by acquiring the knack of making successful use of their respective talents.

The player in farce must be sincere. He must be humorous, yet he cannot learn humour. He must be able to portray trouble, and fear, and worry, and all the other human emotions. This is how he creates interest in the characters—and it is not easy to be funny and serious and dramatic, all, so to say, in one.

Farce is not pantomime, in which the players can get their effects by mere fooling—in farce they have to be absolutely in earnest, truly dramatic, and able to get all the feeling out of certain scenes—say a love scene. At the same time, the funny sides of the situation have to be brought out with the facility with which the conjurer produces his effects. These, in my opinion, are the elements of success in farcical acting.

Finally, the best way to start to learn to play farce is to play in drama. I learned in dramas and melodramas of the type that used to be played at the old Adelphi and Drury Lane. They are the best material on which to train.

Photo Reproduction Co.

Flora Robson

ACTING IN NATURALISTIC DRAMA

FLORA ROBSON, Actress. Appears in plays and films, and is noted for her studies of historical characters

HOW many times when one has been watching the performance of a naturalistic action has one heard a member of the audience say, "But that is not acting, he is just being himself!" This may be a tribute to the actor's particular style, but it is not a true statement; he is, in reality, giving a highly finished performance, every movement and intonation of which is thought out to the last detail.

The most important fact to make clear is that the actor is never being spontaneous or natural; he only *appears* to be. In ordinary life you do not know what you are going to say next, whereas on the stage you do, but you must make it appear spontaneous. However normal and everydayish the dialogue reads in a modern play, immediately the actor has learned the words, it ceases to be natural to him. Also, he may be required to talk natural conversation, but he is in a vast theatre, and he must make his voice heard at the back of the gallery without appearing to be shouting or overacting. To give the effect of naturalness, he must spend infinite trouble trying different tones and expressions for a single word or short sentence.

Your first task on reading a play is to see your part as a whole before you attend to details, and to see it in relation to the other characters. Imagine the play as a symphony. You must determine when your character is the solo instrument and when it is part of the harmony. This is a great help to the producer, who is in the place of a conductor.

If you are the solo instrument, you must claim and hold the attention of the audience and make the members of it focus on you. But it is important, if you are part of the harmony, that you should help to focus the audience's attention on to the central character by listening carefully, and by not distracting their attention.

Take a scene between two people. Sometimes both characters are of equal importance; then the speaker and the reactions of each are important, and the scene is more or less straightforward; but in a scene where one actor is relating something at length, and the other has short interpolations (which are not important except to help to carry the narrative along), then the second actor should subordinate himself by making his reactions slight, by listening and watching, and by slipping in his interpolations quickly on his cues. He can thus avoid distracting, and can help to focus the attention of the audience in the right place. I cannot stress sufficiently the importance of listening to, and looking at, the person who is speaking to you. It helps the audience to listen, and also it helps the other actor enormously—he immediately acts *to* you (instead of *at* you and *to* the audience), which makes for naturalism—and you are always "in" the scene.

Study your part as a whole; study it for contrast. Just as an artist can more easily get his effect by means of a contrasting background, which throws his subject into clear relief, so a dramatist heightens the effect of his scenes by contrasting one scene with another. Bring out these contrasts, and by means of them work up to your big scene, always keeping something in reserve for this climax.

Remember, when you are working out the character of your part, that no person is perfect. The day of the pure white heroine and the coal-black villain passed with the Victorian melodramas. Your part will appear much more naturalistic if it has human faults mixed up in your interpretation; I mean, of course, where the text suggests it, but to make the character just pretty takes away its human values.

It is so important that, whatever part you play, you should understand it and sympathize with it, even if the part is of the blackest villain; but when you play it do not spare its worst characteristics, and above all, do not sentimentalize it.

When you have realized your part as a whole, *learn your words*. This sounds elementary advice, but it is vital to a producer. Some actors think that to know their words by the last week before production is good work, but, believe me, the work does not begin till everyone is word perfect! You must also know what the other actors have to say. If you are busily listening for a cue, there is no by-play between the characters.

Secondly, when you learn your part, do not make the mistake of stressing too many words in a sentence. Particularly, when you have a phrase that has an obscure or involved meaning, if you speak too slowly and underline too many words in an effort to explain it, it becomes almost unintelligible.

The fewer words you stress, the simpler and more natural your words will become.

Thirdly, vary your pace a great deal. Sometimes, race your words, so that an important line stands out in comparison when it is said slowly and weightily. Also, vary your intonations and inflections. When I first learn words aloud, I listen to myself and often find that every line has the same inflection, and very dull it sounds! Cultivate listening to your own voice in private, but *never* listen to yourself on the stage.

In emotional acting, the great pitfall to avoid is to shock or surprise your audience suddenly. If you do not prepare them for an onslaught on their feelings, they will laugh.

I need say only a word about gestures, because in naturalistic plays they are very natural and simple, only they must be neat and slick; don't fumble! Rehearse with your properties wherever possible.

In studying a part, I think it should be conceived objectively, and then played subjectively.

I read the play, and I do not read myself into the part. I see her as the character in the play, or often I connect her with someone in real life who is similar; and occasionally she is a creature of imagination, made up of experiences of chance meetings or from books.

If you observe someone going through an emotional strain you may see certain outward signs; one stiffens about the shoulders, another opens and closes his hands, or his throat muscles contract. These are useful things to notice and copy, but unless you realize the mental agony and are able to understand the emotions that cause these outward signs, your performance will lack its most essential quality.

One of the most important attributes in naturalistic acting is that of seeming to be unconscious of anybody watching or listening. In intimate scenes this gives members of the audience the feeling that they are listening to people who have been left alone together. I quote from a letter of Antoine's criticizing a realistic play by Becque; it had been played by actors in the "rhetorical, high-flown style of old plays." (This quotation is from M. Komisarjevsky's book *Myself and the Theatre*.)

"The important thing in the new Theatre is the total absence of self-consciousness on the part of the characters, as in real life, where people are not forever conscious of what they are saying or doing. Last night we merely saw so many actors strutting and reciting, instead of the people created by Becque. . . .

"Not once did the players look at each other while speaking. In real life you would say: Look at me, damn you! It is to you that I am speaking—to anyone whom you were addressing who behaved as they did. . . ."

In the same letter he says that once when rehearsing a play he could not make an actor even move across the stage towards a table and sit in an armchair without glancing at the auditorium, or striking a special attitude. "I must admit," says he, "that the actor knew his job, but he had lost his simplicity and was incapable of acting as if no one were looking at him. . . . For actors who are tied to the old tradition the stage is a sort of tribune, and not an enclosed spot where something happens."

This reference to "an enclosed spot" inevitably brings up the question of the "fourth wall." I am rather against the theory the application of which makes actors self-consciously turn their backs on the audience, and avoid looking "out." I believe that as long as you are thinking the thoughts of your character, you can look right into the auditorium without looking *at* the audience.

Flora Robson

Alexander Bender

Isabel Jeans

ACTING IN ROMANTIC DRAMA

ISABEL JEANS, Actress. Her favourite parts are Margery Pinchwife in "The Country Wife," and Hypatia in "Misalliance"

SHAKESPEARE, I am told, is the most important romantic dramatist. I made my first appearance in a Shakespeare play as the Third Lady in *Richard II* and walked on in *King Henry VIII* the following year. Since then I have played other characters in Shakespeare's plays.

In writing on such a theme as Acting in Romantic Drama, it is, I think, helpful to find out what specialists have written or said about it. I confess that when I began "to look into" the significance of the word "romantic" and its varied usage, I was greatly surprised by Jacques Barzun's chapter entitled "Romantic"—A Sampling of Modern Usage" in his book *Romanticism and the Modern Ego*, in which I read:

"Romanticism will exist in human nature as long as human nature itself exists. The point is (in imaginative literature) to adopt that form of romanticism which is the mood of the age."—Thomas Hardy, Journal, November, 1880. *The Early Life of Thomas Hardy.*

"The most that the realist can do is to select the character and situations that seem to him to serve best as types of men and life; and his selection differs only in degree, as a rule, from the romanticist's choice of material. . . . At best, then, our terms 'romantic' and 'realistic' can only be vague because they will always be relative."—H. R. Steeves. *Literary Aims and Art.*

But to develop thought on these lines will take me into the World of Literature instead of into the World of the Theatre.

Is acting in Romantic Drama different from acting in any other type of drama? Yes and No. Yes, because (to give one illustration) a greater degree of emotional intensity is needed for its interpretation than for communicating convincingly the thoughts in a play of ideas.

The one is of the heart; the other of the head. But even as I write I realize I have stated a half-truth. If I suggested that depth of emotion is an essential in the portrayal of some of the characters in plays by Bernard Shaw, of whom it is often said that his heart is too rigidly governed by his head, I think I should be just as near to Truth, but not necessarily at its core.

The other day, I asked a friend what he thought was demanded of the actor or actress in Romantic Drama. He replied: Imagination and a sense of Poetry; also a light, musical voice by which, he explained, he meant that the quality of the voice should not be characterized by deep resonance and non-flexibility. I myself believe that the material upon which an actress or an actor works has a direct bearing upon how the technique of interpretation should be applied. The manner in which technical equipment is drawn upon and employed for the interpretation of a comic character is necessarily different from the essentials in acting in, say, a symbolic play that is given a stylized production. I cite an extreme contrast for the purpose of emphasis. Sarah Bernhardt in *The Art of the Theatre,* having made the point that "By means of faith an actor who is badly endowed by nature will captivate a prejudiced audience," proceeds: "Faith will enable an artist to impose upon the public a fresh incarnation of a character already created by an actor of genius, which character, adopted by successive generations, has become the tradition."

Again: "In the theatrical career, as in other careers, there are misfits and failures who take up too much room, speak too loudly, stand bravely before crowds, pose as unappreciated geniuses, and fall victims to absinthe. The public too often confuses them with true artists. But what does it matter. We artists follow our path, so arduous, so full of snares, but so bedecked with flowers. It is our mission to stimulate the minds and move the hearts of men. The poets and dramatists entrust us with the finest products of their art. They place in our trembling but confident hands the quintessence of their minds, the flesh of their flesh, their long-meditated utterances, the generous thoughts they would sow in the heart of crowds, the lesson they would teach society in an entertaining manner, without direct affront to the listener. And under the mask of laughter they extract from a ludicrous situation a new injunction against this or that abuse. And we are the advocates in these proceedings. We alone may communicate instantaneously to the public the ardent faith of the author. It is we who must, with one hand, snatch away the tares, and with the other sow the good seed. Ah! What intense joy steals over the actor when he feels that a trembling audience is hanging on his lips and his looks, while he knows that behind the scenes is a person whose heart is beating quickly, who has taken two years of his life to elaborate what often proves to be a masterpiece; who has erased, corrected, rejected words, sentences, lines; who has so much at stake, his future, sometimes even his daily bread, his glory, his all."

Mr. C. B. Purdom looks at the subject from another angle when he writes: "Romance is idealism in action . . . I place tragedy and romance near together. Both depend upon faith, upon confidence in the destiny of man, upon the conviction that man can save himself. I do not say that romance is in conflict with comedy; for I think that comedy will continue to flourish beside romance. Indeed, comedy will gain when romance returns, for it will get more substance."

My quoted friend, it will be noted, refers to imagination and the poetic spirit. One of the most interesting of our contemporary authors, Mr. W. Somerset Maugham, in his autobiography *The Summing Up* discusses Naturalistic Drama and its development, and expresses the opinion that it may be superseded by Poetic Drama. What is in the mind of those who see in poetry in drama the possibility of the soundest advance of the modern theatre? Matthew Arnold, I think supplies one answer, and I need not apologize for going again to Literature: "Poetry is simply the most delightful and perfect form of utterance that human words can reach. Which of us doubts that imaginative production, uttering itself in such a form as this, is altogether another and a higher thing from imaginative production uttering itself in any of the forms of prose?" But, of course, he supplied the answer before the question was asked.

In expressing my opinions on acting in Romantic Drama I have generalized about the spirit of Drama and merely fringed the given theme. This is because my view is that the actor or actress must, in the first place, have the full equipment of his or her profession—to succeed. That equipment is drawn upon variously and is conditioned by the material that has to be worked upon and communicated to the audience. Players must be interpreters. They need to be creative as well as to be skilled technicians. They require head and heart to be a working duo rather than two individual soloists. "Flesh and blood" is a phrase that is often used of players in the "legitimate" theatre to contrast them with the projected players in the cast of a film. It is intended to emphasize the value of the *human* element in interpretation; but more than the merely physical is needed there should also be the sparks of intellect and revelations of the Spirit of Man. Louis Calvert, a distinguished member of our profession, wrote in his *Problems of the Actor*: "The art of the actor is a most sensitive one, susceptible to every influence varying fads of fashion and thought may bring to bear. It is on the stage that we find the most faithful expression of the moods of thought which are peculiar to each generation; and which make each generation 'modern' and those that have gone before 'old-fashioned'."

Romantic drama can reflect the "mood of the age" of which Hardy speaks and the actor will use not only his technique but also his creative understanding of life to interpret it.

Pollard Crowther

Robert Atkins

ACTING IN SHAKESPEARE'S PLAYS

ROBERT ATKINS, O.B.E., Actor and Stage Director, Open-air Theatre, Regent's Park; Memorial Theatre, Stratford-upon-Avon

IT has often been stated that any actor or actress who wants to be an accomplished delineator of a character in a modern play ought before he or she attempts delineation to have had experience in Shakespearean productions. It is undeniable that actors and actresses in Shakespeare's plays work upon material that can be adequately dealt with from a histrionic and an artistic point of view only by those who can blend the theory and practice of acting. The modern play, with its smart dialogue, its snappy lines, perhaps rich in scintillating wit, and certainly reflective of the moods and modes of expression of the moment, calls for a sophistication that is reminiscent of the life that is lived by people who move in certain circles of Society. There is a technique in modern acting just as there is a specialized technique in acting in Shakespeare's plays. It is easy to exaggerate the importance of technique, notwithstanding the fact that it is a most important essential. Without technique there cannot be adequacy of interpretation. Delineation requires understanding of subtleties. Subtlety is the outcome and crystallization of applied theory. Sarah Bernhardt, in her book *The Art of the Theatre*, revealed that she had a clear understanding of the limitations of technical efficiency: "Whatever I have to impart in the way of anguish, passion, or of joy, comes to me during rehearsal in the very action of the play. There is no need to cast about for an attitude, or a cry, or anything else. You must be able to find what you want on the stage in the excitement created by the general collaboration. . . . Everything must come from suggestion." The sources of suggestion are varied. They are in both the company and the audience.

Actors and actresses work in the realm of creative imagination—if they are first-class exponents of the art that they exercise. It requires a genius to be a versatile actor or actress and an expert delineator in many roles. But something more than creation, which I suggest is of primary importance, is necessary. Aptitude for and ability at imitation are requisites. The player in a modern play may think that imitation is better than creation for the purpose of characterization. The player in a Shakespearean tragedy, or a Restoration comedy, or in Greek drama, cannot go to contemporary life for models. He or she has to create the character imaginatively. The characters must be made to exist in the mind of the interpreter, and their existence must be given verisimilitude of a sort. There is always a danger in attempting to get "near to truth," especially in the theatre: truth to tradition, to convention, to external trappings, or the spirit that is generated within. Many problems can easily be started. Years ago *The Stage* published a leading article on Period Acting. "It was Francisque Sarcey, we think," stated the writer, "who once said that on the stage he liked the natural of art but not the natural of nature. In other words, a play is not just a raw slice of life, and acting is not simply a transfer of speech, movement, and feeling from the street or the room to the stage. If nothing more than that were asked from the actor, then anyone could be an actor. But acting calls for the histrionic gift and for the technical ability to express it. Stage naturalness is not crude nature but the art of seeming to the audience to be natural; and this naturalness has to be, as far as possible, at one and the same time naturalness within the design of the part and naturalness acceptable to the audience. Anyone with any technical knowledge of acting is aware that a piece of acting, whatever its period, shows, if studied from close quarters on the stage, highly accentuated values in much the same way as the facial make-up of the actor is out of perspective from the same angle of vision." Questions that arise out of consideration of period and perspective are important. "The dramatist or the actor," (to quote *The Stage* again)" dealing with a period not his own, can reconstruct more or less from the sources of information open to him. There can be no intimate realization—only this approximate reconstruction. He can show something of historical spirit, and can keep his work free from obvious anachronisms and solecisms. What he cannot do, however flexible and sympathetic his mind and wide his researches, is wholly to project himself into a period not his own. To some extent he is obliged in an old period play to fall back upon convention whether of manner or speech, or both. Blank verse, for example, is a convention, or rather an artistic and poetic medium of expression. It must be spoken in accordance with its structure and cadence. It can be spoken in this way, and very beautifully and dramatically spoken; and it certainly cannot be spoken—unless for the purpose of trying perversely to undo all that it aims at doing—in the highly colloquial way of our street corner talk. Generally, the acting of the period play, if it cannot altogether obtain from the actor the special vitality that he imparts to his work in a play that belongs to his own day, calls upon him for knowledge, insight, imagination, and for a full technical skill able to range from the nice conduct of a clouded cane to a just and fluent delivery of the mighty line of blank verse."

These pertinent points can easily be made to apply to acting in Shakespeare's plays. Type casting, which is common to-day, is in some cases an obstacle that impedes the development of acting talent. Shakespeare's plays offer less scope for the application of modern methods of both casting and acting, assuming, of course, that the attainment of a high standard of artistic interpretation through presentation is desired. Think of either Shakespearean comedy or tragedy. There is a richness of language that is in striking contrast to the paucity of the dialogue of the average modern play. The exquisite delicacy of language that is one characteristic of Shakespeare's plays must be conveyed in acting by the soundness of interpretative technique, plus the spirit that stimulates imagination and gives point and purpose to the interpretation. We live in an age when the simple, direct, and easily understood are features of written expression. Shakespeare's plays have a richness of language that must be thought about, analysed, and understood if significance of meaning is to be extracted from them. Shakespearean dialogue is both sound and sense. Neither can be made to serve its true function unless the actor or actress can arrive at understanding by means of the difficult, the indirect, and the complex. There must be elocution, within the best definition of the word, for the voice is the medium of expression. But although skilful use of the appropriate tones is necessary, elocution is not enough. There must be a sense of the rhythm of language, a sense of the freedom that gives harmony to gesture, and movement that is meaningful though modish. There must be technique suffused by idealism. In other words, and to quote Martita Hunt's "'Macbeth' From the Actor's Point of View" (*The Listener*): "For the actor there are two entirely different points of view on every play—his ideal conception, in theory, when he reads the play (we are assuming that he is the kind of actor who does read a play, and not only his own part), and his very different attitude, in practice, when he is faced with the difficulties of carrying out his conception. If these difficulties can be overcome and an ideal conception ideally carried out, the audience should have that great emotional experience which surely only the theatre can give. I do not imply that a great play may not be conceived ideally in many different ways, provided that it is a genuine interpretation of the author and not the exploitation of an actor's personality or a producer's idiosyncrasy. It is very important in a play like *Macbeth*, where the leading actor carries most of the responsibility of interpretation, that his ideas and the producer's should be the same. Indeed, if a production has not unity of purpose it can never convey to an audience that greater significance, which lies behind the mere action. *Macbeth* can be considered as nothing more than a very exciting murder play, written by a fine poet and dramatist, but it should create a deeper impression, something which one carries away from the theatre, a quickening of the imagination, a spiritual experience."

Robert Atkins

Dorothy Wilding

Dame Sybil Thorndike

ACTING IN TRAGEDY

DAME SYBIL THORNDIKE, LL.D., Manchester and Edinburgh Universities; Actress and Manager

I AM invited to write on "Acting in Tragedy." Now of all things, the most difficult is for an actor to explain the how, why, and wherefore of his craft. Perhaps craft is the wrong word, for every artist should be able to explain the technique of his art, which is craft, but an exposition of the art itself presents great difficulties. The all-important difficulty is that when an artist has formulated what he is trying to do in his art he finds suddenly in the very act of formulation something has become static, lost its fluidity—and he himself has made a leap ahead of what he has put down in black and white.

However, it is on quite selfish grounds that I respond to the invitation, in the hope that I shall be jerked into some greater knowledge by this act of writing down what I think. It will be good for *me*, but perhaps a bit hard on the reader!

To begin with I must state that I object strongly to the labels "a tragic actor," "a comedian," "a straight actor" (whatever that much-used phrase may mean), etc. This labelling is a sign of the times (and perhaps of all times, for it has gone on during the whole of my own lifetime).

It's the easiest way out, the sign of commercialism, and of the idea that "There's no getting anywhere if you don't specialize." I'm not absolutely sure about all the other professions; it may be better for a doctor to specialize in one branch of his subject to the exclusion of the rest, but to the artist it is fatal. To those who say "You won't get anywhere without it," my answer is "It depends where you want to get." If you want quick success, then specialize—adopt one style—metaphorically, if you have a certain style of looks, a fringe, perhaps, stick to it so that the public know you, and go on that way till you tire them out and they want something fresh! In the meantime, you've got into a rut, and you need a lot of character to start somewhere else, and "cut the fringe." Specialization means death, or settling down, the fatal disease. Generalization is the creative way, and the hard way (for the temptation to play the parts for which you seem to be the most suited is great) but you must not be afraid of failure. It is very often the failures, or rather the effort and determination to do the things that don't suit you quite so well, which colour and improve your best work. This is the truth, whatever the critic may tell you.

After this long, but necessary preamble, we come to acting in Tragedy. It's important, first of all, not to confuse Tragedy with Pathos. Pathos is the form of play the English public in their serious moods like best. Comedy, of course, is the English public's real love. Concessions are made occasionally to seriousness, but they have to be on the Pathos level, for Tragedy hurts too much. Of necessity it hurts—it is a revolution, a jarring, a turning of values upside down, and it leaves a sense of the overpowering vastness of life. Integral to the whole is some huge Pity (or is it Mercy?), something too big to be understood, which is deeply felt by both actor and audience to the extent of hurting them both. This is the first essential of Tragedy.

The next essential, and I speak now as an actor, is that you must rise above this feeling, or you are sunk, drowned—the misery of the world is too much for you to bear alone. Get above it into Timelessness (and get above it with your fellow human-beings: a shared misery has value), into the realm of imagination, the mind of God (call it what you prefer) into a place of quiet knowledge where the two opposites, namely, intense feeling and beyond feeling, are co-existent. This must be your attitude of mind when you play Tragedy. Your technique: a flexible voice. If you have three octaves, you are luckier than the person who has only one, but if the person with one octave can use those eight notes in an infinite variety of ways and withal keep sincerity at the back of it, then he is happier than the three-octave player who listens to notes and vocalizes. There are two traps: one, the fear of not being real, and therefore not venturing vocally beyond the drawing-room size playing; the other is that of using the voice as a singer, where tone, not the words, is the important thing and sincerity is lost. One should not confuse sincerity with realism—it's just as easy, and more frequent in our London theatre, to get into "natural" tricks, as it is to get into what are colloquially called "ham" tricks. You can be just as "ham"—insincere and untrue—if you speak realistically as you can if you speak on a larger scale. (There are many traps and the words "Watch and pray that ye enter not into temptation" should be the motto of actors!)

A body flexible enough to take new shapes and forms is also necessary. This is easier for students, because most people nowadays are more "movement" than "speech" conscious.

There is no more to say, and yet there is everything to say. The subject is inexhaustible. Everyone who studies tragedy must work out his or her own salvation with fear and trembling and faith.

Let me finish by quoting *Œdipus* as an example of Tragedy and the way players interpret this to themselves. The story some say is absurd—but that doesn't matter: the hugest things are absurd, viewed realistically. The story is a symbol—to the individual, to the nation, and back to the individual again, and its meaning differs to each, as a ritual act differs.

Let me take one interpretation. A disease is rife in the land. The righteous man, the good-worldly ruler, or the good-worldly nation, desires to stamp it out. He is on a high moral stand. He searches and uncovers the reason for the disease, and, in the end, it comes home to him—he, perhaps unknowingly, is the guilty one—which makes the tragedy high-pitiful. Is this analogous to our world misery? I think so. Greek Tragedy brings home to each of us—nations and individuals alike—a sense of guilt. Our participation in world wrong may be unknowing, but we must humble ourselves to share the guilt and misery of our fellows under a mighty Hand whose ways and path we do not understand. A tragedy is a huge, cosmic, question-mark. Who can solve these great things?

These remarks are one particular actor's way of viewing Tragedy. I don't speak for the whole body of players. Each has his or her own vision—and way.

THE AMATEUR MOVEMENT, PAST AND FUTURE

GEOFFREY WHITWORTH, Founder and Director of the British Drama League. Author of "Father Noah"

THE title "The Past and Future of the Amateur Movement," preliminary as it is to studies on the arts of Theatre and Stage, may seem, and may well be, too ambitious. To write adequately of the past of the Amateur Movement, in the sense in which the term is here used, would be to write the early history of the stage as a whole. For nothing is further from the mark than to regard the amateur actor as an appendage to the stage, which only came into existence with Charles Dickens and the "amateur theatricals" of the mid-Victorian era. Normally, of course, when we speak of the Theatre we are thinking of a highly organized activity whose function it is to present Drama to the public with all the luxury and efficiency of a big commercial undertaking. Nor is it surprising that an art with so wide a popular appeal as that of the Stage should have become associated (as much to its benefit as to its hurt) with commerce, and therefore with professionalism. But at the beginning of things we may be sure that the gulf between amateur and professional did not exist. Just as the modern playwright is either good or bad, so we may assume was the primeval actor; and that was an end of the matter.

Kenneth Collins

GEOFFREY WHITWORTH

The art of acting, like that of pictorial design, is co-eval with civilization, and it is only an accident—the permanency of the rock—that allows us to trace the beginnings of draughtsmanship in the cave dwellings of Palaeolithic times, whereas no physical relic of the prehistoric actor survives. Nevertheless, where Stonehenge or some similar monument persists to remind us of the practice of religious ritual before even the dawn of history, there we may fairly deduce the existence of the actor, since all religious ritual is a kind of "play," even as in the life of children, we find the rudiments of the actor's art spontaneous in the "dressing-up" games of the nursery.

A feeling for the drama, then, and some ability to express it in action, are innate human characteristics. Man, in fact, might be defined as a "dramatic animal" with quite as much reason as Aristotle had for defining him as a "political animal." There are probably more Englishmen alive to-day who could put up a passable show on the stage of a theatre than could hold their own in a debate in the House of Commons. And are there not uncivilized races, like the Bantus in Southern Africa, whom travellers have described as all "born actors"? Let us see, very briefly, how this widespread instinct became canalized, so to speak, within the limits of conscious art; and then refined to such a pitch of specialization as to make inevitable the modern distinction between professional and amateur.

By the fifth century B.C. the Greek Theatre had attained a position that we can recognize as the source from which derives the European theatre as we know it to-day. Already Thespis had demonstrated the superiority of his carefully trained "chorus" in the dramatic celebrations which accompanied the festivals of Dionysus, that famous ritual whence was to evolve the whole classic drama of ancient Greece. This "chorus" was composed almost certainly of amateur performers, but in the later civic festivals of Athens, professionals, employed by the State, assumed the chief individual parts. A group or "caste" of these professional players was allotted to each dramatist entering for the prize given to the best play. Apart from this competitive element, the general organization of the festivals must have been comparable to that of such an amateur but municipal effort as that of the Passion Play at Oberammergau. The idea of the drama as a private enterprise came later, and then only in respect of the comedies of the Greek decadence.

The secular drama of Rome was in the hands, doubtless, of professional companies. It was the remnant of these companies—comedians for the most part—which, scattered northwards after the fall of the Roman Empire, kept alive, through the so-called Dark Ages, the tradition of stage professionalism. But theirs was, for the most part, an art of strolling jugglery and minstrelsy. The serious drama was dead—awaiting its rebirth at the hands of the amateurs, and once again through the inspiration of religion. Throughout the fourteenth and fifteenth centuries it was the Catholic Church in England, France, and Germany that renewed the art of drama by the impulse it gave to the creation of those Miracle and Mystery Plays of which the outstanding examples in our own country are the Guild Cycles of Coventry, Norwich, and York. These Plays were written to popularize the cardinal facts of Old and New Testament history. Conceived in the spirit of religious instruction, they presently took on elements of what would now be known as "entertainment value." From the church they migrated to the market place, to be acted at times of public holiday in much the same way as the local "pageant," which has become so marked a feature of the amateur theatre of modern times.

The story of the transition from the theatre of the Guilds to the theatre of the Elizabethans is of deep interest. It has been told in a fascinating volume by Dr. F. S. Boas, *An Introduction to Tudor Drama*—a book that can be cordially recommended to anyone who is concerned to trace the connexion between the amateur and the professional theatres of the Renaissance. From the researches that have been made generally available in this book, it is clear that the dramatists immediately antecedent to Shakespeare would have found no outlet for their talents had it not been for the help of amateur actors encouraged in their art by Courts, Universities, and Schools. Henry Medwell, the pioneer Tudor playwright, wrote his *Fulgens and Lucres* for production at Morton's Palace at Lambeth in the year 1497; John Heywood *The Play of the Wether* for some similar domestic entertainment a few years later; while *Ralph Roister Doister* was written by the schoolmaster Nicholas Udall probably while he was serving in that capacity under Gardiner, the Bishop of Winchester. The plays of many of the more illustrious Elizabethan dramatists were first performed on the amateur or semi-amateur stage. In fact, it would be no exaggeration to assert that Shakespearean Drama as we know it—not excluding the work of the master himself—would never have come into existence had it not been for the facilities for dramatic experiment that had been provided by the amateur stage of the period.

By the time of Shakespeare several professional companies were, of course, in action, both in London and in the Provinces. The play scene in *Hamlet* shows the princely attitude of the time towards one of these companies of touring players. And the amateur movement of the day—in one of its less exalted manifestations—comes in for some pointed yet not unsympathetic satire in the clown scenes of *A Midsummer Night's Dream*. Bottom and his troupe of "rude mechanicals" suggest that amateur acting was not even then confined to the social strata exemplified by royal courts and seats of learning, but that it had spread, as in our own day, to the ranks of the "workers."

Skipping forwards, we find John Milton writing *Comus* for performance at a courtly Masque at Ludlow in the year 1634. But the Puritan movement killed amateur acting as a popular pastime, and, unlike the drama of the professional stage, it made no recovery for a hundred years or more. It was not till later still that the amateur stage regained any influence upon the progress of the English theatre as a whole.

Throughout the eighteenth century, however, there are records of sporadic amateur activity in various parts of the country. In Exeter, for instance, we know of a Mr. Andrew Bryce who, with the help of a company of players from Bath, built a theatre behind the Guildhall. In 1737 theatrical performances in Exeter were illegal, but in the intervals of publicly advertised "Concerts of Music" the Bath Players would perform a play "merely for their own Improvement and Diversion and without Gain, Hire or Reward." Persons applying to Mr. Bryce for "tooth powder" (by trade he was in fact a printer) paid 2s. and were admitted to the best seats, while 6d. for a corn plaster admitted to the gallery.

Meanwhile, on the continent of Europe, developments were occurring that are comparable with those in England, if in many ways dissimilar in their outcome. In France, for instance, royal patronage of Court drama culminated under Louis XIV in the foundation of the *Comedie française*. This classic institution was the parent and pattern of all those National and Civic Theatres that have become the rule abroad, to the infinite advantage of the European theatre. Dramatic production on the grand scale did not, however, destroy the natural desire felt by every social rank for personal participation in the art of the stage. But amateur acting was frowned on as a pastime for royalty, and Marie Antoinette, who built and equipped a charming Little Theatre at her Palace of Les Trianons, came in for sharp criticism on account of the play-acting tendencies that she indulged there, albeit in private. All through the eighteenth century the Italian drama owed scarcely less to the impromptu enterprise of the amateurs. It is to Germany, however, that we must look for the next link of capital importance between the amateur and the professional stage. In the year 1775 the Duke of Weimar appointed Goethe as Director of his amateur Court Theatre. Goethe filled this post for forty-two years, and thus—though oftentimes in revolt against the petty tasks entailed by his office—the great poet-dramatist had the great advantage during a major portion of his life of the varied experience and practice that only work on the amateur stage, it may be, can afford.

Glimpse of Part of the Auditorium of Marie Antoinette's Theatre, showing her Initials above the Curtain and Restoration of the Stage

We cannot here argue questions of cause and effect, but it must be noted that the admitted decline in intellectual vigour that the drama suffered during the first half of the nineteenth century, coincided with a corresponding failure of amateur effort. Fine actors there were, but few fine plays, till Ibsen, the Norwegian, inaugurated a new era of dramatic creativeness. England felt this influence later than some other countries. But by the first Jubilee of Queen Victoria the revival was beginning. Henry Irving, though wedded to plays of the old school, was significantly knighted in 1893. At Oxford and Cambridge the O.U.D.S. and the A.D.C. were restoring a *rapport* between the stage and university life that had seemed gone beyond recall. This, too, was the hey-day of "amateur theatricals," a movement untouched by intellectual impulse, but still affording evidence of the wide spread of histrionic talent among all classes, and of great service to the charitable funds in whose aid the performances were held. But in America, by the first decade of the twentieth century, the Little Theatre Movement was well on its way, and in Russia, at a country house outside Moscow, Stanislavsky was laying the foundations of an Art Theatre that was to vindicate once more the ability of the amateur to inspire and rejuvenate the art of the professional stage.

STAGE AT OBERAMMERGAU

In the few years immediately preceding the First Great War, there came signs of a new development of amateur drama in England. The success of Miss Horniman's professional "Gaiety Theatre" Company in Manchester must have done much to encourage an interest in intelligent drama in the North of England, and about this time we come upon the foundation of such amateur clubs as the Stockport Garrick Society. To these days must also be ascribed the birth of Sir Barry Jackson's Birmingham Repertory Theatre which began as a small amateur society. A new kind of Village Drama also came into existence about this time as typified by "The Aldbourne Players."

These, and a few other comparable activities, showed which way the wind was blowing, and doubtless amateur dramatic work would have grown in volume and efficiency in the ordinary course of progress. But I think it unlikely that, but for that War, we should have been faced with anything like the flood of amateur effort and accomplishment that was so notable a phenomenon of post-War years.

The First Great War, a turning point in world history with consequences that we have lived to deplore, appeared in its more immediate effects to have destroyed the European Theatre as the repository of a Fine Art. This applies in a special degree to our own country where no State-endowed theatre exists to maintain artistic standards in periods of crisis or unusual depression. During the War itself our professional stage was given over to the provision of "entertainment" in the most trivial sense of the word. By so doing it fulfilled a necessary function, but the drama as a living art thereby suffered severely. In 1918, when things had almost reached rock bottom, few people could have foreseen that we were in fact on the eve of a renaissance of dramatic idealism (if not always of accomplishment) which has had no parallel since the age of Tudor Drama.

The movement began very humbly and very simply, inspired to some extent by two bright lights in the wartime darkness: (1) the heroic enterprise of Miss Lilian Baylis whereby the "Old Vic" established itself as a centre of Shakespearean production in South London; (2) the unique service rendered to our troops in France by Miss Lena Ashwell who, from the germ of a "Concert Party," evolved a theatrical company which proved that plays of high artistic standard were, in the long run, appreciable to the full by an audience of "Tommies." The same discovery was being made by small groups of dramatic enthusiasts here and there at home. Early in 1919 I came into contact with one such group attached to the Vickers-Armstrong Works at Crayford in Kent, and thus my eyes were opened to the possibilities inherent in the drama viewed not from the angle of commercialized entertainment but from that of personal expression and self-culture.

The story of the British Drama League, which was founded in the same year, is really the story of the Amateur Movement, which, since 1918 has transformed the theatrical scene. The League began in the most modest circumstances, but with high ambitions, not as itself a play-producing organization, but, in the words of its prospectus, with the sole object of assisting the development of the Art of the Theatre and of promoting a right relation between Drama and the Life of the Community. From the start, the League set its face against any cleavage between the professional and the amateur stage. Its first committee, under the Chairmanship of Mr. Harley Granville-Barker, included the names of several leaders of the professional theatre. Among its members there have always figured a goodly number of professional actors, playwrights, and theatre managers. As a result of this policy, and of the support given to it by the profession, the League has done much to secure that friendly feeling between professional and amateur which is so welcome a feature of our dramatic life. Even the so-called "commercial theatre" has come to recognize that the amateur stage is a useful ally as a training-ground for young actors, as a fruitful field for the discovery of new playwrights, and last but not least, as an incentive to intelligent theatre-going.

Content, at first, to offer a central focus and clearing-house for dramatic activities of every kind, the League, as it grew, was able to initiate various more positive forms of service. With the assistance of the Carnegie United Kingdom Trust, it formed a Dramatic Library for the use of its members. This Library contains over 25,000 volumes, among them many reference books of great value. "Drama Schools" are organized from time to time in various parts of the country, a monthly journal, *Drama*, is published, and Village Drama is specially catered for by a Village Drama Section, which continues the work of the Village Drama Society, which, founded by Miss Mary Kelly at about the same time as the League, was incorporated with the League in 1932. Already some 2,500 societies had joined the League, among them being the Scottish Community Drama Association.

These figures are in themselves sufficiently impressive. But it must be remembered that there are probably at least an equal number of societies and smaller dramatic groups that are unattached to any parent body, in addition to the many amateur operatic societies that enjoy membership of the National Operatic and Dramatic Association. Individual membership of all these bodies must run into hundreds of thousands, and it is not too much to say that there is scarcely a district in Great Britain to-day which, in one way or another, is untouched by the Movement.

If the First Great War had a stimulating effect on the drama in this country, the Second Great War proved even more influential in the same respect. For the first time in our history the State woke up to the necessity of providing Theatre, both for the Forces and for those who stayed at home. E.N.S.A., from the very beginning of hostilities, offered entertainment of a more or less frivolous kind for the soldiers, both in England and overseas. A few months later the Council for the Encouragement of Music and the Arts—familiarly known as C.E.M.A.—was founded under the auspices of the Ministry of Education. This organization provided cultural amenities of a high standard in painting, music, and drama. The Theatre Royal, Bristol, was rescued from demolition, and five or six excellent dramatic companies were sent on tour throughout the country. They visited the smaller rather than the larger centres, and many people who had never before seen a stage play were suddenly confronted with carefully selected examples of dramatic art. The response was overwhelming, and when the company departed from any locality it left behind it a new and fervent desire for more and more drama.

Almost at the same time the Service of Youth, also under the auspices of the Ministry of Education, was started. Thousands of youth groups came into being, and one of the most popular of group activities was the acting of plays. While most of the larger amateur societies closed down for the war period, new and smaller ones took their place. The standard of performance was not invariably high, but it was surprising what enthusiasm achieved, while towards the end of the War many of the older and more established societies revived. During the "blitzes" amateurs continued their work of spiritual salvage, which was recognized, perhaps for the first time, as a benefit of national importance to the community.

Most surprisingly, local education authorities woke up to the need of dramatic instruction to assist these newly-formed groups. Supported by the Carnegie United Kingdom Trust, rural community councils and local education authorities began to appoint county drama advisors who organized local efforts and provided just that training which is so necessary for those who aspire to be leaders and teachers of amateur drama. This educational impetus has clearly come to stay.

All this activity naturally involved a new call on the services of the British Drama League. At the end of the War its membership had risen to over 6,000, of which 5,000 were affiliated amateur drama groups. Its library was issuing as many as 16,000 reading sets annually and over 15,000 single copies of plays to its members.

Miss Gwen Carlier's Setting for Episode 5, "Shakespeare," at the Crescent Theatre, Birmingham
Photo, Crescent Theatre

We have seen how continuous is the record of amateur drama throughout the ages. This new revival is not, therefore, to be regarded as miraculous or unprecedented. It is natural, however, that one should seek some explanation for its sudden emergence at a time when conditions might well have been thought to be particularly unfavourable to anything of the kind.

The explanation is to be found, as I believe, in

a spontaneous and inevitable reaction against other tendencies that are flagrant in the world. The moral exhaustion that was the aftermath of the War has left half mankind at the mercy of the mechanical-economic elements in modern civilization. These elements have given us, it is true, certain alleviations from themselves. The motor car takes the town-dweller into the country with an ease and celerity hitherto unknown. Wireless and radio have opened up for the multitude a new field of dramatic enjoyment, albeit at one or two removes. But these last are purely passive pleasures, and a little tainted at the source. In the main we are still the victims of an impulse which, if pushed to its logical conclusion, would deny to us all that sense of personal vitality which is a prime condition of happiness. Here Drama comes to the rescue. It provides just the needed antidote to the poison of the Machine. On the stage a free wind of the spirit blows. And thither, unconscious often of the motive that drives us, we turn for the refreshment of an Art that is almost Nature, since its medium is the Bodies and Souls of Men.

Statistics of the number of amateur dramatic organizations give no idea of the variety of circumstance and method that characterizes the Movement. It is a far cry from the sophisticated refinement of such a society as the "Manchester Unnamed" to the small club-room in an East End slum where a company of boy scouts are playing, for the first time in their lives perhaps, some simple farce or melodrama. And then, again, there is the "school play" to be found in educational establishments of every class and type. These plays take place often enough at the time of the end-of-term celebrations, though sometimes we find that play-acting is introduced as part of the normal curriculum as an aid to the teaching of History or Literature. Though this "dramatic method in education" is widely practised, I have sometimes thought it strange that it is not in more frequent use as a means to the learning of foreign languages. There are plays in all the important foreign languages that are admirably adapted to class work from day to day.

SETTING FOR A PRODUCTION OF "HAMLET" BY THE RADLEY COLLEGE A.D.S., DESIGNED BY R. M. SIMPSON, PRODUCED BY A. K. BOYD

But the relation, as a whole, of drama to national education merits a chapter to itself, and members specially interested in this aspect of the subject may be referred to the admirable survey published by H.M. Board of Education in 1927 under the title of "Report of the Adult Education Committee on Drama in Adult Education." The publication of this Report is itself good evidence of the important place that the Art of the Theatre has regained in the estimation of officialdom.

And what, it may be asked, of the Future? That numerically the Movement can continue to grow at the same rate as during the past few years may be doubted, though when one considers the vast masses of people still untouched, it would be rash to set limits to possible expansion. For amateur drama is not a thing that appeals only to amateur actors. The stage is the focus of many talents, and the painter, the man or woman with a literary turn, the amateur mechanic, can all find work to do, and plenty of fun in the doing of it. That the Movement will continue to grow is, therefore, certain. What is more difficult to diagnose are the possibilities it holds for progress on the artistic side.

Hitherto the great defect of amateur acting has been its lack of any real and impartial criticism. Whenever an amateur production has been passably good (and sometimes even when it has been execrable) the easy praise of friends and relations has dropped a rosy veil over all shortcomings. But the growing popularity of competitive festivals is doing much to counteract this vicious tendency.

The highest art may not often be found as the result of competition. But, at least, it is a safeguard against the worst; and there is no doubt that the general standard of amateur playing has vastly improved among those societies that have taken part in the various competitive events now organized, notably by the British Drama League and by the Federation of Women's Institutes. The League Festival takes place annually, and culminates in a "Final Festival," in London, which is held in the month of May, when the Howard de Walden Cup is presented to the best of the five teams appearing. These teams have been chosen in turn by a series of eliminating contests throughout the five areas into which Great Britain is divided for the purpose. Out of over five hundred competing teams only a few, naturally, can appear at the Area Finals and the Final of all. But the most valuable part of the Festival is not to be found in these "star" performances, but rather in the detailed criticism that is given by impartial adjudicators at every stage.

Unfortunately, competitive organization can, as a general rule, deal only with the one-act play, but latterly the Drama League has instituted a full-length play festival which may do something to prevent an undue preoccupation with the "one-acter." This indeed is unlikely to occur in the case of established societies with their own following and, perhaps, their own Little Theatre. To such as these festival work will always remain but one incident in a full season's programme. In any case, the reproduction of a West End success will be wisely avoided by the progressive society, not because a West End success is necessarily unworthy of their attention, but because it will be rightly felt that it is the amateur's special privilege to experiment with plays that are not commonly seen elsewhere.

Finally, as the permanent exponent of dramatic art, the professional theatre must always hold its own in large towns. But in smaller places, or in suburban areas where the professional theatre cannot live, the field open to the amateur is unending. It is on his ability to provide entertainment for a more general public than he has hitherto attempted to reach that his ultimate justification must be claimed and found in days to come.

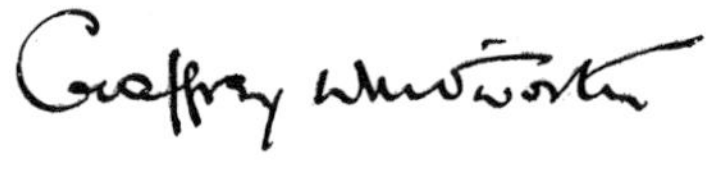

H. J. Whitlock & Sons, Ltd.

D. Kilham Roberts

AMATEURS, PLAYWRIGHTS AND PRODUCTIONS

D. KILHAM ROBERTS, M.A., Barrister-at-Law, Secretary-General, The Incorporated Society of Authors, Playwrights and Composers; Hon. Adviser, The League of British Dramatists

TO the man in the audience it must seem odd that the relations between two groups of individuals so mutually dependent as are those who write plays and those who perform them—especially if the latter are amateurs—should be marred to so large an extent by indifference and even, in some cases, active hostility. It would not be unreasonable to have supposed that in the interests of their own material welfare, if for no higher motive, each would endeavour to appreciate the other's position and point of view, and so avoid much of the misunderstanding that at present exists.

The situation is one for which both groups are to blame. Dramatists who can count on a West-end or Broadway run for almost any play they write have been inclined to regard the Amateur Theatre with a superior scorn, which, had they taken the trouble to attend the amateur performances of some of their works, they would have found was as unjustified as it was insufferable. Such dramatists regard the amateur society merely as a provider of what are in the gross satisfactory, if individually comparatively insignificant, windfalls.

There are, of course, even among playwrights of standing, a large number of exceptions to whom the Amateur Theatre means something more. Many, indeed, among our more far-sighted dramatists see in it and in the whole Little Theatre Movement the theatre of the future—the ultimate stronghold of the stage against the encroachment of the screen. But even they, even those public-spirited authors who give up valuable time to such work as adjudication at British Drama League Festivals, although they have faith in the Amateur Theatre as a movement and admiration for what it has achieved in the face of overwhelming odds, have hard things to say about the extraordinary absence of ordinary commercial morality which still pervades it.

Most of the larger and more progressive amateur societies are, of course, above reproach in this respect. They recognize the necessity for obtaining the permission of the author of a play before that play is publicly performed. They appreciate, what many amateurs apparently fail to appreciate, that to perform an author's work without his authority, and without payment of the fee required, is as dishonest morally and legally as it is to travel on a railway without buying a ticket.

So long as a play remains in copyright, which is for the duration of its author's life and for fifty years afterwards, it is private property; and until that time has expired the owner of the copyright has, in the words of the Copyright Act, "the sole right to produce or reproduce the work or any substantial part thereof in any material form whatsoever, to perform . . . the work . . . in public"—or to exploit or make use of it in any way. The Act contains another provision which is often overlooked and which might with advantage be mentioned here. It is to the effect that any person who, for his private profit, permits a theatre or other place of entertainment to be used for the performance in public of a work without the consent of the owner of the copyright is also guilty of infringement, unless he was not aware and had no reasonable ground for suspecting that the performance would be an infringement.

Amateurs and owners of halls would also be well advised to remember that the plaintiff in a successful action of infringement, following an unauthorized performance, is normally awarded an injunction, damages, and costs, and to bear in mind the fact that the two latter items jointly are often more than ten times the amount in return for which they could have obtained the necessary authority to perform the play had they applied for it before the performance.

A further point that is not widely enough known is that a play reading is in law a "performance" of the play, and may not, unless it is "private and domestic" in character, be given without permission.

A large proportion of those responsible for what may be termed casual amateur performances, such as performances organized at schools or on behalf of charity, are, incredible as it may seem, certainly blissfully unaware that an author's play cannot be appropriated with impunity; but the frequency with which an injured tone is adopted when the impending performance is discovered and the fee demanded provides striking evidence of the extraordinary inability of ordinary people to understand the principle of property as applied to something less tangible than an oak table. Even more shocking are the cases of vicars and head mistresses who, conscious of the fact that what they are proposing to do is both illegal and immoral, try to evade payment of the author's fee by keeping their performance as dark a secret as possible. It does not seem to occur to them that playwrights no less than wheelwrights have to live on the proceeds of what they create, and that playwrights can no more afford to allow free use of their plays than theatrical costumiers of their costumes. Nor have those responsible for amateur performances, the proceeds from which are to be devoted to some charity, the slightest justification for assuming that the author of the play concerned will be any more willing to forgo his fee than the costumiers or the printers of the programme. Even if the charity is one in which the author is likely to be interested the proper procedure is to leave it to him to decide what sum, if any, he will contribute. He is far more likely to be generous if no attempt is made to force his hand.

One very real difficulty with which amateurs have often had to contend has been that of discovering to whom they should address inquiries in connexion with the play which they wish to perform. Generally, when the play is published, a note on the fly-leaf provides the necessary particulars. In the absence of such a note a letter to the publishers will usually elicit the name and address of the copyright owner or his agent. Failing that, the best course is to communicate with the League of British Dramatists, 84 Drayton Gardens, London, S.W.10, of which nearly all practising playwrights are members. The League will also in most cases be able to furnish information as to dates on which recent plays are likely to become available for amateur performance; for it must be remembered that, especially in the case of plays which have had or are to have professional runs of tours, the manager has usually insisted on the inclusion of a clause in the contract forbidding the release of the play for performance by amateurs until a certain specified date.

In conclusion, I would again emphasize that the important thing is for amateurs of all kinds to get their permission before they give or even announce their performances. Only when this becomes a rigid rule will dramatists as a whole become convinced that there are no longer grounds for their traditional attitude of mistrust. When that time comes, I have no hesitation in saying, amateurs will find dramatists ready enough to treat them with the sympathy and consideration they expect, and to show the practical interest in the Amateur Movement which is essential if it is to be a movement forward.

D. Kilham Roberts

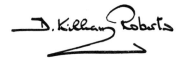

B

BROADCASTING AND THE THEATRE

BUSINESS ORGANIZATION AND MANAGEMENT

STARTING A SOCIETY
THE SECRETARY AND HIS WORK
THE ACTING MANAGER
THE TREASURER'S DUTIES
ADVERTISING AND PUBLICITY

Charles Nicol, Glasgow

JOSEPH MACLEOD

BROADCASTING AND THE THEATRE

JOSEPH MACLEOD, Former Announcer, B.B.C., Author of "The New Soviet Theatre," "Actors Across the Volga," etc.

THE fundamental difference between a radio play and a stage play lies in the separation of performers from audience. This separation gives radio drama both advantages and disadvantages in relation to the theatre.

The worst disadvantage is that the audience is scattered and cannot play its normal part in the performance. Listeners may laugh, but cannot by doing so help a comedian with his timing. They may be deeply stirred, but the tragic actor never feels their emotion and can draw no strength from it. In his grief or fear or jealousy he is a pin-point of humanity, not the quivering voice of hundreds.

Television extends our methods of broadcasting; in its absence the player remains deprived of several acting tools: limbs, face, bodily relationship to other players. Charm in a charming figure must somehow be centred in the voice. Grace turns into a matter of vowel and consonant. On the other side, a sinister appearance has to be suggested by the vocal cords. All these factors throw a special strain on some of an actor's physical developments and quite disregard others. This would not matter much, if characters were mere types; but there are characters in drama, as in life, whose outward surface belies their inner nature: a heart of gold behind a harsh voice, or a vicious resentment of mankind lurking under an attractive one. In such cases the radio actor's tone has to attempt complexities almost impossible.

The author or adapter soon finds the limitations of the radio. He must plan for the ear only. It is true that some playwrights are more sensitive to sound than sight. Ostrovsky is said to have listened to his own first nights out of sight of the stage, in order to judge the performance of the players. Bernard Shaw, at any rate in his later plays, places the interplay of thought in words and the changing of emotion in sounds above the mechanics of the visual playwright. The radio playwright has a chance to extend this latest development of the stage; but he has no visual stagecraft to rely upon at all. His climaxes cannot be expressed by sudden exits or entrances. Ernest in full mourning for his imaginary friend Bunbury misses the rich comic effect Wilde planned for the stage. W. J. Turner's man in a diver's suit because eating the popomack has given him an offensive smell would not be funny on the air. Clever production of reactions from the other characters certainly might momentarily amuse the listener, but not for long, and not as vividly as it amuses a stage audience. For laughter is largely the result of *tempo* and the ear has to kindle the imagination before the vision amuses. That peculiarly "radiogenic" humour heard in ITMA depends to some extent on a quick response due to familiarity.

For the same reason, crowd scenes on the air are seldom effective. The ear lacking visual aid to selection fails to sort out quick and confused sounds.

Scenery and lighting also are lacking; and with these, much of the easiest method of establishing or intensifying "atmosphere." A good stage set, well lit, can be emotional as well as realistic. On the air such atmosphere must be provided by a narrator, or by suggestion through music, or sound effects. The margin of error in the last two is great owing to the different emotional or associational values put by different listeners on a Sibelius symphony or a dripping tap. In narration also there is a variety of reactions to any one voice. The opening narration, which sets the stage, is comparable with the rise of a curtain before people in the audience have quite relinquished their own lives and entered into those on the stage. Hence staff announcers are frequently used for this function; whereas actors' voices of certain quality can prepare a more "stagey" atmosphere, as, for instance, to introduce crook plays.

Lastly, although it is possible to give perspective to the voice, by the use of different microphones, or by standing speakers at varying distances from one microphone, or by inserting an artificial "echo" to give hollowness for ghost scenes or certain outdoor effects, nevertheless, the range of these is restricted. During the Second Great War British broadcasting changed from the American method of using several studios of varying resonance, to the German method of "multiple microphones," that is to say, several microphones in a large single studio screened from one another. This does not mean, however, that the producer "conducts" the performance. Positions and intonations are planned beforehand. The performance operates by cue-lights. Most British producers no longer assume personal control of the mixer panel. Their work is finished when the transmission light comes on steady red, just as a stage producer's is, or ideally should be, finished, when the curtain rises.

These very disadvantages, however, contain in themselves advantages from the invisibility of the performers. The burden of meaning falls on the spoken word: and words are very ready to undertake this burden.

The listener's ear, which in many educated people's lives to-day is apt to lag behind the eye as a means of receiving impressions and communications, has grown more sensitive since radio entered the home. If radio drama gives a possibility of more naturalistic speech, or half-speech of grunt, sigh, mumble, or gurgle, than is possible in an auditorium, so does it demand a greater accuracy in the use of words. The difference is noticeable when the undistinguished dialogue of a Hollywood sound track is broadcast. Lacking the facial "registering" of emotion for which the dialogue was written, the listener finds the result thin and the silences meaningless. On the other hand, poetic dialogue comes into its own. Accuracy of epithet or metaphor, the utterly "right" word, are able to carry full force because of the lack of sight. Undistracted, the ear ministers to the brain's associations. Alone, or in a small intimate circle, the listener's memories and subconscious motives have full play. Archibald MacLeish's superb radio play *The Fall of a City* in 1937 showed the effectiveness of verse as a radio medium, provided it is not mere verse for study.

This quickening of listeners' imagination can be utilized in other ways peculiar to radio.

First, time may become fluid. The cinema technique of the "flashback" to a previous experience or epoch, sometimes possible on the stage though apt to be clumsy, can be extended on the air till a character is living in several periods at once. This is frequently done in "feature" productions, that is to say, actuality or documentary programmes, where a narrator or historical personage travels backwards or forwards through several centuries. On the air he can even gather fellow travellers from several ages as he goes. On the stage this would result in a mere animated museum.

Space too can be fluid. The ends of the earth can be evoked in a few seconds, faster even than is possible on the screen. And so can character. A man can change his whole imagined appearance, costume, face, even his body, if not as fast as thought, at any rate as fast as speech. He may grow wings or turn into a snowman or a tree. There is no limit to fantasy on the air. On stage or screen such changes are tricks: the audience are suspicious of them, ceasing to "suspend their disbelief." On the air they do not seem to be tricks, because the listener himself is performing them in his head. Or a voice can even be just a voice, without a defined character although for psychological reasons it is rare that a voice without a face does not set up some impression of personality, usually visual, in the listener's imagination.

Similarly, places, scenery, nature, can become personified to an extent only dreamed of by the most stylish of classical poets. A tree, river, country, period, idea, or tool can speak with its own voice. On a more realistic plane, too, the radio has opportunities for locality denied to the stage. The very first play ever written for British broadcasting, *Danger*, by Richard Hughes, in January, 1924, was located in a coal mine in utter darkness after an explosion. No other dramatic form could have attempted this.

The most important of radio's advantages in drama is that of communicating a thought-process. On the stage, except in highly stylized productions, the "aside" jars on a modern audience. Out of its realistic convention the audience awakes to the fact of performance, and the full force of the spoken thought fails. On the air this is not so. The microphone can be made to "pan" like a cine-camera inside the very mind of a man or woman. Either the character speaks in a low confidential tone close to the microphone; or, synthetically, thoughts become actualized, vocal, re-enacting remembered incidents or creating dreams. Nor is this limited to plays specially written for the purpose. Works of great authors with a deep insight into the human mind, like Shakespeare's or Ibsen's, sometimes acquire a deeper performance from the very absence of visual qualities, despite the visual conditions for which they were designed. This may be because the listener is undisturbed by the reactions of his neighbours; or, because of some predisposition of the eye in a theatre, views a character like Gregers Werle from the angle of whatever other character most appeals to the particular spectator. Such identification is not so easy on the air, where the mind tends to forget characters which are not actually speaking. Concentration on each character in turn allows of greater depth in the understanding of them.

Indeed, there are few limits to the range of the microphone's curiosity, in time, space, or intensity. Life, whether human or animal, chemistry, physics, and all the branches of science are at its disposal as dramatic material. The pity is that its rewards do not attract the most celebrated authors to write for it, except occasionally. One live performance is the normal; two are fairly frequent; three or more are rare. The radio script writer is, therefore, much in the position of the playwright in the early nineteenth century who seldom expected royalties on more than a very few performances. As a result, radio scripts are generally written by staff authors who are craftsmen more than creative artists; and the greater portion of radio drama consists of adaptations from stage or bookshelf.

Nevertheless, in the hands of creative artists more interested in new mediums than in financial results, the radio drama is capable of big things. One of its conveniences is its length, which may be anything from fifteen minutes' duration to two hours, after which the ear gets tired. The "chronicle" or episodic play, so tiresome to British playgoers though a favourite in Soviet Russia, is specially suited to broadcasting. The "serial," too, since its try-out in *The Count of Monte Cristo* in 1938 attracted thousands of listeners to radio drama, just as the cowboy or crook serial attracted thousands to the early picture palace. During the Second Great War these two forms fused together in a serial called *Front Line Family*, modelled on the Constanduros *English Family Robinson* of 1938. This was a remarkable piece of radio drama. Intended for listeners overseas to hear what life was like in Britain, it ran every day throughout the War. Authors, producers, actors, actresses, came and went—but the story and the family continued. It was the story of an ordinary family, part English, part Scottish, and the ordinary experiences they enjoyed or endured. Under different authors, different aspects of the characters emerged—but they were the same people. At one period adventure became a little too prominent, and the story turned into a melodrama. Another change of author, however, and the even tenor was resumed. Quite simple, completely sincere, sometimes a little sentimental, often deeply moving, it was in the aptest form a rich exploration, by the dramatic muse, of the lives of ordinary people.

Radio drama is the property of the ordinary people, and serves them best. There are neither stalls nor boxes. It belongs to everybody. There is neither greasepaint nor tinsel. It performs in the heart. There is no sense of that festivity which has accompanied theatrical performances since before the days of Aeschylus, for it takes place among normal familiar everyday things and people: in the home.

Joseph Macleod.

BUSINESS ORGANIZATION and MANAGEMENT

H. P. HOLLINGDRAKE, REGINALD A. RAWLINGS and
A. H. SEXTON, Director National Operatic and Dramatic Society

INTRODUCTION

JAMES R. GREGSON

AN amateur society that cannot exist without a subsidy is a failure; so also is the society that cannot make a profit, or cover expenses, out of the public sales of its performances. The most experimental amateur theatre should be self-supporting. But it is on the selling side that most amateur societies experience failure, even though they have the advantage of local goodwill. The Amateur Movement kept the theatre and the stage alive in many provincial areas during the bleak period between the two Great Wars and, although they have no longer to call on an army of ticket-selling helpers, the problem of selling drama is as acute and important as ever. Most amateur societies have dropped the undignified form of appeal of "Please buy this because it's ours and we're friends of yours," but they still hesitate to adopt the forthright attitude of "Buy this because it's worth buying." That hesitancy must go. If the Amateur Movement is to play its part in a Dramatic Renaissance, as it did in the nineteen-twenties, it must tackle, wholeheartedly and scientifically, this problem of selling.

On local goodwill it may bank with certainty. The West End theatre has its "star" with a following. It has also first call upon certain well-known and popular playwrights whose works have a definite appeal. These advantages do not, however, ensure success in every case, and they are not as constant a factor in the success of the amateur theatre as local patriotism can be, if it is rightly fostered.

Sound salesmanship, in other words, intelligent and live business direction, gains and holds local patriotism and support. "Direction" implies a "management" that begins at the beginning and does not concern itself merely with preparing or auditing a balance sheet. The first essential of good salesmanship is to have something good to sell. To all amateur societies I would say—

Do not be afraid of giving your public the best—the best plays of every time and type, and the best presentation of them within your powers and resources. Let your programme be as varied and catholic as possible. Do not be exclusively high brow, low brow, middle brow, or any other brow. Do not specialize in dead masters and make your theatre a museum. Do not become obsessed with "light entertainment" or try to compete with the music-hall. Do not concentrate on modern morbidists and turn your stage into an operating theatre. Do not attach yourself to any particular "school," or you will find your public playing truant. In your selection of plays, look neither for literary merit first nor for bizarre dramatic technique first, second, or third. Go for the play, tragedy or comedy, that fulfils the first purpose of the theatre, that fires and releases the emotions, and, fusing your audience either by tears or laughter, makes them as gods, seeing all, comprehending all, and while the curtain is up, forgetting everything about themselves and the life they have temporarily left behind them. In short, give your public a bit of everything except a label to hang round your neck. Keep them guessing about what you will tackle next. Better to die of shock than boredom!

James R. Gregson

This means that you will have to keep your eyes wide open for new and rising playwrights. Do not wait until a dramatist is an established success before you tackle his work. Do not follow too slavishly, or at too great distance, any mode or movement. Try to get in first. Be prepared to take a risk with a new writer—especially if he is a "local." Try to build "regional" drama. Reflect upon the way in which the experimentalism of the Irish Players has enriched our dramatic literature. It may be your good fortune, your high privilege, to discover a new Sean O'Casey and to make your stage his apprentice-laboratory. You can afford the risk much better than the West End professional manager. It is easier for you than it was for C. B. Cochran with Eugene O'Neill, or Sir Barry Jackson with Eden Phillpotts.

Extend this experimentalism. Keep an eye open not only for new playwrights, but also for new forms and themes and new ways of presenting them. Before the Second Great War, the "living newspaper" made its first appearance. During the War, the "documentary" was introduced. The possibilities of these and others have still to be fully exploited and developed.

Lack of money need never cripple your scenic experiments. Radio and film, combined with human-actor presentation, give ample scope for invention and for making the traffic of the theatre even more fluid and fast-moving than anything we have yet seen—even more supple than the stage for which Shakespeare wrote.

I once ran an amateur theatre where my programme for one season included nine plays of Shakespeare, Ibsen's "Peer Gynt" and "A Doll's House," plays by Strindberg, Shelley, Sudermann, and Maeterlinck, modern English comedies, and operas by Verdi and Ethel Smythe. The productions lacked precision and finish—perhaps almost everything except vigour and life. We began with half-empty houses of puzzled slum-dwellers who had seen little real theatre; we finished with full houses, extended runs, and a growing clientele of playgoers from other parts of the city and from the towns outside it.

One of the most successful little theatres in the North—amateur, of course—made a profit of over £200 in one season with a programme that included plays by Shaw, Beaumont and Fletcher, Clemence Dane, Capek, and the first amateur production of two comedies by new playwrights. Another season opened with a new first play by a local author, then produced Sheridan's "The Rivals," and followed with a thriller, a modern farce, a burlesque of Victorian melodrama, a French fantasy (specially translated for the society) and a Shakespearian production. (That society began its activities in a hired hall and later owned its own theatre without either debts or debentures.)

Programmes of this quality are not only easy to sell but also to advertise because you can tell the truth about them, and truth is a sound foundation of publicity. Tell your audience as much as you can about your wares, but avoid creating the impression that you are educating them. Do not tell them too much and do not raise unfounded expectations. Let them know truthfully that they can reasonably expect to be interested, amused, and excited. In short, make your theatre a playhouse and advertise it as such. Business and Art and a little artfulness must go hand in hand if the Amateur Movement is to continue to fulfil the promise of its childhood and to play its full part—a leading role, perhaps—in what every lover of the theatre hopes for in the future, another, and an even greater, English Drama Renaissance.

James R. Gregson.

STARTING A SOCIETY

Several factors must be reckoned with before a new amateur society can come into being with reasonable hopes of success.

Enthusiasm and artistic capacity are dealt with elsewhere; finance and administration are equally important, yet neglect or mismanagement in these two departments is not uncommon.

Few amateur societies have what is known as "legal entity"—they cannot sue or be sued except through their members collectively or individually. It is an indictable offence, in British law, to be "without visible means of support," and though there are cumbrous means by which creditors may obtain their rights from the members of a society, those means usually reflect badly on the society and often unfairly on individuals. Outside the amateur stage, few ventures start without capital or tangible assets. It cannot be other than commercially immoral for a company of amateurs to set about the formation of an operatic or dramatic society (particularly the former with its heavy costs) without sound backing of assets or firm guarantees from substantial persons. Before the first show contracts will have to be entered into with traders, theatre proprietors, rights holders, etc., and the slogan of "all right on the night," bad as it is for the cast, is worse still for the treasurer.

There are several kinds of support or guarantee: in the case of smaller dramatic societies, especially in rural districts, these are adequately provided by local interest, curiosity, or the patronage of the "nobility and gentry"; whilst those societies, also, which are anchored to a particular church or chapel and give their performances in their own schoolrooms rent free under benefit of clergy may be said to enjoy comparative immunity from liability to disaster through the assured support of their own friends and parishioners. For it is an odd fact that there is yet a vast number of people of average intelligence whose consciences forbid the sinful temptation of the theatre but permit, if they do not actually compel, their enjoyment of *Our Miss Gibbs*, or some other ghost of a bygone gaiety, in their parish schoolroom, provided that it is labelled an "Entertainment" in aid of some parochial fund.

It is, then, the large, full-size operatic and dramatic societies which remain to be considered, and whose means of support are most in need of examination. It would be idle to pretend, as it would be impossible to acquire, a full knowledge of the financial methods and results of all the larger societies in the United Kingdom. Many of them, particularly on the operatic side, contribute substantial sums annually to local or national charities, and judged by these figures they would appear to be financially sound. But enough is known to enable one critic at all events to state boldly that many of these excellent results are due more to good luck than to good management. Consider for a moment a typical example.

An operatic society of 70 acting members enters into signed contracts by its committee to rent a theatre, pay acting rights, hire scenery and costumes, and engage a producer, the total liabilities amounting to £800. There are no reserve funds, and no subscribers except, it may be, 50 patrons or vice-presidents at half-a-guinea apiece. A system of ticket-hawking by the acting members is forced upon them, involving traps for the unwary by the Entertainments Tax authorities later on, but beyond this there is no other visible means of support or guarantee that the costs of production will be met on the due date. All that is possible is to place implicit faith in a fickle public to pay into the box office sufficient funds to prevent disaster. Is "commercial immorality" too harsh a term to apply to trading ventures of this sort? And, if not, what is the remedy? Criticism should be constructive as well as candid.

The remedy is to convert an uncertain and unreliable audience into a reliable and permanent one by enrolling annual subscribers of fixed amounts entitling them to the corresponding value in booked seats for the performances. The amount subscribed should not be less than 75 per cent of the total estimated expenses, and this sum will be in normal circumstances ample, together with the cash taken at the theatre doors, to meet all liabilities and leave a balance in hand for disposal.

As it may be doubted whether the remedy suggested can be carried into practical application, let it be said plainly that it can be and has been for over 30 years by many of the largest and oldest operatic societies in the kingdom. The subscriptions are for four or six seats; and any combination of these alternatives is permissible for family parties or other groups; for example, eight seats are secured by two subscriptions for four seats; ten seats by one subscription for four seats, and one for six seats. The seats may be booked on any one night or spread over the period of the performances.

The reason for the popularity of this system is that whilst subscribers pay nothing extra for their seats they have the privilege of booking them before the plans are open to the general public, and the seats are guaranteed.

The result is, therefore, attained of securing a permanent audience in the stalls and dress circle with the additional security of having a comfortable sum in the bank before the curtain rises on the opening night.

The advantages of the system, both to the society and the subscribers, must be obvious; what may not be so conspicuously obvious is the protection provided for the society's trade creditors.

Good Mrs. Beeton in her excellent book of cookery recipes was ever careful to leave little to chance in the ingredients she deemed necessary for the proper composition of her culinary masterpieces, except it might be some simple seasonings "to taste." We shall do well to be equally careful to omit or overlook no essential or desirable ingredient in the formation of an amateur operatic or dramatic society; and it is the purpose here to offer to those who may have such a project in mind some helpful suggestions that have been proved by the test of long experience.

It will be convenient to assume that an operatic society is contemplated, as, although some modifications in detail may be possible in the case of a dramatic society, the principle remains the same. For example, an operatic society usually gives one big production for six nights once a year in a fully equipped theatre, whereas a dramatic society may give one or more plays for three nights apiece in a suitable hall with a fit-up stage. Hence the formation of an operatic society with a personnel of 50 or 60 acting members is a much larger and more costly venture than that of a dramatic society, and requires handling on a larger scale. It is a matter of proportion and not of principle.

The two main ingredients are, beyond any question, first the amateur artists themselves or a nucleus from which a group or society could be developed; and, second, an adequate number of local persons willing or anxious to support them financially. The vital need for this second ingredient cannot be too strongly emphasized. These two essentials must exist before any progress or development is possible, and it would not be profitable to discuss which of the two is the greater—for if one be the greater the other must be the lesser; better that they should be deemed equal and interdependent. That is to say, and to lay down as an axiom, that unless there is sufficient talent available of a quality that collectively under competent coaching would merit the support of the public, or, on the other hand, assuming the talent is available, unless the public support expressed in terms of annual subscriptions is adequate, the project should be abandoned.

It will be noted that in defining the word talent to mean talent of definite stage value and of definite box-office value, the qualification has been induced by the knowledge that the public of our time resents, and refuses to support, entertainments of inferior merit and has long since demanded performances from the amateur which, in their ensemble of *décor* and technique, are excelled only by the London stage itself. Hence, to adapt to the subject Sir Richard Terry's aphorism on singing, there is a great distinction between the urge to act and the ability to act, and it is only those who have highly developed both the urge and the ability who are seriously to be considered.

Assume now that the talent is available and that diplomatic inquiries have revealed some measure of interest amongst the leading citizens and notables of the town with promises of support; the next step must be the tentative inception of the society by means of a resolution passed at an *ad hoc* meeting of persons *invited to attend* by the promoters of the venture, one of whom would act as temporary secretary. This method has a great advantage over an advertised town's meeting in that it excludes the almost predictable election of a committee composed of utterly useless people, or at all events the wrong people. The resolution might well be in this form—

"*That it is desirable to establish an amateur operatic (dramatic) society in* (*name of town*) *and that, subject to adequate financial support being secured by the registration of annual subscribers, this meeting pledges itself thereto.*"

If that resolution is carried, it should be further resolved whether or not the society is to be constituted upon a charitable basis; that is to say, are *the whole* of the profits from its performances to be devoted to charities or, alternatively, is the group to be "partly educational" (note that it is the audience (not the players) which must be "educated") and profit-making eliminated? If not, no exemption from Entertainments Duty can be obtained. A further alternative is for the venture to be free and untrammelled by the dictates of the Commissioners of Customs and Excise and to work only for the good of the movement, to build up reserves, and to be charitable or educational or just entertaining, as funds and one's own policy permit.

The selection of the first committee is of the greatest importance and the utmost care should be given to it. Opinions may differ as to the wisdom of making definite appointments at the preliminary meeting, but, provided there are available persons of known ability and energy for the work that lies ahead, it would seem to be prudent to enrol them at once with power to add such others as may be deemed desirable if and when the project matures.

The preliminary meeting would then be adjourned for three weeks or a month to enable the secretary (*pro tem.*) to draw up a circular letter setting out the aims and objects of the proposed society and inviting the addressee to become an annual subscriber. It should be pointed out that until the response to the invitations is known no further progress can be made, and a definite date should be fixed for the receipt of replies. The letter should bear the names, as signatories, of the chairman of the preliminary meeting and the secretary *pro tem.*, and have a tear-off slip at the foot suitably printed for the use of the addressee.

As this is written with a keen desire to make it helpful in small as well as large matters, and as the success of the venture depends entirely upon the success of the appeal letter, a few general hints to the secretary will not be out of place at this point. To be effective the letter should have what is known as "pull"—that is, it must have a personal appeal to the recipient. Begin your first sentence and most of the others with the word "you" and not "I" or "We," and use short paragraphs instead of long ones. Let it be either printed, in clear plain type from one fount for all sizes of letter, or duplicated on good, but not expensive, paper, quarto, or foolscap size. Letter postage ($2\frac{1}{2}$d.) should be paid. The extra cost will be money well spent. So much advertising matter, catchpenny proposals, "accounts rendered," and other distressing printed circulars are daily delivered through letter boxes that scant attention, if any, is given to halfpenny or penny postal "junk." Your letter will be useless unless the recipient reads it. Remember, too, that there is a right and a wrong time for the posting and receipt of letters, and if in doubt, put yourself into the position of the addressee and view the problem from *his* angle. For instance, the circular letter you propose to send out is in the nature of a begging letter; at all events, it is a request for a money subscription. Clearly, it would be unfortunate if it was delivered to a business man at the end of a tiresome day. Letters of this kind should arrive by the first morning delivery and, for choice, in the middle of a week.

To illustrate, the appeal letter might be worded thus—

Dear Sir (or Madam),

You may be interested to hear of a movement in the town to form an amateur operatic society to present annually at the .... Theatre a musical play or light opera with a full company of local principals and chorus.

The advantages of such a society are many and varied, giving opportunity for the expression and development of local talent, social expansion, and the raising of funds for deserving causes.

You will realize, however, that to establish a society of this kind on a sound basis adequate support must be assured; already we have many promises, including His Worship the Mayor, Sir.................................... Dr. .... (etc., etc.), and we are still further encouraged by a unanimous resolution passed at a preliminary meeting held at .... on .... that an operatic society should be formed, provided support be forthcoming.

May we, therefore, invite you to join us by becoming an annual subscriber to the society, if or when formed, and to be good enough to signify your decision on the attached slip not later than...

Yours faithfully,

. . . .
Chairman of the Preliminary Meeting.

. . . .
Hon. Secretary (*pro tem.*).

Tear off

. . . .

I am (am not) willing to become an annual subscriber to the proposed...Amateur Operatic Society of an amount not exceeding £ s. d. which will entitle me to booked seats to that value in each year.

Name (Mr., Mrs. or Miss) . . . .
Address . . . .
. . . .

We will assume that in response to the appeal letter sufficient pledges of financial support have now been received. By the word sufficient is meant a number varying according to the estimated all-in cost of an average production under local conditions and bearing a substantial proportion thereto. For it can with reasonable confidence be predicted that if the society develops on right lines the number of subscribers will steadily increase as the date of the performances approaches.

The acting secretary will now summon a further meeting and to save expense this can be done by advertisement in the local Press as an invitation to all interested persons to attend. There is the additional advantage that a reporter will probably be sent to "cover" the meeting, which is the start of the publicity campaign.

At that meeting the chairman, or the acting secretary, will give a report or précis of what has taken place up to that date and will announce the result of the circularization. He should also, for the benefit of those who were not present at the first meeting, reiterate the aims and objects of the society without undue prolixity. After which the following resolution should be proposed, seconded, and carried formally—

> "That a society to be known as The .... Amateur Operatic Society for the performance of operas, musical plays, and similar works (in aid of local charities or with "partly educational objects"?) be established."

From that moment the society comes into being.

No further constructive work remains to be done at that meeting, for, if my advice has been taken, the chairman will be able to announce that the nucleus of a committee has already been appointed at the earlier meeting and that additional members and officers for the first year will be selected by them. The opportunity should, however, be taken to enrol more subscribers amongst those present, as there may be many to whom the circular letter has not been sent, or who have hesitated to reply.

The nucleus committee should meet immediately to elect a chairman, to appoint officers, and to co-opt additional committee men, if necessary. Note: *avoid large committees.* The usual officers are—

President	Hon. Treasurer
Vice-President	Hon. Secretary
Hon. Musical Director (or Conductor)	Hon. Acting (or Business) Manager
Hon. Stage Manager	

The Auditor, whether honorary or paid, is *not* an officer. Some societies, for reasons of their own, sub-divide some of the duties of their officers and appoint one or more of the following—

Business Secretary	Programme Secretary
Correspondence Secretary	Chorus Master (as distinct from Conductor)
Patronage Secretary	
Publicity Manager, and the like	

Little can be said in favour of this system; on the business side the multiplicity of officials or semi-officials tends to the overlapping of duties, which at best are difficult to separate, and on the musical side productions have been marred by the Conductor's unfamiliarity with the work as rehearsed by the Chorus Master in collaboration with the Producer. Much better is it to appoint a competent Secretary to undertake the whole of the business management, with a capable Assistant Secretary for dictation, typing, and committee routine; and the Conductor should be his own Chorus Master.

The President and Vice-President may quite usefully be figure heads, though not necessarily; they should both be persons of local eminence or distinction to attest the *bona fide* status of the society.

The Treasurer holds a position in an amateur society to which there is no professional counterpart, but he appears through long custom to have survived as a link between the Acting Manager and the society's bankers. Originally he acted as the accountant to the society, but modern methods have so simplified all book-keeping that it would add very little to the sum total of the secretarial work. On the other hand, a Treasurer has to keep a guard on all moneys paid out as well as those paid in to the bank, and in some societies he gives the Acting Manager assistance in checking up the nightly final return at the theatre, or the receipts from acting members and others for ticket vouchers sold in advance. It will be found convenient to appoint as Hon. Treasurer an official of the local bank at which the society's account is kept.

The Stage Manager is concerned wholly with the rehearsal and staging of the show, and in a well-ordered society he should be under the supervision of the committee in matters of expenditure.

With regard to the Secretary and Acting Manager, experience has proved that the duties of these two officials—particularly where a long list of subscribers has to be handled—are so interlocked that there is substantial advantage in their being entrusted to one man and not two, the Secretary becoming a dual officer as "Hon. Secretary and Acting Manager." It follows that the Secretary cannot also be an acting member on the stage; and indeed it may be laid down that a Secretary never should be. On the principle that "a cobbler should stick to his last," no man, however gifted, can be a success on both sides of the curtain at once. This rule should *never* be broken in an operatic society.

The Committee, when completed, should not exceed 10 members in all, including the officers, and this number gives ample opportunity for the acting members to be directly represented upon it—a useful provision, effecting a liaison between the rank and file and the governing body. It should be understood that members of Committee and officers hold their appointments from year to year, that is from their election until the close of the next Annual General Meeting at which they are re-elected or their successors appointed.

At their first Meeting the Committee must take steps to draw up their Rules and Constitution, and to obtain the requisite number of acting members. If sufficient applications have not already been received the Secretary should be instructed to insert an advertisement in the local paper—

> "..................Amateur Operatic Society has vacancies for good voices in all parts. Applications *in writing only* to the Secretary, Mr.................. (address).................."

Note the words "in writing only," especially if the Secretary is a married man!

The determination of the Rules is best dealt with by a sub-committee in the first instance, as it demands great care and concentration, expert guidance if at all possible, and skill in drafting not unworthy of a lawyer. Here space will only permit one or two practical hints on which reliance can be placed—

1. The Constitution must state clearly whether the society is a charitable organization, and, if so, that *the whole* of its profits (if any) will be devoted to charity, or is "partly educational" and not founded for the making of profit, if exemption from Entertainment Duty is sought.

2. That the Committee, and not the acting members, shall select and cast the works selected for production.

3. That before admission as acting members *all* applicants must submit to an audition before the *full Committee*.

4. That all music rehearsals shall be under the sole control of the Hon. Musical Director and all stage rehearsals under the sole control of the coach.

(This rule prevents unpleasant incidents between the Conductor and Producer in the matter of metronome tempi as rehearsed before staging begins. Remember that many amateur conductors are choir masters rather than chorus masters and are apt to forget that a musical comedy is not an oratorio!)

5. That acting members must attend not less than 75 per cent of the rehearsals in order to take part in the performances.

6. That any matter not provided for in the Rules as drawn up shall be dealt with by the Committee.

THE SECRETARY AND HIS WORK

The secretary is the most important official in a well-ordered amateur society, and, whether paid or unpaid, he ranks in responsibility equally with the producer.

That this is not yet generally realized is proved by the frequency with which societies announce a change of secretary. The obvious and not unfair inference, after making all allowances for unforeseen difficulties, is that secretarial appointments are far too lightly made and given to men of no outstanding qualifications for the position, with the result that each year there are many resignations from those who have discovered the real nature of the task that is allotted to them.

The ideal secretary is a born organizer; cool, clear-headed, and methodical in all his work; one whose instinct in a critical or difficult situation instantly senses the "next best thing" to be done and restores order out of incipient chaos. He must know something of ordinary business methods and office routine, be able to conduct the society's correspondence in clear and grammatical English, and record the proceedings at committee meetings in his minute book. In addition, he should have tact, courtesy without servility, and an innate and constant love for his work and the society he serves.

There are such secretaries up and down the country; quiet men working unobtrusively, but splendidly, for sheer love of their hobby. Hence, it is difficult to be sympathetic towards societies with troubles that are largely of their own making through the selection of the wrong type of person as their principal and most responsible officer. Further, it may reasonably be suspected that the appointment of men who are either incompetent or unwilling to undertake the whole of the secretarial duties is the reason why those duties in many societies are subdivided amongst a number of semi-officials with impressive titles. If there is one officer whose value to his society increases in proportion to his length of service it is surely the secretary, and there can be no gain, but definite loss, by replacements every two or three years.

Let the selection of the secretary, therefore, be made with the greatest possible care and understanding, for upon it will depend the smooth working and a good deal of the success of the society's affairs. Select, if possible, a man who has ample leisure, no other serious hobby, and his own office staff.

In the hope that they may be found useful by those who are in the earlier stages of their secretarial career a few notes—gleanings from a long experience—are offered.

The secretary should remember that he is the official spokesman or mouthpiece of the society, and that he owes his position to the acting members in annual meeting, but derives his authority from the committee. He has a duty to both. He is not the servant of the committee, but its representative, through whom it acts, issues orders, and controls the affairs of the society.

All official letters, therefore, on behalf of the society should be signed by the secretary, and should be worded, "I am authorized (or directed) by the committee to . . ." A secretary will do well not to sign important letters unless or until he has the authority of the committee to do so. Copies of all letters, however unimportant they may appear to be, should be made and filed. The official notepaper should be post 4to, size 10 in. × 8 in., with square envelopes to match, $5\frac{1}{4}$ in. × $4\frac{1}{4}$ in., the letter being folded twice only. The heading should be neatly set out, with the name of the society in plain bold type and other matter in smaller sizes of the same fount. The name of the secretary and his address for correspondence should be prominent.

A sound system of filing letters should be adopted and maintained. Unfiled correspondence should not be allowed to accumulate. At the end of each season it is a great advantage to re-sort the letters for final storage under subject headings, and to number and index them for easy reference.

A loose-leaf minute book with numbered pages is better than a bound book. Minutes should be numbered and indexed.

In recording minutes scrupulous accuracy is required, as much may depend subsequently upon the actual wording of a resolution in the minute book, and an ambiguous phrase may have awkward consequences. Minutes should not be elaborated into a précis of the arguments and discussions at a committee meeting, but in important or controversial matters a short summary of the debate may, with advantage, be recorded.

The following skeleton will serve as a guide—

Minutes of a Committee Meeting
held at............on.........the............of............19...

PRESENT: Mr. A. B. in the Chair; Messrs. C. D., E. F., G. H.

MINUTES: (1) The Minutes of the last Committee Meeting were read, approved, and signed.

CORRESPONDENCE: (2) (*a*) Read letter from Messrs. X, & Co., submitting samples of cheap printing.
RESOLVED: That the offer be not entertained; and, further, that all orders for printing shall be placed, as far as possible, with local firms.
(*b*) Read Secretary's reply to Messrs. Y. Z. & Co. as instructed under Minute 10 of the previous Meeting.
RESOLVED: That the reply be approved.

THEATRE RENT: (3) The Secretary reported his interview with Mr. M. with regard to the rent of the Frivolity Theatre, and that a renewal of the previous contract was offered.
RESOLVED: That the Secretary be empowered to accept the offer and to sign the appropriate contract.

Make a habit of reading *all* correspondence, both letters received and those sent out, at committee meetings. The secretary writes in the name and at the direction of his colleagues, and it is courteous to let them hear how their instructions have been carried out. It also has a stimulating effect on the secretary's prose style.

A reputation for promptitude in replying to correspondence should be earned. Any person who has taken the trouble to write is entitled to the courtesy of an acknowledgment, if an immediate and complete reply is impossible; just as a secretary has the right to expect an acknowledgment of any information or assistance he has been able to give to another society. The secretary who pleads that he has not had time to write or type a three-line postcard will not be a great success.

In a large society where there are many subscribers in addition to acting members it is desirable for the secretary to have a supply of stock printed postcards to enable him to deal promptly with routine matters that do not require personal letters, such as notices of committee meetings, acknowledgments of applications for auditions, changes of address or resignations. A useful card for the last two is worded—

> "I have to acknowledge the receipt of your letter, and to state that your instructions have been carried out.
>
> ....
>
> Hon. Secretary."

This wording discloses nothing to the curious, and is a courteous and sufficient reply.

I have given merely an outline of a secretary's duties: many details must be left to suggest themselves, but the underlying principle is the same, whether the society be small or large. The aim of every secretary should be to be known as "the man who never forgets anything." He should keep a memorandum book and whenever a relevant thought occurs to him, jot it down at once.

Finally, *all documents* should be dated.

THE ACTING MANAGER

The acting manager is the official or representative of the society who is placed in control of the auditorium, or "the front of the house," as it is usually called. He is responsible for all arrangements for booking seats, whatever system may be most suitable; for the cash receipts at the box office and pay boxes; for the sale of programmes; and for the nightly "return" or complete statement of receipts at each performance.

He is in supreme command of "the house" from the theatre doors to the curtain, just as the stage manager is in command behind it. This is a strict rule that must not be infringed, and it is worth while elaborating or illustrating it, for unless it is fully understood friction and unpleasantness are bound to ensue. The theatre is divided into two separate and distinct portions, the auditorium and the stage, the pass doors communicating between them forming a barrier through which there is no passage from either side *without permission.* That is to say, the acting manager has no power to authorize any person to pass from the auditorium to the stage without the express knowledge and consent of the stage manager, nor can the latter grant permission for any person to pass from the stage or dressing rooms into the auditorium without the knowledge and consent of the acting manager. This rule must be scrupulously observed. The only exception to it is the personal privilege accorded to all officials of the society, who, if they are wise, will not avail themselves of it over-liberally.

To be a success as an acting manager it is necessary to realize that the society presenting the play or opera, and therefore dependent upon an audience for its existence, is in the position of a seller and not a buyer; and that the acting manager is the salesman. Upon him rests the responsibility of advertising his wares attractively and making them easy of access. Leaving for the present the subject of advertising, it is to the seating accommodation and the method of selling it that special attention should be concentrated. Whatever system of selling tickets of admission may be adopted, or tested as an experiment, one indispensable feature of it must be the ease and comfort with which a willing purchaser may be enabled to witness the entertainment. Finical rules or a suspicion of red tape methods must be avoided, not only in the booking of tickets of admission, but also in the theatre itself. Remember that each occupant of a seat is your guest, and not a mere number; and that a guest should be welcomed and not irritated or dragooned. It is usual to have a few voluntary assistants in a full-size theatre—not to supersede the regular theatre staff—but to undertake the sale of programmes, especially if they are of the modern souvenir type. Ten or a dozen smart stewards (with a chief steward in charge) in evening dress, distributed throughout the theatre, have been known to realize £100 by the sale of programmes during a week's performances (without matinée) in a Lancashire theatre. Some societies appoint a bevy of girls dressed *à la mode* or in the costume of the opera for the same purpose, but, for reasons that prudence forbids me to disclose, they have not proved in general experience so successful as their male competitors. The acting manager should appoint one of the stewards to organize the sale of programmes, i.e. to take responsibility for receiving and checking deliveries from the printers, to issue supplies nightly for sale, to tally programmes unsold, and to hand over the cash receipts to the acting manager or hon. treasurer.

Before I deal with the actual booking of seats I will refer to two important duties for which the acting manager is responsible: (1) the issue of "paper" and (2) the nightly "return." The latter is the record that is kept in duplicate of the total receipts of each performance. It is analysed in meticulous detail for every part of the theatre. Whether Entertainments Tax is payable or not, the return must account for every seat that is occupied at each performance and the price paid for it, the total agreeing with the total number of seats in the theatre, less the unoccupied and complimentary seats. Here note that, unless the tax is not payable, the tickets for the latter must be stamped "COMPLIMENTARY" across the face and the counterfoils must also be so stamped. A rubber stamp is generally used. To "paper the house" is to issue at the discretion of the acting manager a sufficient number of free passes for a performance where it is obvious, from the booking plans or local knowledge, that otherwise the company will play to a house so thin as to imperil the success of the entertainment. Only experience will guide the amateur as to the extent to which "papering" is politic: if it is too meagre it is of little use, but if it is over-lavish or indiscriminate it defeats its object by encouraging the professional "deadheads." It is a sound principle when issuing complimentary tickets to send them only to such persons as can be relied upon to use them and to appreciate the courtesy. Such institutions, for example, as the local infirmary, nursing homes, orphanages, and district nursing hostels should always be included in the "free list"; and I would also suggest to the acting manager that a couple of stalls—more if available—tactfully presented to the G.P.O. telephone operators through their lady supervisor "for services rendered" will always be welcomed—and repaid. If, as often happens, considerable papering is necessary on the Monday night of a week's run, a couple of seats allotted to each of the acting members will ensure a warmer audience than a chance collection of pay-box dodgers.

The acting manager must, amongst his multiple duties, see that reservations are made for the local Press on the opening night, and that the representatives are supplied with any information or items of public interest that it is desired to publish.

One or two useful hints may be offered to the inexperienced—

Ascertain from the stage manager *before opening* the approximate times of the intervals and the final curtain. You are sure to be asked.

Make notes each night of the *actual* times of ringing up, etc.

If possible—and it often is—ascertain the location of a doctor in the audience in case of need before or behind the curtain. Many doctors volunteer this information on arrival for their own convenience in anticipation of a telephone call.

Remember that your brief authority ends on the last night of the production: it is much better to exercise tact and leave the theatre staff to deal with any unpleasantness where personal or legal rights may be involved. But on all other matters your authority, though brief, is complete.

Having outlined the general nature of the duties of the acting manager, we must now pay attention to details. His main job is the business of selling and allotting space in the theatre or hall in which the production is taking place; otherwise, the booking of the seats. Audiences are fickle at all times, particularly those that patronize amateur shows, and the really prudent acting manager must make such arrangements for booking as will give the least possible trouble and inconvenience to all concerned.

Mainly, the problem is one of handling a large body of subscribers, each of whom is entitled to an agreed number of seats for the performances. Where, perhaps, 500 subscribers, all having rights and privileges, have to be pleased, what is the acting manager to do? He must deal as fairly as possible with each one. There must be no primitive "first come, first served" method. Unseemly rushes and ill-tempered queues of subscribers on inclement evenings are unnecessary. I offer here the details of a method that has stood the test of over 30 years in practice. Its basis is a ballot. I assume that 500 subscribers pay 30s. each annually for six seats at 5s. each, and that bookings may be made for any one performance in the week or spread over the full week if necessary. These subscribers are privileged to book seats before the plans are open to the general public; so a week before the booking dates a ballot is conducted.

A specimen circular letter that can be used is given in the next column.

Each subscriber's name is written on a small card and the cards are placed in a suitable bag. Corresponding numbers are placed in another bag. Double or multiple subscriptions demand a like number of members' cards in their appropriate bag. Each subscription is, therefore, guaranteed a number. Names and numbers are then drawn out of the respective bags, and the numbers are recorded on the prepared vouchers made out to subscribers. These have already been arranged in alphabetical order, and each member of the committee present has to deal with a section.

It is essential that such a ballot should be openly conducted by officers and acting members, with, if possible, a representative of the local Press. It would be better still if two of the subscribers themselves could draw the names and numbers.

——— Operatic Society

———

November, 19

"———————"

at the

Grand Theatre, ———, December 4th to 9th

DEAR SIR OR MADAM,

THE BALLOT FOR THE ORDER OF BOOKING SEATS WILL BE HELD ON ————————, AT THE ——— HOTEL, AT 6.30 p.m., AND A BOOKING VOUCHER STATING THE NUMBER YOU HAVE DRAWN WILL BE POSTED TO YOU THE SAME EVENING.

IT IS NOT NECESSARY FOR SUBSCRIBERS TO ATTEND THE BALLOT.

YOUR SUBSCRIPTION SHOULD BE PAID WHEN YOU BOOK YOUR SEATS ON ——— IN EXCHANGE FOR THE TICKETS TO WHICH YOU ARE ENTITLED, AND NOT BEFORE.

PLEASE NOTE THAT THE BOOKING WILL TAKE PLACE AT THE ————————

PLEASE NOTE ALSO THAT THERE WILL BE NO SEATS AVAILABLE FOR SUBSCRIBERS FOR THE MONDAY PERFORMANCE.

IN ORDER TO PREVENT ANY POSSIBLE DISAPPOINTMENT, SUBSCRIBERS ARE RESPECTFULLY REMINDED THAT THE SOCIETY DOES NOT ISSUE THEATRE TICKETS UNLESS SUBSCRIPTIONS ARE PAID.

THE AMOUNT OF YOUR SUBSCRIPTION IS —— ENTITLING YOU TO — SEATS IN THE DRESS CIRCLE OR STALLS AS AVAILABLE AT THE TIME OF BOOKING.

Yours faithfully,

————————

Hon. Acting Manager.

Addressed envelopes are ready for the insertion of the vouchers, and they are immediately sent out by post. Good organization and previous preparation will easily ensure this being done on the one evening.

——— AMATEUR OPERATIC SOCIETY

"——————————"

AT

THE GRAND THEATRE

—————————— 19

VOUCHER FOR SIX SEATS IN THE DRESS CIRCLE OR STALLS

——— Hon. Acting Manager.

This Voucher will not admit to the Theatre, but must be exchanged for Tickets as per the following instructions—

The Seat Plan will be open to Subscribers at ———— —————————— on ———— —————————— from ———— and on —————————— from ———— to ————.

As the Seat Plan will be open to the Public on THURSDAY, the ————, Seats cannot be guaranteed for Subscribers unless booked before that date.

SEATS MUST BE BOOKED IN THE ORDER OF THE NUMBERS BALLOTED FOR AND ACCORDING TO THE TIME TABLE ON THE ANNEXED SHEET.

YOUR NUMBER IS [ ]

These booking vouchers are the official instructions to the acting manager or his agents to issue to the subscribers six seat tickets each at the time, date, and place fixed for the booking, and the numbers drawn in the ballot show the order of precedence in which subscribers may book seats. On the booking voucher is printed a time-table of the approximate time at which it will be the turn of the subscriber to book. Subscribers with double or multiple subscriptions are permitted to book the whole of their seats on the lowest number drawn.

This scheme does not guarantee that seats will be available for any particular evening's performance, and those who draw high numbers in the ballot will have little or no chance of securing seats for the popular Friday or Saturday nights. It may be found that a few subscribers whose names are at the end of the list are unable to book seats for the only evening on which they can be present. Their subscriptions should be suspended for the season, and not treated as resignations.

MONDAY, ——————

NUMBERS		TIMES OF BOOKING A.M.
1 to 25	between	10.0 and 10.30
26 to 50	,,	10.30 ,, 11.0
51 to 75	,,	11.0 ,, 11.30

The acting manager should make it a hard and fast rule that subscribers must pay their subscriptions at the time of the booking, the tickets issued being treated as receipts. The omission of this simplest of precautions is responsible for far too many societies having to present annual balance sheets showing too many "unpaid" or outstanding subscriptions.

Finally, the good acting manager must be the nearest approach to a superman that it is possible to find. He must have three essential qualities that are all too rarely found in combination—infinite tact, unfailing presence of mind, and an unconquerable patience.

THE TREASURER'S DUTIES

In keeping the accounts of an amateur theatrical society there are two essential functions of the accounts to be kept in view: (1) that the accounts should disclose at any time the exact balance of cash in hand, and (2) after each production the treasurer should be able to produce a clear statement of accounts, so analysed that the finances of each separate section of the society's activities can be seen at a glance.

It is advisable that all moneys received be

paid into the bank without delay, and that all payments, except those that fall strictly within the bounds of petty cash, be made by cheque. Not only does adherence to this plan enable the auditors of the society to check the accounts easily, but it safeguards the treasurer himself.

A ledger is not an essential part of a small society's accounting system. An analysed cash book for receipts, another analysed book for payments, and a petty cash book are all that are necessary. A receipt should be given for all money received, even if it is merely received from another official of the society. From the counterfoils of the receipts the treasurer enters up his Receipts Book, placing the total amount received in the Total column and then extending the item into the appropriate analysis column. As the money is paid into the bank the Total column should be ruled off and the appropriate entry made in the Bank column.

All major payments should be made by cheque and a receipt obtained. The Expenditure Book should be entered up from the counterfoils of the cheque book, each item going first into the Total column and then extended into the analysis columns, as in the case of the receipts. Only payments made by cheque must be entered in this book, and as all payments into the bank are carried to the left-hand column from the Receipts Book, the treasurer can at any time see from his Expenditure Book exactly what balance remains to the society's credit at the bank.

As far as possible the treasurer should be careful to see that he obtains a receipt for all items of expenditure, and it is a good plan for him to have receipt vouchers in hand so that he can obtain receipts for incidental items that are paid through petty cash. The Petty Cash Book should be analysed in the same way as the Cash Book kept for cheque payments. The Sundries column should never be allowed to assume large proportions; if it does there is something lacking in the analysis. The treasurer should never keep more than a pre-arranged amount of petty cash in hand, and when the balance becomes low a cheque should be drawn for replenishment. Small amounts of cash received should never be taken into credit of the petty cash, but should be paid into the bank in accordance with the general scheme.

Receipts and vouchers of all kinds should be carefully preserved, and for the convenience of the auditors arranged in the same order as the items they refer to occur in the books. The treasurer should call for the Bank Pass Book periodically and compare the balance shown there with that appearing in his own accounts; and whenever an audit is to be conducted the bank should be asked to send a balance certificate direct to the auditors.

When the final accounts of a production are to be presented the treasurer should draw up a tabulated statement of accounts from his three books. The Petty Cash Book and cheque Expenditure Book should be combined in total and analysis columns and shown in conjunction with the totals of the Receipts Book, so that receipts and expenditure in respect of such items as programmes, etc., are clearly shown. Comparisons of the current accounts with those of previous years are interesting and useful to the committee, and the treasurer will do well to present such a statement whenever possible. The accounts should be audited and certified by the auditors before they are issued to the members in general.

RECEIPTS BOOK

Date	To Bank	Date	Received from	Total	Subscriptions	Tickets	Programme Sales	Refreshments

EXPENDITURE BOOK

Date	At Bank	Date	Paid to	Total	Rent	Printing	Royalties	Costumes

—— AMATEUR DRAMATIC SOCIETY

STATEMENT OF ACCOUNTS FOR THE YEAR 1948

	Total			1948	Spring Production			1948	Autumn Production			1948
Receipts—	£	s.	d.	£	£	s.	d.	£	£	s.	d.	£
Subscriptions	36	15	–	34								
Members' Bookings	60	11	–	56	35	12	6	29	24	8	6	27
Public Bookings	163	12	6	140	84	8	6	69	79	4	–	71
Programme Advertisements	10	10	–	10	5	5	–	5	5	5	–	5
Programme Sales	12	13	4	11	7	3	2	6	5	10	2	5
Refreshment Sales	17	8	6	19	10	1	–	10	7	7	6	9
Cloakroom Receipts	5	4	3	5	3	2	3	3	2	2	–	2
Loan of Costumes	11	–	–	8								
Sundries	1	4	–	1		13	6	1		10	6	
Total Receipts	£318	18	7	284	£146	5	11	123	£124	7	8	119
Expenditure—												
Rent of Hall	58	–	–	58	29	–	–	29	29	–	–	29
Rehearsal Rooms	36	–	–	46	23	–	–	23	23	–	–	23
Scenery Expenditure	16	18	–	12	8	18	–	7	8	–	–	5
Hire of Equipment	15	–	–	15	7	10	–	8	7	10	–	7
Stage Hands' Wages	10	–	–	10	5	4	–	5	4	16	–	5
Royalties	16	16	–	20	10	10	–	13	6	6	–	7
Libretti and Books	5	5	–	8	3	–	–	5	2	5	–	3
Hire of Costumes, etc.	28	8	6	14	18	4	6	8	10	4	–	6
Costumes Purchased	18	10	–	25	10	–	–	13	8	10	–	12
Carriage	2	1	–	1	2	1	–					1
Advertising	18	10	–	20	10	10	–	11	8	–	–	9
Printing	18	–	–	14	10	2	–	7	7	18	–	7
Refreshment Purchases	10	2	3	12	6	–	–	7	4	2	3	5
Producer's Expenses	8	–	–	4	5	3	–	2	2	17	–	2
Secretary's Expenses	6	1	–	4								
Cheque Book and Postages	4	4	6	3								
Sundries	4	3	–	3	2	1	–	2	2	2	–	1
Total Expenditure	£285	19	3	269	£151	3	6	140	£124	10	3	122
BALANCE	32	19	4	15	– 4	17	7	– 17	– =	2	7	– 3

Extract

	£	s.	d.
Cash Balance b/f	28	4	6
Balance, 1948	32	19	4
	£61	3	10

Programmes—	£	s.	d.	£	s.	d.
Sales	12	13	4			
Advertisement	10	10	–			
				23	3	4
Printing				7	10	–
				£15	13	4

Refreshments—	£	s.	d.
Sales	17	8	6
Purchases	10	2	3
	£7	6	3

ADVERTISING AND PUBLICITY

A useful record which may be compiled, either by the treasurer or by the acting manager, is an analysis of the sales of differently priced seats for each production shown as a percentage of the seats available. Different kinds of production may attract different types of audience, and it may be found that it is easier to fill the more expensive seats at an operatic production than at a straight play, or vice versa, or that comedy attracts a better paying audience than heavier types of play. If an analysis similar to that shown is compiled for a series of productions the committee will have valuable information to guide them in deciding the prices they can fix for the seats, and the most advantageous number of seats to be provided at each price.

The question of financial success or failure leads to a consideration of advertising. The best advertisement a society can have is a good reputation. If the public have learned to recognize that they can buy tickets for a society's productions, not with the feeling that they are supporting a charity, but with the confident expectation that they will be getting value for money, the success of the society is practically assured. However, some form of advertising is essential for every production. This matter may be left to the secretary, or a special publicity secretary may be appointed. Advertising is expensive. A definite sum of money to cover all advertising expenses should be voted by the committee; and it is the publicity secretary's job to draw up a plan of action.

Publicity should begin as soon as the play has been definitely settled. Local newspapers are usually willing to insert a paragraph in their news columns provided it is attractively written and concise. The members of the society themselves can do a great deal of useful work by talking about the forthcoming production.

As the date of the production draws near the actual direct advertising must be considered. The newspaper advertisements should be as large and as bold as possible. The essential parts of the advertisement are the title of the play, which should appear in the boldest type; the name of the society; the date, time, and place of the production; the prices of the seats, and where they may be booked. Do not forget to send complimentary tickets to, and to reserve seats on the opening night for, the Press. Before posters are printed the publicity secretary should interview a local firm to ensure that the posters can be exhibited in prominent positions at reasonable rates.

Smaller bills to be displayed in show windows are another valuable and comparatively inexpensive form of publicity. They should be printed in neat type in quiet, attractive colours.

—— AMATEUR DRAMATIC SOCIETY

ANALYSIS OF SALES OF SEATS, 1948–49

Price	Spring, 1948			Autumn, 1948			Spring, 1949			Autumn, 1949		
	Available	Sold	%	Available	Sold	%	Available	Sold	%	Available	Sold	%
1s. 3d.	1,000	950	95	1,000	850	85	600	580	97	800	760	95
2s. 4d.	1,200	950	79	1,200	1,100	92	1,400	1,100	79	1,250	1,000	80
3s. 6d.	600	500	83	600	550	92	800	540	68	750	500	67

Beware of starting the final intensive advertising too early. News paragraphs and members' conversation will have prepared the public for the society's announcements, but little ticket selling will take place earlier than a week before the opening date of the production. Public memory is short, and ten days or a fortnight before the first performance is quite early enough for the posters and bills to appear.

Special novelty advertising is often useful, particularly if the bookings are slow, or if performances have actually started and are not well supported. The publicity secretary who has the slightest grounds for suspecting that some special effort may be necessary would be wise to think out and keep in reserve some such idea to stimulate a flagging public interest.

Since one of the chief traits of the good business man is adaptability, the suggestions that have been given on Business Organization and Management can be usefully adapted by all secretaries and other officials to the requirements of their particular societies.

The ultimate responsibility for the running of every properly organized society rests upon its committee. The secretary, the treasurer, and all the other officials derive their authority from, and act on behalf of, the society's committee. If the committee have been really alive to their responsibilities and have taken their proper place and interest in all phases of the society's activities, there will be no crisis if an official suddenly fails them. The feeling of confidence that knowledge of the ability to cope with such an emergency engenders is the best possible indication that the business organization of a society rests upon a sure foundation.

C

CENSORSHIP

CHILDREN'S THEATRE

CHORAL SPEAKING

CONVENTION AND CONVENTIONALITY

COSTUMING, HISTORIC STAGE

- OVERTURE
- THE GREEKS
- THE ROMANS
- THE SAXONS
- THE NORMANS
- THE PLANTAGENETS
- THE THREE EDWARDS
- RICHARD OF BORDEAUX
- THE THREE HENRIES
- YORKIST
- HENRY VII
- TUDOR
- SHAKESPEARE'S ENGLAND
- CHARLES THE FIRST
- PURITANISM
- RESTORATION
- DUTCH WILLIAM
- GEORGE II
- THE MAN OF FASHION
- EMPIRE AND THE DANDIES
- THE CRINOLINE, 1850–60
- GROSVENOR GALLERY, 1870
- NOAH'S ARK, 1880
- THE NINETIES
- THE CLERGY AT MASS
- CLERGY—CHOIR AND STREET

CRITICAL FACULTY, THE

CRITICISM, ASPECTS OF

- THE CRITIC AND THE AMATEUR
- ADVICE TO INTENDING CRITICS

CENSORSHIP

HAROLD DOWNS, Lecturer on Drama and Literature; Adjudicator

CENSORSHIP law goes back to the Theatres Act of 1843, a significant year in the history of the English theatre. Another was 1737 when Walpole's Act was passed. The "Origin of the Present Control Over Theatres and Stage Plays" is admirably explained in Report from the Joint Select Committee of the House of Lords and the House of Commons on the Stage Plays (Censorship) together with the Proceedings of the Committee, Minutes of Evidence, and Appendices, published in 1909. Interesting and important alike, it remains an illuminating Bluebook for serious study when attempts are being made to sift relevant material for the formulation of judgment on contemporary problems that are rooted in the writing, producing, and acting of modern plays. The explanation reads:

> The modern English drama may be considered to have had its rise in the period of the Renaissance, and a censorship over the performance of stage plays has existed since that time. In the reign of Henry VIII the amusements of the Court were under the control of a Master of the Revels. From that date to the time of the Commonwealth, when all theatres were suppressed by law, writers of plays were subject to the authority either of the Master of the Revels, or of the Privy Council, or of the Court of Star Chamber. It is not certain at what date the Lord Chamberlain first began to exercise a direct censorship over stage plays, but the records of his Office show that as early as 1628 the Lord Chamberlain, either personally or through the Master of the Revels, who was his officer, licensed theatres and closed them, and exercised a general supervision over the work of the dramatists.
>
> These powers sprang from the Royal Prerogative, but in 1737 the censorship became a statutory function of the Lord Chamberlain. The Act of 10 George II, c. 28 (An Act to explain and amend so much of an Act, made in the twelfth year of the reign of Queen Anne, intituled, An Act for reducing the laws relating to rogues, vagabonds, sturdy beggars and vagrants, into one Act of Parliament; and for the more effectual punishing such rogues, vagabonds, sturdy beggars and vagrants, and sending them whither they ought to be sent, as relates to common players of Interludes) was carried through Parliament in that year by Sir Robert Walpole, in order to restrain the political and personal satire which was then prevalent on the stage, which the Government of the day found embarrassing, and which the censorship as it then existed was found ineffective to curb. There stands on record a strong protest by Lord Chesterfield against the powers which this measure conferred. The Statute constituted the Lord Chamberlain Licenser of Theatres within the City and liberties of Westminster, and wherever the Sovereign might reside. It required a copy of every new play to be sent to him not less than fourteen days before the proposed performance. It empowered him to prohibit, at any time and anywhere in Great Britain, the performance of any play, and it imposed heavy penalties on those who should perform any play in an unlicensed theatre, or any prohibited play, or any new play without the sanction of the Lord Chamberlain or of Letters Patent from the Crown. On the passing of this Act, although not required by it to do so, the Lord Chamberlain appointed and "swore in" a Licenser or Examiner of Plays, with a salary of £400 a year, to act under him, and also appointed a deputy. The office of Examiner of Plays has existed continuously from that time to this.

Here, it will be gathered, is the explanation of why, recurringly, actors and actresses are referred to as rogues and vagabonds. The legal obligation, even to this day, is:

> A copy of every new stage play, and of every addition to an old play, must be sent to the Lord Chamberlain by the manager who proposes to produce it, at least seven days before it is intended to be performed, accompanied by a fee to be fixed by the Lord Chamberlain, not being more than two guineas. The Lord Chamberlain may prohibit the acting of any play or any part of a play, even if it has been licensed, "anywhere in Great Britain, or in such theatres as he shall specify, either absolutely or for such time as he shall think fit." The Statute of 1737 conferred upon the Lord Chamberlain an unfettered power of veto, with no indication of the grounds upon which he was to act; when the Bill of 1843 was passing through the House of Lords, words were inserted on the suggestion of Lord Campbell restricting though vaguely, his powers of prohibition to cases in which "he shall be of opinion that it is fitting for the preservation of good manners, decorum or of the public peace so to do." These wide words form the only provision which now gives statutory direction to the operation of the Censorship.
>
> A stage play is defined in the Theatres Act, as being "taken to include every tragedy, comedy, farce, opera, burletta, interlude, melodrama, pantomime, or other entertainment of the stage, or any part thereof"; with a partial exemption for performances at fairs. Adequate penalties are imposed for infractions. The Act applies to Scotland, but not to Ireland.

This quotation is from the official Report. It

furnishes voluminous evidence which brings out the pros and cons of the censorship.

The law of censorship confronts some people with problems that are not easily soluble, although literary genius of our age, George Bernard Shaw, considers that he himself solved them years ago. When I invited Mr. Shaw to contribute the article on the censorship to THEATRE AND STAGE he declined the invitation in this characteristically Shavian reply:

> . . . what you ask me for is quite out of the question. I have no time to write over again what I have already written in seven volumes. You can quote as much as you like; but not another word will you get from me on a subject that I have exhausted and a problem that I have definitely solved.

A renewed invitation was declined in Shavianism intensified. I intend, however, to take full advantage of Mr. Shaw's generous offer and to quote from his well known Preface to *Widowers' Houses*. Mr. Shaw is firmly convinced that he has solved the problem of the censorship. The trouble is that many men and women will not think as he thinks or behave as he would have them behave. Censorship problems arising out of man's submission to his creative urge have increased rather than diminished with the revolutionary changes that have been introduced into the theories of the government of peoples during the past quarter of a century or so. A glance backward will bring disturbing reminders.

> Paris, during the German occupation (pointed out an editorial note in *Theatre Arts*, Dec., 1944) could say nothing on its stages that might offend the German war-lords. Contemporary playwrights were suspect, but the classics evidently were considered safe. And so the story comes from liberated France (reported by George Slocombe in the New York *Herald Tribune*) that André Barsacq produced *Antigone* in a modern version by Jean Anouilh two months before Paris was set free. Though ostensibly merely a retelling in modern dress of the story of the Greek maiden who refused to obey the harsh laws of the dictator-king of Thebes, every line was freighted with "resistance," with passionate revolt against the brutal and ruthless oppressors. Yet the Gestapo let it pass. The theatre which would have been punished for defying the dictator in terms of a new play, said its say by way of Sophocles. For the theatre-minded, there is always a playwright available, even when contemporary voices are silenced.

That legislative restrictions imposed centuries ago are still with us is, in a sense, evidence of the potency of playwrights. Any attempt to get the censorship in perspective must take into consideration Walpole's administration and its work, which was, undoubtedly, corrupt. Three P's—Press, Pulpit, and Playwrighting—might have continued on a plane of equality—if the writers of plays had been less incisive, less critical, less cogent in their expressions of opinion on aspects of public life. The playwrights of the day, however, were too outspoken, too fearless, too destructive of official administration and its manifestations in terms of public life and of the lives of human beings. There were, as there always are, some who wanted to express thought irrespective of where expression led them, and some who wished to stifle thought even though they could not prevent its creation. Free thought and its expression gained ground and had their reflection in the world of the theatre, where licence tended to outstrip liberty, and profanity rather than profundity held sway. The Theatres Act was regulative in influence. The Tudor Period, characterized by relative order and common sense, maintained censorship that did not seek arbitrarily to differentiate between theatre and pulpit, or Press and theatre. The theatre, in short, was not an exception. But when Walpole was in a position to wield political power the politicians were sensitive to the necessities of self-protection. As parliamentarians they laid themselves open to adverse criticism by their parliamentary acts which sought to smother criticism. Otherwise the Lord Chamberlain's privileged power might have passed into the licensing laws. Walpole's Act aimed at strengthening the line of demarcation between the theatre and other institutions. The outcome was the Act of 1843 which both repealed Walpole's Act and created the regulations by which the contemporary theatre must function. With modifications made through local government acts, it remains in force. The treatment is less harsh, but it is none the less handicapping in its repressive incidence. Mr. Shaw states the facts and emphasizes them in his Preface to *Widowers' Houses*. Mr. Shaw more than thirty years ago wrote:

> In 1737, Henry Fielding, the greatest practising dramatist, with the single exception of Shakespeare, produced by England between the Middle Ages and the nineteenth century, devoted his genius to the task of

exposing and destroying parliamentary corruption, then at its height. Walpole, unable to govern without corruption, promptly gagged the stage by a censorship which is in full force at the present moment. Fielding, driven out of the trade of Molière and Aristophanes, took to that of Cervantes; and since then the English novel has been one of the glories of literature, whilst the English drama has been its disgrace. The extinguisher which Walpole dropped on Fielding descends on me in the form of the Queen's Reader of Plays, a gentleman who robs, insults, and suppresses me as irresistibly as if he were the Tsar of Russia and I the meanest of his subjects. The robbery takes the form of making me pay him two guineas for reading every play of mine that exceeds one act in length. I do not want him to read it (at least officially: personally he is welcome); on the contrary, I strenuously resent that impertinence on his part. But I must submit in order to obtain from him an insolent and insufferable document, which I cannot read without boiling of the blood, certifying that in his opinion—*his* opinion!—my play "does not in its general tendency contain anything immoral or otherwise improper for the stage," and that the Lord Chamberlain therefore "allows" its performance (confound his impudence!). In spite of this certificate he still retains his right, as an ordinary citizen, to prosecute me, or instigate some other citizen to prosecute me, for an outrage on public morals if he should change his mind later on. Besides, if he really protects the public against my immorality, why does not the public pay him for the service? The policeman does not look to the thief for his wages, but to the honest man whom he protects against the thief. And yet, if I refuse to pay, this tyrant can practically ruin any manager who produces my play in defiance of him. If, having been paid, he is afraid to license the play: that is, if he is more afraid of the clamor of the opponents of my opinions than of their supporters, then he can suppress it, and impose a mulct of £50 on everybody who takes part in a representation of it, from the gasman to the principal tragedian. And there is no getting rid of him. Since he lives, not at the expense of the taxpayer, but by blackmailing the author, no political party would gain ten votes by abolishing him. Private political influence cannot touch him; for such private influence, moving only at the promptings of individual benevolence to individuals, makes nice little places to job nice little people into instead of doing away with them. Nay, I myself, though I know that the Queen's Reader of Plays is necessarily an odious and mischievous official, and that if I were appointed to his post (which I shall probably apply for at the next vacancy) I could no more help being odious and mischievous than a ramrod could if it were stuck into the wheels of a steam engine, am loth to stir up the question lest the Press, having now lost all tradition of liberty, and being able to conceive no alternative to a Queen's Reader of Plays but a County Council's Reader or some other sevenheaded devil to replace the oneheaded one, should make the remedy worse than the disease. Thus I cling to the Censorship as many Radicals cling to the House of Lords or the Throne, or as domineering women shun masterful men, and marry weak and amiable ones. Until the nation is prepared for Freedom of the Stage on the same terms as it now enjoys Freedom of the Press, by allowing the dramatist and manager to perform anything they please and take the consequences before the ordinary law as authors and editors do, I shall cherish the Queen's Reader as the apple of my eye. I once thought of organizing a Petition of Right from all the managers and authors to the Prime Minister; but as it was obvious that nine out out of ten of these victims of oppression, far from daring to offend their despot, would promptly extol him as the most salutary of English institutions, and spread themselves with unctuous flattery on the perfectly irrelevant question of his estimable personal character, I abandoned the notion. What is more, many of them, in taking this safe course, would be pursuing a sound business policy, since the managers and authors to whom the existing system has brought success not only have no incentive to change it for another which would expose them to wider competition, but have for the most part the greatest dread of the "New" ideas which the abolition of the Censorship would let loose on the stage. And so long live the Queen's Reader of Plays!

And the King's Reader of Plays, also! One of Mr. Shaw's shrewd interpreters, the controversial Mr. St. John Ervine, once wrote of the Censor of Plays: "The custodian of the *status quo*; he is the guardian of existing morality; and his duty may be summarily described as that of resisting all attempts to dislocate or change the current moral system until such dislocation or change has received the sanction of society."

Questions spring to mind. Is the censor an able custodian? Is existing morality worthy of the censor's guardianship? In the interests of progress, is it desirable to resist *all* attempts to dislocate or change the current moral system until such dislocation or change has received the sanction of society? Would a distribution of censorship power be advantageous? Ought feminine opinion to be reflected in censorship decisions? I quote again from Mr. Shaw's Preface.

No doubt all plays which deal sincerely with humanity must wound the monstrous conceit which it is the business of romance to flatter. But here we are confronted, not only with the comedy and tragedy of individual character and destiny, but with those social horrors which arise from the fact that the average homebred Englishman, however honorable and goodnatured he may be in his private capacity, is, as a citizen, a wretched creature who, whilst clamouring for a gratuitous millennium, will shut his eyes to the most villainous abuses if the remedy threatens to add another penny in the pound to the rates and taxes which he has to be half cheated, half coerced into paying. In Widowers' Houses I have shewn middle class respectability and younger son gentility fattening on the poverty of the slum as flies fatten on filth. That is not a pleasant theme.

Modern plays, some theatregoers affirm, should fulfil a purpose removed from that attempted by some present-day dramatists. War, its aftermath, contemporary problems—these often stifle criticism and curtail liberties. As the Censorship of Stage Plays has existed since the period of the Renaissance, in which modern English drama had its rise, cogent arguments have been advanced in favour of the abolition of an institution which is antagonistic to the democratic spirit of the twentieth century.

The Bluebook from which I have quoted points out that since the passing of the Theatres Act, 1843, on three occasions "Committees of the House of Commons have considered the provisions and application of the law relating to the Lord Chamberlain's Censorship for plays, though on each of those occasions the question of the licensing of plays was little more than incidental." Conflicting opinions were expressed before the 1909 Committee. No statutory effect was given to recommendations. Nevertheless its influence on the administration of the Censorship has been appreciable, and since that time there have been few occasions on which serious controversy has arisen over the exercise of the Lord Chamberlain's veto. None the less, it should be noted that on 16th April, 1913, the House of Commons, without a division, passed a motion which, *inter alia*, called for revision in the process of censorship—but, as no legislation was introduced, it was not put into effect.

Since those days we have, perhaps, become wiser. We accept responsibilities which a few decades ago we shirked. Despite Mr. St. John Ervine's contentions, there is no doubt that the Censorship does not always succeed in making impossible the production of the meretricious and harmful. For example, the Censorship machinery is obviously defective in its working when one of His Majesty's judges found it necessary to point out on one occasion, years ago, that "people who cannot get the leave of the Censor to produce plays in the ordinary way are able, apparently, as the law stands, to produce them . . . privately by subscriptions or by some way in which, apparently, they cannot be stopped." Further, problems arise out of production and performance. A play script can mean one thing; interpretation of it in performance another. A final quotation from Mr. Shaw's Preface stimulates thought on this aspect of the subject:

"It is quite possible for a piece to enjoy the most sensational success on the basis of a complete misunderstanding of its philosophy: indeed, it is not too much to say that it is only by a capacity for succeeding in spite of its philosophy that a dramatic work of serious poetic import can become popular."

One deduction is that there is real need for a Censorship that is even more rigorous. On the other hand, there is the indisputable fact that the approval of the Censor is no guarantee that that which is approved is perfect or that its production or performance will not be harmful.

Education through ordinary channels, by the Press, through books, repertory theatres, and playgoers clubs, has brought change and improvement. Abolition of the Censorship would please some and displease others. Dramatists who believe that "until someone can prove to us that we have arrived at finality in truth the stage is one of the greatest means of expressing the discoveries in truth" (Zangwill) would probably indulge their critical faculty, both destructively and constructively, to a greater extent than at present if there were no Censorship. The entertainment-seeking public might or might not wish the stage to become a popular medium for the expression of "discoveries in truth." Their wishes could be determined. In the past the Censorship has banned plays by Shaw, Granville, Barker, Oscar Wilde, Ibsen, Brieux, Strindberg, Schnitzler, Pirandello, and others—significant names in dramatic literature. Would abolition necessarily effect adversely playwrights and their plays or the "existing morality" of the playgoing public? The First Great War and the Second Great War altered many values, and the significance of alteration cannot yet be fully appraised.

CHILDREN'S THEATRE

JOHN BOURNE, Author of " The Unhappy Clown," " Crack o' th' Whip," and other plays; Editor of " Eight New Plays for Boys and Girls" and " The Junior Theatre "

MUCH advice has been offered by clever philosophers, school teachers, and students of psychology on the subject of the child-actor and the plays he should perform. I do not wish to trespass on the province of the experts, or to put forward fresh theories; I write merely as an ex-child who has suffered, as a parent whose offspring has confounded his theories, and as a writer whose plays seem to amuse Little People in spite of the Sophisticated.

While collecting a number of plays for publication I have constantly been struck by the divisions of opinion that apparently exist among the people who write for children. One section writes "down" to what it obviously thinks is the child's very restricted need—and becomes patronizingly silly; another seeks to educate the child through play-acting—and becomes horribly dull; a third section recognizes that the child is highly imaginative and wants to "do a play," mainly for the purpose of dressing-up and pretending to be somebody else and also to live temporarily in another world.

The first section churns out flat plays about priggish princesses, fatuous fairies, and goody-goody children who are always sweet and kind. The second section generally takes an historical text, or points a superb moral, sometimes in very blank verse. The third section accepts the child mind on its own wide basis with a full realization that colour and action—and a certain amount of naughtiness—have greater potentialities in young hands than pompous language and high-minded moralizings.

The children's field in dramatic work is a big one. The Boy Scouts have a department devoted exclusively to it, and so have the Girl Guides, who organize competitive festivals in London and the provinces. Some of the county organizations have annual non-competitive children's festivals, and there is a Juvenile Drama Committee of the British Drama League, which advises on plays and stagecraft in general. In this last connexion lists of plays suitable for boys and girls have been compiled. The National Association of Boys' and Girls' Clubs does much to encourage dramatic work; and so do the Y.W.C.A. and Y.M.C.A., although the enterprise of the last two organizations is naturally confined to young people who hardly come under the title of "children." There are very few schools that do not include at least one play a year in their activities, and many church organizations now look kindly on such work.

The problem of competitive work by children's groups is a knotty one. On the whole, I believe that the disappointment which comes to all but the winning teams more than offsets any enterprise which competitions encourage. There can be no standard of comparison where children are concerned, unless they all play the same piece and are all pretty much of the same age. Non-competitive festivals, at which the adjudication is constructive and good-humoured, are great fun, and can do much to spur children on to better effort—but the children must be able to appreciate the adjudicator; arty young women and "precious" young men should be avoided.

Because of the widespread interest in children's plays, publishers are paying increased attention to them. Some firms specialize in books of plays for young people of all ages. The shelves of the British Drama League Library have a wide selection of children's plays on them. Undoubtedly, the best plays for children are those in which there is plenty of action and which lend themselves to costuming.

Although the child's mind is immature, children are shrewd enough to know whether a play is suitable for them or not. The fact that they do not take to a play is sufficient indication that they will not act it satisfactorily. For that reason it is wise to allow the would-be actors to have a voice in choosing the play they are to perform. One thing children dislike is to have anything they are to "play at" foisted on to them against their will.

When it comes to *producing* the play—strong

measures must be taken. The grave educationist who asserted that children were born actors and did not need teaching gave expression to a generalization which might be applied to *extempore* performances in the nursery, or to a charade, but which would have poor results on a stage before an audience. The technique of the stage has to be considered in the school-theatre almost as much as in any other, and the less the young actors are allowed to rely on the indulgence of their audiences the better. If the children are to grow up to be efficient members of dramatic societies, there seems to be no reason why the good work should not be begun as early as possible. In any case, it is unfair to leave a public performance to genius or chance.

In producing children's plays it is essential to avoid discouraging the mimetic instinct which children, by reason of their simplicity of outlook, undoubtedly possess. They should be allowed to interpret their parts in their own way, with much more elasticity than is permitted to grown-ups. The latter's interpretation is often merely a copy of somebody else whom they have seen in the part, whereas the child is nearly always original. The producer of a children's play, therefore, will be well advised to confine his efforts to general stage principles, such as audibility, positions, movements, and the outline of the play rather than to much interference with characterization. While the producer must keep a strong hand on the production as a whole, and must always have the final say, he must never be a martinet. No child can, or should, be frightened into playing a part in a way that is foreign to its nature. But every child will react to appreciation, and, if consulted rather than dictated to, will readily eradicate faults.

Good casting is, of course, extremely important. Here, again, the consultative method will get the best results. The one aim of the producer should be to fit the young players into the parts to which they are instinctively drawn. Unlike grown-ups, they rarely want to play "leads," and jealousies are minor and easily suppressed. Children love to assist the producer and stage manager *behind the scenes*, and should be encouraged to do so, even to the extent of taking their opinions without necessarily accepting them. There seems to be no reason why children should not be trained and encouraged to be producers as much as to be players.

Too much emphasis on the spoken word often ruins a children's play, and that is why an elocution mistress does not always make the best producer. Elocution is immensely valuable; but it is not one-quarter the art of acting. Thousands of children have been "put off" Shakespeare for life because they were taught to "elocute" him.

As "dressing-up" is the keynote of all successful children's performances, every effort should be made to keep the young actors interested in matters of costume. If they are old enough to make their own dresses, they should be allowed to do so, and should be told the "reason why" of the costume. They will be found to be resourceful both in matters of dress and stage "props." Boys seem to be able to find anything from a rope to a scaffold-pole at short notice! Girls like to be taken into account, particularly over the *colours* of their costumes, and are just as keen to help with the boys' costumes as with their own.

There is no need to worry about their enthusiasm; there is no sport or game that will hold them like acting. Rehearsals are just as big a thrill to them as are actual performances, and, as the modern child is more assertive than his parents ever dared to be, stage fright is practically a thing of the past.

Above all, it should be remembered that children are rarely at their best when they appear on the stage *as children*. The whole reason for their love of acting is that it gives them a chance to be somebody or something outside themselves —fairies, dolls, animals, pirates, Red Indians, statesmen—anything but everyday children. The worst acted play by children I have ever seen was one in which all the characters were schoolboys and schoolgirls; the best—surprising as it may seem—was the trial scene from Bernard Shaw's *Saint Joan*!

John Bourne

Douglas

Edwin C. White

CHORAL SPEAKING

EDWIN C. WHITE, Author of "Problems of Acting and Play Production"

CHORAL speaking is a method of interpreting verse or prose by a chorus of many voices speaking in unison, in harmony, or in contrast. Its practice demonstrates that certain kinds of written language need more than a solo voice for full vocalization and interpretation. Although choral speaking has a long history its revival is comparatively recent, and in its experimental stages, in spite of many notable achievements and successes. At its best, it provides both speakers and listeners with an experience both exciting and intense.

Properly approached, it is essentially a method of interpretation, and not merely an arbitrary device for the employment of many voices and the display of vocal and choral skill. Its purpose should be the full revelation of the intentions of the verse or prose selected. Therefore care should be exercised in the choice of material for choral vocalization. The discipline that is necessary in choral speaking renders it an invaluable method by which to train speakers. Whether speaking in unison or in harmony, speakers are impelled to accept uniformity of speed, intonation, and rhythm. There must also be absolute agreement upon such matters as volume, purpose, and climax. Individual opinion and taste must give way to common acceptance of purpose, and all speaking in a choir must conform to a single authority as singers and instrumentalists obey the control of the conductor of choir or orchestra.

In the preliminary practice of choral speaking a conductor possessing authority is essential. He will control speed, volume, crescendo, or diminuendo, and insist on uniformity of rhythm. With beginners his authority may be arbitrary, but it should not be long before agreement upon all matters is achieved after general discussion or, perhaps better still, when experiments have been made. Valid experiments, however, are not possible until skill has been achieved by the individuals taking part in collective vocalization. When the ability to speak together at determined speed, with uniformity of rhythm, emphasis, and modulation has been gained, it is possible to discuss the relative effectiveness of variations, and the members of the group may be able to give expression to the appropriateness of different methods of speaking the selected passages.

It is conventional to divide choirs into three sections according to individual types of voice: high, medium, and low; or, as more usually expressed, light, medium, and heavy. It is often desirable before doing this to practise speaking in unison, and to examine the effects which many voices speaking in unison achieve. Passages of prose or verse which express purely personal points of view should never be chosen for choral speaking. When the material is impersonal or general, with the emotion general, not individual, it is appropriate for the use of a choir.

The concluding passages of the chase in Masefield's *Reynard the Fox* make an excellent exercise in unison speaking from

"Three hundred yards and the worst was past"

to the moment we hear that

"The earth was stopped; it was filled with stones."

This passage is marked by a clear and definite rhythm. As it develops it gives scope for considerable variations of speed, great contrasts in volume, crescendo, and diminuendo; and the climax is one of intense pathos. The speaking of this and similar passages impresses both speakers and listeners with the power of interpretation gained by the use of massed voices. The passage specified may be regarded as over-long for early study, but it is unnecessary to interpret the whole of it at first. It can, with advantage, be studied sectionally. Then the poet's method is more readily observed and students appreciate the deviations of movement that lead to the climax. From this appreciation they more easily determine the appropriate vocalization for interpreting the intentions of the narrative. Sometimes the poet turns aside from his concentration upon the fox to describe the countryside, but always description has reference to the plight of the fox; it threatens danger or holds out hope. Sometimes attention is directed to the pursuers who are always presented in vivid contrast to the pursued. The contrasts in this poem are vivid and varied, and provide opportunities of comparable vividness and contrast in vocalization.

Passages from the Bible, especially the Psalms, are suitable for group speaking. Antiphonal interpretation of the Psalms has been established over many generations, and, although the separate parts are actually spoken in unison, the choir is divided into two parts which reflect both harmony and contrast. The speaking of Psalms antiphonally gives invaluable practice, especially in the essential skill of preserving rhythm after a silence. When choirs sing the Psalms this is not a difficulty because the music demands and aids this. With speech, however, the task is not simple. Over a whole Psalm there is a uniformity of rhythm that must be preserved by the speakers. This demands considerable practice, but its achievement is essential, for a Psalm is a unity. Repetition is a quality of its structure and its rhythm, which antiphonal speech must preserve.

When the choir is divided into three or more parts; when, as is frequently the case, words and phrases are spoken by few or even by a single voice, the difficulty of preserving rhythm is increased. Unless each member of the choir has attained a proper sense of rhythm, the result is a disconnected and disrupted interpretation that affects the emotional quality of the whole poem or prose passage.

The purpose of a three-part choir may be clearly discovered by the study of a passage such as Isaiah XI, verses 1 to 10. Experiment will illustrate how the qualities of the "rod out of the stem of Jesse" will be emphasized by the varying groups of vocal colour; the striking contrasts will be revealed by the contrasting voices, and the climax attained by the massing of all vocal effort in a grand triumphant finale. In this passage, too, the use of a single dominating voice can be attempted for the opening line, with a contrasting, but equally dominating, voice for the second, followed in the third line by a quiet resonant treble voice leading to the employment of each group separately for the next three lines. To experiment with three-part choirs intensifies excitement as interpretation reveals the true intent and meaning of the words.

Far more complicated is *The Golden and Leaden Echo* by Manley Hopkins, but when its interpretation is achieved the experience is impressive. For most readers the meaning of this poem remains vague; for many it has no meaning. A thought is gleaned here and there, but the poem as a whole seems to lack both form and meaning.

Some years ago I was privileged to hear a group of verse speakers studying and experimenting with this poem. At first no one was able to understand it. Under most able direction the rhythm was first mastered. Then experiments were made with the use of groups of voices. Single voices were used for this word, two voices for that; phrases and sentences were spoken by heavy, light, or medium voices; contrasts were noted; emotional effects of this or that moment were interpreted experimentally; gradually, the significance of certain words and the phrases became clear, which, in turn, gave more and more meaning to the whole. At last, after many rejections and re-trials, excitement was great as for all present, a great poetic expression was revealed in thrilling splendour.

Rules for the achievement of interpretation cannot reasonably be stated dogmatically. Only by intense and most careful experiment, the patient testing of colour against colour, of voice against voice, can appropriate vocalization be realized.

One defect in choral speaking is to make it over-conventional. In the desire to give speech to the various sections of the choir, the speaking may easily become artificial. The passage spoken must not be interrupted by change of voices merely to give speech to this or that group. Voices must be used purposefully, changes must be made only for reasons of emotion or emphasis to clarify the text to speakers and listeners.

Individuals in a choir should always speak naturally, keeping their own natural pitch and register.

Once I heard a choir speak to a set pattern of pitch. The result was intoning which in itself interestingly illustrated amazing control and discipline, but attention was focused upon the method of speaking; skill in the maintenance of the pattern evoked admiration, but the poem itself was lost in the device of speaking.

Intoning has an emotional effect as may be appreciated in certain church services, but as a method of interpretation it should be used only when it is specifically appropriate. Choral speaking must never be characterized by a display of vocal gymnastics, however skilful. It must be used purposefully to clarify meaning. To achieve this, natural speech is essential. Individual voices must blend. Only when special emphasis is required by the language should a special quality of voice stand out.

Perhaps this explains why few men take part in choral speaking, and why many prefer to exclude men from the speaking choir. Unless there is a proper balance between men's and women's voices, there cannot be that adequate and proper blending of tone and pitch which achieves success in the choral rendering of verse or prose. Nevertheless, I think that men could play their part in the development of this method of interpretation. For certain types of lyrical verse, a women's voice, it is true, more readily interprets quality of both tone and emotion; but this is not true of all types of verse or prose. Virile and majestic passages in the Bible, the vigorous and manly narratives of Masefield, and such poems as "Hymn Sung by Shepherds" from *In the Holy Nativity of Our Lord God* in which the chorus are shepherds, can best be interpreted by male voices, or by blending male and female voices in response to varying emotions and intention of language.

Because choral speaking has been mainly developed by women, poets, and especially dramatists, have written for women choirs. Gordon Bottomley and T. S. Eliot are outstanding examples. Both have appreciated the lyric and dramatic qualities and value of this new art, and have introduced interesting choruses for women into their plays.

In *Singing Sands* Gordon Bottomley provides a chorus of eight women—a chorus of waves. These women, dressed in clinging green, with large sweeping sleeves, range themselves across the front of the acting space. The chorus speaks and moves rhythmically to suggest waves, and behind it is the scenic representation of the mouth of a cave and rocks. Finally, the waves open out and group about the space to reveal to the audience the characters of the play entering between the rocks and moving towards the mouth of the cave. The chorus is not merely an introduction to the play and its characters, or a commentary upon the action, but is dramatic providing balance and poise in the development of the drama. For vocalization the greatest care and control are required; control of pitch, tone, speed, rhythm, emphasis, and strength. All taking part must be conscious of the effects desired and the means of attainment. Effort to obtain the required dramatic significance of the chorus is a most valuable experiment and experience. *Singing Sands* is an impressive play for women to study and perform. Its lyrical verse is beautiful to speak, and the chorus fascinates. In addition to the practice in vocalization and movement that it gives, it can be used effectively for a careful study of repose. The chorus must acquire graceful and rhythmic movement. Those taking part must attain a high degree of control in repose, for on the stage it provides a background to the principal characters when it is not active in developing the play.

To T. S. Eliot, we owe the most important contribution to modern verse drama and to the use of the chorus. Both *The Rock* and *Murder in the Cathedral* illustrate the power of verse as a vehicle of dramatic expression and make considerable use of the chorus.

The chorus of the Women of Canterbury in *Murder in the Cathedral* presents an interesting dramatic task for the choral-speaking group. In the choruses we hear, vocalized, the thoughts of common humanity, of oppressed humanity, of humanity suffering from fear, want and insecurity. By courtesy we allow these thoughts to be spoken by the Women of Canterbury of Becket's time, but we know them to be the expression of the incoherent masses of to-day and every day. For the first time in drama Eliot has given character to the many-headed mob; not merely to the few Women of Canterbury, but to the millions of struggling common people throughout the world. Only a chorus of many voices can bring singleness of purpose and expression to this many-voiced mass, and Eliot, understanding the power of this new medium of interpretation, employs it with masterly skill.

The theme underlying the surging murmurings is the bitter and astonishing realization of "Living and partly living." If "To be or not to be" is an expression of utter weariness, the like of which is not to be found anywhere else in our literature, it must also be granted that nowhere else in literature can be found an expression of greater bitterness than this "Living and partly living" of the Women of Canterbury. This cry, first spoken perhaps, by a single voice capable of giving vital articulation to such a pregnant thought, is in its repetitions caught up by more and more voices, until finally it becomes the despondent, bitter wail of all.

The chorus is a dynamic *character* in the play in conflict with other characters: Priests and Thomas Becket. It develops with the movement of the play and reflects influences both of the time and of the other characters. It is a representation of a mass of individuals, and it is the mass that we see rather than individuals. The individuals are so submerged by the mass that they can scarcely be considered to possess either personality or form. They are, individually, vague and shapeless. As individuals they are nought; as a mass they are both a force to be heard and a people to suffer through the wranglings of the great. "They speak better than they know." Their wisdom is intuitive; not rationalized. The effect of their wisdom is emotional. We see their suffering and hear their longings, and our sympathy reaches out to them.

Strong temptation to give personality to the individuals of the chorus must be resisted. They must remain as voices, as individual or group voices that give dynamic personality to the mass. It is dynamic in its realizations of hardships, injustices, joys and pains, fears and terrors. Through all these comes the tragic realization of "Living and partly living," and the repeated and vigorous demand: "Clear the air! clean the sky! wash the wind! take stone from stone and wash them."

The individuals of this potent chorus of humanity are of little importance; attention must be focused on the mass realization, the mass aspiration, and most important, the mass determination.

This massed chorus is a challenge to the conventional method of dividing choirs into groups of voices according to voice colour, and of grouping each separate voice quality. For interpretation here the blending of voices into harmonious unity is undesirable. The emotion to be effected is created not by beautiful and pleasing sound, but by purging the mind of satisfaction and content by the weight of a terrifying spectacle and rhythm laden with bitterness.

There must be grouping of speakers, but it should not be achieved by the conventional differentiation of light, medium, and dark voices and the groups must not be separated. Spontaneity of speech coming from an ever-changing section of the mass must be achieved.

The Women of Canterbury chorus is a complex character of major importance in the play, and some of its complexity, in both characterization and purpose, may be noted in the contrasting rhythms of its various sections or speeches. Choirs should make a special study of these various rhythms and understand the reasons for both the changes and their effects. The method of interpretation will be varied to conform to the content and purpose of the speech as in similar speeches delivered by other characters. The opening stanzas are informative about aspects of place and person; they contain historical and social comment, and philosophical argument. Contrast these with the stanza beginning; "We do not wish anything to happen," and it is clear that now the chorus takes on a more important role, an active part in the development of the play. It is no longer used merely to give information and to make comment. It assumes that personality, already noted, and has become definitely dramatic in purpose. This dramatic purpose imposes on the speakers the necessity of seeming to be natural and spontaneous.

Eliot has observed the lyric and dramatic value of choral speaking and has reflected in his characterization of the masses the spirit of the twentieth century. He has passed on the task of interpretation to the speakers of verse, demanding from them a skill never before imposed upon speaker or actor. When speakers have acquired the skill that is equal to the adequate performance of the task, they leave upon the mind an unforgettable experience.

Edwin C. White.

Robert G. Newton

CONVENTION and CONVENTIONALITY

ROBERT G. NEWTON, Adviser, Middlesex County Drama Committee; Author of "Acting Improvised"

THE moment we can say of something "Everybody's doing it": that is the moment when we should be most careful. When an activity becomes a movement, it is taken up by people whose enthusiasm exceeds their understanding, and wherever enthusiasm is ahead of understanding, over-seriousness and imitation arise. Now there is little doubt that, as far as dramatics are concerned, "Everybody is doing it": dramatics are being taken up on all sides by people whose splendid enthusiasm is far ahead of their understanding of the art. As a result, the Amateur Movement is, through over-seriousness, apt to lose its sense of humour, and to rely too much on imitation. This is dangerous, because it means that the amateur theatre will become too respectable, too conventional, and the theatre suffers considerably if it becomes too conventional. An excess of this on people whose enthusiasm for drama exceeds their understanding of it blinds them to the significance of the dramatic moment and dramatic convention, the appreciation of which is the basis of theatrical understanding.

The importance of dramatic convention cannot be overstated because theatrical performance is not a photographic reproduction of life. Even the most realistic play, like *Strange Orchestra* or *The Corn is Green*, is performed in a theatre without a fourth wall and with the audience seated in an auditorium, all of which immediately introduce an element of unreality. Komisarjevsky says: "Nothing on the stage can be natural, because the theatre is an Art form and therefore inventive." It is in a way unfortunate that the Amateur Movement should have grown up at a time when realism or near realism was the dominating dramatic form. Hence the criticism, "How very natural," became the highest praise. The general approach to a piece of dramatic work was that "So-and-so would not behave in such-and-such a way." Great attention was paid to detail, and there was evidence of considerable observation, but frequently that was all. At drama schools I have often asked for criticism of a scene that has been rehearsed, and in nearly every case this has been connected with details of observation and only rarely with the dramatic purpose of the scene. "Mrs. Biggs posted her letter without stamping it," or "Mr. Speedwell never picked up his hat before leaving the room"—this sort of criticism is common. How comparatively rare is a criticism such as, "If Mrs. Biggs plays her 'big scene' centre stage how will she be able to dominate the scene when Mr. Speedwell comes on?" Or, "Why on earth does not Mr. Speedwell accelerate the pace when he comes on in the second scene, seeing that the play has changed from the convention of comedy to that of farce?" There is, in other words, a strong tendency to think realistically, but only a limited one to think theatrically. The latter, which is as important as the former, depends on two things: sensitiveness to the dramatic moment, and a feeling for the conventions in which a play is written.

To make this clearer, the terms "dramatic moment" and "convention" need amplification. To have a sense for interpreting a "dramatic moment" is in the first place an instinct, but it is one that can be developed by all who have a true feeling for the theatre. The essence of giving correct emphasis to a dramatic moment is, first, the realization that in drama words in action are more important than words. Since everything that takes place upon a stage is meant to be seen as well as heard, movement and pantomime are as significant as dialogue. Secondly, situation, created by contrast and conflict, is the life-blood of drama. A situation may be created by a course of events or by psychological developments, but without situation there is no drama. Sense of the "dramatic moment" is linked to a capacity for spotting situations: not so much the big obvious ones, but the little ones by means of which the big moments are built up. These must be expressed in action; mental action or physical action, and wherever possible the latter should illustrate the former. Their interpretation should be satisfying to the eyes and ears of the audience, and it should, in addition, give them a pleasure that is purely dramatic. In brief, a feeling for the "dramatic moment" is a feeling for the right thing done in the right way at precisely the right moment, "precisely" being the operative word.

Convention is one of the most important elements of a theatre. It is, however, an unfortunate word: exaggeration might be more accurate. The convention in which a play is written is conditioned roughly by the degree of exaggeration away from realism. If the exaggeration is *emotional*, we have the conventions of drama, tragedy, and melodrama. If, however, the exaggeration is intellectual, we have the conventions of light comedy, comedy, and farce. Although the emotion is more exaggerated, or bigger if you prefer it, in *King Lear* (a tragedy) than in *Journey's End* (a realistic play) the interpretation of both plays must be based upon truth. There must be truth even in a melodrama like *East Lynne*, otherwise melodrama becomes burlesque. A play like *Charley's Aunt* is based upon truth; in this case the incongruity of a man dressed up as a woman. Since it is the incongruous aspect that is emphasized, the play develops from one ludicrous *situation* to another and is, therefore, a farce.

A word must be said about what have been called the intellectual exaggerations which are, in fact, the comedy conventions. It is palpably absurd to describe an admirable farce like *See How they Run* as intellectual. The point is this. In all the comedy conventions, or intellectual exaggerations as they have been termed, it is fatal to the author's purpose that the audience should *feel*. Since the challenge in every case, even when the material is ridiculous, is more to reason than to emotion, in the playing pace is most important; the audience must not have time to feel.

Owing to the over-powering influence of "realism," many believe that an actual reproduction of life should be the aim of every stage performance. Such people are unaware that realism is a comparatively late intruder in the theatre. In countries where the classical influence was strong, the rules governing dramatic form were strict: tragedies were tragedies and comedies comedies. In England, ever since the medieval mystery plays, theatrical pieces have been written in various conventions. It is quite normal to find tragedy and farce side by side in an Elizabethan play. Owing to the growth of the scientific spirit, and with it the introduction of realism, modern dramatic forms are not as crude as they were. As a result the changes from convention to convention are more subtle, and therefore have to be handled more skilfully by modern producers. Many producers treat any play that is written in prose, and that deals with quite ordinary people, as though it were necessarily naturalistic. This is often a mistake. How fatuous it would be to attempt to play Barrie's *The Admirable Crichton* as if it were a photograph of life; the conventions of romance, melodrama, and high comedy are all found in this play. How much more entertaining would be the performances of many of Shaw's plays, if producers had emphasized the farcical passages inherent in them.

Conventionality is not important to the theatre, but convention most certainly is. An appreciation of this, plus a feeling for "the dramatic moment," are essential. Hence the slogan, "Think and feel Theatrically," cannot be insisted upon too strongly.

Henry Wykes

MARY KELLY

HISTORIC STAGE COSTUMING

NEVIL TRUMAN, Author of " Historic Costuming," " The Pageant of Nottinghamshire," etc.

INTRODUCTION

MARY KELLY

STAGE costuming is the most fascinating job, and one that can absorb the enthusiast almost, if not quite, as much as lighting. The two, of course, work hand in hand nowadays, for the lighting artist can transform any material, and work magic with what has been made. They get together at once over choice of materials and colours, which are made to vary very much under the modern treatment by lighting—a subject in itself. The wardrobe mistress who has these modern methods of lighting to help out her ideas and enhance her effects is a lucky woman indeed.

Roughly speaking, the main things to consider in costuming are Character, Colour, and Line. I have put character first since the others join in expressing it. The costumes must help, with every other detail of the production, to express its meaning as a whole, and the meaning of each individual character in its place in the play. Now, from 13 *years' experience of hiring costumes, I have learnt that this idea does not come easily to the individual amateur actor and actress, whose main object is to make himself and herself as lovely as possible; and they are urgent with their producer to "let them hire their own." Silks and satins they must wear, the longest of plumes, the greatest abundance of jewels, and —with the ladies—the dress must be suited to "a small blonde with blue eyes," or "a tall brunette with gray." The gentlemen, too, on being asked for measurements, are apt to add an inch or two to their stature.*

It is a hard task for the producer to make his supremacy felt over his cast, especially over the small blonde with blue eyes, in the matter of costume, but it must be done if his costume is going to be part of his play—part of his expression—and not a contradiction of it.

It should never be hard to find a wardrobe mistress, for women generally have far more sense of colour and form than they can use in ordinary life; and the wardrobe mistress must help him in making the players understand that character, colour, and line in costume count infinitely more than the surface of the material, which does not get much farther than the stalls. If she and her myrmidons are keen enough to start dyeing and stencilling, then they have all power in their hands. There is nothing so saddening as to wander about the furniture shops, looking for a good piece of material suitable for Philip the Second of Spain, or Tamberlaine the Great, and to be told "Oh no, Moddom, that kind of material is not being used now!" But if you can buy a piece of hessian or sheeting, and at home go to your dye tub and your paint pots—well, there you are! Through the boiling of your stuff alone you increase its beauty, and if you want it stiff, a hard hessian, sized and stencilled, is excellent.

Colour is like music—full of infinite tones and supertones of meaning and symbolism. It will speak alone in the entry of a group of mourners, or of a company of lords and ladies to a poverty-stricken peasant group. It has a great deal to say, and you must be able to hear it. Producers, particularly of pageants, often say: "Oh, let's have plenty of colour!" but they seldom use their colour in contrast and harmony. In such work one has to study the colours used at each period (and each has a different range), the dyes used by the peasantry, the middle classes, and so on. Your grouping in crowd work cries out for strong contrasts in colour, used boldly: and so used it is nearer truth than the usual amateur stage crowd, which looks like mixed fruit drops jumping up and down. There are power and vigour in such massing of colour, and you will never come to an end of learning about it.

Line is vitally important, for it speaks as clearly as colour: long flowing lines that give dignity, age, or a kind of completion; ceaselessly moving lines that give fantasy and spirit; comfortable lines of plump prosperity, and so on. Your materials and form of dress give you these, and here we see how little surface matters, for if you can get a lovely line with a drapery of sheeting, why should you use satin? Velvet, of the richer materials, is of real value, because of the deep contralto notes it gives, and because it clings to the ground in movement, and also because it alone will combine with cotton. What really give the line to material are the respective strengths of warp and weft, and if you find the balance you want best in the cheaper materials, choose them rather than the richer.

Study your period thoroughly and then forget it a little; the essentials will come back and the useless part will drop out. And do not forget in this study the pattern design of the time, for it jars very much on an intelligent audience to see this all wrong.

A knowledge of design in general is necessary, even to get the very forms of the dresses in accord with the play, and pattern design, for the painting of whole dresses, or borders and ornaments, or their addition in appliqué, needs a great deal of attention. The good use of pattern against solid material will all help towards the thing that really makes your costume live, and that is what your producer will be asking of you—contrast.

Contrast is really at the back of dress design for the stage; by contrast you make your characters stand out or fall back at your wish. If you have a principal to be hidden, dress him uniformly with other characters—if he is to stand alone, give him the strongest contrast possible. Hamlet's inky black is an obvious instance of the latter.

The stylization of costume and all kinds of symbolism are a necessary and interesting study, leading to a sure knowledge of what is absolutely essential to make a costume speak in unmistakable terms. As in all arts, you have to know everything about your medium and subject before you can leave anything out; nothing is more difficult than simplicity; and much that covers itself with the name of "stylization" is mere nonsense. But there is a great power in it when it is used with true imagination, and not merely as a stunt.

Make, in any case, for the real essentials of dress, for the right line, for both colour and pattern to have the force they should have, and for a subtle sense of harmonies and control in their use.

This I will say in conclusion—the costuming of plays is one of the finest jobs that a producer can give to a fellow-worker, and it leads on and on to an endless interest and delight.

Mary Kelly

OVERTURE

The age-old story of this still mysterious world contains no pages more fascinating than those which reveal how men and women have clothed themselves, with what devices they have decorated their limbs, in what gay colours they have arrayed their bodies, and into what fantastic shapes they have twisted and twirled the forms their Creator gave them.

Ever since the day when Eve made a girdle from the leaves of the nearest tree, Woman has sought to attract and delight her Adam with similar tricks, and if today she no longer is content with the simple beauties of Nature and must call in to her aid the developments of an artificial and mechanical age, her aim is, nevertheless, the same as that of her first parent.

NEVIL TRUMAN

To-day clothes have returned to their first precedent. In Eden it was Woman who was the adorned and decorated one. Her spell of supremacy over Man was short-lived. Adam imitated her leafy garment and outshone her speedily. For eighteen hundred years of the Christian Era Man was the more brilliantly costumed. Taking another leaf from Nature's book, he gazed with awakened eyes on the animals and birds, and discovered that to the males were given the brightest colours, the gayest shapes, and the most impressive forms.

Woman, whilst she was but little behind in the race for sartorial supremacy, never outran her partner and won that race until the last of the Georges dazzled Europe with the massiveness of an intellect that could devise an eight-inch shoe buckle.

Prince Florizel also made fashionable the black suit—and men have mourned ever since—though whether for the suit or for the character of its inventor we leave the historians to decide.

Woman now heads the bill. Her shape alternately swells and slims, lengthens and diminishes, according as her fancy takes her—and Man in his sober duns, greys, and blacks, looks on admiringly. Perhaps the wheel will turn again. There are signs, in the cautious revival of colour and shape, that modern man is tired of being the uninteresting foil to woman, and we may yet see him again arrayed in all the glory of the rainbow.

Adown the procession of the ages flit many famous people. The history of costume conjures up for us the figures of great men and women. Indeed, it is impossible to separate the two. Who can think of Cardinal Wolsey without his bright red cape and biretta? Who remembers Queen Elizabeth without her great lace ruff? Indeed, the clothes have become the symbols of the people; and the lesser has usurped the place of the greater. What is Wellington but a pair of boots, or Gladstone but a travelling bag? Raleigh with his cloak, Henry VIII with his falsely broad shoulders, King Charles with his feathered hat, Lord Byron with his open collar, James the First in his padded plus fours—we cannot recall the men without their clothes. The clothes *are* the men. They stamp their personalities upon us.

Then are not clothes a fascinating part of history and of life? Will not their study well repay us in forming a prelude to our understanding of human nature, without which knowledge it is impossible to advance far in the battle of life? Let us then to business.

As clear-cut a description of the different periods as is possible with such a complex and pliable subject as costume will be given. In order to make reference quick and easy, the dress of each reign or period will be summarized in tabular form in each article, preceded by fuller descriptions and illustrations. It will thus be possible, once the descriptive matter has been mastered, for the reader to turn to the summary and immediately to grasp what is wanted without having to re-read the whole chapter, as is the custom with most costume books. Indeed, writers on this subject are notoriously vague, and it is by no means easy to select the dress of a special epoch readily from current works. Writers have great reluctance to date the costumes sufficiently precisely. This springs partly from the undoubted fact that dress changes so imperceptibly and gradually—being advanced in the larger centres of population, and old-fashioned in the country places—that it is never safe to dogmatize too severely as to what was or was not worn at any given date.

Woman of the Period of Elizabeth

Nevertheless, the amateur actor is not expected to be an antiquary. He is expected to appear in a costume that is correct. I will give the normal type of dress of its date, without the "buts" and "ifs" of the archaeologist. The risk of dogmatizing must, therefore, be incurred in the interests of practicality. This risk is really slight when it is borne in mind that the purpose of the costume is to please a theatre audience, which is never so critical as the members of a learned society. People to-day, with the spread of education, know broadly what costumes are "right," and they naturally resent the production of a period play that is not in the main correctly costumed. Bearing these points in mind, all that is necessary will be given.

We must remember that what the medieval mind loved above all things was colour. The people of the Middle Ages had a sound artistic sense that seems to have sprung naturally from them. It was partly due, no doubt, to the fact that they were a race of craftsmen. The coming of the machine struck a deadly blow at craftsmanship, and men turned to the machine-made article which resulted in the machine-made mind. Luckily, there is to-day a revolt from the mastery of the machine and the domination of the trade designer. This is all to the good. We are returning to our earlier good taste and the dressing of any play should be prepared on an ordered scheme of colour.

Have as much colour as you can by all means, but avoid harsh and clashing effects. The cast of a play may indeed be dressed in clashing colours, provided that they do not appear together on the stage. Lovely effects can be obtained by blending the minor characters in different shades of the same colour, whilst making the leading characters outstanding with vivid contrasts. Nothing looks better than to have retainers dressed alike, whilst medieval crowds may be as bright and variegated as possible, and little attention need be paid to avoiding clashing, if a goodly proportion of browns and greys are included for the menfolk. The right use of black as a foil and an accentuator should be recollected.

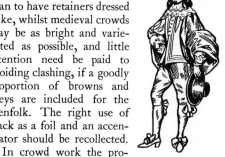

Man of the Period of Charles I

In crowd work the producer should mark the places where he desires his supers to stand having regard to their dress colours. For this he must have full knowledge of the colours of the dresses that will be provided. He can then allot them in mind from the start, and it will be easy at each rehearsal to get the characters into the places they take for the actual performances.

THE GREEKS

During the 2,500 years of Greece's power costume varied, and in the earlier period was so scanty as to be useless for stage purposes. The Greeks knew the advantage of sun and air reaching the skin, and their clothes were designed so as to allow for this, and also to give great freedom for athletic exercises—two points that we should do well to imitate to-day. The great Greek dramas of the classical period range from 550 B.C. to 322 B.C., and were acted in the great open-air theatres, usually semi-circular, though sometimes circular. Greek clothes depended for their beauty on simplicity of line and gracefulness of folds and draping. It is this period which is wanted for theatrical purposes and which is here described.

The *Doric Chiton* (men and women) was a tunic made from a rectangle one foot longer than the wearer's height and of width twice the distance from finger tip to finger tip with arms outstretched. It was made of wool, and the favourite colours were purple, red, saffron, and blue. To adjust it, the extra foot in length was first folded over, then the long rectangle was folded in half and draped round the body with the fold on the left side. Back and front were caught together with pins at the shoulders, and it was girdled at the waist with a slight overhang there. Thus two loopholes were left at either side for the arms to pass through. The length was shortened by pulling it over the girdle to form a blouse called the Kolpos. The arms were left bare. The loose ends at the right side were not fastened together, but were left free for exercise; for theatre purposes these should be stitched together. The overfold may be embroidered with Greek Key and other designs and the loose end (on the right side) should be weighted with beads. This end should fall slightly lower than the overfold edge on the left side.

The *Ionic Chiton* (men and women) was a similar tunic without the overfold at the top, but made of linen or cotton, and larger and fuller, showing more folds. It was also distinguished by

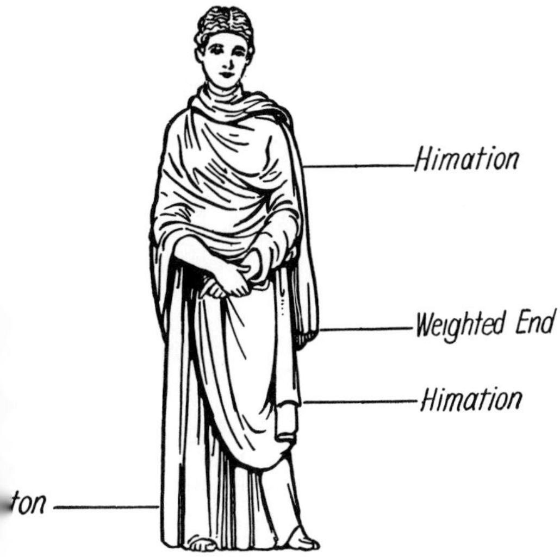

GREEK WOMAN (Indoors)

having sleeves made by holding the back and front of the chiton together at intervals with small pins at the arm openings. An overfold was sometimes, but rarely, added.

Skirts must not be worn under these tunics, as the limbs must show in outline, and the draping should be done with the greatest care. It was one of the chief duties of the slaves to adjust these beautifully.

The *Super Tunic* (men and women) reached to the waist and was worn for extra clothing. Generally speaking, the tunics of the men were shorter than those of the women.

The *Pallium* (men) was a large cloak worn by philosophers, who also wore the Tribon, a rough cloak of black or brown.

SLEEVE OF IONIC TUNIC

The *Peplum* (men and women) was about 4 yds. long by 2 yds. wide, and was passed twice round the body under the arms. It was then brought up over the shoulders, and secured by closely winding it about the body, or it was pulled over the head. The latter was the case when there was mourning.

Girdles (women) went across the shoulders and breasts diagonally with the Ionic tunic, and round the hips several times. Later, they went round the body, higher than the waist and just below the breasts.

The *Himation* (men and women) was a large rectangle of white wool, draped over the left arm and shoulder, across the back, and under or over the right shoulder. Its weighted end was thrown over the left shoulder or the left forearm.

The *Chlamys* (men) was a small mantle for travelling, riding, and war, fastened by a fibula (pin-brooch) on the right shoulder or in front. It was made of wool. It covered the left arm, leaving the right arm bare, and was often weighted at all four corners. It was extensively worn by youths. A good size is 5 ft. by 3 ft.

The *Diplois* (women) or doubled mantle was folded at a third of its width and caught up on the right shoulder with a brooch at some distance from the ends, which fell in zig-zag folds. It was wound tightly round the body under the left shoulder.

The *Peplos* (women) was a veil of woollen stuff that could envelop the whole figure if thrown over the head. It was a shawl with an overfold at the top, and was worn, with a girdle, beneath the left arm and fastened with tapes on the right shoulder so that the overfold covers the body to the waist.

The *Strophion* (women) was a kind of corset with three bands—one round the hips, one at the waist line, and one under the bust.

Women wore their tunics to floor level and even below and had to walk with a pushing stride. Old men wore them to their feet, but younger men wore them shorter. The borders of the

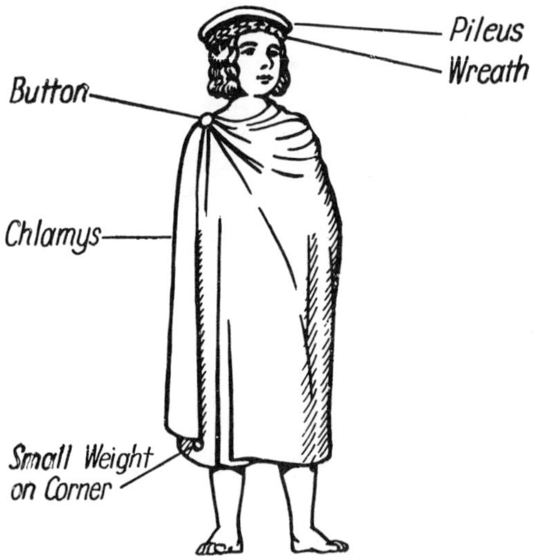

GREEK BOY

tunics and the corners of the cloaks were decorated, whilst spots, stars, and birds were often embroidered all over the fabric. Simple sandals were worn by the men, also shoes of soft ornamental leather, and boots. Boots were high to the middle of the calf, laced up the front, and turned over at the top for the richer folk.

Sandals were also worn by the women, and had thick leather soles, ankle straps, and an ornamental piece on the instep. Coloured leather shoes, laced on the instep, were also used.

The men wore their hair short and curly and curling tongs were used if required, a finish being given by the use of a fillet round the head across the brow. Short beards were the mark of the older men.

The women's hair was waved and curled, and dressed in a knot of plaits or curls high above the nape of the neck and projecting well beyond it. It was *always* parted in the middle. Sometimes the hair was placed on a metal frame attached by bands over the head. White (not gold) bands round the hair are allowable, and girls may wear a wreath of flowers.

The *Petasus* (men) was a wide felt hat with a low round crown and ear flaps, to which tying strings were fastened. When not in use, it was borne on the shoulders at the back by the strings. It was worn only when travelling, and was similar to the medieval pilgrims' or palmers' hats made familiar by the opera *Tannhäuser*. The *Pileus* (men) was a tight fitting cone shaped hat.

The *Himation* (women) served the purpose of a hat when thrown over the head on the rare occasions when women travelled, a fold being carried from the body over the head. The women also wore dazzling veils of white cotton or other (then) expensive material. Actual hats are rare and can be ignored.

The women wore a great profusion of jewels—combs, pins, hair nets, and brooches, which were ornamented with gold mounts; bracelets of gold or silver; necklaces of beaded fringe on plain bands, armlets, anklets, etc. The Gold Room of

THE PETASUS PEASANT'S HOOD

the British Museum furnishes many excellent examples of this fine work. The men wore rings and sometimes carried walking sticks.

Peasants wore short and plain *Tunics* with few folds (scanty) and with short sleeves.

The *Cloak* was a rough oblong for travelling and wet weather.

The *Hood* had a short point, giving a "gnome" effect, and was made from thick brown felt or cloth. Artisans and crowds can be bareheaded.

The *Carbatina* were of soft leather, put under the foot, but 2 in. wider all round so that the surrounding portions could be drawn up and over the foot by lacing to cover the toes and heel.

Puttees were linen straps swathed round the legs like modern puttees, but without the modern thin and regular strip.

Slaves may be richly dressed, if their owners please, and should have closely cropped hair.

Courtesans carried hand mirrors. The Greeks used flame coloured wedding veils, held on by gold fillets in the key design, with a golden girdle, but no wedding ring was worn.

For *Dances*, garlands and wreaths were used, and the colour for funerals was white. In the military dances the men still wore the cuirass, crested helmet, and leg-greaves, made of gold, brass, steel, or tin. Skins of animals, sometimes gilded, were stretched over the cuirass and helmet. The armour should be worn over a short tunic, the greaves over the bare skin. The feet were either bare or sandalled. This armour was certainly old fashioned and retained for ceremonial dancing only. Every Greek was most wisely compelled to dance until he was thirty years old, this being another instance of the wise rules of physical culture then current. In war, bows and arrows were used with spears, and swords were worn under the left armpit. Further light on the costume of the period may be gained at the British Museum—especially the Elgin Marbles.

SUMMARY

MEN

Dress

Doric Chiton or Tunic.
Ionic Chiton or Tunic.
Super Tunic. Pallium—a large cloak. Peplum—an outer wrap. Tribon—Black or Brown Cloak.
Belt of leather.
Himation—an outdoor cloak.
Chlamys—a short cloak.

Hair

Curly and short. Fillet on head. Short beards.

Hat

Petasus of wide felt with cords.
Pileus—a tight round cap.

Feet

Sandals. High-laced boots and soft leather shoes.

Legs

Bare.

GREEK ARTISAN

Jewels

Finger rings. Walking sticks. No armlets or anklets.

WOMEN

Dress

Doric Chiton or Tunic with overfold.
Ionic Chiton or Tunic without overfold, sleeved.
Super Tunic.
Peplum—an outer wrap.
Girdle.
Himation—an outdoor cloak.
Diplois—a doubled mantle.
Peplos—a shawl-veil.
Strophion—a corset.

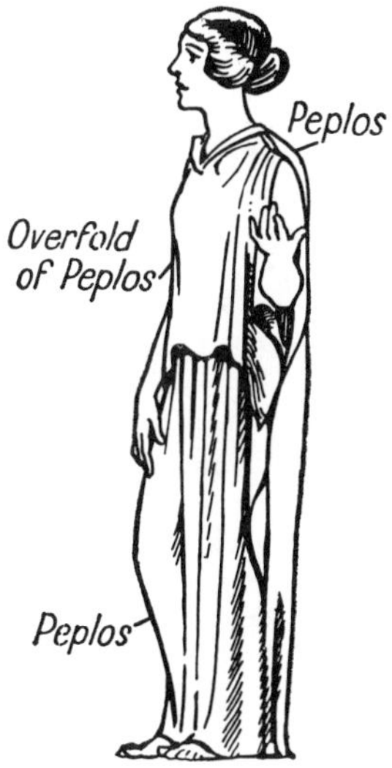

GREEK GIRL

Hair

Waved or curled.
Middle parting.
White bands round.
Flower wreaths for girls.

Hat

Fold of the Himation.
White veil.
Hats very rare.

Feet

Sandals. Coloured leather laced shoes.

Jewels

Gold and silver mounted bracelets, necklaces, pins, brooches.

PEASANTS

Dress

Chiton or Tunic, very plain.
Simple cloak.

Hair

Rough and short.

Hat

Hood of soft leather

Feet

Carbatina of soft leather.

Legs

Linen puttees.

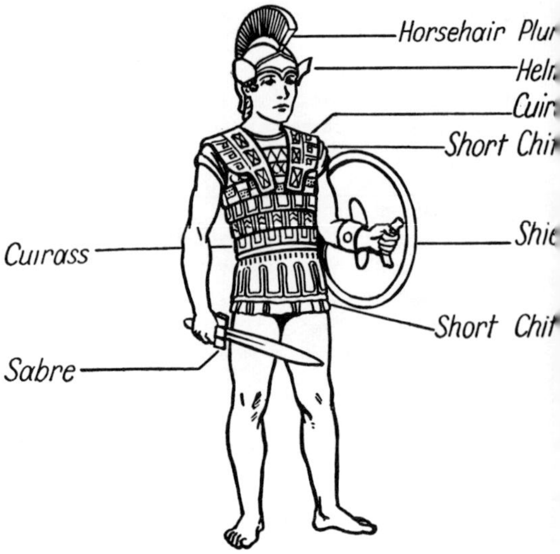

SOLDIER

THE ROMANS

The Romans set great store on physical perfection in order to produce as perfect a race as possible for the good of the State, which was pre-eminent in the minds of the nation before the Empire fell into decadence owing to excessive luxury and pleasure-seeking. Their dress, consequently, was loose and free, and whilst they were rather more fully clad than the Greeks, there was plenty of space allowed for sun and wind to reach the skin. Sports were often indulged in whilst the athletes were naked, and this also applied to the races and other games played during the great annual festival of the Saturnalia. The Romans, as the conquerors of the then known world, had great dignity and sense of power, and this too was reflected in the lines of their dresses, which were flowing, dignified, and of full length. They had elaborate sumptuary rules—as to what colour and decoration might be worn by particular classes of people. The classes were clearly marked, being divided into the court circle of Patricians (the Nobles), the Government Officials, such as Senators, Magistrates, and Priests, and the Common People. In addition, there were the military, by whom the people set much store, and the gladiators, who were the public entertainers, who, though they might be popular, were an unfortunate class, being doomed to early decease.

The Roman Republic began in 509 B.C. and became an Empire in 31 B.C. It collapsed in A.D. 324 when Constantine the Great transferred his capital to Byzantium, which he renamed Constantinople, and the Sack of Rome put the finishing touch to this epoch. Cicero and Caesar flourished from 106 B.C. to 44 B.C. and it is this time that is mostly in demand for stage purposes.

The principal dress for men was the Tunic and the Toga; for women it was the Stola.

The *Tunic* (men). The Tunic can be seen to-day, scarcely altered from Roman days, in the Dalmatic worn by the deacon at High Mass. It was of wool, in its natural yellowish shade, but later sumptuary laws allowed colour. Its length was a matter of taste, but those who wore it to the feet with sleeves to the wrist were thought effeminate. Two pieces of material were sewn together at the sides and top to form a shirt with short sleeves. Normally it reached to the calf, or half way down the thigh. It was drawn up under a girdle, at option. The *Tunica Palmata* worn by generals at triumphs was covered by palms embroidered in gold. The *Tunica Laticlavia*, worn by consuls, senators, and priests, had two broad bands (Clavi) of purple, which encircled the neck opening and ran down to the hem in front centre. Similar narrow bands from shoulder to hem, back and front, were allotted to the knights. No girdle was worn with the banded tunic.

The *Toga* (men) worn out of doors over the tunic, was a large cumbersome white woollen cloak. About eighteen feet by seven, it was semicircular in shape to enable its two ends to clear exactly the floor back and front. To wear, place the straight edge, at about a third of its length, on the left shoulder, letting the shorter end fall on the ground in front. Carry the rest of the straight edge across the back and under the right arm. Take the remainder (in front of the body), not at its edge, but about a third of the way down its depth, and let this upper part fall over the front. Gather the bulk now in front and carry it over the left shoulder. The fallen over straight edge now forms a kind of pocket (*sinus*) or loop which can be tightened by pulling up the left shoulder piece. In this was kept the handkerchief, etc. Later the toga was made of silk. It was never used during mourning.

Under the Empire (31 B.C.–A.D. 476) togas were of scarlet, purple, and violet, but by law white was the correct hue.

The *Toga Praetexata*, worn by magistrates, priests, and censors, was bordered with purple. Freeborn boys under 14 years of age, girls till marriage, and the later emperors wore this. The *Toga Picta* worn by generals was of purple cloth embroidered with gold stars, and was worn on state occasions also by emperors and consuls. The *Toga Candida* worn by candidates for public office was made pure white by chalking, and as much of the body as possible was exposed. The common toga, called *Toga Virilis*, as worn by all men, was of white wool. Children wore togas.

The *Lacerna* (men and women) was an outer mantle worn over the toga. At first it was brown or black and only used by the poor and soldiers. Later it was generally adopted and when red was called a Birrhus. It was short, sleeveless, open at the sides, and could have a hood called a Cucullus. It was fastened by a brooch on the right shoulder.

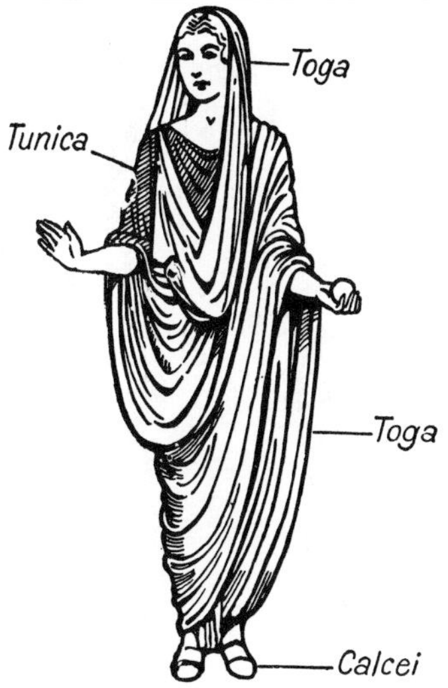

ROMAN LADY

The *Paenula* (men and women) was a thick woollen travelling cloak, large and circular, with only a neck opening. It was like a full chasuble worn at Mass and was the origin of this vestment. Occasionally left open down the front, it was lifted over the arms each side.

The *Stola* (women) was an Ionic Chiton, i.e. a long tunic fastened along the upper arm by costly brooches to form sleeves. Long and loose, it was essentially an aristocratic garment. It differed from the Greek tunic in having a wide flounce (*instita*) at the bottom and was pulled up under the girdle at the hips. Three loops on each arm are enough. It need not have sleeves. It can be any colour and embroidered, the fabric being wool, silk, or linen.

The *Zona* (women) was a girdle wound round the body under the breasts and at the waist and hips, with long knotted ends hanging to the ground in front.

The *Palla* (women) was a shawl wrap worn over the Stola. It was a rectangle or square of wool worn across the back and over both arms.

The *Pallium* (women) was a cloth cloak with

ROMAN PRIESTESS EMPEROR HADRIAN

woven intertwining floral designs, bordered with fringe. Like the palla, it could be placed over the head and was shawl-like.

The *Toga* (women) was worn in early times by women only; later it became the badge of freed slaves and prostitutes, so no respectable matrons would use it.

Sandals had a strap between the big toe and the rest, four cross-over straps, and two upright ones at the heel.

Soleae were slippers of leather or matting with straps, only in the house worn.

Calcei were street shoes covering the upper foot and laced or strapped. Senators' shoes were higher cut and patricians' and magistrates' shoes were of the richest leather, ornamented with gold and silver.

The *Pero* was a boot of rough leather or untanned hide, worn in early times by senators. From 157 B.C. senators, however, wore high black boots with a silver or ivory "C" or crescent-shaped ornament above the heel behind the ankle.

Caligae were stout shoes with spiked soles for soldiers.

The colours yellow, white, and green were forbidden in men's shoes.

The *Phaecassium* (women) was a white leather boot covering the whole foot. Occasionally it was worn by effeminate men.

The men's legs were bare and the women's legs did not show.

Sandals (men and women) of open leather work were worn in the house. A strap was passed between the big toe and the rest. There were about four fairly broad straps—loops on one side and ends on the other—tied at the top, and the "lacing" could be covered with a patterned leather or metal "tongue." In addition to these horizontal straps, there were two upright ones at the heel.

HAIR

Men's hair was worn longer earlier; in the bulk of the period men's hair was short, curly or waved, and a short curled beard was common. The emperors, except Marcus Aurelius, were nearly all clean shaven. Priests wore a band of ribbon.

Women's hair was curled, waved, and false hair was dressed in broad plaits, whilst a band of ribbon was bound round maidens' heads, and the staid and respectable adult women, including priestesses.

The *Caul* (women) was a gold wire hair net, pearled, jewelled, and even embroidered—a fashion continually cropping up through the centuries.

Men mostly went bareheaded; the back of the toga could be drawn over.

The *Causia* was the same as the Greek Petasus—a broad brimmed, low crowned hat with ear flaps, like a Pilgrim's hat of the Middle Ages. It was used by the upper classes when travelling.

The *Pileus* was a tightly fitting cone shaped hat worn by the commoners and freed slaves, specially at the Saturnalia.

Laurel Wreaths (men) were awarded to the military for their triumphs, and Julius Caesar had special licence always to wear one.

Gold Coronets, high in the front, narrowing at the sides and back, were worn by emperors and kings.

Women wore diadems set with diamonds, sapphires, emeralds, opals, and garnets, and the younger ones used floral wreaths. The shawl garments were used as head coverings, but hats as such did not exist.

A signet ring was a man's sole jewel and intaglio rings were used as seals.

The *Bulla* (boys) was a golden ball hung on the necks of boys up to 14 years old. It was sometimes heart shaped, and contained charms.

Great profusion of elaborate jewellery was worn by women—necklaces, bracelets, pins, nets, fillets, diadems, and long ear-rings set with stones; twisted gold wire rings and armlets. Serpent bracelets; large-headed pins for the hair; the umbrella and fan may here be mentioned as carried by fashionable women.

Peasants wore a plain tunic, and the *Toga Sordida* or *Pulla*, which was of black or brown with a *Hood* and *Cape* like those of the Greeks or the Medieval Englishman.

Carbatina were similar to the Greek, being of soft leather 2 in. wider than the foot, drawn up over it by lacing to cover heel and toe.

Reference to the British Museum will provide information on the costume, ornaments, and

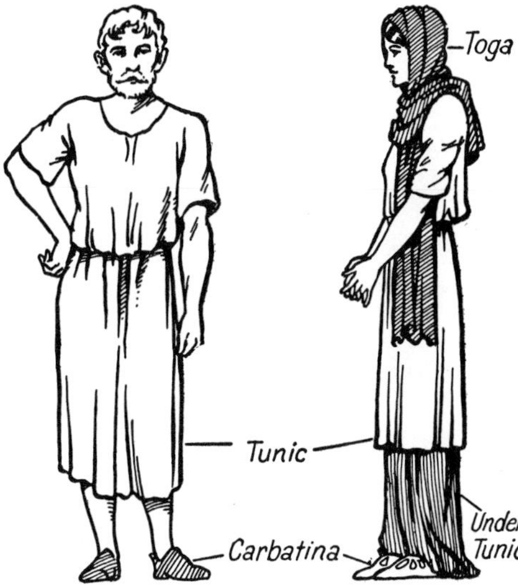

ROMAN PEASANTS

living habits of the Romans, who, like the Greeks, attached much importance to the value of physical development.

SUMMARY

MEN

Dress

Tunic—a woollen shirt.
Toga—a woollen cloak of many types for outdoors.
Lacerna—a dark outer mantle and optional hood.
Paenula—a travelling cloak.

Legs

Bare.

Feet

Sandals.
Soleae—house slippers.
Calcei—street shoes.
Pero—Patrician's shoes.
Caligae—Soldiers' spiked shoes.

Hair

Short curled hair and beard. Longer earlier.
Emperors mostly clean shaven.

Hats

None mostly
Petasus or Causia (see Greeks)—a broad brimmed travel hat.
Pileus—cone shaped.
Back of the Toga.
Laurel wreaths for triumphs and Caesar.
Gold coronet for emperors.

Jewels

Signet ring only. Intaglio rings as seals.
Bulla—gold pendant for boys.

WOMEN

Dress

Stola—an Ionic Chiton (see Greeks), with wide flounce, sleeves or without sleeves.
Zona of Fascia—a girdle.
Palla—a shawl.

Dress—contd.

Pallium—a flowered cloak.
Toga—a cloak in early times only.
Paenula—a travelling cloak.
Lacerna—a dark outer mantle.

Feet

Sandals.
Phaecasium—of white leather.
Shoes and slippers like men's, only finer.

Hair

Curled, waved, false, broad plaits.
Caul—a gold hair net.
Veil.

Hats

Diadems and wreaths.

Jewels

Rings, necklaces, bracelets, ear-rings, diadems, pins, nets, fillets. The umbrella and fan.

PEASANTS

Dress

Toga Sordida or Toga Pulla—brown or black cloak tunic.

Hat

Hood and Cape (see Greeks).

Feet

Carbatina (see Greeks).

THE SAXONS

The Saxons existed from about A.D. 460 to A.D. 1066 for my purpose, and one immediately conjures up visions of the Bayeux Tapestry. Yet the Saxons and Normans were by no means as awkward as they look in that piece of needlework, and their reputation for angularity must be attributed to Queen Matilda and her ladies who made this embroidery. The Saxons were perpetually harried by invaders—Danes, Scots, Northmen, Normans—and it is a wonder they had time to devote to the niceties of dress at all.

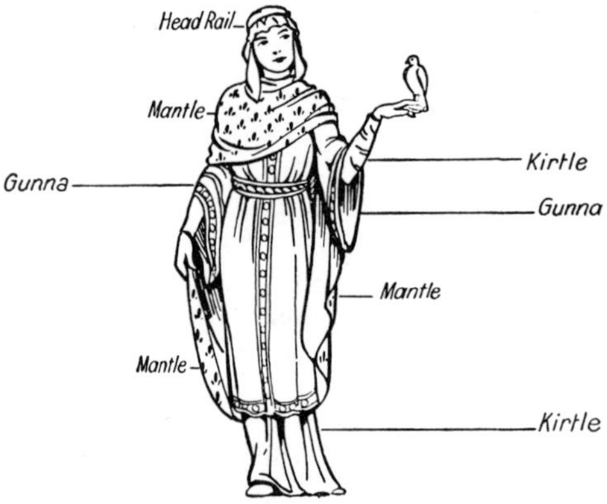

SAXON WOMAN

Clothes were made from linen, silk, and wool, often fur lined and embroidered in gold. Colourings were simple, and tended to favour browns. Clothes were thick, and a somewhat stocky appearance was given to the figure owing to their volume. The shape of the body was not revealed as in later times.

In some ways Saxon dress resembles ancient Greek in its general outline, though our colder climate made Saxon clothes more bulky, of thicker material, and, as a result, less graceful.

The *Under Tunic* (men) was of knee length and made of linen. The *Outer Tunic* (men) was of knee length, but had long sleeves that were wrinkled up over the arm, which they exceeded in length. It was slit at the sides from the hips downwards, to allow freedom.

The *Kirtle* (women) was an inner tunic with the same long sleeves, whilst the *Gunna* (women) was an outer tunic like the men's but had short sleeves. Its skirt was tucked into a belt on the right side.

It will be noted that only the men's long sleeves were visible, whilst the women's short sleeves on the outer tunic showed and the longer sleeves of the kirtle also appeared from the elbow downwards. Thus the women revealed two sleeves, the men only one.

There was not much difference in the cut of

the tunics of either sex, but the women's were slightly longer. A *Girdle* or *Belt* encircled the waist.

The *Mantle* (men) was cut something like chasuble—elliptical or circular, and was fastened on the right shoulder by a brooch or pin, or gathered through a ring. It was short and circular or long and straight.

Trousers (men) were long and loose, rather full, and wrinkled in much the same way as the sleeves, but on a lesser scale. They were cross gartered to the knee and the trousers reached to mid thigh,

SAXON PEASANT

from the foot. Cloth stockings were, alternatively, worn.

Men wore low leather *shoes*, with a fastening at the side or in front. Socks or stockings of cloth were worn.

Women's *shoes* were tied or buckled at the ankles.

Hair (men) included a full beard with two-forked ends. The hair was long and unconfined, parted from crown to forehead, and curled in ringlets. A big moustache was included, and the whole presented a vivid contrast to the closely cropped Normans when they came over.

Hair (women) was loose or braided, whilst fillets of material were worn by the better classes, but often the hair was hidden under the head rail (head covering). It was also worn in two plaits hanging down on either side of the front of the body.

Caps (men) were made of skins or cloth and were small and pointed, not unlike a cap of liberty or a Greek cap.

The *Head Rail* (women), later to be called a *Wimple*, was a large white linen or coloured square, about $2\frac{1}{2}$ by $\frac{3}{4}$yd. in size, which was drawn over the head from the left to the right shoulder, under the chin, and then around the back of the neck to the right shoulder. Over this was worn a circlet of gold, which was narrow. The same thing for an unmarried girl was called a *Snood*. It completely hid all hair from view, save where the long hanging plaits were worn.

Besides the golden circlet mentioned, the women wore large circular ear-rings, necklaces,

SAXON PEASANT

rings, bracelets of the precious metals, and they were skilful embroideresses, working in threads, which harmonized with the coloured material of the kirtle or tunica, and it was the purpose of showing this embroidery and colour to their best advantage that led to the custom of tucking up a corner of the gunna into the belt. The furs worn included sable, beaver, cat, fox, and lamb.

The men's *armour* was composed of mail in chains, rings, or scales sewn sometimes on to leather, at others hung over a leather jerkin. The shield had a six inch boss projecting from its centre, and was kite shaped as in the Bayeux Tapestry, or circular in the more old fashioned North.

Sir Walter Scott was a careful writer, and he has a brilliant passage descriptive of the costume of this period. The Anglo-Saxon aristocrat had "long yellow hair, equally divided on the top of his head and upon his brow, and combed down on each side to the length of his shoulders. His dress was a tunic of forest green, trimmed at the throat and cuffs with what was called minever, a kind of fur, inferior to ermine, and formed, it is believed, of the skins of the grey squirrel. This doublet hung unbuttoned over a close dress of scarlet, which was set tight to his body; he had breeches of the same, but they did not reach below the lower part of his thigh, leaving the knee exposed. His feet had sandals of the same fashion as the peasants, but of finer materials and secured in the front with gold clasps. He had bracelets of gold upon his arms, and a broad collar of the same precious metal about his neck . . . Behind his seat was hung a scarlet cloth cloak,

Saxon Noble

lined with fur, and a cap of the same material richly embroidered, which completed the dress of the opulent landowner when he chose to go forth."

From the word "Gunna" comes "Gown." Sir Walter Scott has an equally interesting passage about the Anglo-Saxon noblewoman.

"Her locks," he says, "were braided with gems and being worn at full length intimated the noble and free born conditions of the maiden." (Here I think Scott describes the hair of the younger women only, for, as I have written already, women's hair was nearly always carefully concealed under the head rail.) "A golden chain, to which was attached a small reliquary, hung round her neck.

"She wore a bracelet on her arms, which were bare. Her dress was an under gown and kirtle of pale sea green silk, over which hung a loose robe, which reached to the ground, having very wide sleeves, which came down, however, very little below the elbow. This robe was crimson, and manufactured out of the finest wool. A veil of silk, interwoven with gold, was attached to the upper part of it, which could be, at the wearer's pleasure, either drawn over the face or bosom, after the Spanish fashion, or disposed as a sort of drapery round the shoulders."

Considering that Sir Walter Scott wrote over a century ago, when antiquarian questions received scant attention (apart from Classical ruins) it is surprising how accurate his description of

Saxon Lady

Saxon costume is, and *Ivanhoe* throws quite a vivid light on the manners and customs of this period. Scott was, of course, the pioneer of the modern love for the antique and the respect for the work of our ancestors in Britain.

The moustaches of the men were grown as long as nature allowed, and it was the absence of this feature that led King Harold's spies to assume that the clean shaven army of William the Conqueror were not soldiers but merely monks. The Conqueror took a dislike to these over prolific hirsute adornments, and ordered the Saxons (or at any rate those about him) to be clean shaven.

The Saxon peasant wore clothes of the simplest cut possible, in view of the fact that his wife had to make them in her spare time. A sleeved close jacket of skin reached from the throat to the knees, with a narrow neck opening just sufficient to admit the passage of the head without leaving too wide a gap to admit cold and wet. His sandals were bound with leathern thongs and a roll of leather was twisted round the legs to the calf, leaving the knees bare. This bandaging and cross gartering of the legs, over stocking or trousers, is a distinctive feature of Saxon times.

The practice of making sleeves much too long and wrinkling them up was a practical one, for it gave additional warmth through the extra thickness, and in winter the hands could be withdrawn completely into the sleeve, which thus served the purpose of the modern glove.

The edges of the tunics can be embroidered in coloured thread or wool to form a border of decoration, and this border can be carried up around the slits that appeared at each side from the hip downward (for the men) to allow freedom of movement, the tunic being rather closely fitting.

The Bayeux Tapestry is a good guide to the dresses, but some elementary knowledge of the clothes that were worn is necessary in order to distinguish the various garments from each other. Unfortunately, the Bayeux Tapestry is not easy to reproduce in illustration. The best illustrations of it are the enlarged coloured prints that may be

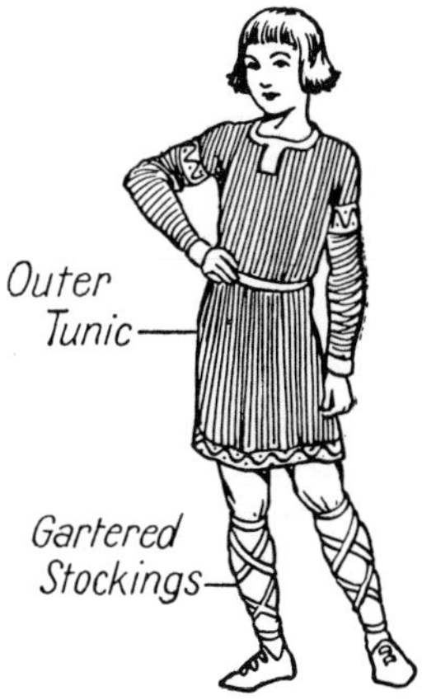

SAXON YOUTH

seen in many museums in London and the country. The small photos of the Tapestry sold at the Victoria and Albert Museum will not serve the purpose of anyone making costumes in this style.

SUMMARY

MEN

Dress

Under tunic.
Outer tunic with long sleeves, slit at sides.
Girdle.
Mantle, circular or straight, fastened on shoulder.

Legs

Trousers, long and loose and wrinkled.
Cross garterings.

Feet

Low leather shoes.
Socks or stockings.

Hair

Full bi-forked beard. Heavy moustache. Long, curled hair, mid parted.

Hats

Skin or cloth "Liberty" caps.

Armour

Mail of various types. Kite-shaped or circular shield with large centre boss.

WOMEN

Dress

Kirtle—an inner tunic with long sleeves.
Gunna—an outer tunic with short sleeves. Skirt tucked into belt.
Girdle.

Feet

Shoes tied or buckled at ankles.

Hair

Loose or braided for youth and peasants.
Head rail for the others, concealing hair.

Hair—contd.
Fillets of material.

Hats
Head rail.
Circlets, mainly golden.

Jewels
Large round ear-rings, bracelets, rings, necklaces.

PEASANTS

Dress
Sleeved close tunic. Narrow neck opening.

Feet
Leather sandals, thonged.

Legs
Leather bandages, or cross gartering.

THE NORMANS

Owing to the perpetual battles that William the Conqueror and his successors had to undertake in order to subdue a country that did not welcome the Normans, there was little change in dress during the Norman period. Men's minds being upon war were not inclined to waste time in designing costumes, and of what use was it for the ladies to think of something fresh when their lords were almost always on service?

NORMAN NOBLE

The basis of the clothes was a shirt which was close fitting and reached to the ankles, but its simplicity was relieved by its having the edge banded and embroidered with gold, while the large hanging cloak added a decorative and spacious appearance to the costume. The cloak was fastened by a massive brooch, often of elaborate design, in precious metal or humbler substance. The type of design was similar to the well known (though earlier) Alfred jewel.

Clothes were lined and adorned with fur—ermine, squirrel, marten, goat, and rabbit being favourites.

WILLIAM I

The men seem to have taken over the ways of the women in the matter of the length of their tunic sleeves, for the outer tunic now has short sleeves, and the inner one, long sleeves. Both were knee length and embroidered.

The *Outer Tunic* (men) had short wide sleeves of elbow length, with embroidered edges. The *Inner Tunic* (men) was of white, with long wrinkled sleeves projecting over the hand if extended. This white tunic shows round the neck, where the wider opening of the outer tunic was V-shaped. This close neck hole was bordered with embroidery or it might be V-shaped, about five inches deep. It was either belted or closely fitted the knees, and, if the latter, had slits at either side to allow free movement. The *Mantle* was a knee-length cape, rectangular or semi-circular, fastened on the right shoulder or in the front. It was like the Saxon mantle, except that it was slightly larger, and was kept together with a brooch. The women dressed like the Saxon women and the Norman men, in two tunics (the kirtle and the gunna), now called the chemise and the gown. The *Chemise* was of white linen, with a long skirt and long wrinkled sleeves.

The *Gown* had a loose elbow-length sleeve and a skirt of three-quarter length and often even longer.

WILLIAM II

The men's tunic sleeves became so long that they were turned back over the wrists.

The women's tunics were laced up the back so as to make the front fit smoothly to the figure.

Cloaks (women) were lined with fur, and hung from the shoulders by straps across the bosom.

1100–1150

The *Bliaud* (women) was a long smock-like gown with a laced bodice of elastic fabric. The skirt was full and straight, and was bound by a wide belt. *Girdles* were either a wide strip of cloth richly embroidered or a long silken rope wound round the waist, with tasselled ends, which hung in front almost down to the hem of the gown. The pendulous cuff increased so much that the sleeve had to be knotted on itself to prevent it trailing on the ground. Clothes became longer.

Chausses (men) were trousers of wool, tight to the ankle. The legs were wound to the knee with strips of leather or cloth, which was sometimes banded at the knee and/or the ankle. Linen breeches, like pyjamas, were fastened with a running string at the hem.

There is much confusion in costume books between breeches and chausses. Breeches, no matter what their length, were always hung from the waist downwards, being fastened by a running string. They were close fitting, or loose, according to taste, and if loose were brought close to the leg by cross strapping from the knee to the ankle. The length varied from what were our modern "shorts" to ankle length. Shorts were loose enough to enable them to be caught up at the sides of the thighs and pinned to the upper waist line part.

Chausses were stockings and were drawn from the foot upwards, and this distinction between the two garments should make clear the different cut and use of the two. The hose gradually became longer and more closely fitting and were very wide at the thigh so that the breeches could be tucked into them. Old drawings show that these stockings were tied to the waist string of the breeches in front by a tape. Again, some drawings show that even when the "shorts" variety was adopted they could be gathered in at the knee to prevent draughts blowing upwards.

Shoes (men) were of black leather with narrow bands of embroidery along the top and down the instep. Red, yellow, blue, and green shoes were also used, and their tops rolled over to the ankle. In William II's day (1087–1100) the shoes became pointed, and were stuffed with wool at the point. In the reign of Stephen (1134–54) the tops of the shoes went much higher, and were rolled back so as to show the brilliant lining. Stockings, which became common about 1100, were made of say, which was a kind of worsted cloth.

Hair (men) was during the reign of William I short, and clean shaven faces were *de rigueur*, but this custom only lasted a short time and the nation went back to the pre-Conquest customs of longer hair. By William II's time the hair and beard were worn quite long again.

Hair (women) was simply coiled at the back of the head, and in curls about the face. It was

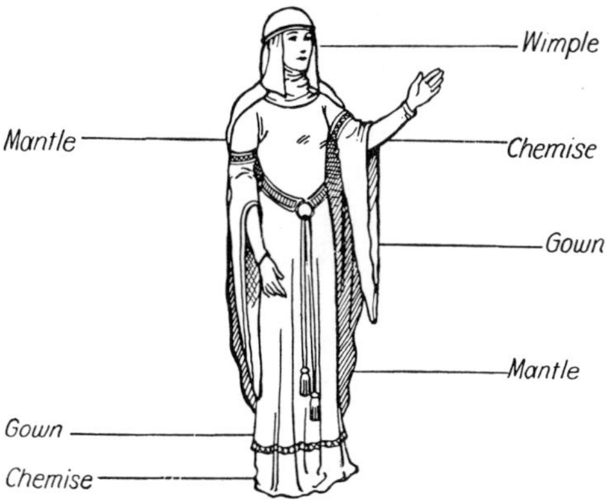

NORMAN LADY

still hidden by the head rail (now called a wimple). By Henry I's time (1100–35) the hair was no longer hidden, and long braids which were intertwined with coloured ribbons became fashionable. The ends might be bound with strips of silk instead, and about 1135 the wimple went out.

The *Hood* (men) was warm, and of cloth, but tight *Caps* of cloth were also worn. These were brimless or were peaked in the centre of the crown (the "gnome" variety again).

The *Wimple* (women) was the Saxon head rail. It was a square of material, generally white, which was wound round the head and throat. Some women preferred to expose the hair even in early Norman times, and this became normal in Henry I's time, when the wimple went out, about 1135.

Down to the end of the fourteenth century it

was the common custom to be bareheaded—a healthy practice which has come again into fashion in our own times. Hoods were worn mainly when travelling and in inclement weather. A similar use applies to the wimple and it is not entirely necessary to provide headgear to be accurate. Hoods and wimples appear and re-appear right down the centuries in varying forms and have lasted right down to the present day in academic and monastic dress. Conversely, it will be observed, as this treatise progresses, how in

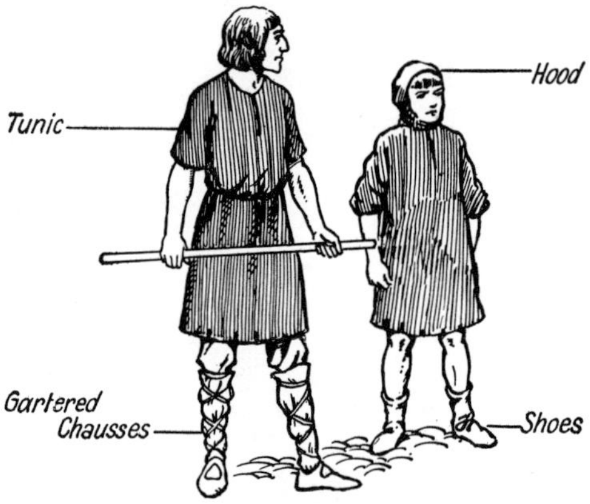

NORMAN PEASANTS

later centuries—the seventeenth and eighteenth—the reverse principle was adopted and instead of men and women going bareheaded out of doors, they wore their hats indoors as well as outside.

For the peasants, canvas and fustian were popular. As in all ages, the peasants disregarded the extremes of fashion when they were exaggerated in cut. This is only to be expected; firstly, because they had not the money to spend on the latest fashions, and, secondly, because such exaggerations nearly always got in the way during work, and only the rich, who had little manual work to perform, could tolerate such clothes. This refers specially to the points appended to clothes and shoes, and to the extreme length of dresses.

Hats and caps were of felt. Trousers were loose.

Costume in Norman times was in the main quite simple for all classes. The rich imported fabrics, and adorned the native English woollens with needlework, pearls, and other precious stones, a fashion that followed the more advanced culture across the Channel. It should be borne in mind, however much we are inclined to resent the Norman invasion, that Norman culture and Norman learning were definitely in advance of the Saxon, and though the Conqueror's methods were stern, he and his descendants introduced many benefits in government and living.

In stage work this distinction between the cultured Norman and the less polished Saxon can be made with advantage.

The Crusaders had a reflex effect in the introduction, by the returning warriors, of Eastern fabrics and decorations, and the lengthening of dresses, which became voluminous, like those of the East.

The Girdle comes into great prominence during the first half of the twelfth century, and may be said to be a distinguishing mark of this period. Mittens were in use. The wimple is sometimes known as the couvre-chef. The favourite colours of early Norman times were red, blue, and green.

With the advent of the long sleeves, which touched the ground, men found a way out of the difficulty of being unable to use their hands by making a slit in the sleeve at the place where the opening ought to be, that is, at the elbow, through which the arm was put, the rest of the sleeve hanging down. This interesting relic still remains in the academic gowns of masters in our universities.

When braids came into fashion, those women who were not well favoured by Nature did not shrink from using artificial plaits for the purpose.

Macbeth is sometimes costumed in early Norman style, though that usually adopted is a kind of legendary British and Saxon combined. Its main features are described in the chapter on the Saxons, but for the braided hair, and the long sweeping sleeves customary for Lady Macbeth and her womenfolk, the Norman dresses are sufficiently accurate. Indeed, there was at first little change between the Saxon and the Conqueror's fashions.

In fashioning the ample cloaks to the shoulders large circular brooches or rings should be used. These give scope for fine decorative touches.

Deep borders of ornament on the tunics were embroidered, woven or appliqué at the neck, wrists, and hem, and sometimes there was also a band of decoration round the upper arm.

SUMMARY

MEN

Dress

Outer tunic with short sleeves.
Inner tunic with long sleeves.
Mantle, fastened on shoulder.
Belt.

Legs

Chausses—wool trousers.
Leather or cloth bandages.

Feet

Leather shoes, black or coloured and embroidered.
Later they have high rolled tops.

Hair

William I—clean shaven.
William II—long hair and beard.

Hats

Hood—gnome-like.
Cap—peaked in centre, brimless.

WOMEN

Dress

Chemise—long skirt and sleeves, white linen; Gown—elbow sleeves } William I

Cloaks—fur lined, straps on shoulders } William II

Bliaud—a smock-gown laced; Girdles; Long knotted sleeves to gowns } 1100–1150

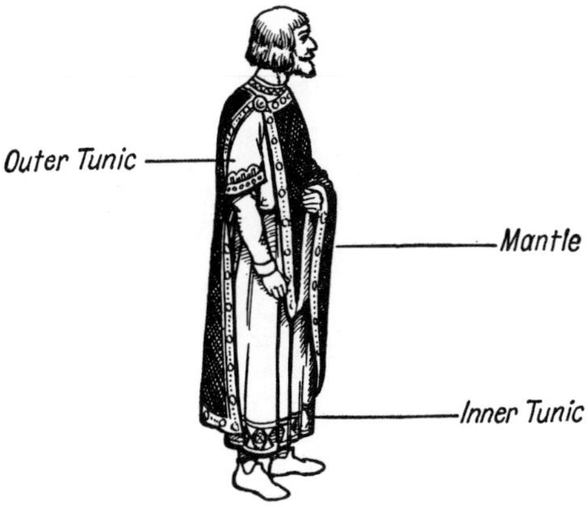

NORMAN NOBLE

Hair

Coiled at back, curls in front—hidden by wimple (William I and II).
Long braids (1100–1150).

Hats

Wimple till 1135 round head and throat.

PEASANTS

Dress

Fustian or canvas.
Hats and caps of felt.
Loose trousers.

THE PLANTAGENETS

Oriental fashions began to affect European styles and introduced delightful new materials for dresses. These new materials, rather than any very marked alteration in cut, constituted the new models.

I now deal with the period from 1154–1272—the reigns of Kings Henry II, Richard I, John, and Henry III. The constant travels of Richard I in the Crusades familiarized his people with the gorgeous fabrics of the East, and great luxury resulted. They brought back with them the Dalmatica. Another factor was the wearing of steel armour that readily rusted in every shower. To obviate rust the Surcoat was invented to cover the armour. It is in this period that the Capuchon, or hood, first appears, and it lasts through many centuries in one form or another; indeed, for a long time it remained almost unchanged, and we may say that it has persisted to our own day in the clothes of the monks and friars.

Garments became more voluminous and were

embroidered. A favourite pattern was that of circles overlapping each other, which appeared on garments and shoes; when on the latter the embroidery was in gold.

Many new materials appeared. Of these were Burnet, a brown cloth; Bysine, a fine cloth of cotton or flax for mantles; Ray, a striped Flemish cloth; and Damask, which took its name from the city of its origin—Damascus. It was the rich stuff that is known by that name even to-day. Peasants wore a coarse brown cloth called Burel, a thicker cloth called Byrrhus, sheepskin leather named Basil, and a rough cloth termed Brocella. It is curious that all these names begin with the same letter.

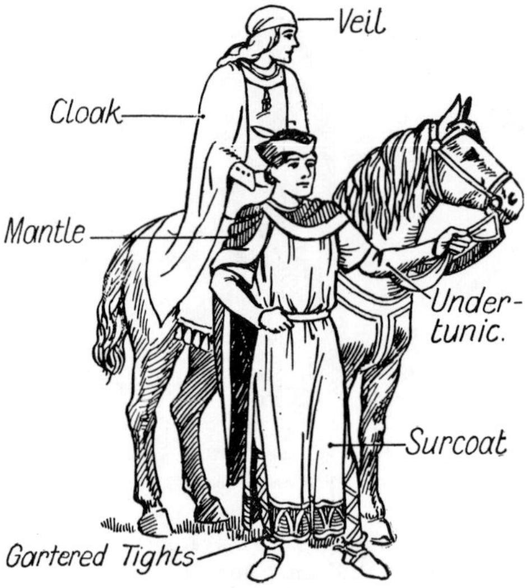

NOBLES

Under Henry III, when the Crusaders returned, the Eastern materials came into rapid vogue, and had many delightful names, such as Baudekin, Checklatoun, Ciclatoun, and Tissue. All these were silk woven with gold thread and many coloured. Sarcinet was a thinner silk. The Tennysonian "Samite" was a similar gold-woven silk, rather like Satin. Gauze was known. Gowns and mantles were brought over from Italy, and all were richly lined with fur, for the badly heated rooms of the period were cold and draughty.

The effect of all this sudden magnificence tended to make the gayer folk try to wear everything at once, and this caused garments to become both numerous and bulky; indeed the age is known as the age of draperies. At the same time, the cut was simple and dignified on the whole, and did not attain to the fantastic shapes made fashionable by the clever and artistic Richard of Bordeaux.

HENRY II and RICHARD I

The *Dalmatica* was shirt-like, being a loose-sleeved, full-length tunic, worn over the *Under-tunic*, which was of equal length, but had close-fitting, tight sleeves.

The *Mantle* was worn over all, and was voluminous and made from fine Flemish cloths or rich Italian silks.

JOHN

The *Surcoat*, which came into prominence first in King John's reign, was a full length garment, sleeveless, and with wide arm-openings. It had a slit from the bottom edge to the waist in front to give freedom in walking and riding. (This slit may be omitted.) Not yet are coats of arms emblazoned on the surcoat. It was belted in leather with a buckle and a long tongue falling in front. The whole was worn over.

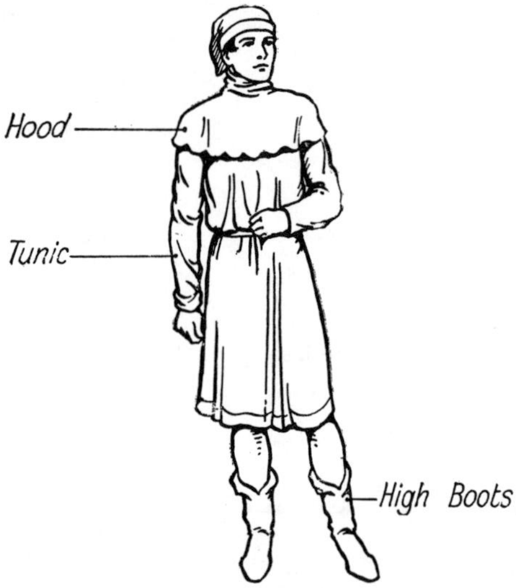

MIDDLE CLASS

The *Long Tunic*, which reached to just below the knees, had sleeves, either tight or loose.

The Capa was a large mantle with a hood that could be drawn over the head when needed. It was made of wool.

The *Balandrana* could be worn over all these, and was simply a large cloak, It was worn, like the hood, when travelling.

HENRY III

The *Surcoat*, which first appeared in John's reign, now became fashionable, and was as already described under that reign. It was worn over

The *Tunic*, which was either tight sleeved or loose sleeved, as in the previous reign, was of full length. The sleeves, if loose, should flow.

The *Cloak* was circular, fur-lined, and made of silk. It should be capacious. The furs in vogue were marten, beaver, badger, sable, and squirrel.

The *Capuchon* was a hood attached to a short cape that covered the shoulders, fitting neatly over the chest, arms, and back. Its bottom edge was sometimes cut in semi-circles.

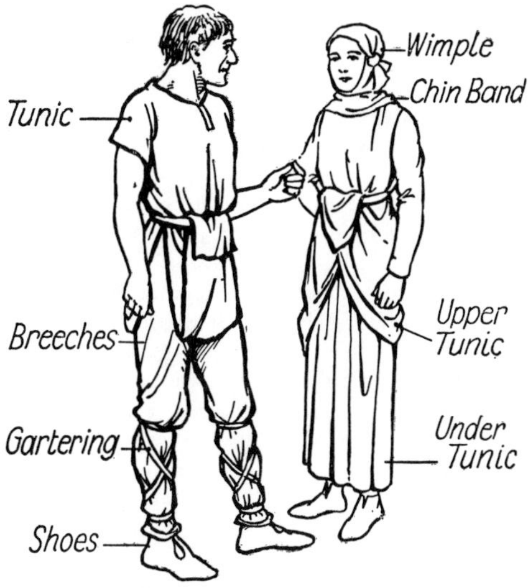

PEASANTS

The short *Upper Tunic*, which is common to all reigns, was worn more especially by older men and was Tabard-shaped; that is, it was slit right down each side, it fell straightly down back and front, and was gathered in by a belt, so that many folds appeared.

WOMEN OF ALL REIGNS

The *Gown* was loose, with sleeves cut close from the elbow to the wrist, at which appeared a row of small buttons. The sleeves should extend well below the wrists, so that wrinkles appear throughout their length.

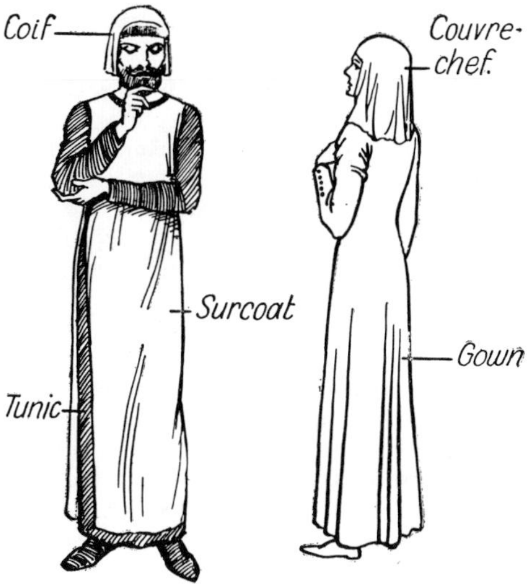

DOCTOR AND NURSE

The *Belt* was in silk or leather, with a good buckle and long tongue like those of the men.

The *Aumônière* came in during Henry III's time, and was of silk or cloth bag hung from the belt at the left side.

The *Mantle* was a long cloak simply cut, left open in front, and tied across the chest by cords, which were attached to the mantle by handsome metal clasps.

The Men wore *breeches*, but, owing to the length of the tunics, these did not show. Stockings appeared in the earlier reigns, and in Henry III's time close-fitting tights came in.

The men wore *shoes* that were slightly pointed in the earlier reigns, but in Henry III's time these became much sharper, the point, of course, extending in front either from the big or the middle toe.

The women's shoes were similar, but the points were shorter. They should be of leather and well-fitting. Another version is a rather blunt toe, long enough to be bent back over the foot. They were fastened by one button above the ankle. High boots to the calf may be used. Both kinds were rolled over at the top.

The men were generally clean shaven, though a few had short beards. The hair was curled, and occasionally a fillet was worn over the brow.

The women's hair, though much hidden by the wimple, was more elaborate in treatment. It was parted in the middle, and the plaits were gathered into two bags, one each side of the face. These were sometimes again covered by the *Couvre-Chef*, which was a veil. These bags could be richly jewelled or netted in an elaborate pattern.

The men wore tall crowned *hats* with brims which were turned up at the back and which ran forward to a point at the front. A long quill was stuck into the side. It will be recognized from this description and that of the Capuchon that we have reached the age of Robin Hood of Sherwood Forest. *Conical caps* were also worn. They were of the sugar-loaf variety and were not too tall. The *coif* (really a peasant's cap) was worn by the better class when hunting, probably because as it was close fitting it did not catch the wind. Further, it could not be wrenched off when the hunters were passing under trees in the forest. The coif was white and fitted the head closely. It came down at the back and was tied under the chin with strings or it was without strings. The coif lasts well into Jacobean times as part of a judge's official dress.

The *Wimple* and *Chin Band* (women) was in two pieces of white linen. One was bound round the forehead and secured by the other, which went under the chin. They were pinned together at the top. The former should be pinned at the back. This is a most becoming fashion, especially for older folk with double chins. It is seen to-day in most of the orders of nuns, though many of them have spoilt its beauty by unduly stiffening and starching the wimple and chin band.

Peasants wore, as usual, the always serviceable tunic and hose, with a coif or hood. It was a neat and warm dress that did not get in the way when the peasants were at work. They also wore breeches, which were loose and full to the knee, and tied round the waist with a string. The hose were fastened to the breeches by similar strings tied to the waist.

For their feet the peasants wore what were oddly called *Startups* or *Peros*. We came across the Pero in the chapter on Roman dress, and it is the same thing in this reign. They were high shoes, laced in the front, and the soles were pegged with wooden pegs that were similar, in principle, to those used in modern football boots. Considering the normal state of the floor of the living rooms in this period a little elevation from it was quite desirable! The rushes covered many unpleasant things!

Gloves were of gauntlet type. The wealthy had the backs richly jewelled. This custom led in time to the back being embroidered instead of jewelled, though the bishops retained their jewelled gloves to comparatively recent times. The poor had to be content with woollen mittens.

During the Crusades, with so many men away from home, there was little incentive to the women to dress themselves radiantly, and their costumes changed but little, but with the return of the warriors things took on a brighter hue. Cut, colour, and fabric became more elaborate and more gay.

In Henry II's time tights were fastened with cross garterings, which ended in a tassel below the knee. Shoes were of coloured leather, not black, and had golden stripes or patterns upon them.

SUMMARY

MEN

Dress

Dalmatica — long sleeved Undertunic — tight sleeved Mantle—voluminous	Henry II and Richard I
Belted surcoat Very long tunic Capa—large hooded mantle Balandrana—wide cloak	John

Dress—contd.

Surcoat—leather belted Tunic—tight or loose sleeved Cloak—fur lined, circular Capuchon—hood and cape	Henry III
Short upper tunic, Tabard shape Gloves	All reigns

Legs

Breeches—did not show } Richard I and John
Stockings—hardly seen under tunic } Richard I and John

Tights—close fitting (Henry III).

Feet

Shoes slightly pointed (Richard I and John).
Shoes sharply pointed (Henry III).

Hair

Clean shaven. Short beards sometimes.
Hair curled, sometimes a fillet on brow.

Hats

Tall crowned, brim turned up at back and pointed at front.
Conical caps.
Coif when hunting.

WOMEN

Dress

Gown—loose with sleeves close from elbow to wrist and long rows of buttons.
Belt—silk or leather.
Aumônière—a bag at the belt (Henry III).

Dress—contd.

Mantle—long cloak, open in front, cords across chest, fur lined.
Gloves—jewelled.

Feet

Shoes less pointed than men's. Well fitting in leather.
High boots.

Hair

Middle parting.
Two hair nets at sides over bags, jewelled sometimes.

Hats

Wimple and chin band.
Couvre-chef—a veil.

PEASANTS

Dress

Tunics and hose.
Coif or hood of felt.
Breeches.

Shoes

Startups or Peros (*vide* Romans)—high shoes, front laced.
Soles—wooden pegged.

THE THREE EDWARDS

Tired of the voluminous and clumsy garments of the past age, men revolted during the reigns of the three Edwards, and adopted a closely cut, tight fitting costume. Women, too, had their own rebellion, this time in the matter of the hair, which had been carefully hidden from view. They displayed it to the public admiration, and their choice of gowns became more beautiful with the greater facilities of range now offered. The sumptuary laws were enacted in 1363 and were a curious attempt to control personal extravagance. Their enforcement was not altogether a success. The people found a way round the law.

Stamped velvets and rich brocades, in conventional patterns, which contrasted with shining satins, were introduced.

EDWARD I

The *Cotehardie* (men) was the new mode. It was a close fitting garment like a coat. It reached to the knees and was fastened by a waist belt. Its front was slit and fastened with buttons and a row of buttons fastened the sleeves from elbow to wrist. The sleeves were closely fitted to the arm and at the elbow a long hanging sleeve fell nearly to the ground. It could be bordered with fur.

The *Surcoat* (men) was the same as before, but heraldic designs appeared upon it in embroidered work.

Tights (men) were worn with the cotehardie, and the effect was quite different from the previous reign, the men wearing a clean-cut sparse costume.

The *Mantle* (men and women) alone remained in generous width and length as of old.

The *Kirtle* (women) closely fitted the body and

was often laced, with tight sleeves buttoned from elbow to wrist. Over it was

The *Loose Gown* (women) of a different colour from the kirtle but with a lining that matched the kirtle. Its sleeves were quite long and loose, and there could be a train. It was confined by

The *Girdle*, which was slung from the hips.

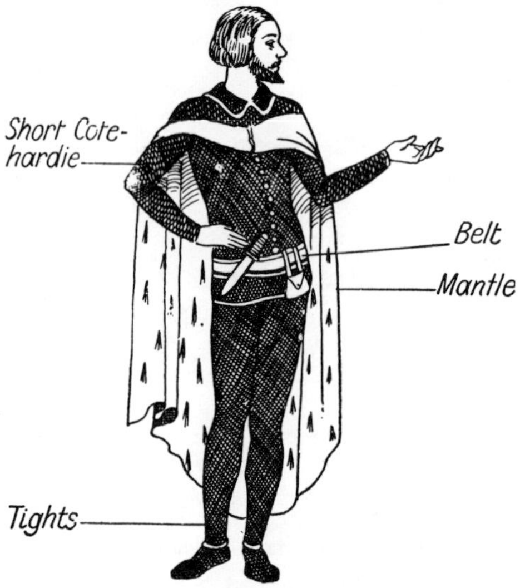

MAN—EDWARD III

The over-gown was pulled through the girdle in front so as to show the kirtle. A two-colour effect was given by the combined frocks—one shade for kirtle, skirt front and sleeves, and gown lining, the other for the gown exterior.

EDWARD II AND III

The *Cotehardie* (men) was the same, but was parti-coloured vertically.

The *Belt* carried a pouch and dagger.

The *Cape* (men) was either long or short as taste dictated. It was edged and collared in fur, and buttoned at the neck.

The *Full Gown* (women) was the same as before, except that *Tippets* were worn from 1350 to 1380. These were long strips of cloth or fur fastened just above the elbow to the sleeves. Before these came in the sleeves were wide and long.

The *Kirtle* (women) was worn under the gown as before.

The *Cyclas* (women) was used in Edward II's reign only, and was a tight surcoat. It was shorter in front than behind, and had no sleeves.

Tights (men), parti-coloured to match the cotehardie, gave prominence to the legs. Bi-coloration was either single colour to each leg or the two shades were combined on each leg, vertically divided. The shades must alternate with those of the cotehardie, i.e. if the latter is red on the right and green on the left, then the tights must be green on the right and red on the left. It was a fashion that no doubt owed its inspiration to the growing popularity of heraldry. We have already noted that coats of arms began to adorn the surcoat in Edward I's reign.

These parti-coloured tights came in during the reigns of Edward II and Edward III only.

Dark leather shoes with longer points than before were worn by men and women, the latter's being less sharp.

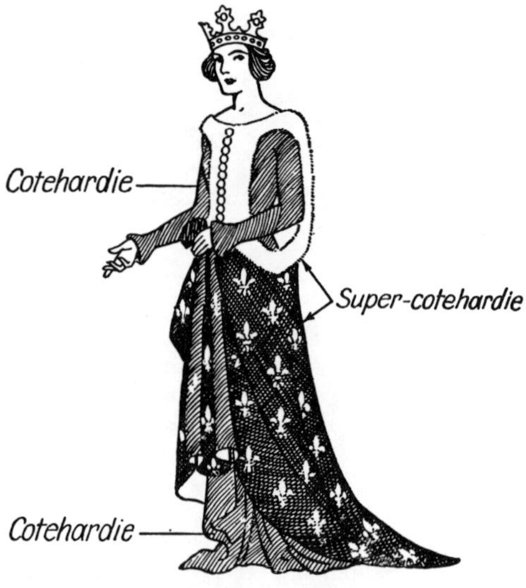

A LADY, 1350-60

The men's hair was long and bushy in Edward I's time. During Edward II's and III's reigns it was still bushy, but was cut round and curled. Faces were clean shaven, but old men wore a beard parted into two curling points.

The women's hair in Edward I's time was parted in the middle and bunched on either side of the face in a bag or net, and was dressed over the ears.

In the time of Edward II and Edward III girls wore two plaits and placed the gorget under them. The women of this date still wore the hair in side nets.

The *Beaver*, worn by men in Edward I's reign, was a hat with a turned up brim and a tall crown with a somewhat ridiculous feather in front. It was placed on top of the

Hood or *Capuchon* (men), which was the same as before, except that the

Liripipe (men) was now part of it. This was an exaggeration of the original peak to the hood, and attained a great length. A good general length is sufficient to drop on the shoulder, though it was often so long that it could be wound round the neck like a scarf.

The beaver hat was optional. If worn, it should be in conjunction with the hood.

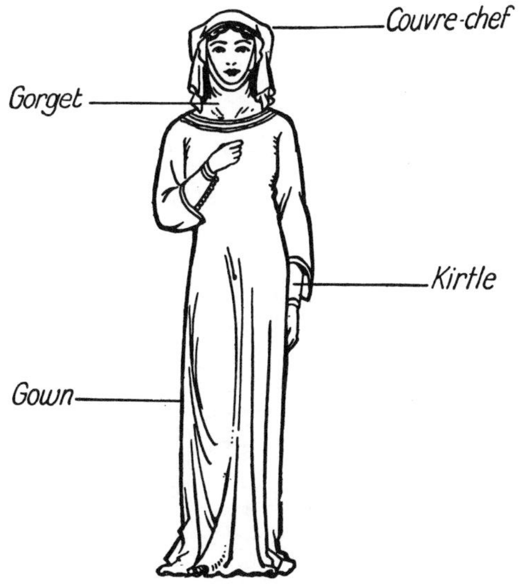

LADY DE COBHAM, 1320 (COBHAM)

The *Gorget* (women) is another name for the chin band, which was a linen band drawn over the head, with another under the chin.

The *Wimple* (women) remained as before but was now worn by the older women. Also it was dyed yellow.

Caps were richly varied, a popular one being the

Spanish Turban (women), in which the forehead band was widened and stiffened, not unlike the modern Russian tiara one sees in pictures of the massacred Russian Royal Family.

In Edward III's reign the men had the liripipe

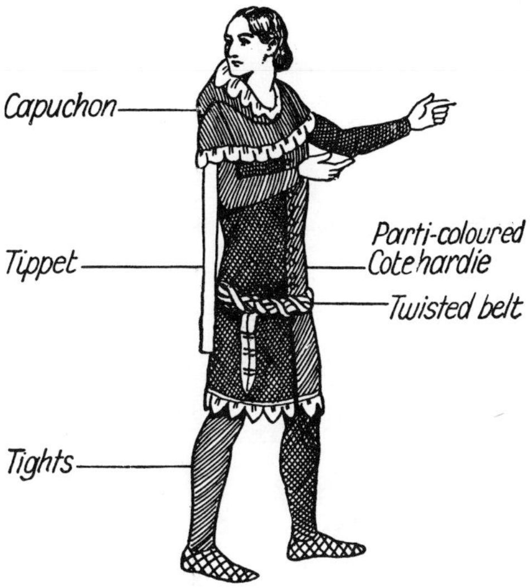

MAN, ABOUT 1350

attached to the hood, as before, but it was longer. It was even longer than floor length, in which case it was knotted to clear the floor, or was wound round the head, with the end tucked in or draped about the shoulders. It was in this case a scarf attached to a hat.

The women wore gorget and wimple of fine lawn. Silk ribbon fillets bound round the brow were popular, as were also the side nets for the hair as before, the nets being made in gold work and jewelled.

The peasants still remained much the same, but the Sumptuary Laws checked any originality in costume as far as they were concerned, and no peasant wore fur. The materials for his dresses were mostly coarse grained cloth, chiefly brown.

To all garments of this period "dagging" was done. This consisted of scalloping or cutting the edges of the clothes into points, semicircles, or irregular pieces resembling leaves.

SUMMARY

MEN (EDWARD I)

Dress

Cotehardie—tight knee-length coat. Tight sleeves with strip from elbow to ground attached. Belt.
Surcoat—now heraldic.
Mantle—still long.

Legs

Tights.

Feet

Dark leather shoes, with longer points.

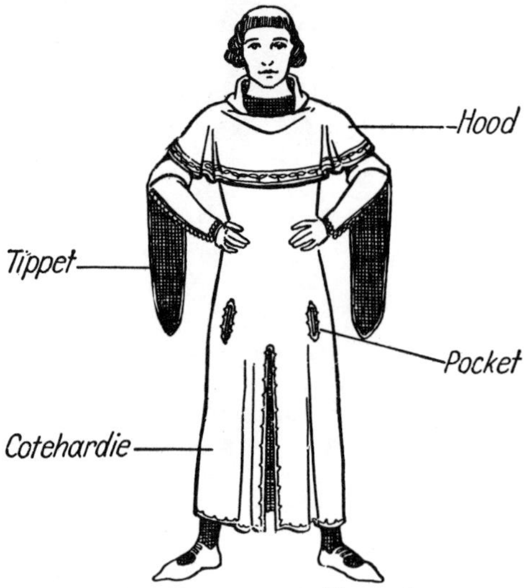

ALAN FLEMING, 1361 (NEWARK)

Hair

Long and bushy.

Hats

Beaver with turn up brim, tall crown, feather. Hood or capuchon with liripipe, with or without beaver top.

WOMEN (EDWARD I)

Dress

Kirtle—close fit, laced, long tight sleeves, buttoned from elbow to wrist.

Dress—contd.

Loose gown—over the above. Train. Long hanging sleeves. Lined.
Girdle—on hips. Gown pulled up in front to show kirtle.
Mantle.

EARLY CHAPERON

Feet

Shoes less pointed than men's.

Hair

Parted middle, over ears in bunches.

Hats

Gorget and fillet—linen band on head and under chin.
Wimple—added for older women, coloured yellow.
Caps—endless.
Couvre-chef—a veil.
Spanish turban with stiff band on forehead.

SIDE NET CAP

MEN (EDWARD II AND III)

Dress

Cotehardie—parti-coloured, with tippets.
Belt at waist with pouch and dagger.
Capes—long or short. Collar and edge furred.
Buttons at neck.

Legs
Tights now parti-coloured.

Hair
Bushy, cut round, curled. Clean shaven. Old men wore bi-forked beards.

SPANISH TURBAN, 1300 (LINCOLN)

Hats
Liripipe to hood.

WOMEN (EDWARD II AND III)

Dress
Cotehardie—long gored skirt, tight sleeves, back laced, hip belt, low neck, not parti-coloured.

Dress—contd.
Super cotehardie—long, loose, sleeveless, large armholes.
Full gown—sometimes trained, with tippets—long strips—and wide elbow sleeves, over a
Kirtle—tight sleeves.
Cyclas—tight sleeveless surcoat, shorter in front (Edward II only).

Hair
Girls—two braids, gorget under them.
Women—two side bunches netted.

Hats
Gorget and wimple of fine lawn.
Silk ribbon fillets.
Gold side nets.
Couvre-chef—a veil.

MAN'S BEAVER HAT

RICHARD OF BORDEAUX

The pendulum again swings. During the three Edwards men revolted against long trailing skirts and their clothes became curtailed. In Richard II's reign they adopted a sort of compromise, and wore short dresses with trailing sleeves. The clever young king was much in advance of his day in his peace policies, but he loved display of a less harmful sort than war, that is, in pageantry and costume. It became an age of extravagance in dress, in material, cut, and adornment. Dagging was applied to everything. This was the scalloping, or circular, or leaf-shaped cutting to the edges of the cloths, producing an effect like the mantling that surrounds a shield of arms. Parti-colouring continued, and increased to such an extent that a really smart man never dreamed of wearing two shoes alike. But it was in the headgear of the women that design really attained its height. The simple wimple swelled out; the side hair nets did the like, and we arrive at the beautiful, reticulated head dress, and the "Juliet" caul.

The standard dresses are the houppelande overcoat and the Zouave-like super cotehardie jacket. Buttons were sewn on in great profusion, but it should be remembered that these were bead shaped, and not the modern flat buttons. Trains were much in vogue, and the ladies' skirts were gored to form a wide, many-folded frock. Peasants wore much the same as before, and paid little attention to the fashions with the exceptions that they scalloped the edges of capes and skirts and used bright colour in the stockings and breeches of their "best clothes."

The *Cotehardie* (men and women) (see summary), was adopted by the women as well as the men and was now jewelled.

The *Tabard* (men) is the heraldic surcoat also already described. Since the arms of the wearer were embroidered upon it, it became a kind of visiting card, since everyone who was anyone understood heraldry.

The *Houppelande* (men and women) was also called a pelicon, and was an overcoat worn over the cotehardie. It had a high bell-shaped collar, standing stiffly up round the neck, and long, full sleeves with dagged edges, cut like surplice

sleeves. It was a full-length dress, buttoned down its entire length with many small buttons set closely together. It could also be buttoned for a few inches down the collar, with the rest not buttoned. One side was slashed from knee to hem. It was lined occasionally with fur, but more often with a contrasting colour, and the sleeves were turned back at the wrist so as to show this lining. The back part often trailed on the floor. The tight fitted sleeves of the cotehardie showed under the houppelande sleeves where their upper part was cut away. The collar was similarly rolled, in which case the two top buttons were unfastened. Young men wore a houppelande that stopped abruptly just below the waist, the skirt becoming a mere frill, but the sleeves were as long as in the other type. This looked rather odd, the huge sleeves, almost sweeping the floor, being stuck on to a tight little jacket, with tights.

The *Cloak* (men) was fastened on the right shoulder.

The *Baldrick* (men) was a gaily embroidered or chased metal belt, from which hung the *Gipciere*, a purse-pouch suspended by two straps. The belt was narrow. One end fell in front, and was often in leather. It also supported a finely chased or carved dagger, or this was worn on a separate ribbon or chain.

Tippets (women) continued in fashion. They were long strips of material reaching from elbow to knee, and they were set in an over sleeve that ended just above the elbow.

Mantles (women) were simple, as before, open in front, and fastened by two silk cords across the chest.

The *Surcoat* or *Super Cotehardie* (women) (see summary) was worn over the cotehardie. In front, its edges nearly met, and later revealed a narrow front, pointed at the bottom, and adorned with a few buttons. It was a sleeveless waistcoat. This garment came in during the end of Edward III's reign, and continued until the end of Henry IV's reign.

The *Gown* (women) was long and loose, but had the favourite tight sleeves, buttoned at the

HOUPPELANDES

wrist, and overhanging the back of the hand. It also had a V or a square cut neck.

Tights were parti-coloured, each leg being different, or each leg itself was divided vertically into two colours.

Crakowes, shoes worn by men and women of this period, took their name from the Polish city of

Cracow. Like much else they were exaggerated as much as six inches long in their points. To stiffen this projection, they were stuffed or wired at the end. They were laced, buckled, or buttoned, but the women's were rather shorter than the men's. In bad weather they were protected out of doors by the

Poulaines, which were wooden clogs with the same pointed toe pieces. These shoes were so extended that it became necessary in the interests of traffic congestion to pass laws limiting their length!

Men wore their hair fairly long, and, since the King's was a pale gold, dyes were used to secure the same shade! Forked beards, with moustaches, were worn by older men. The brow was bound with a golden fillet decorated with flowers in enamel—a pretty custom. The women plucked their eyebrows, and shaved the backs of their necks in the manner of our own century. Their hair was stuffed into the two side bags called the reticulated head-dress. These now be-

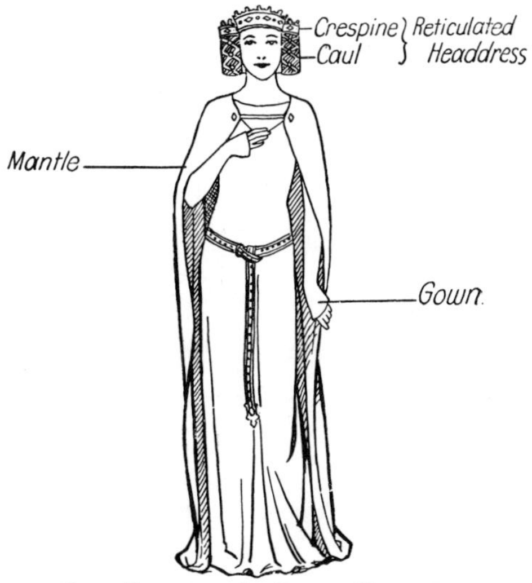

LADY BURTON, 1382, LITTLE CASTERTON

came stiff wire cages on either side of the face, joined together by a decorated band called a *Crespine*, which went along the top of the head in front as a forehead band.

The *Dorelet* (women) was a caul of gold net worn all over the head with the hair tucked underneath it. It was of the "Juliet" type.

The *Nebule* (women) was a cylindrical roll of wire net, worn at first on top of the head, and later also on sides of the face. Its date is 1350–1380.

The *Turban* (men) was what its name implies. It had a cloth crown with dagged ends, which overlapped the edge slightly.

The *Cap* (men) was rounded and brimless, but

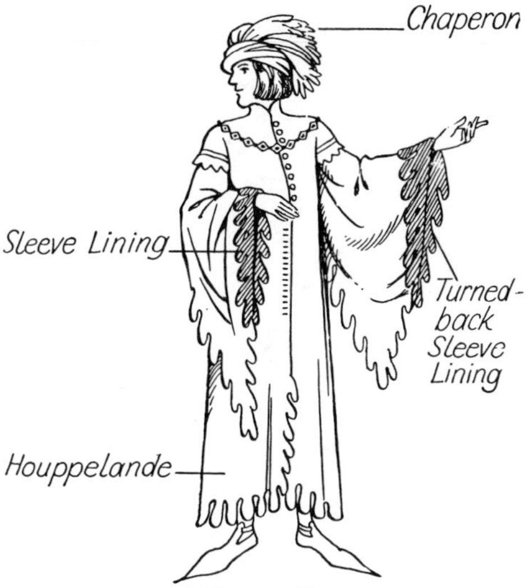

A DAGGED DRESS

it was not a skull-cap. It stood up like a fez, and was the favourite for young men, who decorated it with an ostrich feather, at the side.

The *Chaperon* (men) effected the greatest transformation from the original hood shape in which it was still made. The men decided to put their heads through the face opening, leaving the cape part, which used to cover the shoulders, to form a huge rosette at the side. It was secured in place by twisting the now long liripipe round it. The liripipe was also used as a scarf round the neck. It was originally merely the peak of the hood.

The *Capuchon* (women) was the hood of yore and retained its old shape for women, being a cape, to which was attached a close head-covering, ending in a peak at the back of the head. The head cover was turned up over the head in bad weather, but otherwise it could be worn hanging at the back of the neck. In its original shape, it is still the correct style of academic hood, and is now so worn by many graduates, though the eighteenth-century wigs caused the head opening to widen considerably, with the result commonly seen to-day of a graduate wearing his hood half-way down his back instead of on his shoulders.

The *Fillet* (women) was a narrow strip of linen round the forehead and was worn with the *Gorget* (women), which was a strip of linen passed round the throat several times and fastened to the hair above the ears, where it was also kept in place by the fillet.

There was plenty of variety in design, though the essentials were retained; materials were of the richest; velvets, silks, and fine linens, with sweeping trains, and the graceful floating veils of gauze or thicker material. Jewellery was finely wrought, and colourings were vivid. The parti-coloured men's dress formed effective foils to the women's simpler two-colour schemes whilst the firm, straight limbs of the young men in their tights contrasted well with the long, heavy folds and wide skirts of their women folk.

SUMMARY

MEN (RICHARD II)

Dress

Cotehardie, jewelled.
Tabard—an heraldic surcoat.

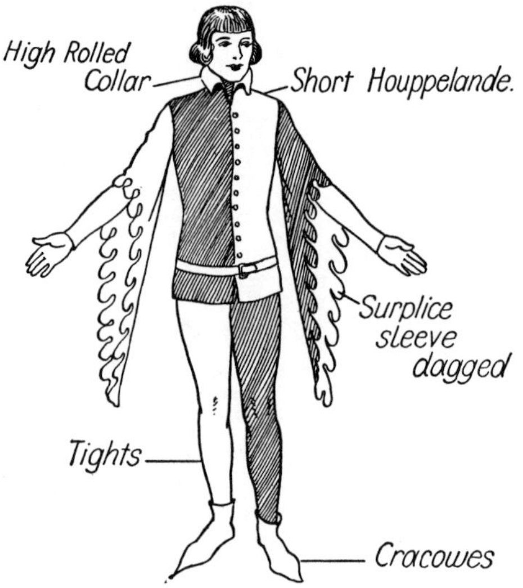

A Gallant

Houppelande—long full sleeves, high bell-shaped collar, many buttons, very long or very short, side slashed.
Cloak—on right shoulder.
Gipciere—pouch on two straps from belt.
Baldrick—narrow belt, end falls in front.
Dagger, jewelled—on ribbon or chain.

Legs

Tights.

Feet

Crakowes—shoes, 6 in. long, stuffed or wired points.
Poulaines—wooden clogs with pointed toe.

Hair

Long, often dyed yellow. Moustache. Forked beard.
Fillet on brow in gold and enamel flowers.

Hats

Turban—cloth crown, dagged ends overlap edge.
Cap—round, brimless, with one ostrich feather.
Chaperon—hood with head put through face opening, the cape made into rosette, the liripipe knotted round as scarf or hat band.

Jewels

Huge rings, heavy chains, great elaboration.

WOMEN (RICHARD II)

Dress

Houppelande—as men.
Tippet—strips from elbow to knee, attached to an oversleeve.
Mantle—as before.
Cotehardie—long gored skirt, long tight sleeves, back laced, hip belt, low neck, parti-coloured.
Surcoat—fur edged and lined, sleeveless, wide armholes, cut away sides, waist length, parti-colour.
Gown—long, loose. Tight sleeves buttoned at wrist. V neck.

Feet

Crakowes—shoes less pointed than the men's. Laced, buckled, or buttoned.

Hair

Back of neck shaved, eyebrows plucked.
Reticulated—netted side bags and crespine (forehead band).
Dorelet—gold net caul.
Nebule—wire cylinder round face.

Hats

Capuchon—a hood as before.
Fillet and gorget—as before. For country folk.

Jewels

Gloves, rings, chains. Great profusion.

PEASANTS (MEN)

Dress

Tunic—long, loose, belted. Dagged skirt and cape.

Hat

Capuchon.
Slouched hat. "Robin Hood" type.

Legs

Chausses, thick, bright coloured.

Feet

Black cloth or felt boots.

PEASANTS (WOMEN)

Dress

Gown. Sometimes front laced and turned up over knees, long tight sleeves.
Underskirt—striped horizontally. Plain cotehardie.
Cotehardie—plain. Aprons.

Hair

No nebule or dorelet. Pigtail or two braids for girls.

Hats

Veil or wimple. Slouch hat.
Conical felt hat over wimple.

Feet

Coloured stockings. Leather shoes.

THE THREE HENRIES

Richard of Bordeaux, who is sneered at by some historians, was wise beyond his time; he had a fixed policy of peace, and in this he gave his long-suffering people a welcome period of relief between the sword rattling Edward III and the equally militaristic Henry of Lancaster. During Richard's reign the people had time to cultivate the arts and culture of peace, and their costumes reflected this fact by their brilliance of colour and design, and by the new modes that were introduced. England, thrust back into the gloom of almost perpetual war under the three Henries, had little time to invent new fashions, and continued the old, though women had a wide range of new hats. Sugar loaves, horns, hearts, steeples—all were pressed into the service of millinery. Dress tended to become slightly more solid with the almost constant wearing of the ankle length Houppelande.

The *Cotehardie* (men and women) was becoming old-fashioned for men. It was a garment with a wide gored skirt, long tight sleeves, a hip belt, and it was laced at the back or made loose enough to slip on without lacing (though that mode was becoming out of date). It had a low neck and was parti-coloured.

The *Super Cotehardie* (women) was still the vogue, but was now fur-edged as well as fur-lined, the edging showing all round the garment from neck to waist, and at the back. It was a sleeveless coatee, with wide armholes and a cutaway front.

The *Houppelande* (men and women) could be worn long or short (the latter for young men). It had the same wide sleeves as before, the collar had become even higher, and was rolled over at the top. The main difference was that dagging was going out: it was retained only on the cuff, which was made wide enough to fold into regular pleats within the belt. In the later period the wide open sleeves were displaced by the bag sleeve, which was made full at the top to below the elbow, from where it gradually narrowed to the wrist, where it was gathered into a deep cuff by a button, or put into a simple wrist band.

The *Baldrick* (men) was another distinctive note. It was a long loop of cloth or leather, hung with small bells all round. It was worn diagonally over the left shoulder, and fell to the right

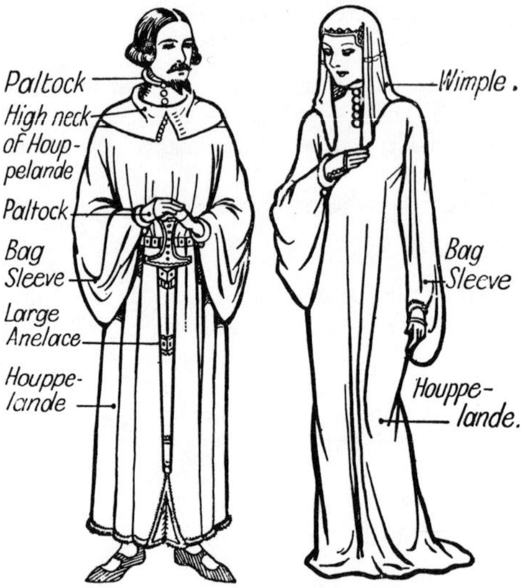

Civilians 1400 (Silbrook)

knee at front and back. In Henry VI's reign this gave way to an horizontal belt, which had small bells only across its front.

Tights (men) were parti-coloured.

Shoes also caught the parti-colour infection, and no decently dressed gallant dreamt of going about with two shoes that matched in colour. They had to agree with the shades of the rest of the costume. The tops were long enough to roll back to show the coloured lining, which had to agree with the general colour scheme. The long points continued until Henry VI's time, when they were replaced by shorter toes, on shoes laced at the sides. For bad weather the wooden clogs called *Poulaines* were still required. No difference from the previous period was made in the women's shoes.

The *Hair* (men) was now closely cropped, being completely shaved at the back of the neck and over the ears—a fashion that may still be seen, somewhat modified, to-day. The older men wore pointed, rather Vandyk-like, beards, but these had two curled points instead of the single one we recognize as the true Vandyk. The women's hair was seen only through the gold net bags or cauls, and often little enough showed then if a heavy veil or other contraption was added. It was not just put into these cauls in any manner; contemporary pictures prove that it was carefully plaited before insertion into the net.

Hats were varied. We have the old *Turban* (men), which was extensively worn in the reigns of Henry IV and V. It was a round cloth crown with dagged ends overlapping the edge. It was a large, clumsy looking headgear, and the ragged end, which flapped about on top or at the side, gave an effect not unlike a cock's comb.

The *Roundlet* (men) was the distinctive Henry IV hat. It had a small stiffened rolling brim with a draped crown and a long streamer, which was broad, and hung from the crown right down the side of the body. It was so long that it could be looped up and fastened to the skirt by a

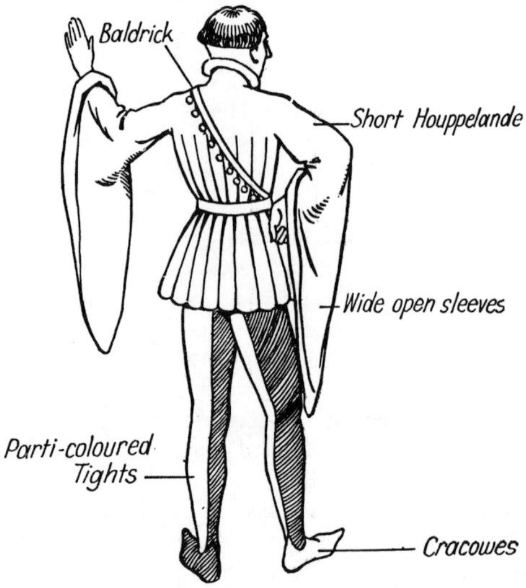

A Young Man (Henry V)

brooch or clasp, though a more moderate version reached to the shoulder only.

The *Sugar-loaf* (men) was a brimless oval cap and was popular under Henry V, specially for young men; it was a kind of elongated fez, often of white.

The *Hood* (men) was cut as of yore, but the

face opening was now edged with fur, which indicated that the inside was also similarly lined. It was, when worn, usually shown over the head, and was not hung on the back of the shoulders.

The *Tall Hat* (men) had a turned up brim, which was cut out into squares.

The *Hood* (men and women) was the same as before, but it was usually worn by country folk and the poorer classes.

The *Hennin* (women) was a tall sugar-loaf or steeple shaped cone of buckram, covered with silk or brocade. The end was not yet sharply pointed, but was rounded, and the whole was covered with a floating veil hanging over the back. The weight of this head-dress, which hung backwards, would have tipped it over but for the *Frontlet*, which was designed to balance it, and was made of a deep band of black velvet, rectangular shaped, covering the top of the head and falling on either side of the face to the shoulders. The hennin was lined with thin steel or wire netting forming a close

ARCHITECT, 1440 (ROUEN)

fitting cap for the head, and in this way it was kept on. Long floating *Veils* of white gauze were worn with all the head-dresses of this period (save the hood) at will, but they were not needed for the horned and heart hats, though they were usually worn. The veil must accompany the hennin always.

The *Horned* head-dress had many varieties and modifications, but the earliest form consisted of two horns of wire foundation, sticking outwards and upwards from the sides of the head. The beginnings of this style were found in the *reticulated* head-dress that was made from two cylinders in gold net worn on each side of the face. These cylinders were now elongated to an inordinate

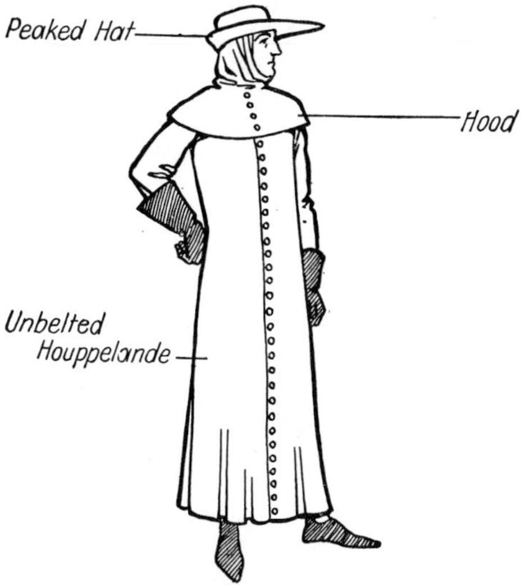

HENRY IV PERIOD

length and curved so that they resembled the Viking helmets of many centuries previously. The patterns on these horns were many. They were formed by plaiting and twisting the gold wire or by covering the horns with brocade and silk, and even twisting material round them. Another variety was to retain the *reticulated* side bags and to place on top of them two side horns of curved wire from which hung the veil, the top of the wire being covered by the edge of the veil, which was brought over as a valance. A more solid effect was given by enlarging the crespine till it became a kind of toque placed over the veil, which was worn over the side bags. The toque was embroidered and jewelled, as were the side bags and the horns when the horns were made of solid material.

The *Crespine* was the metal connecting band over the forehead between the two side bags.

The next step was to alter the shape of the horns and first to make them point directly upwards instead of outwards. This *Forked* the hat and heightened it, and it was accompanied by a modified hennin, in which the round pointed end was cut off, leaving a short roll with a flat end. All were attached to the caul-cap on the head, the flat-ended short hennin pointing out at the back of the head, the cap covering it, and the horns standing above it. A veil was pinned at the front, where it met the centre of the forehead, and was drawn over the ends of the horns and floated down the back of the head, but the veil did not cover the pattern of the horns.

The *Heart* shape hat was immortalized by Sir John Tenniel in his drawings of the Duchess in *Alice in Wonderland.* The hair was padded and stuffed till it attained considerable height; it was placed in nets, and the curved part of the heart shape was covered with the veil.

The *Turban* was an enormously inflated caul, i.e. netted cap, into which the hair was placed.

SUMMARY

MEN

Dress

Cotehardie.

Houppelande—long or short, long wide sleeves, higher collar, regular pleats, geometrical designs.

Henry VI Period

Houppelande with bag sleeve—leg of mutton shape, deep cuff or plain wrist band. Dagged cuff.

Cloak.

Baldrick—belt hung with small bells, worn diagonally over left shoulder.

Baldrick—belt with bells across front, worn horizontally (Henry VI)

Legs

Tights—parti-coloured.

Feet

Shoes—long pointed. Top turned back to show lining. Parti-coloured.

Turban (Henry VI)

Shoes—shorter toes, laced at sides (Henry VI).
Poulaines—wooden clogs.

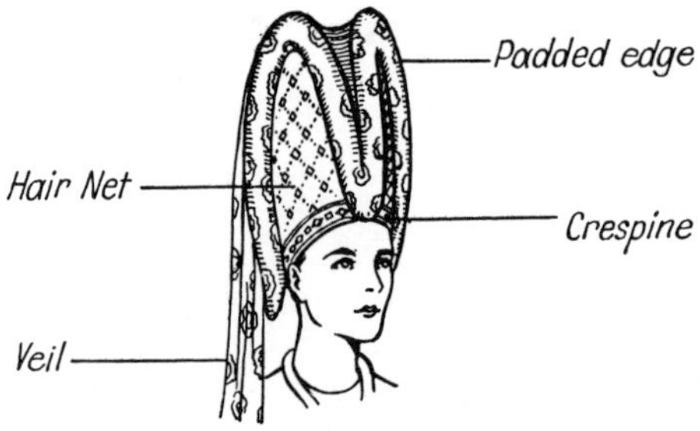

Forked Hat (1435)

Hair

Short—cut close, shaved at back and over ears.

Beards—short, Vandyk shaped; but in two curls for older man.

Hats

Roundlet—small round with stiff rolling brim, draped crown, long broad streamer over side (Henry IV).

Turban—cloth crown, dagged ends overlap edge (Henry IV and V).

Roundlet

Sugar-loaf—brimless oval (Henry V).

Hood—fur-edged round face opening.

Tall—turned up brim cut in square scallops.

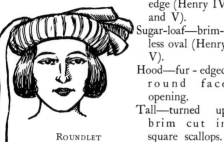

WOMEN

Dress

Houppelande—as above.

Cotehardie and super cotehardie.

Mantle—as before, strings across chest.

High-waisted gown—long gored skirt, belt high up, trained, V-neck fur-edged.

Feet

Cracowes—slightly pointed, laced, buckled, or buttoned.

Hair

All concealed under the gold net cap.

Horned Head-dress

Hats

Reticulated—netted side bags or side wings.

Hood—for country folk.

Hennin—sugar loaf, with frontlet and veil.

Horned—at sides with crespine and veil.

Forked—pointless roll back of head with horns upright above head, no frontlet.

Heart—heart shaped frame and veil.

Turban—inflated caul, no veil or frontlet.

Frontlet—black velvet strip hanging to shoulders either side of face.

YORKIST

The years from 1461 to 1485—the brief age of authority of the Yorkist Kings, Edward IV, Edward V, and Richard III, were not years of great change in costume, though they immortalized themselves by the startling codpiece, and are chiefly remembered for the ladies high-waisted gown. Hats remained as original as ever, the principal features being the delightful Butterfly for the women and the endless variety of low crowned hats for the men. There was no sign of any sobering down of the rather freakish outlines and the extraordinary silhouettes of both male and female fashions. This modification was gradually to come about under Henry VII.

The *Doublet* (men) was worn to hip length only, but it had been developed by padding on the breast and back, the material being gathered into formal fluted folds and confined by the belt. The collar continued to be high, but was open at the front. The sleeves were tight, and extended to the wrist, but a hanging sleeve was added at will, with an elbow opening, through which the inner sleeve and arm were thrust, leaving the rest of the

King Richard III

outer sleeve to dangle. After 1480 hanging sleeves became longer, and were often loosely looped together behind the back. At this date slashing came in, and revealed the embroidered shirt at the elbows and shoulders. The shoulders were artificially raised by padding, and the front of the doublet was opened to show the shirt, and loosely laced across the V.

The *Jerkin* (men) was also hip length. It could be extended to the middle of the thighs. but its

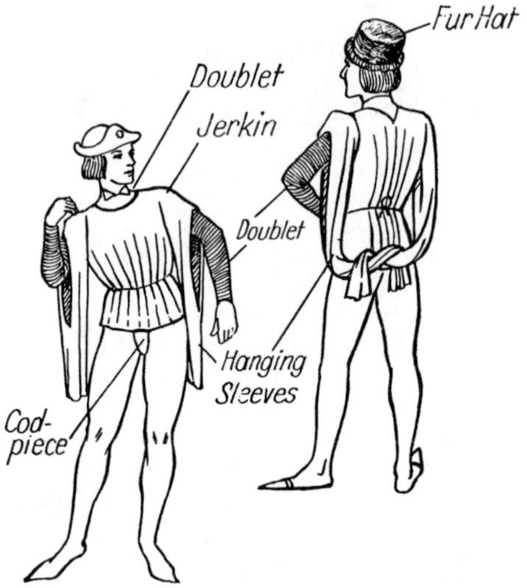

YORKIST MEN, 1480

sleeves were roomy and loose at the wrist, and were slit down the front seam to form long hanging sleeves. The slashings became much longer and larger, and often extended from the shoulder almost to the wrist, where in the earlier reigns they gave mere glimpses of the shirt.

The *Gown* (men) was the houppelande slightly modified. *Cloaks* (men) were sometimes worn, chiefly by older people.

The *Shirt* (men) came into its own, and was richly embroidered in black and red silk and (later) in gold thread. For the first time it had a definite neck band.

Tights (men) had the codpiece added, though it had not the elaboration of the codpiece of the Tudor period. This codpiece was a stuffed small bag placed at the fork of the tights and fastened up by laced "points" or strings.

The *Houppelande* (women) was modified slightly and became tighter and more shaped to the body. Towards the end of this period it moulded the bust.

The *High-waisted Gown* (women) was the almost universal dress. It had a wide, gored skirt, with a train, and long, tight sleeves coming well over the wrist and hands, where it widened into a square cut cuff. It was trimmed with fur round the skirt bottom and the neck opening, and was finished off with a broad belt. The materials used were beautiful damask and tapestry patterns in brocade and rich silks of conventional design, which are still popular in our church furnishings. The pineapple, pomegranate, vine, and grape, together with leaves that are familiar on English trees, were utilized for these designs.

The principal changes were in the neck opening, which in 1460 was round, and which, in 1480, had become square. In the latter form it was so wide that it almost bared the shoulders and gave that "slipping off" impression which so much intrigued the early Victorian men.

Shoes (men) had the toes stuffed with moss and hay and were the familiar *Poulaines*. From 1470

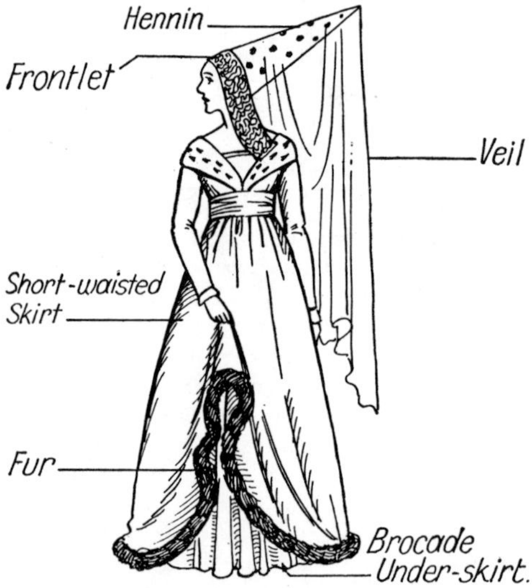

THE HIGH-WAISTED DRESS

to 1480 the points were of immense lengths, and finished in a long needle point, which was sometimes pinned back over the shoe for convenience.

Hair (men) was bobbed in an attractive fashion, but the bowl crop of Henry V had definitely gone out of favour. The dandy wore his hair long over the forehead, even longer over

YORKIST LADIES, 1450

94

(G.2477)

the neck and nearly to the shoulders. The parting was in the middle.

Hair (women) displayed little, but it must not be assumed that because the veil and enormous head gear had most of it, it was bundled up and stuffed into the gold net cauls. Contemporary illustrations show that the hair was carefully braided in square-crossing patterns.

Hats (men) were varied. The crowns were high or low; the brims narrow or broad. A conical hat was like a Turk's fez or, when longer, became a sugar loaf shape. The bycocket was pointed and pulled down in front, with a turned-up brim at the back, and was rather like the modern felt Trilby, with the exception that there was no dent in the top of the crown. It was mostly favoured by the sober, who dared not wear the more fashionable small caps. Tall, upright, single ostrich feathers in front or at the back added to the fantasy. Jewelled hat bands

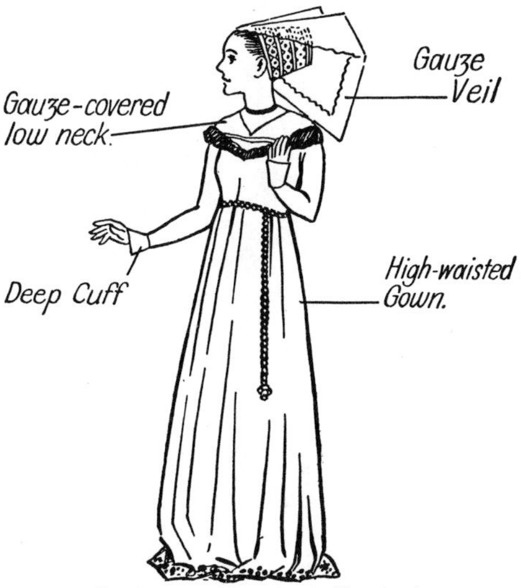

BUTTERFLY HAT, 1478 (OULTON)

and brooches kept the shape together, and maintained the turned-up brim for the wealthy. After 1475 a kind of "smoking cap," like the caps of the Victorians, was worn. It had a deep turn-up all round. The most popular types were the sugar-loaf and the low cap with turn-up.

Hats (women) were as elaborate as before.

A new type was the charming butterfly headdress, which was worn between 1450 and 1480. This was a floating gauze veil stretched over wires, which were tilted at the back of the head at an angle of 45 degrees. The gold net cap enclosed the hair, and was often placed at the extreme back of the head. It revealed the front hair, which was brushed back from the forehead.

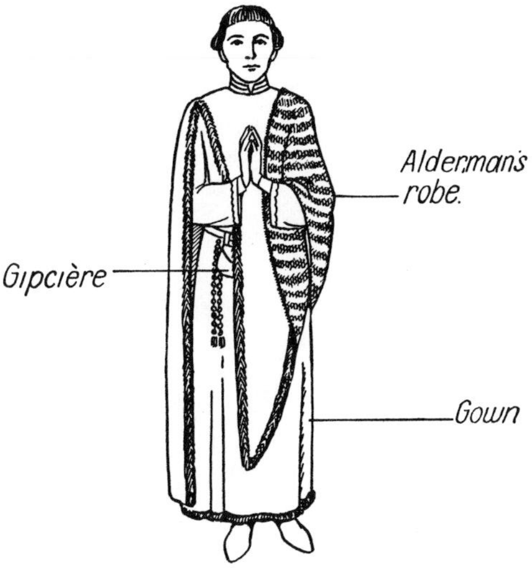

ALDERMAN FIELD, 1474 (LONDON)

The frontlet sometimes covered this front hair, but it was made of white gauze instead of black velvet.

Another new type was the barbe, which was worn by older women. It was a veil over the head and sides of the face, with a kind of linen bib worn above or below the chin and covering the upper part of the chest. It was attached to a chin band, and was pleated in formal folds vertically. The whole gave a nun-like appearance. Ladies of the upper class covered the chin; others wore the band under the chin.

It is customary to dress this period in the acutely pointed steeple hats that are so familiar in manuscripts and illuminations, but in England this is not strictly correct. The genuine steeple was extensively worn on the Continent, but it was not popular in England. Perhaps the English women felt that its sharp point emphasized their own angularities. The steeple in our own country was generally rounded off at the end to make an elongated sugar loaf hat without the acute angled point. From all these hats floated the gauze or linen veils that were attached to the front. A small loop of string or material was seen exactly in the centre of the forehead. It rested on the bare skin, and is thought to have been placed there for convenience in pulling on the headdress.

The beehive hat was a truncated sugar loaf with little gradation, and was smaller at the top of the crown. It was covered with a veil, which was tucked in closely to the hat.

Walking sticks began to be fashionable for the men.

SUMMARY

MEN

Dress

Doublet to 1480—padded, fluted, hip length, high open collar, close and/or hanging sleeves to wrist.

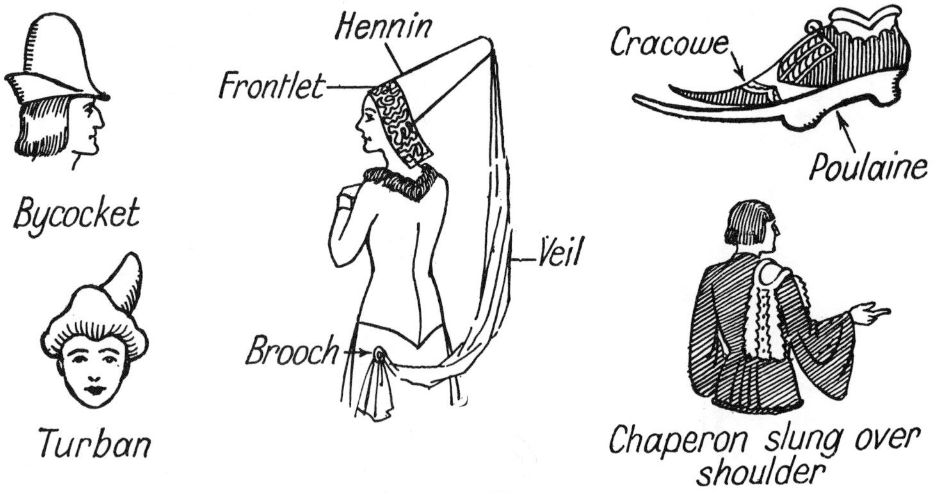

Doublet from 1480—open down breast, loosely laced across, high padded shoulders, shirt shows at slashes of elbow and shoulders.

Jerkin—hip and mid-thigh length, roomy sleeves, loose at wrist, slit down front seam to make long hanging sleeve, looped behind.

Gown—modified houppelande.

Cloaks—rare.

Shirt with neckband—embroidered 1480 onwards.

Legs

Tights and codpiece.

Feet

Immense needle points 1470–80, then fade out.

Stuffed toes.

Poulaines.

Hair

Long over forehead and nearly to shoulders.

Bobbed.

No bowl crops.

Hats

Crowned—high or low.

Brimmed—narrow or broad.

Conical—fez or long sugar loaf.

Tall upright ostrich feather, front or back.

Bycocket—"Robin Hood" type.

Jewelled hat bands and brooches.

"Smoking caps" with deep turn-up, after 1475.

WOMEN

Dress

Houppelande—tighter and, later, moulded to form.

High waisted gown—neck 1460 round; neck 1480 square, almost bare shoulders. Long right sleeves, widened at wrist to square cuff. Broad belt, fur trimming.

Hair

Concealed under hat, but braided to show through.

THE BARBE

Hats

Forked with veil.
Beehive with veil.
Butterfly 1450–80 with veil and/or frontlet.
Hennin 1460–70 or steeple, not sharp pointed, with veil.
Wimple for windows.

Hats—contd.

Barbe—wimple with linen bib and chin band, vertically pleated.

PEASANTS

As in previous reign.

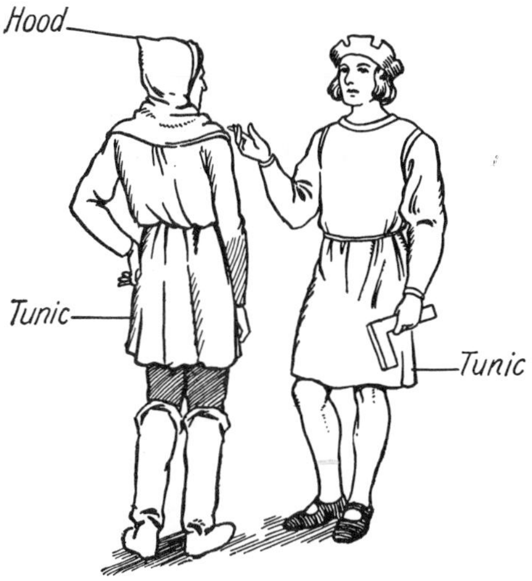

CRAFTSMEN

HENRY VII

The rise of the wool merchants created a new and wealthy middle class which dressed soberly but richly, avoided the more advanced styles, but attained much dignity by the use of fine materials and fur trimmings.

From 1485 to 1509, the period of the reign of the new Tudor king, dignity returned to fashion with the long gown and chain and the gable hat, and continued throughout the whole of the Tudor line's rule, with slight returns to the freakish in the more exaggerated modes of Henry the Eighth and Elizabeth, though the general modes retained their dignity. Costume was symbolic of the Tudor monarchs themselves since all (with the exception of the young Edward VI) had greatness in no small measure, and despite the tempestuous outbursts of the royal Blue Beard and the Virgin Queen, they always managed to keep their personal dignity.

It was a period that became increasingly prosperous, for there were no wars, and the nation had time and money with which to develop its civilization. There sprang up a new race of nobles whose claims to peerage, like those of our own day, depended on money instead of on birth and breeding. This position was reflected in the increased gorgeousness of materials and designs for clothes. Rich silks, figured brocades and damasks, stamped velvets and cloth of gold, were imported from Italy and the East, and jewellery became massive and finely wrought, especially in ladies' girdles and pendants and the brooches in men's hats.

The new note was in the increased importance of the white shirt, richly embroidered in black and white thread, and even in colours, and in the stomacher or waistcoat, which was of brocade. The ladies originated the gable hat and abandoned the fantastic wired shapes of the Lancastrian and

Yorkist times. Slashings began to appear, somewhat timidly, in Henry VII's reign. On the whole, costuming in this reign was sober and restrained, and thoroughly sound. It was during the reign of his son, who spent his father's savings, and then robbed the Church for more, that clothing became really extravagant and less dignified and quiet.

HENRY VII

The *Linen Shirt* (men) was gathered at the neck into pleats and embroidered with red and black thread. It showed through the slashings of the stomacher and from elbow to wrist if the stomacher had no sleeves.

The *Stomacher* (men) was of patterned fabric, rich and elaborate, with its floral design conventionalized and outlined in gold thread. It reached from the chest, where it was square cut at the neck, to the waist, where it was laced or tied to the tights.

The *Doublet* (men), worn over the stomacher, was close fitting, and quilted, as in the previous reigns, but was open down the front in a V-shape and loosely laced across, thus showing the stomacher. It had a short hip-covering skirt, or a slightly longer skirt, and its sleeves were slashed at the elbow and hung down from there loosely, again revealing the stomacher (if sleeved) or the shirt sleeves. The doublet sleeves were close from elbow to shoulder.

The *Jerkin* (men) was occasionally worn over the doublet, and had either no sleeves or wide or hanging sleeves. These garments were held to the waist by a narrow *Sash.*

The *Gown* (men) was the characteristic note of this age, and was long, but the sleeves had become mere cylindrical rolls of cloth with lengthwise arm openings. A broad square cut collar extended down the back and continued along the edges of the front in revers faced with silk or fur.

The *Petti-cote* (men) was a shorter version of the long coat.

The *Gown* (women) was long, and made from rich silks with a broad square cut neck outlined with bands of embroidery. A train was added by the upper classes. The sleeves were close at the top and wide at the elbow and banded, often with fur. It was the custom to lift the skirt to show the under dress of rich material, generally figured. The gown was occasionally fur-lined.

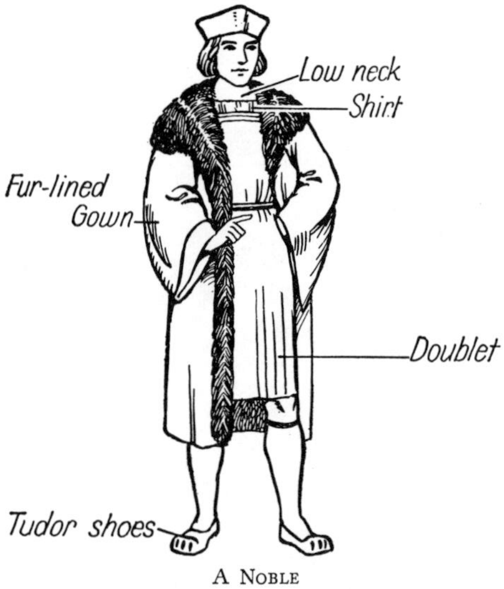

A NOBLE

The *Chemise* (women) was white and pleated, and showed above the neck opening of the gown.

The *Underdress* was on the same cut as the over-gown, but was of figured damask or woven tapestry or cut velvet, but the pattern was fairly simple as the split opening of the over-gown did not come into fashion until Henry VIII's time,

A Tudor Merchant and His Wife

so that until then the under-gown was not permanently displayed.

The *Cloak* (women) was full and ample, and had open sleeves, which were necessary owing to the bulky lines of the clothes that were worn under it.

Tights (men) were of fabric, silk or velvet, cut on the cross. Dandies wore striped tights, which had slashed and puffed knees. A curious mode was to have a different material and colour at the hips, and this was slashed and sometimes attached to the body of the garment by loose lacings. Through all these slashings showed the underclothes of white, which were slightly pulled through to form little puffs.

Shoes were of velvet or leather with bulbous rounded toes, and were sometimes slashed to show the coloured feet beneath them.

Hair (men) was worn flowing to the shoulders, and was usually parted in the middle. *Hair* (women) was also parted in the middle, but only a small portion was visible in front of the forehead, as the rest of the head was completely covered by the headdress.

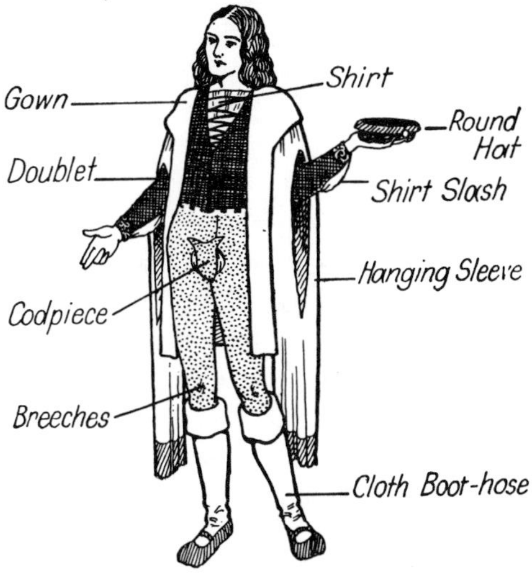

A Young Man

Hats (men) were of velvet in two shapes. One had the brim turned up on all sides and the four corners pinched together to form a square cap —an early form of the biretta now worn by the clergy. The other had a broad brim, turned up but without cornering, to which were added feathers turning backwards. This type was worn over a close-fitting cap.

Hats (women). The Gable or Kennel type was the characteristic piece, and was in three sections. The first was a white coif or close-fitting cap, over which was placed a piece of material in silk, velvet, or embroidered cloth,

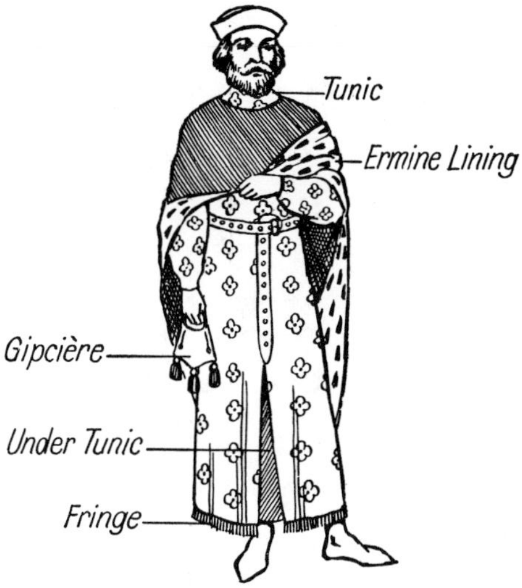

Gentleman, 1450-1500 (All Saints, York)

nearly always black. It was stiffened like a roof or tent so that it hung in a point at the top and angles at the sides, and there were strings at the sides with which to tie back the hanging ends from the neck. A stiff band of material embroidered on its front edge with pearls was added to the whole, to show in front. It, too, was stiffened and bent in the centre and placed over the coif. The coif was first, the pearl band next, and then the black, embroidered veiling.

Another type was the Franco-Flemish, which was simpler in outline, Made of dark material, it covered the head and sides of the face with ample folds. It had a bright lining, which was turned back on the top of the head in front to add a note of colour.

Older women wore the pleated barbe of linen with a plain arched linen hood faintly dipping in front of the forehead (the precursor of the Mary Queen of Scots hat). This was put on over a stiffened front, or the material itself was stiffened and hung over the face and outward on the shoulders. The *Barbe* was a kind of pleated bib, covering the chest up to the chin and occasionally extending over the chin.

MERCHANT CLASS

Jewellery (men) was principally shown in the massive and beautiful neck chains that hung, like a modern mayor's official chain, from each shoulder in a wide curve across breast and back. Pendants were added. These were crosses and other designs with a touch of the Renaissance, such as allegorical figures of cupids, arabesques, and conventionalized natural forms. Rings and belts were also of gold, and all the jewellery was heavy and massive to harmonize with the heavy and massive lines of the clothes worn. A thin, delicate piece of goldsmith's work would have looked tawdry and out of place.

Jewellery (women) was chiefly centred in the long waist chain with a long hanging end reaching three-quarters of the way down the skirt. From it depended a large round pendant. Elaborate crosses with pearl drops at the ends were used as brooches on the breast. Occasionally brooches adorned the men's hats. Rings were large and square.

Peasants wore much the same type of clothes but in plainer materials and simpler cut. Stockings were of white wool, and slipper-shoes of leather were popular. Outer cloaks were worn by wealthy citizens only. Shirts were of coarse, unbleached linen of a grey-brown shade with turn-down collars, or upstanding collars cut away slightly in front. The main robe was cassock-like and girdled with a belt. Working class people wore a shorter tunic.

SUMMARY

MEN

Dress

Linen shirt—pleated at neck, embroidered black and white thread, shows through slashed points of

Stomacher—sleeve optional, patterned fabric waistcoat, from chest to waist, where it is laced or tied to tights.

Doublet—over stomacher, close fit, quilted, open in front to show stomacher, short skirt, close sleeves to elbow. From elbow to wrist reveals shirt or stomacher sleeves.

Jerkin—hip length, sleeves hanging, or wide, or none.

Sash—narrow.

Gown—long; sleeves cloth cylinders with long arm slits, broad square collar with front revers.

Petti-cote—short version of long coat.

Legs

Tights—fabric with codpiece, striped, slashed and puffed knee, hips different colour.

Feet

Shoes—velvet or leather, bun toed, slight slashings and puffs.

Hair

Flowing to shoulders. Square cut. Beard rare.

Hats

Turn-up brim, four corners pinched together.

Broad heavy brim with back-turning feathers over skull cap.

Jewellery

Gold chains with pendants (see also Women).

WOMEN

Dress

Chemise—pleated white, shows above gown.
Gown—long, rich silk, broad square neck outlined with embroidery band, train. Sleeve close at top, wide at elbow and hand, fur banded. Tight bodice, Lift to show—
Underdress—costly figured material.
Cloak—full and ample, open sleeves.

Hair

Parted middle and brushed back, only visible in front.

Hats

Gable—white coif, over which black silk or velvet stiffened like sloping roof, and stiff band of material pearl embroidered. Side strings to tie back from neck.
Franco-Flemish—ample dark veil on head and shoulders, turned back on top to show gay lining.
Barbe—pleated linen with plain arched linen hood, slight front dip, on stiffening over head and shoulders, with barbe-pleated bib on chest.

Jewellery

Long belts, with pendants, necklaces, and rings, massive and finely wrought for both sexes, and pendants.

Elizabeth of York

TUDOR

Fashions designed to subdue the uncouth shape of Henry VIII were adopted by his flattering courtiers, and as he was surrounded by a *nouveau-riche* nobility swollen with the loot of the despoiled monasteries, there was more ostentation than good taste.

We come to the years 1509 to 1558.

More clothes were visible.

The *Shirt* (men) was white and had frills at the wrist and neck, with the breast embroidered chiefly in red and black or even gold, where it showed. It had sleeves sufficiently large to allow them to be pulled through the slashings of the outer garments to make the puffed "blistering." Under Queen Mary a Spanish ruff was added.

The *Doublet* (men) was of knee length, with large slit sleeves and a full pleated skirt. The shoulders, eked out with padding, were extremely broad. The slits were vertical and regular, their ends being closed with jewelled brooches for the rich. The doublet was fastened down the front to the waist; below was left unfastened It was fur-lined, and the lining showed at the bottom of the skirt. Under Queen Mary the shape became more self-fitting and padding went out of favour. The skirt had a pleated effect. Over it was worn the *Jerkin* (men), which was of ankle length for old men; others wore it to just above the knees. It was an overcoat, with a huge wide collar and furlined revers down the front. It could be sleeveless, have a half-sleeve formed of one large puff from shoulder to elbow, or a hanging sleeve from the elbow.

The *Vest* (men) was worn only when the doublet was cut low in the chest to display the vest. It was of elaborately embroidered velvet or brocade and was sleeveless.

The *Belt* (men) had become a mere sash.

The *Cape* (men) was circular to just below

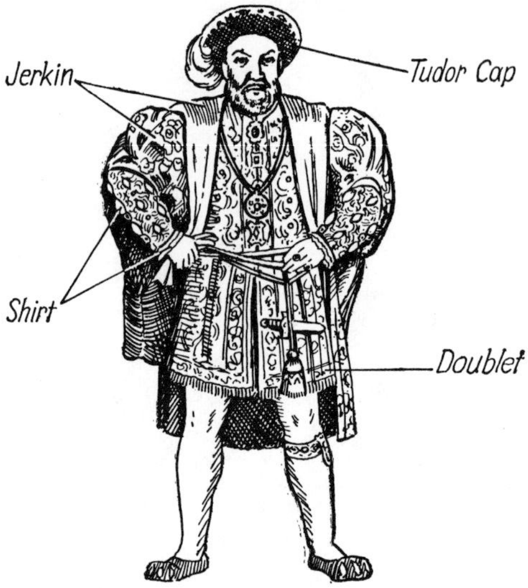

HENRY VIII

the waist, and banded with several lines of horizontal braiding at the edge.

Stays (women) were of leather or bone and with the *Hoop* (women), which was bell-shaped, formed the foundation for the tight and smooth outer garments.

The *Chemise* (women) was embroidered; a good deal of it showed when it covered the chest, as the bodice was low and square.

The *Petticoat* (women) was a most important garment, and was of brocaded velvet or silk, with large symmetrical designs of fruit and leaves. It was stretched tightly over the hoop, and its pattern matched the undersleeves of the gown.

The *Gown* (women) was bell-shaped, with a skirt open from waist to hem in an inverted V shape. The waist was gored and the long padded bodice went to a point below the waist line. The square cut neck was low and showed the bare skin unless the chemise was worn gathered up to the neck. The lined bodice was fastened at the back, and as its shoulder seams were long the armhole was not in its natural place, but about two inches down the arm, where a distinct line was shown. These sleeves were wide at the elbow and banded with fur or velvet; thus was disclosed the tight undersleeve, which at the elbow became a huge puff or "bishop" sleeve. The undersleeve matched the petticoat. Under Queen Mary the low neck disappeared in favour of a high cut bodice with an open collar to just below the throat; its edges were turned back, and spread out on either side of the throat and over the back.

The *Partlet* (women) was a fine linen neck-filling, with the older fashioned square cut neck.

The *Breeches* (men) were puffed and slashed like the doublet, and had a codpiece, which showed where the doublet was unfastened. They were worn under the doublet. The codpiece was a padded flap at the fork of the legs. It was tied with ribbons called "points," with the white shirt pulled through at each side to show.

Stockings (men) were for the first time of silk, but of a thicker silk than modern stockings.

QUEEN MARY, 1541 (LONDON)

Shoes (men and women) became more natural in shape, though they were still bun toed. They covered the instep and had a series of slits lengthways through which different coloured materials were pulled.

Hair (men) was short. Men were clean shaven

or a short fringe of beard, with similar whiskers, was worn. The King's hair was red.

Hair (women) was parted in the middle, or less often braided, but only the front portion was visible. Under Queen Mary it was puffed out instead of being flattened, and more was seen by thrusting back the hat.

Hats (men) were the black velvet square cap, familiarized by Sir Thomas More and Holbein. The velvet skull cap and Henry Tudor cap were also black. The latter was a circle of stiffened velvet gathered into a narrow brim. It is still worn by doctors in the universities. If one side only was turned up, a jewel held the single turn-up. If all sides were turned up, then they were regularly jewelled all round. A long, curling ostrich feather was placed across the front or slightly at the side, and the crown was flat. The Marian cap was gathered into a head band and had no brim.

Hats (women) were of two kinds—the Gable

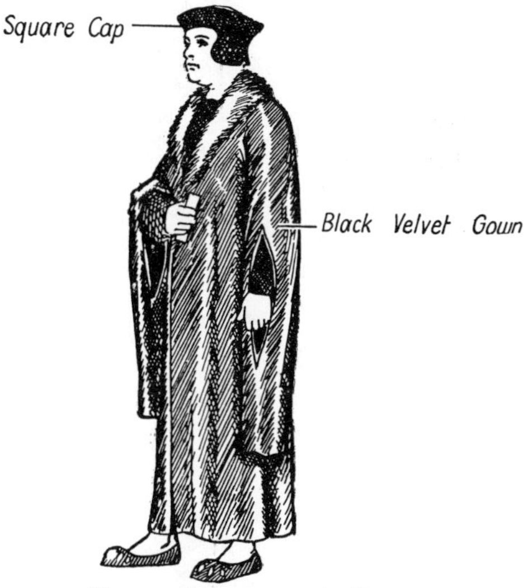

THOMAS CROMWELL, 1537 (LONDON)

and the French Hood. Both were elaborate, and consisted of three or four different pieces.

The *Gable Hat* (women) first had a strip of brown or black silk crossed over the forehead and sewn across in stripes. This showed beneath the gable point. Next the stiff white hood, or coif, which was jewelled in front about two or three inches wide (or the jewelled piece was separate) was worn.

Later was worn a long bag of velvet or satin, usually black, which was sewn to the cap, and the whole was covered with a rectangular piece of material long enough to form the gable or sloped roof part on top of the head, with falls on

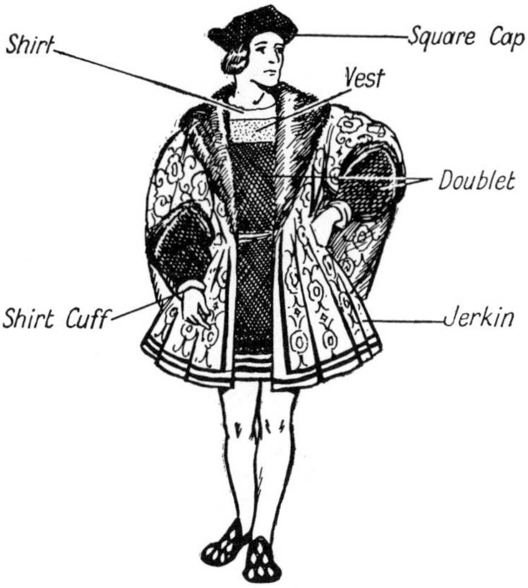

DR. ZELLE (BRUSSELS)

either side of the face. The pendant pieces had strings attached for the purpose of tying the sides back on themselves so that the ends were facing upwards and nearly reaching the first slope of the gable. Subsequently, these ends were permanently sewn upwards in the same position. The strings might also be used to fasten the ends together by passing the ends of the strings under the chin. The material of this piece was velvet, silk, or embroidered fabric. Stiffening was used to maintain the acute angles in position.

The *French Hood* (women) came in under Queen Mary. First was worn a flat frill of gold net or white lawn. Over this and behind it was a two-inch wide stiff band of velvet or satin, edged with pearls and covering and curling round the ears. The velvet bag was added as before, or a short veil was fastened to the back of the head. This type of hat revealed more of the face. Under Queen Mary the headdress became less stiff and elaborate, and was a simple black velvet cap set far back on the head with a slight peak over the forehead. A velvet strip hung from the back.

A jewelled *Girdle* (women) surrounded the waist and hung down for a good length in front, finishing with a beautifully designed piece of goldsmith's work in the form of a pendant, ball, or cross. This was large and richly jewelled. From the men's girdles hung short daggers which were for ornament rather than use.

SUMMARY

MEN

Dress

Shirt—white, frilled wrist and neck, embroidered breast, large sleeves. Under Mary a ruff added.

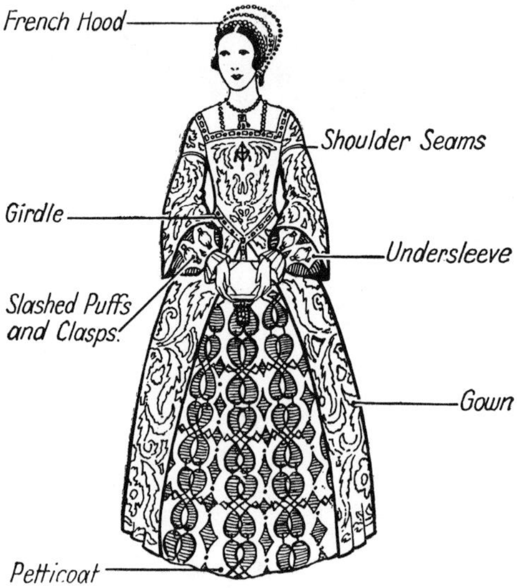

PRINCESS ELIZABETH, 1546 (HAMPTON COURT)

Doublet—knee length, large slit sleeves, full pleated skirt, fur lined, wide shoulders. Under Mary closer fit, and less padding.

Jerkin—long or short fur-lined coat, huge flat collar and revers, sleeveless or one large puff, knee length, open in front.

Vest—sleeveless, embroidered velvet or brocade, worn if doublet cut low enough to show it.

Cape—(Mary only) circular to just below waist.

Belt—a sash.

Legs

Breeches—puffed and slashed, codpiece.

Stockings—thick silk.

Feet

Shoes—more natural, cover instep.

Hair

Short, clean shaven, short fringe beard and whiskers.

Hats

Black velvet square cap.

Velvet skull cap

THE GABLE HOOD, 1525

Stiff velvet circle in narrow brim, one or all sides turned up, jewel, flat crown, feather across front.

WOMEN

Dress

Stays—bone or leather.

Hoop—bell-shaped.

Chemise—embroidered.

Petticoat—stretched, large pattern, matched undersleeves.

Gown—bell-shape, skirt open in front from waist, gored waist, lined and padded bodice long and pointed. Square, low neck, back laced. Shoulder seams long so armhole is two inches down arm. Sleeves wide at elbow with broad fur or velvet bands. Tight under sleeves of fabric.

Dress—contd.

(Mary only) bodice cut high, collar open to below throat and spread out each side and at back.

Partlet—(Mary only) linen, filling in neck.

Hair

Mid parted or braided, only seen in front. Under Mary puffed and more seen.

Hats

Gable—1st strip, brown or black silk; 2nd, stiff white coif or hood jewelled; 3rd, long black velvet or satin bag; 4th, black silk, velvet or embroidered strip.

French hood—(Mary only) 1st flat, gold net or lawn frill; 2nd, stiff velvet or satin pearled band; 3rd, velvet bag or short veil on back of head.

Cap—(Mary only) simple black velvet on back of head, peak on forehead, velvet strip hung behind.

PEASANTS

MEN

Dress

Plain cloth or serge, no blisters.

Shirts—unbleached linen or calico, narrow turn-down collars.

Mantle or gown—only for rich citizens.

Legs

Breeches—two puffs to knee.

Stockings—wool, often white.

Feet

Shoes—leather, slipper shaped.

Hats

Low crowned felt, wide brim.

Flat cloth cap.

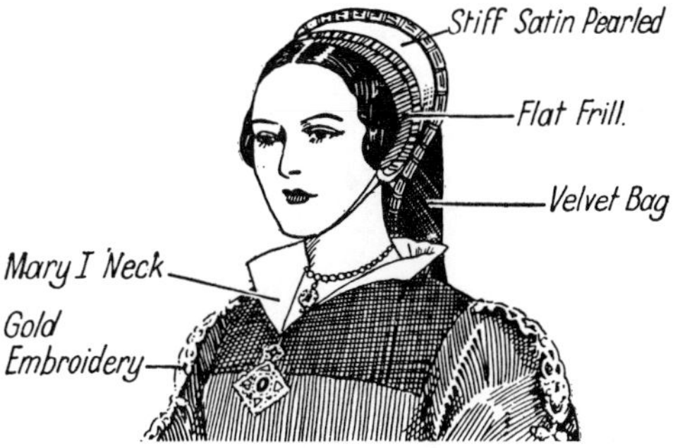

THE FRENCH HOOD, 1541

WOMEN

Dress

Coarse serge or cloth, dark blue being mostly worn.

Gown—tight, long bodice, tight sleeves, back laced. Skirt split to show petticoat. Girls had short skirts pleated to bodice.

Petticoat—aporn.

Legs

Stockings—gray wool.

Feet

Felt or leather shoes.

SHAKESPEARE'S ENGLAND

Gloriana, outwardly, was nothing but a walking wardrobe—a mass of wires, stays, and struts to which were fastened the stiff barbaric clothes that almost disguised the fact that she had a human form. She wore a ginger wig, and the only parts of her skin not covered by clothes were effectively concealed under a coat of raddle.

ELIZABETHAN

The *Spanish Cape* (men) was circular, with a high collar, and was banded along its outer edge with braids.

The *Italian Doublet* closely fitted the body from neck to just below the waist, where it ended in a short frill. It was boned and padded so that the front edge was curved outwards to a point below the waist, which looked like, and was called, a peascod. The armhole was outlined with a padded crescent-shaped epaulet, and at first the sleeves (which were of a different colour) were tight, long, and slashed, but later they were not slashed. The wrist finished with a frill or turned back linen cuff, lace edged, and the sleeve could at option be split to show the under sleeve. The tunic was buttoned down the centre, and could be opened to disclose the vest, in which case it was reversed with a different colour. It had a high collar.

The *Ruff* (men) was starched yellow. It folded into figure eight shape and encircled the neck.

The *Collar* (men) was of white linen turned down or square and wired, but these two latter

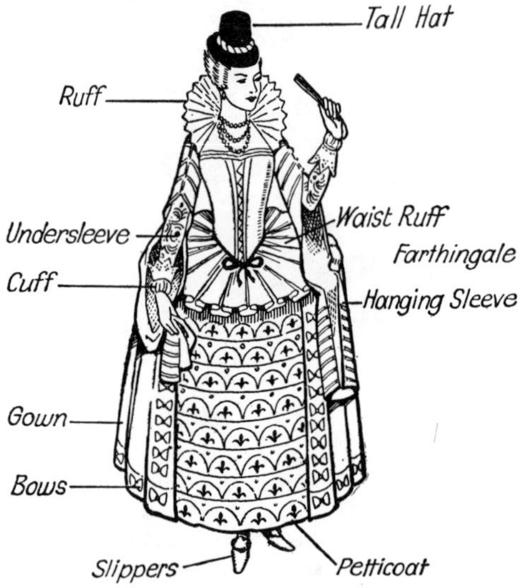

ELIZABETHAN LADY

alternatives to the ruff really became general in James I's time.

The women wore a linen *Chemise*, a leather or whalebone *Corset*, and a huge wheel or hoop of whalebone called a *Farthingale*, which was attached just below the waist. Over this several *Petticoats* and two *Gowns* were worn. The cut of the gowns was fuller, but, as in the previous reign, they had hanging sleeves of lawn and cambric, or lace, stuck to the armhole of the under robe, and with a deep point to the bodice.

The *Ruff* (women) was of cambric or lawn, plain or lace edged, and if it was very large it had to be underpropped with bones. The enormous upstanding lace collar, wired to stand up at the back of the neck, came in at the close of the reign, about 1580. There was another late variant of the circular ruff. It parted in the middle and formed a semi-circle or a heart-shape on back and shoulders only.

The *Trunk Hose* (men) were really breeches, much slashed, puffed, and padded. They were almost circular. They ended at mid thigh and were "paned" with decorative vertical bands. With these might be worn *Canions* (men), which were tight shorts to the knee, over which the stocking was taken. They were padded. If the trunk hose and canions were worn they were in one garment and the stockings were separate. If they were not, then the trunk hose were worn with stockings tight, which came farther up the leg, well above the knee.

Stockings (men) were long and came above the knee. If no canions were worn, the stockings came nearly to the fork, and were joined on to the trunk hose breeches.

Shoes (men) had a high instep, buckled or rosetted, and were made in velvet, leather, or cloth.

Slippers (women) were of velvet or satin, which necessitated the 2 in. to 7 in. thick cork-soled *Chopines* (women) to be added for street wear.

The *Hair* (men) was long and brushed back. They wore a pointed beard and moustache. A dandy wore on his shoulder one love lock which was delicately tied with a ribbon!

Hair (women) was curled and frizzed and dyed golden. It was worn high on the forehead and away from the sides of the face.

Hats (men) were round or flat with soft crowns

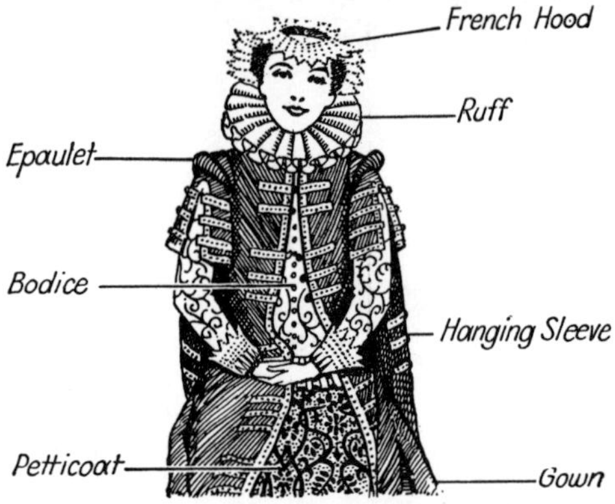

LADY PEMBROKE, 1614

and narrow brims and a feather. A gold lace or twisted cord went round the crown. Felt, beaver, sarcenet, and velvet were the materials.

The *French Hood* (women) was much the same as in the previous reign.

The *Tall Hat* (women) was exactly like the

men's tall hat—shallow brimmed, high crowned, and with a twist of material round the crown. About 1590 the veil of the French Hood was wired into arches behind the shoulders. Smaller bonnets were also worn.

JAMES I

Breeches (men) became looser and longer, and covered the knee, where they were buttoned or ribbon-tied, though the older circular type of trunk hose continued to be fashionable.

The *Ruff* (men) was succeeded by the *Whisk* (men), a stiff semi-circular collar of lace, square in front, and wired out. The ruff remained popular, but it was not so modish. The remainder of the costume was as before.

The *Collar* (women) changed from the circular

SIR WALTER RALEIGH AND SON, 1602

ruff to the wired lace or cambric collar standing up at the back of the neck and attached to the open neck on each side in front. It was dyed different shades, and was circular, except in front, where it was square cut. Another form, a heart shape, was in two circles at the back. This type was popularized by Elizabeth, but it became more general and smaller in James I's reign.

The *Waist Ruff* (women) came in at the close of Elizabeth's reign, and was a box pleated rectangle, tied round the waist with a bow in front and resting on the horizontal part of the skirt, which was upheld by the farthingale.

The *Petticoat* (women) was of satin, and short enough to disclose the feet in their dainty satin slippers.

The *Gown* (women) had a low cut square neck opening, and tight sleeves to the elbow, from

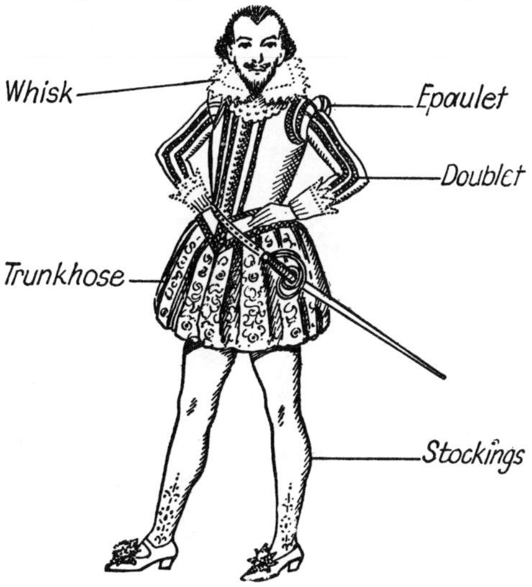

RICHARD SACKVILLE, LORD DORSET, 1616

which dangled long streamers–relics of the hanging sleeves. The bodice was cylindrical and pointed, all creases being removed by the corset, and the skirt opened in front to reveal the satin petticoat. The undersleeves, which showed from elbow to wrist, were ruffed at the waist with small frills or were finished with cambric cuffs stitched in coloured and black thread or with lace cuffs—both were of the turn-back type.

Shoes (men and women) were ribbon rosetted, and the women also wore rosettes of lace.

Hair (men) was worn half-way down the neck, and was brushed back. It had the almost invariable addition of a short pointed beard and a small tuft, not joined to the beard, just below the lip, and moustaches were slightly pointed.

Hair (women) was dressed high and backwards from the face.

The *Tall Crowned Hat* (men and women) was of small black felt with a high crown and small brim, a cord or twisted material round the crown, and a feather starting in front and fastened with a jewel at the side. The men also wore a beaver hat with a white plume erect behind it.

Jewellery. Many necklaces, chiefly pearl, for the women, and gold chains with large rings for men. The folding fan made its appearance for the first time and displaced the flag type fan.

SUMMARY

MEN (ELIZABETH)

Dress

Spanish Cape—high collar.

Italian Doublet—close fit, small frill below waist, padded and boned to form curved convex shape pointed downwards. Sleeves differed in colour and split to show undersleeve. Tight, long, slashed sleeve and turnback cuff, armhole covered by epaulet. High collar, buttoned down centre or open to show vest. Vertical embroidered panels.

QUEEN ELIZABETH, 1600

Ruff—yellow starched linen, figure eight shape.

Collar—white linen, turned down or square and wired.

Legs

Trunk Hose—round breeches, very full at top, end at mid-thigh; slashed, puffed, padded.

Canions—shorts, padded (1570 on).

Stockings—long to above knee.

Feet

Shoes—high instep, buckled or rosetted, leather, velvet, or cloth.

Hair

Long, brushed back, pointed beard, moustache slight. Love lock on one shoulder, ribbon tied.

Hats

Round or flat, soft crown, narrow brim, feathered, gold lace or twisted cord round crown. Felt, beaver, sarcenet or velvet.

WOMEN (ELIZABETH)

Dress

Corset—leather or whalebone.

Farthingale—huge bone wheel below waist.

Petticoats—several. Chemise—linen.

Two Gowns—hanging sleeves of lawn or cambric to underdress; general style as Henry VIII, long point to bodice.

Ruff—cambric or lawn, plain or lace edged, underpropped if large: (1) circular; (2) semi-circular; (3) upstanding at back, round or heart shaped.

JAMES I'S DAUGHTER, QUEEN OF BOHEMIA, C. 1620

Feet

Slippers—velvet or satin.

Chopines—cork soled over shoes.

Hair

Curled, dyed, frizzed, high on forehead and clear of sides of face.

Hats

French Hood—as Mary's reign.
Tall Hat—shallow brim, high crown as men.

Jewels

Chains, pins, scented embroidered gloves, lace or silk handkerchiefs, flag-shaped fans in hand or girdle, masks for street and theatre.

MEN (JAMES I)

Dress

Breeches—loose, cover knees where buttoned or ribbon tied.
Rest, as above, but less slashes and padding.
Whisk—a standing collar vice ruff.

Feet

Shoes—ribbon rosetted.

Hair

Half down neck; pointed beard; lip tuft; moustache; brushed back hair.

Hat

Tall crowned, wide brimmed.
Beaver hats with white plume erect at back.

WOMEN (JAMES I)

Dress

Collar—wired lace or cambric dyed. Fans out behind.
Waist Ruff—box pleat, tied above farthingale.
Farthingale—huge bone wheel below waist.

Dress—contd.

Petticoat—satin, shows feet.
Gown—low cut square neck, open cylinder bodice, tight sleeves to elbow; from there streamers, open skirt in front to show petticoat; undersleeves to wrist where ruffed or with cambric or lace cuffs.

JAMES I'S QUEEN

Feet

Shoes—lace rosetted.

Hair

High dressed.

Hats

Same as men, high crowned felt. No caps.

Jewels

Necklaces—many. Folding fan first arrived.

CHARLES THE FIRST

King Charles the First was an artist and a saint. He was one of the earliest of our monarchs to live a pure home life, and his devotion to the historic Church cost him his life. He was one of the most cultured men in Europe, and his art collections in London and Windsor for the most part happily remain with us. As the patron of Vandyk and Rubens he has earned undying gratitude. The fashions during his reign became less awkward and more graceful and easy, and the gentlemen knew how to wear their clothes to advantage. It was a thoroughly artistic period. King Charles the First as a gentleman and a man of culture knew how to wear his clothes with an air and a manner.

The *Doublet* (men) was busked with bones and was corset-like. Until 1632 it had a pointed waist, with four to six vertical slits on the breast and back. The sleeves were close-fitting and plain, but another type had the sleeve close from wrist to elbow, where it widened into a large puff, which was paned to show the linen shirt. Paning was a series of strips of material with gaps vertically cut between. After 1628 the doublet became deeper and less pointed, and was loose fitting with only a slight point in front. The epaulets, which were slight at first, disappeared during the reign. After 1645 the jacket became skimpy and reached to just above the hips, leaving a gap to show the shirt, which was pulled out. It had no waist.

The shortening of the doublet and the practice of leaving the lower half unbuttoned allowed the white shirt to show below it at the waist. In

CHILDREN OF CHARLES I (LONDON)

Charles II's reign it became shorter still, and turned into an "Eton jacket." Simultaneously with this curtailment, which occurred about 1645, the breeches changed into full, loose, tubular trousers like modern "shorts." They were edged with lace or ribbon bows at the waist, the knees, and down the side seams.

"Tassets" was the name given to the small skirts of the doublet.

The *Breeches* (men) were fastened by points, i.e. a row of bows at the waist. Trunk hose remained only for pages, and in State robes.

In 1620 they had a high waist and full knickers to just above the knee. In 1628 they reached to below the knee, and were gartered with a large bow or rosette, and buttoned all down the side. If the lower buttons above the knee were unfastened they disclosed the linen lining. In 1640 they had become full and open, i.e. tubular, and were unconfined at the knee, or they were close at the knee, and finished with ribbons. The waist dropped to just over the hips so that the full shirt bulged out above them and between them and the now short doublet. This was a precursor of the Charles II costume.

The *Jerkin* (men) was sleeveless or had hanging sleeves. In leather, as the buff coat, it was laced up the front and sometimes had loose sleeves to match, or close stuff sleeves striped with braid or lace horizontally or vertically. It was a military garment.

The *Coat* (men) was cassock-shaped, and reached to midthigh. It had wide sleeves, the cuff being turned up broadly. It was worn during evenings.

The *Cloak* (men) became longer and fuller, and reached at least to the knee, sometimes lower, and was draped over the arm.

The *Gown* (men) was of the type still worn by chancellors and lord mayors, and was worn by older men.

The *Bodice* (women) up to 1630 had a deep point and a wasp waist. After that date it was

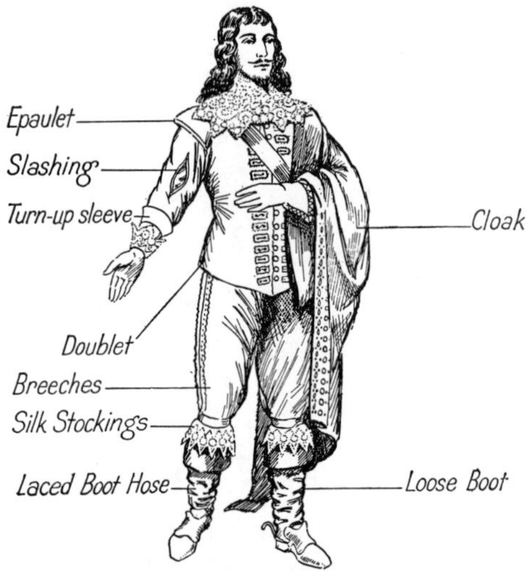

LORD PETERBOROUGH, 1635

low-necked, with a high waist and skirt tabs like the men's doublets, and was worn over a round pointed stomacher, which matched. The sleeves were at first close to the wrist and followed the man's fashions by developing into large puffs, or they were leg-of-mutton types with slashings. The commonest form was in one puff to below the elbow, and, later, to the elbow only, the bare arm showing in either case.

Charles I and His Queen

(G.2477)

The *Skirt* (women) was gathered at the waist and hung loosely. It had, at option, the reversed V opening, in which case the *Petticoat* (women) showed when the skirt opened in a front Λ, but otherwise it did not, as the fashion of raising the upper skirt to show the under-robe had gone out.

The *Gown* (older women) was close at the throat and fitted the body, after the type of Lady Pembroke. The skirt was full.

Silk stockings were popular, and the men wore enormous boots, which necessitated *Boot Hose* (men) of material edged deeply with lace, which fell over the boot top. The more economical wore *Boot Hose Tops*, which had no calves; the boot covered the rest. Garters, finished with a great bow at the side, or large rosettes in coloured ribbon were prominent.

Spurred boots were almost *de rigueur*. Their tops were folded down and over. Some wide-spreading top-boots had their tops so loose that they formed a cup all round. All had square heels. Red heels for evening wear remained the mark of the aristocrat. The wide tops came in about 1640.

QUEEN HENRIETTA MARIA (LONDON)

Men wore their hair off the brow and to one side and level with the jaw till 1628, but afterwards it lengthened and they had a fringe on the brow. The vandyk-pointed beard remained until 1640, but was then displaced by the chin tuft, which began in 1630 and lasted till 1645. Moustaches were brushed upwards.

The women wore their hair brushed back off the face and tied into a bun at the back. On the forehead was a fringe, or kiss curls were worn there. Ringlets appeared and, as the reign proceeded, they were worn longer. At first they were mere bunches at each side of the face, but in the end they became long corkscrew curls. Pearl

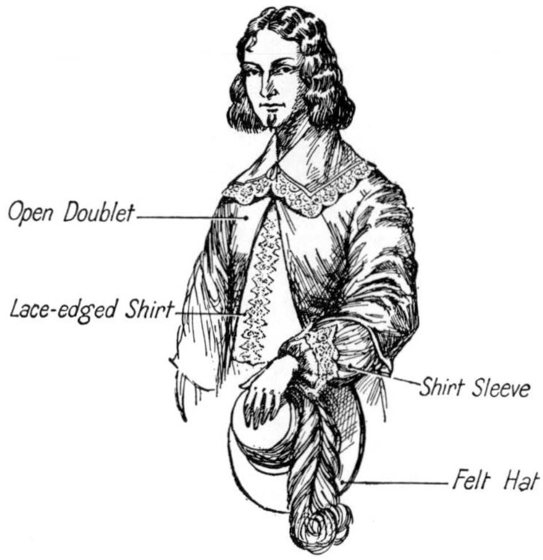

SIR RICHARD FANSHAWE, 1644

ropes adorned the head. Jewellery was much less profuse and consequently more tasteful.

The *Sombrero* (men) of black felt, loose and wide brimmed, with one side turned up, and with a fairly high crown, is well known. One or two ostrich feathers adorned it at one side, or a hat band was formed of the cut ends of ostrich feathers. After 1640 the Puritan type began to be worn, the crown became higher and the brim narrower, and the whole appearance was marred.

The *Montero* (men) was a cap used for sport, and had a loose, adaptable brim, which could be turned either up or down at taste. The women were usually bareheaded, though they occasionally wore a loose gauze veil or a loose hood. The Cavalier hat was used only for riding.

The high felt hat was almost universally worn at the end of Charles I's reign and (robbed of its feather and ribbon) by the Puritans.

Cleanliness was a feature of the Carolean Court. In consequence, linen played an important part. Lovely lace collars were wired into various shapes. The old whisk was succeeded by the

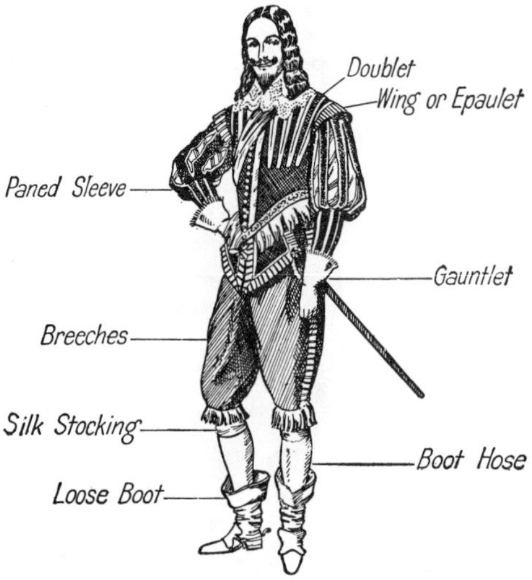

KING CHARLES I (LONDON)

Falling Ruff (men), which was the old ruff lying down instead of standing up. This became the *Falling Band* (men), which was a collar of the same shape but without the gathers of the ruff. Both hung from the throat to the shoulders, the band being wider and deeper. After 1640 they shrank in size. Cuffs were deep and turned up over the doublet sleeve. The sword was suspended by a broad waist sash, worn horizontally, or from the *Baldrick*, or sword belt, hung diagonally over the right shoulder.

Up to 1635 the women wore the *fan-shaped* wired-up ruffs, as before. Older women still wore the *cart-wheel ruff* of the reigns of Elizabeth and James I. After 1630 the *broad falling collar*, like the men's, came in, and, like theirs, it was made of linen or lace. Later, the broad falling collar with the *upstanding fan collar* was worn. From 1635 the low neck was covered with a neckerchief folded diagonally, and by 1650 the neck line had become horizontal and presented that appearance of the bodice falling off altogether which was so much loved by the early Victorians.

SUMMARY

MEN

Dress

Doublet—pointed waist, busked. Vertical slits front and back. Close sleeves or close wrist to elbow, then wide puff, paned below to show shirt. Looser and less pointed later. Epaulets disappeared gradually. Skirt shortened to hips later.

Breeches—row of bows at waist. In 1620 high waist and knickers above knee. In 1628 knickers below knee. In 1640 "shorts," open and fuller.

Shirt—linen. When doublet shortened to hips, the shirt showed in bulge there.

Jerkin—sleeveless or hanging sleeves. Leather front laced. Loose sleeves, matching or striped, optional.

Coat—loose, cassock-like to mid-thigh with wide sleeve and broad turn-up cuff for evening wear.

Cloak—full to knee or lower.

Gown—like Chancellor's for older man.

Legs

Silk stockings. Boot hose, edged lace deeply.
Boot hose tops, without calf.
Garters—great bow below knee or rosette.

Feet

Spurred boots, top folded down.
Wide spreading top-boots, high square heels.
Red heels for dress wear.

Hair

Off brow one side, level with jaw. Later, lengthened with a fringe. Vandyke beard to 1640. Chin tuft 1630–40. Moustache brushed up.

Linen

The whisk collar to 1630.
Falling ruff.
Falling band.
Deep turn-up cuffs.
Sash broad over waist, or shoulder belt-baldrick for sword.

Hats

Sombrero—high crown, wide brim cocked. Ostrich feathers or feather hat band.

High conical crown, narrow brim later.

Montero—cap with reversible brim for sport.

Fur cap—close fitting.

WOMEN

Dress

Bodice—deep pointed wasp waist, and stomacher.

After 1630 low neck, high waist; skirt tabs like doublet, and round stomacher to match.

Sleeves—close to wrist or puffed, as men, or leg-of-mutton, slashed. Later, one puff to below elbow, then to above elbow unslashed. Bare arm.

Skirt—waist gathered, opening optional, hung loose.

Petticoat—showed at opening of skirt. Often unseen.

Gowns—older women, close throat, fitted body, full skirt.

Hair

Off face to bun at back. Head fringe or kiss curls. Ringlets. Corkscrew curls. Pearls.

Hats

Mostly bare heads. Loose gauze veil. Loose hood. Cavalier hat for riding.

Linen

Fan-shape wired ruffs as before to 1635.

Cart-wheel ruff for older women.

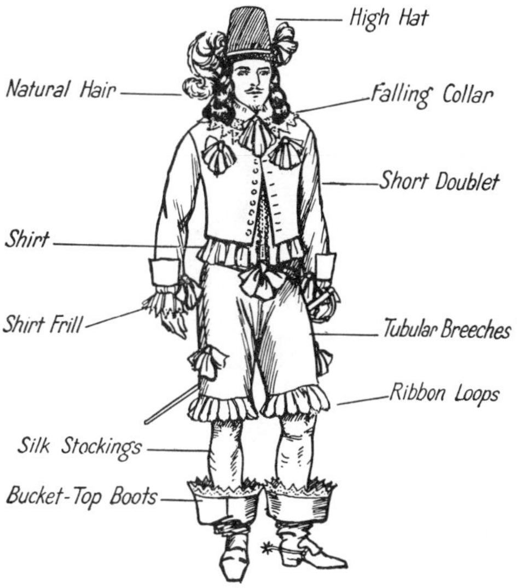

GENTLEMAN OF 1645

Broad falling collar. Falling collar and/or upstanding collar.

Square kerchief over neck opening.

Horizontal opening after 1650.

PURITANISM

Puritanism has gained more credit than is its due, owing to the extremely inaccurate historians of the Victorian era who had a habit of making their history fit their politics. What is regarded by the man in the street as the age of liberty and freedom was, in reality, quite the reverse. The dates are from 1649 to 1660. When the dictatorship began to lose its grip and men looked for freedom through the return of the king, the strict Puritan modes began to be ignored.

England was under the domination of a crude, brutal, and unrefined man—that of the Dictator Cromwell. The effect was that everyone had to conform to the standard pattern. Dress, as a result, became harsh and plain, like its exponents, and it lacked all grace of colour, shape, and design.

The modes, stripped of every atom of charm, remained the same as at the end of the reign of the Martyr King, but the extreme of Puritan dress was affected chiefly by the more fanatical types epitomized as "Roundheads." Others avoided the strictly cropped head, and the favoured few of Cromwell's entourage wore what they liked. A General Harrison, though he was a Puritan, at a reception appeared in scarlet trimmed with silver lace and ribbons. This was exceptional. Most men wore their hair fairly long and brushed in any style.

All ribbons, lace, and embroideries were abandoned. Materials were of muddy brown, funereal black, and other shades that were reminiscent of dirt and mud.

The *Doublet* (men), robbed of its point and shape, became a badly fitting sack.

The *Breeches* (men) were quite plain, and had no decorated bands up the sides. They were gathered into a band at the knee.

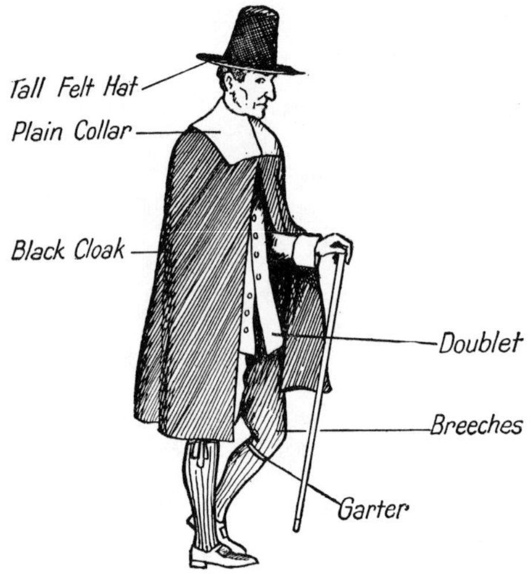

The *Shirt* (men) did not show except where the deep, plain, white linen cuff was turned up over the sleeves of the doublet or jerkin.

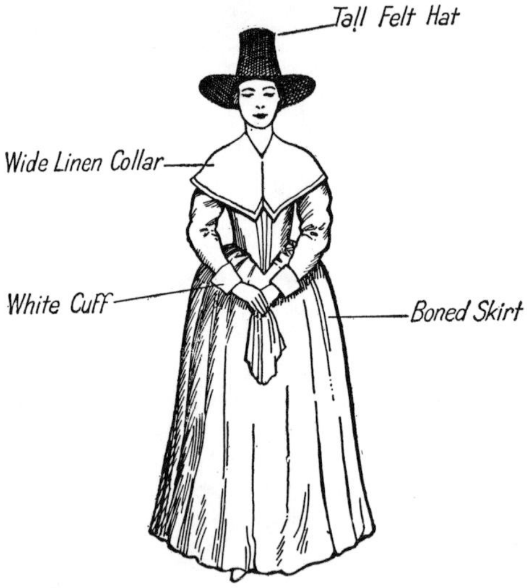

The *Coat* (men) was like a cassock, and fell to the middle of the thigh. It had fairly wide sleeves to enable it to go over the inner sleeves of the rest of the costume.

The *Gown* (men) was still worn by the older men, and was much the same as that of a modern lord mayor's, except that it had no bands of metal lace or other decoration.

The *Bodice* (women) had a square cut, fairly low neck, but not as low as in Royalist times. It had a straight waistband, and the pointed shapes were abandoned. The square tabs into which the skirt of the bodice was cut in the preceding reign were discontinued, save, oddly enough, for one solitary tab, which, like a tail, hung on in the middle of the back. The sleeves were plain and close fitting, though sleeves of elbow length were

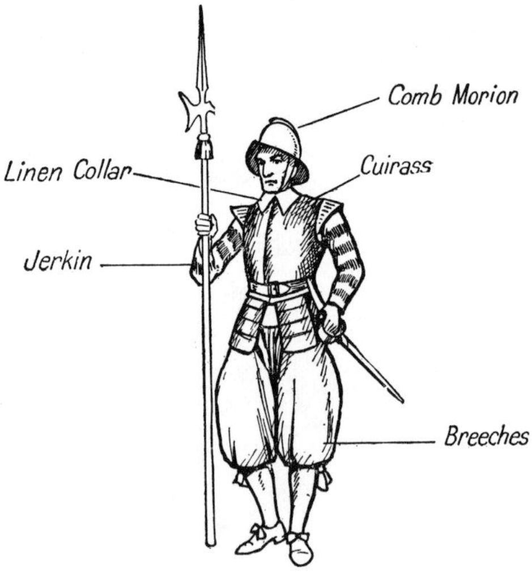

worn by the more "abandoned" women—chiefly working class.

The *Skirt* (women) was plain. It was gathered into the waist by a band and was somewhat loose in cut. The ʌ opening, which used to reveal the petticoat in the King's time, was considered indelicate.

The *Apron* (woman) was of plain linen of the usual type.

The *Gown* (women) was the older women's garment and was made as previously.

The period gives no assistance to the artist who has to design its costumes, but if pearl and oyster greys or pleasant cinnamon browns are contrasted with the large spaces of white linen in apron, kerchief, collar, and cuffs, a suitable effect can be obtained.

The men wore plain black cloth or wool stockings of thick material, and women rosettes to their shoes. Red heels were abolished.

Very wide tops of black leather or brown were put on the thigh boots, and shoes with plain metal buckles—perhaps even silver—were worn. They were much like modern court shoes with square buckles about half an inch in breadth.

Close-cropped hair was the mark of the extremely righteous and of the fanatic, but the bulk of the men refused to comply with this custom and wore their hair fairly long to about the top of the nape of the neck. It was parted in the middle and was roughly brushed. Faces were clean shaven. The women dressed their hair straightly and plainly, and hid most of it under the white linen caps. No curls or pearls helped to make the hair more beautiful.

It was an age of linen.

Plain square-cut collars like immense Eton collars were worn by men and women alike.

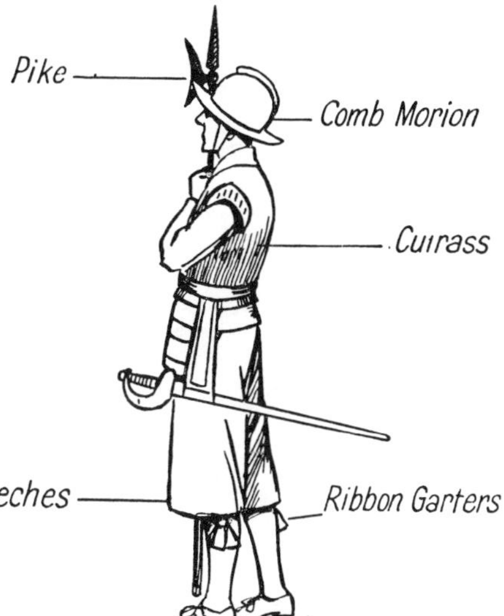

They were of the falling band type of the previous reign, but lay flatter on the body. Deep linen cuffs were turned back over the wrists. No lace was used. The square white kerchief was folded diagonally, as before, over the breast and shoulders, and gave a V opening effect to the neck. The collars were wide at first, but towards the close of the revolutionary period they shrank in size.

The hat *par excellence* was the comic black felt with a high crown and a narrow brim. Older men wore close fitting skull-shaped caps. The women wore the linen coif or skull-cap, rather more of a mob-cap cut than the men's, and

over this the Puritan high-crowned men's hat. Black silk hoods were popular; sometimes they were attached to a full length cape over the shoulders.

No jewellery of any kind was worn. Market baskets in wicker, oval in shape, with circular handles, are effective properties, and tall plain walking sticks with, perhaps, a plain silver knob may be used by the men.

People affected dour and severe expressions to denote the lack of humour and graciousness of their outlook. This should be observed in stage work of this period.

Women for the most part still went about bareheaded, though the Puritans considered this immodest. Hats should, therefore, be worn in representations of the early part of this period but not towards its latter end. Lace caps were also worn by the more daring or the more conservative, and it is probable that country folk still wore what they possessed, no matter whether it was "Royalist" in style or not. The use of the tall hat worn over the lace or linen cap can be seen in remote parts of Wales to this very day.

The Puritan regime originated no new styles of dress, but merely modified the modes of Royalist days. Everything was sobered down—there

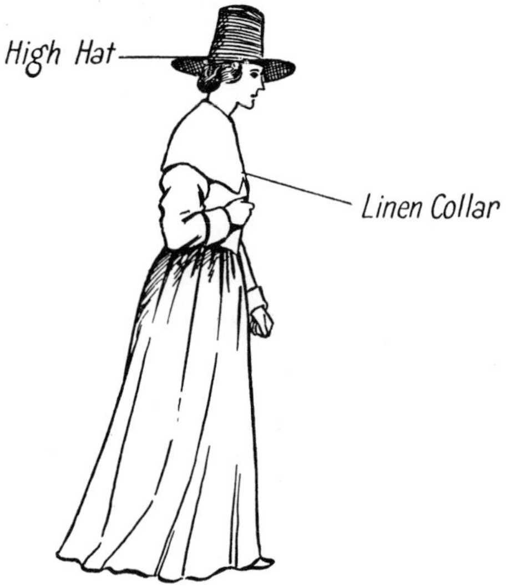

was no lace, there were no ribbons or feathers; plain linen instead of fine lace, straight lines instead of curves were the vogue. The ruff was generally abandoned, although it was in its simpler form of a falling band lace collar.

At the same time, the governing faction wore what they liked. I have instanced the case of the Puritan General Harrison. Another similar case was that of the Protector Cromwell's daughter, who, according to her portrait in the National Portrait Gallery, London, in 1658 was dressed in the height of the French fashion. The date of this painting should be borne in mind. After the execution of the king the Puritan Party was in the ascendancy, and the Roundhead fashions were dominant. After some years of Oliver's iron rule the nation (which had never approved of the King's martyrdom) made its feelings felt more strongly, and a definite move towards the restoration of the monarchy began. Elizabeth Cromwell's portrait was painted only two years before the King came into his own again: men were looking towards France, where resided the Queen Mother, and their thoughts were reflected in their clothes. Presbyterian fashions fell into definite dislike and disuse, and were replaced by clothes common to the rest of the Royalist States of Europe, in herald of the approaching dawn of liberty, which was to break into day with the return of the Merry Monarch.

SUMMARY

MEN

Dress

Doublet—plain and fairly loose fitting.
Breeches—plain, no decoration, band at knee.
Shirt—not showing, save at turn-up cuff.
Jerkin—for soldiers and artisans.
Coat—loose, cassock-like to mid-thigh, fairly wide sleeve, turn-up cuff.
Cloak—plain, not very full, to mid-thigh.
Gown—for older men like a mayor's.

Legs

Cloth stockings or woollen.

Feet

Thigh boots—wide tops.
Shoes with plain silver or metal buckles.

Hair

Close cropped.
Clean shaven.
Long to back of head and mid-parted.

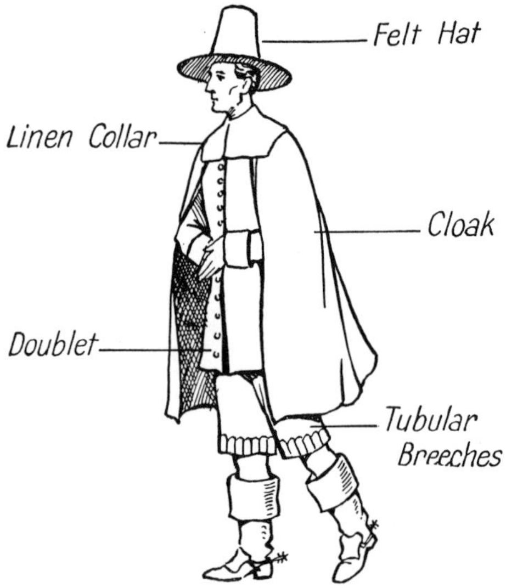

Linen

Plain linen collars, falling band type, square cut.
Deep linen cuffs, turned back over sleeve.

Hats

Broad brim, high crown, black felt.
Caps for old men.

WOMEN

Dress

Bodice—square, lowish neck, straight waistband, no square tabs, save one in centre of back.
Sleeves—plain and close fitting.
Skirt—waist gathered, no ∧ opening.
Petticoat—unseen.
Apron—plain linen.
Gowns—for older women.

Legs

Shoe rosettes permitted.

Hair

Straight dressed, no curls or pearls.

Linen

Wide collars, square cut, no lace.
Later collars shrank in size.
Kerchief square, folded diagonally over neck opening.
Broad linen cuffs.

Hats

Black silk hoods, sometimes attached to
Full length capes.
Linen coifs or caps.
Black felt broad brim and high crown. Can be worn with or without coif.

Jewellery

None.

RESTORATION

Restoration of the monarchy meant also restoration of artistry in dress, and the general relief at the cessation of the Republican Autocracy caused expansion in design and gaiety in colour. The period divided itself sharply into two sections of men's costume. In the beginning it continued the "Eton jacket" style, where it left off under Charles I, but instead of the "Shorts" came the kilt-like petticoat breeches. This ended with the importation of the "Persian Vest," which was a long, heavily braided cassock-like coat which was worn during the rest of Charles II's reign and that of his brother. This is one of the most revolutionary changes ever to occur in juxtaposition, the complete outline changing from a figure sharply divided by the waistbelt, to one which had no marked waist line. This section covers 1660 to 1689.

The Doublet (men) became short, like an Eton jacket, and was left open in front. It had short sleeves to just below the elbow, where they were finished with a deep fringe of looped ribbon. The sleeve had a front opening till 1665, but afterwards was turned up from the elbow in a close-buttoned cuff. It followed therefore that—

The *Shirt* (men) showed greatly. It was puffed out over the waist and through the sleeve

EARLY RESTORATION MAN

slits. Ribbon tied till 1680, it had deep lace ruffles at the wrists, and a ruche or frill at the breast-opening, towards the close of its popularity.

The *Collar* (men) continued as the falling band till 1670, but afterwards became a mere bib on the breast with the corners rounded. At the end of this period the collar as such ceased to be worn, and the neckcloth, which was a scarf tied at the throat to form a cravat with falling ends, lace edged, took its place.

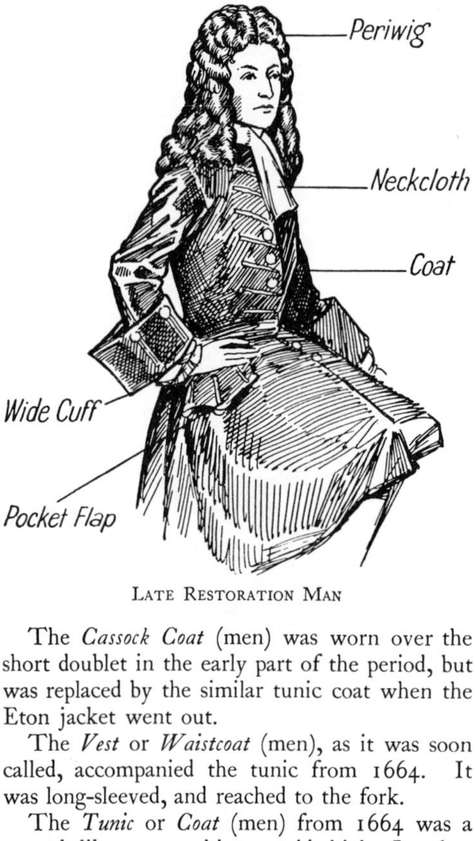

LATE RESTORATION MAN

The *Cassock Coat* (men) was worn over the short doublet in the early part of the period, but was replaced by the similar tunic coat when the Eton jacket went out.

The *Vest* or *Waistcoat* (men), as it was soon called, accompanied the tunic from 1664. It was long-sleeved, and reached to the fork.

The *Tunic* or *Coat* (men) from 1664 was a cassock-like coat reaching to mid-thigh. In 1670 it reached to below the knee, and it had elbow sleeves finished with broad turned-up cuffs. It was slit up each side and at the back. These slits, as well as the front, were trimmed heavily in the frogging manner with dummy buttons and buttonholes. The resultant horizontal effect on a long coat was the distinguishing mark of the bulk of the Restoration period.

Cloaks (men) were used for travelling, but were not used continuously with day dress as they were in the previous reign. The hat and cloak romance had vanished.

Petticoat Breeches (men) were at first much like kilts, and in the sixties they had ribbon loops at the waist, hem, and sides. In the seventies, they reached only to mid-thigh, and after then they were replaced by full breeches gartered at the knee. Breeches became narrower in the eighties. In the nineties they were plain and tight-fitting, and strapped below the knee with a buckle or six buttons. They were made either of black velvet or material of a colour that matched the rest of the suit.

The *Bodice* (women) took the shape of the corset under it, the shoulders being bare. The less daring veiled this expanse of skin with a scarf, or pulled up the chemise to fill the hiatus. The bodice was either laced at the back or fastened in front, generally the former. It had elbow sleeves, sometimes slashed in front, and a row of bows adorned the front of the bodice. The sleeves were puffed till 1670, and then

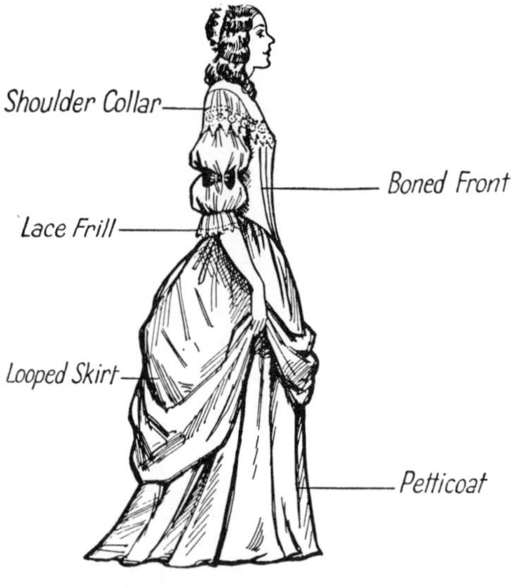

became loose and tubular in shape. Throughout the period they were often of shoulder length only. The end of the sleeve was finished with a row of ribbon loops. Instead of the former deep collar, the lace edging to the neck became a mere border.

The *Skirt* (women) had a front Λ, which was

CHARLES II AND HIS QUEEN

tied back by bows or clasps right along. Another mode was to pull back the skirt and to fasten it at the back. This disclosed the differently coloured lining, which the former method did not.

The *Petticoat* (women), which showed prominently, was decorated with embroidery or other patterns.

Gowns (women) in 1680 incorporated the bodice and skirt in a one-piece garment.

Boot Hose and *Boot Hose Tops* have previously been described.

Stirrup Hose widened above the knee, and were fastened to the petticoat breeches by ribbon points. Often a second pair was worn over them. Their wide tops dropped over the garters and below the knee, and were finished with a deep, full flounce of lace or linen. A separate valance of linen or lace was popular between 1660 and 1670. These knee frills went with the petticoat breeches kilt costume, but not with the later

A Family, 1688

cassock-coat costume. After 1680, with the advent of coat and vest, the knee ribbons vanished and the stockings were rolled over the breeches. After 1690 there was no rolling, but the stocking was drawn above the knee.

The *Jack Boot* (men) had a square shaped cuff-like top above the knee and a square toe. These high boots were characteristic of the age. From 1670 they were laced up the front.

Spatter Dashes (men) were, as their appropriate name denotes, leggings worn with shoes from 1690 onwards.

Shoes of black, with prominent upstanding tongues, came in during 1680, but red heels were

Nell Gwynn

worn for evening dress occasions only. Particularly to be noted is the disappearance of rosettes, their place being taken by a stiff butterfly bow on the shoe. Shoe buckles were also worn from 1680.

In the sixties the women wore high-heeled *Louis Shoes* with taper toes, which were made of satin, needlework, or brocade, the instep being finished with a buckle or a bow.

Mules (women) were slippers with high heels and cut-away sides, so that only the toe and instep were covered over.

Buskins (women), worn for riding, were made of leather or satin.

The *men* were clean-shaven, though here and there the chin tuft still lingered amongst the older men who had not changed. The moustache became a mere thread from the nostrils to the corners of the lips—a fashion popularized by Charles II. The great novelty was the introduction of the *Periwig* (men), which fashion the King brought over after his European travels. It was, of course, worn purely as an artificial covering, and there was no attempt to make it look like natural hair. The head was shaved to accommodate the erection, which was quite graceful. In its early stages it was an irregular mass of curly hair reaching to the shoulders, but later it became formalized into rather stiff cork-screw curls and was a more solid looking mass. This change took place in the seventies.

Three distinct changes marked the *Women*. In the sixties their hair was puffed above the ears and wires held it well away from the cheeks at each side. By the seventies the wires had been dropped, and the side curls were quite close to the face. Ten years later a centre parting heralded the approach of the Queen Anne styles.

In the beginning of this period the steeple crowned felt hat remained, but a new variety was introduced with a flat crown and wide brims, something like a Harrow or Boater hat of to-day. It was stiffened. Plumes and ribbon decoration remained popular until the eighties.

The women still went about bare-headed, but when they needed a covering they wore a loose silk hood or a simple kerchief (countrywomen almost always wore one or other of these types when they wanted hats). For riding purposes men's hats were worn, or rather hats similar to the men's—wide-brimmed felt with a feather or ribbon bunch trimmings.

SUMMARY

MEN

Dress

Doublet.—Short Eton, open front, short sleeves to below elbow with deep fringe looped ribbons. Front opening to sleeve till 1665; after that sleeve turned up at elbow in close buttoned cuff.

Shirt.—Early, bulged at waist and showing front. Ribbon tied to 1680. Deep wrist ruffles. Ruche or frill at opening.

Collar.—Falling band square cut to 1670. Then breast bib with round corners. Then neckcloth.

Cassock coat.—Worn over short doublet.

Vest or waistcoat.—1664 on. Long-sleeved to fork. Over it was

Tunic or Coat.—Long cassock coat to mid-thigh; 1670 to below knee with elbow sleeves and broad turn-up cuff. Slit up to hip each side and back. Dummy button trimmed.

Cloak.—Mainly travelling.

Petticoat breeches.—Kilt-like. In 1660 ribbon loops at waist, hem, and sides; 1670 to mid-thigh. Afterwards full breeches, knee-gartered. Narrower in 1680. In 1690 plain tight strapped below knee, with buckle or buttons. Black velvet or match suit.

Legs

Boot hose and boot hose tops till 1680.

Stirrup hose.—Widened at knee. Fastened to Petti-breeches by points. Often two pairs worn. Wide tops drooped over garters in flounce below knee.

Lace or linen valance 1660–70. After 1680 no knee ribbon and stocking rolled over breech. After 1690's no roll and stocking was drawn above knee.

Feet

Jack boot.—Square cuff top above knee. Square toe. 1670 onwards laced.

Spatter dashes.—Leggings worn with shoes 1690 onwards.

Black shoes with upstanding tongues to 1680 (red heels for dress). No rosettes, but butterfly ribbon bows. Shoe buckles 1680 onwards.

Hair

Clean-shaven. Thread moustache.

Periwig. Irregular in 1660's; corkscrew formal in 1670's.

Hats

Steeple crown in 1660's.

Low flat crown (Boater). 1665–75. Plumes and ribbons to 1680.

WOMEN

Dress

Bodice.—Corset, bare shoulders, or scarf or chemise covers, back laced or front fastened. Bows in front. Elbow sleeves, some front slashed. Puffs to 1670, then loose tubes. Elbow fringe of ribbon loops. Often shoulder length sleeves. Lace border to low neck.

Skirt.—Front ∧ tied back by bows or clasps or fastened behind to show lining.

Petticoat.

Gowns.—One-piece version of above in 1680. Deep collars for older folk.

Feet

High Louis heels, taper toes, satin, brocade, or needlework. Instep buckle or bow.

Mules.—High heel, only toe and instep covered.

Buskins.—For riding. Tall. Satin or leather.

Hair

1660. Puffed above ears. Corkscrews wired away from cheeks.

1670. Side curls close to face. Mop of curls over head or forehead.

1680. Centre parting.

Hats

Bare mostly.

Kerchiefs. Loose hoods.

For riding—men's hats.

DUTCH WILLIAM

Dutch fashions affected English modes when William of Orange took over, in right of his wife, the throne vacated by her father, James II. They modified our clothes by making them more precise in cut, with carefully pressed seams and stiffly arranged folds, instead of the more natural shapes into which materials had hitherto fallen: the domination of the tailor over the seamstress and of the triumph of formalism over Nature began. It was a swing away from the French fashions, brought over by Charles II and James II after their long sojourn abroad, to the Flemish styles to which the new sovereigns, as Prince and Princess of Orange, had been accustomed.

GENTLEMAN WITH MUFF

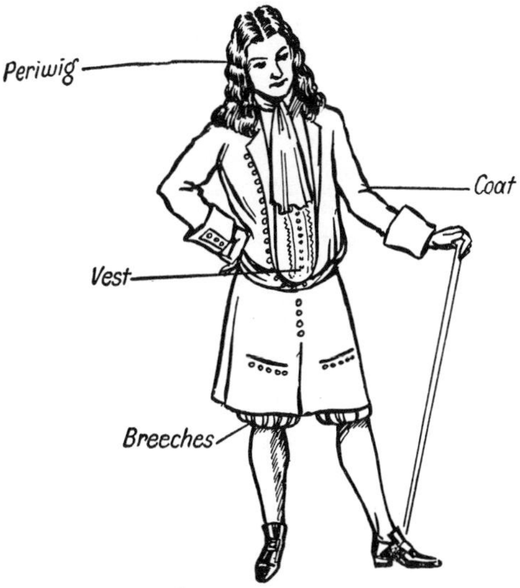

GENTLEMAN, 1680

William III's reign was from 1689 to 1702, Anne ruled from then till 1714, and George I till 1727.

A distinction may be drawn between the broad outlines of the clothes of the gentry and those of the commons—

Gentry	Commons
Wide sleeves	Closer sleeves
Coat knee length	Coat below knee
Cocked hat	Uncocked hat

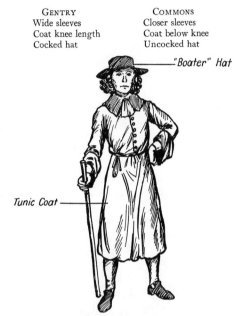

A Working Man, 1688–1711

The style for men at the latter part of the Restoration period remained in force. Skirts were made wider, sleeve cuffs broader, the wig was fuller, and the petticoat breeches gave place to tighter-fitting varieties, which reached below the knee. The flat Boater hat became a cocked hat by turning up two of its sides, and buckles replaced rosettes and bows on the shoes.

The snuff box began to be seen. It does not reach its zenith until the time of the middle Georges.

Both *coat* and *waistcoat* (men) were richly embroidered, and the button-holes were elaborately frogged. Waistcoats were made of Calimanco, which was a material of wool or linen weave, faced on one side with satin, on which a rich design was worked.

The full *sleeve* (women) was replaced by a tighter sleeve, ending in a cuff above the elbow. Beneath this appeared the under sleeve of lace or lawn, with a ruffle springing from the gather at the forearm.

The waist-line was straight, not pointed, and often concealed by small decorative aprons. In Anne's time more flounces and frills were developed, and the skirt became bell-shaped by the addition of the circular hoop.

Flowered materials and sprigged designs came in about this time, and for riding purposes the women adopted men's dress styles, including their hats, wigs, and coats.

The age favoured well-fed, rounded appearances, and to assist Nature, when she was not naturally inclined to mould the face into the desired shape, artificial aids, called "plumpers," were supplied and worn. This fashion accounts for the universally well-fed appearance of the ladies in portraits of the Queen Anne period.

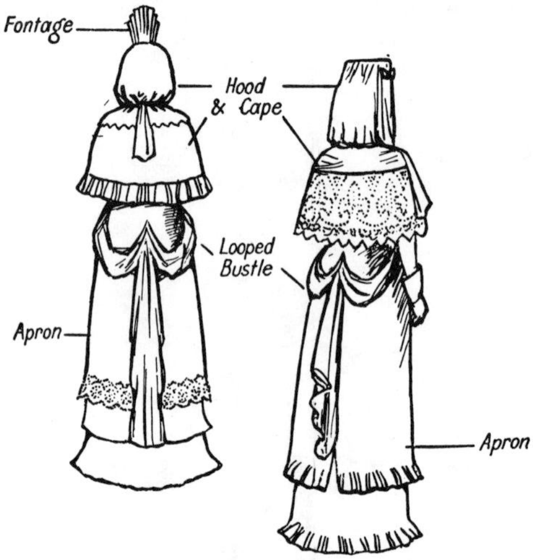

Ladies Outdoors, 1696

The fashion for wide skirts had a reflex action on the furniture of the day: wide-seated chairs came in. Getting through doorways was not easily managed, as houses, unlike furniture, were less readily adaptable to current modes. To pass through a doorway a lady had to depress her hoop by folding it in front or lifting it at the sides. When sitting down she had also to be careful.

The back part of the hoop had to be "sat upon" from the bottom so that it doubled up under the person.

Women, too, wore the same styles, but thought of a fresh hair-dressing. This was a high wired erection, placed on the top of the head, and giving considerable extra height to the wearer, when the hair was carried over it.

The men also devised fresh head-wear. This took the form of the *Ramillies wig*, which was a powdered, brushed-back peruke, with the hair puffed out at the sides, and at the back a long queue, fastened with black bows at its top and bottom. During the reigns of both William and Anne no real changes in clothes occurred, but there were these changes in the hair of the men and the hats of both sexes. If they indicate that in those days the head was esteemed more than the body, it is a good sign, but it is difficult to

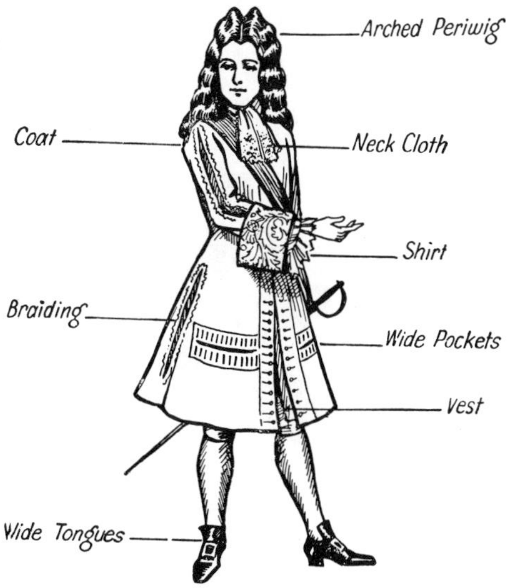

LOUIS XIV, 1694

be convinced of the truth of so flattering an explanation.

The wig became larger, higher, and fuller, and its cost was so high that stealing it was profitable, though risky; indeed men had their wigs snatched off their own heads in the street.

The *Commode* (women) was an erection of wired lace placed upon the top of the head in tiers, three or four in all, rising above each other. They diminished in width as they rose, and at the sides had long lappets of lace, which fell over the shoulders.

George I's reign brought scarcely any change in fashion. The full periwig had been displaced

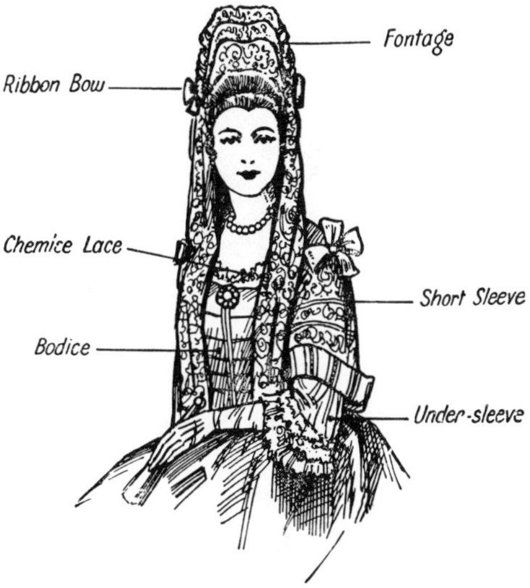

QUEEN MARY II, 1694

by the Ramillies and other shorter wigs powdered white, but they were still a modern justice's full bottomed wig in that they had front lappets over each shoulder, finishing with a tied loop of hair. The coats were flared even fuller than before and worn buttoned only at the waist. This caused the upper part to bulge outwards. Shoe buckles were larger.

The principal change in women's dress was the disappearance of the stiff front "V" of the bodice in favour of a bodice that was close fitting and boned, but had a scarcely perceptible dip in the front of the waist-line, which was thus nearly straight. The "V" having gone, the bodice was the same colour and material all round. The commode or frontage was replaced by the mob cap.

SUMMARY

MEN

Dress

Collar—neck-cloth or cravat. Brussels lace. Ends passed through waistcoat button-holes. Very long. Geneva bands, smaller than above.

LADY. QUEEN ANNE

Tunic or coat—as before, but open to show waistcoat, skirts were wider, cuffs broader. In Anne's reign skirt shortened; cuff revers were still larger, and lace ruffles; skirt wired out.

Waistcoat—as before, but with pockets in Anne's reign.

Breeches—petticoat breeches replaced by tighter ones to below knee.

Cloak—winter and travel.

Muffs—small round.

Legs

Stockings drawn over breeches, sometimes to mid-thigh. In Anne's reign they were still above the knee, but gartered below it, and mainly blue or red.

Feet

Buckles instead of rosettes to shoes. In Anne's reign red heels, small buckles, and square toes.

Hair

Periwig—higher and fuller than before.

No moustache or beard.

Ramillies wig—Anne's reign. White, brushed back, and puffed at sides. Long pigtail plaited. Black bow top and bottom of queue.

Hats

Felt "boater," but with two sides turned up. Ribbon bows. Often carried under arm. In Anne's reign three turn-ups and laced with gold or silver galoon; sometimes feather edge.

LADY. GEORGE I

Jewellery

Snuff boxes. Amber- or gold-topped canes. Masks.

WOMEN

Dress

Bodice—higher neck, tight sleeve. Cuff above elbow. Lace or lawn ruffles below. Long gloves. Round neck opening wide. Stiff "V" front, laced across. Under George I no "V."

Skirt—front "V" showed petticoat. Looped round body in front, and hung on loose folds behind as panniers.

Petticoat—in Anne's reign widened and touched the ground; frilled.

Hoop—bell-shaped; 1710 on, widening till 1740.

Dress—contd.

Cape—short black, deep frill.

Apron—small black silk.

Hair

Brushed up on wire frame to give height. In Anne's reign less high and more natural.

Hats

Hood—usually without commode.

Lace shawl or

Commode or frontage—upright lace in tiers, pleated. Long lappets over shoulders. In Anne's reign became lower and gradually displaced by

Mob caps—lace or linen, frilled.

GEORGE II

George II's reign lasted from 1727 to 1760 and was distinguished by the cult of the "pastoral," which caused a rage for the imitation shepherds and shepherdesses that are familiar to us in Dresden china. It was a prettily dressed period almost all the time. The ladies' skirts were braided, quilted in diagonals, and richly embroidered, and the *motifs* included flowers, fruit, and even animals. The men's coats and waistcoats were marvels of beautiful embroidery and delightfully coloured silks and satins, garnished with gold and silver threads and sequins. Ribbed silks were worn, and the effect of men allowing themselves to wear cheerful and bright colours, with artistic designs upon them, was seen almost for the last time.

SIR BENJAMIN KEENE, K.B., 1730–50

CAPTAIN CORAM, 1740

Powder and patches summarize the epoch, and the patches (which were worn high up on the cheek or near the eyes) were made in an extraordinary range of subjects. Even coaches and horses and the cabriolet were popular. The commoner variety was the simple dot. Slender canes of elegant wood and massive round gold knobs were carried by the men, and the periwig was put away for ever. The people no longer dressed alike; the new fashions gave scope for originality in treatment, and the personality of the wearer was reflected in his or her clothes.

ROUBILIAC, *c.* 1740

In the early part of the reign the men presented the same appearance as in that of George I. They wore the widely flared skirted coat, with its long row of buttons down one edge, only one or two being brought into actual use in order to produce a bulging effect above the waist, where the coat fell outwards. About 1750 the coat shrank into a more closely fitting style, and was slightly cut away at the sides, and the waistcoat became shorter. Great elegance was given to both by the trimming of their vertical edges. Velvets as well as silks and satins were fashionable.

A change also came over the women's frocks. In the beginning of the reign women wore widely belled hoops, but in the 'forties, owing to their increasing inconvenience, they were suppressed in front, the sides only being left belled out in panniers. This style also failing to give sufficient ease, the panniers themselves were abolished; they had almost gone by the end of the reign.

The *Collar* (men) was in the form of a neckcloth or cravat with lace ends. Plain ones were also worn, their ends being tucked under the waistcoat.

The *Coat* (men) was widely flared and was sometimes wired out. It had small buttons right down its edge, and was buttoned there with only one or two buttons. There was no collar, or occasionally a small turn-over collar was attached. The cuff revers were wide and reached nearly to the elbow; the sleeve reached nearly to the wrist, where the shirt showed in a puff, frilled or lace-edged.

The *Waistcoat* (men) was long and pocketed, and the pockets were decorated round their edges. It had as many small buttons, closely set as the coat, and reached nearly to the knees.

LADY CHATHAM, 1750

Breeches (men) were fairly tight, and reached to the knee, where they were gathered into a plain band, which was buckled or buttoned.

Muffs (men) were worn in the street. They were small and round, and made of fur.

The *Hoop* (women) was the foundation of women's dress and ranged over various shapes.

In 1735 it was bell-shaped and large. In 1745 the front part of the hoop was narrowed so that the skirt touched the body, but the side parts were as wide as ever and formed panniers.

Over the hoop was placed the *Petticoat*, and over this the sacque and over-skirt. Two variations were allowed. A bodice and over-skirt to match could be worn, in which case there was no "V" opening in front to disclose a contrasting skirt, or the sacque could be worn over the bodice and skirt, in which case a "V" was formed by the sacque, which disclosed the bodice and skirt, which (themselves matching) contrasted with the sacque. The *Sacque* (women) was a long, loose gown of considerable fullness to allow it to go over the hoop. It hung from the shoulders and was close-sleeved to the elbows, where frills showed. It was heavily gathered (later box pleated) at the back, so that long folds of material

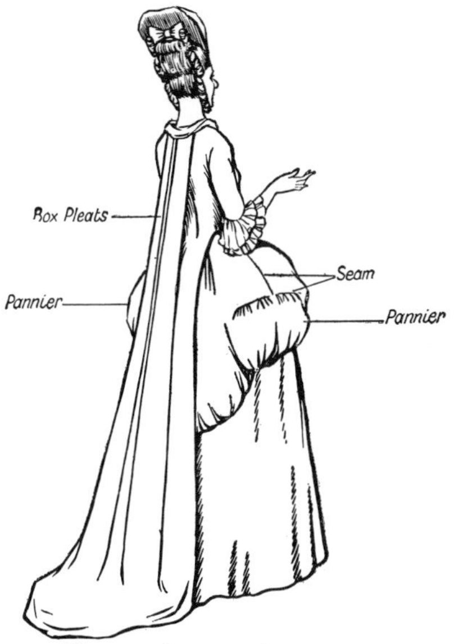

WATTEAU PLEATED SACQUE, 1760

swept down from the neck to the ground. These gathers allowed the material to widen out at the waist-line to cover the panniers. The sacque did not meet in front, but parted at the sides to disclose the under-garment. Its front edge was trimmed with sewing or metal lace or ribbon. A small frill appeared round the neck, which was slightly low.

The *Bodice* (women) was boned and had a square low neck, lace-frilled. There might be a slight point at the waist, but the general impression given was that of a straight waist.

Skirts (women) were all rather shorter than previously.

Aprons (women) were much worn for orna-

MR. AND MISS LLOYD, 1752–59

ment. They were made of silks and satins. They might be plain or tucked, and they were circular in cut.

A fashion set in for white stockings, which soon displaced the coloured stockings previously worn. The gentlemen pulled them over the breeches, where they were fastened by garters, over which they were rolled, so that the garters did not show.

The men wore square buckles of silver on their shoes, which had upstanding, square-ended tongues and low heels. The women had high heels and pointed toes to their shoes.

The periwig disappeared in favour of the bag wig. This was a white-powdered wig, with its side pieces brought round in front and tied with bows of ribbon. They were long enough to rest on the collar part of the coat. About 1750 these front pieces were curtailed, and their place was taken by tight formal side curls in horizontal rows —say three. Both forms had a queue. The latter was tied with a black ribbon, which was brought round the neck to the front, where it was made into a large bow fastened with a diamond brooch called a solitaire.

KEVENHULLER HAT

The women did not wear wigs, but dressed their own hair smoothly and closely to the head and confined it in the mob cap.

The *Chapeau Bras* (men) was a small three-cornered felt hat, sometimes edged with braid or with feather trimming of the fringe type, such as is still seen on the hats of sheriffs and mayors. The feathers were ostrich fronds. Though this hat was worn upon the head, as a hat is intended to be worn, it was also often—more often than not—carried under the arm, hence its name.

The *Kevenhuller* (men) was a three-cornered hat that had high turn-up brims with a peak coming in front. They appeared in 1740, and were always banded along the edges with gold braid or other material. They were as shown in the accompanying illustration.

When no wig was worn the shaven head was protected by a turban, but this was only indoor *négligé*.

The ladies looked charming in a variety of styles, of which the *Mob Cap* was the favourite. Made of linen or lace, it had a small frill, and was tied with ribbons, cherry and pale or royal blue being the colours most favoured. When made capaciously, they came down the sides of the face and were tied under the chin. The commode entirely disappeared.

Hoods were also worn in black silk or colours.

Tiny *Straw Hats* with wide brims gave a dairy-maid effect. They were tied under the chin with streamer ribbons, and the underneath parts of the wide brims were decorated with artificial flowers.

SUMMARY

MEN

Dress

- Collar—neck-cloth or cravat. Lace ends, or plain with ends tucked under waistcoat.
- Coat. Small buttons right down side. Mid-calf length. Fastened only at waist, bulging above and below. Little or no collar rever. Very wide cuff revers nearly to elbow. Flared wired skirt. After 1750 flares cease, and sleeve nearly to waist.
- Waistcoat—long, pocketed, many buttons. Nearly to knees.
- Breeches—fairly tight knee-length, where banded.
- Muffs—small round.
- Shirt—loose sleeves frilled.

Legs

- Stockings rolled over breeches. Mainly white.

Feet

- Square buckled shoes.

Hair

- White bag wig. Queue fastened by black satin tie, joined in front with bow and diamond-brooched. Side lappets till 1750, then side curls.

Hats

- Chapeau Bras—very small tricorne, carried under arm.
- Kevenhuller—very high cocked tricorne, banded on edge. About 1750.
- Turban—without wig.

WOMEN

Dress

- Hoop—1735, bell-shaped; 1745, suppressed in front; 1755, smaller all round; 1760, almost gone.
- Sacque—long, loose gown, open in front, hangs from shoulder to ground loosely. Gathered in folds over hoop. Panniers.
- Petticoat—over the hoop. Shows in front in early period.

At Court, 1760

Dress—contd.

Bodice—square open neck, laced frilled. Boned body. Slight point at waist.
Over skirt—panniered at sides. Shorter than before.
The "V" effect may be given by the sacque or the bodice at option.
Aprons—plain or tucked, long or knee-length.

Legs

White stockings.

Feet

Shoes—high heels, pointed toes.

Hair

Smooth and close to head.

Hats

Mob cap with frill. Lace. Also, if fuller, tied under chin.
Lappets—two lace streamers falling from top of head to shoulders.
Straw hats—very small and flat. Flowers under brim. Streamers. Hoods.

THE MAN OF FASHION

Elaboration has set in to such an extent that most of my space will be occupied by a carefully tabulated summary, and only a brief account of the less obvious forms of dress will be given. The period dates from 1760 to 1820—the long reign of Farmer George III, who personally did not influence the fashions. This age of solid prosperity was reflected not only in substantial houses but also in the heavy and massive cut of the clothes and the rich, thick, heavily embroidered materials of which they were made.

In the early part the fashionable young man, called a Macaroni, achieved fantastic results by exaggeration. His wig towered high above him, and on top of it was sometimes perched a tiny tricorne hat that had to be raised by his sword or cane. He wore two fobs to his waistcoat, carried a jewelled snuff box, a gold knobbed amber cane with a tassel, and a diamond hilted sword. His coat was tight and short like his vest, and his breeches were well moulded to his form.

The *Coat* (men) tended to change from the square cut ends to a cut away, which became much like our Morning Coat. The collar got higher and higher, the cuff rever went out of fashion, and double breasted (D.B. in Summary) coats came in about 1780. The stiffened flares of coat and vest disappeared, and the vest lost its long skirts in 1780. *Overcoats* had at first flat, wide collars, sometimes double, and these developed into the double and treble collared capes that are familiar in coaching pictures. The *Shirt* had at first a double frill down its front opening, and this, in 1800, became a stiff pouter pigeon single frill, or a white bow neck cloth

LORD KILMOREY, BY GAINSBOROUGH

finished off the shirt. For indoor wear a dressing-gown-like coat, called a nightdress, was worn with a turban to cover the head when it was relieved from the hot and heavy wig. *Stockings* (men) were at first coloured, as before; in 1780 white ones came in, and continued until 1800 when black ones were the mode. *Top Boots* (men) were used for riding only until 1780 when they were adopted for walking as well. In 1790 the *Hessian Boot* (men) was introduced. It was a short, close-fitting boot, which came up to the knee, and was finished with a tassel in front.

Wigs (men) remained, but with modifications, and in 1790 went out in favour of natural hair, which was worn long, curly, and brushed back like Nelson's. In 1800 it was shorter but curled

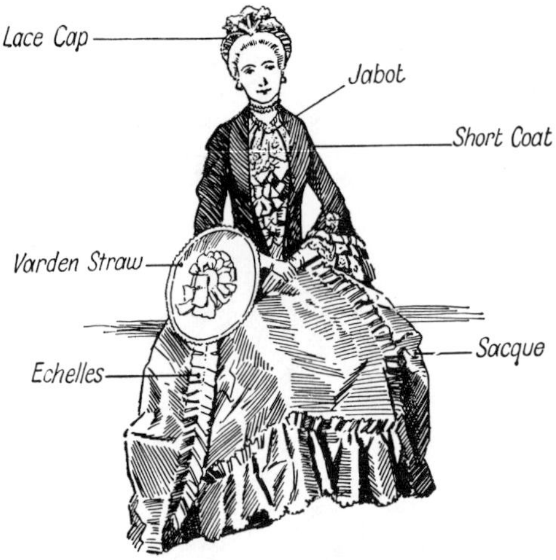

MRS. OSWALD, C. 1770

STREET SCENE, 1778

all over. The *Sword* was discouraged and by the eighties had ceased to be worn.

Women's dress changed little save in the shape of the hoop, which gradually lessened till it went out in 1790, when a complete change was made by the one-piece dress, which heralded the approaching Empire style with its armpit waist. Apart from Caps, head coverings were unpopular until the nineties, when Straws in many shapes were popular, ceding place to huge Turbans in 1800.

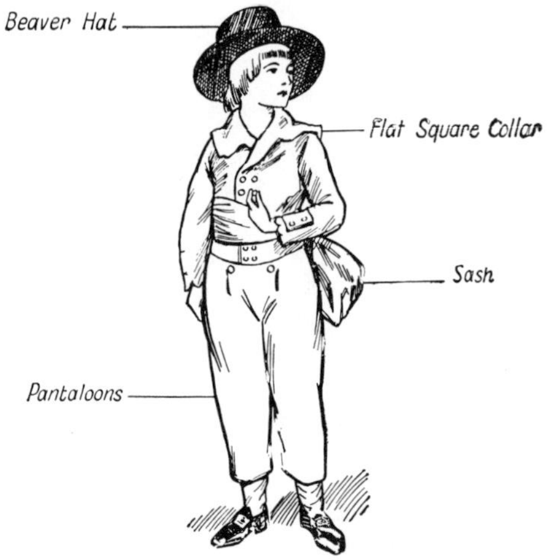

LORD ALTHORP, 1886

LADY CAROLINE HOWARD AS A CHILD, 1779

Though the bodices were cut low, the hiatus was bridged by fichus and scarves. The *Polonese* (women) was a Sacque which instead of having straight front edges, curved these away to the back. Echelle trimming to both garments, consisting of a row of tiny bows down the front edge, was widely popular.

Hair (women) was piled high on the head in an oval shape eked out by wire frames in the seventies; but in the eighties and nineties it lost its height and widened out with masses of curls on top and long locks of curled hair behind or pulled over the front of the shoulders. In 1800 it became ugly and clumsy, with a front curled fringe, a heavy chignon, and long ringlets at the rear.

Hats (women) were diverse from 1790. The wide Gainsborough straw was familiar, also the Dolly Varden milkmaid straw with flatter brims. In 1800 hideous Turbans and coal scuttle straws were worn. The latter had huge peaks in front and little back part, and presented a lop-sided view, little of the face being visible.

The *Buffon* (women) was a fichu, puffed out pouter-wise on the chest, and gathered in at the waist. It gave a goitre-like effect to the throat.

SUMMARY

MEN

	1770	1780	1790	1800
DRESS COAT . .	Curved tails. Close sleeve. Small cuff. Small or no collar rever. Less pocket flap. Very short for beaus.	Cut away. Short square back collar, or D.B. with large lapels, and square tails. Big cuff, not to wrist, showed shirt sleeve.	High collar to ears. Cuff to wrist showed only shirt frill.	Tight sleeves. Cut-away. D.B.
VEST . .	Sleeved. Skirts unstiffened. Buttoned at waist only. (Others not fastened.)	Short skirtless square cut or D.B. with large pointed lapels outside coat. Buttoned all down.	Same.	Striped.
OVERCOAT .	Large cuff. Flat wide collar (often double collar).	Capes instead of collar.		
SHIRT .	Double frill *jabot* showed through unfastened vest.			Pouter frill or white bow. High cheek collar.
BREECHES .	Hardly seen under long vest and coat.	Skin tight for riding. Bunch of ribbon or buckle at knee.	Breeches or tight pantaloons (trousers) buttoned below calf.	Black pantaloons and breeches.
NIGHTDRESS	A *négligé* indoor dressing gown coat.	Same.		
LEGS				
STOCKINGS.	Gold and silver clocks for State. Black silk usual. Rolled over knee.	White. Under breeches at knee.	White.	Black.
FEET				
SHOES . . .	Small oval buckle. Red heel. Rosettes.	Large square buckle or strings. No red heels save for Court.		
SPATTERDASHES	Long gaiters.		Short spats.	
TOP BOOTS	For riding.	For walking also.		Heavy turnover
HESSIANS			Short close fitting boot to knee, where tasselled.	Same.
HAIR				
RAMMILLIE	Wig as before.	Single broad roll all round.		
PIGTAIL .	Spiral black ribbon case behind.			
WHITE .	Two horizontal side curls very high for beau.			

SUMMARY (*continued*)

MEN

	1770	1780	1790	1800
NATURAL .		Powdered.	Long curly, brushed back.	Short curly all over.
HATS				
TRICORNE .	Laced. Braided. Feather fringed.	No feather fringe.		
BICORNE .	Rare.	Common. Worn long or short ways.	Same.	Worn short ways.
KEVENHULLER	High front peak as before.	Same.	Same.	
NIVERNOIS	Tiny tricorne for beau.			
WIDE QUAKER		Common.		
TALL BEAVER		Tapering crown.	Straight crown.	Like modern "Topper."
NIGHT CAP	For *néglig*é in absence of wig.	Same.		
LINEN				
CRAVAT .	Falling ends.	Plain folded stock or *jabot* of lace.	Choker knotted in front. Very high.	Same.
SLEEVES .	Ruffled lace shirt.	Same.	Small frill.	Unseen.
WIG RIBBON	Loose on shoulders and pinned under throat. Black.			
WHITE BOW	Muslin in huge front bat's-wing bow for beau.			
JEWELS .	Sword losing favour. Tasselled canes, knobbed. Muffs. Snuff boxes.	No sword. Same. Same.	Same. Same. Same.	Same. Same, plainer. No muffs. Fobs.

WOMEN

	1770	1780	1790	1800
DRESS				
BODICE .	Open laced or not. Corset shape. Stomacher. Echelle—front bows. Elbow sleeve flounced. Bell sleeve.	Long, close sleeve.		Tight one-piece dress Tight elbow sleeve. Armpit waist. Wide skirts. Square neck. V neck bare to shoulders. Fairly wide.
SKIRT .	Ankle length. Front open. Full gather at hips. Bustle starts. Three frills.	Trains optional.		
OVERCOATS		Short.		Long, fur edged.
PETTICOAT		Quilted.	Quilted.	Very thin and tight
HOOP .	Two side hoops.	Bustle, not hoop.	Bustle disappeared.	
SACQUE .	Open to ground or to waist. Pleated edges. Rear box pleat. Three bustles on hoop.	Pleats sewn flat, down to waist.		
POLONESE .	Sacque with front curving away to back.			
RIDING .	As men.			Hooded, fur edged.
CLOAKS .	Armholed.	Same.		
CAPES .	Long ends in front.	Same.		

SUMMARY (*continued*)

WOMEN

	1770	1780	1790	1800
FEET SHOES .	High heels for evening. Generally lower. Ribbon ties, rosettes, buckles.	Round toes.	Flat, heelless. Satin. Tiny front bow. Ballet shoe with sandal ribbons.	Same.
HAIR . .	High, egg shape, Chignon and nape ringlets.	Broad and flat. Full curls on crown and very long lair behind.	Broad and less high. Same.	Curled. Front fringe. Chignon and long rear ringlets.
HATS . .	Lace or linen caps with long lappets at rear, very large, frilled edges. Mobs. Dairymaid straws.	Same. Calash—large hooped hood.	Gainsborough. Dolly Varden straw. Turbans. Same.	Coal scuttle. Straws feathered. Beaver "Topper." Long ostrich plumed Turbans.
LINEN .	Fichus and scarves. Narrow lace frill above bodice. Deep sleeve ruffles. Long gloves, mittens, muffs.	Same. Same. Same.	Buffo nfichu till 1795; afterwards broad frilled collars. Same.	Lace scarves. Same.

EMPIRE AND THE DANDIES

Revolution affected the fashions by a sudden reversion to Classical modes. Instead of the balloon effect, women adopted sylph-like outlines. To so great an extent were these desired, that petticoats became things of the past, and in order to imitate Greek and Roman statues frocks were damped before they were put on. Men were unable to vie with this classicism, but the tight craze influenced them to the extent that they damped their pantaloons before putting them on and then dried them, thus making them skin tight.

Great simplicity characterized woman's charming costume. White was extensively worn, and embroidery and trimming were discarded. The dress depended on charm of outline and purity of line—a fashion difficult for all but the youngest figures.

Towards the end of the period the Gigot or leg-of-mutton sleeve was invented, and with the near approach of Victoria to the throne this was divided into several puffs by bands down the arm. The style was called "François Premier," as it was a revival of the male sleeve of that reign.

EMPIRE, MEN, 1802–1813

The *Coat* had broad swallow-tails, and was

A SPORTSMAN, 1814

cut away squarely above the waist with a double breast adorned with large brass or gilt buttons.

For evening wear even finer buttons of crystal silver and gold were used. It had a high collar and a tight sleeve coming well down to the back of the hand, where peeped out a narrow band of linen. Blue, dark brown, and bottle green were the usual shades.

The *Vest* was short and square cut, with smal

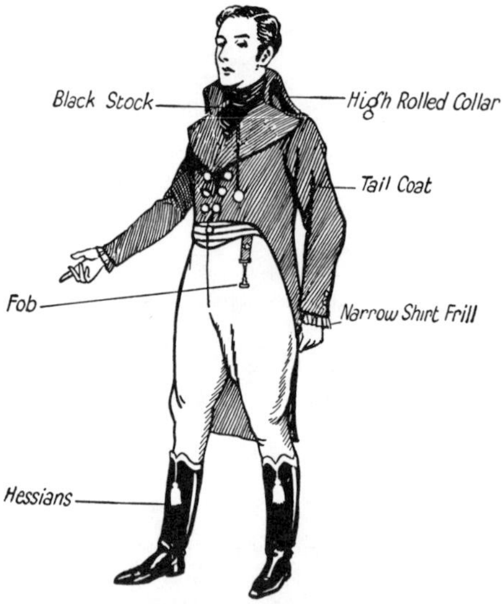

EMPIRE PERIOD MAN

lapels, no longer overlapping the coat. Beau Brummell laid down the rule that buff or light shades were correct for the morning, and white alone was permissible at night. The waistcoat was single-breasted.

Pantaloons were trousers, tight, and reaching to the middle of the calf. They were buttoned at the side, where the calf narrows into the ankle. Their sides were braided in semi-military fashion, and black was essential at night, though lighter shades were worn at other times.

Breeches were made of buckskin and were alternative to pantaloons.

REGENCY MEN, 1813–1837

The same *Coat* was worn, but its colours were blue, grey, and buff. The collar became higher and the lapels broader, whilst the sleeve had a small puff at the top. In Sailor William's time, velvet collars and cuffs were added, and in 1825 appeared the Frock Coat in dark blue or brown, with a high rolled collar and fur edging along the bottom.

The *Vest* was the same, but was striped, or checks were made by appliquéing on thin silk strands in yellow. *Breeches* ceased to be worn for everyday use under William IV, and *Trousers* took their place. They were strapped under the instep and braided at the sides at option. *Pantaloons* continued in use. *Peg-top Trousers* were not beautiful, and gave scope to the fun-makers. They were full at the waist, and tapered to the ankle, where they were tight. Vertical striped materials, as well as plainer ones, were used for them.

The *Stock*, of fine linen, was lightly starched and put on over the throat, wound round the neck once or twice in careful creases, and then tied over in cravat fashion in front, where it was pinned or otherwise steadied. Black silk was also worn for it.

The *Shirt* was frilled and starched in front, and had a high collar, which was carefully turned over the stock. The Byron collar showed the neck without the stock, but was not common. Under William IV overcoats were made with long capes reaching to the waist.

Tall high square *Beaver Hats*, in various shades of black, grey, and biscuit, were worn. They were furry, not smooth like a modern top hat. They curved inwards in the middle of the crown, and the brim was rolled at the sides rather more than it is to-day.

The *Hair* was brushed out at the sides, and faces were clean shaven.

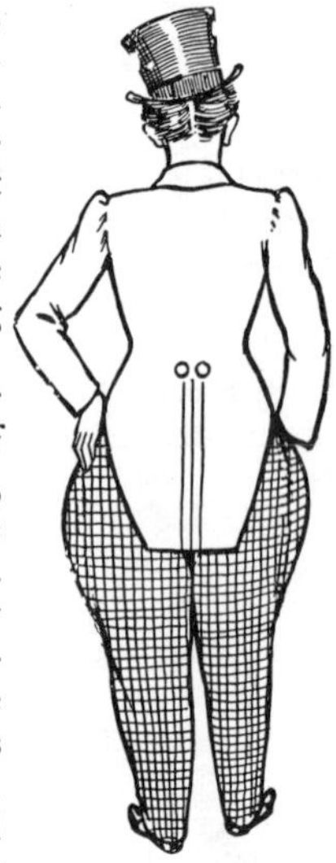

PEG-TOP TROUSERS

EMPIRE WOMEN, 1802–1813

The *Empire Gown* had short tight sleeves reaching only half-way down the upper arm, and finished with long gloves, which were coloured to match the shoes; its armpit waist was girdled by a narrow ribbon with long ends fringed. The neck was cut low, and scarves were worn. The skirt was smooth in front without gathers, the necessary fullness to enable the wearer to move being given by gathers at the back. It was laced up the back, and designed to reveal the natural outlines as much as possible. It was, therefore, made of the thinnest of materials—muslin and lawn—and its whiteness was unrelieved by any trimming or embroidery. A petticoat might be worn, but as this hid the limbs it was often abandoned. For out of doors a *Pelisse* of thin silk was allowed, but it afforded little warmth to an already too thin costume. It had sleeves, and was a short mantle. Parasols, gloves, reticules, and scarves completed the toilette.

The *Hair* was worn in Classical fashion, piled high on the head in a tapering cone bound round with ribbons. *Turbans* of velvet, silk, crepe, and muslin attained voluminous proportions, and were made rather ridiculous by the large single ostrich feather, which curled outwards over the face, or at the side, but chiefly in front.

EMPIRE PERIOD WOMAN

REGENCY WOMEN 1813–1837

The *Bodice* had its waist shifted lower to the normal waist-line, where it had a rather broad belt of the same material as the costume. The waist was also pointed a little. The shoulder seam dropped to below its proper place, thus baring the shoulders, while the sleeve filled out into a "Bishop" type. Diagonal pleats and tucks were given to the bodice. With William IV came the leg-of-mutton sleeve, wide from shoulder to elbow, from which it became tight to the wrist. Soon after its appearance it was divided into double puffs by a ribbon tied on half way, and just before the close (about 1835) of the period it was further divided into several puffs. To prevent the bodice falling off the bare shoulders yokes were introduced. These were made of muslin at first, but this proving to be not sufficiently substantial, yokes of the same material as the dress were made.

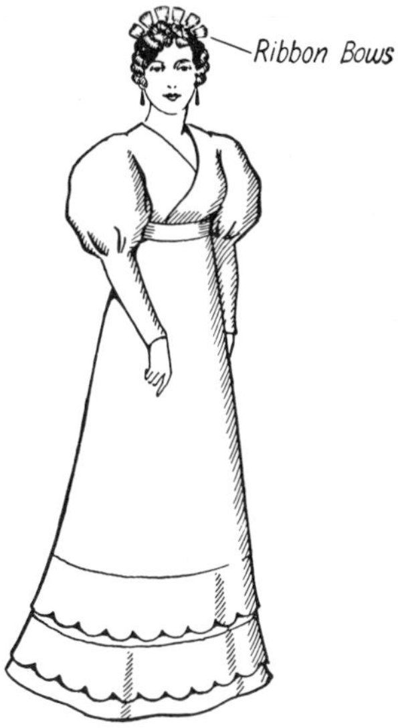

THE LEG-OF-MUTTON SLEEVE, 1830

It was an age of crude, strong colouring, and magentas, gamboges, violets, resedas, and emeralds dazzled the eyes of the traveller in Regent Street and Carlton House Terrace.

Like the bodice, the *Skirt* became fuller and wider at the bottom, and it was shortened to ankle length under William IV. To aid in this fattening process, the *Petticoat* was restored to favour and was stiffened or made of thick material in order to hold out the skirt.

The foundation of the bodice was a *Corset*, over which it was loosely draped.

The *Pelisse* did not remain unaffected by the general enlargement. It cast off its thin silks, and was wadded or quilted to present a stiffer and more ungainly appearance.

Shoes remained small, but were more practical than formerly; the old velvets went out in favour of leather and black glazed material. The type for indoors was that of the ballet shoe, tied with ribbons crossed in front and fastened behind.

Hair was rather charming. It was parted in the centre and neatly brushed down there to flourish into clusters of curls at the sides and over the forehead. Several formal ribbon bows were added at the top.

Hats were in straw, with large brims, adorned with feathers, and worn at the back of the head like the bonnets. Ribbons and flowers were impartially used on both hats and bonnets. The latter had flowers under the brim and ribbons across the top to tie below the chin in a bow and falling ends. The Coal-scuttle hat was made on a foundation covered in silk, or of straw. At first the angle of the poke rose sharply, but later the angle ceased and the slope from back to front was by a gradual rise.

SUMMARY

MEN, EMPIRE

Dress

Coat—cut away, square tails. Double-breasted high collar. Tight sleeve. Blue dark brown, bottle green.

A Lady of 1826

Vest—short. Small lapels. Morning, buff or light; evening, white. Single-breasted.

Pantaloons—calf-length trousers. Tight. Buttoned below calf. Braided sides. Black for evening.

Or Breeches—buckskin.

Stock—linen.

Legs

Striped silk stockings for evening.

Feet

Hessians—short close-fitting boot to knee, where tasselled. Worn with pantaloons.

Top Boots—worn with breeches.

Shoes—black, worn with pantaloons.

Hair

Frizzed out at sides. Clean-shaven.

Hats

Opera for evening.

Beaver for day. Tall square.

WOMEN, EMPIRE

Dress

Empire Gown—white muslin or lawn. No decoration. Armpit waist. Low bodice. Skirt not full in front, slight gathers behind. Back laced. Sleeve tight to upper arm. Waist ribbon.

Petticoat—none, or extremely thin.

Pelisse—sleeved mantlet, thin silk, for outdoors.

Gloves—long to above elbow. Coloured to match shoes.

Reticule—handbag.

Scarves.

Feet

Slippers—low-heeled, velvet.

Hair

Classical, piled high and wound round with ribbon bands.

Hats

Wide straw. Turbans of velvet, silk, crepe, muslin.

MEN, 1813–1837

Dress

Coat—buff, blue, grey. High collar, broad lapels. Cut-away tails. Double-breasted. Long sleeve, puffed at top. High waist. Brass buttons. For William IV, velvet collars and cuffs. 1825 onwards, frock coat, dark blue or brown. Fur bottom band. High roll fur collar.

Vest—as before, striped or checked.

Pantaloons—as before.

Dress—contd.

Breeches—as before (except for riding), not worn under William IV.

Trousers—strapped under instep, 1830 onwards.

Peg-tops—trousers full at waist, tight at ankle.

Stock—linen or black silk neckcloth. Tied as cravat.

Shirt—frilled. High collar turned over stock.

Overcoat—under William IV long capes to waist.

Fob—watch pendant.

Legs and Feet

As before.

Hair

Short. Full at sides, brushed over to eyes. Side whiskers. Bushy in front. Under William IV centre parted occasionally.

Hats

High beaver.

WOMEN, 1813–1837

Dress

Bodice—short pointed waist. Shoulder seam drops. Larger sleeve, diagonal pleats and tucks. Evening, bare shoulders. Under William IV, leg-of-mutton sleeve to elbow, tight to wrist, or double puffs. Later,

Dress—contd.

many puffs. Muslin yokes, later matching dress. Normal waist-line. Belt. Yokes first of muslin, of material towards close.

Skirt—round and full. Ankle length under William IV.

Petticoat—stiff to hold out skirt.

Corset.

Pelisse—wadded and thicker.

Feet

Shoes—stouter, leather, black glaze.

Hair

Centre parting. Curl clusters forehead and sides. Ribbon bows.

A BOY

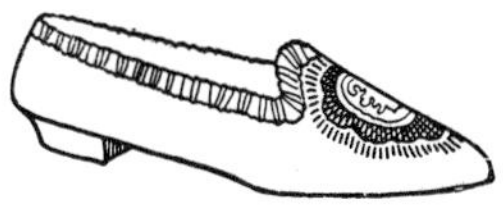

SHOE, 1800

Hats

Straw—large brim, large feathers, ribbons, flowers.

Bonnet—coal-scuttle, straw or silk covered. Sharp angle first, later less acute. Trimmed under front.

THE CRINOLINE, 1850–60

The pageant of clothes has ended. Gone are the lovely colours and resplendent materials which men delighted to wear; gone, too, the gracefully formed fashions of the women. The era of the machine, the age of materialism, both in thought and in action, have arrived.

Until the invention of the steel-ringed crinoline it was necessary—in order to make the skirt swell to the desired balloon-like proportions—to wear petticoats which had to be padded with horsehair to prevent them dropping into their natural folds. A skirt had to be about ten yards round at the bottom, and a tulle dress of four skirts, ruched, took 1,100 yards of material. Thin gauze-like materials were worn and were cheap. Each frock had many flounces. In 1850 the number was from 15 to 25. The effect of these flounces in the filmiest materials was rather charming, but a frock could be worn only once if it was made of tulle, as it depended entirely on its freshness for its effect.

The popular materials were *crêpe de Chine* organdie muslins, tarlatan, and satin.

The flounces were made of lace, muslin, and tarlatan over silk of the same colour. These flounces matched the frock or contrasted with it.

The men began to look very much as they look to-day. The frock coat costume was much worn; also a lounge suit, which had the lower front corners of the coat rounded off and a small opening at the neck instead of the modern long revers. The lounge suit could be made in light colours. A popular material was one with a plaid effect; it had horizontal and vertical, rather widely placed stripes. With the lounge suit was worn a bowler or a top hat. The latter should

THE FLOUNCED SKIRT, 1856

be used with the frock coat. The trousers were often of plaid and the coat and vest were plain—or a dark coat was worn with light trousers. For evening dress a tail coat, with a low-cut vest showing much starched shirt (which had a small frill) and a huge white bow tie, was correct. The cravat was worn for day wear, but the large bow tie made of wide material was more popular. The lounge coat might be left open. "Swells" often had their waistcoats and coats cut low, and their coats with wide revers to show plenty of shirt, the latter fastened with two pearl buttons.

The *Skirt* was wide and had many flounces, but, later, the hoop was lowered so that the dress fitted at the hips, and the flounces were superseded by a single frill at the hem of the skirt. This was towards the end of the sixties. From 1860 onwards the skirt was often drawn up in four places to display underneath the petticoat, which became more decorative.

After my lady had put on her lace-trimmed *Drawers*, she got into her *Under Petticoat*, which was lined and corded with horsehair, and had a straw plait in the hem to make it stand out. The *Petticoats* had then to be managed. Several of these were sewn into one band for convenience: they must have been difficult to wash. The order of the petticoats was—

1st. A flannel one.
2nd. A horsehair padded one $3\frac{1}{2}$ yards wide.
3rd. One of Indian calico stiffened with cords.
4th. A wheel of thick plaited horsehair.
5th. A starched muslin one with three flounces.
6th. A starched muslin one.
7th. Another of the same kind.
8th. The *Frock*.

The *Bodice* (women), fairly roomy and balloon-like, was gathered in at the waist into a band. The sleeves were narrow at the shoulder, but swelled out in a large open bell at the elbow. It had many flounces, and to it was attached the

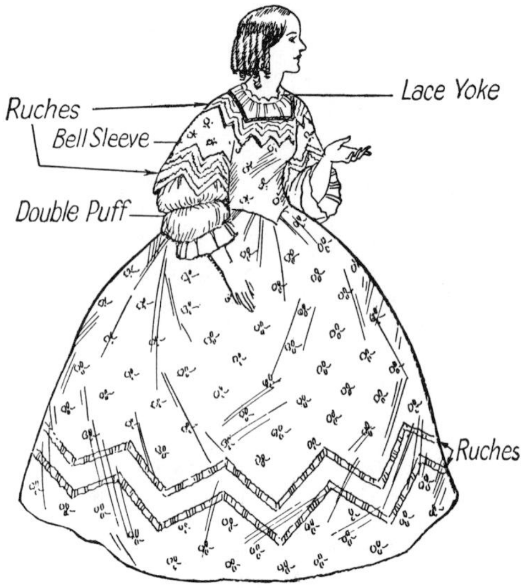

THE BELL SLEEVE, 1858

under sleeve, of white thin material, which was balloon-shaped and gathered at the wrist into a frill. The neck was open a little, and adorned with a narrow lace collar or a bertha of ribbon, ruches, or embroidery. Checks and stripes were in vogue, and the colours tended to be rather "strong."

A curiously masculine effect was given when for indoor wear about the house the short coat was introduced from Russian sources. It soon developed into the *Zouave Jacket* (women), which was worn with a *Waistcoat* (women).

This Zouave jacket was really a bodice open in the front and worn over a contrasting waistcoat, which showed there. It was braided and embroidered and decorated with large buttons—the larger the more daring—and the vest had to be as "stunning" as possible. The Zouave had long sleeves, which were cut open to the elbow.

Owing to the wide sleeves it was impossible to get into a cloak or overcoat. Shawls and mantillas were consequently adopted. The former were square and of cashmere or shot silk, which was always a lovely shade. They were heavily fringed and embroidered by hand in coloured silks.

Small muffs were carried, and the evening frock had a low neck which made it appear to be slipping off the shoulders.

Profusion of hair marked the period. Beards,

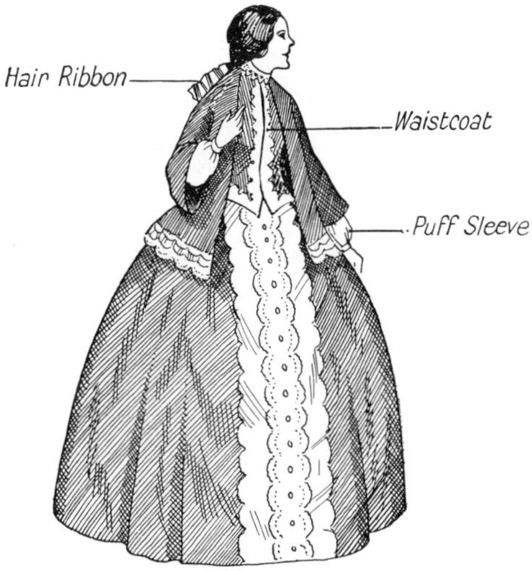

ZOUAVE JACKET, 1854

side whiskers, and heads were frizzed out and curly. An imperial could be worn, but it was not common till towards the end of the period when the Emperor Napoleon III was imitated.

Women smoothly parted their hair in the middle, drew it tightly across the head into a net bag behind, and allowed side clusters to appear to frame the face. At night a wreath of artificial flowers—roses mainly—in circular shape was worn, rather off the head, or it might have a point at the front to form a wreath of the type associated with classical victors.

The silk top hat was worn on all occasions, with lounge suits or frock coats. At evening

OUTDOOR LOOPED DRESS, 1860

the opera hat was indispensable to the smart man. The bowler hat, though rather different from that of to-day, first made its appearance. It was worn on informal occasions, had a short straight brim, a bell-shaped fairly low crown, with a knob on the top. A straw boater, exactly in the modern shape, was also worn by bus drivers, etc. Workmen wore a curious round fur cap, square in outline, and the carpenter's square paper cap was often seen. The top hat could be smooth or furry, and was tall and narrow in the crown. Another type had a larger crown, which curved inwards at its middle and out again at the top, but it was somewhat foreign. Mourning bands of felt were put on when required, and their widths varied.

The *Poke Bonnet* was extensively worn, but shared its popularity with the much-reviled *Round Hat* or *Leghorn*. Both were made of straw. The bonnet was a coal-scuttle shape, with broad ribbons passing from the top down the sides and tied under the chin, from which the broad ends hung for a considerable length. The under part of the brim, which framed the face, was trimmed with flowers, and the outer crown was also adorned with these or with ribbons and laces. It was correct to wear the bonnet as much off the head as possible, a lot of the smoothly bandolined mid-parted hair being seen. Under the bonnet matrons wore a white cap of lace or material trimmed with ribbon. The round hat was simple and large. It caught the wind very much, and strings by which it could be held down in a gale were attached in front. The customary trimming was a single ostrich feather curled round the crown, or a broad band of ribbon with two tails behind. It could be turned up at each side.

Heavy gold jewellery, in the form of watch-chains, looped into both waistcoat pockets, began to be worn by the men. Fobs were also used. The women had necklets and rings, also the chatelaine, which was a buckle-hook fastened to the waist at the left side. It had several short chains, to which were attached articles of everyday use, such as scissors, buttonhooks, paper-knives, etc.

SUMMARY

MEN

Coat. Frock or light or plaid, with rounded edges and high neck.

Vest. Short, opened high. Single breasted, braid edged.

POKE BONNET

Tie. Bow or Ascot cravat. Black stock rare.

Trousers. Tight, checked, striped, dark with light coat.

Boots. Elastic sided. Low heels. Black.

Beard. Side whiskers. Moustache, Imperial. Thick bushy hair.

Hats

Silk Topper. White, grey, or black. High.

Straw Boater.

Bowler. Bell-shaped crown, tight-rolled brim. Black, white, fawn. Knob on top.

Jewellery. Heavy gold watch-chains. Fobs.

THE REDUCED FIGURE, 1868

WOMEN

Bodice. Balloon-like Pagoda sleeve, narrow shoulder, and large open bell at elbow. Many-flounced. Open neck. Lace collar or bertha of ribbon, ruches, embroidery. For evening, low neck to shoulders.

Undersleeve. White light material from elbow, getting larger till 1860, when it was steel hooped.

Blouses. White, attached to skirt by ribbon braces and sashes.

Zouave. Bodice open in front over contrasting vest. Long sleeves cut open to elbow.

Vest. Worn with Zouave coat. Cut like a man's.

Shawls. Square cashmere, *crêpe de Chine*, embroidered in silk and heavily fringed. No cloaks were possible.

Mantilla. Velvet, lace, taffeta.

Skirt. Wide, many-flounced. Later it fitted at the hips when hoop lowered and no flounces. From 1860 skirt was drawn up in four places to show petticoat.

Petticoats. Seven worn, horsehair stuffed and padded to give width until crinoline of steel wire replaced stuffing and then fewer petticoats were worn. From 1860 onwards the outer petticoat was coloured.

Drawers. Long, trimmed with lace.

Flounces. Many. Lace-trimmed, scalloped, gauffered, plaited, fringed, looped, festooned.

Boots. Elastic sides. Black cloth.

Slippers. No heels.

Hair

Mid-parted. Smooth on top, bun at back, side clusters. Girls wore long braids wound about ears. Wreaths for evening.

Hats

Poke Bonnet. Straw, ribbon tied under chin. Flower trimmed.

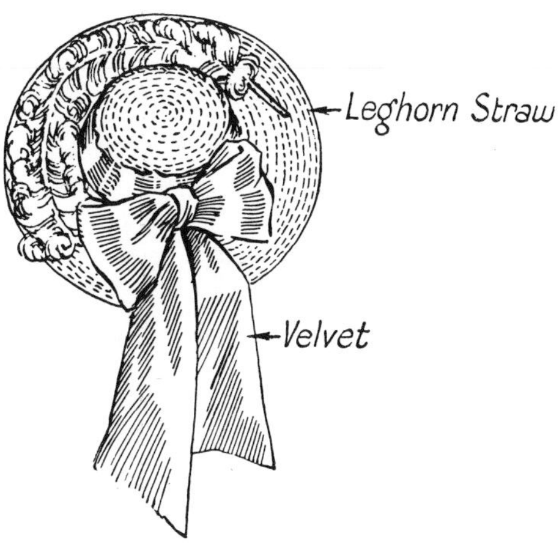

ROUND HAT

Leghorns. Large round hats of straw, ostrich feathered.

Caps. Worn under bonnet by elders, white lace, ribbon trimmed.

GROSVENOR GALLERY, 1870

Aestheticism, though it was much ridiculed, was really a step in the right direction, for it laid emphasis on a beauty that had wellnigh been forgotten amidst the horrors of mid-Victorian prosperity. Its leader and chief apostle was the brilliant author and playwright, Oscar Wilde, whose epigrams and good birth took him easily into the front rank of Society and brought him hosts of imitators. The author of *Lady Windermere's Fan* achieved enormous success with his plays and has attained immortality as the Poet in Gilbert and Sullivan's skit on the craze—*Patience*—quite apart from the intrinsic merit of his own works. The period is the Eighteen Seventies.

The "Greenery-Yallery, Grosvenor-Gallery, Aesthetic Young Man" was so termed because of the breakaway from the current crude colouring and patterning of dress materials in the seventies in favour of sage greens, yellows, cinnamons, and peacock blues. It was a revolt from the cult of the primary colour.

With this was coupled a search for beauty in the blue-and-white porcelain of Japan, the many-hued shades of the peacock, the light oval Oriental hand fan, and a general thirst for the antique in furniture and fittings with a recall to the work of the Old Masters of Italian painting. All this was to the good, as comparison of this fashion with the contemporary unreformed bustle and bust proves. The movement never became widespread; it was killed by ridicule. Yet being confined to thinkers, artists, and an inner circle of high society, it did not affect the great mass of the people to any extent. Its chief importance to the student of dress is that it was the first herald of a new dawn of real beauty and a much-needed harking back to the antique. It finds its permanent place in theatrical and social history with the large output

AESTHETIC REVIVALS, 1877

of plays in the seventies that need to be dressed sympathetically.

The hallmarks of the true devotee (it affected women's clothes more than men's) were the puffed sleeve, the low neck, and the absence of the bustle.

The sleeve might form a huge puff at the shoulder, from whence it descended in the normal tight sleeve to the wrist: this style was common to the decade. Again, a revival of the French *François Premier* sleeve, with its many puffs right down the whole length of the sleeve, gathered in with narrow velvet ribbons, was popular. It had previously been worn at the beginning of Victoria's reign; the Queen is seen wearing such a sleeve in the well-known painting of her first Council meeting. Two puffs to the elbow and then a straight sleeve were also worn. The neck (which normally was high cut) was, with the Aesthetes, a low one, edged with a narrow frill. This V opening might be cut still lower down the bodice, the opening being filled in with gathered muslin, but still baring an adequate portion of the chest.

In the hair, too, the Aesthetes showed commendable courage. They broke away from the hideous chignon, and took up ancient Classical Greek modes. In these the hair was piled fairly high at the back of the head in an upward pointing cone, strung round at intervals with braids of ribbon. On the forehead a natural wave replaced the frizz of the "Philistine" (a Philistine was one who did not favour the craze). Even loose hair long was worn by the daring, or it might be piled high on the head, brushed back, and finished in a knot in the style of Madame Pompadour.

Care should be taken with the settings to include bric-à-brac. Japanese and Chinese porcelains, huge bowls, oval paper or silk fans with bamboo handles, china elephants, and peacock feathers are typical. Good pictures should

"GROSVENOR GALLERY," 1882

be used, for the pre-Raphaelites were the exponents of aesthetic principles. The women of Rossetti, Burne-Jones, William Morris, and Holman Hunt are all of this type, and Morris is outstanding for his strenuous advocacy of the necessity to lay emphasis on craftsmanship.

Apart from the artists were the rank and file of the decade, and some account of the costume of the seventies must be given.

Men were dressed in the frock coat, tight trousers, and top hat. Latitude was allowed in the country and amongst the lower orders. This took the form of lounge suits and different hats.

The *Frock Coat* (men) had thin lapels, often covered with velvet. It was single or double-breasted, and was usually worn fully buttoned. To leave the coat unfastened was not good style. It was given grace of shape by well defining the waist.

The *Lounge Coat* (men) had either cut-away or square corners, and was short. Extremists had the skirts flared, but gentlemen did not. The two buttons, which originally held the sword-belt in place, were still stitched on to the lounge coat, as well (of course) as on the frock coat.

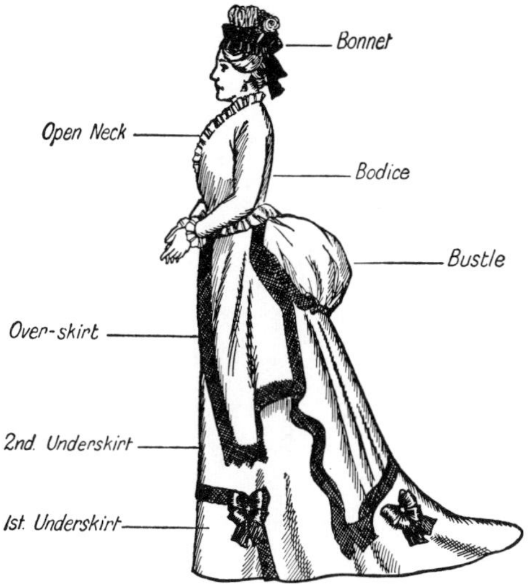

DAY DRESS, 1873

The *Waistcoat* (men) was made with a narrow V opening and cut high, though there were instances where the opposite was the case, and the vest was cut extremely low.

The *Tie* was cravat-like, and was made broad, but it was tied in a sailor knot or pulled through a gold tie ring.

Trousers (men) were narrow, but not skin tight. Bell bottoms were introduced. Trousers were generally light in shade and almost always checked or plaided. The check was not a series of small squares as to-day; the material was crossed with thin stripes.

The *Bodice* (women) was tightly stretched

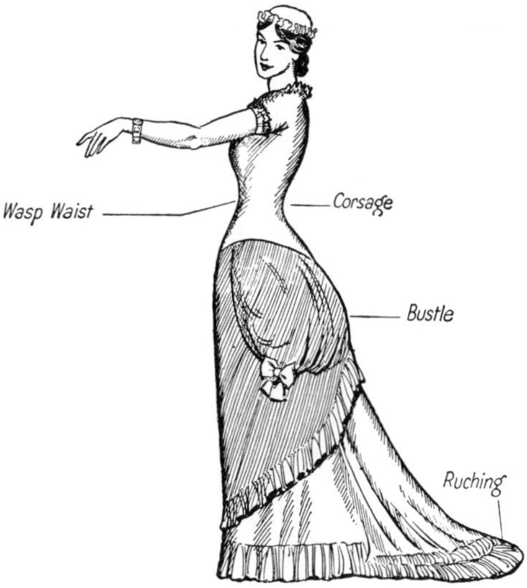

BALL DRESS, 1877

over a corset and of hour-glass shape. If one could possibly squeeze into a 19-in. waist one was in the height of fashion. For evening wear no sleeves were worn, a string of material or ribbon finishing off the armhole. For day wear long tight sleeves reached to the wrist, where they were finished with a narrow frill. The neck, which was low for evening wear, was high during the day and gathered into a frill or a plain band at the top.

The *Skirt* (women) fell to the ground, where it swept up the dust. A long train was added at night, and a short train during the daytime. The skirt followed the natural figure, and was tight-fitting over the hips. At about the knees it widened into a wide skirt, finished with a broad flounce, or with two or three flounces at the hem.

The *Overskirt* (women) was generally made up with the skirt, but appeared like a separate garment, especially when made of contrasting material. It hung down to just below the knees in front, was slightly drawn up at the sides, and loosely folded at the back over a bustle, the wire frame of which held out the skirt. The wired bustle went out in 1877 but left a slight bunch behind.

THE MAN-WOMAN, 1877

Overcoats (women) were of different types. One just like a man's was worn. It was of ground length, with a broad waist belt and large buttons, and it had a short hood at the back, lined with silk. It was generally double-breasted, but could be single-breasted, and could also be worn of three-quarter length. Plaids were popular.

A *Short Coat* (Women) with a flared skirt at the waist and broad lapels with broad velvet collar and cuffs and a double-breasted fastening was more favoured by matrons. More stately matrons wore a three-quarter length velvet or fur coat with a broad fur-edging all round and also on the cuffs.

Men's *hair* was brushed outwards and upwards from every possible portion of the façade. Long beards, side whiskers, middle or side partings—and the wonderful Dundreary moustache—added to their range of choice. The Dundreary moustache was a "dragon" type, like two large capital S's.

Women adopted the hideous chignon, which was made as large as possible and tucked into a thick fish net at the back. The hair was brushed away from the face and was rather flat on the crown, with a fringe over the forehead, giving an untidy frizzy effect. Round the chignon (which was a wire cage inserted under the hair) were coiled masses of hair in thick plaits, and ribbons or lace caps, with trimmings, were almost compulsory for all right-thinking females over the age of 21 years.

Men wore almost everywhere and always the top *hat*, which was higher and narrower than it is to-day. It had a narrow front and rear brim, larger at the sides, but deeply curved round. The line of the side of the hat was also semi-circular, not straight. In the country, bowler, cloth, and straw hats were worn (tradesmen wore these, though the majority wore the topper). The

AN 1877 SWELL

topper was not then a class distinction. The bowler was almost like our own, but had a higher bell crown and the brim was shaped like the top hat brim.

Women did their best to look charming in small toques trimmed with ribbons and feathers. They had low bell-shaped crowns and short brims.

SUMMARY

MEN

Dress

Overcoat, heavy to ankles. Broad belt. Short hood at back. D.B.

Frock coat, thin lapels. S.B. or D.B. Velvet collar. Waisted.

Lounge coats, cut away or square corners. Short. Two buttons at back. Slightly flounced skirts.

Waistcoat, cut high at neck.

Legs

Trousers, narrow. Checked. Bell bottoms sometimes. Light colour.

Feet

Boots, side elastic insets or buttoned at side. Low heels. Laced shoes occasionally.

Hair

Dundreary moustache. Side whiskers. Long beards. Mid or side parting, well brushed-out thick hair.

Hats

Top hat, black, white, fawn. Silk or beaver. Well curved brim, narrow front and back.

Cloth, bowler shape.

Bowler, informal. High bell crown, narrow well-curled brim.

Straw; seaside and country use only.

WOMEN

Dress

Bodice. Hour-glass corset shape. Twenty-inch waist. Tight, long sleeves. Frill or band fits neck.

Skirt, ground length. Train. Natural outline. Close fitting to half way, then widened. Hem flounce.

Overskirt. Apron fashion in front carried up at sides. At back fell in loose folds on bustle. Bustle lessened, 1877.

Overcoat, as men, in plaid. Ground or three-quarter length. Velvet three-quarter length. Broad fur edge and cuff.

Short coat. Flared skirt at waist. D.B. Broad lapels. Broad velvet cuff and collar.

Feet

Boots, elastic insets. Shoes.

Hair

Brushed back off face. Chignon in rear. Heavy plaits coiled. Lace caps for all married women. Mid-parted and loose, not covering nape. Forehead fringe.

Hats

Toques, feather or ribbon trimmed. Bell-shaped crown. Short brim.

NOAH'S ARK, 1880

As drawn by Tenniel *Alice in Wonderland* immediately conjures up a vision of the period.

During the eighties of the last century the all-prevailing bustle ceased to dominate the female figure. It dwindled until it became a mere sash and bow at the back, and in this form it was rather more tolerable than it was at the height of its development in the previous decade. The seventies were possibly the most hideous years for women's dress in any age and any land.

The period now under review has been immortalized by the charming drawings of George du Maurier, the talented father of a talented son—Sir Gerald du Maurier. A true artist, George du Maurier managed to make his ladies look pleasant. When his period is known there is realization of how great an artist he must have been—and with what an imaginative touch he used his pencil.

My lady still looked like an hour-glass, and much damage to health must have been caused by the tight lacing that was required in order to make nature fit the prevailing modes. Man's hirsute features and potato-bag contours, caused by his shapeless coats and trousers, were a fitting foil to the extraordinary appearance of his womenfolk.

The bustle was worn until the eighties. The

fashionable modified it, and it dwindled into the form of a huge bow and sash at the back without the wire cage that used to stuff out the form into a most unnatural shape.

The overskirt was drawn higher than before. In the seventies it was about three-quarter length or half-length; in the eighties it was only

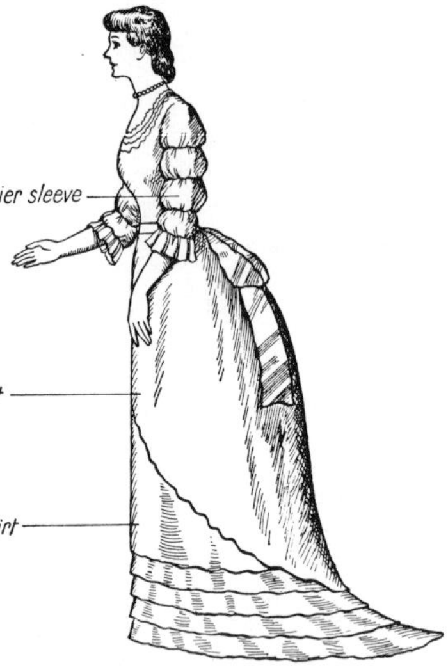

YOUNG GIRL'S EVENING FROCK, 1882

quarter-length and, being parted immediately and carried round to the back, was scarcely seen in front.

To the eighties must be given the credit of perfecting the wasp waist and creating the Noah's Ark figure. Numerous little buttons in vertical rows completed the illusion. The Great Flood idea was reflected in the houses of severe brick with the plainest of doors and windows, and no grace of outline or beauty of design.

It was a prurient and prudish age. Bathing gowns were flounced and frilled and covered the body.

Man continued much as before. His features, covered by masses of bushy hair that bristled out in side whiskers, long beards, and tremendous moustaches, were rarely seen. His trousers were a couple of creased and crumpled objects that might be described as tubes. Similar tubes, though more shapely, covered his head. He wore his hat in the House of Parliament and in the club, and he carried it into ladies' drawing-rooms when he called for afternoon tea, and he took his opera hat into their ballrooms at night. Even in bed he wore a night cap!

Sir John Tenniel has immortalized the period in *Alice in Wonderland* where the queens, with their enormous netted chignons and their many-ruched skirts, are typical of the Age of Hideousness of the seventies and the early eighties.

Man looked best in his long, waisted, *Overcoat*, of three-quarter or longer length, with its broader revers and its side pockets with flaps.

The *Frock Coat* or *Tail Coat* was worn by nearly everyone.

His *Trousers*, coming right down to the instep, were narrow and fairly tight.

His *Lounge Suit* was baggy and creased. It had no waist. The corners were rounded or squarely cut, and the rever was fairly deep.

His *Waistcoat* was cut high to show at the

EVENING GOWN, 1882

neck only a small V, through which appeared an enormously wide and massive tie of sailor knot variety, or a cravat of dark silk.

His *Collars* varied. The really smart man wore a single choker collar, which gave him a clerical appearance. Most men wore a double collar with long pointed ends that were tucked under the coat, like those worn by butlers, and the bow tie when worn with this had its ends tucked under the collar. Evening dress was almost identical with our own, except for the tighter trousers, and dinner jackets, which were introduced in 1880, were not worn very much. A velvet smoking jacket could be used instead for formal evening wear. White waistcoats were worn by the smart; others wore black.

The modern differentiation between the tail coat and the frock coat, the former being more formal than the latter, had not been made, and either was worn.

The *Norfolk Jacket* appeared about 1885 for sports wear, and was made in tweeds, with two box pleats vertically down back and front to give play to the arms. A belt to match was attached to the coat by loops.

The *Bodice* (women) was corset-shaped, with a V point in front below the waist. As every crease had to be banished the waist was cut in

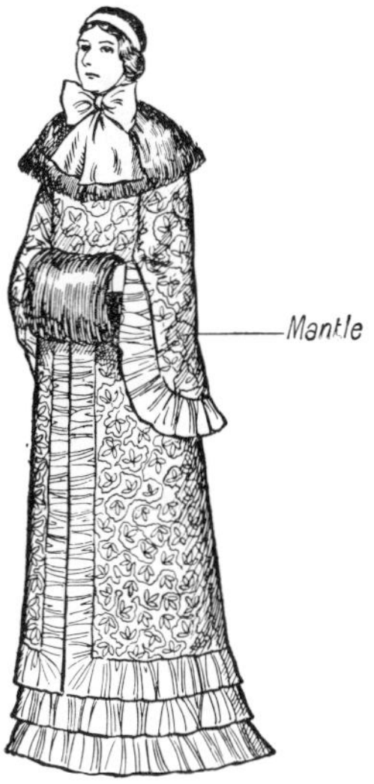

A Matron, 1882

sections, and the lining was shaped exactly to match, the two being stitched together, and the various sections [then united so that wrinkles or puckers were possible. The sleeves were usually tight and fitted smoothly without wrinkles into the armholes. At the elbow they were frilled. For day wear the sleeve was prolonged to the wrist and frilled there. A single shoulder puff, or the many-puffed *François Premier* sleeve, was also worn. The high neck was frilled, and the square yoked bodice was filled in with other material of a lighter type or to match the main fabric. Ruchings and frills were applied. Low necks were customary for evenings.

A Young Matron, 1882

The *Skirt* (women) fitted well at the hips, and was kept close to the figure to the knees, from which it widened, and for evenings it was trained. It was elaborately decorated, sometimes with rows of ruchings, sometimes with several frills at the hem or even over the whole of the skirt.

The *Overskirt* (women) continued to be in bustle form, but it was not too exaggerated in shape. It was parted immediately below the point of the bodice, carried round to the back, and there draped in a bunch over the bustle, from whence it trailed downwards over the back of the skirt. It was occasionally fastened with large bows. In this way the overskirt covered the hips in front only. A more graceful type was the overskirt that hung down in front to about half way, and was carried to the back, which it almost covered. At the back of the waist a huge bow sash was tied. Its ends hung right down nearly to the ground. The effect was less rigid.

The *Coat* (women) gave the real Noah's Ark

effect. It was creaseless and well defined in its curves, and adorned with numerous small buttons in one or two vertical rows. It had side pockets, and was about half-length. Fairly large muffs were worn, but they were circular in shape or nearly so. Sealskin was fashionable for these short coats, and sealskin or bearskin capes coming well over the shoulders, where they finished, were also worn.

A BUSINESS MAN, 1882

Men wore the ubiquitous *topper*, either high or low. If low, it was not a "John Bull" hat but tapered upwards. For the country, sport, and informal wear *cloth hats* of tweed were worn, especially for travelling. *Bowlers* with low bell crowns and curled brims were in the main worn by the lower classes only, though they, too, wore the topper.

Bonnets were of straw or of material for matrons. They were trimmed with lace, bows, ribbons, and, rather rarely, with flowers. Low bell-crowned *Hats*, with widish brims turned up, were popular, and were trimmed with ostrich feathers curled round the hatband. Young girls wore *Picture Hats* made in soft materials, with low crowns and wide brims, rather flimsily shaped and adorned with ribbon bands or flowers.

The "Kaiser" moustache with upcurling ends but rather thinner, also the "Bismarck" variety, where the ends drooped downwards, were worn. Young men were clean shaven, though many wore large beards, as did practically every older man. Side whiskers and bushy hair untidily brushed were in the mode.

Women's hair was not beautiful. Dressed low on the crown and carried well down the nape of the neck in plaited braids, it looked as though it had been flattened by a heavy hat. A small frizzy fringe covered the forehead. Mid-partings were often worn. There was a tendency to puff out the hair more at the sides; previously it had severely pulled-in sides and plastered effects.

SUMMARY

MEN

Dress

Overcoat. Long. Waisted. Broader revers. Side pockets with flaps.

Frock coat or Tail coat. Waisted.

Lounge coat. Loose and baggy. Rounded or square corners. Fairly deep rever. Waistcoat square ended. Norfolk jacket box pleated.

Legs

Trousers. Tight.

Feet

Boots. Narrow points or square ends. Cloth or elastic sides.

Linen

Collar. High single choker. Turn down double with points (butler).

Cravat. Dark silk with tie-pin.

Sailor knot tie, with tie-ring. Very broad.

Hat

Topper. Tall or low.

Cloth. In checked tweed.

Bowler. Low bell crown. Curled brim.

Hair

Beards. Side whiskers. Clean shaven. Kaiser moustache. *Ad lib* generally.

WOMEN

Dress

Bodice. Corset shaped, creaseless. Pointed in front at waist. Tight sleeves to elbow, where frilled. *François Premier* sleeves. High neck frilled. Square corsage filled muslin or lace. Low neck evening. Single puff sleeves.

Skirt. Many frilled or ruched in horizontals. Train at night only.

Overskirt. Huge bow, with long ends at back. Short overskirt parted in front carried over hips to back. Bustles.

Coat. Tight-fitting corset shape. Many buttons down front in single or double lines vertically. Side pockets. Capes, shoulders only.

Muffs. Moderately large. Round.

Hair

Low in front with fringe. Long loose knot at nape. Mid-parting. Slight side puffs.

Hats

Bonnets of fabrics or material. Flowers rare.

Hats. Bell crown low. Rather wide brim turned up. Feather-trimmed round band.

For Shopping, 1882

Picture hats. Wide brims, low crowns. Soft material. Ribbon band and flowers.

THE NINETIES

The nineties introduced an improvement on the previous decade. The bustle vanished; clothes differentiated married and single women.

Children, until the later Georges, were miniature replicas of their parents; then they really blossomed in the rather comic fancy dress into which the late Victorians put them. The "Little Lord Fauntleroy" costume was popularized through the sickly sentiment of Mrs. Burnett's story. The child went about in a kind of travesty of a Charles the First dress, without its natural manliness. Victorian children had to do as they were told, and when they finally rebelled there was much lamentation at the loss of the long hair that went with this dress.

Little boys also wore other fancy dresses, such as the sailor suit, complete with wide brimmed round straw hat, which was a replica of the uniform worn by Her Majesty's seamen. Another creation (in England) was the more natural Scottish costume, which had the merit of picturesqueness without femininity.

The late Victorians were so busy piling up money out of trade, extending their vast Empire, and generally dictating to the whole of Europe through their indomitable leader, the Queen, that they had little time to think about dress. The men remained uniformly undistinguished and ungainly in their costume, which changed but little from that of the previous decade.

In this history of costume it will be noticed that, whereas until George IV each reign embraced a single style, or at most two styles, of dress, when the nineteenth century is reached the changes are so rapid that I am compelled to treat them in periods of ten years at a time. This is in the main due to the decline in the wearing capacities of dress materials, and the poorness of the dyes used. Cheapness became desired everywhere, with the result that materials were made without regard to their lasting qualities, and the aniline dyes, freshly discovered, tended to rot the materials. In consequence, clothes wore out more rapidly, necessitating new ones, and there was no reason why the opportunity should not be taken to have a complete change in style.

The most significant change among the men

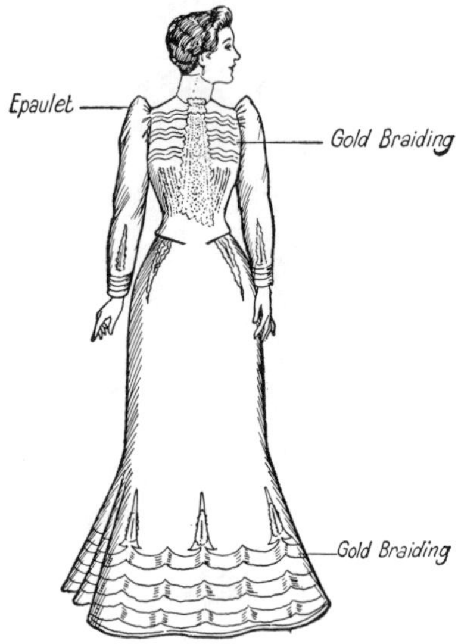

QUEEN MARY'S DAY DRESS, 1893

was the disappearance with the European War of the Norfolk Jacket and its replacement by the loudly checked sports coats. The dinner jacket was the only really new feature, and is said to have been invented at Monte Carlo because the tail coat caused strain when worn for long hours at a stretch at the gaming tables. Until the death of Edward VII it was never worn for formal evening parties. It was confined to the domestic hearth, where it replaced the black velvet smoking jacket of similar, though looser, cut.

The other innovation was brown boots, which gradually were allowed for street wear, black previously being *de rigueur*.

In our own times men have revolted against the cloak of drabness and uniformity that has paralysed all attempts to make their costume pleasing ever since the time of the Prince Regent. No longer are blacks and browns essential, but blues, greens, and purples are used for suits, and the "extras" are even gayer. Sweaters and pullovers of knitted wool are worn in every conceivable colour, and fresh, clear tones in the primary colours everywhere please the eye. This colour revival had previously extended to the ties and silk handkerchiefs, which still are the vogue, though there is room for improvement in getting still brighter colours for actual suiting materials.

The bustle finally vanished in 1891, when the SKIRT was made to fit closely at the hips, billowing out in a bell shape by means of many gores. Called an umbrella skirt, it was trimmed with guipure and braids of elaborate patterns, placed vertically at intervals down the skirt, and the same trimming was put horizontally on the bodice to match. In 1908 appeared the Hobble Skirt, from which all fullness had been taken away. It made quick walking impossible, only the shortest steps being allowed by the scanty material.

A BALL DRESS, 1893

To remedy this, the skirt was later slit at the sides, which was considered altogether too daring. In the 1900's spotted nets and muslins were worn over coloured silks.

The BODICE retained the Noah's Ark bust and fitted tightly by means of gores and pleats. It had a high collar, sometimes edged with a small frill. It was hooked at the back or the front and, if the latter, the fastenings were concealed with lace falls, which might also encircle the neck.

SLEEVES (women) varied. At first they were close-fitting to the wrist, and at the shoulders had peaked epaulets. formed by a puff in the material. These developed into the leg of mutton sleeves with huge shoulder puffs narrowing into a sleeve tight to the wrist. This was a revival of Georgian modes, and occurred in 1893. Finally, about 1895, the tight sleeve was abandoned in favour of one that was full right down and took the name of Bishop's sleeve owing to its likeness to the wide sleeves of the episcopal rochet.

Since the bodice fitted tightly and was brought down in front in a slight peak, no BELTS were required until its shape changed in 1908, when the gap between bodice and skirt was covered by a sash or fairly broad belt. A masculine version

DAY DRESS, 1892

came in with a shirt-blouse, stiff linen collar, and man's straw boater hat, worn with a tweed skirt.

For outer coverings, the popular coat was half-length and flounced out behind by means of gores. It was edged with a narrow band of fur at the neck and wrists, and buttoned down the centre with large bone buttons. Sealskin coats of the same cut were desired by women, but costly full-length fur coats were worn only by the very wealthy. Longer overcoats were also worn, but they were less popular except for older people.

For EVENING DRESS (women) the same styles, slightly modified, were current. For instance, the arms were bare, and covered by long white kid gloves to just above the elbow. The sleeve

EVENING DRESS, 1908

retained only its large shoulder puff, or even none at all but a single ribbon strap. Short trains were added to the skirts, which were gathered in flat pleats at the back to provide the necessary fullness for them. Necks were low and circular or square cut, with or without a lace frill. Artificial seed pearl trimming sometimes created beautiful effects in narrow borders.

HATS were of straw, with medium-sized brims, trimmed with a feather or with wired upstanding bows. After 1908 they were more severe, with large, flat, black velvet bows, and a bird's wing, the whole being put on rather flatly. Bonnets were extensively worn. Thick spotted net VEILS worn with either hats or bonnets, covered the face, but towards the middle of the Edwardian reign veils went out.

HAIR (women) was brushed back from the face in a puff called Pompadour after the famous friend of Louis XV. It was twisted into a top-knot at the back of the head, slightly towards the crown.

On the whole, English costume, until Victoria's Reign, was beautiful, serviceable, and artistic. Men's clothes were equally so for a rather shorter time, until George IV struck a death blow by his persistent habit of wearing black.

We end with Queen Victoria. Her death was the end of an epoch, and it is significant of her essential greatness that the farther we get away from her times, the greater grows her reputation One thing she did not achieve—beauty in dress, and this may partly have been due to the indifferent attitude that she herself displayed towards her own costume.

The study of clothes is fascinating. Love of them is inherent in the human frame, and they will probably remain our delight until the end of time.

SUMMARY

MEN

Dress

Norfolk Jacket as before, till 1914.
Sports Coats after 1914 loose, checked.
Frock Coat as before.

Afternoon Frock, 1897

Lounge Coat as before.
Overcoat as before.
Vest, straight bottom, S.B.
Ties. Loose long-ended bows over collar; small bows under collar flaps; sailor knots.

Evening Dress

Velvet Jacket. Informal.

Dinner Jacket. Informal till 1911, with black tie and vest.
Tail Coat with white tie, black or white vest.
Collars. Butterfly wing replaced high single; double turnover; "Butler's" low, points under coat.

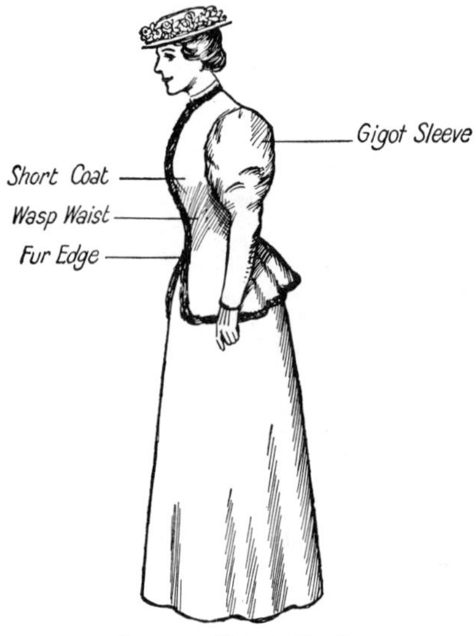

Autumn Costume, 1894

Legs

Trousers, narrow. Mostly pin striped. Black.

Feet

Boots—brown worn in street; black usual.

Hats

Topper—fairly tall.
Bowler—low crown.

Hair

As you please.

WOMEN

Dress

Bodice. Rather tight Noah's Ark shape bust, high collar. Guipure and braid trimmed horizontally. Front or back hooked. Lace falls in front. 1908 high waisted. Berthas. Sashes. Lace plastrons and *motifs*.

Skirt. Fitted hips closely. Many gores to make bell shape till 1908. Rows of braid at bottom. 1908 hobble. 1911 slit at sides. Spotted nets over silks.

Sleeves. Large. At first small epaulets. 1893 leg of mutton. 1895 Bishop, with different colour and made to bodice.

Jackets. Half-length, below waist. Fur-edged neck and wrists. Buttoned (front, gored).

Belt. None till 1908.

Evening Dress

Large puff sleeves at shoulders. Bare arms; short trains; low necks; panels inserted down front. Lace frill to neck. Skirt gathered in flat pleats at back.

Hats

Straw; medium brim. Trimmed bows or feathers.

Bonnets.

Wide straw after 1908. Wing trimmed or wired bows.

Veils. Thick spotted.

Hair

Pompadour with topknot.

CHILDREN

Lord Fauntleroy

Velvet jackets and short trousers. Wide hanging sash-belt. Wide lace collar. An imitation of Charles I period. White silk shirt. Rosetted sleeves.

Sailors

Miniature able-bodied seamen.

Scotsmen

Miniature Highlanders. Kilts, sporran, velvet cut away coat, silver buttoned. Stockings. Bare knees. Glengarry bonnet.

THE CLERGY AT MASS

Ecclesiastical costume, more than any other type, is most often wrongly shown on the stage. It falls into three categories, according to whether it is worn for Mass, for choir services, or for the street and home. It is further subdivided by the persons, cardinals, bishops, or priests, who wear it. Throughout the Middle Ages ecclesiastical costume met with little change, but there have been modifications during modern times, and there is an interlude from the Reformation until the middle of Victoria's reign during which certain garments fell into disuse. The modern Roman Church in addition to medieval vestments wears new garments derived from late Italian sources. It is important that care should be taken to depict the clergy correctly; travesties of clothes are introduced by some pageant masters and stage producers.

The *Cassock* is a ground-length, close-sleeved coat, double-breasted, fastening with a single button at the shoulder and another at the waist, and made of black cloth, except for bishops, who wear magenta or purple, and cardinals, who wear scarlet. It has a shoulder cape without a hood, and about 1850 became a single-breasted garment fastened down the centre with numerous small buttons. In modern times bishops and cardinals wear it piped with their respective colours, along the cape edge, the cassock vertical edge, and with the buttons in colour.

The *Alb* is a ground length white shirt with loose sleeves to enable it to slip over the cassock.

The *Stole* is a long strip of embroidered or coloured silk or other material, about 2½ in. wide, and reaching to just below the knee. It is tucked in by the girdle at the waist and worn in different ways by the various orders. A bishop wears his straight down, a priest crosses it over the breast, and a deacon has it over the left shoulder and loosely tied under the right arm at the waist, the ends hanging down the right side of the body.

The *Amice* is an oblong piece of linen, 36 in. by 24 in., to which two tapes are attached at the upper corners. It is placed behind the neck and shoulders. The tapes are carried round the neck to the front, across the back and round the waist in front, where they are tied. It has an oblong

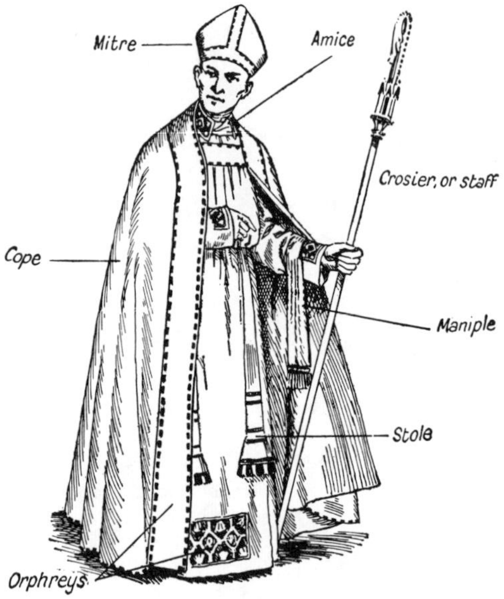

Bishop (Solemn Services)

patch of embroidery, called an apparel, appliquéd at back of neck.

The *Girdle* is a linen woven rope tied round alb and stole at the waist.

The *Maniple* is a miniature stole about 3½ ft. long worn on the left arm at the wrist.

The *Chasuble*, when placed straight out on a table, is vesica shaped, that is the shape of two Gothic arches placed together with their points outwards and meeting each other at a straight line drawn just below their chords. It is, in other words, an oval shape with its longer ends sharply pointed. It is adorned in a Y shape, with bands of embroidery back and front at the seams, which are called orphreys. They may also take the shape of a cross on the back and a pillar on the front, this type being late Medieval. It should be fairly full, hang in good folds, and be made of light silk, with a hole for the neck.

A set of Mass vestments (chasuble, stole, maniple) should match in material and embroidery. Its colours are restricted to red, green, violet, and white, with black for funerals, and gold, or yellow as an optional shade, for other occasions. In the Middle Ages colour restrictions were few, and almost any colour or combination of shades is permissible.

The *Dalmatic* is a tunic with sleeves reaching to the forearm, and having two vertical bands of embroidery (orphreys) down front and back, joined by two horizontal bands. Like all the Mass vestments it is a survival from Classical times, and follows the lines of the Roman tunica. It is fringed along its edges.

The *Tunicle* is a similar garment to the dalmatic, except that it has its two vertical bands joined by one short horizontal band of embroidery at the top.

Gloves were at first of white silk with jewels on the back and wide tasselled gauntlets. To-day they are of coloured silk. In Georgian times they

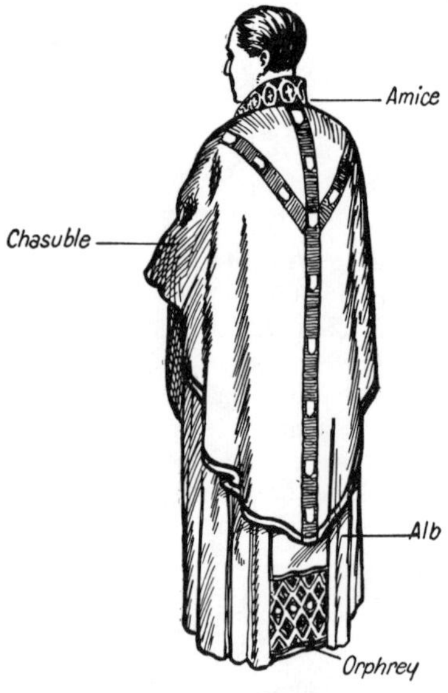

Priest at Mass

were of white or lavender, with gauntlets fringed with gold bullion.

The *Pallium* is of white lamb's wool, adorned with crosses in gold or purple, about 1½ in. wide, with about five crosses on the pendant portion hanging down in front of the chasuble, and four on the shoulder parts. It is worn over the shoulders, and hangs down in front in a loose tie.

The *Pastoral Staff* or *Crosier* may be of ivory, gold, silver, ebony, or other decorated material, in the shape of a shepherd's crook, and of Gothic or Renaissance design. Just below the crook a linen scarf, long enough to cover that part of the staff that is held by hand, is hung from a metal ring. It is designed to protect the finely wrought work from damage by the hands. The bishop bears it with his left hand.

The *Archbishop's Cross* is a processional cross about 8 ft. high, made of similar materials to the crosier. It is borne in the left hand.

Both staff and cross may be carried by chaplains, in which case they hold it in front of them with both hands. The bishop merely carries it in his left hand so that he may bless the people with his right hand.

The *Mitre* is a hat of silk or velvet and con-

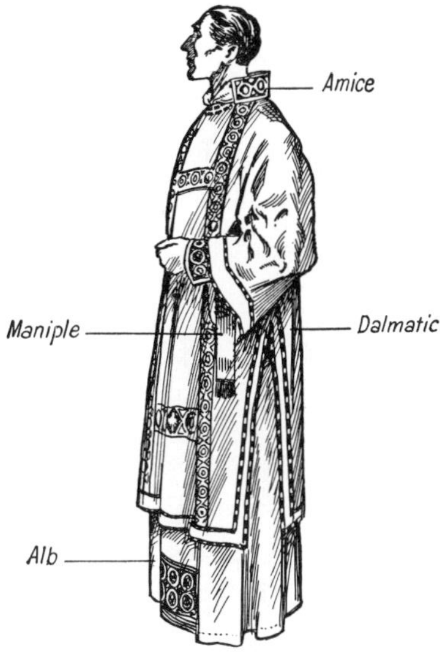

DEACON (SOLEMN SERVICES)

tains an inner cap, in front and at the back of which are placed triangular upstanding pieces of material decorated with bands of embroidery and jewelled.

At funerals the bishop wears a plain white linen or silk mitre; on other occasions a decorated coloured one; on great feasts one plated with gold and jewels.

The bishop's *Ring* is generally of amethyst. It was worn on the middle finger of the right hand in the Middle Ages, but is now worn on the third finger.

THE PAENULA (CLASSICAL CHASUBLE)

The order in which these clothes are put on is—

Cassock.
Amice.
Alb.
Stole.
Girdle.
Maniple.
Chasuble, or dalmatic or tunicle.

The bishop wears, over the alb and under the chasuble, thin silk dalmatic and tunicle without embroidery—generally of golden colour.

A medieval bishop wore stockings of linen, later of silk, and shoes, at first of open work, but later, in the fourteenth century, fastened with strings and adorned with a Y-shaped band like the chasuble band.

If clergy are represented in connexion with a High Mass the priest is assisted by a deacon and a subdeacon. All wear vestments of the same colour and design.

If late Renaissance vestments are required, the

chasuble is cut away at the sides and curved like a fiddle back and the sleeves of dalmatic and tunicle become merely large epaulets hanging about 6 in. over the shoulders.

Mass vestments are rarely worn in the street, nor are dalmatics, tunicles, copes, and mitres, except in religious processions.

REFORMATION TO MID-VICTORIAN

The Mass vestments and the almuce fell into disuse after Elizabeth's time. Mitres and crosiers were worn until Charles II's time. Copes continued to be worn throughout in cathedrals mainly. Bishops retained their gloves, white or lavender, fringed with gold bullion.

Episcopal pectoral crosses do not come in till Victorian times.

ACOLYTES and servers at Mass wore cassocks and albs with amices up to the Reformation, and from 1900 onwards they wear either an alb or a cotta—which is a waist length surplice with tight sleeves to just below the elbow—edged with lace at option.

Bishops, if not celebrating, may attend at Mass in cope and mitre. These are also worn for processions, whether in church or in street.

SUMMARY

FOR MASS

Cardinals may be either bishops or priests, and wear the clothes of those orders at Mass.

Priests

Cassocks—black, double-breasted; single-breasted since 1850.

SERVERS

Alb—long white ground length shirt.
Stole—long embroidered shoulder strip. Crossed in front.
Amice—linen oblong.
Girdle—linen rope.
Maniple—small stole on arm.
Chasuble—elliptical silk cloak.

Bishops

The same with the addition of—
Mitre—cap with triangular revers.
Gloves—gauntleted.
Pastoral staff—shepherd's crook.
Processional cross borne before him at option.
Stole is not crossed in front.
Dalmatic, Tunicle } of thin silk.
Ring—right middle finger—amethyst.

Deacons

The same as priests, save for a dalmatic instead of a chasuble, and stole worn over left shoulder under right arm.

Subdeacons

The same as priests, save for a tunicle instead of chasuble and no stole.

Archbishops

Same as bishops plus *Pallium*—white wool strip, and use pastoral staff and processional cross together.

RELIGIOUS ORDERS

Benedictine Monks

Tunic, ankle length, sleeved. Cowl (large loose gown, hanging sleeves, and hood). Scapular (an apron, back and front, circular neck hole, sleeved or sleeveless) replaces cowl when at work. All black.

Cistercian Monks

As Benedictines, but very long sleeves to cowl. White tunic and cowl. Black scapular.

Cluniac Monks

As Benedictines, but cowl is bell-shaped, ankle-length, and slit at sides for arms. Brown in France, black in Germany.

Premonstratensian Canons

White tunic, rochet, biretta, and almuce.

Austin Canons

Tunic. White rochet girdled, tight sleeves. Cloak with small hood.

Franciscan Friars

At first brown tunic. later grey. White cord girdle. Hood, long, pointed, to waist.

Dominican Friars

White tunic, hood, and scapular. Black cloak and hood.

Carmelite Friars

Black tunic, hood, and scapular. White cloak and hood.

Abbesses

Long cowl girdled, loose-sleeved cassock. Under this tight-fitting sleeves of under dress. Barbe or chin cloth. Mantle cope-shaped. Veil. Ring optional.

Abbots

As their order. Some privileged to wear a mitre. All had pastoral staff. Ring optional.

Rosaries were worn by all orders on the girdle, and cassocks were double-breasted. Modern religious habits still unchanged unless the order is modern. For Parliament, long cape open at front, slight train.

CLERGY—CHOIR AND STREET

By choir dress is meant the vestments that are worn at the daily services other than the Mass. In the Medieval period services included matins and evensong, or vespers, besides the "little hours," which were similar, but shorter, services of psalms and readings held at stated intervals during the day. They are still held by religious orders and Roman secular clergy.

By Sacramental vestments other than the Mass are meant the dresses worn for baptisms, confirmations, marriages, and funerals. For these the same garments are worn, but the stole replaces the almuce or the tippet and hood. For solemn services of all kinds, both priests and bishops wear a cope, and the bishop his mitre.

CHOIR DRESS

The *Cassock* has been described.

The *Surplice* is of linen, reaching below the knees, and has wide, open sleeves of the shape that the name denotes. At the neck it is gathered into a circular band, which is rather wider than the neck itself. In the Middle Ages the surplice was made full, with beautiful folds, and with long sleeves. In Tudor times a fashion came in to make the sleeves identical both back and front so that their edges were true to each other. Previously the front edge was less than the rear edge, and the style was more graceful.

The *Almuce* was a dark cloth hood lined with fur, with long ends hanging down in front over the surplice, and with a roll collar. It came in about the thirteenth century, mainly for warmth in the then unheated churches. The fur part was worn outside, canons and dignitaries having grey fur, usually squirrel. The *Tippet*, in the fifteenth century, took the form of a scarf, still worn cloth-side inwards, but with a sable-fur lining turned back and rolled over from the inner edge as it lay on the body. In summer the lining was of silk. All graduates wore it. Lesser clergy wore, instead of an almuce, a tippet and hood of black cloth. The *Hood* should be of medieval shape, which was a full cape covering the shoulders, with a small peaked hood attached to its back. This shape is much more beautiful than that of the modern hood, which has degenerated in a curious fashion owing to the wearing of wigs in later times. The wigs would not allow the narrow natural opening of the hood to pass over them, so the openings were widened, with the result that the hood gradually came to rest half way down the back. The cape portion was narrowed till it became a mere string round the neck, the original fullness being relegated to a formal appendage on the back. To-day it is being increasingly worn in its older and more comely shape.

The *Cope* is a semi-circular piece of silk, highly decorated with bands, called *orphreys*, right along the straight edge, and with a "hood" on the back. This hood has become merely a formal semi-circular piece of velvet, decorated with embroidery. The cope is fastened in front, just across the chest, with a clasp, called a morse. This is of material, except for bishops, who are allowed to wear morses of precious metal.

Priest (Choir Services)

BISHOPS

The *Cassock* should be of magenta or purple, double-breasted until 1850, when it became single-breasted.

The *Almuce* must be of grey fur in winter and silk in summer. Bishops in Medieval times often wore, first, the surplice and then the *Rochet* over it. The rochet was a long white linen shirt not quite as long as an alb, with loose, but not balloon sleeves. The cassock sleeve was usually turned up over it to form a dark band at the wrist. In the eighteenth century, until about 1900, the sleeves became balloon-shaped by stiffening the material, which was of lawn, till it burgeoned out in the ridiculous shape that was so often caricatured. The sleeves were attached to the chimere, which otherwise disappeared. This ballooning has passed away now, and the bishops have returned to the older type. The *Chimere* was a silk overcoat of ground length, open in front all the way down. In modern times it is sometimes held together across the chest by a string. It has no sleeves, and when the white rochet sleeves are pulled through it, it gives the well-known "magpie" effect. No academic hoods should be worn with the chimere; they are often incorrectly added. Its colour is black satin or silk, but red ones are worn on certain high days. Bishops wear either cope and mitre or rochet and chimere, but never a combination.

Italian Prelate (Choir Services)

The *Square Cap* was at first of loose black cloth or velvet, its seams forming four ridges along the top, not accentuated, and it fitted with ear-flaps closely to the head. In Charles I's time it developed into the "Bishop Andrewes Cap" by widening the upper portion till it became a loose, square shape attached to a band, which fitted

BISHOPS

As Cardinal In Choir and Processions At Mass Outdoors

(G.2477)

the head. In the universities this process of thinning the height and widening the sides was developed until it became the modern graduate's cap, which is a mere "mortar-board" of stiff cardboard covered with cloth, and square in shape, fitted on to a stiff skull cap, longer at the back than the front, and with a long tassel on top. The tassel must be worn hanging over the front side, and *not* at the back. Another development that came about in the seventeenth century was away from the wide, loose type of Bishop Andrewes to the stiff close fit of the *Biretta*. This is now worn by most modern clergy. It has its seams turned into stiff, high, semi-circular ridges on three (not four) sides of the top, and is collapsible. The side that has no seam ridge must be worn on the wearer's left. This is easy to remember when it is borne in mind that to take it off with the right hand requires a

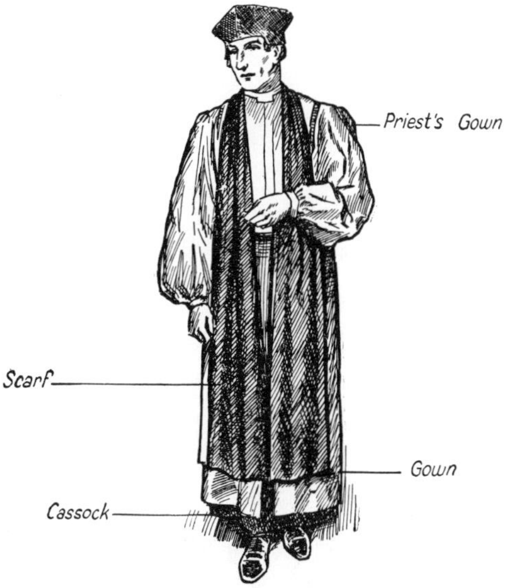

Priest (Walking Dress)

ridge to clasp. In the Middle Ages a skull cap, rather full on top, was alternatively worn.

Hats, whether mitres or biretta types, are worn at services during readings and psalms, but not during prayers; also on ingress and egress to the choir.

The *Mitre* has already been described.

IN THE STREET

During Medieval times the clergy were somewhat lax about wearing strictly clerical costume, and often dressed as laymen. During the Medieval period and down to George III's day the customary outdoor dress was cassock, gown, hood, and square cap. Graduates also added

Bishop (Walking Dress)

the tippet. In Georgian times the square cap gave way to the wig, and the gown blossomed out into full bishop sleeves. The cassock was fastened by a broad waist band, and bands instead of the neckcloth or cravat were added at the neck. The cassock was of silk, at any rate for the richer clergy. The hood and tippet were not worn out of doors.

At the end of the eighteenth century this ancient street dress was abandoned, and the clergy wore dress similar to that of other professional men. This consisted of breeches, and a black, cut-away coat, a white collar and neckcloth, and a top hat, the wide brims of which were tied with side strings to the fabric. This costume has been retained to our own day by bishops, but not by ordinary clergy.

The Roman Catholic clergy dressed as laymen from Elizabeth's day till Victoria's, after which they followed the Anglican clergy in dress.

Street dress for priests changed in Victorian times into frock coat and trousers. The head-gear varied. A silk hat was worn till about the 90's, then a clerical flat hat till about 1914, then a black felt trilby to our own time. The frock coat has died out save on formal occasions, when it, or a cut-away morning coat and striped trousers, may be worn.

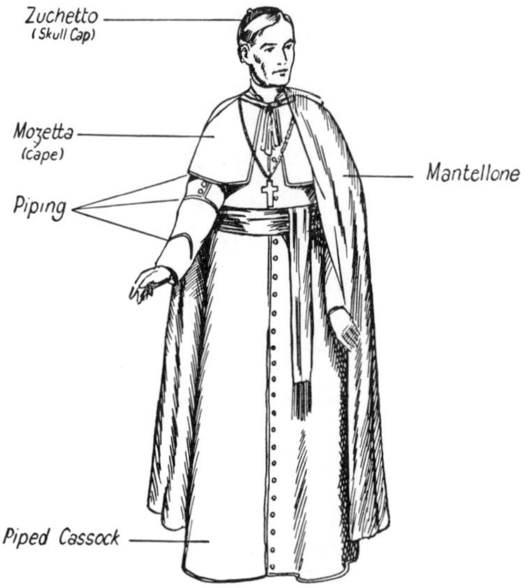

Italian Prelate (Walking Dress)

Neck-wear followed lay custom till early Victorian times, when a white neckcloth was worn; later it changed to a white bow tie. The modern Roman dog-collar came in about 1807. Below it was worn a stock instead of a tie. The stock was made of black for priests, magenta or purple for bishops, and scarlet for cardinals.

MODERN ROMAN DRESS

For bishops and cardinals an informal full dress consists of a black cassock buttoned and piped with colour—magenta for bishops, scarlet for cardinals. Many Anglican bishops follow the same custom. The cassock is single-breasted, with numerous buttons right down the centre, and with a shoulder cape, also piped, as are the cassock edges and the sleeve edges. This costume is worn both in the British Empire and in other countries. It is less noticeable in a modern world than the more beautiful but more striking full dress scarlet or magenta, which is reserved for choir services, processions, indoor state occasions such as receptions, levees, and public occasions generally.

Full dress consists of cassock and cape, with a train all in magenta for bishops and in scarlet for cardinals.

Modern Italian modifications of the ancient dress are worn by Roman Catholic bishops. Thus the chimere is now the mantelletta—a knee-length, wider, and looser garment. The bishops wear skull caps called zucchetos under their birettas. All are of magenta—those for cardinals are of scarlet. The cassock has a train, and lace-edged cottas supplant the surplices. Pectoral crosses depend from long chains of green cord or gold, and are fastened at the neck, the chain hanging in two loops on the breast. Over all and during travel a great caped cloak with narrow collar is worn. On occasions of great ceremony the *cappa magna* (a hooded and caped trained cloak) is used.

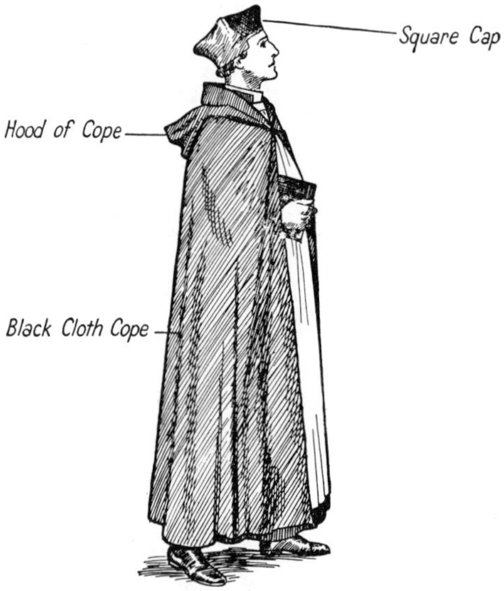

Priest (Outdoor Services)

SUMMARY

FOR CHOIR

Priests

Cassock.
Surplice.
Almuce, or tippet and hood
Cope—optional.
Square cap or biretta.

Bishops

Cassock.
Grey fur almuce.
Surplice and/or rochet, with
chimere and square cap, Bishop Andrewes cap or biretta, or cope and mitre.

FOR SACRAMENTS (EXCEPT MASS)

Bishops and priests wear a stole, instead of almuce or tippet and hood. For state and solemn sacraments both may wear a cope as well.

FOR STREET

Priests

Cassock.
Gown.
Tippet.
Square cap—black cloth.

Bishops

Cassock.
Chimere.
Scarf or tippet—sable-lined.
Square cap—black velvet.

THE CRITICAL FACULTY

IVOR BROWN, Author of "Book of Words," "Parties of the Play," "Brown Studios," etc.

EVERY actor is a critic—of the other fellow or the rival team; and sometimes he is a very good critic, for he speaks of what he knows and of what he has learned by suffering, and spins no theories out of book-lore. But his point of view is often rather limited; he is so interested in the technique of expression that he overlooks the thing expressed or intended to be expressed. In my contacts with professional actors I have found them acute critics of detail in performance, but indifferent judges of the play as a whole. (Naturally such a sweeping statement must allow for exceptions. The shrewder actors often help a dramatist with suggestions before production.)

MR. IVOR BROWN

This criticism of the actor-as-critic is less true of the amateur than of the professional stage, or at any rate it is less true of the more ambitious corner of the amateur stage, where I believe there is real feeling for drama in its totality and not merely a jealous computation of personal opportunities offered and missed. Moreover, the best kind of amateur puts up with a reasonable censure far better than the professional, who simply reads criticisms with a hungry eye for epithets; if he does not find "admirable" or "brilliant" he is apt to dismiss the notice with contempt. On the other hand, during rehearsal he has to put up with continuous criticism from his producer and, in some cases, this is frank and even harsh. One or two of our leading professional producers indulge in methods of criticism that no amateur company would tolerate.

Amateur actors get little newspaper criticism of value. In London there are so many groups competing for attention that newspapers have, for the most part, given up the job of noticing their efforts. There is neither space nor staff to cope with them after the considerable demands of the professional stage have been met. The societies most likely to get good newspaper criticism are those in a town large enough to own a good local Press. Here there will probably be a competent theatrical journalist who will have time and space at his disposal. Amateurs in small towns or villages that have only a weekly paper receive the usually flattering attentions of a reporter who cannot be expected to have special knowledge or strict standards of assessment. It is much better fun for him to go to a play than to attend a public meeting and record its round of speeches and so everything in the dramatic garden is apt to be lovely in his eyes. This kind of journalistic attention is doubtless pleasant to the amateur exhibitionist; it assists publicity and may help the box-office at the next performance; but it is of no use to the amateur as theatrical worker.

At the same time the amateur societies which perform in the big Festivals of Community Drama receive expert and detailed criticism from the judges after their performances in the initial and intermediate stages of the Festivals. This is criticism of the very best kind, practical observations by practical workers in the theatre. It would be asking too much of human nature to expect the critic always to be right and the actor always to agree; but the competitors always get something to think and argue over, and it is one great merit of the Festivals that they provide these opportunities for public assessment and subsequent privy discussion.

But Festival performances are only a tiny fraction of the myriad amateur productions that are given throughout the year. For these other and far more numerous occasions the British Drama League and other organizations provide, for affiliated societies and at a small fee, a competent critic who will give a considered verdict at the end of the evening. These facilities are considerably used in the London area; naturally there is less employment of visiting critics in the country, where the travelling expenses will be larger and the amount of time involved may make it harder to procure the right man or woman.

Without doubt this supply of qualified criticism is one of the most useful of the many services supplied by the League and it is desirable that every ambitious society should make use of it. The expenditure on criticism should not be regarded as a luxurious extra; it should be regarded as essential to the health of the society. I suggest that, where the local newspaper criticism is no more than a form of amiable reporting, the amateur groups should ask the editors to print instead the opinions (or a summary of the opinions) expressed by the qualified visiting critic. The editor might even be coaxed into paying for this copy, as he would have to pay his own reporter for the job, and in that case the expenses of the visiting critic would be met or diminished. The visiting critic presumably has "a name" in his own line of business and speaks with authority; hence his copy would be better for the local paper than an unsigned description by a reporter who may be an excellent all-round journalist but cannot be blamed for a certain innocence about the theatre.

There is scope also for mutual exchange of criticism between amateur societies that are of similar ambition and achievement. Complimentary seats might be sent to the leading members of a neighbouring group with an invitation to express their opinions later upon the merits of the production; preferably this would be done in a written report. The judged would subsequently visit the other society in the capacity of judges and report in due course. Such a situation would need tactful handling; but, where both societies are animated by the real spirit of community drama, I see no reason why the system should not be of practical value. It may be that some members of the Movement, who are not naturally actors but have a deep attachment to the theatre, a clear comprehension of dramatic values, and a ready means of self-expression, will wish to devote themselves more and more to critical activities of this kind.

The number of people who can get up immediately after a performance and deliver, by word of mouth, a well-arranged, proportioned, and articulate criticism must be small. There are good speakers who are not good critics and good critics who are not good speakers; a bad speech will destroy the value of a good criticism. It would be optimistic to expect a constant supply of people enjoying the double qualification. But there is no essential need for immediate judgment. The amateur society, which has invited a visit from one of the amateur critics whom I have just described, should be ready to distribute typed copies of his verdict a day or two after the event, if, as is likely, he is unwilling to get up and speak *ex tempore*. Besides, if he has to be stern, it is more agreeable to be so on paper, when he can consider his words carefully. There is less chance then of the rash phrase which he himself would subsequently regret.

In any case criticism, through the Press, the visiting deputies of the British Drama League, or through local initiative, is essential to the vitality of the Amateur Movement. It will show a poor spirit in the Movement if it does not ask for frank and frequent comment or resents it when given. But I have far larger opinions of the Movement than to expect pettiness of outlook, and I await the time when the supply of expert criticism will be organized on a really wide scale.

Ivor Brown.

ASPECTS OF CRITICISM

S. R. LITTLEWOOD, Past President, Critics' Circle; Author, "Dramatic Criticism"; Editor, "The Stage"

ALL sorts of misconceptions about criticism must first be set right. Then, and not till then, it may be useful to discuss its uses to the professional and the amateur theatre, and to those who are working for either or both out of sincere love for the art of the stage.

The hardiest of these misconceptions is a belief that the critic is at once a judge and a servant of the theatre—that he belongs to the theatre and has a responsibility to it. This cannot be too emphatically denied. Of the random essayist—a source of much excellent criticism—it is palpably untrue. It is no less so of the professional critic—the accredited practitioner in the "craft and mystery" of journalism, who uses the theatre as his material. For him, as for all, the word "critic" implies judgment—that is to say, he is empowered to give judgment if he wishes to do so. Anyone who has worked in a newspaper office knows that there are countless writers who are not allowed to do this. The "critic" is so called because he is distinguished from these. But it does not mean that he is in duty bound to give a considered verdict upon—or even pay attention to—anything which does not interest him, or which he does not think will interest his readers. So long as he satisfies them—and in the long run this includes every point of efficiency—he is absolutely free. He can omit all judgment whatever, if he thinks the play or performance is not worth it. He can regard what he has seen from any standpoint—that of his own personal impression, that of the general public or some portion of it, or that of a reader as opposed to a playgoer, or that of some fancied ideal or temperament. Anything like persistent unfairness will, of course, soon bring its revenges. But this is only because the critic, like the actor, dramatist, and manager, must give the public either what they want or what he can teach them to want.

The old and much-vexed question of the complimentary ticket does not alter the state of affairs in the slightest. It has been hammered out again and again, both in public and private—always with the same result. The complimentary seat is a courtesy for which the theatre finds it convenient to arrange. That is all. There is probably not a critic in the world who would not rather fill a seat which has been paid for. But in that case—as has been shown by experiment—he would only wish to go, like the public, to plays which he knew would please him. The effect would be that only a few theatres would get any notices at all.

On one famous occasion—the production of *The Morals of Marcus* at the Garrick Theatre in 1906—no complimentary tickets were issued. There were no notices anywhere. The play, which was not at all a bad one, struggled on for a time; but very soon arrived an "S.O.S." from the management, imploring any sort of reference, hostile or otherwise. So the critics returned—at any rate, some of them—and all was comparatively well. Another reason for the complimentary seat is that any candid reference is legally uninvited, and therefore actionable, without it. The fact thus emerges that, so far from the complimentary seat entailing an obligation to praise, the exact opposite is the truth. Most managers know as well as the critics themselves that mere puffery is dull and does no one any good.

Having cleared away, to some extent, the ever-harmful fallacy that critics are in any sense parasites of the theatre, we can come back along the line and recognize that only the critic who loves the theatre is worth anything at all; also that, as a journalistic ambassador, he is of immense importance. He brings, in the first place, publicity—and to the professional theatre publicity is the very breath of life. Indeed, it might almost be described, from the Kantian point of view, as the "thing in itself." One way or another, the essence of all is show. Even to the amateur, from the most practical standpoint, full houses for a week may make all the difference between carrying on or giving up. This admitted, it is no less vital that the interest created in the theatre by an understanding critic—as compared with some other aids in this direction—is on the side of intelligence. When he is not actually creative, he conveys ideas and discoveries to people who would otherwise never have thought or even heard about them. Also, a good and sympathetic critic not only inspires the public with his own enthusiasm; he gives priceless encouragement to dramatists, players, and producers.

This creation of a general interest in the theatre by choosing it as a theme can illuminate as well as interpret. It is, to my mind, a far more important element of criticism than the mere delivery of an *ex cathedra* verdict upon the merits of this or that play, favourable or adverse. I count the immediate decision upon something which is either obvious or a question of taste as a very secondary matter. Nothing is easier than to go to a play and to say whether one has enjoyed it or not. With nine plays out of ten, even on larger grounds, it is clear enough whether a good or a bad piece of work has been forthcoming, and where it and the company have succeeded or failed. The question as to which section of the public the play will please or otherwise is a little more complicated, but simple enough to any playgoer of experience—after production. These affairs are for commonplace minds. It is not there that the call for men of genius in criticism has arrived and been sometimes so remarkably responded to.

IBSEN AND THE CRITICS

A common charge against criticism as an art is that great dramatists have not been awarded immediate and universal honour by all critics—that Ibsen, for instance, was pilloried by Clement Scott, just as Wagner was by many of the music critics in his early days. But this is only to say that one critic of a flamboyantly emotional and romantic temperament had the courage to express his sincere feelings at a particular time. As a matter of fact, it would be difficult to find an author who owed more to English criticism than Ibsen. The very productions against which Clement Scott fulminated were promoted by a fellow-critic, J. T. Grein. The translation used was made by another fellow-critic, the late William Archer, who had taken the trouble to learn Norwegian so as to confirm his faith at a time when very few other people in this country knew Ibsen's name. Even now there are thousands of quite reckonable folk—I do not happen to be one of them—who look upon Ibsen as a "dated" author. Supposing that Scott was definitely wrong—and on some points he certainly was—how much better that he should have honestly represented his temperament and period, waving its tattered banners to the last! His vituperations against *Ghosts* and *A Doll's House* are excellent reading still, just because they were sincere. They mean something.

ARCHER, WALKLEY, SHAW

So utterly wrong is the idea that critics are to be judged by the impersonal correctness of their judgments that in my own pretty long experience I have found those the best and most useful to the theatre who have been strongest in their aversions and most pronounced in their fallibilities. Scott was by no means the only "sinner" in this respect. William Archer, though he acclaimed Ibsen, had a strangely inconsistent prejudice against the Elizabethans. He considered them for the most part over-praised melodramatists; though *The Green Goddess*, by which he himself was to make a fortune at the close of his life, was frank melodrama from beginning to end. When someone suggested to Walkley that he should learn German so as to be able to read Schiller in the original, his reply will be recognized as probably authentic by all who knew him. It was to the effect that one of the reasons for his not learning German was that he could the better avoid Schiller in the original. So, too, with Shaw. Though his dramatic criticisms are among the most entertaining things he has written, his views on romantic drama are by no means always to be trusted, and much that he writes upon acting is false and over-stressed. Yet these three critics—however human and fallible—did an invaluable work by building up an interest in the theatre among well-educated and thinking people. It would be difficult to calculate the number of young men and women of the early 'nineties who were brought into the theatre by reading Archer, Walkley, and Shaw. They said to themselves that here was a new world of discovery—something that interested men of intelligence and charm—and they became playgoers. They made a public through which the later Pinero, the Barrie, the Shaw plays, and everything good that has followed became possible.

OLD CRITICS AND NEW

I was just starting criticism at the time, and can vouch for the truth of this. When I began, Clement Scott was still the dictator of the front of the house. He used to have a box, whilst the other critics had to be content with stalls. The pit and gallery used to watch his face to see whether the play was going to succeed or not. Their confidence was not altogether misplaced for a theatre in which drawing-room melodrama on the Sardou plan was still the staple fare, verging to other products of the all-dominant French stage, from *Two Little Vagabonds* at the Princess's to *A Night Out* at the Vaudeville. It was not ideas that filled the close-printed "column-and-a-bit" which appeared next morning from Clement Scott's pencil. It was a glowing reflection of the excitements of the evening; a detailed, lively summary of the plot, with or without reminiscences of the generally Parisian original; a vivid, frank, and instructive criticism of the acting, character by character and act by act, followed by an equally careful and appreciative recognition of the "production," with notes on each scene. To finish up with would come a clear and more or less reliable estimate of the play's value to the playgoing world that Clement Scott knew. Those criticisms of Scott's—which were models to most of the daily paper critics scattered beneath him—were, to my mind, not to be despised. They brought people in flocks to the theatre. They have not lived, but they served their day. Apart from his fluency, ready emotion, and knowledge of the theatre, he was not a man of high attainments. But he was an enthusiast; he claimed space and prominence for the theatre in his paper. He paved the way for the new type of man better suited for dealing with the new type of play.

With the arrival of Ibsen and of his influence on the stage of the world, the days of the old-fashioned criticism were done. A subtle perception of the author's meaning took the place of reams of homage to the player. A knowledge of the classics and of the French adaptation-market was just not enough. Not only Scott, but all the old-fashioned critics—fine scholars, some of them, like Joseph Knight, with his vast beard, and kindly Moy Thomas—found themselves outclassed by young men who had not a tithe of their knowledge of the theatre, but were able to dash off in a line or two an idea of the play, which was what mattered when plays began to have ideas, and to leave the acting and the tric-trac of the stage more or less to take care of itself. To read Walkley's early criticisms as "Spec" is to realize the change and its importance. Meanwhile, the weekly and the monthly reviews began to pay an attention to dramatic criticism that had never been called for before. Even so, save for Walkley's subsequent weekly article in *The Times*, English criticism has produced nothing comparable to that of the French *feuilletonistes*—nothing combining wit, theatrical knowledge, scholarship, charm of personality, and sound judgment as Sarcey and Lemaître combined them. This may be partly because dramatic criticism has never been with us a matter of training and tradition as it always has been in France. We have no National Theatre, no Ministry of Fine Art, nothing to give the theatre an academic permanence and dignity.

NEWS AGAINST VIEWS

Since those days professional dramatic criticism has changed completely. In place of the long, detailed survey, conscientiously going through an entire play and cast—good, bad, and in between—the method started by Walkley has spread almost universally. Only a few very old-fashioned daily papers—and they mostly in the provinces—would think nowadays of devoting over a column to the most important production of the night before. So far as London daily papers are concerned, even if the will and the space were there, the writing or dictating of a notice of that length after the performance has become by no means so simple a matter as it might seem. Nearly all newspapers go to press so early now that for the larger circulations notices have to be written during the "show." In a large proportion of cases, what the playgoing public gets is an impression of the first act and a guess at what follows, confirmed by telephone afterwards—or, possibly, corrected, if it has been grossly wide of the mark. Also "news" has become not only a clamant but an unassailable competitor, so much so that first-night criticism, crashing in at the last moment, has to be treated as news and for its news-value. This has inevitably resulted in the replacing of helpful criticism in some quarters by "snappy" paragraphs of personal or other superficial gossip. Or it necessitates some extravagant expression of praise or blame, sufficiently sensational to make it good for a headline and flattering the ignorance of a public incapable of appreciating anything better. This tendency is, unfortunately, spreading to the evening papers, where news, social gossip, domestic chit-chat, and pictures encroach more and more. Meanwhile the periodical reviews have faded almost completely from power. Their place has been taken to a great extent by the Sunday papers.

FIRST NIGHT CRITICISM

None the less, with all this against it, I can say from an intimate knowledge of forty years that first-night, professional criticism was at least never more influential than it is now. Considering the difficulties, I doubt if it was ever done more ably. How easy, by comparison, it used to be, may be gathered from the fact that in my own early days a notice did not have to be delivered before one o'clock in the morning. It was possible not only to collect one's thoughts, but to enjoy a leisurely supper after the play, before sitting down to write in comfort. It means a good deal that there are more young University men who have entered upon dramatic criticism as a career than there ever were, and that critics are now organized into a body—the Critics' Circle—whose activities for the welfare of the theatre in its relation to journalism have won respect on both sides of the footlights. The rise in importance of the old "libraries" and new ticket-agencies, whose decisions on doubtful plays are strongly influenced by morrow-morn criticism, and the arrival of the "press-agent," whose very natural concentration of focus needs perpetual adjustment, have both enhanced the need for independent opinion. But, as I have said, his duty as an honest tipster upon "winners" and "flops" is not in my view by any means the critic's chief function.

So my advice is, when you see criticism that you do not care for—whether you agree with it or not is a minor matter—do not "shoot the man at the piano" until you are quite sure he is not playing a tune he is forced to play on an instrument not of his choosing. Each public gets the dramatic criticism it deserves. If in your particular paper you see tendencies that distress you—if you see "snappy pars" about the private lives of actresses and topics of that sort put in front of thoughtful work for the theatre as an art—write in to the editor and protest. You will help the critic to do what he is—if he is worth his salt—wishing to do all the time. Let the intelligent public make itself into an active majority and it may come up to the intelligent critic in time to support and follow him.

VALUE OF CRITICISM

My more recent experiences as an editor have only confirmed my beliefs as a critic. My duties in connexion with *The Stage* have given me in many ways a more intimate view of the value of criticism to the professional actor and actress than was possible during close upon half a century of service to the general public. It has been part of my task to see that every new play or important new production throughout Great Britain and Ireland, not to mention the United States, the Dominions, and elsewhere, has as much justice done to it as is possible in the circumstances. I have found on all hands not only an eager response and frequently a welcome to sincere and justified criticism, but also a demand for more knowledge of technique, of tradition, of dramatic literature, and of new possibilities of every kind. It comes from an ever-growing body of amateur and would-be professional workers. In this the critic can be both a learner and an instructor, without neglecting his primary duty as a recorder of aims and achievements. Up to the present the crop of good, living plays likely to endure has been disappointing. The vast mass of endeavour has been, on the one side, in the direction of trivial variety-entertainment, which does not call for extended critical treatment, and, on the other, in that of over-stressed sophistication. I have found a strong tendency to neglect sound popular classics in favour of things cheaply exotic with a limited human appeal. This is, after all, only natural to young, ardent, but comparatively inexperienced practitioners. All the more is the well-informed critic of broad sympathy and knowledge likely to be useful.

A largely prevalent notion that the theatrical profession is against criticism has been encouraged, I am afraid, by one or two isolated expressions of angry fancy. They have been prompted, one gathers, by equally isolated examples of aggressive, pompous, and sometimes admittedly, unfair judgment. But there are exceptions to every rule. The majority of critics, as represented by the Critics' Circle, founded thirty-two years ago under the presidency of William Archer, whom every section of the theatrical world regarded with respect, work whole-heartedly for the betterment of art, and in entire sympathy, as many happy occasions have shown, with dramatists, actors, actresses, managers, and the public, whom all serve.

THE CRITIC AND THE AMATEUR

I have dealt with professional, daily newspaper dramatic criticism in its relation to the professional theatre. I am now going to make a few suggestions as to the value and uses of criticism to the amateur actor and producer. I need not say the amateur dramatist. This is because—more's the pity!—there is no such person. At any rate, I have not yet discovered him or her. I have found people willing and eager to act, produce, prompt, paint scenery, make properties, print programmes, look after the lighting, punch tickets at the box-office, scrub the floor, do anything in and about the theatre for sheer love of it, demanding neither fame nor fortune nor hope of recognition of any kind. But I have never yet found anyone who wrote good plays contentedly for the love of it, without hope of fame, or money, or social advancement, or the training that would ultimately bring these commodities. The very existence of the law of copyright shows that while everything else connected with the theatre may be a pleasure, the writing of plays is regarded as a form of activity demanding a reward so consistently that the State has to be called upon to enforce payment. The British Drama League, which refuses amateur status to actors receiving fees, even if these are less than the expenses entailed, does not even envisage the possibility of a playwright refusing to be paid. It is, of course, conceivable that the genuine amateur playwright does lurk modestly somewhere—exclusive of the waiving of rights to a charity, the experimental adventure, or the gratuitous performance of a play which would have no money value anyhow. But the fact just stands that the amateur playwright has both officially and in my own experience no existence. I am going to leave it at that. If a reason needs to be suggested, I should say that acting is at once the pursuance of a natural instinct, flattering to self-love, and a healthful and often delightful recreation, and that the other practical activities I have mentioned can be capital fun. On the other hand, the supplying of ideas, characters, and dialogue without getting any credit for it would be living by proxy and looking into happiness through other men's eyes.

My own private view of the amateur stage is that it includes all that is done for joy in the work itself, and not for exploitation. I should include many enterprises which do not come authoritatively under the amateur label—part-time repertory companies, for instance, like those of the Maddermarket at Norwich and of the Bath Citizen House Players. These semi-amateur repertory companies have been, and still are, immensely important seeding-grounds for the new professional theatre now springing to life again everywhere after the temporary deluge of cinema and radio competition. In my opinion—not unsupported, I think, by that of most watchers of the town and country stage—they represent the most vital element of all in the creative life of the theatre of our time.

As with every other section of theatrical life the amateur stage developed enormously and was of infinite use during the Second Great War. Wherever the Forces were stationed there was an undoubted drawing-together of the professional and the amateur. With performances by units in the jungle and the desert, in Indian palaces and on board ship, there was obviously little to choose between the amateur who would have been a professional if he had stayed in civil life, and the professional who was perforce for the time being an amateur. In Britain itself the extent to which close on 200 repertory theatres and the new civic theatres at Bradford, Cheltenham, and elsewhere, were founded upon amateur effort is beyond calculation. So far as criticism is concerned, no amateur worth his or her salt would wish to be judged by anything but a professional standard. The critic, on the other hand, should obviously know how to be instructive and inspiring without being disheartening. As a matter of fact, I have found that for the amateur actor and actress an accomplished amateur critic is peculiarly suited—it is an excellent way to learn the craft, as Walkley found—and the amateur critic, having nothing to lose, seldoms errs on the side of leniency. But alas!—the amateur critic worthy of the name is almost as rare as the amateur dramatist!

ROUTINE WORK

In the pre-War days of the actor-manager the amateur stage was, as many of us remember only too well, almost wholly imitative and therefore hardly worth critical notice. We had a galaxy of accepted dramatists on the professional stage—very occasionally added to by some managerial "discovery"—whose plays were regularly produced at appropriate West-End theatres, then went on tour, were finally "released" for amateur performance, and were duly presented by a cluster of well-known amateur clubs. This routine phase of amateur play production is by no means dead. Though the actor-manager is no more, the ever-growing number of amateur "Dramatic and Operatic Societies" belonging to banks and business houses still rush for every successful musical play and popular comedy as it becomes available. They still keep up the traditions of Gilbert and Sullivan, and afford a stable income to the author of any old play which has a long cast of fairly equal and easy character parts. We have not done with *Tilly of Bloomsbury* yet!

All this is very harmless and I think on the whole beneficial. It interests vast numbers of young folk in the theatre. As a critic, however, I cannot pretend that I want to spend my scanty spare time seeing well-meaning but necessarily indifferent echoes of successes which have already registered themselves. There is no new idea to write about in them. With all the goodwill in the world, one has more important things to do than to implant possibly vain hopes in the breast of this or that estimable young person by saying that he—or she—bears a remote likeness to some familiar original.

The outlook is altogether different in regard to the creative amateur, who has been responsible for nearly everything that is worth while on our present-day stage. From Stanislavsky and the Moscow Art Theatre, Antoine's Théâtre Libre, the New York Theatre Guild, and our own Independent Theatre and Stage Society—amateur in spirit for all their professional casts—to the host of organizations now gathered under the British Drama League's banner, what our stage and the stage of the world owes to work that has been done without thought of profit is incalculable. In a class by itself must be set the revolution occasioned in every kind of classic production by that really great man of our period, Mr. William Poel. I often feel we do not sufficiently recognize to what an extent it should be a matter of pride to all concerned in present-day theatrical art just that they have been his contemporaries.

CREATIVE AMATEURS

It is in the fostering of amateur creation of this order that criticism has had and still has a great task to perform. Take Mr. Poel, for instance, and the productions of his Elizabethan Stage Society, which happened to coincide with my early days as a critic. From the standpoint of popular interest—a standpoint which some modern newspapers regard with a kind of statistical reverence, apportioning their attention in exact ratio to the numbers present—they were of no value whatever. Here were a few hundred rather crankish people gathered in a City hall seeing performances utterly at variance with every canon of popular attractiveness, in a dim light and to the accompaniment of obsolete musical instruments. If there had been no critics impelled to let the world know that at the back of it all was something which was right where everything else was wrong, nothing more would have happened.

Happily, however, a few critics were so impressed that they defied their own professional interests by writing quite a deal about Mr. Poel. The result was that, though he himself benefited not at all—not being of an exploitatory turn of mind—his ideas gradually spread. He proved, in a phrase actually used by Granville-Barker, "good to steal from." So did Gordon Craig —whom I would include in my encomiums were it not that I know he would resent ferociously being referred to as having anything to do with "amateurs." Among others Reinhardt was inspired by both Craig and Poel to make profitable havoc of accepted conventions in theatres little and big. So it came about that although only a comparative handful of enthusiasts saw those early productions of Poel and Craig—Poel's were presented at an average cost of £150 each, much of which came out of his own pockets—no Shakespearean or classic production of any kind would be tolerated nowadays which does not owe some quality to them.

THE MIRACLE PLAY

This is not only in the theatre. The Poel production of *Everyman*—till then only known to scholars—by an entirely amateur company in Charterhouse churchyard, was taken round the country and to America by Sir Philip Ben Greet. It established a modern "miracle-play" tradition, which made C. B. Cochran's great show at Olympia possible, and has had recent fruit in such exquisite things as Charles Claye's *Joyous Pageant of the Holy Nativity* (another wholly amateur production), played to crowded audiences in every kind of building, from cathedral to music-hall. Incidentally, through the comparative accident of supplying a handy title to the late Joseph Dent for his already contemplated library, Mr. Poel's re-discovery of *Everyman* after five centuries added a new "household word" to the language.

In none of these achievements can critics claim the credit for initiative. But even granted the utmost determination on the part of men like Poel and Craig the work could never have gone on without critical encouragement. There is also this to be remembered. Though the playgoing world in general saw very little of Mr. Poel's efforts—or of Craig's for that matter—a standard of taste had been created among the critics themselves. However much one disagreed with some things—such as the appearance of girls in men's characters, which could hardly be excused by the contrary practice on Shakespeare's stage—every Poel production was an inextinguishable memory to all who saw it. Whether wholly satisfactory or not each one was an event in their artistic lives. In this way, ever since, no one has been able to present a stupid and mangled spectacular hash by way of a Shakespearean revival and "get away with it."

I need not, assuredly, go through the long list of all the amateur movements that have owed their wider influence upon the theatre in general to intelligent and sympathetic criticism. One way or another the revealing of practically every new vista that has opened, and is opening yet, has been due to this *entente* between the creative amateur and such critics as are not content with the mere recording of self-evident success. It was so from the early days of the Independent Theatre to the arrival of Shaw as a "commercial dramatist." It was so from the starting of the little amateur group which foreran the Abbey Theatre in Dublin to the presenting of Synge's *Playboy of the Western World* and O'Casey's *Juno and the Paycock*. It was so from the founding of the Mermaid Society by a critic, Philip Carr, to its direct outcome in Sir Nigel Playfair's management at the Lyric, Hammersmith. In all of these and countless other enterprises that began with faith and led—some of them—to fortune, the apostolate of critics has been undeniable.

PIONEERS AND THE PRESS

It is happening still all over the country, wherever there is an amateur or semi-amateur theatre doing the kind of work those pioneers of other days set in front of them. But it is not happening to the extent that one would wish. This is partly because dramatic endeavour—above all amateur endeavour—is getting more and more localized, while newspaper interest is being more and more centralized. I often feel that the more adventurous kind of amateur theatre in a provincial town has a much harder struggle than it need, because the local newspapers have not the hold they used to have and do not pay the same amount of attention to the theatre. Again and again I have been impressed by this on journeying to a provincial town to see a performance of genuine importance from an artistic point of view. I have opened the local paper and have found columns and columns of palpable "blurb" about stale American films, which have already been done to death elsewhere and have no local bearing whatever. I have often found hardly a line about some native product of the theatre—a thing, possibly, of beauty and of genius.

LOCAL CRITICISM

It is difficult to know how this state of affairs is to be remedied. The fault may be—and I am afraid often is—that of the newspapers themselves. Some of them are certainly run on unenlightened principles. At the same time I feel that it is often due to a lack of recognition on the part of the theatre's own management of the importance of local criticism. I have known young theatre-managers—especially those who have not experienced what it is to rough it with a small touring company—settle in a town and imagine that the local Pressmen are going to form a worshipping choir immediately and of their own accord. This is, it must be emphasized, not their habit. Before these "chartered libertines" show respect their tendency is to demand respect. If the editors themselves can be wooed and won to forget the inevitable commercial preponderance of other attractions, well and good. It has been done miraculously in some instances. But even when the local critic is a young fellow whose knowledge is assumed rather than acquired, it is for the manager to go down on his knees and thank Heaven fasting for a good journalist's love. The junior reporter is never to be despised. He may be proprietor in a year or two. At the worst he also can learn—and like it.

When all else fails there is no questioning the value of the critical programme—or theatre magazine—though I see no reason why this should be entirely devoted to "fan" biographies, as it practically always is in this country. The precedent of Lessing is rarely followed, except in some University magazines, where we do get a certain amount of candid analysis of the play and its treatment. I myself am a great believer in amateur critics for amateur actors. But the theatre magazine cannot, and never will, replace the unhampered criticism of an independent newspaper. This is preferable not only because it is in a position to administer reproof but because it can dare to be far more outspoken in its praise. Strange though it may seem, the older and more powerful and experienced the critic the kinder he generally is. The best arrangement is when a little body of theatre-folk and local critics are all working and dreaming and hoping together, moved by a common bond of love of the theatre and of their native or adopted home. It leads to that pride in common achievement which is one of the chief delights in theatre-work of all kinds. This was one of the happy characteristics of the old Horniman days in Manchester. Beneath all the grime of the black-faced old city one felt that it was good "in that dawn to be alive." In the circumstances, how easy to forgive an apparent forgetfulness that what Manchester thought to-day England had thought some three-hundred-odd years before!

Those joyous memories throw a certain light upon a question which is often put to me, as to whether it is advisable for critics and actors and producers to meet together, or whether they should be kept, as it were, in separate cells, tapping at the wall to let each other know that someone is there. Of course, all that idea about isolation is sheer nonsense. It is generally a mere excuse invented to avoid having to meet an unwelcome personality. Nothing that conduces to love and knowledge of the theatre can possibly do any harm. The notion has sometimes been put forward on the ground that the critic must keep his judgment clear from all favouritism or its opposite. Stuff and nonsense! This fallacy about impersonal judgment I have already dealt with in some detail. I need only repeat here that judgment—in the law-court sense, as if the actor or dramatist had committed a crime—is the experienced and able critic's easiest, least important, and least effective task. What is good will be good, what is bad will be bad, and what is indifferent will remain indifferent, whatever he says to the contrary effect.

FALSE THEORY

It has been said that when one knows the player off the stage illusion is destroyed. A futile theory! It argues simply lack of ability on the part of the actor and of imagination on the part of the critic. Could one get a finer proof of illusion than Lamb's description of the art of Munden—of Munden who "stood wondering, among the commonplace materials of life, like primeval man with the sun and stars about him"? In Lamb's immortal essay—and Lamb had been a professional dramatic critic on the *Morning Post*—Munden is transfigured to an extent probably out of all proportion to his real merits as a comedian. These were considerable but not superhuman. The same thing happened with Deburau in Jules Janin's monograph, where we are told that when Deburau put up his coat-collar his critic felt that it was raining. But Lamb was an intimate crony of Munden's, who had caused an exhilarating mug of beer to be passed through the orchestra to Charles, his friend. Janin and Deburau were on terms of equally close acquaintance.

The critics, players, and dramatists who have been quoted as most rigorous in their choice of friends have been, to my knowledge, the opposite in reality. Archer used openly to boast of keeping away from actors; but to those he liked he was a devoted comrade and he owed much to them, both in ideas and practical help. Irving did not cultivate the society of young paragraphists in his later years, but he loved talking up to any hour of the night with his old critical friends.

So, too, with the theory that criticisms should not be read by their subjects. This also comes in most handily for an actor or dramatist or producer who has read every word but would rather it were not known that he had. All asseverances must, in courtesy, be taken at their face value; but, let him tell the truth or not, the man who is not keen and human enough to go to bed with his notices is not likely to be of much use in the theatre, or out of it.

ADVICE TO INTENDING CRITICS

Having tried to suggest the usefulness of good criticism to the theatre, I must now approach the most ticklish task of all. I must try to express the value of the theatre to the journalist, and, if possible, proffer some morsels of advice to the young playgoer who wants to take up dramatic criticism professionally.

I have found among young friends a remarkable desire to go in for dramatic criticism as a profession. There is, of course, the obvious notion that it is a wholly pleasurable calling. Some of them think that there is no work entailed, no experience called for, no responsibility—that it is just having a good time and being paid for it. These fallacies I have, I hope, sufficiently dealt with elsewhere. But there are more serious spirits to whom dramatic criticism appeals as one of the new and important vocations. There are many young men and women to whom the theatre revealed itself in the war-years as something entirely new—a great and living art, likely to become more so, and one to which they would be prepared to devote their lives in whatever capacity their abilities find a suitable outlet. It may mean something that the universities are beginning to wake up, and a Chair of Drama at Oxford was suggested, ironically enough, by a trip of its delegates to America at the expense of Sir Alexander Korda, the film-magnate!

It would be easy, of course, to answer such a demand with the hackneyed old rejoinder that the "intending critic" would do best to intend nothing of the kind. But this, I am afraid, is not my attitude. I myself have devoted the better part of a lifetime to the work. Though there are many things in my career that I regret, this choice is not one of them. As a branch of journalism, dramatic criticism has an outlook upon both Life and Art together afforded by no other. Partly, perhaps, for that reason, it has employed some of the finest minds ever devoted to the service of newspapers. I say "newspapers" advisedly; for I must start with a note of warning to those young people—and how many they are!—who want to begin at the end. They want to rush into "volume form." They would air opinions before they have had the experience which can alone make those opinions of any great value. They are apt to look with the impatience of youth upon what they consider "mere journalism." Such must be told frankly that, whatever future they contemplate, unless they are ready to learn how to be competent journalists and to take a pride in being so, they had better leave dramatic criticism—as a profession—alone.

It is all very well to talk of essays in periodicals, of collected excerpts, and of footnotes to biography. These have their rightful place on the desk and bookshelf, together with speeches, sermons, table-talk, and a mass of other accidental literature. I myself have found the writing of books on all kinds of subjects pleasant and profitable. The re-publishing of newspaper criticism itself, when it is spontaneously demanded, is a valuable recognition. But in the main the one thing that matters practically to the theatre and to the critic as a professional man is active and accredited newspaper embassage. Nearly all the critics whose work has been worth putting into covers—from Lamb and Hazlitt onwards—learned their job as newspaper representatives. This is largely because criticism of the stage must be focused at a particular time, upon which a whole crowd of influences are concentrated. In this it differs from that of books and pictures. They can be treated just as well—if not better—centuries after. With them the critic does not need to catch, and react to, an effect which can only arrive at a certain moment, in a living environment which will never happen again.

It may be said that some famous dramatic criticism is based upon memories hoarded over years. I have failed, however, to find a single instance in which anything more than a dim, scrappy reminiscence is supplied by these belated and isolated pronouncements. When they are of any use, they are nearly always the ultimate form of ideas which had first registered themselves, and been duly set down, long before. Even if this were not so, I should be sorry to advise any young man to go in for professional criticism with no other hope than that of leaving behind him tributes to a remote past, or of publishing these when he is in his dotage. The odds are that they would never be published at all. He would have died of starvation meanwhile.

Another difficulty is with the equally large, if not still larger, number of young people who want to be critics just so that they may become playwrights. Here example is a little divided. There are undoubtedly some, though comparatively few, good playwrights who have also been good critics. These tempt us to forget the many indifferent critics who have been indifferent playwrights, and might have done much better in either vocation if they had begun with it and stuck to it. The problem must, I think, be allowed to solve itself. Nothing will stop a man of real creative genius—or, indeed, anybody else—from writing plays. It is good and natural that this should be so. The successful dramatist's reward is so great that something must be radically wrong about anyone concerned with writing and the stage who does not make the attempt early in his or her career. Walkley used to aver that he had never written a play; but this was with a twinkle of the eye, and he never said that he had never tried. In later life, as a busy and well-paid official, he simply had not the time. Shaw was an acted and well-known dramatist long before he became a dramatic critic. Archer was writing plays all his life—not to his immediate advantage, in spite of his luck at the finish. I remember talking with the late James Welch in his dressing-room on the first night of the afterwards successful farce, *When Knights Were Bold.* The play was not going too well. He put this down to the apathetic demeanour of the critics present. "I know those —— critics," he exclaimed, shaking his fist in the direction of the auditorium; "disappointed dramatists, every man jack of them!"

PLAYWRIGHTS

Allowing for some heated exaggeration, the taunt had at that time a basis of truth. But I do not think it would hold good to anything like so great an extent now. At most, not more than three new plays were then produced in the West End each week; so that dramatic criticism for a single paper could not be described as a whole-time occupation, and salaries were commensurately small. Nowadays, with a new play nearly every night and often more of them than one, a dramatic critic has at least twice as much work to do as he used to have. Also, without any fabulous prospects, a moderate living is to be made out of it. This being so, only fierce ambition, extreme toil, and miraculous versatility can couple the writing of good plays and of good, regular, everyday criticism. Even when the double event is achieved, one or the other—if not both—must suffer. It is possible, to be sure, for the dramatist with critical experience to keep on writing articles and book-reviews, as do Mr. St. John Ervine and Mr. Ashley Dukes. But both of these old colleagues of mine were tentative dramatists before they were critics, and both have wisely given up the daily practice of criticism.

So I would say to the young man who looks upon criticism just as a stepping-stone to playwriting, that he has got things the wrong way round. If he has not yet made a vigorous start at playwriting, no amount of critical practice will ever light the creative spark. He must recognize, like many good and even great men, that he was not born to be a dramatist. If, in these circumstances, he still goes into criticism with the idea that it will, by some sort of magic, change him into one, he will only meet with frustration and probable unhappiness.

If, on the other hand, he has already begun to turn out plays of even the faintest promise and is conscious of power to write more, a spell of criticism may help. But even then he will have to reckon with the more and more exacting and competitive labours of modern newspaper life. There is considerable danger that he may not be able to get out from what will seem to him drudgery to do the work he wants to do. I have seen this happen. It is, if anything, a more painful spectacle than the other. For the born dramatist, the stage itself seems to me a much better training-ground than criticism, especially as modern repertory theatres offer chances more varied than any known to the elder generation, so many of whose young people had to eat their hearts out in everlasting tours of third-rate melodramas. The experience to be got in helping to stage a round of classics with a struggling semi-amateur company is likely to be more useful to the budding dramatist than anything he will learn in a newspaper office, which will tend to make him—as it should—a critic instead. The all-important thing for him, either way, is that there should be as many outlying adventures between whiles, at home and abroad, as he has pluck to enter upon. The less literary these are, so much the better.

THE BORN CRITIC

I can come now to that curiously rare personage—the man or woman who is a born dramatic critic—that is to say, a born journalist with a love of, and instinct for, the theatre, untainted with personal vanity or idle delusions of other kinds. To anyone who answers this description and needs to know how to become a dramatic critic, there is no question as to the first essential. It is that he should make himself an expert newspaper-man. The difference between the competent critic and the amateur is not that he goes to theatres and sees plays. Everybody does that. It is that he is able to turn out on the spot —or at an office immediately afterwards—a clear, bright, and accurate assessment, which has an interest and character and entertainment-value of its own and is something that everyone will want to read. He must be at once lively and judicious, and be so at break-neck speed and with every sentence and paragraph formulated as it comes to an exact number of words. This rapid blending of character and truth, the seizing of salient points, and the exercise of imagination capable of conveying ideas into immediate print cannot be managed without experience. How is that experience to be got?

NEWSPAPER WORK

My own feeling is that by far the best way for the young would-be critic to find this experience is by taking the theatre for granted and beginning with general newspaper work. The all-round journalist who is, and is known to be, keen about the theatre will get his opportunity long before the exclusively theatrical student. He will also be more likely to make good with it than the man who has still to acquire a sense of proportional values and other instinctive promptings which come naturally to the trained mind and hand. I myself went through the provincial "mill"; and owe an incalculable deal to it. I had done practically everything on the editorial side of newspapers, both in town and country, before I was given my first appointment as dramatic critic for a London daily. It was on the strength of a notice of the first performance of Forbes-Robertson's *Hamlet* at the Lyceum, written from the third row standing behind the gallery. Granted wide reading and ardent playgoing—without which there would be no hope for him at all—I do not think the intending critic who takes the trouble to be a journalist first need fear missing a few seasons of specialized theatrical knowledge. This will come soon enough. I can assure him that after twenty or thirty years he will find that he knows, if anything, too much. To keep young of heart and in sympathy with the supposed new movements which are always cropping up he will have to be constantly deciding what it is best to pretend to have forgotten.

I am often asked whether a university training is a good thing for an intending critic. Of course it is. It is so particularly just now, when not only Oxford and Cambridge, but London University and others, are paying a remarkable amount of attention to the theatre, both officially and otherwise. I do not believe in specializing too early. The groundwork—classical and modern—must be broad and thorough. All the lectures on dramatic theory—inspiring though they may sometimes be—will not replace sound scholarship and the mastery of at least three languages. Meanwhile, to be in the swim of the theatre-"groups" is a great thing. The Oxford University Dramatic Society and kindred amateur clubs elsewhere have borne notable fruit among critics as well as among actors and dramatists. They will, I think, do so still more. It is to be remembered, however, that journalism has to be learned afterwards just the same, with or without a university degree. This is the shock in store. The undergraduate essay, with its parade of borrowed views, its assumption of knowledge, and its fear of expressing sincere and simple-hearted enthusiasm, is generally an exact example of how dramatic criticism should not be written.

SINCERITY

We will suppose, then, that some young friend has been to a university, has had some drilling in journalism, has gone about the world just as much as his pocket and temperament have made possible, and is being given his chance in the theatre. Some little hints born of long service may be useful. The chief of these is that he should resist any temptation to sneer, or to court cheap notoriety by those spiteful epigrams which are so easily concocted. They help nobody. They do not instruct old playgoers or make new ones. In the end they are certain to bring their revenges upon the critic himself. At the same time absolute candour, sincerity, and independence are essential. I have always remembered the dictum of one of my earliest and most respected editors. "Say just what you like, my boy," he used to tell me, "so long as you sincerely think it and have reason for the faith that is in you. I don't mind who it is you go for. All I ask is that you should be glad if the play is a good one and sorry if it is not." How natural and reasonable a point of view it seems! Yet I have again and again known young critics—and not only young ones—hailing some ghastly failure with delight as giving them scope for throwing paper-pellets with impunity. This sort of thing only gets dramatic criticism into disrepute without betraying an attractive personality in the critic.

More than any other—on account of its vitally practical effect—dramatic criticism should be constructive rather than destructive. If destruction is deserved, criticism is all the more deadly in its power when it is known that the critic is a true lover of the theatre and not given to unnecessary attack. By constructive criticism I mean that which encourages good and struggling work, builds up reputations by persistent interest, interprets ideas that might be misunderstood, creates in the reader a wish for what is best in the theatre, and offers the suggestion of new possibilities. Young critics may be warned against a kind of "constructive" criticism which is boring to everybody and of no use to the theatre. This is the bringing in of niggling and purely technical matters—little points of setting, construction, or stage-management which would often be far better dealt with in a letter to, or talk with, the producer, playwright, or actor. This is the besetting sin of many young academic critics, desirous of revealing a nascent understanding of playcraft. I have always found it well to keep in mind that in the newspaper one is writing not for the theatrical manager but for the public, most of whom will not even see the play and are only confused by contention over trifles.

IMPRESSIONISTIC OR INFORMATIVE?

To those who have practised dramatic criticism for any length of time there is a very plain answer to the long-vexed question as to whether it should be impressionistic or informative. It must be both. I have no patience with some current criticism which purports to be so exclusively impressionistic that it conveys no idea of what the play is about, whether or not it is worth seeing, what kind of production it is, or who appeared in it and in what characters. This is not criticism. It is just tomfoolery. It lives only in circumstances definitely hostile to the theatre.

The older I grow the more I find it advisable and possible to rely on my own sub-conscious impressions. I have found these to be always right, as against any argued or external representation to the contrary. I do not believe in thinking out my notice during the play—as so many have to do. I believe in being an absolutely natural playgoer up to the fall of the curtain; then, an absolutely unnatural journalist. With impressions collected, good journalism demands that one should be just as informative as time and space permit.

I have a great belief in telling "the story." This is not, however, as so many think, "the story of the play"; but a story of one's own choosing and forming and telling, corresponding to that of the play but entirely different in its emphasis. One cannot set it down too strongly that the incidents of a play are not events. They never happened; and a record of them is the dullest of dull reading. What has happened is that a certain number of people have gathered together and, by the arts of the dramatist, actor, designer, and musician, should have been moved to various emotions and, perhaps, have received some intellectual enlightenment. This achievement—or lack of it—is what the critic has to convey before he can do anything else. His story has to suggest in a few lines, to a cold and unprepared reader, an effect it has taken the people on the stage three hours to produce.

This may seem a humble beginning of dramatic criticism; but, as a matter of fact, the expression of a play in its quiddity is as difficult as it is important. The young critic who has learnt to do this one little thing well is already far from being a useless monopolist of the newspaper office's complimentary pleasures.

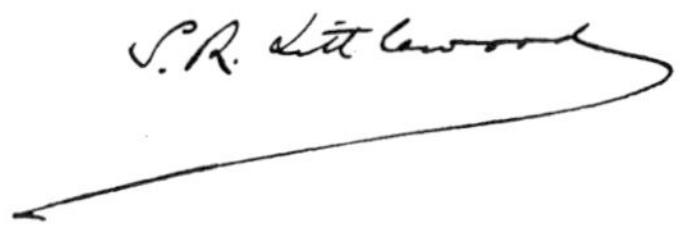

D

DANCING, BALLET

- THE DANCER
- THE CHOREOGRAPHER
- PRACTICAL POINTS IN BALLET PRODUCTION

DANCING, STAGE

- THE DANCER AND HER AUDIENCE
- LIGHTER FORMS OF DANCING
- OPERA—CABARET—COMPETITIONS
- THE GOVERNANCE OF THE DANCE IN ENGLAND

DRAMA AS EDUCATION

- THE STUDY OF ACTED DRAMA
- AUTHENTIC DRAMA OF THE THEATRE
- PLACE OF DRAMA IN SCHOOLS
- DRAMA AS A YOUTH CLUB ACTIVITY
- THE STAGE-PLAY DOCUMENTARY
- ORGANIZATION OF A PLAYWRIGHTS' CLUB
- ACTING PLAYS IN FOREIGN LANGUAGES

DRAMA IN THE CO-OPERATIVE MOVEMENT

DRAMA, RELIGIOUS

DRAMATIC TECHNIQUE

- LIMITATIONS
- THE WELL-MADE PLAY
- SOME MODERN TENDENCIES
- THE ONE-ACT PLAY
- ON PLAYS FOR CHILDREN

Houston Rogers

MADAME MARIE RAMBERT

BALLET DANCING

ARNOLD L. HASKELL, Author of " Ballet: A complete guide to appreciation "

INTRODUCTION

Madame MARIE RAMBERT

LOOKING back upon the glories and achievements of the Russian Ballet it would be an easy thing to say that with the death of Diaghileff ballet itself died. Indeed, in its final days his ballet showed none of the signs of vitality that mark a living art. Pure dancing, the life of ballet, was too often sacrificed to unsuitable music and startling decorative effect, beguiling the mind and diverting attention from the essential art. The quality of dancing must necessarily deteriorate as ballet relies more and more for its effect on music and décor: the result is a vicious circle. Diaghileff possessed such extraordinary personal gifts that to the end he could still present works with an excellent semblance of significance, to be criticized only by appealing to the earlier Diaghileff. But with his death the position changed. No one could continue his work without his prestige, above all without his wizardry in binding music and décor to some conception always just a little ahead of general experience. The hope for ballet in our day—it has had lean periods before—is to concentrate on the pure art of dancing, leaving aside complications of theme and presentation. Here Diaghileff himself showed the way by the knowledge he has given us of the greatest of choreographers, Petipa. We must not confound the glamour and lavish presentation of such ballets as "Swan Lake" and "The Sleeping Princess" with their essential simplicity of intention. They are conceived solely for the glory of the dancer, to reveal beauty in line and movement; the music is easy to grasp; the costumes increase the beauty of movement and line. Strip them of glamorous presentation, change ballet dress for practice frock, use piano for orchestra, the beauty still remains, so that the performer gains new power at every rendering and the artist who can execute this is master of every type of dance. To save ballet we must gain this idea of dancing as the art in itself, apart from costume, and even from music. In the past, when ballet was at a low ebb, it was saved by the art and appeal of some individual dancer who gave it new direction: the fame of Taglioni made the male dancer a mere lifter of his partner until Nijinsky showed the glory the male role could be. A choreographer can only work through the dancers he has at hand. To return to simplicity of idea combined with perfection of technical execution may be to mark time, but it is all that can be done until the new direction is revealed from its natural source in the inspiration of the dancers themselves.

Another important factor is that the theatrical public undergoes a process of training parallel with that of the performers. In Russia the audience was highly trained to appreciate the most subtle technical distinctions between its favourites: it was out of the question that personal charm should cover imperfect technique. The audience knew in detail the classic ballet of Petipa, and its appreciation was trained by seeing the set dances of his work executed by many different artists. Diaghileff had behind him all the tradition of the Maryinsky Theatre, but out of Russia his progress was too rapid and his visits to each capital too brief to train an expert audience. Moreover, no guidance was given by the Press, for ballet was reviewed by music or art critics who naturally emphasized their own interests at the expense of the whole.

Ballet will live if sound dancing lives, so that if anything is to be sacrificed to the economic needs of the moment it must not be the dancing. It is, indeed, perfectly easy to conceive of dancing, of movement, as an independent art that requires neither costume nor music to set it off. Theatrically, this might be somewhat arid and monotonous, save to a highly-specialized audience used to the beauty of line and to the subtleties that the acting of the whole body can express, but it is perfectly logical and understandable. It is that conception that the present-day dancer must bear in mind, a sense of power in what he can do, and not the feeling that may so easily arise, that it is not worth while continuing without a full symphony orchestra and a gorgeous setting à la Bakst. This does throw a greater onus on the dancer, concentrate all the attention on him, but it also gives him greater opportunities.

I wrote the foregoing in October, 1933, *when the most enthusiastic supporter of English Ballet would not have dared to predict the events of the ensuing years. At that time the first season of the de Basil Ballets Russes at the Alhambra had just come to a triumphal conclusion, and our own native ballet was beginning to find its feet. No one could then have foretold how firmly ballet was to establish itself in this country so that its popularity to-day is greater than it has ever been during its whole history. Even more important than the dancers who have emerged during this period is the fact that English Ballet has produced its own choreographers and designers.*

We may well be proud of what has been achieved, and "the economic needs of the moment" no longer govern every step in our progress. But standards remain the same, and we must still remember that it is ballet itself that matters, not all the trimmings and trappings in which it may be set.

For this reason knowledgeable and level-headed criticism becomes more and more important, and, properly directed, can be of the greatest use both to the ballet and the ballet public.

At the time this article was first written, I was asked to introduce Mr. Arnold L. Haskell's series, "Theatrical Dancing." He was the first critic in England to write about ballet with a full knowledge and, moreover, love of his subject. To-day his name is too well-known among ballet-goers for me to need to introduce him again.

Marie Rambert.

THE DANCER

The writer on dancing is handicapped over the writer on any other branch of theatrical art in the ability to make himself clear by the fact that it is not possible as with the drama to quote from a text or to indicate dramatic action or even gesture and movement, save in technical language that would only prove illuminating to the professional. Dancing, like the English law, is built up on precedent and tradition, so that it is constantly necessary to refer to such and such an artist or such and such a ballet. Dancing is a plastic art and no amount of reading can replace watching the practice of it. My sole object, therefore, is to supplement the knowledge of those who have seen but a few performances, and by a careful analysis to provide them with certain critical standards, and I hope with a keener enjoyment of a great and intricate art, that it is so easy to misunderstand or not to understand at all.

ARNOLD HASKELL, FROM THE DRAWING BY CECILE WALTON
Courtesy Drummond Young

Dancing, perhaps more than any other art, is dependent upon tradition, especially the particular branch of dancing, known as ballet, which is the subject of this study. While in the whole of dramatic art tradition is valuable, in the art of ballet it is vital, for although there are many known methods, chiefly German at the present day, of keeping a written record of a ballet, very much in the manner of a musical score, in actual practice this has rarely been done owing to its immense technical difficulties, and works have been handed down from generation to generation by memory. The ballet "Giselle," for instance, the oldest in any current repertoire, was first presented at the Paris Opera in 1832 and was revived in London in 1932, where it was put on by the old Russian *maître de ballet* Sergéef, who carried it in his memory. It must have undergone changes, and each successive ballerina who undertook this most brilliant of roles has undoubtedly left something of herself in it; Grisi and her contemporaries, Karsavina, Pavlova, and finally Spessiva. And yet from the evidence of old prints and contemporary records it has come down to us practically unchanged, Pavlova alone making one startling innovation by appearing in a Greek tunic in the second act instead of the customary tarlatan. I shall make it my aim in this study to keep on practical topics the whole time, but, as I have shown, tradition in ballet is essential and is certainly practical and relevant. I shall have to make frequent historical allusions in order to trace the origins of the dance as we know it to-day. Every dancer is something of an antiquarian and historian. Every dancer loves those quaint early Victorian prints of Taglioni, Grisi, Grahn, Cerrito, Elssler, and their peers. This is not sentimentality, but something much stronger and finer, something that has kept alive a costly and highly complex art in the most trying times. Dancing can no more die than can walking or running, but ballet, its most highly developed form technically, is in constant danger. There are still some who question whether the ballet form is worth preserving at all, and it has certainly suffered under the onslaughts of movements from Germany that have invaded the school curriculum, though no forms of dancing could be more unsuitable educationally. I shall avoid controversy or the expression of any too personal opinion, but in its proper place I shall give the full case for ballet, both as an art and as a training, as against Greek dancing, the modern dance, and various "natural" methods. In any case I shall deal with ballet first and at considerable length, because practically every form of stage dancing at the present day is born from it, and our interest is in the theatre, rather than in the concert hall or the village green.

I shall first deal with a subject common to all dancing, "The Dancer and Her Attributes," with the economics of dancing, the position of the male dancer, and finally with the dancer's mission. I shall then leave the performer to discuss ballet and its composition, and I shall try to situate it in the arts. Before leaving ballet I shall trace its moods and developments through the last century. Every other topic that I shall discuss after that, acrobatic dancing, musical comedy, or the advanced modern schools, will have a direct bearing on what has gone before. In my analysis of choreography ("the art of creating movement in ballet") I shall make use of much material that has been put at my disposal

Tamara Karsavina in "Petrouchka"

by Fokine, creator of so many dance masterpieces. This material, hitherto unpublished, is of immense value not only on account of Fokine's genius but because of the position he occupies halfway between the old and the new. It will show clearly the artistic genesis of the Russian ballet, admittedly the peak of theatrical dancing.

THE DANCER AND HER ATTRIBUTES

In our first consideration, before we go into any detail, either historical or actual, or discuss different schools of dancing, we are on common ground. The dancer, whether in ballet, concert or music hall, requires much the same attributes. There are certain questions that I as a critic of dancing invariably ask myself when I see a dancer for the first time. The answer to those questions will give us certain critical standards.

The first vital point is the dancer's body. Just as in passing judgment on a violinist it would be perfectly legitimate criticism to say that it was impossible to judge of his merits as the tone of his instrument was too bad, so with the dancer it would be perfectly legitimate to say: "Miss X may have good technique and plenty of feeling, but we could not judge, for she is bow-legged, her back is far from straight, and she squints." I purposely mentioned the squint because I feel that facial beauty is a real consideration in stage dancing. I remember an old *balletomane* saying to me once: "I always look at their faces. I can invariably tell a good dancer that way." It was, of course, a paradox, but there was an element of truth in it. A fine head and neck, well set on the shoulders and carried with dignity, is one of the characteristics of the Russian school dancer—however brilliant the footwork it will not compensate for that. Ballet dancing should aim at complete coordination and harmony, and not at the acrobatic exploitation of footwork. While the singer aims at pleasing through the ear, she may and often does look unprepossessing; the dancer's appeal is to the eye, and therefore looks are essential. It is remarkable, however, to what an extent the ballet training improves the whole physical appearance. I can remember one of our finest dancers as a bandy-legged child whose sole object in taking up dancing was to rectify this defect; she started at eight years old and by thirteen she was so expert that Serge Diaghileff took her into his company and roles were created for her. To-day she is world-famed. This shows the great value of ballet training from a remedial point of view. Only the big head is a fatal flaw, as Diaghileff invariably pointed out.

Natural grace is an essential. To many people, unused to the study of dancing, "graceful" is the indispensable adjective to "dancer." In actual fact this is by no means always the case. I very much doubt if training can provide it. For twenty dancers who can beat a perfect *entrechat*, scarcely one can walk across the stage to take up a position in a graceful or impressive manner. Training will develop natural grace, it can bluff the tyro into believing it exists where it is absent, but will never make up for it, and it is this quality that may just make the difference between two highly technical performers. Ballet training, while it gives perfect control of movement, if it is misused, frequently results in a stiffness and definite lack of grace. Great teaching preserves natural grace, poor teaching kills it.

NATURAL ATTRIBUTES

When considering personality, temperament, and intelligence we are again dealing with natural attributes, the first two of which are exceedingly difficult to define in a positive manner, but their absence is so noticeable that it may cause the first-class technician to spend all her days in the chorus, while her friend, much less good in the classroom, is entrusted with solo after solo. Personality or glamour is more than *brio*, temperament, or the American "sex appeal." It is a combination of all these, yet it contains poise and serenity. Whenever a dancer is called a second Pavlova you can be sure that she lacks it. There is no "second" possible in such a case; it is the triumph of the individual.

Many dancers arrive at their schools with individuality, and through uninspired teaching rapidly lose it, only to become part of a collective personality, a *corps de ballet*. The full expression of a personality is only possible to the finished technician. The pupil will be too worried with detail to be able to express anything at all.

One definition of personality in ballet is when the intelligence clearly commands the movements of the muscles.

Temperament is equally difficult to define in a positive manner. It does not mean the noisy stamping and handclapping of the typical pseudo-Spanish dancer or the making of "scenes" off stage. It is an aspect of personality, and I only mention it here because an accusation that you will still hear made against English dancers is that they are lacking in temperament. I disagree with this on the whole, and believe it to arise chiefly on account of the fact that tradition in England is still in its infancy, and also from a total misunderstanding of the implications of the word. The French and Italian dancers of to-day would seem far more lacking in temperament, which, used in this sense, I would define as the power, often unconscious, of being able to get across the footlights the reality of what is only a convention. Pavlova in the "Dying Swan" was a supreme example, dancing it in such a manner that one could not analyse the movements in the general feeling of sorrow. This was something far greater than acting ability. It was something inborn, the power to gain contact with an audience. I remember once the thrilling experience of watching from the wings Pavlova dancing the "Bacchanal." The proximity increased the effect, made it almost overpowering, in spite of the loss of all lighting illusions. Here was the embodiment of Bacchic youth, even in the way in which she received the plaudits when the dance had ceased; yet the moment the curtain fell and contact with the audience was cut off the transformation was startling and pathetic; all that remained was an insignificant and a weary woman, young in build but old in her expression, almost the pathetic figure in Vicki Baum's *Grand Hotel.* These then are things that are difficult to write about, and that cannot be learned, but they are the things that make the great artist, and we must understand them if we are to understand the make up of the great dance artist. They are all included in that much misused word "genius."

MUSICAL SENSE

One would imagine that the dancer would require a more than ordinarily developed sense of music. With the great virtuoso this is undoubtedly the case, but in practice with the general run of dancers it is not so. That great English dancer, Lydia Sokolova, gained her first big chance in the ballet because having been originally trained as a pianist, she was able to understand and to carry in her head the intricate counting of Ravel's *Daphnis and Chloe*, where others, who might have been assigned the part, were completely at sea. I believe that a fine musical sense, a perception that is of *tempo* and not an aesthetic appreciation, which is irrelevant here, is one of those small details, almost impossible to analyse, which make the difference between the good dancer and the great dancer; a difference that is so subtle that it would not be possible to say that the less good performer was in any sense out of time. It is just that little difference that produces in the audience the feeling of complete confidence in the performer.

Acting in dancing covers an exceedingly wide range, from a mere indication of atmosphere in such a ballet as *Les Sylphides*, where a toothy grin would destroy everything, to the definite portrayal of a sadistic Georgian queen, *Thamar*. It is important to realize at once that the acting, or mime, as it is called, is an integral part of the whole movement, the facial muscles playing their part in the dance as much as the legs or the arm muscles. In *Giselle*, for instance, there is a famous scene of insanity before the unfortunate heroine commits suicide. Now a realistic rendering of insanity, however brilliantly done, would be hopelessly out of place. Yet every time I see that particular scene I am harrowed by it as by the real thing. Pavlova's rendering of it was unforgettable; put it into the middle of a stage play where a mad scene was required, and it might well make the public laugh. Why?

Tamara Toumanova
Photo by Brewster

Because ballet is a convention, and, once that convention has been accepted, it is perfectly possible to be realistic within it, or perhaps to be more easily understandable I should have said there is ballet-truth like any other truth. Let us analyse this convention as it applies to the ballet *Giselle*. The plot is simple: the village maiden, thinking that she has been betrayed by her lover, goes mad, seizes his sword and falls on it before she can be prevented. What is the truth in life? Impossible to say; but she might well have been ugly, have had a slight squint, and a suspicion of bandy leg. She would most certainly have chosen another method of exit, in spite of the fact that gas ovens were not yet known.

What is the truth on the stage? It depends on the dramatist, but with such a subject he would most certainly never have resisted a long speech, centre of the stage, couched in language that no village maid would use in the circumstances. That also if it were competently written would have its truth.

Now the ballet convention is that people express themselves in movement, not in word, and that that expression in movement is governed entirely in *tempo* and duration by certain music that is being played, music that may possibly express something of the action, but that at this particular period most certainly did nothing more than mark the time. The whole portrayal of madness therefore must be restrained by music and by the actual dance that has been arranged; also it must be exceedingly direct and simple, because a story is being told without the use of words. The dance before the scene of madness and after is the same if described in technical terms, but the *ballerina* must suggest in the second dance that it is being performed mechanically by a brain that can no longer co-ordinate muscular movement; that it is a question of reflex and not of will. If the second dance truly contrasts with the first, then there is realism within our convention and the audience will be thrilled and moved. The acting required of the dancer, an ability that is generally missing, is perhaps at the bottom of all highly disciplined movement on the stage. The high standard of ballet acting that is sometimes required, and its extreme difficulty, can be gauged when I state that in Balanchine's *Songes*, at one moment when the *ballerina* is already on her points she must tip toe out of the room as a child does. A truly extraordinary blend of realism within our convention. The role, however, was designed for an unusually fine balletic actress, Toumanova, who succeeded to perfection. An experienced producer once told me that he would be able to produce a certain actress in a short time because she had been trained as a dancer, and so knew what to do with her hands. In the films to-day Deborah Kerr and Katherine Hepburn are clearly ballet trained. Zorina and Belita show the value of such training. All those actresses belonging to a certain generation, whom we admire on account of their "school," have had a foundation of ballet training. Also, I am firmly convinced that dancing is the essential training for film acting, and it is a noticeable fact to someone used to watching ballet that the film star has with few exceptions little conception of movement.

The whole of the theatre is a convention, and the branch known as ballet has the strictest rules. Master those rules and while you may never become a great dancer, acting, whether film or stage, will be more accessible to you.

It is impossible to discuss the role that intelligence plays in any artistic creation. I doubt whether it plays a great role. So long as the dancer is possessed of presence of mind that is all that is necessary. Emergencies are frequent, shoes slip off, costumes are torn, the stage is slippery and quick thinking is essential. The audience must never notice.

I regard general artistic knowledge and education as highly important for the dancer, and I can name dancers of some merit who have definitely failed through lack of it. The Imperial Ballet School of St. Petersburg provided a thorough general curriculum for its pupils, an education that would put to shame that of the average secondary school. The result has borne fruit all over the world to-day. The St. Petersburg and Moscow dancers, widely scattered, have been able to produce ballet, and to foster the understanding of modern art and music. They have created ballet, and not just danced in it. Fokine, Nijinsky, Massine, and others are all products of this magnificent education. The average English dancer stranded from her school would be quite incapable of arranging a dance, let alone choosing suitable music or character costume. Karsavina has told me how when preparing a romantic role she studied the literature and iconography of her subject at length in order to live it convincingly.

The average English dance pupil knows her technique reasonably well, and that is about all. Of music she will know a little Chopin, a little Delibes, and perhaps some Tchaikovsky; of painting nil, while her practical ideas on period costume will be of the vaguest. If she arranges a dance it is fairly safe to say that it will be a *pizzicato* Pierrette of sorts.

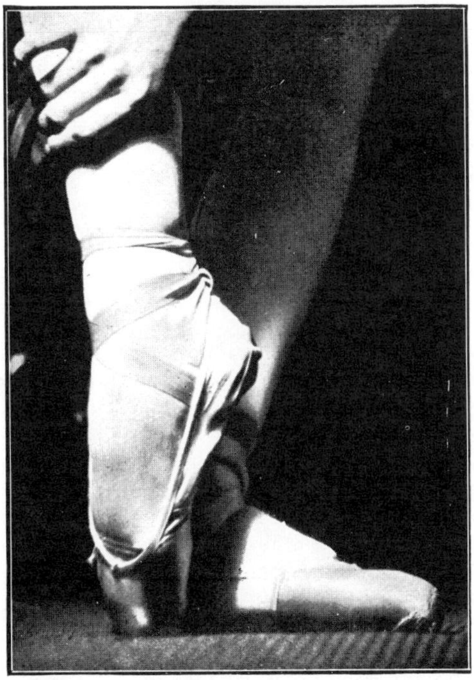

TOUMANOVA'S "POINTS"
Photo by Brewster

If the dancer is to be anything more than a machine she need have no great intelligence, but she must take an active interest in literature, music, and especially the plastic arts. This may sound far-fetched to the little girl delighted with her first clean *pirouette*, but it is vital, and it is the lack of that which is proving such a handicap to our English dancing. I have mentioned above that acting in ballet is frequently nothing more than the suggestion of atmosphere to an audience. Anything so subtle as that can scarcely come from instinct alone; it is only culture that can supply the necessary starting point. The producer may shriek at the *coryphée* in *Les Sylphides*, "Be romantic," but she will still be content with a sickly smile, which she imagines is the real thing; while all the time she requires a background of the Romantic Movement in music, literature, and painting. This is not a far-fetched statement, for in practice it has given us a Tamara Karsavina.

I would say to the young dancer that her lessons at school are as much a part of her training as the *barre*, that is if she wishes to become an artist of the dance.

As can be seen by the list, the attributes required by the dancer set such a high standard that only a few can expect to be chosen out of the many who set out. Here it is important to clear up a common misunderstanding that has been broadcast by a lay Press. I refer to the use of the term *Russian ballerina* as applied to any moderately competent dancer. In all countries where there is a dancing tradition and consequently a state opera, *ballerina* is not merely a complimentary term but denotes a special official rank gained by apprenticeship, examination, and work before the public. It will be realized how rare was this distinction when I state that in Imperial Russia, the country *par excellence* of fine dancing, there were but a handful of *prima ballerinas* at any one period; in our own times Kshesinskaya, Preobrajenska, Pavlova, Trefilova, Karsavina, and, just before the end, Spessiva. Each one of these six was so technically perfect that the subject would not even be questioned, but each had some particular distinguishing genius, which I will discuss when I come to the varying types of ballet. It is necessary to stress this point because a kindly but misinformed Press so frequently cheapens the art of dancing by making high distinction appear too frequent and easy. For every *ballerina* or dancer of genius I could name ten front-rank pianists, violinists, or actresses.

The Soviet Ballet continues the great Russian tradition.

In Britain our one undisputed *ballerina* is Margot Fonteyn, who has earned the name through her interpretation of the great classical roles in *Giselle*, *Coppélia*, *The Swan Lake*, and *Casse-Noisette*. Like most great classicists, she has a wide range that takes in Fokine romanticism as well as contemporary creations.

There is one vital thing to realize: it is more important to have a company with an artistic personality of its own than a solo star with a background. Nothing can damage ballet more than the indiscriminate worship of individuals. Fonteyn as *ballerina* is a creation of Sadler's Wells, a part of the company as well as being its brightest ornament.

THE DANCER AND HER OPPORTUNITIES

In countries such as France, Denmark, or Russia, where there is a state academy, the problems of the would-be *ballerina* are far simpler. From admission, through graduation, right up to retirement when she receives a pension, her training and livelihood are the concern of the state. In Britain it is different.

Take the child whose parents decide to turn her into a dancer. If they are prudent they will wait until she is about 8 years old or even later. The story of the necessity of intensive early training is a dangerous fallacy that is responsible for the ugly development of superfluous muscle. They will then take her to a good school and let her attend classes once or twice a week until the teacher advises them that she is sufficiently developed to attend daily. They will, if they are wise, pay great attention to her general education in the directions I have already indicated. They should most certainly take her to see as many performances of ballet as possible.

Now consider all this from a practical point of view. The cost entailed will be that of a biweekly class for two years, allowing for holidays, followed by a daily class for about two years.

After that she may be fitted to earn a living. These direct charges are inexpensive, and, moreover, no responsible teacher will turn away a really promising pupil through lack of money.

Look into a typical classroom and follow the fortunes of twenty pupils, children whose parents are full of thoughts of future Pavlovas. Of those twenty, five may get married too soon to attempt a career. Who can say whether their dancing has helped them there? Five may be utter failures, whose dancing has probably aided them in being a little more gracious in ordinary life. The other ten will go on the stage in some branch or other of the profession. One of them may find fame and fortune in musical comedy. I can remember June as the most promising pupil in the academy that produced Dolin and Markova. The majority will drift into the chorus and find really hard work but a fair living there. Occasionally in some classroom there will be a girl who is remarkably talented and ambitious to continue in ballet. Her path will be hard, the work will often be the main reward. There is but one Sadler's Wells, there are many aspirants.

This view may be a depressing one for the beginner, but I can honestly say of the many girls whose careers I have watched that there is scarcely one who has not benefited physically and materially by the training, and who is not far better equipped to take up some branch of the theatrical profession. Dancing is undoubtedly the basis of all art where disciplined gesture is required, and the film companies want girls who are able to move correctly. If the production side of the theatre is the pupil's ambition, the dancing class again, with its disciplined movement, is the right training. No one has ever been able to handle a stage crowd with greater genius than Fokine in *Petrouchka*, while Mamoulian, producer of *Porgy* and other films, has shown the value of a choreographic approach to the theatre. There is also a large future for the person who can invent a small ensemble for cabaret or music hall.

Finally, there is a class of dancer that I have not yet dealt with because she is the exception.

In England concert dancing is quite exceptional; Argentina alone has appeared with real success. Economically on paper this form of dancing should have a future, dispensing as it does with the greatest expense of all, the orchestra, but in practice it is not the case. It requires unusual gifts for an artist to keep an audience interested for a whole evening by her own unaided efforts, gifts that are somewhat outside those that I have mentioned. She must be definitely creative, with a strong literary bias, and a vast range of mood. The concert artist is all too often a dancer who seeks self-expression outside ballet discipline. For one Duncan, an undisciplined genius, there are dozens of little girls who skip about in flowing drapery banging cymbals, and whose concerts are patronized by indulgent friends and relatives. The concert dancer, in fact, is as rare as the Ruth Draper or Cornelia Otis Skinner; her art is closely related to theirs. She is born rather than made, and it is an ambition that must be dismissed at once from the mind of the pupil. The stage encourages the brilliant individual, but

ALICIA MARKOVA
Photo by Brewster

it thinks in terms of the team. The team must have its captain, but he, too, is part of a whole and is enhanced by the whole. The Pavlova of the *Dying Swan*, a concert dance, was only made possible by the Pavlova of *Giselle*, the most brilliant part of a whole of some hundred people, whose pattern led the eye to her. Also the ballet solo is so arranged that it comes to an end while the public is still entranced and awaiting more. The longest solo that I can think of lasts some four or five minutes.

THE MALE DANCER

In this economic consideration of dancing I have hitherto considered only the girl's chances. With regard to work in serious ballet, the position is much the same, with this difference, in favour of the boy pupil, that the number of male students is exceedingly small, so that there is generally work to be had for a boy that a girl of the same ability and standing could not get. This accident of numbers has all too often the most unfortunate effect of making the young male dancer so conceited that all progress in his work is rapidly at a standstill. As I write I can think of many promising careers ruined through such a cause. The damage is, however, still greater, for this inevitably

PEARL ARGYLE
Courtesy "Dancing Times"

prejudices people against the career of dancing for a man.

In the history of the ballet the male dancer fulfilled an important role until the advent of Taglioni, when he became merely a lifter, only to rise again into prominence with that genius Nijinsky.

In the hey-day of the Russian Ballet, when there existed a galaxy of brilliant women, Petipa, the first modern choreographer, rarely set a prominent dance for a male in any of his ballets, where the male merely danced to rest his partner, to lift her, and to prepare her next triumphant entrance. The male was also entrusted with grotesque character parts and national dances.

It is with the Diaghileff régime, with Fokine and Nijinsky, that we have a succession of fine male roles: The Rose, The Moor in *Petrouchka*, The Faun, the Mazurka in *Les Sylphides*, the Slave in *Sheherazade*, the Harlequin in *Carnaval*, etc. This greater predominance of the Male was fully justified by its artistic results. It gave balance and contrast. There has always been in England considerable prejudice against the male dancer on the grounds of effeminacy. The effeminate male dancer is a bad dancer. The fine male dancer must be as virile as the boxer or footballer, but, unlike either, his great strength must be hidden by graceful movement. His whole type of movement is a strong contrast to the woman's. In *Les Sylphides* it is true that he is longhaired and clad in a velvet jacket but the dance with its elevation is essentially masculine, while the clothes belong to a romantic conception. Hair was worn in that fashion in Florence at a period when men were exceedingly virile. The whole misconception is a confusion between romanticism and effeminacy. The monotony of the average pantomime ballet, where nothing but women appear, shows the absolute artistic necessity for the male. It was a stroke of genius to put the one man in *Les Sylphides* and so turn the sentimental into the romantic.

The man, too, is invariably the creator in ballet, and with the exception of Nijinska, every Russian choreographist of note has been a man: Petipa, Fokine, Nijinsky, Massine, Balanchine, all have been dancers, and without them ballet would not exist.

There is an excellent career for the virile man, the true athlete, in ballet. For the effeminate there is no place at all.

The enthusiasm of the confirmed *balletomane* may sound preposterous to the person who goes to the ballet as a light diversion after a heavy dinner, but I maintain in all seriousness that the dancer has a mission far more important than to provide light entertainment, or even the laudable one of transporting an audience temporarily. *The dancer is the finest agent for fostering and propagating the musical and decorative arts of a country that exists at the present day.* At the risk of being tedious I will give a shortened list of those famous painters and musicians, who have been made known to a wider public through the instrumentality of dancers. The list is amazing, and is eloquent testimony to the permanent value of ballet to any country. It is also significant that during the past twenty-five years ballet, which was in former years the flighty young sister of opera, has appealed to the composer far more than opera as a medium of expression.

Music. Almost all the Russian music that is so popular to-day was brought to Western Europe on the "points" of Karsavina and her colleagues; by Fokine, Nijinsky and Massine. Rimsky-Korsakov, Tcherepnin, Borodin, Igor Stravinsky, entirely a ballet discovery, Prokofiev. The French: Auric, Poulenc, Milhaud, and the English composers, Vaughan Williams (*Job*), Walton (*Façade*, *The Quest*), Lambert (*Romeo and Juliet*, *Adam and Eve*, *Pomona*, *Horoscope*), Berners (*Triumph of Neptune*, *Luna Park*, etc.), Bliss (*Checkmate* and *The Miracle in the Gorbals*), and there are many omitted for the sake of brevity.

Art. Alexandre Benois, one of the greatest theatrical designers of all time and inspirer of Bakst, who has played a role in heightening the colour scheme of theatrical and industrial art that is nothing short of revolutionary; Picasso who announced the far-reaching cubist revolution in the Ballet *Parade*, Derain, Matisse, Braque, and in fact the entire Paris School; in England, John Armstrong, Edward Wolfe, Vanessa Bell, Gwendolyn Raverat, Duncan Grant, Edward Burra, Rex Whistler, Oliver Messel, Leslie Hurry.

LEON WOIZIKOVSKI IN COTILLON

Photo by Brewster

A glance at such lists as these must make the dancer proud of his opportunities and must convince the layman that ballet is all-important, a living force in the art life of the nation.

Finally, it is necessary to stress that in order to bring about all this, a serious education is essential for the dancer since bad taste is a good deal easier to spread than good.

THE CHOREOGRAPHER

The whole success or failure of ballet depends on the delicate adjustment of those elements of which it is composed; The Music; The Décor; The Literary and Dramatic; The Dancing. Different periods have stressed one or more of these elements at the expense of the whole, with the result that ballet has come very near to extinction at times, but such is its vitality that it has lived on. In England, immediately before the advent of Diaghileff, ballet was regarded as a light after-dinner entertainment, to which one could drop in at any time, or as the poor relation of opera, which made it bearable to the unmusical and the inartistic. Yet when we look at the composition of the opera, the same as ballet save for the important substitution of the human voice for the dancing, we see how much more perfect the ballet is *in practice* as an art form. Opera is a spectacle that is designed to appeal to the ear and the eye. Theoretically and on rare occasions, it may do so, but in actual fact the singer's whole training is diametrically opposed to grace in movement or to dramatic ability within the particular convention. It must be difficult enough to find the singer with the voice for the particular role, but if her attributes must also be those I have previously discussed, it would never be possible to present an opera at all. The result is that opera is not true to its own convention, save in the rare case of a Chaliapine, while ballet is now as a rule consistent in practice as well as in theory. It took the genius of a Diaghileff to realize to the full all that ballet could contain, and to force that realization on the cultured public of Europe, so that at the present day the young composer and painter finds his inspiration in ballet rather than in opera.

For our own practical purposes here modern ballet has its beginnings with Diaghileff as the directing brain, literally the G.H.Q. of the diverse arts, Alexander Benois, and, later, Bakst for the *décor*, various romantic composers for the music, and Fokine, Karsavina, and Nijinsky for the dancing, which had already been perfected by the wonderful system of the Imperial Schools, and which was now used to its fullest advantage as part of a fine art form. If any of these partners is the predominant one it is dancing, in the sense that ballet being a theatrical art basically, "the dance is the thing," and it is the dance that has formed the link with tradition and that has given us continuity since the days of Louis XIV. It was for the dance that the whole expensive machinery was set into motion and it was for the dance that composers wrote their music and artists designed their costumes. It was the whim of a dancer with shapely legs, La Camargo, which gave us the beginnings of our modern ballet costume and influenced the whole progress of our art. It is important to insist on these points because immediately the dance assumes an inferior position to the other elements, we are faced with the perfectly logical position that marionettes would serve the producers as vehicles for their music and *décors* fully as well. When the dance takes on an undue position we are still left with ballet, though it may possibly be bad ballet. I can, in fact, perfectly well conceive of the dance unaided by artist or musician as an art form, delighting by its purity of line, much as a fine drawing does, although I can see that it would appeal to too few as a theatrical entertainment. It is a point, however, to be borne in mind; at one extreme the triumph of the individual, worth while only as long as the individual is worth while; at the other extreme the complete degradation of the individual, who assumes the position of a puppet. The Greeks, who were wiser in these things than we are, gave to the Muse of dancing, Terpsichore, a position of great importance. This being the case, let us discuss the dancing and the dance arrangement first. We have already covered the subject from another aspect, that of the dancer.

Dancing as we understand it in a theatrical sense is organized movement, undertaken to express either something definite, yet something that words cannot express, or to arouse emotion in a far more subtle manner by its contrasting lines. We are on difficult ground here, and this needs some elaboration. Aesthetics have a definite physiological foundation depending as they do upon the mechanism of the eye. There are certain lines which, based upon the laws of optics, "soothe" the eye, while others are obviously irritating and difficult to look upon. This would also apply in the case of colour. Certain papers published by the French Académie des Sciences, outlining the experiments of the Russian sculptor-scientist Yourievitch, make this assumption appear perfectly reasonable, and certainly help us in our appreciation of dancing. According to Yourievitch, the movement culminating in the pose known as an *arabesque* is pleasing for the definite optical reason that the line from the back of the head to the tip of the toe, the gentle slope, is one of the lines that it is easiest for the eye to take in and caress, while the angles formed by the legs and the trunk of the body form a contrast that draws attention to the gentle slope and saves it from monotony. Whether these complicated experiments are correct or not, this conclusion seems entirely reasonable and is helpful.

Dancing in ballet, however, does not depend on one individual or on such a simple combination of line. To take a helpful analogy, the dancer is a note, the ballet a whole score; or better still the dancer is a simple melody, the ballet a complicated orchestration where several things are going on at once. The role of the choreographer, the actual creator of that part of ballet which consists of movement, is to *orchestrate dancing*. His place in the arts is half-way between that of the musician and of the painter of large groups. He differs from the first because his means of expression are plastic, from the second because it is not static, and the group is merely the climax, the full stop to his phrase. In practice he cannot create ideally because he must work in harmony with his music and with the actual physical material assigned to him. He is akin to the painter again when he thinks in terms of *ballerina* and *corps de ballet*; the relation between foreground and background. It has been argued that the ideal ballet should consist of mass movement with no definite foreground, but I am quite unable to see the point of this. It may produce exceedingly moving results. Mass movement well handled invariably does, but it is only one possibility of an art that should have unlimited possibilities. It is merely another form of the old theatrical argument about the merits and demerits of the "star" system. In ballet practice it is always the "star" who has developed choreography and has been the inspiration of the whole system. The ideal composition of a ballet company from a choreographic point of view is a *corps de ballet* so competent technically that any

KARSAVINA IN "THE SWAN LAKE"

one of its members could dance a leading role, but with sufficient outstanding personalities to act as fuel for inspiration. This was the case in the heyday of the early Diaghileff ballet, it was the case with its successor, de Basil's Ballets Russes de Monte Carlo, it is the case with our own Sadler's Wells. The reason that choreography was not developed to any great extent over a long period of time in the Pavlova Company was due to the inevitable abuse of the "star" system, one genius in surroundings that existed only to centre attention on her. We have in such a case the whole machinery of ballet to exploit what is virtually the concert dance or *divertissement.*

MARKOVA IN "THE SWAN LAKE"
Photo by Brewster

The inspiration of Anna Pavlova has fired thousands of girls with ambition that should bear fruit, and it has given thousands of us memories that we shall always cherish. It has certainly advanced dancing in that way, but it has played a minor role, out of proportion with its fame in the development of orchestrated dancing ballet.

The great French *maître de ballet,* Noverre, in his historic letters, has given us some indications of what is expected of the choreographer, and the gist of what he says is surprisingly modern and applicable to present-day conditions.

He postulates a knowledge of painting and art history; "his art has in view the same subject as theirs; a sound knowledge of musical composition." "The choice of good music is as essential to the dance as the choice of words and phrases to the orator." Again on the same subject: "He, the choreographer, will furnish the composer with the principal points of his action." He sees a necessity for a smattering of geometry, another link with the painter. Most important of all, a point that is so frequently neglected in ballet composition, contact with life itself is essential, a contact that has been lost since the days of Noverre himself until found once more by Fokine, whose choreography and ideals need a section on their own. Noverre advises the choreographer to study the jealous man and observe the shades of difference on his face, for, "if the grand passions are suited to tragedy they are no less necessary to pantomime," the very basis of tragedy. The remoteness of ballet choreography to humanity is one of the chief points against this form of dancing that is made by the exponents of other forms of the art. As I have shown, it has been foreseen by a great *maître de ballet* and put into practice by another, long before these objections were raised.

So many, then, are the attributes required by the choreographer, in excess even of those required by the dancer, that it is not surprising that there are few who even make the attempt, and in the whole history of the dance only three or four outstanding names arise, Petipa, Fokine, Nijinsky, and Massine being the great Russian masters, and Ashton, de Valois, and Helpmann the English. It is this fact that gives us the greatest cause of apprehension for the future of ballet, but where there is good dancing material—and it is abundant at the present-day—there are great hopes that someone new to make them dance for us will be forthcoming.

There are two conceptions of ballet music; as a mere rhythmic accompaniment, irrespective of its own intrinsic merits or its mood; as an actual "partner" both in mood and movement. The first conception, the old one, produced much that was admirable (Debussy and Tchaikovsky, greatest of all dance composers), but much more that is unplayable to-day, such as that of Minkus and Pugno, and that is utterly unworthy of the fine choreography that was arranged for it, or of the attention of sensitive and intelligent people. The old we might conveniently label as "ballet music," bearing in mind the exceptions, the new as "music" with no qualification. Fokine and Isadora Duncan altered that entire position and proved that it was possible to dance to the classics, not only with no disrespect but in a manner that would enhance their prestige. The change that took place in the whole position of ballet can well be imagined when it is realized that before the Fokine reforms it was sacrilege to dance to anything but "ballet music," while afterwards Beethoven himself was open to the choreographer. This meant an entirely new public to supplement the "tired business man," and also led to the co-operation of the serious composer such as Stravinsky. This threw a far greater onus on the choreographer, who must now study mood and atmosphere as well as rhythm, and a complex rhythm that was no longer a straightforward accompaniment. At its worst it meant the dictatorship of the composer, and the dancers were completely lost (the puppet situation I have mentioned); at its very best such an harmonious whole as the De Falla-Massine-Picasso *Three Cornered Hat*.

These incursions into theory and recent history are definitely of a practical nature. They cover a curriculum that every pupil should know, if ballet is to be considered as more than a series of difficult, but meaningless, movements.

DÉCOR AND BALLET

Costume has had a close link with the development of dancing and yet in one limited sense it is the least important feature of ballet. From the public point of view, the box office, it is perhaps the most important.

The whole aim of the decorative artist is as close a co-operation as possible with the choreographer, so that he will stress the choreographer's design and never confuse it. He may have remarkable ideas on paper, but he must always bear

PAVLOVA IN AN "ARABESQUE"

in mind the fact that his costumes are to be worn by people in violent motion, and that therefore they must be light and well balanced. What is more logical than the conventional ballet skirt that spreads itself out and balances the dancer like the rim of a top? It is a design that has been evolved by experience. Costumes in mica or other rigid material may make an admirable theatrical effect, when the dancers are static, but so hamper their movements as to be bad designs. Of all the sketches that are carried out by enterprising young artists for ballet, over half are impracticable from the first. Let us take some definite examples. Balanchine's *Cat* was one of the most popular of the late Diaghileff ballets. Its great costume and scenic feature was the material in which the designs were executed, mica and oil cloth. Well-lit upon the rise of the curtain, the effect was truly amazing. However, once the action began, the oil cloth was so slippery that the ballerina had to tip her shoes with rubber, naturally handicapping her movements considerably. This seems an illogical intrusion of the artist, and however effective it may have been, I would call it a bad *décor*. We have another example in the costumes by André Masson for Massine's masterpiece *Les Présages*. Here, though the colouring seems to me harmonious, the dancer's arms are covered with a woollen material that rucks up in movement, concealing a naturally beautiful line and giving the comical illusion of long-sleeved underwear that undoubtedly damages an impressive sight.

* DIAGHILEFF AT V. POLUNIN'S SCENIC STUDIO WITH PICASSO AND POLUNIN
(*Copyright V. Polunin*)

* MASSINE WITH THE ARTIST AT V. POLUNIN'S SCENIC STUDIO
(*Copyright V. Polunin*)

In the history of the Diaghileff ballet the changes that *décor* has undergone have altered the whole of the decorative art of the theatre. It was Diaghileff's aim to anticipate public taste, so that an artist would be dropped, seemingly capriciously at the height of his success, but actually in a manner that probably conserved public interest in him far longer than otherwise would have been the case. When, in an interview after the War, Diaghileff was asked about the revival of his early ballet successes, he said that if they were revived, all the colours would need intensifying in order for them to live up to the memory of the public's first startled shock.

Early ballet scenery was built on a solid scale, semi-realistic, semi-fantastic, having little relation to the action. To-day it might appeal to us as having the quaint charm of an old print—that is all.

Alexandre Benois played the great role in harmonizing costume and *décor* and bringing them into partnership with the rest. Painter, historian, and expert on the French 18th century, which had a profound influence on all his work, he was associated with Diaghileff from the beginning and played a major role in the creation of the ballet as we know it to-day. It was Bakst, however, who caused the real world revolution, changed sober tints into pure bright colour and started the craze for the Russian decorative art that we see in such companies as the Chauve-Souris. Yet Bakst is not to me typically Russian, and Russian art is actually far less exotic. Bakst has synthetized

* I am grateful to Mr. V. Polunin for his kindness in allowing me to reproduce here for the first time these rare photographs.—A. L. H.

and exaggerated Russian decorative characteristics. He has stressed the Oriental. At his best he has produced masterpieces such as *Sheherazade* and *Thamar*; at his worst he is nearly vulgar, but he always retains an admirable sense of the theatre. Among the most interesting Russian artists employed by Diaghileff were Goncharova and Larionov, who combined a modern inventive outlook with tradition. Larionov I believe to be one of the greatest of all stage designers with a latitude ranging from the legendary *Children's Tales* to the final Diaghileff creation *The Fox*. He has had a profound influence on his fellow artists, including Picasso, and has never received the public recognition due to him as did Bakst. He is undoubtedly the superior of the two.

It was only natural after the Oriental riot of colour of a Bakst that Diaghileff should turn to the calm logic of the French. It is rare that a fine easel artist finds success in the theatre, the qualities required being so different, but in Pablo Picasso and André Derain great artists were found who could subordinate their art to an ensemble. France alone, perhaps, can produce perfect collaboration between her different artists. There is a sensitive atmosphere in Paris that brings about parallel movements in art and synchronizes them. It is for that reason alone that Paris has been the headquarters of ballet, for French dancers are exceedingly mediocre; not one has ever joined the Diaghileff troupe, and our audiences in England are far less capricious and more understanding.

The last pre-war decorative phase is exceedingly interesting. Just as cubism originally turned to ballet in *Parade* in order to assert itself with a large public, so now has *surréalisme* with results that are far more beautiful than on canvas. *Jeux d'Enfants*, by Juana Miro, suggests endless new possibilities for *décor* by the artists of this School, for with their aims an atmosphere of fantasy can be created in the most extraordinary manner and the dancers and *décor* become one picture—the ideal of the scenic artist.

With our British ballet it is impossible to speak of decorative *phases*. Until the war period *décor* was the weakest factor in our ballet; there have been important works by Leslie Hurry (*Hamlet*, and *Swan Lake*), Edward Burra (*Miracle in the Gorbals*), and John Piper (*The Quest*).

LITERATURE AND BALLET

From the moment that ballet attempts to tell a story the literary element is present in some degree, but, as ballet seeks to tell in movement what cannot be expressed in words, literature plays a subordinate role. There, where it predominates and long programme notes are essential for understanding and enjoyment, the choreographer has clearly failed in his intention.

If we follow the historical development of the theme or story in ballet we will better realize the position, and the differences between the old and the modern.

In the romantic period of the 1830's, the grand days of Taglioni, the subject would be based on a plot by Scott, Byron, Gautier, or Schiller, and require development in several acts, development laid down by precedent, as in opera; so much given to *pas d'action* that actually develops the story; so much to formal dances with the ballerina's *adagio* occurring at a definite time of the evening.

In the original Russian Ballet the story comes from fairy tale or legend: *The Sleeping Princess*, *Aladdin*, *Casse-Noisette*, *The Little Humpbacked Horse*, etc. Again it is presented in a conventional manner: fine *divertissements* bound together by *pas d'action*. The story may seem complicated and require elaborate programme notes, but actually this is not the case because it is generally known from childhood by the entire audience, and is in any case of no importance whatsoever, being merely a peg upon which to hang so many dances. There is no question of an harmonious whole. Two such ballets in severely curtailed form are popular to-day: *Aurora's Wedding*, consisting of the finest dances from *The Sleeping Princess*, and *The Swan Lake*, which is a slice out of a long and elaborate plot which, curiously enough, concerns dual personality, and was originally performed by two ballerinas—an idea that was hailed as strikingly modern in the ballet *Anna-Anna*. (The heroine of *The Swan Lake* is "Odette-Odilia.")

It did not seem in any way strange or sacrilegious to hack these works about. On the contrary, it probably preserved their beautiful choreography since the adaptations were made at a time when classicism was less popular than at the present-day. The modern attitude towards art exists in these old-fashioned works, for just as the modern painter says: "The line's the thing, not the subject," and hails Ingres, the painter of innumerable "subject" pictures, as his inspiration, so here the dance is the thing and the subject of no more importance than in an Ingres painting. It might be completely abstract for all the importance it has. And so the seeming extremes meet and with no paradox or involved reasoning.

With Fokine the idea of harmony predominates. Ballet is shortened, drama marches with movement, and music becomes important and cannot be abbreviated. Ballet has a *theme*, which becomes self-evident in the dancing, rather than a *plot*. The music aids in creating the atmosphere: *Sylphides*, the dancing of sylphs in a wood, a picture by Corot, the wonderful transformation of the technical into pure poetry; *Carnaval*, *Commedia dell' Arte*, the soul of tragedy and comedy; *Petrouchka*, the first great drama of the new ballet, a drama that contains everything as we watch its progress, and it contains everything just because the story can be told in three or four lines of print, leaving its true meaning to action. At the moment we are concerned with the dramatic element alone. First the *ballerina* is a technical dancer, with one act in which she has a heavy dramatic role, about something definite that can therefore be expressed in words (*Giselle*). Next she becomes a "conveyer" of atmosphere, subtle and restrained; mime is no longer conventional and the whole movement of the body becomes mime. The narrative poem gives way to the sonnet. Kurt Jooss, one of the finest of the Central European dancers, said in an interview during 1933 that mime should not be taught apart, as the whole of dancing is mime, a law that he lays down as one of the discoveries of his method. It was, as we shall see, discovered by Fokine in the first decade of this century.

Nijinsky dispenses still more with a set story to give us an analysis of moods: *L'Après-Midi d'un Faune*, sensuality; *Jeux*, flirtation; *Sacre du Printemps*, the primitive in man. After Fokine, and especially in the final Diaghileff period, ballet finds once again a closer approach to literature, which has now changed from poetry to satire: *The House Party*, *The Blue Train*, the latter no longer a study of flirtation with sport as its setting, but a satire on tennis itself, golf, and the popular Riviera resort. One thing has become certain, such ballets, dealing with the craze of the moment, are soon out of date, while Fokine created for always.

There is another interesting point, that of "Ballet realism," a belief in the particular convention of the art. Much of the later Diaghileff ballet was not true to its own convention. In *Le Fils Prodigue*, for instance, there is a small low structure, which is indicated to us as a gate early in the ballet. Later it is completely ignored. This is, in fact, as bad as if in a realistic drama a character were to come not through the door, but over the footlights and through "the fourth wall."

I have had many scenarios sent to me, some as detailed as a novel. They are a complete waste of time. As we have seen, the finest ballet may be inspired by a line or two of poetry—

"Je suis le spectre de la rose
Que tu portais hier au bal."

or from a nursery legend or story. Only the man of letters living in an atmosphere of ballet, and thinking in terms of dancers, has a place in the creation of ballet.

In practice it is difficult to say exactly how a ballet is created, that is to say in what order events occur, as in each case circumstances vary so that it would be difficult for the collaborators themselves always to be sure. In most cases it is definitely the choreographer, who wishes to exploit some particular emotion and who seeks the music, either already in existence or generally to be commissioned.

The chance origin of Nijinska's *The Blue Train* is interesting, for the influence of this work persists in all the lighter forms of dancing, although itself it is dated and dead. Jean Cocteau happening to pass by the dressing rooms of a French theatre saw Dolin perform some acrobatics, the unusual and striking feature being the fact that they were performed definitely with a classical *plastique*, that is with the movements of a ballet dancer. It is safe to say that ballet is always born in the shadow of the theatre.

THE RUSSIAN CLASSICAL BALLET

It is always well at the outset of any subject to discuss and define the "classical" period, which sets a standard by which the other periods can be measured. I have not been privileged to assist at the Maryinsky Theatre spectacles, but what follows is not entirely hearsay, for the great dancers of the Diaghileff days were Maryinsky trained and the tradition has persisted and can be clearly felt. Also it is impossible to discuss Fokine without understanding what it was that he evolved from, and how the St. Petersburg Ballet itself became truly Russian. People talk glibly of Russian Ballet and the Russian School with no clear idea of what it really implies, and of how the journey via France and Italy affected our art.

Dancing had found its way to Russia long before there was any State-supported institution, and the Imperial Ballet first owed its being to the Court performances of troupes belonging to wealthy private Maecenas. But as is the case with everything new to a country, inspiration had to come from abroad; such famous masters as Didelot and Perrot brought French methods to St. Petersburg in the early part of the last century. But the real Russian Ballet, as we know it, was brought to Russia by two foreigners who subsequently adopted Russian nationality, Johannsen, a Dane, pupil of the Bournonvilles, who were pupils of Vestris (that is one line of succession of the Russian School), and Petipa, a Frenchman, a native of Marseilles. Both were professors in the schools and developed the actual dancing technique; while Petipa was also the father of modern choreography. Apart from these permanent residents, all the great dancers came as guest artists, including the Italians with such dancers as Zucchi, Brianza, who afterwards taught Karsavina for a season, Limido, Legnani, and Cecchetti, the great *maestro*, who afterwards joined the Imperial Schools as a teacher, and subsequently the Diaghileff ballet, and who has left behind him, especially in this country, so rich a legacy. It will be seen then that St. Petersburg was a rallying point for dancers, and as is natural it was able to take the best from each school, the grace of the French with the strength and technical repertoire of the Italians. Such method superimposed on the Russian physique after a time gives us the Russian School of Ballet, with its large, noble movements, its fine, proud carriage of the head, its avoidance of bulging and ungainly muscles and its freedom from mere acrobatism disguised as dancing. The Russian School has sometimes been called "the true French School that the French themselves have forgotten." Be that so or not, its origin is polyglot. That is a point to be remembered when we clamour for British Ballet. Art can know no patriotism in its small, limited sense, and it takes some generations for ballet to become indigenous. We have as yet to produce an English ballet tradition. All the time we may be creating it, but I fear not, for we have not yet the necessary machinery that has existed in ballet's three homes: France, Italy, and Russia.

"Classicism" here must not be confused with the attempt to revive the Greek dance, which has found so much favour in England, where under the influence of Duncan, groups of girls in tunics pose loosely round the Parthenon and are photographed.

"It would be impossible to find an organization which has given to the world more *classical* dancers of different and varying talents than the Imperial Russian Ballet."

It is with these words that Valerian Svetloff, the great Russian critic, begins his exceedingly interesting study of Anna Pavlova. It is the word "classical" in this phrase that strikes me most. Kshesinskaya, Trefilova, Pavlova, Karsavina, Egorova, Preobrajenska, all have this one thing in common; they are "classical" dancers, though in every other respect they differ, each having a clearly defined personality. Fortunately, the majority are now teaching and have formed the dancers of to-day in their image. Trefilova was the classical dancer *par excellence*, an inspired interpreter of Tchaikovsky; Pavlova was more dream-like, more sentimental, using the word in its best sense, while Karsavina has made her name rather in the Fokine Ballet as a romantic actress of power and versatility, and Preobrajenska, who has given so many dancers, including Baronova and Toumanova, to the contemporary stage, excels in the humorous and in mimique. Each one of these great artists is entirely different, yet each one has this common grounding of "classicism," and it is this classicism that has permitted each dancer to express her particular personality. It is interesting, therefore, to inquire into the exact nature of this classicism without which the dancer of the ballerina class cannot exist. I do not intend to treat the question from a dance technique point of view, but from a wider and more easily understood aspect. The word can easily be translated without any reference to the sister arts, though, as it will be seen without much difficulty, classicism in painting, music, and ballet are very closely connected.

Firstly, I would translate "classicism" very freely to mean "pure dancing" (Noverre has said

KARSAVINA IN "GISELLE"

in his famous letters: "Pure dancing is like the mother tongue"), the "classical dancer" to mean a dancer of perfect technique who has sought no short cuts to proficiency, and the "classical ballet" as a ballet designed first and last for the dancer. Such definitions are necessarily incomplete, but they give us an approach to the truth, which we can reach by elaborating them. Firstly, by "pure dancing" I mean that dancing which has been based on the five positions, which produces long, graceful lines, and which is neither acrobatic nor in any way violent and lacking in dignity. The classical dancer has a definite system, built up by years of study, and it is only when this system has been thoroughly learned, has become a second nature, that the dancer is ready to be seen by the public. The opponent of classicism shows great ignorance of the subject by the argument that the *pirouette*, *pas de chat*, etc., are monotonous and meaningless, and that the modern public requires something significant. Apart from the sheer abstract beauty of a well executed step, a quality that is entirely missing in what the opponents of classicism would give us as a substitute, the classical dance can be full of character. The steps of a dance are like the musical notes, they are limited in number, and the effect depends on how those notes are combined and executed. The arguments used by the modern school of painting, arguments with which I am for the most part in thorough agreement, cannot be applied in the case of ballet. The arguments of the modernist painter are naturally based upon his media of canvas and paint, while in ballet the medium is the human body, and however justified deformation may be on the canvas, it is out of the question in dancing. The mistake that is always made by the opponents of ballet dancing, and I am speaking of dancing here and not ballet, arises either from a totally incorrect view of what is actually happening, or from the fact that they have never seen a first-class *ballerina* dance. They make the great mistake of thinking that the dancer is expressing "classicism," instead of taking it as it really is, that classicism is helping the dancer to express herself. They would probably understand the argument if applied to the pianist or violinist, and if the word "classicism" were replaced by "school." Just as without "correct fingering" no would-be pianist, however bright the fire of genius burned within him, would be able to express himself, so it is with the dancer. Once the technique has been conquered, the artist can express his personality. He may specialize in Bach, Beethoven, or Chopin, and what is more, he may interpret his chosen composer in a manner that has never been tried before. This is much more the case with the dancer, who is not bound down to such a great extent by the choreographist. The whole Russian School of Dancing is the gradual result of the interpretation of the Italian and French methods of dancing by such purely Russian dancers as Vera Trefilova. A simple *pirouette* may be danced by any number of dancers of equal technical ability, and produce an equal number of entirely different sensations. Firstly, it may be danced by the brilliant technician, and beyond the admiration her virtuosity calls for, it may leave the spectator cold and bored; a certain tightness in the movements may make it vulgar and irritating; it may be taken poetically, aristocratically, passionately, mischievously, in as many different manners as there are differences of character. There is nothing great about the *pirouette* itself; it is merely a note in a melody, a step in a choreographic creation, yet it can be made great by a great executant, and from an abstract point of view it is a thing of intense beauty. Ballet, like every art, requires close study. It is not the mere idle entertainment that some would have it. Taken as such, without a knowledge of the technique or an analysis of the art of the *prima ballerina*, it may quite conceivably be less exciting than the more immediately obvious dances that are offered to us daily.

The eccentric ballet that has departed from classical dancing leaves little chance to the *prima ballerina* to excel or express her personality, and that is one of its many drawbacks as a form of art. It destroys the dancer.

I have stated that classical ballet was ballet designed first and last for the dancer. In saying this I am both explicit as to its nature and at the same time vague. I have stated its most essential characteristic, but it needs further explanation to find out what constitutes good classical ballet. The old-fashioned ballet was a singularly stereotyped and unimaginative affair, based upon symmetry. In spite, however, of all its drawbacks, its lack of intelligence, and its many ridiculous features, it possessed one solid virtue—it gave the dancer an opportunity to shine, and its movements were a definite help to the dancer's physical development. It could in no way be taken as an artistic whole. Movements could be taken separately, criticized, and appreciated from a point of view of abstract beauty. The music of such ballets was often as worthless as swing and resembled it from the point of view of simplicity of rhythm and utter vapidity.

Such was the classical ballet at its worst. At its best it was different, really expressing something. The finest artists in the country, men such as Korovin, Golovin, Roerich, Benois, Anisfeld, designed costumes that were a help, and not a hindrance as is so often the case to-day, and the music was composed by such a genius as Tchaikovsky, music both beautiful in melody and easy for the dancer to follow, and the choreography magnificently created by the father of Russian Ballet, Petipa.

Such productions were few, but that is in no way a criticism of a system that could produce

VERA TREFILOVA IN "ARABESQUE"
Photo by Manuel

its own remedy from within itself, and in Fokine's evolution those classical principles that have formed the great artists of the dance were in no way dispensed with; they were and still are retained as the basis of ballet.

One of the greatest dangers of classicism is an abuse of virtuosity, an insistence on quantity rather than quality. There is nothing more contrary to the spirit of classical dancing and of Petipa himself than this acrobatism, this insistence on a record number of *fouettés*, or *pirouettes*, with a complete disregard of the music or the finish of those steps. The whole beauty of the *pirouette* or *fouetté* consists not in their number but in their crispness and their finish. I have explained the terms "classicism in dancing," "classical dancers," and "classical ballet," and have also stated that all the great dancers have been classical dancers, but there is another and more difficult point that yet remains to be explained. Karsavina is a classical dancer, yet by nature she is essentially dramatic; Pavlova was a classical dancer, yet by nature a romantic. Preobrajenska is a classical dancer and yet by nature a mime or a comedienne. Up to now I have used the term "classical" to denote training, and it has therefore been common to all great dancers, and in order to explain something of their art I have to find another term descriptive of their temperament. But there is such a thing as a classicism of temperament, and it is thus that I would class the late Vera Trefilova, the true type of classical ballerina of the Maryinsky period and whose performance in *The Sleeping Princess* at the Alhambra set a "ballerina standard" for history. She was a classical dancer both by training and temperament. She could perform a record number of *fouettés*, but each one was perfection, about each one there would be style and finish. The spectator was not so much amazed by their quantity as by their remarkable purity. He did not sit, restless and counting, wondering whether she would ever get through—and I have done so with countless dancers—he was too enthralled by the amazing beauty of line.

The celebrated thirty-two *fouettés* of *Le Lac des Cygnes* are artistically unnecessary, if not actually ridiculous, and one is always struck with that fact, save when such a dancer as Vera Trefilova is the dancer. So classical a role only appears in all its beauty when a ballerina who is classical in feeling as well as in technique performs. In ballet, perhaps far more than in music, the temperament of the artist binds him to the interpretation of the works of certain composers. Each of the great dancers, in spite of the magnitude of her repertoire, becomes associated with a certain type of role, and for that reason comparisons can be drawn that are detrimental to no one. One's preference will generally depend upon one's own temperament.

Vera Trefilova in a Tchaikovsky Ballet was Russian Ballet at its highest, and I lay stress on her performances because I believe her to be the greatest classical *dancer* we have seen in London, one who has set a definite standard for all time.

The Russian periods of Russian Ballet have lasted but an exceedingly short time. Rapidly, from its Italian origins, ballet becomes truly Russian. Its first step is a change that implies no loss of nationality; then speedily it absorbs the culture of modern Paris; for a short time it retains its character; then the desire to please the foreign public transforms it, and Russian Ballet is no more, and we must think in terms of Diaghileff ballet. In all there are but two brief periods: the birth of the Russian style, and its evolution from the classical to the romantic. The history of Russian Ballet has been one crowded hour; it has altered almost every branch of art that has come into contact with it. In the brief years in which it lasted it produced such a wealth of talent that one talks of the Diaghileff era in art.

FOKINE AND MODERN BALLET

I cannot do better here than give Fokine's own "five points" on his ideas for ballet production. Everyone connected with dancing should learn them by heart. They constitute the most important utterance on ballet that has ever been written. It is also a fine tribute to Fokine as the true creator of the modern art of ballet. The points were made in a letter to *The Times*, dated 6th July, 1914, before dilettantism had attracted attention, and when Fokine had already been putting them into practice for nearly ten years. This is the practical advice of a practical man.

"The misconceptions are these. That some mistake this new school of art (The New Russian Ballet), which has arisen only during the last seven years, for the traditional ballet which continues to exist in the Imperial Theatres of St. Petersburg and Moscow, and others mistake it for the development of the principles of Isadora Duncan; while as a matter of fact the new Russian ballet is sharply differentiated by its principles both from the older ballet and from the art of that great dancer.

"The older ballet developed the form of so-called "classical dancing," consciously preferring to every other form the artificial form of dancing, on the point of the toe with the feet turned out, in short bodices, with the figure tightly laced in stays and with a strictly established system of steps, gestures, and attitudes. Miss Duncan established an entirely opposite form of her own.

"Every form of dancing is good in so far as it expresses the content or subject with which the dance deals, and that form is the most natural which is most suited to the purpose of the dancer. No one form of dancing should be accepted once and for all. Borrowing its subject from the most various historical periods, the ballet must create forms corresponding to the various periods represented. I am not speaking of ethnographical or archaeological exactitude, but of the corresponding of the style of the dancing and gestures with the style of the period represented. In the course of the ages man has repeatedly changed his plastic language and expressed his joys and sorrows and all his emotions under a great variety of forms, often of extreme beauty. For man is infinitely various and the manifold expressiveness of his gestures cannot be reduced to a single formula.

"The art of the old ballet turned its back on life and on all the other arts and shut itself up in a narrow circle of tradition. According to the old method of producing a ballet, the ballet master composed his dances by combining certain well-established movements and poses, and for his mimetic scenes he used a conventional system of gesticulation and endeavoured by gestures of the dancers' hands according to established rules to convey the plot of the ballet to the spectators.

"In the new ballet, on the other hand, the dramatic action is expressed by dances and mimetics in which the whole body plays a part. In order to create a stylistic picture the ballet master of the new school has to study in the first place the national dances of the nation represented, dances differing immensely from nation to nation, and often expressing the spirit of a whole race; and in the second place, the art and literature of the period in which the scene is laid. The new ballet, while recognizing the excellence both of the older ballet and of the dancing of Isadora Duncan in every case in which they are suitable to the subject to be treated, refuses to accept any one form as final and exclusive.

"Not to form combinations of ready made and established dance steps but to create in each case a new form corresponding to the subject, the most expressive form possible for the representation of the period and the character of the nation represented—that is the first rule of the new ballet.

"The second rule is that dancing and mimetic gesture have no meaning in a ballet unless they serve as an expression of dramatic action, and they must not be used as a mere *divertissement** or entertainment having no connexion with the scheme of the whole ballet.

* Concert dance.

"The third rule is that the new ballet admits the use of conventional gesture only where it is required by the style of the ballet, and in all other cases endeavours to replace gestures of the hands by mimetics of the whole body. Man can be, and should be, expressive from head to foot.

"The fourth rule is the expressiveness of groups and of *ensemble* dancing. In the older ballet the

MICHAEL FOKINE

dancers were arranged in groups only for the purpose of ornament, and the ballet master was not concerned with the expression of any sentiment in groups of characters or in *ensemble* dancing. The new ballet on the other hand, in developing the principles of expressiveness, advances from the expressiveness of the face to the expressiveness of the whole body, and from the expressiveness of the individual body to the expressiveness of a group of bodies and the expressiveness of the combined dancing of a crowd.

"The fifth rule is the alliance of dancing with the other arts. The new ballet refusing to be the slave either of music or of scenic decoration, and recognizing the alliance of the arts only on the condition of complete equality, allows perfect freedom both to the scenic artist and to the musician. In contradistinction to the old ballet it does not demand "ballet music" from the composer as an accompaniment to dancing; it accepts music of every kind, provided only that it is good and expressive. It does not demand of the scenic artist that he should array the ballerinas in short skirts and pink slippers. It does not impose any specific "ballet" conditions on the composer or the decorative artist but gives complete liberty to their creative powers.

"No artist can tell to what extent his work is the result of the influence of others and to what extent it is his own. I cannot therefore judge to what extent the influence of the old traditions is preserved in the new ballet and how much the new ideals of Miss Duncan are reflected in it."

Finally, I am able to clear up the point touched upon above after many conversations and much correspondence, Michael Fokine's attitude towards Isadora Duncan, and what is more important still to the history of the modern dance, the true extent of her influence on him, for though he might be inclined to belittle this, his replies are so obviously reasonable and true that there can be little doubt that he is entirely correct. They naturally repeat some of the "five points," but repetition is important and it is full time that Fokine was given the credit due to him in full. In any case it is only outside dancing circles that the myth of Duncan's immense influence on the early Russian Ballet has survived. The question came to a head with a letter from Diaghileff published in Propert's *Russian Ballet*, 1921-1929. The passage says—

"I knew Isadora well at St. Petersburg and was present with Fokine at her first debuts. Fokine was mad about her dancing and the influences of Duncan on him lay at the base of all his creative work." Coming from Diaghileff such a statement should be final, but it is made in so sweeping a manner, and is so contradictory to what one has heard from others of Fokine's contemporaries, and more important still from what can be deduced from a comparison of his works and Duncan's that it can be dismissed. It may well have been prompted by some purely personal reason. Fokine himself replies to this in a letter to me—

"Diaghileff could not have made such a statement sincerely. He knew better than anyone the great difference between the New Russian Ballet created by me and my various reforms and the natural dance to which Duncan tended. He saw my rehearsals and watched me compose. He knew perfectly well that 90 per cent of my compositions are totally contrary to Duncan's ideas.

"When I talk about Diaghileff I want you to understand that I am a great admirer of his and I realize and know from my own experience what he has done, better than anyone else. He was a genius as a propagandist for art and as an organizer of artists; he was something more besides, but he was no more a creator of ballet in the sense of a choreographist than he was a painter or musician. Those that give him any other position are of no value. They deny his real and immense achievements for which all who love art and beauty should be grateful. Many books have recently given an entirely false impression. I hope that you will not carry on these legends but give true history.

"To return to Isadora Duncan. Let us contrast our viewpoints. She stood for the freedom of the body from clothes; I believe in the obedience of the costume to the movements of the body and its proper adaptation to style period. She had one plastic conception for all periods and nationalities, while I am essentially interested in the difference of the movements of each individual person. She, for instance, had the same form of dance for Wagner, Gluck, Chopin, the Spanish dances of Moszkovski, and the waltzes of Strauss. The national character is absent; only ancient Greece existed for her, as if it were adaptable in its form to all periods. For me art is very closely united with the time, place, and nationality of its creation, and without this approach art loses a great deal.

"I have always been a great admirer of Duncan. The reaction against the unnaturalness of the ballet, the freedom of the body from tight clothes, the inspired simplified dance all came from Duncan. But why should we be limited to naturalness? Is not our art the development of nature to its highest forms? It is impossible for a dancer not to know how to walk and run naturally, but it is equally impossible to be limited only to walking and running. One must explore further into the developments of body movement of a child. The child is beautiful. But what relation has that to art? If we were all to be like children, would that be enough? Movement is complicated and has wisdom. It was created by the centuries, by human history."

Almost on the first occasion we met, Fokine outlined to me the artistic credo that led to the ballet as we know it at the present day. I will add, the ballet at its best, for it was while disavowing some of the later Diaghileff productions that were on just then in Paris that the conversation came about. It touched closely on the question of Duncan's influence—

"Early in my career the unnaturalness, the lack of justification, the psychological untruths of the ballet so disillusioned me that I began to study for another career, that of a painter. It was only when I was appointed a teacher in the theatrical school that I began to realize with my pupils the direction of my new tendencies—towards a 'ballet realism,' towards the notion that on the very foundation of the dance should be placed sincere emotional movement, that no matter how obscure, fantastic, and unrealistic the form of the dance may seem, it must have its roots in the truth of life. Duncan too realized this, though I had already carried out some of my reforms before I saw her. I remember well going to see her with Diaghileff. I had already been engaged by him then. I became most enthusiastic because I realized that here were the very elements that I preached. I found all the expressiveness, simplicity, and naturalness that I hoped for in my own colleagues. With that initial conception there is some similarity in our aims, but there is still greater dissimilarity and our actual methods could not be more different. My Russian, Egyptian, and Oriental Ballets, my romantic works such as *Le Spectre de la Rose*, *Carnaval*, and *Les Sylphides*, still given every season, have nothing in common with her. The resemblances are in the ballets *Daphnis and Chloe*, *Narcissus and Echo*, the bacchanals from *Cleopatra* * and *Tannhäuser*. We studied the same vases in the same museums; but even here her dance is free, my dance is stylized and my movements are highly complex. The similarity lies in plastic and the design of poses. I am very happy that in the treatment of ancient Greek themes—her chosen terrain—I have something in common with her, just as

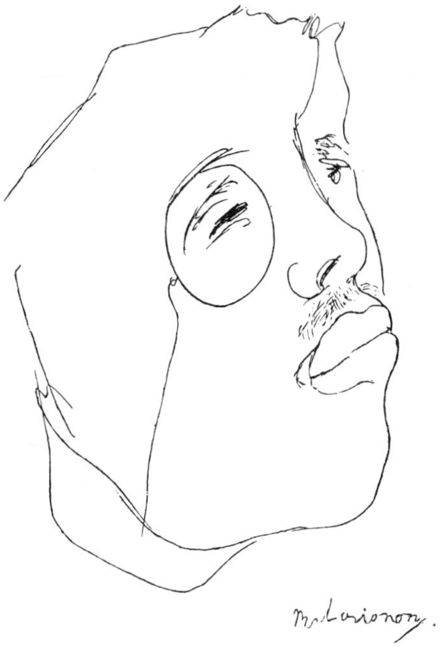

DIAGHILEFF, FROM A DRAWING BY LARIONOV
(Arnold L. Haskell: Collection)

I am delighted to differ in other periods and moods.

"The most competent witnesses of my work are not those who knew only the Diaghileff ballet but members of the Imperial Theatres."

* Known to us as Pavlova's famous "Bacchanal."

NIJINSKY, MASSINE, AND BRITISH CHOREOGRAPHY

In our historical survey we have reached the climax of Fokine's evolution. The dance has developed and altered in character since his leadership, but changes have been more or less superficial. He has established once and for all ballet as we see it at the present day.

After Fokine, we come to the man who made his name in Fokine's own ballets and who thereby greatly altered the status of the male dancer, who previously had been little more than a lifter and foil since the days of Taglioni. Nijinsky as a dancer may well have affected the future of ballet far more deeply than Nijinsky as choreographer. Owing to a combination of private circumstances, culminating in his tragic "death" as a dancer, we have seen but three of his works, *Le Sacre du Printemps*, *Jeux*, and *L'Après-Midi d'un Faune*, and only the last survives in the current repertoire. One other work, *Tyl Eulenspiegel*, to music by Strauss, was produced in the United States. These four ballets, then, and some unfinished projects, are the only works of this now almost legendary figure, and it is not easy to gauge his influence in choreography as a whole, though it has certainly been far more extensive than the actual amount or quality of work done, and curiously enough in an entirely opposite direction from the ballets in which he made his great name. His theories, not fully matured at the time of his retirement from dancing, are somewhat complex and negative when explained in words and he certainly lacked the ability to put them into practice. Some quotations from Mme. Nijinska's life of her husband will help to reveal his ideas, which will be clearer to anyone who has seen *L'Après-Midi d'un Faune*.

TAMARA TOUMANOVA IN FOKINE'S "LES SYLPHIDES"

"Nijinsky made a very definite distinction between movement and the dance, which is a combination of movements. It was clear to him that the first and most important thing is to express an idea through movement, as a writer through words, as a musician through notes on a scale.

"Nijinsky treated movement literally, as the poet the word. He eliminated the floating, sinuous gestures, the half gestures, and every unnecessary move. He allowed only definitely rhythmic and absolutely essential steps, as in verse one only uses the words needed to express the idea without rhetoric or embroidery for its own sake. He established a prosody of movement, one single movement for a single action."

While his "new technique" has been adapted and used from time to time, it has caused no real revolution in dancing. The classical technique that gave Nijinsky himself his art still reigns supreme. It was, however, in the practical demonstration of the facts that the choreographer should not be restricted in his use of movement and that there were not two distinct categories of movement: (*a*) beautiful, graceful, (*b*) jerky, ugly, inharmonious, and that the second group should never in any circumstances be used, that he was a genuine pioneer. His ballets once again shook the spectator out of his complacency, and made him see the intimate relationship between ballet, drama, and those vital emotions and ideas that could not be expressed by any other medium. In Fokine's *Petrouchka* there was a mighty moving drama that went deep into primitive fears and emotions, to witchcraft, jealousy, and the fear of being locked up. Its form was such that many may not have realized its true depth.

Alexandra Danilova in Massine's "Le Beau Danube"

Riabouchinska and Massine in Massine's "Scuola di Ballo"

Nijinsky's work "shocked" and made one take stock once again. He, too, had vital things to show, in *Sacre du Printemps*, the youth of the world, in *Jeux*, the modern conception of love, flirtation, the youth of individuals, and in *L'Après-Midi d'un Faune*, the true and essential archaic Greece: to quote the great Rodin: "The perfect personification of the ideals of the beauty of the old Greeks."

Had I been writing of Massine, Nijinsky's immediate successor both as dancer and choreographer, before 1932 when he began a new career, my attitude would have been entirely different. I would have spoken of him as the creator of several first-class works and as someone worthy to continue a great tradition. After the production of *Jeux d'Enfants*, *La Symphonie Fantastique*, and *Choreartium*, and after some fifteen years of work on a high level indeed, Massine shows himself to be like his predecessors—a great innovator, a creative artist who has freed the dance still further from the many restrictions that prejudice has placed upon it. Fokine's *Sylphides* was obviously pure dancing, with no plot or story, but the ballet was arranged to definite *dances* by Chopin. *Les Présages*, Massine's first great symphonic work (Tchaikovsky's Fifth Symphony), had a definite symbolism, and, moreover, this composer was closely connected with ballet, and the music is essentially balletic. It is a different matter with Brahms's Fourth Symphony. Here the choreographer was dealing with abstract music, and not only courting the practical danger of offending susceptibilities, but also the artistic one of putting into

Pearl Argyle in Frederick Ashton's "Lady of Shalott" (from a film)

the form of action ideas totally hostile to the composer. He set himself a gigantic task, a partnership with Brahms, and by his success showed to many that dancing, pure dancing, movement for the sake of its intrinsic beauty and significance, has no limitations. While I believe that for reasons of "timing" symphonic ballet has no future, especially as a general practice, I would like to quote that great musical critic, Ernest Newman, who has never shown himself particularly sympathetic to ballet, and who, so to speak, holds a watching brief for Brahms.

"Massine showed the common sense we might have expected of him when he put aside all thought of reading a story into Brahms's symphony and decided to approach it as music pure and simple. . . . If music is to be ruled out

Pearl Argyle in Frederick Ashton's "Lady of Shalott" (from a film)

from ballet when it is 'pure' music, what justification is there for *Les Sylphides* for example? There is no more programme in Chopin's music than there is in that of Brahms; yet the enduring success of *Les Sylphides* proves that choreographic figures can be devised that are felt to be not in the least alien to the spirit and the build of this music. We are bound to grant, I think, that there is nothing *a priori* incongruous in the mating of 'pure' music, whether that of Brahms or of any other composer, with the lines and masses and movements of the ballet. . . . The only question is to what extent the choreographer has succeeded."

After an interesting discussion on nationality, in which he justifies Massine for a non-German interpretation, he goes on to say:

"What has Massine done with the remainder

of the symphony? Here I can only wonder at the lack of imagination that prevents some people from seeing the points of genius with which Massine's choreographic score, so to call it, positively bristles. There can, of course, be no question of a translation of the 'meaning' of this music as a whole into terms of another art: this kind of music is just itself, the expression of something to which there is no real equivalent in any other art. But if there is no equivalent, surely there can be parallelisms; surely certain elements in the musical design can be counterparted in choreographic design, certain gestures of the music, certain softenings and hardenings of the colours can be suggested quite well in the more objective medium. I found myself profoundly interested in watching these correspondences, many of which gave me a fresh respect for Massine's genius. Unfortunately, as I have remarked before in a similar connexion, there is no way of making these correspondences clear to the reader without quoting the musical passages in question side by side with photographs of the particular moments of the ballet with which they are associated. But how any musical listener in the audience who knows the Brahms score and has any imagination at all could fail to perceive these extraordinary parallelisms I confess myself unable to understand.

"The opening entry of these two figures, for instance, with their curious gliding, undulating motion seemed to me as perfect a translation into visible motion of the well-known dip and rise of the first phrase in the violins as could possibly be conceived. I could cite similar felicities of parallelism by the hundred; the sense of the musical design conveyed for instance by the entry of the same two figures each time the first subject of the symphony assumed a leading part in the structure, the subtle distinctions invariably made in choreography between the basic elements in the music and the transitional passages—between the bones as it were and the cartilages—the curious correspondence between harshness in the harmonies and musical colours and angularities or violences in the gestures, and so on. In the finale, which, as the reader no doubt knows, is in *passacaglia* form—a series of variations upon a ground figure—Massine seems to me to have done wonders. He typifies the commanding main theme by six black figures that persist through the whole movement as the ground bass itself persists in music; and he intensifies or thins out the action and the groupings in accordance with the changing texture of the variations." (*The Sunday Times*, 29th Oct., 1933.)

MARGOT FONTEYN IN "NOCTURNE"
Courtesy "Dancing Times"

BRITISH CHOREOGRAPHY

There could be no more extraordinary tribute to the progress and achievement of British ballet than the fact that about twenty years ago this article contained small mention of British choreography, while to-day it would be comically incomplete without it. We are not so much concerned with those achievements as such but with the direction they have taken.

Our ballet is in the direct European tradition, the technique that it traces is the same as that of Moscow or the Paris Opera, and those teachers who have made the present generation of Sadler's

Wells dancers are the pupils of Cecchetti, Legat, and other great figures in Russian Ballet. There was never any doubt that the British turned out admirable dancing material. Pavlova had proved it and Diaghileff himself, even more convincingly, with such names as Sokolova, de Valois, Savina, Markova, and Dolin. There were, however, several doubts as to the possibilities of British choreography. For a long time that art had seemed the monopoly of a handful of Russians; Fokine, Massine, Balanchine, and Nijinsky.

Marie Rambert launched the first important choreographer in Frederick Ashton, whose *Capriol Suite* so delighted Pavlova that she commissioned a work from him. Unfortunately, she died before this could be carried out. Of all our British choreographers Frederick Ashton is the most in the great Russian tradition; i.e. in the contrasting tendencies between movement for the sake of movement and dance drama he is nearer the first. His works are many since *Capriol Suite* heralded his discovery. From them I would single out the witty *Les Rendez-vous*, the harrowing *Dante Sonata*, the tender *Nocturne*, and perfectly balanced *Wise Virgins*. Another critic might make a totally different selection.

I would point out to the student of the past few years who is familiar with choreography through the work of Sadler's Wells only, and there are many such, that Ashton is our "school" man, a safe model to follow.

"Nocturne"—Curtain Fall
Courtesy G. B. L. Wilson

Ninette de Valois occupies with Serge Diaghileff an altogether unique position in ballet as the director and animator of a great enterprise. What concerns us here, however, is her work as a choreographer. De Valois has produced not only the most heroic of our ballets, but also the most national. *Job*, to Vaughan Williams's noble score, the ballet that not only made her fame but also launched our whole enterprise, is an evocation of the Bible story as seen through the eyes of Blake. De Valois excels in such evocations; *The Rake's*

Progress gives us Hogarth, *The Prospect Before Us* Rowlandson. This is a dangerous method save in the hands of an expert because it can so rapidly degenerate into the *tableau vivant.* De Valois' musicianship and her thorough understanding of the painters concerned have obviated that risk. Her *Checkmate,* a balletic game of chess to music by Bliss, is an outstanding work, and in a lighter vein *The Gods Go a'Begging* and *Promenade* are ornaments to any repertoire.

Our newest choreographer Robert Helpmann approaches ballet through the drama. His outlook is extremely personal, so personal that he is a dangerous model to follow. In each of his ballets he has tackled some fresh problem. In *Comus* he blends speech and movement, paying tribute to the one time national art form, the masque. In *Hamlet* he gives us balletic criticism based on the words "Perchance to Dream," and avoiding the pitfalls of making a Shakespeare play into a ballet. In *Miracle in the Gorbals* he presents a sordid realistic present-day drama and finds real and moving beauty in a slum.

No company has had three such choreographers working with it at one time, and there is no doubt that the dancers have greatly widened their scope. It is possible to say that British dancers, behind the Russians in their technical attack, excel in depicting character.

So far I have dealt with Sadler's Wells alone. Marie Rambert, a great pioneer and the first to discover and launch Ashton, continues her great work of discovery. Andrée Howard, a member of her original company, has created works of great sensitivity, *Death and the Maiden*, *Lady into Fox* for Marie Rambert, and *Le Festin de l'Araignée* for Sadler's Wells. Antony Tudor who produced many ballets for Rambert, including *Jardin aux Lilas*, is prominent as a choreographer in the U.S.A. Among her young choreographers are Frank Staff and Walter Gore. Her great work continues.

In the twenty years since the first edition of THEATRE AND STAGE, British ballet has definitely entered into the main stream of ballet tradition, sharing with Russia both the taste and the ability for ballet.

PRACTICAL POINTS IN BALLET PRODUCTION

Having given an historical survey of modern ballet, I will conclude the subject with some practical considerations that will be of use to those who intend to give dance recitals or to fit solo dances and small unambitious numbers into a production, and also with some advice to those who think of taking up ballet dancing as a career. There is ample need for such advice, I am convinced, judging from the many letters I receive weekly, and the shows, by pupils, I have witnessed.

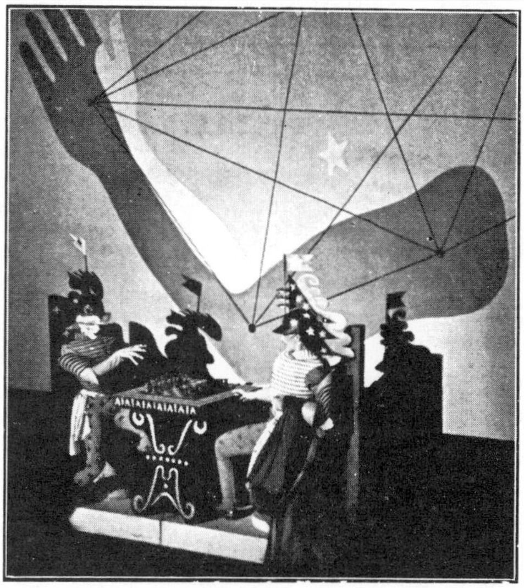

CHECKMATE
Photo Merlyn Severn. Courtesy "Dancing Times"

There are various obvious points that I will not dwell upon. It is certain that anyone who intends to arrange dances, or to perform them, will have to have some few years' experience of dancing, and will, therefore, have realized the type of stage that is needed, the condition of its surface, and such eminently practical details; but my first point they may well not realize (many professionals do not): it is that it takes a genius to keep an audience interested in a solo for more than *one minute* or so. Too many untrained people give dance recitals in which they "express themselves." Let them realize that Anna Pavlova, great genius as she was, whose every movement was interesting, did not rely upon herself entirely unaided for an evening's performance and that her famous solos, including *The Swan*, *The Californian Poppy*, and *The Dragonfly*, lasted for only two minutes. Realization of that fact should have a chastening effect on those who expect the public to look at them dancing their own creations to their own costumes for anything up to two hours. Few dancers are ever justified in giving recitals at all, and then *not* because they have insufficient technique to fit into a ballet company, which is the underlying reason in ninety-nine cases out of a hundred.

We have seen that in the whole history of modern choreography, there are not a dozen outstanding names Therefore, it is evident that the beginner should play for safety, and not for originality. This is not a defeatist counsel. If the real creative mind be there, it will develop all the better for a cautious beginning. Your true choreographer is usually a dancer of parts, for creation comes to the brain through the body, and cannot originate purely in the brain. My practical points are—

1. Do not attempt to create, to arrange, or to produce a dance, much less a ballet, unless you yourself are a dancer of some experience. Ideas for ballets from non-dancers are nearly always so much waste paper.

2. Think in the terms of the material you have to handle. Even the biggest choreographer must do this. With mediocre material you will present a mediocre work, but you may bluff to a certain extent by limiting the range of movement. Nevertheless, remember that it takes a great artist to stand still or to walk across the stage with meaning, so that a comparatively easy technical exercise that savours of the class-room is more effective than extreme simplicity, and for some unknown reason it always impresses an audience when a dancer gets up, however laboriously, on to her points.

3. Avoid symbolism or satire. It takes a great choreographer and a great dancer to succeed with either. The nearer your humour is to the broad lines of clowning, the more obvious it is, the more successful you will be. Ballet can be extremely subtle, but all through its history there are notable clown and character parts, from *La Fille mal Gardée* and *The Sleeping Princess* to *Scuola di Ballo* and *Beau Danube*.

4. Avoid at all costs, and I say so with feeling as I have suffered from it more than most, frenzied rushing to and fro on bare feet, cymbal-banging, pipe-holding, waving cheap coloured scarves in the air. Barefoot dancing requires all the discipline that many years of experience can give. I can remember few barefoot dances that were not utterly ridiculous and only one that was truly great, Pavlova's "Bacchanal."

5. Choose music that is not vague and indefinite, something that is melodious, and that falls into the class of good ballet music: Delibes, Tchaikovsky, Drigo, Strauss. Such music will help both audience and dancers.

6. With non-expert dancers, the question of costume is of first importance, for costume not only helps the dancer, but diverts the attention of the audience. For this reason, ballet practice dress is a traditional black tunic, which shows up in merciless fashion every fault. The choreographer of a small production should aim at a pleasing stage picture, and use curtains rather than a set.

7. Finally, from three to five minutes is ample time for any amateur ballet, just as one minute is long enough for any solo. This somewhat negative advice is all that can conscientiously be given. Were it followed, many a school performance would be less of an ordeal.

Earlier I dealt with the economics of dancing. This will have allowed the intending dancer to see, that from that point of view at any rate, the rewards are few and the way is hard. The first essential for the young dancer is a good school. Even the dancer of genius will be ruined by faulty training, both physical and psychological. The girls' school atmosphere, that spirit of fair play that says: "X has been here longest, so that she must have the best role in the school performance" is inappropriate in a dancing class. The class must not try to turn out a competent machine, but a dancer of personality who is different from her fellow pupils. All too often the exceedingly promising child is retarded from shining at the expense of her elders. That is the great fault of our English dancing. A certain amount of jealousy, while it may be bad in school, is necessary in the development of an artist. We must not confuse character training with the making of artists, but if the character is in question, then ultimately it will surely benefit from the hard work and the sacrifices that are involved. The team spirit must give way to individualism if we are ever to produce more than useful members of a *corps de ballet.* After all, children are individuals, and although they must be disciplined, their individuality must not be destroyed. There are a hundred different subtle shades in the making of a movement, and it is the manner in which that movement is made that gives personality, so that even in the technical training respect must be shown for personal rhythm. It may not be generally realized that, just as with singing, there are in dancing certain well defined divisions parallel to soprano, contralto, bass, tenor, though these divisions are on the whole dictated by temperament rather than physique. To force a dancer into the wrong division is to ruin her. These divisions are—

Classical. This is the ballerina, *première danseuse* division. At its extreme it means brilliant, sparkling, technical dancing in the works of such a choreographer as Petipa, though it is used erroneously to include the romanticism of Fokine in *Sylphides.* Classicism calls for a conventionalized mime, and for a powerful personality that can dominate a large company and hold an audience for a considerable time. The true classical dancer can, as far as actual dancing is concerned, perform absolutely anything, so that a classical training is the background for all work.

Demi-Caractère. The difference between this and the preceding division lies in the spirit and the acting rather than in the dancing, which may well be fully as technical. *Demi-caractère* is more naturalistic in the sense that the dancer portrays a role, and interprets it closely; she is not just the eternal ballerina in whatever circumstances, with a series of set dances and an *adagio* as a climax. An admirable example of *demi-caractère* is Columbine in Fokine's *Carnaval,* the very spirit of mischief and flirtation, or the young girl in *Le Spectre de la Rose,* dreaming of her first dance. It is the *demi-caractère* dance that is the most usual in concerts and school recitals, and it is perhaps more suitable to the English temperament than pure classicism.

Caractère. This denotes National dancing that has been "balletized" for the stage, and all the various buffoon roles that are a tradition in *ballet.*

BALLET IN THE LITTLE THEATRE

If one thing is quite certain it is that the production of any form of ballet is completely beyond the powers of the untrained amateur, but the trained amateur can put on a pleasing work if he bear certain principles in mind. Ballet on a small scale is ideal for the Little Theatre Movement, and should find many exponents, because the commercial ballet stage cannot possibly absorb all the competently trained dancers who are yearly turned out of the various dancing schools, and who, if they do not wish to go into musical comedy, cabaret, or revue, can find no sphere for their activities. Indeed, the adoption of such unpaid work might not be an unwise move in the end, as in every type of musical show a dance producer with some imagination is needed, and at present such a person scarcely exists, judging by the results I have seen. The small ballet production would be the ideal training ground.

All the practical advice that I have to offer, through watching innumerable productions, [illegible] the germ of the idea to its successful presentation, may sound negative, but it deals with the producer's attitude and approach to his work, and it is that initial point of view that can make or mar the whole thing.

There are first of all certain purely material considerations that a little common sense will soon decide, questions of the space available, and the quality of the dancers. The best choreographer in the world may use a small stage to immense advantage, but he cannot make it hold many more dancers than the tyro can use, and also he can do little with an untrained troupe. It is axiomatic, however, that the poorer the producer the better his dancers must be. If the producer has no great choice of material, I would advise him, all things being equal, to make the most prominent use of the best looking girls, bearing in mind that ballet is a spectacle for the eye, and even in the most serious production physical beauty can blind one to a quantity of faults. When dealing with the attributes of the dancer, I placed beauty, using the term in its widest sense, as the first essential, and said that it is only when there is something displeasing about the head or the body that people stare in a hypnotic fashion at the feet.

When the producer has selected his company,

and knows something of their capacities from repeated auditions in various types of work, there are two distinct ways of looking at his contemplated ballet. The first is to attempt a new form of movement or combination of movements, and to be really creative, a sculptor in human form; the second is to bring a fresh point of view to the dressing up of conventional movement, so as to

"LES MASQUES" AT THE BALLET CLUB
Photo by Pollard Crowther

produce a pleasing theatrical spectacle. The inexperienced producer must dismiss the first from his mind from the start, and that without considering himself in any way disgraced, for only five persons at the most have given anything at all to the dance during the past thirty years or so, as the apprenticeship required is so severe that the ambition to write a best selling novel or to become a Royal Academician is more easily attained. Too many inexperienced producers, however, have foundered through imagining that such a thing is within their grasp. On such occasions they have given displays of so-called modernism that are painful to look upon. To be truly a pioneer in any form of art it is necessary to have absorbed all the wisdom of the academician, with no loss of one's own personality.

There are in practice various approaches to choreography, which, by its nature, is a compound of the various arts; part dancing, part music, part decorative art, akin to painting, part drama.

When thinking of the many ballets I have seen created it is not always possible to say from which direction the form of inspiration has come. Usually in a stable company with its entourage of painters and musicians the idea has been picked out of the air, so to speak, and is the result of endless discussion and rediscussion, so that by the time there is anything to be seen no one can quite remember how it all originated. An organized "muddle" of this kind is not for the amateur.

The good choreographer almost invariably takes his initial inspiration from the music, that is the actual form that the dancing is to take. Few amateurs will be in a position to commission special music, so that the first problem will be one of selection. The points he must remember here are: duration, period and atmosphere, variety, and rhythm. Only a skilled musician will dare to tamper with a score for ballet purposes, and then that is most inadvisable, so that bearing in mind the fact that an orchestra is out of the question, and that a good chamber combination is also expensive and difficult to find, it is best to look for piano music. My advice here is not to select anything already well known, which places too great an onus on the choreographer, as the audience has already some mental image of the meaning of the music, and will not

"LYSISTRATA" AT THE BALLET CLUB
Photo by Pollard Crowther

readily accept a new one. To write a ballet around Rachmaninoff's famous prelude, for instance, is to court disaster. At the same time it is necessary to select music that will lend itself to a definite programme and that has a rhythm that the young dancer can memorize. Nothing mars a work more than the obvious counting of beats.

If the approach is through art, the inspiration of a certain painter's work, it is necessary to make a thorough translation; by this I mean a practical realization of the medium. It is not enough to give a few poses from the selected pictures, however accurate; to do that, is to produce *tableaux vivants.* It is necessary to paint with your dancers innumerable pictures in the style of your artist. The ballet consists not in the static poses that are given you as your point of departure, but in the transition from pose to pose. Nearly every painter's work will lend itself to ballet, if that point is borne in mind. Another difficulty is the mating of painter and composer. Period is the most obvious clue, romantic to romantic, classical to classical. More subtle combinations are possible, but they require immense tact and knowledge. This whole pictorial approach is usually inadvisable; it is wiser to find the composer first.

The final approach is the dramatic. It is obviously easier to hold one's audience when there is some small dramatic situation or story to unfold. The inexperienced cannot grasp an audience by his use of pure movement. The story must be simple and self-evident. It must not on any account rely on programme notes. It must not be a story where the situation depends on a spoken word. I have received scenarios that are so complicated as to be quite impossible of realization. *Atmosphere and not plot is the essential.* There is a vast field in fairy tale and legend. Folk lore lends itself to a particular style, and is dangerous, if that style is not thoroughly mastered. It is legitimate to take a Greek legend and to transpose it into conventional ballet, but in that case the transposition must be complete. There is nothing worse than pseudo-Greek, bare feet, scarf-waving, and the like.

This same question of accuracy arises in any ballet based on national dancing. The onus of knowing correct dancing, costume, and music is on the producer, as well as the onus of finding some original angle of presentation. His task is doubled, and while, in most cases, sinuous movement will suggest the Orient to an equally untrained audience, and sword-dancing and kilts Scotland, such bluff is a poor, unworthy thing for any self-respecting producer.

The student of ballet with a three or four years' training will know a vast sequence of steps, which should give him an adequate vocabulary, if he avoids the dangers I have indicated.

With regard to costumes, apart from their intrinsic merits, they must be light and easy to dance in. The conventional ballet skirt is the

"LYSISTRATA" AT THE BALLET CLUB
Photo by Pollard Crowther

product of centuries of experiment. Its origin came about through such practical reasons. It helps in turning, like the rim of a top; it leaves freedom to the legs; and in design, as far as colour is concerned, it permits of infinite variation. Whether or not it is adopted must depend on the legs of the performers. The clever designer will have his dancers in mind the entire time. *Costume can accentuate or hide physical defects.* The arms, the trunk, and the legs can be lengthened or shortened by skilful study. It is not enough to knock off a series of spirited drawings. Too many amateur and even professional designers leave it at that. If there must be a choice between the artist who is vague and the dressmaker, the dressmaker is the more valuable. Only a designer who understands practical dressmaking, the choice of materials, and the actual cutting has any *raison d'être* in the theatre. All the finest designers, such as Natalie Goncharova, have supervised the actual making of the costume from the first sketch of the general aspect, through the successive stages of detailed tracings, up to the cutting and sewing.

Most small producers will use curtains for scenery, and by skilful draping they are always superior to cheap or inadequate scenery. When Pavlova used curtains for the famous *Dying Swan* the effect was always vastly superior to the poorly painted lake background that was sometimes used. Curtains and a plain white backcloth, well lit, will produce a variety of effects. They can be draped to represent trees or columns, and used in a variety of ways to represent the "feel" of bifferent periods. In any case, on a small stage the screens so often used for scenery are only too often in the way of movement, and by their use it is exceedingly difficult to suggest any perspective. They usually have the effect of making the dancers appear large and cumbersome.

Avoid unnecessary props. It requires great experience to handle them to music, and veils, flowers, Pipes of Pan, and the like have a way of falling to the ground and attracting the gaze of the company and the audience, until someone has the presence of mind to kick them out of the way. Mime or acting should be simple, but not conventional, save in a conventional ballet. Ballet, like every other art, has its realism, and no one can be moved to anything but amusement by the hand-on-heart type of thing. There are many other ways of suggesting love.

"Les Sylphides" at the Ballet Club
Showing the perspective that can be obtained on a small stage by the use of curtains and backcloth
Photo by Pollard Crowther

This whole question of mime is extremely complex; many, I would say the majority of practised professionals, never master it at all. There is one point that I must stress. The choreographer must bear in mind the fact that mime is not superimposed upon dance movement; it is a definite part of it; that is to say, the body as well as the face must express the particular emotion. Every muscle movement in the face is a part of the dance. If this were realized, the meaningless toothy grin that disfigures so much dancing would disappear. It is definitely part of the producer-choreographer's job to watch these things. The Ballet Club, although a professional theatre with an experienced company, shows what can be done with ballet on an intimate and unambitious scale, and it has definitely proved that ballet has its place in the Little Theatre Movement. Its success, I believe, is largely due to the fact that it started round a school, and that its company was recruited from that school. Ballet requires an infinite number of rehearsals, and parts cannot be taken home and learned. Ballet also requires the greatest team-work and discipline. A group of girls who have always danced together, even if only in class, may show better results in a shorter time than more brilliant individuals gathered here and there. In a school, rehearsal can be a definite part of the curriculum. If each of our numberless schools had their rehearsal clubs, quite apart from the annual pupils' show, much valuable work could be accomplished.

I am aware that throughout I have given counsels of prudence, counsels lacking in ambition or adventure. I have done so deliberately to discourage a vain search for originality.

When the choreographer is able to produce truly original works he will not need my hints or anyone else's. Meanwhile many dancers with the means at hand can please their audiences, enjoy themselves, and, by learning, assist actively in the great ballet revival that is now taking place in England.

STAGE DANCING

PHILIP J. S. RICHARDSON, Editor, " The Dancing Times "

MR. ARNOLD HASKELL has dealt, almost exclusively, in THEATRE AND STAGE, with what is popularly known as "ballet" dancing. This is the highest form of spectacular dancing, and it is possible that many readers will wonder why so much space should be devoted to such a difficult phase of the Art. The reason is that a high percentage of all spectacular dancing has for its basic technique the same technique as is required of the ballet dancer. This indebtedness to classical dancing is particularly noticeable in modern musical comedy work in which the dances entrusted to the chorus to-day are frequently of the nature of ballet in their conception, and sometimes include difficult work *sur les pointes.*

ALICIA MARKOVA
Former *prima ballerina assoluta* at La Scala, Milan, in an " arabesque "
Courtesy Maurice Seymour

THE DANCER AND HER AUDIENCE

Before we proceed to consider any other form of spectacular dancing, whether it be based on the ballet or not, it will be as well to say a few words about the relationship that exists between the dancer and her audience.

There are many forms of dancing, but for the moment let us divide all dancing into two groups —personal dancing and spectacular dancing. By "personal" dancing I mean all those forms of dancing that we do for *our own* personal gratification. This would include ballroom dancing and all dancing for purposes of physical culture. On the other hand, by "spectacular" dancing I mean all that dancing, generally performed on a stage or other specially prepared space, which is done for the entertainment *of the spectator.* It is spectacular dancing that I intend to discuss.

The term "spectacular dancing" (including the music which accompanies it) implies three things: the dancer, the audience, and some link between the two. This link consists of the organs of hearing and seeing. All that can come across the footlights from the stage to the audience are waves of sound and waves of light that impinge upon the ears and eyes of the spectator. Everything that a dancer wishes to convey to her audience can be entrusted to these waves by an artist who knows her business, and can be received by a spectator *who is prepared to do his share of the work.*

Here we come to the first important point that must be appreciated by every dancer who hopes to make a successful appearance before the public. The work does not rest entirely with the dancer —the spectator has to do his part. He must not be content to let these waves of sound and light just reach him . . . he must encourage them to penetrate as deeply into his understanding as they can, and the depth of their penetration depends not only on their nature as sent out by the dancer, but also to a considerable extent on the artistic susceptibilities of the spectator at the moment of reception. If a dancer's work is worth thinking about, it can only be appreciated to its full extent by an audience that is prepared to think, and as that act of thinking stirs up the higher aesthetic faculties of the spectator he or she is liable to brain fag just as much as the dancer is liable to bodily fatigue.

"Les Présages"
A scene from Massine's ballet, composed to the music of Tchaikovsky's Fifth Symphony, presented by "Les Ballets Russes de Monte Carlo" at the Alhambra

Great care must be taken, therefore, to see that the programme is not too long, that it is suitable for the type of audience before whom it is to be presented, and that the items are presented in the most advantageous order.

The "symphonic" ballets, *Les Présages* and *Choreartium*, produced by Massine at the Alhambra, require a considerable amount of concentration on the part of the spectator if they are to be appreciated to the fullest extent. It would be inadvisable, therefore, to place them both upon the same programme, and it would be foolish to present them either in a "revue" or in the middle of a variety programme when the mind of the spectator is not attuned to the atmosphere of such ballets. Dance turns that are given at cabaret entertainments in restaurants and are generally seen by people who have already spent three hours in a theatre should be so "light" in conception that they demand no over-deep thought on the part of the audience.

Dancing has been defined as the outward expression in co-ordinate rhythmic movement of an inward emotion felt by the dancer. If we accept this broad definition a difficulty under which the spectacular dancer labours is at once apparent. The spectacular dancer has to express emotions that she may not really feel. She may have to be gay when she has no real cause for gaiety; she may have to be sad when she is seeing the whole world in colours of the rose; she may have to move in the atmosphere of the seventeenth century when she is an extremely up-to-date member of the twentieth. And so there is a danger that her dancing may not be truthful and that she will not be conveying to her audience truth" to which I have referred may be broken. One is by the use of wrong music. There is something untruthful about a Polish National Dance done to Hungarian music. Historical inaccuracies should be guarded against, and, conversely, historical accuracy sought.

It is, therefore, essential that the message sent forth by the dancer to her audience shall convey

"LES SYLPHIDES"
Fokine's famous ballet danced to Chopin's music, as presented by the Sadler's Wells Ballet Company
Photo by J. W. Debenham

that sense of truth which is one of the most important attributes of her work. It is, therefore, most essential that this defect be remedied. The young dancer must realize from the beginning that the spectacular dance must be imbued with a certain number of the qualities of the personal dance, and she must educate herself to be able to feel, as far as is possible, the emotions that the part demands, for if she does not feel them to *some* extent she cannot expect the spectator to feel them to *any* extent at all.

There are other ways in which this "sense of a sense of truth. It must also convey what I will call a sense of power. By this I mean that the dancer must give the impression that she could, if she liked, do far more. She must never appear to have touched the limits of her technique. A sense of power can be shown by a young dancer every whit as well as by an experienced ballerina. It is shown by one who has never shirked the drudgery of practice. It simply means that, as far as you have progressed, you are mistress of your technique. . . . be that technique what we call Elementary or Advanced. Let me try to explain more fully what I mean. I have never timed how long a dancer can hold an *arabesque*, but supposing she can do this in the classroom for three seconds without wobbling, then on the stage she must never hold it for more than two seconds at the longest. If she holds it for the full time the audience knows, as she begins to wobble, that she has reached the limit of her powers; if, however, she deliberately passes from the still firmly held *arabesque* into another pose her full powers are not revealed, and she conveys the impression that she is a complete mistress of poise. This is what I call a sense of power, and it applies to many things besides *arabesques*. If in the classroom you can just do an *entrechat six*, then attempt to do no more than a perfect *four* in public. You have no idea how many dancers ruin the effect of their dancing by attempting things that are on the extreme confines of their powers.

I have explained to you how your dance, if it is to appeal to your audience, must convey what I have called a sense of power and a sense of truth. It must also convey a sense of design—that surely is a fact so obvious that it scarcely needs enlarging upon, for a dance with no design is not worthy of the name of dance at all. I was originally going to write a sense of beauty, but I think the word "design" is better, for the eccentric and the humorous dance may appeal and yet have no "beauty" as we commonly understand that word.

Further, in countless instances, when the dance tells a definite tale or interprets a definite idea, when it is a "story dance," it must also convey a sense of meaning. Such instances are to be found in ballets like *Petrouchka*, *Coppélia*, or *Comus*, and in practically every character and demi-character number that occurs to you.

In all cases, then, whether your dance is a dance of meaning, a story dance, or not, it is essential that in its execution you should convey to your audience this sense of power, truth, and design to which I have referred—but if your dance tells no story—if it is just pure dancing such as we see in *Les Sylphides*—if it depends upon its sense of design for its existence, then to convey a sense of power and of truth is even more necessary in order that the absence of meaning may be atoned for. These types of dances require that the performer should be a complete mistress of the technique that she uses. They require at least a budding artist to execute them and a real artist to arrange them. They are like copperplate writing; if there is the least flaw in a curve they are marred. They are so difficult because unless they are absolutely perfect, the sense of power and of design is lost, and as

TATIANA RIABOUCHINSKA
As "The Dancer" in the Fokine ballet "Petrouchka"

they have no story in the ordinary acceptance of the word, they have, therefore, by the time they reach their audience, no message to carry at all. Therefore, whenever you present a dance of this nature, let it be so simple that it is well within the powers of the performer. Remember what I said about the sense of power—it is the margin between what you do and what you could do. We see many solos that convey no sense of power at all because they are crammed full of difficult steps that absorb every atom of the performer's ability, and leave her floundering in an endeavour to stretch that ability more than is possible.

LIGHTER FORMS OF DANCING

Dancing, being a living art, is constantly changing. The basic technique remains the same, but the texture and shape of the art which clothes that technique alters just as frequently as do the fashions of ladies' dresses. It is extremely sensitive to the dominating idea of the moment. Over a hundred and twenty years ago the wave of romanticism that swept the world and brought forth the novels of Sir Walter Scott and Victor Hugo and the poems of Heine found its echo in dancing in the romantic ballet *La Sylphide* and the popularity of the valse. More than twenty-five years ago the hectic days of the Armistice gave birth to the "ugly" period of the Diaghileff Ballet, an orgy of highly syncopated "tap" work, and the eccentric phase of the foxtrot.

In no way are these changes in "world thought" so irrevocably registered as in that form of dancing which is called "musical comedy" or "revue." Indeed to some extent it is more progressive in its changes than is the ballet, for though the construction of new ballets may show continual alterations, it is quite possible for the old style (such as *Giselle*) to be revived with great success, whereas the style of ten years ago in musical comedy could never be renewed, except as a curiosity such as the resuscitation of the *Can-can.*

I am using the term "musical comedy dancing," I should point out, in a broad sense to include the dancing not only of the chorus and the principals in musical comedy proper but also that type of dancing which is done by troupes in revues and as "turns" in a variety bill or cabaret.

Not many years ago the principal assets of a dancer who aspired to this type of work were a pretty face, a good figure, a well shaped pair of legs, and ability to kick high, do the splits, and execute a *pas de basque.*

To-day the dancer who seeks work in musical comedy must be exceedingly versatile and have had a thorough training. She must have gone through a course of limbering and stretching, and must have a good working knowledge of the technique of classical dancing—up to a certain point. In addition, she must be familiar with syncopated "tap" and "buck" steps and be able to do side, front, and hitch kicks with ease and lightness.

AN EARLY DEVELOPMENT OF MUSICAL COMEDY WORK
Helen Burnell and chorus in *The House that Jack Built*
The Stage Photo Co.

It was probably about the end of 1927 or the beginning of 1928 that the usual rather vapid "ensemble" work by the chorus in musical comedy gave way to something better and more artistic, and the girl who had apparently "wasted" her time learning the classical technique suddenly came into her own.

On the other hand, work that may be described as almost pure ballet was entrusted to the chorus in that great Alhambra success, *Waltzes from Vienna*, and all the members of that chorus were highly trained classical dancers. They were entrusted with such steps as *entrechat six*, *sissones*, *cabrioles*, and *grands jetés en tournant*. That work, of course, was somewhat exceptional, and would not be required of the dancers in musical comedy as a rule.

"WALTZES FROM VIENNA"
The chorus in this musical play at the Alhambra were all highly trained ballet dancers
Photo by Eric Gray

Albertina Rasch with her famous troupes in the United States set the lead, and the example was soon followed in this country by up-to-date producers. Movements and steps hitherto left for the classical ballet were introduced, and some call was also made, particularly when "strong" work was required, on the so-called Central European methods of Mary Wigman and von Laban. The chorus dancing to accompany Sonnie Hale's famous song, "Dance Little Lady," in C. B. Cochran's revue, *This Year of Grace*, and the work of Helen Burnell and chorus in the song " My Heart is Saying " from the Jack Hulbert revue *The House that Jack Built*, were early examples of Central European influence in this country.

More recently the light opera *Gay Rosalinda*, based on Strauss's *Die Fledermaus* has shown us some beautiful ballet work arranged by Wendy Toye, who was herself a well known classical dancer.

A phase of dancing that is exceedingly popular in musical comedy and revue is that usually known as "troupe" dancing. This is performed by a troupe of girls, usually eight, but sometimes as many as sixteen or twenty in number. In this case all the members of the troupe execute the same steps simultaneously.

Some years ago the "Palace Girls" were a troupe of this character and became world-famous. The secret of their particular success was the way in which the whole company moved as one person.

An American "Adagio" Pair
Virginia Haglin and Clayton Kendall

When they turned, they turned together; when they marched in line, the line was absolutely straight; when they kicked every foot was raised the same height from the ground; and when they did tap work their beats were clean and clear. It was nothing but a thorough training, constant rehearsal, and a wonderful enthusiasm for their work that brought about this result.

"Tap" work, which is used a great deal to-day, has greatly changed during the past few years. In many ways it is possible that this is one of the oldest forms of dancing, but it comes to us from

Contortionism
Renée Joliffe, well known in London pantomime

so many sources and through so many countries that its origin cannot be clearly defined.

In England we go back, at any rate within comparatively recent times, to the clog dancing of Lancashire, in which a wooden sole and heel were used. Later came the "jink" or heel with loose metal plate substituted for the wooden heel. Then followed the long or flap shoe dancing, as done by the famous Dan Leno. But years have passed since the days of the old clog dancing contests in which the lower limbs only came into play, and the judges sat under the stage in order that they might hear the beats. "Buck" dancing, introduced to us from the coloured folk of America, has exercised an immense influence on this type of work.

To-day tap work is frequently known as "rhythm dancing," and the development during the past few years has been very great. "Floor walloping," as step work was called in the old days, appealed only to the ear. To-day troupe and solo work of this type must appeal to the eye as well, and it must be full of touches of humour and the unexpected. It must never be too obvious —even the appeal to the ear must not be made by tapping out the obvious beats. It is the "off beat" and the secondary rhythm that must be looked for. And yet, though "Lancashire Clog" and "Buck Dancing" are back numbers, the old steps still form the basis of the new technique.

A solo tap or rhythm dancer can make his steps as complicated as he is able to, but in the case of troupes, in order to preserve a "sense of power" the steps must be much simpler so that they may be done together with mathematical exactitude. For the same reason, better work can be done by a team of eight than by a team of sixteen.

"Acrobatic" dancing is a term that is popularly used to denote all those forms of dancing that are allied to acrobatics. I shall continue to use it, although, strictly speaking, it refers only to dancing in which one performer springs off another one's shoulders. In the popular sense, however, it includes what are technically called by such names as "Eccentric Dancing," "Contortion Dancing," "Tumbling," and "Legmania." This form of dancing seems to go back either to the Arabs or to the Circus. The best performers on the stage all seem to have learned their business in the circus, and the names they use for the various movements are frequently different from those used by teachers of dancing. An endeavour is being made to straighten out this difference by a few of the leading teachers, in conjunction with some of the principal stage performers.

When this sort of work is presented as a *dancing act* care should be taken that it is made as artistic as possible and that the posturing, contortionism, tumbling, and acrobatics should be harmoniously blended with some beautiful dancing movements.

It was clearly proved when the Children and Young Persons Act was discussed in Committee that there is no danger to the young child learning this type of dancing *provided the teacher knows her business.*

Miss Zelia Raye in her book *Rational Limbering* says: "There should be a controlled freedom in dancing. The old method has always been to get the muscles tightened up like steel, which must naturally hinder all supple movement. Any authority on physical culture knows the value of pliable muscles. The stretching and limbering exercises form the ground work to all acrobatics. Hand stands, cart-wheels, tinsecas, back bends, splits, etc., are within the average dancer's capabilities, and give the thrill of achievement apart from keeping the student in a state of physical fitness."

A Cabaret Duet
By Wendy Toye and Fred Franklin at Grosvenor House
Photo by A. & L. Elstob

In the case of acrobatic dancing couples—what the Americans call an "adagio" team—it may be taken as a *sine qua non* that the girl has had a ballet training and is able to do *pointe* work in addition to her acrobatic acquirements. The thorough ballet training assures that whenever her partner lifts her or holds her on high her body, arms, and legs will always fall in a graceful pose. The toe dancing gives finish to her work and increased height.

Methods of practice differ considerably, and no hard and fast rule can be laid down. Some use the ropes and other appliances of the gymnasium, trying out difficult poses with a waist band, which is attached to a rope suspended from the roof, and thus preventing a nasty fall. Others content themselves with thick mats to break any unexpected tumble.

Acrobatic dancing has changed during the last few years. It used to be acrobatics with little dancing, but to-day the team that does not dance as well as "stunt" does not go very far.

OPERA—CABARET—COMPETITIONS

In many of the well known operas, such as *Faust*, *Carmen*, and *Aïda*, there are ballets, and from time to time when these operas are given someone is called upon to arrange the dances. This is not quite such a straightforward or easy matter as it may appear to be, and a considerable amount of historical knowledge is wanted. For if, as is usually the case, the opera is presented on the old familiar lines, it is essential that the ballet should follow the style that is traditionally associated with that particular opera.

When the Royal Opera Syndicate, in 1933, entrusted the production of the ballet in *Faust* to the Association of Operatic Dancing, now The Royal Academy of Dancing, that Association, although it numbers several well-known choreographers amongst its members, preferred to send to the Paris Opera for M. Leo Staats so that it might have the choreography traditionally associated with that particular opera.

ALL ENGLAND COMPETITION
Pupils of the Hammond School of Chester win the Cabaret Troupe Section

During recent years the Sadler's Wells Ballet has made frequent appearances with the Sadler's Wells Opera Company, one notable occasion being in Smetana's *The Bartered Bride*.

Producers who are called upon to arrange any dance that may have to be included in some "straight" play—such, for instance, as the "Minuet" in *School for Scandal*, must always be careful that their arrangement is in full accord with the period of the play. In a London production of a musical play—not a musical *comedy*—of which the period was about one hundred years ago, a dancer was made to execute a ballet dance with *modern arm movements* such as one saw in some of the later Diaghileff productions. If, on the other hand, the musical play is a musical comedy, historical accuracy, though desirable if possible, is not essential.

In such plays as *The Mikado*, *The Geisha*, and *San Toy*, where there is a certain amount of dancing by Japanese or Chinese characters, accurate national dances of those countries are not expected—the Chinese or Japanese atmosphere should merely be suggested. The same attitude may be safely adopted in the case of all Eastern dances, but when the dances of countries in, say, Western Europe have to be executed they should be correct.

ALL ENGLAND COMPETITION
Pupils of the Ripman School of London win the Group Section
Photo by Peter North

Of these perhaps the most difficult are the dances of Spain. These should always be referred to someone who has an intimate knowledge of Spanish dances; otherwise one runs the danger of seeing, for instance, a classical dance done by a performer in peasant costume or vice versa.

When producing what is popularly known as a "cabaret" entertainment—that is, a series of short "turns" given as a rule on a ball-room floor, usually rather late in the evening—the producer should bear in mind that his audience only want to be amused in the lightest possible way, and that they do not wish to see dancing that requires a lot of thought on the part of the spectator to understand it properly. A troupe of eight doing ensemble and tap work is the ideal opening number. "Adagio" acts and single turns of an eccentric or contortionist nature are always popular. If there are to be several items, all should not be dancing turns; some sort of contrast should be introduced. Stage waits must be avoided, and, if the dancing has to be done on a ball-room floor, the shoes of the dancers should be treated with some form of rubber solution to prevent slipping. With certain audiences a straightforward exhibition of modern ball-room dancing done exceedingly well is welcomed. This also serves to make a happy contrast with other dance turns. On these occasions unless the lighting facilities are exceptional, it is frequently advisable to have "full house lights" and not to attempt to make use of indifferent "spots."

As my subject is theatrical dancing, it is desirable for me to refer to the dances that are presented at numerous theatrical dancing competitions.

The principal one is the "All England Stage Dancing Competition," held during the first three months of each year in aid of the "Sunshine Homes for Blind Babies." It is sometimes referred to as the "Sunshine Competition." Next in importance is the Stage Dancing Section at the annual Blackpool Dance Festival, held during

MADAME ADELINE GENÉE

President of the Royal Academy of Dancing on her last appearance at the Coliseum in 1933

Photo by Lenare

May, when over a thousand different dances are seen on the stage of the handsome Opera House in that popular resort. In addition, many of the musical festivals and eisteddfods, held all over the country, include a Stage Dancing Section.

At these competitions the competitors are grouped into classes according to age. The dances are divided according to "Style" into Classical (ballet), Greek, or Natural Movement, National, Character, Demi-character, and Musical Comedy or Cabaret. They are also further divided into Solos, Duets, and Groups.

When arranging a dance for one of these competitions it is essential strictly to carry out the conditions. For instance, in the Classical section a purely technical or ballet dance should be given without any suggestion of character or demi-character work, and in that section usually labelled "Group" and qualified with the statement, "Any style except Cabaret or Musical Comedy," care should be taken to avoid simultaneous ensemble and tap work that is usually associated with revue or cabaret: the arranger should endeavour to produce a miniature ballet.

Every dance in a competition has a time limit, which varies from a minute and a half to two minutes for solos, and from two to five minutes for duets or groups. This time limit must be strictly adhered to, otherwise disqualification may ensue. Sometimes this limitation involves a "cut" in the music. The "cut" should be made only by someone who thoroughly understands music. To a person with a musical ear it is as bad to make a faulty "cut" in music as it would be to omit a line of poetry from a verse without paying any attention to the sense.

In the "National" section of a stage dancing competition the adjudicators look for the traditional national dance done to correct music and in a true costume. The national dances of Ireland are, perhaps, the most sinned against in this section. In the jig instead of seeing the true Irish jig one is frequently presented with an elaborate dance by a dancer who wears a costume that no Irish dancer ever wore.

It is essential that a dance for a competition should be arranged so that it is well within the powers of the person who will have to execute it. The adjudicators prefer to see simple steps brilliantly done to a number filled with difficult *enchainements* that the performer cannot do.

These Stage Dancing Competitions have been the means of discovering talent that otherwise might never have been noticed.

A number of performers who are well known to the ballet public to-day were first heard of in such events. Among these may be mentioned Margot Fonteyn, Pamela May, Wendy Toye, Harold Turner, and Frederic Franklin.

TAP WORK

The "Eight Step Sisters," whose beats were frequently heard in broadcasts

Photo by B.B.C.

ENSEMBLE OR TROUPE WORK

The Alfred Haines Dancers showing how all must move alike

THE GOVERNANCE OF THE DANCE IN ENGLAND

It has occurred to me that, in this brief treatment of stage dancing, a useful purpose will be served if I give an account of the various bodies which, to some extent, control the teaching of dancing in England.

It should be made clear that it is not absolutely necessary for a would-be dancer to join one of these bodies or to pass their examinations, though to do so will be found a great help. In the case, however, of a student who is hoping to become a teacher they will be found almost indispensable.

It is gradually being realized by education authorities that dancing properly taught can be used in the general education of the young child to help in her physical and mental development. But to do this with success it is necessary that the teacher of dancing should be well educated and, in addition to her dancing knowledge, know something about psychology, anatomy, hygiene, and the kindred arts of music and design. The Royal Academy of Dancing has a syllabus for such would-be teachers and arranges a course of lectures and classes. By this means it is hoped to produce in a few years' time a number of teachers who have a sound knowledge of dancing and who can satisfy the pedagogic requirements of the Ministry of Education. When one remembers that there are in this country about six million children between the ages of six and fifteen years who have to be educated, it will be realized what very great possibilities there are in this direction.

Until about twenty-five years ago we had a mere handful of English teachers who could be

A Scene from "Job"
The famous ballet set to music by Vaughan Williams with *décor* after the drawings by William Blake, produced by the Vic-Wells Company
Photo by J. W. Debenham

relied upon to teach the correct technique. English dancers who wished to progress had therefore to go to a foreign teacher, who might be in this country one month and out of it the next to wherever his engagements chanced to take him. This lack of sound English teachers was due to the absence in this country of any Royal or State-aided school that could be turned to as a criterion of what was right and what was wrong. As long as Russia, Italy, France, and Denmark had their famous endowed schools in Leningrad, Milan, Paris, and Copenhagen, there was no excuse for bad teaching in those countries, and, conversely, until we established some such school in this country there was no guarantee that our teachers were correct.

Feeling that no assistance could be hoped for from the government, a few far-seeing teachers banded themselves together in an endeavour to supply the omission, and as a result there are now several bodies that place the correct technique of dancing within the reach of all.

I mention the Royal Academy of Dancing, which has the honour of being under the Patronage of Her Majesty Queen Mary and of holding a Royal Charter granted by King George V. This body makes it its duty to preserve and to teach the traditional "Classical" or "Ballet" technique, which is the basis of nearly all dancing. It is controlled by a Council of which that famous dancer Madame Adeline Genée is the President, and Madame Thamar Karsavina and Miss Phyllis Bedells members.

Membership of the Academy is gained by passing its Elementary Examination. Once that has been negotiated the member is expected to

A Scene from "Coppelia"
A production of the Vic-Wells Company. Madame Lydia Lopokova as "Swanilda" is in the centre
Photo by J. W. Debenham

MEMBERS OF THE ROYAL ACADEMY OF DANCING
A production of "The Debutante" at the Coliseum
Photo by Lenare

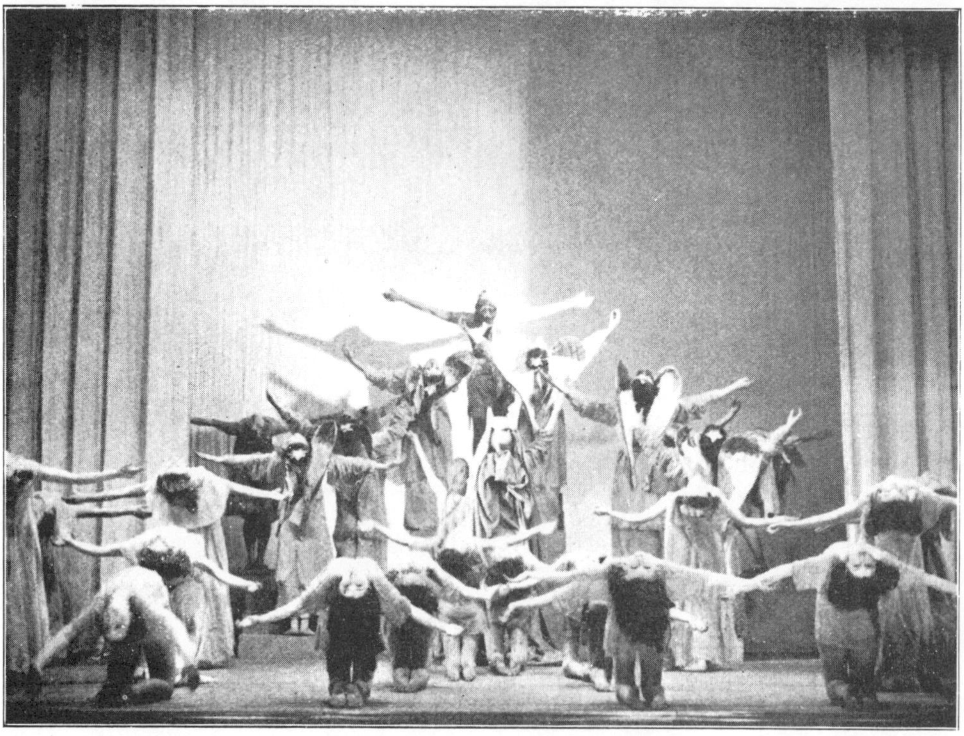

PRODUCED BY ONE OF THE BALLET CLUBS
The final tableau in the ballet "Apocalypse," arranged by Majorie Middleton and produced to music specially composed by Leighton Lucas
Photo T. Knight

take subsequent examinations, known as the "Intermediate," the "Advanced," and the "Solo Seal," which are of increasing degrees of difficulty. There is also a special Examination for Teachers. The Academy has over two thousand members, and an engagement as an assistant in a dancing school is frequently contingent upon the candidate having passed one or more of the Academy's Examinations.

Its activities include numerous free classes or lectures for the benefit of its members, and several times a year are held specially graded Examinations for Children, for which there are about ten thousand candidates annually. The offices of the Association are at 154 Holland Park Avenue, London, W.11.

Working on somewhat similar lines to those of the Academy the Cecchetti Society was founded about two years later for the purpose of perpetuating the method of teaching ballet dancing used by that famous teacher, Enrico Cecchetti, who was for many years associated either with the Imperial School in Leningrad or the Diaghileff Ballet. The method adopted is perhaps slightly different from that in use by the R.A.D., and it is beyond my province to discuss here which is the better. It may be stated, however, that many dancers and teachers have found it useful to study both systems. The Cecchetti Society has been incorporated in the Imperial Society of Teachers of Dancing, and is known as the "Classical Ballet" Branch of that Society.

BALLET ON THE FILMS
Moira Shearer, one of the leading dancers of the Sadler's Wells Company, as she appeared in the ballet in "Red Shoes"

The Imperial Society of Teachers of Dancing, with headquarters at 70 Gloucester Place, London, W.1, is the largest association of dance *teachers* in the world. It has about three thousand members, but a high percentage of these belong to its ball-room branch only. Of particular interest to readers of THEATRE AND STAGE are its Classical Ballet Branch and its Stage Branch. In the latter full attention is devoted to all those phases of stage dancing that do not actually come under the heading of "Classical Ballet"—such as "tap," "acrobatic," and "musical comedy" work. The Society also has branches devoted to "Operatic" and "Greek" dancing. The syllabus for these two branches is based on those of the R.A.D. and the Greek Association respectively.

The Greek Dance Association was founded by Miss Ruby Ginner a number of years ago, and has its headquarters at 7a Ebury Street, London, S.W.1. This association is more or less indispensable to anyone who wishes to take up the teaching of this style of dancing, which now finds so much favour in the High Schools of the country. For the theatrical dancer its importance is not so great.

In addition to the associations and societies that I have named there are others that do good work in their own particular spheres, but in the majority of cases most of their activities are devoted to ballroom work. Nine times out of ten merit alone will enable a girl to make her way as a dancer, but she will find membership of an appropriate organization of great help—especially if she wishes to become a teacher.

It is undoubtedly owing to the hard work that has been accomplished by these bodies during the past ten years or so that English dancing has gained in reputation.

The value of the work that these associations have done is already recognized abroad, and on several occasions the R.A.D. and the Classical Ballet Branch of the Imperial Society have sent their examiners to South Africa, and Australia.

Practically all the societies and associations, in addition to the many free classes given during the course of the year, hold, generally during the summer months, a "Week" of special lectures and classes, at which instruction is given to their members by some of the most famous teachers in the world.

These associations are not "employment agencies," but, nevertheless, membership frequently brings the young dancer into contact with those who have it in their power to give engagements or at any rate to provide auditions. Often an entertainment is staged at which budding talent can be seen. Now and then is stage managed or organized a bigger event, such as the visit to the Royal Theatre, Copenhagen, by an English ballet company, which was arranged by the R.A.D.

During the past few years a number of ballet clubs has sprung into existence in many of our large towns. These afford the amateur an excellent opportunity of learning something about the professional side of dancing. Each of these clubs is open to amateurs as well as to members of the profession. At frequent intervals meetings are held at which lectures by well-known authorities take place and classes are given in the rudimentary technique. Very often a club will stage a public performance once a year in which those amateur members who have shown some promise are permitted to appear alongside the professionals. The Production Club which is attached to the Royal Academy of Dancing is one of the most important of these clubs and it has already held several recitals at West End theatres. The Edinburgh Ballet Club has also done some very good work and there are clubs in Bristol, Manchester, Liverpool, and Bournemouth. Care should be taken when joining a club that it is a real ballet club and not merely an activity of one particular school.

DRAMA AS EDUCATION

T. G. WILLIAMS, M.A., F.R.Hist.S. Author of "Main Currents of Social and Industrial Change," "The Peopled Kingdom," "The History of Commerce"

SINCE Mr. Granville Barker in 1921 "drafted a bill" for an Exemplary Theatre, and in the preamble urged the educational claims of acting in schools, much light has flooded the boards of the amateur stage. "You don't expect me," said his Minister of Education to the Man of the Theatre in *The Exemplary Theatre*, "to encourage you to go round muddling up my teachers' minds . . . with talk about the civic importance of the theatre, and the psychological necessity for the development of the histrionic instinct in children. I enjoy a good play, well-acted; so do they. Don't spoil it for us. I admit a certain absolute educative value in music. I haven't yet admitted it in the drama, have I?" "If you didn't teach some form of drama in schools," retorted the M. of T., "you couldn't teach anything at all . . . But I'll promise to be not at all exigent about what you do teach as long as you'll give it its rightful name, and not disguise it as gymnastics, or as some Cinderella branch of literature."

THE STUDY OF ACTED DRAMA

What then are the educational claims of acted drama, as distinct from the recreational? The question can be asked without conveying any implication that the former transcend the latter, and without suggesting a false dichotomy of school activity. Leisure is the budding time of the human spirit, when the sap rises and feeds the swelling fruit-buds. It has claims on youth that are neglected only at the risk of a warped and stunted personality, an "expense of spirit in a waste of shame." But notwithstanding this, the claims of recreation are capable of being distinguished from those that belong to the more formal and systematic activities of school life, and the question now to be considered is what place the study of drama, approached not as a literary form but in action and practice, may claim to hold in the educative process.

Looked at from the individual standpoint, the values of acted drama are to be found in an acquired illumination and an inward endowment. "Not to know the relative disposition of things is the state of slaves or children," wrote Newman; "to have mapped out the Universe is the boast, or at least the ambition, of Philosophy." The Universe to be mapped out by the actor is the universe of experience, of character, of incident, of situation, of human relationships, of emotion. He studies the interplay of human ambitions, the breadth and the depth of love and jealousy and cruelty and misunderstanding. He explores the springs of human folly, and seeks to find the fountains of laughter and of joy. His Universe includes the vast regions above and below the plane of conscious living, which he investigates by eliminating from the totality of effects those that arise from the known and calculable aspects of experience, and considering only the remainder. Those psychic and spiritual aspects of experience that form so large a part of life, being inward and personal, press for outward concrete interpretation with an even greater insistence than the actual and the factual as they appear in the light of common day.

There is an important element of truth in the assertion that the only interpretation possible for an actor is the interpretation of himself, that he cannot get outside his own skin. The Hamlet or the Caliban that he renders is the Hamlet-constituent or the Caliban-constituent of his own organic self. According to this view, all acting is self-expression. But there is here need for caution, since every virtue has the defect of its quality. Self-expression may easily pass over into self-assertion, and the urge to be "individual" may encourage the development of affected mannerisms. An acting technique that is merely imitative may well lead to such unfortunate results. But where there is a high sensibility and intelligence there can be no danger; for no satisfaction can be got by an actor capable of genuine feeling and independent thought from the act of presenting the merely external aspects of a character. His expression, if it is to be of *himself*, and yet of the playwright's creation, demands that a process of alchemy in the crucible of the mind should have been carried out to its conclusion. Consider what this process is.

ACTING TECHNIQUE

The actor, in the preliminary study of his part, applies his intelligence to probe deeply into the thoughts and emotions of the character, and to reflect these thoughts and feelings in words and tones that seem to echo them. With every repetition of his part in rehearsal he reaches to a finer understanding and appreciation of it, to a closer identity with it, and to a more perfect articulation of his own movement and utterance with the rest of the action. Eventually, in a moment of intense excitement, when the sensibility is caught up to a pitch of illumination that clarifies and simplifies all as in a lightning flash, the personation that the actor is attempting passes over into experience, the emotion formerly simulated is now felt, and his voice, his gestures, his countenance reflect no longer a merely feigned and counterfeit motion of the spirit; rather do they now "show virtue her own feature, scorn her own image and the very age and body of the time his form and pressure." Thereupon, when the moment of excitement is passed, the mind as intelligence looks back in silence and repose upon its experience as upon an emotion recollected in tranquillity, reflects upon the incident or the situation that gave birth to it, and works it up as an element in consciousness.

There is here a full and complete synthesis of mental states. The active principle of the actor's will first directs and focuses attention on a character, a situation, an incident. The intelligence subjects it to an analysis, a reconstruction, to lay bare the plan and purpose of it, its motivation, its relationships. Finally, the actor, usually in a flash, apprehends the part emotionally. In that instant he adds something to his experience; the horizons of his life are extended; his mind has become a more sensitive instrument of living; his capacity for volition, for thought, and for feeling is increased.

Hitherto we have been considering only the personal values to be derived from the effort to interpret a part in an acted play. But the social values are not to be overlooked. If we regard the matter from the standpoint of the school as a community, one of the most important features of play production is the opportunity it presents and the demand it makes for co-operative effort. The art of drama is composite, requiring for its highest expression a contribution from all the arts. Its appeal is at once to the eye and the ear, to the intellect, the emotions, and the imagination. It calls for an understanding of the principles of architectural composition and structural design, pattern and colour, speech and music, dance and rhythmical movement. The artistic crafts are summoned to lend their aid in a hundred directions, and in theatrical technique no practical expedient that scientific invention suggests is overlooked.

All these are contributory to the effort of giving concrete presentation to a discernment of truth and beauty arising in the mind of the playwright and expressed in words according to certain accepted conventions governing dramatic form and stage performance. In the establishment of such conventions of the theatre ideally every collaborator is concerned to an equal degree: the scene designer, the stage mechanic, the electrician, the maker-up, the costumier, the librarian, the musician, the producer, the actors, the playwright. There is here no hierarchy, no aristocracy. The theatre is a commonwealth of equal participants.

SOCIAL INFLUENCE

It follows, therefore, that the practice of acted drama has a powerful social influence. It has been pointed out that music, poetry, and painting are arts that can come to their fullest expression in communication from one solitary mind to another. They are "mono-emotional." But inasmuch as acted drama calls for the co-working in one place and to one end of so many people behind the scenes, on the stage, and "in the front of the house," with many contributory endeavours in the same direction extending over weeks or perhaps months previously, drama is unrivalled among the arts as a stimulant of social activity. It requires, moreover, if it is to produce its full effects, a charged atmosphere, such as often results from the assemblage of a number of people in receptive mood and for the moment in a state of "release." But it is not only on the day of a performance that the harvest of social values in acted drama is garnered. In all the preparatory work the same influences have been operative, uniting and cementing, breaking down reserves and inhibitions, building up loyalties, sympathies, and traditions.

Furthermore, drama gives opportunity for education by "doing," and engages more fully than any other educational device the activity of the pupil. But here we must distinguish sharply between acted drama and drama as literature. It is no more consonant with the nature of drama that it should be studied only by means of the printed word than that a sonata should be read silently from a score. No play will yield a tithe of the dramatic values that it possesses unless it is interpreted in action. A play begins to render up its meaning only when it is reflected back to an audience through the mind of the actor, as the richness of light is perceived only when it is "fractured" in a prism. Many an obscure passage in a Shakespearean play, on which commentators speculate, in the intense illumination of imaginative acting presents no difficulty at all. The study of Dramatic Literature—drama, so to speak, in repose—will yield its own values, but these are not to be confused with the values that are to be derived from the study of drama in and through action. The former are mainly intellectual and critical values, the product of direct reason, patiently acquired by the use of the logical processes of analysis, classification, comparison. The viewpoint is detached, and the values are expressed in terms of objective knowledge. The latter are principally aesthetic and dynamic values, depending on emotional response, limited by subjective factors, and emerging as creative impulse.

THE LITTLE THEATRE
L.C.C. City Literary Institute

It is also important to distinguish between the practice of the art of acted drama, in conformity with the established conventions of stage technique on the one hand, and the use of dramatization as a method of teaching on the other. The distinction lies principally in the end in view. In the dramatization, for example, of historical episodes as a method of impressing facts, the purpose is not artistic at all. There is no subjective experience clamouring for aesthetic expression. There is no emotional exaltation. Dramatization is a merely practical adaptation of means to an end, like the manipulation of a pair of compasses to describe a circle of a given diameter. The teacher's purpose in dramatizing the incidents of the story of Wat Tyler or of the Five Members or of Florence Nightingale is to impress facts on the memory through a medium other than the printed book, and to vivify history by making it visual. In dramatization we have certainly most of the raw materials of dramatic art: dialogue, properties, costume, setting, gesture, characterization. But though many of the elements of dramatic technique are employed, they are combined in a totally different way. Little attention is paid, for example, to design or plot, since it is the succession of incident that is of greatest moment, and dramatization generally proceeds on the line of a chronicle. Moreover, there is as a rule no audience, and the essential aspect of art as communication is therefore absent.

LEARNING THROUGH ACTIVITY

For a long time past, educationists have stressed the importance of learning through activity, and the trend of recent research in psychology confirms the view that the learning process is extremely complex. Books are useful only up to a point; knowledge derived from books or acquired with the aid of books has to be followed by the adjustment of individuality to the external world of natural objects, of human society, and of the moral order. These three worlds, nature, society, and morality, every man has to explore, and to bring into relation with each other and to his own self before he can be said to be educated. The process of adjustment we call experience, and it consists partly in organizing the subjective life in relation to a given external environment and in moulding this environment to forms that answer to the demands of the subjective life. In childhood, adolescence, and manhood the adjustment proceeds continuously in all three directions at once. The effort involves the discipline of trial and error; it calls for the employment of every function of conscious life, willing, thinking, feeling. The new shaping of the environment is a creative act, guided by imagination, and requiring often the exercise of practical skill. Only thus may the system of the three worlds of external nature, human relationships, and the moral order be understood and organically related to the self.

The study of acted drama is unrivalled as a basis for this many-sided activity. It helps to give the student command of language, the most important medium of communication, and supplies him with standards of excellence in the adjustment of language to thought and sensibility that we call literature. It trains him in the art of speech, perhaps of all elements of his everyday social conduct that which is of greatest moment, inasmuch as it sets its stamp indelibly upon him and fits or mars him for certain activities in society. Furthermore, the stage is a school in which the actor can study human conduct in a thousand varied aspects. He can enter into a world of passions and sorrows and ambitions lying outside the narrow orbit of his own experience. Thereby his vision is enlarged and his sensibilities are quickened. The actor is constantly cultivating his aesthetic appreciation, schooling his taste and deepening his perceptions of the harmonies of colour, sound, and form. He aims, too, at physical fitness achieved through strict observance of the laws of personal hygiene. He learns how to achieve poise of body and of spirit, expressed in the balanced rhythm and economy of movement and in a vigorous co-ordination of mood, gesture, and speech.

EXERCISE OF IMAGINATION

There is no device in educational method that gives greater scope than acted drama for the exercise of imagination. Every play is an essay in interpretation. Into this interpretation must enter the personality of the actor, his conception of character and incident formed by a study of the play, and the means he has devised for embodying the conception in forms belonging to theatrical art so that the play may "get across." This is a complex task demanding imaginative insight into the efficacy of symbols and conventions, the limits of naturalism, and the adaptation of means to ends. While the skilful actor never forgets that he has an audience that is potentially a partner in the creation of illusion, he uses every device that his imagination suggests in order to facilitate acceptance of his lath and canvas box as a parcel of the hard core of the world. He must understand the laws of perspective and architectural structure so that no disproportion may detract from the illusion. He must study colour values in relation to costume and lighting. In a hundred directions, he may utilize any mechanical skill he may possess in designing and making properties that will help the interpretation he wishes to suggest.

In conclusion, acted drama belongs not to any one stage in the educational process, but to all. It is just as much in place in the nursery as in the Secondary School, in the University as in the Evening Institute. For its material is human life and the means it employs are the specifically human attributes of speech and gesture, thought and emotion. By these means the "ego" expresses itself and adjusts itself to its surroundings: two functions that are necessary for its very existence.

DRAMA IN THE CURRICULUM

It remains to consider the place of acted drama in the curriculum of an educational institution. An initial practical difficulty lies in the fact that school grading is usually an horizontal stratification. The more homogeneous the constitution of a particular form of boys or girls in intellectual ripeness and personal qualities, the less varied the material available for the purposes of acted drama. For ordinary teaching purposes this horizontal stratification is expedient; for acted drama a vertical stratification might be preferable. A group, the members of which were diversified in age and physique and mental development, would provide greater possibilities of suitable casting. From this it follows that the unit for the successful practice of acted drama is the whole school rather than the single form.

There is the further difficulty of computing quantitatively or qualitatively the results of a year's study of "drama in action." There are no scales in which to weigh achievement, and anyhow the values at which the teaching should aim are for the most part comprised of imponderables. Furthermore, the art of drama being practised co-operatively, individual achievement has no meaning apart from the performance of a group. Certain of the difficulties, e.g. the over-crowded time-tables, the inexperience of the average form-master or class-teacher in play production, the large size of the classes, the lack of empty floor space in the class-room, are capable of being removed, and are already absent in the design and the organization of some up-to-date schools. But in general such disabilities are so formidable that they effectually keep acted drama out of the "educational" time-table, and cause it to be relegated to the status of an extraneous and semi-recreational or even ceremonial activity. It is possible that most school plays produced for some annual occasion have been selected by a member of the staff with a view to the parent public that is to be pleased than to the pupils who are to be trained. For the annual play stands as a rule in no organic relation to the school curriculum, and few of the hard-ridden form masters or mistresses can, out of the couple of "periods" a week in which they have to cover an examination syllabus, afford time to rehearse a play, and to distil patiently from it the values that it may possess for a liberal education. The preparation of the play may have a considerable social value for the pupil-players, who are thereby brought into a new relation with their teachers, but there is, in the conditions of average school life, little possibility of developing the practice of amateur acting and accumulating the resources available to the players as there is, for example, in amateur dramatic societies with an adult membership.

AUTHENTIC DRAMA OF THE THEATRE

Any amateur dramatic society assembled to discuss the choice of its next play is faced with difficulties of two principal kinds. In the first place there are the obvious limitations set on its choice by the extent of its membership, the proportion of men and women, their range of ages, their experience of acting, their general education, the material resources of the society, the available stage accommodation and equipment, the variety of social accomplishments among the acting members, their knowledge of the theatre acquired as playgoers, the relation of the society to the community from which the members are drawn, the frequency of its productions, the character and intelligence of the probable and possible audiences, the ability of the producer: all these circumstances will be present in the minds of those who have been entrusted with the task of selecting the play. Between the extreme limits of the unrehearsed acted charades of a Christmas party and the full-dress performances of a first-class amateur repertory company, with its developed resources and established audience, there are hundreds of intermediate agencies of play production. In the second place, the choice of play will be governed by a consideration of the ends in view. Plays may be rehearsed and produced for a variety of possible motives. A group of village youths and maidens will join under the leadership of the local schoolmaster to present a "sketch" in the church hall, the proceeds to be devoted to the Cottage Hospital. With a parallel motive a number of Mayfair débutantes and their entourage of eligible young men will present, at a *matinée* in a fashionable London theatre, some pageantry giving opportunity for the display of youth, beauty, and gallantry. Westminster School has continued since its foundation its long tradition of acted Latin plays, which are a contribution to the study of Latinity and a part of the classical curriculum, while in the university dramatic societies the motive is pre-eminently cultural, the exercise of an art that may add a grace to life and give opportunity for the expansion of personality and the deepening of emotional sensibility.

We shall probably agree that some of the ends that play-acting societies have in view are spurious. In particular, the society which exists primarily for the production of the propagandist play in which dramatic values are secondary cannot be said to be using drama for a legitimate purpose. Nor is it any more legitimate to use the stage for mere spectacle, or for the exploiting of pretty figures, faces, and fashions.

SOUND PRINCIPLES

In general, however, the popularity of amateur acting is based on sound principles and answers to certain permanent characteristics of our human nature: our love of make-believe, our delight in a well-told story, the pleasure we find in watching colourful motion, our interest in the interplay of thoughts, passions, and fancies that are as threads drawn out of our own experience of life and woven into new patterns. To see and hear the presentation of a human story, perfectly blended in word and action, made concrete and actual, albeit projected in a world of illusion, transcending yet reflecting the forms and features of life, and lifting us up in an exaltation of spirit to a new sense of beauty and rhythmic order: this is the authentic drama of the theatre.

The play is the universe of circumstance which, by implied agreement between players and playgoers, is to limit for the brief traffic of the stage the range of action, thought, and emotion. Such a universe may be narrowly circumscribed in space and time, as within the four walls of a scullery, "between the soup and the savoury," or it may stretch to the confines of a mighty kingdom,

> Jumping o'er times;
> Turning the accomplishment of many years
> Into an hour-glass.

ACTION OF THE PLAY

The action of the play may arise from the elemental facts of human experience, common to peasant and peer, and entering into our daily observation and conversation: love, hate, fear, want, satisfaction, weariness, ambition, cruelty, loyalty. Or it may spring from more subtle and tenuous reactions to life.

It is clear therefore that the question "What is a good play?" will be difficult to answer. In fact the "goodness" of a play is always relative to circumstances. It may be easier to answer what is a suitable play for a given group of actors, to be presented on a given stage, and before a given audience. But it may at least be laid down that no play is worth an hour's rehearsal that fails to provide a vehicle for acting, and, since acting is an interpretative art that uses human nature as its material, the play must portray fundamental human character or become merely a surface presentation of conventional morality. The characters to be delineated should not too far exceed the range of knowledge, experience, and emotional sensibility possessed by the actors.

Furthermore, the action of the play should be such as would permit of its representation on a stage of given shape and dimensions and with given appliances. But by means of capable and imaginative production, the limits of possibility might indeed be extended to an indefinite degree. A symbolic rather than a naturalistic setting would enable many difficulties to be surmounted, provided only that the acting too was in the same mood. Inasmuch as all stage technique demands the use of conventions and symbols, the only question is one of scale. The more primitive the stage machinery, the greater the necessity for adopting a symbolic treatment.

Another important consideration in the selecting of plays for acting is the character of the dialogue. Drawing-room wit would not come smoothly off the tongue of a farm labourer, nor could he cast off his rustic heaviness to the extent of being able to catch the swift missile of repartee and throw it nimbly back. The choice of poetic drama would be unwise for actors who had not enjoyed a literary training and whose voices were uncultivated. The dialect play ought to be attempted only by actors who were native to its idiom and intonation. These considerations are, however, negative. The only positive consideration that can be suggested is that out of a number of otherwise equally eligible plays those should be chosen which offer the English language in forms that are calculated to enrich the everyday speech of the actors. Parts that require the use of barbarous speech will not yield the same personal values as dialogue that puts at the disposal of the actor, for his own subsequent use, a more delicate instrument of expression.

Finally, there is the problem of the audience. To select a play with no regard for the character of those who are to see it performed is to forget one of the most fundamental aspects not only of dramatic but of all artistic expression.

All art is communication. In the beginning the mind of the artist is suddenly taken with the apprehension of some fresh aspect of beauty. This he fastens upon imaginatively, arresting it in some palpable symbol lest it escape him again. But while it is yet in his mind, there is no art. Art results only when the artist, circumscribing himself within the conventions of a medium of expression, communicates his idea to another mind. Only when he has called up an answering response in that other has art been created. Note that the medium of communication must be an instrument of both intelligences. For should the artist express his idea in terms that are totally incomprehensible to others, while he may satisfy himself, he has failed to call into being, in a mind outside his own, an equivalent conception.

Anything that will destroy inertia and encourage a spirit of active participation by the play-going public will help to establish fruitful traditions. Supported by these, the actor need not take so many chances. He can disregard the casual playgoer with his changeful appetite and concentrate on a public with which he has already collaborated. To acquire a habit is to economize effort and to release energy for new experiments in conduct. Habits of thought and behaviour shared by the members of an institution crystallize into traditions that store up experience. A similar economy results from the establishment of a community of interest between actor and audience.

It may be observed here that this problem of the relation between players and public scarcely arises except in the modern professional theatre. For in its origin drama was essentially a communal affair. In primitive communities of to-day it still keeps this character. Being an expression of social and religious life and proper to the great occasions when the interest of everyone is involved, participation is wide and the distinction between actor and audience narrow.

PLACE OF DRAMA IN SCHOOLS

It is not often that the inclusion of drama as a school subject is advocated, and it is just as well. For side by side with Geography, Algebra, French and a score of other customary subjects, drama would prove to be a wayward companion, impatient of rule and discipline and reluctant to keep its place in a tidy time-table. Reference to a "subject" in a school curriculum normally implies a certain quantum of knowledge or a certain degree of technical skill which has to be assimilated or acquired before the subject can be said to have been "done" and the way cleared for the next stage in the process of learning. In this sense drama can hardly claim to be accorded a place in the curriculum. In the broadest sense, drama is a school of good and cultured behaviour, marked by self-possession, resourcefulness in reacting to a new situation, the cultivation of personality and sympathetic understanding of others. It belongs therefore to the education of the whole man and is an element in all training that touches on human values.

In any case the whole tendency of curriculum-making in the schools is to-day away from the demarcation of knowledge and skills into "subjects," and the teacher's task is tending rather to be considered as the organization of experience for the pupil. Where the teaching method is that of "theme" or "project" study, enabling the child to follow his own bent to a great extent, and emancipating him from the severe limits of a time-table, the possibilities of using drama as one among several school disciplines are much increased. No longer fettered to a place at a desk, the child can be practised in comely and graceful posture and movement and will have occasions for courteous speech which will compare very favourably with the artificial conditions imposed on the serried routes of large classes. Unhappily, the full emancipation of the child must await the rebuilding of our schools. Until then we may rejoice that no new school is likely to be erected which does not make at least some provision for free activity, including a stage and some simple accessories.

THE LATE REV. STEWART D. HEADLAM
Founder of the Stewart Headlam Shakespeare Association

THE NURSERY SCHOOL

In the Nursery School, drama is an aspect of imaginative play, chiefly the play of make-believe. Even a child of three will want to intensify his enjoyment of such a story as that of the Three Bears, when it is told or read to him, by appropriate action: knocking like Goldilocks at the door, mimicking the manner of Father, Mother, and Baby Bear's utterance, and so forth. The same child, playing at "shopping" will allocate spaces along a blank wall for the butcher and baker and the Post Office, and will run errands suggested by his own imagination. The teacher's task is to create opportunity to aid this imaginative play. Toys are after all, at any rate many of them, from the point of view of the child, dramatic properties. In these modern days the town child of nursery school age will engage in mock conversations with friends real and imaginary over a toy telephone, and invent dialogue and emotional expression (for example, laughter and surprise) which is full of the substance of drama. A child thus experimenting with language will show a natural delight at each new acquisition of power and with total absence of self-consciousness repeat his "effects" over and over again. He is indeed a born actor, and needs only scope and companionship for his talent to enable him to find himself confidently on the expanding stage of his little world.

THE PRIMARY SCHOOL

In the average primary school with its large classes necessitating more or less formal methods of discipline, its overcrowded curriculum and its generally antiquated building allowing but little scope for self-activity, the prospect of using drama as a normal adjunct of teaching may seem to be remote. Yet class-teachers of initiative and enterprise have triumphed over such difficulties. It is not so much a question of adding "drama" to the curriculum as of using the device of dramatization to vitalize the teaching, and to counter the tendency for the teacher-pupil relationship to degenerate into a static speaker-listener relationship. It may be an advantage that the primary school class teacher is usually more of a general practitioner than a specialist, for when this is so the tyranny of the "subject" and of the time-table is less formidable than it is for his colleague at the secondary school.

Historical episodes, including stories from biblical history, will furnish ample material for dramatization, and our ballad literature provides many suitable passages of narrative which can be recast into the form of dialogue. The possibilities of "acted ballads" are now recognized among teachers who look for new methods of speech practice combined with action and emotional expression. The newspaper, reflecting so many aspects of the human comedy, is another prolific source of dramatic material. Exercise in improvised acting and dialogue on a given theme (with independent groups working on the same material) gives some surprisingly good results, a comparison of which will give opportunity for some elementary instruction on the technique of drama.

THE SECONDARY SCHOOL

In the Norwood Report (*Curriculum and Examinations in Secondary Schools*) published in 1941, a reference is made to the growing interest in speech training, and the opinion is expressed that it is not as yet practicable to propose that every school should have an expert "in speech training" on its staff. If that be so, it would follow that to have an expert in dramatic production on the staff is still less practicable. In practice the possibility of organizing acted drama in a secondary school depends on the chance of someone with experience and enthusiasm being available and willing to sacrifice time and energy for an extra-school activity. Even in such conditions there are schools which have achieved notable successes in their annual presentations of plays.

The pressure of work for examinations and scholarships puts narrow limits upon the freedom necessary for the serious practice of dramatic art. Yet there are aspects of the study of drama which can and do find a place in the secondary school. Dramatic writing is a department of literature and the history of drama will have a prominent place in any syllabus. The study of dramatic criticism is inseparable from the general study of literary form. There is an encouraging development of play-reading circles to supplement the work of the class-room. The virtual disappearance of the theatre as a cultural institution over many parts of Great Britain has meant that countless numbers of people are without experience of the living drama. There are, however, a few favoured places where the theatre survives, and it may be expected that the Arts Council of Great Britain will reintroduce the art of the theatre in towns which have almost forgotten it. Meanwhile commendable efforts are being made here and there (for example, in London, Malvern, Stratford, and Bristol) to enable school children from municipal schools to see performances of standard plays done by professional trainees (for example, those taking courses at the Royal Academy of Dramatic Art). These have been enthusiastically received, and whether looked at from the standpoint of the children or the trainees, the results cannot be other than good as long as the right plays are chosen.

THE EVENING INSTITUTE

In contrast with the slower advance of the practice of acted drama in the day schools, the growing interest in acted drama in evening institutes is most marked. In the conditions of modern business life, opportunity for an individual interpretation of experience is usually denied. Work for livelihood is for most people mechanized, standardized, and rationalized. No personal reactions can as a rule be permitted to disturb the smooth dispatch of business or factory routine. But at the end of every business day there comes release, and the spirit naturally seeks a freer *milieu* in which personal choice and original interpretation is possible. The acting drama class in the evening institute provides this opportunity more readily than any other organization.

Whether in junior or senior evening institutes the classes formed for the study of acted drama consist of students who have voluntarily selected this aspect of study rather than another out of the general time-table of courses. They have done so because they are already drawn to the drama and have for one reason or another come to look upon the study and the practice of it as answering to the particular need of which they are conscious. A fortuitous assembly of such people will quickly, under the tactful handling of an expert instructor, gather up a corporate enthusiasm. Meeting for a common and well-understood purpose, there are fewer competing claims on time and energy to be resisted. Usually there is sufficient directing and administrative capacity available in the group to which definite functions can be delegated. Moreover, the material is diversified. There are wide limits of age, social experience, powers of speech and general knowledge, and usually there are varieties of developed skill in the arts and crafts ready to be called upon for service. Work on the play is usually part of the activity of a class that is engaged on the study of Dramatic Literature, and is included as an integral part of the syllabus. The class meets normally for two hours weekly throughout a session of, say, thirty-six weeks. There is time for a pretty thorough study of dramatic structure, literary values, social and other implications of the play, and the place of the play in the evolution of dramatic technique. The students are meantime being trained in proper habits of speech production, and are using the play as a basis for their exercises. Furthermore, the " dramatic class " is an important focus of the social life of the Institute, and its productions offer occasion for pleasant foregatherings of the general body of the students and their friends.

The important place that acted drama has come to occupy in the curriculum of the Evening Institute is due principally to the advocacy of the late Rev. Stewart D. Headlam, who was convinced of the cultural value of the theatre and of its importance as a religious, social, and educational force. He fought down the prejudice that regarded play-acting as degenerate idling, and contributed greatly to the renaissance of popular drama that has been so marked a feature of national life in recent years. The introduction of the study of acted drama, and particularly of Shakespeare, into the Evening Institutes of London is directly traceable to his championship of its claims, and the Stewart Headlam Shakespeare Association of London is a fitting memorial to his courageous espousal of the cause.

DRAMA AS A YOUTH CLUB ACTIVITY

The Youth Club, membership of which is technically limited to the years which lie between the school-leaving age and twenty, has become part of the accepted educational machinery of Great Britain. An increasing number of full-time trained leaders enter the service of the clubs, which passed rapidly beyond the somewhat negative attitude summed up by the phrase "keeping young people off the streets" and moved towards a more positive function of providing the opportunity and stimulus of adventures in self-expression and creative living at the intellectual, moral, and emotional level of adolescence.

By common consent, drama has been recognized as one of the most, if not actually the most, valuable activities of the club. It calls for the co-operation of many talents. The practice of dramatic art can be enjoyed at many levels. It has a technique or techniques the mastery of which implies a valuable and sustained discipline of mind and body. It provides an outlet for repressed natures in an atmosphere of release and sympathetic human understanding. It promotes a sense of unity among all the members by bringing them together from time to time as audience. Further, there is a natural transition from behaviour on the stage to behaviour in ordinary life. In the matter of speech, gesture, movement, manners, and the wearing of clothes the stage can be a school of life. Lastly, it is often through drama that those who have a capacity for leadership mark themselves out. Co-operation, discipline, freedom, manners, initiative: these are among the highest values which adolescent education can provide.

Notwithstanding the efforts which are made by those who direct the training of youth leaders to get dramatic activities in the clubs organized on sound progressive lines, we too often find that the first impulse is to assemble a group, select a play, cast it, and begin rehearsals forthwith. It is a shortsighted policy, and many of the potential values of drama as a medium of education are thereby lost. Herbert Read in *Education through Art* distinguishes four varieties of the play-instinct in children, leading respectively through feeling towards drama, through sensation towards design, through intuition towards dance and music, and through thought towards craft. Of these the fundamental variety of play is drama since it "involves craft, design and dance as necessary co-operative activities." This suggests that drama should grow not so much out of a play, but out of play, the play of make-believe, the play of dressing-up, the play of mimicry. Words, much less a set form of words to be memorized, are not essential in the first beginnings. Mime based on individual occupational movement, characterization, and emotional expression, and then developed as group-mime, offers a sound foundation. The silent mime can afterwards be given a musical or spoken accompaniment as in spoken and acted ballad, the speaker and actor being separate persons.

IMPROVISATIONS

The next stage is that of improvised dialogue, the charade, acted book-title and other varieties engaging the activity not only of a small chosen cast, but of every member of the group in turn. This is the stage of speech and action combined. The need for the learning of the specific technique of speaking and acting will before long become apparent, and with sympathetic encouragement and the exercise of some ingenuity in the devising of exercises which are seen at once to have point and purpose as well as entertainment value, the systematic cultivation of the voice and the study of the elements of acting can be begun. It is important that the exercise should be shared equally. A situation can be analysed into its simplest elements: opening a door or a letter, sitting down on a chair, picking up a handkerchief, greeting a visitor, giving an order, and so forth. Each action can be performed in a variety of moods and attitudes, in lightheartedness or depression, in fear or confidence, in boredom or ecstasy, in real or feigned politeness. Since the actor can represent rich man, poor man, beggar man, thief, and a thousand other human types, it is clear that the permutations and combinations are inexhaustible.

The exercises need not and should not always be impromptu. If announced in advance they provide an excellent opportunity for rudimentary efforts in casting by those who come forward as leaders. It will be found, moreover, that sketches will be written and the whole business of presentation freshly thought out by the groups of two, three, or half a dozen which usually suffice. In this phase of the practice of dramatic art, it is essential that originality be encouraged. Sketches, revues, pantomimes can all be devised by young people in their 'teens, using popular melodies with fresh words for songs and choruses.

PLAY READING

The best approach to play production in the full sense is probably through the regular practice of play-reading. This is not merely a matter of sitting in a half-circle and reading in turn. The play-reading in some measure calls for the art of the producer, who will be responsible for the choice of play, the distribution of parts, the cuts and the preparatory analysis of the play without which guidance much of value will be lost. It is to be recommended that all who according to the script are present in the scene should rise from their seats whether they have words to read or not. As a beginning it may be sufficient if they do not move away from before their chairs, but a practised play-reading team will without apparent effort achieve a simple grouping and even use gesture and stage business though with book in hand.

It is not here proposed to carry the discussion to the full production of acted plays in the club. But it may be as well to utter a warning against exhibitionism which in the years of adolescence is often a besetting sin. Since the stage play offers so ready a means of egotistical display, the youth club leader will be especially careful to emphasize other aspects. The best corrective is undoubtedly an insistence on the acquirement of an adequate technique, for it is the exhibitionists who are most tempted to be impatient of true dramatic standards.

THE STAGE-PLAY DOCUMENTARY

During the last two years of the Second Great War, workers in the field of A.B.C.A. (Army Bureau of Current Affairs) realized that stage drama, rendered infinitely more flexible and expressive by the use of a technique of production which employed every kind of mechanical device known to cinema and radio, could be turned into a powerful instrument for the discussion of urgent social, economic, and political problems. Therewith a new form of documentary came into existence. Already A.B.C.A. had abandoned the academic analysis, the dissertation and the exposition after the manner of the college lecture-room as unsuitable for the conditions of army life, and had substituted a more informal method of discussion with whatever visual aids were available. Much was thereby achieved in the direction of making clear to those who were serving in the Forces the fundamental issues of the time and of providing them with material on which they could form intelligent opinions. But even so, many were unresponsive. The problems discussed seemed to be remote and needed a more dynamic presentation if their bearing on life was to be fully comprehended. In the effort to achieve this, a new technique of the stage and an enlarged dramatic purpose were developed.

THE MEANING OF DOCUMENTARY

Paul Rotha, discussing in *Documentary Film*, the nature of this modern art-form, defined it as "the use of the film medium to interpret creatively and in social terms the life of the people as it exists in reality." John Grierson saw in the documentary uses of the radio and the film new ways of educating public opinion in a democracy. The purpose of each was to show "how men live and should live and where the creative forces that fill men's honest needs reside." There seems to be no good reason why the drama of the stage should not make its contribution to the same purpose. Indeed, the actor, holding the mirror up to nature, has always attempted an interpretation of life. The difference is one of range and potential.

In the new technique of stage presentation worked out by A.B.C.A. play-units, the fullest use was made of mechanical contrivances with suggestions for both broadcasting and film technique. The latter is the medium *par excellence* for the animated chart or diagram with its moving arrows, its expanding or contracting outlines and its living arithmetic of figures and isotypes. It can punch home to the dullest consciousness with irresistible effect the time-space relationships which lie at the root of so many questions of public policy. It can present contrasts with trenchant force or with subtle suggestion, can alter scale and perspective and jumping through time with flash-backs and flash-forwards can work with devastating effect on our imaginations. Radio, too, is capable of quick surprises, surging climaxes and fade-outs, though its medium is nothing but sound. It is the greatest exponent of the device of "noises off."

Here then was a new instrument ripe for exploitation in the interests of a more vital civic consciousness. It is, if we consider the matter sympathetically, not surprising that the normal state of mind of the average citizen is one of perplexity. He is aware that there are powerful forces at work in the world shaping his destiny, but he has not as a rule been trained in the difficult processes of social analysis, and he therefore too often gives an otiose assent to conclusions offered to him through the agencies whereby opinion is canalized and used to impel public policy. The operation of the forces conditioning his life is mostly indirect. The train of causation is long and complex. Factors are involved which lie outside normal experience. Small wonder, therefore, that the man in the street knows hardly more than that the problem is there for him. He is impatient of academic expositions which aim at explaining the problem, because explanation so often implies apology and acceptance of the supposedly inevitable.

DISCUSSION THROUGH DOCUMENTARY

One important virtue of documentary, whether of the cinema or of the stage, is in its power to suggest *becoming*. Its function is not so much to present actuality as to penetrate to the meaning behind actuality. It is not sufficient to be descriptive and factual; documentary demands a dramatic interpretation, a creative reconstruction, even though always using natural material. Thus, through the medium it supplies, discussion becomes, as it were, stereoscopic, three-dimensional, giving the illusion of life. The sequences are related not so much to a plot or a story as to a theme. The characters are types rather than individuals because the theme centres not in the actions and destiny of a particular human being but in the fortunes of a social or political group. If there is in it an element of the spectacular, it derives from the miracle of the obvious. Its romance is the romance which "brings up the 8.15" each morning. In its creative presentation of the scene, documentary looks before and after; it sees the present in the womb of the past, the future in the womb of the present. Its values are not static but dynamic.

Drama has always served as a vehicle for the communication and discussion of ideas. In its very nature it presupposes the existence of a conflict in which human destinies are involved. It presents the issue in the form of some concrete problem which calls for a solution. Herein is the crux of the dramatic situation, and hence arises the tension which engages our intelligence or tears our emotions to tatters. The conflict or dissonance may be of character, or principle, or loyalty; it may be the opposition of wills or of humours; it may rest merely upon the contradiction between the actual and the supposed, between what is known or experienced by one person and what by another. Every play thus presents a problem, though not all are called problem plays. The difference may be expressed by saying that the problem play touches on an issue felt to be within the range of present personal experience rather than on an issue that belongs to universal experience. In any case a resolution of the conflict has to be found, valid for the purposes of the drama, though not necessarily valid in the light of history or of absolute truth or morality.

In the stage-play documentary, the dramatic method is used with a difference. There is no time for the slow building up of the situation as in the ampler business of the traditional theatre. It demands a quick-fire technique which raises the dramatic tension to the *n*th degree. To discuss the production of documentary in terms of "sets" is hardly possible, inasmuch as the background to the action is not set but fluid. The A.B.C.A. play-unit producers were not averse to using all the aids which up-to-date psychological science suggested. They were not propagandists, but, notwithstanding, the modern arts of propaganda, with their seeking after mass-effects, were contributory. Lighting and colour values were exploited to the full, with spots and black-outs for emphasis and change of direction, while music reinforced the mood.

A.B.C.A. PLAY-UNITS

The earliest of the productions of the A.B.C.A. play-units were *What's Wrong with the Germans* and *United we Stand* (a contrast between the structure and history of the League of Nations and those of the United States of America), both dating from 1943. There followed in the next year *Lend Lease, or The Great Swap*, and *The Japanese Way*. It is natural that in 1945 attention should have been turned to problems of reconstruction at home. *Where Do We Go From Here?* was an analysis of the problems of employment before, during, and after the War. These plays were all based on Army Bureau of Current Affairs pamphlets, which had already been discussed by most of the members of the Services audiences for whom the plays were originally written. Thus there was already some general acquaintance with the topic in hand.

The extraordinarily enthusiastic reception given by Service audiences to the A.B.C.A. plays suggests the question: "Has the stage-documentary any prospects in the town theatre?" One's answer will depend to some extent on the estimate one is prepared to put on the average intelligence of the greater public. There is much to indicate that agencies of entertainment and recreation such as the B.B.C. and E.N.S.A. set the common denominator too low. It is too large a question to discuss here, but it may safely be stated that whatever attitude the commercial theatre adopts towards documentary on the stage, it will find its development mainly in repertory and the communally-owned theatre.

ORGANIZATION OF A PLAYWRIGHTS' CLUB

It is strange that hitherto there has been so little organic relation between the actor and the playwright. And yet the potentialities of such co-operation will be immediately apparent to anyone who thinks of the matter. The drama of the professional stage is indeed sometimes the product of close accord. Shakespeare was, and Noel Coward is, an actor-playwright. In the minds of such men plays have often taken on their shape and structure in and through the business of acting. Many other dramatists have constructed plays round the personality of an actor or actress, in direct relation to a specific demand, with the stage itself and the character of the playgoers concretely in view. But in general most writing of plays is done at the study table, and few of the writers have any opportunity of bringing their work to a practical and decisive test. The great majority must perforce accept a verdict based on a reading of the manuscript. In consequence, literary values are easily confused with acting values. Probably this accounts for the great proportion of failures among the plays that are accepted and produced in the theatres, and for the immense wastage of good plays that remain in manuscript form, their acting possibilities not realized.

In the Amateur Movement there is, however, an excellent opportunity for bringing the work of playwright and actor into a fruitful relation. Wherever a strong amateur dramatic society has gathered some substantial measure of support from players and playgoers, there should be found the conditions necessary for the formation of a

Playwrights' Club, working in co-ordination with it. Many among the actors as well as many among the members of the audience need only the encouragement and stimulus that are given by such an opportunity in order to attempt dramatic creation. The knowledge that any serious effort will at least be paid the compliment of being given a careful reading by players cast for the parts, and that it may possibly earn the still greater compliment of being properly rehearsed and produced, is an incentive of the greatest value. My purpose is to set forth some of the practical considerations that experience has shown to be important in the conduct of the activities of a Playwrights' Club organized in close relation with a play-producing society.

MEMBERSHIP

Membership of the Playwrights' Club will be of two kinds: (1) author; (2) associate. The associate members will in general constitute the critical audience, having themselves no inclination to write, but contributing nevertheless by constructive comment and discussion to the work of dramatic creation. The subscriptions payable by members need not be large, because the expenses of running the Club will be trivial. But the writer-members will enjoy the greater privileges, the associate members being much in the position of patients who lend themselves to treatment for experimental purposes. It is appropriate, therefore, that the playwrights proper should pay a much higher subscription than the rest.

PROCEDURE AT MEETINGS

A description of the general procedure will suggest what officers will be required. Meetings will be held, say, fortnightly or monthly. Before each meeting the typed manuscript of the play or plays to be read must be multigraphed, so that separate copies are available for each member of the cast with two or three over. The manuscript must be in correct format.

In the preparation of the typescript a standard form should be prescribed. Quarto sheets of fairly thick paper will be found to be the most convenient in handling. All typing should, of course, be on one side only and double-spaced. There should be a generous margin, say of 2 in., on the left, and the pages should not be too crowded at top and bottom. The act and scene should be indicated on every page at the top right corner, and, in addition, the pages should be numbered consecutively. The names of characters, description of settings, stage directions, indications of "business," entrances and exits, and all such instructions ought to be picked out by underlining in red ink; for the names of characters capitals only should be used. The acts should be bound separately, each set of folios being provided with a title page giving the name of the play, the number of the act and scenes, and the author's name and address. The whole should be contained in some kind of portfolio which would allow of the extraction of one act at a time. Attention to small details of this kind will be found to add considerably to the pleasure and effectiveness of the reading, and will, moreover, be of material advantage if and when the play comes to be marketed.

Author members with experience of acting will in rotation take over the responsibility of casting, but associate members may be called on in turn to render service as readers. Each member of the cast will read the whole play in advance of the meeting. The "caster," or pseudo-producer whom we shall for convenience call simply the producer, will sit with the readers to call the acts and scenes and to read out the stage directions.

The reading cast will sit in a semi-circle facing the audience, the members of which should be provided with notebooks and pencils. It is not necessary that a stage should be used, unless the audience is large. An ordinary room, furnished with chairs and a table or two, is usually sufficient. The producer reads: "*Act* I. *Scene* I. *The curtain rises and reveals a stockbroker's office . . . The telephone bell rings. Enter the Junior Clerk, a . . . young man of twenty.*" Whereupon Mr. Brown, cast as the Junior Clerk, stands up book in hand, comes forward a step or two and reads his lines. Similarly, with each "entrance." Each reader remains standing until his "exit," when he sits down again. There is little "business" except such as can be improvised by a reader, book in hand. So the reading goes on to the end of the play.

The discussion will follow immediately after the reading of the play, a rigid time-table being set, in order to ensure that, in the event of the meeting being called to consider more than one play, none shall be crowded out. The producer will preside over the discussion, which should range over such matters as plot-structure, characterization, dialogue, motivation, atmosphere, acting-values, and so forth. The producer will make rapid notes of the points raised and attempt to sum up the general verdict. The author, too, is usually present and will join in the discussion, but occasionally it is found that the author will prefer anonymity at this stage. If so, there is no reason why his wishes should not be respected.

THE QUESTION OF PRODUCTION

When a reasonable number of plays has been in this way read and discussed, the question of production will probably arise. This will be the most difficult part of the work of the Club. It is likely that only a few plays will in the opinion of the members merit production in their original form. Plays that after reading have been considered to have merit sufficient to justify production will next be re-considered by a panel of the most experienced actor-members who will have the producer's summing up of the discussions before them, and a final choice will then be made. It is necessary that there should be a considerable degree of unanimity at this stage, because the play must be enthusiastically produced if it is to have a fair chance.

The value of co-ordination with a play-producing society is now obvious. Many members of the Playwrights' Club will also probably be active in the work of the parent Dramatic Society, and therefore in a position to recommend that the chosen play be produced as a part of the regular season's programme. The rules of the Club will give the members the right to arrange for a production of the play in any way that is deemed expedient, and the playwright-laureate will not be entitled to withhold his consent. Nor will he, of course, charge the Club a royalty. In certain circumstances, the licence of the Lord Chamberlain may first have to be obtained.

The question of the expense involved in the production of an original play needs to be carefully considered. Cheapness ought not to be allowed to weigh heavily in favour of one play as compared with another that might necessitate greater expenditure on costumes and properties. Ideally, plays should be chosen for production on their intrinsic merits only, and the Committee should be resourceful enough to discover or invent ways and means of presenting the plays of their choice without unreasonable stinting. For such a purpose, a reserve fund might be built up gradually, and in a difficult situation the author might be allowed to guarantee the Club against any loss incurred beyond an agreed sum. Much would depend, however, on the relations between the Playwrights' Club and the parent Society if such existed. Should the Playwrights' Club have no backing such as a successful dramatic society might give, it must needs proceed more cautiously, and endeavour to extend its associate membership.

Nothing has here been stated about some of the more specialized arts of the playwright, for example, the writing of film scenarios and of radio plays. Eventually it is probable that sections of the members of the Playwrights' Club will be formed for mutual aid in acquiring the technique of such writing. But it must be remembered that the method of the reading-circle is far less suitable a process for the discovery of good work of these specialized kinds, where mechanical contrivances play such an extremely important part.

THE LIBRARY

The Club, as it develops, will doubtless soon devise other means of serving its members. For example, it may gather a collection of books on the craft of the dramatic author, on criticism, on the arts of the stage, and so forth; the collection should also include the works of the principal dramatists. The books will be placed in charge of a librarian who will issue them to members, but never without a written receipt. The librarian, too, will keep a file of copies of plays submitted by members and read at the Club's meetings.

A further service may be offered in the shape of advice on agency. A sub-committee set up to collect information regarding the legal and financial aspect of the marketing of dramatic rights will gradually acquire expert knowledge of which other members may avail themselves. Contacts will be gradually established with agents, producers, and managers, and the inexpert individual member will enjoy some protection from his association with the rest.

EXERCISES FOR BEGINNERS

While it does so much for the practised writer, the Club would do well to give some thought to the question of the best method of encouraging first and early steps in dramatic writing. It may be found that an evening devoted to the reading and criticism of a number of miniature and apprentice attempts to dramatize a given theme, say, an historical episode, or a fable of Aesop, or a *cause célèbre* agreed upon in advance may yield good results. Here the plot and the characters are given and the exercise will be in devising structure and dialogue. At another time the general idea only may be suggested, the writers being left to invent the characters, the *mise en scène*, and the rest. A useful elementary exercise would be to take a conversational chapter in a novel and to recast it in dramatic dialogue. A more difficult exercise would be to devise an alternative last act to a given play. All such efforts, however limited in intention, should be read at the meetings of the society and considered as seriously as full-fledged work. For the Playwrights' Club will not be wise to forget that it has an educational function to perform, and that such early encouragement may produce rich dividends in due course.

The following suggestions for a draft constitution are offered in the hope that they may save organizers a little time and serve as a framework to which details may be added to meet special conditions. It will conduce to smoothness and efficiency if a copy of the full constitution is handed to every member at the time of joining.

SUGGESTIONS FOR A CONSTITUTION

Name. The name of the Club shall be "The . . . . . . Playwrights' Club."

Objects. The objects of the Club shall be to provide members with the opportunity of hearing their plays read and discussed, and on certain conditions of having them performed in public. The Club shall, in addition, give to members advice on the marketing of plays.

Membership and Subscriptions. Membership of the Club shall be open to . . . . . . and shall be of two kinds: (1) author membership, (2) associate membership. The subscription shall be . . . . . . per annum for author members and . . . . . . per annum for associate members.

Officers and Committee. The Officers of the Club shall be as follows: President, Vice-Presidents, Honorary Secretary, Honorary Treasurer. The Committee shall consist of the above and . . . . . . other members, elected at the Annual General Meeting.

Meetings. Ordinary Meetings shall be held at . . . . . . on . . . . . .

Submission of Plays for Reading. Each member shall be permitted to deposit with the Secretary one play at a time. Readings of plays shall be arranged in order of submission, except as otherwise decided by the Committee in special circumstances. No member shall be allowed to submit a second or subsequent play whilst one of his plays is still on the waiting list. Plays must be typed in regular format, of which particulars may be obtained from the Secretary.

Casting of Plays for Readings. The Committee shall appoint a panel of members who shall in rotation be entrusted with the responsibility of casting plays for reading. One member of the panel shall undertake the casting of all plays to be read at any one meeting. The casting shall be done at least two weeks before the date fixed for reading. The author shall provide a sufficient number of copies of the play and shall allow one copy to remain in the hands of the Secretary for the use of the Committee for a period of . . . . . . months after a reading. Should the author so desire, he may request that the play should be read by one member only, nominated by himself.

Selection of Plays for Production. The Committee shall take note of plays which on reading appear in their opinion to merit production. These plays may be further submitted to a competent adjudicator for a considered opinion, but the Committee reserves the right to an independent judgment and its decision regarding production shall be final.

The Production of Plays. The Committee shall appoint for the purposes of each separate production a Producer, and such other officers as may be considered necessary. These shall be drawn from the membership of the Club. The casting of plays chosen for production shall be jointly undertaken by author and producer. It shall be permissible with the consent of the Committee to invite persons who are not members of the Club to undertake acting parts.

Expenses of Production. The expenses of production shall as a rule be borne by the Club, but should the production of a play which is otherwise suitable be vetoed solely on the ground of probable expense, it shall be permissible for the author to guarantee a sum sufficient to enable the play to be produced.

Annual General Meeting. The Annual General Meeting shall be held in . . . . . . of each year. Its business will be to receive the report of the Honorary Secretary, to receive and adopt the statement of accounts, to elect officers, to discuss matters affecting the welfare of the Club, and to consider amendments of the rules of which notice has been submitted in writing to the Secretary by any member not less than three weeks before the date of the meeting, and thereupon communicated to all members together with the notice convening the meeting.

Special General Meeting. A Special General Meeting shall be called at any time at the request of not less than . . . . . . members of the Club.

Quorum. . . . . . . members shall form a quorum at a General Meeting, and . . . . . . members at a meeting of the Committee.

Accounts. The Honorary Treasurer shall open an account in the name of the Club at the . . . . . . Bank. All receipts should be paid in to this account. Withdrawals of more than £ . . . shall require the joint signatures of the President and Honorary Treasurer.

In the event of the dissolution of the Club any funds in hand shall be paid over for the benefit of the . . . . . Hospital.

Since a knowledge of practical stage craft is essential to the writer of plays, this aspect of the playwright's art cannot be neglected. The Club will, therefore, encourage to the full the study of the architecture and equipment of the stage, including lighting and background effects. Perhaps the best plan is to establish a special section known as the Model Theatre group, and so provide opportunity for those among the general members who have a practical rather than a literary talent to make their contribution to the common effort, which is the creation of drama. The playwright as he works needs to watch the play of his characters not merely through the typed lines of his manuscript but in the sound on the three-dimensional stage. He has to consider the position of exits and entrances, the placing of chairs, tables, windows, telephones, light-switches, and a hundred other details which affect the action. To enable him to decide on such matters, he requires to use a scale model of the setting, and may well enlist the co-operation of the model theatre group to provide one.

Fortunately, efforts made in this direction are cumulative. In course of time, a number of models will have been made and these will be placed at the disposal of any member engaged on the writing of a play.

Another direction of development may be the formation of a Puppet or Marionette Theatre group. This group will function independently by writing and producing its own plays. Notwithstanding this, the practice of the art of puppetry is one way of developing a sense of drama, and the effort to render a situation in terms of the miniature stage with animated models must have a stimulating influence upon one who aspires to write for the living stage.

ACTING PLAYS IN FOREIGN LANGUAGES

While for the great majority of English people plays written in a foreign language must become known, if at all, in translations, it will be readily granted that, when the conditions requisite for production in the original form obtain, it is infinitely preferable that foreign plays should be so presented. We are not considering at the moment school or after-school exercises in conversation based on "dramatic" sketches specially devised to enlarge the vocabulary or to illustrate the use of idioms, such as the familiar dialogues associated with the process of "brushing-up" one's French or German. These have obviously little or nothing to do with drama. Nor are we here concerned even with plays of full construction if they be written *primarily* with a view to language study and have no pretensions to belong to the accepted dramatic literature of a foreign people. The drama contemplated in this article is the body of legitimate drama, consisting of plays written for production in the theatre under ordinary conditions. We are also not considering plays brought to this country by foreign companies; we have in mind foreign plays presented to English audiences by English players.

It may be allowed that a principal intention in the rehearsal and presentation of plays in a foreign language may nevertheless be linguistic study, and such an object is perfectly compatible with a serious dramatic purpose. Indeed, such productions must ultimately stand or fall by the ordinary criteria of acted drama. From the standpoint of the audience the language question is of secondary import; dramatic values are the primary consideration. In every respect the production has to be up to standard. If there be shortcomings in regard to dramatic essentials, the failure is, in fact, more, not less, pronounced by reason that a less familiar medium of speech is used. To create and to hold the dramatic illusion while using a foreign tongue may well be a more than usually difficult task. The actor cannot rely as confidently as in an English play on the receptivity and collaboration of his audience. Some of the finer shades of meaning will inevitably be missed, and some of the subtler by-play will be ineffective. For that reason the injunction of Irving: "To be natural, your acting must be broader than Nature" is specially applicable here.

From the standpoint of the players, linguistic considerations have far greater importance. For them the conning of a part, the constant repetition of speeches that should be rendered with effortless ease, and the instantaneous picking-up of cues, must result in a great accession of fluency and ease. But the gain is by no means confined to the mechanics of speech, the more facile articulation of the speech organs. Being employed in dramatic utterance, the foreign idiom acquires for the players a dynamic quality, charged with power. Emotional response is always surer and quicker than intellectual response. Teachers who have freed themselves from academic methods and are acquainted with modern psychological research nowadays make the fullest use of this principle in their practice. To say that *j'ai faim* is French for *I am hungry* engages the apperceptive memory only—an intellectual process involving the recognition of *faim* as a substantive and *hungry* as an adjective in the respective idioms. But to simulate somehow the distress of hunger as in an acted play is to call forth an emotional response that is more automatic in its working and accords better with the nature of the origins of speech as a reflex operation of mind. Thus acquired, the knowledge of the idiom *j'ai faim* becomes an aspect of experience, something vital and organic, and is no longer a lifeless, synthetic product reconstructed from the elements of a grammarian's analysis.

LANGUAGE AND CULTURE

But there are other and more fundamental advantages that accrue from the study of foreign drama in action. To present a foreign play is to unshutter a window opening on the culture that produced it. Language itself is the most important cultural product of any race or nation. In its words and in its structural forms the history of the people is crystallized. Anatole France once said that a dictionary is the Universe in alphabetical order; it may equally be said to be an index of the cultural traditions of a people. But a play is more than the expression of thoughts and emotions in words. It is based on certain conventions of gesture and behaviour, perfectly understood by the audience for which it was originally written. These conventions reflect a particular form of social, economic, and political organization. The pervading moral code is the climate in which they flourish. Much of the play's significance is allusive rather than expressed in words, and therefore it will yield its full meaning only to those who are familiar with the *genus loci.* If the action of the play touch heroic events, it will necessarily reflect the pride or the humility of the nation, and body forth a vision of its hopes and aspirations. Even if its purpose be to present only a commonplace situation, it will in so doing reflect those aspects of life and livelihood, those habitual modes of conduct and ways of thinking that the nation in her heroic moments has striven to preserve and to perpetuate. Understanding begets sympathy, and through sympathy we reach out to humanity. The play is a document and the close study of it may yield to the thoughtful actor the franchise of a wider culture than that of his own country. If the amateur stage is to be regarded as having anything more than an entertainment value for those who interest themselves in it, the contribution it is capable of making towards a broader outlook upon humanity cannot be despised.

TRANSLATION INVOLVES LOSS

Some of the values of a foreign play might doubtless be realized if it were rendered in translation. But a considerable part of its meaning would surely be lost. In the passage from the mind of the dramatist to his manuscript, from his manuscript to the mind of the translator, from *his* mind to *his* manuscript, from this manuscript to the mind of the player, from the player's mind to the speech and traffic of the stage, and from this again to the mind of the audience through their eyes and ears, how many transitions, what perilous hazards, and how great the certainty that at each of the several stages of the transition some of the quality of the dramatist's apprehension of truth and beauty must escape! Even in the most competent translation the original association-values of words are lost completely. Along with these association-values there escapes a certain emotional aura which was part of the "meaning" that the dramatist wished to convey. The words of the translation, they, too, in their turn carry their particular association-values, and to each of them is attached an emotional savour of its own. The results, therefore, cannot but be different. And this is particularly the case when we are considering the rendering into a foreign idiom of dramatic writing that is from its nature strongly charged with emotional intensity.

All acting of plays in a foreign tongue is conditioned by one circumstance of paramount importance: that the medium of communication, being relatively unfamiliar, calls for an intellectual effort on the part of the audience that is considerably greater than would be required for any English play. Unusual concentration is necessary. It may therefore be legitimate and indeed a measure of prudence to afford the auditors every assistance that can result from a simplification of the action. There are dangers involved in the attempt to achieve naturalism. To begin with, the properties ordinarily at the disposal of an amateur group of limited resources are hardly likely to assist the illusion. A backcloth designed to represent an avenue through an English park cannot be made to serve for a Corsican vista, and although it may be easily possible for the French Count to arrange to be seen reading a Paris newspaper as the curtain goes up, or for the producer to have the walls plastered with Italian railway posters, it will be found difficult to carry out the whole scheme on a realistic basis. There will always be someone in the audience who notices that such-and-such door-handles are never seen in Germany. It is therefore better to aim at an impressionistic technique, using only a few simple but unmistakable and unchallengeable effects.

CURTAINS

Possibly the most satisfactory method is to play in a curtained stage. The foreign play will be presented as a rule in a small theatre before a limited audience. In these circumstances realism is out of the question and failure will probably attend any attempt to achieve it by an elaborate scheme of production. The auditors are, by hypothesis, people of more than average education and culture, and will readily accept the conventional limitations that the players impose upon themselves.

The players, as has already been suggested, should aim at creating broad effects, easily apprehended. It is poster art rather than the art of the old Dutch masters which suggests the method. The playing should be simple and direct, even deliberately negligent of the finer shades if by a more thoroughgoing action and characterization the language difficulty can be overcome. While it is an axiom that the players should never overlook the presence of an audience, it is particularly necessary in the acting of foreign plays to ensure that the points get home. This is something requiring great acting skill and imagination. It calls, too, for the exercise of the most careful restraint. It is inevitable that the *tempo* should be slower than in the acting of plays in the native tongue and in consequence the temptations to indulge in fussy "business" are correspondingly greater. Accordingly the producer should endeavour to obtain precise and palpable effects by the employment of the simplest of devices and the avoidance of loose and incoherent movement and gesture.

ACTED TRANSLATIONS

The question arises whether the loss of some of the finer points in acting does not entail a greater sacrifice than would be suffered by the rendering of the play in translation. This can only be decided in view of all the circumstances. It may well be that, notwithstanding the impossibility of retaining in a translation the full significance of the original play, it will in a more familiar guise still keep so much of its dramatic value as to make it worthy of study and production. Only in translation, indeed, are we ever likely to see acted by English people (except in certain schools) Greek and Latin plays, or those examples of Scandinavian, Russian, or Czechoslovakian dramatic craftsmanship that have so great a significance in the history of modern dramatic structure and stagecraft. In general, however, it may be said that, given a reasonable linguistic facility on the part of the actors and the audience, the potential values of foreign plays can be realized most adequately when they are rendered in the native idiom of the dramatist.

In practice, those who present plays in foreign languages to general audiences in this country make a concession to their shortcomings in regard to any language but their own by supplying along with the programme a more or less detailed analysis of the plot. This was the practice of Sacha Guitry when he presented his French comedies in London theatres, and the example was followed by the German players from Aachen who performed the *Urfaust* in London, Oxford, and Cambridge on the occasion of the Goethe Centenary in 1932. It was usual also for Sarah Bernhardt, who used no language but French during her seasons in England more than fifty years ago, to afford her audiences similar assistance, though it is allowed that her consummate artistry rendered quite unnecessary any such adventitious aid to interpretation. It could, therefore, not be considered derogatory, especially if playing to an unacademic audience, if an amateur company should make a similar concession. But it is hardly necessary to suggest that when an account of the action is supplied it should be given in the language of the play that is to be performed. Dignity demands at least so much.

LINGUISTIC COMPETENCE

Whether it be due to ineffective methods of teaching in this country, or to the fact that our insularity deprives us of opportunity, or whether it be due to a certain lofty indifference and laziness, it is certainly true that the conditions which would make possible the adequate presentation of foreign drama by amateurs in the original are only occasionally found. For this presupposes a fair linguistic competence. Bernard Shaw many years ago made an honest confession of his deficiencies as a linguist, modestly but erroneously adding that his disability seemed to be most humiliatingly exceptional. "My colleagues sit at French plays, German plays, and Italian plays, laughing at all the jokes, thrilling with all the fine sentiments, and obviously understanding the finest shades of the language; whilst I, unless I have read the play beforehand, or asked somebody during the interval what it is about, must either struggle with a sixpenny 'synopsis,' which invariably misses the real point of the drama, or else sit with a guilty conscience and a blank countenance, drawing the most extravagantly wrong inferences from the dumb show of the piece. . . . On the whole, I came off best at the theatre in such a case as that of *Magda*, where I began by reading the synopsis, then picked up a little of the play in French at Daly's Theatre, then a little more in Italian at Drury Lane, then a little more in German from the book, and finally looked at Duse and was illuminated beyond all the powers of all the books and languages on earth."

While many of us would recognize ourselves in this description, it is fortunately not necessary to suppose that the amateur stage in England must limit itself to English plays. In most of our Universities there are French, German, Italian, and Spanish Clubs, consisting of undergraduates and members of the lecturing staff, and there is usually a potential audience among the students and the cultivated members of the public in the neighbourhood. In the larger towns, too, there are language clubs and circles; for example, those affiliated to the *Alliance Française*, consisting of those who are keeping alive a long-standing interest and are extending their knowledge by means of regular lectures and discussions in a foreign language. The meetings of such clubs are frequently enlivened by the presentation of plays. In the higher forms of Secondary Schools, where language teaching follows up-to-date methods, the possibility is equally present. The study of foreign drama in action is becoming an important feature of the curriculum of Adult Evening Institutes where the cultural values of foreign languages are kept prominently in view.

SUITABLE PLAYS

There is no lack of suitable plays since there is the whole body of dramatic literature to choose from. A search through the file of programmes of foreign plays presented during a period of two or three years at a certain Adult Educational Institution yields the following: In French—*Le Juif Polonais* (Erckmann et Chatrian), *Après Moi* (Bernstein), *Papillon* (Bernstein), *Les Cloches Cassées* (Greville), *Maître Corbeau* (Raymond et Ordonneau), *L'Eté de Saint-Martin* (Meihhac et Halévy), *Dr. Knock* (Jules Romains), *Les Boulinard* (Ordonneau et Valabrègue), *Les Précieuses Ridicules* (Molière), *Les Petites Godin* (Ordonneau et Chivot), *La Poudre aux Yeux* (Veber), *Le Voyage de Monsieur Perrichon* (Labiche), *L'Extra* (Labiche); in German—*Szenen aus Faust* (Goethe), *Die Geschwister* (Goethe), *Minna von Barnhelm* (Lessing), *Kleptomanie* (Hartung), *Die Andere Seite* (Sherriff—being the German version of *Journey's End*); in Italian—*Festa di Beneficenza* (Niccodemi), *Lumiè di Sicilia* (Pirandello), *La Locandiera* (Goldoni); in Spanish—*Las de Cain*, *La Peubla de las Mujeres*, *Herida de Muerte*, *La Esposa y la Chismosa* (all by Los Quintero).

DRAMA IN THE CO-OPERATIVE MOVEMENT

JOHN BOURNE, Adjudicator; Lecturer at Co-operative Drama Schools; Midlands Pageant-Master " Co-operative Century "; Author of " Drama for Co-operators "

Of newer movements in amateur drama, the activities of the Co-operative societies have developed significantly. There is a Co-operative society in practically every city and town. Many have their own halls; these, in some places, are the best equipped theatres in the district.

THE THEATRE AT THE CO-OPERATIVE COLLEGE, STANFORD HALL, LEICESTERSHIRE

As a rule, Co-operative drama is in the hands of education committees, youth clubs, and women's guilds associated with each Co-operative society. So numerous are these various drama groups that seven sectional drama associations (acting as foster-parents) have been formed to cover England Scotland, and Wales. At the top is the National Co-operative Drama Association. Unlike other national organizations, which have more or less led the way, the N.C.D.A. came into being mainly at the instigation of the local and sectional associations which had felt the need of a headquarters.

The three types of drama groups are similar to (*a*) the usual mixed groups of adults; (*b*) the club that appeals to young people aged 16 to 20 years; and (*c*) those women's institutes which do not include men in their activities. The first two—in addition to other performances—organize their own festivals and enter "open" drama competitions. The drama groups of the women's guilds give most of their performances at guild meetings. They also hold festivals strictly confined to guild members.

All three joined hands in many places in 1944 when the Co-operative Movement celebrated its Centenary with a pageant *Co-operative Century*; written by Dr. L. du Garde Peach. Although the three sections generally work separately, they are of considerable value to each other in matters of personnel and equipment.

The Co-operative Union is very much alive to the needs of the drama groups and encourages them by literature and courses at summer schools. Local Co-operative education committees arrange lectures and week-end schools, and support the drama groups financially. The People's Entertainment Society began with Co-operators.

The Co-operative Movement owns the best-equipped Little Theatre in Great Britain. It is at Stanford Hall, Leicestershire—once the home of a millionaire, and now a Co-operative college. The theatre is all-electric and has every modern device, including an organ, cinema projectors, and up-to-date stage lighting.

Is Co-operative drama different from other amateur drama? Yes, it is a "plus" drama—the various groups follow the same methods as those of their prototypes in other fields. In addition, there is a leaning towards experiment and plays of "social significance." The Co-operative Movement has its own philosophy, and plays which bear on it are encouraged. It would, however, be quite unsound to allege that the drama enthusiasts are merely propagandists. Indeed, there are within the Movement those who feel that the drama groups should be more actively propagandist.

On the whole, the plays performed by Co-operators are similar to those chosen by other amateurs, if only because few plays are written that fit exactly Co-operative ideology. Co-operators, too, are fully aware of the danger of blatant propaganda. They realize that a restricted drama would be inimical to the general education and culture they strive to attain.

The National Co-operative Drama Association correlates much scattered activity. Co-operative drama festivals will develop increasingly into national, perhaps international, demonstration. The Co-operative colleges and schools foster a wider dramatic education. The plays that emerge are the plays that Co-operators seek. Better trained amateurs graduate from the youth clubs. Co-operative halls, better equipped, may easily develop into a chain of Little Theatres.

Admittedly, the standard of acting is not generally high, mainly because Co-operative drama is young. Organization, personnel, exist; and, in the background, the schools and colleges have enormous potentialities. As an educational, cultural, and social force, Co-operative drama should, in course of time, pay a high dividend.

Ramsey & Muspratt

E. MARTIN BROWNE

RELIGIOUS DRAMA, PAST AND FUTURE

E. MARTIN BROWNE, Director, The Pilgrim Players

IN this age of specialists, it is inevitable that the arts, like everything else, should suffer classification. But the term "Religious Drama" has done disservice both to drama and to religion. It has caused the theatre-folk to forget that their art is religious in origin, and that any drama that is truly drama is in some sense allied to religion from which it sprang. Hence the actor has tended at times to become just a craftsman using tricks of a trade, omitting to recreate at every performance the human character which is for him the mirror of the divine. Hence the parson and the devotee have tended to regard drama as a means to the end of promoting or teaching their particular brand of faith, denying it the intrinsic life which belongs to it as an art.

But since we are familiar, for good or ill, with the title, we had better define "Religious Drama" in the first place as drama dealing with the relationships between God and Man, and more especially with that relationship as shown in the Bible and in Christian history. The startlingly swift and widespread revival of this kind of drama in the past thirty years has indeed given it enough importance to make it worth study, especially as its modern growth seems only to be just beginning.

Before speaking of the twentieth century we must go back to the Middle Ages, for a comparison with what happened then is too illuminating to be omitted. From the ninth century to the sixteenth, a drama of the Church grew up in Europe. It began in the church itself, and as part of the Mass, with the minor ecclesiastics as the actors. But parallel with this worship-drama there grew a popular religious drama, wherein the guilds and other bodies portrayed in their own tongue the Mysteries of the Faith. In England this took place mostly on "pageants," special double-decker wagons which were drawn from street to street. It was a festival occasion, once or twice a year: the players were therefore all "amateurs," though they were paid small sums for playing; and there was a healthy rivalry between the teams such as subsists at a modern drama festival. This did not, here any more than in ancient Greece, destroy the essentially religious character of the undertaking or diminish the devotion which inspired it.

We have, however, to remember that that age was an "age of faith": the bulk of the population were unquestioning believers in the religion which the dramas presented. Our own age is very different: not ten per cent of our present population can be definitely claimed as believers in Christianity. Where the medieval dramatist took his audience's faith for granted, and was therefore able to portray the most profound matters in the most naïve terms, and to mix them with scenes of realism from the lives of contemporary people, without causing any one concern, his modern successor is much more circumscribed. His actors are playing to a world that is not with them, however much it would like to be: and accordingly they must present things another way.

The modern development of religious drama began, like the medieval, within the Church and as a popular movement. It was not the hierarchy who started it: the parish priest wanted to show his people what the stories which he read and told to them were like in action: the Sunday School teachers found that their children could create for themselves a convincing picture of the Bible story by playing their own version of it. At the same time, actors of the professional theatre, which had grown up so independent of its religious origins, found themselves drawn back to these profound subjects that Puritanism had debarred them from representing, and William Poel's revival of *Everyman* was the first of an increasing series. Nugent Monck, at Norwich, leading an amateur company in work of the highest standard, persisted in spite of threats of prosecution for blasphemy, in doing the old "mysteries." These pioneers awoke England to her heritage in religious drama.

It was, however, the Bishop of Chichester who really put it "on the map." As Dean of Canterbury, he caused Masefield, Holst, and Ricketts to collaborate in the creation of *The Coming of Christ*

(1928) for performance in Canterbury Cathedral itself: and this presentation in the Mother Church did more than anything else to open the way for the general use of religious drama. He followed with the creation of the Friends of Canterbury Cathedral, first of many such bodies, which held from 1930 onwards an annual festival of the arts, including a new play specially written each year by an author of the first rank. On his appointment to Chichester, he created the post of Director of Religious Drama for the Diocese. This was the first official recognition of the integration of drama into the life of the Church; it was followed by several other similar appointments, and by the creation of committees for drama in many church organizations. By 1939 it could be said that what the individual enthusiasts had begun was established as the policy of the whole body.

Meanwhile, the breaking of the long divorce between Stage and Church had proceeded apace. The most important landmark in this was the success of *Murder in the Cathedral* (1935), which Eliot originally wrote for the Canterbury Festival, and which, transferred to the little Mercury Theatre, in London, attained a long run and wide acceptance in theatres all over this country and America. This was significant in two ways: it meant that the modern poets, setting out to write for the theatre after a lapse of centuries, were attracted by religious themes; and it showed the theatres that there was at their disposal an audience new to them and wanting a different kind of fare from the usual. In the years between the first success of *Murder in the Cathedral* and 1939, several other plays of note appeared for this audience, and since then it has not been neglected, even during the stress of the Second Great War. Bridie's apocryphal

THE ROCK AND CHORUS OF THE CHURCH
Before the altar, in the final scene of *The Rock*, T. S. Eliot's "revue" of church-building at Sadler's Wells, 1934
Photo by Pollard Crowther

plays of Tobias, Jonah and Susanna on the lighter side, Dorothy Sayers' *The Zeal of Thy House* on the heavier, are some of the most popular examples.

During the War activity increased rather than diminished. First of all, the travelling companies, which took drama to millions who had never experienced it before, were the purveyors of religious plays. These were the Pilgrim Players, who, working as a community for a Tommy's pay, started in November, 1939, to take such plays all over the country. *Tobias and the Angel*, *Murder in the Cathedral*, *Noah*, were interspersed with plays specially written and with seasonal plays at Christmas and Easter. The audiences reached were more various than had ever been touched before, and the effect was quick and widespread. One result was the formation of the Adelphi Players, who extended the same kind of work; another the following up of the Pilgrim initiative by the amateurs in the places they visited.

For, of course, the amateur movement in religious drama has been growing by leaps and bounds. Here, even more than in secular drama, people have been creating their own plays: most of them poor enough in quality, naturally, since most of their authors know nothing about the dramatist's craft, even if they have a spice of his art, but many of them sincerely trying to bring to new life the familiar subjects. In 1929 a small group of enthusiasts formed the Religious Drama Society, which has grown into the national body for advice and help in all matters connected with religious drama. It has its headquarters at S.P.C.K. House, Northumberland Avenue, London, W.C.2, and for a subscription of 10s. provides library and advice facilities and runs schools and conferences for its members. Regional bodies affiliated to it are all over the country.

A notable experiment was Sheffield. As a result of Pilgrim visits there, the Association of Christian Communities asked the Religious Drama Society in 1943 to send an expert to report on the possibility of working in the city. Miss Pamela Keily, an ex-Pilgrim, went for a month and stayed. She is Adviser on Religious Drama to the Association. Half her salary is paid by grant from the local education authority, and she conducts classes and productions with groups both young and adult from every quarter and denomination of the city. Fine work has been produced; but even more important is the educative effect which can be clearly seen by any visitor to this remarkable experiment.

Religious drama has been an important feature of broadcasting. Dorothy Sayers was commissioned to write a Life of Christ in twelve plays.

"DEATH STANDS IN THE GATEWAY"
From "The Acts of Saint Richard," by E. Werge-Oram, before the Bishop's Palace, Chichester, 1933
Photo by Malcolm McNeille, Chichester

The result was *The Man Born to be King*. It marked an epoch in religious broadcasting, both because the Drama Department of the B.B.C. voted it the finest play of the year, which puts religious work on its proper parity with the rest of dramatic art, and because it was able, since the visual was excluded, to represent the Protagonist. The Lord Chamberlain's licence still prevents this on the stage, and there were objectors to it on "the air," but what was achieved by Miss Sayers was proof that it could be done to the benefit of religion and art alike.

The future obviously holds plenty of scope for religious drama. New plays, produced at the Mercury Theatre since 1945, are largely on religious themes. Many great projects all over the country are additional proof that the Church is awake to the claims and the value of this most essentially religious of the arts. It may be well to conclude this article by trying to assess what are the qualities which religious drama needs.

First, now as in the Middle Ages, a passionate assumption of the mind of the believer. People come to it for faith, and you cannot give them what they want if you cannot assume it yourself. This is true of all acting, but most of all of religious acting. Some who in real life have faith cannot convey it because they do not feel it with passion: some who do not have it can convey it because their imagination allows them to enter into it: but either must come to it free from selfish preoccupations, and willing to state directly and with some of the fervour of the prophets, what they stand for. Take a couple of examples. Gordon Bottomley's St. Peter in one of the finest of Cathedral plays (*The Acts of St. Peter*, written for Exeter), goes to his death saying:

> This God Who is great, yet can make himself small and helpless . . .
> This Jesus you have, sisters . . .
> He is all things, you have no need of me.

And Eliot in *The Rock* asks the caustic question:

> Do you need to be told that even such modest attainments
> As you can boast in the way of polite society
> Will hardly survive the Faith to which they owe their significance?

These are the sayings of believers, just as the act of the simplest shepherd who kneels at the Crib is an act of faith.

Second are the qualities of style and imagination. The play treats of eternal things; they are not easily or happily confined within the bounds of naturalism. Some plays, like the medieval ones, show them as if they happened in the writer's own day; others try to interpret them as history; others again in the formal or symbolic guises of poetry. But to all these needs to be brought the clear and vivid imagination which rescues the familiar from dead convention and lets it shine forth anew with the light of its eternal truth, seen again in terms which we could understand.

The Choice of a Play. Many of the most successful religious plays done by amateurs are written or made for their particular occasion. They seldom "travel," being dependent for their effect on local conditions and personalities. If the would-be producer is looking for a script among those published, he will do well to join and consult the Religious Drama Society, which has the standard library and the widest knowledge of plays.

These fall into five rough categories. First, there are the plays which either use the words of the Bible, or attempt to reproduce the Bible stories in their original setting. Of these, the most notable are the works of Mona Swann, in which the psalms and other folk-hymns are used for choral speaking. This gives a fine chance for community playing and brings the Bible to life as the story of a people with a mission. Added to the plays proper are tableaux and mimes, popular with many companies of beginners and for those who delight in decorative effect. Most notable of these is Charles Claye's famous Chelsea Pageant, *The Joyous Pageant of the Nativity.*

Next come the plays which, in order to bring the Bible into contact with our own life, transfer its setting to a contemporary one. This is what the medieval Mysteries did unconsciously: the Shephard who

> sought with my dogs
> all Horbury Shrogs

in the Wakefield play was looking in Yorkshire for the Christ-Child without any sense of incongruity. The modern play does it consciously, for we have what we call "a sense of period," but none the less it often succeeds in giving new life to the too familiar. Sheila Kaye-Smith has made Nativity and Passion Plays on this model, and Norman Nicholson has translated the story of Elijah to his native Cumberland in *The Old Man of the Mountains.* Many other examples might be cited.

A third group is that of historical plays on Christian life, both in the past and the present.

Great plays in this class are *Murder in the Cathedral* and *The Zeal of Thy House,* and the most difficult of all its types, the missionary play, has been well done by Charles Williams in *The House of the Octopus* and more simply by F. H. Wiseman in *Glorious Odyssey*. There is great scope here for development; and plays on current affairs are made by groups for themselves, notably under Oliver Wilkinson at Glasgow Community House, not uninfluenced by the new documentary drama.

The symbolic has always been a natural type of treatment for religious themes, and modern moralities comparable to the medieval *Everyman* have been produced. Dorothy Sayers did a Faust play just before the War: Ronald Duncan's *This Way to the Tomb!* succeeded in combining with ultra-modern satire a medieval morality-masque. These are a few of many attempts to relate the Absolute to the contemporary by means of symbol.

Last comes the category of plays which deal realistically with modern life in terms of a religious outlook. Here we are weakest: the outlook is perhaps not clear enough on many matters to enable plays to be written on them—for a dramatist has to know what he thinks! Eliot's *The Family Reunion* was an important attempt to do this in verse: the plays in prose which can be compared to it are almost non-existent. They will doubtless come: such plays as *Outward Bound* and *Glorious Morning* are forerunners, one may hope, of clearer work in this kind.

RONALD DUNCAN'S "THIS WAY TO THE TOMB!" AT THE MERCURY THEATRE
Courtesy Derek Beck

PRODUCTION

The producer is appointed and his play chosen. He has now to cast and plan his production. In the former task, he will be actuated by most of the same motives as his secular brethren, but also by one or two that apply only to religious drama. His play, especially if it be on a New Testament subject, is mainly concerned with spiritual matters, and needs actors who understand them. The actress who, at rehearsal, in preparation for her first entrance as an angel, nonchalantly placed her handbag on the altar, was obviously miscast for the part, as her performance proved. But the opposite mistake is equally dangerous. To cast the best girl in the village for the Madonna, although she has a flat voice and no chin, is to bring the Christmas story into contempt. The actors, especially of the chief parts, must both have the Christian outlook (not necessarily in an orthodox form) and be able to express it in a positive and attractive manner.

"THE ACTS OF SAINT RICHARD" AT CHICHESTER

Against an old wall of the Bishop's Palace. This open air stage was only 18′ by 12′ on top, but slopes of the full width on all four sides greatly increased the playing space and gave dignity and variety to movement and grouping. The use of a banner as backing to a scene may be noted. This photograph was taken from the side at an actual performance.

Photo by Malcolm McNeille, Chichester

One other recommendation should be made a rule. *No names* should be given in religious productions. This rule of anonymity has been adopted with success in some secular companies, notably the Maddermarket Theatre at Norwich. In sacred plays it is essential, both to place the players in the right atmosphere and also to communicate the nature of their offering to the audience. "And here we offer and present unto Thee, O Lord, ourselves, our souls and bodies, to be a reasonable, holy and lively sacrifice unto Thee." There are to be no big- or small-part actors, no "stars," no "building up" of individual parts; the play is one offering made by all, without thought of self, yet all giving of their best.

The planning of the production needs the same kind of care as does that of a secular play. A "production-copy" must be made; the words and "business" of each actor progressively imagined and written down; the necessary properties and scenery and costumes put in hand. In making the "production-copy," the religious producer needs to realize that, though the *tempo* of his play may be smoother and more even, and some forms of violent emotion (anger, for instance, or loud laughter) may not occur, the structure of the play must still be dramatic, the climaxes must still be built up, the characters still be clearly defined. So he may avoid the dullness of many religious productions, which have no form nor character.

It has been noted that naturalism is not wanted in religious drama. In particular, the exact sense of *place*, such as is given by a drawing-room or kitchen set to a domestic comedy, is scarcely ever desirable. The tendency of the religious play is rather to parallel the Elizabethan method, wherein the stage is always a stage—a platform set in the midst of the audience, who never regarded it as a picture of somewhere else (as we regard the proscenium-frame scene). The location of scenes is either undefined or is altered in the audience's imagination by the advent of different sets of characters and their talk. Only a rude shelter, for instance, will stand for the stable, and the characters will not play all the time inside it; but it will be clear, when Joseph says—

> But we must gather all our gear,
> Such poor garments as we wear,
> And put them in a package,

that he is inside the building; and equally from:

> Ah, Lord, but the weather is cold,
> The fearfullest freeze that ever I felt,

that he is outside.

As this type of play seeks to draw its audience into common feeling with itself, many producers go further, and jump the boundaries not only of place on the stage but also of the stage itself.

"The Coming of Christ" in Lancing College Chapel

A natural stage of great beauty, dressed solely with banners, shields, and fine costumes by the late Charles Ricketts, R.A. All the actors were boys. Spot lighting only.

Characters enter at the back or sides of the auditorium; and "journeys" are made through the audience; sometimes speeches are made to or by characters over the audience' heads. This method needs to be used with discretion. It may confuse the spectator, and may bring the actor so close to him as to destroy the illusion of character, especially with inexperienced actors who cannot keep "in the part" under such a strain. But in the main it has great value, and is in the tradition of religious drama we inherit from the Middle Ages, where we find Herod directed to "rage in the pageant (-wagon) and in the street also."

The attitude to religious drama above described finds natural expression in the production of a play in church. It is only in the last few years that many churches have been opened to plays, and there is still a considerable body of objectors. Accordingly, those responsible for a play in church have a special obligation laid on them to ensure that worship is not interfered with, that reverent behaviour is maintained, and that the performance is made, by the care and hard work of all concerned, worthy of the sacred building.

"DISARM" IN ST. ANNE'S, SOHO

A platform was built over the choir stalls. This picture was taken with the church lights on, but the effect of the spot-lighting can be seen; the dimly-lit figures in the background are ghosts.

Photo by Pollard Crowther

Further, it must be realized that here conditions are entirely different from those of the theatre. The play must fit into the church, using the architecture of the building and not altering it in any noticeable particular. No front curtain or scenery should be allowed, for these turn the church into a hall. Any curtaining at the sides and back must be hung on *taut* wire or rods and must be as little prominent as possible. It is desirable that a back curtain, if used in an

Anglican church, should at some time be withdrawn to show the altar. The platform must be high enough to enable the congregation to see (craning of necks is not conducive to devotion), which usually means about the height of the pew-tops; at this level it is not too noticeable when empty. It will often be found useful to build *slopes* instead of steps leading to the platform, especially at the back; this gives greater freedom of movement at all speeds.

Without a front curtain, all entrances and exits have to be made in view of the audience. This renders the choice of plays more difficult, since only those made or adapted for such treatment will serve. There are, however, an increasing number of such plays being written; and those others which do not depend for effect on the tableau type of "curtain" can often be adapted by the producer. Still tableaux, which necessitate a front curtain, should not be given in church, unless it has a screen into which curtaining can be introduced without spoiling its appearance.

As scenery is denied, the visual effect of the production is made by the players seen against the dark and spacious background of the church. This is a beautiful and mystical effect. It is obtained by the use of concentrated lighting, covering only the acting area. Thus, the players appear out of darkness, play their parts glowing in light against vast spaces of dimness, and fade again. Spotlights are of course the main source of such light; they may be concealed behind pillars or woodwork, and must be on dimmer-control to get the right effect. These points are illustrated by the accompanying photographs.

Another device useful in church production is *multiple* stages. The old Mystery Plays were played thus on the Continent; they had a "station" or small stage for each scene or group of characters. Modern multiple staging is not so elaborate; three or four stages are placed in different parts of the church and the drama passes between them, sometimes taking place on two, or even three, at once. For examples of this see Nos. 3, 4, and 5 in Sheldon Plays (S.P.C.K.).

The rehearsal period for a religious play will reveal a number of inhibitions in some players' minds. They must be helped to overcome their shyness at giving life to what in their minds has hitherto been a mystery, veiled from close examination. And, towards the end, they will need just the same pressure as secular players do, to gain speed and smoothness. The lack of this final stage of rehearsal has spoiled many a religious play.

Meanwhile, preparation should also have been going on "in front." Religious drama is new, and audiences need to be told what they will see and how to approach it. If the play is in a church, there is the seating question. Seats may not be sold, but may be reserved free of charge, and it is the writer's experience that if anyone will undertake the task of booking all the seats in the church, they will be amply repaid by happy congregations and increased collections. Pews are not comfortable, and people appreciate being relieved of a long wait in them before the play begins. If, however, any of the congregation must be seated early, suitable music should be provided to beguile the time.

Religious drama, even more than secular, depends for its success upon the willing co-operation of all concerned; and it is a large part of the producer's task to commend the play and his plans for it to his fellow-workers in such sort that they will give of their best to the perfecting of a beauty worthy of its subject. It should be entertainment in the highest sense, in that the audience receives an enriching experience: and this should lead to a response which may develop into a new and vital worship.

DRAMATIC TECHNIQUE

HERMON OULD, Author of "The Art of the Play," "Ada Wodderspoon," "New Plays from Old Stories," "The Dance of Life," "The Moon Rides High," "John Galsworthy," etc.

NO handbook, rules, prohibitions, examples, or hard work will make a playwright of one who was born without the dramatic instinct; but given the instinct, he may derive profit from examining the principles which inspired the work of playwrights who have succeeded in their art, even though the scrutiny should lead to his scorning their principles and disregarding their practice. The playwright of genius will almost inevitably find a way of his own, and if he has anything worth saying to say, will proceed by trial and error until he achieves his goal by inventing the technique most congenial to his mind. The would-be playwright whose talent falls short of genius, however, will not be forgiven his blunders. The least that will be expected of him is a reasonably close acquaintance with the canons and limitations of his art.

LIMITATIONS

It should be borne in mind that the drama, unlike other "creative" arts, is largely dependent upon a number of factors outside the control of the artist. A painter sees his picture exactly as he has painted it: no other personality intrudes between the work and its creator. He can watch its progress, shape it and change it, and bring it to a completion which, whatever its shortcomings, is what he alone has accomplished. Even the composer of music has a fairly close control of his medium; and although one interpretation of a work may differ from another, the range of possible variation is more or less fixed by an immutable notation and a system of marking which can be as lavish as the composer desires. The dramatist is much less happily circumstanced, and the aspiring playwright would be well advised to envisage some of the limitations that hedge his craft about.

To start with, the most important part of his medium is that unknown quantity, the human being. It is safe to say that except in those cases where parts have been written especially for particular actors, no playwright has ever seen a role played precisely as he conceived it. Unlike the novelist, whose characters are fixed for ever in his mind, the playwright must be prepared to see the creatures of his imagination in some degree distorted, however intelligently the actor interprets the part. The more vividly he has imagined a character, the more is he likely to be shocked when he sees it played. Physically, the actor will falsify his inward vision; the actor's voice will seem unfamiliar to his inward ear; the actor's personality, however skilfully adapted, will only approximately resemble the personality of the character as he, the author, conceived it.

Nevertheless, to write parts for particular actors is open to serious practical and artistic objections. Practical, because except in the rarest cases a dramatist cannot command the services of a particular actor even for his leading role, and it would be a piece of incredibly good luck if he had the services of a whole company at his disposal. Even repertory companies, like Miss Horniman's pre-War Gaiety Theatre at Manchester, or Stanislavsky's Moscow Art Theatre, or the present Liverpool Repertory Theatre, are only relatively permanent: their personnel is in a state of flux and one season's cast differs substantially from the next. Artistically, the practice is almost indefensible, and is only to be recommended to playwrights whose gift for creating character is so slender that it needs the personality or peculiarities of a particular actor to stimulate it. A role adapted to the personality of one actor is likely to be lifeless when interpreted by another.

Secondly, although in ideal conditions the setting of a play may conform almost exactly with the intentions of the author, conditions are so rarely ideal that one must be prepared to accept a compromise. The room which has existed in the author's mind during the process of creation will probably only resemble very superficially the room which the scene-painter and stage carpenter place before him at the dress rehearsal. The mountains, glaciers, caverns, and

Swaine

Hermon Ould

hilltops which have served as the background to the author's imagination will take on entirely different appearances as soon as they have been fitted to the limitations of a stage by a scenic artist with his own personality to express.

THE PRODUCER

Thirdly, between the author and the play looms the producer. Now, the producer in the modern theatre plays almost as important a part as the financial backer himself. The backer may determine the policy of the theatre, but, the play once chosen, no dictator could be more dictatorial than the producer. The author, if sufficiently prominent, or lucky, will be consulted about the cast and may, if he unites pluck with luck, have some chance of expressing an opinion at rehearsals; but his power of veto is somewhat academic and his choice of actors is in any case limited by financial and other considerations. Moreover, in most theatres, certain actors and actresses seem to have a divine right to jobs and often lay what appear to be undeniable claims to leading roles.

But even if the cast is an ideal one, the producer will not necessarily handle it in a way which commends itself to the author. Most producers—and rightly—have theories of their own which they wish to exploit, tricks of production which they wish to try out, ideas about lighting, and so forth; and although all these factors may be intensely interesting in themselves, they remove the play further and further away from the author's control, leaving him almost as detached an onlooker as the dramatic critic.

Fourthly, an even more important collaborator than the producer, the actor, and the scene-designer, is the audience. It is self-evident that a play does not rightly exist until it is produced on the stage of a theatre; it is scarcely less axiomatic that it does not exist in the fullest sense until it has been played before an audience. Not only is there a subtle psychological bond which links performers with public and determines in what degree a production is successful or not; but the chief aim of the producer's art is to calculate the effect which certain factors—actions, movements, inflections, tricks of lighting, timings, silences, and a myriad others—will have upon an audience, and until these have been tried out and have succeeded the work of the producer cannot be said to have passed the test.

The art of the theatre is largely the art of "making an effect," and presupposes an audience. If *rapport* between players and public is not established soon after the rise of the curtain, the play is in danger of never coming to life. Remembering the variability of audiences, their incomprehensible uncertainty—enthusiastically alive to-day and inexorably dead to-morrow—we shall recognize the importance of their contribution to the dramatist's art. An audience is not interested in intentions: it judges by results and ought not to be asked to make allowances. It has no time for reflection until the curtain descends: effects, therefore, however subtle, must not be ambiguous. Whatever esoteric meanings may be there for subsequent discovery, they must carry a face-value meaning which is not subsequently belied.

From all this it is clear that the drama is a co-operative art in which the author plays an important, but not the only, part. The author who wishes to control the expression of his art, who shrinks from the contaminating hand of another artist, should leave the drama alone and save himself much irritation, despair, and heartache. But once the importance of the four collaborators with the author—actor, scene-designer, producer, and audience—is admitted and accepted, the would-be playwright may consider some of the principles which go to the making of a play.

UNITY

A play, like any other work of art, must be an harmonious whole; however diverse its parts, they must be so related that an effect of unity is produced. The modern dramatist does not trouble himself about the Aristotelian "unities" of time and space, which decreed that the action of a play should be continuous and the scene constant—and, indeed, the practice of the Greeks themselves only superficially adhered to them. Unity of a more important and subtler order is demanded, depending on a nice sense of proportion and a feeling for what is relevant. It is not necessarily much concerned with the division of a play into accurately measured acts: a play can be in one, two, three, four, or five acts, or in a series of scenes of odd lengths, and either succeed or fail in attaining unity. Mr. Bernard Shaw's *Getting Married* is not divided into acts or scenes at all; its action is continuous and its setting unchanging, but it is doubtful whether it thereby achieves an effect of unity. Ibsen's *Peer Gynt*, on the other hand, which follows its hero's life from boyhood to old manhood, through scenes of the utmost diversity, is a unified whole.

Unity, then, is a mental or spiritual quality, dependent for its attainment upon the sensitiveness and conscience of the artist. Actions or speeches dragged into a play in order to make an effect not inherent in the development of the theme destroy its unity; and fantasy and farce are no less subject to this rule than so-called realistic drama. The apparent irrelevancies of farce must be as carefully selected as the superficially more logical action, or they will destroy the flow essential to a successful farce. Fantasy follows laws of its own, but they are *laws*, and the waywardness of fantasy is only apparent, not real. There is no inconsequence about Housman's and Granville-Barker's *Prunella*.

CONFLICT

All arts have their dogmas. The drama is beset by them, and if the high panjandrums who invent or support them could have their way, the drama would become one of the most rigid and limited of arts instead of what it is by nature, one of the most fluid and diverse. One of the most persistently repeated dicta is that drama, all drama, is conflict. Brunetière[1] was probably the first to utter it, but it has been repeated over and over again by people who have never heard of that distinguished French critic. It is only a half-truth. Many famous plays exemplify it; as many more give it the lie. In any play there are bound to be various currents which run counter to one another, and presumably no play exists in which the hero steers a course entirely free from obstacles. But to deny the right of existence to plays which are not based on conflict is to set up an arbitrary and stultifying limitation to the scope of the drama.

The most that can be justly claimed is that conflict determines the course of more plots than any other single relationship; but it would no more be true to say that drama cannot exist without conflict than it would be to claim that all conflict is drama. A quarrel on the stage, as in life, may be an extremely tedious and undramatic affair; ten minutes of carefully pointed dialogue, in which there is no hint of conflict, may be intensely dramatic. Drama may show one man in antagonism to another, or one idea in antagonism to another, or man in conflict with the state, or in conflict with the world, or Hamlet-like, in conflict with himself; but it may also show, and be no less dramatic in the showing, man progressing from one state of mind to another, from one emotional state to another; it can show man passing from ignorance to knowledge, from foolishness to wisdom; it can picture phases of society humorously, vindictively, satirically, or approvingly, and can pillory the foibles and stupidities of the age by showing them the reflection of themselves. It can inspire by showing heroism in which the element of conflict has no place, and a love passage unmarred by differences that is as dramatic and as stimulating as a passage of arms.

Conflict, then, although often an important ingredient of drama, is not an essential ingredient; there are many first-class plays in which it has no place and there will be many more when playwrights refuse to be bound by rules-of-thumb and shibboleths invented by well-meaning but often limited theoreticians.

ACTION

"Actions speak louder than words" is almost a truism in the theatre; but the word "action" as it concerns the drama has been much misunderstood. It is true that drama without action is almost a contradiction in terms. A play in which nothing happened would be unthinkable; a play in which there were long stretches of inaction would be undramatic and boring. But action does not necessarily mean, as it is often alleged to mean by those who are readier to use clichés than to think for themselves, physical movement. Complete immobility is often dramatic, and physical movement is often lacking in dramatic significance. Physical movement on the stage should be used sparingly, more sparingly, indeed, than it is used in real life. So many of our movements in daily life are aimless and our gestures meaningless. Watch people at home,

[1] Ferdinand Brunetière: *Etudes Critiques.*

or in a restaurant, in the street or in a railway carriage, and you will be amazed by the physical restlessness which characterizes many of them. Their hands fidget; they pat their hair, finger their faces, adjust their clothing, cross and uncross their legs; they move from one place to another for no apparent reason and indulge in gestures which seem to bear no relation to what they are saying or thinking. The psycho-analyst would no doubt deduce peculiar and interesting facts from all these apparently inconsequent activities; but as the average member of an audience is not a psycho-analyst, the actor who employs a gesture or makes a movement which does not immediately convey a recognizable meaning is not only wasteful in his technique but is actively misleading. A meaningless gesture is not merely useless; it is positively harmful and destructive of continuity. Continuity is a word which has been used before in these pages and will no doubt be used again, for it relates to one of the essential attributes of dramatic art. However broken up the action of a play may be, the dramatic thread, like the thread of life, must remain intact or theatrical suicide will be committed. When the curtain falls on an act or a scene, or a black-out brings about a pause in the physical action, the complex of emotions or ideas which the dramatist has aroused in the audience must go on working, perhaps consciously, perhaps subconsciously, so that when the time comes for the curtain to rise again the public's mind is alert and expectant. Indeed, the action of a play might almost be said to take place in the mind of the spectator.

Dramatic action, then, does not necessarily imply physical movement, although physical movement is sometimes involved in it. If John crosses to the window for no ostensible reason, the movement may be necessary for stage-grouping or for some other purpose known to the producer, but it has nothing to do with dramatic action. If, however, John, having just confessed that he is bankrupt, crosses to the window in such a way as to awaken in the audience's mind the thought that he is about to throw himself out, that is dramatic action, because it carries the emotional plot one step further. If Jane, accused of murder, stands transfixed and speechless, that very immobility is dramatic, expressing innocence or guilt as the author decrees.

In a word, dramatic action is the movement from one mental or emotional state to another, and no play, however quiet, however lyrical, however spectacular, can exist without it.

THE WELL-MADE PLAY

The following pages are concerned primarily with what has come to be regarded as the well-made play, the play, that is to say, which conforms to certain reasonable rules and does not seek to break away from accepted practice. Later something will be said about experimental forms; here we will confine ourselves to plays which are, loosely speaking, realistic or naturalistic. The adjective is, of course, inexact, for no play, however photographically it reproduces the material seeming of real life, is even remotely realistic. Selection, dove-tailing, and telescoping are not only artistically commendable, but practically unavoidable. Nevertheless, it is possible so to present plays on the stage that they assume a semblance of real life—plays in which the characters are recognizably human and comport themselves in much the same manner as men and women comport themselves in the world around us; plays in which nothing happens that might not conceivably happen in real life; plays, in brief, which endeavour to depict life faithfully as in a mirror which is not intended to distort but to reflect.

A good play is organic, like a human being; not put together, like a machine. A machine is designed to fulfil a specific function—to cut paper, to weave cloth, to haul cargo; a human being is a community—a skeleton, a complex of correlated organs, a nervous system, a muscular system, all working in harmony, plus that unknown quantity called personality which makes one human being essentially different from all others; in a word, a human being is designed to *live.* A play may be constructed according to all the rules of dramatic technique and yet fail to come to life; it may break all the rules and yet, because the author has imbued it with vitality, it may transcend them and become a living work of art.

The first essential of a good play is that it should be alive, bearing within it the principle of growth. The playwright conceives an idea which germinates first of all in his mind, and afterwards, when the embryo is sufficiently advanced, it may be handled and shaped into a play. Before the aspiring author troubles his brain about dramatic construction (the skeleton, shall we say) he must be convinced that he has a play to write and is not merely inspired by the wish to have written a play. A vague impulse towards creation is not enough. The desire must be definite and dynamic and must be supported by the conviction that he has something acceptable to express and the innate power to express it. The impulse may spring from many equally legitimate sources, some of which we will now consider.

THE SITUATION

A common point of departure is a striking situation; for example, John, after having married Jane, discovers that she had been married before he knew her and had concealed the knowledge from him, possibly for shameful reasons, possibly out of consideration for his peace of mind. Situation enough, here, to set a playwright going. The first husband, believed by Jane to be dead and therefore properly dumb, turns up. Or a child by the first husband, carefully committed to the keeping of a trusted friend or retainer, makes his or her unexpected appearance, to the astonishment of John and the dismay and shame of Jane. Or, worse still, the banished son of the first husband may chance upon the daughter of the second, in Italy, shall we say, and, all unsuspecting the relationship, fall in love with her. The possible developments are many and various and hundreds of plays, good and bad, have been born of a situation no more pregnant.

For plays of this kind the French have a special predilection, and the names of Bernstein, Scribe, Sardou, Hervieu, and many others spring to the mind; but they have no monopoly, and Schnitzler, Sudermann, Henry Arthur Jones, Pinero, Oscar Wilde, and many of their contemporaries were similarly stimulated; moreover, as many of the succeeding generation have availed themselves of much the same expedients, it may be assumed that the play of situation still has a good deal of life in it. Noel Coward's *Easy Virtue* is a play of situation, so is *The Vortex*; so, with a difference, is *Private Lives*, the difference consisting in the deliberate pattern-making of this play which distinguishes it from the more or less natural development of the average good play of situation.

An indispensable condition of a dramatic situation is plausibility; this achieved, the complications and permutations may be as many and ingenious as the theme allows; without it, ingenuity is wasted. An author must not ask his audience to believe in a situation inherently impossible as the price of an evening's ingeniously resolved complication. Even situations which are highly improbable should be resorted to sparingly, and then only if the author is sure that he has skill enough to make them convincing. At one time the wildest absurdities of coincidence and purblindness seem to have been accepted in the theatre; but to-day verisimilitude is demanded of plays which claim to be realistic. Misunderstandings which would be explained away in five minutes of real life are not allowed to occupy 2½ hours' traffic of the stage; parents are not permitted to recognize at first sight offspring from whom they have been separated for upwards of twenty years in order to pander to the sentimental notion that because blood is thicker than water it is therefore endowed with abnormal powers of divination.

A DISTINCTION

It is necessary to distinguish between situation and story. Every play is, in a sense, a story, if a story may be defined as a series of connected happenings. Pinero's *The Second Mrs. Tanqueray* has an easily related story; Galsworthy's tragic demonstration of the impersonality of Justice, in the play bearing that title, has a story; plays as essentially of the theatre as Chekhov's have stories; even a play like Shaw's *Misalliance* has a story, and there is no intrinsic reason why certain plays should have been conceived as plays rather than as novels. But of the works mentioned only one—*The Second Mrs. Tanqueray*—could be properly described as a play of situation. Theatrically speaking, a situation is a number of circumstances which, taken separately, have no dramatic significance, but, taken in relation to one another, form a combination which is, in itself, pregnant with dramatic possibilities. The fact that John married Jane; the fact that Jane had been previously married and had lost sight of her husband, believing him to be dead; the fact that the son of Jane by her first husband should meet and become enamoured of her daughter by her second husband—none of these facts, taken separately, is dramatic; combined, they make a situation which contains the very essence of drama.

Nor must story be confused with plot. A plot is the inter-related material out of which a play is built. A story narrates how Beta follows Alpha and Delta follows Gamma until Omega is reached and the narrative comes to an end. But a plot deals with Omega's structural relation to Delta, and Delta's to Gamma, and so on through all the units of construction.

Allied to the play of situation is the thriller. As the chief aim of a thriller is to shock by surprise, it may perhaps be assumed that the invention of a suitable instrument for administering the required shock is the most productive source of plays of this kind. The old dramatic law, that the audience should never be kept in the dark concerning the playwright's intentions, which never possessed the validity with which it was invested by the theorists, is completely discountenanced by the writer of thrillers. The author of one kind of thriller would, indeed, feel that he had failed in his task if the audience even suspected who the real criminal was before the final curtain was about to descend. Most of the usual practices of the normal play hold good for the thriller, tightened and heightened; suspense is even more breath-bating, tension even more taut, the denouement an even greater relief; but character-drawing claims little attention and psychology goes a-begging.

PLAYS OF CHARACTER

Another source of inspiration is character. Sometimes a character, or a group of characters, will assault an author's mind and clamour to be put into a play. The author thus assailed would be well advised to give his assailants an opportunity of disclosing whether they are psychologically interesting and dramatically effective. A play devoted to the exploitation of a single character is often interesting, but it is only justified if it fulfils the fundamental dramatic requirements. As many well-known plays would appear to have come into existence on account of the vitality of a single character—Eugene O'Neill's *Anna Christie*, St. John Ervine's *Jane Clegg*, H. A. Vachell's *Quinneys*', Ibsen's *Hedda Gabler* and *John Gabriel Borkman*, not to mention *Hamlet*—there would seem to be no inherent objection to the practice. It is, nevertheless, fraught with dangers from which only particularly skilled dramatists are likely to be immune.

CRITICAL ALOOFNESS

Some authors have declared that their characters, once conceived, take the law into their own hands. Such a statement need not be taken too literally; it may be due to parental pride or more probably to a misgrasp of what really happens. It is true that the vitality of some characters is so immense that more than common care is needed to keep it within bounds. When an author claims that a character has taken the law into its own hands, probably what has really happened is that the author, following the line of least resistance, has not been sufficiently detached from his offspring, but has allowed its development to pursue too facile a course. However enamoured the dramatist may be of his character, a certain critical aloofness is absolutely essential. A character in a novel may perhaps be allowed to run riot for a few pages and be brought back by the scruff of the neck before going too far; in a play such dallying is indefensible.

A character which has sufficient vitality to force itself upon an author's consciousness is likely to need firm handling. It must not be given its head, nor be allowed to impose its will upon the author until the author is properly convinced. Bearing in mind that a play is, first of all, action in logical continuity, every speech which a character wishes to utter, every movement which a character wishes to make, must be minutely scrutinized before it is allowed to pass. Words and movements may be perfectly "in character" and yet serve no dramatic purpose; and as it is one of the fundamental laws of drama that anything which does not help, hinders, irrelevancies born of character, however delightful in themselves, must be pitilessly sacrificed. Irrelevant emotion must be suppressed, irrelevant epigrams scattered to the winds. No character in a well-made play is important enough to be allowed to destroy the balance of the whole conception with impunity. Dramatic purpose should always take precedence over character.

Another danger, of which the practised dramatist is only too aware, but which the novice may overlook, is that, however exactly and lovingly a character has been conceived, the actor has not yet been born who could embody it on the stage. A compromise is inevitable; and bearing this in mind, the temptation to sacrifice drama for the sake of character-drawing may be lessened.

SUBTLETIES OF PSYCHOLOGY

But if subtleties of characterization must be employed sparingly, subtleties of psychology need only be limited by the author's insight into human conduct and his capacity for expressing it in dramatic form. What may be called the psychological make-up of *Hedda Gabler* might be revealed almost equally well by, say, Mrs. Patrick Campbell or Miss Jean Forbes-Robertson; but it would be impossible, after seeing both interpretations, to say with conviction which of the two Heddas was likelier to approximate to Ibsen's own; indeed, it would be safer to assume that neither of them bore the slightest resemblance to Hedda as conceived by him.

However, if the play born of a character, or of a group of characters, is surrounded with pitfalls from which the play of situation is free, it is some compensation to know that it is on a much higher plane and is, at its best, of supreme interest and significance; for no faculty of the dramatist is more valuable than that which enables him to show mankind the image of itself and to throw light on the mysterious sources of human behaviour. The power to draw character, plus the power to analyse and express psychological reactions, is the dramatist's most precious gift, without which his art would be that admirable but lesser thing, craft.

An author may be tormented by a social problem and wish to body it forth in dramatic form. Most of the plays of Bernard Shaw belong admittedly to this class, and many of John Galsworthy's. Brieux, Ibsen, Strindberg, Eugene O'Neill, and numerous other dramatists have written successful plays that were inspired by a desire to reform the world, and this impulse towards creation is at least as serviceable as any other, and more likely than most to result in a play worth seeing.

A great deal of nonsense has been written about propaganda in art, and the drama in particular has suffered from generalizations which would rigidly exclude all didacticism from the realm of the theatre. The very roots of the theatre are imbedded in the passion to instruct. Leaving the great Greeks out of consideration, our own theatre would not have come into existence if it had not been for an urgent desire to display the history and teachings of the Christian religion in dramatic form; the early "Mystery" and "Morality" plays have no other origin. Because the chief function of the theatre in these days is to entertain—using the word in a liberal sense—we are losing sight of the fact that by thus confining it we are attempting to warp its natural growth and to limit its appeal. It may be relatively true that within the charmed circle of West-End theatres propaganda is taboo; but the Theatre, luckily, is not circumscribed by the dictates of commercialism, but is subject to laws of its own, and, although its growth may be for a time artificially stimulated in one direction and dwarfed in another, soon or late it will readjust itself, break down barriers, and follow the lines of development inherent in its own nature.

PROPAGANDA AND INSPIRATION

Propaganda, or the desire to plead a particular cause, is, then, a legitimate source of inspiration; but obviously the propagandist must be the servant of the dramatist and not the master. Indeed, it might almost be said that the source of inspiration must be forgotten as soon as the play is under way. The realization that the Law, however theoretically just, bears more hardly upon the poor than upon the rich, probably inspired Galsworthy to write *The Silver Box*; but once having set out to write the play he concentrated his attention on the development of plot and character in such a manner as to secure the greatest possible dramatic effect, and was only subconsciously aware of the moral he wished to draw. *Ghosts* would never have been written if Ibsen had not wished to demonstrate what he deemed (wrongly, it appears) to be a biological law of heredity: that the excesses of the father are visited on the son. But the play is innocent of any direct propagandist statements. The story unfolds itself, inevitably, to its tragic ending, and points its own moral. If the biology implicit in *Ghosts* is unscientific, the play is the more apt an example of rightly-planned propagandist drama, because its power and truth as a play are in no way invalidated by the falseness of its biological premises. For the duration of the play we accept them; our emotions are stirred and our moral senses aroused in precisely the same degree *as if* the incidents placed before us were ungainsayable; and that is all that can be asked of any play. *Ghosts* is unlikely ever to fail to make its appeal, because it is so deftly constructed to secure its dramatic effect that the onlooker is willing to suspend judgment. Ibsen, in this and other plays, proves himself to have mastered propaganda as a source of dramatic inspiration. Bernard Shaw, on the other hand, lacking Ibsen's architectural sense and having less concern with posterity than with his own castigable generation, has nearly always put propaganda first and art second and thereby run the risk of indelibly labelling his plays with the date of their production. The flogging of dead horses is neither a dramatic nor an edifying spectacle, and plays which *explicitly* attack abuses that have ceased to afflict us are bound eventually to sink into oblivion. Some of Shaw's early plays have already met their doom, and he would probably be the first to admit, indeed to claim, that having served their purpose the proper place for them is the museum library.

It all boils down to this: the dramatist who is moved by righteous indignation to attack or by enthusiasm to glorify, should make sure that these admirable emotions have not taken possession of him, but are well under his control.

THE WELL-MADE PLAY

The structure of the well-made play has a certain skeleton-like rigidity, but is capable, like a skeleton, of assuming a number of different forms. A play may be in three, four, or five acts, and be subdivided into as many scenes, so long as the emphases are right. It is all a question of proportion and rhythm. There is a certain geometrical proportion about the three-act form which gives it an initial advantage over more complicated mediums. It is, as it were, a triptych with a central act of great weight and significance, balanced on the one hand by a first act of exposition and awakening interest, and on the other hand by a third act devoted to the resolving of complexes, the unravelling of tangled skeins, the tying of loose ends.

THE THREE-ACT FORM

Perhaps it is this obvious symmetry which makes the three-act form appear to be the most suitable form for artificial comedy, especially in these days when intricacies of plot—which might properly claim four or five acts—are discountenanced. The triple form lends itself more readily to the weaving of a play of light texture and readily assimilable pattern than the solider four-act structure; and the five-act play has gone out of fashion since two hours came to be regarded as the maximum duration of an evening's theatrical entertainment. But there is no inherent reason why an artificial comedy should not be in four acts or in as many acts as the author can handle.

A playwright may start out with a definite scheme in his mind, or he may shape his material as he goes. There is no golden rule. The temperament of one author favours one method, the temperament of another the other. But whichever course the playwright adopts, the result must be a structure whose parts relate logically to the whole. Whether it is desirable to work to a scenario is again an open question which can only be answered according to the idiosyncrasies of the author. Edward Knoblock placed it on record that he worked to a scenario of the most elaborate kind, with all the entrances and exits scrupulously planned, the substance of each scene not only barely indicated but described in detail, with the drift of the dialogue outlined, and the division into scenes and acts carefully schemed. *Kismet* came to birth in this manner. The scenario for *Kismet* occupies some thirty pages of print. This brief extract gives an idea of the method—

> Hajji is brought by the Guard, followed by Shopkeepers and a Crowd, in which is the Guide of Scene I.
> Hajji accused by Shopkeeper I.
> Shopkeeper II bearing No. I witness.
> Hajji protests.
> Meant to pay. Excitement of new clothes made him forget.

Produces money.
Where did he get his money?
Sheikh of desert.
They all laugh.
Sheikh of desert does not give money.
Sheikhs are outlaws, robbers.
Not allowed in town.

There can be no doubt that with a scenario as completely schemed as this many snares are avoided. False trails are not likely to be followed and the author will not find that his plot ends in a *cul de sac*. Many of the most prominent exponents of the well-made play have invariably worked to a scenario; many no less prominent, including John Galsworthy, whose plays are certainly no less taut than Edward Knoblock's, did not; and it cannot be said that Galsworthy's plays were more wasteful or tentative in construction than, say, Sardou's.

MAKING A START

When the practices of successful dramatists are so divergent, it would obviously be absurd to lay down laws; but it may, perhaps, be said that no competent play was ever written by an author who did not start out with some definite situation, character, plot, or "message" to exploit, and although an elaborate scheme of construction is manifestly not essential, the beginner would be well-advised to have a possible climax and winding-up in his mind before he has been long at work on a play. First and second acts which lead nowhere must be the experience of many beginners, and tame or supererogatory last acts have wrought the downfall of many plays.

The business of a first act is to awaken interest and maintain a feeling of expectancy until the fall of the curtain. The chief characters must be introduced as early as possible, if not in person at any rate by arousing interest in them. And as a corollary of this, it should be remembered that characters who play an unimportant part in the main theme of the play should not be allowed to attain too great a prominence. The balance of many plays has been destroyed by small parts attracting more attention than principal parts, a defect due sometimes to the author, but more often to the actor.

As it cannot be assumed that the audience will be perfectly receptive at the rise of the curtain, the earliest moments of a play should not contain matter of vital importance. It would be unwise to allow essential facts or relationships to be divulged as soon as the curtain goes up and then left to be assumed. Late-comers, like other sinners, should be left to their well-deserved punishment; but even those who are present at the opening of a play are apt to have their minds so full of irrelevant matters that the effort of concentration required for taking in a new set of relationships inevitably absorbs some moments. The wise playwright allows a few minutes of quiet, relevant action to occupy the mind of the audience while the process of focusing the attention is taking place. Even the most attentive member of an audience will be endeavouring to take in the physical details of the scene as soon as the drawing of the curtains discloses it, and while his eyes are thus busy, his ears are only partly alert. An exception may be made of startling openings such as a pistol shot, a scream, or some other catastrophic happening designed to arrest the attention; but it is only a certain kind of play—broadly the thriller—that is likely to employ a device of this kind. There is no fundamental reason why a play should not open with a moment of tenseness or excitement which is gradually resolved to tranquillity during the length of its three or four acts, but it will be discovered in practice that a play produces a more satisfying effect upon an audience if it starts quietly and rises by a series of small crises until it reaches a fitting climax.

RELATIONSHIP OF CHARACTER

Having satisfactorily opened, the playwright's task is to reveal as briefly and naturally as possible the relationship of one character to another, to awaken interest in them and their doings, and to keep the attention occupied until the end of the act.

The intermediate acts are concerned with the development of the theme and the increasing of tension. New characters must only be introduced if they bring new light to the situation, and although new aspects of the main problem or theme may be given, and are indeed expected, it would be fatal to introduce a new one, however unimportant. The plot of a play may be retrospective—Ibsen's *Rosmersholm* is the classic example of this kind of play; or it may be chronological, event following event before one's eyes with scarcely a glance at events which happened before the curtain rose for the first time—Galsworthy's *The Silver Box* is a good example of this kind of play. But whether retrospective or chronological, the same rule applies: intermediate acts must increase the tension and only relevant new material may be introduced.

The last act of the well-made play is the most difficult of all. The first act allows the author's fancy to roam more or less at will, with the sure and certain knowledge that he has two or three more acts to follow in which he may tie up loose ends, correlate his material and justify the ways of playwright to audience. The intermediate acts screw down his mind more exactingly to the task; the last act condemns or acquits him. In the last act a clean sweep must be made of all apparent irrelevancies; light must be shed on all obscurities; and when the curtain descends inexorably for the last time, the audience must be satisfied that poetic justice has been done. All doubts and misgivings which have been generated during the play must be dissipated; ambiguous actions which may have been necessary for the unfolding of the plot must now be properly explained, and however unexpected the upshot of the play may be, it must be acceptable to a normally intelligent audience. To do all this and yet never let the purely dramatic content flag is the difficult task of the last act. Explanations, if required, must be skilfully insinuated between lines, thrown off incidentally in the flow of natural dialogue; and although the end, when it comes, must seem inevitable, it must not be foreshadowed so clearly that tension is relaxed and the audience receives the impression that it is being told something that it already knew.

DANGER OF ANTICLIMAX

Generalizing, it may be said that the penultimate act should contain the biggest scene of a well-made play, but if something of essential interest is not held over for the last act, something which, perhaps, gives a new twist to the material, or throws yet further light on it, or in some other way intensifies the drama, the danger of anticlimax can hardly be avoided. It is permissible, and even desirable, to allow a quiet ending to follow an intense situation—climax does not necessarily imply cataclysm; but the quiet is the quiet which is intended to allow an audience breathing space after unaccustomed tension, and not the dullness born of exhausted interest.

ATMOSPHERE

The atmosphere of a play, its nervous system, is very largely a matter of right preparation, and like almost every other department of dramatic technique is intimately concerned with the exclusion of irrelevancies. Everybody knows that however consummately well the atmosphere of a scene has been built up, a cat unexpectedly finding its way on to the stage will destroy it in the twinkling of an eye. The most perfectly prepared climax, the most scrupulously timed love scene, the most delicately contrived fantasy, will be dissipated by an irrelevant sneeze, on or off the stage. Such calamities as these are beyond the control of the dramatist and of the actors, but the author is not infrequently guilty of irrelevancies scarcely less disastrous which some blind spot in his mentality prevents him from seeing. Most common of all is the irresistible joke. "A laugh is never wasted," a well-known dramatist once said—a generalization which should be disregarded by all but the most immovably established of authors. An ill-timed laugh is not only wasted: it is an irrelevance which may destroy a play, dissipating atmosphere which has taken many minutes to generate and cannot be recaptured.

An obvious way of creating atmosphere is by placing the acting in the right setting. Warmth of feeling, passion or hot-house emotion, would have a hard fight against a setting—shall we say the office of a mining engineer?—which gave no suggestion of emotion. The elements should be used sparingly—thunder-storms, howling wind, and noisy rain, legitimate adjuncts of the drama though they be, are apt to prove less impressive on the stage than in the mind of the dramatist. It is so easy to miscalculate mechanical effects that the playwright should be chary of counting on their aid. The rain which fell incessantly during the greater part of Somerset Maugham's *Rain* as produced in London, the drums which beat an endless tattoo in Eugene O'Neill's *The Emperor Jones*, were doubtless designed to exercise a hypnotic influence upon the minds of the audience, but only partially succeeded in doing so; on many minds the effect was one of irritation, amounting in some cases to exasperation.

The soundest method of producing the right atmosphere is through the medium of the dialogue, by the careful selection of the right words, the right sentiments, the right moments for silence, and above all, by ruthlessly excluding any words, sentiments, or movements which detract from the desired atmosphere. Remembering that the drama is ultimately enacted in the mind of the beholder, the playwright will suggest to the beholder's mind only those ideas and emotions which build up the atmosphere he wishes to create.

CHARACTERIZATION AND DIALOGUE

Dialogue being by far the most important factor in the expression of character, it would be absurd to treat one independently of the other. The physical actions which reveal character are crude in comparison with the subtleties which can be revealed by the spoken word.

As we are discussing the well-made play, we may dismiss any consideration of plays which do not aim at presenting characters more or less recognizable as living human beings. The "humours" of eighteenth century comedy do not here concern us, nor are we for the moment dealing with modernist drama which, in some of its developments, has abandoned character-drawing. In the modern well-made play characters are expected to behave like human beings. The capacity to create character is either innate or non-existent: it cannot be acquired. But even the capacity to create character is useless without the skill to present it convincingly on the stage; and it is there that craft, which *can* be acquired, comes in. The character having come to birth in the dramatist's mind, he must brood upon it ceaselessly until he knows all about it—its past as well as its present and its possible future. He must know just how far it can go in all directions, how it is likely to express itself, as well as what it is likely to do, what, in fact, its potentialities are. It is not necessary that a character should be slavishly consistent—consistency is an attribute of types; but if it is inconsistent, its inconsistency must be made convincing to an audience; it must be explained and not be left to be taken for granted.

The first words uttered by a character must be true to the whole conception, and the more they can reveal of the character without sacrificing credibility, the better. Let us imagine that a play opens with Mary, John, and Jane discovered.

> MARY. Did you hear a knock?
> JOHN. Yes; it was the postman.
> JANE. I wonder who the letter is for.

What characteristics are revealed by this perfectly natural conversation? None at all. The speeches might be interchanged without loss of verisimilitude, John's being given to Jane, and Jane's to Mary, and so on. Suppose the speeches had been as follows—

> MARY. Jane, dear, that was a knock; didn't you hear it?
> JOHN. Post. Late as usual.
> JANE. There's not likely to be a letter for me.

Not much, but something of the peculiarities of the three personages is revealed. We suspect that Mary is possibly mildly affectionate but petulant; that John is not of an entirely equable temper, and that optimism is not likely to be Jane's strong point. Other, stronger, indications of character could easily be fitted into three opening speeches announcing the coming of the postman. Gradually, as the play proceeds, it is less necessary to be so exacting; the character once established, any speech that is "in character" is permissible, but the more explicitly the dialogue reveals the unique qualities of each character, the more likely is the performance to be what the author intended. In the best plays every sentence adds to our knowledge of character, intensifies our interest, and enhances our awareness of personality.

SPEECH AND REALITY

Dialogue in the well-made play is not realistic. Phonographically recorded speech is not dialogue. Nobody desires to hear on the stage the loose, meandering, disjointed, inconsequent, *unco-ordinated* speech of daily life. It is the dramatist's task to invent a form of speech which, while consciously significant, gives the semblance of reality. The modern masters of dialogue—Shaw, Galsworthy, Somerset Maugham, for example—employ a form of speech which in no sense reflects the conversation we hear about us. Open any play of Shaw's at any page and you will find that, however easily it runs, the dialogue is in the best sense literary and not colloquial.

> HOTCHKISS. I find you merely ridiculous as a preacher, because you keep referring me to place and documents and alleged occurrences in which, as a matter of fact, I don't believe. I don't believe in anything but my own will and my own pride and honour.
> (*Getting Married.*)

Galsworthy, more restrained than Shaw, is no less literary in the sense in which the word is used here. A famous passage, famous as much for its dramatic effectiveness as for its bitter content, is Stephen More's extempore attack on the mob.

> MORE. You are here by the law that governs the action of all mobs—the law of Force. By that law, you can do what you like to this body of mine. . . . You—Mob—are the most contemptible thing under the sun. When you walk the street, God goes in. . . .

This is not realistic speech, but it is dramatic speech. Nobody would be likely to say, even in the heat of indignation: "You are the thing that pelts the weak; kicks women; howls down free speech." But listening to these words in the theatre, they strike no discordant note, because the intensity of the drama has been brought to such a pitch that the mind is prepared for them.

SOME MODERN TENDENCIES

The convention of the well-made play, which came into existence only during the latter part of the nineteenth century, has been losing ground ever since the psychological upheaval of which two Great Wars were either the cause or the expression. The neat compactness of the realistic play, however significant in content, seemed an inadequate vehicle for the tumultuous emotions and feverish groping of a generation whose ideals had been shattered by cataclysms so stupendous that all standards of conduct and all bases of judgment had to be reconsidered.

Most of the established playwrights continued in the technique which they had perfected, for any deviation from the normal is regarded with disfavour by those who have come to accept a convention; others clung to the principal features of their method, but showed their awareness of changing conditions by somewhat tentative innovations. The symbolism of *The Skin Game* and *The Forest*, and the somewhat cinematographic technique of *Escape*, are indications of Galsworthy's responsiveness to post-war tendencies. But it was the new-comers, and particularly in Germany, who more deliberately cast off the shackles of the realistic method and endeavoured to create new forms. Some of them were entirely unsuccessful; some produced, as if by chance, interesting works which remain without progeny; and some evolved new methods which enabled them to extend the scope of theatrical art and enrich our knowledge of human nature.

EXPRESSIONISM

Theorizing was rife, and among the many new words which came into existence "Expressionism" was the most employed and the least understood. It was apt to be used to connote all forms of dramatic art save the realistic; dramatists as diverse as Pirandello, the Čapeks, Ernst Toller, and George Kaiser were lumped together indiscriminately, and with some dramatic critics the word became a term of abuse. Few plays could be justly labelled expressionist. One of the most famous, George Kaiser's *Gas*, may be taken as a good specimen of the method, exemplifying both its weakness and its strength. The expressionist endeavours to show you *the thing in itself*, shorn of such impedimenta as character-drawing, realistic local colour or normal plausibility. He does not aim at creating human characters; his object is rather to create a series of platonic ideas and show them in relation to one another. For this reason the *dramatis personae* are not given names, for that would particularize them: they are labelled in such a way as to indicate their status or function. In *Gas* we have The Engineer, The Gentleman in White, The Billionaire's Son, The Mother, and so forth. "Gas" presumably symbolizes those formulae in modern civilization which appear to work, forces which make for material success yet lead to spiritual disaster. The play opens with the appearance to The Clerk of The Gentleman in White, who may be taken as a symbol of terror. There is eventually an explosion; the factory is razed to the ground; thousands of workers are maimed or killed. The Billionaire's Son (the idealist), beholding the ruins (Europe after War), seeks to build anew, discarding the old formulae, but The Engineer will not admit any fault in his calculations. There are exciting scenes which give scope for the rapid interplay of conflicting ideas, and the climax comes when the workers, having to choose between The Billionaire's Son (the idealist) and The Engineer (purveyor of old destructive ideas), again choose the latter, acclaiming, as is the way of mobs, the one whom they had formerly reviled.

This bald *résumé* of the plot is not fair to the play, but it may serve to show how the expressionist method works. Generally speaking, it does not lend itself to subtlety; the symbolism is apt to be obvious lest it should be misunderstood, and in denying himself the right to exploit the infinite varieties of human personality, the expressionist robs himself of one of the most potent ingredients of the dramatist's magic brew.

ERNST TOLLER

Ernst Toller, in *Masse Mensch* ("Masses and Men"), also employed an expressionist technique and showed what could be done with the method in the hands of an author with an unfailing sense of the dramatic. Here again the persons of the play were not characterized—each of them was a symbol, a force, an idea; but the flaming intensity of the dialogue, rising frequently to poetry of a high order, and the vividness of imagination in developing the theme, made characterization unnecessary.

But expressionism, rightly so-called, is obviously limited in its applicability, and it is doubtful if any playwrights are now employing it exclusively. Like cubism in the plastic arts, its influence has outlasted itself: the course of many of the most significant playwrights would have been quite different if expressionism had never existed. Its chief virtue is that it pointed out one way of escape from the bonds of realism; many others have since been discovered.

Toller himself never wrote another entirely expressionist play; nor did he ever write another realistic play. In *Hoppla, wir leben!* ("Hoppla!") a play about the Berlin revolution of 1919, he made use of a mixture which, in the hands of a producer of genuis, Erwin Piscator, was brilliantly effective. There is not space here even to mention the many innovations which he introduced into his play. Scenes which are relatively realistic are interspersed with "cinematographic interludes," showing the uprising of the people, factories with streams of workers, and so on. One act is set in a hotel, of which all the rooms are visible to the audience, the light darting about from one room to another as the action shifts; another scene shows a number of prison cells, and curious mechanical devices were invented to show the means by which prisoners communicated with one another. The dialogue, never entirely realistic, sometimes breaks all bounds and becomes frankly rhapsodical. The chief character, Karl Thomas, dazed by the world in which he finds himself after some years' incarceration, soliloquizes aloud—

> When others creep into the shadowy bosom of the night,
> I see murderers lurking everywhere, the evil workings
> of their brains exposed to my gaze . . .
> I have lost my hold on the world.
> The world has lost its hold on me.

It is, perhaps, in this matter of dialogue that the revulsion from realism is the strongest, and it would be fairly safe to prophesy that the days of attempted verisimilitude in language are numbered. Its best early exponents in England—Stanley Houghton, Elizabeth Baker, Harold Brighouse, for example—wear a somewhat old-fashioned air nowadays; and even the artistic compromise effected by such authors as Galsworthy, Granville-Barker, Somerset Maugham, whose feeling for words forbade them to reflect too faithfully the language of common speech, is unlikely to hold sway much longer. A language which was once at the service of Shakespeare, Marlowe, Beaumont and Fletcher, Dryden, Congreve, Goldsmith, and Sheridan, will not forever tolerate a convention which clips its wings, stunts its growth, and limits its medium of expression to a common denominator imposed by the unenlightened and inarticulate. Poets will victoriously enter the theatre again when it is realized that without them the theatre is a body without a soul. Meantime, they are creeping in by the back entrances.

SEAN O'CASEY

There is Sean O'Casey, for instance. Having achieved success with two or three realistic plays, in which the poet was for the most part in shackles, he disclosed his hand in *The Silver Tassie.* For perhaps two-thirds of its length it is naturalistic, but the second act is openly poetic

—some would say expressionistic. In this we are shown War, not as it physically was, but made manifest by language intensified and heightened to express the *emotion* of war. And when the soldiers come in from fatigue, they do not address one another in the unrevealing speech of exhausted tommies, but chantwise:

FOURTH SOLDIER. Twelve blasted hours of ammunition transport fatigue!
FIRST SOLDIER. Twelve weary hours.
SECOND SOLDIER. And wasting hours.
THIRD SOLDIER. And hot and heavy hours.
FIRST SOLDIER. Toiling and thinking to build the wall of force that blocks the way from here to home.

Chants and rhythmic speech make up the whole of the act.

SECOND SOLDIER.
God, unchanging, heart-sicken'd, shuddering,
Gathereth the darkness of the night sky
To mask His paling countenance from
The blood dance of His self-slaying children.
THIRD SOLDIER.
Stems of light shoot through the darkness,
Fierce flowering to green and crimson star-shells,
Glowering their eyes of hate where once
Danced the gentle star of Bethlehem.

The last act, superficially realistic, also snaps its bonds, and, mingled with normal speech, we find a passage in free verse like this—

HARRY. Life came and took away the half of life.
TEDDY. Life took from me the half he left with you.
HARRY. The Lord hath given and the Lord hath taken away.
TEDDY. Blessed be the name of the Lord.

Sean O'Casey's later play, *Within the Gates*, outstrips even *The Silver Tassie* in its disregard of literal verisimilitude. Formal scenery, formalized costumes; chorus and solo songs; symbolism and realism, poetry and plain prose, all have their place in a work which is likely to be permanent in English drama. O'Casey has now left the realistic drama behind him, and his latest plays, such as *Red Roses for Me* and *Oak Leaves and Lavender*, are as "literary" in their expression as the so-called poetic drama.

EUGENE O'NEILL

In America experiments of varying degrees of importance have been made, more in staging than in writing, notably by Elmer Rice who, in *The Adding Machine*, used a somewhat confused medium to inveigh against an age which threatens to make machines of men. The play was a mixture of realism, expressionism, and something neither one nor the other but vaguely poetic or fantastic. The transition from one plane to another was not convincingly fused or contrasted, but there is much that is theatrically effective in the play; the work of an alert mind, keenly aware of the needs of theatrical expression.

But it is Eugene O'Neill who stands head and shoulders above all other American dramatists, for the originality of his ideas, the venturesomeness of his technique, his superb vitality, and astonishing versatility. Even his earliest plays, nominally naturalistic, show signs of impatience with the medium, and quite soon he threw over conventional forms without apology and steered a course of his own. *The Emperor Jones* is far removed from the well-made play, and *The Hairy Ape* might legitimately be called expressionistic. Its hero, a gigantic stoker on an ocean liner, is no normal human being, but the embodiment of brute power, proud of itself and aware of its own importance. The language employed is not that of ordinary human beings; it is based on Yankee slang raised almost to poetry. Thus—

Sure, only for me everything stops. It all goes dead, get me! De noise and smoke and all the engines movin' de woild, dey stop. Dere ain't nothin' no more! Dat's what I'm sayin'. Everything else dat makes de woild move, somep'n makes it move. It can't move without somep'n else, see? Den yuh get down to me. I'm at the bottom, get me? Dere ain't nothin' foithur. I'm de end! I'm de start! I start somep'n and de woild moves. It—dat's me! De new dat's moidern de old. I'm de ting in coal dat makes it boin; I'm steam and oil for de engines; I'm de ting in noise dat makes you hear it; I'm smoke and express trains and steamers and factory whistles; I'm de ting in gold that makes it money.

Since *The Hairy Ape* O'Neill has gone from experiment to experiment, each of them interesting though not all of them successful. Perhaps the most significant is the introduction of spoken thoughts in *Strange Interlude*. The suggestion that this is merely a revival of the aside and the soliloquy, conventions which were abandoned with the advent of the naturalistic play, is superficial. The naive interjections of which the old asides consisted bear no relation to the method by which O'Neill enables the audience to follow the intricate ramifications of his characters' thoughts and to share in the omniscience of the author. In plays where the psychological content is paramount, the method has a great deal to recommend it, and it is improbable that *Strange Interlude* will be the last play of its kind.

Every play by O'Neill since *Strange Interlude* has disregarded conventional forms; *Lazarus Laughed*, *Mourning Becomes Electra*, and *Ah, Wilderness* all break new ground.

FRENCH INNOVATORS

Expressionism has not found many converts in France, though even there its influence has not been negligible. More significant pioneering has been done, however, by authors who have taken other paths. H. R. Lenormand, for instance, far from showing any tendency to disregard the subtleties of characterization, has probed deep into the sources of behaviour and found inspiration in the theories of psycho-analysis. The art of Jean-Jacques Bernard is even further removed from expressionism. His plays are remarkable for their delicacy.

His plots have an artful simplicity which might lead the unwary to assume that they are almost childishly ingenuous. In reality, his work abounds in over-tones which can only be heard if the ear is attuned to the delicacy of his medium. He has been credited with basing his work on a *théorie du silence*, but has properly repudiated the suggestion on the grounds that no artist works to a theory but follows the dictates of his artistic conscience. He believes that the theatre is above all the art of the unexpressed, and the action of his plays might almost be said to take place between the speeches. "The theatre has no worse enemy than literature," he once said; literature "expresses and dilutes what should only be suggested," a statement that reveals misunderstanding of the function of literature, but indicates Jean-Jacques Bernard's attitude to the theatre.

French playwrights show that respect for tradition which is typical of the French attitude to literature, and few radical experiments are made by them. Cocteau, whose *The Eagle has Two Heads* exploits a pseudo-romantic symbolism, is the most likely to startle us by throwing conventions overboard. His mind is still the most original in the French theatre.

Several others who might usefully have engaged our attention are Pirandello, whose explorations into the nature of reality are perhaps less evidence of a desire to reform the drama than of a preoccupation with psychology, and the brothers Čapek, whose *The Insect Play*, an elaborate allegory of post-War Europe, was improbably designed to open up new theatrical paths; these and others—Jean Cocteau, C. K. Munro, W. B. Yeats, Philip Barry, for instance—have demonstrated that the well-made conventionally-constructed play is not the be-all and end-all of drama.

A PERSONAL NOTE

To avoid the charge of disingenuousness, I may perhaps be permitted to add a short note concerning some of my own plays. *The Black Virgin* (1921) is a play of intensive symbolism. The title itself is derived from the curious fact that the peasants in the little Bavarian town where the play is set used to blacken the images of the virgin inside and outside their houses in imitation of church images which had grown black with the grime and soot of ages. "That is how it is with us here," says Lena, the chief character; "we collect habits and customs by mistake or misfortune and then we worship them." Briefly, the symbolism of the play is two-fold: each character symbolizes a force, a tendency, an attitude, and the entire action is an allegory of the political and social forces at work a few years after the First Great War. *The Dance of Life* (1923) uses symbols also, but what gave it novelty was the employment of two planes of consciousness. Wishing to express the bewildered post-war psychology of disillusioned youth, I followed not only the physical doings of my hero but also introduced scenes which disclosed the workings of his mind; the symbols chosen were, like all symbols, arbitrary, but I hope self-explanatory. In *The Piper Laughs* (1925), an independent sequel, the same method was adopted, I believe, more consistently. It has been said that the non-realistic scenes in these plays represent the subconscious mind of my hero, and although this is not strictly accurate, it gives a hint of what I was driving at. An experiment of another order was made in *The Moon Rides High* (1925). Here I selected words and rhythms designed to create certain moods; the dialogue, therefore, although it "speaks" easily enough, is for the most part a convention, neither naturalistic nor poetic. As the protagonist is a man whose mind becomes somewhat unhinged, I permitted myself another innovation. My hero, by the intensity of his imagination, built up the images of two persons, mistaking them for real. To him they *were* real, and as the play from one point of view was primarily concerned with an attempt to reveal the state of his mind, it seemed to me logical that the figments of his imagination should be made manifest on the stage, visible and audible to the public as they were to my hero. I was informed by theatrical wiseacres, with many years' commercial experience behind them, that this device would not "get over"; production proved them wrong.

THE ONE-ACT PLAY

The one-act play has been described as the Cinderella of the theatre, a modest, neglected creature, driven to the kitchen while her less comely but more fortunate sisters, the full-length plays, were displayed for the admiration of the town. If this description was apt in the past, it is even more apt in the present, for the fairy tale has run its traditional course, and the one-act play, once despised and neglected, is now received in the highest places; only in the commercial theatre is the welcome dubious. At one time it was used as a stop-gap, before or after the main fare—a curtain-raiser to keep the pit amused while the late-coming gentry shuffled to their seats, or an after-piece thrown in to make up the three hours or more which theatre-goers at one time claimed as their right. These short plays were not taken very seriously, and it was a rare event if an actor of recognized attainment took part in them. But they had uses apart from those mentioned: they provided an opportunity for small-part actors to play modest leads, and they enabled budding playwrights to try their prentice hands at something less ambitious than a full-length play. Their value was, in a word, utilitarian and had little to do with art.

With the dropping of the curtain-raiser and the abolition of the after-piece, the one-acter was driven from the commercial theatre; but so far from suffering from this neglect, it has shown an ever-increasing vitality and has now established itself as an art-form with as legitimate a claim to recognition in drama as the short story has in literature. Needless to say, there are innumerable one-acters with no greater claim to artistic consideration than the majority of short stories contributed to the popular magazines. Written to a formula dictated by public demand, they achieve or fail to achieve their object, but should not be judged seriously as works of art.

The range of the one-acter is, for various reasons, considerably greater than that of the full-length play. For example, whereas a play designed to fill an evening must keep approximately to a given length, the one-acter may properly occupy the five-minutes mete for a revue sketch or the sixty to eighty minutes necessary to reveal a character as complex as Miss Julie. The form of the one-acter is freer than that of the full-length play. It may be neat and rigid, but it may also be wayward and flexible. So long as it does not deny the fundamental principles of drama, it may employ an almost infinite variety of forms, exploit an almost infinite variety of themes and methods. An audience will give its suffrage to a half-hour experiment which, expanded to two-and-a-half hours, it might find intolerable. Let us recall some of the possible forms of the one-acter.

THE STRAIGHT PLAY

In this category may be classed the greater number of short plays whose technique resembles in most respects the technique of the well-made long play. The characterization is much the same, but more speedily built up; the atmosphere is generated in much the same way; the laws which govern the dialogue of the long play govern the short play with even greater severity, but they are the same laws. Only in the matter of structure is there any radical difference.

A one-acter may be many things; but it is not a long play cut down. The approach is different. Even a fairly long one-acter has no time for the leisurely exposition tolerated in a full-length play. It is, as always, a question of right proportions. If the play is to take a quarter of an hour in performance, exposition must occupy no more than a minute or two; even a half-hour play cannot afford to spend more than a few preliminary minutes in which to set the stage for the story which is to be unfolded. Contact with the audience must be made at once, and no time ought to be lost in establishing not only the appropriate atmosphere but even the nature of the theme. How quickly Synge, in that masterpiece, *Riders to the Sea*, reveals the burden of the play! The curtain rises on a fisherman's cottage kitchen. The audience is allowed to take in the details which reveal the nature of the scene—the nets, the oilskins, spinning-wheel, and perhaps to feel some curiosity concerning the new planks standing against the wall. A girl enters and asks in a low voice which is in itself portentous: "Where is she?" and the reply: "She's lying down, God help her, and maybe sleeping, if she's able," adds further to the sense of calamity. Another second or two pass, and then we find that the newcomer has brought with her "a shirt and a plain stocking were got off a drowned man in Donegal." The mind is thus prepared for the piling on of woe and the inevitably tragic climax.

Riders to the Sea is, like perhaps the majority of one-acters, a story; but the one-act play has no time to relate a story showing all the incidents in the order in which they happened: the method of projection is almost inevitably retrospective. The play is, in itself, a climax—dramatic tension in a state of dissolution—during which all the antecedent causes are revealed. The story thus brought to light is not necessarily an intricate one; but it must be sufficiently complex to make the *dénouement* interesting. The plot of *Riders to the Sea* is simplicity itself; it is the story of Maurya and of her six sons, all of whom are given one by one to the sea. The gradual revelation of this series of calamities, of which only the last actually takes place during the course of the play, produces an effect of profound tragedy, greater, probably, because more concentrated, than if each successive drowning had been shown to us over the three hours of a full-length play.

Synge's masterpiece cannot be taken as a typical example of the straight play, however, because the dialogue, ostensibly naturalistic, is as far removed from realism as poetry is from prose. The poignancy of the play is at least as much due to the beauty of its language as to the touching history it tells. Not every writer of peasant plays can reveal the souls of his characters in cadences like these—

MAURYA (*raising her head and speaking as if she did not see the people around her*); They're all gone now, and there isn't anything more the sea can do to me. . . . I'll have no call now to be up crying and praying when the wind breaks from the south, and you can hear the surf is in the east, and the surf is in the west, making a great stir with the two noises, and they hitting one on the other. I'll have no call now to be going down and getting Holy Water in the dark nights after Samhain, and I won't care what way the sea is when the other women will be keening. . . .

It's a great rest I'll have now, and great sleeping in the long nights after Samhain, if it's only a bit of wet flour we do have to eat, and maybe a fish that would be stinking.

If Synge stands alone in this respect, many other authors of one-acters, probably not uninfluenced by him, have evolved a form of dialogue, a sort of heightened prose, which resembles his. There are passages in Mr. J. A. Ferguson's *Campbell of Kilmohr*, which would stand comparison with Synge, and George Reston Malloch, Gilbert Cannan, Constance Holme, Dorothy Una Ratcliffe, and Padraic Pearse, among others, have followed in the tradition. But good, straight prose, approximating to the speech in use by the class depicted, is a sufficiently serviceable instrument, and those who are not drawn by an inner urge to express themselves according to a quasi-poetic formula, would be wise to avoid it. They will have the good companionship of such authors as Harold Brighouse, St. John Ervine, Stanley Houghton, A. A. Milne, Pinero, H. A. Jones, and many more.

THE POETIC PLAY

The author of the poetic play, because at the outset he disowns realism by writing in verse, is released from many of the restrictions which bind the realist. Relieved of the necessity of reflecting current speech, he is not compelled to attain visual verisimilitude either. Gordon Bottomley may with propriety open his play *King Lear's Wife* with Merryn, waiting-woman to Queen Hygd, praying aloud—

> Shield me from rotting cancers and from madness:
> Shield me from sudden death, worse than two death-beds;
> Let me not lie like this unwanted queen . . .

what time the queen herself is lying asleep in bed. In a realistic play such disregard of the probabilities would not be tolerated. Soliloquies and asides, banished from the well-made play, are readily accepted with all the other conventions which belong to poetic drama. When, in Mr. Laurence Binyon's one-act tragedy, Œnone, in pursuit of Paris, finds him vanished, we are not surprised that she should break into audible lamentation—

> Alone and dying in this darkness, oh,
> Where have I driven him? Where lies he now,
> Fainting, perhaps, and fallen on the rocks?

We should have been more surprised if she had kept her grief to herself. Among poets closely acquainted with the modern theatre—notably W. B. Yeats, John Drinkwater, John Masefield—there is a tendency to avoid soliloquies and asides, but the abandonment of these conventions is probably due to unconscious subservience to modern theatrical usage rather than to any inherent objection to the conventions as such. John Drinkwater himself, in his finest one-act play, *X = 0*, threw verisimilitude to the winds at the most tense moment of the tragedy, when Pronax, returning to the Greek tent and finding his friend slain, addresses the heavens—

> . . . gods! . . . what, friend . . . Salvius, Salvius, . . .
> Dead . . . it is done . . . it is done. There is judgment made . . .
> Beauty is broken . . . and there on the Trojan wall
> One too shall come . . . one too shall come . . .

THE FANTASY

Not far removed from the poetic play is the fantasy, whether written in prose or verse. The fantasy, disregarding the restraints laid upon the imagination of the realist, imposes limits of another order upon the author's muse. His vision may be rangeless, but his play will not be effective unless he restricts its field of action. From his abundance he must select only what is relevant and congruous. Among the most successful workers in this medium is Lord Dunsany, who has created a world of his own, peopled with characters as indubitably Dunsanian as Galsworthy's characters are indubitably English. All that we have any right to ask of them is that they should be true to their own inborn characteristics, to behave like Dunsanians and speak Dunsanese. A world even more remote from the world around us is that created by Maurice Maeterlinck, a world of half-lights, where shadowy half-human creatures live in an atmosphere of foreboding. These little plays—*pour marionettes*, as the author expressly states—offer great opportunities to imaginative producers capable of identifying themselves with the Maeterlinckian mind, but are a snare to would-be imitators. Any play in the Maeterlinck manner is apt to seem like a parody of the master. Even Oscar Wilde, who, consciously or unconsciously, employed a similar technique in his one-act tragedy *Salome*, barely escaped from the danger of being unconsciously humorous.

Success in fantasy can only be achieved by those whose minds find natural expression in fantasy, an individual vision above all being essential. Good and successful plays have been written in the manner of masters of the realistic school; poetic plays directly traceable to the influence of Shakespeare are innumerable, and many of them admirable. But plays written in emulation of Dunsany or Maeterlinck, or of Barrie at his most whimsical, are almost inevitably spineless failures. The tricks and mannerisms may be seized, but the inward conviction which gives them life is far to seek.

THE HUMOROUS PLAY

The one-act form lends itself particularly well to the humorous subject. A joke is the better for not being long-drawn-out, and brevity we know is the soul of wit. If comedy usually demands the shapeliness of the three-act structure for its happiest expression, many a farce which has been spread over an evening would have been better compressed into forty-five minutes. A humorous one-acter may be a picture of a certain section of society, pleasurable less for the story it tells than for the pointedness of the observation it displays; it may be nothing more than a satirical comment—an anecdote designed to call attention to some social anomaly or to foibles which are better ridiculed in an amusing skit than scourged in a polemical tract. H. R. Rubinstein contrived to pack much trenchant criticism of the theatre and theatre-goers into the five one-acters which he collectively called *What's Wrong with the Drama?* Miss Gertrude Jennings has pilloried numerous odd but ever-present social nuisances in a series of amusing and somewhat acidulated little plays. Barrie has given some of his most significant work in the form of one-act comedies, including *Shall We Join the Ladies?* whose cynicism gives the lie to much of his own sentimental philosophy. Shaw has found the one-act play a conveniently elastic vessel for containing ideas which seemed too slight for full-length plays, and between *How He Lied to Her Husband* and *A Village Wooing* has run the gamut from true comedy to preposterous farce.

EXPERIMENTERS

Venturesomeness in technique has not been particularly characteristic of the writers of one-acters. The range of expression open to them—from strictest comedy to wildest farce, from rigid realism to unbridled fantasy; tragedy, satire, history, religion, mysticism; grand guignol thrills and Cranford charm—has been so great that the need to expand the medium has perhaps not made itself felt. But here and there, following in the footsteps of experimenters in longer forms, we find authors who venture outside the established conventions. The human mind has served as the setting for more than one short play, of which Evreinov's *The Theatre of the Soul* is perhaps the best known. Miles Malleson's "fantastic scrap," *The Little White Thought*, in which all the characters are thoughts—The Thought of Somebody Else's Wealth, The Thought of the Girl he Loves, and so on—disporting themselves in a chamber hung in rich black curtains, was one of the earliest examples, and H. F. Rubinstein's *Insomnia*, with The Ego, Memory, Conscience, and the like as *dramatis personae*, is another entertaining example of the same technique. Clifford Bax, in a little play called *Prelude and Fugue*, anticipated the technique of Eugene O'Neill's *Strange Interlude* by making the two characters speak their thoughts aloud. And doubtless there have been other experimenters. But the most suggestive contribution to the technique of the one-act play is probably W. B. Yeats's *Four Plays for Dancers*. Finding the conditions of the modern theatre uncongenial, Yeats went back to the "Noh" plays of aristocratic Japan, and his four plays were written with the express intention of dispensing with the trappings of the ordinary theatre. They were written to be performed without scenery, in a room or any small place where two or three are gathered together, the actors either wearing masks or painting their faces to resemble masks. Here are the preliminary instructions to the first of the plays, *At the Hawk's Well*—

> The stage is any bare space before a wall, against which stands a patterned screen. A drum and a gong and a zither have been laid close to the screen before the play begins. If necessary, they can be carried in, after the audience is seated, by the First Musician. . . . The First Musician carries with him a folded black cloth and goes to the centre of the stage towards the front and stands motionless, the folded cloth hanging from between his hands.

The cloth is slowly unfolded and folded again to denote that the play has begun, and at the end of the play the same simple ceremony is repeated. Plays like these of Yeats's, strange in theme and written in verse which is in itself an incantation, are no doubt peculiarly suitable for this kind of stylized production; but the method is roughly that which has held the traditional stages of Japan and China for many centuries and its possibilities might well be further investigated by playwrights weary of the kind of theatrical production which leaves nothing to the imagination of the audience.

ON PLAYS FOR CHILDREN

Plays for children are of many kinds and there is no space here to deal with them all. The kind written with one eye on the parents and both on the box-office is not my present concern; ostensibly written for children, it is usually entirely unsuited to the child mind: the humour, except when it is knockabout, is generally directed at the adult members of the audience; the sentiment is perfunctory or trite and expressed with such a lack of conviction that children do not take it seriously; the setting is usually tawdry and the music cheap. There are exceptions to these generalizations, of which the classic examples are Barrie's *Peter Pan* and Maeterlinck's *The Blue Bird*, both of which have been prolific of imitators; but these are outside the scope of this article. I want to write about plays which can be acted by children for children or for such grown-ups as still delight in simplicity.

SOCIAL VALUE

The social value of such plays is becoming

more and more recognized. The normal child is a natural actor. Left to themselves, children will create a world of make-believe which is to them momentarily as real as the world of the senses. It is a matter of common observation that children will accept any convention that is properly presented to them and "Let's pretend" is a cliché of the nursery. Little boys and girls, playing at kings and queens, need no more than a chair for a throne, a table-cloth for a robe, a toasting-fork for a sceptre. "There's nothing either good or bad, but thinking makes it so." I once saw a little street urchin puff up his cheek and assume an air of great suffering: "Coo, I ain't 'arf got a toothache," he whimpered to his friend, who entered into the spirit of the game and at once offered to pull out the offending molar.

A normal child's vitality is staggering in its abundance and the need for imaginative expression is so urgent that if it is not properly provided for it inevitably finds an undesirable outlet. The child, father to the man, has a streak of exhibitionism which should be given an opportunity to expend itself innocuously. The instinct is healthy enough and is probably ineradicable. It is a commonplace of the animal kingdom—peacocks strut for their own self-glory and to the delight of their hens; the male of most species displays itself for the admiration of the female and the female has its own ways of calling attention to itself. Babies with rattle or spoon will exert great strength to announce their prowess; boys and girls at play derive as much satisfaction from the exhibition of their own superiority as from the enjoyment of the game as such; while children of a larger growth, in test matches, tennis tournaments, boxing displays, Brooklands competitions, and Olympic Games, show no less zest.

DRAMA AND EDUCATION

The current theory which looks to education to draw out the latent qualities of the child could have no more devoted handmaid than the drama, and it is not surprising that the more enlightened schools treat the study and acting of plays as a part of their usual curriculum. Shakespeare, the victim of unintelligent cramming, may presently find his right place in the theatre, performed before audiences consisting of adults who have no recollections of painful hours devoted to parsing and analysing purple passages, but recall pleasant hours when their dramatic instincts were stimulated by acting in plays within their emotional and intellectual grasp.

SUBJECTS

When the young actors have not yet reached their teens or are still in them, plays of modern life are better avoided. Plays which involve historical or fanciful costumes have several advantages: (*a*) children like dressing up—they are apt to shed their self-consciousness with their everyday clothes; (*b*) to impersonate characters far removed from daily life is a greater stimulus to the imagination than to impersonate the people one sees every day—the latter is likely to degenerate into imitation or caricature; (*c*) whereas a child of eight may convincingly play the part of a king, a councillor, a witch, or a popular traditional hero, a strong element of absurdity has to be forcibly eliminated from one's mind before one can accept an eight-year-old aping a grown-up of our own time and country. Plays about children of their own age are not open to this objection; but it will be found in practice that much as children like to read school-stories, projecting themselves into hair-breadth escapes in which they identify themselves with the heroes and heroines, when they come to act they prefer to detach themselves from the daily round, the common task. . . .

The number of available subjects is almost unlimited. History provides many of the most attractive. Kings and queens, adventurers and pioneers; heroes who have fought against great odds and won; poor boys who have become rich and famous; girls who have sacrificed themselves for some great cause—these are characters which every ordinary child aspires to play; and, conversely, wily and finally defeated chancellors, villains who are in due course properly thwarted; wicked queens who meet a deserved doom; conspirators who conspire to their own undoing—children are just as eager to impersonate these undesirables, thereby healthily expelling from their systems such incipient cupidity, spitefulness, or sadism as might otherwise be suppressed and develop into a morbid complex. For however sincerely children may admire virtue and heroism, they are nonetheless attracted to the opposites.

This dual delight is shown in a play which a small friend of mine, aged ten, wrote and sent to me in the hope that I would "publish it." It is called *Edward the Black Prince* and bears this verse on the title-page—

> Once in the court of Edward III
> was born a baby
> not fat nor slim
> and this is
> the story
> I am going to tell of him.

The young author shows throughout that he is on the side of the angels, but, alas, the most vivid scenes are those which reveal a delight in violence. The opening is comparatively tame.

EDWARD III. Now I will begin. I am going to make war with France, I will not lose my possessions (the court starts up with amazement) why what is the matter with ye now gentles all, ye look fair baron Royon as one who has sat on a hornets nest,

QUEEN PHILIPPA. But sure this is so sudden where will you get money for the war

EDWARD III. Ah dame I will get money right enough, I'll get it from Parliament or the church, never you fear.

But in the next scene things begin to move. The Black Prince informs "Sarlisbury" that, the French having wronged us, "now we are going to wrong them the dog ha ha ha ha ha," whereupon Sir Richard: "I love to think of their blood upon my sword."

Against this blood-thirstiness, however, it is only fair to quote the piety—

SALISBURY. We will need plenty of rest tonight
ROYON. Ay, and plenty of prayers
BLACK PRINCE. That is right we sure will.

This last phrase, it will be observed, employs modern idiom in the manner of the fashionable school of historic drama.

The average child, at least until the age of adolescence, is rarely able to appreciate psychological subtlety, and in taking historical incidents for converting into plays, the author would be wasting time and skill if he attempted to invest the *dramatis personae* with the finer shades of characterization. Without injuring his conception, he will find it possible to build up convincing personalities from which the more obscure or questionable features have been excised. Leave these for later study to reveal to the inquiring child. So long as the characters are not actually falsified, it is well, in choosing historical figures, to endow them with a set of easily assimilable characteristics and to place them in circumstances which will most vividly display them.

Traditional stories, legends, and fairy tales are perennially popular and provide even greater opportunities than historical subjects. It is a mistake to imagine that the modern child is only interested in aeroplanes, the wireless, detective exploits, and gangsters. My own experience has proved the contrary. New fairy tales are slow to take root, but the old are as popular as ever. They appeal to something fundamental, and even little boys who have supped on cinema excitements will quickly shed their sense of superiority if understandingly handled. Fairy tales offer chances to imaginative children to appear larger than life: the wonders of Aladdin's cave are thrown open to them; they are permitted to revel in fantasies which school-life and home-life deny them; they may engage in exploits which give them a sense of power and achievement; chivalry is encouraged, and obstacles which seemed insurmountable are always overcome in the end.

TECHNIQUE

The technique of the play for children is not essentially different from the technique of the play for adults; but there are certain special limitations which should be borne in mind. The dramatist should not be too conscious of the fact that he is writing for child-actors—that might lead to the unforgivable sin of "writing down," which children rightly resent; but it would be just as absurd to write above their heads, employing words which they are not likely to understand or turns of expression which would convey nothing to them. Children are only too ready to roll off rounded rhetorical phrases from Shakespeare and Holy Writ without having the least idea of their purport. It should be an instructor's first task to see that no child utters words or phrases which it does not understand; and no playwright who has any claim at all to write for children needs to be told what words and phrases may be legitimately put into their mouths. Slang and other jargon should be used sparingly; and foreign words calculated to make a child self-conscious are better eliminated; but these exceptions apart, the author will find that there is an almost boundless richness of language open to him, and it is his own lack of skill, and not the young actor's, if he finds that his dialogue fails to trip easily from the tongue.

The length of a play for children is determined by practical considerations. The child's staying-power being less than the adult's, full-length plays are undesirable, except in the case of episodic or pageant plays in which each section is virtually a separate play; and even in these cases special care should be taken that children are not allowed to become over-tired, waiting for their turn and lingering in a state of excitement long after their own particular episode has been disposed of. Ordinarily, a play should not take longer than an hour-and-a-half in performance; this, with intervals and such habitual irrelevancies as speech-making, makes a sufficiently long entertainment, long enough for the children taking part and long enough for the children in the audience, whose power of concentration is not likely to be equal to more. For similar reasons, plays should be broken up into shorter lengths than plays for adults demand. Long acts are an excessive tax upon the young actor's powers of endurance unless they are divided into two or three scenes. Plays which are not expected to provide the main fare, may be of any length ranging from fifteen to sixty minutes, and forty-five minutes seems to be particularly suitable—not too long for the concentrated attention of a youthful audience, nor for the histrionic staying-power of youthful actors, and a manageable length for rehearsals.

REHEARSALS

A word on rehearsals. When the producer is also a teacher, he must not take an unfair advantage of his position of authority. The production of a play, even when it forms part of the normal school curriculum, is a communal activity in which the producer is only one, if an important one, of the participators. Perhaps its chief value is that it encourages the team spirit, and this would be almost nullified if the producer should don the mantle of a dictator instead of working hand in glove with the young actors, drawing out their special gifts, offering encouragement whenever possible and never damping enthusiasm. In the long run the producer of a children's play, like the producer of any play, must be autocratic, but the producer with tact and understanding always persuades and never coerces, leaving the budding actor with the impression that his inspiration is entirely from within.

PARTS

Some children will inevitably display more talent than others and the producer must guard against exploiting them unduly; that would be a double offence—an offence against the talented children themselves, and an offence against the other children who might develop a sense of inferiority. In most plays expressly designed for children there are numerous characters, of varying degrees of importance, and if the less talented are given roles which demand less skill and play them adequately, there is little danger of their feeling slighted. It would be advisable also to see that the more brilliant children are sometimes made to play unimportant parts. If the producer, taking the children into his confidence, explains that every part is really as important as every other part; that one could not exist without the other; that leading roles depend for their effectiveness upon the "feeding" which they receive from minor roles; that the success of the play as a whole is the important thing and not the success of individual actors, he will find a quick response and ready loyalty. Let the most talented youngster in the troupe see how his own cleverness trickles away ineffectively when some unready maiden fails to come in sharply on her cue, and he will soon realize how interdependent the members of the company are—and doubtless the unready maiden will be no less aware!

Arising out of this, young people are, generally speaking, fairly quick at learning their lines; where they are apt to fail is in learning their cues. Ugly gaps between set speeches are a commonplace of children's performances. It should be impressed upon them that cues are as important as lines and should be learnt as assiduously. It is almost as important to remember that a cue is sometimes a cue for silence: children, in their eagerness to demonstrate that they have not forgotten their words, are loth to allow a pause to follow a speech. The producer should be at pains to explain the significance of a pause, so that the child, when the time comes, will instinctively wait for the required length of time. When it is possible to do so without destroying the required dramatic effect, it is a good idea to fill in a silence with some movement, however slight, which may itself serve as a cue. The fixed blank expression which is prone to disfigure the face of the child actor who has nothing either to say or to do is to be avoided at all costs.

SCENERY

The subject of scenery scarcely comes within my purview, but I should like to put in a word on behalf of curtains or conventional settings. Painted scenery for school performances, or for performances by boy scouts, girl guides, and the other bodies that specialize in children's plays, is hardly ever satisfactory. There is rarely money enough to pay for scenery to be specially painted, and when hired it is generally nondescript, uninspired and uninspiring, out-of-date, and completely lacking in imagination. When, as is the case at some enlightened schools, there are youthful carpenters, designers, painters, and seamstresses, who are ready to lend a hand, special scenery has a great deal to be said for it; but failing this, curtains, perhaps an occasional "flat" or screen, provide all that is necessary for a background. Appropriate costumes, the right "properties," a few pieces of real or imitation tapestry, will give plenty of scope for colourful stage-pictures, and the neutral character of curtains will at any rate ensure that the wrong ideas are not conveyed to the audience. If the required atmosphere cannot be produced by good diction, convincing acting, imaginative costumes, and artfully insinuated music, the lame attempts of hack scene-painters are not going to be of much use. The simpler the setting the more vividly must the playwright perform his share of the task. However distantly, he must follow in the footsteps of Shakespeare, whose language, unsupported by carpenter and scene-painter, brought the forest of Arden, Cleopatra's barge, and the pomp and circumstance of the courts to the bare boards of the Globe Theatre.

Hermon Ould

F

FESTIVALS AND COMPETITIONS

Andrew Paterson

John Bourne

FESTIVALS AND COMPETITIONS

JOHN BOURNE, Adjudicator; Playwright; Director of Plays, Little Theatre, Leicester, 1944-45; Editor, "New Plays Quarterly;" Author of "Thousands of Actors," "Teach Yourself Amateur Acting," etc.

THERE is no more invigorating experience in amateur drama than to enter a festival or competition. Viewed from the right angle it draws out the best that is in a society and gives the members a definite status. Whether they win or lose it spurs them on to better work, and by bringing them into contact with others in the same craft, gives them a wider sense of the New Amateur Movement, which is as different from the old amateur theatricals as Noel Coward is from Henry Arthur Jones.

METHODS OF APPROACH

One can nearly always tell the difference between those societies that are a law unto themselves and those that knock up against their fellows in festivals and competitions. The former, when not precluded by their constitution from entering, are generally either snobs or incompetents; the latter, even when they are inexperienced, have a way of challenging criticism and interest that makes for better entertainment, and leaves one, if not satisfied, at least with the idea that they have had the edges taken off them in their own theatre.

Before the Second Great War, festivals and competitions were growing rapidly. The entries for the British Drama League's National Festival of Community Drama, which began in 1926, had risen from seven to 600. Its offshoot, the Scottish Community Drama Festival, had strongly developed. Independent festivals of one-act or full-length plays, generally of a week's duration, were annual events in a dozen English towns. They were so popular that entries had to be restricted. Nearly all these events ceased during the Second Great War; but they have been reborn and are now more numerous than ever. In 1947 and 1948 the British Drama League organized a national festival of full-length plays; but it was then suspended for a year. In 1948, the League evolved a New Plan for its national festival of one-act plays whereby locally-run festivals could, if they wished, become a preliminary stage in the national festival. This plan introduced several entirely new features including the non-announcement of marks and "places," and the inclusion of non-competitive festivals in which the option was given to entrants to go forward to the next round or not.

During the War, festivals were organized in connexion with the women's institutes, youth clubs, rural community councils, the Co-operative Movement, and other associations. Some of the big music and drama festivals, notably Brighton, continued with greatly increased support. So, too, did the Welsh "Drama Weeks" —generally devoted to full-length plays. The schools certainly did not stop; and as the Ministry of Education favours the inclusion of a stage in every newly-built school, development of schools' festivals is certain.

New drama clubs are eager to test themselves in festival work. They, as well as the "old hands" will find it beneficial to approach the subject in the right perspective.

Several organizations, including the B.D.L., the S.C.D.A., local Guilds and the International One-Act Play Theatre, have arranged playwriting competitions. Since most competitions and festivals have to rely on the one-act play, these moves to encourage the dramatist are extremely valuable and should be followed by societies looking for original work.

While a good old play should always be preferred to a bad new play, no art that does not welcome fresh ideas can live. The playwright is as important to the theatre as the actor. The adjudicator, wearied by the constant repetition of hackneyed plays, is eager to study new material, which should be carefully chosen. Drama clubs should not "fall" for a play merely because it is by a local author or a friendly supporter or the wife of the president. They will be wise to have every new play "vetted" by an independent and knowledgeable critic.

To enter a competition merely for the sake of scoring off somebody else, or for the sake of winning a trophy (and particularly a money prize) is contemptuous. It is merely bringing a society to the level of a man throwing darts in a public bar for the honour of gaining a pint of beer or a little credit "on the slate." That is why the word "festival" is preferable to "competition"; it implies a friendly attempt to succeed rather than a fight to a finish.

There are some amateurs who believe that competitive work is beneath their dignity; others that it interferes with their season's programme. Some think that the competitive spirit itself is bad and should not be connected with art; others, that they "are not good enough" and must leave competitions to the more experienced. None of these excuses seems to me to be valid. The dignified are sometimes so good that their entry would be a great incentive to those who would meet them (and is therefore a duty), and sometimes so bad that a test of their dignity would be an eye-opening experience. Those who complain that competitions interfere with their season's work seldom realize that an entry would greatly enhance the interest of their programme. The play entered could be performed before their own club first and would then be keenly followed throughout the competition. Those who say a restricted competitive spirit is bad for art are usually insincere; their art is so precious that it will not stand the strain. The timid ones have my sympathy, but I hope to help them to change their inferiority complex into an asset.

Most of the trouble in competitions and festivals is caused by people—committees, producers, playwrights, actors, and even adjudicators—who take part without properly studying rules or aims. At the beginning of the season such societies say "Oh, I suppose we had better rehearse a one-act play for such-and-such competition," and sometimes they argue "Well, why bother? Why not enter with Act II of the full length play we are doing for the hospital?" They then proceed to do one or the other in the same manner as if they were playing it as part of an ordinary programme, and without regard to specific points for which the adjudicator is appointed to watch. I have had irate individuals tackle me after an adjudication because they have lost marks on a particular point when five minutes' reading of the rules in the first place would have shown them that it was inevitable. It is a curious thing about many amateurs that they simply cannot bring themselves to adopt the same attitude towards rules that they would, say, towards a tennis tournament. And not rules only, but the scope and purpose of the particular competition. Yet this is the first thing they should think of if they wish to get the best out of such work.

Different competitions—different aims and rules. For example, the British Drama League Community Theatre Festival has a different basis of marking from that of the Women's Institutes' Competitions. Yet teams will enter both with the same play and the same methods, and expect to reach the same point in each. In the Women's Institutes and certain village festivals, judges do not object to men's parts being played by women. I have even seen a woman Othello; but such casting would be almost bound to lose marks in a more open contest.

The attitude towards children's plays is frequently at fault. Elocution mistresses have an unfortunate habit of trying to show off their pupils in something that is hackneyed or quite outside the scope of a competition, forgetting that to "elocute" is one thing, to act another.

The question of the performance of excerpts from full-length plays needs more serious consideration than it receives. An excerpt is much more difficult to judge than a complete one-act play. The B.D.L. rules urge entrants to remember that excerpts that are complete in themselves are "desirable." Yet I have had to judge the middle act of *Dear Brutus* (which looks ridiculous divorced from Act I and Act III) and the first act of *A Marriage of Convenience* in which the principal character of the play does not appear! The first act of *The Silver Box* consists largely in leading up to the main idea; to see it by itself is most unsatisfactory. How can one award marks for "dramatic value" of something that is incomplete? There are, of course, excerpts that can stand by themselves; for example, the first act of *Outward Bound*, Act II of *The Kingdom of God*, the Trial Scene from *Saint Joan*, and certain sections of Shakespeare. On the whole, however, an excerpt is a risk, and the performance of it is frequently evidence that a team has not concentrated on the festival but has merely entered part of a play that has been worked at for another purpose. Audiences do not like excerpts, which mean incomplete entertainment for them. Therefore, if you are only half entertaining your audience you are losing valuable contact and hampering your acting.

The first thing, therefore, to do in approaching a competition is to read with a critical eye the explanatory details that are sent out by the organizers. Is there a particular requirement of the organizers? Are they looking for experiments in production and new plays? Do they favour the spectacular or the simple in presentation? Is the balance on the side of plays with big or small casts? Is the adjudication personal to the judge or on a marking system? Have the rules changed since last year? (They generally have in some particular, occasionally shifting the keynote of the festival.) All these, and other, questions need to be asked at the outset. Subsequently I hope to point the way to the best methods of fitting into the various organizations and generally how to appeal to an adjudicator.

Rules and aims are often vague and inadequately expressed. The ideal is to get these cut and dried before entrants begin to rehearse. They should not be left to the discretion of the adjudicator or a committee. In my opinion, the Scottish Community Drama Association has evolved by far the best festival organization. Entrants, adjudicators, and organizing committees know exactly what is expected of them from start to finish.

In connexion with the New Plan of the B.D.L., an excellent handbook has been issued which thoroughly goes into details of organization, finance, the purpose of the festival, and the method of adjudication.

Competitive or non-competitive festivals? Which achieve the more? Ideally, the non-competitive system—in which performances are criticized but not "placed"—creates a happier spirit. But there is no tangible incentive, and the standard of non-competitive festivals tends to be on a comparatively lower level. Audiences

A Scene from "The Kingdom of God" as played in the Final of the National Festival of Community Drama

This photograph was taken by *The Times* from the Circle during the actual performance

unquestionably prefer the element of competition; and, although the winning of cups and trophies ought not to be the primary aim, much kudos and satisfaction are gained by competing groups, if adjudication is in experienced hands.

So long as these trophies are regarded as incentives to good work, only good can come of efforts to win them. But the really important thing about festivals and competitions is that they provide the only considered criticism that societies get throughout the whole of the year. As a rule, the local Press is afraid to criticize in case it offends (a reflection on the players as well as the newspapers), or is unable to do so because there is no competent critic on the staff. If it were not for festivals and competitions, many societies would carry on for a whole lifetime without ever being judged impartially. Competitive work, therefore, is worth more than the haphazard attention it too often gets. It is also highly specialized, and the special methods of approach that are essential to success need to be understood.

I have deliberately used the word "approach" because some societies before they enter give too little thought to festivals and competitions. After the adjudication there are all sorts of excuses. "I *never* read rules," said one person to me as though that statement completely vindicated her viewpoint. Dozens of people, when criticized, have said, "Oh, but I didn't notice that point in the rules." Whether the battle of Waterloo was won on the playing fields of Eton I do not know, but success in dramatic competitions is certainly half won by those people who know all about their goal before they attempt to reach it.

GETTING TO WORK ON THE PLAY

When an amateur dramatic society has decided to enter a festival or competition, and has carefully studied the rules and aims, the next thing to do is to find the play that will suit the cast at the producer's disposal. Also it must fit the society and fit the festival. The advice may appear to be extraordinarily trite; yet I have known societies choose a play that was damned from the start because it was not in keeping with an organization that sought to develop "the progressive element in the amateur theatre" or had some similar aim.

One of the best produced comedies I have adjudicated lost heavily on this score. In a music-hall, or in a competition that had no special purpose, it would have done well, but it did not fit that particular festival. There was nothing progressive about it, and it was an old piece. It made few demands on the producer; it was in doubtful taste; it did nothing to show that the society had troubled to give other than a slick show of sorts. On the same programme was a new and worth-while play that was somewhat patchy in performance. It had a large and difficult cast, and its production called for creative work. The costumes, setting, and lighting had to be specially thought out. The result was that it was placed before the better-played comedy.

WORTH WHILE PLAYS

What the adjudicator looks for in such a festival is not merely a piece of bright entertainment (although that is welcome) but an effort that has more or less successfully made all-round demands on author, producer, and actors. Therefore, choose a play you can wrestle with; one with something worth while in it. A poor play will never be successful in performance, however well it is played. A badly written or loosely constructed play hampers actors and producer in their efforts. No competent adjudicator will pass a bad play. He will give high marks for purely technical points, but the lack of spirit, atmosphere, and dramatic effort of the whole will not earn marks. He will be bored by the play, and bored by futile attempts to camouflage it.

Do not misunderstand me—I am not arguing in favour of highbrow themes. The slightest idea, if it is soundly carried out, may make a first-rate play. What slighter idea could you find than that of *The Cab*? In this play a man is given half-a-crown to order a conveyance for bringing his wife's gammy-legged relation from the station. He spends the money on beer, and has to take the old man home on a wheelbarrow. The Author does not waste a word in the dialogue, and keeps the action going from the rise to the fall of the curtain.

To find a suitable new play needs effort and enterprise. Much help can be gained from reviews. Secretaries of societies should ask publishers to put their names on their mailing list so that early intimation of forthcoming books may be received. The British Drama League Library is invaluable not only because it contains all the latest plays, but also because the librarian has first-rate knowledge that she is always ready to impart. It is also wise to keep in touch with authors whose plays usually suit the society.

Certain local Guilds and similar federations have smaller libraries of their own. A valuable publication is *New Plays Quarterly*—the only journal in the world which concentrates entirely on plays. Four or five new one-act plays, each decided upon by an Advisory Board, are printed in each number; and a new full-length play is sent to subscribers annually. Between issues, there is a Supplement containing details of every one-act and full-length play issued by British publishers, thus forming a complete and handy record which saves societies wading through catalogues, and helps them immensely in their search.

Many societies, such as B.D.L. groups, Y.M.C.A. clubs, W.I. circles, and Youth movements are affiliated to their own national association which has drama advisers or special committees either to offer advice or to put groups with similar ideas in touch with each other. The Co-operative Movement has a national drama association with sectional drama associations that cover England, Scotland, and Wales. Societies connected with these or similar associations gain much knowledge and avoid isolation if they keep in touch with their own headquarters. Guilds and federations of societies in given areas do valuable work by concentrating on affiliated groups in their own field. They should attend festivals outside their own districts and learn all they can about plays, adjudication, and festival work.

When you have decided on your play, the next thing is to decide on whether you are going to have an amateur or professional producer. My advice is to ignore the categories, as such, and to rely on the man or woman whose work you know and believe in. It is better to have a competent amateur producer than to pay a small fee for a fourth-rate professional. On the other hand, a competent professional is invaluable. Before engaging him, however, make certain that he knows festival and competition requirements. Do not be misled by high-sounding publicity on his part. If all other things are equal—choose the amateur. The probability is that he has no axe to grind, and, as the competition is an amateur competition, you will have the satisfaction of knowing that you have worked in complete harmony with the spirit of the organization.

MAIN ESSENTIALS

Producers should, of course, realize the difference between producing a one-act play and a full length play. Whichever they decide to produce for a festival or competition, they also have specifically to consider the adjudicator. Unlike the audience, who often judge the production at the winning post, the adjudicator watches the work from the start. Final "curtains" of themselves do not win trophies. Attack and speed (not necessarily rapidity) are the main essentials in producing a one-act play. Once the production has become dull, there is seldom time left to undo the harm and to lift it back again to a satisfactory plane of quality.

The full-length play permits of greater development of character. The plot is likely to unfold itself more gradually, and there are more climaxes that need to be built *up* and then held.

The biggest fault I have noticed in festival work is that productions do not seize and hold the essential *style* of a play. Farces are played as comedies, and serious drama is treated as comedy. Each style demands a different approach, different speed, and a different form of attack. If you are in the wrong vein, the adjudicator will notice it at once.

Try to understand the adjudicator. Being human, he will have tastes and theories, although the ideal adjudicator will keep his ideas fluid and will approach a performance without "leanings." He should, indeed, be quite indifferent to the fact that he has seen the play before. "How does the play act *to-night*?" should be his principal question. Nevertheless, it does no harm to have knowledge of an adjudicator's previous adjudications, and to have read what he has written about them. From what I have written here you may be sure that I would not become enthusiastic over a badly written and carelessly constructed play. Yet I would not allow my feelings about the play, as written, to detract from such stagecraft and acting qualities as you might bring to bear on it. You would lose marks only in the sections in which you deserved to lose them.

Much of the actual presentation will depend on whether you are playing in curtains or not. Nearly all festivals now insist on curtain settings.

Therefore a handicrafts section of your society can be of immense value. What is needed is not great ability in scene painting or stage decoration, but imagination, coupled with artistic sense in giving to the stage those little touches and additions that convey an atmosphere in keeping with the play. What can be done in this respect is wonderful. I have seen an ordinary set of curtains made to give an impression of a Chinese garden merely by simple lighting effects and inexpensive odds and ends that had been touched up by an artist who had thought in terms of impressionism rather than naturalism. The illustration shows how an elaborate terrace can be suggested by simple means. The pillars are straight-hung curtains; the low wall consists of sugar-boxes tightly covered with sheets.

Finally—and above all—make up your minds to fit into the organization of the festival or competition. Have a self-contained entry, ready to go straight into the programme. Do not expect from the organizers things that they have not promised, and do not send notes to the adjudicator "explaining" this and that about your play. If you can help another team, do so; otherwise it is better to keep out of the way. And if when the adjudication is at an end you have lost, go out with a smile, and at least give the impression that you believe the adjudicator was right! That is what is known as The Festival Spirit.

ORGANIZING A FESTIVAL

Committees and organizers always have to undertake a lot of work for which they get little credit. When a dramatic festival or competition has to be organized all sorts of difficult people have to be "managed."

Sometimes one person alone can do the work. The usual way is to appoint a committee, of which there are two effective kinds. One is a body consisting of representatives of the societies that enter for the festival; the other is a group of people who are independent of the entrants. There is a third kind, which is a combination of the other two, but, while not ruling it out, it is to be avoided because it opens the door to charges—generally unfounded—of favouritism.

My own opinion, based on experiences of all kinds of committees in London and the provinces, is that a fully representative committee is the best. The independent committee is inclined to be too much involved in the wheels of organization, and is tempted to be dictatorial. The fully representative committee has its drawbacks, since it may be unwieldy and, occasionally, unpractical; but it does not lack enthusiasm, and it is always out to help itself—which means, paradoxically, to help that community of societies whose main idea is not mere numbers and figures and methods, but good dramatic performances. Some of the happiest committee work of which I have had experience has been that in which half a dozen societies have got together and organized their own festival. Each was given a sense of the difficulties of the others, the whole organization was a dovetailed effort, and lasting friendships were made. Some of the unhappiest times I have had have been as a member of a committee more or less remote from the entrants. We moved those concerned about like pawns, and wondered afterwards why so few of them entered the following year.

However, finance is the first thing to consider. In this connexion keep the entrance fee as low as possible. If the average society has to pay more than half-a-guinea in addition to the royalty on the play that is to be produced, it may be reluctant to enter. By far the best arrangement is to relieve entrants of paying royalties. Nothing appeals to them so strongly as the fact that, apart from the entrance fee, they need not spend another penny on their production.

Programmes can pay for themselves—by advertisements and by the charge that is made for them. It is nearly always possible to obtain a few donations towards a festival, since it is of interest to educationists and people who want to foster the community spirit. Even the Customs and Excise authorities have it in their discretion to exempt a festival (on the ground that it is "educational") from Entertainments Tax, provided the adjudication is made a definite item in the programme and that there is no *entr'acte* music, mechanical or otherwise. This exemption must be applied for well in advance.

When booking the hall make sure that it is licensed for dramatic performances. If it is not, the manager must apply to the local justices for an occasional licence. If any children are to take part during the evening it is necessary to ask the magistrates' permission for them to appear. If, as frequently happens, a play is to be performed for the first time in public it must be licensed by the Lord Chamberlain. It is best to put the onus of licensing on the society that is to produce it. The society may pass this on to the author, but whoever meets the obligation must apply for a form of application to the Lord Chamberlain (St. James's Palace, London, S.W.1) at least a fortnight in advance of the performance. The fee is a guinea for a one-act play; two guineas for a full-length play. In law, the responsibility lies with the manager of the hall or theatre, as it is to him, and not the society, or the author, that the Lord Chamberlain eventually issues the licence. All managers, however, will expect you to see that this matter is put in hand for them. In any case, you cannot expect them to pay for the licence.

Aims and rules of the festival should be carefully considered and explained simply and forthrightly. Do not mince words or evade issues. To do so will lead to trouble. Collect all the information available from other organizations. The points that need to be clarified are (*a*) the definition of the word "amateur"; (*b*) the playing-time and the setting-time; (*c*) whether a player may perform for more than one society and whether a society may enter more than one play; (*d*) the definition of the "new" play; (*e*) the minimum and maximum number of players that may appear in any play.

Teams should be told, upon entering, the dimensions of the stage, the colour of the curtain-set (preferably neutral), details of the lighting equipment, and what props and furniture are available. Teams should be told quite frankly at the outset that they must provide any distinctive and peculiar props or furniture that are essential for their own productions. The furniture provided by the committee should be items that are common to all, or that can reasonably be expected to be found in the average hall—such as tables, chairs, and a settee.

Places on the programme can generally be arranged to suit the plays; otherwise the best way is to ballot. Someone, who is independent of all the teams should be appointed stage director for the purpose of timing and controlling arrangements while the curtain is down.

Two other points need careful consideration in arranging a festival: (1) adjudication and (2) publicity. In certain competitions the adjudicator is chosen by a body that is independent of the local committee. Even so, the opinion of the local organization counts, and should be expressed. The best adjudicator is the man or woman who first and foremost has a judicial mind and *knows the movement from the inside.* A great many people know a great deal about drama in general, and a still larger number know one or two aspects only of it. In competitions and festivals we are not concerned with generalizations on the one hand or side-issues on the other. It is undesirable, for example, to appoint as a judge of rural drama a man whose whole life has been spent on the West End stage. Similarly, it is not helpful, in connexion with a festival the aim of which is to encourage the progressive spirit in the amateur theatre, to appoint as adjudicator an old "pro." who is full of prejudices and out-of-date ideas, or a young "pro." full of "arty" theories. It is still worse to appoint somebody who patronizingly talks down to "these amateurs." I do not believe that anyone ought to judge an amateur festival who has never been in close contact with the Amateur Movement, or who does not know the one-act play (and many professionals do not), or who is an expert in one branch of drama only—such as elocution, lighting, or playwriting. The adjudicators who are wanted are the well-read people with broad sympathies, judicial minds, experience of the work, and the ability to express themselves along the lines of the aims and scope of the particular effort that they are judging and trying to help.

Publicity for a festival is slightly different from that adopted in connexion with other dramatic work. There is more "news" in it for the Press. Frequently, the dramatic reputation of a town or village is at stake. If a local team is sent forward to a County or London Final the fact is worth recording. The Press should, therefore, be encouraged to watch for this from the start. Local trophies also help, and in many parts of the country the Press is the first to assist in this direction by offering one. Civic authorities can be approached. The adjudicator's name has been known to be an attraction, and his photograph may be reproduced in the local papers. Educationists and people who are interested in "the Drama" will support a festival, although they may hesitate to patronize one society's performance. Production of the work of a local playwright is an additional draw. The publicity section of the committee should emphasize the fact, and study other plays to ascertain if there is anything novel or specially interesting about them. I have never seen a programme of four one-act plays about which I could not write something in relation to the authors or the origins or the plots or the settings. Are they prize-winning plays? Are they new? Do they demand some special "effect"? Is there an actor in the festival who has an unusual part? Is the programme all comedy, or all thrills, or does it contain something of everything? These and many other questions, with their answers, will provide valuable publicity material.

Finally, the best way to run a festival is to be enthusiastic about it. Make it a festival in the full sense of the term. Then you will discover that you have learned much, lost nothing, and that you are eager to continue the work of making "hempen home-spuns" into finer cloth.

THE ONE-ACT PLAY

A study of the one-act play and its essential differences from the full-length play is of the utmost importance to all who take part in festivals or competitions. Author, actor, producer, scene designer—all must realize that they are dealing in a special medium of expression before they can reasonably hope for success.

The author has a maximum of forty minutes during which to present a complete idea. Obviously that idea must not be one that needs a slow process in working up an atmosphere or that necessitates great elaboration of detail. From the moment the curtain goes up to the time of its final fall there must not be a wasted word or action. That is not to say that the author's idea need be trivial. All the one-act plays of such writers as Barrie, St. John Ervine, F. Sladen-Smith, Harold Brighouse, and Philip Johnson have ideas that are bigger than those of many full-length plays. What all these and other successful writers of one-act plays realize is that they cannot handle more than a *phase* of life in the time. They therefore keep their plays, each with a simple central theme, within bounds. You cannot portray a life-story in a one-act play; indeed the most successful plays are those in which the actual playing period more or less coincides with that which the play suggests. Occasionally an author will hit upon a method of presenting years in minutes—as in Thornton Wilder's *The Long Christmas Dinner*—but it is rarely happy in performance. Even Mr. Wilder's play is apt to become a tiresome procession.

The division of a one-act play into two or more scenes is risky. It tends to create scrappiness, hinders the making of atmosphere, and breaks dramatic continuity. Barrie's *The Old Lady Shows Her Medals* and St. John Ervine's *She Was No Lady* overcome the difficulties solely because they were written by playwrights who possess a full knowledge of stage technique. Each scene leads directly to the next, and the lowering of the curtain actually heightens the effect. But Barries and Ervines are few, and the novitiate dramatist will do well to avoid writing his plays in scenes until he can write *one* scene satisfactorily. Generally speaking, those authors who write one-act plays in a number of scenes have missed their province; they ought to be writing for the screen.

It should be remembered by authors that one-act plays are rarely performed except in festivals and competitions in which curtain settings only may be used. Therefore, if an author wants his play to be widely performed it is useless to introduce scenes that look ridiculous in curtains. Surprising things can be done, and the accompanying illustration shows how such a difficult subject as the outside of a country inn can be conveyed without the use of "flats." But there are limits. You cannot satisfactorily suggest a railway station or the deck of a ship in this way unless you have modern lighting equipment and expert advice. Even then the work must be done with great skill and rehearsed with the utmost care—essentials that are impossibilities in a competition in the average hall.

In a sentence the ideal one-act play is a concise, unbroken expression of a simple idea untrammelled by side issues and unnecessary elaborations. It is not a three-act play condensed, or a thing so empty that the use of the word "sketch" to define it is applicable. It can be about anything —life or death, fairies or insects, historical characters or robots, and it can be in any vein—poetic, comic, experimental, or "straight." But when the curtain falls the audience must be sure that what they have seen is complete, and not a mere chapter of something else. Mr. H. G. Wells has likened the one-act play to the short story. Shakespeare made Hamlet give some wise instructions to the one-act players before they performed so successfully before the King. "Suit the action to the word, the word to the action " was the very essence of the argument.

If I were asked to mention half a dozen examples of recent one-act plays that apply the theories I have expressed and that do not demand a special technique, I would name *Exit* (Cyril Roberts); *The Man Who Wouldn't go to Heaven* (F. Sladen-Smith); *The Cab* (John Taylor); *It's Autumn Now* (Philip Johnson); *Fumed Oak* (Noel Coward); and *Count Albany* (Donald Carswell). For experimentalists I commend *Symphonie Pathétique* (Sydney Box); *Singing Sands* (Gordon Bottomley); *Masks* (Patricia Chown); *They Move On* (Gregory Page); *Man is Omega* (Nora Ratcliff); and the plays of Sudermann and Thornton Wilder. Among the best costume plays are those of F. Sladen-Smith, Clifford Bax, A. J. Talbot, and T. B. Morris. And there is always Chekhov.

There is a temptation to use the one-act form as a medium for propaganda. It fits nicely into certain functions, such as a semi-political "evening" or an annual meeting of a social institution. In "open" festival work, however, the propaganda play can be a danger. Logically, there is nothing against it if *the drama of the play is not less in value than the propaganda.* Many competitors with propaganda plays forget that they are participants in a *drama* festival and not a general election.

Cloth of a Different Colour is used for the Door. The Windows are painted on Cardboard and attached to the Curtains. The Signpost has a Heavy Base

Whilst the foregoing advice is primarily offered to the would-be playwright, much of it may be taken to heart by play-choosing committees. Difficulties are increased and marks are lost when a play for competitive work is chosen (*a*) that is awkward to fit into a festival programme; (*b*) that wastes time and dramatic tension by being divided up into a number of scenes; and (*c*) that invites adverse criticism because it has been written with no acceptance of basic principles.

Producers, I hope, will realize that the points I have made about conciseness and attack will need to be emphasized by them in performance. The pace of a one-act play is much more important than that of its bigger brother. With a full-length play the audience may get used to a certain amount of slowness during the course of the evening; with the one-act play there is no time to regain atmosphere once it is lost.

The making of the points in the plot of a one-act play requires the utmost care. Most of them can be made only once. Likewise, the characterization must be extremely clean-cut. Nobody must be in doubt about the characters in the play after their first entry. In many one-act plays characters have only a few lines to say, and make but brief appearances. Hence full value must be got out of words; movements must be deliberate, and make-up must be more than usually indicative of character.

In every direction the work is intensive, and the scenic designer's task is intensive on new lines. I have already referred to the need for imagination in curtain settings. There is a further need—the additions to curtain backgrounds must be handled so that they take on a relative importance. Note the signpost in the illustration. Without it the scene would simply be the outside of an inn; with it, we are made to realize that Ye Olde Boar's Head is near cross-roads at a definite point; and we are given a sense of the outdoor. The names on the signpost may be used to account for the dialect of the players; or to reveal how far the highwayman has travelled when he arrives; or to suggest that the inn is in a lonely district.

These are touches which, in a short play, compensate for the lack of explanatory details. Also, they make a much greater appeal to the mind of the audience than that made by hurriedly-joined "flats" and realistic "effects."

Even if playwrights, actors, producers, and scene designers do not agree with all my conclusions, I shall not have failed if I have provoked them to make a closer study of the one-act play. Too often it has been regarded as a trivial form of art merely because of its brevity, but, since brevity is the soul of wit and conciseness is a rarely found virtue, the one-act play cannot be dismissed so airily. One does not despise a diamond because it is a small gem.

ADJUDICATION

However well organized a festival or competition is, and however brilliantly the plays are produced and acted, an incompetent adjudicator can upset "the apple-cart." Adjudication is a delicate job. Human nature being what it is, there can be no such thing as popularity when you are judging other people.

People engaged in dramatic work develop an extraordinary acidity after the mildest of judgments. They nearly always forget the kind things that one has said. One line of adverse comment in a written criticism will weigh more with them than five pages of praise. Yet the work is entertaining and worth while. It keeps the judge's mind active, and if he is anything of an idealist and knows his job, he will get an immense satisfaction in helping his fellows to do better work. What should be his qualifications?

Primarily—the critical faculty; and by that I mean the real thing, including the ability to give it expression, either by word of mouth or in writing. Many people can nag about a play, can pull it to pieces or become enthusiastic over the parts that stir their particular souls, but the true critic will judge good and bad relatively, will praise as well as blame, and will always give reasons for his statements. His reasons will be based on knowledge gained by wide reading and personal investigation—not necessarily *practice* in each department, otherwise he would have to be a playwright, elocutionist, producer, actor, lighting expert, costume designer, scene painter, and so on. True, he must have been in close touch with the work of all these (particularly of the producer). If he has practical knowledge so much the better—if he can see good in other people's work.

But a man can judge a play without ever having tried to write one, just as an editor need not necessarily be a brilliant reporter.

The best critics and adjudicators are those who "live" in the world of the theatre—amateur and professional—and who have absorbed its spirit, purpose, and difficulties, yet have kept their heads. The worst adjudicators are one-sided people with pet theories, enthusiasms, and prejudices, who judge everything (with supreme conceit) from a personal angle instead of trying to discover how far author, actor, and producer have co-operated towards a given end.

Many people have told me that they would dislike to be adjudicators, but some of them have ambitions in that direction. They fail to realize, however, that an adjudicator ought to be a person who has demonstrated in some other way that he is qualified to judge other people. The best way to prove to organizers of festivals and competitions that one has the necessary ability is to express it in writing or speaking. No person who cannot speak in public, or who cannot write analytically, will ever make a competent adjudicator. A complete understanding of the movement one is to judge is essential, and it must be "inside" knowledge.

Therefore, if any of my readers has it in mind to become an adjudicator, let him mix himself up with any dramatic enterprise he can find, particularly studying a wide variety of methods of production. He should take every opportunity to assist in the production of a play, and eventually take on the job himself. He should study the methods of experienced adjudicators, attend festivals, assist in their organization, and become associated with a newspaper, magazine, or society in connexion with which he can demonstrate by writing and speaking that he has a balanced mind and the critical faculty. He will have to begin in a small way at each stage. It would be invaluable to associate himself with a repertory company and to do any odd job that comes his way. To get into newspaper work he should begin by writing criticisms and offering them merely as specimens to the nearest editor. Drama schools and courses of study will help; but personal experience of the staging of plays is most important. His first adjudication (perhaps of a minor competition) will provide him with a recommendation (or otherwise) for additional work.

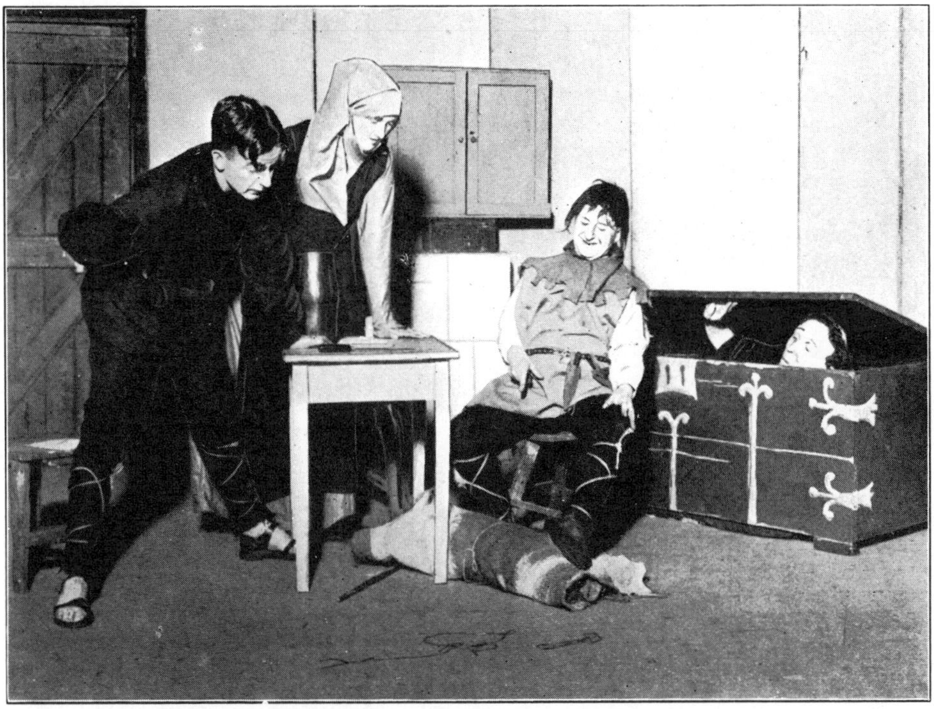

A SCENE FROM "THE DEVIL AMONG THE SKINS," BY ERNEST GOODWIN
With this play the British Drama League Festival was won by the Liverpool Playgoers Club
Photo Frederick Hopwood

A Guild of Drama Adjudicators was formed in 1946. It has done much, by way of instructional courses and examinations, to raise the standard of adjudication. The members are classified as either Associates or fully qualified. The former are reviewed at intervals and made full members when their experience and ability warrants advancement. The B.D.L., S.C.D.A. and other bodies recognize the Guild and have agreed to the conditions and minimum terms of engagement it has worked out.

An actual performance, seen through the adjudicator's eyes, is different from that seen by the audience, who merely wish to be entertained. The adjudicator is present primarily to study technique. He will, of course, look beyond that, and in his marks take into consideration the spirit, sincerity, and personality of the players. Sometimes these things outweigh technique; therefore one cannot be cut and dried in one's system. True drama is, at its roots, a spiritual thing—and no marking method in the world can allot percentages for emotional qualities. Still, a system is necessary, although it can never be applied to dramatic work in the same way that a system of judging can be applied to a more materialistic effort.

My own method is to work with a large sheet of stiff paper prepared for each performance. I rule this sheet into as many divisions as there are sections in which marks have to be awarded. While the performance is in progress, I rapidly jot down in the divisions the points I must consider afterwards and upon which I shall have to comment in the spoken or written report. The reason I use a large sheet of paper is that I can drop on to the sections instantly, and can then pencil in my notes without taking my eyes off the stage since I have accustomed myself (and it is not difficult) to write without following the pencil with my eyes. If I hear a phrase in the play I want specifically to refer to I take the gist of it down in shorthand.

When the curtain falls I re-write the whole sheet neatly if it needs it, and allot marks to the various sections. *I do not add these up until the last play has been performed;* and I do not refer to them until the close of the evening's performances. When I have finished marking the last play I add up all the marks. In this way the performances place *themselves* in order; yet each play is judged on its own merits according to a general standard rather than the standard of that particular evening. Within five minutes of the final curtain I have, all ready, a set of notes from which I can speak, and many others from which I can prepare a more intimate written report.

The spoken adjudication calls for tact and restraint. The temptation is to make a speech that will entertain the audience, whereas the true purpose of the adjudication is to analyse the work that has been done, and to help the teams.

The best thing is to keep strictly to the headings under which the organizers have invited you to adjudicate, and to omit irrelevancies and merely personal side issues.

The emphasis should be on positive rather than negative judgments. If, for example, the stage is overloaded with properties you may be tempted to say "The stage was hopelessly cluttered up and reminded me of a second-hand furniture shop." That would be true; but it would be much more helpful and more acceptable to the team to say "If the settee had been placed at the side, and the small table and two of the chairs dispensed with, there would have been more space for the actors and the stage would have looked better."

In the written criticism it is best to summarize briefly what you have said on the stage, and then to add some of the more personal and technical points that would not interest a general audience. It is best to avoid announcing marks, since these are liable to slight adjustment when you are correlating one evening's marking with the whole competition. (In the New Plan of the B.D.L. festival, the announcement of marks is prohibited.) It is a good idea to end on a word of thanks to the audience for listening so attentively (they always do if you are good-humoured) and to make it clear that your decision must stand. My last words always are, "Ladies and gentlemen, I would remind you that although I am not infallible, I am—on this occasion—*final.*" And then I remove myself rapidly from the stage!

L

LAW IN THE THEATRE

ENTERTAINMENTS TAX
THE LAW OF COPYRIGHT
EMPLOYMENT OF CHILDREN IN THEATRES
SUNDAY PERFORMANCES
THE LICENSING OF THEATRES
INSURANCE
LOTTERIES, LICENCES, LIBEL
CONTRACTS

LIGHTING, STAGE

AUDITORIA AND STAGES
LAMPS
LIGHTING APPARATUS
DIMMERS
STAGE SWITCHBOARDS
COLOUR
PROSCENIUM STAGE AND LIGHTING INSTALLATION
COMPARATIVE EXAMPLES OF STAGE LAY-OUTS
LIGHTING METHODS
SPECIAL EFFECTS

LIGHTING APPARATUS AND SCENIC EQUIPMENT

SMALL ACCESSORIES AND DIMMERS
CURTAIN SURROUNDS
SIDE CURTAINS AND BACKCLOTH

LAW IN THE THEATRE

DUDLEY S. PAGE, Author of "The Law of the Amateur Stage" and
H. SAMUELS, M.A., Barrister-at-Law

THIS section deals with aspects of the Law that affect amateur theatrical societies, i.e., with entertainments tax, copyright, employment of children, Sunday performances, licences, insurance, lotteries and libel.

ENTERTAINMENTS TAX

When Entertainments Tax was first introduced into this country, in 1916, certain provisos were included in the Act, and in various amendments since that year, for the benefit of charitable entertainments and entertainments provided for partly educational purposes that are not conducted for profit.

Purely charitable entertainments, which are governed by Sect. 6 (4) of the Finance Act 1924, may be divided into entertainments—

(1) Promoted by Societies of a permanent character, and

(2) Of a casual or isolated character.

Of the two, the former class is the more important, in that it applies to entertainments organized by permanent Operatic and Dramatic Societies giving their productions periodically, one, two, or more each year, and working under a properly organized constitution.

In all such cases applications for exemption are regulated by the percentage that the profits bear to the expenses. These percentages vary from the amount of the tax levied on the first production to a maximum of 25 per cent on later productions, but the maximum is not wholly reached until after the seventh entertainment.

Claims by Societies for exemption from Entertainments Duty under this Section of the Act are ordinarily decided in accordance with certain rules that have been drawn up by the Commissioners. These rules form no part of the Act itself, but have been framed by the Commissioners for the purpose of ensuring uniformity in dealing with such claims, and for providing certain forms of application applicable to varying cases. The rules themselves are embodied in the Commissioners Leaflet No. 16, which is as follows—

1. If such a Society has not already held any entertainments, whether for charity or otherwise, its FIRST entertainment will be provisionally exempted from duty if a guarantee is given that the donation to charity will be not less than the amount of the duty remitted.

2. Its SECOND entertainment will be provisionally exempted if a guarantee is given that the donations to charity as a result of the two entertainments will be not less than the duty remitted on the first, plus 20 per cent of the gross receipts from the second.

3. The THIRD entertainment will be provisionally exempted if a guarantee is given that the donations to charity as a result of the three entertainments will be not less than the duty remitted on the first, plus 20 per cent of the gross receipts from the second, plus 25 per cent of the gross receipts from the third.

4. The FOURTH entertainment will be exempted if the donations to charity as a result of the three previous entertainments have been not less than the amount of the duty chargeable in respect of the first entertainment, plus 20 per cent of the gross receipts from the second, plus 25 per cent of the gross receipts from the third.

5. The FIFTH entertainment will be exempted if either—

(*a*) the aggregate donations to charity from the three previous entertainments have been not less than 20 per cent of the gross receipts from the second, plus 25 per cent of the gross receipts from the third and fourth; or

(*b*) the aggregate donations to charity from the four previous entertainments have been not less than the amount of duty chargeable in respect of the first entertainment, plus 20 per cent of the gross receipts from the second, plus 25 per cent of gross receipts from the third and fourth.

6. The SIXTH entertainment will be exempted if either—

(*a*) the aggregate donations to charity from the three previous entertainments have been not less than 25 per cent of the aggregate gross receipts; or

(*b*) the aggregate donations to charity from the four previous entertainments have been not less than 20 per cent of the gross receipts from the second entertainment, plus 25 per cent of the gross receipts from the third, fourth, and fifth; or

(*c*) the aggregate donations to charity from the five previous entertainments have been not less than the amount of the duty chargeable in respect of the first entertainment, plus 20 per cent of the gross receipts from the second, plus 25 per cent of the gross receipts from the third, fourth, and fifth.

7. The SEVENTH entertainment will be exempted if either—

(*a*) the aggregate donations to charity from the three or four previous entertainments have been not less than 25 per cent of the aggregate gross receipts; or

(*b*) the aggregate donations to charity from the five previous entertainments have been not less than 20 per cent of the gross receipts from the second entertainment, plus 25 per cent of the gross receipts from the third, fourth, fifth, and sixth.

8. SUBSEQUENT entertainments will be exempted if the aggregate donations to charity from the previous three or four or five entertainments have been not less than 25 per cent of the aggregate gross receipts.

If the Society which makes the claim has already held one or more entertainments, for charity or otherwise, it will be treated under the above rules as far as applicable but any Society which is unable to obtain exemption under the foregoing rules for a forthcoming entertainment may be granted provisional exemption if a guarantee is given that the resulting donation to charity will be not less than 25 per cent of the gross receipts.

If the guarantees required by Rules 1, 2, and 3, are not forthcoming, duty must be paid, but the Commissioners will be prepared to consider applications for repayment of the duty when it can be shown that such repayment will enable the Society to fulfil the conditions in respect of which a guarantee was required; provided that at least 14 days before the entertainment, either application for exemption has been made or notice of intention to claim repayment under this rule has been given.

The condition that the whole of the net proceeds must be devoted to charitable or philanthropic purposes will be interpreted as allowing the three following items to be charged against the gross receipts—

(*a*) a reasonable amount carried forward as a working balance to meet the preliminary expenses of the next performance, provided that the Society has passed a rule, that, if it is dissolved, any balance in hand shall be given to charity.

(*b*) the annual subscription to a Central Association to which the Society concerned is affiliated;

(*c*) refreshments to the performers at a cost not exceeding 1s. a head per performance.

It will be noted that under Rules 1, 2, and 3, the exemption is not only *provisional*, but also subject to a guarantee. Rule No. 4 omits both these conditions, so that if your first three entertainments have attained the percentages required, your fourth and subsequent shows would be exempted, *ipso facto*, and without guarantee. But directly you fail to reach the percentage required, your exemption would again become provisional and subject to guarantee.

Applications for exemption in cases arising under the above rules should usually be made to The Secretary, H.M. Customs & Excise, Custom House, London, E.C.3, and must be made at least fourteen days before the date of the entertainment. Failure to observe this time limit will invalidate any application.

The appropriate forms for all such applications may be obtained from the Secretary's office, as aforesaid, or from any Customs and Excise office.

The regulations that apply to entertainments of a casual or isolated character (Class 2) differ materially from those in Class I set out above.

As regards charitable entertainments of a

casual or isolated character, exemption is granted in cases where the Commissioners of Customs and Excise are satisfied that the whole of the takings of an entertainment are devoted to philanthropic or charitable purposes without any charge on the takings for any expenses of the entertainment.

An application must in all cases be made for decision as to whether exemption is allowable, and should be sent in as long as possible before the date of the entertainment, but in any case not later than fourteen clear days before that date. A form of application, E.D.12, may be obtained from any Customs and Excise Office or from the Secretary, H.M. Customs and Excise, City Gate House, 39–45 Finsbury Square, London, E.C.2. If the Commissioners are satisfied as to the facts, a certificate will be issued authorizing the entertainment to be given free of Duty, subject to the production in due course, if required, of satisfactory evidence of the disposal of the takings. Unless exemption has been obtained before the entertainment, duty must be paid in the proper manner.

Exemption is not allowable in any case where any of the expenses, however small, are paid out of the takings of the entertainment or are defrayed out of the funds towards the benefit of which the takings of the entertainments are devoted, but if the expenses of the entertainment are met by donations from other sources given for the express purpose, this fact will not disqualify the entertainment for exemption.

(The expression "takings of the entertainment" includes not only all money taken for admission, but also all takings from any source whatever in connexion with the entertainment; for example, money taken for insertion of advertisements in programmes, takings from the sale of programmes or of refreshments or of articles exhibited for sale at the entertainment, takings of side-shows, etc. The actual takings for refreshments, side-shows, games, etc., must be included in gross in the takings of the entertainment, and exemption is not allowable in any case where only the net profits from these sources are included in the takings. Similarly, the expression "expenses of the entertainment" includes expenses of all kinds in connexion with the entertainment and its side-shows, etc.)

Apart from those entertainments which are in a position to claim exemption from tax as falling within either Class I or Class II above, *repayment* of tax which has already been paid may be claimed in certain cases, namely where the Commissioners of Customs and Excise are satisfied that the whole of the net proceeds of the entertainment are devoted to philanthropic or charitable purposes and the whole of the expenses of the entertainment do not exceed 50 per cent of the receipts.

Except as provided for below, duty must be paid by means of stamped tickets. Application for repayment of the Duty paid must be made to the Commissioners on a prescribed form, numbered E.D.13, and must be accompanied in every case by the portions of the stamped tickets retained by the proprietor.

In any case where the Commissioners are satisfied, on previous application being made to them, that there is a reasonable probability that the expenses will not exceed 50 per cent of the receipts, they will be prepared, for the sake of convenience, to allow the proprietor of the entertainment to dispense with the use of stamped tickets subject to the deposit of a sum of money sufficient to cover the probable amount of Duty in case it should prove, when accounts of the entertainment are furnished, that repayment of the Duty would not have been allowable in law. Application for this arrangement should be made as long as possible before the date of the entertainment on a prescribed form, numbered E.D.14. Stamped tickets must be used unless the application has been granted and the necessary authority received.

If the entertainment is given in a place of regular entertainment the proprietor of which holds a standing authority from the Commissioners for dispensing with stamped tickets and paying the Entertainments Duty on the basis of weekly returns of payments for admission, the Duty on the entertainment must be included by him in his returns. Application for the repayment of the duty paid must be made on the prescribed form, numbered E.D.13.

The expression "receipts" includes not only all money received for admission but also all receipts from any source whatever in connexion with the entertainment; for example, money received for the insertion of advertisements in programmes, receipts from the sale of programmes or of refreshments or of articles exhibited for sale at the entertainment, receipts from side-shows, etc. Similarly, the expression "expenses" includes expenses of all kinds in connexion with the entertainment and its side-shows, etc.

With regard to such items in an entertainment as refreshments, side-shows, games, etc., the expenses of all such items, together with the receipts in respect of them, must be included in gross in the accounts of the entertainment, and repayment of the Duty is not allowable in any case where only the net profits from these sources are included in the receipts.

Copies of the above-mentioned are obtainable from any Customs and Excise Office or from the Secretary, H.M. Customs and Excise, City Gate House, Finsbury Square, London, E.C.2.

THE LAW OF COPYRIGHT

Copyright is defined in Section 1 (2) of The Copyright Act, 1911, which now governs the law on the subject, as being the sole right of the author or composer of every original literary, dramatic, musical, and artistic work to reproduce his work to the exclusion of every one else for the period therein specified. It creates virtually a monopoly to that person in the product of his brain, and reserves to him the fruits of his labour.

The time specified in the Act subsists for the period of the author's life and fifty years after his death, and in the case of collective works, such as opera or musical comedy, in which the music, dialogue, and lyrics are distinct contributions of two or more persons, the fifty years does not begin to run until after the death of the survivor.

Parliament, therefore, has been far more generous to the owners of copyright than to the holders of patent rights, which latter extend for the comparatively short period of fourteen years only.

It is not surprising, therefore, to find that the copyright in many classic works, the authors or composers of which have been dead many years, still subsists.

A striking instance is to be found in the Gilbert and Sullivan operas, in which the music and libretto are distinct contributions. The copyright in these did not expire until fifty years after the death of Sir Arthur Sullivan, and as he died in 1900 the copyright in these works expired in 1950.

But apart from these interesting and comparatively little known facts, the law of copyright has an intimate bearing on the administration of most operatic and dramatic societies.

Perhaps the most frequent question that arises is: What constitutes infringement of copyright? Here we are confronted with a real difficulty, for the Act itself, whilst it defines in a general way what constitutes infringement, leaves us to guess whether any given case comes within the purview of that definition or not.

The matter is dealt with in Section 2 of the Act, which reads—

> "Copyright in a work shall be deemed to be infringed by any person who, without the consent of the owner of the copyright, does anything the sole right to do which is by the Act conferred on the owner of the copyright."

That is certainly non-committal, not to say vague, and it is not surprising to find that much litigation has taken place upon the interpretation of the Section.

The most useful interpretation is to be found in the leading case of *Duck* v. *Bates* (1884), in which it was held that in order to constitute infringement there must be a representation that will injure the author's right to fees. A more recent review of the whole matter was made in *Performing Right Society* v. *Gillette Industries, Ltd.*, (1943) in which it was decided that a performance given only to employees of a particular factory was not a private performance.

But, generally speaking, the test is whether the reproduction is of a *private* or *public* character, and here again it is not always easy to define a distinct line of demarcation between the two.

Obviously, a purely domestic performance of a play given in one's own home without any charge of any sort, would be a *private* reproduction, and would not constitute an infringement. But directly the element of payment enters into the business, the performance takes on something of a public character, even though those present may be there by invitation. Nor need the payment necessarily be the price of a seat; for, to quote the preamble to The Sunday Observance Act of 1780, there may be "many subtle and crafty contrivances," which, although quite innocently conceived, might render the performance one of a public character. For instance, admission by purchase of a programme; the supply of refreshments at more than the customary rates; the payment of one or more of those taking part; the issuing of invitations in the Press or the taking of a voluntary collection from those present, are all cases that transform an otherwise domestic and private performance into one of a public character, and thereby constitute an infringement.

All these cases have already formed the subject of prosecutions, not necessarily under the Copyright Act, but also under other Acts regulating the theatre, but the test is the same, and would apply equally to infringement of copyright, even though the performances take place in a private house. Of course, if they were given in a public building, the danger would be infinitely greater, and might, in addition, involve trouble with the licensees of theatres or Entertainment Tax authorities.

I have dealt almost exclusively with the production and performance of stage plays, but there are many reading circles throughout the country that confine their activities to the reading of stage plays, and these are also intimately concerned with the law of copyright.

Here, again, the test would seem to be whether the reading of stage plays would constitute a public entertainment, or whether it is a purely domestic concern.

Any such reading circle that comprised a large number of people other than those actually reading parts, might constitute an infringement, particularly if any charge were made for admission. The matter, however, was much simplified by a special arrangement that the Incorporated Society of Authors made to govern such cases. By this arrangement the Society agreed that no fees shall be payable in respect of any private play reading that is confined only to its own members or their guests, providing no money is taken at the doors and the attendance present, excluding the cast of readers, consists of not more than fifty persons.

This arrangement certainly gives a fairly wide scope for the reading of plays, and so long as the rule is strictly followed, no infringement would be likely to occur.

Some publishers and controllers of performing rights have followed this rule, and in some cases they will agree to an extension of the number of persons present, subject to a payment of half the royalties.

To summarize the matter, the following rules should be observed—

1. The reading should be undertaken only by members of the circle or their guests.

2. No money must be taken for admission in any form, in subscriptions, collections, sale of programmes, or otherwise.

3. The attendance present, exclusive of cast, must not exceed fifty persons.

4. The play must be read from the published copy, and no scenery or properties must be brought into use, nor must any action be portrayed.

5. No public announcement of the reading must appear in the Press or otherwise.

The penalties of infringement of copyright are severe, and apply not only to the actual promoters of the performance, but also to any persons permitting the use of a theatre or place of entertainment for such a performance, unless he can prove that he had no ground for suspecting that an infringement of copyright was taking place.

The author's remedy for infringement may be either by civil action or, in the case of entertainment for personal profit, by summary conviction at petty sessions, which latter involves a fine not exceeding £50, and even, in the case of subsequent offences by the same person, to imprisonment with or without hard labour, not exceeding two months.

From the foregoing, it will be seen that the law on the subject of copyright presents many pitfalls to the unwary, and, having regard to the somewhat uncertain state of the law, it behoves all those promoting entertainments of any kind to exercise caution. There are no hard and fast rules to guide one, and each case must depend upon its own particular circumstances. But the suggestions offered may help amateurs to decide upon the merits of any case with which they may be concerned.

Happily, authors are not usually vindictive, and they do not rush into prosecutions, but amateurs should not suppose that because they can name societies that have come within the infringements herein suggested and escaped prosecution, that they were *not* infringements, or even that they may be as lucky as those societies.

After all, it is mean and contemptible to rob an author of his fees, even by clever subterfuge, or by taking the chance that one may never be found out.

EMPLOYMENT OF CHILDREN IN THEATRES

It frequently happens that amateur societies, both operatic and dramatic, find it necessary to employ children in their productions; indeed throughout the year productions entirely by children, sometimes of quite tender years, are given. In all such cases, the law has defined certain requirements for the protection of those who are too young to protect themselves, but there are, I presume, few people outside legal circles who have much knowledge of what those requirements consist.

We are not so much concerned with the requirements that are applicable to cases on the professional stage, where children are exploited for personal gain, but it may be stated briefly that those requirements comprise an application to the local education authority, which may grant a licence if the authority is satisfied that the child is fit to take part in the entertainment or series of entertainments, and that proper provision has been made to secure his health and kind treatment. Even so, such licence would be subject to the rules prescribed by the Ministry of Education. These include the production of birth certificates, photographs, medical certificates, reports on educational attainments, hours of employment, provisions for school attendance and recreation, and appointment of responsible guardians.

This is truly a formidable list, but there are, I believe, many instances among amateur entertainments in which this method of procedure is adopted, where a knowledge of the simple alternatives provided by Act of Parliament would attain the same object and save a good deal of time and trouble.

I will therefore deal only with those requirements that are applicable to cases in which the entertainment is organized for charity, as distinct from those that are organized on a professional basis, although both are governed by the same Act, namely, The Children and Young Persons Act, 1933, which incorporates and amends similar provisions hitherto provided in The Children and Young Persons Act, 1932, and the Education Act, 1921.

By Section 22 of The Children and Young Persons Act, 1933, it is provided as follows—

(1) Subject to the provisions of this Section a child shall not, except under and in accordance with the provisions of a licence granted and in force thereunder, take part in any entertainment in connection with which any charge, whether for admission or not, is made to any of the audience; and every person who causes or procures a child, or being his parent or guardian, allows him to take part in any entertainment in contravention of this Section, shall, on summary conviction, be liable to a fine not exceeding five pounds, or, in the case of a second or subsequent offence, not exceeding twenty pounds.

(2) Subject as hereinafter provided and without prejudice to the provisions of this part of this Act and any by-laws made thereunder with respect to employment, a licence under this Section shall not be necessary for a child to take part in an entertainment if—

(*a*) he has not during the preceding six months taken part on more than six occasions in entertainments in connection with which any such charge as aforesaid was made; and

(*b*) the net proceeds of the entertainment are devoted to purposes other than the private profit of the promoters:

Provided that this subsection shall not apply in the case of an entertainment given in premises which are licensed for the sale of any intoxicating liquor unless either

(i) those premises are also licensed for the public performance of stage plays or for public music, singing or dancing; or

(ii) special authority for the child to take part in the entertainment has been granted in writing under the hands of two Justices of the Peace.

It will be noted that the Act does not apply in the case of an occasional entertainment not promoted for private profit, so that an entertainment promoted for charity is exempt from the provisions of the Act, provided the entertainment takes place in premises other than those licensed for the sale of intoxicating liquor.

But in the case of all such entertainments held

on premises that are licensed for the sale of intoxicating liquor, unless they are also licensed for the performance of stage plays or for public music, singing or dancing, the requirements of the Act must be observed.

There is, however, a simple method of getting over the difficulty. This is set out in the Act, and adoption of it entails obtaining the consent of two Justices of the Peace as referred to in subsection (2) (i) of the Act.

It may be presumed that in nearly every case one or more of the promoters will be acquainted with two Magistrates from whom a certificate can be obtained. Since there is no statutory form for such certificate, the following formula is suggested—

> "We, the undersigned, two of his Majesty's Justices of the Peace for the *(here state the County Borough or Magisterial Division in which the entertainment takes place)*, being informed that an entertainment is to be held by *(here state name of Society or persons promoting the entertainment)* in the *(here state place)* on *(here state date or dates)* in which children being girls under the age of 16 or boys under the age of 14 are taking part, and being satisfied that such entertainment is promoted in aid of charity and that proper provisions are being made for the comfort and safety of the children, hereby certify that such entertainment shall be exempt from the provisions of Section 22 of The Children and Young Persons Act, 1933.

Have such a document as this typed on foolscap and obtain the signatures of two Magistrates at the foot thereof. But since Magistrates will probably want to be satisfied that they have the power to sign, and since they may not always be familiar with the Act, it will be desirable to inform them of the requirements beforehand and to refer them to the section of the Act authorizing this procedure. Such certificate, when obtained, should be available during the performance for production if required to any police officer.

Promoters of entertainments will be well advised when in any doubt whatever to obtain such a certificate.

It should be noted that omission to comply with the requirements of the Act renders any offending person liable on summary conviction to a fine not exceeding £5, and in certain cases in which life or limb is endangered, such penalties could amount to as much as £50.

Reference must be made to the responsibility resting on the promoters of entertainments and proprietors of licensed premises for the safety of children *attending* public performances, as distinct from those taking part. Section 12 (i) of the Act is as follows—

> "Where there is provided in any building an entertainment for children, or an entertainment at which the majority of persons attending are children, then, if the number of children attending the entertainment exceeds one hundred, it shall be the duty of the person providing the entertainment to station and keep stationed wherever necessary a sufficient number of adult attendants, properly instructed as to their duties, to prevent more children or other persons being admitted to the building, or to any part thereof, than the building or part can properly accommodate, and to control the movement of the children and other persons admitted while entering and leaving the building or any part thereof and to take all other reasonable precautions for the safety of the children."

The responsibility falls not only on the promoters, but also on the proprietor of the premises. The penalties for breach of this necessary provision for the safety of children are heavy, and render an offending person liable on summary conviction to a fine not exceeding £50 for a first offence and £100 for a subsequent offence. An offence might also involve a revocation of the licence applicable to such premises. It behoves all those responsible in such cases to comply with the requirements of the Act.

SUNDAY PERFORMANCES

If the Sunday Observance Act, 1780, were to be interpreted from a strictly legal point of view, there would be no need for any article upon the subject, for in that case there could be no such thing as a Sunday performance. Moreover, it must not be assumed that because Sunday performances generally, and many possibly within the reader's own knowledge, take place in all parts of the country, that they are necessarily legal, but rather that the authorities have allowed a certain judicial elasticity in the interpretation of the Act, and that so long as no undue liberties are taken, nothing serious need happen.

The Act is described in the preamble as "An Act for preventing certain Abuses and Profanations on the Lord's Day called Sunday," and whilst it deals with a variety of such abuses and profanations, we are concerned mainly with Section 1 of the Act relating to public entertainments, by which it is enacted as follows—

> That any house, room or other place which shall be opened or used for publick entertainment or amusement or for publickly debating on any subject whatsoever, upon any part of the Lord's Day called Sunday, and to which persons shall be admitted by the payment of money or by tickets sold for money, shall be deemed a disorderly house or place; and the keeper of such house, room or place shall forfeit the sum of two hundred pounds for every day that such house, room or place shall be opened or used as aforesaid on the Lord's Day to such person as will sue for the same, and be otherwise punishable as the law direct, in cases of disorderly houses; and the person managing or conducting such entertainment or amusement on the Lord's Day, or acting as master of the ceremonies there, or as moderator, president, or chairman of any such meetings for publick debate on the Lord's Day, shall likewise for every such offence forfeit the sum of one hundred pounds to such person as will sue for the same; and every door-keeper, servant or other person who shall collect or receive money or tickets from persons assembling at such house, room, or place on the Lord's Day, or who shall deliver out tickets for admitting persons to such house, room or place on the Lord's Day, shall also forfeit the sum of fifty pounds to such person as will sue for the same.

It will be noted that the test to be applied is similar to that required in the case of infringement of Copyright, and to bring a particular case within the Section, it must be a performance open to the *public on payment of admission.* As we have already seen in the law of Copyright, it is not always an easy matter to determine precisely when a given case ceases to be a purely domestic affair and when it becomes a public entertainment, nor is it any easier to determine always what constitutes payment for admission.

It has been held that the mere payment of artistes constitutes a *public* entertainment, and certainly any general announcement such as bills displayed publicly, or advertisements appearing in the Press, would be prima facie evidence of the public nature of the entertainment.

Payment of money at the door would in itself be sufficient presumptive evidence that the entertainment was of a public character, and therefore an offence would be committed. Moreover, payment by admission cannot be evaded by subterfuge, for Section 2 of the Act anticipates what are described as the *many subtle and crafty contrivances* of persons who attempt to evade the Section, and puts its own interpretation upon the word "admission."

Under this definition, admission by payment includes cases in which refreshments are supplied at more than the usual rates, or in which the entertainment is provided by subscribers or contributors to the expenses, or even to admission by the purchase of a programme.

It would seem difficult, therefore, to conceive anything other than a purely domestic entertainment that would not infringe the provisions of the Act. But there is a way out of the dilemma, and one that has the authority of a leading case on the subject, which we will now consider.

The Act, as we have seen, provides that there must be *payment by admission* in one or other of the methods referred to. Therefore it follows that a *free entertainment* would not constitute an infringement. But of what use, it will be asked, is a free entertainment to the promoters, who may be wanting to raise money for charity, and who may be put to considerable expense in promoting the entertainment?

Happily the case of *Williams* v. *Wright* (1897, 13 L.R. 551), helps us considerably, for by that case it was held that since the Act does not stipulate that the free admission shall include a seat, and so long as there is a reasonable part of the house open to free admission, it is permissible to make a charge for seats in the rest of the house.

The ruling, therefore, is simply this, that so long as nobody is *compelled* to pay, you are not infringing the Act.

None the less, it behoves you to be careful, for whilst under the ruling in this case you may be all right under the Sunday Observance Act, there may be difficulties arising under the Theatres Act, 1843, for under this Act the Licensing Authority has power to attach to every theatre licence adequate rules for ensuring the proper conduct of the theatre, and not infrequently one of those rules is that the theatre shall not be open on Sundays or Good Friday. But, of course, this applies only to entertainments that take place in a building licensed for the performance of stage plays.

With reference to the performance of stage plays in London under the administration of the Lord Chamberlain, these are usually held by groups forming themselves into Clubs or Societies, and if bona fide established for the private performances of stage plays, the Lord Chamberlain permits such productions subject to certain conditions. Here then we have the anomaly that whilst such productions may be illegal under the Sunday Observance Act or the Theatres Act, they have a semi-official sanction by reason of the rules issued by that official.

It is under these rules that the Sunday play-producing societies in the Lord Chamberlain's administrative area conduct their performances.

The rules comprise the following conditions—

1. The Society must be bona fide established for the private performance of stage plays.

2. Admission must be by ticket procurable only by members of the Society presenting the proposed play, and under no circumstances shall money be taken or tickets supplied at the Theatre.

3. No payment, direct or indirect, beyond an honorarium for expenses shall be paid for the services of those taking part.

4. No intoxicating liquor shall be sold or supplied whilst the Theatre is being used on Sunday.

5. No performances shall be permitted on Christmas Day or Good Friday.

A copy of these conditions can be obtained by application to the Lord Chamberlain's office, St. James's Palace, London, S.W.1.

Sunday cinema performances, which do not much concern us, are now specially controlled by the Sunday Entertainments Act, 1932, which makes special provision for all such performances. But up to the passing of that Act all such performances were absolutely illegal.

It is desirable in concluding this article to warn all those who promote Sunday entertainments to exercise care, for the penalties for infringement are particularly severe, ranging as they do to a fine of £200 against the proprietor of the place of entertainment; £100 each for the promoters; and £50 for each attendant on duty, and the fines can be imposed for every occasion on which the offence is committed.

Proceedings, moreover, can be instituted by a common informer, which means that, in addition to the police, any private individual can take such proceedings and recover the penalties. However, lest such persons should conceive this to be an easy means of making money, it is as well to remind them that the Crown has power under the Remission of Penalties Act, 1875, to remit the penalty in whole or in part, but the costs against the defendant might none the less be a heavy burden to bear.

THE LICENSING OF THEATRES

It is a curious fact that the laws in this country relating to the stage should be governed principally by an Act that is nearly 100 years old, namely, The Theatres Act, 1843, which, so far as its main provisions are concerned, still controls the regulation of the theatres. But although the Act may be old, it must not be forgotten that it was designed mainly to protect the public, particularly in regard to the licensing of theatres for stage plays and to prevent the danger of places inadequately constructed being used as places of public entertainment.

Section 2 of that Act is the one with which we are mainly concerned in regard to the licensing of theatres. That Section provides as follows—

> It shall not be lawful for any person to have or keep any house or other place of public resort in Great Britain, for the public performance of stage plays, without a licence as thereinafter provided, and every person who shall offend against this enactment shall be liable to forfeit such sum as shall be awarded by the Court, not exceeding Twenty Pounds for every day on which such house or place shall have been so kept open by him for the purpose aforesaid, without legal authority.

When we consider some of the cases in which prosecutions have occurred, I think it will be agreed that the provisions of the Act are essential.

A difficulty arises in determining what is "a place of public resort," and here again, as in other matters relating to the Law of the Theatre, the test is similar to that referred to in previous articles on the Law of Copyright, Performance of Children in Theatres, and Sunday Performances. As in those cases, it is impossible to lay down any hard and fast rule, as the interpretation of the law depends upon the circumstances in any particular case.

A purely domestic entertainment held in a private house and restricted solely to the promoters' own guests would not, of course, be a public performance, and no licence would therefore be required. But the line between the *domestic* and the *public* is very thin. For instance, in spite of the fact that an entertainment might take place in a private house and be restricted to an audience present by invitation, it might none the less become a public place of entertainment in certain circumstances; if, for instance, a charge was made to those invited, or any public announcement was made of the proposed entertainment, or a collection was taken among the audience, or payment was made to any artistes taking part.

Any or all of these might convert an otherwise domestic performance into one of a public character.

There is a well-known case, known as *Shelley* v. *Bethell* (1883, 48 J.P. 244), upon this subject. Shelley gave a performance in a private theatre fitted up by himself on his own property, admission being by invitation and the payment of £1 1s. The performance was held to be a public performance, although it was established that the promoters derived no benefit whatever from it, the proceeds being handed to charity. Mr. Justice Mathew, in his summing up in that case, declared as follows: "It is the *inviting* of the public to attend the performance of such plays, *and whether on payment or not, matters not*."

A similar case occurred more recently in the prosecution of the Bath Citizen House Players, who were also convicted under this same Section of the Act. In that case the defendant gave a performance of a passion play in her private theatre, admission to which was by invitation tickets only. No one was admitted without a ticket, and there was no charge for admission, but none the less a conviction was recorded, which conviction was subsequently confirmed on appeal to Quarter Sessions.

In another case the owner of a small theatre, known as the Gate Theatre Studio, was prosecuted for a similar offence. The defence put forward in that case was that the building was run as a club and that only members and friends of members were admitted, but here again the Court recorded a conviction.

Such cases as these may appear at first glance to be arbitrary, but no doubt the adjudicators have in mind in all these cases the defects of the building in the matter of precaution against danger by fire or panic, and the inadequate construction of the building in the way of exits.

It will be seen, therefore, that to use an unlicensed building, even in your own home, may sometimes have serious consequences, but those consequences might be infinitely more serious to the promoters in the event of loss of life through fire or panic if the place were unlicensed, for it could conceivably be held that the omission to obtain such a licence had led to the consequent loss of life. Since people are frequently careless in their provision for the safety of others, it is highly desirable that adequate precautions should be taken.

The Act therefore applies to all buildings, whether private buildings or not, which are used for the purpose of public entertainment, and since the line of demarcation is finely drawn, one might almost say that it applies also in many cases to private entertainments.

Strangely enough, the Act does not apply to entertainments that take place in tents or public booths such as those erected in fairs and places of that description, and, indeed, the Justices have no jurisdiction at all to grant a licence for such places, even were it required.

In order to obtain a licence for the performance of stage plays, it is necessary to make an application to the proper authority, namely, the County or Borough Council within whose area the building is situate, but in practice County or Borough Councils invariably delegate their powers, as provided in the Act, to the local Justices, before whom the application should be made.

The Clerk to the Magistrates should be approached for the purpose of ascertaining, first, whether such powers have been delegated, and, secondly, to give him notice of the proposed application.

In the event of the building being within the administrative area of the Lord Chamberlain, that is, within the parliamentary boundaries of the City of London and the City of Westminster, and of the Borough of Finsbury and Marylebone, the Tower Hamlets, Lambeth, and Southwark, the application must be made to that official, and should be addressed to the Lord Chamberlain's Office, St. James's Palace, London, S.W.1. In granting a licence, the authorities will require the applicants to obtain a bond in themselves and two sureties for such sum as they may deem adequate, the purpose of which bond is to ensure the due observation of the rules governing the licence.

The authorities under Section 9 of the Act have power to attach proper rules for ensuring the proper conduct of a theatre, such as restricting its use on Sundays or certain other days, and regulating the hours of opening, etc. The fees payable are not excessive.

The granting of a Theatre licence carries with it the right to sell intoxicating liquor on application to the Inland Revenue Authorities. In these days, however, the Magistrates not infrequently grant the Theatre licence conditionally that there shall be no application made for a drink licence.

Of course, the Magistrates also satisfy themselves before granting any licence that the building is adequately constructed and provided with proper fire appliances and exits. In the London area controlled by the Lord Chamberlain, these requirements are stringent.

If an occasional licence is required for the production of a stage play for one or more evenings only, the application should be for an occasional licence to cover the period required. All stage play licences, whether occasional or otherwise, must be granted to the responsible owner or manager of the premises, and not to the promoters of the play.

The penalty for (1) acting any part in a play for hire, or (2) causing or allowing this, in a place which is not licensed as above, is £10 a day. If any admission fee is charged or the place is one where liquor may lawfully be sold, the actor is deemed to be acting for hire. In any proceedings the onus is on the person charged with the offence to prove that the premises were duly licensed.

INSURANCE

Apart from those larger and more important legal matters that have already been dealt with in THEATRE AND STAGE, there are other matters of rather less importance that arise occasionally in the administration of theatrical societies.

The most frequent of these is, perhaps, the matter of insurance, and it is, indeed, a matter about which few societies trouble themselves. But the time may none the less arise when they might wish they had. There are risks taken in every production against which any prudent business man would protect himself. It should, therefore, be the duty of every secretary to bring these risks to the notice of his committee, and thus at least relieve himself of any personal blame in the event of a claim or a loss arising.

Among the risks that might arise under the heading of insurance are the following: employer's liability; personal injuries to members of the audience; loss through unavoidable cancellation of performances, and loss or damage to scenery or costumes by fire or water.

The Workmen's Compensation Acts ceased to operate from 5th July, 1948, but since many societies employ persons, whether paid producers or stage hands, in the course of production, the liabilities of employers in the matter of injuries suffered by employees must be borne in mind.

An employer has the duty at Common Law to provide a safe work place, safe appliances and a safe system of work. As regards persons under 18, his duties are still higher—he must see that they are properly instructed as to the dangers arising from any risky work, and if necessary, provide competent supervision until they are adequately instructed. If an employee who suffers an injury which he can successfully establish to have been wholly or partly due to the employer's failure to carry out any such duty, his claim against his employer will succeed.

Then comes the question of liability towards members of the audience. The latter are in the position of invitees, and are entitled to look to those responsible for the performance to use reasonable care to prevent injuries arising from any unusual danger which the latter know or ought to know. This duty comprises seeing that the premises are safe, and also that the performance does not involve risk. As regards the former, a visitor can entertain a claim for injury caused by bad lighting, a slippery floor, a defective railing, or a stampede caused by insufficient gangway space. As to the latter, the manager must, for example, provide a tight-rope dancer performing at the head of the audience with a net in case of a fall and must, where firearms are used on the stage, take care as to the loading and the kind of ammunition supplied. An example of a case on the other side of the line occurred where a dancer who was a member of a variety show produced by Elsie and Doris Waters was giving a high kicking performance when the heel of her shoe flew off, hitting someone in the audience. Here no liability was held to attach to the producers because they had no reason to apprehend this danger.

Having dealt with personal injuries to employees and members of the audience, let us consider the risk occasioned by unavoidable cancellation of performances. Such cases have arisen within the knowledge of most of us, and might, of course, arise again. I refer more particularly to cancellation caused by destruction of the theatre by fire, epidemic disease, royal demise, national or local calamity, strike, earthquake, civil commotion, failure of light or power, illness of principals and, lastly, the strike of any sufficient number of members of the company.

All these risks happen suddenly and cannot be avoided, but the loss arising from such contingencies can and should be avoided by insurance, for the loss would be considerable in most cases, and, again, the liability would fall upon those responsible for the production. Insurance can be effected through any insurance broker, and should cover the total estimated expenditure of the production. The takings of any performances that might have already taken place would, of course, have to be deducted from the claim. The rates are naturally somewhat heavy, but if a society is affiliated to a central association such as The National Operatic and Dramatic Association or the British Drama League, which has a specially appointed broker, the rates are considerably less than those quoted in isolated cases.

With regard to open-air performances, galas, pageants, etc., there is always the added risk of loss arising from rain. This risk can also be the subject of insurance, but this class of insurance depends upon the amount of the rainfall, and the premiums vary according to the amount stipulated. The premiums are fairly heavy, and although the rainfall might be sufficient completely to ruin the show it might none the less be insufficient to reach the stipulated amount as recorded by the rain gauge.

Unless there is an express agreement or understanding to that effect a society is not liable as employer for the loss of the belongings of an actor or other person employed by them. In the case of *Deyong & Sherbourne* (1946) an actor claimed the value of an overcoat stolen from the dressing room, but his contention that it was an implied term in his agreement with the producer that the latter should use proper care to safeguard the actor's belongings failed and his claim was dismissed.

A final risk might arise in the case of loss or damage to costumes or scenery by fire or water, and either in the theatre or in transit. Many of the costumiers and scenic artists undertake this risk themselves, either in whole or in part, but care should be taken to see that the risk is set out in the contract for hire of costumes or scenery, and to what extent it covers the risk. It would certainly extend to damage by water occasioned in quelling fire, but probably would not extend to damage occasioned by rain or storm in transit.

In conclusion, it cannot be too emphatically stated that the risks here enumerated are real. All can be covered, and those who are wise will take the prudent course and insure. Those societies affiliated to a central association can obtain fullest particulars and rates of each class of insurance by writing to the official broker, and, as already stated, will be able to acquire terms considerably lower than those usually quoted for insurance against isolated contingencies.

If you are not so affiliated you will be wise to become so without delay, for this in itself is a form of insurance, in that it protects the amateur stage in general and your society in particular. Indeed the saving that would arise from these insurance facilities alone would probably be more than sufficient to pay the annual subscription.

LOTTERIES, LICENCES, LIBEL

I will now concern myself in some detail with the consideration of a few important matters that bear indirectly upon the Amateur Stage, and that occasionally arise in the administration of Operatic and Dramatic Societies.

LOTTERIES

A lottery, sweep, draw, lucky dip, or other ingenious variation is frequently the resort of harassed Committees to make up financial losses on a production or to replenish the depleted treasury after a season's working.

As a general principle, it may be said that all games of chance are illegal. Even games or competitions in which the element of skill may be said to enter would probably be held to be illegal if the element of skill be so remote as to render it a mere guessing competition. The test to be applied to all such cases is whether the particular contest is one in which there is a real and not imaginary element of skill, or whether its solution depends on pure chance.

The law of lotteries is governed by the Betting and Lotteries Act, 1934, which lays it down as a general principle that lotteries are unlawful. The Act creates a number of offences which are punishable either on summary conviction or indictment, the penalties in the former case being a fine of £100 maximum for a first offence and a fine of £200 maximum and/or 3 months imprisonment for a second offence, and in the case of indictment £500 (maximum) fine for a first offence, and £750 fine and/or one year's imprisonment for a second offence. The offences include printing, selling, distributing, or advertising lottery tickets, printing or publishing advertisements of a lottery, using premises or allowing them to be used for the purpose of a lottery.

As we all know, an ordinary sweepstake is illegal, but many promoters fondly imagine that if they announce on the face of the ticket that the money paid is a voluntary contribution to the funds, or that the ticket is a receipt for a subscription, they take their scheme out of the purview of the Act. Again the prize may be a motor-car with a stipulation on the ticket that the winner shall pay one shilling for the car before delivery. Both methods are equally useless.

Other devices, such as the distribution of prizes among members of the audience who occupy certain lucky seats, or who have purchased a numbered programme with a chance of drawing prizes, are all lotteries, and the fact that the prizes have been given and not purchased out of the proceeds makes no difference.

Such devices, however ingenious they may be, would not, in any circumstances, render an otherwise illegal competition legal. The law on the subject, however foolish it may be or however much we may resent it, is not to be defeated by any subterfuges such as these.

From the foregoing it will be seen that the only way to bring a scheme within the law is to see that the solution depends unequivocably upon skill, or, alternatively, to find some exception (referred to in the Act) that may have been authorized by law.

With regard to the first of these alternatives, the following may be suggested as being perfectly legal competitions, namely—

(1) Estimating the number of people attending or paying for admission.

(2) The placing of a given number of persons, posters, plays, etc., in order of popularity.

(3) Arranging a short sentence illustrating a selected word.

(4) Cross-word puzzles (as the law stands at present), but not limericks.

Regarding cross-word puzzles, I have always felt that if these were seriously contested, those where the alternative words run into so many thousands of variations as to reduce the whole thing to a matter of pure chance, would be held to be illegal.

The 1934 Act lays it down that it is an offence to conduct in or through any newspaper, or in connexion with any trade or business or the sale of any article to the public,

(*a*) any competition in which prizes are offered for forecasts of the result either of a future event, or of a past event the result of which is not yet ascertained or not yet generally known;

(*b*) any other competition success in which does not depend to a substantial degree upon the exercise of skill.

One instance under the second alternative is to be found in the Art Unions Act of 1846, which is still in force. That was an Act to protect certain voluntary Associations formed under the name of Art Unions for the purchase of paintings, drawings, or other works of art to be afterwards allotted and distributed, by chance or otherwise, among the several members, subscribers, or contributors forming such Associations, or for raising sums of money by subscription or contributions to be allotted and distributed by chance or otherwise as prizes.

The Act further proceeds to protect such Unions and their members from any offences that might be deemed to come within the provisions of the several Acts of Parliament passed for the prevention of lotteries, and which might render such persons liable to certain pains and penalties imposed by those Acts. It is first necessary that such Associations should obtain a Royal Charter for their incorporation, which is, of course, not always easy, and is certainly somewhat costly. Moreover, the Charter can be withdrawn wherever it shall appear that such Association is perverted for the purposes of this Act. But the Act certainly seems to open possibilities which are not generally known.

There are other specific exceptions allowed by the 1934 Act from the general rule making lotteries illegal. These are

(1) small lotteries incidental to certain entertainments;

(2) private lotteries confined to the members of one society or organization.

As to (1) a lottery which is merely incidental to a bazaar, sale of work, fête, or other entertainment of a similar character is not unlawful provided it complies with the following conditions—

(*a*) the whole proceeds of the entertainment (including the proceeds of the lottery) after deducting—

(i) the expenses of the entertainment, excluding expenses incurred in connexion with the lottery; and

(ii) the expenses incurred in printing tickets in the lottery; and

(iii) such sum not exceeding ten pounds as the promoters think fit to appropriate on account of any expense incurred by them in purchasing prizes, must be devoted to purposes other than private gain;

(*b*) none of the prizes may be money prizes;

(*c*) tickets or chances may not be sold or issued, nor may the result be declared, except on the premises on which the entertainment takes place and during the progress of the entertainment; and

(*d*) the facilities afforded for participating in lotteries may not be the only, or the only substantial, inducement to persons to attend the entertainment.

As to (2) a "private lottery" is not unlawful if it complies with the following conditions—

(*a*) It must be a lottery in Great Britain which is promoted for, and in which the sale of tickets or chances by the promoters is confined to, either—

(i) members of one society established and conducted for purposes not connected with gaming, wagering or lotteries; or

(ii) persons all of whom work on the same premises; or

(iii) persons all of whom reside on the same premises,

and which is promoted by persons each of whom is a person to whom under the foregoing provisions tickets or chances may be sold by the promoters and, in the case of a lottery promoted for the members of a society, is a person authorized in writing by the governing body of the society to promote the lottery.

"Society" includes a club, institution, organization or other association of persons.

(*b*) The whole proceeds, after deducting only expenses incurred for printing and stationery, must be devoted to the provision of prizes for purchasers of tickets or chances. In the case of a lottery promoted for the members of a society, however, they may be devoted either to the provision of prizes as above or to purposes of the society or partly to one and partly to the other;

(*c*) there may not be exhibited, published, or distributed any written notice or advertisement of the lottery other than—

(i) a notice thereof exhibited on the premises of the society for whose members it is promoted or on the premises on which the persons for whom it is promoted work or reside; and

(ii) such announcement or advertisement as is contained in the tickets, (*d*) the price of every ticket or chance shall be the same, and the price of any ticket shall be stated on the ticket;

(*e*) every ticket shall bear upon its face the names and address of each of the promoters, a statement of the persons to whom the sale of tickets or chances by the promoters is restricted; and a statement that no prize won in the lottery shall be paid or delivered by the promoters to any person other than the person to whom the winning ticket or chance was sold by them. No prize shall be paid or delivered except in accordance with that statement;

(*f*) no ticket or chance may be issued or allotted by the promoters except by way of sale and upon receipt of the full price, and no money or valuable thing so received by a promoter may in any circumstances be returned; and

(*g*) no tickets in the lottery may be sent through the post.

Of course the whole question of lotteries frequently depends upon the attitude of the local authorities upon these matters, for many sweepstakes take place all over the country, particularly on the Derby, to which the authorities turn a blind eye, especially when they are promoted in a small way by clubs, institutions, or societies.

But care should be taken in all cases by those promoting any such scheme, for the consequences are unpleasant and the penalties severe.

LIQUOR LICENCES

In all cases in which a special liquor licence is required or an extension of an existing licence for the purpose of any entertainment connected with the activities of an Operatic or Dramatic Society, application can be made to the Local Justices of the town or district in which the premises are situate.

If the premises are already licensed, the application will be for an extension of the existing licence beyond the permitted hours. If the premises are not licensed at all, the application is for an occasional licence to cover the time required by the occasion. No special form of notice is required other than a letter to the Superintendent of Police for the district, giving notice of the intention to make the application, setting out the name and address of the applicant, and the place and occasion in respect of which the licence is required. The Magistrates' official consent to the application must be forwarded to the collector of Customs and Excise with the necessary remittance, in most cases 10s. a day.

Such licences as these are readily obtainable as a rule, but the application should be made at least a week before it is actually required, so as to give time for the necessary regulations to be observed.

UNIFORMS ON THE STAGE

By the Uniforms Act, 1894, it is enacted as follows—

It shall not be lawful for any person not serving in His Majesty's Military Forces to wear without His Majesty's permission the uniform of any of those forces or any dress having the appearance or bearing any of the regimental or other distinctive marks of any such uniform.

By Section 2 (1) of the Act it is provided that this enactment shall not prevent any person from wearing any uniform or dress in the course of any stage play performed in any place duly licensed or authorized for the public performance of such plays, or in the course of a musical or circus performance, or in the course of a bona fide military representation.

The Act itself is of course designed to prevent His Majesty's uniform being brought into contempt or ridicule, but the special provisions of Section 2, as will be noted, exempt all stage productions in premises duly licensed for the production of stage plays.

By the Police Act, 1919, a similar provision is made with regard to the uniforms of the Police.

LICENSING OF PLAYS

New plays and additions to old ones must be submitted to the Lord Chamberlain for his approval before being acted for hire in any theatre.

In the case of a play which has not been so licensed, a penalty of £50 may be imposed on any person who for hire acts or presents a part or causes it to be acted or presented, and the theatre licence is also liable to be revoked or suspended. (Here again a charge for admission or the sale of liquor brings the provision into force.)

It is not a defence that the person charged was not personally present at the performance.

The unauthorized introduction by a performer into a licensed play of some extra expression or "gag" does not of itself turn the play into an unlicensed play so as to make the person presenting the play liable to be prosecuted.

THE LAW OF LIBEL

Actors and others responsible for performances to which the public are admitted are in a different position from ordinary private persons so far as action for defamation is concerned. They are placed somewhat similarly to people who are actively engaged in politics or other public walks of life. Anyone who goes on the stage may be freely criticized, and the actor has no right of action however unjust or severe or inaccurate the criticism may be so long as the critic is giving honest expression to his views and not indulging in abuse under the cloak of criticism. It matters not whether the criticism is made in the Press or by members of the audience in the theatre. So far as the latter is concerned, however, while members of the audience have the right to express their disapproval of a performance by hissing, they must not make such a noise as to prevent others from hearing what is going on on the stage. If two or more persons go to the theatre with the intention of hissing, they may be liable for a conspiracy, and if three or more persons so act in combination, it may amount to a disorder or a riot.

It is always open to an actor who can establish that criticism is malevolent or exceeding the bounds of fair opinion to take action for defamation, for in that case the defendent will be unable to rely on the defence of "fair comment."

Again, no one has a right to attack the private character or private life of an actor under the guise of fair comment, since these are not matters of public interest.

So far as the actor's position *vis-à-vis* the producer and the manager of the performance is concerned, the printing of the names of actors on the playbill in the wrong order has been held sometimes to be a ground for claiming damages for defamation.

CONTRACTS

The law relating to contracts is, of course, a comprehensive subject, but one that frequently arises in the administration of Operatic and Dramatic Societies.

Certain contracts must be under seal, but as these are hardly within my scope for present purposes I will confine consideration of the subject to those termed "simple contracts," such as those for the engagement of a producer, hire of costumes or scenery, or for the use of a theatre, as distinguished from contracts under seal.

It is not absolutely essential, except in certain cases with which we are not concerned, that the contract should be in writing, but since it might not always be easy to produce evidence of actual agreement between the parties by parole evidence, the prudent secretary will see to it that all his contracts are reduced to writing, which will thus provide evidence of the actual terms of the agreement.

It should be noted that in all the forms of simple contract with which we are likely to be concerned, there must be some consideration, present or future, for the services to be rendered, for a contract without consideration is absolutely void unless it is made under seal.

Again, all contracts, simple or otherwise, are void if the consideration specified is for services that are illegal, immoral, or unreasonable.

For our purpose the word "consideration" means a monetary consideration, although it need not always be so; for instance, a promise to marry is valid consideration, and also a gift to wife or child, in which the consideration is "natural love and affection."

We will now consider contracts from the point of view of an offer made and an acceptance received. A contract with these requirements observed is actionable if it is broken by one party against the other. Every contract involves two parties, that is the promiser and the promisee, and there must be an expression of common intention reduceable to a simple matter of offer and acceptance, for every contract springs from the initial acceptance of an offer. For instance, a producer says in effect: "I will produce your show for an inclusive fee of 50 guineas." In reply to that you say "I will accept your offer of 50 guineas to produce our show." That forms a contract, whether in writing or not, but as I have pointed out, it is desirable that it should always be reduced to writing.

In practice, of course, it must extend further than just the offer and the acceptance; that is to say, it must specify the actual dates and times of production, and any special conditions agreed between the parties.

The contract may arise from correspondence, which is all-sufficient to prove a contract, although, of course, such letters should be stamped with the necessary stamp duty, which is usually 6d.

Both parties are then bound equally to carry out their obligations, even though the terms are by way of correspondence and not reduced to legal terminology. It must be noted that in cases of contracts the terms should be unambiguous so as to exclude differences of opinion as to the intentions of the parties nor must there be any conditions that have not been definitely accepted, otherwise it may be impossible to show that the parties have made any contract at all.

Further, it must be quite clear that the acceptance of an offer made is complete, either by a legal form of agreement or by correspondence, or by some overt act or words spoken, which are evidence of an intention to accept. This rule of law is clearly defined in a judgment of Lord Justice Bowen, in a well-known case in the following terms—

> One cannot doubt that, as an ordinary rule of law, an acceptance of an offer made ought to be notified to the person who made the offer, in order that the two minds may come together. Unless this is so the two minds may be apart, and there is not that consensus which is necessary according to the rules of English law to make a contract. But there is this clear gloss to be made upon that doctrine that as notification of acceptance is required for the benefit of the person who makes the offer, the person who makes the offer may dispense with notice to himself if he thinks it desirable to do so; and I suppose there can be no doubt that where a person in an offer made by him to another person expressly or impliedly intimates a particular mode of acceptance as sufficient to make the bargain binding, it is only necessary for the other person to whom such offer is made to follow the indicated mode of acceptance; and, if the person making the offer expressly or impliedly intimates in his offer that it will be sufficient to act on the proposal without communicating acceptance of it to himself, performance of the condition is a sufficient acceptance without notification.

In all cases in which an acceptance of an offer is made by post the offer remains open and cannot be avoided until the receipt of the acceptance in the ordinary course of post, although this rule would not necessarily apply in cases where inevitable delay has occurred. But such cases would be rare in these days, and would, of course, depend in each case upon the merits or circumstances.

But it is an undeniable principle of the law of contract that an offer of a bargain by one person to another imposes no obligation upon the former until it is accepted by the latter according to the terms in which the offer was made. Any qualification of or departure from these terms invalidates the offer unless it be agreed to by the person who made it; therefore acceptance must be absolute and must correspond in every respect with the terms of the offer.

With regard particularly to contracts for the hire of scenery or costumes, so far as the amateur stage is concerned, or at least so far as those societies affiliated to the National Operatic and Dramatic Association are concerned, these have been rendered very much easier by the adoption of a simple form of agreement approved by the National Association on one side and the Theatrical Traders' Association on the other. When this form is in general use all that will be needed after agreement to the terms will be to fill in the necessary details.

The contract also provides for various forms of insurance and other matters not usually thought of by the society.

Theatre contracts must of necessity vary. In some cases the contract provides for the hire of a theatre or a hall, whereas in others the contract is based on the usual professional form of taking the theatre on a percentage basis.

In the former case the observations regarding contracts generally will apply.

In the latter case the theatre proprietor usually has a printed form, which sets out the terms and conditions of the contract. These printed forms usually contain the following conditions—

1. The name and dates of the production.
2. The rate of percentage to the theatre and the company respectively.
3. The theatre to provide usual lighting, band, working staff, one set of daybills, usual newspaper advertisements, etc.
4. The society to provide the production and full and efficient company, including musical director; to pay authors' and composers' fees and

to provide scenery, costumes, pictorial and letterpress printing.

5. No understudy or deputy to be permitted except for good and sufficient cause.

6. A barring clause not to appear within a certain radius, if insisted upon.

7. The agreement to be null and void in the event of the theatre being closed in consequence of any public calamity, royal demise, epidemic, fire, or act of God, or any cause whatsoever not within the power of, or occasioned by, the proprietors.

8. *Matinées* not to be curtailed but given fully as at night.

9. No children shall perform without special licences as provided by Act of Parliament.

10. A schedule of printing required to be provided by the society.

Any other conditions that may be peculiar to the circumstances of an amateur society should also be inserted, for it cannot be too clearly emphasized that although these theatre contracts are stereotyped documents their use is by no means a mere matter of form, and each condition should be studied carefully and considered in the light of its effect upon the society, for any disputes that might arise afterwards may lead to serious consequences.

Happily, disputes of this nature are rare, and, as a rule, can be adjusted by arbitration. But the careful secretary will see that his contract leaves no ambiguity.

Shelburne Studios

Robert Nesbitt

STAGE LIGHTING

FREDERICK BENTHAM, Inventor of the Light Console. Author of "Stage Lighting"

INTRODUCTION

ROBERT NESBITT

THE literature of the stage, producers, actors, perhaps in a lesser degree playwrights, and the relatively non-critical members of theatrical audiences tend increasingly to exaggerate the undoubted importance of stage lighting. My theory is that stage lighting, admittedly an essential component of modern theatrical presentation, is but a part, and as such it should never be used to overpower other indispensable and effective components.

What are the purposes of stage lighting? Ask specialists in the theatre this question, and their replies are certain to vary according to their line of specialization. The experimenter who wishes to exploit its potentialities to get the maximum amount of theatrical effect from the standpoint of spectacle will, in all probability, hold different opinions on relative values from those held by the man who insists that "the play's the thing," and, therefore, is capable of holding the attention of an audience without the aid of scenic and lighting effects.

The history of stage lighting is the story of development from the primitive to the complex; of the harnessing of scientific knowledge to theatrical purposes. The modern trend, most significantly, is away from the overall lighting provided by magazine battens and lengths. This is recognized. It can, I think, be enforced by recalling salient points of my own productions.

It will be noted in my productions that the principal lighting is derived from high-power sources, my design being to ensure that magazine battens play only a subsidiary part. These sources, 1,000–2,000 watts, except for cyclorama work, are rarely open floods, but acting area floods, pageant lanterns, and mirror spots in which concentrated beams with relatively sharp edges and without stray lights are produced.

Additional details will be illuminating.

Acting area floods, as at the London Coliseum, hang in rows over the stage, and even over the orchestra, to provide for the apron—that all-important first nine feet down stage. Front lighting, from the circle battery, is by mirror spotlights. These are used almost as floods, but the optical system ensures accuracy in focusing the light clear of backcloths, cyclorama, and auditorium. Often this circle battery makes it possible to dispense with footlights. For side-lighting relief I use pageant lanterns and 2 kW. soft-edge spots in the sides of the auditorium; also back stage as vertical boomerangs each with several lanterns in the wings. With this equipment I can light, with high intensity, specific areas of the stage and simultaneously leave other areas dark, contrast colour with colour, and thus secure an interesting pattern of highlights and shadows, expressive control of the light rays being a considerable aid to "atmosphere."

One pertinent and practical point should, I think, be emphasized.

Lanterns should not be located permanently. Notwithstanding the large number I have installed at various theatres, I rearrange them for each production in accordance with my conception of the requirements of the scenery and grouping which I consider to be the inescapable essentials. This means practical and artistic planning. I plan the lighting ahead, and the layout is conditioned by the production, which I think of as primary. In other words, the installation does not dictate how the lighting shall be planned. The result is that I seldom employ three-colour lighting equipment on the cyclorama. If only a blue sky is required, it is pointless to introduce banks of floods in three colours to use up available hanging space and to increase expenditure. Some people find irresistible the temptation to manipulate colour for the sheer sake of manipulation. Colour lighting and modern stage lighting are not synonymous terms. Colour must be kept in its proper place and used discreetly, or it becomes tedious and makes for monotony. The main contribution, in my opinion, should be made by the pale tints such as 36 *Surprise Pink or* 50 *to* 54 *Pale Golds. Rich colour light becomes increasingly effective in inverse proportion to the frequency of its use.*

Control is also of the greatest importance.

The value of the most elaborate combination of lighting equipment can be heavily depreciated by difficulties of control. A direct operated switchboard can be 20 *ft. or more long. As it is obviously unwieldy to work, and impossible to place satisfactorily, it is not surprising that expert ingenuity has been exercised to produce a thoroughly satisfactory alternative. It is of course, the Light Console which I am pleased to be able to claim I was the first to use.*

As the producer of many London Palladium and other big musical shows, I can testify to the advantages of having a lighting system literally under the operator's fingers. From his vantage point he (*or she*) *sees the stage as the audience sees it—this is of immense practical value. Association here introduces the name of Frederick Bentham, the author of the special articles on Stage Lighting published in this edition of* THEATRE AND STAGE.

Mr. Bentham invented the Light Console—after the most exacting and concentrated work. His position in the Research Department of the Strand Electric Co., Ltd., has enabled him to take full advantage of scientific experiments carried out by him and his colleagues. It is not surprising, therefore, that he has been responsible for many new designs, including Mirror Spots, Pageant Lanterns, and Acting Areas. Mr. Bentham has additional qualifications to express, authoritatively, opinions on modern stage lighting. He is engineer, designer, artist. He has worked with me at the London Palladium when the total connected load has been 1,800 *amperes. Contrast this with the example furnished by him in his treatment of "Comparative Examples of Stage Layouts" in which he refers to an installation with a total of only* 15 *amperes. But although Mr. Bentham is expert and pioneer alike, emphatically he is not a faddist. He begins by stressing the importance of an appropriate building in which to perform. He is aware of the developments in modern apparatus and of the increase in the variety and scope for which research and modern manufacturing processes are responsible. He is broad-minded in his attitude towards stage lighting. He tells what can be done with modern stage lighting, and states the basic principles that must be applied to secure the best results, taking into account, however, the human element which precludes infallibility but which is assisted to make ever nearer approaches to perfection by the simplification of apparatus and equipment. Personal taste is reflected in specific aims and the methods by which it is sought to realize them.*

Mr. Bentham in his systematic presentation of the principles of stage lighting and the possibilities of their application takes into consideration modern tendencies, stimulates interest, and furnishes practical guidance on how to make the most of lighting in the theatre, irrespective of whether the workers in it are primarily concerned with opera, ballet, musical, straight, propaganda, documentary, or any other type of play.

Robert Nesbitt

AUTHOR'S NOTE. *When Harold Ridge and F. S. Aldred wrote on "Modern Stage Lighting" in the first edition of* THEATRE AND STAGE *they were practising as independent consulting stage lighting engineers. They have retired, and, as far as I am aware, they have no successors, the stage lighting engineers that I know being associated with commercial firms. I myself have spent sixteen years in the Research Department of The Strand Electric and Engineering Co., and, perhaps inevitably, my opinions on stage apparatus have been, are, and will be incorporated, directly and indirectly, in the Company's range of apparatus. All the photographs reproduced to illustrate my articles are of Strand Electric models, except where otherwise acknowledged, but the opinions expressed are my own. The use of apparatus and the ways in which they may be combined as an installation, etc., must be a matter of personal evaluation and not commercial policy. Further, each of my opinions is just as likely to create either agreement or disagreement among specialists either inside or outside that firm. This much I think it is desirable to state in the interests of both honesty and clarity, as, in present circumstances, it is unlikely that the exposition of any specialist in this field could be completely independent.*

AUDITORIA AND STAGES

STAGE lighting must, unlike other forms of lighting, conceal more than it reveals. One piece of scenery lit by a spotlight may appear as a complete setting; one piece of scenery lit by a general flood of light from footlights and battens will certainly appear as one piece of scenery.

FREDERICK BENTHAM

The would-be stage lighting artist, amateur or professional, is well advised not to restrict his lighting activities to the stage. One difficulty is to obtain sufficient practice in the art in order to get the feel of lighting so that thoughts and emotions find ready expression. If the stage is looked upon as the only place where any form of practice is obtained, then usually, either the stage is kept waiting while the artist experiments or he will be too polite and have to curb his ideas.

We should take a poor view of the actor who had not troubled to prepare his part before arriving at rehearsal. What would be said to the musician who arrived with only the faintest notion of the technique of his instrument? Yet the blunderings that go on, even in professional circles, when the lighting rehearsal takes place are extraordinary. Granted that the set is being lit for the first time, that the stage may be strange and the switchboard out of sight in the wings; the fact remains that there is no excuse for lack of knowledge of what happens when two colours mix additively or subtractively, or of the light distribution and intensity that may reasonably be expected from a particular piece of lighting equipment.

The mystery that surrounds colour mixing and the effect of colour on colour can be broken by a few simple experiments made at home. The feel of plastic or directional lighting can be obtained by moving two or three 100-watt lamps in boxes, from one position to another, lighting trees and bushes in the garden. The effects of light of all kinds—the sky, the sun through the trees—should be observed in much the same way as the painter observes them. Inspiration is far more likely to come from outside, than inside, the theatre.

A model theatre is an unrivalled aid to proficiency. Every lighting artist should have one. With its aid, unlimited practice and experiment can take place in private. Here lighting can be related to experimental sets, curtains, and cyclorama as an end in itself and not merely to the prospective production at the theatre. The man whose task it is to light a series of chamber sets can seek wider horizons in his model theatre.

The accompaniment of suitable music by changes of lighting on dimmers (colour music), variations on curtains, or on a suitable setting, not only helps one to think in light and to mix one's colours instinctively, but also to engage in a most satisfying pastime. Another useful exercise can be performed to a radio performance of any Shakespeare play. One is able to prepare a suitable permanent set with variations and lighting layout in advance. As the play proceeds along its course, which because of cuts is an unpredictable one, each scene has to be set and lit on the instant.

MODEL THEATRE

Unlike many other experts, I hold that the lighting of a model theatre should be a miniature of the full-size theatre in layout, though not in the actual lanterns used. For a proscenium opening of twenty-four inches a low voltage of 6 volts from a transformer is suitable. A little skill and ingenuity can provide floods, spots, and battens, which, though not furnished with scale exteriors, provide scale lighting. For dimming, 6- and 16-ohm wireless rheostats are ideal. This is not mere theory: at one time I possessed a model theatre the homemade switchboard of which contained eighty-seven dimmers complete with electrical master-dimming. It began as a theatre with only three dimmers! The scene designer is not ashamed of his models. Let's have no more: "Try an 8—make it a 4—no! What about a 3? Yes! make it a 36!'

The lighting artist, aided by my treatment of the subject and more especially by his own practice, will be able to enter the theatre or hall equipped to think in terms of light, but there will still be the snag of electricity. It is more than likely that readers will be unable to develop an interest in 3-phase, 50-cycle supplies, balancing, earthing, etc., and yet lighting ideals have to be reconciled with the laws of electricity before they can be put into practice.

Generally, authors in dealing with the subject begin their exposition with a simplified description of the various components and processes in a direct current (D.C.) circuit, most of which lend themselves to simple description. However, alternating current (A.C.) has almost completely replaced D.C., except for a few specialized applications. Alternating current is far more convenient for practical distribution, but not, unfortunately, for simplified description. The adage about a little knowledge has pertinence in these days of high voltage (230-400) A.C., as a mistake in the temporary connexions to a lantern may lead to a serious, even fatal, shock. The days when completely unskilled amateurs could construct their own dimmers out of drain-pipes filled with washing soda are gone. My intention is not to contend that only qualified electricians can take part in the art of stage lighting but to stress the need for every amateur society to enrol a qualified man to oversee its electrical activities, for there are men with the necessary technical experience who are willing to make their contribution. Most stage productions employ a considerable quantity of temporary wiring, and it is common sense to ensure that it is carried out in a safe manner. Assuming the presence of a knowledgeable electrician, amateur or professional, in the background, I do not propose to explain electrical terms and I shall use the minimum consistent with clarity.

LIGHTING EQUIPMENT

The story of the lighting equipment will be found to develop naturally from the lamps commercially obtainable, through the means of controlling them optically and electrically, thence to their application to particular stages and to effects. As the stage is a limited market, it is seldom possible to begin with the effect required and to work back to a special lamp. Throughout the short history of stage lighting it is seen that this order is imposed. It was impossible until comparatively recently to project a beam of light, intensity being obtained by repetition of low-power sources. A line of these at the front edge of the stage with vertical rows behind the wings (lengths) and horizontal rows (battens) behind the overhead borders, originated during oil days, persisted in gas days, and even later when electricity gained acceptance. Footlights, battens, and lengths then became hallowed by tradition. Indeed, the Russian Ballet at Covent Garden Opera House just before the Second Great War, in spite of lavish equipment, preferred to rely on lighting that departed very little from the tradition imposed by small source battens and footlights, a fault which, happily, was not repeated by the Sadler's Wells Company on the same stage. With this form of lighting the aim could be only an evenly lighted, shadowless stage, shadows and perspective being painted on the flat scenery. Spectacular results were obtained by this use of perspective, though the whole set could have looked "right" from only one seat—that of The Patron.

SCENE-CHANGING

It is interesting to speculate whether the horizontal lines of flat cloths, cut cloths, borders, wings, etc., were the result of the methods of lighting that were adopted or were dictated by the need for an easy method of changing the scene. In any case the principal method of scene-changing, with horizontal rows of scene battens and grid, is basically the same to-day as it was then. Unless care is exercised, this pattern is imposed, willy-nilly, on the lighting equipment. About the only equipment one can be certain of finding in any theatre is a grid with its complement of scenery and lighting battens, plus the footlight.

Aggravating is the way borders, and consequently battens, still appear in halls, even where there is no scenery grid, or the slightest chance of flying scenery owing to the lack of height. The excuse often made is that of sight lines, but a lot of the trouble is caused by the commercial firms that supply stage-lighting equipment. Of two to-day, one began as a supplier of West End theatres, the other as a specialist in colour lighting of cinema stages. Both have expanded their practice, but in so far as a firm can be said to have a style their origins are betrayed in their work and ideas. The tendency has, therefore, been to regard amateur installations as a kind of reach-me-down version of the commercial stage, either legitimate theatre or cinema. Naturally, amateurs and little theatres with little money to spend have found themselves with an installation based on the commercial irreducible minimum: magazine footlight and battens together with a dimmer board, or even an absurdity such as two battens, a footlight, and no dimmers, funds having run out. Such installations represent a considerable expenditure of money. Similarly, switch and dimmer boards have been unsatisfactory, employing cut-down versions of the framework and shafting of larger boards. However, apparatus designed especially for the amateur is becoming available.

If the lighting apparatus of pre-War days was unsatisfactory, what of the halls in which amateurs were (and are!) expected to perform? Although such torments are familiar I must refer to the hall in which, before turning professional, I obtained my first experience. It seated 400 on a flat floor; the acoustics and sight lines could scarcely have been worse. Not only was there no wing space, but also the walls angled in, reducing the available stage width up-stage. No height above the proscenium was provided, and what height there was, was reduced by the interposition of a low ceiling over the last third of the stage's depth. The footlight and batten were switched on on opposite sides of the stage! Concerted action by all the amateur societies in the neighbourhood, after many years' agitation, resulted in modification.

Reduction in height up-stage, involving the rear wall, is common, as is the occupation of valuable wing space by a pair of rooms labelled "Dressing Rooms." The stage in a modern town hall (1,000 seats), completed just before the War, is spoiled by a first-floor passage bracketed out from the rear stage wall.

REAR STAGE WALL

Heating pipes and radiators seem to be introduced at the first opportunity. When a new hall is being built, a constant vigil is necessary to ensure that the rear stage wall is free of doors, panelling, hot-water pipes, ventilation trunking, electric conduit, etc. A rear wall unadorned can be plastered and given a finish of matt white distemper, and thus become a cyclorama. Happy indeed is the company that works in a hall with such a cyclorama rear wall!

Many stages are ruined by antagonistic roofing. Irrespective of flying scenery, it is important for sufficient height to be available to get the lighting equipment out of the way. A "pitched" roof, unless the side walls are built unusually high, will cut down the scenery wings and borders at the very point where the demands of sight lines insist on extra height. Tricky enough where the slope is across the stage, these things are made even worse when a third slope is formed by the roof from the back wall. It is incredible that any one should make such a mistake, but within twenty minutes' walk of where I write there is a social hall with just this fault.

It is difficult to get an architect to understand that the stage is a workshop demanding standards of finish quite different from the rest of the hall. Where, as is often the case, the stage is required for ceremonial purposes or for concerts, a suitable setting must hide the workshop. Curtains, light movable panels, etc., can easily form a temporary background dignified enough for the Mayor, Brigadier X, and other personalities at the prize-giving.

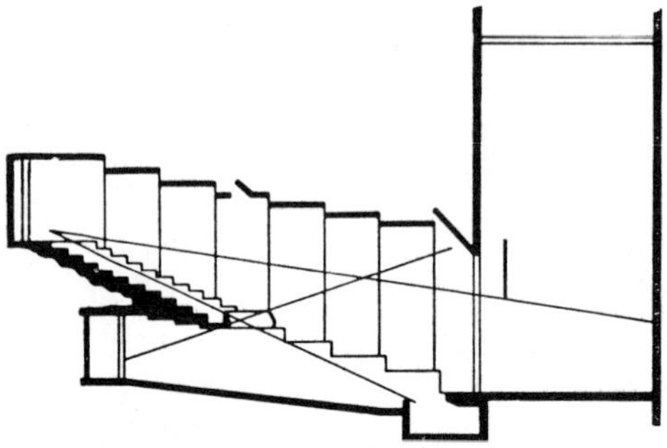

FIG. 1. SECTION SINGLE TIER AUDITORIUM

Stage design apart, halls are commonly spoilt for the production of plays by being expected to double the part of a dance hall. The flat floor is thoroughly unsuitable: unacceptable sight lines and acoustics are the result. The alternative to the multi-purpose hall is usually conceived as a concert-dance hall with a separate theatre. For the provision of this, with few exceptions, whether at the civic centre or the village community centre, funds are not available. The real solution lies in providing one hall, to serve both music and the drama, with properly stepped seating, and an adjoining exhibition gallery, with a flat dance floor. Dancing in a fine room with the walls hung with pictures comprising current exhibitions is not only possible but also a delightful way of introducing art to people who might not otherwise see it. Two lofty halls with elaborate seating, etc., are thus avoided, and additional time for rehearsal may be allocated to productions in the main hall: production in the most lavishly equipped theatre can be robbed of pleasure and effectiveness if there has not been adequate time to rehearse on the actual stage. The absolute minimum is two rehearsal nights, the first to fit up scenery and lighting and to rehearse the changes; the second for a full-dress rehearsal.

Amateurs reflecting on the shortcomings of the halls in which they find themselves are often liable to say: "If only we had a real theatre!" Too often the glamour that surrounds the professional theatre, the West End, obscures their defects, about which, in my opinion, we are too tolerant. The older theatres are seen through a haze of tradition. The fact that Garrick walked the boards excuses a grid that will not fly scenery without tumbling. No amount of historic association is adequate compensation for bad sight lines and acoustics. On the other hand, some find merit in a theatre simply because it is relatively new. The so-called *modern* theatre often provides a stage just as cramped as that of an older theatre, and auditorium sight lines that represent very little improvement. Often the main difference is a padded seat and a doubled price for pit and gallery. While reducing the number of circle tiers from three or four to two, the commercial theatre demands increased seating capacity and the modern deep circle is the result. The angle from the upper circle is steep, and the back rows are a long way from the stage. In order to make the expensive theatre site pay, perhaps twice as many seats are required than the site can carry if the show is to be the thing.

A concert hall where only half the orchestra could be heard properly would not pass without criticism, yet commonly in the theatre only two-thirds of the audience get a satisfactory view of the stage and less than one half a good view. The high value of West End sites seems to me to provide an excellent reason for more theatres in the suburbs. Suburban theatres might be municipally owned, for—why should local authorities restrict their activities to music and dancing? A good theatre is just as important as a public park or library. It will be found that seating roughly 1,000, a stalls floor and one circle, in conjunction with a 30 ft. proscenium opening, are the limit for good sight lines (Fig. 1). The proscenium opening is important, 30 ft. for drama, but at least 40 ft. for opera and ballet. The Sadler's Wells

Ballet at the New Theatre during the Second Great War provided a fine example of the limitations imposed by a small stage, and the orchestra overflowed into the stage boxes. It is commonly suggested that any State or municipally-subsidized theatre is unnecessary. The truth is that the site and building for a theatre, democratically designed to give everyone a good view, is so expensive that it constitutes an impossible dead weight—hence the present-day cramped, overloaded site.

Looking over the plans of a number of modern theatres, I have come to the conclusion that the architect often overlooks the fact that his high proscenium arch is much reduced by masking. The design may show 26 ft. to the arch or 22 ft. to the underside of the pelmet, but this invariably has to be reduced by a proscenium border or false proscenium to about 16 ft. at the most. Immediately, most of the backcloth is cut off from the view of the upper circle (Fig. 2).

The mounting and launching of a play demand sufficient financial outlay without involving also the incubus of a theatre. The municipal park is not expected to show a profit in £ s. d.; why, then, should the theatre building?

The trend in monopoly conditions in the commercial theatre suggests another reason for municipal competition. Grant the logic of a municipal theatre, then let it be properly designed, making sure that the current production does not use a cyclorama because it does not require one and not because there isn't one: that the mounting and lighting of the play meet aesthetic considerations and are not imposed by physical limitations. It will be found that needs are modest, and that the ideal civic theatre does not resemble the Red Army Theatre, Moscow, the Paris Opera House, or the Radio City Music Hall, New York.

However, speculation is not my province except in so far as I shall have constantly to show that stage lighting is not a subject that can be studied in isolation. Stage lighting is inextricably bound up with the building, the play, the scenery, the actors: in a word—"the show."

LAMPS

The electric lamp is a device for turning electric power into light. This is obvious, but what is often not realized is that the electric lamp so far devised is inefficient. Almost all the power supplied to an electric motor is turned into motion and to an electric fire into heat: in the electric lamp less than 2 per cent of the energy is converted to light; the rest becomes heat, the presence of which explains the bulky lamphouses and large bulbs used in the theatre. Many theatre

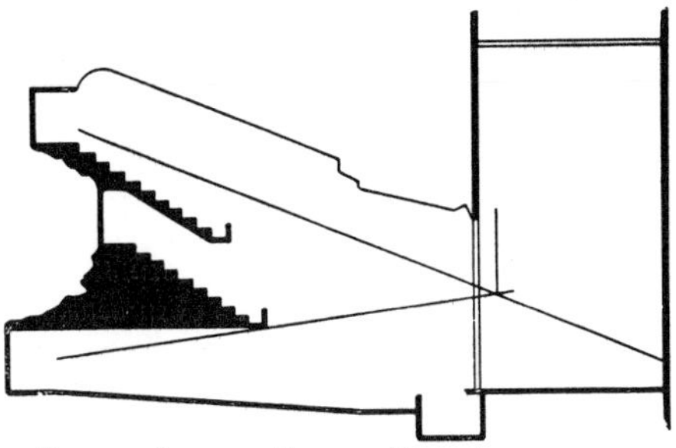

FIG. 2. SECTION DOUBLE TIER AUDITORIUM

people seem to think this bulk is the result of carelessness or oversight by the designer. "If you can produce the light of a 1,000-watt spot from a small lantern the size of a 100-watt spot, then you will have got something!" This production is possible to-day, but it brings limitations that nullify any advantage gained: short life of lamp, one burning position, and so on.

Which lamp to employ for a particular purpose is fundamental for the designer of stage lighting equipment. What is not obvious is the importance of choice to the buyer and user of the equipment. If funds will permit replacement of a lamp only once every 1,000 hours, then to buy a lantern requiring a high efficiency lamp with an official life of 100 hours, however tempting the demonstration may be, will be absurd—hence my general treatment of lamps and their characteristics.

ELECTRICAL TERMS

The various electro-technical terms used must be fully understood. The one without which it is impossible to think in stage lighting is *watts*. Lamps, lanterns, and dimmers are referred to as of so many watts. Briefly, the watt is the term that covers the power consumed in an electric circuit at any moment. A 1,000-watt fire or lamp consumes ten times the power of a 100-watt lamp; and if a circuit consuming 1,000 watts is kept alive for one hour, then the result is a power consumption of one Board of Trade unit. The unit—1,000 watts for one hour—(one kilowatt hour) is what registers on the company's meter.

The power (watts) in a circuit is the product of electricity of certain pressure (volts) flowing at a certain rate (amperes). The pressure in volts is highly important. When lamps and dimmers are ordered the voltage needs to be given. Usual voltages for lighting are 200, 210, 220, 230, 240, and 250; of these, 230 and 240 are the commonest, 230 being the official standard. Even voltages of 100 and 110 are not uncommon.

VOLTAGES

It may be asked: What useful purpose do all these voltages serve in this small country? The answer is : They are far from useful, and are a legacy from the innumerable small supply undertakings of early days. Just as the main line railways had to standardize on one track and loading gauge, so there is need for the standardization of supply companies' voltage which, ultimately, will be 230. Much lower voltages, such as 12 or 6 for car lighting, are common for special purposes. The lower the voltage, the higher the current in amperes, however, and amperes dictate the size of wiring and its accessories. A 100-watt 6-volt lamp needs a much heavier flex than a 100-watt 200-volt lamp: the former takes a current of nearly 17 amperes, the latter only half an ampere. This effect being so marked, even with such small wattages, it is not surprising that where large loads have to be fed from a power station at a distance, every opportunity is taken to raise the voltage, and thereby to reduce the amperes and the size of cables. Transforming of electricity from one voltage to another, like its generation, requires motion which is supplied by an electric motor rotating a dynamo. This arrangement is costly, cumbersome, and, incidentally, noisy, so the motion is nowadays applied to the electricity itself—hence alternating current, which has now almost completely supplanted direct current, except for specific uses.

Direct current (D.C.) gives a continuous flow from the positive terminal to the negative; in alternating current (A.C.) the direction of flow is reversed, generally 50 times a second (50 cycles), in so accurate a manner that it can be used to drive a clock without an escapement motion. Static devices are now easily possible to convert high voltage low current to low voltage high current, whenever required. These devices are known as *transformers*.

Some metals, such as silver and copper, conduct electricity well, and are known as *conductors*. A wire of a good conductor will offer resistance to the passage of the electricity if it is of insufficient diameter to carry the requisite amperes. The energy absorbed, which depends on the length of the wire, is converted into heat. Where this is done intentionally, wires of low conductivity, such as iron or nickel chrome, are used to keep the length of wire short. Materials such as rubber, paper, porcelain, and bakelite do not conduct electricity, and are known as *insulators*.

An electric circuit must always consist of a complete loop so that the current can return to the battery or dynamo whence it came.

The source of light in the common lamp is a resistance in the shape of a filament of fine tungsten wire heated to white heat, in which 94 per cent of the energy emitted represents heat and the remainder light. To prevent oxygen in the air which is necessary for combustion, reaching the filament, a glass bulb from which the air has been exhausted (the vacuum lamp) encloses the filament, which, running at high temperature, gradually evaporates and is deposited on the bulb. This becomes noticeable as blackening on the bulb. Simultaneously the thinner filament carries less current, and gives less and less light until the filament fails altogether.

GAS-FILLED LAMPS

The higher the temperature at which the filament is run, the better the efficiency of the lamp and the whiter the light emitted. To slow down the evaporation of the filament and to enable it to run at the higher temperatures, the bulb is filled with an inert gas (usually nitrogen), which provides some obstruction to the molecules that leave the filament. These gas-filled lamps are easily recognized by their whiter light; the energy emitted is 8 per cent of the light. Filament temperature is related to the thickness of the filament and benefits lamps of a high wattage. Thus, a lamp of 1,000 watts will not give ten times the light of a 100-watt lamp, as one might suppose from the power used, but fourteen times owing to its greater efficiency. Moreover, the light is whiter.

Efficiency, therefore, is not merely a matter for the engineer, but also of importance in so far as quality and colour of light are concerned to the stage lighting expert. Such efficiency is expressed as *lumens* (a unit of light) per watt (L/W). A lamp with an efficiency of 19 L/W is a lamp plus when compared with one that gives 12 L/W only, these being the efficiency figures for a 1,000-watt and a 100-watt lamp respectively. All lamps, gas-filled or vacuum, suffer a diminution of light output with age, their light changing from white to yellow. The makers, therefore, give a life figure in hours during which the deterioration is not pronounced; in the case of domestic lamps or general service lamps it is 1,000 hours. It is possible to use a lamp beyond this period, maybe for years, but to do so is not a matter for self-congratulation. Such a lamp gives a travesty of white light, and when it is used behind blue filters practically no light may be emitted for the power expended. Lamps in the blue circuits are the most critical. The practice of waiting for a lamp to fail before replacing it, is shortsighted. Many installations for which new apparatus is contemplated require only a good clean and a new set of lamps.

More light may be obtained from lamps for special purposes by running the filaments at a higher temperature and rating them as short life, sometimes as low as fifty hours or less. Combined with this is an increase of efficiency obtained by bunching the filament close together so that it becomes almost a solid source of light. The bulb may also be shaped in such a way that optical lenses and reflectors can be brought close to the filament. The bulb, particularly at the point where it is cemented to the lamp cap, is vulnerable to heat, and the condition is aggravated when the lamp is suspended cap up. To keep this part as cool as possible, a long neck and mica baffles are needed in the larger wattage lamps (Fig. 3). If, then, a lamp is designed without a long neck in order to be compact, it follows that there must be a prohibition on burning cap up (Fig. 4). Similarly, a lamp with a narrow tubular bulb (Fig. 5) can be burnt only vertically cap down; otherwise a blister will form on the part of the glass wall nearest and over the filament.

LAMP CAPS

The lamp cap serves two purposes: (1) to supply current, often considerable, to the filament; and (2) to provide a rigid fixing for the lamp. Because of the second reason even small lamps on the stage are not fitted with the bayonet cap-holder common in the home, as the spring contacts of this holder allow too much wobble. A range of screw holders is used to allow the lamp to be held firmly. These holders are known as Edison screws, and are made in various sizes: Miniature Edison Screw (M.E.S.), used in pocket torches; Small Edison Screw (S.E.S.); Edison Screw (E.S.) for lamps of 100 watts or so; and Goliath Edison Screw (G.E.S.) for lamps of 500 watts and over. Even these caps are not sufficiently accurate for apparatus in which the exact location of the filament, relative to the optical system, is all-important. Here pre-focus types of caps and holders, familiar to some in home cinema projectors are used. Three types only are employed in the theatre: Medium Pre-focus, equivalent to E.S.; Large Pre-focus, equivalent to G.E.S.; and Bipost. The first two may be fitted at a slight extra cost to any projection lamp in exchange for its standard cap, but the last named needs a special lamp assembly. The Bipost (Fig. 6) is of a size which I suspect owes its origin to the large wattage lamps, 3,000 or 5,000 watts and 110-volt supplies common in film studios. These lamps need very large currents in amperes and to supply them through the lamp cap was a problem. The Bipost cap resembles a large two-pin plug, and, though it can be supplied for wattages as low as 500, it is rather an anachronism below 2,000 watts, on the score of both size and price!

OPERATING VOLTAGE

As the filament temperature is important if the lamp is to have its rated life and efficiency, the pressure in volts applied to the lamp is also important. Every lamp is manufactured to work on one voltage only; higher voltage will increase the light output but decreases the life, and, conversely, lower voltage will decrease the light but prolong the life. This is generally known, but it is not commonly understood how little voltage variation is needed to play havoc with the lamp. A 5 per cent increase in volts decreases the lamp life 40 per cent, and 5 per cent decrease in volts reduces the light output by 18 per cent. Putting a 240-volt lamp on 200-volt mains involves over 40 per cent loss of light. He who merely knows his supply voltage as "200 and something—can't remember exactly," may be unpleasantly surprised. Voltage problems make touring of equipment unsatisfactory. Two sets of lamps may be carried, 110 volt and 230 or 240; and half-a-dozen voltages may be encountered. Some towns get, literally, a brighter performance than others!

Particular types of lamps, all commonly used in stage lighting apparatus, may now be considered in detail. The efficiency figures in lumens per watt (L/W) are for the 200/250-volt range unless stated otherwise.

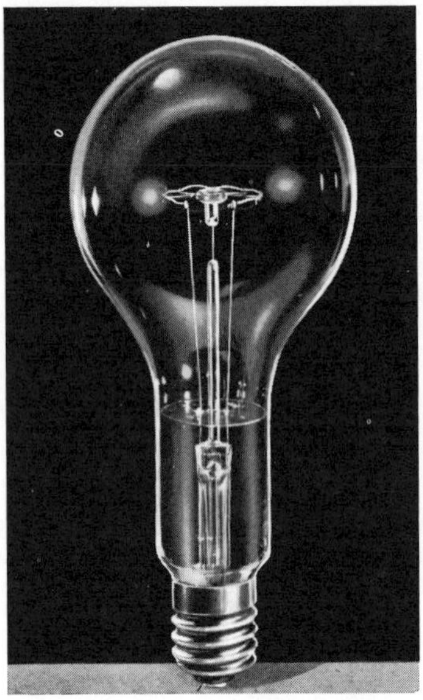

FIG. 3. OSRAM 500-WATT G/S LAMP
(General Electric Co. Ltd.)

GENERAL LIGHTING SERVICE LAMPS

The usual abbreviation is G/S lamps. This class (Fig. 3) is the most familiar and includes the ordinary domestic lamps. Only 200-, 300-, 500-, 1,000-, and 1,500-watt sizes are used in stage lighting. The 200 and 1,500, both rather cumbersome, are seldom employed. These lamps have a wreath-shaped filament and burn in any position. For stage work, it is usually desirable to specify "angle burning" lamps, in which the filament is shaped and supported to enable it better to withstand the shocks of stage work. There is no extra charge, and the life of both filaments is 1,000 hours. The efficiency of the 500- and 1,000-watt lamps is 17 and 19 lumens per watt respectively. For general lighting service below 200 watts, the theatre has a special class, manufactured by the G.E.C. and Ediswan firms for certain, and, perhaps, by others.

FIG. 4. OSRAM 1,000-WATT B.I. LAMP
(General Electric Co. Ltd.)

THEATRE BATTEN LAMPS

Sometimes known as Samoiloff lamps, these are made in 60-, 100-, and 150-watt sizes, E.S. caps. The filament centres are the same distance from the lamp caps, and the bulbs are the same size as that of the domestic 100-watt G/S lamp. The lamps are more expensive than corresponding domestic lamps, but interchangeability may make the extra worth while. In any case, the normal bulb size of the 150-watt lamp is unwieldy for stage purposes. The filament is wreath-shaped and may be burnt in any position. Efficiency is about 11 lumens per watt for the 60-watt and 13 L/W for the 150-watt, and the life of all is 1,000 hours.

Where it is desired to use standard G/S lamps for these wattages, they should be recapped E.S.

PROJECTOR LAMPS

ROUND BULB CLASS B.1

These lamps (Fig. 4) are made in 100-, 250-, 500-, and 1,000-watt sizes, the first two with an E.S. cap, and the others with a G.E.S. or Large Pre-focus cap. The 100-watt lamp is seldom used on the stage. All the lamps have a "bunch" filament, and the filament centres (also bulb sizes) are the same in the 500-watt and 1,000-watt lamps, which are interchangeable. The filament, as its title implies, is a bunched compact source of light, and the bulb, almost devoid of a neck, makes it handy in shape. The life is 800 hours, and the lamp may not be burnt with the cap within 45° of vertical over the bulb. Efficiency of the 500-watt is 14.5 L/W and of the 1,000-watt 16 L/W; less than the corresponding efficiencies of the G/S lamps.

PROJECTOR LAMPS

ROUND BULB CLASS B.2

In these lamps bunch filament is fitted in the standard G/S bulb, which enables the lamp to burn in any position, but the large bulb with neck is inconvenient.

PROJECTOR LAMPS

TUBULAR BULB CLASS A.1

These lamps (Fig. 5) are made in 100-, 250-, 500-, 1,000-, and 1,500-watt sizes. The cap arrangements correspond to those of the B.1 round bulb lamps, but only in the 1,000-watt size do the filament centres make the lamps of the two classes readily interchangeable. For this reason and because of their fragile filament construction, the 100-, 250-, and 500-watt sizes are seldom used in theatre work; of the other two, the 1,000-watt is the more popular. A grid filament is mounted in a tubular bulb, which makes a compact source with a pronounced light distribution from the two faces of the grid as compared with the four edges. The filament is run at a higher temperature than the previous lamp classes, and gives an efficiency of 22 lumens per watt in the 1,000-watt size. The life is 100 hours and there is an absolute veto on any burning position except vertical cap down. A slight tilt of 20° either side of the vertical seems, however, to be all right! When it is tilted too much, the tubular bulb develops a blister.

The filament formation in various makes of projector lamps, particularly A.1 tubulars, differs somewhat. For example, Philips and Osram (G.E.C.) filaments are slightly smaller in area and more nearly square than others. For Mazda (BTH) lamps slightly higher lumen figures are published and may be explained by the life

FIG. 5. OSRAM 1,000-WATT A.I. LAMP
(General Electric Co. Ltd.)

figures: the BTH. 100 hours is stated as maximum and the G.E.C. as average.

PROJECTOR LAMPS

CINEMA STUDIO CLASS

These lamps (Fig. 6) are made in 1,000-, 2,000-, 3,000-, and 5,000-watt sizes; but only the 2,000-watt is used on the stage. An almost square grid filament is fitted in a round bulb so that the lamp can be burnt at any angle—between vertical cap down and horizontal. The efficiency is 24 lumens per watt and the approximate life 100 hours. A G.E.S. cap is standard, but a Large Pre-focus could be fitted. An almost similar lamp known as the Bipost is obtainable. The filament is, more or less, the same, but its supports and bulb design are of the different construction that is demanded by the Bipost cap. The price of a 1,000-watt Bipost lamp is twice that of the corresponding B.1 or A.1 projection lamp.

PROJECTOR LAMPS. LOW VOLTAGE

The commonest is the A.1 tubular lamp, known as the "30-volt, 30-amp." The cap is G.E.S. or Large Pre-focus, and the filament centre renders it interchangeable with the other 1,000 projector lamps. The filament is beautifully compact and gives an almost solid square of light. As the result of the low voltage is higher current, thicker filament, and increased permissible filament temperature, an efficiency of 28.5 lumens per watt, with a life of 100 hours, burning vertical cap up, is not surprising. The 30-volt, 250-watt A.1 tubular E.S. or Medium Pre-focus cap is a good source with an efficiency of 25 lumens per watt. It is, more or less, interchangeable with the mains voltage 250-watt lamps with an efficiency of 17 L/W. The life of both is 100 hours.

Another most useful low-voltage lamp is the

FIG. 6. OSRAM 2,000-WATT BIPOST LAMP
(General Electric Co. Ltd.)

24-volt, 240-watt Round Bulb Projector (Aircraft Landing Lamp), fitted with a medium Pre-focus cap. This lamp, which has an efficiency of 24 lumens per watt and a life of 50 hours, is a neat source of light that can be tilted, but for stage lighting purposes it is well to under-run it slightly to increase its life, though decreasing its efficiency to 20 L/W. The range of 12-volt car

FIG. 7. 36-WATT LOW VOLTAGE SPOT

lamps also has possibilities, the 36-watt V filament and the 60- and 100-watt line filaments being commonly used. In the latter two sizes the S.E.S. cap should be ordered in place of the standard Small Bayonet; otherwise there will be lampholder troubles. Fig. 7 shows a spotlight only 3 in. by 5 in., using a 36-watt car lamp.

NON-FILAMENT LAMPS

The commonest classes of lamps—those employing an incandescent filament as light-source have been considered. There remain two other forms of lamp. One, the Carbon Arc, may be said to have had a glorious past—it was the first electric light; the other, the Discharge Lamp, holds the key to the future. Both have only limited application to the theatre, especially the amateur theatre, and will not be treated in detail.

THE CARBON ARC

This consists of two sticks of carbon, one connected to the positive terminal and the other to the negative of the supply. These sticks are brought together to touch for a moment and then moved a short distance apart; thereupon an electric flame or arc is formed between the carbons. The result is to form an intense white-hot crater on the positive carbon. Exposed to the air, the carbon burns away, the positive with the crater faster than the negative. To compensate for this and to keep the light centre constant as the carbons are fed (usually by hand-operated knob), the positive carbon is larger in diameter than the negative (Fig. 8A).

The carbon arc is one of the specialist applications where direct current is advantageous. It can, however, be operated on alternating current. The A.C. arc uses two identical carbons, and the light source is the tips of both carbons and a ball of gas between the two. The A.C. arc is not as directional as the D.C. and is, therefore, not so efficient for use with elaborate optical systems as is the latter. The arc *must* be wired in series with a resistance or choke as a current limiting device. The technical reader will note in the possibility of the efficient choke instead of a resistance on A.C., a compensation for loss of efficiency in the non-directional A.C. arc itself.

Fig. 8A. Carbon Arc Mechanism

Amateurs are unlikely to require an arc projector; even in the professional theatre its application is restricted to the powerful following spots beloved of music-hall stars and some others. At one time, more and more current was used in an attempt to get more light, but nowadays the tendency is to use more elaborate optical systems, thereby making better use of the light. Such modern systems are easily recognizable from the clear-cut circles of light projected on to the stage. An example of the latest type of F.O.H. following spot is shown in Fig. 8B.

Skill is required of the operator to keep the carbons burning satisfactorily, especially on A.C.; sometimes, as in film projectors, automatic motor-driven feeds are fitted.

DISCHARGE LAMPS

Except for a few specialist applications, discharge lamps have not been used on the stage. Nevertheless, the filament lamp has been exploited almost to the limit, and it is from the discharge type of lamp that future developments are likely to come. It is of interest, therefore, briefly to survey their record.

The first general application took the form of the tubes used for signs generally described as Neon lighting. In these a high voltage (6,000 or so) current jumps from an electrode at one end of the tube to the other, the tube being filled with a gas that is rendered luminescent by the discharge. Dependent on the gas, a few colours were produced; neon gave red, mercury vapour blue, and so on. Improvements were brought about mainly in conjunction with the mercury vapour filling by coating the tube with powders which, owing to the phenomena of fluorescence, gave a fine range of colours. Fluorescence (described in "Colour") provides a method whereby light can be produced coloured without resort to wasteful filters. A few years before the Second Great War

Fig. 8B. Mirror Arc Spotlight

another discharge lamp was introduced in street lighting. The lamps were fitted with means for automatically heating the electrodes before the discharge struck up. The pre-heating enabled

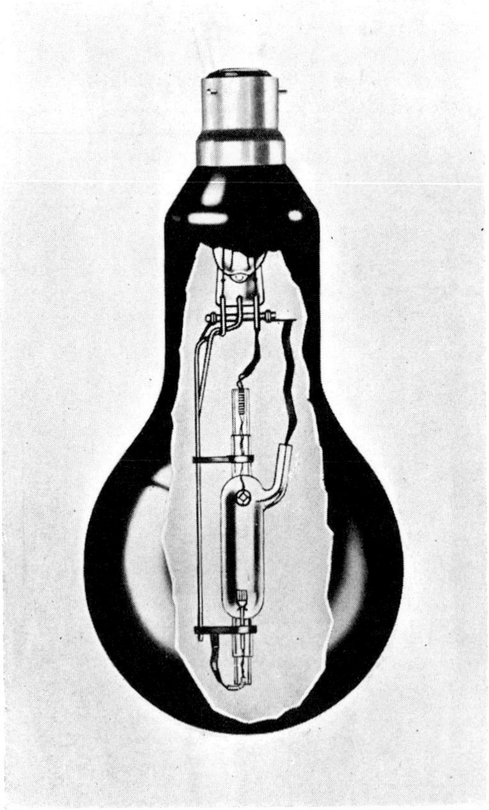

FIG. 9. MERCRA 125-WATT BLACK LAMP
(*The British Thomson-Houston Co. Ltd.*)

normal voltages of 200 and the like to be used. This type of lamp is known as the "hot cathode" in contrast to the cold cathode sign tubing.

With these two basic methods and the possibility of using different voltages, different gas fillings and gas pressures, in conjunction with complete or partial change of colour by fluorescence, a whole new world of infinite possibilities seems to be ahead. In any case, a striking advance has been made in efficiency and the discharge lamp more nearly approaches cold light. Consequently, 30-40 lumens per watt and a life of double the corresponding filament lamp are usual.

In addition to these two types, there are the 5 ft. fluorescent tube and the extra high pressure projector lamps with a source 5 × 2.5 mm., a wattage of 500, and an efficiency of 50 L/W.

Extensive use of discharge lamps on the stage has been retarded by the difficulty of dimming and the colour of the light from the projector types. Electrical dimming is possible with the sign type mercury vapour fluorescent tube, and is effective for ballroom and similar decorative lighting, but not wholly satisfactory for the exacting demands of the stage. The extra high voltage is another drawback. The projector-type lamps cannot be dimmed and the colour of the light, though an improvement on early street lighting lamps, is not sufficiently white.

The discharge lamps used on the stage for special effects are the 400-watt tubular mercury vapour street lighting lamp, G.E.S. cap; the 125-watt and 80-watt mercury vapour lamp with pearl bulb and 3-pin B.C. holder, the last two lamps being also obtainable with black glass ultra-violet filter bulbs (Fig. 9).

All these lamps operate off 200–260 volts A.C., but *must* be supplied from a circuit with a suitable choke. The 3-pin B.C. holder prevents insertion of the lamp in an ordinary non-choked lighting circuit. The lamps take three minutes or so to attain full brightness, and, when switched off, require to cool before they will strike up again. Therefore, great care must be taken to ensure that any circuit of these lamps is not broken accidentally or switched off, that the plugs do not come apart, etc. If a mishap occurs, the lamp can be switched on again, but it will not light until it—not the stage—is ready.

D.C. Mains. Where the electric supply is direct current, it will not be possible to use static transformers, and thus the use of low-voltage lamps as an economical proposition will be prevented. Furthermore, as discharge lamps require a rotary converter, an unpleasant complication, they can be ruled out.

On a D.C. supply, the carbon arc is far more satisfactory than on A.C. and, given careful attention, it can be used where an extra bright source is required, also with a special heat-resisting glass filter to provide ultra-violet radiation. Filament lamps of the same voltage as the supply (G/S, A.1, B.1 and B.2, etc.) are equally satisfactory on D.C. and A.C.

LIGHTING APPARATUS

It is customary to divide stage lighting apparatus into four main classes: magazine equipment (footlights and battens); floodlights; spotlights; optical lanterns (effects projectors). This deceptive division will not be adopted here. There is little difference between some spotlights and a narrow angle flood, and a magazine batten is but a collective expression for a lot of baby floodlights that are joined together. The real clue to the light distribution and utility of a lantern for a particular purpose (its characteristics) is given by the optical system.

When the optical system is used for classification, apparatus, beginning with the simplest, is grouped as follows:

(1) Lamp non-adjustable in relation to reflector giving fixed light distribution: floodlights and magazine equipment.

(2) Lamp adjustable to lens and/or reflector, giving variable light distribution: focus-lanterns and soft edge spots.

(3) Precision optical systems: spotlights and effects projectors.

The first requirement for all three classes is a method that describes the light distribution. Some lanterns spread their light profusely; others give such a narrow beam that even at a distance they only just cover a man; some give a definite beam with clear-cut edges; others fade away gradually at the edges. A simple description of what may be expected is given as the beam angle and the cut-off angle.

If we put a lamp in a simple black box with one side open, then light will emerge and can be directed on to a backcloth; it will, however, be cut off at the points where the box edges obstruct or cut off the filament from the backcloth; beyond these edges there will be no light. We have achieved primitive control of the light, and the angle, with the lamp as its apex, between which the light is cut off, is appropriately called the "cut-off angle" (Fig. 10).

The next step is to place a suitable reflector behind the lamp and to redirect forward the light, which would otherwise be absorbed, as a beam. We may then have two lots of light on the backcloth; the direct light from the lamp (the cut-off angle) and a further patch of brighter light, perhaps, in the centre, thrown by the reflected beam. The angle which this beam makes to the lamp is known as the "beam angle" (Fig. 11).

These methods, somewhat rough and ready,

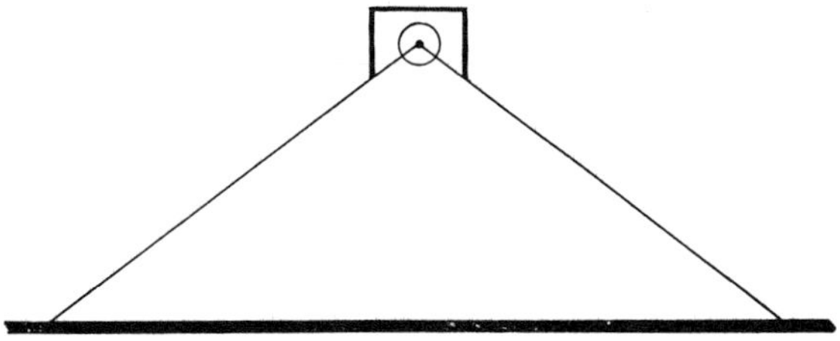

FIG. 10. CUT-OFF ANGLE

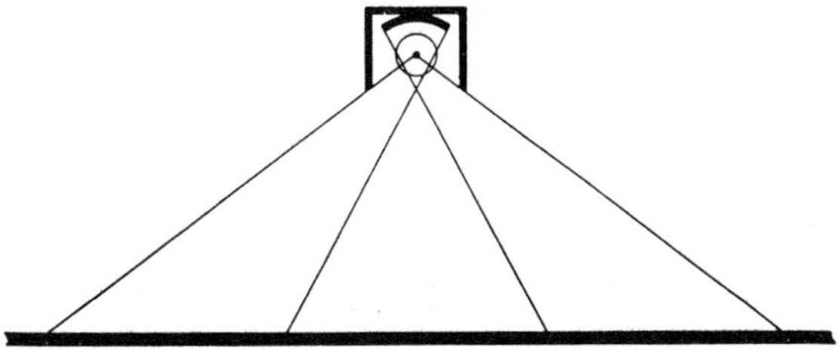

FIG. 11. BEAM ANGLE

are in common use among illuminating engineers and will be found of great practical use. Beam angle 100°, or beam angle variable between 10° and 40°, tells us at once what to expect, especially when combined with the cut-off angle. A lantern with a beam angle and cut-off of 30° has clear-cut edges; whereas beam angle 30° and cut-off angle 100° indicate a general flood of light getting stronger in the centre.

These angles as stated by the manufacturers are not guesswork; to the eye the beam angle may merge imperceptibly into the cut-off angle, but a photometer is used and the intensity measured. The official definitions are:

CUT-OFF ANGLE. *This is the angle of the direct light from the lamp, and is determined by the edges of the lantern or by special devices, such as spill rings*

BEAM ANGLE. *This is defined in the case of a symmetric lantern as the total angular width between the limits at which the illumination produced on a surface normal to the axis of the beam is one-tenth of the maximum* (Fig. 11).

Beyond the edges of the cut-off angle should be absolute darkness. In badly designed lanterns this result is not achieved: ghost light and stray light may be present. The former is light, reflected internally, which passes through the front lens or aperture of the lantern and appears as a low intensity phantom somewhere on the stage, a ring of light from a reflector edge or lampholder, etc. Stray light, however, leaks direct from the lamphouse via ill-fitting access doors and badly baffled ventilation apertures. Such defects should be looked for, when a lantern is being bought, as they can be extremely annoying. Stray light may not only illuminate something that is unwanted, but also draw the attention of the audience to the position of the lantern in use—the hall-mark of bad lighting.

Next may be considered in detail what can legitimately be expected from the three classes of equipment—the floodlights, the focus lanterns, and the precision optical projectors.

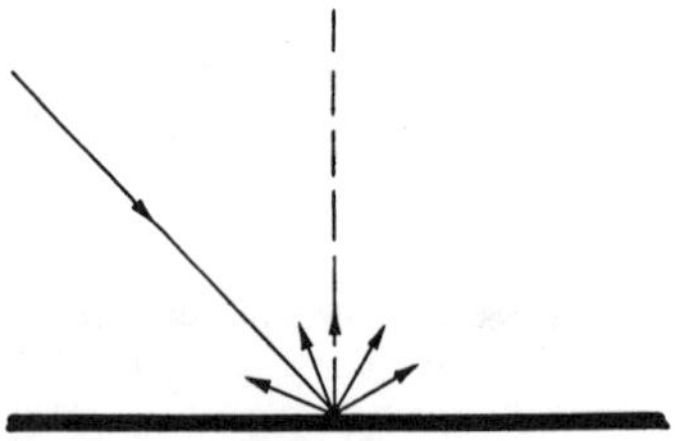

FIG. 12. DIFFUSE REFLECTION

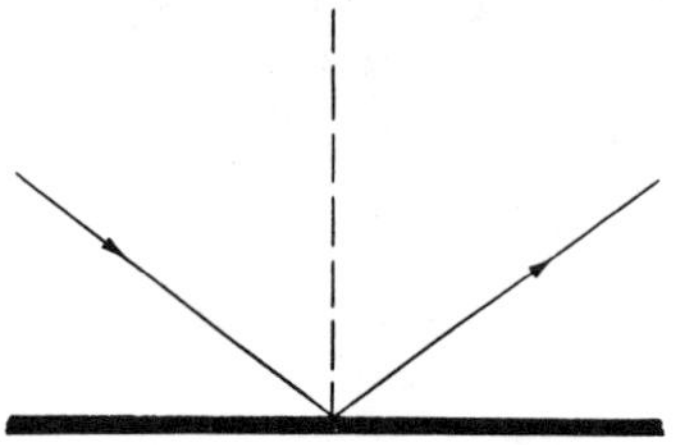

FIG. 13. SPECULAR REFLECTION

REFLECTION

The basic principle common to floodlights is reflection. If instead of having a black interior, a simple box floodlight is painted matt white, we get a simple reflector of the diffusing type. Reflecting surfaces range from white blotting paper to silvered glass mirror. Probably these two dissimilar surfaces reflect exactly the same amount of light, but in the first a beam of light striking the surface is scattered in all directions (Fig. 12) and in the second redirected at an angle corresponding to that of the incident beam (Fig. 13). The latter type of reflection is known as "regular" or "specular" reflection. To describe a surface we need to know both the total reflection factor and the proportion specularly reflected. Taking a few of the commoner reflector materials, we get the following comparative percentages:

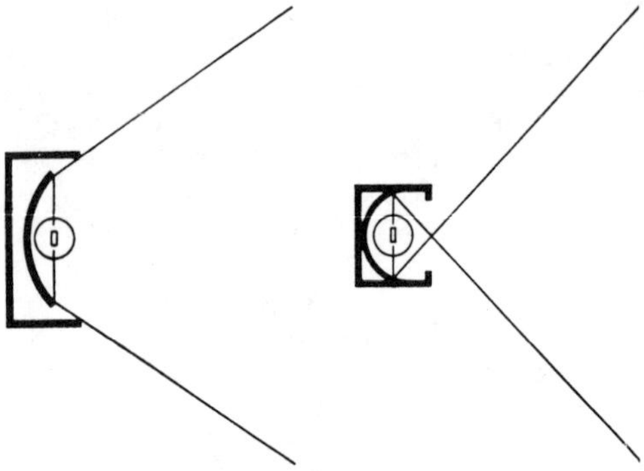

FIG. 14. LANTERN APERTURE AND BEAM SPREAD

Material	Total Reflection Factor	Proportion Specularly Reflected
	per cent	per cent
Silver-backed mirror glass	80–85	80–85
Surface silver on brass	85	85
Stainless steel . . .	57–60	50
Chromium plate . .	60–65	55–60
Anodized aluminium .	84	83
White blotting paper .	80	0

Most reflectors used in stage lanterns are formed in varied curves for two reasons: (1) by curving the reflector a large angle of light is collected from the lamp without too great a reflector diameter; (2) by variation of the curved surface the light can be redistributed to give the required beam angle. It may be thought that the second reason is only important for a lantern that gives a narrow beam, and that for a wide angle beam the diffusing reflector is better. Such is seldom the case in practice. Fig. 14 shows how by shaping the reflector so that the beam crosses, more light is passed without requiring an unduly large colour frame and filter.

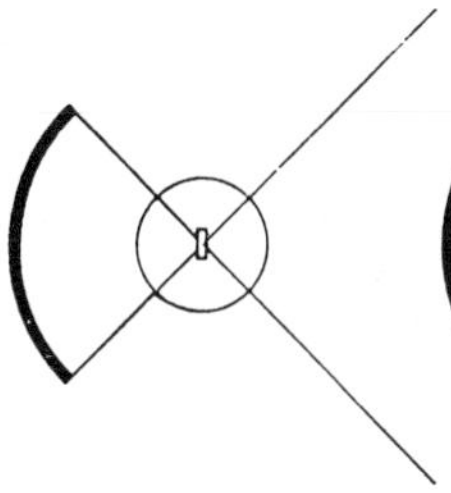

Fig. 15A. Spherical Reflector

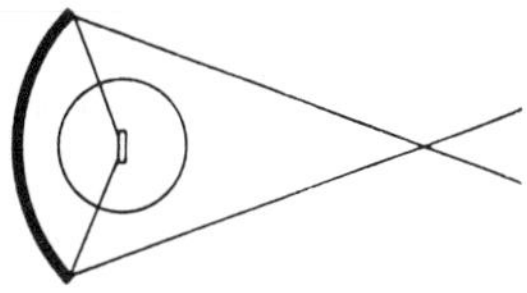

Fig. 15B. Spherical Reflector

Reflectors generally conform to three mathematical forms, known as *spherical, parabolic*, and *elliptical*. With these types the lamp can be so positioned that the spherical reflects the light back through the filament (Fig. 15A); the parabolic collects the light and redirects it as a parallel beam (Fig. 16); the elliptical brings the light to a second focus (Fig. 17). Variation is also possible by moving the lamp relative to the reflector. To bring the lamp nearer the spherical (Fig. 15B) causes the beam to cross farther out instead of at the filament, and even, ultimately, to become a parallel beam. Owing to the size of the light source, these results cannot be achieved exactly in practice: study Fig. 18 to understand

Fig. 16. Parabolic Reflector

what happens to the parallel beam. The amount of light collected from the filament, and used, is known as the "solid angle." Because collection is in three dimensions, the amount of light gained by the good solid angle as against the bad one is considerable; the second of the two diagrams (Fig. 19) collects four times the light of the first.

If silvered glass is used as the best reflector, what will the light look like when it impinges on a white surface? As the lamp filament, assuming an A.1 lamp, is in grid formation, all reflections will contain this formation in some degree, and we shall see various magnifications of this grid, at best distorted to look like streaks (termed "filament striation"). This striation may be removed by the use of a reflecting surface less regular than silvered glass, or glass with an uneven surface may be used instead of plate. Glasses of this type that are commonly silvered are: Cathedral, with a slightly rough rolled surface; Sunray, with a hammered surface, giving the effect of innumerable little ball lenses. There are many intermediate glasses that can be used. Cathedral is most suitable for narrow beams, Sunray for wide.

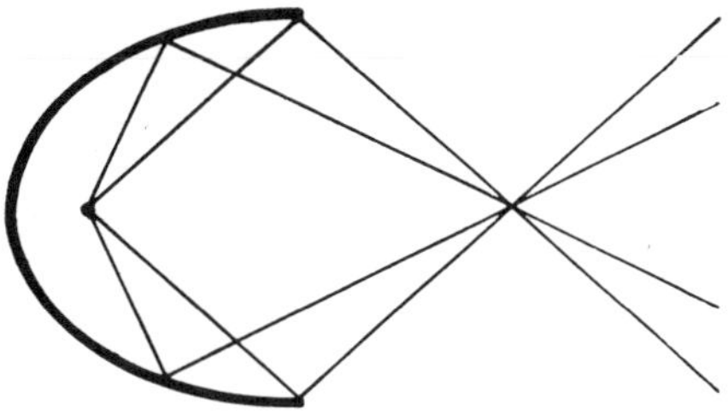

Fig. 17. Elliptical Reflector

Another form of reflector relies not on silvering but on complete internal prismatic reflection. When built up individually, as in a lighthouse lantern, this system is ideal, and there is nothing to deteriorate: commercially produced as small moulded reflectors, they lose some of their efficiency because of the limitations of the moulding process.

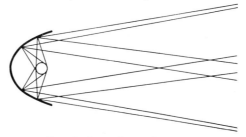

Fig. 18. Large Light Source and Parabolic Reflector

A lot of nonsense is talked about the fragility of

reflectors. The fixing should be properly designed, and there are glass lamps inside which are more fragile than any reflector. Glass affords subtlety in choosing the right degree of striation breakup, and has magnificent reflection factors. Glass reflectors require resilvering every three to five years when they are used at close range to high wattage lamps in concentrating optical systems. The process is simple and cheap. Metal reflectors would require resurfacing or plating within the same period. The future of metal reflectors may be bound up in the development of anodized aluminium rather than in plating.

GENERAL STAGE FLOODS

These are made in three sizes for:

(*a*) 60–150-watt lamps;
(*b*) 300–500-watt;
(*c*) 1,000-watt.

The 1,000-watt is definitely a flood for the large stage. If it is well designed each size

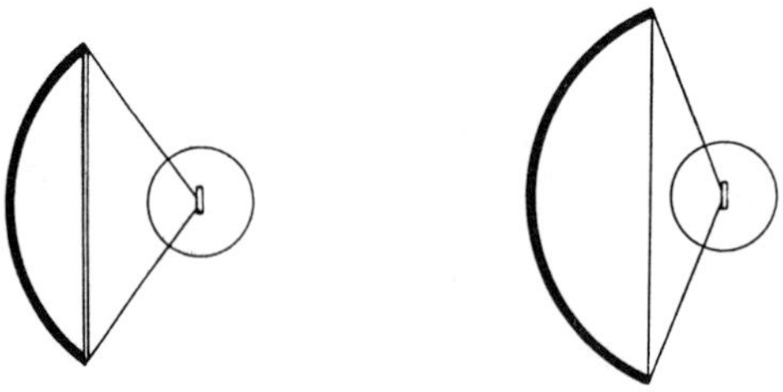

FIG. 19. COMPARATIVE SOLID ANGLES

should be able to take, without alteration, either of two reflectors, giving a medium angle 50° beam and a wide angle 100° beam. The cut-off angle will be constant round about 100°. All floods should be fitted with tilting fork and locking wheels. The fork can be used for suspension, with or without special clamp, or inserted in a telescopic stand. Colour frames, runners, proper ventilation, and robust construction are important (Figs. 20A and 21).

The purpose of the alternative light distribution given by the two reflectors is to add to the flexibility and efficiency of the unit. For close range work, lighting backings, etc., the wide-angle reflector is needed; for acting area lighting from battens it will be an advantage to have a more localized beam that is unlikely to strike the backcloth or cyclorama. In extreme cases, it may be necessary to reduce the cut-off angle to more nearly that of the 50° reflector; special hoods

FIG. 20A. 60–150-WATT BABY FLOOD

or funnels will then be inserted in the colour runners (Fig. 20B).

All sizes of floods are commonly mounted on a barrel as a flood batten, each flood being independently adjustable. The baby flood and its reflector are often made up into magazine equipment.

MAGAZINE EQUIPMENT

In magazine equipment (Fig. 22), the individual baby floods become compartments in one

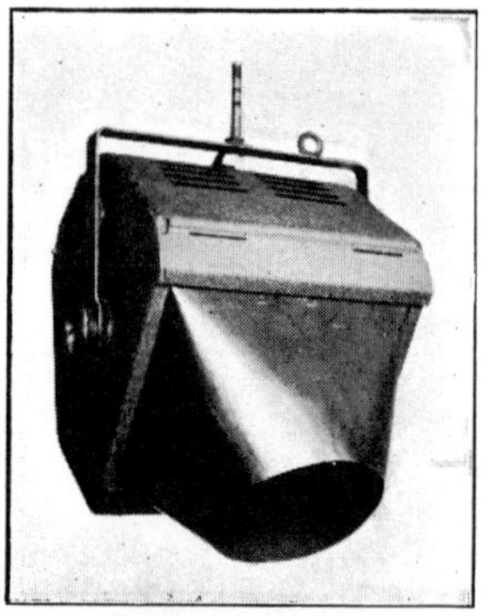

FIG. 20B. BABY FLOOD WITH FUNNEL ATTACHMENT

housing. The lamps are mounted at various centres from six inches upwards; nine inches, giving opportunity to employ a large reflector, is a good figure.

Two main types of housing are used: one throwing light upward as footlight or ground row; the other throwing light downwards as battens. The same medium angle and wide angle reflectors are common to both, but variation in housing is needed to cope with ventilation in the two burning positions. Ventilation that produces a current of air between the colour medium and the lamp is important.

Fig. 21. 500-watt Flood

For standard batten work the medium angle reflector is used, the direct light from the lamp lighting at close range the adjacent border, while the main beam is projected on the actors below (Fig. 23(*a*)). For cyclorama work, the wide-angle reflector is required to give even illumination and mixing of colours (Fig. 23 (*b*)). The footlight seldom requires anything but the wide-angle reflector as it has to light actors down-stage at close range. Further, it is undesirable that it should project light at a distance on the up-stage scenery and cyclorama. The cut-off angle is particularly important in a footlight, as light must not stray on to the pelmet or proscenium border.

Ground row or bottom lighting to a cyclorama or a backcloth can be carried out by the same unit. Large cycloramas are catered for by two rows carried one above the other. Castors are often fitted to a ground row to make it easily removable: the term "trucks" is applied to these units.

ACTING AREA FLOODS

The vertical acting area flood (Fig. 24A) is extensively used in spectacular productions. The lanterns utilize a 1,000-watt G/S lamp in a large diameter concentrating reflector, beam angles of 26° or 45° being usual. The front of the lantern is fitted with spill rings or other means to intercept the direct light of the lamp: the cut-off angle thus becomes the same as that of the beam (Fig. 24B.)

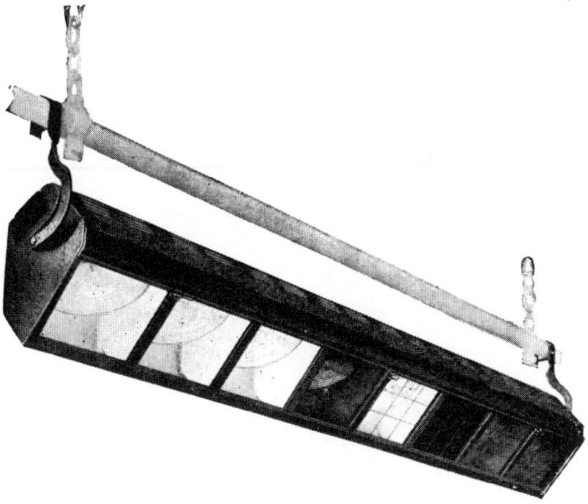

Fig. 22. 60–150-watt Magazine Batten

These lanterns are often massed as battens or hung singly or in pairs between 6 ft. sections of magazine batten.

CYCLORAMA FLOODS

The cylindrical German pattern taking a 1,000-watt tubular line filament lamp has

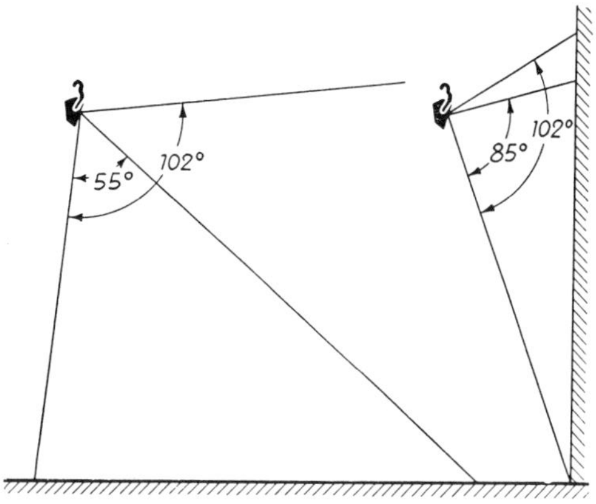

Fig. 23. Light Distribution (*a*) Medium, (*b*) Wide, Angle Batten

largely been superseded by the British circular flood taking a 500-watt G/S lamp (illustrated in a bank on page 345). Whatever the relative merits may be, there can be no doubt that for the flat type of cyclorama common here, the latter is considerably more efficient.

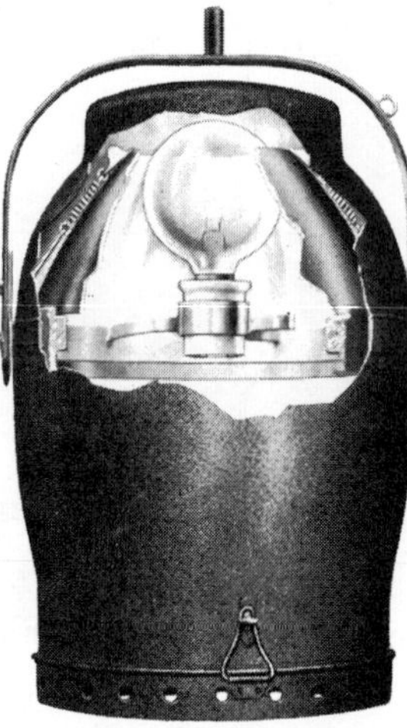

FIG. 24A. 1,000-WATT ACTING AREA FLOOD CUT AWAY TO SHOW REFLECTOR

PARALLEL BEAM LANTERNS

The parallel beam lantern might be classed as a *spot* but for the fact that the beam angle is scarcely adjustable. The lantern takes a 1,000-watt lamp, and by means of a 10-in. diameter

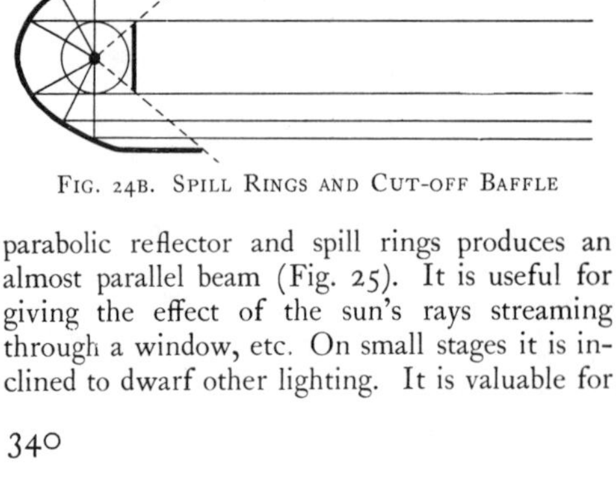

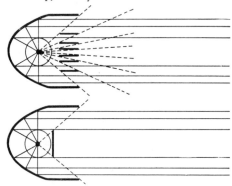

FIG. 24B. SPILL RINGS AND CUT-OFF BAFFLE

parabolic reflector and spill rings produces an almost parallel beam (Fig. 25). It is useful for giving the effect of the sun's rays streaming through a window, etc. On small stages it is inclined to dwarf other lighting. It is valuable for spotting in outdoor or indoor pageants, when it is often called a Pageant lantern.

A model for small-stage work takes a 36-watt 12 volt lamp with built-in transformer.

FIG. 25. 1,000-WATT PARALLEL BEAM PAGEANT LANTERN

REFRACTION

When light passes from one translucent material to another its path is bent or refracted: from air to water, air to glass, or one kind of glass to another. The amount of the refraction depends both on the material and on the angle at which the ray strikes it. By shaping a block of glass we get that valuable device for light control, the lens. Some of these shapes are complex, but in general stage lighting a few simple types are all that are required. The diagram shows a plano-convex

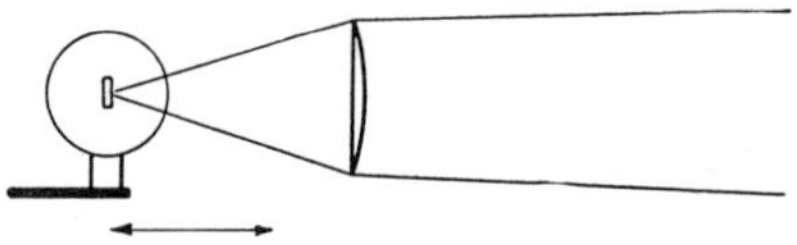

FIG. 26. P.C. LENS GIVING PARALLEL BEAM

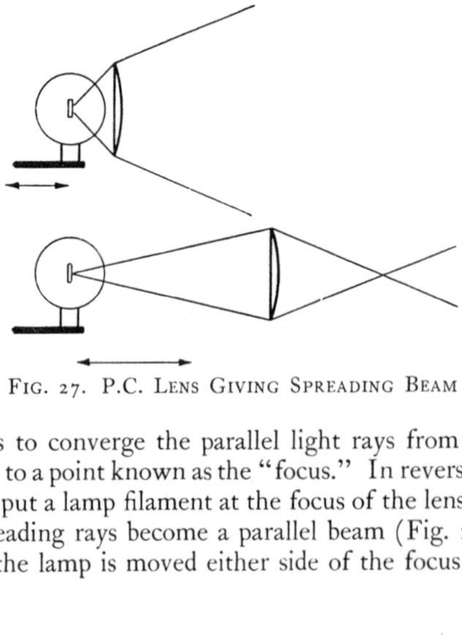

FIG. 27. P.C. LENS GIVING SPREADING BEAM

lens to converge the parallel light rays from the sun to a point known as the "focus." In reverse, if we put a lamp filament at the focus of the lens, its spreading rays become a parallel beam (Fig. 26). If the lamp is moved either side of the focus the beams will spread (Fig. 27) in one instance "beyond the focus" by crossing first. A lens can be designed for almost any focal length; a 6-in. diameter × 20-in. focus (the diameter is always given first) is almost flat, whereas a 6-in. × 8-in. focus is quite thick at the centre. The shorter focus lenses are commonly used for focus lanterns in stage work in order to confine the length of lantern to reasonable limits and to collect as large a solid angle of light for redistribution as possible.

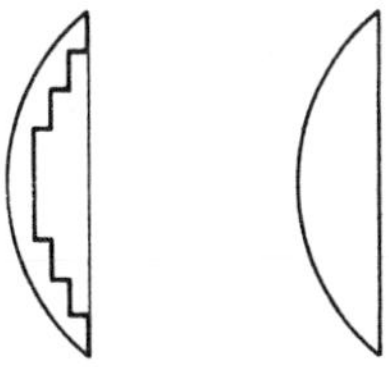

FIG. 28. STEP LENS AND PLANO CONVEX COMPARED

Short focus lenses have the drawback that the light must pass through a thick section of glass in the centre; this cuts down the amount of light passed and for reasons given under "Colour" (page 364) introduces coloration. When a lamp filament is at the focus behind a lens, various-sized images of the filament as with a reflector,

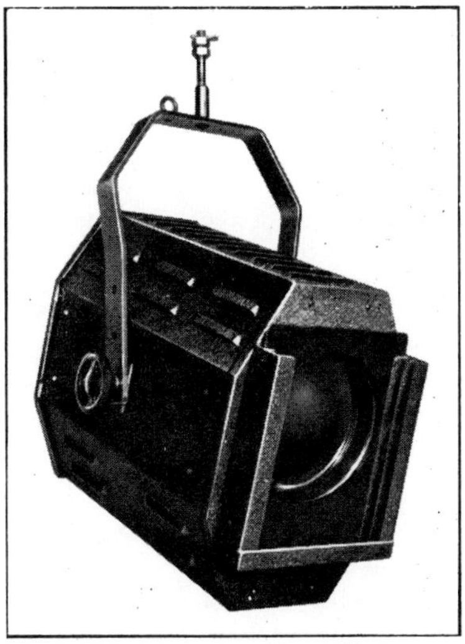

FIG. 29A. 1,000-WATT FOCUS LANTERN

are projected; if these are covered with coloured striation as well as with the ordinary kind, the result can be objectionable. Therefore, the thick parts of the lens are often cut away in a series of concentric steps so that even the centre is comparatively thin. Such lenses are known as "Step" or "Fresnel" (after the inventor) lenses (Fig. 28).

FOCUS LANTERNS

The focus lantern is the commonest type in the theatre to-day; it is usually referred to under

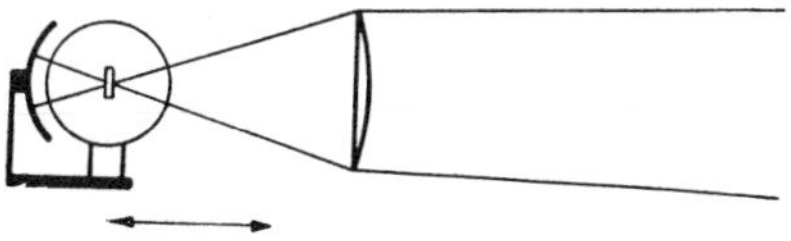

FIG. 29B. FOCUS LANTERN OPTICAL SYSTEM

the misnomer "spotlight" or "spot" (Fig. 29A). Wattages of 250, 500, and 1,000 are usual.

As lanterns are basically the same, a description of the 1,000-watt will serve for all. In this lantern the lamp is carried on a movable tray behind a 6-in. × 10-in. plano-convex or a 6-in. × 9-in. step lens. At the focus point almost a parallel beam is produced, and a somewhat crude image of the lamp filament is projected. It follows that the filament of the lamp (commonly a B.1) should be nicely adjusted to centre on the lens, if a pre-focus holder is not fitted. Behind the lamp is a small spherical reflector (usually of metal) to redirect lamp rays, which would otherwise be wasted, back through the filament (Fig.

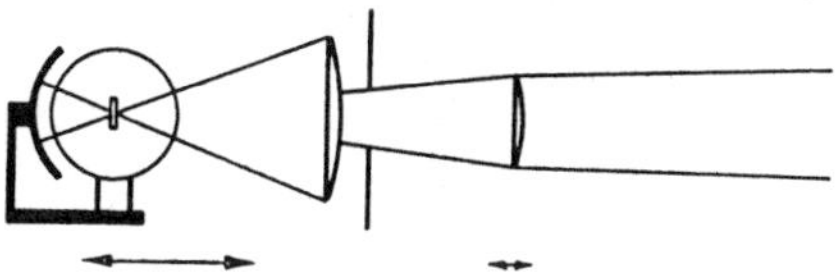

FIG. 30. SPOTTING ATTACHMENT OPTICAL SYSTEM

29B). When the lantern is being adjusted, this second weaker filament image can easily be seen, and it should be set so that it fills the gaps between the direct filament image. As the tray carrying lamp and reflector is moved forward towards the lens, the unpleasant filament image enlarges and vanishes, leaving a pool of light with clear edges. The beam angle is variable from 11° to 42°, filament striation being present up to about 16°. The cut-off angle is the same as that of the beam.

This type of lantern does not give a clear-cut small spot; its results are more those of a medium to narrow angle adjustable flood with defined edges. For clear-cut spotting, a supplementary lens attachment, known as a "spotting attachment," is fitted. The main lens now becomes the condenser and the extra one the objective (Fig. 30). The objective focuses the edges of an adjustable diaphragm in the attachment and not the lamp filament. As the diagram shows, much light is lost in the process. Therefore, where any real intensity is required, a precision spotlight is advised.

Exactly the same focus lantern optical system is used in what are usually described as Soft Edge Spots, with which type the collection and redirection of as much light as possible is the principal aim. Both lens and reflector are increased in diameter in order to collect a large solid angle, and for the same reason the focus of the lens,

FIG. 31. 2-KW SOFT EDGE SPOT

aided by its step construction, has been reduced. At least a 10-in. diameter lens is usual (Fig. 31). The large illuminated lens is inclined to give slight ghost light, and the beam has a softer edge than the standard focus lantern. Both these factors restrict application somewhat, but for special purposes on large stages high intensity is valuable. The lamps usually employed are 2,000-watt cinema studio class. The beam angle is variable between 10° and 45°.

PRECISION OPTICAL PROJECTORS

The lanterns already described have depended (with the exception of the spotting attachment) on magnified images of the lamp filament, which gives a series of circular pools of light. Complete control over the shape of the beam is obtained by bringing the filament image to a focus at a position behind a variable gate, the gate and projected image being further focused by an objective lens.

The best known example of this principle is used in the slide lantern. Fig. 32 shows a short

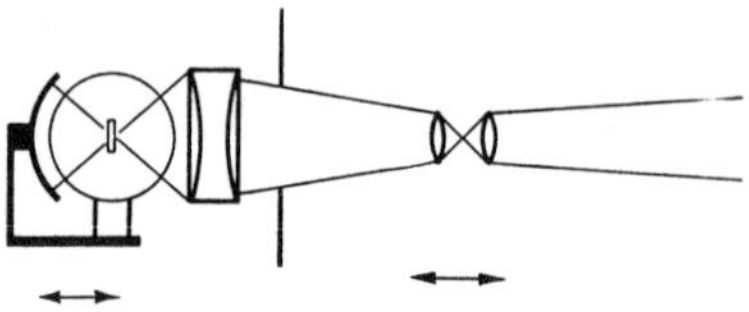

FIG. 32. EFFECTS LANTERN OPTICAL SYSTEM

focus condenser, consisting of two plano-convex lenses, ball to ball, focusing the filament image upon the gate where the lantern slide is inserted. This slide is next focused by an objective lens, and thereby projected on the screen. The objective is a compound lens, a slide being sensitive to distortion. By using objectives of different focal lengths, variation in picture size and length of projection throw can be obtained.

The Optical Effects projector used for projecting clouds, flames, and even scenery, on the stage employs this system. In many instances the slide is a moving disc or something similar. When a cloud effect is projected from the side of the stage, a 3-in. focus objective may be used; if it is projected from the gallery in a theatre, perhaps 20-in. focus will be required.

For spotlighting, a less high degree of definition is needed, and there is no fragile slide to be spoiled by heat; therefore steps can be taken to collect and focus more light. For this purpose reflection can be more satisfactory than condenser

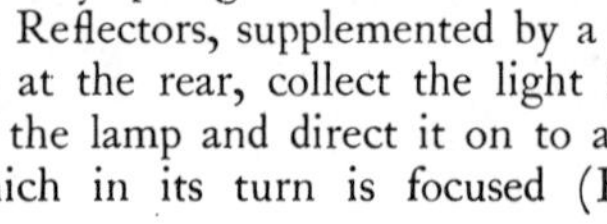

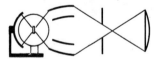

FIG. 33. STELMAR OPTICAL SYSTEM

lenses; the result is the Stelmar spot or the Mirror spot. The Stelmar was the first precision high intensity spotlight to be used in the English theatre. Reflectors, supplemented by a spherical reflector at the rear, collect the light from the front of the lamp and direct it on to a variable gate which in its turn is focused (Fig. 33).

Some lanterns that employ this system are on long front-of-house throws from the roof of Stratford-on-Avon Memorial Theatre and the Covent Garden Opera House.

A shorter lantern is obtained in the Mirror

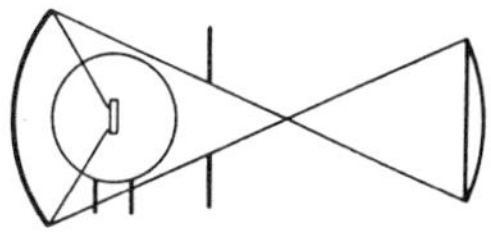

FIG. 34A. MIRROR SPOT OPTICAL SYSTEM

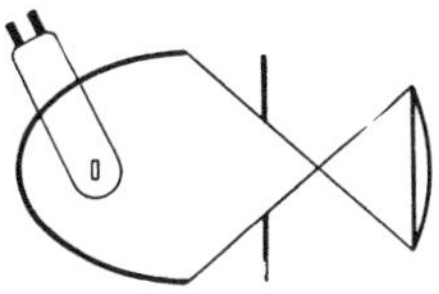

FIG. 34B. MIRROR SPOT OPTICAL SYSTEM

spot, the light being collected by a large diameter mirror at the back of the lamp and redirected to the gate which is focused by the objective (Fig. 34A). Light intensity is increased three times or more when the same lamp is used in the Mirror spot instead of in the simple focus lantern optical system. Mirror spots can take A.1 or B.1 1,000-watt lamps. A special model is obtainable only for A.1 tubular lamps in which advantage is taken of the tubular bulb to bring the reflector closer to the lamp filament, thus further improving the solid angle of light collected. A baby Mirror spot for the small stage is also available.

FIG. 35. SKELETON MIRROR SPOT, FOR USE IN CIRCLE FRONT HOUSINGS

In conjunction with a special tubular lamp, burning cap upwards, the Americans carried this system to its logical conclusion by enclosing the lamp in the reflector (Fig. 34B).

Beam angles in the Mirror spot are variable between 3° and 19°. For wider spreads, up to 30° on short throws, a short focus double objective lens is used. The size of spot is obtained by adjustments at the gate, which consists of four independently moving shutters or a variable iris diaphragm for circular spots. By moving the lamp or reflector, more light can be passed through the gate when it is set for small apertures. Most regular or irregular shaped objects can be picked out exactly with the Mirror spot. It is the ideal front-of-house spotlight, as the light can be adjusted to cut off along the footlight and up-stage to miss the cyclorama. When numbers of these Mirror spots are installed in a special housing, usually on the circle front as in the London Coliseum and Palladium, then opportunity is taken to simplify construction by omitting the individual housings to each lantern. Fig. 35 shows one of these skeleton mirror spots; the lens, gate, lamp, and mirror can be clearly seen.

All precision optical projectors need most careful adjustment and centring of the various parts of the optical system unless pre-focus lampholders are fitted. Therefore, these should always be specified.

REMOTE COLOUR CHANGE

When lanterns are placed in positions that are inaccessible during a performance, remote methods of changing the colour filters are of great value. Such lanterns are the front-of-house spots on the circle front or in the roof, and, perhaps, banks of acting area floods on the stage for spectacular productions. Tracker wire can be used, but, undoubtedly, electric methods are preferable, the lantern and its colour-change mechanism being merely attached to a flexible lead. One method is the electro-magnetic in which an energized solenoid coil attracts a plunger and draws up the colour semaphore-wise (Fig. 36).

FIG. 36. ELECTRO-MAGNETIC REMOTE COLOUR CHANGE

Four colours are commonly fitted, though much can be done with two; and even one, a colour and white, is useful. The mechanism for moving the colours electrically is expensive for lanterns with lenses of 6-in. diameter or over. Two or three lanterns can be purchased for the price of one fitted with electric colour-change. In the professional theatre, where banks of a dozen or more lanterns are fitted to the front of the circle, space impels this form of colour-change; on the other hand, amateurs do well when they consider doubling the lanterns.

A little ingenuity produces colour-change facilities. The 1,000-watt focus lantern in Fig. 29A can have the springs in the side runners removed, thus making possible the dropping of a metal colour frame into the front and back runners respectively. The frames will require weighting slightly, and runner sides must be extended to act as guides for the withdrawn position. Tracker wires from these frames pass over pulleys fixed above the lanterns. Provided no ambitious run, involving long lengths of wire and many corners, is attempted, this device is satisfactory. No elaborate control is needed: but just a loop and two hooks—colour in, colour out. If the proscenium cannot be pierced, cords can be brought down each side wall and operated. Even though subtle colour-changing cues are not possible, colour changes between the acts, for instance, are advantageous. By careful selection of filters and with two frames white and three colours can be obtained.

MAINTENANCE

It cannot be too strongly emphasized that all lighting equipment must be regularly cleaned: even reflectors and lenses are sometimes neglected. A film of dust changes the characteristics of both.

All reflectors, lamp bulbs, and colour filters should be dusted and polished once a fortnight, and every three months lamp bulbs, reflectors, and lenses should be removed, washed in soap and water, dried, and polished. At the same time, lamps should be examined for age—the blackening of the bulb is a handy guide—and the silvering of the reflectors of precision spots checked.

DIMMERS

When "dimmer" is referred to in the theatre the reference is to a device inserted in the electrical circuit. However, the possibility of variable shutters in front of the light source cannot be overlooked. The electrical method (the more usual) involves the reduction of the normal line voltage applied to the lamp or lamps. This reduction is commonly made by inserting a variable resistance in series with the lamp to vary the voltage between that of the mains (200–250) and 32, at which point the filament just glows and may be switched off as the final step.

LIQUID DIMMERS

The resistance itself may be liquid or metallic. The former is rare in professional circles, but it still appeals to amateurs on account of its simple construction (Fig. 38). It is the only dimmer that amateurs can make easily—a drainpipe, a fixed metal plate at the bottom, a moving metal plate at the end of a flex, and a solution of washing soda, the wattage controlled varying with the amount of the soda. Ingenuity can provide a useful winch or lever control for the moving electrode.

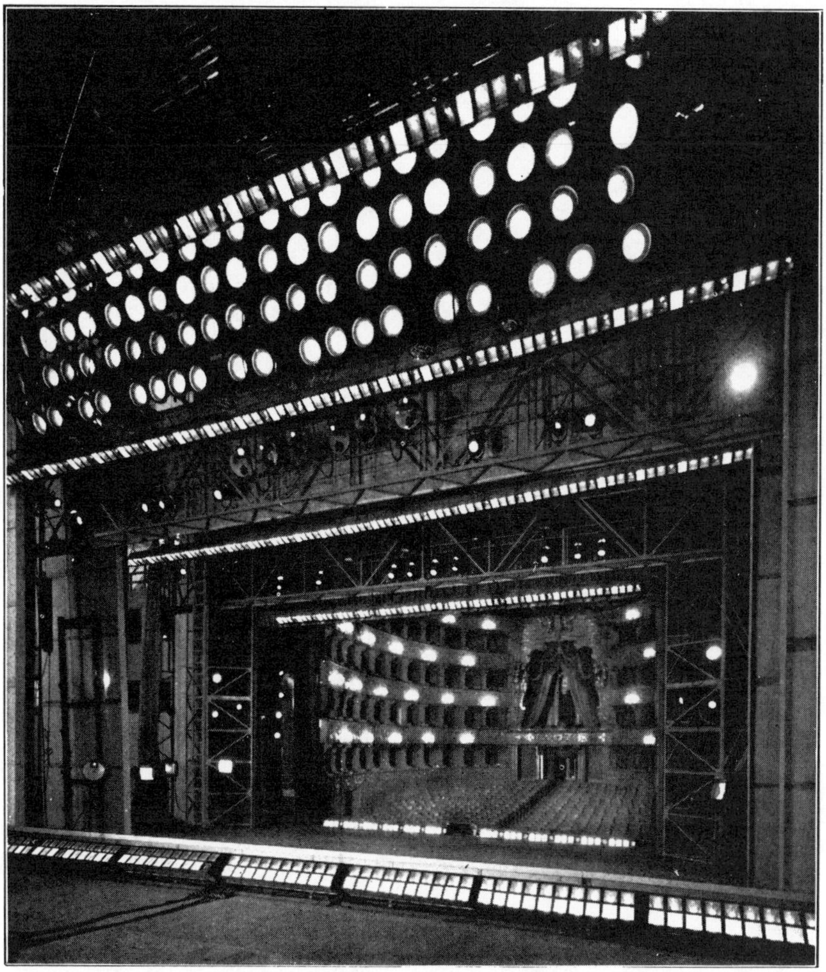

FIG. 37. THE NATIONAL OPERA HOUSE, S. CARLOS, LISBON, PORTUGAL

View from back of stage looking towards the auditorium. Complete British stage lighting equipment exported and installed in 1940. Magazine battens and footlight; 3-colour cyclorama bank and groundrow trucks (in the foreground); cloud effects projectors; acting area and wing floods, mirror spots on two lighting bridges; 2-kW soft edge spots on mobile towers; boomerangs; remote colour change high-tensity F.O.H. spots concealed in auditorium cornice.

The whole is controlled from the author's Light Console (*see* Figs. 61 and 62) placed on a movable platform in the orchestral pit.

When liquid dimmers are used, as there is a tendency for the surroundings of the pots themselves to become damp, they should never be mounted on or over the stage, but placed under the stage and partitioned off, allowing only the electrical expert to have access to them. The electrodes can be operated from the stage above by cords or tracker wire, but care must be taken to attach the wires with porcelain insulators. The simplicity of construction of the liquid dimmer is more than offset by the extreme care that must be

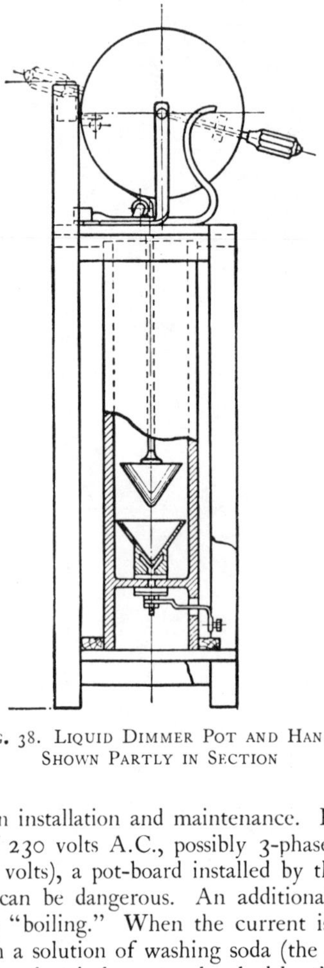

FIG. 38. LIQUID DIMMER POT AND HANDLE SHOWN PARTLY IN SECTION

taken in installation and maintenance. In these days of 230 volts A.C., possibly 3-phase (equal to 400 volts), a pot-board installed by the non-expert can be dangerous. An additional drawback is "boiling." When the current is passed through a solution of washing soda (the electrolyte), the electrical energy absorbed by the resistance is turned into heat, and the solution may boil. If the two electrodes are separated a little, to give a slight reduction in the light of the circuit, jumping of the movable electrode (even when quite heavy) may take place and the light flicker. For similar reasons the two electrodes must always be short-circuited by a switch when in contact (the full on position). There are other drawbacks, such as evaporation. As there are now many efficient and reasonably-priced metallic dimmers available I think amateurs should avoid liquid dimmers. The operator of a pot-board and the operator of a metallic board stand in somewhat the same relationship as the driver of a steam locomotive and the driver of an electric one.

SLIDER DIMMERS

The simplest form of metallic dimmer is known as "the slider." It consists of a former, such as a vitreous enamelled tube or rectangular slate, on which nickel-copper resistance wire is wound, and a sliding contact (the slider) bridges the gap between the wound surface and the square rod on which it moves. A terminal is fitted on one end of the resistance wire and another on the rod. Thus, by moving the slider backward and forward, more or less resistance is tapped off. The resistance wire is clamped by a band at each end. When the slider is at the end that includes the terminal, all resistance is cut out. Similarly, a dead spot can be arranged at the other end. This simple form of sliding resistance, although common in electrical engineering, is seldom used in stage lighting, the principal reason being the excessive length of tube required to accommodate the resistance wire that is necessary to cope with the great voltage range needed to dim a lamp properly. This is obviated by mounting two tubes side by side and causing the slider to bridge the gap between them, thus connecting various lengths of both tubes in series, the terminals being on the resistance coils. These double sliders provide a useful facility when such dimmers are toured. By fitting a movable plug to give the series arrangment described, or a parallel

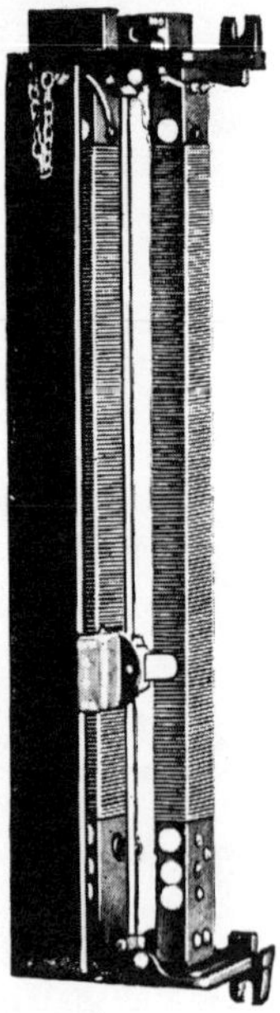

FIG. 39. SLIDER DIMMER

connexion of the coils, the dimmer can be used on the low-voltage (100) high-current range as well as on the more usual high-voltage low-current range. For normal use this plug is a waste of money.

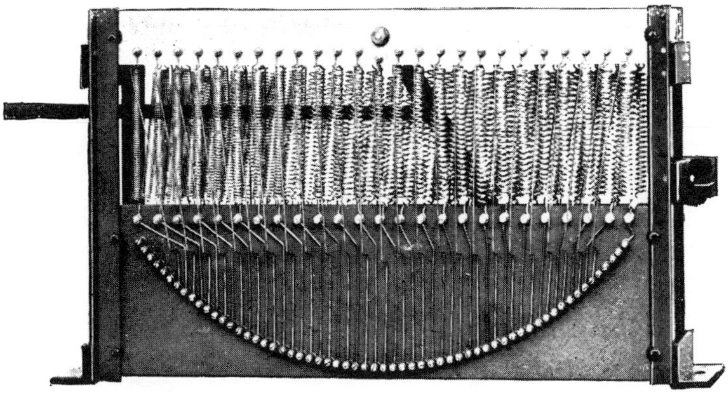

FIG. 40. OPEN COIL RESISTANCE DIMMER

The slider contact direct on the wire is not an ideal electrical arrangement, and the problem of a good contact, not too free and not too stiff, is still, to my mind, far from perfectly solved. This is a matter which the prospective purchaser should keep well in mind. He should insist on practical trial, both with the dimmer cold and after it has been slightly on check with its load for half an hour. As with the liquid dimmer, the energy absorbed by the resistance is turned into heat and the wire expands; unless neatly wound, the slider may squeak or even stick. A too-loose slider annoys. When the dimmer is mounted vertically, the slider may shake down half an inch or more. Owing to the contact arrangements, it is inconvenient to operate these dimmers through a panel (see "Dead front boards," page 354), and, therefore, they carry their own guards, one of which is shown removed in Fig. 39.

A final word on the subject. Often the slider contact is carried on a lead screw or worm drive, operated from a handle. This device imposes a slow-speed dimmer travel, and is not the slightest use for stage purposes.

Slider dimmers are manufactured for various wattages from 60 to 3,000; but I would put the limits as 250 to 2,000, and keep to 500 and 1,000 sizes, whenever possible. In the small sizes the wire is too fine to be completely satisfactory for direct contact, and the large wattage dimmers are far too cumbersome. A slider dimmer varies in its dimensions according to its wattage.

It will be gathered that I am not enamoured of slider dimmers. The slider was early in the field as a smooth and flickerless dimmer, but should have been supplanted long since by the multi-contact dimmer. It survives because it is the only dimmer that is compact and complete with operating knob, fixing lugs, and cover. The multi-contact dimmer has hitherto needed an elaborate supporting framework and shafting for the operating lever, etc., making it expensive in comparison with the slider type. But I shall try to show this need not be.

MULTI-CONTACT DIMMER

Broadly speaking, each turn of the wire in a slider dimmer is a contact, but in this context the word "contact" is used more strictly. The contact is solely concerned with the good conduction of electricity, and the resistance wire is connected to that contact.

FIG. 41. ELEMENT TYPE RESISTANCE DIMMER

Multi-contact dimmers take various forms. Most of them use stud contacts, which may be mounted in a complete circle or as two segments of a circle mounted side by side (Fig. 40). The actual resistance wire is coiled or wound on formers; tappings are taken from appropriate points on the resistances to the contacts. In the circular dimmer the wiper arm bridges studs directly opposite each other on the circumference. In the segmental (rectangular) dimmer the wiper arm bridges the gap between the two parallel rows of contacts, in a similar manner to that in which the pairs of windings are bridged in the slider dimmer. The dimmer assembly, complete with wiper arm, contacts, and resistances, is known as a "dimmer plate." Eighty or a hundred contacts are usual: the latter should be adopted.

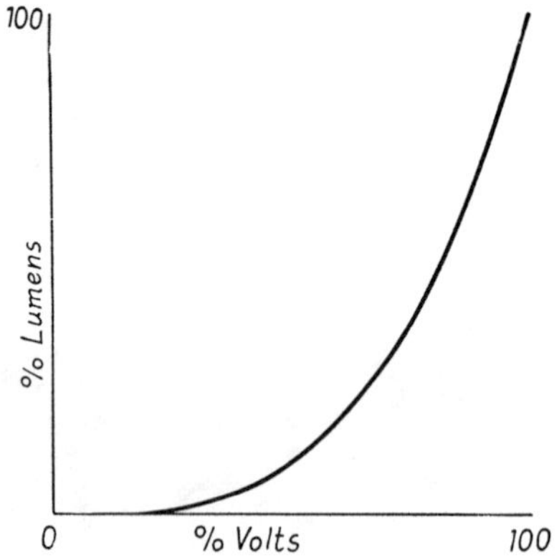

Fig. 42. Volts-lumens Curves

The dimmer, with the resistance wound on formers as elements (Fig. 41) has much to commend it when compared with the open-coil type. The smaller gauges of wire used on most dimmers need this support, and, further, more tappings can be taken off at any point instead of being limited to the top and bottom of a coil. This last, combined with the fact that clearances need not be so great, much reduces the overall size of the element dimmer.

When 100 contacts are used, the light of the lamp or lamps must be reduced in 100 imperceptible light steps from full on to a point where it can be switched off without detection. For finest results a dimmer should be wound exactly for one load only at one voltage. The selection of the resistance to give the voltage drop between each contact is not simple. It might be supposed that on a 230-volt circuit 100 steps dropping 2 volts at a time would be suitable. Unfortunately, as will have been gathered from page 329, the

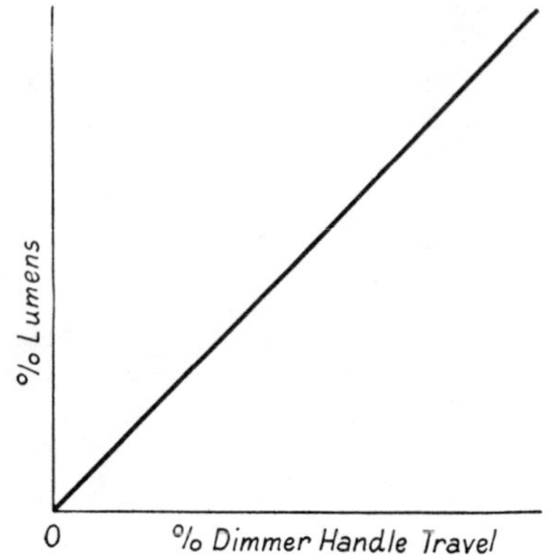

Fig. 43. Ideal Dimmer Travel-lumens Curve

relationship of voltage to light output is not straightforward. A 25 per cent reduction in volts gives roughly a 60 per cent reduction in light (Fig. 42); therefore 2-volt steps will give a pronounced jump in the top part of the dimmer travel and too little change later on. It is desirable to be able to relate the travel of the dimmer

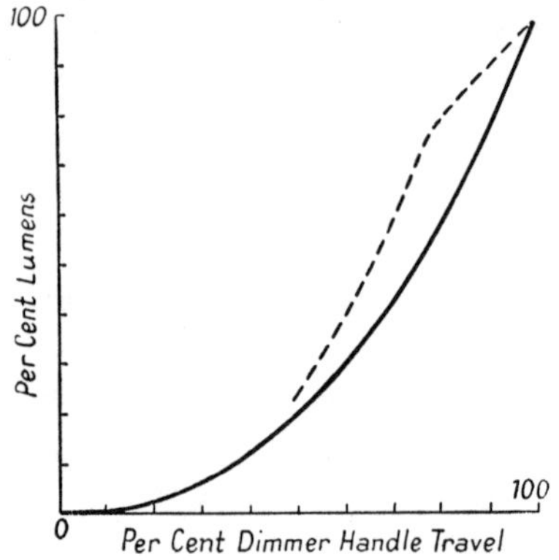

Fig. 44.

handle to the amount of light emitted by the lamp; ideally 50 per cent dimmer travel should give 50 per cent light (Fig. 43). By adjusting the voltage steps between each contact this can be achieved, but a much greater number of contacts than the 100, which are economical, are needed; otherwise there is bad flickering. Compromise is necessary. Fig. 44 represents the results from a well-arranged standard dimmer. This curve will give reasonable results, even on the smaller wattage theatre batten lamps. Messrs. Ridge & Aldred devised a dimmer that gave a curve nearer a straight line for cyclorama work (dotted line in Fig. 44), but it tends to give a flicker for lamps of less than 500 watts.

Light jumps or flicker in the small hall or theatre must be seriously considered because (1) the smaller wattage lamps are more susceptible to flicker; the thicker filaments of the bigger wattages have a slight time-lag before responding in temperature to voltage variation: (2) the smaller the hall, the closer the audience to the stage and less the number of lamps comprising a particular batten. A good, but exacting, test is to bring in slowly from blackout a row of 100-watt blue lamps at the bottom of a cyclorama.

It is possible for dimmers to be wound to allow a variation of wattage of $\pm$ $33\frac{1}{3}$ per cent, common ones being 750-watt $\pm$, giving a wattage range of 500–1,000 watts, and 1,500-watt $\pm$, giving 1,000 watts to 2,000 watts. This arrangement involves a compromise winding, which is effective provided lamps below 250 watts each are not used.

The expression "+ or —" is not used by me here, the limits of variation being given; for example, a 750-watt $\pm$ is described as a "500/1,000-watt dimmer" and a 1,500-watt $\pm$ as "1/2,000-watt." As the volts dropped at each contact depend in a resistance dimmer on the current forming the load, a 500/1,000-watt dimmer, though dimming both 500 watts or 1,000 watts properly, will not dim them in the same dimmer handle travel. The heavier the current, the more the obstruction offered by the resistance; the position of the dimmer handle for 50 per cent light will differ in each case. Stated another way, if we have one 500-watt lamp on check at some intermediate position, the addition of another 500-watt lamp to the dimmer will cause a reduction of the light from the first lamp. On a 230-volt supply, the lamp volts need not be reduced below 32 before the wiper arm passes on to the dead contacts forming the "Off" position: this is just as well, as Fig. 44 shows. (A warning: make sure that the 100-contact dimmer has all these devoted to resistance steps: the contacts for the full "On" and "Off" positions must be additional.)

A slider dimmer cannot provide the careful matching of dimmer travel to lamplight that is possible on the contact dimmer plate; the most

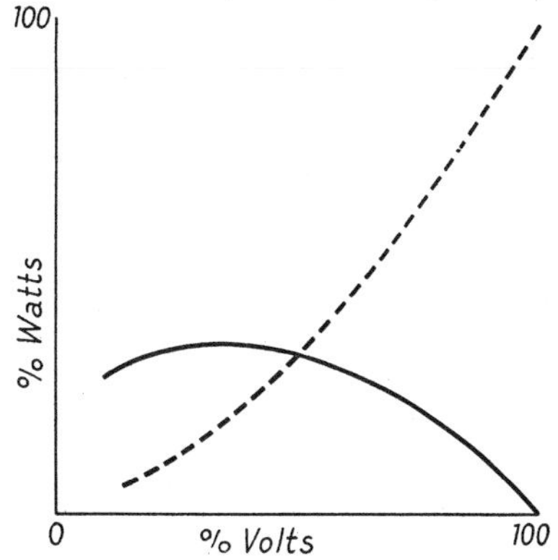

FIG. 45. HEAT LOSS CURVES

that can be done is to wind the slider formers in sections with, perhaps, four different gauges of resistance wire. The rectangular dimmer plate can be operated (Fig. 41) by a handle fitted to an extension of the wiper arm beyond the pivot. This is not possible with the circular dimmer plate, which is, therefore, unsuitable for use in the unit-type dimmer board described in page 357.

HEAT LOSSES

All resistance dimmers convert into heat the energy they absorb in order to dim the lamp or lamps; their surroundings must, therefore, be well ventilated. The process is not so wasteful as it sounds. For example, when the lamp volts are reduced 50 per cent the same amount of power is not consumed by the combination of lamps and dimmer whether the lamp is full on or half-dimmed. To introduce resistance in a circuit reduces both the voltage to the lamp and the current in the circuit. Fig. 45 shows the relationship of reduction of lamp volts to watts (power) in the circuit. The dotted line shows the amount of power dissipated by the lamp itself for the corresponding reduction in volts. For example, when the dimmer reduces the volts to the lamp by

50 per cent, the power in the circuit (watts) is reduced to 70 per cent, of which 50 per cent is dissipated by the dimmer and 50 per cent by the lamp. At 25 per cent volts the watts are reduced to nearly 48 per cent, of which 75 per cent is dissipated by the dimmer and 25 per cent by the lamp.

TRANSFORMER DIMMERS

The dimmers already described, whether liquid or metallic, have depended on the introduction of more or less resistance in the lamp circuit for their operation. The extensive use of alternating current now allows the use of transformer-type dimmers, which employ reactance for dimming, the voltage reduction being independent of the amount of current in the circuit. Whereas the resistance dimmer set at a position to reduce the voltage 50 per cent requires a definite load (wattage) to achieve this reduction; the transformer dimmer, when set at the 50 per cent position, gives 50 per cent of the mains voltage loaded either lightly or heavily. Strictly, the 50 per cent is there even when not loaded and this applies to any intermediate position to which the dimmer may be set.

Such transformer dimmers take many forms, but the commonest is the multi-tapped auto-transformer. This usually consists of a core of

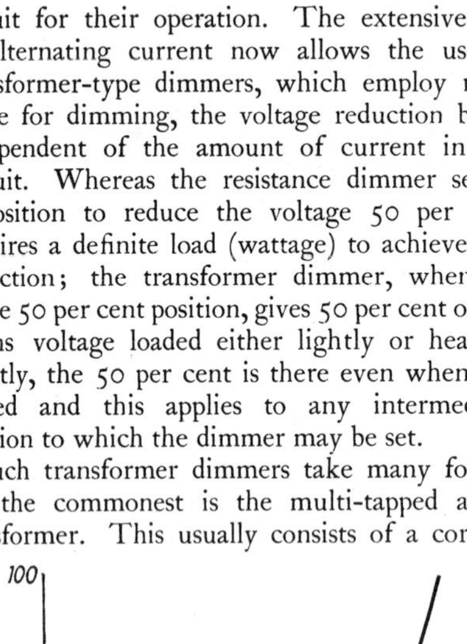

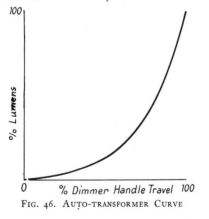

FIG. 46. AUTO-TRANSFORMER CURVE

laminated iron in the shape of a ring, round which is wound enamelled (insulated) wire in tight formation. A contact path along the wire, either inside or outside the ring, is cleared by removing the enamel. Along this path a wiper contact passes. When the two ends of the winding are connected to the mains, any voltage between zero and that of the mains can be tapped off by the wiper. As the number of turns is above 200, and the wiper

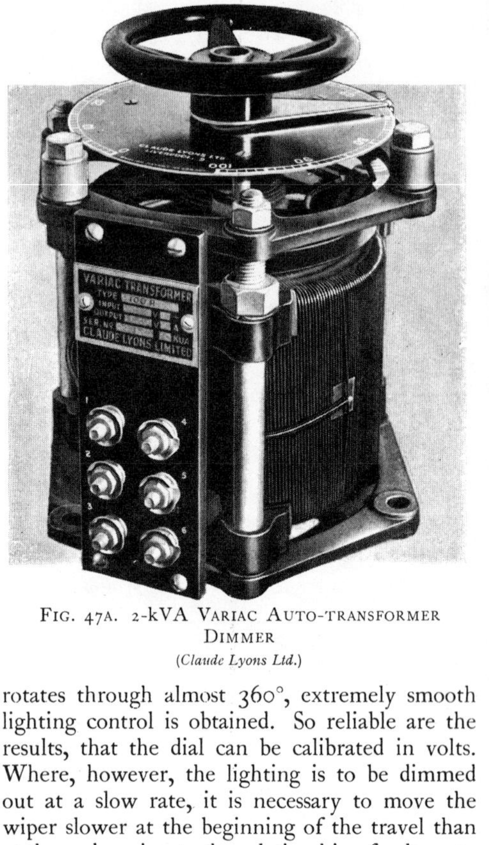

FIG. 47A. 2-kVA VARIAC AUTO-TRANSFORMER DIMMER
(*Claude Lyons Ltd.*)

rotates through almost 360°, extremely smooth lighting control is obtained. So reliable are the results, that the dial can be calibrated in volts. Where, however, the lighting is to be dimmed out at a slow rate, it is necessary to move the wiper slower at the beginning of the travel than at the end, owing to the relationship of voltage to light, the curve being shown in Fig. 46.

One of the neatest and best known of the variable tapped auto-transformers is the Variac (Fig. 47A). In another form, the Gresham (Fig. 47B), the contact is made via a commutator instead of direct on the wire. It is important to remember that when a transformer dimmer is described, for example, as 7 kW, the meaning is that any load up to that figure can be regulated. Further, most transformers can be overloaded 50 per cent for short periods, so that a 7 kW transformer can be employed on a 10.5 kW load for a few moments at a time.

Some designs provide a number of separate wiper contacts to tap off several dimmer circuits from a single transformer winding and assembly.

FIG. 47B. MAGNETIC CLUTCH DRIVEN TRANSFORMER DIMMER

Developments on these lines may reduce the cost, and space occupied, per dimmer way.

It will have been noted that contact in some transformer dimmers is made on to the wire as in a slider dimmer. However, the reasons why this is bad practice in resistance dimmers do not apply here, as there is no question of energy being dissipated as heat. Unless the auto-transformer is badly overloaded, the winding remains comparatively cool, and, therefore, perfectly tight. The loading of auto-transformers is usually given in kVA. As it is impossible to furnish a simple explanation of the difference between a kVA and a kW, in the present context the expressions can best be considered as interchangeable.

An important technical aspect of the auto-transformer dimmer is considered in a note at the end of page 363.

Transformer dimmers have one great drawback—high initial cost. Their use is, therefore, restricted to circuits such as stage plugs where the variable load factor is important. An ideal use of these dimmers is as master dimmers, and where funds permit they will be found to give superb control in this position. A suitable circuit is given on page 363 (Fig. 65). The importance of these new forms of dimmer cannot be stressed too much as they represent the logical use of A.C. current, and it is in this direction that future development lies.

Another form of A.C. dimmer is known as the *saturable choke*. This dimmer is rather difficult to explain in non-technical language. Briefly, the effect of the magnetic iron core, which is the backbone of any transformer, is countered by applying a greater or lesser amount of D.C. in a special winding. Fig. 48 conveys this idea. Normally, the volts from A to B drop from 230 to 0; consequently, there is no light in the lamps. As more D.C. is applied to terminals C and D, less voltage is dropped between A and B, and the lamps increase in brightness. The D.C. current required is very much less than the actual current in the lamp circuit. The D.C. may be supplied through an orthodox dimmer from a rectifier (to convert

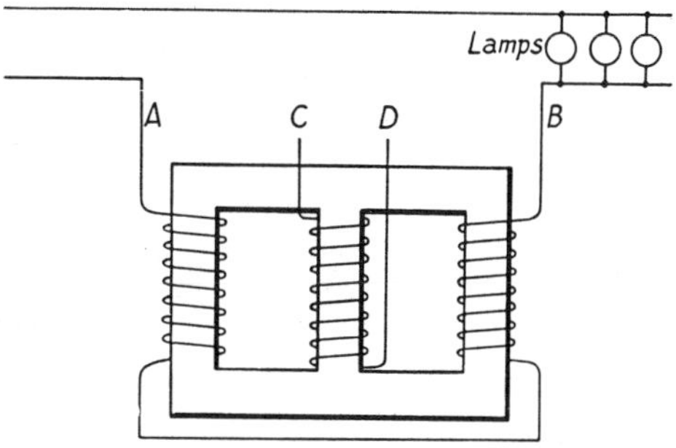

FIG. 48. SATURABLE CHOKE DIMMER

A.C. to D.C.) or through an electronic circuit, such as the BTH Thyratron valve in which the prime mover is a small knob, radio fashion, which regulates the current passed by the valve grid.

SHUTTER DIMMERS

One of the commonest types of shutter dimmers is the iris diaphragm attachment (Fig.

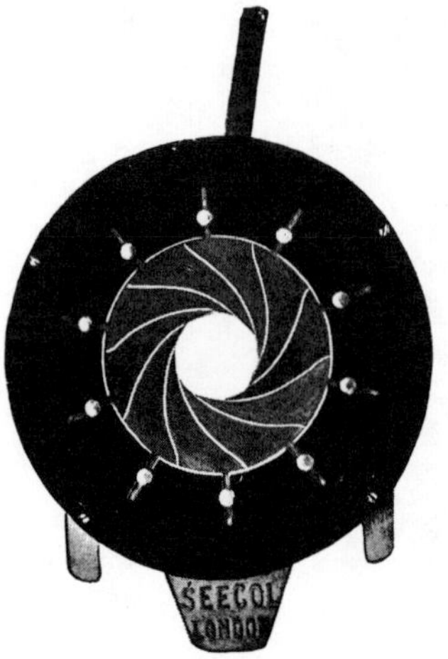

FIG. 49. IRIS DIAPHRAGM

49), fitted to the front of a focus lantern. As the aperture is gradually closed the light is dimmed, often contrary to the wish of the purchaser, who wishes the size of the spot beam to be reduced. As the effective diameter of the lens is reduced by this device, the light passed is also reduced.

Germans used shutters in front of their large 3,000-watt cyclorama floods to avoid the change of colour emitted from the lamp filament as the voltage is reduced. Behind a blue filter the red-orange glow of the dimmed filament prevents a true blue being obtained at low intensities with the filters in common use on the stage. Producers elsewhere consider themselves lucky when they have a cyclorama, and are, therefore, not, as yet, so sensitive.

Shutters are likely to come into their own when discharge lamps operated from a system of remote control are used for cyclorama lighting in the theatre. An earlier arrival will probably be the Extra High Pressure Mercury Lamp for scene and effects projection, the dimming shutters being operated by hand.

Note for D.C. Mains. Liquid and metallic resistance dimmers can be used on D.C. as well as A.C. The addition of a quick break spring contact at the point where the wiper arm runs off the resistance contact studs on to the "Off" studs, is required for D.C. This is essential, as D.C. arcs badly, and unless a circuit is broken instantaneously such arcing burns away the stud contacts.

Any attempt to make the transformer dimmer work on D.C. will merely result in a blown fuse. Except for the introduction of one-third + or —, variable load dimmers on D.C. have to

FIG. 50. PORTABLE SLIDER DIMMER BOARD, 6 WAYS

consist of several plates with switches to connect them in parallel, all the wiper arms being mechanically connected to the same operating lever. The correct number of plates has to be switched in to suit the load to be dimmed. The liquid dimmer is practical on D.C., and, by adding more or less washing soda, the electrolyte can be matched to the requirements of the particular show.

STAGE SWITCHBOARDS

The expression "stage switchboard" is rather a misnomer. Switches are the least important, dimmers of primary importance. "Dimmer board" is a better term. Often the non-committal expression "stage-board," which is adopted here, is used. Stage-boards are either direct-operated or remote-controlled. The former have the dimmers mounted immediately behind the operating levers; the latter work dimmers at a distance by tracker wires or purely electrical means. Remote control is expensive—a fact which prevents its use by amateurs and little theatres. Therefore, direct operation will be considered first and at greater length.

Direct-operated boards may use either slider dimmers or contact dimmers. Fig. 50 shows slider dimmers mounted to make a stage-board, in this case portable. Each dimmer feeds a plug socket to which the temporary connexions are brought. In the example there are six dimmers. One of the first problems of the operator is how to move several dimmer knobs at once. Sometimes a rod is kept handy, but pushing several stiff slider knobs by a rod under them is not easy, especially if with those that have to be moved are one or two that must remain stationary. Fig. 51, also of a portable board, shows an attempt to overcome these difficulties. Each of the slider dimmer knobs is made off to an endless tracker wire, which, passing over pulleys, is fixed to a grooved wheel carrying the operating handle. The handles and wheels are mounted on a shaft to which they may be screwed for master operation by a wheel at the end of the shaft. However effective the arrangement is, it is costly and removes the initial reason for using slider dimmers—cheapness.

MECHANICAL INTERLOCKING

Now consider the contact dimmer stage-board. Hitherto, this has been bulky, expensive, and generally unsuitable for small stages. Before I describe a new improved type, I shall explain previous practice.

FIG. 51. PORTABLE INTERLOCKING BOARD, 6 WAYS

The contact dimmer has always been built into what may be termed "mechanical interlocking boards" (Fig. 52 and Fig. 54). The dimmers are mounted in tiers on a built-up frame, usually of angle and channel iron, each tier of dimmers being connected by links to a row of handles pivoted on a shaft. Handles may be operated singly or locked to their shaft for operation by a master control at the end. In the cheaper boards the handles screw to their shaft, but self-release handles which slip at the end of travel are available. Similarly, the master wheels may have an alternative slow-motion worm drive.

The larger boards have four tiers and the very large ones have their shafts in each tier split into two sections. The various sections are then provided with gearing so that the shafts can be driven from a grand master worm wheel located in the centre of the board (Fig. 53). In the professional theatre, shafts are often allocated to individual colour groups. However, the installations now considered will not lend themselves to this practice. The dimmer operating links work through slots in a sheet-metal panel, thus keeping the "live" dimmers out of reach.

FIG. 52. SCREW DOWN (BRACKET) HANDLE SWITCH AND DIMMER BOARD WITH SLOW MOTION MASTER WHEELS

In most English boards the circuit switches and fuses are mounted on panels of insulating material carried on the frame over the top tier of dimmers (Fig. 54). The switches are then, as far as possible, fixed in rows and at centres to correspond with their dimmers. Switches are either of the Bakelite tumbler type or the back-of-board type operated through a slot from a lever in front. In either case there is no unshielded live metal on the front of the board, and all wiring and connexions are behind the panel, which is then known as "dead front."

A type of board, with a completely flat sheet-metal front, originated in U.S.A., makes a neat-looking job. However, the shafts are there, though they are concealed behind the sheet-metal face, where cleaning is likely to be overlooked. In these boards it is usual to find each circuit switch mounted adjacent to its dimmer. This may have the drawback of increasing the vertical centres of the all-important dimmer handles.

The circuit switches in both kinds of board were originally single-way switches, the function of which was to render the particular circuit dead. Recently several, and sometimes all, switches have been of the three-position or 2-way-and-off type. When the switch is in the "Up" position, the circuit is connected to the busbar fed by the master blackout switch; in the "Down" position it is connected to a permanently live busbar.

The master blackout may be a mechanically operated switch on the back of the board, or remote from the stage and operated by an electro-magnet, only the small magnet coil-switch being on the board. This arrangement is desirable owing to noise of operation where the blackout switch is large. In the professional theatres that employ the colour shaft grouping there is a separate master blackout contactor switch to each colour, these in their turn being connected by 2-way-and-off switches either to a master black-out switch or to a live busbar.

MECHANICAL *v.* ELECTRICAL INTERLOCKING

The mechanical interlocking board has many faults and limitations.

(1) All the shafts, bearings, operating levers, gearing, etc., render an elaborate framework and skilled fitting essential. Even the simplest

form of board therefore, costs at least three times as much as the actual contact dimmers themselves.

(2) Owing to the barrier provided by the shafts, access to the dimmers must be provided behind the board, thereby adding 1 ft. 6 in. to the depth taken up by the board.

(3) Master dimming is not proportional.

(4) Mechanical interlocking is illogical on an electrical switchboard.

individual dimmer handles down; in the electrical interlock only the master dimmer handle moves, just as operation of the master blackout switch leaves the individual switches "On."

The proportional dimming given by the electrical master method ensures proper balanced lighting at all times. For example, in a scene where the cyclorama is lit by 50 per cent blue and the acting area by spotlights at 100 per cent, a slow dim (check) on the mechanical board gives

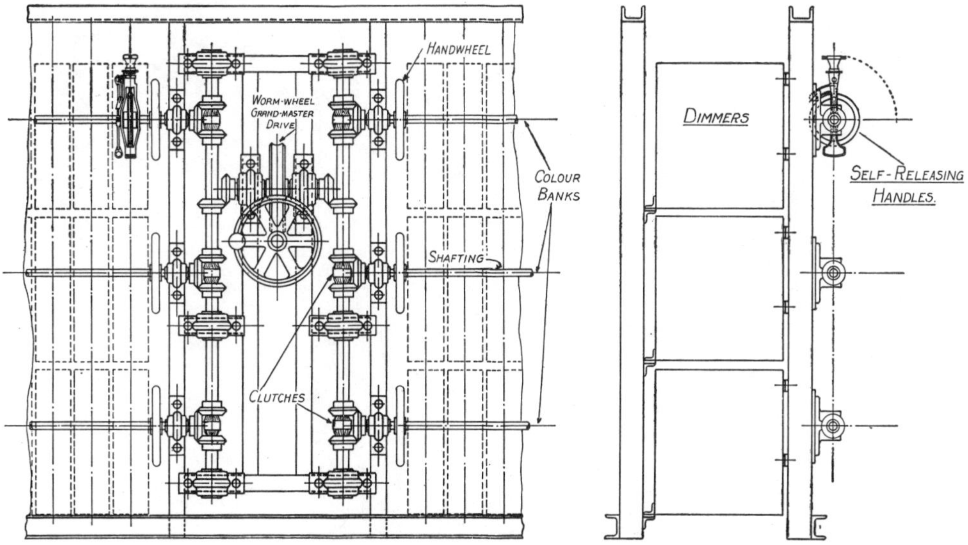

FIG. 53. GRAND MASTER CROSS-CONTROL GEAR

Consider the fourth point in greater detail. Fig. 55 shows a typical stage-board circuit as used hitherto. The circuit switches, 2-way-and-off pattern, can be made to connect the various lighting circuits so that they are fed direct from the mains or from a large master blackout switch. In short, the switches can be *electrically* interlocked. The dimmers, however, are mechanically interlocked by a shaft (the dotted line) as already described. In the second, Fig. 56, the dimmers are arranged so that by operation of 2-way switches they can be connected to a large master dimmer. In other words, both the circuit switches and the dimmers are electrically interlocked and no mechanical gearing is required. In the mechanical interlock a general dim by operation of the master wheel brings all the

a completely black cyclorama at a turn of the wheel while the spots are still at 50 per cent; half a turn on the electrical master dimmer brings the cyclorama to 25 per cent and the spots to 50 per cent, the lighting remaining properly balanced. Examples in colour mixing confirm this: a bright grey cyclorama, made up of blue 100 per cent, green 80 per cent, and red 50 per cent, with half a turn of the mechancial master, changes to blue 50 per cent, green 30 per cent, and red 0 per cent—from grey to dull blue-green. A master dimmer when moved to 50 per cent reduces blue to 50 per cent, green to 40 per cent, and red to 25 per cent, giving the correct change from bright grey to dull grey. In the case of an orange cyclorama, red 100 per cent, green 50 per cent, the former makes a change from bright orange to dull red, and the latter a change from bright orange to dull orange.

So far general dimming out of lighting has been considered, but the electrical master also scores in reverse. It is frequently required to bring in at one movement several individual dimmers to various check positions—75 per cent, 50 per cent, 40 per cent, and so on, to give a balanced effect. This is a most difficult operation on the mechanical boards because as the master wheel is turned, the various dimmers have, in their turn, to be unlocked at the proper positions. When the electrical master method is adopted, the job is easy. The various dimmers are set to the positions required while the master dimmer is "Off" and all that is needed at cue is to turn up the master dimmer.

Neither system by itself will perform all required lighting manoeuvres, but on balance the electrical master is much the better. Why, then, has such a completely logical system not been standardized? After all, no one carried out master blackouts by mechanically interlocking the switches! The Cambridge Festival Theatre had such a system years ago, and it has cropped up in various small theatres (mainly amateur), one example being the Cambridge A.D.C. in 1937. It has lacked general acceptance largely because stage lighting manufacturers' have maintained a policy of designing their gear mainly for the professional theatre and cinema; thus the amateur and small theatres have had to use makeshifts. Much valuable space on small stages has been occupied by stageboards giving facilities limited and out of proportion to their large bulk and cost. Thus standardization of the electrical master board has depended on the professional theatres.

The main reason for the adoption there years ago and the continuing use of the mechanical

FIG. 54. GRAND MASTER CROSS-CONTROL BOARD; 92 DIMMERS ARE DIRECT-OPERATED

interlocking system is explained by the great difficulty of designing a master dimmer that will cope with the large diversity of loads that may be connected to it. Such a dimmer at one moment will have to dim 20 kW and shortly afterwards merely 1.5 kW, and so on. Only since the introduction of reliable dimmers of the auto-transformer type employing voltage regulation just before the Second Great War has electrical master dimming on a large scale been possible. New design *all electric* boards may increasingly be used in the professional theatre. Such voltage regulators are expensive when compared with the cost of corresponding resistance dimmers and expense may make them impossible for most amateurs. However, as load diversity is not usually so marked in their case, resistance master dimmers can be used sucessfully.

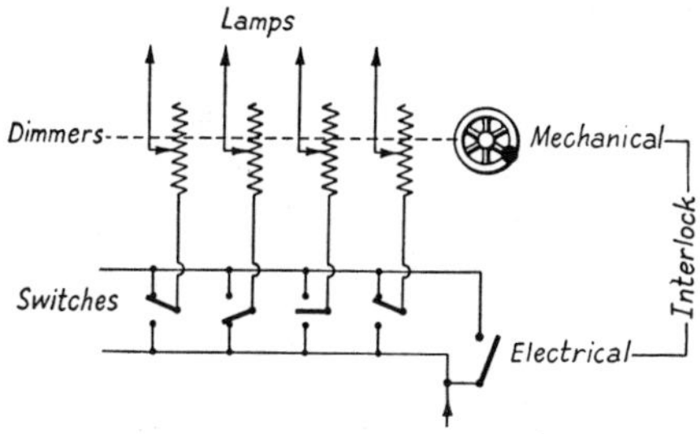

Fig. 55. Schematic Diagram of Mechanical Interlocking Board

UNIT DIMMER BOARDS

Recently I investigated the possibility of a unit system of dimmer boards for amateur stages and small theatres. This system, which is based on electrical mastering, would have to be produced on a large scale. The prime essential of the system is the reduction of cost by ensuring repetition of a few unit parts, which are:

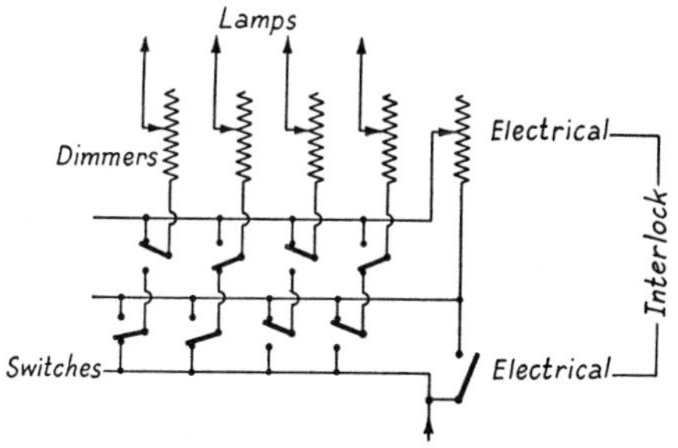

Fig. 56. Schematic Diagram of Electrical Interlocking Board

(*a*) Standard Dimmer Unit (Fig. 58). This is arranged so that any winding up to 3,000 watts can be fitted. Carried as part of the dimmer is a panel through which the operating handle (an extension of the wiper arm) projects. A 15-amp. circuit fuse, a 2-way switch wired in series with the dimmer, a scale giving dimmer positions and circuit label, are mounted on the dimmer panel.

Fig. 57. Suggested Unit Board   Fig. 58. Dimmer Unit

(*b*) Standard Master Dimmer Unit. This has the same dimensions as the dimmer mentioned above, but the winding can be made to take a total load of 6 kW with the variation necessary in a master dimmer.

(*c*) Unit Frame (Fig. 57). This is of light metal construction and is arranged to take eight standard dimmers. The frame is complete with a wiring trough along the lower rear edge. The sides are fitted with perforated metal guards. Dimmers are inserted in the frame, fixed, and wired from the front. The only space behind the board that is needed is two or three inches air space for ventilation.

(*d*) Base Unit. A 12-in. plinth with vent holes to obviate placing the above unit direct on the floor.

(*e*) Neutral Box. This is 8-way and arranged to take either fuse or links as the supply arrangements may demand. The box can be mounted on the end of the standard frame or on the wall adjacent to it.

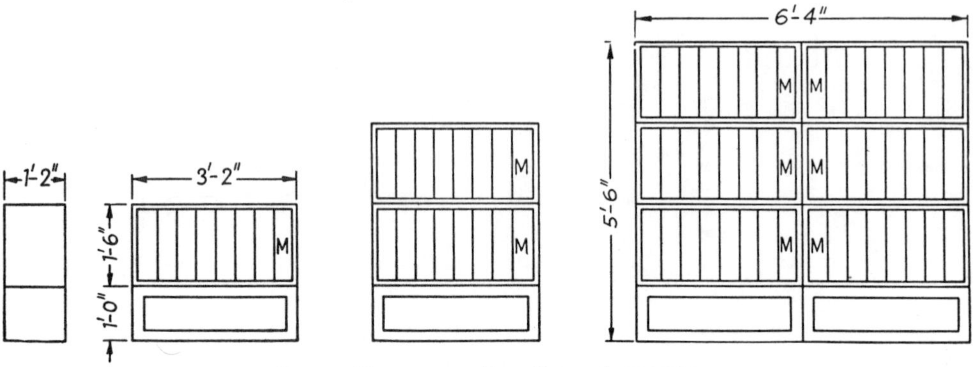

FIG. 59. DIAGRAMS OF UNIT BOARD ASSEMBLIES

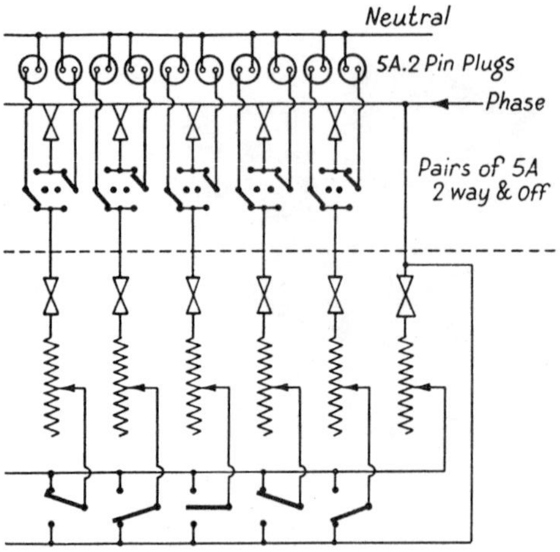

FIG. 60. FLEXIBLE BOARD CIRCUIT

(*f*) Plugging Unit. This is not an essential part of the board, but its use enables one set of seven dimmers to serve fourteen lighting circuits (Fig. 60).

The photographs give a good idea of the various parts, both separately and assembled to form a complete board. The aim has been to avoid the expense of boards specially designed and built for each particular stage; also to allow extension from time to time as funds permit. The minimum frame possible provides for 8 ways, i.e. 7 circuit dimmers and a master (Fig. 59). The next stage is two 8-way frames on top of each other, providing 14 circuit dimmers and 2 masters; then three, one on top of the other; followed by four 8-way unit frames (two pairs side by side) giving 28 circuit dimmers and 4 masters, the masters being placed adjacent to one another to allow of easy collective operation. Six unit frames in pairs side by side give 42 ways and 6 masters, though for this size transformer mastering should be adopted, if possible. Where funds do not permit or the lighting installation require it, each 8-way unit need not be occupied by its full complement of dimmers, the spaces being provided with blank panels. Only three connexions are made to each dimmer, so that insertion is easy. Further, incomplete frames can be made up to the full complement by hiring the standard dimmer units when a special production demands it.

Even if the Cabinet board is unobtainable the system of electric interlock can be applied to existing components. Contact dimmers (element type) can be mounted vertically and their arms extended to form handles (Fig. 41) instead of being operated by a link (Fig. 40). These dimmers to be mounted on a frame with slotted metal front panel and two-way switches on a panel above. Mastering is by a larger dimmer or a Variac.

A similar set up of seven slider dimmers and a master would when wired as Fig. 60, be much less costly than a seven-way mechanical interlock board.

FLEXIBLE BOARDS

Although the ideal arrangement is to have a separate dimmer for every stage lighting circuit, as in the professional theatre, it is rather expensive for amateurs, who will find it feasible to economize by making each dimmer serve at least two lighting circuits. Fig. 60 shows how, by means of two 5-amp. 2-way-and-off switches, two circuits may be connected to one dimmer, or one to the mains direct and one to the dimmer, etc. The diagram shows the circuit used in the standard plugging unit. It is in the plugging and switching arrangements that amateurs can exercise their ingenuity. As they are merely assemblies of commercial plugs, sockets, fuses, and switches, amateurs may prefer to make up this part of the board themselves. One 8-way unit frame and its dimmers can be the basis for reasonable stage control. Great care should be taken in selecting the various dimmer wattages in relation to the various lighting loads in order to obtain the greatest flexibility. Incidentally, this kind of stage-board, where a set of dimmers is made to serve more than its own number of lighting circuits, is known as a *flexible* board. The boards illustrated in Figs. 94 to 97 are unit boards, some of which are flexible, matched to the installations.

In a flexible board either the dimmers may terminate in fixed plugs into which lighting circuits on wander leads are plugged, or the dimmer leads may wander and the lighting be fixed. Where the dimmers are live fed from a master dimmer, the latter arrangement should not be adopted. It is always better for the dead leads rather than the live leads to do the wandering.

REMOTE-CONTROLLED BOARDS

All remote-control boards are much more expensive than direct-operated boards. Whatever the system, it consists of a miniature board operating on the equivalent of a direct-operated board placed at a distance; the action required, whether mechanical or electrical, is an extra charge to be met.

The main reason for the adoption of remote control is the large stage installation where there are more dimmer handles than can conveniently be reached and worked by one operator. This is usually taken to mean 100 dimmer ways or over. I would place this total much lower, and say that above 60 dimmers a direct-operated board is no longer handy. I do not deny that one man with a 120-way direct-operated board and suitable electrical mastering can work most cues likely to be required, but such a board leaves no margin for the future. An operator who cannot see the stage as the audience sees it, is greatly handicapped. Development of stage lighting will call for far more movement, which, however, will have to take place with finesse. The lighting installation must be played upon by an artist; all suggestions of "working the lighting" are quite alien to the ultimate progress of this art. Sometimes the lighting changes will, for dramatic effect, be required to draw attention to themselves, but, at other times, the operator will move dimmer after dimmer throughout the show without the audience being aware of his activities; the lighting contribution will, nevertheless, have been made.

As the large installation was the first to have remote control, it was not surprising to find it common in the great opera houses of the Continent, in particular in Germany. The Germans used neat regulators attached to the dimmers by the most elaborate mechanical systems relying on tracker wire. For an electric board electric methods are far more appropriate and, further, a properly designed fully-electric remote control relies on flexible cable connexion between the miniature panel and the dimmers themselves.

For remote control purposes the dimmers may be divided into families, each with its variable speed motor-driven shafting to which individual

Fig. 61. Strand Light Console

Fig. 62. Remote Controlled Dimmer Bank

The Light Console above controls 108 dimmers. It is an early model; to-day a similar sized console with three keyboards would operate 216 dimmers. The dimmer bank is for 108 dimmers of the resistance and auto-transformer type. The electro-magnetically operated circuit switches are mounted on the panel behind the dimmers.

dimmers are connected by electro-magnetic clutches to travel in either direction. The photograph shows a remote-controlled dimmer bank with clutch-driven resistance and transformer dimmers (Fig. 62). Circuit switches are operated by electro-magnets and the grouping and supplying of current to switches, clutches, and motors is carried out by a relay board (on extreme left).

This kind of dimmer bank is operated remotely from a console or desk (Fig. 61), under the Light Console system I have invented. By adopting the keyboards and stop-keys of the organ instead of knobs and levers the fingers can be used independently instead of requiring a hand to work a particular circuit lever.

The console is connected to its dimmer bank by 15 volt D.C. action requiring a multi core cable in a $1\frac{1}{2}$ in. flexible metallic hose. A detachable plug can be fitted (Fig. 63) and the console moved to several positions. There are at the time of going to press four theatre installations in England and two on the Continent. A further console of 216 dimmers is under construction by Strand Electric for Drury Lane Theatre.

So complete and expressive is the control given that it has been played upon as a colour organ both in Lisbon and in Earl's Court Exhibition Hall, London, as the central feature of the *Daily Mail* Ideal Home Exhibition. For a full description of the Light Console as a colour organ readers are referred to *Coloured Light*, by Adrian B. Klein (1937 edition published by the Technical Press, London).

Another interesting system of remote control is of American origin, and was supplied to the Odeon Cinema, Leicester Square (Fig. 64). This board, which consists of small potentiometer controls about the size of a radio volume control, operates through the thyratron valve a saturable choke dimmer. By repeating the small knobs, each change can be "preset" with absolute accuracy and repeated from a master control. Acting on saturable chokes, it provides variable load dimmer control to a limited extent. There are no moving parts in the remote dimmer bank.

There have been various refinements in valve dimmer control in the United States which have tended to remove the slight time lag inherent in the response of a saturable choke and also to improve the variable load factor.

One method of doing this is to omit the choke and use the valve directly to govern the voltage fed to the lamps. The crucial matter is current and we in Britain are better off in this respect than the Americans as our mains voltage is double theirs. The Strand Electric have made an

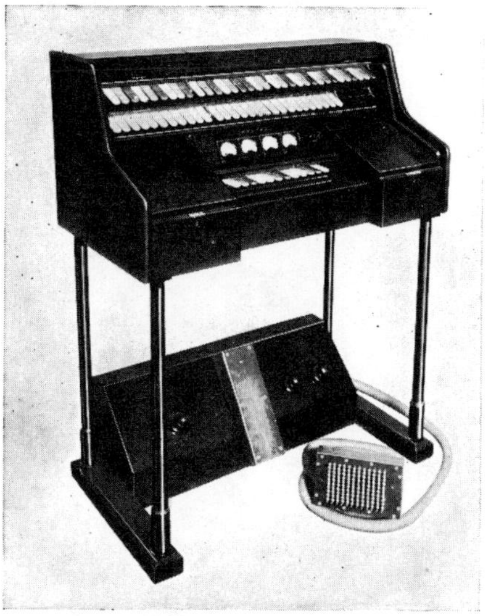

FIG. 63. 60-WAY LIGHT CONSOLE AND MULTI-WAY PLUG

experimental direct valve board, and if tests are satisfactory the preset system will be possible where costs have until now compelled the use of large direct-operated boards.

Probably the highest manifestation of the valve preset board is that designed by George Izenour and installed in Yale University theatre. There is a control desk with a set of rehearsal levers, master faders, etc., and there are 10 presets which can be set up on an auxiliary board. This model for 44 dimmer ways is very compact, but this feature will, in my opinion, be lost in a large installation of 100 or 200 ways.

The Light Console employs certain limited preset aids but it is really quite different from any preset system. It relies on an artist using the controls to paint the stage with light for the drama rather than to move dimmers to previously plotted numerical positions.

Fully automatic dimmer boards can be designed for many purposes, the main limits being

Fig. 64. BTH Thyratron Reactor Two Scene Preset Dimmer Control in Alhambra Odeon, London

The actual Switch Panel is 73 inches wide × 40 inches high (52 Dimmer Ways)

economic. Unskilled hands can produce colours stationary or in moving cycles in a foolproof manner. These are valuable in cinemas, ballrooms, and exhibitions where unskilled labour may be expected. However, in my opinion, they have no place in the theatre, where electricians should take a pride in knowing their craft. We should not think much of an orchestra which allowed its pianist to use a pianola.

PLACING THE STAGE-BOARD

Undoubtedly, the place for the stage-board is out in the auditorium, where the operator can see the stage as the audience sees it. When the Light Console, Luminous Panel, Light Desk, or some other (but not all) remote-control systems are used, this is easy. Even direct-operated boards have been so placed when the number of dimmers is small, as, for example, in the orchestra pit of the Rudolf Steiner Hall, London, or in the special gallery at the back of the London Theatre Studio. Problems of communication between board operator and the other lighting men do not exist during the show. Amateurs, however, are advised to place their boards so that the stage can be easily visited during intervals or rehearsals. In their case, it may well be that the switchboard operator is the only one who is really *au fait* with their installation and its adjustment. Never place a direct-operated board far away from the stage as the wiring between it and the stage will be costly.

When an auditorium position is impossible the best place for the board is against the proscenium wall. On very small stages this will be difficult to realize unless the board is of a type that does not require rear space. For amateur work it is better to have the board on stage floor level, not on a perch. In the position recommended (Fig. 97), a view of the down-stage is obtained through the first wing and a view of at least some part of the cyclorama can be obtained whatever the setting. Though the tendency is to put the stage-board on the same side as the stage manager, I cannot see any justification for this practice. Any signals between board and a stage manager are better given by lights and buzzers. On a small stage it is a definite drawback to have both the board men and the stage manager trying to peep through the same restricted space. They must occupy opposite sides of the stage; the stage manager should have first refusal of the side nearer the dressing-rooms, but hard cash will probably insist on the nearness of the stage-board to the supply authorities' mains being the governing factor. Should the size of the board on the plan of the stage not allow the proscenium wall position, then a site in the wings will be required, in which case the board must be on the same side as the stage manager as all kinds of signals may

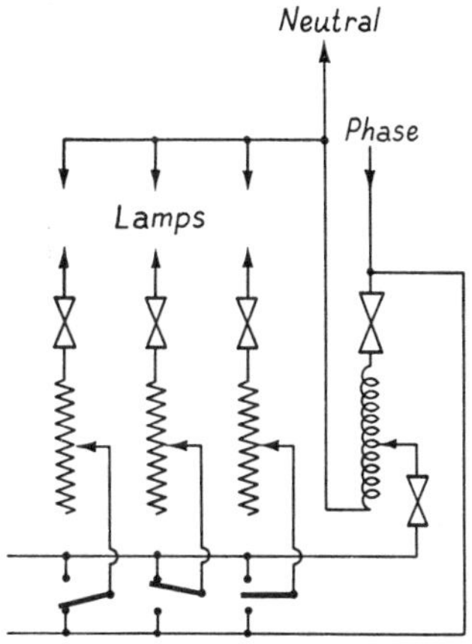

FIG. 65. TRANSFORMER MASTER CIRCUIT

be necessary, since the acting area will be out of sight when box sets are used.

Note for the D.C. Mains and 110-*volt A.C. Mains.* The unit board system described depends on standardization for its success; it is not, therefore, available for D.C. mains. On 100- or 110-volt A.C., there will be double the current, and, therefore, only restricted application to the smaller stages will be possible, the mechanical interlocking system being, perforce, adopted for the rest.

Technical Note on Wiring of Stage-board. All dimmers should be wired in the phase or live side. The practice of putting them in the neutral is inexcusable; switches, even when fitted to stage-boards, are seldom used and working takes place on the dimmers. If, then, the dimmer is in the neutral, a stage hand may receive an indication by the extinction of his lamp that its plug socket is dead when it is fully alive.

Where auto-transformer dimmers are used it is essential to see that the return side of the lamp circuit is connected to the neutral; otherwise the "lights out" position of the auto-transformer will correspond to phase on both pins of the plug! Also H.R.C. fuses must be inserted between the winding and the phase line, and not between it and the neutral. Fig. 65 shows a suitable circuit with a transformer dimmer as master. Some licensing authorities require that written application shall be made for permission to use auto-transformers.

COLOUR

That white light is the sensation of viewing several coloured lights simultaneously, and that coloured light is something *less than* white light, must be firmly fixed in the mind. A spotlight with a blue filter is a spotlight minus, not a spotlight plus.

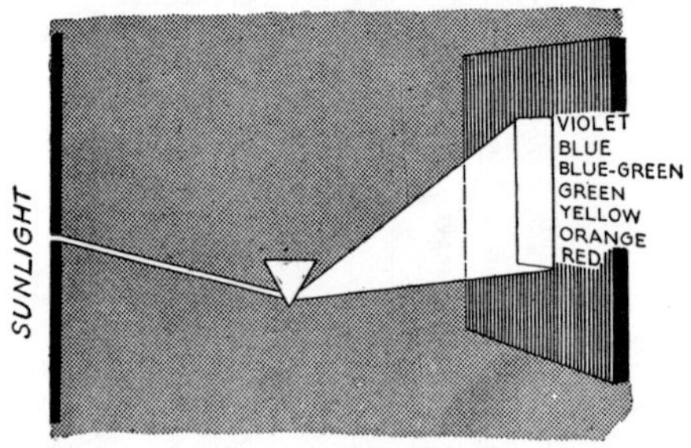

FIG. 66. THE PRISM

If white light is passed through a narrow slit and thence through a prism (Fig. 66) refraction takes place, and a band of coloured light, the spectrum, appears. Seven prominent colours are seen: red, orange, yellow, green, blue-green, blue, and violet. Hundreds of different hues make up the apparently continuous band. The spectrum band is a series of images of the slit side by side, each one in a slightly different hue. What we see as a wide red band is a number of very narrow bands of differing reds.

The explanation is that light is a small section of the great range of radiation, part of which is known as "wireless waves." Light waves are very much shorter than these and each variation in wavelength gives the eye a sensation of strong colour. The more different wavelengths (colours) that are seen at one time, the nearer to the sensation of white we get.

The red waves are relatively long, the violet short, and the intermediate colours form steps between these extremes. Each wavelength is refracted by the prism to a different extent; hence the series of coloured images of the slit forming the continuous spectrum.

Sorting the wavelength by passing the colours from glass to air is not the only method. White light can be passed through a very fine mesh or grating and a spectrum produced. This method is known as "diffraction," and has the advantage that, unlike the prismatic spectrum, the colours are spaced without distortion.

Both prisms, or diffraction gratings, may be made into an instrument known as a *spectroscope*, which looks like a small telescope. With its aid, one can see the spectrum instantly (Fig. 72).

Beyond the visible colours there is invisible radiation: at the red end, the infra-red wavelengths; at the blue end, the ultra-violet. Both these ranges, though invisible to the human eye, can be photographed. Furthermore, the ultra-violet can be converted by chemical action into visible longer waves—the phenomena of fluorescence. Ultra-violet is not one wavelength, but a whole series, and in its shorter wavelengths is extremely dangerous to the eye. Fortunately, these dangerous wavelengths are not required for stage effects, and can be stopped by a sheet of ordinary glass.

COLOUR FILTERS

The simplest method of obtaining colour is to suppress the unwanted colours. Dyed gelatine mediums do this precisely. They filter away the unwanted colours, the energy of which is promptly turned to heat by the filter. A good green filter inserted in front of the spectroscope blacks out the ends of the spectrum, leaving only the broad green band (Fig. 73A). A very pale-green filter may pass a little of all colours, but the green is strong and dominant (Fig. 73B). As colours absorbed by a filter represent wasted light, filters designed for the stage aim at suppressing the minimum number of wavebands. A red will probably be allowed to pass a little orange as well (Fig. 74A); certainly an orange will pass red, orange, yellow, and green (Fig. 74B).

It is now necessary for readers to have a chart of colour filter samples for reference. It is impossible to reproduce the colours satisfactorily;

further, reproduction would not allow the colours to be superimposed. Colour cards giving the samples can be obtained from stage suppliers. As the Strand Electric Cinemoid (a new plastic) range and numbers have been adopted by the principal firms as the British standard for the stage, a producer no longer needs to call for a 32, expecting blue and seeing red.

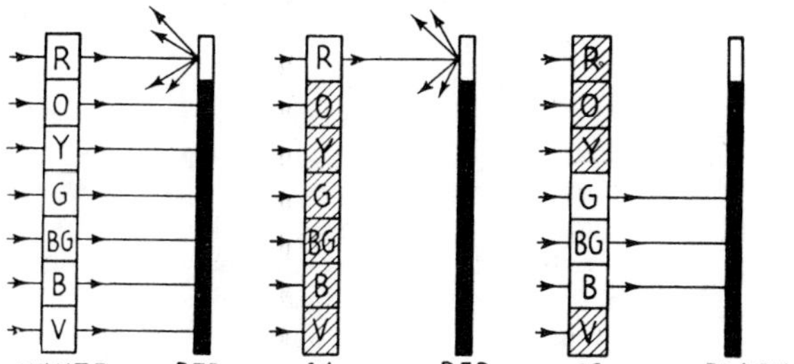

FIG. 67. REFLECTION OF COLOURED LIGHT FROM PIGMENTS

PIGMENTS

Just as a gelatine filter suppresses some colours of the spectrum, so a painted or dyed object may do the same. A pillar-box is red, not by conversion of white light into red, but by the absorption of all colours, except red, which is then diffusely reflected into the eye. It follows that the pillar-box must be lit either by white light or red light. A blue-green (No. 16) light produced by removing all spectrum colours, except blue-green and its neighbours, will not contain any light that can be reflected by the pillar-box, with the result that it appears black (Fig. 67). Unless trick effects such as the Samoiloff (*see* page 413) are deliberately required the colours which the dresses or scenery reflect must always be present in the light that illuminates them. The eye cannot see the colour of the pillar-box at very low intensities, even if the light is white. In bright starlight the pillar-box appears black; this, the Purkinje effect as it is called, will crop up again on page 397.

SUBTRACTIVE MIXING

Between forty and fifty standard gelatine or Cinemoid filters are available in the colour chart. About half are saturated colours, which absorb some part of the spectrum completely. The remainder are the paler colours, which merely require a decreased brightness in some parts of the spectrum. No. 36 Lavender (Surprise Pink) reduces the green region slightly, thus stressing any reds and blues it is used on. No. 3 Straw reduces the blue region, thereby giving the light a warmer tone.

The total may seem to be large but when reference is made to the chart, it may be found wanting. Any one particular about colours, as lighting artists should be, will be far from satisfied with the greens available, to quote only one example. However, the solution is easy: filters may be combined in one frame, thus subtracting the parts of the spectrum that are not common to both. For example, a 26 mauve passing red and blue may be combined with a 16 blue-green passing blue and green; the light resulting will be a blue, the colour common to both filters (Fig. 68). This subtractive colour-mixing follows similar lines to the mixing of pigments. When plotting the mixture it is better to write down 26 – 16, as the plus sign for additive mixture will be required later.

As with pigments, so with filters: the more the colours combine, the more colours will be subtracted until black is obtained. The joy of colour combinations is that experiments are easy to undertake at home. Further, the opportunity is created to express one's tastes in colour; after all, few artists are content to use colour neat as they buy it in tubes.

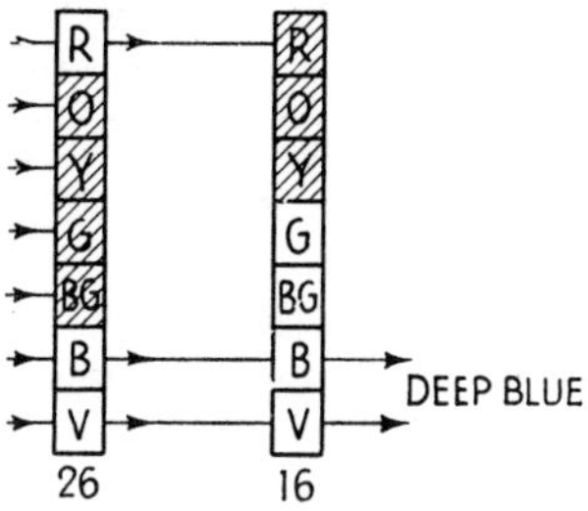

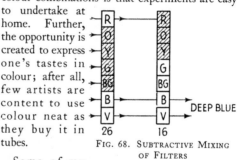

FIG. 68. SUBTRACTIVE MIXING OF FILTERS

Some of my favourite subtractive mixtures are:

50 orange — 11 or 12 rose = blood orange
10 pink — 4 amber = sunset (or flame)
8 salmon — 2 amber = flame
19 blue — 1 yellow
16 blue-green — 24 green } Compare these greens
50 yellow — 17 steel
54 pink — 17 steel
36 pink — 50 yellow } Compare these greys with No. 60
36 pink — 17 steel
36 pink — 3 straw } Compare these with 36 Surprise Pink or lavender

BROKEN COLOUR

Subtractive mixing also leads to a most important effect that I cannot recollect having seen in the theatre other than accidentally or in my own work. This technique I call "broken" colour. It consists of placing two or more filters behind each other in such a way that the colour can be seen separately and combined. A circle can be removed from the centre of one filter or triangular filters combined. Some of these are

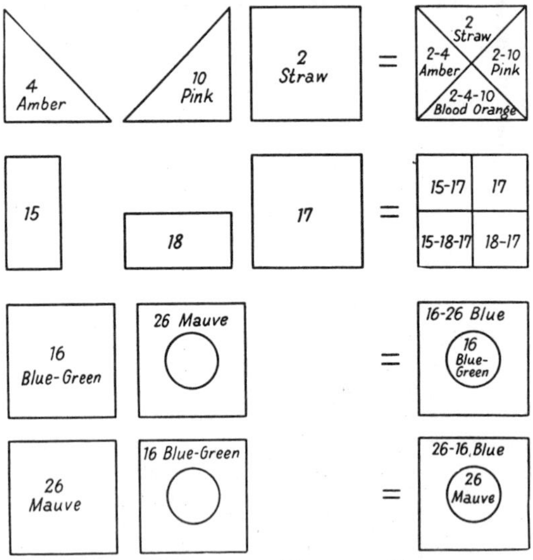

FIG. 69. SUBTRACTIVE MIXING OF FILTERS
BROKEN COLOUR

shown in Fig. 69; a sheet of No. 2 amber with triangles of 4 and 10 imposed and placed in front of a focus lantern gives a broken beam of four colours. This method is valuable in many applications, which are treated under "Lighting Methods" and "Special Effects."

ADDITIVE MIXING

Pass from consideration of the subtraction of colour by mixing two or more filters, or by the projection of coloured light on to a different colour pigment, to the result of adding two coloured lights.

If a red (No. 6) circle of light and a green (No. 39) circle of light from another spotlight are allowed to overlap the result will be yellow. If the colours are red (No. 6) and blue-green (No. 16), the result will be white. These results reveal the fact that the laws of subtractive or pigment mixing do not apply. Indeed, it would be strange if they did, since the exact opposite of the process is involved. For centuries colour-mixing has been synonymous with the mixing of pigments: add yellow to blue to get green; the three primaries are red, yellow, and blue (Fig. 75, *f.p.* 368). This is now known to be based on a false idea: colours have hitherto been subtracted. Take the seven principal colours of the spectrum as pigments, mix them together, and the result is black. Do the same with coloured light, and the result is white. What, then, are the primary colours?

Experiment in mixing coloured light shows that there are three colours that cannot be produced by mixing. They are red, green, and deep blue (Fig. 76, *f.p.* 368). When these three are mixed in varying proportions any other saturated colour in the spectrum is obtained, and also colours, such as mauve and magenta, outside the spectrum, as follows.

Adding green to red = Light red, orange, yellow.
Adding green to blue = Medium blue, light blue, blue-green.
Adding red to blue = Violet, mauve, magenta.

For stage purposes, filters covering rather a wide band of the spectrum are used to avoid wastage of light: No. 6 red, No. 39 green, and No. 20 blue. As indicated in "Lamps," there is not a great deal of blue in the spectrum emitted by the gasfilled lamp; to assist this colour at least double wattage has to be employed. The colour wheel or triangle (Figs. 70 and 71) is a guide as to what may be expected when the three primary colours are mixed on dimmers. The colours midway between the primaries are known as the "secondaries," and a little thought will show these to be the primary colours for pigments. A secondary like yellow, composed of red plus green at full strength, will be twice as bright as each of the primaries by itself.

When red, green, and blue are mixed, the result is as near white as the slightly deficient blue will permit. This result gives a clue to the method of obtaining tints of the various saturated

ADDITIVE COLOUR MIXING SCHEDULE

HUES

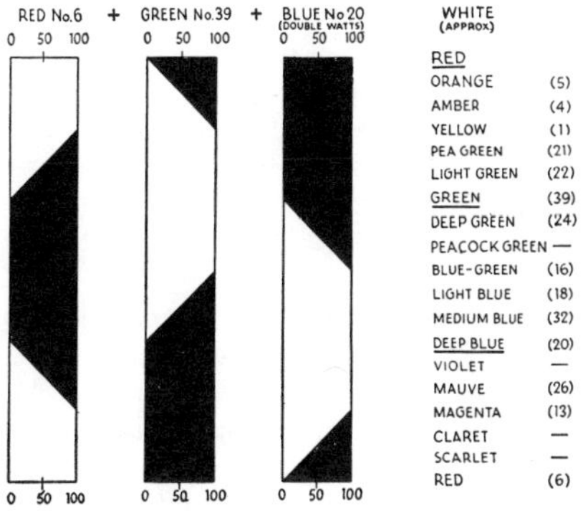

TINTS

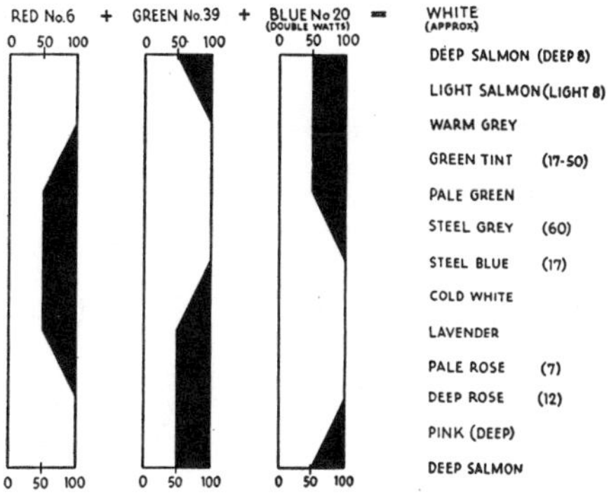

COLOUR FILTER SCHEDULE

List of standard stage filters (Strand Electric) in colour order as in the chart and numerical order for reference.

White	Clear . .	30		Deep rose . .	12
	Light frost . .	31		Magenta . .	13
	Heavy . .	29	Red	Red (Primary) .	6
Yellow	Pale yellow .	50		Ruby . .	14
	Yellow . .	1		Mauve . .	26
Amber	Straw . .	3		Purple . .	25
	Light amber .	2	Blue	Steel blue . .	17
	Medium amber .	4		Pale blue . .	40
	Deep amber .	33		Light blue . .	18
	Salmon (Amber-pink) . .	8		Medium blue .	32
				Dark blue . .	19
Orange	Orange . .	5		Deep blue (Primary) .	20
	Deep orange .	5A			
Pink	Gold tint . .	51		Peacock blue .	15
	Pale gold . .	52		Blue-green . .	16
	Pale salmon .	53	Green	Pea-green . .	21
	Middle salmon .	9		Moss green .	22
	Light rose . .	7		Light green .	23
	Pale rose . .	54		Primary green .	39
	Lavender (Surprise pink) .	36		Dark green .	24
	Middle rose .	10	Neutral	Chocolate tint .	55
	Dark pink . .	11		Pale chocolate .	56
				Pale grey . .	60

1. Yellow	21. Pea green
2. Light amber	22. Moss green
3. Straw	23. Light green
4. Medium amber	24. Dark green
5. Orange	25. Purple
5A. Deep orange	26. Mauve
6. Red (Primary)	29. Heavy frost
7. Light rose	30. Clear
8. Salmon (Amber-pink)	31. Light frost
9. Middle salmon	32. Medium blue
10. Middle rose	33. Deep amber
11. Dark pink	36. Lavender (Surprise pink)
12. Deep rose	39. Primary green
13. Magenta	40. Pale blue
14. Ruby	50. Pale yellow
15. Peacock blue	51. Gold tint
16. Blue-green	52. Pale gold
17. Steel blue	53. Pale salmon
18. Light blue	54. Salmon tint
19. Dark blue	55. Chocolate tint
20. Deep blue (Primary)	56. Pale chocolate
	60. Pale grey

colours: merely add some of the remaining colour to suit. Thus to light blue (100 per cent blue, 50 per cent green) add a little red to get pale blue: to magenta (red 100 per cent, blue 100 per cent) some green to produce rose pink.

With three dimmers it is possible to produce the intermediate colours given in the schedule.

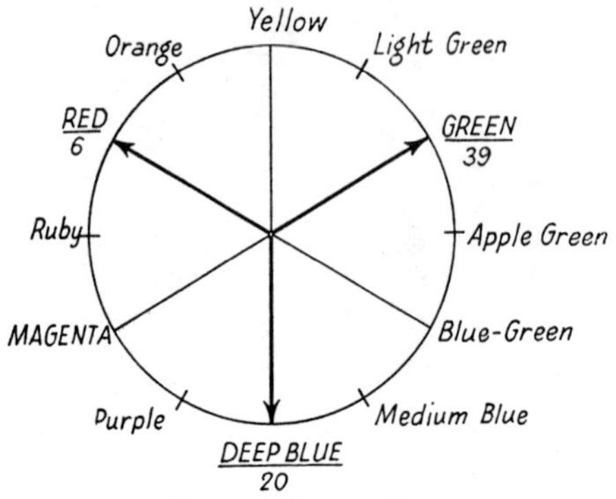

FIG. 70. COLOUR CIRCLE

The percentages are the probable corresponding handle positions on an average dimmer. The matches given are approximate only, and are what are known as sensation matches.

Colour-mixing will be found to be fascinating, and after a little practice the operator will find it easy to produce any colour required. Not only will he have won this skill, but he will also have gained a new insight into colour in all its applications.

COMPLEMENTARY COLOURS

If equal amounts of any two colours opposite to each other on the wheel or triangle are mixed, the result is white. Any such pairs of colours, red and blue-green, yellow and blue, green and magenta, are known as "complementary." If either of these pairs is a pigment, as yellow light on blue paint, the result is black. Any pair of complementary colours can be used, but, except in a few instances, the stage filters are very impure: As No. 1 yellow actually passes a little blue it does not "behave" according to the book. The colours that are reasonably pure are: No. 14 red, No. 6 red, No. 39 green, No. 16 blue-green, No. 20 blue, No. 26 mauve. Any one who wishes to go deeply into colour experiments, for their own sake as apart from stage applications, is advised to use the accurate Wratten filters supplied by Kodak (*see* page 371).

A warning note on sensation matches needs to be struck: the eye can easily be tricked. A No. 19 blue can be made to look like a No. 20 by adding a little red; a No. 6 red can be matched to a No. 14 red by adding a little blue; both will pass muster until the blue is used to turn red pigment black or the red to turn blue pigment into black. The slight addition of red in the first instance and blue in the second will modify the result.

An extreme example of the unsatisfactory results of sensation matching when used to light pigments is produced by sodium lighting. Most people have seen sodium discharge lighting used in some streets—the lamp emits its light in a narrow yellow spectrum band and only yellow objects are reflected under it, the rest appearing grey and black. Suppose for some peculiar reason this light has to be imitated on the stage: by mixing red and green a perfect sensation match is obtained, but as soon as the light is thrown on to coloured objects, not only yellows but also reds and greens will appear. Further, stage amber filters will not be much help as all pass red, and some a fair amount of green in addition to yellow.

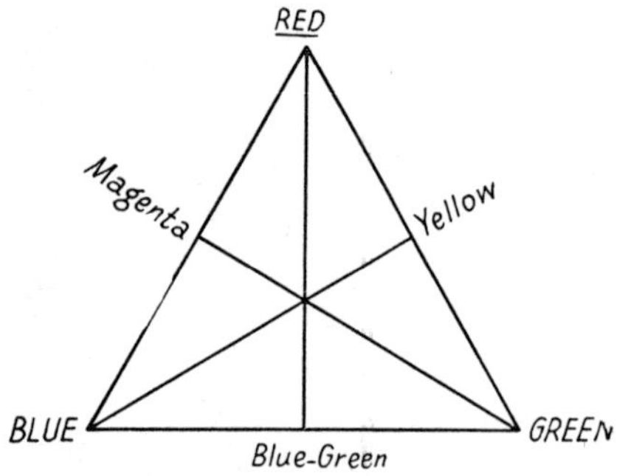

FIG. 71. COLOUR TRIANGLE

CONTRAST

The perception of colour depends very much on the presence of contrasting colours. A stage lit evenly in red soon loses its redness, and is interpreted as a kind of fatiguing pink. The same red seen as a small contrasting patch on a blue stage seems to be an entirely different colour.

FIG. 72. WHITE LIGHT SPECTRUM

FIG. 73A. GREEN FILTER

FIG. 73B. PALE GREEN FILTER

FIG. 74A. RED FILTER

FIG. 74B. ORANGE FILTER

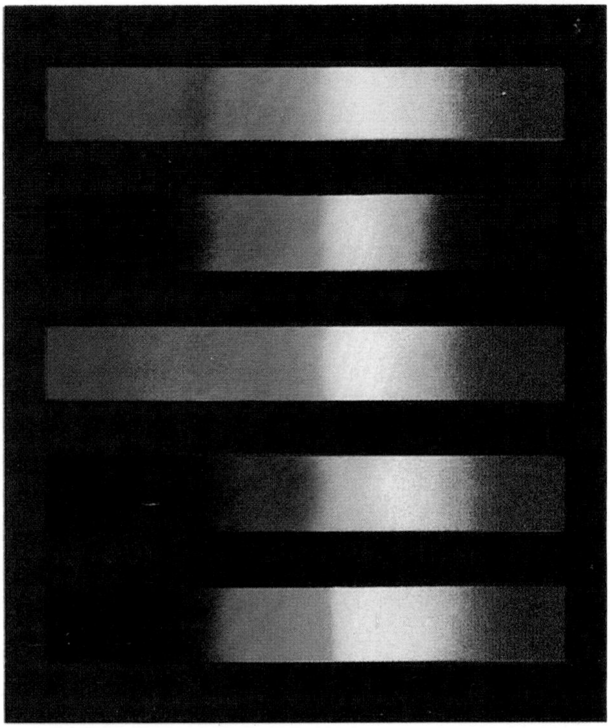

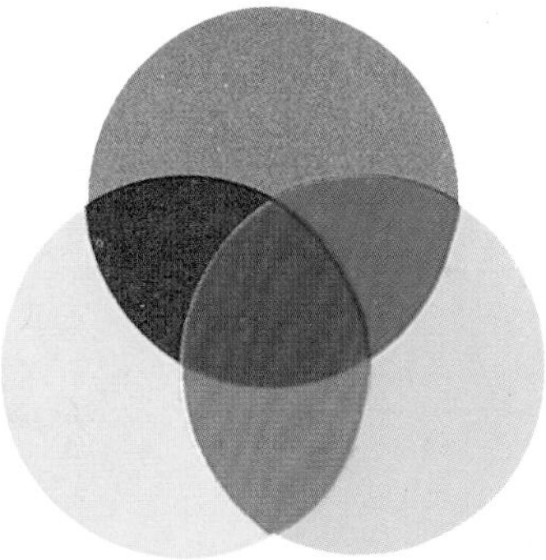

FIG. 75
SUBTRACTIVE COLOUR MIXTURE

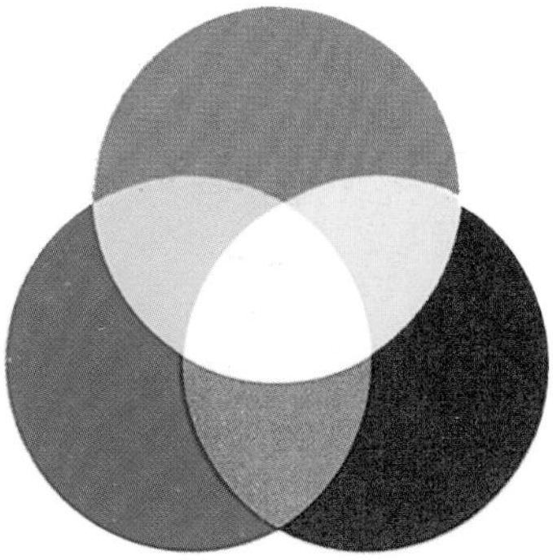

FIG. 76
ADDITIVE COLOUR MIXTURE

COLOUR FILTERS AND COLOUR MIXING

Colour that is to appear rich or vivid must be confined to small patches and high lights. There may be instances in moonlight effects or the Samoiloff complementary colour trick lighting when the lack of colour contrast may be valuable. There can be no rigid rules in this matter: how much of a colour and what contrasts to use make stage lighting a field for the artist. Colour mixing, additive or subtractive, requires only common sense and practice, but the application of the colours when mixed is quite another thing.

A THEORY OF COLOUR VISION

Convincing deceptions such as presenting red and green to the eye for yellow (two very different wavelengths offered as a third), lead to speculation on the nature of colour vision.

Many theories explain colour vision. As none really ties up with any physiological findings, the one that is simplest and accounts for the phenomena encountered may be chosen.

The colour theory of Thomas Young (who lived in the early nineteenth century) is that there are three sets of colour sensitive equipment (nerves, if you like) associated with the eye. The first is sensitive to the wavelengths in the red region of the spectrum; the second to the green region; and the third to the blue. None of these is exactly sensitive to its own region only, but tends to overlap, reacting more and more weakly as the wavelengths get into the domain of their neighbours. Thus a yellow light stimulates the red and green nerves to some extent, sending a message to the brain the same as that sent when red and green are employed. Yellow and its complement blue stimulate all three sets and give white.

The theory also accounts for colour fatigue, a striking demonstration of which can be given on a cyclorama. Put the red and green dimmers to full, and the result is yellow. Do this again, but give the eye a minute of green cyclorama first, and the result is an orange. Repeat, but give the eye a minute of red and the result is a light green. This different colour for an identical mixture suggests that the colour-registering apparatus of the eye or brain gets tired in use, probably not in a physical sense, but similar to the way in which a full-up stage seems to be bright after a half-checked stage but soon loses some of its initial effect on the eye.

Colour fatigue suggests a way in which the colour of a stage may be emphasized or not: a blue footlight on the act drop if a stage very red in appearance is required to follow, a red footlight if the red, as for the Samoiloff trick, is not to draw much attention to itself.

CYCLORAMA COLOUR MIXING

A system such as the three primary colours in which any colour can be mixed from the switchboard is valuable, but it should not be assumed that its use follows automatically. If the cyclorama is to appear dark blue or light blue for a number of weeks, it is rather wasteful to leave a red circuit idle and the green on half, only the blue being used full up. This is emphasized when the equipment is hired or toured for a production that needs limited sky effects.

Even for repertory theatres it is worth while to consider the season's likely programme in order to discover how many plays will demand a red cyclorama and how many a green. We can assume that such colours are useful at the bottom of the cyclorama in the ground row, but a green or red top cyclorama must be rare.

The commonest colours for the top cyclorama are dark blue, various blues up to light blue, greys, blue greens, ambers, mauves, and pinks. All these can be obtained by another combination of mixing colours, ensuring that the commonest colours utilize as much of the available watts as possible.

The colours I use are No. 5A orange, No. 16 blue-green and No. 20 blue (No. 19 if double wattage is not available for the blue circuit). With this arrangement light blue is two circuits full up, No. 20 (100 per cent), No. 16 (100 per cent) instead of No. 20 (100 per cent), No. 39 green (50 per cent). A range of important greys (warm or cold) is obtained by adding some 5A to this mixture. Pinks and mauves are obtained by mixing the 5A and 20 in varying proportions; ambers by mixing 5A and 16.

FLUORESCENCE

The description so far has been of colours obtained by filtering out the unwanted colour wavelengths or by presenting two wavelengths to create a sensation of a third colour, the wavelength of which is not present. Fluorescence changes the light of one wavelength into another *longer* wavelength. This effect is usually taken to concern the conversion of invisible ultra-violet rays into visible light, but is equally applicable to the conversion of (say) blue light into orange colour (Fig. 77). Certain substances will fluoresce in varying colours when lit by the near ultra-

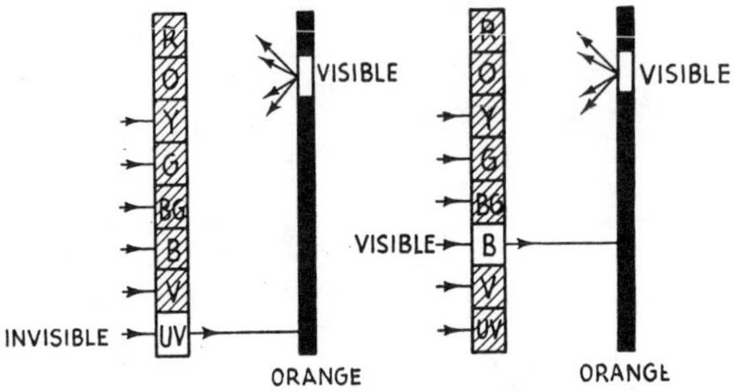

FIG. 77. PRODUCTION OF COLOUR BY FLUORESCENCE

violet (U.V.) rays immediately beyond the visible spectrum; others when lit by the dangerous very short ultra-violet rays farther beyond. These latter rays can be stopped by a sheet of clear glass, and as they are dangerous, glass will be used to filter any of the sources of U.V., effects being confined to those produced by the near ultra-violet.

The usual source of U.V. is the so-called "black lamp" (Fig. 9), a discharge lamp which gets its name from its black glass bulb. This bulb serves two purposes: (1) the glass filters off the dangerous short wave U.V.; (2) the black filters off nearly all visible light. This lamp, fitted in a 150-watt baby flood, is a good and convenient source of light.

Fluorescent chemicals are usually supplied in solution as paints, dyes, and make-up for stage purposes. Varied colours, all of which appear to be of great depth and intensity under U.V., are available. The two in commonest use are, probably, the invisible green and the invisible blue. Both have great beauty under U.V., although they are invisible under white light. They are applied as a colourless liquid. Other colours are visible under white light, but gain in depth under U.V. or are transformed from a garish horror into something sublime. Some colours have a slight afterglow when the activating light is extinguished. More important still, some colours are rather expensive and a few exceedingly costly.

The principal use of fluorescence on the stage is for trick effects, but apart from these, fluorescent powders are valuable, when coated to discharge lamp bulbs and tubes, as a method of providing pleasing colours. The stage applications are considered in "Fluorescent Effects," page 412. Fluorescence is not limited to special chemical paints: many things fluoresce to a greater or lesser degree—teeth (real, not artificial), skin, and the eyeball, for example. The fluorescence of the latter gives a slightly hazy feeling to the person under U.V. light and leads him to believe that his eyes are being burned. This, the experts say, is unsound, provided the black glass bulb to the lamp is intact. Out of the 220 colours in the British Colour Council's chart, several fluoresce slightly—two numbers very strongly.

FILTER MATERIALS

The actual colour filters can take the following forms: (A) lacquer or lamp dip; (B) china spray; (C) dyed gelatine sheets; (D) dyed plastic sheet; (E) coloured glass. A, B, and E are available when simple lampholders and bare lamps are required. The lamp lacquer or lamp dip is a liquid supplied in many of the colours of the gelatine colour chart. The lamps, dipped into the liquid while burning, must be vacuum lamps; gasfilled lamps develop too much heat, and burn the lacquer rapidly. Gasfilled lamps up to 100 watts, coated with a coloured china spray in a few pastel shades, are supplied. Natural colour glass bulb lamps are also available in the lower wattages, but very little light is emitted. In all these coloured lamps the colours are poor, particularly in the blues.

Dyed gelatine in a convenient cheap commercial form is sold by most stage lighting suppliers. It is ideal for rehearsal work or for productions designed for two or three performances only. For longer runs, or for cyclorama three-colour lighting where the same colours may be used, if only intermittently, for many months, the more durable plastic materials are recommended. One of the great drawbacks of gelatine, apart from its general fragility, is its characteristic of absorbing the moisture of its surroundings. If left unused in a lantern for a few nights, it goes limp and is spoiled; any stock not kept at an even dry temperature is as bad. For accurate colour experiments, the fine range of scientific gelatine Wratten filters supplied by Kodak is well worth the greatly increased cost which prohibits their use on the stage. For mechanical strength, Wratten filters can be obtained mounted between optical glasses.

Several plastic sheet filters are on the market; all are stronger mechanically than gelatine, and more or less impervious to moisture. Plastic filters known as Cinemoid have been designed for the stage in as complete a range of colours as the gelatines. Moreover, they are fireproof: this is important, as the licensing authorities will pass only fireproof filters. The supplier's specification should be examined and the material tested with a lighted match. If it is fireproof, it will produce a gas which extinguishes the flame as quickly as it appears. These plastic materials have rather complicated names which are concealed under a trade name such as Cinemoid. Unsuitable materials on the market drop burning material to the floor when the test is performed. Cinemoid is more expensive than gelatine, but where any degree of permanence is required, money is well spent on it.

The development of plastics has tended to eliminate, to a great extent, the glass filter problem. Glass is ideal as a permanent filter, but, unfortunately, colours are limited and cannot do just what is required for the stage. Blues are bad, and all colours absorb far more light than the dyed filters. The fact that the German Schwarbe system of cyclorama lighting used glass filters in seven colours instead of three is an indication of the difficulties of glass.

As an ultra-violet filter glass is supreme, and takes the form either of a black glass bulb for a small discharge lamp or of a moulded heat-resisting plate filter for use in front of long throw arc projectors.

Experience of stage colour filters gained during the Second Great War should be discarded. Owing to drastic shortages of certain dyes, many colours—particularly blues and pinks—went off colour: blues became greenish, for example. In providing the colour standards for the new Cinemoid range, I have tried to correct these defects. Inaccuracies in the spectrum bands transmitted can have bad effects on three-colour mixing and complementary colour effects.

PROSCENIUM STAGE AND LIGHTING INSTALLATION

It cannot be too strongly stressed that a grid for flying scenery does not make a theatre. To be of use it must have considerable height and it is, therefore, expensive. Further, it is not easy without skilled labour to make good use of flying facilities. On the list of priorities it can be placed very low indeed. There are examples in civic centres of a grid and flying space, but the auditorium has a flat floor. The money spent on the grid would have been far better spent in making provision for the audience to see the stage properly. There is no point in lighting a stage unless the light, after striking the actors and setting, can be reflected into the eyes of all the members of the audience.

It is, unfortunately, seldom that the ideal hall dedicated solely to dramatic performances is attained. Often the building has to serve as an assembly hall, class-room, ball-room, concert hall, theatre, etc., and before it is finished there has been conflict between those who demanded a flat floor and those who wanted a stepped or raked floor. Invariably the flat floor advocates have won. Thus the drama is handicapped by bad sight lines and acoustics. An attempt is made to remedy this by increasing the height of the stage floor, and in this way the evil multi-purpose hall has come into existence. When, in addition, the stage floor is raked and the rear wall is covered with oak panelling, perhaps garnished with gilt radiators and a centre door, conditions are all but impossible. Oddly, given a few simple provisions, the sight lines are potentially better than those of most commercial theatres with their two or three tiers. The hall I have in mind may have seating accomodation for from 200 to 1,000; above this total a hall constructed on multi-purpose lines becomes unsuitable for drama, although not for ballet, which usually benefits by expansive surroundings. If more than 1,000 seats are required, resort must be made to separate halls, a large-scale concert hall and a smaller-scale theatre, as at Wolverhampton.

SIGHT LINES AND SEATING

In any auditorium that seats over 100 people the rear seats will require to be raised. Assuming the seating area to be roughly a rectangle (the front corners will be angled) about twice as deep as it is wide, then half the seats should be raised. Of the raised group, the rear half might be provided with fixed and the front half with movable rostrums. In a compromise, two rows of seats a step are permissible, each step being 6 in. high in the movable sections and 9 in. in the fixed. For example, a hall with twenty rows of seats will have ten rows raised; six on three steps rising 6 in. at a time and four on two steps rising 9 in., the total rise being 3 ft. only for (say) 300 seats (15 in a row) less the front corners (Fig. 78). A 3-ft. rise does not demand a stepped gangway, but merely a little ingenuity in arranging the steps for access. In this example the whole set of rostrums could be removable, though I am in favour of a fixed nucleus inside of which the removable rostrums can be stored. The flexibility imparted, even to a hall used solely as a private theatre, by having a good portion of flat floor available on occasion repays the extra trouble of making removable rostrums. Where money is the primary consideration, the difference made by this slight stepping, though far short of the ideal, will be surprising. To see the show comes before cushions and soft seats.

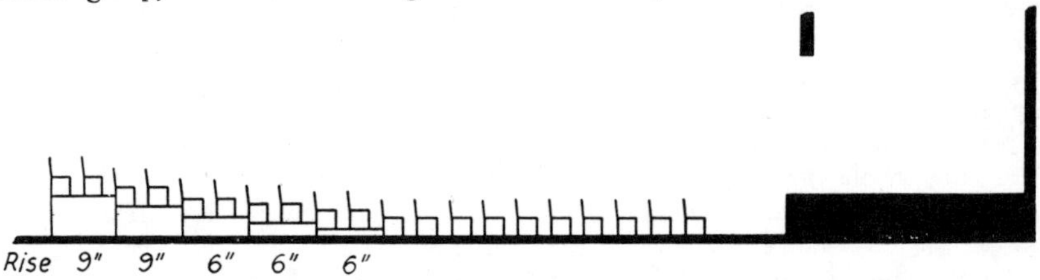

FIG. 78. SEATING ARRANGEMENT (SECTION) FOR SMALL HALL

Restriction to a flat floor is inexcusable even in a multi-purpose hall. A 1,000-seater (Fig. 79) will possess a small straight balcony—no horseshoes, please—under which will be the permanent stepped section (black in the figure) with the more elaborate access needed owing to the height of (say) 5–6 ft. In front of the permanent section will be the removable steps (shaded) to be stored in the former when not in use. Thus three-quarters of the stalls floor can be cleared for dancing, etc., the fixed seating and steps being available for sitting out and watching the cabaret; it is not pleasant to dance under a balcony, anyway. The balcony above will be available as a base from which temporary lighting can be projected on to the dancers.

When *every* member of the audience has been provided with a seat where he or she can see the major part of the stage, including the backcloth, then a grid and elaborate machinery for flying scenery can be considered. The stage forms a complete picture, and if it contains only one actor and no scenery, all of it should be seen.

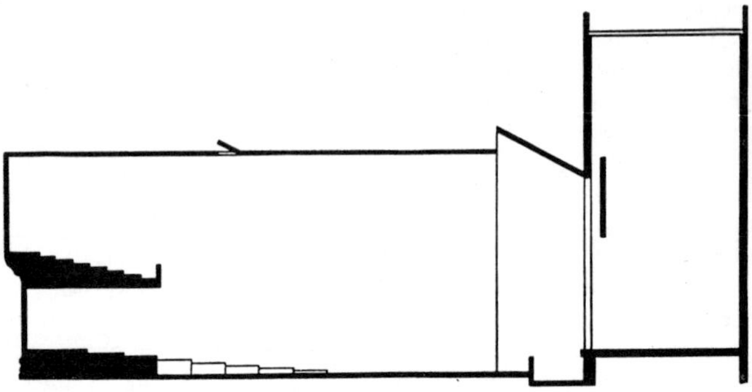
FIG. 79. SEATING ARRANGEMENT (SECTION) FOR LARGE HALL

STAGE LAYOUT

Now consider the design of the stage and the layout of the masking that will be essential, even for an empty stage. The stage floor must be level and about 3 ft. above the lowest point of the floor of the stalls. The rear wall must be flat finished with Keene's cement painted matt white, and should extend as far into the wings and above the stage as possible. This wall becomes an elementary, but none the less effective, cyclorama. It follows from the sight lines that a pitched roof is not suitable for the stage, since this will give the greatest height to the cyclorama in the centre where it is least wanted.

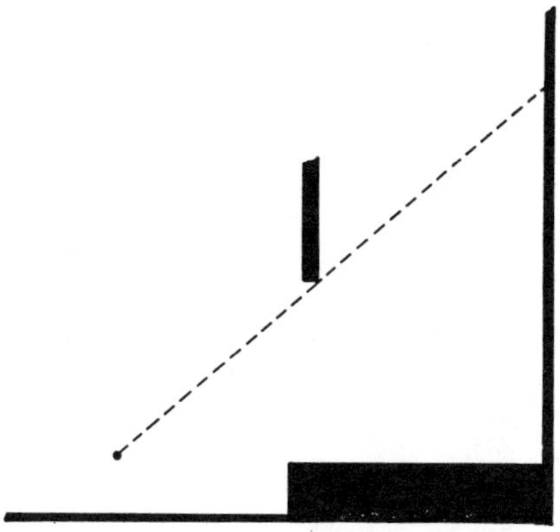

FIG. 80. SIGHT LINE WITHOUT BORDERS

The proscenium opening should not be made too large as either it will be costly to fill with setting or it will have to be masked in with the almost equally costly false proscenium, often seen in the theatre. Width is better obtained by a fore stage in front of the proscenium opening. For a hall that may be required for orchestral concerts a large proscenium opening is desirable. This can be arranged by making the proscenium sides as sliding doors, capable of decreasing the opening by a further third, and by dropping in a pelmet. The fore stage will also be useful in concerts.

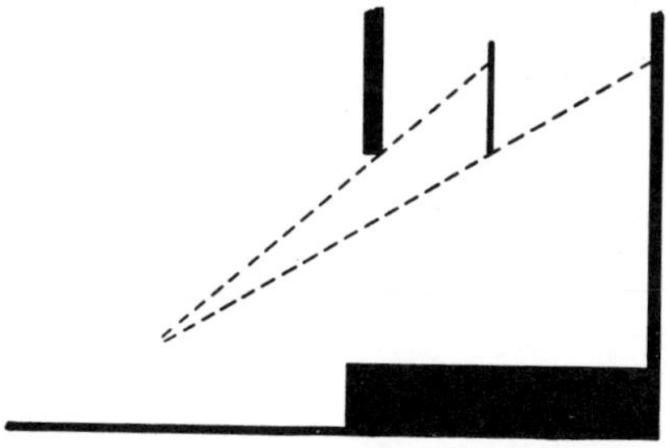

FIG. 81. SIGHT LINE WITH ONE BORDER

In the smaller buildings the stage itself ought to be roughly as deep as the proscenium is wide. Greater width will make up for lack of depth, but not vice versa. There should be plenty of wing space, on both sides, level with the stage floor: a depth of one half of the proscenium opening to each side.

The ratio of the height of the proscenium to the width ought to be such as to make a nicely proportioned opening, such as 2 to 3. Height is taken to mean to the underside of the pelmet, if fitted. About 10 ft. is the minimum height; usually the scenery will be about 1 ft. 6 in. higher than the opening. Thus, 10 ft. 6 in. × 16 ft. opening 12 ft. scenery flats, 12 ft. 6 in. × 20 ft. opening 14 ft. flats; on a larger scale 16 ft. × 30 ft. opening 18 ft. flats. These figures are rough guides only, and exact information is obtained from setting out the various sight lines, as in the examples given in Figs. 94 and 97. Even though the vast majority of productions, at any rate, on the smaller stages, rely on the simpler scenery obtaining its effect from suggestion, it will be well to arrange the stage so that a realistic box set can be put on if desired. Simplification should be dictated by artistic or, alas! financial considerations.

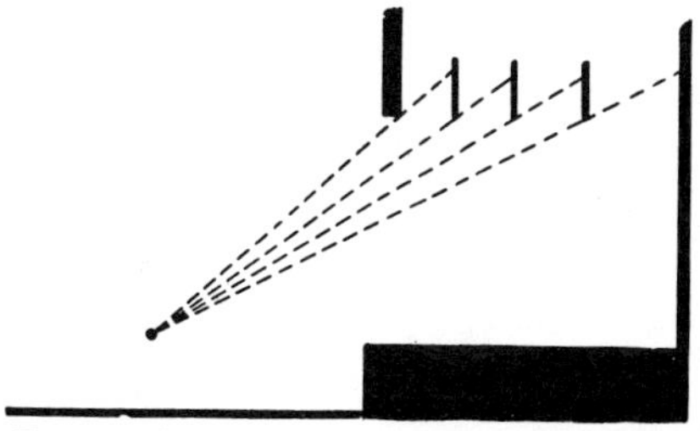

FIG. 82. SIGHT LINE WITH THREE BORDERS

STAGE MASKING

Next consider the minimum masking that is necessary to clothe the stage. An empty stage, not a naked stage, presents the great test. With a white cyclorama back wall, right wings, left wings, and overhead have to be taken into consideration. Overhead raises the most vexed question, although it usually concerns only the front half of the seating. Ideally, the vertical sight line from the front row should include nothing but cyclorama beyond the proscenium opening (Fig. 80), but the ideal is unlikely to be attained. Next, a single deep border (Fig. 81) would be Utopian—in this context! Probably there will be three borders (Fig. 82), which will immediately complicate the lighting installation. Methods of masking have been responsible for the rows and rows of lighting battens of which the theatre is only just being relieved. A batten will be needed behind the proscenium opening for the acting area and also the up-stage border for the cyclorama. Such lighting will leave borders Nos. 2 and 3 quite dark and cause a ghastly shadow to be thrown by No. 1 into the bargain (Fig. 83). Even if lighting equipment for Nos. 2 and 3 can be afforded, balancing the lighting intensities will be troublesome—and all merely in order to use the traditional masking borders which will not look right in the exterior sets, and in the interiors, which form the majority of settings, they will ruin every set, no matter how good.

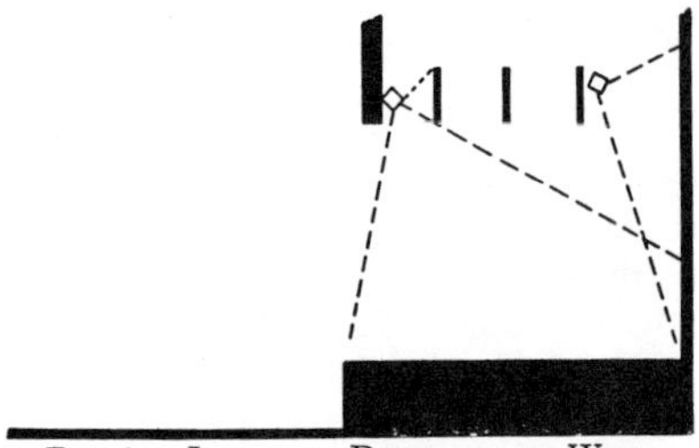

FIG. 83. LIGHTING DIFFICULTIES WITH THREE BORDERS

The solution is to provide a false ceiling to extend over, roughly, two-thirds the acting area (Fig. 84). The cyclorama lighting can be mounted over the up-stage edge of the ceiling and the acting area batten under the down-stage edge behind the proscenium. On smaller stages, sets will almost always be regular in shape, since there will be little space to spare. The curtains, flats, etc., can be fixed to the off-stage edge of the ceiling. In most cases it will be an advantage to run a track along this edge to carry a number of standard curtain widths which can be opened or rolled up for the insertion of doors and windows. The ceiling should be constructed of three-ply wood on a suitable frame, and fixed rigidly, thus helping to support any flats that are placed against it.

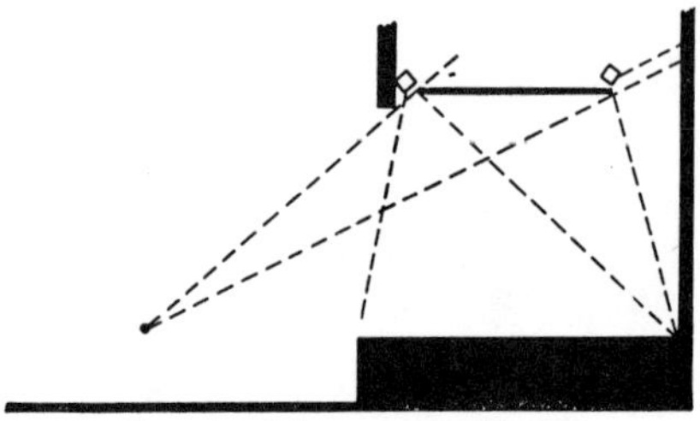

FIG. 84. MASKING BY CEILING

It may be found advantageous to make the ceiling into a permanent setting by the addition of two columns at the up-stage corners of the ceiling (Fig. 85). With curtains along the sides and the plain cyclorama at the back, this set can, if properly proportioned, look handsome for prizegivings and other occasions from which drama will be excluded. If the architect is

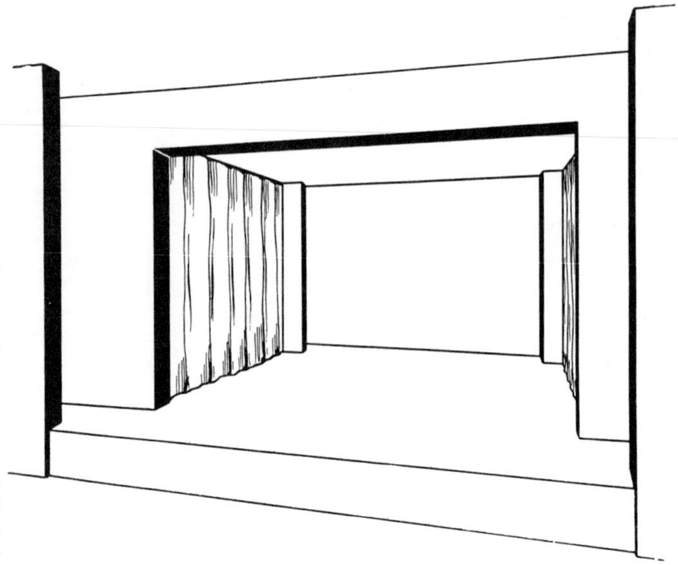

FIG. 85. STAGE WITH CEILING MASKING FOR INTERIORS

inclined to quibble at a plain back wall in such a prominent position, let him examine the treatment of the lecture theatres in the R.I.B.A. building, London. When such a permanent setting is provided, there is no reason why a hard plaster ceiling should not be used, but whether it is of plaster or plywood, the acoustics will benefit. To place flats along the edges of the ceiling enables a box set of the utmost realism to be provided. Then with a few curtains and simple pieces of scenery all Shakespeare can be staged to provide excitement for the eye as well as the ear. In serving the needs of lighting, that great bugbear of amateur stagecraft—rigging the ceiling—has been abolished.

Interiors have been in mind. What of exteriors? Here a convention has to be adopted—unavoidable in any case owing to the restrictions of a small stage. Further, there must be no attempt to employ realism, except up-stage beyond the ceiling where a painted ground row and profile trees can be set. These will dress the whole stage, in spite of the neutral ceiling and masking used down-stage. For exterior scenes, curtain wings, or, better still, flats nearly parallel to the proscenium (Fig. 86) will be more effective than the boxing-in used for interiors. Where flats are used, they must not be painted or shaped as trees, etc.: the essence of success is to set the picture in front of the cyclorama, then the masking will not draw attention to itself. The pieces used in front of the cyclorama may be painted in any style. *See also* the photographs, Fig. 100.

These principles can be applied equally well to medium-sized stages, i.e. about 14 ft. high by 20 ft. wide by 20 ft. deep. For these it may be advantageous, if height permits, to make the ceiling fold and hang vertically as a border. The down-stage lighting batten and the pelmet must be capable of movement in order to allow greater flexibility in scenery height. Unless the stage is deep, it is better to carry out height adjustment from a pelmet, in front of the house tabs rather than from a proscenium border up-stage of the tabs. Such a proscenium border tends to bring No. 1 batten too far up-stage: on a shallow stage every inch counts. Variation in stage

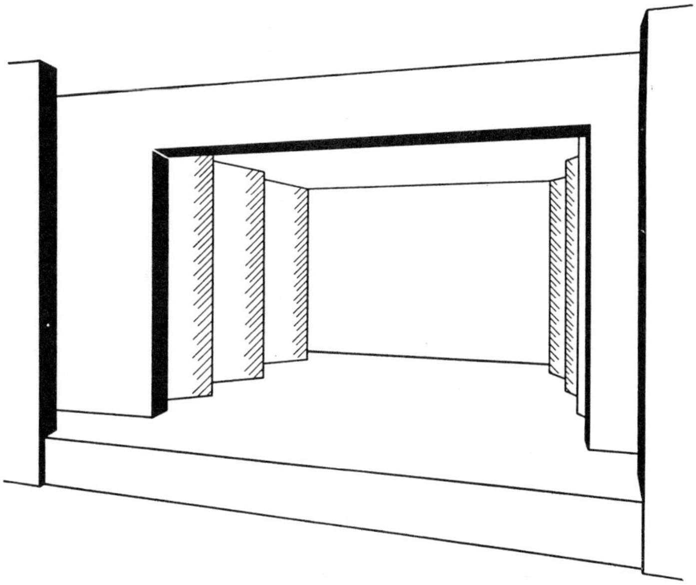

FIG. 86. STAGE WITH CEILING MASKING FOR EXTERIORS

height is essential for all but the smallest stages. Cottages 16 ft. high can be tolerated only in very large theatres. It will be best for the pelmet to be raised out of view for the tall sets and dropped in for the others. Another movable ceiling arrangement is suggested under Example D in "Comparative Examples" pages 380–392, in which part of the ceiling pivots to form a border.

LIGHTING IN SECTION

Concentration can now be on lighting. First (but only just) comes the lighting of the actor; and, secondly, the lighting of the set. As far as possible, the apparatus for these two functions should be kept entirely separate from one another. Compromise is inevitable, especially on the small stage. The best place from which to light an actor to reveal his features and yet to provide some, but not excessive, modelling is the auditorium.

The aim is not attained by using either footlights, thereby spraying the background with the same light; or battens immediately overhead, with consequent disastrous results from the modelling point of view.

Focus lanterns or mirror spots out in the front of house near the side walls will light the actors, at any rate, down-stage. The beams will be crossed so that combined with a suitable downward angle they will not hit the cyclorama when it is in use. The framing shutters of mirror spots in this position will be valuable, since the light can be accurately fitted to the acting area. With focus lanterns, a part of the circle is liable to appear where unwanted, unless the lantern is focused down with consequent defects in the area covered. As the number of F.O.H. spots is increased, some will be placed in the ceiling on the theatre centre line. This position is difficult to define, owing to the great variations of ceiling or beam heights. Generally, a steeper angle of throw than 35° being inadvisable, a retreat farther from the stage and a more costly lantern to compensate for increased length of throw may be unavoidable. A focus lantern may be used here with more success than at the side; nevertheless the mirror spot is the real auditorium lantern.

At the next position, immediately behind and over the proscenium opening, known as No. 1 batten, the lighting units will serve the actors up to centre stage and be required to light the setting down-stage of the cyclorama. No. 1 batten will,

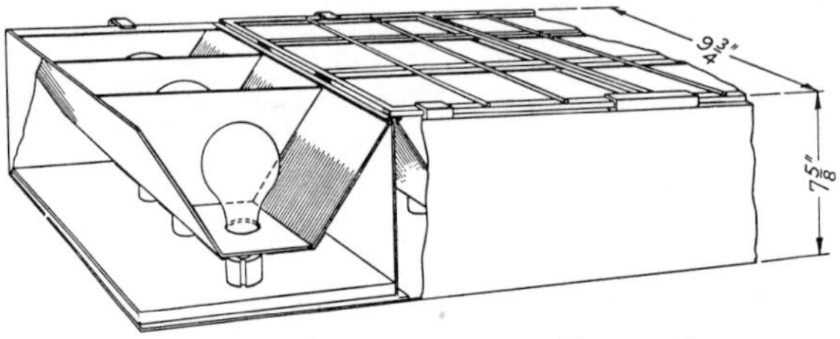

FIG. 88. PARALLEL COMPARTMENT GROUND ROW

therefore, be a mixture of focus lanterns and floods. The focus lanterns will be less powerful than those in the F.O.H., as they have less distance to throw, for example, 1,000-watt focus lanterns in the auditorium, then 500-watt on No. 1 batten. The floods will vary in wattage according to the size of the stage, the minimum being 100- or 150-watt and the maximum 500-watt. To bridge the gap between the rather cumbersome 500-watt size with a 300-watt lamp and the baby 150-watt, a double unit of the latter can be used. Where the stage is sufficiently large, 6-ft. lengths of magazine batten (the compartments of which are virtually the same baby

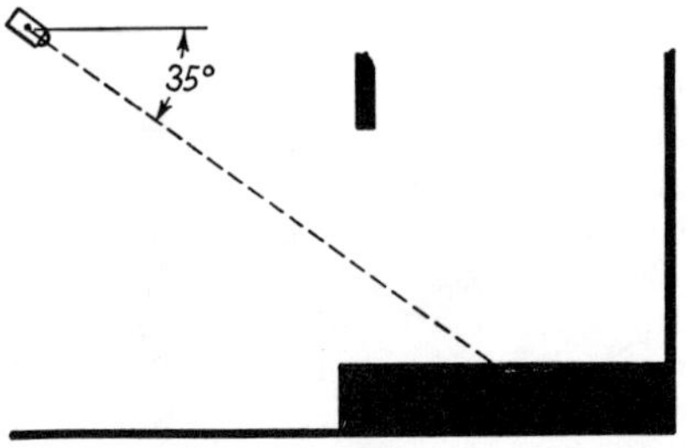

FIG. 87. F.O.H. LIGHTING ANGLE FOR SPOTLIGHTS

floods) can be substituted with advantage, the focus lanterns hanging between the lengths. This is not done on small stages, as the directional possibilities of the individual baby floods especially when they are combined with the hood attachment are useful in overcoming shadow problems.

Medium angle reflectors fitted to the baby floods or magazine lengths enable the main beam to be kept clear of the cyclorama upon which only the direct light of the lamps spills.

This question of direct light on the cyclorama is important, even where a play demands interiors only. There may be windows in the rear wall of the set and these may appear as patches of light on the cyclorama when it acts as a backing. Night scenes with lighted interior are especially troublesome. This is where a No. 1 batten, with the individually swivelled baby floods, will be valuable, particularly on small stages where these troubles are much aggravated. The primary aim of the floods on No. 1 batten is to light any part of the setting down-stage of the cyclorama; they also provide a general wash of light behind the accents of the focus lanterns. Any pronounced colouring for night effects, etc., comes from these floods. The focus lanterns may be spaced out at regular intervals across the stage, but where there are only two, then these will be the extreme ends of the battens, i.e. about level with the sides of the proscenium opening. On larger stages the height may require additional focus lanterns to be placed lower down, just behind the proscenium, on adjustable brackets in order to secure better lighting angles. These lanterns are usually known as "perches" and can be considered as extensions of No. 1 batten.

No. 2 batten will hang or be carried over the up-stage edge of the fixed ceiling, and be devoted to the cyclorama only. In the smaller stages triple baby flood units will be used, worked up as expense permits and size demands through a magazine batten to a bank of 500-watt floods. Here, on the cyclorama, three-colour mixing comes into its own. Therefore, there will be three circuits, and floods or battens will be fitted with wide-angle reflectors.

Possible additions to the basic stage equipment can now be considered. One of the first of these is the provision of three-colour lighting at the bottom of the cyclorama. In its simplest and cheapest form this is a length of 2 in. × 1 in. wiring trough with E.S. holders, the lamps being of the coloured china sprayed type 60- or 100-watt. No exciting colour mixing will come out of this arrangement, but it will be better than nothing. A magazine ground row, or footlight, is the correct thing to use: some designs combine the two functions in the same unit. It is important that the ground row should not be closer to the cyclorama than 24 in. to its front edge. This not only prevents spottiness at the bottom, but also gives the reflector some chance, however small, to throw its light up and at the cyclorama. To cope with very close ranges, a unit with parallel compartments (Fig. 88) can be used, but the result is bound to be rather a makeshift.

When there are three dimmers to the top and three to the bottom, I suggest No. 5A deep amber, No. 16 blue-green, and No. 20 blue should be used at the top instead of the orthodox No. 6 red, No. 36 green, and No. 20 blue, which, however, should be retained at the bottom. The reasons for this were discussed under "colour-mixing" in "Colour" page 369.

Concealment is important, particularly when an empty stage effect is required. Ideally, the ground row ought to be mounted out of sight, below stage level, in a pit covered, on occasion, by removable sections of the floor. Alternatively, a ground row in 6-ft. lengths can be movable and placed on the stage floor, thus making them available for other purposes. Where money is important, it is undesirable that this equipment should be reserved for one job. The portable sections of ground row can be used to light door or window backings to interior sets, or even as a footlight. When a pit cannot be provided, the ground row can be concealed by an inclined plane. This is merely a long narrow plywood flat, one edge of which rests on the floor down-stage of the lighting ground row and the other is propped up so that the plane makes an angle of 35° or less with the stage (Fig. 89). This inclined plane is painted matt white, and will automatically pick up the top cyclorama lighting in a shade of the original colour. The effect is most satisfying and overcomes the need for a painted wall row or a line of hills, etc., in circumstances where something neutral is required.

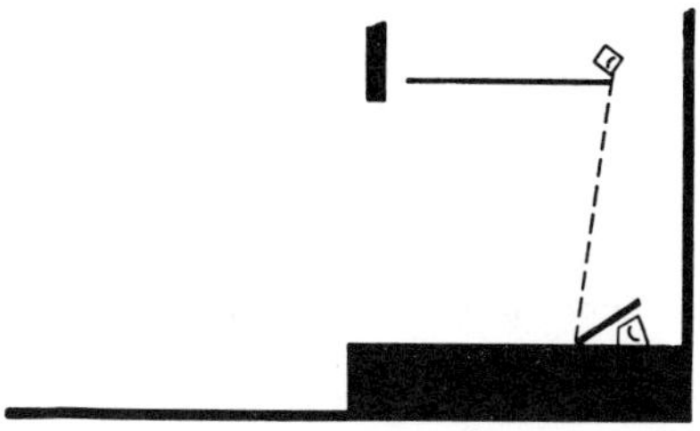

FIG. 89. INCLINED PLANE MASKING LIGHTING GROUND ROW

On medium-sized stages some vertical acting area floods carried on a No. 2 batten half-way up-stage will be useful; these will be 150- or 500-watt depending on the scale. After fairly considerable equipment has been acquired, a footlight can be contemplated. I hope I have made it clear that its priority is very low. A footlight is useful, but expensive, and, unlike focus lanterns, floods, and dimmers, can be discarded. Its functions, except in West End "leg shows," are subtle, and far more shows are ruined by over-use of it than by lack of it. Its main purpose is to soften the facial shadows caused by overhead units or front of house units throwing at too steep an angle. It is invariably too bright, causing actors' shadows on the back of interior sets, plus scenery shadows when the cyclorama is used. In theory, this is overcome by mounting the footlight so that a rising shadow is thrown by the edge of the footlight ramp (Fig. 90A). This shadow includes the cyclorama, but causes a bad shadow line on the side walls of a box set and on curtains, etc., set about centre stage. Usually, the kinds of stage in mind are not deep enough to give the rising-shadow theory a chance, and it will be better to mount the footlight (Fig. 90B). Any woodwork or ramp between the up-stage edge of the footlight and the stage floor must be black.

The length of the footlight should be only 75 per cent of the total width of the proscenium opening. Compartments will have 60-watt lamps and wide angle, or even no reflectors in many instances. It can be wired for two or three circuits. As already

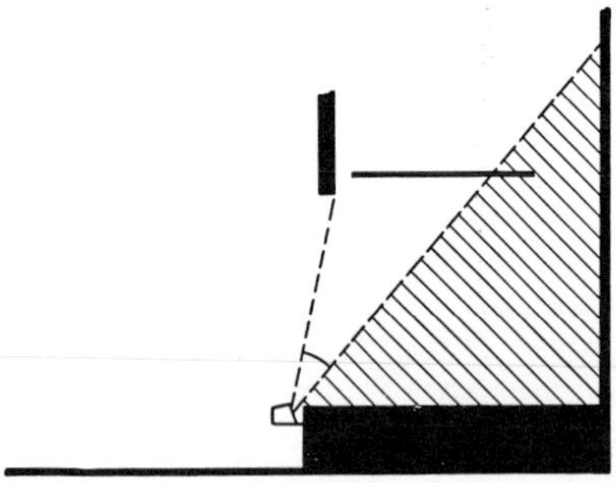

FIG. 90A. RISING SHADOW FOOTLIGHT THEORY

explained, the footlight can often double the part of ground row. For small stages where some footlight correction is absolutely necessary because of enforced high mounting of the auditorium focus lanterns, a cheap remedy will be the opal architectural strip-lamp in 3-ft. or 4-ft. lengths. A single line of these can be mounted in a simple metal hood and carried from brackets along the front of the stage. The lamps will be wired with a dimmer as a single circuit. A touch of this light brought in on the dimmer will be sufficient for most purposes, no colour filters being required. This type of lamp, owing to its shape, will not throw shadows of verticals (actors) on the cyclorama.

When a fore stage is used, footlights must be able to vanish and leave a clean stage front. Various methods ranging from elaborate mechanical lifts or rotating devices to striking by hand are adopted. Bear in mind, however, the priority of the footlights when considering costs. The footlight in the stage lighting installation is similar to the cushion on the seat—a refinement

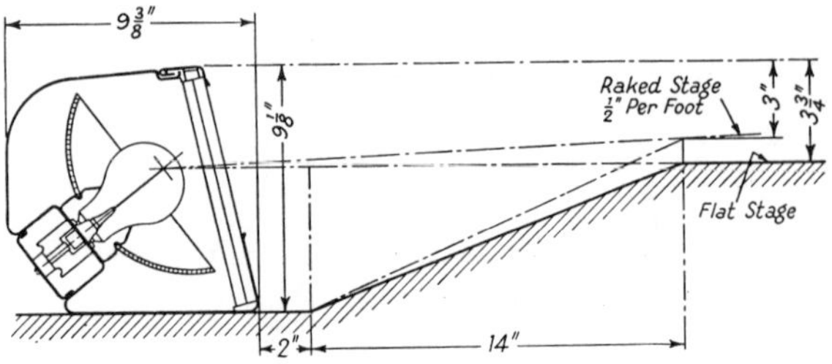

FIG. 90B. SECTION OF FOOTLIGHT AND RAMP

that must come after essentials. On small stages, where floor space is valuable, the footlight can be carried on removable brackets over the front edge of the stage without a ramp (Fig. 91).

LIGHTING IN PLAN

To assess exactly how many lanterns ought to be used in the F.O.H., No. 1 batten for cyclorama, and so on, it is necessary to consider the installation from the plan view. The vertical aspect must always come first; otherwise a diagram that shows the acting area plan is liable to be covered perfectly by the circles thrown by the various lanterns, when in practice the angle at which the circles of light are projected may be of little use for their primary purpose—facial illumination. Taking into consideration and in detail the coverage of focus lanterns, spotlights,

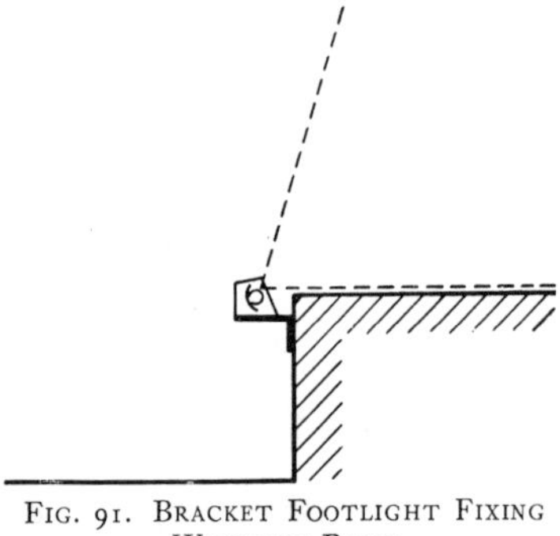

FIG. 91. BRACKET FOOTLIGHT FIXING WITHOUT RAMP

and narrow-angle acting area floods, the stage falls into distinct areas down-stage, centre stage, and up-stage, which are subdivided into Left,

Centre, and Right respectively. Left and right are from the actors' point of view facing the audience, known as Actor's Left and Actor's Right. Thus there are Left Centre (L.C.), Down Right (D.R.), Up Centre (U.C.), and so on (Fig. 92).

It would be convenient if lighting could be

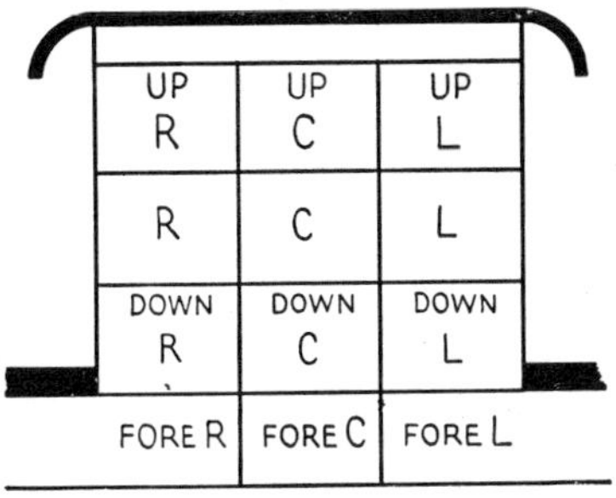

FIG. 92. REFERENCE PLAN FOR PRINCIPAL STAGE AREAS

located according to this formula; then, we should have a further narrow division beyond the up-stage area, best labelled "No-Man's Land," where the lighting for cyclorama and its scenery falls. On a small stage the best that can be aimed at for lighting, is down-stage and up-stage. Thus, with the minimum gear, two spots in the auditorium will cross their beams and light Down Left and Down Right, overlapping in the centre. The two spots on No. 1 batten attend to Up Left and Up Right in the same way. The next step is to add a centre spot in the auditorium, giving Centre, Down Left, and Down Right, the last two crossing beams as before. If No. 1 batten can be treated in the same way, then the auditorium spot becomes Down Centre. The next additions are designed to give a change of colour to these areas, beginning with the most important Down Centre—hence one focus lamp left and right, but two in the centre. The change of colour takes place on dimmers during a scene and is, therefore, not made possible by mechanical means, however elaborate.

This system is applied until there are two spotlights for each of the stage areas and also some unattached ones. Often the centre and up-stage areas receive assistance from vertical acting areas in a second batten over centre stage. However, this is vertical light, and, in any case, when interiors are in question, the ceiling prevents the use of battens other than No. 1. This is a good reason for concentrating main acting area lighting forces here and in the auditorium. A full spot batten will have spots, two to each of the centre and up-stage areas (i.e. twelve spots). The lighting artist will not earmark his spots rigidly for these areas, but will bear in mind that a proportion of his spots will be confined to semi-flooding duties; the fewer spots there are, the higher the proportion.

If there are a dozen spots in No. 1 batten and also "perch" spots, the scene lighting will be a fabric of spotting carefully built up and balanced. This end should not be attempted on a small stage, even if the number of spots is available, as actors moving about the stage at such close ranges tend to intercept beams intended for other areas. Broad effects are better. They require simpler equipment, and the idea behind them is far more likely to get over. The wonderful mosaic built up over several days, using vast numbers of spots, all at individual check positions, is really appreciated only by the producer who carried it out. Perches are useful in throwing characters into relief, but can be used only on stages with height.

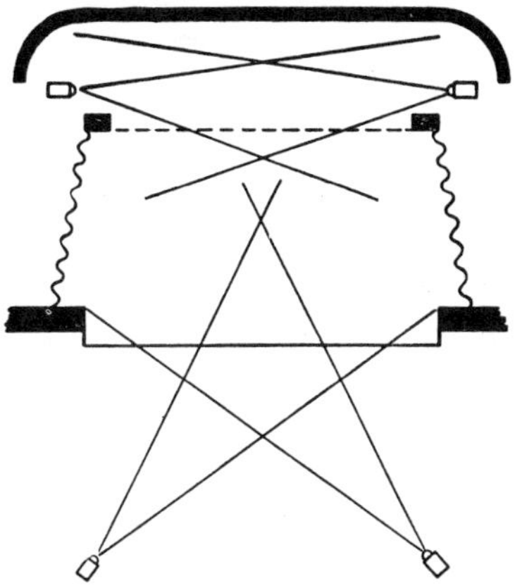

FIG. 93A. LIGHTING UP STAGE WHEN CEILING IS USED

On small stages, actors will have to use the "No-Man's Land" in front of the cyclorama. Frequently spotlights placed high in the wings, or at the ends of the cyclorama batten, will serve very well to light this region, since the actor will not walk on sideways and will, therefore, be facing the spot on the opposite side (Fig. 93A). Larger stages will have spots on the end of the cyclorama batten and No. 2 batten for this purpose. Backings to doorways will be lit by baby floods hanging over the door: a common fault is to use a flood from the side projecting a distracting shadow of the actor.

Where a fore stage is used, it becomes another area to be lit and so there are Fore Left, Fore Centre, and Fore Right, though it may be necessary to make do with two lanterns.

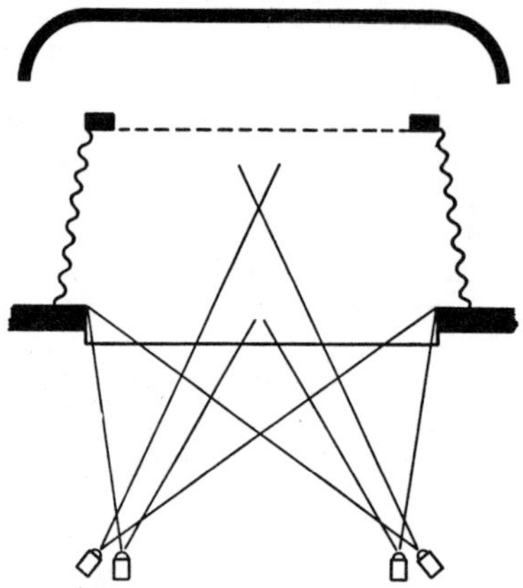

FIG. 93B. LIGHTING THE DOWN STAGE CORNERS

Note on Crossing Beams. References are made to the crossing of beams from spotlights or focus lanterns: the Left spot lights the right-hand side of the stage. While writing, I had in mind the small stage with limited height and space. In these circumstances, there are two main problems: (1) how to get the light to spread quickly, and (2) what to do about shadows on scenery and cyclorama. However much the blue lighting of the cyclorama is increased, in, for example, a day exterior, direct light that may be thrown from a spotlight can never be swamped. The result may be an unpleasant circle of light, and, certainly, actors' shadows.

By crossing the beams, the shadows are projected to the sides of the stage where, even in a box set, they are not so noticeable. As the stage increases in size, more liberty can be taken in this matter. Usually the crossed beam lights the actor from the more important "on stage" aspect. Sometimes, when important action takes place in the down-stage corners of the stage, it is necessary to take steps to counter the too directional effect of the crossed beam, and a supplementary, less powerful, spot is used (Fig. 93B).

COMPARATIVE EXAMPLES OF STAGE LAY-OUTS

All the plans detailed here are drawn to the same scale and although no really large stage is shown, there is a remarkable variation in size from Example A to Example G. Each one of these stages may, on occasion, have to mount the same play!

Scale related to physical dimensions is obvious to most people; scale in lighting is less obvious but equally important. While, in view of the enormous lighting intensities that have to be suggested in a daylight scene, it is desirable to employ the highest intensities, it is possible to use small wattages provided *all* the lighting is in scale. *All* is important; even the house lighting must be in scale. When comparing the following details of installations, the scale, which is not necessarily tied to the size of the stage, should be kept in mind.

The apparatus must be thought of as mobile, particularly in the earlier examples, and shifted to suit a particular production. For example, the floods behind the proscenium might, on occasion, be grouped to one side of the stage instead of being equally spaced.

In all the examples the minimum current required is given; whenever new mains are being installed, considerable margin must be allowed for future extension or for the use of additional dimmer boards and equipment hired for special productions.

Summary of Comparative Examples

A. Total load	3,300 watts.	Lighting circuits	7;	dimmers	7
B. Total load	6,700 watts.	Lighting circuits	7;	dimmers	7
C. Total load	9,750 watts.	Lighting circuits	18;	dimmers	11
D. Total load	16,500 watts.	Lighting circuits	30;	dimmers	20
E. Total load	26,040 watts.	Lighting circuits	28;	dimmers	28
F. Total load	60,860 watts.	Lighting circuits	47;	dimmers	47
G. Total load	182,600 watts.	Lighting circuits	109;	dimmers	109

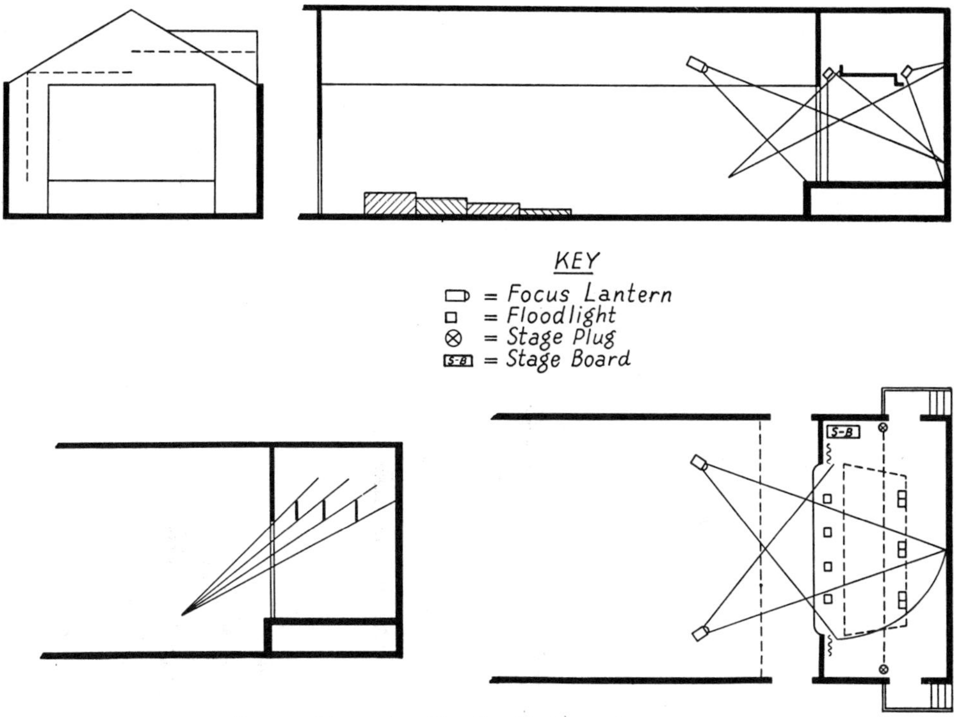

FIG. 94. TEMPORARY HUT FIT UP STAGE INSTALLATION

EXAMPLE A

This is an absolute minimum installation planned on a small scale as a nucleus for a small stage or a travelling fit-up with extreme limitation on current, the total required being under 15 amps. at 230 volts.

The stage in the diagram is based on the plan shown on page 40 of *Community Centres* (H.M. Stationery Office) which utilizes standard huts as a temporary measure. The maximum possible proscenium opening is 16 ft. by 9 ft.; a door is provided on both sides of the stage without which the stage would be unworkable and even with it extensive use of scenery and furniture is impossible, though the ceiling masking and white rear wall will be some compensation. The proscenium arch, stage lighting, and switchboard could be removable, leaving a completely open platform for concerts.

		Total
FRONT OF HOUSE		
Two 500-watt focus lanterns; (6 in. diameter lens and simple hand colour change from gangway if possible.)	2 dimmers 500-watt	1,000 watts
No. 1 BATTEN		
Four 100-watt medium angle baby floods; (Wired 1 and 3 one circuit; 2 and 4 the other.)	2 dimmers 200-watt	400 watts
CYCLORAMA BATTEN		
Three 150-watt wide-angle twin baby floods;	2 dimmers 450-watt	900 watts
STAGE PLUGS		
Two 5-amp. B.S. 3-pin, one each side of stage;	1 dimmer 250/500-watt	500 watts
Two 5-amp. B.S. 3-pin, one each side of stage switched only		500 watts
	7 dimmers	3,300 watts

STAGE BOARD

One unit cabinet with 7 dimmers and a 3,000-watt master; minimum mains 15-amp.

ACCESSORIES

Set of four funnel attachments for floods on No. 1 batten.

One 150-watt baby flood with alternative wide and medium angle reflectors and a funnel attachment.

One 250-watt baby spot for general stage duties.

EXAMPLE B

This is another minimum equipment for a stage with ceiling masking similar to that in Example A, but larger in scale. With such an installation, which forms a fine nucleus on which to build, much interesting work can be done. It can easily compete in cost with that well-known white elephant minimum—two magazine battens, a magazine footlight, and no dimmers!

		Total
FRONT OF HOUSE		
Two 1,000-watt focus lanterns; (With simple hand colour change from gangway, if possible.)	2 dimmers 1,000-watt	2,000 watts
No. 1 BATTEN		
Six 150-watt medium angle baby floods;	2 dimmers 450-watt	900 watts
CYCLORAMA BATTEN		
Six 300-watt wide-angle floods;	2 dimmers 900-watt	1,800 watts
STAGE PLUGS		
Two 5-amp. B.S. 3-pin, one each side of stage;	1 dimmer 500/1,000-watt	1,000 watts
Two 5-amp. B.S. 3-pin, one each side of stage switched only	.	1,000 watts
	7 dimmers	6,700 watts

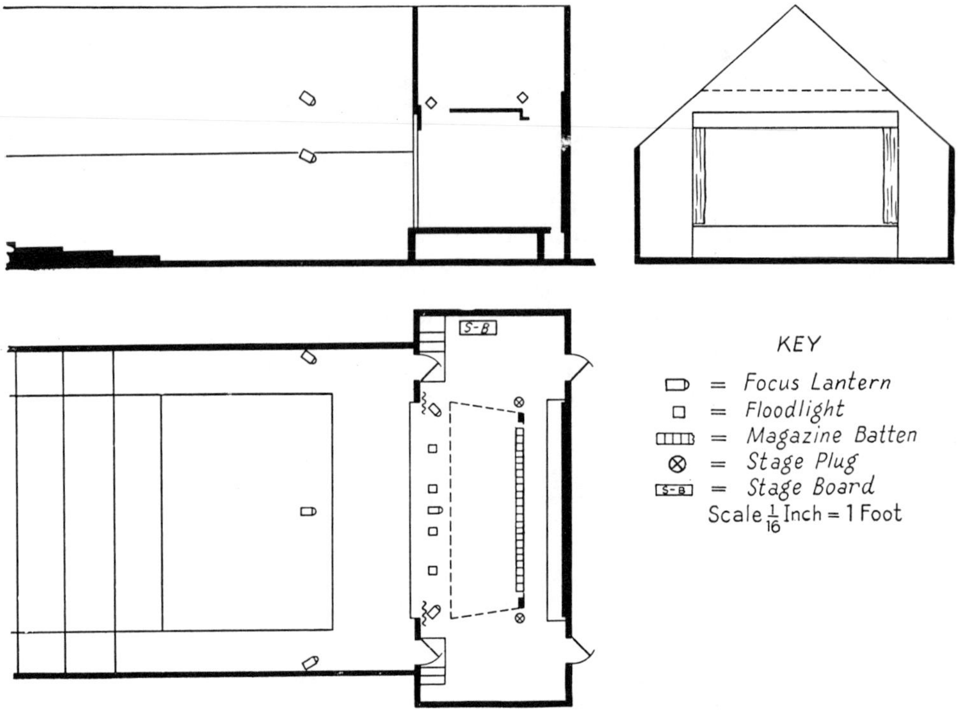

FIG. 95. THE QUESTORS THEATRE, EALING, INSTALLATION

STAGE BOARD

One unit cabinet with 7 dimmers and a 6,000-watt master; minimum mains 30-amp.

ACCESSORIES

Set of six funnel attachments for floods on No. 1 batten.
Two 150-watt baby floods with alternative wide- and medium-angle reflectors and funnel attachments.
Two 250-watt baby spots for general stage duties.

EXAMPLE C

The plan on the opposite page is of an amateur theatre that has employed for the past twelve years or so the ceiling masking advocated in these pages. The theatre belongs to The Questors, Ealing, Middlesex, a flourishing company whose productions are ambitious and varied. From the beginning money was "very tight," and the conversion of an unsuitable mission hall into an attractive theatre was the work of the players and supporters. Their scenery is designed, painted, and built by members of the company. (*See* photographs, Fig. 100.)

For present purposes I have based my example on the installation as it was about 1939, and have stated the commercial equipment that is obtainable to-day. Items marked with an asterisk* including the switchboard with its liquid dimmers were constructed by the amateurs.

		Total
FRONT OF HOUSE		
Two 500-watt focus lanterns (Left and Right); (Fitted with mechanical colour change.)	2 circuits 500-watt	1,500 watts
One 500-watt focus lantern (Centre);	1 circuit 500-watt	
No. 1 BATTEN		
Four 100-watt medium angle baby floods;	2 circuits 200-watt	1,150 watts
Three 250-watt baby spots (focus lanterns); (The baby spots are at the centre and ends of the batten.)	3 circuits 250-watt	
CYCLORAMA TOP*		
15- ft. wide-angle 150-watt wide-angle magazine batten;	1 circuit 1,500-watt 2 circuits 750-watt	3,000 watts
(The colours are orange 5A, blue-green 16, and blue 20 for the double circuit.)		
CYCLORAMA PIT*		
15-ft. parallel type magazine equipment; blue 60-watt	1 circuit 900-watt	2,100 watts
red and green 40-watt	2 circuits 600-watt	
(Owing to the close range, this special equipment (Fig. 88) is specified.)		
STAGE PLUGS		
Four 5- amp. (two Left, two Right);	4 circuits 500-watt	2,000 watts
	18 circuits	9,750 watts

STAGE BOARD* (Flexible Type)

Two unit cabinets and 14-way inter-plugging panel; minimum mains, 40-amp.
The cyclorama top has three dimmers, one 1,500-watt and two 750-watt; for the remainder, six 250/500-watt and two 500/1,000-watt are suitable. Allowing for two master dimmers, there will be room on the board for three extra dimmers.

ACCESSORIES*

Set of four funnel attachments for the floods on No. 1 batten.
One 150-watt baby flood with medium angle reflector and funnel attachment.
One 150-watt baby flood with wide angle reflector.
One 250-watt baby focus lantern.
One 500-watt focus lantern.

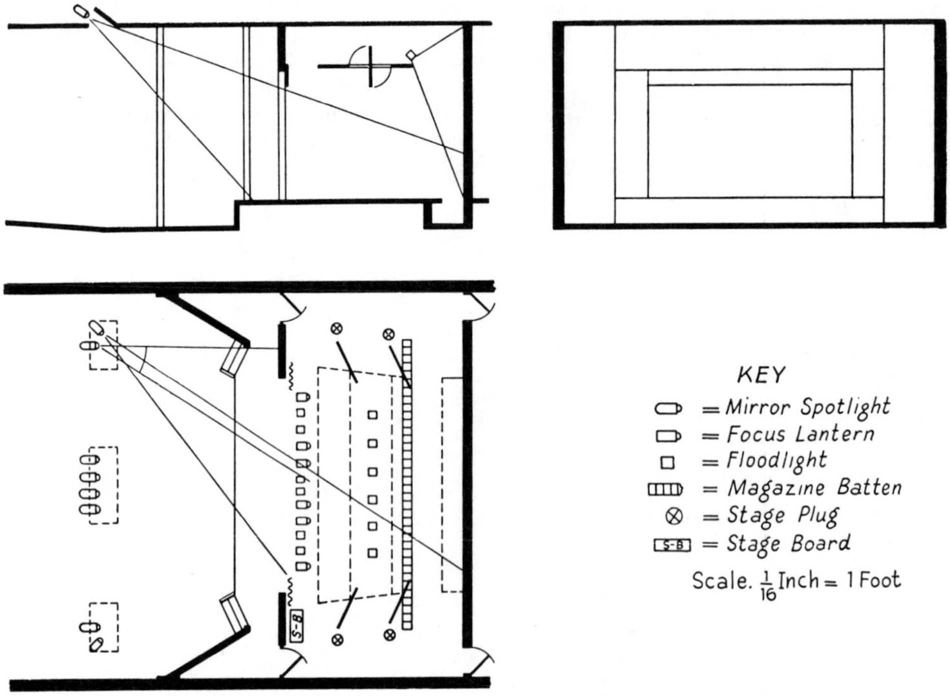

FIG. 96. A LITTLE THEATRE WITH FORE STAGE (*See also* Figs. 85 and 86)

EXAMPLE D

Although this stage is larger than that of Example C, the lighting remains small in scale. The numbers of units have, however, been increased to give the lighting facilities of a fully-equipped theatre. Owing to the increased depth of stage, opportunity has been taken to introduce another lighting batten by pivoting the ceiling. Such a device allows the use of curtain traverses at half stage. This theatre is planned to economize space, but, at the same time, to allow a considerable amount of movement for the dance.

		Total
FRONT OF HOUSE		
Four 250-watt mirror spots (Left and Right);	4 circuits 250-watt	
Four 250-watt mirror spots (Centre);	4 circuits 250-watt	2,000 watts
(The Left and Right spots should have some kind of remote colour change.)		
No. 1 BATTEN		
Six 250-watt focus lanterns;	6 circuits 250-watt	
Six 150-watt medium angle baby floods;	2 circuits 450-watt	2,400 watts
No. 2 BATTEN		
Six 150-watt medium angle baby floods;	2 circuits 450-watt	900 watts
(Funnel attachments to be fitted when required as Acting Areas.)		
CYCLORAMA TOP		
27-ft. 150-watt wide-angle magazine batten;	1 dimmer 2,700-watt 2 dimmers 1,350-watt	5,400 watts
CYCLORAMA PIT		
18-ft. wide-angle magazine ground row blue (150-watt);	1 dimmer 1,200-watt	
red and green (100-watt);	2 dimmers 800-watt	2,800 watts
(By means of extension leads under the stage, this ground row can be used as a footlight when required.)		
STAGE PLUGS		
Three-5 amp. (Left);	3 circuits 500-watt	
Three-5 amp. (Right);	3 circuits 500-watt	3,000 watts
	30 circuits	16,500 watts

STAGE BOARD

Three unit cabinets combined to take 20 dimmers, one transformer master dimmer, and a 16-way interplugging panel. Remote-controlled contactor switch for master blackout. Minimum main 70-amp.

Six dimmers are wound especially for the cyclorama and permanently connected to it in order to get the best colour mixing and freedom from all flicker on these sensitive lamps. This item, 8,200 watts, can go on one phase, if a balance is required. The remaining 14 dimmers for the flexible section of the board will comprise nine 250/500-watt and five 500/1,000-watt.

The transformer master will be an expensive, though ideal, arrangement. An alternative board, using resistance masters, and blackout switch on wall adjacent to board instead of remote contactor, is three unit cabinets combined to take 21 dimmers, three master dimmers, and a 16-way interplugging panel.

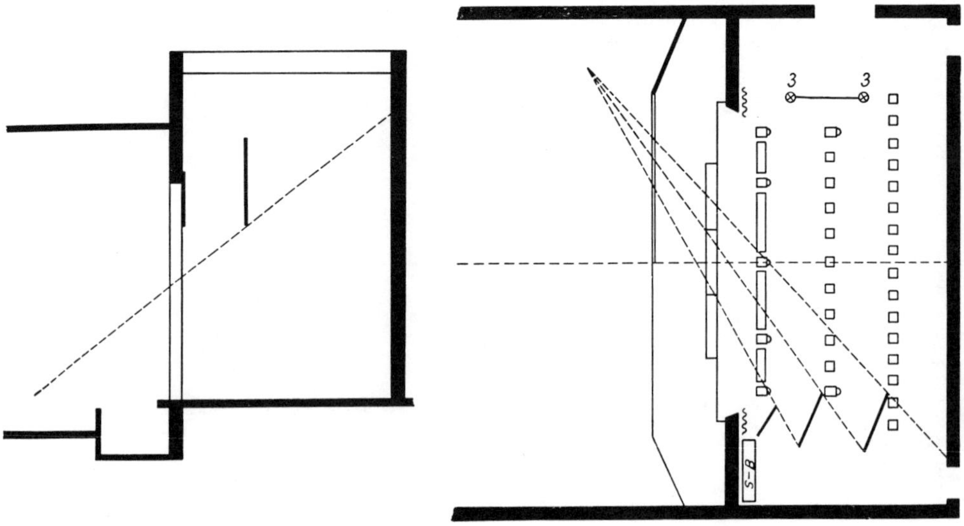

FIG. 97. A SCHOOL STAGE ALSO USED AS COMMUNITY HALL
(Scale $\frac{1}{16}$ inch = 1 Foot)

EXAMPLE E

This plan is based on the plan for a school community centre stage given in *Community Centres* (H.M. Stationery Office). The position of one of the doors in the back wall has been altered to allow the use of a flat cyclorama. The size and proportions of the stage are a great advance on the previous examples. Both the Arts Council and the National Council of Social Service in their schemes advocate stages of similar dimensions. This size is large enough for most normal productions, but not so large that amateurs find themselves forced to make large-scale, and therefore expensive, scenery.

The stage is not sufficiently high to allow flying of scenery, but it will permit the flying of a ceiling piece out of the way when borders are required. To do anything more than this would, in any case, require expensive equipment that would be difficult for amateurs to handle. A fire curtain, which might be evaded in a hall like this for occasional use as a theatre, would certainly be needed were provision for flying scenery to be made.

The lighting in this example and in Example F are intended for direct comparison, the installation being small and full respectively for the same size stage.

		Total
FRONT OF HOUSE		
Three 1,000-watt focus lanterns; (Concealed in auditorium ceiling)	3 dimmers 1,000-watt	3,000 watts
FOOTLIGHT		
Three 6-ft. lengths of 60-watt wide-angle magazine; (To be carried from removable brackets over front edge of stage. Wiring from dimmers to run to plugs on the front of stage and up-stage so that the footlight can be used as cyclorama bottom lighting.)	3 dimmers 480-watt	1,440 watts
No. 1 BATTEN		
Two 6-ft. and two 3-ft. lengths of medium-angle 100-watt magazine batten;	3 dimmers 800-watt	4,900 watts
Five 500-watt focus lanterns (between the above);	5 dimmers 500-watt	
No. 2 BATTEN		
Eight 150-watt medium-angle floods;	2 dimmers 600-watt	2,700 watts
Two 500-watt focus lanterns;	2 dimmers 500-watt	
One 500-watt medium-angle flood;	1 dimmer 500-watt	
The two focus lanterns will usually be fixed at each end of the batten; the 500-watt flood will be used at any position. All floods can be fitted with funnel attachments when the cyclorama is in use.		
CYCLORAMA TOP		
Sixteen 500-watt wide-angle floods;	2 dimmers 2,000-watt 1 dimmer 4,000-watt	8,000 watts
(This arrangement, using high-efficiency lamps, offers the most inexpensive method of lighting a cyclorama of this size, when space allows a reasonable throw for the lanterns.)		
STAGE PLUGS		
Six 5-amp. (pairs in parallel but separately switched) Left;	3 dimmers 500/1,000-watt	6,000 watts
Six 5-amp. (pairs in parallel but separately switched) Right;	3 dimmers 500/1,000-watt	
	28 dimmers	26,040 watts

STAGE BOARD

Four unit cabinets combined to give 28 dimmers with 4 resistance masters; minimum main 113-amp. Board position on a rostrum at stage level.

SUSPENSION FOR HANGING EQUIPMENT

All overhead battens are carried from winch suspensions and are fitted with flexible tails to enable the equipment to be lowered within 4 ft. of the stage floor for cleaning and adjustment.

ACCESSORIES

Apart from lanterns hired for particular productions or carried by visiting companies, this stage ought to possess:

One 1,000-watt focus lantern on telescopic stand.
One 500-watt focus lantern.
Four 500-watt wide-angle floods on telescopic stands.
Three 150-watt baby floods with alternative reflectors and funnels.

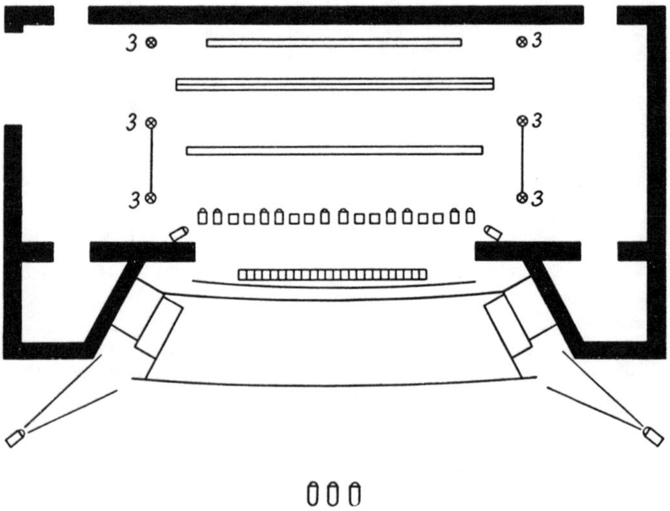

FIG. 98. STAGE FOR COMMUNITY CENTRE (ARTS COUNCIL)
Scale $\frac{1}{16}$ inch = 1 Foot)

EXAMPLE F

The plan is of similar dimensions to that of Example E, but is based on that put forward by the Arts Council for an Arts Centre. The stage is to be equipped with fire curtain and grid for flying scenery. A 40-ft. scenery tower is proposed; this dimension should be from stage floor to grid. There will be additional height to the roof and lantern above the grid.

The lighting installation for such a stage should be somewhat lavish, as there will be touring ballet in addition to the drama to light.

		Total
FRONT OF HOUSE		
Three 1,000-watt mirror spots (Centre);	3 dimmers 1,000-watt	
Two 1,000-watt focus lanterns (Left and Right);	2 dimmers 1,000-watt	5,000 watts
(The Centre spots to be concealed in the ceiling; the others can be carried by removable brackets on the side walls.)		
FOOTLIGHT		
18 ft. of wide-angle 60-watt magazine;	1 dimmer 480-watt 4 dimmers 240-watt	1,440 watts
(Wired one circuit complete across the stage, one half Left, one half Right, one Centre and one Ends. Footlight to be arranged to disappear, leaving the stage flat.)		
PERCHES		
Two 1,000-watt focus lanterns; (One each side of the proscenium arch.)	2 dimmers 1,000-watt	2,000 watts
No. 1 BATTEN		
Ten 1,000-watt focus lanterns;	10 dimmers 1,000-watt	
Eight 500-watt medium-angle floods;	4 dimmers 1,000-watt	14,000 watts
(The floods are wired in pairs A and B Left, C and D Right. For ballet, four extra floods are substituted for some of the spots, thus making the batten three-colour.)		
No. 2 BATTEN		
28 ft. of medium-angle 100-watt magazine;	3 dimmers 1,200-watt	3,600 watts
CYCLORAMA TOP		
60 ft. of wide-angle 150-watt magazine in two rows;	1 dimmer 6,000-watt 2 dimmers 3,000-watt	12,000 watts
CYCLORAMA GROUND ROW		
Four 6-ft. lengths of wide-angle magazine; blue 150-watt; red and green 60-watt. (Movable lengths on castors.)	1 dimmer 1,500-watt 2 dimmers 660-watt	2,820 watts
STAGE PLUGS		
Six 15-amp. plugs (pairs in parallel but separately switched) Left;	1 dimmer 1/2,000-watt 2 dimmers 500/1,000-watt	
Six 15-amp. plugs (pairs in parallel but separately switched) Right;	1 dimmer 1/2,000-watt 2 dimmers 500/1,000-watt	8,000 watts
FLY PLUGS		
Six 15-amp. plugs (pairs in parallel but separately switched) Left;	1 dimmer 1/2,000-watt 2 dimmers 500/1,000-watt	
Six 15-amp. plugs (pairs in parallel but separately switched) Right;	1 dimmer 1/2,000-watt 2 dimmers 500/1,000-watt	8,000 watts
INDEPENDENTS		
One plug each side of stage and flys, four in all, switched only.		4,000 watts
	47 dimmers	60,860 watts

STAGE BOARD

50-way (3 spare) grand master interlocking board or similar model with electro-interlock. Blackouts by remote-operated contactor switches. Board to be carried on a perch platform. Special effects connexion point to be provided for touring switchboards.

SUSPENSION OF HANGING EQUIPMENT

If, as is probable, the stage is equipped with counterweight flying gear, then the overhead lighting battens will be carried from this.

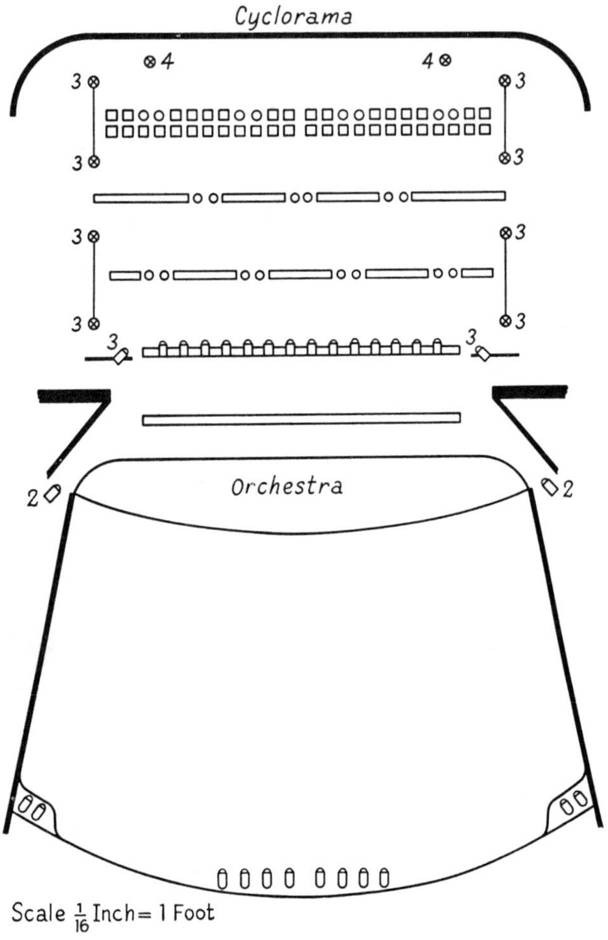

FIG. 99. MUNICIPAL THEATRE

NOTE: Although the acting area floods are shown hanging between lengths of magazine battens there is much to be said for complete battens with the floods on an adjacent barrel. The loss of the grid flying line is offset by the greater flexibility in positioning the floods. Magazine battens should be connected by plugs in the flys so that their dimmers can be released if necessary.

EXAMPLE G

MUNICIPAL THEATRE

This theatre is intended mainly for professional use. The stage and its equipment are on a sufficiently large scale to take full ballet and opera companies without cramping them. Nevertheless, the stage, with its 36-ft. proscenium opening and 32-ft. depth, is not particularly large and extravagant; it is small if we think of some municipal theatres on the Continent. The lighting installation detailed does not differ much from a number of first-rank commercial theatres in London and the provinces. To give everyone a good view, however, the seating is confined to stalls and one circle (Fig. 1, page 326), thereby reducing earning capacity and making a subsidy essential.

		Total
FRONT OF HOUSE (all fitted with remote colour change)		
AUDITORIUM CEILING		
Eight 1,000-watt mirror spots;	8 dimmers 1,000-watt	16,000 watts
ENDS OF CIRCLE FRONT		
Four 1,000-watt mirror spots;	4 dimmers 1,000-watt	
ENDS OF ORCHESTRA		
Four 1,000-watt focus lanterns;	4 dimmers 1,000-watt	
FOOTLIGHT		
30-ft. wide-angle 100-watt magazine;	8 dimmers 500-watt	4,000 watts
(Wired eight circuits, two Left and two Right; two Centre and two Ends. Mounted to disappear.)		
PERCHES		
Four 1,000-watt focus lanterns;	4 dimmers 1,000-watt	8,000 watts
Two 2,000-watt soft-edge spots;	2 dimmers 2,000-watt	
(Mounted on a light movable frame with ladder to move on and off stage; this frame can also carry the tormentor masking.)		
No. 1 BATTEN		
30-ft. medium-angle 150-watt magazine;	8 dimmers 750-watt	20,000 watts
Fourteen 1,000-watt focus lanterns;	14 dimmers 1,000-watt	
(The magazine batten and spot batten are suspended on separate but adjacent lines so that they can be used independently. The perches and battens may be combined with a counterweighted bridge, the whole somewhat as Fig. 37, rendering access for adjustment and colour change easy. The magazine batten is wired in the same way as the footlight.)		
No. 2 BATTEN		
24-ft. medium-angle 150-watt magazine;	4 dimmers 1,200-watt	12,800 watts
Eight 1,000-watt acting area floods (50°);	4 dimmers 2,000-watt	
(Floods are wired in pairs. They dim in pairs but are switched separately.)		
No. 3 BATTEN		
24-ft. medium-angle 150-watt magazine;	4 dimmers 1,200-watt	10,800 watts
Six 1,000-watt acting area floods (50°);	2 dimmers 2,000-watt	
	2 dimmers 1,000-watt	
CYCLORAMA TOP		
Forty 1,000-watt wide-angle floods;	8 dimmers 5,000-watt	48,000 watts
Eight 1,000-watt acting area floods (28°);	4 dimmers 2,000-watt	
(The cyclorama is intended for three-colour mixing with double the number of the dimmers to the blue. The red and green circuits are wired Left and Right; the blues Centre and Ends.)		
CYCLORAMA BOTTOM		
30-ft. wide-angle 150-watt magazine ground row;	4 dimmers 1,500-watt	6,000 watts
(If not in a pit, then in 12-ft. lengths mounted on castors with special plug points to feed them.)		

STAGE PLUGS

Six plugs (pairs in parallel) Down Left; . .	3 dimmers 1/2000 watt . . .	24,000 watts
Six plugs (pairs in parallel) Down Right; . .	" " . . .	"
Six plugs (pairs in parallel) Up Left; . .	" " . . .	"
Six plugs (pairs in parallel) Up Right; . .	" " . . .	"

(Stage and fly plugs dim in pairs but are separately switched)

FLY PLUGS

Six plugs (pairs in parallel) Down Left; . .	3 dimmers 1/2000 watt . . .	24,000 watts
Six plugs (pairs in parallel) Down Right; . .	" " . . .	"
Six plugs (pairs in parallel) Up Left; . .	" " . . .	"
Six plugs (pairs in parallel) Up Right; . .	" " . . .	"

INDEPENDENTS

Eight plugs variously situated. Switched only;		8,000 watts

FLOAT SPOTS

Two plug points in footlight ramp;	. 1 dimmer 500/1,000-watt . . .	1,000 watts
	109 dimmers . . .	182,600 watts

STAGE BOARD

For a stage of this size a remote control is essential. In my opinion the light console, with a plug point in the stalls from rehearsal and alternative points in a F.O.H. lighting box and on the stage for the actual performance, is ideal; but failing this, then, an electro interlock or grand master board on a perch on the side of the stage.

FRONT OF HOUSE ARC SPOTS

A theatre such as this should have two or three mirror arc spotlights in a room at the back of the circle for following artistes in certain classes of production.

ACCESSORIES

These will be numerous, and mainly acquired for particular productions. Touring companies will have their special equipment, which should be connected to the house board controlled stage plugs instead of their portable boards. The fine array of hanging equipment will make unnecessary a lot of fitting up. I would like to see in such a theatre most productions re-lit, apart from special effects, in terms of the theatre's own equipment. Unless this is done, all productions tend to get lighting on the lowest level; i.e. the minimum amount that can be toured and fitted up in the other theatres of the tour.

Technical Note to Electricians. The question of balance over either a 3-wire single phase or a 4-wire 3-phase system arises. Examples A, B, and C have small loads that exempt them from this requirement. Examples F and G need to be balanced over 3 phases. Examples D and E will probably form part of a group of buildings, community centre, youth college, or school, where some other load can surely be found for the third phase.

Where unskilled labour is usual, safety must come before mere paper balancing which is all that it can be in stage lighting. With two phases, the stage floor and temporary extensions can be balanced against the hanging equipment.

LIGHTING METHODS

When the stage is equipped with one of the basic installations detailed in "Comparative Examples of Stage Layouts," above, how is it used for a particular production? The lighting must be considered in the early days and before a decision is reached on the possibility and manner of mounting the play. It would be absurd to select a play that could not be cast. Similarly, the stage and its lighting equipment must be suitable for the specific play. The principal handicaps from the setting viewpoint is the furniture and properties rather than the scenery. Not only a piano or a settee but chairs and fragile crockery require space. *Hamlet*, with sixteen or more scenes, may be much easier to put on a small stage than a modern drawing-room play with only one change of scene. The most exacting lighting arrangements may be required for the realistic single box set because the audience is familiar with the scene; anything may happen to shadows, colours, etc., in remote Elsinore, but not in present-dayLondon.

Modification in the basic installation is possible for a particular production; that apparatus need always be used from the position it is found, should not be the rule. If the play demands it, take down all the spotlights and use them, throwing backwards from up-stage to down. In halls or theatres where there is a skilled electrician, his character can be analysed from his reactions to the removal of lanterns from their usual positions. Permanent installation may be supplemented by special equipment hired for a particular production, though cost will keep this to the minimum. The mains must be capable of taking the extra load and there should be something to which connexion can be made.

At this stage it will be well to decide who will be responsible for the lighting. Often the producer reserves this for himself, but, in my opinion, this tradition is bad, as bad as that of the producer who plays a leading part in his own production. The producer must co-ordinate and direct the work of artists in every department, acting, music, scenery, and lighting. "Artist" is the operative word: the electrician could design the lighting if he were not, as so often seems to be the case, merely a technician. Lighting, like the setting, requires a designer, and the two can, logically, be done by one man. Yet how few scene designers train themselves to light their own sets? Relatively few, probably because of the electricity bugbear. A scene designer does not need exhaustive knowledge of the mechanics of the craft: he can safely leave such things to the scene builders and stage carpenters. Likewise, he can leave electricity to the electrician, but he must know how to paint—with light.

The play having been decided, the lighting artist, whether he will also be scenic artist or not, studies his part and consults with himself, or another, on the relationship of the setting to the lighting. He will attend some rehearsals to enable him to know the location of business and groupings long before lighting rehearsal. Under the direction of the producer, he, like the actors and as an artist, has liberty to interpret. He will have decided what lanterns will be used and where; also the colour filters and the possible changes. Some may have been tested on the model setting in his model theatre.

When the play is performed, the lighting artist will have to decide whether to work the dimmer board himself or not. I am strongly of the view that he should: it is only by actually working a board that real contact with the lighting can be established. In local centres and amateur theatres this is usually possible, but if the lighting artist is not an electrician himself his work should be examined, from this point of view by one who is: In some of the larger town halls and professional theatres the electrician will sternly discourage amateur operators of the switchboard. This attitude springs from a variety of reasons, mostly illogical and, therefore, impossible to combat.

Irrespective of the presence or absence of back stage friction, the switchboard design and position may make it advisable for the lighting artist to direct from F.O.H. where the effects can be seen.

SCENERY AND LIGHTING REHEARSAL

The scenery is fitted up and the lanterns are coloured and focused on the positions required. Specific effects and changes are tried and plotted; but I do not favour going through the scenes over and over again, trying to fit in the changes without the actors. Some repetition is inevitable in the professional theatre, where the play is just "another play," but with amateurs the play is *the* play and the scenery and lighting are registered in their proper context. Amateurs are a team rather than a collection of specialist departments that seems to be unavoidable in the larger professional theatres.

Further, lighting should not be reduced to so many cues, carried out on signals from the stage manager. The switchboard operator must take part in the play; only where the stage cannot be seen should the signal method be adopted.

LIGHTING PLOT

Plotting differs from man to man. Some take down in detail; others rely principally on

Act I. Interior

Fig. 100. Act II. Exterior. Questors Theatre, Ealing. Production of "Arms and The Man" by Bernard Shaw

Both the interior and the exterior use the same permanent ceiling masking

memories. Actors have to memorize their parts and business; why not others? The plot, particularly when it is complicated for a large flexible board—should be arranged so that its layout strikes the eye. It should not consist of line upon line of close writing: a solid page. An effective method is to put the cue line, action, or signal boldly in the left-hand column, and to have vertical columns across the page for the principal groups of apparatus: front of house spots; spot batten; cyclorama. For these, recognized abbreviations are preferable: F.O.H., SPOTS, CYC., etc. The names used in the plot should correspond to the labelling on the board. If the board calls the cyclorama batten "No. 3 batten," then "No. 3 batt." it is.

Invisible manoeuvres, such as the plugging up of dimmers on flexible boards, which have to be done before a cue takes place, should be noted on a separate line between the last cue and the next. The left-hand column should have a dash which arrests the attention more effectively than the word "Prepare."

LIGHTING METHODS

To cover as much ground as possible I do not intend to consider lighting effects in relation to a particular play or scene. My general remarks and hints begin with Realism because such effects are more commonly called for and as we proceed it will become apparent that the boundary between Realism and Impressionism or any other of the "isms" is even less clear in lighting than in *décor*.

It cannot be too often stressed that the lighting for any scene must be dominated by an idea. The approach must not be: a spot on the armchair for Bill's and Susan's big scene; a spot on the table so that they can see Jimmy's business with the wineglass; pick out the doorway, etc. Last, the sun is put in as a sop to Realism, and is strengthened by additional floods because of the shadows on the backing. In consequence, it is quite out of tone with the rest. There is a type of setting that corresponds to this lighting; that where doors and windows are placed to satisfy the play's demand for entrances, without any conceivable architectural relationship. Such a setting is comparatively rare, but such lighting is too common. The justification offered is usually: "You must have some conventions on the stage."

This is true, but there should be consistency. If all that is required is a number of conventional pools of light for the actors, then the lighting should be quite honest with no half-hearted token sources offered. I do not believe that lighting best serves the actors by ensuring, first, that their faces can be seen. For example, if the characters are affected by heat, then the actors will have less work to do if, the moment the curtain rises, the impression given is of heat.

The idea must "click" immediately the curtain goes up: "It is a lovely day! The sun is streaming through the window. It is good to be alive!"; or "The sun is blazing through the window—one can scarcely breathe"; or "It's jolly cold outside, but my! it is cosy in here." Write in a single sentence the idea behind the lighting for the scene. To do this will automatically colour subsequent activities, even if Aunt Jessica's pincushion has to be picked out with a 1,000-watt spot.

EXTERIORS DAYLIGHT

First, there will be the need for a certain amount of general flooding. Unless the site is a leafy glade the scene will not look right if the light is a mosaic of pools and patches. The worst is noon when the sun is high in the heavens. Fortunately, the sky will have to be "full up," and this will help to counter shadows that are thrown. Here medium-angle beams of floods or magazine equipment can be directed to maximum effect on the acting area and clear of the sky. If there is still too much stray light, the funnel attachments will cut it out.

Any tinting of the acting area might be by Nos. 51–52 at the strongest; generally reds, blues, any circuits that are going, should be "all up."

It must be remembered that electric light is yellow compared with sunlight. Provided there is plenty of light, white is usually safest, with, perhaps, No. 50 where the sun's rays are supposed to be visible. As the intensity available becomes less and less, white becomes dull, and light tinting is needed to create interest.

The most satisfactory noonday effect I have achieved was at the Lisbon Opera, where the scenery and acting area were lit in white. The two bridges shown in the photographs (Fig. 37) enabled most of the colour filters to be removed between the acts. The cyclorama was lit in a medium blue, which, by contrast, warmed the white lighting. Apart from the great installation, a disturbing note is struck in this example by the reference to blue sky. Too often the sky in these latitudes is not blue but more a blue-grey, even

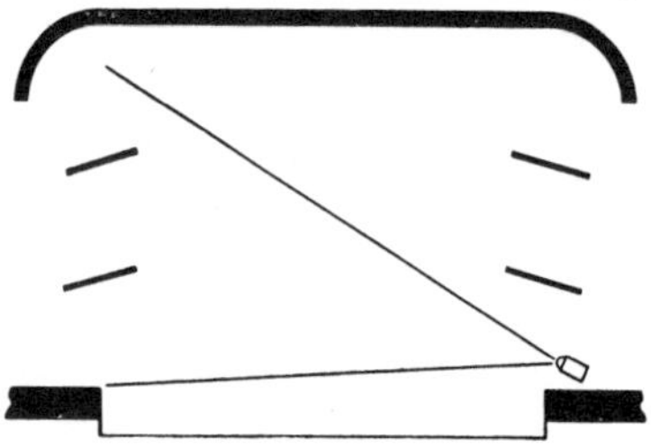

FIG. 101. SUNRISE EFFECT FROM PERCH SPOT

on the finest day. This raises a difficulty: anything like a grey or No. 18 light blue suggests coldness and is not sufficient to warm the white lighting of the acting area. My opinion is that in many instances a point must be stretched in favour of a real blue, such as a No. 32 (or equivalent mixture). This can be toned into warm white at the bottom of the cyclorama by the ground row. The first essential is that the sky shall look attractive—it is a lovely day—not merely matched colour. White lighting on blue painted cloths is unsatisfactory; the blue always looks like grey paint. Light amber or yellow effects should never be used in flood over the cyclorama unless the aim is to convey that the day is unpleasant.

The sky often gains by the introduction of something to break its flat expanse: a few *stationary* fleecy clouds are invaluable; their production, not difficult, is considered in "Special Effects," page 405. Once a few white clouds are on the sky, more freedom in the application of colour is possible.

Early sunlit morning is best suggested by general, diffuse lighting (somewhat cold) from the battens, with directional warm lighting superimposed *from one side*. The earlier the hour, the more coloured is the directional light; the nearer winter, the more the colouring and directional effect will be noticed, the sun being low in the sky. The deepest coloured sunlight is seen on fine but cold winter mornings.

The lighting for cold mornings without sunlight must be as diffuse as possible; anything resembling directional light or shadows must be avoided: probably more footlight correction than usual will be needed. Nos. 17, 60, 55, and 56 and other combinations such as Nos. 17–3, 17–55 are appropriate.

Sunrise and sunset are real "fun" for the lighting expert. These more obvious effects are not difficult. A noonday sky will give far more trouble than a big sunset display. If a play contains both sunrise and sunset, even if they occur in different settings, there should be differentiation. Usually, if given the chance, I assume that the sun is rising off-stage, and focus a lamp (2,000-watt soft edge spot for large stage) on the perch to cover the acting area from one side (Fig. 101). The stage, at first flooded from overhead and slightly from the float in cold light, gradually has this dramatic light brought up across it (Nos. 10–33); the cyclorama top is given a slight blush of reddish pink with a cold ground row. As the scene proceeds, the general lighting increases, overpowering this coloured source, which is then removed. It is one of the few opportunities there are of using strong colour on the acting area in a straight play. Sunset is assumed to take place behind the cyclorama ground row; i.e. in full view of the audience. The most striking clear sky sunsets are possible when red, green, and blue are used in the ground row and 5A, 16, and 20 in the top.

For cloudy sky sunsets it is necessary to use projected clouds, and even a sunburst flood (*see* "Special Effects" page 406); the difficulty is because the cyclorama surface is flat and does not provide any break-up for the light. In changing effects such as these, it is important to keep the cycle of change smooth. A 1,000- or 2,000-watt lamp for the sunrise needs careful dimmer operation. The thick filament takes an appreciable time to warm up. When creeping the dimmer in, one is likely to overdo it, and then the light comes either with a rush as too much light, or so slowly that the cue is missed. Lighting changes must always flow, and any suggestion of bringing up the sun in a couple of minutes at the behest of a cue must be avoided.

EXTERIORS NIGHT

The most tricky provision on a small stage

is that for an inky black sky. It is achieved, not by the absence of light, but by very low intensity No. 20 blue, the dimmer on the bottom stud or two. It is most noticeable how much blacker the sky becomes with this addition of light. Some contrast colour on the foreground, such as might be provided by a street lamp or camp fire, is a

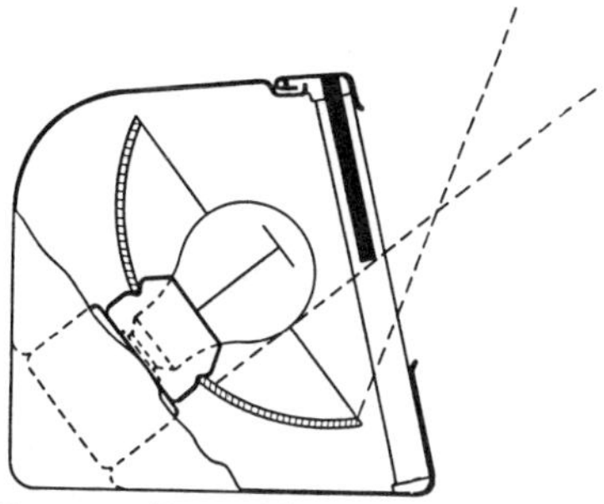

FIG. 102. NIGHT MASKING OF FOOTLIGHT

help. Where such a course is impossible, the alternative is to step up the amount of diffuse blue on the foreground, the point being that the darkness of the sky cannot be conveyed without some intensity comparison. A few stars or a storm cloud greatly help.

A common fault in night scenes is excessive blueness; the theory seems to be that intensity does not matter if colour No. 20 is right. What often happens is that some footlight in light colours, introduced to bring out the faces, throws shadows on the sky, these having to be removed by applying more blue. Frequently, the footlight is fitted with concentrating reflectors, which aggravate this effect. These can be removed altogether from the compartments used for night effects; or the top two-thirds of these colour frames can be blanked out with a mask (Fig. 102).

Moonlight effects are best conveyed by directional rays superimposed on the setting. For large theatres, either the 1,000-watt pageant lantern or the 2,000 soft edge spot (sometimes hung in pairs in special frames from the flys) is commonly used. Smaller stages find a 1,000-watt or a 500-watt focus lantern (with 31 frost) suitable. A flood cannot be used, and a spot cannot be wide focused as the shadows would radiate from this source. The only true solution, where large coverages are required, is the provision of several lanterns, each giving parallel beams. For example, if the setting has a series of wings stage right, each wing will have its moonray lantern, instead of a single flood well off-stage throwing the shadows of the wings in widely conflicting directions (Fig. 103).

The colour of moonlight needs some thought. The blue-green No. 16, labelled "Moonlight blue" in some colour charts, does not in the slightest degree resemble moonlight. Direct moonlight is, under normal conditions, a very low intensity cold white, and its characteristics are the hard shadows giving stark black and white lighting. This white would be best imitated by two steels No 17 or one No. 40, were it not for the Purkinje effect mentioned in "Colour," page 365. This effect intervenes at these low intensities to put colour perception, except the blue, almost, and in starlight completely, out of action. Therefore, the best moonlight effects are obtained from black and white scenery, costumes and make-up, lit through double No. 17 steel-blue filters. Without these, reds and colours show up in such a way that the brain automatically registers cold daylight, not moonlight.

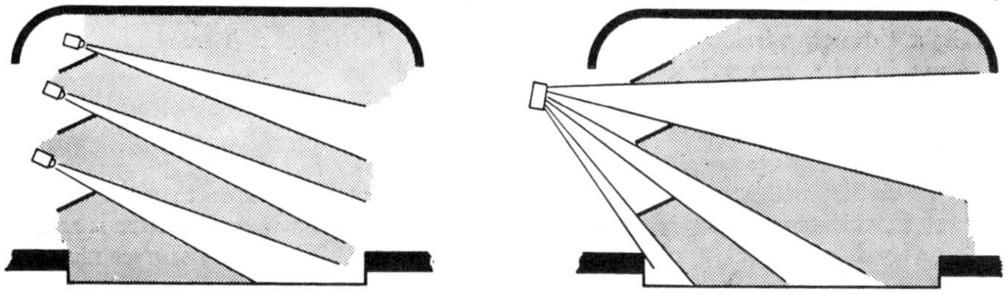

FIG. 103. MOONLIGHT EFFECT

Such a complete change of pigments for one act or scene is seldom feasible. Consequently colour spoiling by filters must be done as far as is practicable without conveying the effect of a riotously blue stage. Any contrast that will emphasize the blue must be avoided. An 18 blue, or better still an 18–17, will effectively suppress most colour, and, at the same time, not look particularly blue, unless it is deliberately contrasted with amber or red lighting. Thus, if the scene is a moonlit village, with glowing lights behind the windows, the temptation to make these orange should be restrained. They must be steel-blue—or natural white. The way orange windows immediately turn the moonlit scene into a Christmas card ought to be an inescapable lesson. The camp fire must err on the cold side for similar reasons: fires are invariably too red on the stage. The problem of showing the moon in person is treated in "Special Effects," page 405.

INTERIORS DAYLIGHT

I assume the presence of a ceiling as there is really no sound excuse for leaving it out when realism is attempted. Even a curtain set is vastly improved when it is used with a ceiling instead of borders. The presence of a ceiling makes it necessary for all the lighting to come from behind the proscenium arch or proscenium border. Again, it is essential to be clear about the dominant idea behind the lighting; to decide upon the source of the natural lighting of the room.

As most of the lighting will have to come from the direction of the audience, it will be necessary to avoid any suggestion that the imaginary source lighting comes from the back of the stage; side windows are obviously the best compromise. Beams of light through windows, as with exteriors, are put in with concentrating lanterns, and not medium- or wide-angle floods. The lighting of backings behind windows needs to be carefully carried out. For up-stage backings, the cyclorama will be best with, perhaps, a painted ground row. Side windows will require their own backings, and considerable care will be required to make the lighting of these tone in with the main backing. As a number of backings can seldom be made to look right with one another, if at all possible there should be some natural reason that will permit the light to stream in without the audience being able to see out—lace or muslin curtains, for example. The wall of the set opposite the window that provides the illumnation will need auxiliary lighting. Where No. 1 batten consists of baby floods, these can be angled to get the desired result. For daylight effects, the ceiling must be lit, though not in appreciable strength. The footlight is sometimes used, but, on the whole, better results are obtained by a baby flood upwards from a perch position. On a large stage this is replaced by a flooded and frosted spot. Unless the walls and the ceiling opposite the window are lit subtly in this way, the lighting never looks right. When there is supposed to be snow on the ground outside, the light must be stronger, and at once the eye will interpret this peculiar light as snow. Such suggestion is often more successful than all the snow backcloths and snow effects.

The focusing and placing of the spotlights for the actors' benefit can now be considered. For day scenes, pools of light must be avoided, and focus lanterns adjusted in flooding terms, well frosted. This lighting will be influenced by the effect lighting which, incidentally, will probably need to be strengthened as more and more acting area lighting comes on.

This method will be heretical to some; "light the acting area first, put in the backgrounds afterwards," is their cry. This teaching is rooted in the doctrine that the actor, not the show, is all-important. Modern stage lighting is not the lighting of actors with focus lanterns instead of magazine battens. It is impossible to convey an idea if it is conceived in terms of lighting superimposed on mere actor illumination. The couple on the sofa must not be lit from just any lantern on the spot batten: it must be the spot which quarrels least in direction with the supposed source of illumination.

INTERIORS NIGHT

It is usually possible to place artificial light sources in such a way that there is an excuse for the lighting. The actual sources must be low in power, about 15 watts, unless they are heavily shaded, and/or tinted. The modern type of tubular fitting gives trouble, as very low wattages are not supplied; pairs of lamps can be connected in series. Whatever is done, glare must be removed or it will rivet the gaze to the exclusion of all else; by contrast the rest of the lighting will appear dim.

An attempt should be made whenever possible,

to light the actors from the fittings that are supposed to provide the illumination. A player who is seated somewhat behind a table lamp may quite well receive good illumination from it. A higher wattage than usual should be used and the side of the shade towards the audience toned down by fitting some neutral filters (55, 56, and 60) inside it. Similarly, firelight should always come from the fire in preference to an elaborate fake-up from perches and spot batten.

Much trouble is caused by using baby float spots for fireglow; baby floods automatically spread. The floods are just as easily concealed as the spots. Where and when the tradition of using a spotlight with a three-inch diameter lens to represent a sheet of flame came from are mysteries. In the same tradition is the use of red for fireglow. Never use a No. 6 red (sometimes known as "fire red") for fire or flame effects. Broken colour should be used: variations in 10–4, 10–5, etc. Where the light of the fire has to be augmented, care should be exercised; the spots on the spot batten should never be allowed to dominate, otherwise the direction of the fireglow will be wrong: to use an acting area flood for this purpose is futile.

The lighting to represent artificial light can be much warmer than that for daylight, and more localized. As a general rule, daylight should be by floods supplemented by focus lanterns; artificial light, focus lanterns supplemented by floods. Keep the top of the set and ceiling dark (Fig. 100: top). Double 51 or 52 are useful for direct light; 3–36 and 2–36 for parts of the set not intended to receive direct light.

The footlight should be at low intensity and arranged to build up slightly where the pools of light from the spots are thrown. Correction can thus be provided, where required. Where there is no footlight, the effect may be got by bracketing a baby flood from the front of the stage. A room lit by oil lamps at table height will never look right if all the light comes from above in the No. 1 spot batten. F.O.H. spots with a low mounting at the sides of the hall can provide ideal facial correction. In larger theatres, these spots are mounted among the stage boxes or where these boxes would be!

It is a great mistake to consider each circuit in a magazine footlight or batten as dedicated to the use of a single colour. Juggling with the colour filters of a circuit can be profitable. Filters can be graded, compartment by compartment, to build up across the stage. In the footlight, lamps can be omitted where some object, a table with a white cloth, for example, will draw too much attention if floodlit at close range by its nearest compartment. Dimmers permit some latitude, except when the footlight or batten is very short. Another device for a small stage is to omit one or two of the normal low wattage (60 or 100) lamps and to insert a 150-watt lamp where extra brightness is required. The whole can then be checked in proportion as required by the dimmer. Always aim to avoid the two extremes, even flat lighting and a lot of detached pools of light. A great deal of practice and a great number of spots would be needed to build up lighting by spots alone.

When realism is not in question, night interiors can be suggested with heavy colours. As an extreme example, a play performed without scenery before black drapes could revel in 8 pink, 7–2, or 7–3, the change in colour being the only way to point the time of day.

In interiors the pattern of the window frames sometimes gets projected on the nocturnal backings. In an attempt to overcome this projection, the backing is flooded with more and more blue to the complete detriment of realism. Covering the windows with grey gauze and using a black backing is one solution when it is supposed to be a dark night outside or when the window is not required to be prominent. The gauze is helpful, even where the backing has to be lit.

Often the room lights have to be extinguished, leaving the room in darkness except for the fire. Inevitably the lighting on the backings, adjusted to tone in with the room lighting, will be too bright. The proper way to carry out this cue is to reduce the backing lighting as the room lights go off. Unless this is done the reverse effect—that of the backings jumping up—will probably be created.

Local authorities will seldom permit real candles, oil lamps, etc., to be introduced, but property fittings for self-contained battery or mains, also property coal, electric, gas, or log fires can be hired. Some of these are good imitations; others are poor. Props should be chosen and reserved well in advance.

Candles are easily imitated by small battery-operated torch bulbs to which a wisp of paper is stuck. A lamp commonly used is known as a "two by one lamp" from its dimensions in inches; there are divers ways of making this suitable. Electric candle lamps are all right when they are concealed by shades or shields.

SUGGESTION

Slavish imitation for the benefit of so-called "Realism" is all very well, but is cause for pleasure when something that cannot be treated realistically on a small stage must be attempted. A life spent in lighting box sets would be excessive restriction for the lighting artist. Every now and then a company ought to give its scenic and lighting men a chance to show off: to put on *The Rumour*, *The Adding Machine*, or some play of their type. Once Realism is discarded, it is often surprising how little scenery and lighting are needed to get the idea over. When such a production is embarked upon, ideas come readily.

An exacting test is the inclusion of one scene that demands suggestion among a number of straightforward sets. The cathedral scene in *The Witch* is illustrative. A cathedral has to be suggested on an 18-ft. by 14-ft. stage. The stage is opened up into the wings as much as possible; all is dark, except for light striking a significant column in the foreground. The need to keep everything as dark as possible may mis-

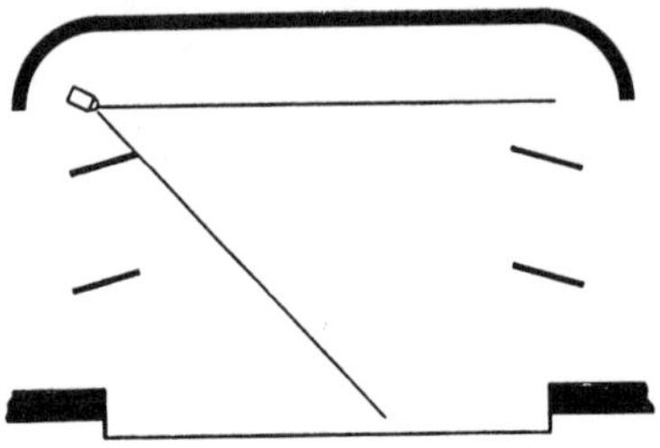

FIG. 104. REAR LIGHTING FOR BALLET

lead; the distant vistas to be found in a cathedral, however dark, must be suggested. To place a faint blue lamp, directly seen here and there, may give the desired effect; something—one cannot tell what and at what distance—is to be seen. Incidentally, the lamp acts as an effective blinder for the dubious surroundings off-stage. The projected suggestion, at very low intensity, of a distant window is another approach.

The light of stained glass windows in the wings off-stage can be suggested by jazz gelatine filter in focus lanterns without their lens. Jazz gelatine varies very much over the sheet and must, in consequence, be carefully selected.

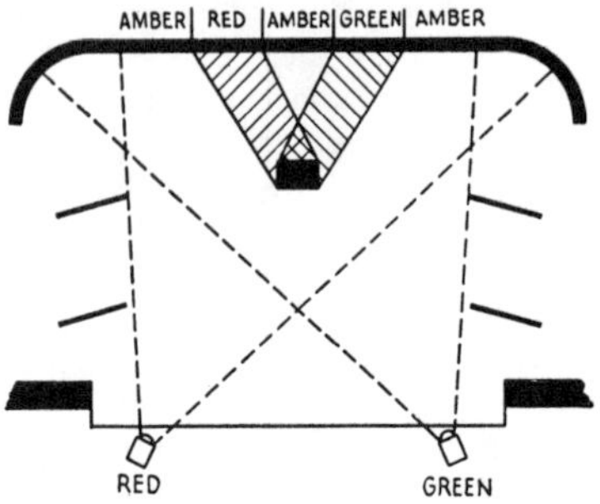

FIG. 105. COLOURED SHADOW EFFECT

LIGHTING FOR THE DANCE

Since facial expression is of secondary importance, the main lighting may well come from the side. Such lighting brings the dancers into relief against the *décor*. Even when front lighting is attempted, it should come from the sides of the auditorium, as modelling is all-important. The lighting of the *Ballet Jooss* is a model of what can be done with slender resources. At the other extreme, the mass of lighting concentrated on one dancer, La Meri, at the Savoy Theatre before the Second Great War, showed how valuable intensity can be to give really exciting colour. All Robert Nesbitt productions are a tribute to intensity and punch of light. Without this punch even the richest colours appear insipid.

Interesting results can be obtained by projecting beams of light from high in the up-stage wings across to the down-stage opposite. This back-to-front effect gilds the dancers in a delightful manner (Fig. 104).

Far more ought to be done to keep the lighting in motion during the ballet; that this is not done is probably attributable to present-day control boards. The operator in his blind position grinding out just a few changes is sufficiently discouraging to prevent more ambitious demands. Lighting changes in ballet have to be tied not only to the action but also to the music; inevitably this necessity means an instrument to play the light. Rhythmic changes are not particularly required in classical ballet, but in symphonic ballet they are essential.

There is a feeling of frustration in Massine's *Choreatium* when the music suddenly soars away from the puny figures on the stage. Only lighting can keep up with these flights. Speculation in this direction leads to realms of colour music, which are beyond present scope.

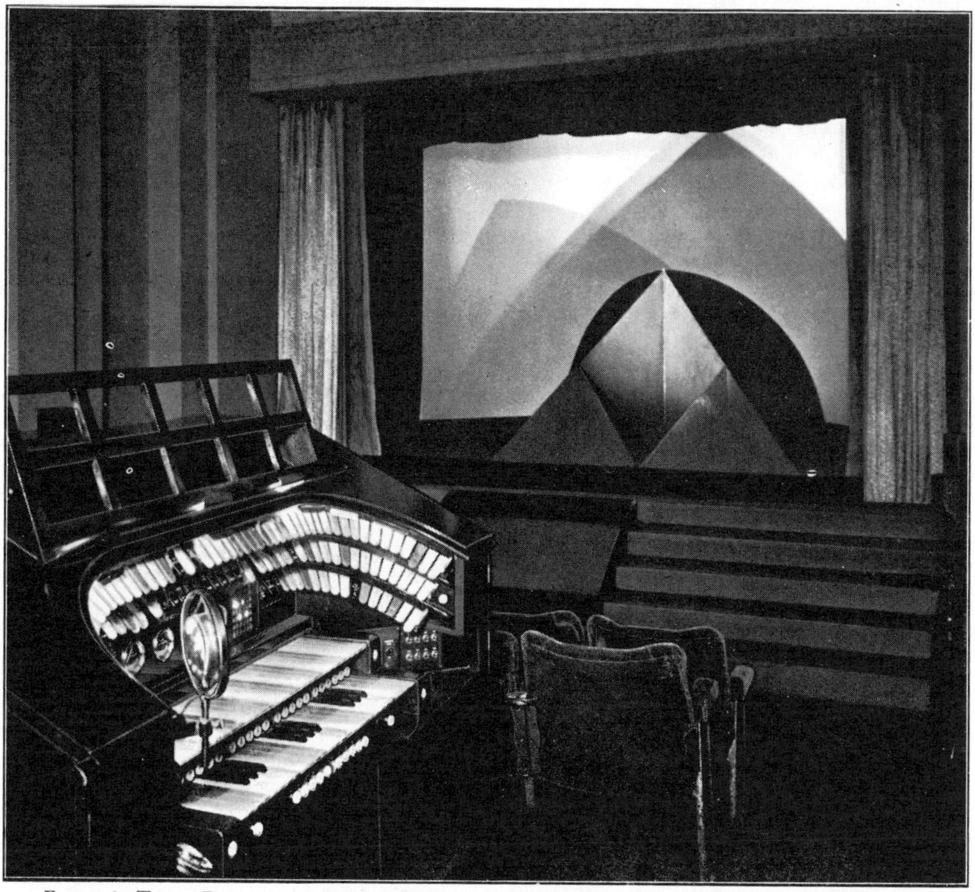

FIG. 106. THREE DIMENSIONAL SHADOW SETTING AND CYCLORAMA. LIGHT CONSOLE IN FOREGROUND

SHADOWS

The dance frequently offers opportunities for the use of enlarged shadows on the background. Shadows of actors and scenery can be effective, particularly when the lanterns are fitted with contrasting colour filters. The lanterns may be concealed in the footlight ramp or mounted in the wings to throw distorted shadows on the cyclorama. If, as in Fig. 105, two lanterns—one 6 and one 39—are employed, the general light where the two mix will be amber, but the shadows will be red and green. Shadows thrown by a multiplicity of coloured sources can be vivid. For really hard definition, focus lanterns with the lenses omitted are used. The setting shown in Fig. 106 is of interest, apart from the shadow effect, as it was built for lighting demonstrations. It consists of a number of geometric shapes which can be put together to make up various three-dimensional formations. The particular arrangement in the photograph is the theme on which I played lighting variations to Tchaikovsky's Fifth Symphony (the ballet *Les Présages*). The variations were played from the Light Console in the foreground to the accompaniment of gramophone records.

LIGHTING THE OPEN STAGE

Where a performance is staged without the use of a proscenium or scenery, only a few screens being permitted, a different technique is needed. No battens, floods, or lighting on or over the stage must be used. The lighting should come entirely from groups of soft edge spots or focus lanterns at the sides of the hall. They must not make a greater angle than 45° with the centre line of the stage, both in a horizontal and a vertical plane. The lanterns must be used as semi-floods, the object being to create a pool of light in which the actors move. The screens and background should not be directly lit, except by the natural diffusion thrown up by the floor of the stage. This ensures that the background seems to be part both of the play and of the hall; there must be no rigid division.

All this assumes that the hall (or church) is pleasing in itself; possibly a place of historic associations. In an unsuitable hall a fit-up proscenium and scenery can be used. Work on the open stage has a fascination all its own. Broad effects and much deeper colour filters will be required than on the proscenium stage. White light ought never to be employed.

FINISH

Apart from artistic considerations, the lighting of a scene should always present a finished look. A glow near wing or border must not be allowed to betray a lantern. Scenery and curtains must be properly backed so that light from behind does not show. Unwanted shadows cannot, but the more obvious ones must be, completely eliminated. Shadows from borders across the scene, projections of window frames on to backings, shadows of actors waiting for their entrance in the wings—these are the results of negligence. Finally, equipment should be properly cleaned and maintained so that it always gives good results.

SPECIAL EFFECTS

In addition to the general lighting effects so far described, there is a range of special effects involving some particular use of equipment. These are almost in the category of illusions or tricks, and need great restraint in their application to prevent degeneration into distracting "stunts." I think the orthodox pre-Second Great War productions of Wagner's *Ring* at Covent Garden probably presented a greater concentration of such effects than any other productions in the theatre. A brief run through the plot may indicate the possibilities—and the snares.

The cycle begins with an orgy of optical effects projectors giving an underwater view of the Rhine. A later scene gives, amid a display of projected clouds on the cyclorama, an example of projected scenery; the distant view of the newly-built Valhalla. At this stage the two giants run off with Freia, guardian of the magic apple-tree, whereupon the gods lose their immortality and grow old and withered—under the influence of mercury vapour discharge lamps. After a visit to the gloomy depths of Nibelheim, things are put right (more or less) and the gods regain their youth. The opera ends with a thunderstorm and the optical projection of a rainbow bridge (a tricky piece of work) to enable the gods to cross the valley into their new home Valhalla. The opera runs continuously without an interval; all changes have to take place as laid down by the music. The opera is a lighting-effect man's paradise—or would be if it were not for the heavy hand of tradition.

The other three operas of the *Ring—Valkyrie*, *Siegfried*, *The Twilight of the Gods*, pursue their way to the accompaniment of clouds, flames, floods, etc., in the catalogue. Such is the realistic approach, brought up to date as far as tradition will allow. Some have had the temerity to suggest that the operas might be much improved if not a single cloud, flame, or drop of water were to appear; to say nothing of sparks from the forge, etc.

The less exalted will run into temptation over the production of Shakespeare—*Macbeth, The Tempest*, and *Midsummer Night's Dream.* I am inclined to think that every now and again an orgy of effects with all the tricks might be fun for all concerned with *The Tempest*, perhaps. For junior school productions there is certainly a lot to be said for overdoing such things; more abandon is likely the farther away the classroom is and the nearer the atmosphere approaches the Fifth of November!

For less melodramatic productions, the difficulty is to blend the special effect into the general background. A moving cloud can be a disturbing distraction; even a stationary cloud can catch the eye. On the other hand, let it be admitted that a flat, clear sky can equally well strike a discordant note. However, there is one restraining brake on one's enthusiasm—the expense of the more realistic effects, even to hire.

OPTICAL PROJECTION

The best known special effects are those that employ an optical projector (Fig. 107). They are known as "optical effects." The projector—usually a 1,000-watt with an A1 tubular lamp—is common to all, the lenses and slide attachments being varied according to effect and throw. The effects include clouds, still or moving; flames; sea waves; scenery slides and others. Most of these are treated in detail below; less expensive makeshifts are described where possible.

Fundamental to all optical effects projection is the need for a rigid fixing; any movement or vibration at the lantern is amplified by the projection throw. In the theatre a perch platform either side of the proscenium is often used. A pair of steps in an unfrequented part of the stage is another device. At Covent Garden a series of rigid perches and a bridge over the proscenium are available. On a small stage, hanging is often the best method, but care must be taken to avoid the lantern being hit by scenery and so set swinging. The steps method is the best where the floor is rigid (only the "on stage" floor should be sprung) as an operator can get at the lantern, and, if need be, stay there to make changes during the scene. A telescopic stand fully extended may not be used unless it is strutted to something rigid. The aim should always be to project the slide or effect from the front on to the screen or cyclorama. Back projection on to a translucent screen takes up too much stage depth and has other drawbacks: the joins between one strip of material and another show; the lantern lens is apt to appear as a flare spot, and more light is absorbed by transmission through a material than by reflection from a surface like hard plaster.

FIG. 107. EFFECTS PROJECTOR

DISTORTION AND FOCUS

Considerable patience and artistry are needed to get the best from an optical effect. It is not a matter of hiring an effect labelled "Wave," connecting it, and focusing. Distortion by the angle at which the effect strikes the cyclorama; masking and choice of lens; clarity or otherwise of focus, and tinting can be used to obtain a fine range of results personal to the operator instead of the stereotyped effect in the box.

It is of prime importance to see that all the lenses and reflectors are thoroughly clean and polished. Next, if the lamp is not fitted with a pre-focus holder, it and its reflector must be adjusted so that the light emerges fairly and squarely from the condenser: the actual rays emerging from it can be seen as a guide. The lamp tray is moved away or towards the condenser, depending on the objective lens combination and the size of slide used. The tray should always be moved backward and forward whenever an effect is set up to see if the light can be improved.

Moving effects consist of a rectangular or circular box with a turntable attachment which, fitting in the lantern runners, enables the effect to be rotated. Stationary slides may be carried either in the orthodox changing slide carrier or in individual metal carrier: both types are actually fitted into a turntable attachment. Use of the turntable device enables the picture to be levelled up when projected at an acute angle from the side of the stage. The effect attachment or the turntable attachment has runners to carry the objective lens. On the stage itself the following short focus lenses will be used:

Narrow angle .	. 9 ft. wide picture at 10 ft.
Wide angle .	. 12 ft. wide picture at 10 ft.
Extra wide angle	. 18 ft. wide picture at 10 ft.

Long focus lenses such as 6-in. giving 5 ft. at 10 ft., may sometimes be required on the stage. Front-of-House throws requiring 12-in. or 14-in. focus lenses will need an auxiliary support to the lens tube.

MASKING AND TINTING

Masks to fit the pictures to the scene may be inserted at two points in the optical systems, in the effects runners (Fig. 108 at B) or in the lantern runners at C. When the mask is at B it can be hard or soft focused along with the subject on the effects slide. At C, the slide and mask can be focused independently, the slide soft, the mask hard, or vice versa.

The cutting of masks to counter distortion by angle of throw and the shape of cyclorama receiving the projection, needs much patience. Experimental masks can be cut in post-card by trial and error; where permanence is needed, the successful one repeated in metal. Black election slides on which white lines can be scratched can be useful. Such a slide, drawn out with some equally

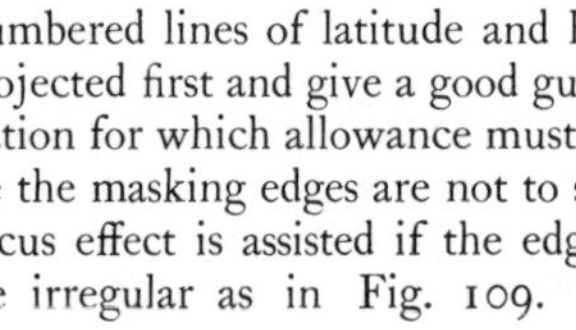

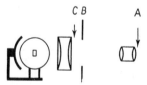

FIG. 108. MASKING AND TINTING POSITIONS IN OPTICAL SYSTEM

spaced numbered lines of latitude and longitude, can be projected first and give a good guide to the compensation for which allowance must be made.

Where the masking edges are not to show, the out of focus effect is assisted if the edges of the mask are irregular as in Fig. 109. Another valuable material which can be used for masking or making designs on mica slides is Photopak (obtainable from photographic suppliers). This dries brown in colour, but is opaque to light. For softening edges and clouding out parts of slides, moist soap can be smeared on lens or slide.

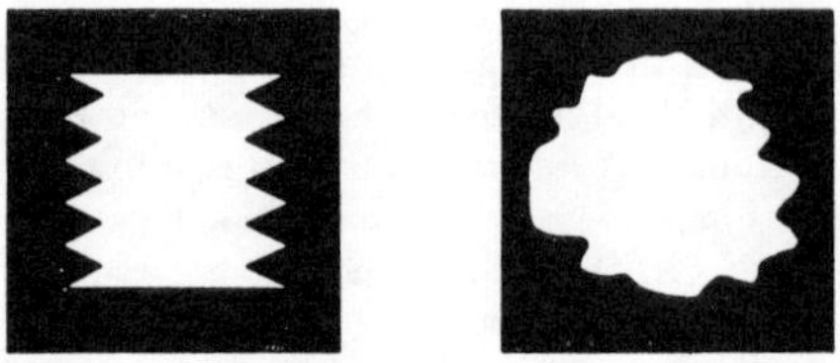

FIG. 109. EXAMPLES OF SOFT EDGE MASKS

Tinting filters can be placed at A, B, or C; but if A is to be used, an auxiliary colour runner should be ordered with the objective lens, as this is not supplied as a matter of course. Positions B and C give an all-over tint or a tint that can be definitely localized to part of the slide by cutting the filter. Position A in front of the objective lens is more subtle in action; by partially covering the lens with the filter, an effect of white merging to colour can be obtained in the picture. The result gives the effect of relief to a flat picture, and, used with moulded glass slides, the results can be interesting.

For most theatre work clockwork is preferred as a motor to drive moving effects. Except in the very rapid effects, there is no noise and steady motion is obtained; also the clockwork motor is cheaper and weighs less. Speed regulation is obtained by a device consisting of rotating wind vanes (Fig. 110). The air offers resistance to these vanes, and by turning them from flat on to edge on, considerable increase of speed is obtained. For still faster speeds, the vanes may be removed altogether. Slow effects, such as clouds, run for several hours; but where the lantern is inaccessible and there is a risk that the motor will run down before the scene is reached, the clock motor can be fitted with an electro-magnetic stop and start operated remotely from a switch and 3.5-volt dry battery. Another method uses an inch or so of fine cotton fastened to one of the vanes; the cotton is tied to a string which, when pulled from below, breaks it and leaves the vane shaft free o revolve.

CLOUD EFFECTS

There are two main types of moving cloud effects; both consist of a circular mica disc in an aluminium case $19\frac{1}{2}$ inches in diameter (Fig. 111). The types are known as "storm cloud" (dark clouds on a light background) and "fleecy" (white clouds on a black background). The discs are hand-painted, and there are several gradations, storm discs varying from very heavy to quite light. The effect must *never be sharply focused*, and a tinting filter, such as 17, 40, or 60, is almost essential. As the background is light, care must be taken that the edges of the projected disc do not show; projecting from the side, well out of focus, this should not cause trouble. The distortion caused by acute angular projection greatly improves the effect. Running very slowly, the denser storm clouds, tinted with filters such as 55, 56, and 60 in combination, make a good mist or fog effect, especially when thrown on to gauze. Storm clouds are suitable for night skies, and with much patience, by cutting a circle of the required distorted shape in the tinting filters, an effect of clouds passing over the moon can be reproduced. This tinting filter goes at C in Fig. 108.

FIG. 110. CLOUD EFFECT DISC AND CLOCKWORK MOTOR

White fleecy clouds are much improved by superimposing the projection from two sets of effects. Not only is more variety obtained thereby, but also the clouds become lighter and wispy. This type of cloud can be more sharply focused than the storm, but nevertheless sharp focusing is to be avoided. Tinting with No. 17 may be necessary to prevent the clouds appearing too warm against a blue sky. Slow speeds are needed, and the effect must not be too bright in contrast to the sky.

Because moving clouds can be distracting, stationary slides often give far better effects. Such still effects must not be obtained by stopping a moving disc, which may be burned thereby, but by using special mica slides. The slides can be hired, or the more venturesome may like to buy the mica with which to make their own with Photopak. The mica must be free of any grease, however slight, before being used, and a cover piece of clear mica bound to the slide to preserve the surface. If complex colour tints, as for sunset clouds, are required, it is better not to colour the slide, but to fit tinting filters to the front of the objective lens. This method provides more lasting colours, greater depth, and the possibility of variation from scene to scene or show to show, using the same slide. The colour frame may be fitted with several overlaid shaped pieces of colour, as in Fig. 69. The result can be a magnificent display of broken colours upon the cloud. Incidentally, the storm cloud giving, as it does, the impression of the sun behind the cloud,

FIG. 111. CLOUD EFFECT

is more suitable as the basic sunset lighting. Using these simple methods, the operator can out-Turner Turner!

The setting sun, with its radiating shafts of light, can be produced by laying a 500-watt flood on its back close to the cyclorama. A complete No. 33 deep amber filter is inserted, together with two-thirds of a No. 11 pink, and on top of this are laid metal strips one inch wide. The resulting arrangement of strips can be cut out of a sheet or soldered to two spacing pieces. Whether the result of these activities is a masterpiece or a distracting eyesore will not depend on any instructions I can give, but on the operator being enough of an artist to follow up my indications.

Where expense is all-important, a simple cloud can be contrived with the aid of a baby flood. The front of the flood is fitted with a sheet of card or stout brown paper; a small portion of this is cut out as a curved slit so that a leak of light is emitted. The lamp in the flood must be clear with a wreath-shaped filament, the image of the filament greatly influencing the shape of light leak or cloud. With a great deal of patience, careful choice of the angle of projection, and suitable tinting, a cloud, which might have come from an optical projector, can be produced at no cost. This result is not produced in five minutes!

STARS

It is hardly possible to suggest an Arabian Nights' sky without stars. In the best circles these are produced by small 15-watt daylight blue lamps mounted behind minute holes in the plaster cyclorama. Each lamp is fitted with an individual thermal flasher, which gives a quick flicker without extinguishing the lamp. Few such stars are needed: five or six are worth while: thirty, as at Stratford-on-Avon, are opulent.

Where this cannot be done, or where a sky alive with stars is needed, then star slides in optical projectors must be used. The slide is merely a piece of zinc in which one can punch *minute* holes to taste. These holes must be confined to the centre of the slide and a medium-angle lens used; otherwise distortion will produce stars like footballs! A tint of 17 or 40 will give whiteness and correct coloration.

Star slides, plus a few of the flickering lamp type, can be convincing. In neither case should real constellations be imitated. For purely decorative effects in spectacular productions, small torch bulbs sewn on to a cloth make a braver, if unreal, show.

FLAMES AND SMOKE

This effect relies on similar principles to those that are applied to clouds, with one important exception: a break-up glass is fitted to the case between the disc and the lens runners. This glass is a slightly rolled cathedral, the object of which is to produce a swirling motion in the flames. Careful focusing is necessary to produce the motion without making the glass or the flame disc too sharp. Flames run faster than clouds, and must be put on with the disc running downwards to counter the reversal of the lens. Discs are painted in colour with more or less smoke predominating; the colour can always be removed for complete smoke by suitable subtractive filters (16–8). This arrangement running slowly has a variety of imaginative applications beyond smoke and flames.

Flames should never be thrown as a flood all over the stage, as the lack of intensity and conflicting directions imparted by the varying planes of the scenery make the effect unrecognizable. Flame effects are better used concentrated on a small section of the scenery or cyclorama. By means of an adjustable lever shutter they can be made to spread from little beginnings. Once again, they must be concentrated so as to appear intense; otherwise the effect will be meaningless.

The disc rotating without the objective lens can give the effect of reflected flame on a window from a fire off-stage. A similar effect may be obtained by waving a bunch of ribbons in front of a flood or spot off-stage, but this is difficult to keep up for long.

A full-scale fire such as that in the final act of Galsworthy's *The Roof* will require many effects projectors for even a medium stage, and the expense may exclude this system. The solution may be to rely on floods, not effects projectors. Where floods are used, the fire has literally to be played upon the dimmer board. There must be at least two sets of floods at each fire point, one held steady and the other brought in and out unevenly on the dimmer. All such floods have broken colour in them with the lighter colours in the flickering ones. Combined with real smoke from smoke boxes and puffs (see below), the results can be exciting; above all, high intensity is there.

Another device is the revolving drum flame. In this a motor-driven drum with flame-coloured apertures revolves round a 500-watt lamp. Put close to the backcloth and mixed with steady floods, the result can be realistic. These drums, working in property beacons on the roof of Shell Mex House, London, when lit up for the first time as part of the Coronation decorations, actually brought the fire brigade out.

Smoke is produced by slow-burning smoke powder in an electrically heated pan; the white smoke is supposed not to tickle the throat. The pan can be hired and plugged into D.C. or A.C. mains. Smoke puffs ready fused and fired electrically are valuable for getting a concentration of smoke quickly. A flash-box fitted with a pair of terminals is also used; a piece of fuse-wire is put across the terminals and covered with special powder. There is a variety of things in the firework line; all have one thing in common—they may travel by goods train only. Therefore, no hasty, last-minute ordering is possible.

For a really convincing blaze the silk flame is best. In this effect, painted silks are mounted over a blower concealed in a trap, the silk being lit by spotlights from beneath. The flame is strikingly real, but should not be used close to actors as the breeze on their clothes "gives the game away." The Wandering Jew burning at the stake in his last scene looks more cold than hot! Such executions are better off-stage, as in *Saint Joan.*

SNOW EFFECT

This is similar in operation to a cloud effect, except that the mica disc is covered with metal foil, punctured with minute holes. The effect should not be used with wide-angle lenses. A tint of 17 is advisable to remove the warmth from the effect; if a wide-angle lens *is* used, a tint of No. 40 will counteract some of the coloration caused by this lens. The effect can be used all over the stage, but the results are better if a gauze can be hung down-stage. Two effects, superimposed on each other, are many times more effective than one. Where this is impossible, a single effect can be improved by inserting a coarse metal break-up gauze between objective lens and disc. Snow is one of the easier effects to use.

RAIN

This effect consists of a disc with ruled lines and a break-up glass in front. As the disc must be black, except for the rain scratches, there is little light to play with. The rain must never be flooded all over the stage or be used with a wide-angle lens. Best results are obtained by locating the rain on part of the cyclorama or front gauze, the rest of the cyclorama being occupied with heavy storm clouds. Tinting with 17 or 40 is essential. This is a difficult effect to use, and often better results are obtained by suggestion. Heavy clouds, or the sunburst effect (described under "clouds") with broken 17 and 40, used inverted high on one side of the cyclorama, may look impressive.

FIG. 112. WAVE EFFECT

WAVE

This is the one effect that is so obvious that it excites comment, even when it is seen by itself. It consists of a rectangular box in which is fitted a stationary slide of the sea as seen from the stern of a ship (Fig. 112). Suspended between the slide and the lens are three slightly muffled glasses which are moved up and down in turn by a clockwork motor. The effect of these is to give so real a rolling motion to the waves that many people find it difficult to believe a film is not used. The most impressive use of this effect is in *Treasure Island*, where the sea is seen over the bulwarks of the *Hispaniola.* When it is properly done, the lanterns are rocked on special stands, thus giving a moving horizon to the sea, and, consequently, the impression of a rolling ship. There are few opportunities for this effect: a possible exception is in *The Tempest*.

The wave effect can be used to give small waves breaking on the shore in the distance. In such circumstances the effect (one is enough)

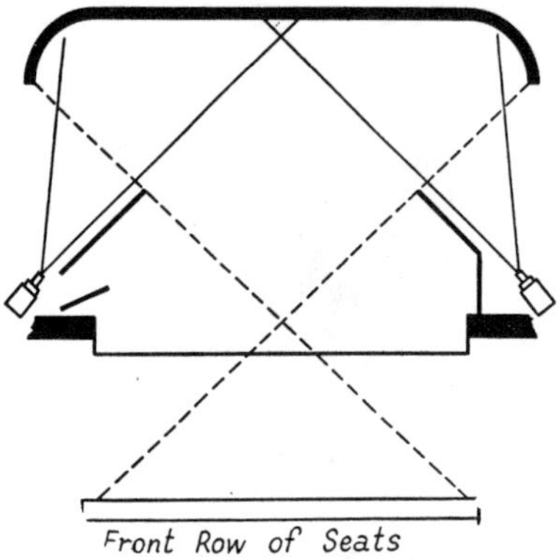

FIG. 113. PLAN OF SCENE PROJECTION ANGLES

is projected from the side on to a ground row. The shore is painted in white or near white; the sea in darker tones. The distorting glasses of the effect cause appreciable movement in the edges of the effect, and the lantern can be so finely adjusted that this movement brings the sea on its down stroke over the white shore. Most realistic impressions of the waves beating against the cliffs can be obtained. The wave effect must be kept well below the horizon; otherwise there will be too much motion in the far distance.

WATER RIPPLE

There are two forms. One resembles the wave in shape and is used to represent the track of the moon on the water; the other, which is much simpler and does not need an optical lantern, merits fuller description. It consists in the smaller size of a 60-watt striplite lamp with a long line filament; in front of this revolves by clockwork a small drum in which a series of irregular horizontal slots is cut. The device is fitted into a narrow box, which can be placed close to the bottom of a ground row. The result is just the right amount of water motion required to put life into an otherwise dead piece of painted water.

OTHER OPTICAL EFFECTS

These include a running water disc which, by means of its turntable front, can be a running river or waterfall; underwater effects, which seldom get a part except in *The Ring* and pantomime; sandstorms which have two discs running in opposite directions and are delightfully murky; a panorama effect showing trees, telegraph poles, and scenery rushing by in a manner that suits burlesque only. The Aurora Borealis also looms larger in effects literature than the number of plays requiring this effect seems to justify.

LIGHTNING

My opinion is that for most lightning cues the flashing of an ordinary batten, with No. 17 or 40 in it, is adequate. The switch of the circuit to be flashed, should preferably be shunted by a push-button momentary contact type. Rocking a quick break switch rapidly is impossible. Essentials are that the lamps should be low wattage, not more than 150-watt, so that they respond quickly to the push and that the push be kept in motion to give a flicker.

Where fork lightning must be seen, an optical effects projector and attachment are used. The attachment consists of a slide and a hand-operated disc with flicker slots. The lantern must pivot easily in its stand and the turntable front must be slack so that subsequent flashes can be rapidly placed at differing angles on different parts of the cyclorama. Considerable rehearsal must be given to this device.

PROJECTED SCENERY

Although elaborate and expensive apparatus is used for this purpose on the Continent, it is possible, particularly on smaller stages, to obtain adequate results from the ordinary effects projector with a 4 in. × 3¼ in. slide. The production of *Julius Caesar* in modern dress at the Embassy Theatre, Swiss Cottage, London, was transferred successfully to His Majesty's Theatre. All backgrounds were projected and the transfer from small to a large stage was compensated by a change of lamp: 1,000-watt A.1 for the Embassy, 30-volt 30-amp. for His Majesty's. Two lanterns were employed on perch platforms, one on either side of the proscenium opening.

Similar methods were used for *War and Peace* at the Phoenix Theatre, London.

To be successful, the essential masking scenery must be planned to allow for passage of the projection rays at a kind angle (Fig. 113). Unless this is done, not only is the distortion of the slide difficult to correct, but also the lens can be made to focus sharply only one part of the picture. Close-range work is impossible except in the most nebulous designs, as wide-angle lenses curve straight lines except in the centre portion of the slide. The lighting of the acting area must be kept absolutely clear of the backcloth, and footlights are out of the question. Slight tinting of the projected picture by use of top lighting often enhances the effect.

Where two lanterns have to be used to obtain sufficient coverage, the problem of the join arises. It is a tricky, though not impossible, business to make this happen behind a central column belonging to the permanent set. It is better not to rely on the projected slide for the sky, this part being blanked off with Photopak. The busy part of the slides are comparatively easy to join, but where there is an overlap or separation of plain sky the join shows badly. The mountains, as in *Peer Gynt,* lend themselves to the omission of the sky (Fig. 114). Here the cyclorama blue at full will provide the sky, the projected slide being merely a black and white mountain pattern. In addition, the cyclorama lighting can always be tilted upwards to keep the lower part of the cyclorama comparatively dark for the projector.

FIG. 114. G.K.P. PROJECTION OF SCENE FROM "PEER GYNT," CONTINENTAL THEATRE

Projected scenery is at its best when no attempt is made to provide a cheap or easily-changed substitute for painted scenery. As in all forms of art, the matter expressed must arise naturally from the medium used: I prefer to forget all about accepted scenery and to allow the designs to evolve from the hints that the lantern will throw out if given a chance. I will give an example of what I mean.

Slides can be made from the hundreds of moulded or patterned clear glass which can be

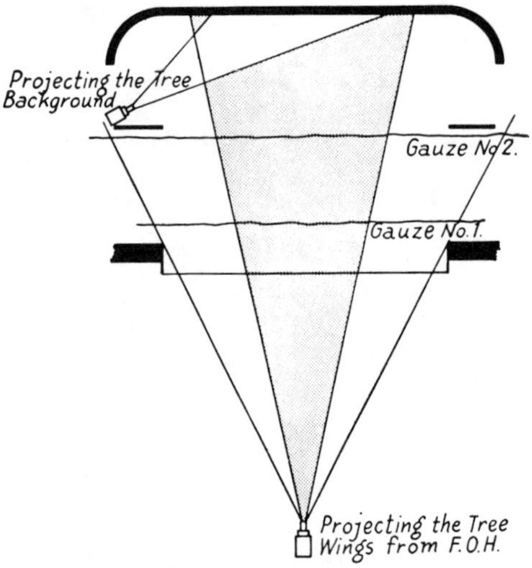

FIG. 115. PROJECTION ON GAUZES, PLAN

obtained from suppliers such as Messrs. Hetley of Soho Square, London. This glass may be slightly rolled, as in cathedral glass, ribbed in various ways, or patterned. If a piece of ribbed glass is inserted in the slide carrier and focused, a series of vertical shaded columns appears. Now place a green filter half across the objective lens and notice how the columns are tinted on one side with green, on the other with white. The columns can be cut off, as required, by placing a suitable cut-out metal stencil in the slide carrier, or even by blanking out part of the moulded glass slide with paint, Photopak, or paper.

For years I demonstrated a forest scene on gauzes to Wagner's *Forest Murmurs*. This scene began as a singularly revolting piece of figured glass of fancy scrolls and thistles like pineapples. By blanking out the centre and such parts as were necessary, fitting a two-thirds 16 filter in front of the objective, and applying just the right amount of focus, tree wings with entwining boughs overhead were produced. The whole result was completely satisfying and right; yet this glass as figured glass was one of the most weird creations I have seen. A projection such as this on to two gauzes, one ten feet up-stage of the other, might easily provide "a wood near Athens" (Fig. 115).

One of the good results of basing one's designs on these glasses is that the temptation to realism can more easily be avoided. The more realistic the slides are, the more the detachment from the actor is stressed. Try a coloured photograph of Venice as a background to *The Merchant of Venice*, and it will be found that the result always stands apart from the foreground.

Another excellent result is the depth in the moulded glass projections and the way that difficulties of colouring are avoided.

As the heat on a lantern slide which may be in use for a half an hour or more is considerable, heat-resisting glass or mica slides have to be used. It is not surprising that paints and dyes fade. A blower effects an improvement, but is noisy and best avoided. Tinting by filters on the objective lens is lasting, and the colours can be changed, if required. This method best suits the glass style of projection.

PROJECTED CURTAINS

Another use for these figured glasses is for curtain patterns. Most amateurs who rely very much on hessian, now and then feel that although this plain material can be beautifully lit, the period really demands a patterned hanging. Hessian can have two figured glasses projected, one from

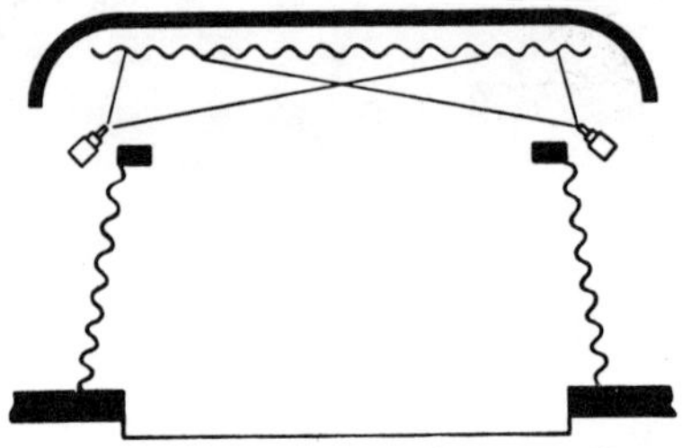

FIG. 116. PROJECTION ON CURTAINS, PLAN

each side of the stage, in slightly differing light colours. If the pattern is not to be too readily recognizable, different glasses are used. The resulting effect is extraordinarily rich and does not betray its origin. Further, the curtain will stand a fair amount of spill light. The patterned light must come from the sides and pick up the folds (Fig. 116), not flatly from the front as is frequently done in the cinema. The same curtain can appear in another act as a plain and completely different material.

VISIONS

Theatrical gauze (mosquito netting) appears to be solid when lit from the front and vanishes altogether when scenery or actors are lit behind it. The secret of success in these vision effects is that the fogging front lighting must be so placed that it does not pass through the gauze to light the regions beyond. Similarly, no light on the vision must be allowed to strike the gauze. A common mistake is to use a magazine batten and footlight to fog the gauze. This light penetrates, and difficulty is experienced in getting the vision to disappear. Except on large stages, it is essential to use narrow beam floods and focus lanterns both for the gauze and the vision.

Properly done, the gauze and vision will, in their turn, vanish absolutely. The best general purpose colour for gauze is grey, which can always be painted with a design. Sometimes gauzes are used one behind the other, the second being a few feet up-stage of the other. The second should be white to make up for transmission through the first; and a different size mesh is needed unless watermark effects are intended. Gauzes may be hung in folds, though these will not vanish altogether. Ethereal effects are obtained by side lighting the folds of one gauze behind the other with, perhaps, a blue lit cyclorama in the background. The two effects in Figs. 117 and 118 are produced from the same gauze setting with different lighting.

FIG. 117. FRONT AND REAR LIGHTING ON GAUZE SETTING

PICTURE EFFECTS

By using a slightly fogged tight gauze downstage of the actors a two-dimensional effect can be produced. The eye is deceived into considering everything beyond the gauze as on its plane. Though a vision when still may be made to disappear perfectly, an actor taking up his position may by his movement betray his presence. To be absolutely safe, a black velvet curtain should hang behind the gauze until the revelation is to take place.

must not be flooded with a high level of ultra-violet, which may bring into prominence the natural, if low intensity, fluorescence of many materials. The skeleton that dances, throwing away his bones, one by one, until he vanishes, will require a black-draped stage and black tights to which the fluorescent bones are hooked. One

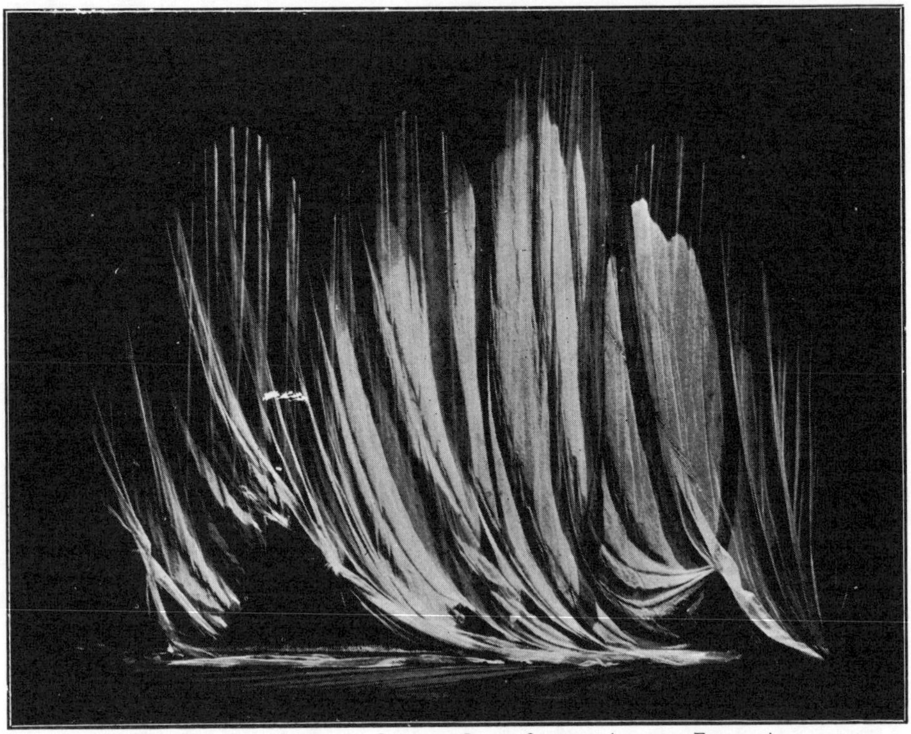

Fig. 118. Rear Lighting Only on Gauze Setting (same as Fig. 117)

FLUORESCENT EFFECTS

Visions, ghosts, and the like can easily be produced with the aid of the invisible ultra-violet rays on fluorescent paints and make-up. However, such effects more easily become, by their close resemblance to the accepted ghost, a burlesque rather than a horror. The spectre with his head tucked underneath his arm and a rapier through his chest (possible under U.V.) is far less likely to terrify than a being slightly abnormal in a way that the mind can feel but not recognize.

When illusions are contemplated, the stage

125-watt lamp in the footlight for a small stage and two for a large will be ample. The skeleton's routine must be arranged so that in no circumstances does a limb from which the bones have been removed pass in front of those that remain.

Another illusion is the reverse of the preceding effect: in this the scenery is treated but the actor is not. For *Golden Toy* at the Coliseum before the Second Great War, the setting included a great fluorescent archway flooded by lamps in footlight and overhead, and backed by a black velvet sky. Lupino Lane ran on stage in a pool of ordinary spotlighting, climbed up a fluorescent rope, hanging from the arch, out of the pool of light, and thereupon vanished: the Indian rope trick!

Fluorescence need not be restricted to the supernatural; as a decorative effect it can be striking. The treated surfaces appearing as actual coloured light producers, not reflectors, give extraordinary rich luminous colours. For these decorative effects the higher the ultra-violet intensity, three or four lamps in the footlights and U.V. floods overhead, the better.

When treating scenery and costumes, the best effects are obtained on white materials. The surface requires to be slightly absorbent; blanket-like materials will eat up the precious liquid. The other extreme, a polished surface, must be avoided, otherwise there will be nothing to key the liquid which will rub off. Doping on a large scale is an unpleasant and tricky business which amateurs are well advised to entrust to firms specializing in this work.

An interesting application is the use of a fluorescent screen for optical effects projection. A 125-watt black lamp is used in place of the usual projector lamp; the invisible light passes through the slide and is focused by the objective lens; the light remains invisible until it strikes the fluorescent screen; there are no rays to betray the source of the projection.

THE SAMOILOFF EFFECT

This, called after its inventor, relies on the use of complementary colours. As pointed out in "Colour," page 365, a lantern fitted with a blue-green filter does not transmit any light wavelengths that can be reflected from a red surface which therefore appears black. Under the red light there is little colour contrast, so the reflected colour is interpreted as a reddish white. Suppose an actor is made up in red and wears a coat of black and blue-green stripes: under the red light he appears as a white man in a black coat; under blue-green light as a black man in a striped coat.

Any pair of complementary colours can be taken from the colour wheel in Fig. 70, but the filters and pigments must be perfect. There are other factors to consider: for example, at first sight yellow and blue complementaries may seem more pleasing, the yellow being more nearly white; but under the blue light the black effect does not get a sufficiently strong contrast. Powdering on top of make-up must be in the same colour as the grease-paint; there is a lot to be said for liquid make-ups.

The colour change need not be sudden; the changes from Winter to Spring to Summer are easily performed on dimmers. The backcloth must be painted with black tree trunks, red flowers, green leaves, etc. Beginning under blue-green light, the scene appears in black and white, colours being spoiled either by absence of their colour in the light or by absence of contrast. As red is gradually added to the blue-green, these defects are remedied and Spring arrives!

LIGHTING APPARATUS and SCENIC EQUIPMENT

ANGUS WILSON, Author of " Scenic Equipment for the Small Stage," "Home-Made Lighting Apparatus for the Amateur Stage" etc.

WHEN you can say you have a good lighting-set half the work in staging your play is done. Everyone knows nowadays the need for good lighting, and most producers could attain it if they had the apparatus. The difficulty is that professionally-made material is expensive and far beyond the reach of small societies, and no group will hire it if they can possibly make it themselves.

HOME-MADE EQUIPMENT

There are sound reasons for making your own set. Flats may have to be hired, because every play needs a different lot, but the same lighting material will do for every play if it is capable of variety in colour and intensity. It can be built up gradually, and it has this further great advantage—it can be made of materials that would not last three months under the nightly wear of the professional theatre. Lastly, there are no appearances to consider—if it works and is safe, it can be as hideously ramshackle as you please, for the audience seldom sees any of it.

ANGUS WILSON

I intend to explain how such apparatus can be made by anyone with a skilful pair of hands and a sound knowledge of electricity.

I warn readers, however, that the greater part of my descriptions applies to lighting-sets that *are not subject to strict inspection by fire authorities.* To many it may seem a waste of time to assume such immunity, but it has been my experience that the majority of *small* societies are able to perform in unlicensed halls, or in halls where the authorities are willing to allow responsible people to carry on unsupervised. In any case, all the apparatus with which I shall deal will be *perfectly safe* if it is made and installed by a competent electrician who applies the precautions that he would usually take when wiring his house. It is mainly the use of wood instead of metal, to which firemen may object, but I shall suggest means of satisfying authorities, except perhaps those of London and some of the larger cities. A few principles must be noted before passing on to practical matters.

PRINCIPLES

If something more than bare illumination is required, stage light must be coloured. The only exception to this rule is the case where the available wattage is just sufficient clearly to show the actors to the audience, and where the addition of colouring would cut off valuable power. Weak lights give a comparatively soft light, which does not need to be toned, but it is not easy to suggest atmosphere or mood without colouring of some kind. Therefore, increase your power if you can, and colour your light.

The next essential is that the rays of light should be so concentrated that they shine on the action and nowhere else. This is a point that cannot be too strongly emphasized. I have seen many otherwise admirable stage pictures ruined by the illumination of the roof above and of the entire proscenium. If every ray shines in the proper direction, so that nothing is lit above the upper edges of the scenery or curtains, the roof will be almost in darkness, and spectators who are in the first few rows of the audience will not notice it unless they look for it. A certain amount of reflected light will be thrown up from the stage floor and the setting, but not enough to matter. Further, no harm will be done by the footlights, unless they are too brilliant.

The greatest advantage of a dark roof is that it needs no borders—those wretched strips of material hung across the stage and known sometimes as "flies"—to hide it. On most small stages all the lighting, except when the backcloth also

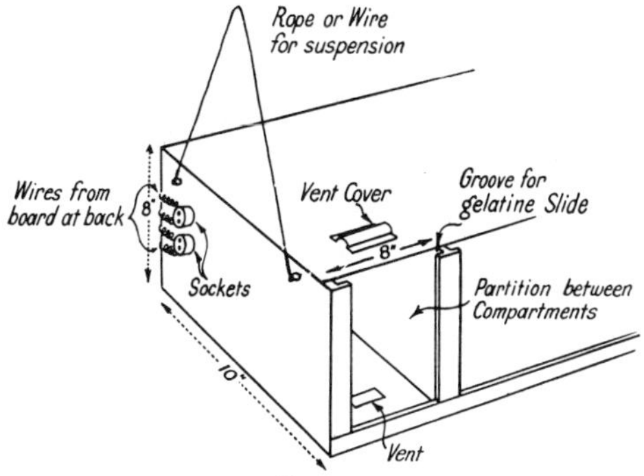

FIG. 1A

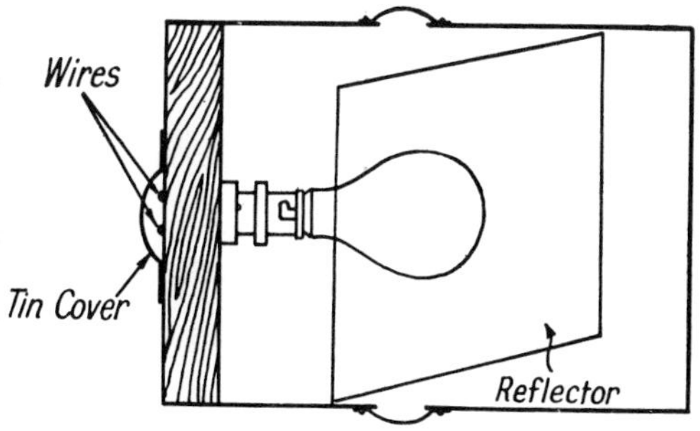

FIG. 1B

is lit, can be done from just behind the proscenium. In the exceptional case, a border will be required to conceal the lit-up roof at the back, but it will not be unduly noticeable if the main lighting shines downwards only.

Concentration can often be combined with another essential—reflection. Amateurs can seldom afford to waste light; yet many of them make no attempt to pick up and to use the rays that shine away from the action. A good reflector above or at the back of a light makes a remarkable difference to its efficiency, and if it acts also as a concentrating shade its value is obvious.

Where should lights be situated? The best place in all cases is just out of the spectator's sight above the proscenium, behind the lower edge of the pelmet. The next best is at the side, as high up as will clear the head of a tall person. If they are any lower, they will shine more strongly on players who are at the sides of the stage than on those in the important centre position. It is only on a deep stage that a second or third row of lights need be hung (perforce concealed by loathsome borders!) farther up towards the back. A backcloth ought to be lit from above and below, but if both positions are impossible, choose the lower one and hide your lights by groundrows or similar pieces. Footlights are easily fitted. They must never be the main source of light but only a corrective to heavy shadows cast by the top lights. I myself have used no footlights for several years, mainly because the trouble of colouring them, and fitting them into the dimming arrangements is more than they are worth. All acting that takes place outside the front curtain-line must have special lighting of its own, and it is here that concentration is absolutely essential. It may not always be possible to prevent light from flooding the whole proscenium, but at least it can be kept off the side walls of the hall and the heads of the front rows of the audience. Tie-beams are useful for hanging outside lights, but the lamps can also be placed on window-ledges. Remember, however, that the farther away they are from the player the less effective they are. This applies to all stage lights—never waste power by hanging a lamp higher than is necessary for purposes of concealment from the spectator.

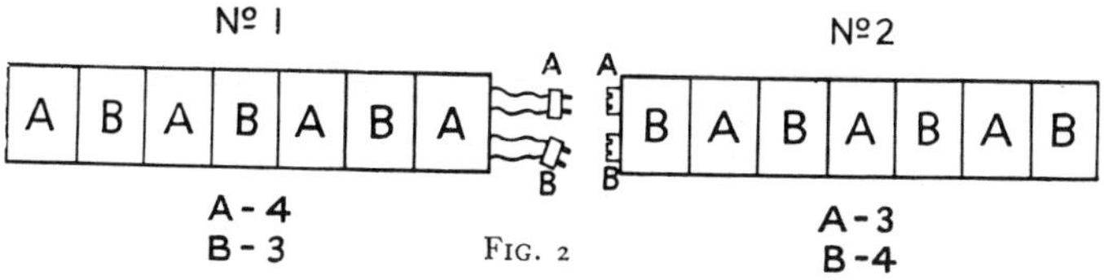

FIG. 2

BATTENS

It has been found for many years that the most convenient way for amateurs to light a stage is to arrange a row of 100-watt or 150-watt lamps behind the pelmet. Lamps of larger power are too expensive to buy and to replace, and smaller ones mean multiplicity of fittings. The problem is how to house these so as to concentrate, reflect, and colour them.

Fig. 1 shows the construction of a batten made of wood. The lamp-holders are mounted on a plank 3 ft. 4 in. by 8 in. by 1 in. (for a 5-lamp batten), the first and last lamp-holders being 4 in. from the ends of the board, and the remainder 8 in. from each other. Use the kind of holder that screws flat on to the wood. The wiring must be done in parallel, and it is essential that each batten should have at least two circuits, each circuit connecting up alternate lamps. A device for varying the number of lamps per circuit when two or more battens are being used is shown in Fig. 2. Suppose there are 7 lamps in No. 1, 4 wired to plug *A* and 3 to plug *B*, and 7 lamps in No. 2, wired to sockets *A* and *B*. If plug *A* is inserted in socket *A* and *B* in *B*, all the 7 *A*'s will be on one circuit, and all the 7 *B*'s on the other. But if the plugs are interchanged, the 4 *A*'s in No. 1 will be circuited with the 4 *B*'s in No. 2, and the other 6 will be together. This change can easily be made between acts or scenes, and if changes of gelatine are also made there is a distinct increase in "flexibility." In 8-lamp battens, 5 of them could be *A*'s and 3 *B*'s, which would make the contrast even greater. Of course, the fuses of both circuits must be able to stand the maximum number of amps.

The wiring that comes out at the back of the board must be covered over with a shield of wood or tin (see Fig. 1B).

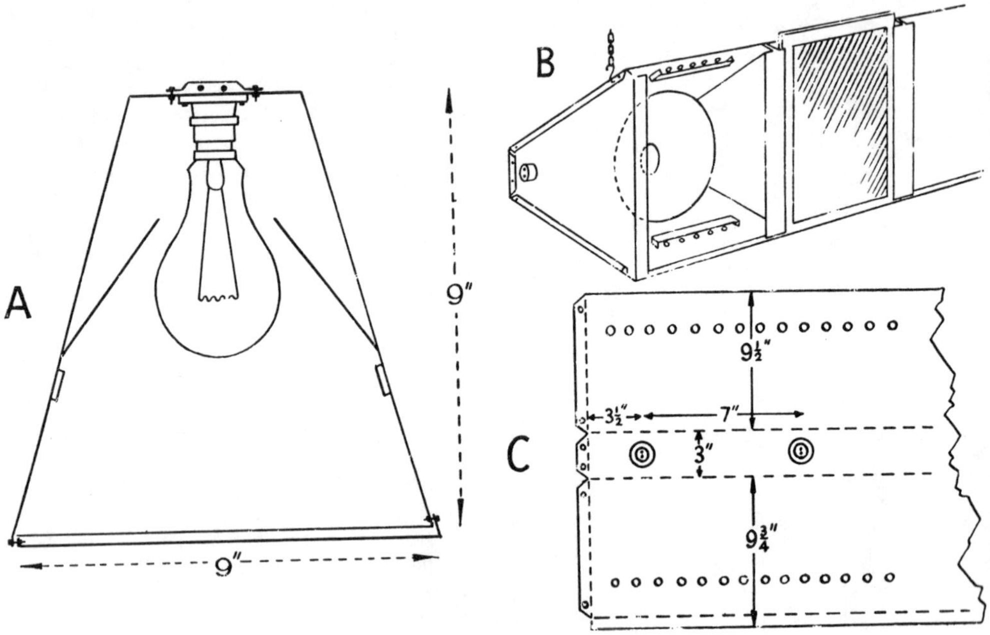

Fig. 3

The remaining box-like framework may be of deal or strong plywood, but too great weight must be guarded against. The depth of the box will depend on the length of the lamps to be used. A 100-watt lamp in its holder is about 6 in. to 6½ in. long, and at least 3 in. ought to be allowed beyond the end of the lamp to ensure concentration and to keep the gelatine reasonably cool. With 150-watt lamps, another inch or inch and a half ought to be allowed.

There is not the remotest danger of fire, using lamps no stronger than 150 or 200 watts, in a well-ventilated wooden batten, but if you feel you must be specially cautious line all inside surfaces with sheet tin or thin galvanized iron.

It is possible to obtain from a wood merchant plywood faced on one side with zinc. This is effective for battens.

However, for the benefit of those who would not be permitted to have any kind of wood near their lights, I will discuss the making of metal battens.

Sheet iron or galvanized iron of the lightest gauge should be used. It is usually stocked in 6-ft. by 2-ft. sheets, a convenient size for our purpose. Do not be alarmed if it seems wobbly in sheet form; when bent, it will be as rigid as is necessary.

Fig. 3 shows the construction. The dimensions given will suit lamps of 100 watts only; for 150-watt lamps at least 1 in. more depth should be allowed—2 in. on total width of sheet. The length of the batten depends on the number of lamps to be used, but a batten longer than 6 ft. would be rather awkward to handle and suspend. It is better to make two short ones. (There is no need for front lighting to go right up to the sides of the stage. On a 20-ft. stage two 6-ft. battens with 7 lamps each, separated by a foot, leave 3 ft. 6 in. on either side, but the lateral spread of the light is such that the sides will be lit almost as well as the centre.) Each is hung by three wires or chains, one at each corner as in *B*, and the third in the centre fixed to the back so that the tilt of the batten can be regulated by pulling up or letting down this chain. The sheet of metal is bent along the dotted lines shown in *C*. The gelatine grooves should not be wider than ¼ in. so that the slides will fit close to the edges. Both end-pieces should be cut so as to project and supply a single groove at either end. The remaining grooves can be made of tin. Holes must be drilled for ventilation and covered over.

The covers for the wires at the back should be attached in such a way that they can be easily removed for wire-inspection. The whole construction can be held together by small nuts and bolts, which are much more convenient than rivets, though the latter make the better job. If galvanized iron is used, the lower inside surface of each compartment, just in front of the reflector, should be painted with dull ("egg-shell") black to prevent light being reflected upwards to the roof.

Note that in Fig. 3 the lamps are at 7-in. centres. This is in order to get the maximum number of lamps into each batten, but there is no reason why you should not have more battens with fewer lamps in each.

BISCUIT-BOX BATTENS

It frequently happens that the standard batten, as described above, is too large and unwieldy

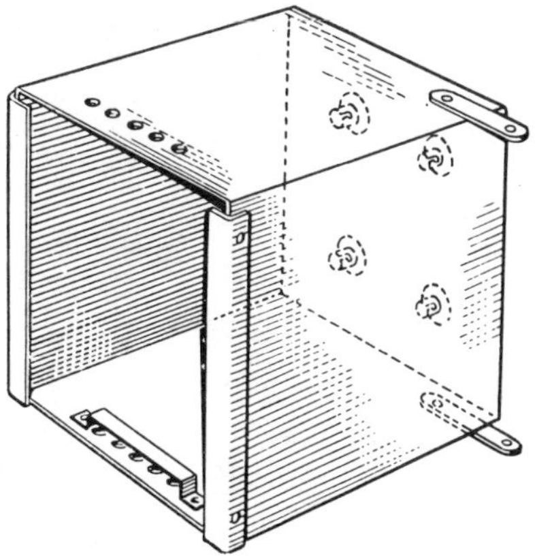

Fig. 4

in proportion to its capacity in watts. A society that takes its lighting set round from stage to stage will economize in labour and space by having battens which are more like groups of floods, i.e. with larger compartments, each holding several lamps. Such a batten is a great advantage when the space behind the proscenium above the front curtain is crowded.

The standard biscuit-tin provides the solution. Fig. 4 shows what has to be done to it. Vents are pierced and covered over; grooves are fitted for gelatine slides; tabs above and below bind each box to its neighbour. All can be attached by bolts or solder. For the lampholders (cord-grip type), holes slightly over 1 in. are cut, and the holders pushed in from outside and held by their shade-rings. If only three are fitted, they should be in a triangle, the single one below. The wiring is in parallel, and can be covered over with a tin casing if desired. As reflectors are too difficult to fit behind so many lamps, the bottom of the tin should be kept highly polished; where reflection is not wanted dull black paint should be applied.

Three battens of five tins each will provide good general lighting for any amateur stage of normal size, and can be wired according to the scheme shown in Fig. 2 to give circuits of variable strength, but note that, since each colour will be more powerful than in normal battens, they must be hung no lower than 10 ft. from stage-level if a patchy effect is to be avoided.

FOOTLIGHTS

Ideally, footlights ought also to be constructed in compartments, on exactly the same lines as

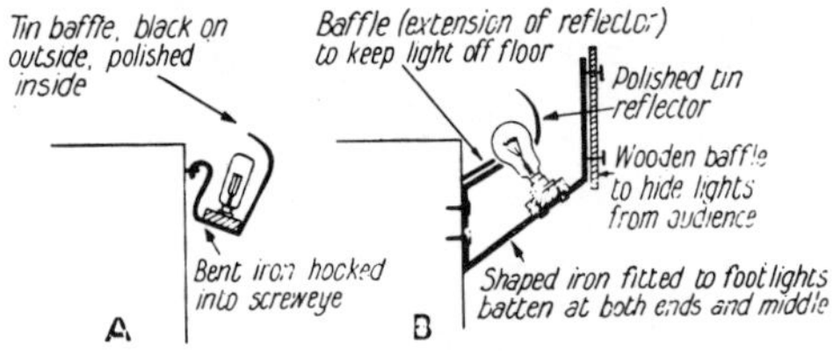

FIG. 5

battens, but not so deep. It frequently happens, however, that they are left to the last or used only occasionally, and many constructors do not feel justified in spending much money on them. There is just one thing they must remember—if the main lights are coloured and capable of being dimmed, the footlights must be the same. If, on the other hand, they are always at the same strength and are always white, they will completely ruin any lighting changes which may occur on the stage.

The most convenient way, short of making proper compartments, is to fix shielded boards as in Fig. 5. Note that a good reflector, made of shiny tin and curving over the top, is particularly necessary if you are using gas-filled lamps. They give out most of their light at the ends, and much of it is wasted if not picked up again and thrown on the stage. Strictly speaking, the arrangement shown in Fig. 5, *B*, is the best for such lamps, but it is difficult to fix and the reflectors are awkward to arrange. It is worth trying, however, if you have only a few lamps to spare and must make the best of them. In both types the reflector goes all the way along.

The greatest drawback of this open type of float is the question of colouring. If you have three circuits you can have red, blue, and green lamps, and can therefore produce nearly any combination by means of dimming. With three circuits you would be wise to use 40-watt vacuums dipped in lacquer and set as closely together as possible in order to avoid patchiness when only one colour is being used, but with only two circuits you must choose which pair of colours you are most likely to need for your play and stick to them throughout the production.

In any case you will need lamps of all three colours, in order to provide for the different lighting schemes of different plays. (It is this that makes gelatines so much more practical than coloured lamps.) If you would rather have fewer lamps of greater power, get 60-watt gas-filled in *natural coloured glass*. (Lamps with the colour sprayed on are obtainable, but the porcelain finish cuts off a lot of light.) They are more expensive, but they are worth it if you do not feel disposed to fix up real compartments.

FLOODS AND FOCUS LAMPS

It is unfortunate that battens and footlights are so much the easiest to make of all lighting apparatus. Amateurs often rest content with them, not knowing that good lighting can be done without them but not without floods and focus lamps. Indeed, many producers start with the latter when they are working out their light-plots and add battens at a later stage, in order to soften the general effect and to lighten shadows and contrasts.

FLOODS

On many modern stages collections of floods, each fitted with 500-watt or 1,000-watt lamps, have taken the place of battens. Any colour mixture can be obtained from three or four of them fitted with the primary colours red, green, and blue, on a dimmer circuit. Amateurs, however, can get an equally good effect from the biscuit-tin battens previously described, and in any case they prefer to use collections of smaller lamps rather than single lamps of high wattage.

Floods have many uses apart from those mentioned—lighting a part of the backcloth, shining through a doorway or other opening on to the stage, giving the effect of sun or moon on a backing outside a window, emphasizing some fairly large part of the stage or acting-area. They can be hung from the back of the proscenium or from off-stage parts of the scenery, or they can be made to stand on their own.

For lamps of over 150 watts, either a professionally-built or a home-made casing on the same lines is essential owing to the great length of the lamps. It is not advisable to make a flood which holds the lamp at right-angles to the throw, as only half the filament is towards the stage, and a reflector gives back only a part of the light from the other half. The need for the lamp to be pointed at the stage means that its casing may have to be from 12 in. to 18 in. deep—a shape that is awkward to make and to suspend.

I consider, therefore, that amateurs are well-advised to fall back once more on the biscuit-box for their floods. A single box, adapted on the lines of Fig. 4, will give 400 watts with 100-watt lamps, or 600 watts from 150-watt lamps, and is simple to construct. For hanging from proscenium or scenery, loops of stiff wire can be soldered on, or small holes punched and threaded with loops of thin wire, but when floods must stand alone, a proper trunnion and stand must be constructed.

The former is a piece of strip-iron from $\frac{1}{2}$ in. to 1 in. wide by $\frac{3}{8}$ in. to $\frac{5}{8}$ in. thick, shaped as in Fig. 6 and long enough, when bent, to allow the tin and its protruding lampholders to turn through an arc of 270 degrees or so. Fig. 6 also shows what is required to fix the trunnion to the box so that the latter can be clamped firm at any angle by tightening the wing-nuts. Bolts with square shoulders must be used but these will soon wear away the soft tin unless a plate of harder metal shown at B is also used. If this plate is bolted on, a ring must be fitted round the square shoulder to keep the heads of the bolts from fouling the trunnion; if the plate is soldered on, the ring is unnecessary.

It is possible to make an adjustable stand with two gauges of gaspiping (the smaller sliding up and down inside the larger) and a weighted box, but the amateur should first study a professional stand and then consider whether he can satisfactorily make such things as the heavy thread of the locking-screw that holds fast the thinner tube. I think he will end by inquiring about the price (not exorbitant) of the professional job!

FOCUS LAMPS

The theory of focus lamps is fully treated in Mr. Bentham's section on "Stage Lighting," so I confine myself to describing how amateurs can make them.

The first essential is the special projector lamp made for this kind of work. I give below a summary of the information supplied in the "Osram" Projector Lamp Catalogue. I believe specifications and prices are standard for all makes of lamp.

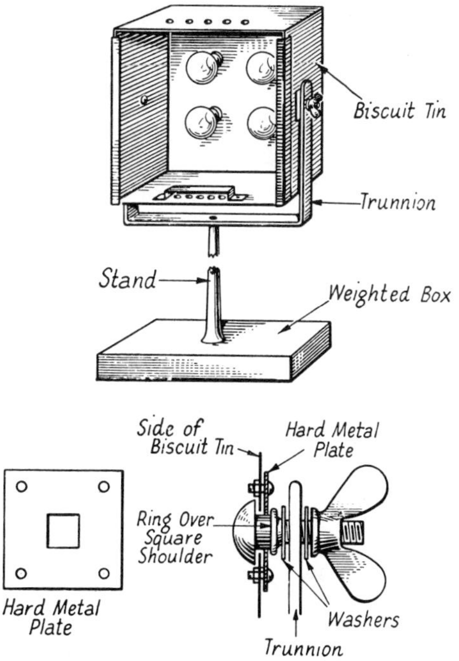

FIG. 6

Class	Shape	Burning Life (hours)	Burning Position	Prices (subject to alteration)	
				500 watts	1,000 watts
A1	Tubular	100	Vertical, cap down	24s.	30s.
B	Round	800	Vertical, cap down	24s.	30s.

There is a 250-watt size, but as it bears heavy purchase-tax, it is not good value for stage work. On the other hand, the B type gives a somewhat less brilliant light than the A1 type, but lasts much longer. I cannot say how time affects these lamps; it is possible that if the burning-life is spread over a number of years the total number of light-hours will be less than the maker's estimate. One thing is certain—Class A 1 is more delicate and is harmed by being burned

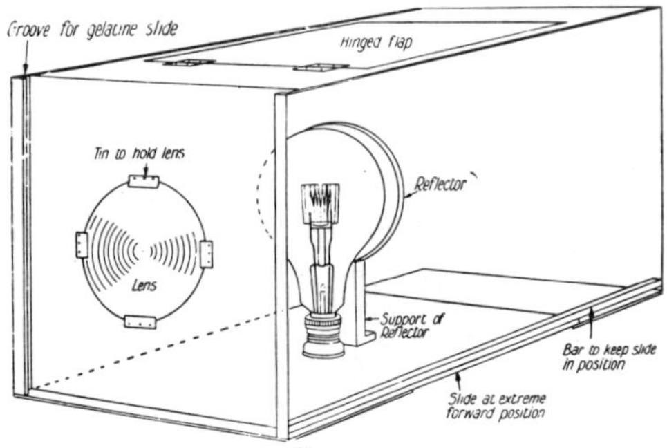

FIG. 7A

at an angle, whereas B can be burned at any angle within 45° of the vertical, cap upwards, and will stand shocks and vibration much better. On the other hand, B is more difficult to arrange in the lantern, since it takes up more room and cannot be brought so near to the lens. The latter must have a longer focal length than for Class A 1.

The lamp-holder for a 500-watt lamp is the Edison Screw (E.S.), batten type.

The next item is the plano-convex lens, or condenser. I have been fortunate in getting several lenses originally made for photographic enlargers for about a few shillings, but abnormal trading conditions have affected the market considerably, and amateurs may have difficulty in obtaining bargains. Try dealers in second-hand photographic supplies in addition to stage-lighting firms. The focal length must be at least 6 in. for a tubular lamp, and 9 in. for a spherical one, and you had better make sure, by experiment with an electric torch, that it gives a sufficiently wide beam of light when the glass of the lamp is as close up to it as it will stand, i.e. not less than 2½ in. With photographic lenses in particular you are liable to find that there is not a great enough widening of the beam-angle when the lamp is moved forward. Get the lens as broad as possible, not less than 4½ in.; 6 in. is a useful size, but 5 in. does almost as well.

The same shops usually stock reflectors, which are silvered glass concave mirrors. These may not stand up to heavy professional use, but will last amateurs a long time. Most stage lighting firms stock a reflector with a brass clip and an adjustable block for mounting, price, say, 7s.

Fig. 7A shows the main point of construction for a lantern made of wood. I have found plywood quite satisfactory if well ventilated above and below so that a constant stream of cool air is passing up round the lamp and behind the lens, but sheet metal makes a stronger job that will pass any inspection. The lamp in a metal lantern can be made to slide by the device shown in Fig. 7B but there are many other ways. The greatest difficulty in this matter of sliding is to prevent light from escaping. In Fig. 7A the lamp is mounted on a slide that covers over the gap below in all positions, the gap being necessary to allow the flex to leave the lamp-holder and to accommodate the handle (which can be a large screweye) by which you do the adjustment. This method can quite well be adapted to a metal lantern.

MAKE A DIAGRAM

It is essential for the constructor to draw a scale diagram before starting work, so that he may work out exactly a number of important points. These are—

(*a*) The centre of the lens, the filament, and the centre of the reflector must be on the same axis.

(*b*) The bulb of the lamp must come no nearer than 2½ in. to the lens in the forward position.

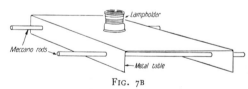

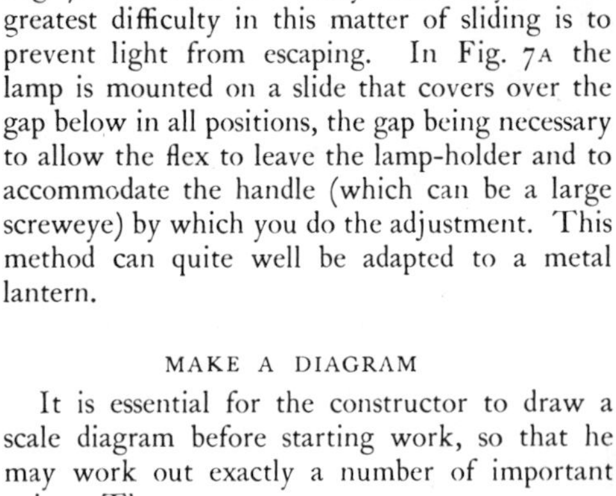

FIG. 7B

(*c*) The back of the reflector and its mounting must be just clear of the back wall of the box.

(*d*) The back position must be fixed so that the filament is at the focal point of the lens, or maybe a little in front.

(*e*) The slide must not let light through.

(*f*) The lamp, in its holder, must have at

least 1 in. clearance of the top of the box, and the same at each side.

(*g*) The sides and bottom must project ¼ in. to allow gelatine grooves to be fitted. Metal boxes must have the sides ¾ in. extra so that ½ in. can be bent over to make grooves.

Dimensions of all lamps are given in the catalogues, so that plans can be drawn before the lamp is bought. An E.S. lamp-holder should, however, be obtained.

In Fig. 7A the lens is fitted on the outside by pieces of tin that keep it pressed against the wood, but it can equally well be inside, the hole in the front of the box being, of course, slightly smaller than the lens. For metal boxes, Fig. 7C shows a rough but effective means of doing the same job, three or four flaps being cut in the edge of the hole, and made to come over the edge of the lens. These are only suggestions.

A flap or sliding panel must be made in the top to allow access to the inside.

No means of ventilation are shown in the diagram. You must drill rows of holes along both sides, top and bottom, and fit light baffles inside. Slots are easier to cut and are equally effective. I recommend, for a 500-watt lamp, a minimum total area of ventilation opening equal to 32 holes, each ¼ in. diameter, distributed so as to ensure the draught already mentioned.

A little experiment will show how near the reflector should be to the lamp. In theory, its focal point should coincide with the filament, but often you have to be content with getting it as near to the lamp as possible. About ¼ in. should be allowed between.

When fixing the lamp-holder to the slide, it often makes things easier to discard the outer casing and porcelain ring. It will work equally well, and as it is inside the box, there is little danger of anything coming into contact with it while the current is on, and so causing a short circuit.

A trunnion and stand can be fitted as for a flood (*see* Fig. 6). If you are hanging it alongside your battens, put in screweyes at various points on top and sides and hang with wires which will enable the tilt to be altered. On a metal box, add tabs with holes in them, and fix these with nuts and bolts.

F.O.H. LIGHTING

A word or two about lighting from the auditorium, known as F.O.H. (Front-of-House) lighting. As I have already indicated, this can be extremely useful as a substitute for footlights, and

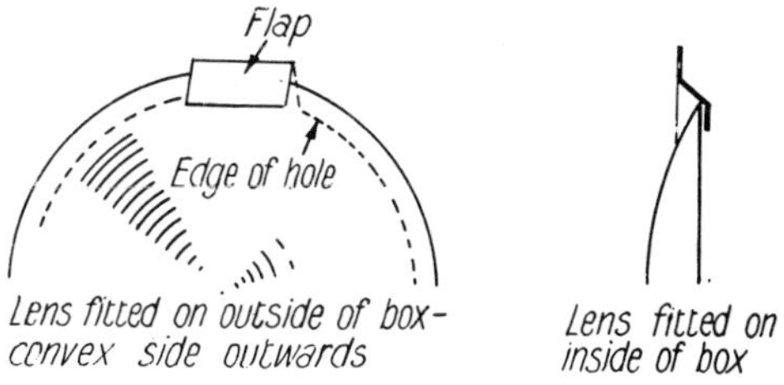

FIG. 7C

is essential when any acting goes on outside the front curtain where the normal stage lighting cannot reach. I have seen a single focus lamp of high power situated behind the back row of the audience and concentrated to cover the proscenium opening and no more, but the resulting light was flat and utterly uninteresting, giving no high-lights or shadows on the players' faces. A much better system is to use two lamps placed nearer the stage on the side walls of the hall. Less power is needed to cover the shorter distance, and, if two different colours are used, the actor's features benefit by better modelling and by coloured shadows.

I would always recommend you to err on the side of strength in deciding what wattage of lamp to get for this type of lighting. The throw is so much longer than from above the stage that 500 watts is liable to be quite ineffective, whereas 1,000 watts, if too strong, can always be reduced by a dark or frosted gelatine or by dimming.

If you do a lot of apron-stage work, you should hang as many focus-lamps as you can afford from the roof of the hall 15–20 ft from the curtain. Better still, see if there is an attic above and if you can, cut openings in the ceiling; if so, house them up there, out of sight of the audience and thus subject to change of direction and gelatine during the performance. Naturally, there must be some way up to this attic from the stage so that the electrician can supervise his lamps; otherwise they would be better hanging in the hall within ladder-reach.

SMALL ACCESSORIES AND DIMMERS

In this section I may seem to be going into rather finicky detail, but it is in the provision of the odds and ends, taken for granted in professional apparatus, that the amateur often fails to finish off his job properly and to make the most of the small amount of light that his finances (or the electric supply of his hall) allow him. The importance of dimmers needs no stressing; everyone nowadays knows that few plays can be artistically lit without them.

STRIPS

Strips are used for odd jobs such as lighting door-backings, or profiles that need to be specially emphasized. They may be anything from 2 ft. to 6 ft. in length, and are simply lengths of wood wired and fitted with lamp-holders. It is not worth while to fit them up as battens, though coloured bulbs are often more effective than white, and some kind of reflector means economy. They can be hung by means of hooks or screweyes. Be sure that your curtains and scenery are light-proof, otherwise the strip will shine through.

REFLECTORS

Reasonably cheap reflectors cannot be bought in small quantities, but amateurs can make quite efficient ones with simple material. Highly polished sheet tin of the lightest gauge reflects nearly all the light it receives provided it is kept in good condition, and it is easy to work.

I have already referred to the necessity on small stages of keeping all light shining downwards only so as not to illuminate the roof and

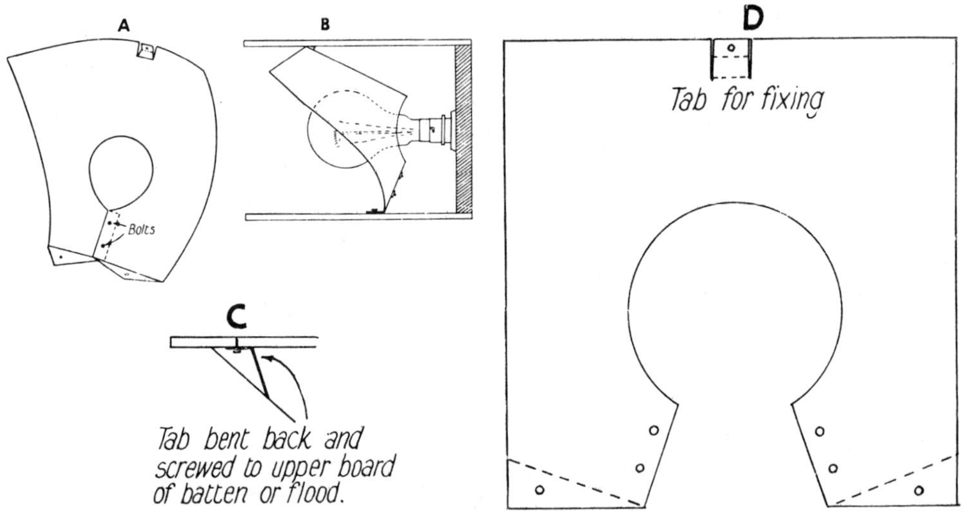

FIG. 8

the top of the backcloth or up-stage scenery. Your efforts at concentration will, therefore, be frustrated if the reflector is shaped so that it sends light upwards, even though the lamp itself is properly shaded. Hence the peculiar shape of the reflector shown in Fig. 8, A. It is made from a sheet of tin about 12 in. by 10 in., according to the size of the compartment, cut as in D, and fitted as in B and C. This is, of course, a rough and easily made type to which many refinements of design can be added, but I have found that it works admirably, and you can make a dozen or two in a short time. Always experiment first with thin cardboard or stiff paper in order to avoid wasting tin.

For the metal batten shown in Fig. 3, you can dispense with compartment partitions, which are rather difficult to fit, and make the reflector do the work, as in Fig. 9, A.

For certain types of flood and batten, such as those that light the backcloth, restricted reflection is not necessary, and you will do better to make your reflectors as shown in Fig. 9, C. Cut your tin, bend it evenly, slip the tongue into the slot, and bend back. Or, if you want to make a neat job, solder the edges together without tongue and slot. The other tongues are for attaching to the inside of the compartment or biscuit-tin. Before you fix it, see that the hole comes just behind the

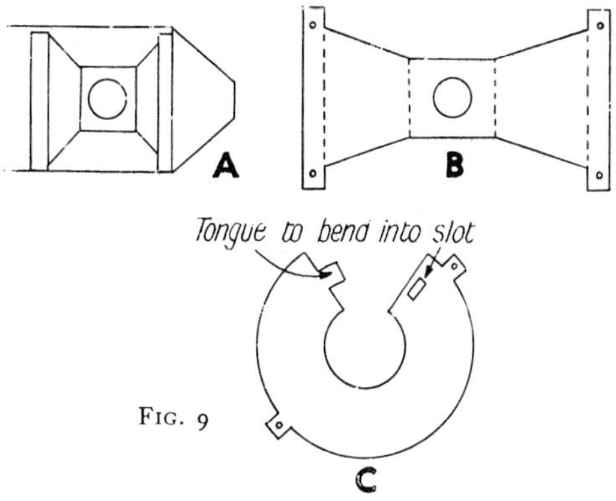

FIG. 9

bulb of the shortest lamp you are likely to use. The tin should not touch the glass.

Reflectors for focus-lamps have already been referred to on page 420, and it is not wise to attempt making your own. If, however, you are hard-pressed for time or money, you would do better to back your projector-lamp with a flat disc of tin than to leave it with nothing.

GELATINES

Send to any of the stage-lighting firms for their colour-card and particulars, and work out for yourself whether it would be more economical to use their "focus-size" (about 8 in. square), or to cut your own from their full-sized sheet (about 22 in. by 17½ in.). It will depend on the size of the opening you wish to cover. It is well to keep the sizes of your compartments, floods, etc., as uniform as you can so that the frames you make to hold the gelatine sheets will fit into any of their grooves; 8 in. square is a good general size.

The frames can be made from metal, plywood, or cardboard, but I have invariably found that cardboard gives less trouble to make. The difficulty with the other materials is that your slides must be perfectly flat, with no projections to catch on the grooves, and there must be room right up into the corners for the gelatine. Consequently, you cannot make your corners firm with nails or bolts. If you have not the tools to do real metalwork and if you do not like the card-board slides described below, get them made in metal to your own requirements by a stage-lighting firm. The Strand Electric Co., Ltd., do them cheaply.

To make the slides shown in Fig. 10, ask tobacconists and radio dealers to sell you their big cartons. (They may be pleased to get rid of them.) Cut out two frames for each slide, each frame in a single piece, and bind on three sides with strong adhesive tape, leaving just a little play so that the gelatine will slip in and out easily. Make the top edge ½ in. wider in order to project above the batten and to allow you to pull the slide out quickly. All other sides should be ¾ in. wide. Cut the gelatine to come within ¼ in. of outside edges, giving a grip of ½ in. You can colour the tape according to the colour of the gelatine, and it is certainly wise to write the name of the colour in large black letters on both sides of the slide. The maximum size of these cardboard slides is 10 in. square if they are to remain firm, but you can strengthen them somewhat by making the borders 1 in. wide or more instead of ¾ in.

DIMMERS

A simple liquid dimmer, on the same principles

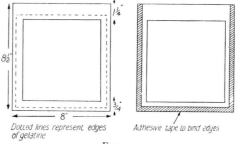

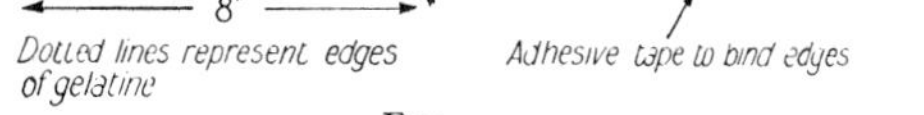

FIG. 10

as those explained in "Stage Lighting," can be made as follows.

Get an ordinary drain-pipe, which is about 2 ft. 3 in. in height, and costs only a small sum of money. You can have it either 4 in. in diameter or 6 in., depending on the amount of current you want to dim. A good plan is to start with one of each, the larger acting if necessary as a master-dimmer for the whole of your lighting. Note that there seem to be several types on the market and one of them must be avoided at all costs. This is the kind of which the base,

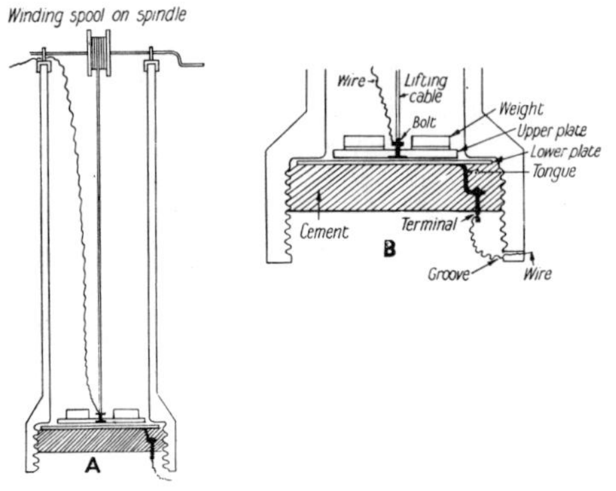

FIG. 11

i.e. the part that bulges, is rather shallow inside, only about 1½ in. deep. You must insist on the type with a base from 3 in. to 4 in. deep so that your concrete filling will get a good grip on the threads. Next get about 1 lb. of cement and some sand. Your dealer will tell you how much. Turn the pipe upside down and cut out of heavy sheet tin or iron a circle that will fit neatly into the base ("lower plate" in Fig. 11, *B*). Cut out a tongue at the edge about ½ in. or ¾ in. wide and bend it up, and then at right angles. Bore a hole in the last part and fit in a terminal. Be careful to see that the top of the terminal will be at least 1 in. clear of the floor when the pipe is standing on its base, and, on the other hand, that between the wire-hole or screw and the lower plate there is room for a 2 in. thickness of cement. In the rim of the base, near the terminal, chip a groove so that the wire will not be squeezed against the floor. If you wish you can fill up the groove again with cement, leaving a hole big enough for the largest flex you are likely to use. Then prepare a perfectly flat disc of tin or iron for the top plate, with a countersunk bolt in the centre hammered well in so that the head does not protrude and keep the plates from making good contact. Under the nut fix lifting cable and flex, and then arrange round it as much weight as you can up to 3 lb. or 4 lb. A thick slab of lead with a large hole in the middle is best; on one of my dimmer-plates I have a coil of old lead gas-piping. The weight should be so distributed that the plate hangs horizontally, but it may be an advantage to have one side coming off the lower plate before the other, thus avoiding the resistance caused by suction.

I have always found cooking salt to be a satisfactory means of increasing the density of the resisting fluid. Start with plain water and add salt till your lights dim out completely when the top plate reaches the surface. If you have to dim different loads without having time to change the solution, the amount of salt must be adjusted to the smallest load. Your heaviest load may then be out before the top plate is half-way up, but you can always wind your wheel very slowly, whereas there is nothing to be done when you find a single light hardly dimmed at all with your plates fully separated.

BACKCLOTH LIGHTING

For the amateur, backcloth lighting is perhaps the most difficult and expensive part of stage lighting. It is essential for artistic work to have something up-stage that will represent the sky in exterior scenes, and, once the apparatus is installed, the constantly recurring expense of painted backgrounds and elaborate scenery can largely be avoided. But it is one of those things that are better left undone than done badly, so you ought to make sure that you can put the money and work into it before starting.

The main drawback is that the light must be strong enough to kill all shadows of players and scenery on the cloth. On a deep stage, with carefully concentrated lighting, shadows can easily be kept off, but most stages that amateurs work on are so shallow that the players are bound to come within 3 ft. or 4 ft. of the back. To neutralize shadows, the light of the cloth must be at least as strong as the sum of the lights that cause them. (Obviously, a focus-lamp directed on the floor or across the stage would not count.) This means that you must have as many lamps at the back as you have in your battens, floods, and footlights, or, at any rate, an equal wattage. Hence the expense.

Another difficulty is in the arrangement of the circuits. If you want sky effect only, you simply put all lamps on one circuit with blue gelatines and leave it at that. But half the fun of backcloth lighting is to bring on such exciting affairs as sunsets and grey dawns, or to cast weird colours over your sky according to the mood of a non-naturalistic play. Thus, if you have decided on a maximum total wattage of, say, 2,000, you will have to set aside at least 500 for your colours, which weakens your foundation blue considerably. Also, when you work out your wiring, and plan to make every third lamp a red or orange, you will realize that there will be gaps in your line of blue when the reds are out.

I think the best way of overcoming this is to separate the blues and the others. Make a batten, which I describe below, for blues only, on one circuit or two, depending on the capacity of your switches and fuses, and then set alongside it either another batten with reds widely spaced, or a number of ordinary floods made so that their light has a wide lateral spread. Put the reds next to the cloth, because they need to show only just on the horizon, as it were, whereas the blue should go as high as possible.

It is not easy to decide how to plan a backcloth batten. The lights must be equally spaced all along the cloth as far as the scenery on either side, and the lamps must be close enough together to make an even line. A large number of 40-watt lamps is better than a small number of 100-watts, but needs more lampholders. Only experiment, with lamps on a cloth and with something to represent the ground-row that you are to work with, will enable you to settle the number, power, and spacing. I mention the ground-row, which is a low piece of scenery representing a range of hills or a garden, because the higher it is the higher you can raise your batten. In Fig. 12, the batten and floods, which stand on specially made supports, are just concealed from the audience, and the cloth gets the full power of their light. If there is a gallery in your hall, lower the light or heighten the ground-row.

The batten is constructed on the same general principles as for front lighting, or rather it is a cross between Figs. 1 and 5, *B*. Since there is not the same need for concentration, it may be no deeper than is necessary to keep the ends of the lamps about 2 in. from the gelatines, and you can omit all partitions between lamps. A good curved reflector coming just behind the bulbs and running the whole length should be fitted. Gelatine slides should be as long as possible, even at the risk of being unstable, since they lie on the edges of the batten and do not carry even their own weight. A sheet of gelatine 22 in. by 17½ in. divided lengthways will make two 22 in. by 8 in. mediums without much further cutting.

For this work I strongly recommend coloured bulbs, in natural glass if you can get a dark enough blue, or dipped in lacquer.

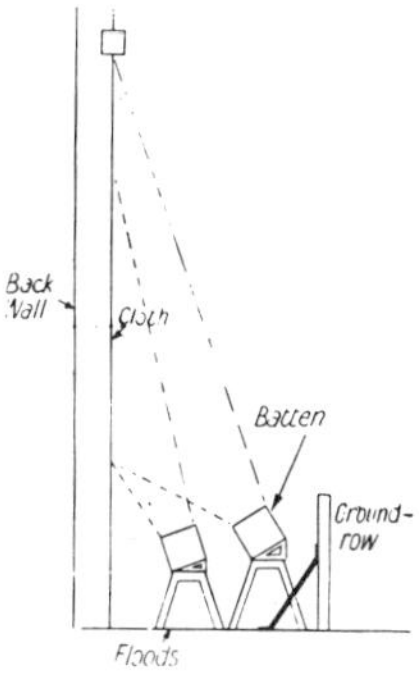

FIG. 12

I have assumed hitherto that all your light is coming from below, but if you can help your lower batten to illuminate the whole cloth, by hanging another behind a border above, so much the better. Make sure, however, that you tilt your battens so that there is not a dark patch half-way up. The upper batten need not be quite so strong as the other, and need usually be blue only, since stage sunsets show in the lower part of the sky only.

CURTAIN SURROUNDS

The history of stage equipment, like that of most other accessories to Art, is full of exaggerated departures from established practice. At the beginning of this century, no Shakespearean production was thought possible without roller backcloths elaborately painted in naturalistic manner, borders representing foliage or heavy oak beams, wings either architectural or arboricultural, and smaller pieces perfect down to the last twig or stone. Nowadays, such things are seen only in remote corners of the country or in burlesques, for in between there was a revolt in favour of curtains and the starkest simplicity for all productions. A sensible compromise has been worked out on the professional stage—solid painted sets for naturalistic plays, curtains and representative small pieces for plays of poetry or the spirit. Now, since amateurs seem to be doomed to do plays of real life, they should never forget that curtains are only a makeshift. It usually happens that they are cheaper and more convenient than flats for most amateur companies, but scenery that gives the impression of solid walls is always preferable if it can be made, stored, and set up on the stage. Such favourable conditions, however, are so often absent that curtains will be for many years the stand-by of the struggling society.

Curtain settings, because of their limited power to create illusion, must be used neatly and intelligently; it is not fair, for example, to surround a bare stage with shoddy and crookedly-hung material and to expect an audience to believe that the scene is a cottage kitchen or the sea-coast of Illyria. Every effort must be made to add such simple scenic pieces as will give a reasonable indication of where the action is supposed to be taking place.

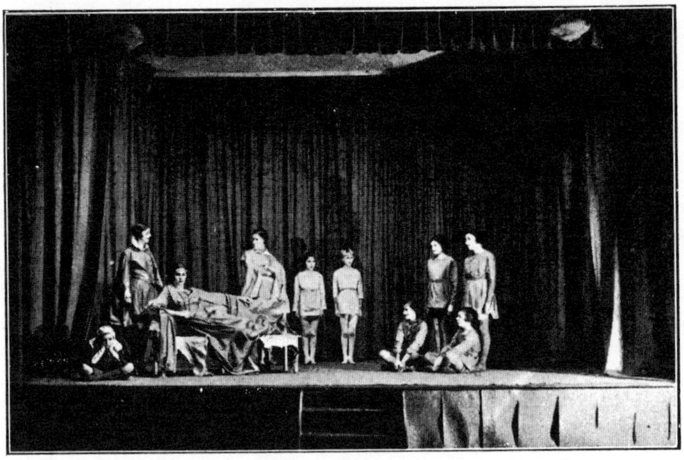

"TWO GENTLEMEN OF VERONA" AT GLOUCESTER HIGH SCHOOL FOR GIRLS

Stage designed by Angus Wilson. Back line of curtains closed. Note the gathering of the material by means of stringed tape. The lighter curtain on the right is the traverse. All curtains go up to the full height possible under the ceiling

MATERIALS

There is normally a wide range of suitable stuffs and the best plan is to get patterns from a store that has large and varied stocks and to choose something that will fit in with the following recommendations—

(*a*) The material must drape well, so that the gathering makes it look richer and heavier than it really is.

(*b*) It should be fairly opaque, so that lights standing behind will not be visible to the audience.

(*c*) Weight should be medium, neither too heavy to handle and stitch, nor too light to hang steadily in draughts.

(*d*) It must be of good enough quality to stand fire-proofing or dyeing.

(*e*) As it has to be folded frequently, it must not crease too permanently. Hanging for an hour or two ought to be enough to smooth it out again.

(*f*) It should not wear *too* well. Provided it keeps a fairly good appearance it should not be so expensive as to prevent future changes and experiments. Audiences like variety.

Velvet is costly, but every society ought to aim at having a set for their more sumptuous interior scenes.

Always get furnishing materials, which wear much better than dress materials. Furnishing sateen has an agreeable sheen under good lighting; bolton sheeting, though dull, is serviceable; hessian is cheapest of all and looks magnificent, but is heavy, difficult to seam, and is far from lightproof; I once got a tough poplin in a wide variety of shades quite cheaply, 50 in. wide, which made lovely surrounds.

It is always a difficult problem to settle the colour when you cannot afford a double set, one light and the other dark. Individual taste must always be the final guide, but it should be remembered that a desire for neutrality may easily lead one to choose colours that are merely dingy, and that it is impossible to find a pleasing shade that will suit perfectly every kind of play. I do not recommend black, since it absorbs a great deal of light and looks too funereal. Dark saxe looks well, and shows up costumes better than a light colour. Silver-grey is more sensitive to coloured lighting than any other, but tarnishes easily.

Perhaps fawn or middle grey will suit most societies. When in doubt, take a light shade—it can always be dyed later on if it gets dirty or is otherwise unsatisfactory. You can often disguise the deficiencies of your curtains by getting cheap coloured muslin and hanging it in front.

In calculating quantities, allowance must be made for half as much width again to ensure ample gathering, though somewhere between this and one-third will pass if money is scarce. Get the stuff 54 in. or wider if you can, as it is best to have your surround in several sections rather than in a few large pieces. This allows windows or doors to be inserted at any point. Thus, a 54-in. strip when gathered will be only 36 in. wide, and an acting-area of 18 ft. and 12 ft. will require fourteen strips, six along the back and four down each side. If the surround were 12 ft. high, 56 yards of material would be needed, but you should always get a few extra yards for spare sections and for odd jobs, such as filling in the gap below a window when you have only a frame and no supporting flat. If you have to use borders, allow for them also. They are of little use less than 2 ft. deep, so split a 9 yd. strip up the middle and you have a couple. You can often dispense with a border if you hang your curtains as high as the ceiling or your framework will allow. Never grudge a few more yards of cloth when they will give your players a background that helps them by being neat and unobtrusive.

"Two Gentlemen of Verona"

Two curtains left at the back to suggest columns. Backcloth is well sewn and tightly stretched, and lit from below stage level. A border was hung during the performance from the batten showing just above tops of curtains. Note side swivel-battens, some closed, some open

MAKING-UP

Sew hems of about 1 in. deep top and bottom, and if your material is light and your stage draughty, insert lengths of chain into the lower hem. Allow about 1 in. per 3 yd. for stretching after the curtains have been hung for a while—the gap below will not last long.

Then get the stringed "Rufflette" tape used for house curtains, and sew it on top of the upper hem. Allow no more than $\frac{1}{2}$ in. of heading, which will remain fairly stiff and upright, whereas a broader heading tends to fall over and reveal the batten or wire behind. By working the tape along the strings the curtain can be gathered to any degree of fullness.

This kind of tape is much better than webbing, as it is fitted with pockets into which special hooks are inserted. These hooks should always be used in preference to rings, as they can be fitted into screweyes, over a wire, or into the runners of any patent track. On no account should you sew on single tapes (grommets) to be tied over the batten or wire. Unless they are no more than 3 in. apart, or you are doing no gathering, the heading falls away in between; it is impossible to slide the curtains sideways as you can do so easily with hooks on a wire or track; you also have to spend valuable time in tying them to the supports.

Now is the time for fire-proofing. This is a precaution that no amateur company, whether inspected or not, should neglect. By far the most satisfactory way, and often cheapest in the long run, is to send your curtains (without the hooks) to a reliable laundry or dry-cleaning firm, as they have space to dry them and will iron them out afterwards. If you can undertake it yourself use the following formula—

Phosphate of Ammonia . .	1 lb.
Chloride of Ammonia . .	2 lb.
Water	1½ gallons

I give it with some diffidence, as there seems to be no perfect solution, all suitable chemicals being liable to rot the material. I have found it fairly satisfactory after a few experiments with small cuttings of the stuff to be proofed. Any saturated solution of borax, alum, or sal ammoniac will prevent curtains from going up in a sudden blaze, and that is all that many authorities require. Under the London County Council all curtains must be of woollen material and proofed as well.

SUSPENSION

You can get a certain amount of variety in your setting by putting door—or window—flats in place of some sections of your curtains, but in quick changes you will find this process much easier if your back line of curtains can be slid along. You can thus make a space for your flat without having to mount a ladder and take down a section. Sections can be fastened to each other by dome fasteners, spring clothes pegs, or safety-pins. A much greater advantage, however, is in being able to pull aside the whole line into the wings, revealing your backcloth as the sky in an exterior scene. You can often leave isolated strips to suggest a colonnade or trees (see photograph on page 427).

There is no method of doing this that will suit

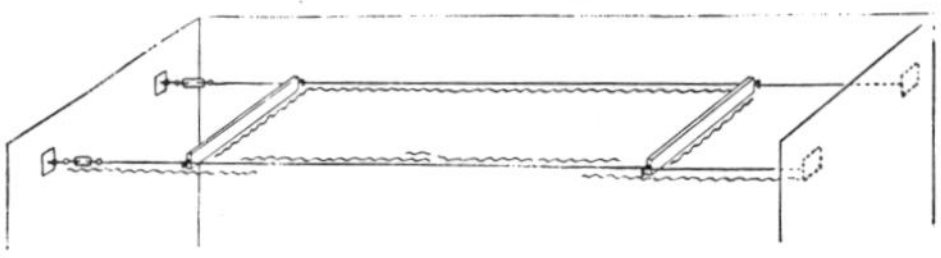

FIG. 13. WAVY LINES INDICATE WHERE SURROUNDS AND FRONT CURTAIN ARE HUNG

every stage, as some walls and roofs can have things screwed and hammered into them, while others are covered with plaster that must not be touched. I shall, therefore, detail as many ways as I know, leaving stage-managers to choose the most suitable.

The most generally satisfactory means is to get a length of wheeled track from a furnishing store and screw it high up on the broad face of a piece of 3 in. by 1 in. timber long enough to go right across the acting-area and about 1 ft. 6 in. beyond on either side. It may often be more convenient to have this batten in two halves, but great care must be taken that the two ends of the

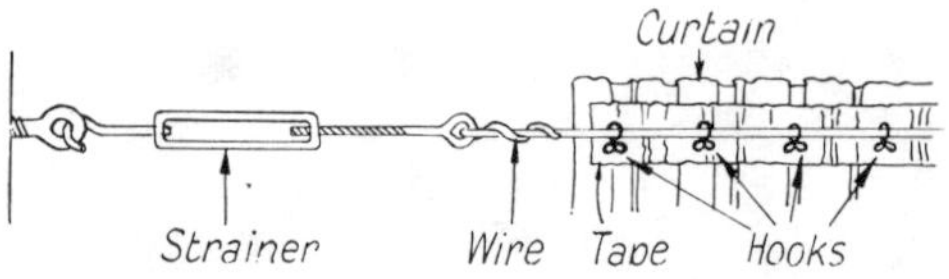

FIG. 14

track meet exactly in the centre so that the wheels will run smoothly over the join.

If your side walls will accommodate screweyes at the height of your curtains, put in a couple of large ones. Get a coil of stranded galvanized $\frac{1}{8}$ in. wire and cut off a length equal to the distance between the eyes. Then buy two strainers (or turnbuckle screws) and unscrew them till they are almost fully extended. Fix the hooks into the eyes and the ends of the wire through the holes at the other ends of the strainers and stretch the wire as tightly as you can by hand before twisting it round on itself at both ends (see Fig. 14). Turn the centre parts of the strainers till the wire is as taut as necessary, and hook on the curtains. The wire may be supported in the centre from above if you do not require the curtains on one half to move over to the other half, but for a span of not more than 16 ft. or 18 ft. a truly tight wire will hold without much sagging all but the heaviest material. You must be sure, however, that the walls or beams into which you screw the eyes are solid, as the strain is considerable. The wire will require further tightening every now and then until fully stretched. (Fig. 13 also shows a method of hanging the side curtains.)

A batten without track will do if you do not want side-to-side movement, and the hooks will engage in a series of screweyes put into the broad face of the wood as near the upper edge as possible. Another advantage of the "Rufflette" tape is that you can move any hook from one pocket to the next to make it come opposite a screweye.

Piping of some kind is often used for curtain hanging. A length of strong gas pipe, if supported in the middle, will cover a span of about 18 ft. In this case hooks are useless, and the special rings made for the stringed tape must be substituted. Make sure the pipe is greased or black-leaded so that the rings will not jam. It is possible to make a framework for curtains from strong electrical conduit, but it needs frequent support, and 8 ft. is about the maximum span of a single length. When the curtains are never moved it is sufficient to have the pipe in a broad hem, or to pin the material over it.

A traverse, or curtain situated about half-way up-stage, is essential in many types of production. Any of the above methods will apply to its erection, but remember that it must meet and overlap in the centre. Two wires are better than one, a curtain on each, allowing them to run a little way past each other, but the best system is still the track. Good makes include among their fittings extra long arms for holding the double track at the overlap. If you are restricted to a single wire, tie together two or three of the rings at the inner ends of the two halves so that the material is heavily bunched, and the lower half of the join will be closed even if the rings do not meet at the top. All these points apply to the front draw-curtain; indeed it is rigged on exactly the same principles, and opened and closed as described above.

SCREENS

Before dealing with the suspension of these curtains on stages that have properly erected frameworks or are fitted with pulleys, lines, and battens, I shall attempt to help those unfortunate people whose scenic background must stand by itself, independent of side or back walls of the stage.

The simplest form is that of the ordinary folding screen. The kind you find in houses is seldom wider than 2 ft. or 3 ft. a wing, and for stage purposes it is better to make them specially. They can be constructed as wide as 4 ft. without being unmanageable, and you can get a surprising variety into the shape of your setting if you make some of the wings only half the width of their partners. A set can be planned as follows: three of 4 and 4, four of 4 and 2, two of 2 and 2. If made of good 2 in. × 1 in. timber they will stand firmly enough at right angles, but the height ought not to be more than 6 ft. or 7 ft., just enough to conceal players standing behind.

They are constructed on the same principles as a plain flat in the article on "Stagecraft," and covered with plywood, hessian, or cardboard. It is convenient, however, to have curtains hanging loose on them, so that the material can be stored separately from the frames, and can be taken off and replaced by a different colour at any time. Head the material with stringed tape as described above, and hang on screweyes or cuphooks (according as you have hooks or rings in the tape) on the top bars of the screens.

To ensure their standing upright, add triangular feet at the back of each, detachable after every performance, with a large hook at the end of each, which will engage in a screweye put into the stage. Many other methods of bracing can be devised.

Make no attempt to mask the tops of the screens with borders, as they are not pretending to be realistic, but are merely something to hide actors and properties. All openings, however, such as doors or windows, must have masking pieces behind, and the "2 and 2" screens are particularly useful for this purpose.

Screens can be effectively used in addition to a plain curtain surround to give an appropriate suggestive background to certain types of non-naturalistic play. Almost any 17th or 18th century play would be greatly helped by screens with the upper edges shaped in graceful curves such as are found in panelling or moulding of the period, and an ingenious designer ought to have no difficulty in devising outlines that will indicate, say, Greece or Tudor England.

SIDE CURTAINS AND BACKCLOTH

The side-curtains are of rather less importance than those at the back, but they, too, present problems. It is essential that they be in sections, as more entries are made from the sides than from the back, and it is here that you want to insert doors and archways.

The curtains can be hung on the battens illustrated in Fig. 13 if you are using wires, but there is no reason why you should not stretch wires instead of battens from back to front, provided you have stout posts at the front of the stage and a usable wall at the back. In ordinary frameworks, the curtains can be hung on the side-battens in the same way as I have described for the back line.

A useful device, however, is the side swivel-batten, illustrated in Fig. 15. The short bars are pivoted beneath the main side-battens by coach-screws, which have a neck that allows a turning movement, and which can be adjusted so that the swing is tight or slack as you wish. Careful calculation is necessary to find the length of the battens, since they must overlap about 3 in. to prevent the audience from seeing into the wings. Four curtains, each gathered to 3 ft., will cover 11 ft. 3 in., three overlaps accounting for the missing 9 in. The curtains, since they do not move along the battens, can be attached in any convenient way.

SCENE FROM "THE SHOEMAKER'S HOLIDAY"
A good example of many scenic errors!

This system has the great advantage of allowing you to have an almost straight line of curtain or a series of fairly wide gaps through which crowds can rush, and it is indispensable for the two-colour arrangement I am about to describe.

I have already mentioned double sets of curtains, light and dark. Obviously, these would be of little use if they could not be quickly interchanged during a short interval or black-out. The swivel battens need only be swung round with a long pole, but the back line will have to be hung on a continuous track, as shown in Fig. 16. Thus, if you want to change your colour, you simply run the curtains (which are made double and hung from extra wide stringed tape) round the end from the front track to the back one. Or, more effective still, if you want to change, for example, from a five-section all-dark line to a pair of light panels and three dark, you run the two end sections round the back, where their light reverse sides will show, and push two dark ones along to take their places. The fact that the light sections are an inch or two farther up-stage will not be noticed, unless the batten and tracks are exposed to view. This scheme is possible only with the patent tracks. The batten must be broad enough to take two tracks and to allow fairly heavy curtains to pass each other without fouling —about 2 in. apart is enough. For a fairly long span, a piece of 2 in. by 2 in. timber will be necessary, but if it is supported at various places it need be only 2 in. by 1 in. The square extensions must be carefully and firmly fitted, and must be right off-stage at either side. You ought to be able to get most of your curtains on to the circular parts of the track when you want to show the backcloth.

BORDERS

Take as much care with these as with the rest. Have them of exactly the same material as the curtains and hang them on a batten, pipe, or taut wire. On no account sling them on a slack cord so that they sag. It is of even greater importance to gather them with as much accuracy as you apply to your curtains. No one need be ashamed of a straight-hung, carefully gathered border, not too brightly lit, and seeming to be an upward continuation of the surround.

If, however, you use concentrated lighting as described in "Lighting Apparatus and Scenic Equipment: Making Your Own Light-battens," you will never need more than one border, unless your stage is unusually deep and your ceiling low, and that will be to hide the ceiling as lit by the backcloth lights. This point is illustrated on page 427.

BACKCLOTH

Every society that wants to do artistic work

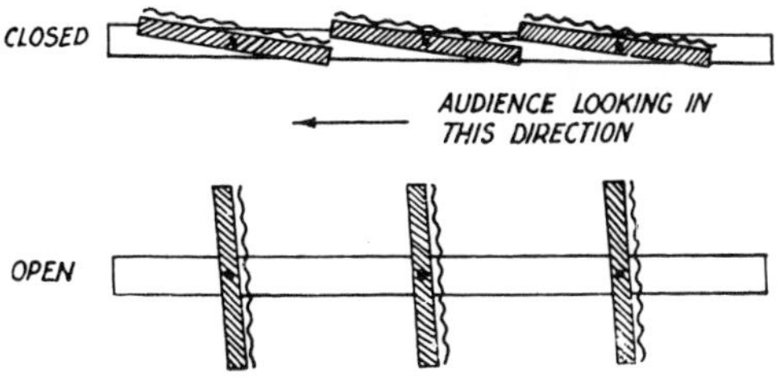

FIG. 15. WAVY LINES INDICATE WHERE CURTAINS WILL BE HUNG

should aim at getting a backcloth. I must, however, repeat my warning that it is waste of money to buy a cloth until you can hang it and light it properly.

The material is unbleached calico of good quality, which can be had in 70 in. or 72 in. widths. Three strips of this width will suffice for many small stages. It makes little difference whether the strips run vertically or horizontally, but I prefer the former because it puts no strain on the seams when the cloth is stretched. Double seams give more strength and show less. The sewing must be done carefully so that no puckers appear, and the worst creases ironed out. The remainder usually disappear when the cloth has

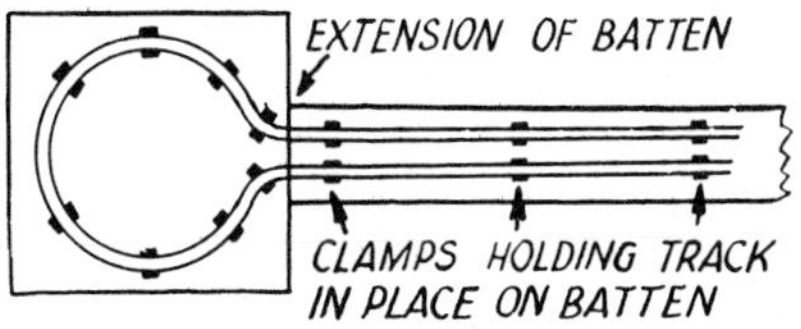

FIG. 16

hung for a few hours, but you must keep careful watch, as a crease or wrinkle establishes the actual distance of the cloth from the spectator's eye, and all illusion of distance is lost. The cloth in the photograph on page 430 shows this fault.

It should now be fitted top and bottom with either upholsterer's webbing or "Rufflette" tape. The latter, since there is to be no gathering, is not absolutely necessary, but is still useful when rings or hooks are to be fixed. A permanent cloth ought to be attached to the top batten, as shown in Fig. 17, that is, the webbing should be held firmly between two 2 in. by $\frac{3}{4}$ in. battens nailed together, but if it has to be removed and replaced frequently, it should be fitted with hooks and these engaged in screweyes on the face of the batten. It is rather difficult to get the tape stretched tightly, and it is as well to work out from the centre, pulling each hook strongly away from the previous one before slipping it into the screweye.

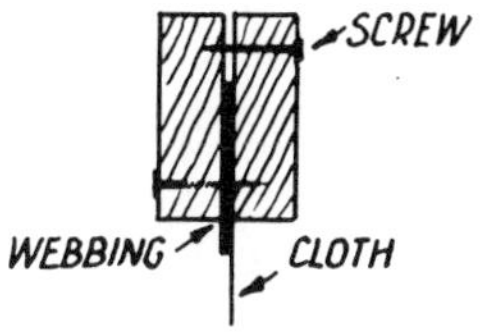

FIG. 17

As the vertical stretching can be done most conveniently from below, put a line of screweyes in the stage below the cloth, arranging them so that a cord can be woven between them and the rings as in Fig. 18. If the cloth is wrinkled in any part, adjustment can easily be effected by working the cord along through rings and eyes. As a groundrow will probably be set up as part of the scenery or to conceal the backcloth lights, the lacing will not be seen. It may sometimes be necessary to do some stretching sideways as well, but safety pins and cord attached to side walls or supports will be sufficient.

I strongly advise societies whose platform is by any means movable to leave a gap of a foot or 18 in. between it and the back wall. The

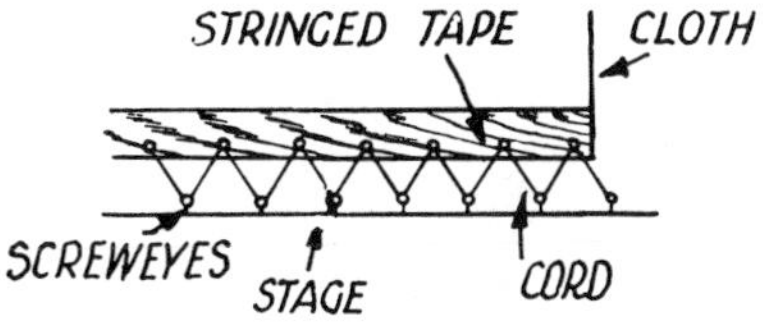

FIG. 18

cloth can then disappear, as it were, into the ground, being laced to the floor, while the lights can be hung on the back edge of the platform. This is what has been done in the stage shown on page 427, and it gives the producer the option of having a groundrow or leaving the stage bare.

Societies working under great financial difficulties are recommended to try the following makeshift. Make a cloth as already described, but of ordinary butter-muslin, middle blue in colour. Though it saves money to dye white muslin at home by cold-water process, it is safer to buy it already dyed, for streaks and blotches ruin the effect.

Such a cloth can be made to do for both exteriors and interiors in a play containing many scenes. The change is made principally by lighting. A garden, for example, can be represented by a flower-bank groundrow behind which lies a row of lamps directed so as to shine up the cloth. The white light on the blue muslin gives a passably good sky effect, as shown in the photograph on page 427. To change the scene to a room, the groundrow and lights are removed, and conventional doors and windows are placed upstage and at the sides. The muslin, being now its own colour, makes a neat background, much preferable to badly-hung curtains.

There are one or two drawbacks. You cannot insert doors, etc., by taking out a section as you can with curtains, so all entrances must be from the sides of the stage. Only windows can face the audience, but the small frame on legs that is often used with curtains will be useless here; it must be a full-sized flat with the window built in or painted on. The areas below and above can be painted to represent the supposed wall of the room.

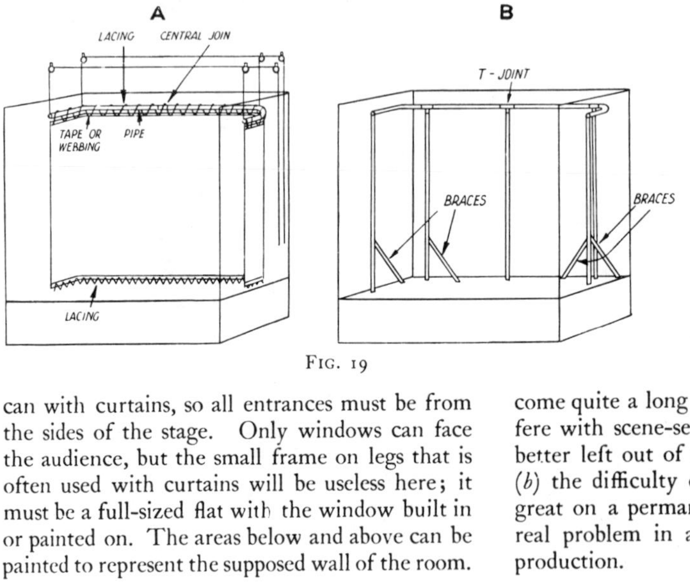

FIG. 19

To return to the cloth. Should the wall behind be of light colour or have anything on it that will show through the transparent material, a second thickness will be required. It need not be carefully prepared; any dark material, if not blotchy, will serve. This ought to have been done on *The Shoemaker's Holiday* stage. But if the wall is fairly smooth and plain, its colour matters little. The lighter it is, the darker must be the blue of the muslin.

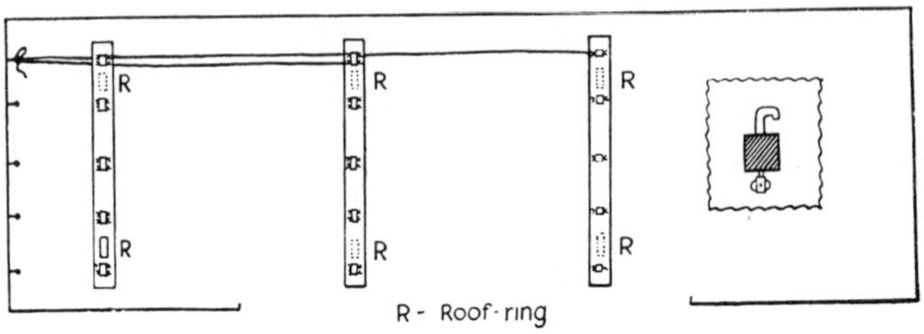

FIG. 20

It is wise to experiment with odd yards of the material in order to get the colour, sewing, and lighting satisfactorily settled. Carefully planned and used, the muslin is quite effective and economical, but it must not be considered a perfect substitute for proper curtains and a calico backcloth.

It may be added that muslin, hung plain or gathered, is an effective auxiliary to all scenic equipment in plays with a vague or poetic atmosphere.

The virtues of the cyclorama, or curved back-cloth, are fully discussed elsewhere in THEATRE AND STAGE, and there is no doubt that it is an exceedingly valuable aid to artistic staging. Its great drawbacks are (*a*) the amount of room it takes up, since its edges come quite a long distance down stage and interfere with scene-setting. The space it encloses is better left out of all calculations of acting-area; (*b*) the difficulty of hanging it. This is not so great on a permanently-equipped stage, but is a real problem in a temporary erection for each production.

If, however, you have a really deep stage, it is worth attempting. Do not try for a completely semi-circular shape; that shown in Fig. 19 is better.

If well slung on lines and pulleys, as in *A*, or well supported, as in *B*, gaspipe or strong conduit holds the cloth from above. It must be bent by an expert metalworker to ensure evenness, and is easier to manage if it is given a firm joint in the centre. Otherwise, it follows the same lines as the ordinary backcloth.

LINES AND PULLEYS

I have often been astonished at how little many amateur societies use the ceiling over their stage. A set of pulleys and lines is of the greatest value in scenic work, since it is frequently possible to hang everything—curtains, backcloth, lighting and proscenium—from the roof, and thus have no trouble with bracing. All borders, etc., can be minutely adjusted so as to hang level, all curtains can be made to reach the floor exactly, and all lights can be lowered so as to give full power while remaining out of the audience's sight. Even when the ceiling is faced with plaster, it is usually possible to pierce through to the joists with a number of large screweyes, about 3 in. broad, with 1½ in. holes, in the positions shown in Fig. 20. You then get two pieces of 2 in. by 2 in. timber, nearly as long as the stage is deep. At distances on each piece corresponding to the positions of the rings you attach hooks or pieces of bent bar-iron (see Fig. 20). Pulleys are screwed into the wood on the lower sides, lines arranged, and the three bars are taken up and hooked into the rings. Some catch or wire binding should be arranged to ensure that the hooks do not slip out. This device is not to be recommended when properly fixed pulleys are possible, but it is valuable when you are performing in a hall not meant for dramatic work, or where the architect's professional pride will not allow rows of pulleys to spoil the appearance of his hall.

A permanent pulley-system is, of course, much superior to any temporary fixtures. When fitting it up get pulleys with wheels about 1½ in. in diameter, and capable of taking, if necessary, a ⅜ in. line. Screw them into the joists as nearly as you can to the arrangement shown in Fig. 21. The row close to the side wall is on the prompt-side of the stage, but on a small stage it might be omitted, provided the lines as they come down from the middle row do not inconvenience players or stage-hands. As pulleys are not expensive I recommend you to have them spaced from back to front at not more than 1 ft. or 1 ft. 3 in. centres, the end ones being about 3 in. from back wall and proscenium respectively. You may need one or two extra down-stage to hold, possibly, lights, pelmet, and front curtain.

Each set must be in perfect alinement, as the lines foul easily. A cleat-bar must be provided on the prompt-wall for tying off, and two sets of transverse lines should be provided if you want to hang your side curtains from the roof. Do not forget that if you remove a batten from its lines you must attach a weight to them in its place, otherwise they will not come down again till angled for.

PERMANENT SET

In some Shakespeare productions an admirable practice has grown up of building a heavy set which remains unchanged throughout the performance. The producer thinks out what arches, stairways, ramps, platforms, etc., he will need, and then with his designer he works them all into a composite set stretching round three sides of the acting area, leaving an irregularly-shaped space clear in the centre. Small movable pieces, such as doors, draped curtains, or furniture, are quickly set wherever they are required during inter-scene blackouts, and the lighting is concentrated on that part of the stage. Thus the action is almost continuous, and if the sight-lines are fairly good the audience will not mind some of the shorter scenes being played rather to one side, or high up, or both. Furthermore, we have ceased to bother in these days if the same sloping platform is successively a part of Elsinore's battlements, an approach to the graveyard, and the stance for Claudius's guards in his banqueting-hall.

I doubt if many amateur groups could bear the considerable expense of money and labour that this type of set involves, but those who can will find it infinitely rewarding. They will also have laid in a stock of timber that will keep them going for several years!

MISCELLANEOUS SCENE-PIECES

A company that does a fair number of non-realistic plays will find it a great advantage to possess a set of scene-pieces that conventionally represent parts of buildings, such as palaces or churches, and are purely formal in outline. Such a set might be made up of 1 large arch, 2 small arches, 4 square pillars, 4 round pillars, platforms, ramps, cubical boxes, sets of steps, etc., as illustrated in Fig. 22. Add to these about half-a-dozen plain flats, and you can use them in an endless series of combinations. Make sure that their sizes are carefully calculated and kept standard with regard to the dimensions of the acting-area, and paint them a light neutral colour. (See illustrations on pages 750 and 759.)

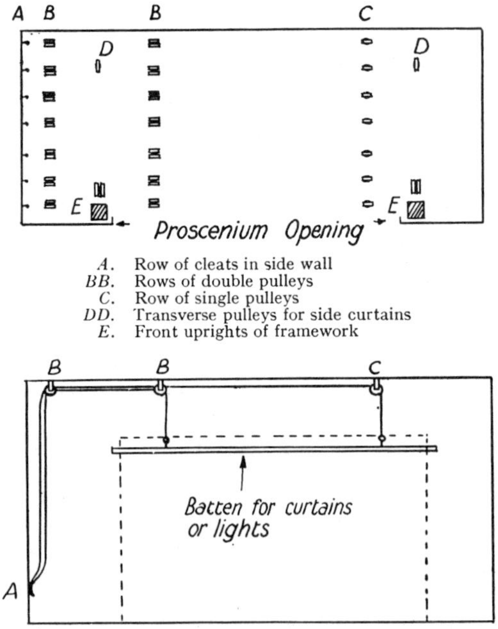

A. Row of cleats in side wall
BB. Rows of double pulleys
C. Row of single pulleys
DD. Transverse pulleys for side curtains
E. Front uprights of framework

FIG. 21. LETTERING CORRESPONDS TO THAT IN DIAGRAM ABOVE
Dotted lines represent proscenium opening

The making of an arch calls for special treatment. There would be no difficulty if it were not essential to supply thickness in order to give the impression of its being part of a wall. The arch with its thickness is made separately and fitted to a flat with a rectangular opening. A framework is made of ½ in. timber, properly braced with blocks or metal brackets, either as a complete rectangle of wood or with a metal sill made of flat iron as in Fig. 23. A piece of plywood is nailed in a curve at sides and top to the inside of the frame, care being taken to see that the arc is true. It may be necessary to fit struts to keep the plywood from bulging in the wrong places. A better way is to cut out pieces of plywood to fit into the corners, in place of the canvas shown in the diagram, but it needs careful work to get the curve accurate. If canvas is used it must be darted to fit the curve when it is taken over the edge, that is, it must have the fullness cut out in triangular shapes. Each flap is then glued down separately, and another strip of the same size as the strip of plywood should be glued on top to make a smooth surface. The whole is then fitted against the opening in the flat, and can be taken out when not in use. The archway shown on page 430 was made in one piece, but the thickness was battered by the third performance.

A square pillar is simply three long narrow flats joined at the edges and cross-braced inside

A column, however, as with all circular things, is more difficult to make. Every scene-builder should be on the lookout for discs of any kind, keg-heads, old wheels, etc. A particularly useful acquisition is a number of the drums on which electric flex is wound—some dealers will gladly give them for nothing—for they are true circles, strongly-made, yet light. To make a column you mount them on a central batten about 2 ft. apart, and tack your covering round the rims, leaving the back open. (Materials for this and other scene-pieces will be discussed later.) A column of 8 ft. or 10 ft. made of flex-drums will stand upright without bracing if weighted at the bottom and put in a safe position on the stage, but it is wiser to brace it. Firms that deal in linoleum will usually give you the strawboard cylinders round which the linoleum is rolled. These, though rather slender for columns, are strong, and useful for all kinds of stage jobs. Three or four of them bound together give an excellent impression of a shafted column in a Gothic cathedral. To make a purely fantastic or highly modern column, try fitting flex-drums on to these cylinders and leaving them with no covering but a good coat of paint.

The remaining pieces, steps, cubes, etc., are better made by a professional joiner, though tea-boxes do quite well for cubes if well reinforced inside and rendered non-creaking. Large stairs can be made collapsible at a small extra cost.

ODD PIECES

Trees. There are several ways of dealing with trees. If your curtains are in sections you can suggest a tree by fixing a tightly gathered strip to the floor and heaping odd bits of stuff round it to represent the spread of the root. A number of such strips, inclined at different angles to the floor, but all apparently leaning in the same general direction, will give a fairly good imitation of a copse exposed to high winds. Lengths of material specially painted like bark can be hung from above in the same way. Strips of paper can be hung from taut wires or string stretched from side to side high up. The paper is fixed to the floor by drawing-pins.

A more satisfactory tree can be made by mounting pieces of stiff material on a 2 in. by 1 in. batten, if necessary. On many stages this type of tree is difficult to fasten, since bracing from behind as for flats always shows to the spectator at the side. Two wires can be stretched tightly between the side walls or the side curtain supports, and the trees pushed up between them; they can be jammed tightly up against the roof if it is within reach; the tops can be fitted with arms that engage in screw eyes on the back curtain support.

If you want a more elaborate tree with real convexity, cut a number of half-rounds in irregular shape as in Fig. 24, nail thin laths the whole length, and cover. A really irregular surface can be obtained by using wire-netting instead of laths, but the half-rounds will have to be more securely fastened to the supporting batten that runs up the back.

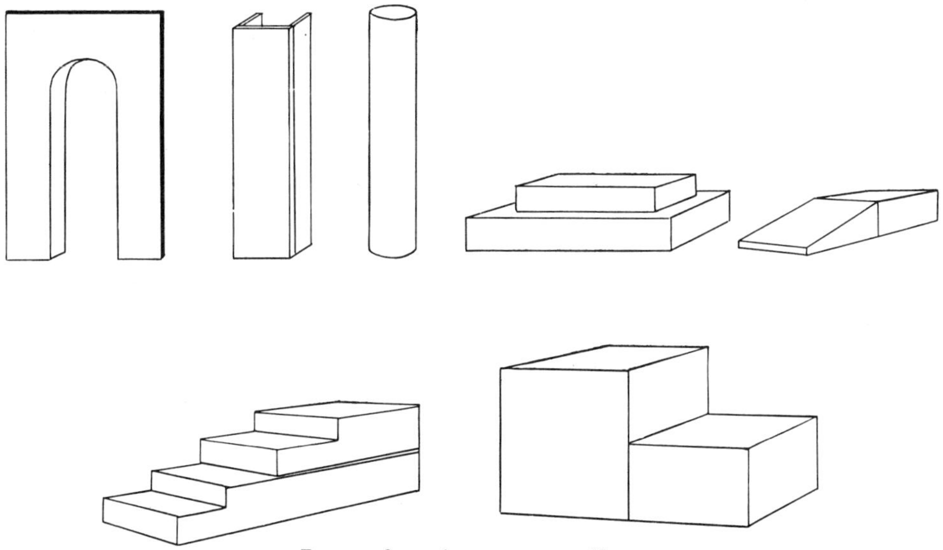

FIG. 22. SOME ARCHITECTURAL UNITS
Platforms and steps in small units capable of being built up. Steps should fit neatly into archways

I do not recommend you to try making foliage, except purely conventional shapes. It is almost impossible to make it convincing without mounting small pieces of canvas on gauze, and it is less trouble to pretend that your trees are of the variety that have no leaves on the first 15 ft. of their trunks. If you make a good job of the latter, the audience will be perfectly content. Branches can easily be counterfeited, provided you do not make them too long and heavy.

Walls. When these have flat tops they are easy, being merely covered frameworks painted. On page 430 is shown a crudely-painted wall of this type, which ought to have had a coping of some kind painted on to give it a finish at the top. If there is foliage or anything else of irregular outline, you must tack on a piece of plywood or cardboard and cut out the irregular edge. Always continue the covering of the framework up on to the extra edging.

Mounds, etc. A common requirement in outdoor scenes is some kind of mound or hillock or log on which players have to sit or walk. The first thing is to make a framework that will bear a reasonable weight. This can be specially made like a stool or low bench, or contrived out of a

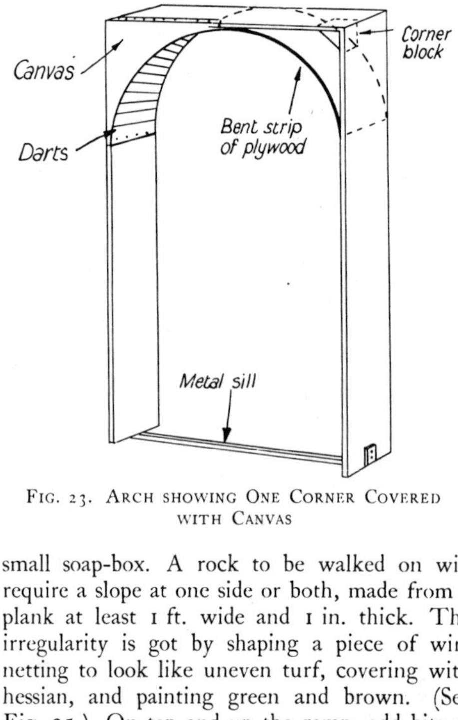

FIG. 23. ARCH SHOWING ONE CORNER COVERED WITH CANVAS

small soap-box. A rock to be walked on will require a slope at one side or both, made from a plank at least 1 ft. wide and 1 in. thick. The irregularity is got by shaping a piece of wire netting to look like uneven turf, covering with hessian, and painting green and brown. (See Fig. 25.) On top and up the ramp, odd bits of sacking can be tacked to continue the unevenness. A log is done on the same principles, with a roughly circular piece of plywood at one end, painted like the cross-section of a tree. Wire-netting can be used for all irregular shapes. A waterfall, for example, can be made as in Fig. 26, being covered with greenish cloth and painted with streaks of silver paint down the front.

Groundrows, essential to most open-air scenes, are merely low pieces of scenery cut in outline to represent distant hills or a skyline of houses. As they are rarely more than 2 ft. or 3 ft. in height, they need not be built with frame and edging separately as for walls. Decide roughly what shape your outline is to be, and make a framework with an irregular upper edge, so

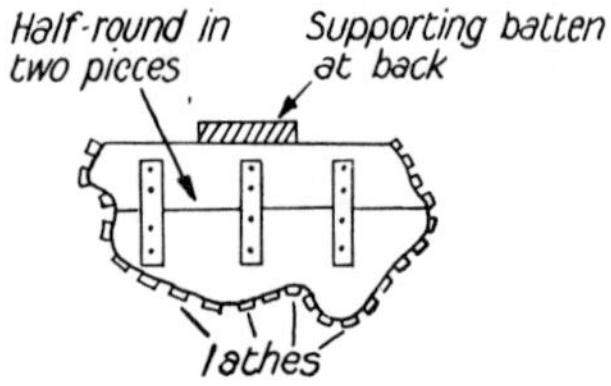

FIG. 24

that every hill or spire that projects more than 6 in. above the general level will have a support to itself. This is not absolutely necessary if you are to use strong plywood as covering, but cardboard requires it. Then paint your covering, nail on, and cut out. Do not forget to supply braces to keep it upright, but take care that they do not interfere with your backcloth lights.

MATERIALS

I have already mentioned a number of the materials that scene-constructors will find useful for these smaller pieces. Wire-netting needs no

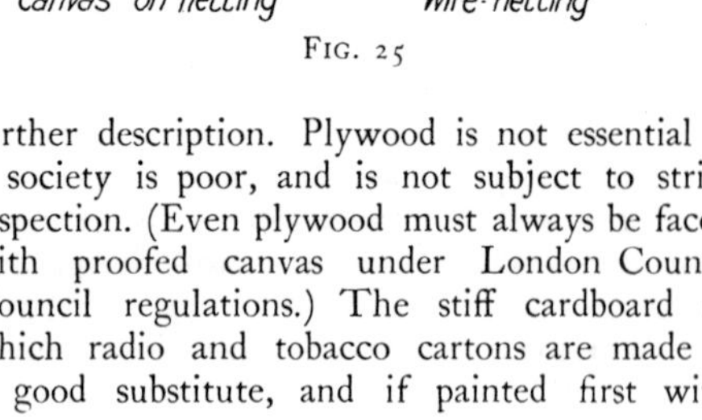

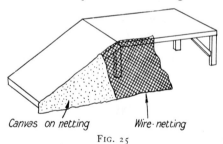

FIG. 25

further description. Plywood is not essential if a society is poor, and is not subject to strict inspection. (Even plywood must always be faced with proofed canvas under London County Council regulations.) The stiff cardboard of which radio and tobacco cartons are made is a good substitute, and if painted first with fireproofing solution is almost incombustible. It is considerably better than strawboard bought at a shop, though you cannot get large pieces free from bends, and it will do for profiles, low walls, trees, and everything except where strength is required, as in arches.

For mounds, old sacking or hessian is best, or

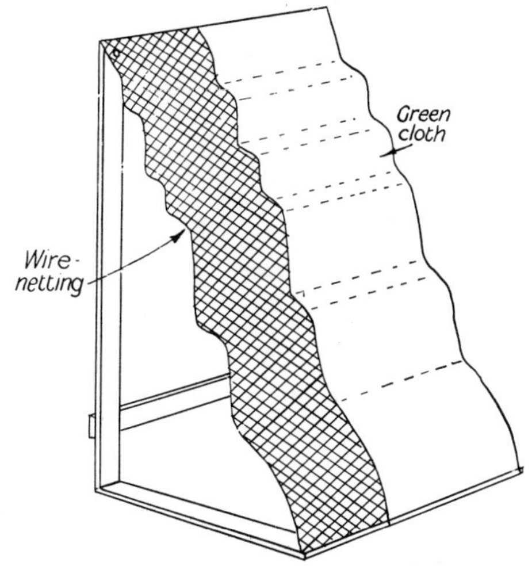

FIG. 26. ROUGH SKETCH OF WATERFALL
Which must have masking pieces, or be filled in with wire-netting and cloth at the sides

old linen blinds will do; for columns cardboard or linoleum (the latter should be carefully fireproofed on both sides and along the edges). I have sometimes, in moments of emergency, used the paper that upholsterers lay under linoleum, or that in which certain bundles of merchandise are wrapped, particularly printers' paper. It is grey on one side and blue on the other, but is not strong enough for any permanent scenery. It must, of course, also be proofed. I do not advise wallpaper for pasting over flats, as it needs careful application and does not look like wallpaper under stage lights. It is better to use your paint-brush.

Fire authorities will pass nothing but canvas-faced plywood, proofed scenic canvas, and timber painted with solution, but all the materials I have described, if carefully treated with proofing mixture, are perfectly safe against the sudden blaze that is the real danger on the stage.

PLATFORM AND EXTENSIONS

Few societies can plan and build the part of the stage on which the actors walk, but they can often adapt what is there already. Gaps at the sides should always be filled in, so that the platform goes from wall to wall, but if there is material for one side only, or if a passage must be left clear as an emergency exit, a complete job should be made of the stage-manager's side rather than that dangerous cavities should be left on both.

Strong tables of approximately the same height as the platform do very well as temporary extensions, or boards on trestles if well screwed down, but packing-cases are unstable, noisy, and difficult to store.

Where extensions are in frequent use, it pays to have a joiner-built sectional framework which can be easily erected, dismantled, and stored. If, for example, an extension 18 ft. × 3 ft. were

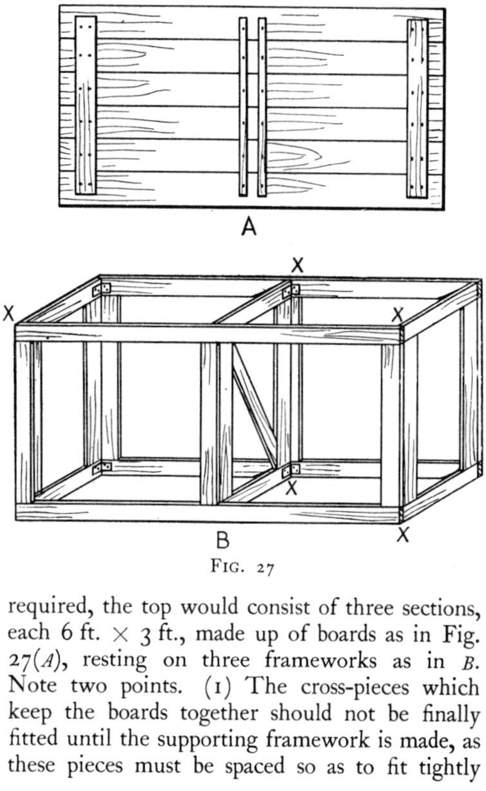

FIG. 27

required, the top would consist of three sections, each 6 ft. × 3 ft., made up of boards as in Fig. 27(*A*), resting on three frameworks as in *B*. Note two points. (1) The cross-pieces which keep the boards together should not be finally fitted until the supporting framework is made, as these pieces must be spaced so as to fit tightly against the corresponding parts of the framework. This saves screwing and bolting (providing the timber does not warp) and gives rigidity. (2) The hinges should be of the "loose-pin" variety, so that it is only necessary to pull out the pins to take the whole thing apart. If, however, these hinges are used only at the points marked *X*, with permanent hinges at the others, each framework will fall into two parts instead of five, and the short sides will fold flat against the long sides.

If you are making an apron-stage, i.e. outside the proscenium arch, make it the full width of the hall, if possible; the extreme ends are useful to a producer for accommodating actors who are not wanted centre-stage, and as places to put permanent doors or screens or odd scene-pieces. This wide apron is often the only way to extend those stages that are boxed in by three solid walls which leave only a minimum playing-area and no wing-spaces. In the same way, if doorways lead off-stage down a flight of steps, try to give the actors at least a place to stand on before entering. Make a platform, 2 ft. to 3 ft. deep and as wide as the doorway, which will fit over the existing steps, and make steps to give access to it. Players, particularly the women during a costume play, will be grateful for it.

Angus Wilson

M

MAKE-UP

THE NEED
THE NECESSARY EQUIPMENT
STRAIGHT MAKE-UP
A "STRAIGHT" MAKE-UP FOR MEN
ALTERATION OF THE FEATURES
MAKE-UP FOR THE BODY AND LIMBS
THE PREPARATION AND USES OF CRÊPE-HAIR
HOW TO MAKE BEARDS, ETC., FROM CRÊPE-HAIR
FOUNDATION BEARDS, ETC.
WIGS, TRANSFORMATIONS, ETC.
LIGHT AND COLOUR IN RELATION TO MAKE-UP
A STUDY OF FACIAL EXPRESSION
COLOUR ATTRIBUTES AS AFFECTED BY STAGE LIGHTING
PHYSIOGNOMY IN RELATION TO MAKE-UP
MAKE-UP AND DRESSING ROOM HINTS
ART IN RELATION TO MAKE-UP
MAKE-UP FOR THE NECK, DISFIGUREMENTS, ETC.
HOW TO MAKE FALSE FEATURES
DESIGNING A CHARACTER MAKE-UP
MAKE-UP FOR NATIONAL TYPES
PRACTICAL MAKE-UP DATA
OLD AGE
RACIAL EXAMPLES

MUSICAL PRODUCTIONS

CHOOSING THE PLAY
CHOOSING THE PRODUCER
AUDITIONS AND CASTING
REHEARSALS AND REHEARSING
SINGING AND DANCING
DRESSING A MUSICAL PLAY
MOUNTING THE PLAY
PROPERTIES
MAKE-UP FOR PRINCIPALS AND CHORUS
THE DRESS REHEARSAL
THE AUDIENCE AND THE PLAY
BEHIND THE SCENES

MUSIC AND THE AMATEUR STAGE

MUSIC IN THE THEATRE

TECHNIQUE OF THE CONDUCTOR
ACCOMMODATING THE VOCAL SETTING
COMBINING THE INSTRUMENTAL AND VOCAL UNITS

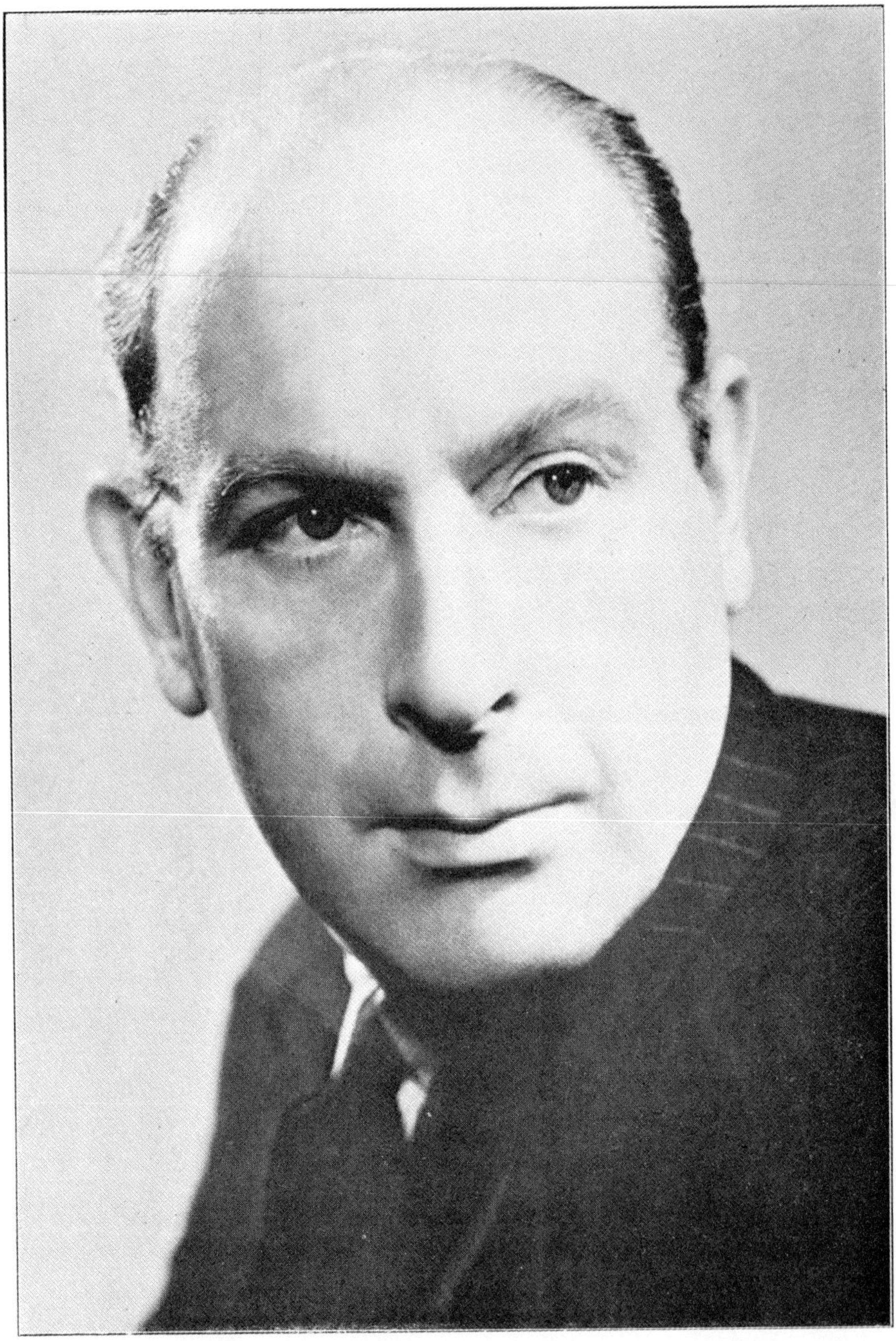

Sir Cedric Hardwicke

MAKE-UP

ALFRED HARTOP, Drama League Teacher of Make-up to Theatre Schools, etc.

INTRODUCTION

SIR CEDRIC HARDWICKE

WHEN I begin the study of a new part it is the make-up on which I chiefly have to concentrate. Many of my friends think I "steal" my features from them. This is not so. If make-up were but a matter of painting and shaping my face to resemble that of somebody I had met, it would be a comparatively easy job. I have to go to infinitely more trouble than that.

I do find, however, that when, gropingly, I begin to visualize a character, the make-up, at first a nebulous shape in my mind, never seems to grow from any conscious effort of my imagination. Often its origins will spring from some small effect that gives me something on which I can build. Thus, when I was considering the make-up for Churdles Ash in "The Farmer's Wife" it occurred to me that an old wig which had been lying, almost forgotten, in a theatrical basket for many years was just the thing for Churdles! From that wig the face underneath seemed to follow naturally.

If it was a wig in Eden Phillpott's play that led to the pictorial development of the character, it might just as easily have been such an odd thing as a carbuncle on the nose. The first glimmering of a make-up is like fumbling with a key at a lock; once the keyhole is found, everything else follows!

Sometimes—but rarely!—a make-up is the result of a happy inspiration. During the earlier rehearsals of "Yellow Sands" I could not form the faintest notion of what Dick Varwell should look like. I was so bad at these rehearsals that I have since heard it was suggested to Sir Barry Jackson that some other actor should be engaged to replace me. Depressed with my inability "to see" the character, I was standing, one morning, at the stage door talking to one of the casual hands employed at the theatre. I found myself watching an odd mannerism he had of stroking a long and straggly moustache. "That's Uncle Dick!" I thought to myself. At the dress rehearsal on the following day my facial make-up was as near his as I dared to get; this, with some of the foulest and oldest of clothes that ever found their way on to a stage, breathed life at last into my conception of Dick Varwell.

Despite this I am convinced that a character solely derived from the imagination is likely to be far more entertaining and amusing than one taken from real life. In life, the appearance of a person has been largely moulded by experiences and inward characteristics; it would indeed be a happy coincidence should these be identical with those of the character to be represented. It is obvious that the face and appearance should be built from what the author tells one about the character.

Good character acting should be like a good painting; not a reproduction, but a criticism. If the only function of an artist was to copy what his eye saw, there would be no need for his art; photography would be much more correct and certainly more detailed. What the artist attempts to accomplish is to illuminate reality with his imagination. Likewise, a successfully portrayed stage character should be an animated picture informed by the imagination of the actor, not an animated photograph!

Even historical characters should not be too accurately represented. Here, however, a difficulty has to be overcome in the minds of the audience who have preconceived ideas—usually culled from unreliable sources!—of what the character should look like. Often the only pictorial knowledge of an historical character is that of portraits and paintings, highly idealized in the first instance and coloured later by years of tradition.

When I played Caesar in Shaw's "Caesar and Cleopatra" my make-up was copied from the bust in the British Museum. One critic said I looked utterly unlike Caesar; another that I seemed to resemble my model more and more as the play progressed!

Some mannerisms and abnormalities are so well known as to be impossible to avoid. No actor can get away from Nelson's one eye and arm. My difficulty when I played Nelson in a film was to lead up to the well known portraits of him painted when he was famous. But what was he like in his younger days before artists had considered him as a subject for their brush?

My Dreyfus was copied from real life—or rather photographs. It had to be.

Once I have decided on a make-up it never changes in the main aspect, although it may, and does, in detail. This, however, is only apparent in the few inches that separate me from my mirror in the dressing room, and would certainly not be observable from the front of the house.

The actor should be accustomed to subtle methods and should always remember that his audience expect and even desire to do some of the work. If the dramatist has done his job well the onlookers will find in his characters and situations what they want to find. Tell them that a character is an old man and they will believe it; but if the actor covers himself with a mass of wrinkles and crepe hair, their attitude will be "Go on, prove it to me!"

If an audience is invited to use its imagination, it will do so, and thus more effectively make-up an actor than the many hours spent in front of the dressing room mirror with grease paints and other accessories. It is not only the actor's make-up but what he does when he is on the stage that is of supreme importance.

There are no hard and fast rules to make-up; everyone must learn for themselves. Thus, the same colour on different complexions will give widely varying results; one must learn by experience and by constant experiment the possibilities of one's own face.

Avoid making the face look like a mask. It is the face underneath the grease paint that has to give expression to the words. Too little make-up is infinitely preferable to too much.

And always remember that make-up alone will never carry conviction to a part. I have seen actors with faces wonderfully disguised to give the impression of old age walk the stage as if they were striplings. I have also seen actors with so little make-up on for a similar character that to look at them you would put them at something less than middle age. Yet because they imitated the mien and the walk of an old man, their performance was much the more convincing of the two.

The more I learn about my job the more I realize it is not what I put on my face, but what I leave off that is going to carry real conviction to an audience.

Imagination is the great thing!

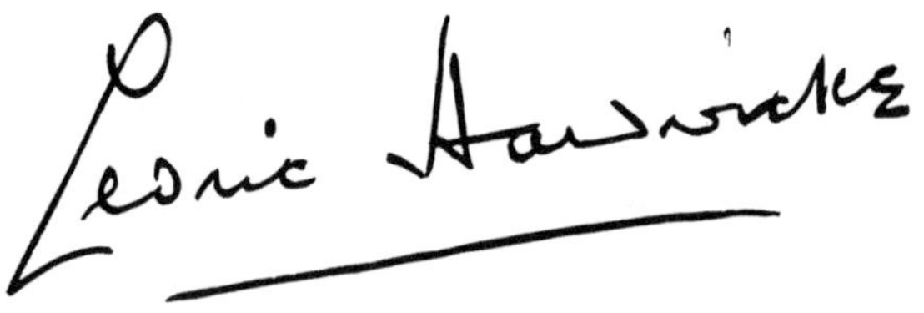

THE NEED

"What beard were I best to play it in?" inquires Bottom the Weaver of Peter Quince the producer, in *A Midsummer Night's Dream* when cast for the part of Pyramus. "I will discharge it in either your straw-colour beard, your orange-tawny beard, your purple-in-grain beard, or your French-crown-colour beard, your perfect yellow." Wherever amateur actors are under rehearsal the question is echoed "How shall I make-up?" and in all probability the echo of Quince will be heard "Why, what you will."

Facial characterization is an ancient art. It is known that masks or false-faces were used by Greek and Roman actors in comedy and tragedy. These masks were moulded and painted and had hair arranged to represent many types of human and animal faces, adaptations of which have been common down to the present day. They were, also, adepts in the preparation and direct application of natural colours to the face and body. It is chiefly along this line that science has evolved the modern cosmetics.

ALFRED HARTOP

Modern methods of stage illumination have changed the whole aspect of make-up; hence the primary need of the uninitiated is to realize the adverse effects of stage lighting on a face that is not made up, and then to acquire a knowledge of the means to correct or neutralize these effects. Making-up is certainly essential for the stage.

Lighting effects are rarely true to Nature. In Nature, light is from above in the open or streaming through a window touching anywhere it can; the rest is reflection and shadow of almost a uniform type. On the stage, however, the performer is confronted by a wall of light from footlights, horizontal shafts from somewhere in the auditorium, floods from wings, batten lights from above; while varying shades of lemon, amber, red, and blue spots add to the diversity. The effect of this intensity is to destroy all natural colour and the natural light and shade, often at the same time creating undesirable false lights and shadows that give the face a featureless appearance. It is, therefore, essential that the normal characteristics of colour and form be restored to the face by refreshing its colour, by lightening the unreal shadows, and by reviving those that we are accustomed to see. These results are obtained by means of correctly placed make-up, the accepted term for which is—"straight make-up." It is of the utmost importance that this aspect of stage make-up should be grasped as early as possible in this progressive study—it is fundamental to the express purpose of the art of make-up; namely, the achievement and fulfilment of natural illusion. The creation of illusion is the basis and aim of all simple or complex "character" types, for their efficiency is judged not as they appear in daylight, or under ordinary conditions, but as they are interpreted by the eyes of an audience under stage lighting qualities. To accomplish this to a marked degree calls for imagination, skill in blending of colours, and the employment of tricks of shading and lining that cannot be learnt quickly.

Stage history reveals that actors of the past made various attempts to discover and employ a suitable medium for make-up purposes. Pigments were used in dry powder form or ground in water or oil, but long ago they were superseded by grease paints that have certainly simplified and extended the scope of application. Grease paints can be easily blended; they are permanent and impervious to perspiration, when they are rightly applied and powdered, the final result being a faithful representation of the clear aspect of natural flesh. A further important advantage is that manufacturers of these paints claim that they are absolutely harmless—entirely free from drying, irritating, or caustic substances, and that their prolonged use has no detrimental effect on the most susceptible skin. These paints are put up in handy "sticks" sealed in hygienic packing.

From grease paints corresponding with the

three primary colours—red, yellow, and blue—and the passive colours—black and white—any desired hue, shade, or tint may be produced by proper admixture, but it would require a degree of skill that can be attributed only to a first-class artist. Although a theoretical knowledge of colour is an advantage the novice in the use of

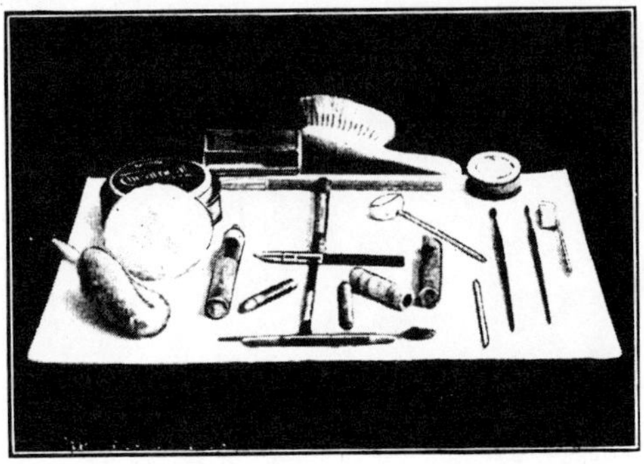

FIG. 1
GREASE PAINTS AND ACCESSORIES

grease paints may find encouragement in the fact that almost every conceivable colour may be obtained ready for use. Roughly, fifty different shades are to be had, each bearing a distinguishing number or name, and as there is a reasonable conformity among the various makers as to shade numbers the following descriptive list may be regarded as general. In order that the list may be a valuable guide to the inexperienced, numerical order gives place to a graded sequence of shade, together with hints on their principal use.

DESCRIPTIVE LIST OF GREASE PAINTS

Flesh Foundation Colours for Ladies—

NO.		
1	Pale . . .	Too pale to use by itself. Useful for blending and high lights.
1½	Light . . .	Also too pale, except when lighting is deep in colour.
2	Medium . .	Best for juveniles and blonde types.
2½	Full . . .	Best for medium types.
3	Florid . . .	Character and blending. For brunettes a creamy tint rather than pink is recommended. Blend a touch of CHROME with No. 2 or 2½.

Flesh Foundation Colours for Men—

NO.		
3	Medium . .	Youthful.
3½	Full . . .	Slightly sunburnt men.
14	Sun Tan . .	Sportsmen.
4	Full Sun Tan .	Sea-faring and soldier types.
4½	Dark „ „ .	Old farmers; outdoor labourers.
13	Chrome Brown	Old fishermen.
15	Full „ „ .	Roman soldiers.
9	Red Brown .	Red Indians and gypsies.
8	Dark Red „ .	Pirates.
7	Brown . .	Mulattoes.
16	Dark Brown .	Creoles.
11	Extra Dark „ .	"Othello" and Moors.
5	Pale Yellow .	Base of many useful blends, also Chinese and Eastern types.
5½	Light „ . .	Oriental.
6	Dull Brown .	Old Age and shading.
6½	Grey „ .	„ „ „ „
10	Yellow „ .	Spanish and Italian.
12	Black . . .	Negroes.
20	White . . .	Clowns; pierrots; whitening hair.
CHROME	. . .	For blending with other foundations, for variety.

Nos. 1, 2, 3 and 4 Carmine for rouging the cheeks; also for lips.
„ 1, 2, 3 and 4 Orange for rouging the cheeks.

LINERS—

Light Grey . .	Eye shading, wrinkles, and shadows.
Dark „ . . .	Eye shading, unshaven face effect.
Light, Mid and Dark Blue . . .	Eye shading and blending.
Light Brown . .	Characteristic shadows.
Dark „ . . .	Characteristic lines; eyebrows and eyelashes.
Lake	Characteristic lines and shadows.
Black	Eyebrows, eyelashes, and blending.
White	High-lights and blending.
Yellow	„ „

THE NECESSARY EQUIPMENT

"The actors are at hand and by their show,
You shall know all that you are like to know."

Some amateur theatrical societies consider it essential to engage the services of an experienced perruquier to make up the whole cast of a production, thus relieving the producer, stage manager, and the players of all anxiety likely to arise in that direction. It cannot be denied that this is the best procedure when the excellence of a production is the chief end in view and when expense is of secondary account. Expert make-up ensures that the whole cast is "balanced"; that is, each individual of the cast will look a part of a general scheme rather than be outstanding because of some incongruity of style or colour. Further, the "character" parts will have the characteristics that are a necessary complement to costume and histrionic ability.

Other societies insist that members, like their professional prototypes, shall provide their own make-up requisites and know how to ply them. Where this rule obtains it is usual to find a deplorable lack of uniformity due to the varying ability of a "cast" to make-up themselves. Many instances have come to my notice where persons making their initial appearance have had no notion whatever of the use of make-up and received help from others whose only notion was to "put a bit of colour on" and let it go at that. Such crude attempts are bound to minimize the effect of appropriate costume and otherwise commendable effort. Real. indifference, I believe, is rare. Fortunately, there is a large percentage of amateurs with sufficient powers of observation and imagination to realize the possibilities of the art of make-up, who take a pride in getting the best possible results by their own effort, and to whom make-up is a fascinating and intriguing study.

Instruction, or what I am apt to term my "gospel" of make-up to amateurs, has been mainly addressed to such through the medium of lectures to Drama Circles, Green Room Clubs, and members of a "cast" who have met together for tuition in their respective needs. In this way, the common and remote difficulties have been anticipated and by easy steps, from simple "straight" to the more complex "character" types, the rudiments of this interesting art have been inculcated to the desired end of a standard in make-up comparable in achievement to other theatrical arts. As in other branches of dramatic art, proficiency can be acquired only by frequent attempts to carry out some form of instruction that will repay in every way the time devoted to a thorough interpretation. It is what you can do rather than what you know that counts, and these attempts need not be irksome, but, on the contrary, a source of pleasure; and they can be made so, especially when tried out in co-operation with other players.

Perhaps the idea of a Make-up Circle is new and one that appeals. If so, why not start one in connexion with the society? There would be no expert's fee for tuition, THEATRE AND STAGE provides all the guidance required; while paints, powder, etc., may be more or less "communal." Evenings spent in this way would be entertaining and instructive, and, furthermore, experience would be quickly gained and facility and speed developed; while the sensitivity to make-up, experienced by many, would soon disappear.

We are now approaching a point where I shall give details of a simple "straight" make-up for trial, but before doing so we must consider the needs of beginners who will not possess grease paints and other requisites; therefore, a preliminary selection, sufficient for general practice, will be made from the Descriptive List, already given. Other shades will be added as required, though from the few selected, foundations for many types are possible when they are used in different combinations.

Women will require grease paints—

STICKS: Nos. 1½, 2½, 5, 9, Chrome, and Carmine 2.

LINERS: Lake, Mid Blue, Dark Brown, and White.

Also a box of Water-cosmetic, dark brown (this is for the eye lashes and eyebrows, but should not be of the indelible or water-resisting variety); a box of dry Rouge de Theatre of a dull medium Carmine. A medium red lip pencil may be added, but it is not essential.

Men will require a rather different range—

STICKS: Nos. 2½, 3 or 3½, 5, 7, 9, Chrome, Carmine 3, and White.

LINERS: Lake, Medium or Dark Grey, and Dark Brown.

A box of brown Mascaro or heating cosmetic, for the hair.

COLD CREAM, of course, will be needed by all. Before grease paint is applied the face should be thoroughly massaged with cold cream so that the pores are well filled. This preparatory process prevents the pores from becoming clogged with colour, provides a lubricating surface for the even spreading of grease paint, and assists in a clean removal of the make-up. There is a variety from which to choose. Further, other kinds of grease may be substituted for cold cream—cocoa-butter, vaseline, etc. The variety known as Theatrical Cold Cream is probably the best, as it can be used both before the application of make-up and also for its removal. Cocoa-butter is popular, and can be obtained in blocks specially prepared for this purpose; many women object to its use, believing that it will cause the growth of hair on the face. They have similar views about vaseline and olive oil. For efficient removal, however, grease of a more solvent kind is desirable, and while any one of those mentioned may be used, preparations known as "Grease-paint Remover" will be found best for quick and thorough cleansing.

Face Powder is applied over grease paint to absorb the grease and to fix the make-up so that it neither smears nor runs; also, powder kills the greasy appearance and attains the semblance of natural flesh. For ordinary purposes of facial make-up the heavily coloured powders are not recommended. The best is undoubtedly that known as "Blending Powder." Being as near transparent as possible and of a neutral shade, it can be applied over any but the darkest make-up without fear of destroying the effect of high lighting and lining. A cheap and efficient substitute is found in ordinary Violet Powder, which is a good absorbent and fairly transparent. Therefore, for our purpose a box of Violet Powder and a small box of Natural and Rachel, for blending with the Violet Powder, will be found best.

Wool Puffs will be required—one of about four or five inches for applying the powder, and a smaller one for applying the rouge. A baby brush or hare's foot is used for brushing off superfluous powder. Two or three orange sticks four and a half inches long are needed for applying dots or lines where required; the extra length prevents obstruction by the hand of the view in the mirror.

Do not omit to get a chamois stump, with a point at each end. These stumps, which have soft and perfectly harmless points, are particularly useful for working about the eyes. The taper style of "pipe cleaners" is handy and can be used for a variety of purposes.

A make-up box will, of course, be necessary. Enamelled tin boxes of various designs, with a mirror in the lid, are obtainable. A satisfactory receptacle, which will readily slip into a larger case, can be made from a cheap small attaché case.

It should be the personal concern of every possessor of a make-up box to keep its contents scrupulously clean, for hygienic reasons, as any irritation or after effects of use are apt to be blamed on the paints, whereas the probable cause is entirely under the user's control. Therefore, make it a rule to use the best materials and to take intelligent care of them. Observance of it will prove to be the best guarantee against any form of detrimental effect.

STRAIGHT MAKE-UP

"On with the motley, and the paint and the powder"—Pagliacci.

The term "Straight" is used to indicate the application of colour in sufficient quantities to counteract the effect of stage lights and to emphasize the features so that they may be seen from any position in the audience.

In some circumstances a simple application will meet the case, as when the lighting is not strong and the audience is near to the performers; when the production is out-of-doors; when presence on the stage is brief and in the background. A simple make-up in such cases consists of an application of cold cream, a good powdering with a flesh coloured powder, the eyebrows darkened a shade, and the whole toned up with a few touches of dry rouge. In all other cases approximating stage conditions a foundation grease paint should be applied to secure lasting results: an even tone for the complexion, the covering of blemishes, the lightening in tone of a dark skin or the deepening of a too fair one, the correction of features by highlights and shading.

We will now give careful consideration to the actual application.

Applying the Foundation. Firstly, the hair should be drawn away from the face and protected from the paint and powder by a net or a band of ribbon tied around the head; also, an overall or cotton dressing gown should be worn to protect the clothing. It is a wise rule to clear the nose before applying anything to the face as the need to use a handkerchief just when the make-up is completed is apt to be annoying. If you find you are sensitive to powder and liable to sneeze, a small wad of cotton-wool pressed into the nostrils will keep the powder out. Now, apply cold cream fairly liberally all over the face and neck, then gently massage it into the skin so that the pores are well filled. This is done with the tips of the fingers or with the aid of a small rubber complexion brush. Give every part, not omitting the eyelids, a fair share of cream, but avoid working it into the hair. This accomplished, wipe off the superfluous cream with towel or soft cloth. Use judgment here as some skins are of a dryer nature than others. In any case, do not leave the face too greasy.

You can now apply the foundation flesh colour, No. 2½, if your colour type is medium; No. 2½ with a tenth of No. 1½ added if you incline to blonde; No. 2½ with a tenth of chrome added if brunette. Make a few streaks across the forehead, one down each side of the nose, a few on each cheek, a sweeping one round the chin, and a few touches under the chin. Begin your new stick of paint by using one side of the tip only. This method will quickly wear the tip to a wedge-like point. This makes the stick less liable to break, the covering area is increased, and the point edge is an excellent aid in lining. The paint should now be smoothed out, with the finger tips, until the face is evenly covered with colour. Again, let me remind you not to work the paint into the hair, but gently to smooth it upward so that the colour fades away just when reaching the hair. Similarly with the chin, smooth the paint downwards until the colour fades away without showing where it ends. Be sure that the hollows of the eyes are covered; that the paint is carried right up to the lashes of the lower eyelid—put a good foundation there; that the ears and the

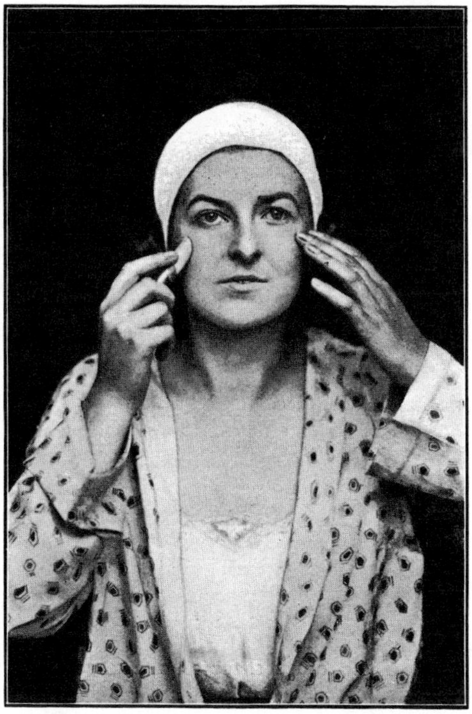

FIG. 2. APPLYING THE FOUNDATION

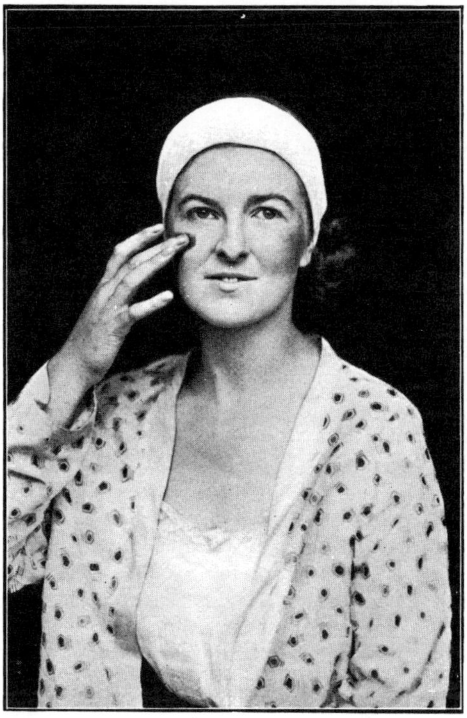

FIG. 3. APPLYING THE ROUGE

(Posed by Miss Bessie Pratt, Bradford A.O.D.S.)

space behind the ears and the neck have all had their share. Here, again, judgment must be brought to bear. The foundation paint should not be applied too heavily, but only as is economically necessary to cover the skin thoroughly and uniformly.

APPLYING THE ROUGE. Next comes the application of rouge, Carmine 2, to tone up the complexion. This must be done with painstaking care. Rouge is a sign-post that attracts the eye of an audience to the part of a face where it is placed, and plays a big part, not only in bringing out the best in your face, but also in improving its contour. Normally it is made to follow the curve of the cheek-bone—in a crescent, the centre of which is below the outer corner of the eye, gradually fading up to the temple, down on to the cheek, well up to the eye, and in to the inner corner of the eye. Keep the colour at its fullest on the cheek-bone and smooth out at all extremes so that there is no obvious joining with the foundation.

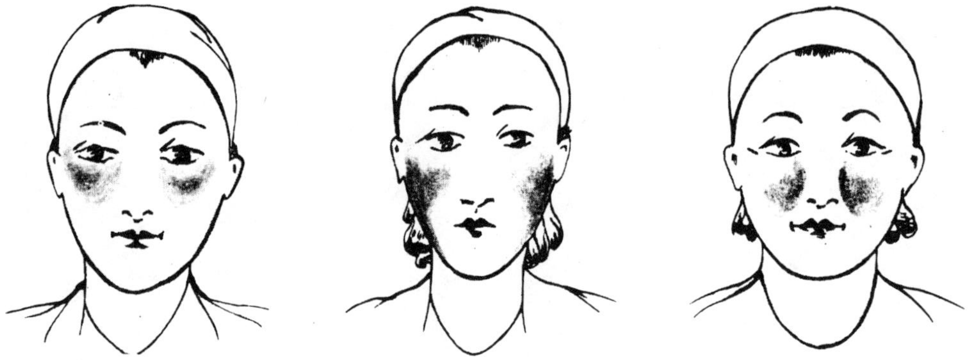

FIG. 4

Differently shaped faces demand consideration of their special needs; therefore, varying placement should be tried until the best way is discovered. Illustratively, should the face be narrow, it can be made to look wider by putting full colour on the outer side of the cheek and running it out to the middle of the face, making it appear wide because the eye is drawn to the brilliance of the sides. On the other hand, if the face is round, broad, or with large cheek and jaw-bones, the reverse treatment is effective—put the rouge inward near the nose and smooth outward so that the fading occurs on the parts that require to be subdued. These tricks can be modified to meet particular needs. Whichever is adopted, avoid the hectic, overdone result, and above all see that the two sides match. When applying, do not get too much on at first; simply make a few light dots in the area, blend, and smooth out with the finger-tips, and add if necessary by touching the fingers on the stick and hence to the face. If you have a dark complexion use Carmine 2 shade with the addition of a touch of Lake and of Chrome.

So far nothing has been done to emphasize the features, or reproduce the natural light and shade that stage lighting destroys. This special aspect of the make-up will next have consideration.

With the rouge shade on the fingers, blend a little with the flesh shade already under the brows, beginning at the inner corner of the eyes and following the sweep of the brows to fade away at the outer corner, thus deepening the tone and creating a natural shadow. Even with strong footlights, darker shades such as green, blue, and brown, carried up so far that they touch the eyebrows, are perfectly obvious as paint to an audience. Therefore, they should be avoided. Now give the ear tips a tinting of the rouge; also, each nostril, the vertical indentation in the centre of the upper lip, and the horizontal one midway between the lower lip and the chin, and, finally, under the chin. A further step can now be taken, the strengthening or slight accentuation of certain features by means of "high lights," or, as the term implies, by the appropriate use of a shade lighter than the flesh shade. Therefore, No. $1\frac{1}{2}$ may be put to use here. Apply a line down the ridge of the nose, then smooth it to appear like a natural reflection of light. Add a touch to the wings of the nose near the cheeks. Run a line at each side of the shadow in the centre of the upper lip, and, if the chin is not too prominent, blend a touch immediately below the shadow under the lower lip.

Pause here and critically examine your work up to this point. If you are satisfied that the general colouring is even and balanced, that the shadows have been placed without blotches or harsh edges, and that the features have been moderately emphasized, it can be assumed that the foundation is well and truly laid.

THE EYES

Attention must now be directed to enhancing the expression of the eyes. This is dependent upon such factors as outline, colour, the attending influences of eyelashes, and the shape and colour of the eyebrows. If these are not taken into consideration the most naturally beautiful eyes would, on a well-lighted stage, appear dwindled in size, faded in colour, sunken, and lifeless. To restore the colour, paint, usually of a colour that matches the natural eye colour, is applied to the eyelids, though, in some cases, a different colour may be more effective. Observation indicates that serviceable colours are limited, and that individual choice should be regulated by general type colouring. For blonde types combining fair skin, blue eyes, fair to mid-brown hair, use light or medium blue. For ash-blonde hair, use light blue, with a line of soft brown on the edge of the lids. For platinum-blonde hair, use a mixture of blue and chrome with a line of soft brown on the edge of the lids. For brown eyes, medium to rather dark brown hair, use medium brown. For blue eyes, dark brown or black hair, use purple—a mixture of blue and red. For brown eyes, auburn to red hair, use chrome and blue with a line of brown on eyelid edges. Grey-brown or grey-blue eyes common to middle-aged persons present a more natural look if the eyelids are painted grey-brown, grey-blue, or grey only. Green shades are recommended by some authorities, but my own experience is that when these are used in sufficient quantity to be effective they invariably give an artificial look to the eyes. Black is too intense for any except coal-black eyes. When, with the aid of the suggestions given, the best colour has been decided, proceed to apply the colour by making a soft line close to the edge of the upper lids, smoothing it upward just to the curved fold at the top of the eyeball—no farther, thus meeting the rouge shading at this point. Extend the colour outward so as to lengthen the eyelids slightly (Fig. 8A illustrates the desired effect). This shading is best done with the tip of the little finger or with one end of the chamois stump. Whatever preconceived notion may be held about the shading of the lower eyelids, I suggest that consideration should be given to the alternative methods treated here. Each is effective under the conditions for which it is prescribed. If you are playing in a small theatre or hall where the audience is quite near and stage lighting is not intense, the simpler method will suffice. With the colour, preferably brown, applied to the upper lids, make a soft shadow under the lower lashes that fades out at the outer corners of the eyes (Fig. 8B). This restores the natural shadow of the eyelashes, but should not be overdone or the effect will be spoilt. Remember that paint under the eyes is much more obvious than it is when it is above them. The alternative method, which is more suitable when playing in a large hall or theatre, can best be dealt with later, along with the eyelashes and brows. These are made darker with water cosmetic, which is applied after the face has been powdered.

APPLYING THE POWDER

In a previous paragraph (Fig. 5) I explained that face powder is necessary to fix the make-up, and, by counteracting the shiny surface caused by the stage lights, to attain the semblance of natural flesh. If you have provided "Blending Powder" it may be applied straight from the box. If, however, you have Violet powder and a small box of Natural or Rachel shade, it will be necessary to mix them to suit your foundation tint. The only reason for mixing is to subdue the whiteness of the Violet powder without destroying its quality of transparency. If you apply the blonde foundation—No. $2\frac{1}{2}$ or $2\frac{1}{2}$ plus No. $1\frac{1}{2}$, then use a powder mixture of $\frac{3}{4}$ Violet and a $\frac{1}{4}$ natural. If the brunette foundation—No. 2½ plus chrome—give the Violet a creamy tint by mixing some Rachel with it. The two should be thoroughly mixed by shaking. A good plan is to sprinkle some powder, sufficient to allow only a thin coating to adhere to the puff, into the box lid, or on a piece of paper. Powder is best applied in

FIG. 5. APPLYING THE POWDER

small quantities; difficulties arise if the puff is too loaded. Use the large puff, and start to powder at the least important part—about the neck and jaws and work upward. Apply with a frequent patting motion, so as not to disturb the paint, over the chin, cheeks, nose, and forehead. Pay special attention to the eyes, as owing to their mobility, their warmth and moistness, it is necessary to fix their colour as permanently as possible. Powder the upper lids with the eyes lightly closed, and to avoid crinkles hold the lids down with the free hand, at the same time raising the brows. In the closed position the under lids are covered by the upper lashes, and often missed. Therefore, open the eyes wide and press the powder well into the corners and around the under folds to the outer corners of the eyes. Another reason why the surround of the eyes should be powdered perfectly dry is that water cosmetic is to be applied next. Application will not be possible if any trace of grease remains. See that the ears, the space behind the ears, and the neck receive their share of powder. Do not hesitate to apply more than sufficient in every nook, crevice, and corner gently patting the face all the time so that the powder is able to absorb every particle of grease. To help this process of absorption the powder should be allowed to stay on the face a few minutes, if time allows, before any attempt is made to brush off the surplus powder. Any little odd job, such as putting paints away, may be done during this brief interval.

Here, it is opportune for me to relate an incident, concerning powder, which occurred during a performance for which I made up the cast. A young lady, showing signs of distress as a result of inflamed, smarting eyes, and a complexion covered with tiny flakes, inquired what I had used that might be the cause. Knowing that I had used nothing that ought not to have been used, I insisted that something outside my responsibility had occurred. Finally, she admitted that her make-up was all right when it was put on, but that, later, because of perspiration, she had powdered again with a powder, the shade of which had taken her fancy, which she found on my table. Unfortunately, it was a powder that I had used for another lady's hair—shampoo powder.

The face is ready now to be brushed with the baby-brush, hare's-foot, or clean puff. Whichever is used, see that no patch of powder is left in the eye corners or in the ears. If the powdering has been adequate, there should be no grease to be seen.

The eyelashes and the brows come next in order for treatment with water cosmetic. This is painted on with the small brush that is supplied with the cake of paint or with a No. 3 camel-hair brush. If the brush is too wet or if too much paint is applied it will run off. Therefore have the paint thick, and paint each hair separately on its top and under sides. In addition, with the camel-hair brush, make a line which will appear as a continuation of the lashes, on each side from the outer side of the upper lashes. Fig. 8c shows that the line is exactly under the extension of the eyelid colour, and is curved outward in the direction of the ear to an extent of about half an inch. Continue with the brush, and draw a fine straight line under the eye to imitate the lower lashes. This is the alternative to shading under the lashes, referred to before powdering, and has the advantage of enlarging the outline to counteract the shrinking effect of lighting. Start the line on the inner side, at a point under where your own lashes begin, continue straight along the edge of the lower lid until it reaches a point under where the lids meet, and then slant up toward the centre

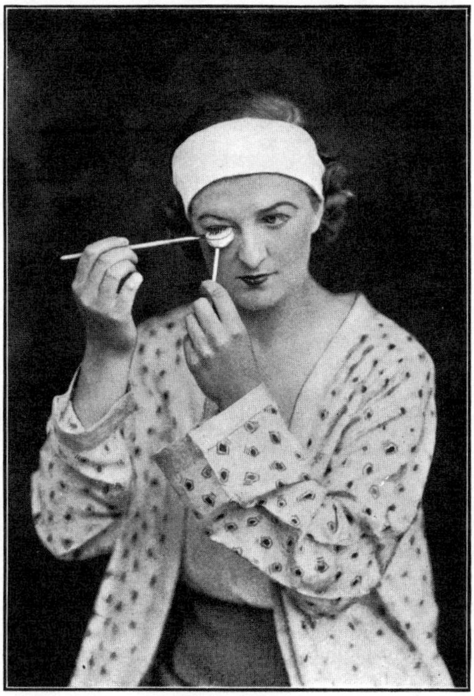

Fig. 6. Applying the Eyelash "Handyman"

of the line coming down from the upper lid. These lines, in effect, extend the corners of the eyes. The eyebrows, if already well defined, only need to have the powder brushed off (a tiny tooth brush or pipe cleaner will serve) to restore their natural colour. If you need to accent them, you may darken and lengthen them with cosmetic to complete the effect of the enlarged eye. Just what you do depends, of course, on the kind of eyebrows you have.

Before leaving the subject of water cosmetic special attention is directed to Fig. 6, where a quick and accurate method of painting the eyelashes with the aid of a support is demonstrated. This appliance or "handyman" simplifies the operation by allowing the eyelids to be quite still during the application of the paint. This makes it impossible for the cosmetic accidentally to stain the eyelid or to enter the eye and cause irritation. The brush is flat and of stiff hog's hair, which gives better control than a soft brush. The handles of both support and brush are long enough to avoid obstruction of the view in the mirror by the hands.

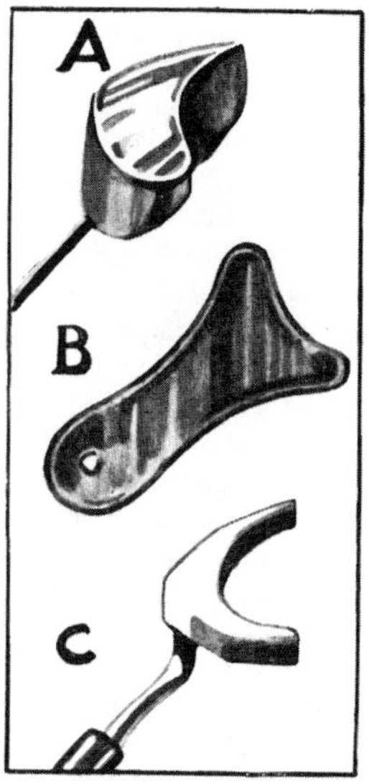

Fig. 7

To use correctly, place the surface of the "handyman" under the lower lashes, then close the eye so that the top lashes also lie flat on the surface, permitting top and bottom lashes to be painted simultaneously.

Fig. 7A gives a closer view of the appliance, which is made from a piece of fine cork, shaped at the front to the curve of the eye, and at the top to the curve of the eyelashes. The top is covered with thin celluloid, and provides a smooth and washable surface for the lashes to rest upon. Fig. 7B shows a more simple form that may be cut to shape from a flat piece of tortoiseshell or similar material. Fig. 7c illustrates one of the professional models that may be purchased at a theatrical stores. The "handyman" can, of course, be used with any colour of either water or grease paint, providing that it is kept clean and that a separate brush is used. It is probably best employed by one person using it upon each of the other members, and it saves time when the cast includes many ladies.

THE LIPS

You may be inclined to wonder why the colouring of the lips was not undertaken at an earlier stage. It is often done when rouging the cheeks—with the same colour—or at any stage before powdering. I have rarely found the results obtained by this method as permanent as when the colouring is applied after other parts of the make-up have been fixed with powder.

The mouth is extremely significant. Its shape lends expression to the whole face. Therefore, it should be treated in such a way as to flatter it, and, also, to ensure that its appearance will not be spoilt by movements, as when singing, speaking, eating, or drinking. For the same reason I advocate the use of special lipstick, which, being made harder than ordinary grease paint, will not smear as readily by such movements of the lips. Before applying the colour, make sure that there is no loose powder between the lips by wiping them lightly with a face cloth, but do not dislodge the foundation paint.

With your lipstick, or grease paint Carmine 2, place a spot of colour at each side of the centre of the upper lip and smooth out with the finger, chamois stump, or blunt end of an orange stick, following the natural contour. Remember that it is the upper lip that controls the shape of the mouth. Therefore, get the outline correct first, then fill in the enclosed space. Slightly emphasize the Cupid's bow curves, keeping them exactly even and leaving the cleft well defined, or they may run together, making the lip appear unduly thick. Carry the outline to the edge of the lip, if Nature has provided one to your liking, but stop just before the extreme corners are reached, leaving the remainder covered with foundation only, because it is there that the colour smudges so easily, and nothing is more unsightly than a blurred look about the mouth corners. The lower lip is treated the same way—first the outline, then fill in smoothly, and extend to the same outward point as the upper lip. Should, however, a fuller appearance of the lips be desired, carry the colour a little beyond the natural edge of the upper lip, or both, as shown in Fig. 8D. On the other hand, keep the colour well within the edge if already too thick (Fig. 8E).

To restore the natural light and shade of the mouth, the upper lip will now require a darker shading of lake, and the lower lip is improved with a touch of No. 1½ to highlight it. A thin powdering will complete the work on your mouth, which may be checked by comparison with Fig. 8.

At this stage, with the lipstick you have just used, the inner corners of the eyes may be defined by placing a dot there with the point of the chamois stump, and then fixed with powder. The use of this dot must be ruled by judgment. Should the eyes be set close to the nose, or if for any other reason you look better without the dot, it is advisable to omit it. When it is introduced be sure that each dot is in the exact relative position and of equal size.

Your "straight" make-up is now finished.

A "STRAIGHT" MAKE-UP FOR MEN

Practically the same methods are used in applying a "straight" make-up for men as those described for women. If the directions already given have been followed, it will be clearly understood that the term "straight" implies the reproducing of natural characteristics, or one's conventional appearance, without any attempt to give the illusion of altered features.

Assuming that the materials previously prescribed for men are at hand, we will briefly consider a few points that are essentially masculine. When ready for making up it is advisable to wear a dressing gown, of washable material, as there is no doubt that the covering provided by one not only protects the clothing from spots of paint and powder, but, also, prevents the possibility of a chill when the actor is only half dressed in a draughty dressing room.

There should be little need to mention, except as a reminder, that the face should be newly shaved—the reason is obvious: grease paint will not cover a stubble beard. The entire surface to be made up will require an application of cold cream, or cocoa-butter, well rubbed into the skin to fill the pores. This done, wipe off all surplus cream with a towel, leaving the skin almost dry.

For the foundation flesh colour No. 3½ will give a healthy, slightly suntanned appearance. Apply by making a few streaks across the lower

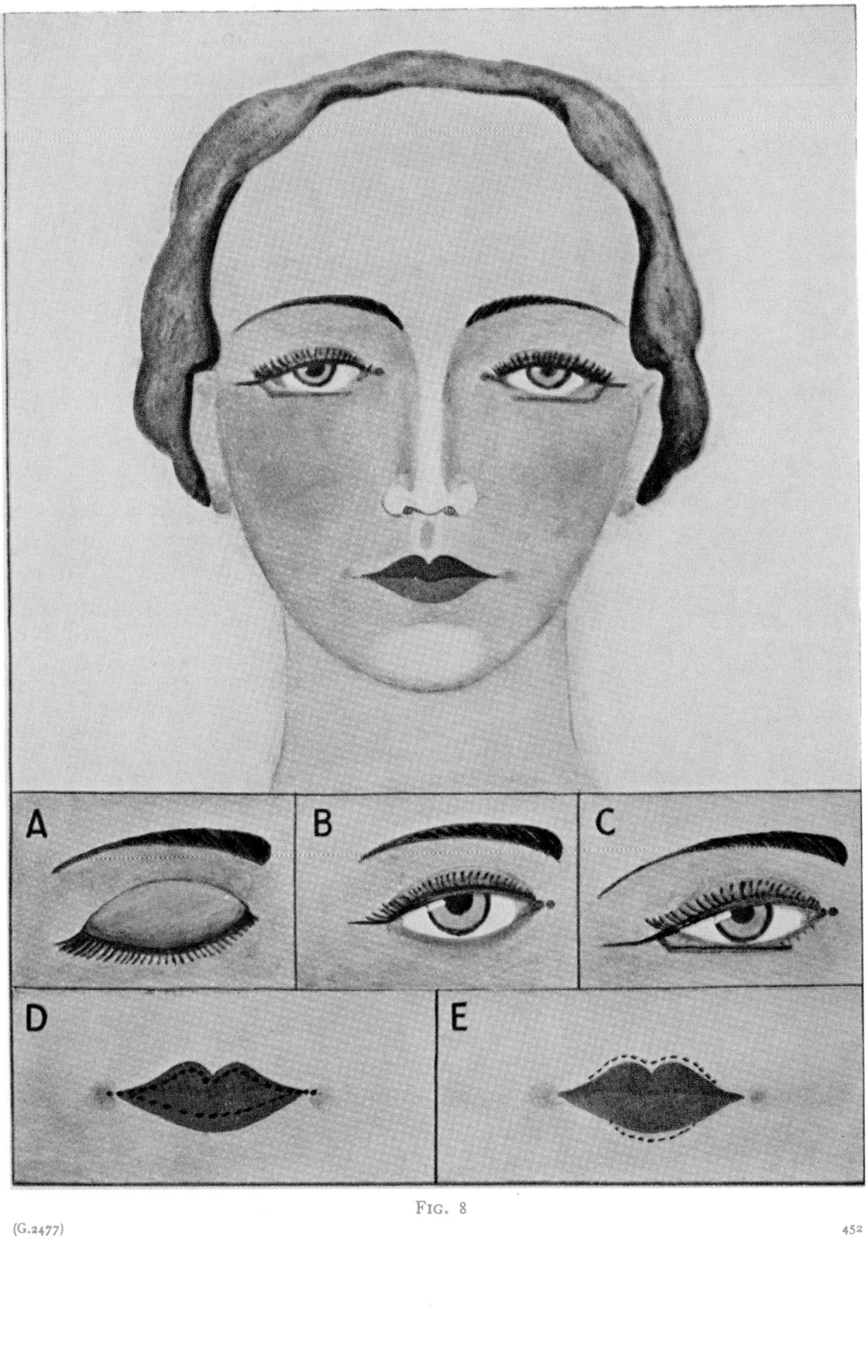

FIG. 8

part of the forehead, down either cheek, over the nose, round the chin, and about the neck. Remember the idea of wearing only one side of the stick so as to produce a wedge-like point, which has the advantage of a larger covering surface, the stick is less liable to break, and the point edge is useful for lining purposes (Fig. 9A).

With the fingers stroke out the paint until a smooth, even, covering is produced. From the lower part of the forehead stroke upward, allowing the colour to fade out at the hair line to avoid a ridge of paint at that point. Cover the eyelids and sockets, giving special attention to the lower lids, for it is a common fault to miss these parts and to produce white patches that destroy the natural appearance of the eyes. Smooth out from the cheeks over the ears, behind the ears down to the neck, and well below the line of the collar from the chin. Use judgment as to the amount necessary to cover the skin thoroughly without being dauby.

The fuller colour of the cheeks is obtained by applying a few touches of No. 9, or if required still darker, No. 9 with a little Carmine 3 added. Place with the finger tips about the cheek bones and spread up towards the temples, backwards to the ears, well up over the lower eyelids, avoiding any noticeable edge where this colour fades out into the foundation. Continuing with the same colour, run a shading under the ridge of the eyebrows and well into the eye corner, taking care to avoid getting any on to the eyelids, as placed there it would give an aged appearance to the eye. Healthy ears are usually of as full a colour as the cheeks; therefore place some over the edges, carrying it down to the tips, or lobes, of the ears. The indentation in the centre of the upper lip may be defined by a shadow of the same colour. In a general way keep the use of this full colour within the limits of a normally healthy appearance.

Observe at this point that the colours applied resemble a typical juvenile complexion, and lack the details that characterize mature manhood. Here, consideration must be given to individual requirements. If a juvenile, or if it is necessary to appear as one, no addition to the foundation is required. Should you, however, have reached an age when shaving is a necessary part of your grooming and your face carries the obvious sign of a darkened skin in the shaving area, then it is in the interests of a correct appearance to reproduce the shaven effect. To do this blend a small amount of grey liner into the foundation, keeping it strictly confined to the necessary area; that is to say, precisely where your beard and moustache would grow. The foundation completed, attention is next given to the needs of the eyes. Here, again, individual requirements should be considered to find the extent to which paint may be used about the eyes without appearing effeminate.

For the juvenile, or where the "part" indicates an uncommonly handsome and debonair impression, a soft blue shading on the eyelids and a fairly distinct outlining of the eyes may be employed to advantage; though in more ordinary instances a grey or brown shading is to be recommended—grey for fair types, brown for medium or dark types.

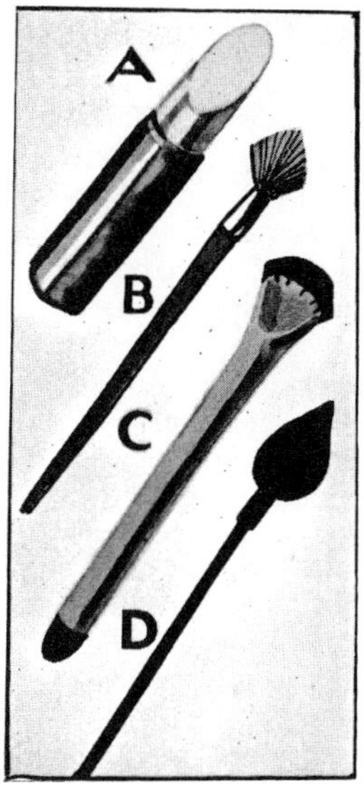

FIG. 9
AIDS TO LINING

Select the colour—say grey—and place a line on the upper eyelids, immediately above the lashes; smooth upward and fade out at the top fold, then extend outward carrying the colour a trifle beyond the outer corners of the eyes. This, in effect, slightly lengthens the eyelids. Reference to Fig. 8A will clear up any doubt about the correct extent of the shading.

The outline of the eyes is emphasized with the dark brown liner. The eyelashes are strengthened by drawing a line along the edges of the upper lids. This is carried out a little at the outer corners to imitate a continuation of the lashes. Fig. 8C shows that this line is exactly under the extensions of the eyelid colour, starting fairly emphatically and diminishing to a mere suggestion. A further line is drawn under each eye to imitate the lower lashes. Starting at a point about a quarter of the width of the eye from the inner corner, draw a straight line along the edge of the lower lid until it reaches a point under where the eyelids meet, and then incline up towards the centre of the line coming down from the upper lid. A tiny dot of carmine is placed at the inner corner of the eyes to lend lustre to them.

The lips should be given a light shading of Carmine 3, the upper one being toned rather darker than the lower. It is usually sufficient to paint the upper lip only, following its natural shape, then to transfer a little to the lower one by pressing the lips firmly together and moving the jaw from side to side so as to rub the lips together. If you feel that it is really necessary to improve the appearance of the mouth by reducing or enlarging it, here is the stage to do it—before powdering. To reduce, use the wedge point of the foundation stick of paint to run along the edge of either lip, or both, thus cutting off the thickness and forming a good shape inside the natural outline. To enlarge, carry the carmine a little beyond the ordinary outline of the upper lip, then pause to see if that is sufficient; it probably will be. Only in extreme cases will it be found necessary to enlarge both lips.

The face is next powdered, either with "Blending Powder" or Violet Powder. The Violet Powder can be used direct or tinted with a Natural shade for juveniles; for older men an addition of Rachel or Sun Tan shade will kill whiteness and produce a creamy tint that will soften the foundation to perfection. Apply with the wool puff, conveying a thin coating round the jaws, first patting it on, then repeating applications until all the painted surface is completely covered up. Observe that the powder dries and fixes the make-up by absorbing the grease; so, in order to assist the process of absorption and ensure the best degree of permanency, powder should be allowed to remain a few minutes before any attempt is made to brush off the surplus. Remove superfluous powder by brushing lightly with a baby brush or the puff, paying special attention to corners that may retain the powder and show as pale patches when on the stage. Many men display an amusing lack of aptitude in wielding a powder puff, but if the eyes are powdered carefully, and as soon as possible, to avoid smearing the rest should be comparatively easy. Do not attempt to apply too much at once, and employ a light patting motion without any suggestion of rubbing that may disturb the paint.

Powder should be removed from the eyelashes and eyebrows, which if sufficiently thick or dark in colour may not require any treatment. Should they, however, require emphasizing it can be done with the brown cosmetic applied with a small stiff brush. If the hair is closely cropped at the temples and around the ears, cosmetic should be applied in just sufficient quantity to simulate the hair line, otherwise, the stage lighting will cause these parts to look perfectly bald. In the event of this being the case be sure that the foundation paint has been carried into this area to kill any paleness of the scalp, then apply the cosmetic lightly with a tooth brush, painting the hair but not the skin beneath. The make-up is now complete.

REMOVAL OF MAKE-UP

Make-up can be removed much more simply than it is applied, yet, to do it thoroughly, without discomforting after effects, a sound method must be employed.

Smear a dab of cold cream or the special variety of "removing cream" over the cheeks and forehead, working it into the paint so as to loosen it, and wipe off with paper tissues or soft cloth. To avoid the bulk of grease and paint entering the eyes leave them until other parts of the face, the neck, and roots of the hair have been thoroughly cleaned by a repetition of cream and wiping. Now, use a clean smear of cream to the eyes, taking care to avoid rubbing it into them. If the paint on the eyelashes is rather obstinate, take hold of them with the cloth between the forefinger and thumb and pull the paint from them. When every trace of paint has been removed the face will still retain a residue of grease, which can, however, be cleared by the use of a sponge, or pad of cotton-wool, dipped in astringent lotion. A good lotion can be cheaply made by mixing one part Witch Hazel and one part Lavender Water or Rose Water. This will kill the grease, close the pores, and leave the face scrupulously clean. The alternative to the use of the lotion is simply to give the face a light powdering to absorb the grease, and to wash with soap and hot water when you arrive home.

The drawing of fine lines with grease paint

colours may be easily accomplished by any of the following methods. A camel hair brush may be dipped in colour that has first been melted, then pressed to a flat edge with the finger and thumb (Fig. 9B). The flat end of an orange-wood stick smeared with colour will answer for very short lines but should be carefully handled when working about the eyes to avoid injury. The utility of a liner can be improved by pressing flat the covering paper at one end, squeezing up more paint to the edge as required (Fig. 9C). Probably the best way for all lining purposes is to cut off a bare half inch from the liner, remove the surrounding paper, and press the piece of paint on to the flat end of a long orange-wood stick. When firmly adhered to the stick the paint can be pressed between the finger and thumb to any desired shape of point, preferably a flat tapering one, as shown in Fig. 9D. This point or edge can instantly be renewed as often as worn down. Sticks of brown, blue, lake, and grey, should be prepared in this way.

BLENDING OF COMPOUND FOUNDATIONS

Assuming that the simple "straight" make-up has been practised and mastered, the scope of our subject may now be extended by a consideration of blending. By this term is meant the discriminate mixing of two or more colours to produce a different one, the product being a compound shade, intended to meet a particular need. For example, it will be found that by mixing together Nos. 5 and 9 a tone can be produced that will exactly match No. 3½. Approximately the same tone is derived from a mixture of Nos. 2½, Chrome, and No. 9. There are other useful mixtures or blends.

Nos.	1½ and 2½	equal	No.	2
,,	1½, 5, and 9	,,	,,	2½ special
,,	2½ and Carmine 2	,,	,,	3
,,	8 and Chrome	,,	,,	14
,,	9 and Chrome	,,	,,	4
,,	8 and 5	,,	,,	4½
,,	9, Chrome, and No. 8	,,	,,	13
,,	8, Chrome, and Carmine 3	,,	,,	15

Consequently, it will be realized that from the limited number of colours in your possession a large variety of foundation flesh tints may be blended that will provide the rosy tint of youth, the ruddy or florid colour of middle age, the sallowness of old age, and practically all racial colourings.

A critical observation of the average natural complexion will reveal that the colour is not an even distribution of a flat shade, but that it is composed of two shades, one over the other; that is to say, a reddish shade superimposed over a background of a pale creamy shade. The aim of make-up being to reproduce a life-likeness as "holding the mirror up to Nature," is it not obvious that a two-colour foundation will give more natural results than a single one?

We have seen that a blend of Nos. 5 and 9 gives the same shade as No. 3½; therefore, it is preferable, in place of using 3½ as a foundation, to use Nos. 5 and 9 in combination, a further advantage being that the result may be varied according to the proportion of light and dark. Undoubtedly, the combined use of these two shades is the medium of a useful range of foundation shades; in fact, judging by its popularity among the "old hands," it would appear to be the panacea for all make-up troubles. It is, however, possible to overrate its importance at the expense of other blends that may be more suitable under certain conditions, as, say, a blend of Nos. 5 and 8, which is equally productive of useful colourings, especially for men of dark type.

The next step in "straight" make-up should be along the lines of a blended foundation, then its advantages will be better appreciated. The first of these is the natural animation that it imparts. Further, the practice in blending will develop a knowledge of colour value and selection, which is essential in "character" make-up. The application of the separate colours is best carried out by first covering the face with the pale shade and then adding the dark shade in such a way as to imitate the flecked appearance of a natural complexion.

Men will start by first applying No. 5 direct from the stick, so that every part of the area to be made up is covered, thinly but evenly. Do not get the idea that because two colours are used double the amount of paint is applied. Only use sufficient to form a pale, clean tone of groundwork, then follow with No. 9 from the stick to the finger tips, and thence to the face. Make no attempt definitely to mix the two shades on the face, but rather get the feeling that the redder shade remains on the surface, thus allowing the paler undercoat to reflect through. The whole area of groundwork should be "topped" by repeated deft touches until just the right tone is arrived at, though varied to result in a semblance of natural light and shade. After a few trials the scope of variation offered by shades combined in this way will be fully realized.

When the compound foundation is complete the make-up proceeds on exactly the same lines as previously described; the cheeks are coloured, shadows are put in, eye colour is added, etc. If the whole application is carried out in the manner described, the result should be a dry, smooth finish of lasting qualities, comparable in effect to the make-up shown in Fig. 10. With practice you will find that this work is all far more simple in execution than it sounds. Make the sequence of features a habit. This will simplify operations and save time. Fifteen minutes is about the time that you will require to allow at your dressing table to put on this really efficient make-up—one that will give you confidence in its correctness to face any audience.

ALTERATION OF THE FEATURES

Compound foundations are serviceable to women. Girls will not improve upon single colour foundation, except for the express purpose of adding a few years to their appearance. For young women No. 5 as a base is slightly too yellow, and should be lightened by mixing with No. 1½ in about equal proportions. The two should be thoroughly mixed before application on the face to produce a creamy tint, and considered as a single base tint over which No. 3 or No. 9 is faintly distributed until the desired tone of complexion is reached; at the same time the scumbled effect should be maintained. Women of middle-age may use No. 5 as a base, and follow with No. 3½ or No. 9 in judicious quantity. The foundation completed, carmine is added to the cheeks, the eyes are coloured, and the make-up is completed and powdered in the usual way. Finally, to tone up the complete make-up, take the dry rouge, and with a hare's foot or small puff give the cheeks a fresh bloom, softening any sharp contrast between foundation and the deeper colour, and toning down any undue paleness about the chin, jaws, or forehead. Always remember that dry rouge must be applied after powdering, and never directly on to grease paint.

Thus far the make-up has proceeded on straightforward lines without making allowance for the special aspect of stage illusion. It should be borne in mind that make-up is the creation of an illusion; that is to say, the natural features and shadows that are obliterated by artificial light must be revived by exaggerating the lines of the features and reproducing the shadows, so that the face will present a natural appearance to the audience. To accomplish this a definite understanding must be arrived at as to how shadows are formed and where they fall, in which connexion important factors are the predominating direction of the light that reaches the face and the distance from which the make-up will be viewed.

The face owes its chief characteristics to its irregularities, which consist of projections and hollows, elevations and depressions, dimples, wrinkles, etc. Imagine, for example, what the effect upon the face would be with a stage illuminated solely by overhead batten lights, which would give a light similar to daylight. Such prominences as the forehead, the ridge of the nose, the cheek bones, the lower lip, and the point of the chin, would first intercept and reflect the vertically falling light, thus producing high lights (the term is used in the sense of implying intense or prominent lights). Hollows or depressions would appear as shaded areas of varying degrees according to the amount of light reaching them; and dimples and wrinkles would appear as high lights separated by graduated shadows.

Under these conditions definite downward shadows would be cast by the main projections of the face, namely, the brows, nose, and chin, which would fall on the eyelids, the upper lip, and the neck. Viewed from the front the light and shade resulting from downward lighting would appear normal, because they present a scheme with which the audience is familiar. If, on the other hand, the direction of the lighting was changed to upward, as in the case of footlights only, the entire scheme of light and shade would be reversed, and would, therefore, present an unfamiliar and distorted aspect of the face, since upward light is never present in real life. Upward

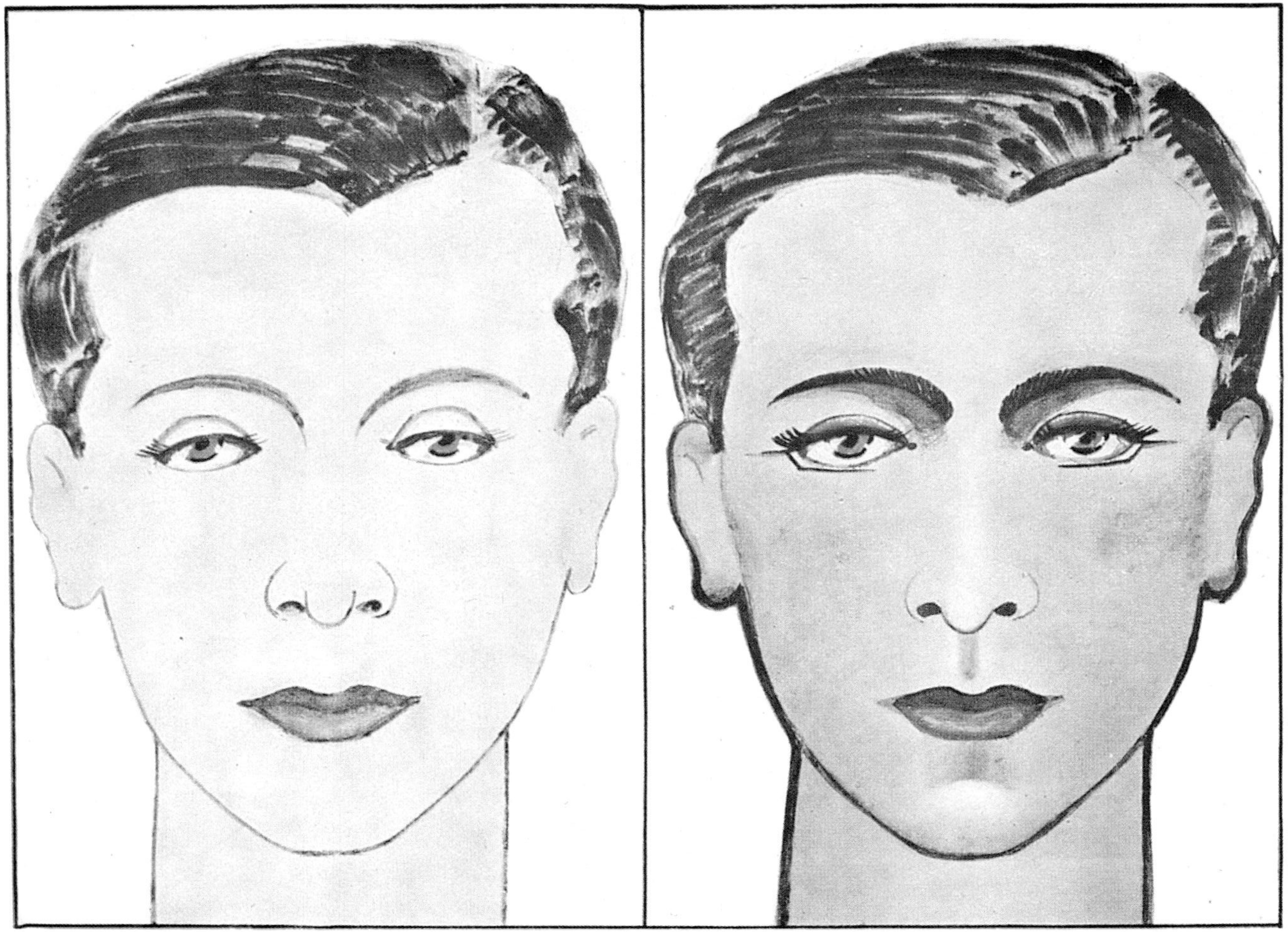

Fig. 10

light, from footlights, creates false high lights on prominences of the face—under the chin, the tips of the ears and nose, and under the eyebrows, thereby eliminating from these positions the shadows that are cast by daylight or downward light.

Generally, it will be found that on amateur stages the lighting consists of a combination of overhead batten lights and footlights, with, probably, a preponderance of footlights, so that it may be assumed that in most cases the strongest light is thrown in an upward direction. Further, the relative position of a person on the stage to the two sources of light needs to be taken into account, for near stage centre the amount of light that reaches the face from each source will be about equal, but as the footlights are approached their effective strength becomes greater, and the amount of top light is reduced. This loss of light balance is explained by the fact that in moving closer to the footlights the face is brought nearer to the source of upward light without being any appreciable distance nearer the source of downward light—because of its height.

With these ideas in mind it is not difficult to ascertain the direction from which the lighting is strongest, and then by appropriate light and shade in the make-up, to tone down false high lights, to fade out false shadows, and, at the same time, to reinstate high lights and shadows on a natural, familiar basis.

Shadows are almost invariably of a similar colour, only darker, to the rest of the face. As they are the result of obstructed light they appear as a darkened area, and are best represented in make-up by a tone somewhat darker than the foundation. Selecting from the colours in hand, this toning down of false high lights and the representation of shadows may be done with No. 9, lake, or light grey, on a pale foundation; or lake, grey, or brown, on a florid foundation. Natural indentations of the chin, the upper lip, and the hollows of the eyes are reproduced in a similar way. Conversely, the strengthening of the features is necessary. Emphasis may be given to the brows, the nose, and chin: the lips may be made more shapely, and the eyes more natural, by high lights of a tone that is lighter than the foundation. No. $1\frac{1}{2}$ should be employed for high-lighting a pale foundation; No. $2\frac{1}{2}$ or 3 on a No. 9/5 or similar compound foundation.

From the foregoing explanation of the formation of high lights and shadows it should be easy to realize the possibilities that a knowledge of light and shade opens out in creating the illusion of altered features. By skilful adaptation of light and shade it is possible to alter the natural appearance of a face to a considerable extent. Applied in the simplest form, light and shade may be employed to correct or improve the features, to change the expression, and to give the appearance of increased age; in fact, it may rightly be said to form the basis of all facial characterization. The alteration of features for the purpose of improving their appearance, or to delineate characteristics or peculiarities not possessed naturally, may be regarded as a first departure from the simple "straight" make-up and a step in the direction of "character" work. Therefore, the following hints on light and shade effects should be carefully noted, though they by no means exhaust the possibilities of this important phase of make-up.

NOTES ON THE ALTERATION OF FEATURES

There are natural characteristics peculiar to a fair face that make a dark make-up unsuitable to it, and vice versa. Consequently, in "straight" parts do not take too many liberties; make up for your type. Obviously, grease paint alone cannot remodel the features; it can only create the illusion of an altered appearance, which, however effective when viewed from the front, is rarely so when the head is turned and the face is seen in profile.

Briefly analysed, the general proportions of a face are approximately equal distances between the hair line and eyebrows; the eyebrows and the nostrils; the nostrils and the tip of the chin. Any definite divergence from this standard will offer ground to work upon. Consider, firstly, the extended effects that may be obtained: the breadth, depth, or angle of any of the facial proportions may be changed by painting a narrow or receding portion lighter, or shading a too broad or prominent portion darker. When a compound foundation is used these changes are made possible by graduating the blending of the colours so as to produce the desired light and shade before the more positive high lights are applied. The forehead, for example, is made to appear broader

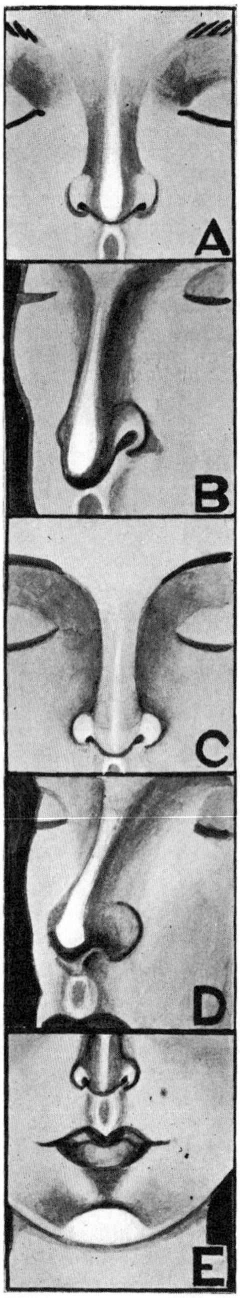

Fig. 11

by applying lighter foundation colour about and above the temples, or made to lose breadth by shading the temples and carrying the shading upwards. The depth may be increased by brushing the hair well back and blending a lighter shade with the foundation close to the hair line or decreased by shading the hair line a little darker and brushing the hair lower down the forehead. The angle of the forehead may be affected by shadowing the upper part so as to give a receding appearance, which is further accentuated by lighting the parts immediately above the eyebrows; and local bulges are brought out by appropriately placed high-lights. A forehead that recedes sharply may be corrected by lighting the receding part, but this effect is somewhat limited by the fact that the upper part of the forehead is a prominence that catches an amount of top light and appears ludicrous if it is too high-lighted. With youthful types it is always advisable to keep the forehead a tone lighter than other parts of the face, as this gives a suggestion of animation to the countenance.

The Nose may be lengthened by blending a high-light of No. 1½ or No. 5 the entire length of the ridge from the bridge down to the tip (Fig. 11a); or a more moderate length may be suggested by a somewhat shorter high-light. If this high-light is supported by shading the sides of the nose darker, the effect is greatly intensified by making the nose appear thinner. (Fig. 11b.) Similar treatment can be applied where the nose is too thick. A nose that is too long or inclined to dip down should be shaded at the tip with No. 9 or lake, as shown in Fig. 11d.

Fig. 11c shows how to increase the general size and prominence of a small nose by shading the cheeks near the nose and high-lighting the wings only, the remainder of the nose being of the foundation tint.

The effect of a Roman type of nose is given by shading the depression between the eyes to give greater depth and high-lighting the ridge to give extra prominence. To alter a high-bridged

Fig. 12

nose, shade the prominent part and leave it devoid of any high-light. A crooked nose may be made straight by applying a straight high-light down the ridge and at the hollow side, subduing the conspicuous side by a supporting shadow. A crooked nose is made by a bent line of high-light on the ridge with corresponding shadows at the sides.

If the tip of the nose turns upward, shade underneath and place a strong high-light, extending upward about one-third the length of the nose above the tip. This applied to a normal nose would make the tip appear to droop over the lip. To make a snub nose shade the ridge nearly to the tip and place a high-light just above the normal tip.

CHEEKS that are inclined to be hollow are filled out by blending a light foundation in the required area, and then by using a somewhat pale shade of rouge, which should be concentrated on the fuller parts. Increased width is given to a thin face by lightening the foundation at the sides. If the cheeks are too full, a soft shading of No. 9, or No. 9 toned a little darker with grey or brown, may be blended under the cheek bones; but it is always advisable to study the effect of shading in this position, as if it is overdone the attempted deception will be obvious. A dimple in the cheek may be suggested by a thin shadow between two small high-lights.

LIPS offer considerable scope for conveying impressions of character traits. The expression of the mouth can be altered to meet special requirements. For instance, an upward slope of the corners lends a more charming and amiable expression; a downward slope produces the opposite or a dejected expression. Small dimples of shading at the mouth corners, supported by small high-lights on the outside, express a smiling mouth.

A receding upper lip can be made to appear more prominent by running a high-light along its edge from corner to corner and then by applying the lip stick heavily beneath it. If the extreme effect is not required, the high-light may be placed so as to emphasize the cupid's bow curves and faded out half-way toward the mouth corners. If the upper lip is wide and flat the vertical indentation in the centre should be shaded with No. 9 with a central line of lake to give depth. The border of the indent is then defined by a vertical line of high light at each side from beneath the nose to the lip edge.

The lower lip can be made to appear more prominent by running a high-light upon its edge to the desired degree.

THE CHIN, if receding, may be brought forward by blending a high-light graduated so that its lightest spot suggests the point of the chin, which may be further emphasized by a shading of No. 9 or rouge immediately below and under the chin, and by another shading mid-way between the chin and the mouth (Fig. 11E). Conversely, to correct a prominent or long chin, or to produce the effect of a receding chin, the most prominent part is shaded and the surrounding parts are toned lighter (Fig. 12A).

Prominence is given to the angle of the JAWBONE by high-lighting at the point of the bone, just below the ear, and shading beneath it, as shown in Fig. 12B. If this angle is too large, put a shading on the point and a high-light to suggest the reduced angle.

CHEEK BONES that are prominent may be made less so by shadowing the point of the bone and toning up the area immediately below (Fig. 12C). Along these lines the width of the face may be varied by high-lighting the cheek bone in different relation to the nose and shadowing the outer parts (Fig. 12D).

EYES that are too deeply set may be improved by careful high-lighting. Using a shade somewhat lighter than the foundation, lighten the outer half of each eye immediately under the eyebrows, and then run a line of the same shade along the full length of the edge of the upper lid. This line brings the eyelid forward, and to be effective the usual eye colour must be placed above it: thus the eyelid will carry two colours, the high-light near the lashes, and the eye colour nearer the fold (Fig. 12E).

MAKE-UP FOR THE BODY AND LIMBS

Now I will deal with a few essentials other than those of the face, for the make-up of other uncovered parts of the body demands consideration and skill. The hands, arms, and shoulders, and in some cases the legs and feet, must be made up to supplement the facial colour and characteristics. With a straight make-up and modern dress, few parts call for attention.

Probably the hands in all cases, taking their conspicuous movements into account, are apt to be noticed and criticized if neglected. Where sleeveless, open-neck, or low-cut garments are worn, parts that are usually covered—the arms, shoulders, neck, and possibly the chest and back —will require their share of suitable colouring.

The right kind of colouring matter to apply will depend upon the required effect, the parts of the body to be made up, and whether such parts are likely to come in contact with anything that will tend to rub the colour off. Grease paint and powder, cold cream and flesh coloured powder, or the sole use of powder, with special adhesive properties, known as "Stage Powder," will suffice for remote parts, but they are not permanent enough for the hands or arms.

Women can hide the adverse effects of occupation or exposure, produce delicate, well-cared-for hands, and the appearance of smooth, unblemished skin, by applying cream paint, which is a coloured cream; cream powder, cream with a proportion of powder mixed with it; or liquid powder (professionally known as wet white), which has a glycerine and distilled water base.

Cream paint or cream powder is satisfactory for occasional applications to small parts, such as the hands or the covering of local skin blemishes, though for larger areas, such as the arms, shoulders, chest, or back, it is advisable to use wet white, as this will cover the skin evenly and will not rub off when it is in contact with clothing or stage properties.

Liquid powder in bottles is obtainable in a variety of shades that correspond with dry powder and grease paint shades, all of which are adaptable to the vagaries of complexion, colour of costume, or lighting colour scheme. There is, also, a dry block or tablet form that only requires to be wetted to make it ready for use.

If it is applied to the hands or arms, supplementary to a straight make-up, white gives a too chilly effect, and is inclined to appear patchy on a reddish skin. Therefore, for a fair or pink skin, the Natural shade will give the best results, and for a dark skin the Rachel shade. Before applying liquid powder to the hands, wash off all dirt or grease. Thoroughly mix the liquid and powder by shaking, then pour a few drops on to a small fine sponge that has been made damp with water, and apply them to the backs of the hands, over the fingers, and up the arms as far as necessary; spread the mixture evenly, yet thinly, into every crevice and crease, and then immediately pat it into the skin with a clean puff or soft handkerchief until it is quite dry. When it is perfectly dry the natural sheen of the skin may be restored by gently rubbing with the palm of the hand. Remove any trace of the powder from the finger nails, which may then be given a coat of nail polish, and, to give the impression of personal neatness to the last detail, treat with a "nail white pencil" at the exposed ends.

Take special note that it is not advisable to apply any liquid powder to the palms or between the fingers as, owing to moisture there, it will not dry thoroughly, and it is liable to rub off, with disastrous results to dark costumes or when it is brought into contact with men's clothing. Attention is drawn to the fact that all forms of liquid powder have a drying effect upon the skin and tend to block the pores. They should not, therefore, be allowed to remain on the skin longer than is absolutely necessary, but should be removed as soon as possible, the skin then being thoroughly cleansed with hot water and soap. Unless the neck, shoulders, and back have blemishes to be hidden, or the skin is of uneven colour, it is preferable to avoid any application to these parts.

Character impressions call for imagination, suggestive effects, and a different choice of materials. Soiled hands, roughened, aged, emaciated, misshapen hands and arms play an important part in character roles, such as housemaids, charwomen, decrepit old women, etc. Simple types, like country girls or workers whose hands one would expect to show signs of their occupation, should not apply liquid powder. The suggestion of reddened skin can be given by applying dry rouge in irregular patches on the backs of the hands, the knuckles, the upperside of the arms, wrist, and elbow bones. Grease paint colours may be used in the same way, but they must be powdered over to avoid smearing.

Reference may now be made to the scope of utility that is offered by artist's water colours for making-up the limbs. A few tubes of these colours help to solve many difficulties. Small quantities of suitable colour wash can be readily mixed with water, or, for preference, glycerine and rose-water can be employed as the liquid base and the necessary amount of water paint can be added. This make-up is easily applied with a sponge or brush, is more permanent than grease paint, and is removed with soap and water.

To get the effect of pale thin hands associated with illness, apply a pale shade of either grease or water paint over the backs of the hands and the forearm; then with grey paint shadow the sides of the fingers and thumb, carry the shadows over the top a little to thin them between the bones in the backs of the hands, and continue around the wrists up the back and front of the forearms to make the tendons there more pronounced. Veins of the hands and arms should be indicated with pale blue or grey; they may also be drawn over water paint or powder with a soft lead pencil.

In the case of healthy old age, the hands retain a normal tone, though they are less shapely. Shadows of Nos. 6, 8, or thin lake will give the suggestion of thin or crooked fingers and hollows, with small high lights placed on the knuckles and the ridges of the hands and wrists. Veining should incline to blue with a touch of high light at enlarged points.

For beggarly and disreputable types, lake between the fingers and brown shadows for all hollows are the most suggestive. A gnarled effect is given to the joints by broken lines of lake, supported with irregular small high lights.

Men playing sun-tanned or weather-beaten types should colour the hands, and, if required, the arms and neck, to match the face; also they should not overlook an application to the scalp if it is naturally inclined to be bald. Whenever it is necessary to have the legs exposed, a liquid wash of a colour that is suitable to depict the character or race should be applied to them. Simple washes that are inexpensive, yet serviceable, can be made from the following harmless colours, which are obtainable at most paint dealers: ARMENIA BOLE gives a fiery sun tan; YELLOW OCHRE, a dull yellow; BURNT SIENNA, a rich copper brown; VANDYCK BROWN, a dark native brown. The colours only need to be mixed with water, to which may be added a tenth part of glycerine. They can be used singly or mixed to produce almost any desired flesh tint, and can be applied with a sponge.

It is by no means a rare occurrence on the stage to see attractive features spoiled by unsightly teeth, which are apt to show with marked emphasis in the light. Obviously, dental treatment is the correct remedy, though discoloured teeth can be concealed and made to appear a desirable white by the application of *Tooth Enamel*, which is obtainable in white and ivory shades. Gold fillings or gold cased teeth may be hidden. The teeth to be treated should first be cleaned and wiped perfectly dry, then they should be painted thinly with enamel with a tiny brush, the lips being held away from the teeth for a few moments to allow the enamel to dry. The enamel may be easily removed with eau-de-Cologne or other spirit, or scraped off with the finger nail.

On the other hand, it is often an advantage to alter the appearance of sound teeth to simulate the discoloured, large, broken, or missing teeth of characters such as aged persons, witches, and a variety of low comedy parts. To "black out" portions or whole teeth paint them with black tooth enamel, which gives a permanent effect and has less unpleasant results than other methods that are sometimes employed. Black or coloured grease paint, lip-stick, or court plaster can be employed if the effect is not required to last long. To enlarge odd teeth, a small piece of gutta-percha or modelling wax can be slightly melted and pressed on to the desired shape.

THE HAIR

As an aid to character parts the need temporarily to alter the style of hair dressing or to change the colour of the hair frequently arises. Substantial alteration to the appearance can be made by parting the hair differently. Change of colour may be effected by using suitably coloured powder, grease paint, hair-cosmetic, water cosmetic, or mascaro.

There are limitations to what may be achieved by powders. Coloured hair-powder may sometimes be employed with advantage to lighten or darken slightly. So-called "fettpuder" ("fat-powder," powder impregnated with oil) will alter the colour and give brightness to dull hair.

When it is necessary to imitate grey hair, either at the temples or over the whole head, an application of white fettpuder, cornflour, liquid

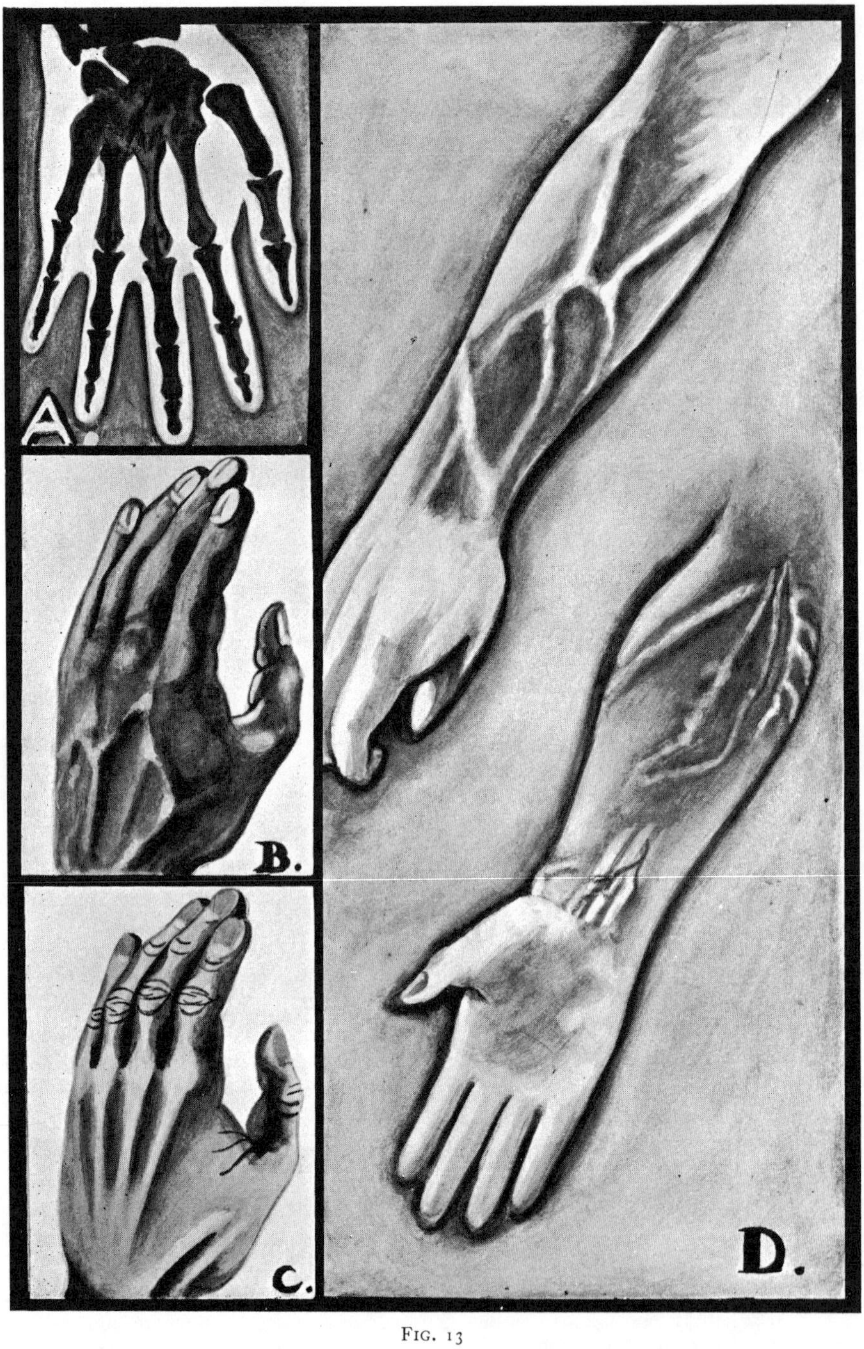

Fig. 13

A. Skeleton of the Hand
B. Veining of Aged Hand
C. Shading and Jointing of Aged Hand
D. Veining and Shading of Forearm

white, or white grease paint will serve. In many cases the use of shampoo powders for this purpose is advantageous because they are easy to clean from the scalp. Remember that there are two kinds, namely, dry shampoo powder, which only requires to be brushed out from the hair; ordinary shampoo powder, which produces a lather when wetted with hot water. Both are practically self-cleaning. Either may be applied with a powder spray or wool puff after the hair has been arranged in the required style.

Liquid white applied with a tooth brush gives a strikingly natural effect, but the hair should be free from oil or grease, otherwise it will not take the liquid. If the hair is greasy, use white grease paint instead, and apply powder over it; at the same time avoid conspicuous streaks or other artificial appearance by gently combing through the hair after the application. Where a perfectly white head of hair is essential to the character portrayal, the only really satisfactory way to obtain the desired effect is to wear a wig. The best substitute would be to give the hair a liberal application of hair fixing cream and to powder it thickly before the cream sets—a messy business to clear up.

Alternatively, grey or light coloured hair may be darkened to any extent. For greasy hair the best preparation to apply is brown or black heating cosmetic—brushed on and removed with oil or grease; for dry hair, dark brown or black mascaro water cosmetic—applied with a brush or sponge and washed off with water. The water cosmetic will give the hair a dull look, but its natural sheen can be restored by the use of a little brilliantine.

Tinsel or metallic powder in silver, bronze, gold, and a variety of other brilliant colours may be used on the hair to produce extreme effects. Aluminium powder gives a silvery brilliance, gold and bronze produce beautiful golden-blond; other colours create fairy-like and fantastic illusions. They should be used only when they are absolutely necessary because of the difficulty in removal from the head and costume.

Whatever treatment is employed to change the hair, colour must be extended to the eyebrows, and in the case of men to the moustache also, to avoid any striking variance. Slight differences are of little account, as naturally the hair on the face is usually lighter than it is on the head. When the hair has been darkened, the eyebrows should be made to match, and if these are not well proportioned they should be extended slightly in order to give increased visibility. This treatment is assisted by applying carmine or lake, which should be allowed to run over the edge slightly, and then painting the hair dark with grease paint, adding, of course, a touch of powder. Water cosmetic may be used instead of grease paint, but in this case it must be applied after powdering.

To match grey hair, first darken the eyebrows, then add streaks of liquid white or white grease paint, start on the inner side, and diminish the amount of white as the outer side is approached.

Aged eyebrows are best suggested by applying white and making them stand out or overhang by rubbing them the wrong way; to complete the aged effect the eyelashes also should be whitened.

THE PREPARATION AND USES OF CRÊPE-HAIR

Of the various arts that are supplementary to theatrical make-up, postiche—the art of the wig-maker—is of supreme importance. The addition of false hair in the shape of the wig, moustache, or beard, often alters the appearance and demeanour of an individual almost beyond recognition, and plays an important part in pageantry and historical plays. A moustache, beard, or wig, singly or in combination, can be, and often is, the deciding factor in the creation and accurate presentation of a character part; the design and colour of the hair identifies, determines, or completes the character.

Sir Cedric Hardwicke, in his introduction, relates how an old wig was the inspiration that led to the pictorial development of Churdles Ash in *The Farmer's Wife*.

Moustaches and beards are made and obtainable, in various forms, ready for fixing, the simplest combined form being constructed on a wire frame, or elastic threads, to fit over the ears for support. These, however, being most unnatural in appearance, are unsuitable for anything but slap-stick comedy. The most natural looking forms have the hair woven on to a foundation of flesh-coloured silk gauze and require to be stuck on the face with spirit gum. Though of excellent appearance, they invariably cause a feeling of stiffness about the jaws that is often detrimental to correct enunciation and freedom of facial expression.

For economy, easy application, comfort in wear, and general good service, there is nothing better for building moustaches, side whiskers,

FIG. 14

short beards, etc., than what is known as crêpe-hair, applied directly on to the face. Crêpe-hair is manufactured from coarse wool or hair of long fibre, such as mohair, horsehair, or oxhair. The hair, is scoured, combed, dyed, and mixed, then spun and plaited into the form of long ropes. The plaiting is done tightly on two strands of thin string, and has the effect of crimping the hair, which retains this crimped or crêpe impression after it is released from the binding strings. It is made in a variety of serviceable solid colours, also in a range of black-grey and brown-grey mixture shades, all of which are sold by the yard in rope form. When seen on the face at a moderate distance, crêpe-hair closely resembles human hair, whilst its easy manipulation and adaptability are a boon to the make-up artist.

Before I explain actual uses and application, it will be helpful to consider the preparation of crêpe-hair from the rope to a condition that is more suitable for shaping into moustaches and beards—a process that requires a little skill that can be acquired only with practice. To assist the preparatory process at least two spring paper clips, 2½ in. or 3 in. wide, are needed, also, for shaping and trimming, a comb and a pair of scissors, preferably the kind used by hairdressers.

Your attention is directed to Fig. 15, which is a photo of actual portions of crêpe-hair at different stages of preparation, together with a few examples of moustaches made from the same hair. Sample A is a portion of hair rope; part of the hair has been released from the plaiting strings to show its fluffy and crimped appearance.

To prepare, begin by cutting a piece of rope 6 in. long. This will provide 12 in. to 16 in. of prepared hair, according to the amount of crimp left in. Remove the plaiting strings by cutting them at short intervals to avoid damage to the hair. Now, with the finger and thumb, gently tease out the hair at one end to a width of about 2½ in., and insert this end into the jaws of one of the spring clips, taking care that all the fibres are gripped (Fig. 14). In opening out a rope it is important to get a correct start. This is best achieved by causing the crimps to side-slip (in a manner similar to opening a fan), the fibres being evenly separated. Be careful to avoid a fracture. Once the opening out is started in this way it is a fairly simple matter to separate the entire length by working away from the clip a few inches at a time, keeping the crimps horizontally straight and the fibres parallel. As soon as the opposite end is reached secure the fibre ends with another clip to prevent any of them going astray when tension is applied to reduce the excessive crimp.

At this stage the hair should have an appearance corresponding to sample B. The next step is to reduce the amount of crimp to a semblance of human hair. Either thoroughly damp the hair, stretch the two clips apart to the extent of 12 in., secure the clips to a board or table with pins, and leave overnight to dry and set, or pin the clips to the board without damping the hair, cover with a damp cloth, and with a hot iron steam the hair without applying any pressure, which would unduly flatten it.

After stretching and setting the hair the clips can be removed. The hair will then be somewhat straighter, resembling sample C, and in the best condition for shaping into any required form. It is usually best to allow a small amount of crimp

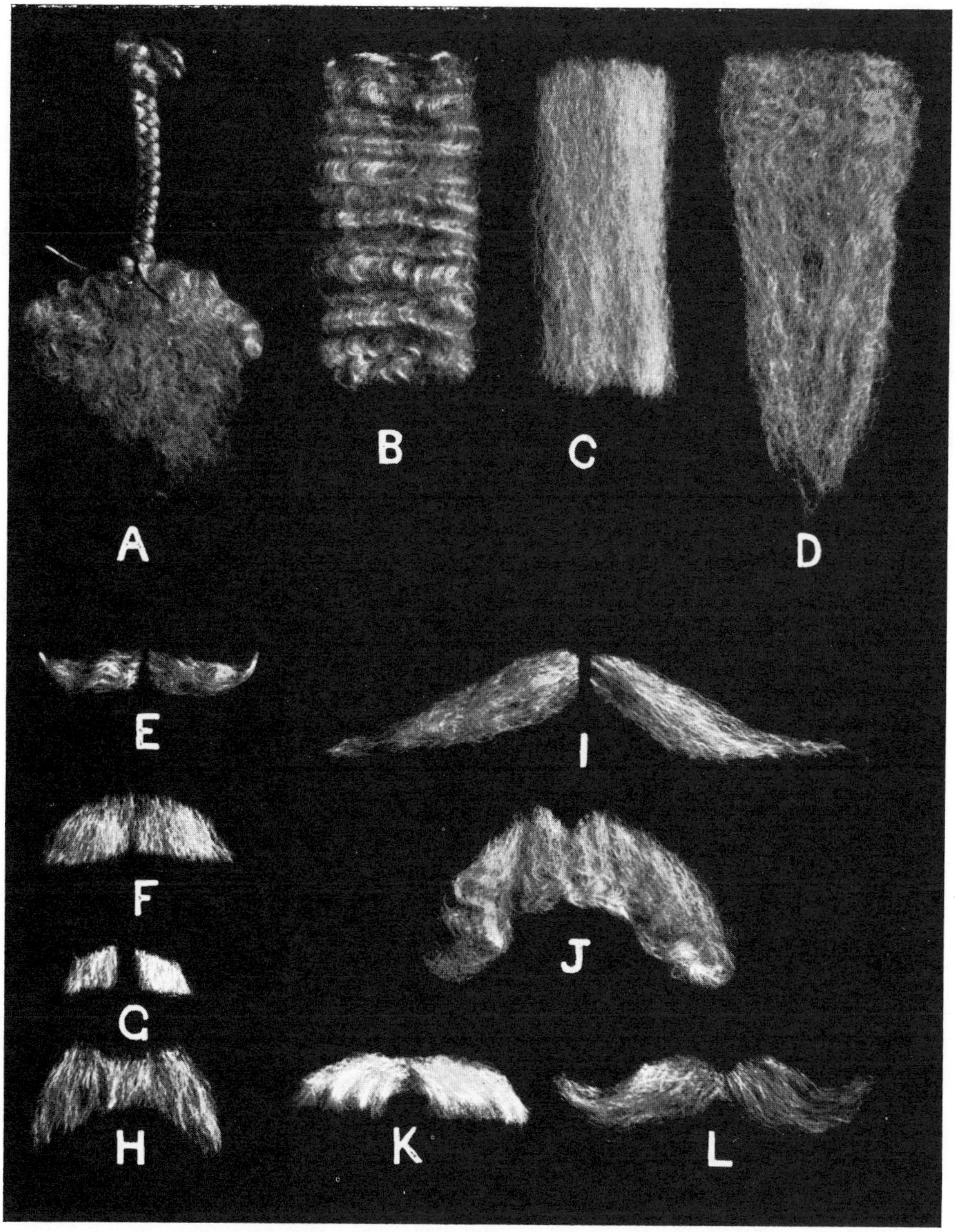

FIG. 15. CRÊPE-HAIR, FOR MAKING MOUSTACHES, BEARDS, ETC.

to remain. This has the effect of interlocking the fibres, whereas if the hair is set perfectly straight the fibres have a tendency to separate and fray when they are cut to a short length. When short portions are required, they should be pulled and broken from the prepared length, instead of cut off. This method provides a tapering end, which is often required for moustaches and pointed beards. Sample D illustrates such a broken piece, which has been teased to its noticeable fullness with a comb.

It is always advisable to anticipate the need to use hair in a make-up and to have it prepared. Guidance in the selection of shades is necessary. If a false moustache or beard is required to match the natural colour of the head, a crêpe-hair somewhat lighter than the natural hair will be needed. It must be taken into account that crêpe-hair does not reflect light to the same degree as natural hair does. Therefore, if the two match in daylight it may be surmised that the false hair will appear much darker on a well-lighted stage. Allowance should also be made for the fact that facial hair is generally lighter than that of the head, so that a false moustache or beard should actually be considerably lighter than the natural hair on the head to make sufficient allowance for these two factors. Obviously, the best place to decide on the right shade is on the stage; otherwise, judgment must be based upon the points just mentioned. If the natural hair is slightly grey, or has been made to appear so with make-up, it can be matched with a grey mixture crêpe-hair from the ranges of black-grey or brown-grey. The brown-grey shades have a fine, soft appearance and are to be preferred if the natural hair has these characteristics, whilst the black-grey is more appropriately used to suggest a strong, wiry growth. Except for dark-skinned characters, such as Negroes, Moors, and some Spanish and Jewish types, the use of black crêpe-hair should be avoided, as when it is in contrast with a pale skin the effect is altogether too bizarre. When it is desired to suggest a black moustache or beard, it is sufficient to use dark brown or reddish-brown; either will be dark enough to match jet black natural hair.

MOUSTACHES

To make a moustache the prepared hair can be used either horizontally or vertically; that is to say, the fibres may run from the centre of the lip outwards to the mouth corners (as seen at E), or run downwards from the nose to the edge of the lip (see F). Type E is made by separating a strand of suitable thickness and by breaking or cutting a strand 2½ in. long. Roll the strand between the palms to make it compact, then broaden it at the centre, and point the ends by twisting with the finger and thumb. Trim the ends off to match, and cut in two exactly at the centre to make a parting, so that a tight lip is avoided. To fix the moustache to the lip whole would result in a tight lip. It is most important that, before fixing, the two edges of the centre cutting should be thinned at the back so that the end of every fibre may be pressed into contact with the fixing gum, and thus held fast. Types of moustaches, like F, G, and H, are made by cutting a bunch of hair, an inch or more long, which is spread open evenly to the width of the lip, and then shaped with the scissors along the top edge, the lower edge being trimmed to the correct length and shape after fixing to the lip. Do not overlook the thinning of the fibres at the back of the top edge before gumming down. Too much stress cannot be laid on the point that the edge of the back layer of fibres should be cut a trifle shorter to form a chisel edge, so that the surface layer may override and adhere to the skin. This applies to all cases where raw cut edges, whether moustaches or beard, have to make contact with the skin. Adoption of this method obviates the risk of edges fraying loose or possibly the whole becoming entirely detached from the face.

Spirit gum or "fixing gum" is required for attaching crêpe-hair, or foundation moustaches, whiskers, beards, etc., to the face. Composed of resinous material dissolved in spirit, it dries rapidly and causes the hair to adhere firmly to the face, though not so tenaciously as to render the removal of the hair difficult when it is no longer required. Spirit gum may be obtained in conical metal containers with a screw stopper with a brush attached. The brush after being immersed in the gum is always ready for use. Spirit gum is also sold in small glass bottles, with or without brush. Pale spirit varnish, often used in place of spirit gum is a satisfactory and an inexpensive substitute. It should be remembered that spirit gum or varnish will not stick anything to a greasy surface. Therefore, the facial make-up must be completed and powdered, and then the parts where hair pieces are to be fixed must be wiped free from grease paint before spirit gum is applied.

To fix a moustache, for instance, the hair having been shaped to the required style in readiness, apply spirit gum to the exact parts of the lip that will be covered with the hair, and allow a few moments for the spirit to evaporate. This will cause the gum to become tacky. Then place the two sections of the moustache into position, leaving a slight triangular space in the centre between them, and press on to the gum with a damp sponge, or towel, until the gum dries and the hair is properly adhered along its full length. This will take only a few moments. Unless care is exercised during the fixing process, gum and hair may stick to the fingers and ruin a piece of good work. Therefore, keep the fingers moist and always use a damp sponge, or towel, for pressing down the hair.

Types of moustaches are so numerous and yet so personal and suggestive in their effect that adequate classification is impossible. Who has not heard of the "Kaiser" moustache, the "Old Bill," "Charlie Chaplin," or "Ronald Colman" type? Guidance is best obtained by the observation and comparison of types of natural growth in living or pictorial form. Almost any natural growth can be imitated, and imaginary types can be devised and executed in crêpe-hair, following the selection and manipulation of suitable hair pieces. Use the hair to the best advantage, and do not be niggardly with it; if a piece fails to meet the case, scrap it and start again.

Small tooth-brush and finely trimmed types present the most difficulty, though they can be produced by handling the crêpe-hair in a different way from that already described. As a preliminary, clip off a small quantity of short fibres and clean every trace of grease from the moustache area of the lip. Using brown-water cosmetic or water-colour, paint the required shape of moustache on the lip, and allow it to dry. Then paint exactly over the shape with spirit gum, and when this is almost dry dab on the chopped hair with a light hand until the shape is re-formed with hair. The result as seen by an audience is difficult to distinguish from a natural growth.

Samples *K* and *L* represent moustaches built up on a gauze foundation, shaped ready for fixing. This form is, generally speaking, the most natural looking, and may be used a number of times if it is handled with reasonable care. Cut the foundation in halves, and fix with spirit gum.

Moustaches may be represented by paint without the addition of hair, but painted moustaches are rarely satisfactory as their flatness is always obvious and their shape alters grotesquely with every movement of the lips. Painting should be confined to comedy characters or those that have a brief presence on the stage; that will be upstage, and, therefore, be seen only imperfectly and in emergency. Solid shapes of black or brown are, in any circumstance, to be avoided. To secure a reasonable semblance of hair, the desired shape is painted on the lip with black or brown grease paint, over which fine lines of lake, carmine, or reddish-brown are painted to suggest the direction of the growth. A few short streaks of high-light complete the effect, which is then powdered.

Along similar lines, natural moustaches are enlarged, altered in shape, or coloured to match the hair of the head when it has been made darker or lighter with make-up. Should a fair moustache have to be made darker, it is advisable to apply the dark shade of paint and then, to relieve the dull tone, to add a few lines of lake; also, if grey is required, the moustache should be darkened before applying white, otherwise the outline will be lost.

Difficulty arises when a natural moustache is inappropriate to the part to be played and some attempt has to be made to conceal it. No method of concealment is as efficient as to shave the moustache off, but as there is usually a reluctance to part with the adornment an alternative must be employed. A heavy and somewhat stiff type cannot be adequately hidden if there is any profile display, as the unnatural bulk of the lip betrays the attempt. A moustache of medium dimensions can be fixed down flat on the lip with a preparation known as "moustache fixer," a gummy compound made up into small sticks. It is somewhat difficult to handle, and should be used sparingly to avoid subsequent trouble when removing it from the hair. Effectually to use it a small piece should be cut off the stick, heated until it becomes soft enough to apply to the moustache, which must be flattened out as much as possible with the aid of a wet orange stick. Sufficient pressure can be applied with the orange stick to make the hairs stick down and use of it will avoid gummy fingers. When the gum is thoroughly dry, cover the gummed hair with a liberal application of the foundation grease paint and powder. As a substitute for this preparation, wet soap, wig joining paste, or spirit gum may be used, with, perhaps, only a little less satisfactory result. For a small and fine moustache, the simplest, and often the most satisfactory, way is to flatten it, before powdering, by generous use of grease paint only. This way is the least liable to result in a stiff upper lip, which, needless to say, can be most uncomfortable when a player is singing or speaking.

1. Preparing the Beard Pieces
2. Fixing the Under-chin Piece
3. The Front-chin Piece in Position.
4. After Trimming

Occasions also arise when a natural growth of short-trimmed side whiskers ("side-boards") is undesirable on the stage. These whiskers may be obliterated in a similar manner to that employed for moustaches, care being taken adequately to cover them with foundation colour and powder, and to create a definite new hair line by painting the hair above a little darker in order to emphasize the contrast.

On the other hand, if side whiskers are necessary, they may be effectively imitated by painting on with black or brown grease paint, relieved by a few lines of warm colour; or they can be made of crêpe-hair and gummed on in front of the ears extending down an inch or so from the hair. To secure a close-trimmed effect, the area to be covered should be cleaned free of grease, painted with spirit gum, which must then be dabbed over with chopped fibres of crêpe-hair. For heavier types, small pieces of hair cut to the required shape and fullness should be pressed on the gummed area, but there must be no perceptible joining with the hair owing to the contrast of colour or difference of thickness. To conceal a joining, the hair pieces should be thinned along the back of the edge to be joined and allowed slightly to overwrap the natural hair. If necessary, the joining can be still better hidden by adding touches of suitable colour so that the natural hair and the artificial merge into each other.

SHAGGY EYEBROWS

Where the need for extra heavy, shaggy, or unkempt eyebrows, has to be met, crêpe-hair can be used to supplement the natural eyebrows. These should, however, be made to suggest the required direction of the growth by brushing them, and the crêpe-hair should be gummed on with the fibres running in the same direction. For instance, if they are brushed upward and supplemented with crêpe-hair that bends to the forehead, a mild, kindly expression is given to the features; on the contrary, if they are brushed downward, with hair added to point in the direction of the eyes, the result suggests ferocity. In extreme cases, it may be necessary partially or entirely to conceal the natural eyebrows before replacing them with false ones. This is done by painting out with foundation colour or by first fixing them down with soap or "moustache fixer" before applying the grease paint and powder.

Whenever small crêpe-hair pieces are required for moustache, side whiskers, or eyebrows, it is an excellent plan to sketch on paper the exact shape in mind and then to select portions from a bulk of prepared hair that have the necessary straight, wavy, or pointed parts to execute the desired style to the best advantage. It is sometimes an advantage, when finally shaping such pieces, to trim them to the exact size before fixing them on the face, so that twin-pieces can more easily be judged to be exactly alike. In other cases, it is better to fix pieces larger than are actually required, the final shape being effected, after fixing, by trimming with sharp scissors.

HOW TO MAKE BEARDS, ETC., FROM CRÊPE-HAIR

The beard is not a mere mass of hair. It is characteristic of the individual and of nationality. Something excessive or ideal may be represented by a beard. It adds to the dignity and character of years. In fact, a beard may be made, with taste and knowledge, the most characteristic part of a make-up.

The best guidance in the selection of a style to convey any character impression is obtained by observation of living models or by reference to pictorial forms. It should be noted, however, that in a full, natural beard, the hair has a peculiarity that depends on the place from which it grows. The hair of the upper lip is more profuse, and, even in the oldest man, is of a darker hue. Again, the hair on the sides of the face grows to a greater length than that which grows from the chin, though this is more especially the character of old age.

When mounting a false beard upon the face, the manner of manipulating prepared crêpe-hair is to some extent governed by the style of beard that is required, and there is ample scope for adaptable artistry. There can be no one system of rules to work by; any method that facilitates the performance and achieves the desired result may be employed.

Fig. 16 provides an example of a typical trimmed beard and illustrates the necessary hair pieces and a well-proved method of mounting direct to the face. Refer to the example (Fig. 16). Assume that the bearded face has to be copied, and examine the details of the beard-line (the outline is over-emphasized to make its position more clear). Note how the beard joins the lower lip at its centre, then curves downward, rising again almost to the corners of the mouth. It then curves down and outward along the cheek, turns upward, and finally ascends in front of the ear to the temple. Begin with about four inches of prepared hair, of full thickness, teased out loosely. At one end open out the hair to form a cup, as shown at A. Fit this opening over the chin and pull the hair into position under the lower lip.

If this method of a single centre piece fails to provide the necessary fullness, the alternative method of using two pieces, as shown at B and C, can be adopted. The beard will then consist of four pieces. Piece B is fixed with gum under the chin as indicated by the line, the portion above the line being bent backward on to the throat. Piece C is then placed into position on the chin, with its top centre close to the lower lip and its sides extended along the jaw. The two side pieces D are added, leaving a space in front of the ears without hair. Join the pieces neatly, and trim to the correct length and shape, care being taken to avoid any bare patches of skin.

Further reference to the four photographs should prove instructive and help to clear up any doubtful points that may arise in actual practice. Note how the short length of prepared crêpe-hair is teased to approximate shape and size with the aid of a comb, and how the under-chin piece B has been placed in position and is being pressed on to the gummed surface with a damp sponge. At the same stage, one-half of the moustache has been roughly mounted. In No. 3 the moustache is seen completed and the front-chin piece C mounted in position before the final trimming. Finally, the combined result of beard, moustache, and eyebrows, reinforced with small pieces of crêpe-hair, is shown.

Beards should always be mounted after the grease paint and powder make-up has been definitely completed, although some margin of the beard area may be left untouched with grease.

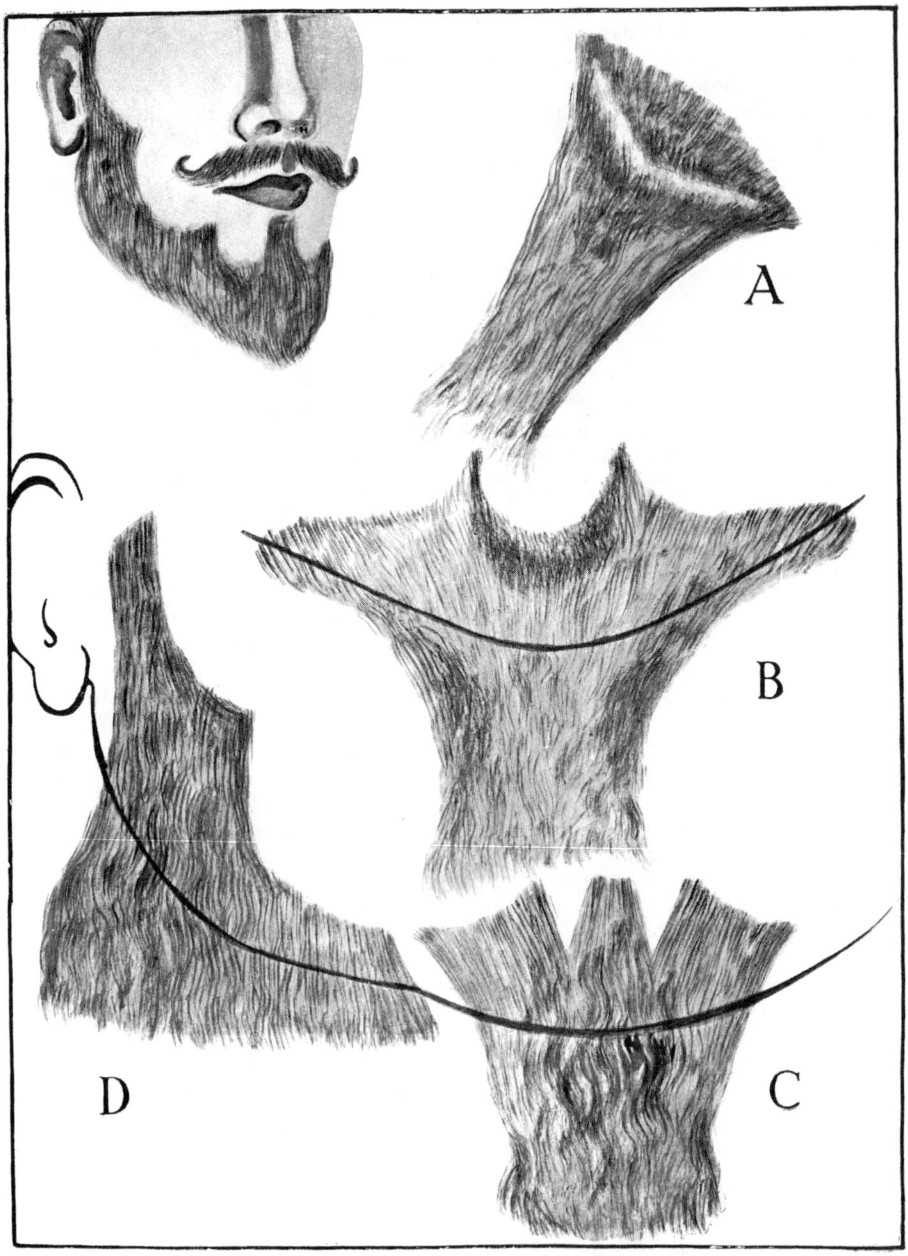

Fig. 16. Mounting a Three or Four Piece Beard

But it should be considered a rule that wherever spirit gum has to be applied the skin should be thoroughly cleaned free of paint; otherwise, the mounting will not be a success. When the hair selected is of a dark colour and the unpainted part of the face is naturally pale, it is advisable to darken the skin with a thin wash of either water-cosmetic or water-colour in order that the whiteness beneath the mounted beard will not shine through by reflecting light from the "foots." Unlike grease, water-colour does not retard the sticking properties of spirit gum.

FOUNDATION BEARDS, ETC.

Although prepared crêpe-hair may be effectively used for close trimmed and short beards in general, it is not advisable to attempt to make long beards from it. Owing to its fineness, crêpe-hair is not sufficiently strong and resilient to be self-supporting. Therefore, a long beard will refract from its natural forward angle and swing with every movement of the jaw. It should be borne in mind that expression in speech results very much from the modulation of the lower lip; and that the rising and falling of the jaw, more especially in singing, add to the motion. I have seen a production in which a player in a serious rôle made the audience laugh because of a patriarchal type of beard, made up of white crêpe-hair, which sagged from the chin to rise and fall in rhythm with the spoken words.

Even for beards of moderate length, that is to say, not more than six inches long, it is an advantage to apply a stiffening agent during the preparation of the hair. Non-greasy hair fixing cream, a mucilage of gum tragacanth or gum arabic, gives the hair a more natural degree of rigidity.

To impregnate the hair a small quantity of cream should be smeared on the palms of the hands and the prepared switch of hair pressed between them. The fibres, whilst in a damp condition, should be separated by combing, and should be allowed to dry; the hair will then be substantially stronger. It is essential that the hair should be combed before drying, otherwise, the fibres will stick together.

When a beard of moderate length is mounted, it is advisable to make the under-chin piece from the strongest hair, as, by so doing, this piece will form a more rigid support for the front and side pieces, and, also, maintain the natural beard angle. Whatever type of beard is worn the naturally correct angle in relation to the face should be aimed at. Judgment will be assisted by obtaining a profile view in the mirror. If the beard is set too far back, the footlights will play on its surface and cause it to appear even still farther back; if it is set too forward the footlights will cast a heavy shadow of it on to the face.

A common fault in mounting crêpe-hair pieces is to leave the edges standing off the face. To avoid this and to produce a naturally thinner hair line between the beard and the face, such edges should be thinned at the back in order to allow surface fibres to make proper contact with the gummed surface of the skin, and pressed flat to the face with a damp sponge. At the same time make certain that the beard area is perfectly free from grease. The edges can be touched up and made to appear thinner by painting fine lines with brown or grey, or with a soft pencil, to suggest the roots of hairs a little beyond the actual hair. Also, to facilitate the binding together of adjacent edges, as, for example, the points of an under-chin and a front piece, a few touches of spirit gum, or fixing cream, may be placed between the two pieces, and the fibres nearest the edges may be made to intermingle by manipulation with the fingers or a comb.

For a curly-haired beard of the negro type, the usual method of preparing crêpe-hair may be modified. In this case, use the hair direct from the rope in its crimped form, tease, and intersperse the fibres into an evenly felted mass, then mount on the face in as large pieces as are practicable, and trim to the desired shape. The best results are obtained by a liberal application of hair, no matter how closely it is trimmed later.

A shaggy, matted, or unkempt appearance can be given to a beard by applying fixing cream, and then deranging and sticking the hair together in appropriate parts.

To suggest stubble or a few days' growth of beard, apply spirit gum over the beard and moustache area, and evenly cover the gummed parts with finely cut hair. This method may be employed over the grease-paint foundation, which must be well powdered before applying the gum.

The best method of removing crêpe-hair moustaches and beards that have been stuck on with spirit gum can now be explained. It is often worth while to preserve for subsequent use hair pieces that have taken time and patience in the making. They should be pulled as gently as possible from the face in order to retain their shape. Cold cream or cocoa-butter is quite effective for counteracting the sticking properties of the gum, and should be well rubbed into the parts where spirit gum has been used, after as much hair as possible has been removed. When the gum is particularly obdurate it may be necessary to apply a little spirit. A small piece of cotton wool saturated with surgical spirit, or methylated spirit, and rubbed on the gummed parts will immediately remove the gum and clean the skin. Spirit is useful to kill grease and to prepare the skin for the application of spirit gum before mounting a moustache or beard; also, there is nothing better for softening and cleaning the gauze foundations of moustaches and beards that have been used a few times and become hard with old gum.

Fig. 17. The Writer as "King Lear"
Bradford Shakespearean Society

For a bushy or long beard it is in all cases preferable to obtain one that has the hair woven or knotted on a permanent foundation of net or gauze, trimmed and dressed ready for fixing. These types of beards can, of course, be obtained from theatrical costumiers and wig makers. The use of foundation hair pieces, whether moustache, beard, or side whiskers, has many advantages; they achieve the most lifelike appearance that can be secured, are easily affixed, and can be used a considerable number of times if reasonable care is taken in removing them.

The best results are obtained when ready-made hair pieces are affixed after other stages of the make-up have been completed and powdered.

When a player is fixing a beard, he should first temporarily place in position on the face the piece or pieces. The exact outline of the foundation edges should be indicated with a pencil mark. This will serve as a guide when the spirit

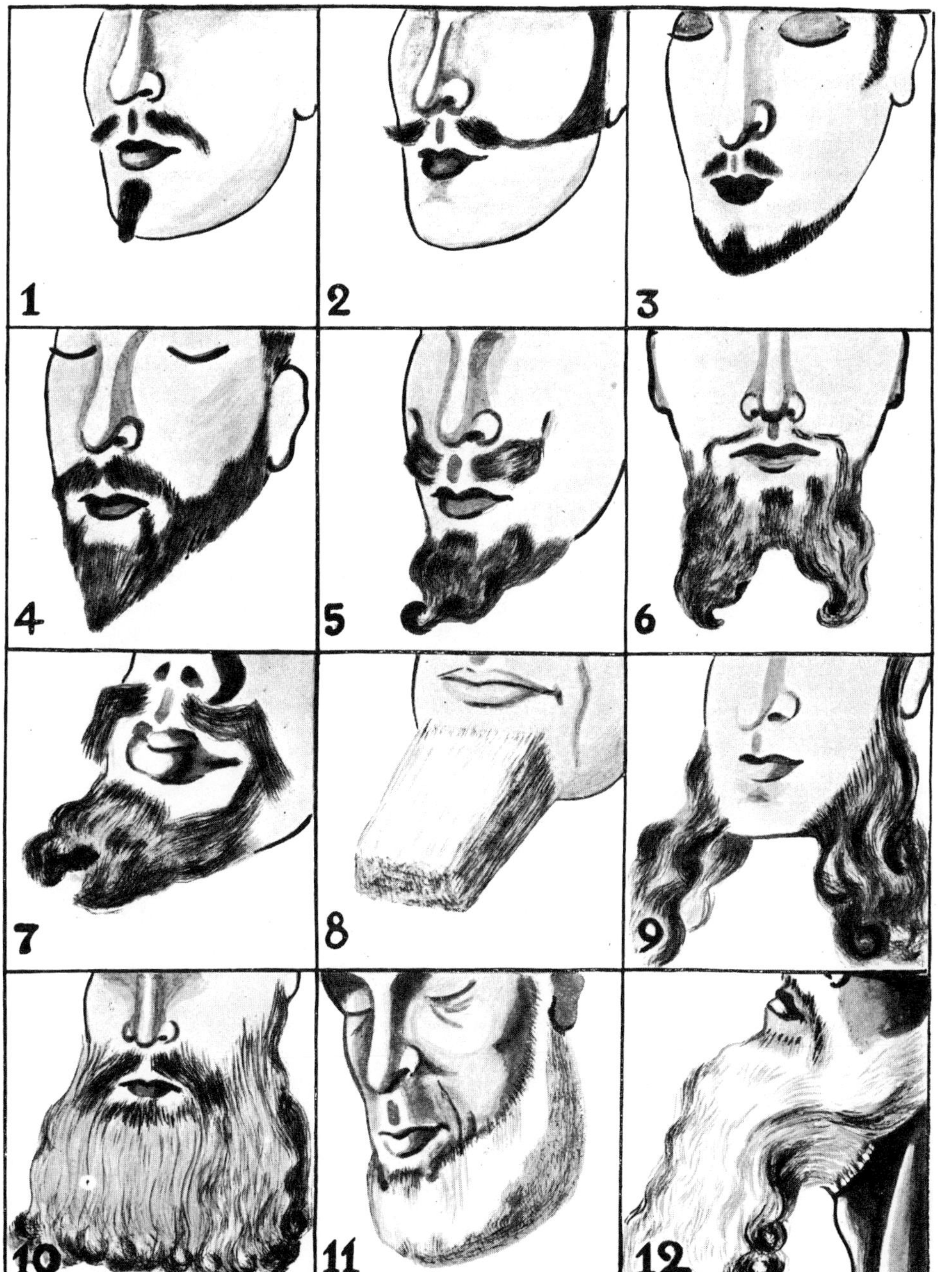

FIG. 18. CHARACTERISTIC TYPES OF BEARDS

gum is applied. All grease should be cleaned from the area with spirit, then the gum should be applied and allowed to dry before the beard is placed, otherwise the gauze will become saturated with gum and dry too hard. When once gauze foundations become boardy, subsequent fixing is more difficult, though they can generally be restored to a pliable condition by a thorough cleaning with spirit. When finally placing the beard give foremost attention to the dip which allows the chin to sink into the foundation to ensure that it sits snugly and in a central position on the chin. Also make sure that the angle is correct. Once the chin portion is properly fitted it is a relatively simple matter to fix the sides. A slight space should be left in front of the ears; then the sides should be pressed and held in position with a damp sponge until they have properly adhered. Take care that foundation edges, both above and under the chin, are firmly gummed down, for often a small gap left unstuck will cause an edge to rip from the face to a considerable extent when the jaw is moved. It is probable that the edges of the beard, especially those on the cheek, will present unnatural and hard lines that will need to be softened. Softening can be done by marking short lines on the face along the line of the edges with a soft lead pencil or with water colour. Another method is to paint along the edge with spirit gum and to dab over with short cuttings of crêpe-hair.

Heavy foundation beards are sometimes equipped with tapes at the top. These are intended to be tied over the head in order to give additional support, and to relieve the drag on the skin that would result if the beard was only gummed on. Obviously, tapes can be employed only when a wig is worn in conjunction with the beard. When they cannot be entirely dispensed with, avoid tying them too tightly, or they may cause pain on the scalp when pressure is increased by movement of the jaw or head.

As a safeguard it is best to remove the tapes and to substitute a piece of elastic about half an inch wide.

Fig. 17 illustrates the combined use of foundation hair pieces and wig.

Fig. 18 provides a few adaptable ideas for characteristic types of beards.

WIGS, TRANSFORMATIONS, ETC.

In many historical plays, Court scenes, and character parts, a wig becomes a necessary and an indispensable part of make-up; in fact, in all cases where a definite change of hair colour, a characteristic style of hairdressing, or the creation of an abnormal type of head, is desired, a wig designed to convey the correct impression must be employed. Wigs of all descriptions—national and period types, Court periwigs and perukes, legal, modern types of full growth or any degree of baldness, eccentric and fantastic character types—are obtainable to meet every conceivable demand.

According to style, wigs are usually made on two main principles. As moderate skill is called for in adjusting a wig so that it will remain unmoved on the head under reasonable stage conditions, consideration of these principles will be helpful.

The simpler styles are those that provide a full head of hair the front part of which forms a fringe over the forehead. The hair is knotted on a cap-shaped foundation of net or calico; and the wig is held in position on the head by spring grips, attached to the foundation at the temples, and a band of elastic at the nape of the neck. This style of wig should not be put on and adjusted until after the face has been made up and powdered, and the natural hair brushed back so that it is completely hidden beneath the wig. The correct way to adjust a wig is to hold the back edge with both hands, to place the front edge in position on the forehead, and then carefully to envelop the head by pulling the elastic band down on to the neck. Should a wig fail to hide completely the natural hair at the temples, behind the ears, or on the neck, so that a contrast in colour is noticeable, the hair will require to be painted to match the wig.

Wigs made on the second and more general principle have, at the front, a flesh tinted silk fabric band, which fits across the forehead to give better security, a closer fit, and a far more natural appearance. Wigs of this type are known as "blender" wigs, probably because it is necessary to blend the forehead band with the complexion make-up so that the edge of the band is not apparent.

Effectually to conceal the join a wig having a

well-fitting blending band is essential. The least slackness will cause the band to lift from the forehead and to break the join. If the band is too tight a roll of flesh will appear whenever the brow is moved. In order to obviate trouble arising from either of these faults it is necessary, in the first place, to supply the wigmaker with accurate head measurements. Secondly, the wig should be tried on in time to remedy any misfit. Should the wig be too large, a centre tuck, or two side tucks, inserted in the foundation at the back will generally give a better fit. The forehead band can be tightened by making small tucks at the temples, exactly at the point where the hair begins. Although, when sending out wigs wigmakers generally supply them too large rather than too small, sometimes a wig is too small. If it cannot be adequately enlarged by removing the elastic grip at the back, a larger wig should be obtained.

Joining-paste (sometimes named wig-paste) is required to fix the blending band to the skin and to hide the edge of the join. This preparation is similar in appearance to grease paint, but is less greasy and possesses adhesive qualities. It is made in different flesh tints, and sold in sticks bearing either its name or Nos. 17, 18, or 19.

A blender-wig is fitted to the head by holding it at the back and adjusting the forehead band to a correct position about the middle of the forehead, the side grips being in line with the front of the ears. Although it is not advisable to put the wig on before making up the face, it is necessary that it should be fitted before the make-up of the forehead is completed, so that the band may be blended with the foundation. The best results are achieved when the operations take the following order. First try on the wig, mark the position of the blending band edge, and then remove the wig. Apply the face make-up, carrying the foundation on the forehead a trifle beyond the limit that will be covered by the wig band, then powder all parts except the forehead. Next, apply a fairly thick coating of joining-paste along the forehead where the join line will fall, adjust the wig, and press flat the joining band so that its edge is fastened with the paste.

Do not pull the wig down too tightly or it may contract the tension, or slip with subsequent movements of the head and spoil a satisfactory joining. To avoid this relieve the tension by bending the neck backwards and raising the brows, before finally making the surface joining.

Now, spread a coating of joining-paste along the edge of the band and smooth out the band until the joining of the fabric and skin is completely hidden, using, perhaps, a touch of grease to avoid the paste sticking to the fingers. Cover the paste joint with foundation grease paint, and carry it up to the hair-line of the wig. The same foundation colour as that used on the skin may appear to be darker on the blender; therefore, the latter should be a trifle paler than the face. The application of powder over the whole forehead will complete the obliteration to perfection.

In extreme cases, where the joining band persists in remaining off the forehead, more drastic measures may be employed. Spirit gum will, of course, fix a band securely, though it should be used sparingly at the temples and allowed to become almost dry before the band is pressed to it. Then saturation and hardness of the fabric of the wig will be avoided. When the wig has been correctly adjusted, a more lifelike appearance may be given to the hair by applying a few touches of brilliantine, and then combing or brushing it after the manner of natural hair. Always remove the wig from the back and turn inside out to prevent a soiled and disarranged condition of the hair.

TOUPEES

The toupee, or toupet, is an ingenious form of semi-wig that is designed more especially for men in order to cover baldness on the top of the head (see Fig. 19 (3)). It is so constructed that the false hair blends with the natural hair, and for this reason the hair of the toupee must match exactly the colour of the natural hair. Naturalness in appearance and lightness in wear are primary features. Moreover, the position of a toupee can be adjusted in several ways to produce dissimilar effects in style of hairdressing. Places are provided on the foundation for the application of an adhesive to hold the toupee securely in position, suitable fixatives being joining-paste or spirit gum.

HAIR PIECE FOR WOMEN

Although, generally speaking, women have not to use wigs to the same extent as men, there will

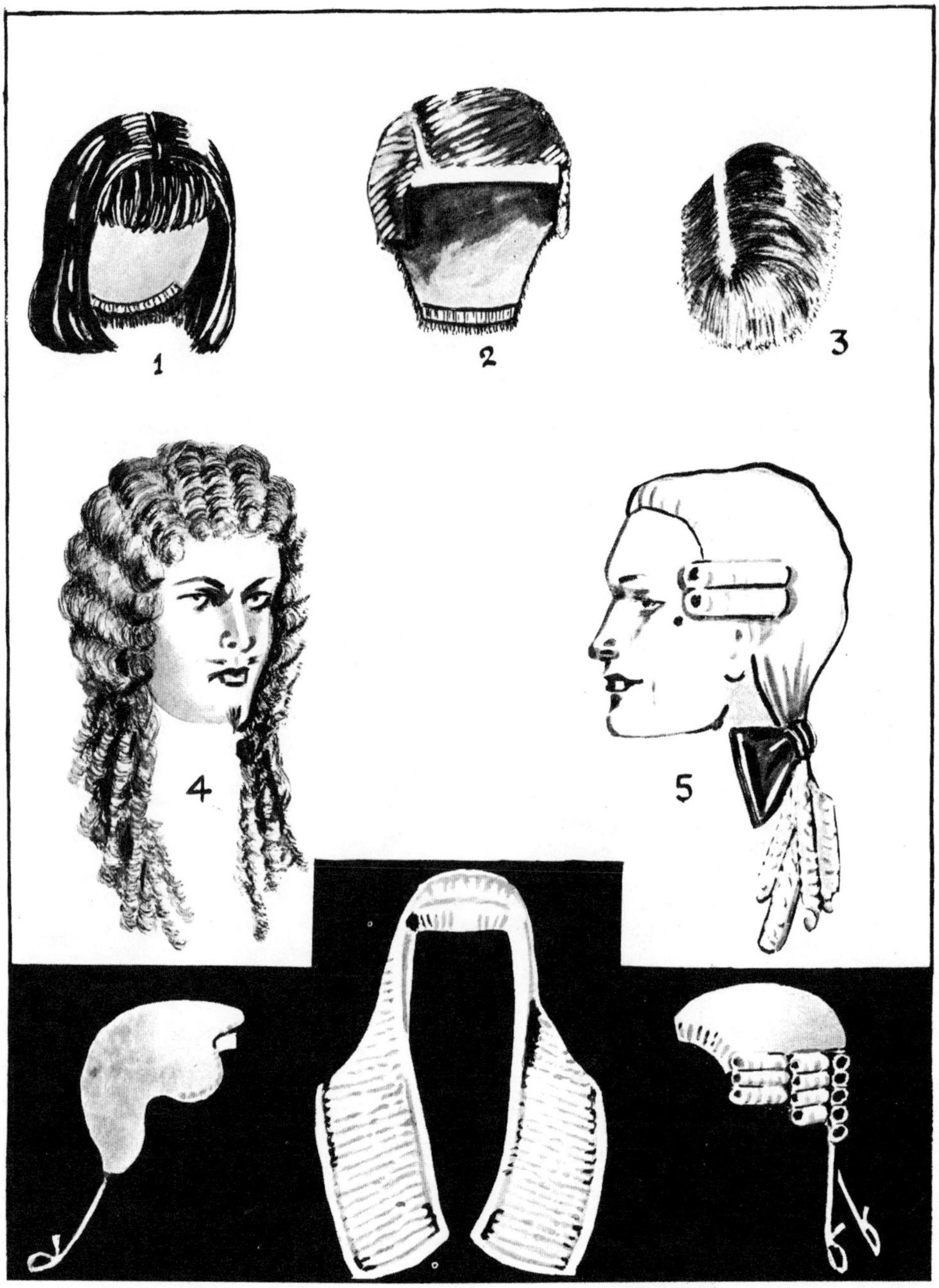

FIG. 19. WIGS FOR MEN

1 Open type of wig
2 Blender type of wig
3. Toupee or toupet
4. A periwig
5. A peruke
Legal types: Bench, Court, Bar

FIG. 20. HAIR PIECES AND WIGS FOR WOMEN

1. A bandeau or frontlet
2. A group of pin-curls
3. Pin waves
4. A simple chignon
5. Long plaits
6. A Court style coiffure
7. A transformation. Blending with natural hair

always be occasions when natural deficiencies of colour, length, or other characteristic will call for supplementary aid to effect a necessary change. Apart from Court wigs, periods, and modern "aged" types (cases which, obviously, necessitate the wearing of a wig) there is a more frequent need to make less elaborate change of hairdressing, mainly in regard to fringes, curls or ringlets, coils or bobs, which are not generally found on bobbed or shingled heads. Many effective changes to the appearance can be made by the use of simple hair pieces that are constructed from crêpe-hair, prepared in the method previously described, or purchased ready made.

Fig. 20 illustrates a few extremely adaptable forms that will solve many hairdressing problems. No. 1 is a waved bandeau, or frontlet, which is useful to add to the front of existing waves.

Pin-curls and waves may be used as side pieces to be worn in front of the ears and against the cheeks; as fringe pieces they are worn on the forehead so as to fall in an attractive manner over the eyes (see 2, 3, and 6).

The chignon is worn on that part of the head between the crown and the nape of the neck; therefore, it is a valuable aid in concealing a shingled head. No. 4 gives a general suggestion, which may be adapted to curls, rolls, or bobs.

The transformation is one of the most popular of heavy forms of postiche. The principle of the construction of a transformation is that the inner part, or crown of the wig, is absent, an outer rim foundation providing the necessary support of the hair. Thus the full effect of a wig, without the discomfort that may be caused by wearing it, is obtained.

LIGHT AND COLOUR IN RELATION TO MAKE-UP

It is well known that daylight reveals things in a manner that cannot be reproduced by any known form of artificial light; the artificial light that will not destroy natural colour remains to be discovered. We must, therefore, be prepared to use judgment that is based upon sound knowledge of the relation of light and colour in order to determine the effect that intensity, direction, and colour of stage lighting will have on any scheme of make-up that is employed.

Many theories of light and colour phenomena have been advanced from time to time by eminent artists and scientists, but there has been much disagreement, into which we need not enter. It will suffice if we confine our inquiry to what is generally acceptable from our point of view.

Light is the physical cause of our sensation of sight. This is proved by the fact that objects are invisible when they are not illuminated by natural or artificial means. The flame of a match can be the origin of some stimulus, to which the name of light is given, which is essential to vision. The great majority of objects themselves emit no light, and are, therefore, known as non-luminous; but some, as, for instance, the sun, have the property of emitting light, and are, therefore, known as luminous. Luminous objects, such as the sun, a lamp, gas flame, electric light, etc., are visible because of their own luminosity, which consists of a number of luminous points from each of which rays of light proceed in divergent directions. Some of these rays reach the eye of an observer and produce vision.

Non-luminous objects are visible only because of the property they have of reflecting and diffusing the light that falls on them from luminous objects. Thus, an object becomes visible by the light that it reflects to the eye of an observer, while its degree of visibility and definition is determined by the nature and size of the reflecting parts, the amount of light falling upon it, and its distance from the eye.

Light-emitting objects appear to increase in size as they increase in brightness. For instance, the sun appears larger when it is shining brightly than when its rays are partially obscured; also, there is an apparent increase in the thickness of an electric filament when its brightness is increased. This is accounted for by the irradiation of the luminous rays, and is, also, common to some degree in objects that only reflect light. Consequently, a bright object, other things being equal, will always appear larger than a dark object of the same size.

It is generally accepted that white light, which is considered as pure light, is composed of all the colours that are found naturally or are made artificially, and can be decomposed into its constituent coloured rays, or its several colours can be recombined into a beam of white light. If a beam of white light is allowed to pass through a glass prism, the light is refracted, or bent and separated into coloured rays, which, when allowed to fall on a screen in a darkened room, produce a beautiful band of colour. This is known as the solar spectrum, and contains every gradation of pure colour in which can easily be recognized the six principal colours—red, orange, yellow, green, blue, and violet.

The difference of colour is due to the different rates of vibration, and, therefore, different wave lengths of the various rays. As we follow the colours from red to violet, the process is similar to playing an octave of music, for colour is to light what pitch is to sound. Red is represented by a low note, violet by a high note.

We have seen how what is known as refraction produces colour by splitting up white light; but the colour of objects we are accustomed to seeing is the result of reflection, as practically all the colour in the world is produced by reflection of light. It should be remembered that colour does not exist in and by itself, but is simply a matter of sensation, that is, an impression produced on the optic nerves of the eye by the nature of the rays of light returned from an object by reflection. In other words, colour arises from the treatment, on the part of an object, of the light that falls upon it.

What we term the natural colours of objects are mainly due to the fact that they return to the eye only certain definite colours out of those that are combined in a beam of white light. Non-luminous objects have the power of extinguishing, or absorbing, the light that enters them. This power is also selective, that is to say, the objects absorb some of the colour rays and reflect others; thus the colour of an object is due to light that it does not absorb, and is returned to the eye. For example, when the light that enters an object is wholly absorbed, the object is black; an object that absorbs all the waves equally, but not totally, is grey; an object that absorbs the various waves unequally is coloured; and if an object can return to the eye all the colours in the same proportions as they exist in white light, it is white. Thus an object that appears to be red under white light is one that has selected the red wavelengths of the light to reflect and absorbed all others.

It should be noted that objects of all colours, illuminated by white light, reflect white light from their exterior surfaces. It is the light which has plunged to a certain depth below the surface, which has been sifted there by selective absorption and then discharged from the object by interior reflection, which, in general, gives the object its colour. Thus a red object selects only red rays to reflect, and, therefore, appears red to the eye.

But the colour of an object also depends upon the nature of the light that falls upon it, because if rays of the colour that it is best fitted to return to the eye are absent, or few in number, the colour will be dim and unsatisfactory. It is a familiar fact that it is impossible to judge the true value of colours when they are seen in artificial light. The reason for this is that they are exposed to light that is lacking in certain rays, and the objects are, therefore, unable to reflect all the colours that would be reflected under normal conditions.

A coloured light is a light that is incomplete; that is to say, it is lacking in one or more of the colours that constitute white light. For instance, if we perceive a red light, it is to be supposed that the other principal colours (blue and yellow) which, combined with red, produce white light, have been subtracted from the white light, and that red is all that remains. Similarly, if a green light is visible, we may conclude that the red rays, from some cause, have been withheld. In other words, whatever colour is visible is a result of its complementary colour being subtracted from pure white light.

It is not to be supposed that colour is a quality that a substance retains under all conditions. If such were the case, an object, for instance, painted green would always remain green, even when exposed to other than white light. We have seen that it can appear green only when green is contained in the light to which it is exposed. The paint serves simply the purpose of absorbing all but the green rays, which are reflected. This can easily be proved if it is exposed to red light. In this case the object will be unable to send out green rays because none has been received, and it will, therefore, appear black.

From what has been stated about the nature of

light, it follows that all artificial colouring processes are simply the production of such a condition on or within the surface of an object that it will reflect or return certain luminous wavelengths—a colour—to the eye and suppress or absorb others. The best method of producing

FIG. 21. FLORENCE GREGSON

these artificial colours upon different surfaces constitutes the art of the painter, the dyer, and the chemist; in fact, all who seek the connexion between the constitution and optical properties of natural and chemical compounds. Such compounds or colouring materials, usually termed "pigments," include dry, earthy substances such as ochre; vegetable, such as indigo and logwood; or animal, such as cochineal; or artificial, which are the products of chemical synthesis. These pigments are made as similar to the spectrum colours as possible, but it is impossible to manufacture a pigment so pure that it will match exactly a spectrum colour.

The pigment theory of colour is based on the assumption that there are three primary colours—red, yellow, and blue—which are independent and separate pigments, differing widely from each other.

MAKE-UP FOR MIDDLE AGE

Between the accomplishment of ordinary "straight" make-up and what may be considered essentially "character" studies, there lies a province of characterization that presents many difficulties to the inexperienced. I refer to the numerous cases that arise where it is necessary for a young player to convey the appearance of increased age. It is by no means easy to get the effect of age upon a youthful face by a few lines and touches of grease paint; and it must not be assumed that age is merely a matter of lines and wrinkles, although, of course, it is much expressed by them.

It is not old age that presents the most difficulties, as in such cases much of the effect can be achieved with the aid of false hair, etc. Actually, the most elusive period to portray is that between thirty and fifty years of age, for changes then are subtle to perceive and still more subtle to simulate. We arrive at a better understanding of how to deal with these cases when we inquire into the gradual changes that take place from youth to advanced age with regard to colour of complexion, form, and expression of features.

Normally, though subject to modification as the result of inheritance, climatic or social environment, and personal habits, change takes place in the colour of the skin. It changes from the rosy tint of youth to become darker and more ruddy during the years of prime age, and fades to a parchment-like sallowness in extreme old age. The soft and velvet texture of the skin gives place to coarseness and wrinkles. There is, also, a diminishing of colour, lustre, and fullness of the eyes, accompanied, in the majority of cases, by evidence of greying and falling of the hair.

The principal changes in form from youth to adulthood are in the shape of the face and the greater prominence of the features that follows expansion of the bones of the face. The face of the adult is lengthened, and a prominent ridge is developed along the course of the eyebrows. Several new characters are given to the countenance by the enlargement of the upper jaw-bone. This has the effect of raising and lengthening the bones of the nose, and of making the cheek-bones project farther. Another effect is to make the angle of the lower jaw recede more towards the ear, and to acquire *more distinctness*.

The form of the face and the feature is only the groundwork of expression. By the habit of expression the countenance is improved or degraded, and the characters of virtue or vice are imprinted.

Everyone is familiar with descriptions of faces such as "What a good face!" "What a wicked face!" "That is an intelligent face!" Without words the face expresses kindness or cruelty, joy or grief, love or hatred, hope or fear, every desire and every emotion—all the multiform life that issues from the brain to dominate and mould the features. In the face we find assembled all the organs of the five senses; nerves sufficiently delicate, and mobile muscles to form one of the most expressive pictures of human nature.

From the foregoing remarks it will be realized that a girl or young woman who is cast for a middle-aged part will find it necessary to age her face by making subtle changes. Character type requires first consideration. If the type to be portrayed is that of a society woman, it may be assumed that she will have retained much of her beauty. The foundation should be a compound of Nos. 5 and 3½ or 9, and the rouge on the cheeks of Carmine 2 or 3, placed not quite so near the eyes as in a straight make-up, thus taking away some of their brilliance, and suggesting a droop in the cheeks. To give the eyes a deeper inset, a rather strong shadow of reddish-grey is placed in the sockets between the eyes and nose, and faded away at the outer corners of the eyebrows. The temples may be shaded, the shading extending down in front of the ears, and also appearing in the hollow between the mouth and chin.

Particular attention is drawn to Figs. 21 and 22, which provide a typical example of how the subtle changes under consideration have been successfully achieved with a minimum of material skilfully applied. Analysed, the type is of a working-class woman, the general expression conveying an impression of a dominating, masterful temperament. Note the accurate shadows in the eye sockets, from the eye corners to the cheek-bones, and the light and shade of the nose and chin. The hair, by its style and suggestion of approaching greyness, is of marked importance.

A STUDY OF FACIAL EXPRESSION

It may not be found easy to reconcile two subjects—probably far apart in the minds of most readers—such as make-up and anatomy of the face, but if the tell-tale facial evidence of character traits is to be understood, it is certain that there is no study more fruitful of instruction,

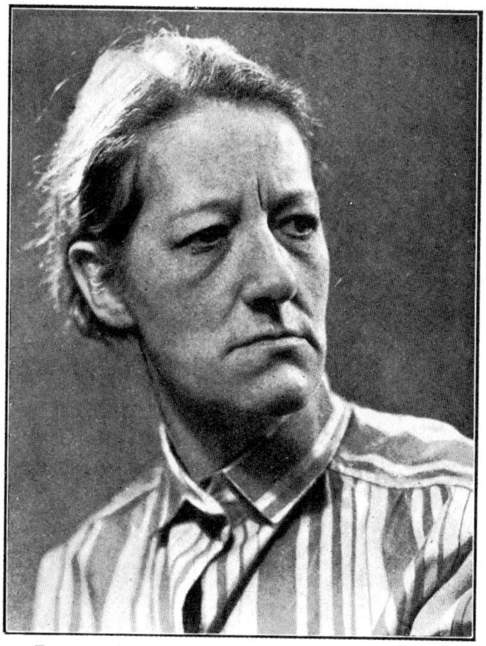

FIG. 22. FLORENCE GREGSON AS MRS. OAKROYD IN "THE GOOD COMPANIONS"

Reproduced by permission of Gaumont British Corporation, Ltd.

or leading to more interesting subjects of inquiry, than that of the structure of the face as the immediate source of expression. By anatomy in its relation to the art of make-up is meant not merely the study of the bones and muscles of the face, but the observation of all the characteristics that distinguish the countenance and constitute form and expression. A knowledge of the subtle changes that take place from youth to age; of the evidence of robust health or sickness; of the peculiarities that are associated with occupation; of the sentiments that prevail in the expression of a face in repose, belongs to this special province as much as does the study of the face when it is affected by emotion. There is as much variety in expression of countenance as in colour, feature, hair, beard, etc.

Viewed in this comprehensive light, anatomy forms a science of great interest, and one that stimulates careful observation, and teaches us to distinguish what is essential to exact expression, that directs attention to appearances on which the effect and force of character delineations depend. Despite the fact that much valuable information on this subject is available, it is neglected and, consequently, character make-up is arrived at by a process of guessing. There is in actuality failure among numerous players who make-up themselves to achieve the characteristics that are necessary to add to the effect of costume and the spoken word. Therefore, there is good reason for emphasizing the importance of a knowledge of the subject. A knowledge of physiognomy, but chiefly a familiar acquaintance with the facial muscles and the peculiarities and effect of their action, is necessary to correct this fault. In the limbs and body, the muscles possessing the power of contraction, and, consequently, of producing motion, are attached to the bones and are distinct and powerful; but as in the face they have merely to operate on the skin, the lips, nostrils, and eyelids, they require less power, and are, therefore, more delicate. This power is not always directly under the control of the will; it is often involuntary, and is inseparably united to the conditions of the mind. When a facial muscle contracts it moves the skin and produces folds, or wrinkles, in the moved skin, which run perpendicularly to the direction of the muscular fibres. Frequently repeated contractions of any one muscle tend to leave their permanent impress upon the countenance. Thus the very spirit by which the body is animated is revealed; the sad gradually acquire the prevailing depressed look of sadness, and the joyous the corresponding permanent smiling look of joyousness. Such expressions constitute a universal language that is understood before a word cheerful or otherwise is spoken, or any indication in the movement of the features of what prevails in the mind is given. By learning the action and the purpose for the action of the facial muscles it is possible to estimate fairly accurately the meaning of the presence of certain wrinkles on the face.

At this stage a few examples, illustrated by the three faces at the top of Fig. 23, will suffice. These show an easy way of learning facial expression. It is based on the teaching of Superville, who uses simple wrinkle lines to express changes of emotion.

1. Horizontal lines suggest calmness, serenity, and nobility. Such lines in architecture convey the idea of calmness and grandeur, which he compares to the cedar tree with its horizontal branches. The straight lines of the eye, the nose, and the mouth in the serene, unruffled countenance, suggest the best human sentiments.

2. Lines directed obliquely upwards and outwards express gaiety, laughter, and lightness as in Chinese architecture. These oblique lines of joy are produced by drawing up the corners of the mouth, as seen in the optimist's expression. This pushes up the cheeks, which in turn push up the outer corners of the eyes, and produce the characteristic crow's-feet of laughter just below the outer corners of the eyes.

3. Lines directed obliquely downwards and outwards reflect sadness, grief, and pain, which Superville likens to the architecture and kind of trees that are usually seen in cemeteries. These lines are produced by drawing down the corners of the mouth, as seen in the pessimist's expression. Wrinkles also develop naturally as the skin loses its elasticity and the flesh shrinks with age. The necessary lining and light and shade to depict a few stages of the change are also shown.

CLASSIFICATION OF COLOURS

All colours may be divided into two groups; namely, simple, or primary, colours, and compound colours.

Simple colours are those that cannot be split up into other colours. In other words, they are fundamental colours, the term being practically synonymous with primary colours; in the pigment theory red, yellow, and blue are included.

Compound colours are those that are obtained by mixing two colours. There are two important groups of compound colours, namely, secondary and tertiary colours.

Secondary colours are produced by mixing primary colours. They are orange, green, and purple. Orange is obtained by mixing red and

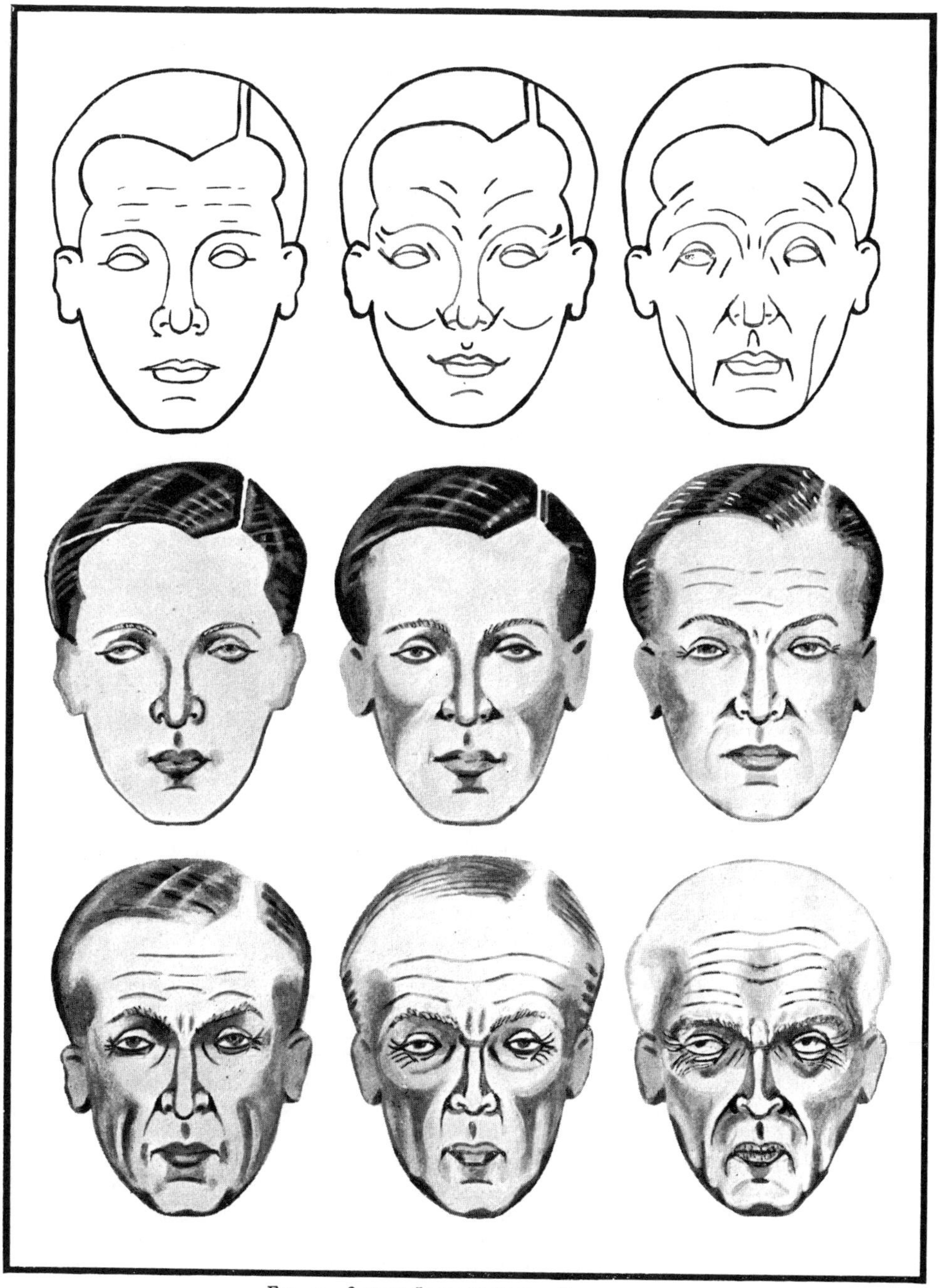

Fig. 23. Simple Lines in Facial Expression

yellow; green by mixing blue and yellow; purple is a mixture of blue and red.

Tertiary colours are russet, citron, and olive. Each is composed of two secondary colours. Russet is obtained by mixing orange and purple; citron is a mixture of orange and green; olive is obtained by mixing green and purple.

A pure, or full, colour may be said to be an unadulterated colour, and the most intense expression of a colour without any addition of black or white being made.

A broken colour is one that is produced by the mixture of two or more pure colours.

Although black and white are not really colours, as they are used in producing shades and tints of colours they are usually spoken of as colours. These two colours and their mixture, which produces grey, also silver and gold, are sometimes termed neutral, or passive, colours.

A shade is a pure colour that is mixed with black. A tint is a pure colour mixed with white.

The tone of a colour is an expression which, in the strict consideration of colour, is confined to the shade and tints of a pure colour. Tone may also be considered as referring to the combined effect of several colours placed in juxtaposition, or to the general effect of a single colour. In either case reference may be made to the prevailing tone, or to such qualities as luminosity, purity, warmth, shade, tint, etc. For instance, it may be said that one colour combination is of a cold tone, that another is warm, etc., or, a single colour may be spoken of as being a deep tone of blue, a warm tone of red, a bright tone of orange, etc.

The hue of colour may be said to be a specific colour that is mixed with a small amount of another colour. Thus, an orange hue of red is made by adding a small amount of orange to a pure red. The term "hue" is sometimes used to refer to that quality which distinguishes one colour, primary or compound, from another. For instance, red differs in hue from green, yellow from orange, etc.

Before passing to a consideration of what may be termed the attributes of different colours, or their behaviour under varying conditions, it is desirable for a user of theatrical cosmetics to be acquainted with the nature and composition of the colouring materials that are employed in their manufacture.

Begin with the simple primary colours of pure red, pure yellow, and pure blue. These are the most important, as all mixtures are secondaries, and from these three, with the aid of black and white, can be obtained every desired shade and tint.

Red. A relatively large number of suitable red colouring substances are available for the colouring of rouges, grease paints, etc. The most important is carmine, which is a product of animal origin obtained from cochineal. In addition, there are some pigments of a mineral character, also a number of suitable coal-tar dyes.

Carmine is a rich, purplish red colour obtained from cochineal—a scale insect that lives in certain species of Cacti, and is found principally in Mexico, Central America, and countries of suitable climate for its cultivation. The dried bodies of this insect contain up to 10 per cent of the colouring matter, called "carminic acid," which is extracted and prepared into powder or liquid of a rich, transparent colour, which fades rapidly in the sun.

Vermilion is a brilliant, durable, red pigment consisting of mercuric sulphide, obtained by grinding the mineral cinnabar to a fine powder, or it is manufactured artificially from mercury and sulphur. The substance is a bright red, tending toward orange. Various shades are made.

Eosine is the name that is applied to various useful synthetic, or aniline, red dyes, which produce somewhat yellowish shades of red or pink.

Carmoisine, another dye used in cosmetics, produces a magenta-red, and is employed as a synthetic substitute for carmine.

Red Lakes are largely made from dyestuffs that are chemically related to alizarine.

In addition to the red colouring matters already dealt with, a number of earthy matters are used as pigments. They owe their colour chiefly to ferric oxide, a perfectly harmless substance that is prepared in a number of forms, and they differ somewhat in colour according to their natural origin and mode of preparation. These are known by different names, such as "Indian red," "Venetian red," "Armenian bole," etc.

Armenian Bole is an earth, coloured brown-red

with ferric oxide, found in Armenia and elsewhere. It gives good flesh tints when diluted with suitable white substances, and is largely employed for making sunburn washes, liquid powders, and grease paints.

Yellow. The yellow pigments consist of ochres, chromes, and sulphides.

Ochres are natural clay, coloured yellow to brown by the presence of ferric oxide. Yellow ochre is a rather dull yellow colour; golden ochre is of a brighter and deeper shade of yellow; dark ochre is of a deeper tone, and may be described as a somewhat greenish brown-yellow. Ochres are extensively used, in conjunction with Armenian bole, for a variety of flesh tints.

Chromes are artificial pigments, consisting of various insoluble metallic salts of chromic acid. Chrome yellow is a chromate of lead.

Blue. The commonest blue pigments are Prussian blue, cobalt blue, and ultramarine.

Prussian Blue is a deep and somewhat greenish shade of blue, obtained by oxidization from green vitriol and potassium. Some authorities regard grease paint coloured with this substance as toxic.

Cobalt Blue is essentially a compound of cobalt oxide with alumina. The purest variety is used for cosmetical purposes, and is innocuous.

Ultramarine was formerly obtained from the rare mineral lapis lazuli, and was expensive. Nowadays good ultramarine is made from kaolin, carbonate of soda, and sulphur. It is cheap, harmless, and extensively used.

White substances are a necessary basis in the manufacture of grease paints and face powder to produce the requisite tints, and as essential vehicles when dyes are employed.

Zinc-white, or pure zinc oxide, is used extensively for the preparation of face powder, liquid powder, and grease paints. It has a soothing and mildly astringent action on the skin.

Kaolin is a fine white clay, or aluminium silicate, used for face powder. It is adherent and a good absorbent.

Talc is a naturally occurring form of magnesium silicate, and, when finely powdered, constitutes "french chalk."

Black pigments, without exception, are chemically similar, and consist of carbon in an amorphous form. Lampblack is the soot formed by burning material rich in carbon, such as mineral oils, naphthaline, etc. It is largely used in the making of chinese or indian ink, kohl, or black eyebrow cosmetic. Charcoal and burnt cork are made by carbonizing wood and bark. "Ivory black" is carbonized ivory or bone.

Brown earths that resemble the ochres are used for darker flesh tints. These earths are sienna and umber. Raw sienna is a light yellowish brown; "burnt sienna" is much brighter and redder in colour. Raw umber is a dark and greenish brown; "burnt umber" has a warmer tone, and is a dark reddish brown.

COLOUR ATTRIBUTES AS AFFECTED BY STAGE LIGHTING

The term "attributes of a colour" is intended to imply certain distinctive qualities and properties of each colour that govern its appropriateness for certain purposes.

Red, orange, and yellow, and combinations in which they predominate, are classified as luminous colours, and are known as warm colours because of their vivid brilliance. Of the three, it may be said that red is the most aggressive. Yellow is a vivid and bright colour, and although it does not possess the strength and warmth of red, it may be said to be the most luminous colour. Combinations of red and yellow, broken with either white or black, provide the majority of the flesh tints and shades that are usually required in make-up.

Green, blue, and violet (complementary colours to the above three), and combinations in which they predominate, are generally considered as cool colours because of their soft, retiring tones. Blue is strong and distinctive, but unlike red, which is warm and aggressive, blue is cold and retiring. In make-up, the direct use of these three colours is limited, though they may be usefully employed in blending and creating contrasts. Care should be taken in applying in its full strength not only red, but also any primary colour on account of the vivid effect that is obtained by the use of unadulterated colours.

The complement of a colour is, theoretically, a colour or colours, which when mixed with it in equal proportions will produce white. It is possible to achieve this result with visible spectrum colours, but impossible with pigments, owing to the imperfection of the colours. A mixture of the primary colours of light will tend to give white light, whereas a mixture of the same pigment colours results in dark grey. There are many pairs of complementary colours, representing the maximum of contrast in hue. The law of contrast is best illustrated when two complementary colours equal in brightness are

SIR CEDRIC HARDWICKE AS DICK VARWELL IN "YELLOW SANDS"
Photo by Pollard Crowther

placed close together; then each complementary enhances to the greatest possible extent the brightness of its companion colour.

Contrast of colours is due to the modifications in the appearance of colours that are caused by the differences in the hue and brightness of adjacent or contiguous colours. If any two colours, differing in hue, are placed together, their difference will be increased, and each of the colours will be slightly tinged, as if mixed with the complementary of the other.

In the case of a pair of colours that differ in degree of brightness, the difference is increased when the two are brought close to each other, or, in other words, the colour that has the greater intensity of hue or brightness has these qualities enhanced; whilst the colour with a lesser degree of similar qualities will have its dullness increased by contrast with the brighter colour. Both a deeply saturated colour and a pale tint of itself, when placed together, are altered considerably; the stronger gains more power and brilliancy, and the weaker appears still feebler by contrast. For example, a pale red tint when placed beside a full red will appear much paler, whilst the full red will gain brightness. All colours in contrast with white appear at their darkest, whilst on a black ground they are seen at their lightest.

The effect of contrast is one of the utmost importance in make-up, and, in fact, in all colour schemes that are employed on the stage, since harmony and visibility, from the point of view of an audience, depend upon such considerations. To arrive at a few practical applications of the foregoing observations on contrast, consider what would be the effect upon the complexion colour and the visibility of the features when a change from light to dark colour of costume or gown is made during the action of a play. Assuming that the colour tone of the make-up was correct in the first instance, the change in contrast between the colour of the face and the gown would, obviously, result in the face appearing considerably paler and the features weaker. An addition of colour tone would be required to remedy this defect. On the other hand, the colour tone required to correspond with a man's red or blue tunic would appear too heavy by contrast with the white collar and shirt-front of evening dress; and would require to be toned down with an application of powder. Further, it is not to be supposed that the same make-up colours harmonize with every colour of costume to the same degree of visibility. A prevailing tone that harmonizes with yellow wearing material will not give the same results in contrast with blue.

To meet this need of appropriate contrast between make-up and colour of costume, the best guidance is derived from a knowledge of the scheme of colour contrast known as "successive contrast." In this connexion an interesting experiment may be made by gazing intently at a red object for a few moments or until the eye becomes fatigued. If the eye is then turned away from the red object towards a white or pale surface, a tint of bluish-green is distinctly seen. This is the accidental contrast colour of red, and is practically the same thing as its complementary colour. This phenomenon is explained by the theory that the eye is furnished with three groups of nerves which, independently, respond to the colour sensations of red, green, and violet. When the gaze is concentrated upon an object of red colour, the red nerves of the retina are highly excited by the red rays, and, on the contrary, the green and violet nerves are not to any great extent called into action. When the impression of the red object is suddenly removed, the green and violet nerves, not being fatigued, respond strongly to the stimulus given to them by the absence of red rays and the presence of light; consequently, as a result of the unusual activity of the green and violet nerves, the eye for a short time receives the impression of blue-green, the complementary of red.

If the same tone of red is repeatedly presented to the eye, the red nerves become fatigued, and fail to interpret the same degree of colour intensity, and, therefore, the colour appears to fade and to become less visible. Should the presentation of red, on the other hand, be followed by a display of blue-green, the eye more readily responds and interprets the second colour at its maximum degree of intensity and visibility, because it is the complementary colour, it may be said, that the eye is expecting to see. The simplest pairs of complementary colours, which are adaptable and most frequently met with, are—

Red . .	Green-blue
Blue . .	Orange-yellow
Green . .	Red-violet
Violet . .	Yellow-green
Yellow . .	Violet-blue

A make-up colour scheme that is devised on these lines will not only achieve harmony of contrast, but also a high degree of natural, unobtrusive visibility. In exactly the same way as the colour scheme of each costume should harmonize with the colour tone of the stage setting, so should make-up be a factor in definite relationship to the general scheme; yet it is too often considered to be of little or no importance. As guidance in this connexion a table of examples, which will meet the majority of women's cases, is given at the foot of this page.

All coloured bodies reflect a certain proportion of white light in addition to their coloured light, and, consequently, suffer a loss of purity in this reflected mixture of white and coloured light. The nearer the surface of an object is to white, the greater is its reflecting power; the darker it is, the less will be the amount of light it can reflect. When the greatest possible degree of purity and richness, that is to say, freedom from white light, combined with a high degree of luminosity, is present in a colour, the effect on the eye is the maximum intensity of hue, or saturation. Colours appear saturated, or, in other words, are stronger, at normal or low intensities of illumination than at high intensities. This means that if a great excess of luminosity or brightness is added to a colour, its intensity of hue, or degree of saturation, is diminished. Consequently, saturation is maintained by an increase in the intensity of hue. Therefore, when stage lighting is strong all colours in make-up should be proportionately heavier.

The modifications or changes that colours undergo when they are illuminated by gas-light or other artificial light must now be considered. Although the improvements that have been made in the development of the white light of the incandescent gas-burner, and in electric lighting,

Costume Dominant Colour	Foundation Tint	Carmine Rouge	Eye Shade	Lip Colour	Powder Tint
Red . .	Cream—No. 2½ chrome .	Carmine 2 .	Green-blue .	Medium . .	Rachael
Blue . .	Cream—No. 2½; No. 5 .	Orange tint .	Gold-brown .	Light . .	Rachael
Green . .	No. 2½	Carmine 3 .	Violet or silver-blue . .	Dark . .	Natural
Violet . .	Cream—No. 2½ No. 5; .	Orange tint .	Green . .	Orange tint .	Rachael
Yellow .	No. 2½	Carmine 2 .	Dark blue .	Medium . .	Natural

have gone a long way towards the equalization of artificial light and daylight, the artificial means still has the effect of changing the hue or appearance of a colour from its characteristic hue in daylight. Artificial light obtained from different sources varies in its composition, and the tone of any particular light depends upon the proportion

Sir Cedric Hardwicke as Moulton Barrett in "The Barretts of Wimpole Street"
Photo by Pollard Crowther

and relative strengths of the colour rays that are present.

Electric light is deficient in blue rays and stronger in its general tone of yellow or red-yellow. Daylight is white, a mixture of all colour rays. Hence it follows that a coloured surface having a predominance of yellow in its composition, loses a considerable quantity of its yellow and appears pale or whitish in artificial light. Pure red, on the other hand, becomes brighter and more intense. Carmines lose their purplish tints and tend toward a purer red; vermilion inclines to a more orange-red. Blues generally suffer in purity and tend to become dull or greyish. Those inclining to a violet cast become more violet-like; but greenish-blues have a strong tendency to become still greener in hue. Violet is much duller and more purplish, and purple inclines to a crimson-red. Greenish-yellow and yellow-greens remain fairly constant to their daylight aspect, but blue-greens become more bluish, and bluish-greys become almost indistinguishable as colour.

From these observations relating to the loss of colour due to the combined effect of the source of intensity of stage lighting, it will be obvious that information of the intensity and prevailing tone of the light and judgment in the application of sufficient colour to neutralize its effect will always be required. White electric light, when used without a colour medium, is of a cold and critical tone, revealing many flaws in careless make-up. When this form of light has to be faced, the foundation should be given a warm tone by the addition of a little extra No. 9, and the rouge perfectly blended in order to avoid sharp contrasts between pale and full colours. For the same reason, shadows and high-lights should merge into the foundation with an imperceptible graduation of tone. A too generous application of full colours should be avoided. Therefore, the cheeks, eyes, and lips will require only a minimum of colour discriminately applied.

COLOURED LIGHT

Obviously, the chief requirement of brilliant stage illumination is to make the actors, costumes, and properties visible to the audience. Combinations of white and coloured light are required to represent the light tints of nature, such as sunlight, twilight, moonlight, etc.; also, to pale or to brighten a scene, transforming it from cold to warm tone, or vice versa. Colour lighting is now recognized as an emotional language, like music, with power to induce and maintain psychological moods in an audience. Suggestive colour is employed as an aid to the creation of the required atmosphere of a play and to give emphasis to the action, whilst gorgeous scenic illusions and effects are produced by the beauty of changing coloured light.

The effect of coloured light is to make still greater changes and modifications in the appearance of colour, whether of costume or make-up. A make-up that would be adequate when playing in white or pale light would need to be almost impressionistic in high-lights and shadows to show up in dark amber or blue light. It is not possible to set down any definite rules to meet a particular colour of light; yet a consideration of the general trend of the changes that take place will assist the necessary judgment when the lighting scheme is known.

Pale tints of straw, pink, or amber, are of a warmer and kinder tone than white, and, therefore, are less critical and do not change colours to any great extent. Intense reds will incline slightly to orange, and blues and greens will be less bright.

Medium and dark red light is aggressive, and will spoil greens and change blue to dark grey. Flesh tints in this colour should incline to cream rather than pink, red should be in sharp contrast, and green-blue or gold-blue should be substituted for dark blue.

Dark amber is drastic in its action; it reduces flesh tints and reds considerably in tone and gives them an orange cast. Blue and greens are completely changed to grey. In these cases it is an advantage to use a paler foundation of a pink tone, carmine-vermilion rouge for cheeks and lips, silver-blue eye shade, with heavy black eyelashes.

When lighting schemes are heavy or bizarre, the audience will not expect to see the same clarity of features and expression, and under these conditions, which are usually of a temporary nature, little change from the usual tone of make-up is advisable. Blue frequently gives the greatest trouble, and when playing in this colour the usual full colours, such as rouge and eye shades, may be omitted and put on for a subsequent scene if this is found necessary owing to a change of lighting.

PHYSIOGNOMY IN RELATION TO MAKE-UP

The real reason for continuing the study of physiognomy is to make clear and comprehensible the conception and the simulation of facial characteristics. Reverting to the analysis and synthesis of facial expression, we are reminded that the prevailing expression of the face in repose constitutes the basis of physiognomy, which is founded upon a study of the anatomy of the face. The conception it is sought to emphasize is one of tremendous practical value. Not only does it lend itself to an understanding of correct light and shade, and the placing of significant lines that conform to, rather than vary with, Nature's own lines, but it also adds force to the controlled action or registration of any particular expression of the face. An understanding of the functioning of the facial muscles cannot fail to help the portrayal of different emotions by facial gesture.

Although the importance of the subject is stressed, it should not be assumed that it is necessary, or even advisable, in any case to attempt to reproduce by make-up a permanent, exaggerated, external manifestation of any emotional quality. It should be clearly understood that a definite discrimination must be made between the permanent evidence in the face at rest and the latent expression, which is only in evidence when the face is in action. For instance, some wrinkles are permanent, whilst the majority are transient, and, obviously, cannot be represented in make-up. A smile, which is considered to be the real basis of facial expression, cannot be made to appear permanent without losing its charm. The chief aim should be to give the face an expressive bias in the direction of the required characteristics, when such do not naturally exist on the player's face, and when it is necessary to accentuate, or add to, the existing natural lines. When this is fully realized, the art of character expression is greatly simplified inasmuch as it is concerned only with the question of how the character should reveal the degree of its outward manifestation.

To understand the action of the muscles of the face it is not necessary for us to know more of their structure than that they are formed of distinct packets of fibres; that they are attached by one end, called the origin, to some point of bone, and by the other end, called the insertion, to the skin of the face, which is moved. These muscular fibres run in a direct line from their fixed origin to their movable insertion in the skin, which, smooth in youth, becomes adorned in later life with the transverse wrinkles of concentrated attention, the vertical wrinkles of reflection, or pain, and with the crow's feet at the corners of the eyes, which suggest a sense of humour. We may accept the opinion of authorities on the subject of anatomy, that the most movable and expressive features are the inner extremity of the eyebrows and the angle of the mouth. Therefore, the simplest classification is to divide the movements of facial expression into (1) the movements of the eyebrows, and (2) the movements of the mouth, and to examine the cause and effect of such movements.

The forehead more than any other part is popularly supposed to be characteristic of the human countenance. It is the centre of thought, a tablet upon which every emotion is distinctly impressed; and the eyebrow itself is an eloquent index to the mind. Someone has called the eyebrow "the rainbow of peace, or the bended bow of discord."

> Yea, this man's brow, like to a title-leaf
> Foretells the nature of a tragic volume.

A chart of the principal muscles involved in expression is shown in Fig. 24, a study of which will lead to a better understanding of one's own features. Notice that there are four muscles attached to the eyebrow (*A, B, C, D*).

A. The Forehead Muscle of Attention. This vertical muscle descends over the forehead, and is inserted into the skin under the eyebrows. The simple action of its front portion is to draw upwards the skin of the eyebrows from below, arching the eyebrows, and causing transverse wrinkles to appear on the forehead. The number or depth of the wrinkles is proportionate to the repetition and intensity of the muscular

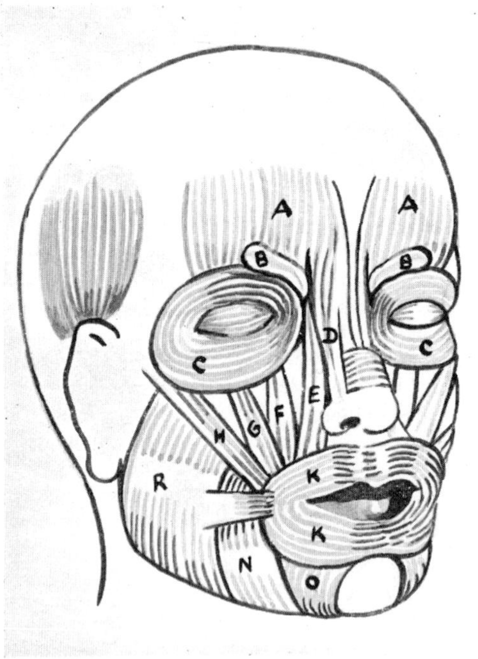

FIG. 24. THE MUSCLES OF THE FACE

A. The Forehead or Frontal Muscle . (*Occipito—frontals*)
B. The Eyebrow Muscle . . . (*Corrugator Supercilii*)
C. The Circular Eye Muscle . . (*Orbicularis palpebrarum*)
D. The Descending Nose Muscle . (*Pyramidalis Nasi*)
E. The Common Lip Raiser Muscle . (*Elevator Alasque Nasi*)
F. A Lip Raising Muscle . . . (*Elevator Labii Proprius*)
G. A Lip Raising Muscle . . . (*Elevator Anguli Oris*)
H. A Lip Raising Muscle . . . (*Zygomaticus Major*)
K. The Circular Lips Muscle . . (*Orbicularis Oris*)
N. The Lip Depresser Muscle . . (*Trangularis Oris*)
O. The Chin Muscle . . . . (*Quadratus Menti*)
R. The Jaw Muscle . . . . (*Patysma Nyoides*)

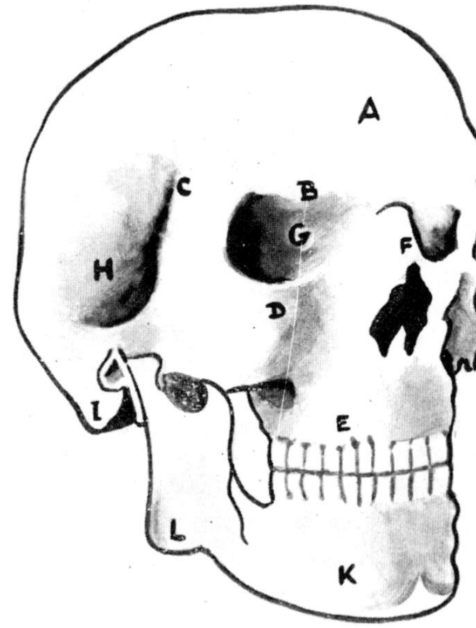

FIG. 25. THE BONES OF THE SKULL

A. The Frontal Bone.
B. The Protuberances formed by the Frontal Sinuses.
C. The Temporal Ridge of the Frontal Bone, on which the form of the Temple depends.
D. The Cheek Bones.
E The Upper Maxillary Bones.
F. The Nasal Bones.
G. The Orbits or Sockets for the Eye-balls. The circle of their margin is formed by the Frontal Bones, the Cheek Bones, and the Maxillary Bones.
H. The Temporal Bones. These hollows are filled with a strong muscle, which passes down, through the arch, to be inserted into the lower jaw-bone.
I. The Mastoid. This is the point into which the mastoid muscles, which give form to the neck, are inserted.
K. The Lower Jaw.
L. The Angle of the Lower Jaw.

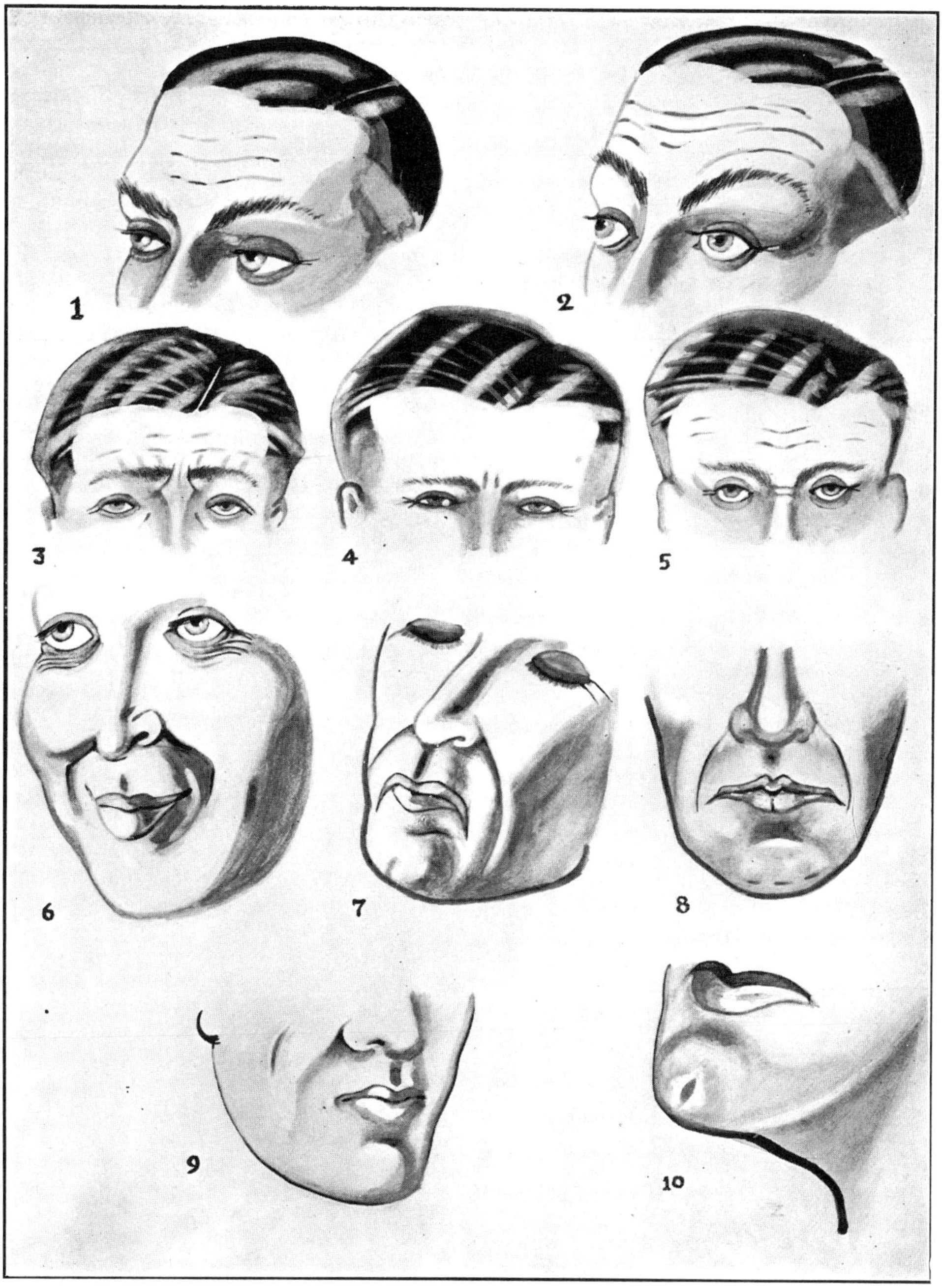

FIG. 26. STUDIES IN EXPRESSION

contraction, which, through the force of habit, becomes largely involuntary. There is a cheerful or an alert and inquiring expression, indicating the faculty of being able to concentrate the attention; also, a susceptibility to surprise and wonder. Darwin says, "Attention, if sudden and close, graduates into surprise, and this into astonishment, and this into stupefied amazement." The effect of the action of this muscle is seen in Fig. 26—1 and 2.

B. The Eyebrow Muscle of Pain. This is said to be the most remarkable muscle of the face. It arises from the frontal bone and, running obliquely upwards, is inserted into the skin about the middle of the eyebrows. It lies nearly transversely, and its action is to draw the eyebrows together with an energetic effect and to knit the skin between them. This forms curved folds at the inner end of the eyebrows and wrinkles above, and there is more or less expression of mental anguish, or painful suffering, as "When pain and anguish wring the brow" (Fig. 26—3).

C. The Eye Muscle of Reflection. Its fibres, being spread in a circular direction upon the margin of the orbit and the eyelids, surround the eye. It is the outer and stronger circle that acts as the direct opponent of the forehead muscle by pulling down the inner end of the eyebrows and generally straightening the curve of them. This action tightens the skin of the forehead, causes the transverse wrinkles to disappear, and produces two vertical wrinkles between the eyebrows. These wrinkles suggest an endeavour to master a difficulty in connexion with thought, and lines drawn here often give to motions of the features in the lower part of the face the expression of a lofty character (Fig. 26—4).

D. The Nose Muscle of Anger. This descends from the forehead muscle, and is attached to the side of the nose. Its action is to draw down the skin between the eyebrows, and, consequently, to lower the inner part of the eyebrows. This action forms between the eyebrows transverse folds and wrinkles that are the evidence of anger, menace, and ferocity (Fig. 26—5).

These four muscles move the eyebrows, and give them all their various inflections.

MUSCLES OF THE LIPS

The fleshy structure of the lips is largely due to a circular muscle that surrounds the mouth. This closes the lips, and is the opponent of many other muscles, which are centred towards the mouth, and which, besides opening it, move the lips in various directions. It is by the successive action and relaxation of these antagonizing muscles that so much and so varied expression is given to the mouth, and a remarkable variety is produced in the lines that mark the features about the upper lip as a direct index to the feelings. These we will consider in order of importance.

H. The Lip Muscle of Laughter. This runs down from the cheek bone, and is inserted into the outer angle of the mouth. Its action is to raise the outer angles of the mouth upwards and outwards. This causes a fold, called the naso-labial fold, to appear. This fold runs from the nose in the direction of the corners of the mouth, convex to the nose above, and concave to the mouth below. By pushing up the cheek the action produces crow's feet under the eye. The effect of a ludicrous idea is to relax the muscles that control the lips and to contract those that oppose them; hence by a stretching of the mouth, and a raising of the cheek to the lower eyelid, a smile is produced (Fig. 26—6).

E and F. The Lip Raiser Muscles of Grief. These two muscles, which arise from the upper jaw, near the orbit, are attached exclusively to the upper lip and raise it. The effect is to alter the shape of the mouth, obliquely downwards and inwards, but the outer angle of the mouth is not raised. The naso-labial fold is thus made strongly concave throughout. The depression of the angle of the mouth gives an air of despondence and languor when it is accompanied by a general relaxation of the features, or, in other words, of the muscles (Fig. 26—7). The muscle indicated at *G* is, also, a lip raiser, but, unlike the last named, it has the power to raise the angle of the mouth.

N. The Lip Depresser of Contempt. This is a comparatively powerful muscle, which arises from the base of the lower jaw, and is inserted into the skin below the angle of the mouth. The effect of its action is to draw the angle obliquely downwards and outwards, and to pull down the lower end of the naso-labial fold, making it deeper. If the action is slight, an expression of sadness is the result; when it is strong and in conjunction with *O*, which arches and elevates the lower lip, there is a contemptuous effect (Fig. 26—8).

K. The Circular Muscle of the Lips. The fibres of this muscle can be traced continuously round the lips, and they have no proper origin. The muscle is affected in various emotions; it yields, both in joy and grief, to the superior force of its counteracting muscles and relaxes pleasantly in smiling. The union of so many muscles at the angle of and below the lips is responsible for the formation, in the child or youth whose face is plump, of the dimple in the cheek or chin. Dimples are considered to be indicative of a kindly, cheerful disposition.

MAKE-UP AND DRESSING ROOM HINTS

An experienced producer once remarked to me that, in his opinion, amateur players were prone to spend, or waste, too much time on making up, and that it was a common cause of curtain delays. He attributed the reason either to insufficient dressing room facilities for making up or lack of ability on the part of the players to put on their make-up with the necessary speed. It is not sufficient to have knowledge, however comprehensive, of the best materials, of colour, form, and line, if reasonable speed in application is not acquired through practice and by experience. Speed is the natural accompaniment of a clear conception of the particular characterization that is required, together with the adoption of method and precision that eliminate needless movements and achieve adequate results in as direct a manner as is possible. This standard of efficiency is attained only when consideration is given to the need of appropriate dressing room facilities, such as lights, tables, and mirrors. When a hall or theatre is equipped with private dressing rooms, players have the liberty to make use of their own devices. On the other hand, it is often the case that players are expected to make up in a single, crowded room, with only one ordinary white light, and with insufficient table and seating accommodation. Under such conditions players may be seen attempting to make up whilst standing, holding a mirror in one hand, and vainly endeavouring to catch a glimmer of light to enable them to get on with the job with the other hand.

It is neither difficult nor expensive to construct a dressing table, complete with mirrors and lights, along the lines suggested by Fig. 27, to accommodate six or eight persons. The table top is covered with white oil-cloth. The mirrors are secured back-to-back, with a light mounted directly above, which illuminates the face, but is not reflected in the mirror.

A few moments spent in orderly preparation for making up often saves many valuable minutes when they are most required. It is an excellent plan to select from the make-up box only those colours and materials that are likely to be required, and to arrange them on a towel spread on the table in front of the mirror. First, make up the face; next dress the hair; then apply wet-white, if required, to the hands and neck. Finally, put on the costume, and note that every detail of it is in order. If for any reason you are pressed for time, remember that the costume is of chief importance, and that it should be put on first; then in the time that is available do the best with the make-up.

FIG. 27. A MAKING-UP TABLE AT THE BRADFORD CIVIC PLAYHOUSE

Difficulty is frequently experienced during dressing and when changes of costume are necessary in passing a garment over the head and at the same time avoiding disarrangement of the hair or wig or, may be, the soiling of the garment through contact with the paint on the face. This difficulty can be overcome by enveloping the head

Sir Cedric Hardwicke as King Magnus in "The Apple Cart"

in a thin muslin bag with an elastic draw that will fasten under the chin. The provision and use, by both men and women, of a head covering of this description facilitate the change and protect both make-up and garment, and if the material is not too thick the wearer can see through it.

For a player on the stage to perspire excessively is a common experience. Excessive perspiration is caused by an overheated atmosphere, exertion in heavy costume or wig, and, in some cases, by nervous tension. Whatever the cause, it is usually so distressing and detrimental to the permanency of a perfect make-up that a few words on the best means of finding even partial relief will be helpful. As a precautionary measure in exceptional cases considerable aid is afforded if the face is sponged over with surgical or methylated spirit, before the application of cold cream. This thoroughly cleanses and closes the pores of the skin. The cold cream that is then applied should be reduced to the minimum. A superior blending powder continues to absorb moisture long after its immediate application, and if it is liberally applied, helps to keep the face dry. The face should never be powdered while it is wet with perspiration. If it is, the powder forms flakes and presents the appearance of a rough, scaly skin. This can be avoided by removing with a piece of blotting paper the beads of perspiration, and then applying a light dusting of powder.

CHANGES IN MAKE-UP

There are occasions when it is necessary to alter the make-up in order to depict a change that takes place in a character during the action of a play. Some alterations are easily made; others require a degree of change that presents many difficulties. As grease paint cannot be spread over a powdered surface, the possibilities of making changes by simply adding more colour or lines are limited. Often the best method of procedure is completely to remove one make-up before attempting to apply another. This is certainly the only course to adopt when two widely different characters are acted by the same player. Every alteration should be anticipated and planned with regard to the nature and extent of the change; at the same time the time that is available for making the alteration should be remembered. Instances arising out of prologues, epilogues, and lapses of time and changes of circumstances between acts are so numerous that it is possible to consider only a few examples of general trend and interest.

Take the well known play, *The Admirable Crichton*, by Sir J. M. Barrie, as one example. It will be remembered that the scene of the first act is a reception room in Mayfair, for which a normal tone of "straight" make-up is all that is required. Act 3, a desert island in the Pacific, finds the same people, after being marooned on the island for two years following the wrecking of their pleasure yacht, living a primitive life.

Granting that sun bathing in the Pacific for two years would have a marked effect upon their appearance, it is obviously necessary in the interests of "atmosphere" to indicate the change. As the time to effect the change is limited to the interval between the acts, part of which must be taken up with a change of costume, the work has to be done with the utmost speed. In order to expedite the change all parts of the body to be exposed in Act 3 should be coloured to the necessary sun-tan before the first act, leaving only the face, neck, and hands for treatment during the brief interval.

A suitable water stain for the limbs can be prepared in the following manner—

Armenian bole	30 parts
Distilled or soft water	60 „
Glycerine	10 „
Gum tragacanth	1 part

The last item must be dissolved in water before adding, or it may be omitted. Apply the liquid with a sponge.

Similar flesh tints, in block or semi-liquid form, are applied with a damp sponge, and are readily removed with soap and water.

The simplest way to add colour to the face is to dab on a somewhat weaker solution of the water stain, taking care to avoid a patchy result. The sponge needs to be rinsed to remove the heavy colour that is used for the body, and applied to the face in a slightly moist condition. If the sponge is not too wet, the powder surface of the original make-up will absorb sufficient colour to depict the changed complexion. Should the eye colour or any characteristic lining be obliterated by the darker wash, it will be necessary to restore it by touching up with the liners.

There are special liners that have not been mentioned. Known as "reform" or "pencil" liners, they are made in pencil form with a grease colour core. They are of a harder consistency than the usual paper-covered liner stick, and are obtainable in the principal liner colours. The extra degree of hardness makes them specially adaptable for retouching, or reforming, any make-up after powdering—sometimes a difficult matter with the softer type. This type of liner following a water colour application provides the best means of restoring the original characteristics.

The last act presents the same people back in Mayfair. It may be assumed that they have retained some evidence of their sojourn abroad. Sufficient alteration is effected by toning down the excessive colour with an application of powder or by damping with a weak, that is to say, well diluted, solution of wet white. Powdering or damping should be followed by a general

Sir Cedric Hardwicke as Captain Shotover in "Heartbreak House"

retouching of eye colour, lip rouge, etc., in order to restore the accentuation of the features.

A second example deals with the numerous cases where it is necessary to convey a changed appearance, due to the passing of time, in a character. In accordance with the lapse of time that is indicated by the action of the play, it is essential to add characteristics of increased age to the original make-up. When it is remembered that in such cases there is the powdered surface to work upon, similar methods to those suggested in the first example will be most convenient. The general tone is made paler by damping the face with a pale water colour, after which shadows about the eyes, cheeks, and temples should be toned in with water colours or reform liners. In the same way, wrinkles are added, and the features are reformed to portray what is considered to be the normal change that has taken place during the interval of years. With a clear conception in mind of the character to be played, develop, as far as possible, the hollows and wrinkles your own face has a tendency to show; and bear in mind, with regard to colour, that hollows and wrinkles when finished should appear to be of the foundation flesh made deeper by the addition of a dark shade. Therefore, if the foundation is of a florid tone, lake darkened with a touch of grey will appear to be natural; if sallow, medium brown will be better. After wrinkle lines have been strengthened, highlight them delicately with a pale flesh tint, or white reform liner; then soften the effect with powder. If the charts of facial expression, namely, Figs. 23, 24, 25, and 26, are well studied, little difficulty will be experienced in correctly placing light, shade, and lines to achieve the changed aspect. In many cases an alteration of the shape of the eyebrows and of the colour of hair with the aid of powder will achieve a pronounced change. For a male character the addition of a moustache, or streaking the moustache with grey, will greatly assist; whilst the whitening of the hair will add a considerable number of years to appearance. One great drawback in whitening the hair of a young man is the fact that it is difficult to disguise the youthful shape of the head, neck, and style of hairdressing. The use of a well-fitting wig is the only satisfactory remedy.

Changes that are outside the scope of these examples are best considered as dual roles. The speediest way to make the desired change is completely to remove the first make-up, to apply a fresh foundation, and to proceed with the new characterization from that point.

THE LARGE CAST

Acting upon the assumption that some readers may be chiefly interested in the subject of make-up from the standpoint of the amateur perruquier, and desirous of using their ability in the making up of other players, I offer a few helpful suggestions on the mass make-up of a large cast when time is limited. It requires organization and time-saving methods to make-up a large chorus when allowable time works out at three minutes a head.

In the first place, provide a firm and comfortable chair facing the table on which make-up materials are systematically arranged and within immediate reach of the right hand.

Cold cream is more quickly applied with a sponge than the fingers.

The foundation should be spread with the fingers of both hands and be followed by the carmine to the cheeks and lips. Next, colour the eyes and darken the eyebrows. Powdering is most speedily done by employing a swan's-down puff about the size of the face. From such a puff powder can be pressed on to the entire face by one application, and the surplus then brushed off.

ART IN RELATION TO MAKE-UP

Fundamentally, the real basis of any "character" make-up is the creation of an illusion by perspective; that is to say, by the art of delineating on a flat surface the true resemblance of an object, as the object appears to the eye from a given distance and situation, by means of correct drawing, light and shade, tones of colour, etc. The measure of success in the delineation of any character depends on the quick grasp and exercise of correct perspective, also of what can well be called the illusion of the eyes. It takes two brains to make a picture, one to paint it, and the other to look at it.

Here the subject of light and shade is continued with a view to removing any lack of understanding of the principles involved, or of the possibilities and limitations that attend inability to apply them in the art of make-up. I am of the opinion that a lack of appreciation and knowledge of the effective use of light and shade is the chief reason why so many players, who make up themselves, fail in their efforts to achieve anything that nearly approaches significant delineation of character. All too often when a character gives scope for the exercise of real make-up art is the simple expedient of adding a few lines, or some whiskers, resorted to, and an attitude of "it's good enough" adopted.

The need for a higher standard of character make-up was authoritatively voiced by the adjudicator at a British Drama League Festival

Competition for societies presenting one-act plays. In criticizing one of the plays, he said that there was a lack of essential atmosphere due to the youthful appearance of an aged character, which should have been corrected by better attention to the make-up of the player. The face is the greatest revealer of character. However valuable clothes and gesture may be, if the face does not convey a corresponding mood the characterization is a failure.

To players with little natural or acquired knowledge and appreciation of art, there is difficulty in grasping essential details, and whilst it is not possible to deal here with the full technical aspect of art, it is possible to select a few elements that will prove of immense value when they are reduced to the simplest mode of application. Following my consideration of the simple alteration of features by light and shade, I now give further examples of a rather more complex nature. These will demonstrate how more extensive changes in appearance can be achieved. At the present stage it is advisable to approach an understanding of these effects in tone values only, apart from any influence of colour. When aiming to attain this specialized work, it is of great help and importance to study the many forms of light and shade compositions that abound in engravings, etchings, portraits, and pictures of finely-drawn faces. A knowledge of what constitutes good composition is best gained by observing, studying, and reflecting on the works of masters. Especially deserving of study are the works of Rembrandt. His paintings and etchings, with their effective handling of light and shade, are object lessons. Beauty and imagination reach out beyond the actual to the ideal. For instance, thousands of artists have drawn portraits of old women. Rembrandt drew the portrait of an old woman, and it is one of the greatest things in the world: not the face of one old woman, but the lovableness, the dignity, sorrow, and other-worldliness of old age of all time. We should never count an hour wasted that is spent on looking at these treasures and learning the lessons they convey.

However entertaining and inciting to effort is the search for, and the creation of, character, remember that it is to be based, and is consequently dependent, upon flesh and bone. One cannot impress too strongly the necessity of knowing the shape and position of the facial bones and the action and effect of the muscles. Behind the muscles of the face lie the bones, which create the permanent form of the face and head, and constitute the skull. Reference again to Fig. 25 will prove helpful in locating the chief prominences and hollows of the face that can be changed in appearance by light and shade to give effectual characterization. Anatomy is not to be displayed; its true use is to inculcate an accurate observation of nature in those slighter characteristics that escape a less learned eye. For example, it should be noticed how a bone, which is near the surface, affects the form. Failure to observe this may lead to the anomaly of attempting to produce a hollow on a surface bone, and the placing of wrinkles in positions that are contrary to natural effects.

Fig. 28A exemplifies this main principle of the illusion of light, shade, and perspective. Notice that it is a simple, familiar composition of three different tones, arranged to form a design of squares, which produces the illusionary effect of cubes or steps. An increase in the angle of inclination at which it is viewed will cause the illusion to be more pronounced.

Fig. 28B teaches the same lesson: a different composition of similar tones resulting in another familiar form—the resemblance of the facial features. From these two examples it may be reasoned that almost every possible form of face can be produced, or remodelled, by the appropriate distribution of light and shade. This possibility permits young players to be made up for elderly characters, older players to appear younger, and it contributes to the creation of an infinite variety of characteristic effects.

Concerning Fig. 28D, it should be observed that tones are graduated, from dark to light, in a way that produces the effect of a convex surface, rising in a round form or sphere, the lighter part, or high-light, being the centre of elevation. Now consider Fig. 28G, where the same graduated shading is applied to an eye and its adjacent parts, giving to the eye a full, forward, and convex appearance. Though a somewhat exaggerated example for the purpose of making the analogy quite clear, it serves to establish a rule that should be exercised whenever it is desired to give a forward aspect to any feature. The width, depth, or angle of the frontal bone may be altered, and prominence given to the eyebrow ridges, the temporal bones, cheek bones, and the angle of the jaw bone or chin. The same rule operates in producing a fullness of the lips or in the filling in of naturally hollow parts, such as the cheeks, temples, or neck.

Fig. 28E is given as an example of the converse graduation of shading, which creates the illusion of a concave, or hollow, surface, like the inner surface of a sphere or ball. An extreme instance of the exercise of this rule is shown in Fig. 28H. Here, again, it is applied to an eye socket, and produces the effect of a concave, or hollow, eye. The same rule offers tremendous scope wherever a hollow needs to be suggested. A sunken appearance of the cheeks, temples, and nose can be effected. The upper or lower lip, or both, can be made to recede and sink back into the mouth.

Fig. 28F shows the illusion of an undulating surface that is suggestive of waves or folds. Here we find a basis, or rule, applicable to a host of effects smaller than those provided for in previous examples. In a similar way, the suggestion of flabby or sagging cheeks is given to perfectly plump ones; folds of flesh are indicated to resemble a double chin or the heavy wrinkles of the forehead and neck. The forehead wrinkles drawn in Fig. 28I are an adaptation of this rule. Here it may be pointed out, with advantage, that a naturally wrinkled face does not present a mass of heavy, dark lines in any kind of light. What is seen are merely folds of skin, separated by shadows cast by the folds, reflecting light. Therefore, it is entirely wrong to represent wrinkles by lines alone. It is done in simple line drawing, like some of the illustrations, but in make-up it should be avoided. From an audience's point of view a wrinkle appears as two ridges of light separated by a graduated shadow, which in its upper portion is lighter than below. When a line is drawn on the forehead to suggest a wrinkle it should be smoothed out almost to the transparent dimensions of a shadow, then high lighted along its lower edge to make the lower portion of the shadow appear darker by contrast. This is done to create the illusion of downward light and to counteract the effect of any false light that floats might reflect on the forehead. A soft line is employed to support and give depth to a shadow at its darkest part, but not as a substitute for the shadow itself. This applies, not only to the forehead wrinkles, but also to all the principal folds that are made by muscular action and the shrinking of the skin.

Soft lines are required to denote the finer wrinkles, such as crow's feet at the corners of the eyes. They must be the only outstanding fine lines of the face, and suggest correct proportion and perspective. The chief aim should be realism, with a minimum of lines. Only those wrinkles and folds that make for action in the face should be indicated. It is reasonable to add that if they are put in the wrong place they will destroy the effect that they are meant to express. Many lines of the face are so fine that they are entirely invisible for the purpose of make-up; therefore omit all wrinkle lines that serve no useful purpose.

Care should be taken to differentiate between the varying textures of skin and fullness of flesh. A fine textured skin on a thin face will need for adequate expression lines of different quality from those for a coarse, heavy face. The folds of a fine skin form closer together and show sharp curves and radiations that are expressive of its quality. A heavy face shows thick folds of flesh, and more ponderous curves of depth and elevation. A fat face develops many more wrinkles, in old age, than does a thin face, which generally exhibits the least signs of old age.

On the subject of lines, Fig. 28C illustrates an illusion that has sufficient adaptability to warrant an explanation. The two straight lines, although of equal length, give the illusion of a difference in length. The apparent difference is caused by the addition of the short lines at each end of the lines. Inverted in the first instance, they make the line appear shorter than in the second instance, where the short lines are extended outwards. In the example of curved lines, the effect of the addition of short lines makes the former appear to be shorter and more round. The placing of inverse short lines at the corners of the eye has a marked narrowing effect; if the short lines extend outwards the eye appears to be broader. Similar lines applied to the corners

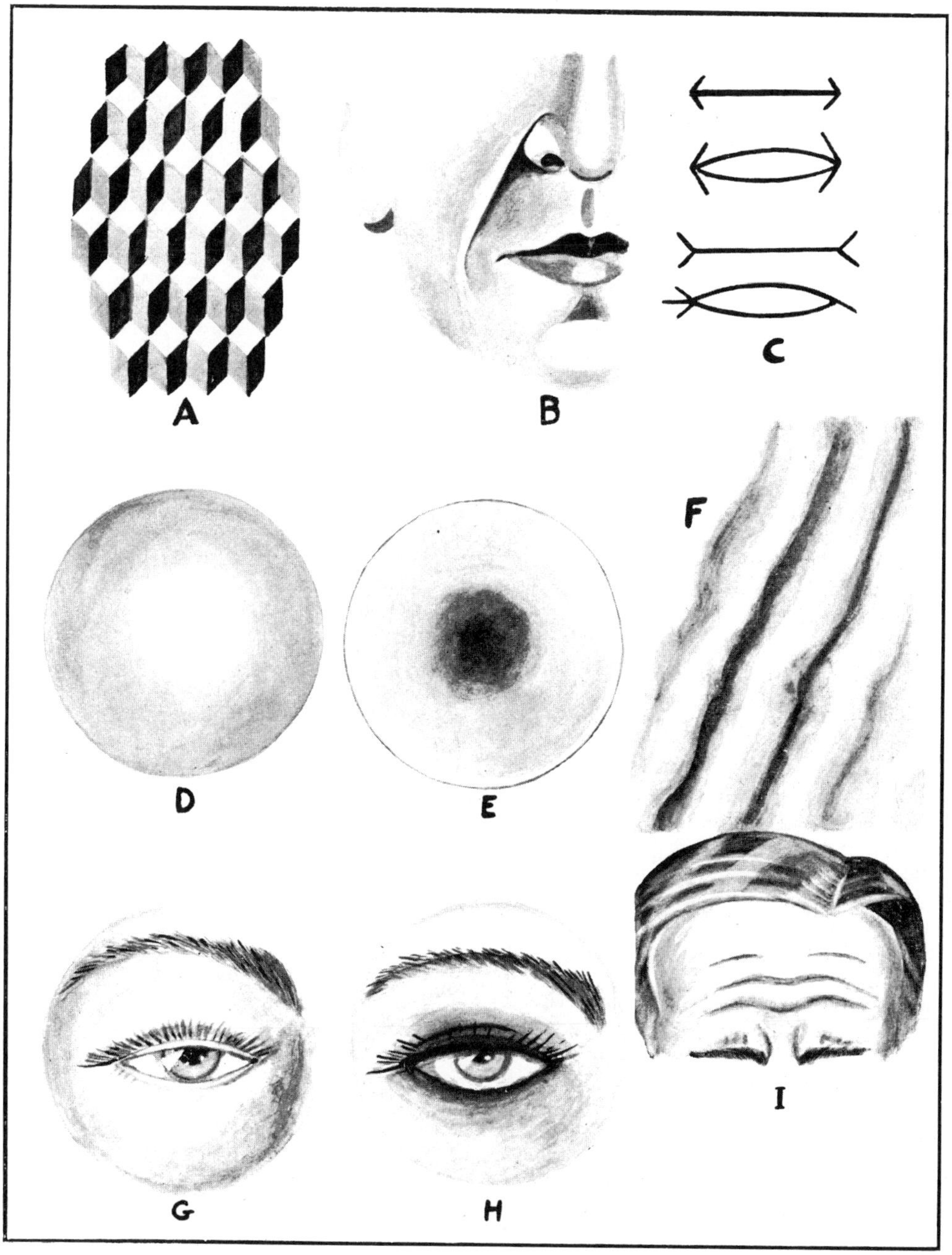

Fig. 28. Examples of Light and Shade

of the mouth have the effect of making it smaller or larger, as desired.

In the practical application of light, shade, and line, the effect of contrast of tones should be borne in mind, for just as shadows have the effect of showing up adjacent parts as high-lights, so do high-lights have the effect of making surrounding parts appear as shadows. There is need for caution in producing high-lights with regard to their positive nature. In general, they should be confined to small areas and not be allowed to run over shaded parts, which would destroy illusion, and make the face appear to be unnaturally pale. Only on rare occasions should white be used to produce high-lights; for example, when it is laid on the top of ground colour it produces the appearance of a muddy or chalky effect. It may be taken as a rule that the darker the foundation the more subdued should be the high-lights.

The distance from which a player and the make-up is viewed by an audience has a direct bearing upon the strength and contrast of any composition of light and shade. In a large theatre strong shadows and pronounced high-light are necessary to show up the modelling of the features that are required by the character. Even then, it is necessary to decide upon the effective range of the make-up—a point that may have to be decided by the producer. Some producers insist upon make-up being heavy enough to be clearly seen at the back row of seats, whilst others are content to have the best aspect seen from the front row. Probably a compromise between the two opinions provides the happy mean, and, failing instructions to the contrary, a considered effort should be made to gauge the effective strength that is sufficient to carry about mid-way.

Character make-up is an art that requires knowledge, patience, and plenty of practice to achieve. There is no fixed rule for style or manner of working. Let your own individual style find its own development by continually learning how to improve, change, or distort a feature in the simplest way. At times, abandon all idea of the stage, and practise entirely for good remodelling of any feature of a character study. This helps to clarify ideas and instruction, and to create an appreciation of the essentials of efficient character delineation.

MAKE-UP FOR THE NECK, DISFIGUREMENTS, ETC.

There is such an obvious connexion between the face and the neck that any character composition will necessarily include consideration of the throat and neck if they are likely to be exposed to view. The wind-pipe and larynx (Adam's apple) and the two muscles that run in an inclined direction from the central hollow of the collar-bone to the back of the ears are mainly in evidence. In a fleshy neck each of these parts will not be noticeable, but when the flesh between them loses its firmness and shrinks the wind-pipe and muscles become more pronounced. A thin neck is generally accompanied by a prominent larynx. The neck varies in general form with the sexes. In a man it is thicker, shorter, and less flexible than it is in a woman. A man's neck is like an inverted cone; that is, it is thickest at the junction of the head and neck, and it tapers downwards to the junction with the shoulders. A woman's neck is cylindrical and of equal thickness throughout its length. As it has greater flexibility, it usually wrinkles and shows signs of age much sooner than that of a man.

The neck is in accordance with the general proportion of a person, long and thin or short and thick, each type being differently affected by old age, illness, or temperament. Hence, it should be assumed that whatever changes are produced in the face will extend to the neck and be of a like character, the semblance of which, in make-up, is created by light and shade.

As an example, if the neck is naturally thin, a flesh tint of paint a tone lighter than that applied to the face gives a fuller appearance. On the other hand, a fat neck is somewhat reduced by the use of a darker tone than that required for the face. In extreme cases it is sometimes advisable to devise a means of hiding, with a high collar, neck-band, or scarf, as much of the neck as possible.

In extreme old age the neck loses every vestige of firmness. It becomes scraggy and has a whole network of wrinkles. To produce a scraggy-looking neck draw two parallel shadow-lines, about one inch apart, leading from the back of the ears down to the central hollow beneath the larynx, at which point they should converge. The space between these parallel shadows should be high-lighted in order to emphasize the shrunken

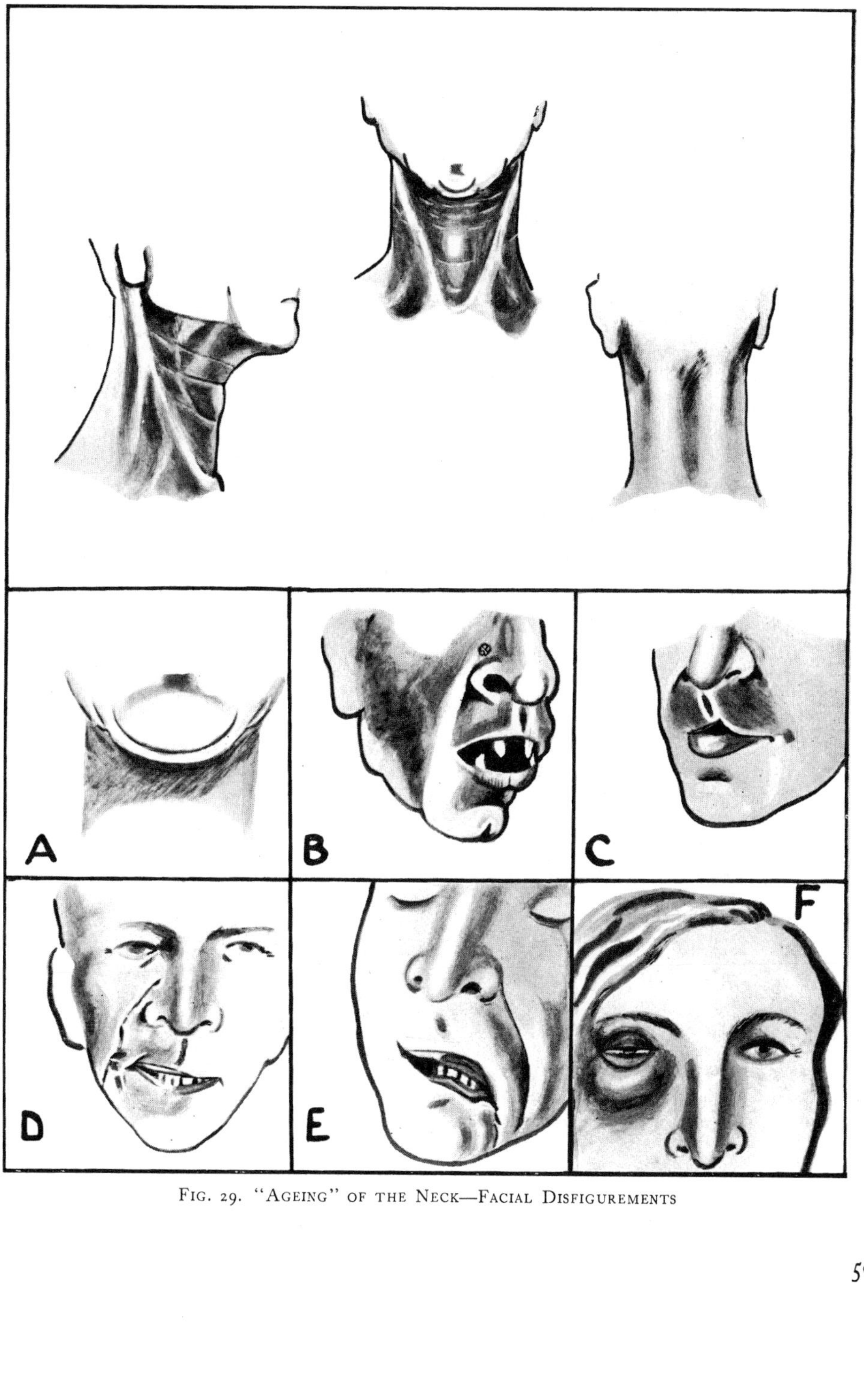

Fig. 29. "Ageing" of the Neck—Facial Disfigurements

effect. Alternatively, a more subdued effect is obtained by simply running the line of high-light only, and omitting the shadows. Another moderately strong shadow leading from just under the point of the chin and fading away at the top of the larynx should be added. There should be the deepest shadow tone at the upper part where the flesh sinks under the bone. The back of the neck should not be overlooked. Shadow the back centre from the base of the skull, and run two supporting ridges of high-light from behind the ears. The side, front, and back views of the neck at Fig. 29 give a good idea of what can be done to obtain effectual alteration.

The double chin is a common feature of the full-faced, jolly type of person, and is frequently required as a particular feature in a given character. The semblance of this type of chin is a useful aid in disguising a youthful throat and chin when a shrunken effect would be inappropriate. To create a double chin, find out where the fold will appear under the tip of the bone by pressing back the flesh of the chin. When the position of the crease is ascertained, relax the skin, mark round the chin with a curved line, and end it in the direction of the mouth corners. A second line, bordering the lower fold of flesh, should be carried just below the jaw bone and curved up on to the centre of the cheeks. The part between the two lines should then be high-lighted to give the effect of fullness below the jaw, which at once suggests the sagging cheeks of advanced age. Note Fig. 29, A.

When it is required to produce a more youthful appearance by hiding a double chin, the order of shading should, of course, be reversed. The fullness under the chin should be shaded to create a more definite jaw line, with a high-light placed at the point to give definition to the chin.

DISFIGUREMENTS

Now consider some of the difficulties that arise when disfigured features, and more or less unsightly concretions on any exposed part of the body, have to be simulated by make-up. These include any change of external appearance for the worse, and comprise moles, warts, birth-marks, bruises, wounds, fresh scars, seared skin, distorted features, indications of ludicrous or grotesque affectation, etc.

A mole is a spot or small permanent protuberance on the skin, usually of a dark brown colour. An imitation is simply painted on, No. 7 Brown being about the right colour to employ.

A wart is a hard and round excrescence on the skin, chiefly on the hands and face, of a reddish flesh colour. For making warts, cotton wool is rolled into small pills, stuck to the chin with spirit gum after the make-up has been powdered, and then tinted with carmine.

Birth-marks (strawberry marks, etc.) are sometimes needed on the cheek or neck. These are defined by a touch of Carmine 3 or Lake; preferably added after powdering to give a more pronounced effect.

Cuts or wounds on the face, hands, or legs should be sketched with Carmine 3 or Lake, and in some cases the addition of a little blue will improve the effect. It is advisable to leave the paint unpowdered so that the suggestion of a fresh wound is conveyed by its brightness. For representing bloodstains on the skin Carmine 1, unpowdered, gives the best impression. Bruises are generally of a blue-black colour, darkest at the point of injury, and fading out into the colour of surrounding skin. In producing the appearance of a bruise, aim at a soft, dull, tone of blue-black or green-black, which should be subdued with a powder finish.

The skin texture can be considerably changed to assist characterization. A freckled complexion is produced by dotting over the foundation tint with a reddish-brown paint before powdering, the same process being extended to the backs of the hands and the arms. Blotchy skin is made by adding faint dabs of reddish colour over the foundation. Coarse, rough skin is obtained by powdering the make-up with a mixture of oatmeal and violet powder. Pock-marked skin is, also, imitated by a fairly heavy foundation of grease paint, with coarse oatmeal applied locally or generally as powder.

Seared skin, presumably resulting from a burn or wound, presents more difficulty, as when the skin is painted it rarely looks convincing. A more effectual plan is to simulate the drawn or puckered skin with thin flexible material, gummed on before applying the foundation paint. For instance, an irregular strip of silk gauze, or stocking net, can be affixed to suggest the desired extent and degree of seared skin, and then covered with foundation paint. Remember that the part treated with spirit gum must be free from grease, and that the gum should be almost dry before the material is pressed on to it, otherwise the material will become saturated and dry hard and tight. As a substitute for the gauze, pale thin rubber, obtainable from a toy balloon, can be used in a similar manner; in fact, because of its elastic quality it is preferable to use rubber in positions that are subject to movement. To avoid a ridge, take care that the edges are properly stuck down and thickly covered with paint.

Another method of creating a basis of irregular skin is to smear "collodion" over the affected area. Collodion is a self-adhesive solution of gun-cotton in ether, which quickly dries in the form of skin when it is spread thinly, though, unlike gummy compounds, it does not become brittle. If you are ingenious, you may devise the creation of a variety of extraneous yet realistic effects. Rubber solution is of a similar nature and can be employed for the same purposes, though it should be applied only after the foundation paint has been well powdered.

Fig. 29, B, provides an example of a grotesque character, which can best be described as hybrid between a man and an animal. It is given as a suggestion of the extent to which light and shade can be exercised to distort the features. The nose with its flat, heavy aspect and the enlarged nostrils is apish. The mouth has a horrid expression, and appears to be always open, with the fang-like teeth showing in a savage grin. This impression is produced by, first, obliterating the natural outline of the lips, foundation paint being used for the purpose. The character lips are then painted with lake outside the margin, and are made the same thickness above, below, and at the sides, with a surround of high-light to make the mouth appear open. Some of the teeth are "black-out" with tooth enamel. Warts are placed in appropriate positions. The ears of this type would stand away from the head and be odd or misshapen.

There is diversity of character in the shape and position of the ears. The delicate feminine ear, the "cauliflower" ear of the pugnacious man; ears flat to the head, standing away, pointed, broadened—all are full of character. Large ears appear smaller if they are kept a tone darker than the rest of the complexion. Small ears are enlarged by running a high-light around the entire rim. A crumpled or "cauliflower" ear is created by adjusting over it a pink elastic band of just sufficient tension to pull the ear into the desired shape. Ears can be fixed flat to the head with spirit gum or made to stand away with a piece of modelling wax; nose-paste provides the best means of making the shape longer, pointed, or broader.

Another disfigurement of Nature that it is sometimes necessary to depict is the harelip—a perpendicular division of one or both lips, but more commonly the upper one, like that of a hare, illustrated in Fig. 29, C. To get this effect, first block out the outline of the upper lip, then create the division on either side of the centre with a lip colour, and at the margin place a high-light, extending towards the centre junction of the nose with the lip.

Scars, or permanent weals in the flesh, caused by wounds of the past, are sometimes essentials. Simple scars are imitated by painting a zig-zag line in the desired position and high-lighting its edges at intervals to give a puckered effect. The colour needs to be determined by the necessary contrast with the flesh tint and the age of the scar. Generally, lake with an occasional touch of blue, meets the case, except on a pale foundation, when a grey or green colour is more suitable. Pronounced scars that distort the features, as shown in Fig. 29, D and E, require a raised, irregular seam of flesh, which is produced with the aid of collodion or silk gauze, then painted over in the same way as the foregoing example. The illusion is made complete by shading and lighting the affected feature as though drawn to the wound. Powder over the painted scar to avoid the result looking too fresh.

Turn to Fig. 29, F, and note another common injury—the "black eye," usually associated with a comedy character. To convey a life-like impression of a bruised eye, it is not sufficient to daub on a quantity of black paint and expect it to carry conviction. Such a crude attempt appears to be like a deep hole in the head; therefore, an effort should be made to achieve a more realistic representation by the artful use of more appropriate colours. Blue, grey, and lake should form the basic colours for toning the darker parts. Apply a dark mixture of these within the margin of the eye socket, allowing the upper eyelid to be the darkest part. Then, to form a swollen pouch of flesh underneath the eye, make a semi-circle about three-quarters of an inch deep of dark-grey shading from the inner corner, under the eye centre, and extending to the outer corner. A high-light of yellow or pale green above this shadow gives the suggestion of puffiness. This pouch under the eye is effective for a dissipated old character or for certain forms of illness.

In the interests of simplicity, a blind eye can be suggested by wearing an eyeshade. Should it, however, be really necessary to portray a permanently closed eye, the difficulty can be overcome by cutting a piece of gauze to the exact size and shape, and fitting it over the eye so that its edges are hidden in the folds of the eyelids. Use as little gum as possible and only at the edges. Cover the gauze thinly with foundation paint, and indicate the closed position of the eyelashes with a thin black or brown line, strong enough to show when the eye is powdered.

HOW TO MAKE FALSE FEATURES

Consideration of the accentuation of facial features has been confined up to this point to the illusionary effects that are obtainable by light and shade. Probably it will have been realized that the exercise of light and shade, although of immense value to the make-up artist, is limited and often inadequate when a pronounced alteration in the shape or size of, say, the nose is absolutely necessary to achieve the full extent of a desired character delineation. Obviously, a definite alteration to the structure of any part of the face can be made only along the lines of an enlargement of that part with the aid of a false contrivance. Further, high-lighting at its best affects the front-face view only; the side aspect can be altered only by employing something to give additional prominence to the features.

Nose putty, or "nose paste," is principally used, as its name implies, to enlarge and remodel the shape of the nose, though it can also be used for a variety of purposes in make-up. Made in the form of sticks, this compound is of a plastic nature, the warmth of the hand being usually sufficient to make it pliable, like putty, in which form it readily adheres to the skin and can be moulded to a nose of any shape that is desired. Its tacky nature, however, makes it difficult to manipulate, but if the fingers are first wetted or slightly greased the putty will be prevented from sticking to them. For the same reason, it is advisable, when shaping the putty on any part of the face, to use a small wax-modelling tool, for this not only avoids a too frequent use of the fingers, but, also, lends considerable aid in obtaining a proper shape and smooth surface of the feature. Always bear in mind that although the fingers and the modelling tool should not be dry too much moisture is apt to make the putty too soft and to destroy its sticking qualities.

Nose putty should be applied direct to the natural skin, which, in order to make the putty adhere properly, must be entirely free from perspiration, cream, or make-up. This is important if the addition is to be made sufficiently secure to remain unmoved throughout a performance.

Fig. 30, A, B, and C, illustrate stages in the method of altering the size and shape of the nose. Sufficient putty to carry out the alteration is cut from the stick, the exact amount required depending upon the type of nose to be produced and the size of the natural one. It will be found that a relatively small amount will affect a considerable difference in the size of the nose. The piece of putty is kneaded with the fingers to a soft, workable consistency, applied along the ridge of the nose, firmly pressed into position, and carefully smoothed out until it assumes the correct shape. Ridges and unsightly edges, which would enable an audience to detect where the nose joined the flesh, must be avoided by working the putty until its surface is level and flowing, and all its edges merge imperceptibly into the skin. When the tip and the sides of the nose are being enlarged, better security is obtained by turning and pressing the lower edges of the putty into the nostrils, at the same time concealing the join. When the nose has to be abnormally large, additional security is secured by applying spirit gum at a few points in the area to which the putty is to be added. This dries quite firmly and is not difficult to remove.

When a satisfactory type of nose has been modelled, do not be discouraged if the first

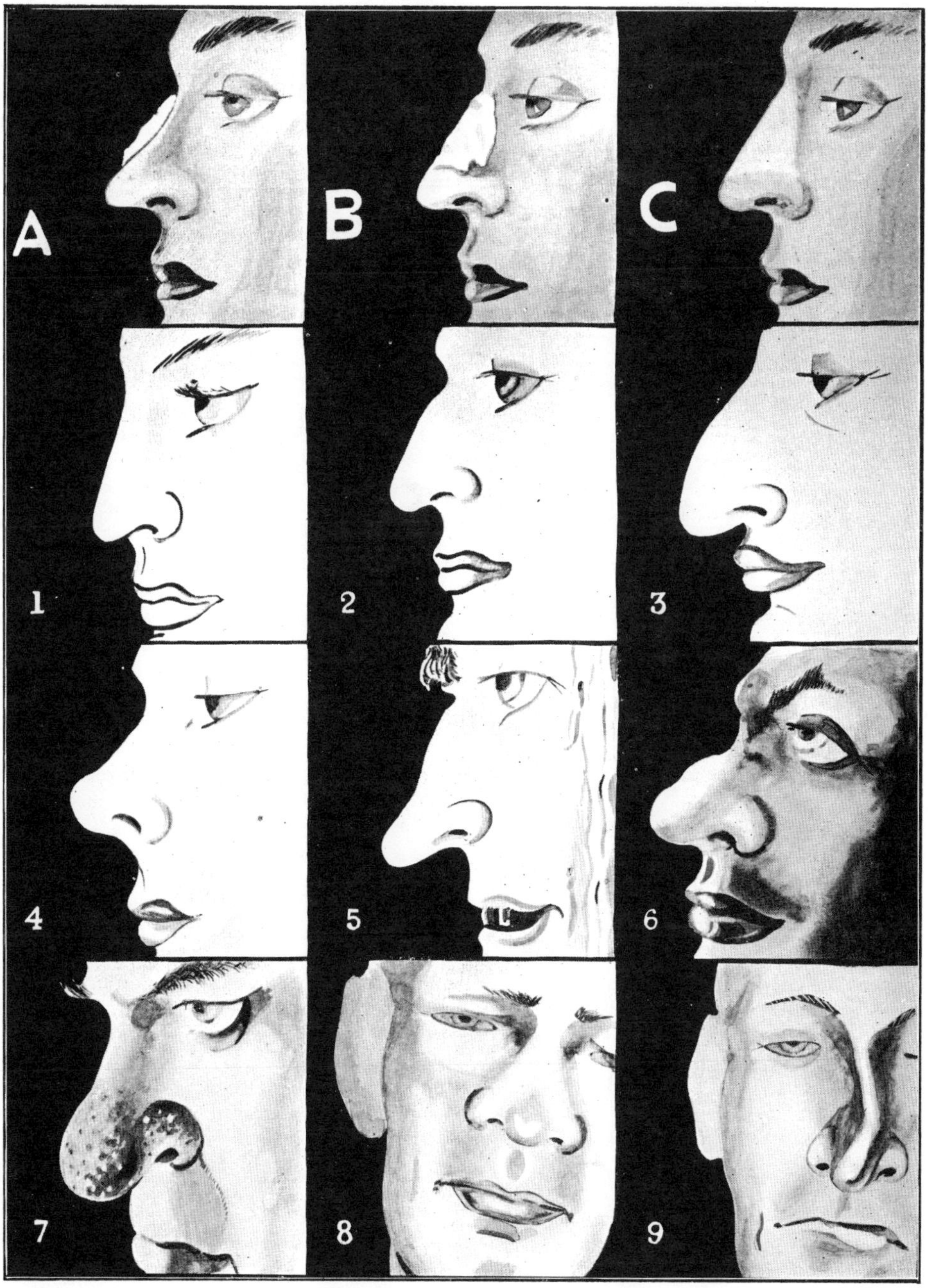

FIG. 30. CHARACTER OF NOSES

1. Grecian
2. Roman
3. Jewish
4. *Retroussé*
5. Pied Piper
6. Bumpkin
7. Toper
8. Bruiser
9. Crooked

attempt is crude, as a little practice will soon prevent crudity; proceed with the general make-up of the face, but leave the colouring of the nose to be done last, as the putty, being of a different colour and texture, will probably require a lighter or darker blend to obtain a hue in harmony with the rest of the face. In applying colour over the putty, no cream should be used or the putty will be made soft, and do not use a stick of paint directly on the nose. Considerable colour will need to be added to hide the putty satisfactorily. Take some foundation grease-paint on the finger tips, the warmth of which will slightly melt it, and gently rub it over the putty nose. This method obviates any risk of pushing the nose out of place or in any way spoiling its construction. Powder, too, must be lightly applied.

In cases where there is considerable difference in colour between the putty and foundation, it is an advantage to colour the putty before application. This can be done during its preparation by kneading with it a small quantity of a strong flesh colour of grease-paint, which, if not excessive, will not be detrimental to the adhesive qualities of the putty. With reasonable care a putty nose can be removed so that its shape is retained for further use; thus the time that would be taken to remodel for a series of performances is saved. Cold cream is all that is required to remove all traces of putty from the skin.

Nose putty offers tremendous scope to the ingenious for the creation of false features other than the nose. It can be employed, for instance, to produce a different shape of chin, to alter the position or prominence of the cheek-bones, to increase the size of the ears or the fatness of the cheeks, and to create bumps and swellings for comedy effects. It is a useful medium to make the skin appear coarse and much wrinkled. When this effect is required, work a small quantity of putty with the foundation colour into a paste and spread a thin layer over the skin, taking care to avoid finger marks. Any wrinkled effect can then be traced with the point of an orange stick, and afterwards, for accentuation, lined with grey, brown, or lake. This is a somewhat difficult process, but with care convincing, life-like effects, especially the fine criss-cross lines about the eyes, can be moulded.

A word of caution about the use of putty for more extensive alterations is necessary. Putty must be employed with discrimination and care, along with recognition that there are circumstances in which its use is inadvisable. Parts like the jaws and cheeks, which are subject to motion or muscular contraction, do not provide an ideal foundation to work upon; hence, the putty, owing to its inflexible nature, is liable to crack and lose shape when a lot of speaking or singing has to be done. Therefore, if there is any likelihood of putty being dislodged by facial expression, or other adverse conditions, it will be wisest to adopt another method.

PADDED FEATURES

Fine gauze, padded with down, wadding, or soft tissue paper, as an alternative, for making false fat cheeks or a nose of the large bulbous type, will produce any bulk without much weight. In the case of the cheeks, the padding of cotton-wool should be cut to shape and the edges thinned down, then placed in position on the face, and held there with a touch of spirit gum. A shaped piece of gauze should then be laid over the padding and gummed down about the edges, care being taken to avoid rucks and creases. The edges should be hidden as much as possible by arranging them close to the nose and ears or so that they are covered with moustache and beard if these have to be worn. A similar result is obtained if cheek pads are made of two layers of gauze, shaped and padded, the whole being held together with collodion or spirit gum and stuck on the face. Pads of this description are easily removed from the face, and can be used a number of times.

Either of these methods of using padded gauze can be employed for creating a large double chin, separate from or in conjunction with a fat neck the fleshy folds of which extend to the back. To make a pad to resemble a neck of this description first cut out a foundation of gauze to the shape of a large-sized collar. Over this foundation arrange three or four lengths of rounded wadding, then, after adding a surface layer of gauze, stitch down to the foundation layer along the edges and between the rows of padding, thus forming the folds. Cut the ends to the correct length required to fit the neck exactly, and attach small hooks and eyes for the purpose of fastening the pad in position with the join under the chin. A neck pad should be adopted only when its upper edge will be hidden at the back by a wig; in fact, wigs that have the neck padding attached as a continuation of the wig foundation, altogether eliminating a join, are obtainable. At the front, the join is covered by the arrangement of the beard, some portion of which can be mounted directly on to the gauze surface of the padding.

The heaviness of nose putty makes its use undesirable when a large coarse nose is necessary. Gauze and cotton-wool can advantageously be substituted for the putty, and handled in a manner that is most adaptable to the conditions. Ready-made substitutes are the excellent imitation noses that are manufactured from waxed linen, or papier-mâché, and suitably coloured. There are, however, a few points to watch when fixing a nose of this type in order to obtain the necessary security and freedom from movement. In the first place, nick the edge in a serrated manner and slightly bend outwards, so that the edge forms a close fitting juncture with the face. Then, to make the false nose fit snugly on the natural member, pack the inside space between them with cotton wool. The nose is finally secured to the skin with spirit gum or adhesive tape.

Bumps on the forehead, a bulging forehead, fat cheeks, long chins, and other oddities can be cut from paper or linen masks and mounted on the face when extremely grotesque faces are required.

The difficulty that is likely to be encountered when constructing gauze covered features is the need to colour them to conform to other parts of the face. It is an advantage to use a gauze as near flesh colour as possible, as this will require only local touches of light, shade, or heightening colour to match the general tone of complexion. In any case, the application of the required colour is best accomplished by rubbing grease-paint on the palm of the hand in order to melt it to some extent. With the aid of a fairly stiff brush the soft colour can then be painted over the gauze surface, or dabbed on with a small sponge. Apply a mere dusting of powder.

PADDED WIGS

It is sometimes necessary for a character to possess an abnormal head, such as a heightened forehead or one of the many forms of elongation or protrusion. This is the case, for example, in eccentric characters such as Mephistopheles, Don Quixote, Falstaff, Mr. Micawber, etc.; also in the creation of fantastic or grotesque characters, and for the absurdities of burlesque. Effects in these categories are obtained with the aid of special wigs padded or otherwise moulded to the required size and shape. The hard types are moulded from papier-mâché or a composition of cork-dust, the hair being attached to the foundation thus provided. The requirements of such characters are well known to any wig maker whose business is to supply theatrical wigs.

TYPES OF NOSES

It is generally admitted that no two noses are alike; that their formation imparts much character to the face and often reveals nationality. Fig. 30 illustrates some typical noses; any of these, and a variety of others, can be imitated by one medium or another. To leave grease-paint unpowdered on the lower half of the nose, whether normal or enlarged with putty, imparts a shiny effect that gives an apparent increase in size, and adds to the realization of a toper type of nose. When enlarging the nose bear in mind that the thickness of the nose is responsible for producing the effect of the eyes being set closer together; to regain correct proportion it is necessary to lengthen the eyes at the outer corners. A flat nose, of the Negro or bruiser type, is probably the most difficult to imitate. To be effective the nose needs to be flattened. This can be done by placing a small piece of kid or silk on the end of the nose, pressed down with a strand of strong silk thread long enough to pass behind the ears and tie behind the head, and adjusted to supply the required pressure. The nose can be made to appear crooked either by high-lighting the ridge at an appropriate angle or by creating a false bent ridge with a little putty.

DESIGNING A CHARACTER MAKE-UP

To give more than ordinary significance to a conventional part, or to play a character convincingly, it is not only necessary to learn the nature of that part or character, but to find appropriate facial expression of its actual soul.

The face is the greatest revealer of character, owing to its ability to change and express ever varying inward moods.

This is the formula that will invariably help to solve your make-up problems when you are given a role to play, whether you are cast for type or faced by a demand to create a type. To cast to type is to choose players for the way they look rather than for their ability to assume characteristics foreign to themselves; in other words, to cast for each part a player who, at least, naturally looks the part: but one-type players do not make versatile character actors. Therefore, every part should be considered in the light of its possibilities for the portrayal of a new personality.

When the actor-knight, Sir Cedric Hardwicke, a worthy example of the dependable character actor, begins the study of a new part he has pointed out that it is the make-up on which he chiefly has to concentrate. I interviewed Sir Cedric in his dressing-room at the St. James's Theatre, London, after seeing his brilliant performance in the record success *The Late Christopher Bean.* He assured me that is precisely what he did in the case of his characterization of the old country doctor's part. His method is to delve into the psychology of the character he is to portray until he really feels that he knows him intimately—that he is a vital living creature, not just a figment of imagination. It was in this way that he so successfully depicted the varied emotions of Dr. Haggett, who, urged by greed, becomes a dishonest and cunning schemer but who regains his old honest self again when he realizes the depth of a woman's faith.

Although deference can be paid to the precept that comparisons are odious, yet comparisons that are afforded by two great actors in their interpretation of the same character are interesting and instructive. How widely different two players can be in the same part and still tell the same story has, in my experience, at any rate, never been more strikingly demonstrated than in the case of the principals in the stage conception, on the one hand, and the screen version, on the other hand, of Christopher Bean. Incidentally, this comparison becomes inevitable when the artists concerned are widely acknowledged to be stars in their respective spheres. Sir Cedric Hardwicke as Dr. Haggett, and Edith Evans as Gwenny (the servant), represented the London stage version: Lionel Barrymore and Marie Dressler, two of America's screen veterans, were in the respective roles in the film version of the play. In each role the personalities were totally different, as were their methods of telling the story; yet both pairs scored success in their own medium and proved that the word "genius" can be applied equally to more than one interpretation of the same role.

The question of creating an outward form that will add extra significance to what a character says or does is all-important and fundamental, and is really the chief aim in make-up art. A player must look the part, and make-up counts for a great deal when it is intelligently designed and efficiently applied.

When a player is cast for a part and the plot and lines have been studied, the first step in approaching a conception of the character to be portrayed is to consider any available source of help. If the play is popular and has been repeatedly performed it is more than likely that the character will have assumed a distinctive appearance and be well known to playgoers. In such cases it becomes as imperative to know the traditional make-up as to know the correct lines, and this can generally be copied from a pictorial record of a former professional, or first-class amateur, production.

Perhaps the author describes the peculiarities of the character he has evolved in his mind. If so, the author should be credited with having a definite idea, and the details of his conception should be produced as nearly as possible. Failing guidance in either of these directions, the player must follow any suggestion of the producer or rely upon his, or her, own imagination and initiative. In the event of the latter necessity, the imagination will need to set to work to create a clear impression of a character and one that fits naturally into the construction of the plot. To the inexperienced player this presents difficulty, but if the problem is attacked by adoption of a method that analyses the part, a method that leaves nothing to chance or guesswork, a helpful conclusion of the temperament as expressed in colour, form, and expression can be drawn. The temperament or personality is the result of the ever-changing influences of life, and is subject to continual change during the varied experiences of life. This is the reason why there are so many and so different personalities, and why temperaments vary so much from moment to moment, from time to time, and from age to age. The mood or prevailing temperament, being the general tone of feeling, forms the basis of the feeling or sentiment that has to be expressed; if the basis is not correctly sensed, it is impossible for the characterization to be correct. Therefore, every new part demands intelligent treatment to achieve sound characterization, which, after all, is the test of good acting.

To analyse a part read it through and try to think of the character as another person who has to speak the words. Imagine what kind of a person would say such things and behave in such a manner. Question what motives and feelings would lie behind the words, and decide if what the character has to do and feel is possible within the limits of the plot. Think what the mental and moral constitution of this person is likely to be; try to reason out something of the past life, for time and experience will have left their marks. Form a mental picture that will help the visualization of the outward indications of the influence of inheritance, climatic or social environment, and personal habits. Something else may be learnt and a more intimate acquaintance gained by knowing exactly what other characters in the play have to say about this imaginary person. Is the character an historical figure? To find out the correct temperament of any characteristic type of individual in any particular age, a study should be made of the recorded life, of the customs and the sentiments of the times; this will be productive of a clearer vision.

When a clear mental conception of characterization has been established it is a wise policy to keep a record of the details as an aid to the maintenance of the clarity of the conception, which should not be allowed to become vague or to be entirely forgotten. The next step is to study oneself and to discover any traits that may be similar to those of the character in mind, noting the qualities that require to be accentuated or subdued, or any that must be acquired. Then try to feel as you imagine the character would feel when speaking the words or in reaction to what is said by other characters.

With a clear idea of the characteristic appearance that is required, turn attention to ways and means of producing the effect. It would be unwise to assume that the ideal make-up can be achieved at a first attempt, especially if that attempt is delayed until the dress rehearsal, when the necessary time and concentration are almost certain to be lacking. Hence, it is always advisable for players who make themselves up to rehearse their make-up, either privately or collectively, in order to put new ideas into practice and to gain facility. Before applying make-up, by the aid of a mirror, observe the face to discover how much its character can be altered by changing the expression of the eyes and mouth, in keeping, of course, with the character of the part. Facial expression can take the part of speech in the expression of thought, but its best use is to add to the effect of the spoken word, so that thereby the thought is made more capable of being felt and correctly interpreted by the audience. Often, however, is not facial expression either omitted or badly created? It is seldom that harmony is maintained between the words and the facial expression that projects a thought or an emotion. It is much more common to have two distinct meanings given, the actual translation of the words giving one meaning and the expression of the face another. These lead to confused understanding.

Remembering that the facial muscles are the basis of facial expression, and that the mobility and readiness for action should be such that they can respond immediately and accurately to the feeling that needs their harmonious co-operation, it is desirable that the maximum of characteristic expression should be attained with as little make-up as possible, for though a thick mask of grease-paint makes disguise easy, the heavier the make-up the more difficult it is to convey sensitive emotional variations by the changing expressions of the face.

A change of hairdressing is often a valuable aid in the alteration of the appearance, but such a change cannot be done at a moment's notice; rather is it a matter for trial and experiment. If it is possible to arrange the natural growth in a way that is suitable to the character, so much the better, for though Nature may seem to be no more than a wig it will prove infinitely more comfortable.

When every effort has been made to look as

much like the part as possible without the aid of any artificial disguise, make-up—nose putty, paint, powder, crêpe hair, etc.—can be brought out and practice with them begun. With paint change the colour tone of the skin, and note the effect. Accentuate the desired characteristics as may be necessary by means of high-lights; subdue others by means of shading. Experiment with the light and shade of the nose to produce a different shape. Paint out the eyebrows and redraw them, altering their form. Cover the lips with foundation colour paint and give them a new outline, neither too large nor too small, but quick to reflect expressions. Put shadows around the eyes, fade the eyelashes, and notice how their brightness is dulled. See if the right expression can be shown with the alteration of a few facial lines. Wrinkle the face, and where the lines naturally appear apply paint to suggest appropriate emphasis. If the eyebrows are raised, the forehead is wrinkled, and attention or surprise is expressed. Transverse wrinkles between the eyes express anger or fierceness; vertical lines express reflection or difficulty. Curved wrinkles at the inner ends of the eyebrows express pain and suffering; hatred if the eyebrows are lowered. Add, if appropriate, a moustache of crêpe hair or a roughly shaped beard.

It may be found difficult to judge the effect of the work as it will appear from a distance; moving away from the mirror provides the perspective necessary to form an accurate idea of the result. A rehearsal of this kind is similar to the work of a painter when he is making preliminary sketches; it helps to get ideas into concrete form. It should be practised until the character is perfectly developed. Should a wig be necessary, draw a sketch of it or find an illustration that will help to explain the style.

Remember that the character of a face depends upon the elemental qualities of form, colour, and expression, and make the characterization as definite as possible in all these qualities. There is as much variety in feature, colour, hair, etc., as there is in expression of countenance; and a little reflection will indicate the necessity for such varieties. The spiritual and the material, the grave, the gay, the healthy, the sick, the aesthetic, the debauched, the old and the young —each has a distinguishing colour and expression.

Although the distinctions between individuals of a particular country are, in many instances, as great as they are between the people of one country compared with another, there are certain forms of head, or casts of feature, or qualities of hair and complexion, which characterize different nations and more particularly different races. How these distinctions have been produced by Nature is a question that need not here be entered upon. Nevertheless, a knowledge of the correct distinctions of racial form and colour is of tremendous importance to the make-up artist. It is for this reason that the chart (Fig. 31) illustrating a few of the varieties of typical faces depending upon national peculiarities is introduced. It will be of assistance in the study of natives who may have to be impersonated.

MAKE-UP FOR NATIONAL TYPES

It was Carlyle who called attention to the fact that there are but two studies: Nature and Human Nature. The study of human nature is as old as humanity itself. That one's occupation and habits stamp their impress on the outward expression was observed and recorded by an Egyptian scribe of the Twelfth Dynasty, perhaps 2000 B.C. This papyrus is now in the British Museum. Aristotle was a devoted student of physiognomy and compared the features and dispositions of men with animals. Hippocrates, the father of medicine, 460 years B.C., refers to the influence of environment in determining disposition, and in the reaction of these on the features.

The sum total of knowledge concerning the variations of human character, obtained through observation and experimentation by students of all times, is prodigious. Important facts relating to it are to be found in all the human sciences. From a study of anthropology we obtain a knowledge of man as an animal; biology explains the living tissue; anatomy and physiology are concerned with the structure and the various functions of his body; psychology examines the operations of his mind; phrenology and physiognomy seek to interpret his character as portrayed in cranial development, and as expressed in his features.

Ethnography is that branch of science which describes the different races of men, their peculiarities of colour and hair, their features, manners,

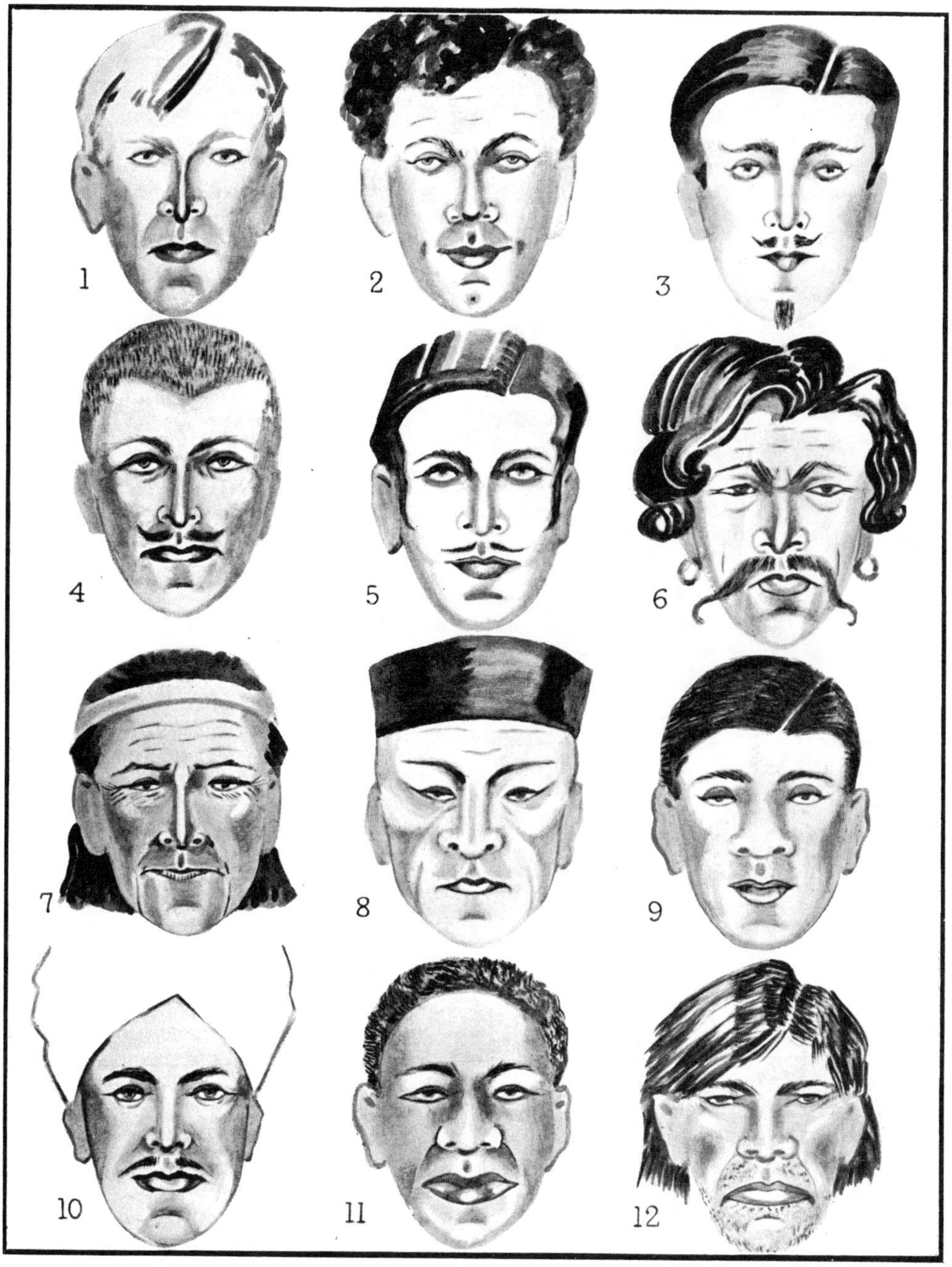

FIG. 31. NATIONAL TYPES

1. Scotch
2. Irish
3. French
4. German
5. Spanish
6. Italian
7. American Indian
8. Chinese
9. Japanese
10. Hindu
11. Negro
12. Mongol Tartar

customs, etc. A knowledge of these factors is essential in the formation of a judgment, this judgment being our analysis of the innumerable character and racial types that most frequently have to be represented on the stage.

The skin, hair, and eyes of all races normally contain a deposit of iron pigment that gives to

Sir Cedric Hardwicke as Charles II in "Nell Gwyn"

A British and Dominions production directed by Herbert Wilcox

them their colouring. The fairer the type the less the pigment that is present; the darker the type the more abundant is the pigmentation. Although from a strictly scientific point of view a racial grouping arranged according to the variations of colour would be considered unsatisfactory, it is, however, usually sufficient for stage purposes to concentrate upon the colour factor, together with the dominant features, the character of hair and the generally familiar cast of face. The following brief survey, based on the relation of these chief factors, will give appreciable aid in acquiring the finesse of national impersonation.

All races in respect of colour can be broadly classified: (1) White, covering a range from the Albino, a race the skin and hair of which are preternaturally white, down the colour scale to brunette; (2) Coloured, typified by the yellow, olive, red, and brown races; (3) Black, comprising brown and black Negroid types. The greatest pigmentation is found in the tropics among African Negroes, East Indians, New Guineans, and the Australian Aborigines, these being practically black. Going north from the tropic, complexions gradually grow lighter, being dark brown in Egypt, light brown in North Africa, deep olive in the Mediterranean, olive in Southern Europe, brunette in Central Europe, blonde in North-West Europe, and a mixed type in America, the American Indian being copper-brown or bronze. In general, the colour of the hair and of the iris of the eye partakes of the colour of the skin, but in all races there spring up occasional varieties.

These three groups, the so-called white, coloured, and black, whilst actually admitting a wide range in colouring of skin and hair, exhibit other distinguishing factors in the quality of hair they possess, and well-marked dissimilarity in form of features. The white group is distinguishable by a soft, flexible, wavy, and flowing quality of hair, as typified by the European blonde, though the variations of colour include flaxen, red, and brown. In this group the forehead in the males has usually a definite prominence over the eye—the so-called "bar of Michael Angelo"; the face is well proportioned and never flattened, and the lips are not everted. Those of the coloured group are characterized by stiff and straight hair, most often brown or black in colour, as represented by the Chinese and the Mongolian types. All these people possess cheek-bones of a greater or lesser degree of prominence. In the black group the hair is of a thick-set, strong, short, curly, or woolly quality, and is generally accompanied by a broad, flat nose. Certain types are difficult to define, but usually the distinction is clear cut. All forms of hair may occur in the same population, where racial admixture has taken place, though normally the variation is slight in the same group.

Of the brief imperfect outline of the great families of mankind that has been presented every phase might be the text of a long essay. In

FIG. 32. AMERICAN INDIAN (SIOUX)

(G.2477)

this, as in other subjects that are supplementary to the main theme of practical make-up, I have attempted only to awaken attention and interest, and to point the way to an observation of the elements on which ingenuity or acumen should be employed. The standard is by no means too high. Your make-up ought to be regarded as something greater than merely a thing incidental to getting ready for the stage; remember it is creating something beautiful, perhaps making a memorable picture, as though on canvas. A high standard, to which efforts must aspire, should be set, the aim being to create a true-to-life and beautiful picture.

PRACTICAL GUIDANCE

With a view to giving as much practical guidance as possible the several phases of instruction will henceforth be passed under review and applied in detail to a range of representative home and foreign types, beginning with the white group of races and working to the other extreme in order of colour index. All the essential details of a straight make-up for both men and women have been dealt with (refer to Figs. 8 and 9) and if, perchance, these have been passed over without trying to turn out presentable efforts based on the instructions given, it will be better to turn back and to master each subject carefully before proceeding. It should be realized in regard to colour data that, in view of the wide dissimilarity in method and intensity of stage lighting, the prescribed colours can be approximate only, and that modifications may be necessary to meet cases that do not conform to a general average of lighting colour and power. For guidance on this point it can be laid down as a general rule that where there is strong light tending to vivid colouring the complexion tone should be somewhat paler and the characteristics drawn more boldly to bring out a clear disclosure and a sharpness of expression in the features.

Teutonic (North Mediterranean) includes English, Anglo-American, Dutch, Germans, Austrians, Danes, Scandinavians, and Norwegians.

English and American straight parts are identical for all practical purposes. Flesh tints Nos. 1½ to 4½ inclusive are used as foundation, the tint varying according to the requirements of the character. Men are usually of healthy and ruddy complexion, with an intelligent and straightforward expression; the hair is generally of a fair to medium brown colour, black hair being in a minority. For youthful roles rely upon No. 3½ as the foundation, appropriately high-lighted with No. 2½, or preferably Nos. 5 and 9, slightly heightened with Carmine 2. The more florid tones of middle-age are best obtained with Nos. 5 and 8 and local touches of Carmine 3. A pale sun-tan tint of powder is advisable.

Bear in mind that the advantage of a compound foundation lies in the variety of different tones that can be obtained by the blending of unequal proportions of each colour, one tone being suitable for one type of complexion, other tones for the ruddier or paler types. Then, again, the necessary graduation of tones from high-light to shadow can be worked in to emphasize or change the contour of the features. The precise tone of the complexion will depend upon the social type, whether the aristocrat, the opulent, the business man, farmer, fisherman, sailor, factory-hand, agricultural or dock labourer, or the down-and-out is being portrayed. A lowering in the social scale, or the effects of association with the unhealthy conditions of life, should be indicated by the dull tone of the colour employed. In a similar way the mood or disposition of a role is at once suggested by colour tone. Thus, a warm and cheerful nature will have a warm and bright tone; a cold, mean, or unscrupulous nature presents a cold, sombre tone of complexion. This cold tone is introduced by the addition of No. 6 or 6½ to a foundation of Nos. 5 and 9, or Nos. 5 and 8; the warm tone is obtained by a somewhat higher proportion of No. 9 in the foundation blend, or by the judicious addition of Carmine.

To wrinkle or not to wrinkle is often a question. Observation informs us that wrinkles in general are much more in evidence in the faces of the restless, the thinkers, the worriers, the emotionalists, the neurotic, and the weather-beaten than in others, the relative amount and degree of these wrinkles suggesting the state of mind or nature of the exposure. On the other hand, freedom from wrinkles is the prerogative of the calm, the spiritual, the saintly, the well-favoured, and well-preserved. When wrinkles are necessary due regard must be given to the natural lines of the face that are created by muscular action. A useful method of locating these lines is to squeeze the eyes shut when applying the pale shade of groundwork. When the eyes are opened the surrounding crow's feet, the frown or laughter lines, will be plainly evident, and can easily be indicated by a darker

ANNA NEAGLE AS NELL GWYN IN "NELL GWYN"
A British and Dominions production directed by Herbert Wilcox

paint. It is, of course, advisable to relax the face before lining in order to prevent smudging. Wrinkles should never be hard and stiff-looking or in the least overdone. Slight undulations of almost transparent lines, appearing dark at the base and fading out at their extremities, and separated by high-lights, are the most natural looking. In all schemes of light, shade, and line do not overlook the subduing effect that powder has upon the grease-paint colours. If this effect is underestimated, it is highly probable that contrasts in colours that appear bold enough before powdering will be partially extinguished, and degenerate into tameness and indifference.

REDUCING AGE

It is by no means a rare occurrence for a player to require to appear younger than he is in a role; and it is not difficult to achieve this result within reasonable limits. If the figure is within desirable bounds, and the limbs are supple, ten to fifteen years may be taken from the face with a good make-up. To do this an advantage is gained if, instead of the usual cold-cream base, a groundwork of pale flesh paint is applied and thoroughly rubbed into the skin. The process has the effect of reducing coarseness of the skin, and producing the appearance of fine texture by filling in enlarged pores and crevices. If there are lines about the eyes, take the forefinger and thumb and slightly stretch the skin, enough to open the crevices, so that the paint can get in and level the surface. Treat the lips in a similar way, extinguishing their natural outline. A tendency of the eyebrows to be too thick or drooping is corrected by blocking out a portion on the underside with paint. The next step is to blend a deeper colour over the groundwork until the desired complexion is attained. For men a mixture of Nos. 2½ and 5 will form the clean undercoat, followed by No. 9. Women should use Nos. 1½ and 5 first, and then No. 3½. To fill out hollows in the cheeks, blend the foundation a tone lighter at these points, subsequently toning them up with Carmine 2, which, in contrast with the darker foundation tone, will have the effect of a high-light without paleness. If the eyes are too deep-set, treat the surrounding skin with just enough Carmine to brighten them, and apply a suitable juvenile eye colour to the upper lids. The lips come next for reshaping with No. 9, darkened with a touch of lake, the upper one being the darker to suggest the shadow. Now give a neat youthful curve to the eyebrows, and, if necessary, darken the hair about the temples. Round off the youthful effect with a natural tinted powder.

A MIDDLE-AGED MAN

For a well-favoured man of 50 years or so, of the business director, stockbroker, banker, or lawyer type, use a foundation of Nos. 5 and 8, high toned with Carmine 3, about the lower parts of the cheeks, extending down to the jaw line, and also on the outer rim and lobe of the ears. If the character is assumed to be accustomed to outdoor exercises, his complexion will tend to be ruddy or tan; if he is not in a healthy condition, a trace of paleness will be evident. With a clear conception of the individual type in mind develop it as far as possible by working on the natural inclination of the face as regards hollows and lines. These should be worked in only sufficiently strong to show up delicately through the powder. There must be no haphazard scattering of lines that may mean anything or nothing; wrinkles should conform to the expression it is desired to convey, namely, in this case, the transverse forehead lines of attention, the vertical lines of reflection, a few crow's feet at the eye corners, normally short naso-labial fold lines, and those indicating a slight droop of the corners of the mouth. The neck, also, will require appropriate hollows or wrinkles, if it is naturally smooth. No. 6 is a most useful flat shade for toning hollows in a medium or inclining to pale foundation, and No. 5 for the high-lights; if it is ruddy or dark, hollows should be toned in with No. 6, then deepened with grey and lake, with high-lights of No. 2½ or No. 3. Do not apply any colour to the eyelids, but define them with a thin line of dark-grey or brown along the edges; the eyebrows should then be painted to look rather bushier and slightly nearer the nose. Alter the character of the mouth by thinning the outline of the upper lip and extending the lower one with No. 9 colour and a touch of lake. Hair going grey about the temples gives a distinguished appearance to this type. White grease paint or wet white, evenly applied with a toothbrush and softened with a dusting of powder, looks natural. Neatly trimmed moustaches are common to this class, and may be of dark grey or matched to the hair of the head.

FARMERS, SAILORS, AND FISHERMEN

Representing the open-air class, these types are assumed to have deeply sunburnt and weather-beaten complexions, entirely free from any trace of sallowness. For farmers No. 4, freshened with No. 9, is a suitable foundation; the bronze-tan of fishermen requires No. 13, and No. 8 on prominent features; for the sailor's wind-and-sun tan use Nos. 4 and 8. Wrinkles and crow's feet about the eyes, suggesting the habit of tightly closing the eyes as a protection against strong sunlight, may be numerous. These are put in with lake, darkened at their deepest points with dark grey or blue, and may extend from the outer corners back to the hair and down over the cheek bones. Small high-lights of No. 3 will make them more emphatic. Finish with sun-tan powder.

Two photographs of typically historical English characters—Charles II and Nell Gwyn—are shown. They are also leading roles in the delightful stage comedy of Pepys, *And So to Bed*, by J. B. Fagan.

PRACTICAL MAKE-UP DATA

Young women, normally, have a clear skin, the hues of a healthy complexion, and bright eyes. Youth renews wasted tissues automatically up to the age of thirty years or so, but afterwards a general slackening of the tension of life begins, and that which happens in the bodily functioning is portrayed first in the face and throat. The slower growth of the skin at this period and later in life brings darker pigmentation, general loosening of the skin from the facial muscles underneath, and less connexion of flesh with bone. Whether the face be thin or fat, this tendency is present, and creases, formed by loose skin, deep crow's feet, and often baggy circles under the eyes appear—hence, the matronly and the elderly, as a rule, are more florid than they are in youth, though complexions vary according to the influence of indoor or outdoor occupation, social scale, health conditions, age, etc.

For young medium-to-fair types No. 2 or 2½ is a satisfactory foundation; better scope for variation in tone is provided by the blending of No. 1½ and No. 5 for the base, over which No. 3½ is subsequently applied and further heightened with Carmine 2. The rouge colour is generally placed high up on the cheeks, beginning under the lower eyelids and sweeping along the upper cheeks straight out to the hair, fading away well above the jaw line. In the case of older women, though, it should be placed lower on the cheeks and carried down to the jaw line to suggest a slight sagging of the flesh.

A WELL-PRESERVED SOCIETY WOMAN

This type is probably the most frequently required characterization in modern plays, and any woman of thirty-five years of age or below who is cast for such a part will need skilful alteration to present a convincing fifty-to-sixty years to the audience and not cause laughter when a married man calls her "mother." In these days of beauty culture, however, a society woman, fifty years of age without grey hairs, and with a youthful figure that has been retained by self-denial and specialist treatment, is quite common. Nevertheless, if the skin has not darkened or become florid, there is a change in texture that is especially noticeable in the neck and hands. In spite of care, the skin of the hands will have shrivelled, the veins will stand out and be a trifle blue, and the flesh will have shrunk away from the bones. It is such points as these that must be taken into consideration when a "grown-old" character is called for—hands, eyes, the muscles of the neck, the gradual thinning of the hair about the temples—with a view to discovering the lines along which one's own features would be likely to develop or shrink according to advancing years.

Begin the make-up with a moderately thin application of No. 5, over which distribute No. 3½. Much of the ageing effect depends upon the way the darker colour is blended in respect of light and shade, the aim in this case being to suggest a slightly different contour due to sinking and drooping in the face. Therefore, the eye-sockets, the sides of the nose, the centre indent of the upper lip, and below the lower one, should be toned slightly darker, whilst the lower part of the forehead over the eyebrows, the cheek-bones, the ridge of the nose, and the point of the chin should be somewhat paler to suggest prominence. Place a soft tone of Carmine 2 on the cheeks, but not quite so near the eyes as in a straight make-up, the aim being to diminish their brightness by shadows. Delicate shadows and wrinkles about the eyes, if artistically done, will suggest age without causing ugliness, as also will one or two vertical frown lines between the eyebrows and a few short shadowy lines across the forehead.

Either No. 6 or light-brown liner No. 28A can be used without danger of overdoing the effect, a touch of lake and light grey being added to obtain further depth. Place a rather deep shadow in the eye sockets between the eye and the nose, a faint one running down in front of each ear; faintly suggest the naso-labial folds, a slight droop at the corners of the mouth, and add a shadow to the hollow between the lower lip and the chin. After painting in the shadows, the eyes can be coloured with a soft shade of grey-blue or grey-brown, applied only to the lower part of the lid so that there may be sufficient contrast between it and the shaded part beneath the eyebrows. Also, outline the eyes with a line of brown run along the edges of both upper and lower lids; this can be done with grease paint before powdering, or with either grease paint or water cosmetic after powdering. The powder should be of a cream tint. After powder has been applied, draw a few fine crow's feet lines at the outer corners of the eyes, with grey darkened at the roots with lake, and one or two curved ones underneath.

There is a sound reason for applying these lines over the powder, this being to overcome the difficulty of drawing lines fine enough, yet sufficiently strong to show through powder. On a powder surface they can be made fine and clear with a sharp liner, then lightly covered with a mere dusting of powder.

Eyebrows that start rather low and arch near the temple to finish with a downward curve, create the haughty look that is often a characteristic of a person with a lorgnette. If there is no natural inclination to an arch, paint out the ends of the brows with foundation grease paint before powdering, and finish the line in the required direction with an eyebrow pencil or water cosmetic after powdering.

In order to avoid painting the throat with shadows and wrinkles, it is advisable to hide as much of it as possible with a band of black silk ribbon or to adorn it with a deep jewelled collar. Beautiful hands, which have the appearance of being cared for, and which are used for calm and delicate movements to convey certain emotions and to supplement speech and facial expressions, generally belong to a person with refined bodily and mental tastes. In this case, the hands, arms, and shoulders should be treated with liquid powder (wet white), preferably of a pale flesh tint, as pure white usually conveys a hard and cold appearance. The hollows between the base of the fingers and the knuckles can then be slightly deepened with a touch of dry rouge, and the veins emphasized by faintly shading them with a soft lead pencil.

A MIDDLE-CLASS WOMAN

This example is of the healthy, normal type, with outdoor life inclinations, though it is not so

FIG. 33. NATIONAL TYPES—WOMEN

1. Irish
2. Dutch
3. German
4. Jewish
5. Spanish
6. Russian
7. Egyptian
8. Japanese
9. Eskimo
10. American Indian
11. Hindu
12. Fijian

well preserved as the exotic occupant of luxuriously sheltered surroundings. The face is slightly dark and ruddy, and has creases and wrinkles that suggest flabby tissues, rather dull eyes, and patches of coarse skin on the lower part of the face and near the hair line. The eyebrows are a trifle heavy, rather high near the nose, then falling away to the outer ends in a steady incline; the hair of the head is mildly tinged with grey.

For the foundation use No. 5 first, then blend No. 9 over it, following the directions about light and shade given in the preceding example, though allowing the general tone to be somewhat darker, with a little extra redness about the hair line and around the jaw from the ear. The purplish hue of Carmine 3 is suitable for the cheeks, but should be judiciously applied. Instate similar shadows, making sure that the eye sockets are strong enough to show as shadows through the powder, and deepen certain of the wrinkles, principally the frown lines, the naso-labial lines, and those at the mouth corners. Further to intensify them, all wrinkles should be faintly high-lighted with No. 2½. The eyelids should be thinly coloured and the eyes outlined with grease paint before the heavy powdering is done; this will give them a faded look, or, if the eyes are naturally dark, omit both the eyelid colour and the outline, thus leaving them to appear small and colourless. If necessary, take away a too-youthful shape of mouth by shading its outline with No. 6 and strengthening the shadow immediately beneath the centre of the lower lip. Powder with a Rachel tint, as this will maintain the high-lights. Finally, re-shape the eyebrows to conform to the character, and then with the aid of white hair-powder give the hair a tinge of grey. Dress the hair to a smooth, tidy coiffure, with a few softening waves.

A VIVACIOUS WOMAN

This is a type of "quips and cranks and wanton wiles, nods and becks and wreathed smiles" that is well-known in comedy. The character should have a warm, pinkish complexion with eyebrows that arch in a semicircle over the eye sockets, and an accentuation of lines resulting from the action of the muscle of laughter. Study Fig. 26/6.

Apply a foundation of No. 3 and all the details of a straight make-up, adding the shadows of middle-age if necessary, but omitting the usual lines of that age, as lines of a different character will be required. The chief wrinkles should be drawn on the cheeks, curving down and out from the sides of the nose for about half an inch, then turning down slightly in the direction of the mouth corners; that is to say, just where a curve appears in a laugh. Should the chin and throat be youthful the effect of a double chin produced according to the directions given with Fig. 29A will be a fitting characteristic. Give the corners of the mouth a slight upward tilt, and line crow's feet, curving from the eye corners down on to the cheeks. Wrinkles on the forehead should be mere suggestions that follow the curve of the eyebrows and disappear in the centre of the forehead. Finish with a pink powder. A merry twinkle is given to the eyes if, in addition to the dot of carmine placed at the inner corner of each eye, another dot is put exactly in the centre of the upper eyelids and a smaller one beneath on the lower eyelids. Do this after powdering in order to gain the utmost brilliancy. It may be considered an advantage to the general effect for this character to possess bright red hair. Providing the player has hair inclining to blonde, its colour can be changed by powdering with red hair-powder, or with Armenian Bole powder.

A COUNTRY WOMAN

This type represents such characters as a farmer's wife, the landlady of a village inn, and many others of the respectable lower class who are accustomed to constant exposure to sun and rain, resulting in a sun-burned and tanned complexion, often accompanied by a generous display of freckles on the face and arms.

No. 13, a reddish-brown, makes a good foundation, along with No. 9 to give plenty of healthy colour to the cheeks, if the character is under forty years of age. For an older character Nos. 5 and 8 will give a rather darker tone, which can be heightened with a little Carmine 3. Shadows, if required to age the player, should be of lake, deepened with grey. As a result of screwing up the eyes in strong sunlight, wrinkles around the eyes will be pronounced and numerous. These lines to show up effectively in contrast with the brown foundation should be put in with lake, and touched with dark blue at their deepest points. Outline the eyes by running a line of dark brown, or thin black, along the edges of both upper and lower eyelids, but omit colouring the eyes. The eyebrows may present a rather overgrown appearance, and should be painted on, the nature of the existing ones being considered. Before applying a creamy tan powder, freckles are imitated on the face, neck, and arms by making irregular dots with a mixture of chrome and No. 8, care being taken that they are spaced enough to allow the foundation to be clearly seen between them.

A CANTANKEROUS WOMAN

This type refers to the definitely sallow and bloodless middle-aged woman of the ill-humoured, old maid variety. The face carries a sour, peevish expression, and is overgrown with untidy hair.

For the foundation use No. 5 to extinguish natural colour; then produce the dull tone of unhealthy skin with No. 6. Use 28A brown for shading and lining. Place a deep shadow of brown and lake in the eye corners near the nose, pinch in the nose with side shadows, which deepen the curve of the wings, and hollow the cheeks with a shadow under the cheek bone. Make two vertical frown lines between the eyebrows, two lines across the nose just between the eyes, and crow's feet that turn up. The naso-labial lines should be deep shadows, running in a straight incline in the direction of the mouth corners, the lips a thin line of dull colour ending with shadow lines that dip straight down. Shade a hollow under the jaw line, extending it behind the ears and on the throat at each side of the larynx. Do not colour or outline the eyes, though a thin line of lake along the edges gives them a slightly inflamed effect; slightly redden the nose towards its tip to suggest a congestion there. Finish with a natural powder. The eyebrows may be scanty and uneven, dipping towards the nose; the hair dull and severely dressed.

OLD AGE

There is another fundamental view of the face that it is needful to be able to express by make-up—old age, the disease from which all races of mankind suffer, the ravages of which neither men nor women can hide or efface. It affects the body and its movements as much as the face. Let me, however, take the latter as the key. Granting that plastic surgeons can perform miracles by face lifting, the fact remains that few women or men are so utterly deluded as to imagine that they can naturally be physically attractive after the age of fifty years. Over fifty there is a definite sagging and a straining, an expression of tiredness and a strained effort to keep going.

This is the keynote of expression that is seen in the group of six faces (Fig. 23), the variations of which should be carefully noted. The first is an average face of a young man about twenty years of age; next is the same man at thirty years; then when about forty years old. The fourth is still the same man advanced to about fifty years; observe the slight development—there is a squareness, a solidity, a little less life in the deeper set eyes; the cheeks are less firm and have a marked tendency to crease; the temples sink slightly, and the hair is thinning. At sixty years of age the cheek-bones are more prominent, the cheeks have hollowed, wrinkles are more numerous and deeper. The last is of particular interest. Here age is seen in the same face, but of seventy or more summers and winters, when all is changed, except the persistent likeness. Notice that the formation of the skull becomes more apparent, due to a lack of flesh and the sinking of it into the hollows and cavities of the bones; the flesh about the eyes sinks into the sockets, causing deeper hollows; the eyelids are heavier, and there is a downward strain of the eyebrows. The muscles of the cheeks and jaws sag, forming stringy folds, which hang over the jaw line and beneath the cleft chin; the lips are shrivelled, with deep wrinkles that enter the mouth. There is an expression of patient steady effort to keep going: it is awake, alert, alive.

Incidentally, it should be recognized that old age does not have the same visible effect on everyone, but that the development will always be a reflection or a confirmation of the prevailing characteristics of earlier days, accentuated by conditions of health and surroundings.

A ROBUST OLD MAN

In this example, assume that the character to be portrayed is a working-class man of about seventy years, enjoying the fruits of a good constitution and an active, well-ordered life. The face is pleasant, yet inclined to be rather fleshy and much wrinkled, the general tone of the skin being darkish, but flushed locally with a touch of redness about the nose, the jaws, and at the sides of the neck. The skin at these points, owing to its closeness to the bone, is blemished with red veins; for that reason, the circulation is not as regular as it is in the rest of the face—hence the blood-vessels become too much congested and show on the surface.

Start the make-up with a groundwork of Nos. 5 and 6 evenly mixed, and spread to obtain a level tone, extinguishing the natural colour and the outline of mouth, eyes, etc., as much as possible. Then with the fingers blend No. 9 over the groundwork to a suitable degree, allowing the forehead to remain somewhat paler in tone than the face below. Here, the art of "ageing" the face with hollows and wrinkles begins, and it cannot be too strongly urged that when finished the light and shade of all hollows and wrinkles should appear as gradations of the same flesh colour, however sharp the contrasts may be. Therefore when working over a florid or tawny foundation, grey and lake, mixed with the foundation, will appear natural as shadow, with a pale pinkish shade as high-light; whilst on a sallow foundation grey and light brown or No. 6½ as shading, with No. 5 for lighting, will result in truer tones.

The large shadows of the cheeks, eye sockets, temples, and throat should be toned in with grey, mixed with the foundation. Bear in mind that shadows cast by downward light have to be imitated, and that such shadows are darker at the upper part immediately beneath a prominent bone. Therefore, blend the deepest colour tone at the upper part of these shadows, and, as you work downwards, make the colour gradually paler until it fades into the foundation colour, which merges into the high-light of another prominent bone below. For instance, the darkest part of the hollows in the cheeks is just under the cheek bones, where the flesh sinks away from the bone, and the shadows fade out before reaching the prominence of the jaw bone. Then, again, in the eye sockets the hollow is deepest at the inner part between the eyes and nose, and fades out over the cheek bones. When the required hollows have been correctly toned in, a touch of lake should be added to some foundation colour, and blended into the deepest part of each hollow to accentuate it.

It is a decided advantage, in the interests of a natural appearance, if the principal wrinkles are first outlined in grey, then touched up with lake and high-light to give relief. Ascertain the correct position of the forehead lines, as far as is possible, from naturally occurring lines and paint in grey; increased in number or degree to the extent that is required by the character. In old age these wrinkles are, as a rule, heavier over the eyebrows, where the flesh has been loosened by the constant contraction of the forehead muscle, but they are fine near the hair line, where the skin is drawn more tightly over the frontal bone. In the type under consideration the two vertical lines between the eyebrows, caused by the frown of reflection and difficulty is strongly marked. These wrinkles are deepest at their base near the nose, and diminish as they ascend to the forehead, but they should not be allowed to intersect the transverse lines of the forehead. The crow's feet are lined next, though, if any difficulty is experienced in making them fine enough, they can be added after powdering. The naso-labial lines, descending from the nose, begin at the curved indent over the nostrils, and the lower end of each line is about half an inch away from the corner of the mouth. Lines droop from the corners of the mouth, and the straighter they descend the harder and meaner is the expression. A shadowy, slightly curved line is placed midway between the lower lip and the most prominent part of the chin.

Coming now to the throat, a deep wrinkle, which is the first fold of a double chin, forms beneath the chin. This line usually makes a curve under the chin; the ends of it ascend over the jawbone, and fade out about the middle of the cheeks, and are often accompanied by a deep cleft at the point of the chin. The neck should be lined with wrinkles, naturally spaced, and converging upwards towards the back of the ears.

Having toned in all the most important wrinkles with grey, it is advisable to accentuate them at appropriate points with an additional shading of reddish-brown, or lake mixed with the foundation colour, along and within the lower edge of all transverse shadow lines. Thus the forehead lines can be deepened in this way to give emphasis at points over the eyebrows; the

Fig. 33A. R. Griffin Without Make-up

crow's feet are deepened near the eyes; the hollow of the chin and the fold beneath are strengthened in the centre.

All vertical lines are treated in a similar manner, but the deepening colour is concentrated on the centre of the grey shadow. Deepen the frown lines at their roots by starting at the bottom and fading the colour upwards. The naso-labial folds are deepest in the region of the nose; therefore apply the colour at those points, on the upper edge of the shadows, allowing them to terminate in grey. Shade the corners of the mouth just where the lines appear to emerge from it; then, in order to reform the mouth, run a shading on the under side of the upper lip, well within the normal margin, and re-shape the lower lip with a light covering of Carmine 3.

When all wrinkles, including those of the neck, have been strengthened enough to allow for the subduing effect that powder will have, they should be correctly high-lighted. Use No. $2\frac{1}{2}$, and with the chisel edge of the stick make a soft line along the lower edge of each wrinkle in the forehead, and, also, of the crow's feet lines. The frown lines require a touch of light between and at each side of them. The high-lights of the naso-labial folds should be soft curves placed over the lines, to appear as though the flesh sagged and caught the light; folds of the double chin and of the throat require a similar effect.

In order to make the eyes appear aged, line

Fig. 33B. R. Griffin as Valentine Wolfe in "Grumpy"

the edges of the lids with lake, put a small high-light on the centre of each upper lid, and reduce the colour of the eyelashes by painting them with No. 5, but not to the extent of making them appear to be white. In keeping with these aged eyes, the brows must be bushy and outstanding. Probably the best way to secure this effect is to gum on false eyebrows of crêpe-hair to match the wig. If the natural brows are bushy enough, however, a good effect is obtained if they are rubbed the wrong way to make them stand out, and then painted with white grease paint or wet white. Assuming that a wig of the blender type is to be worn, the forehead band should be adjusted and painted to correspond with the flesh colour. Use a cream tint of powder. It is of importance to create the appearance of discoloured and decayed teeth in this character by painting sound teeth with special tooth enamel. Do not overlook the make-up of the hands, which should be made to look coarsened and reddened by toil.

Adequately to disguise youthful features, it is often advisable to resort to the use of nose-putty and hair pieces. An excellent example of their effectiveness is shown by the portraits (Fig. 33A and Fig. 33B), though much of the stage illusion is lost in photography owing to the absence of colour and lighting. Both the straight and character portraits are of Ronald Griffin, producer to the Leeds Eyebrow Club, and were taken at the same sitting. The chief details of the make-up to which attention is drawn are: the nose is built up with nose-putty to a shape that lends a different character to the face; a perfect fitting wig, the forehead band of which is so neatly joined and blended to the skin that it is almost imperceptible; the beard and moustache, whilst adding appreciable breadth to the face, have every appearance of a natural growth, and are in perfect unison with the style of the wig—by no means an unimportant consideration. The foundation is a blend of Nos. 5 and 8, and the general scheme of shade and line a modification of the preceding example.

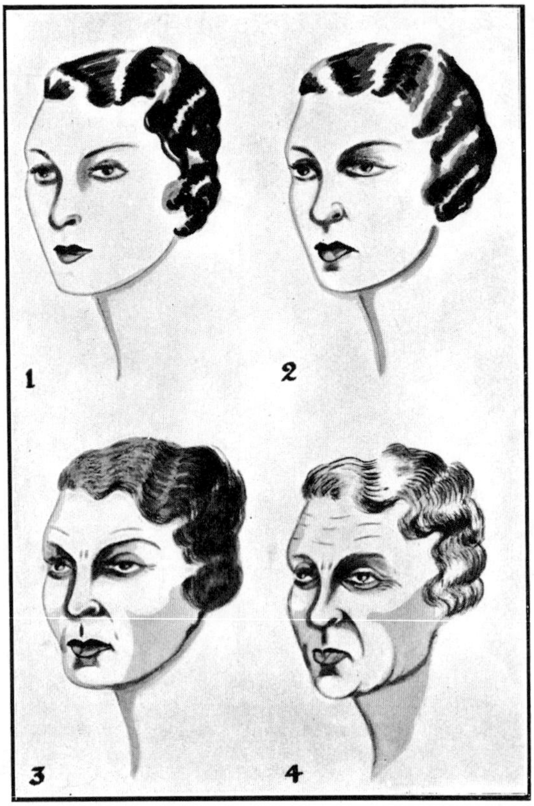

Fig. 34. Advanced Age Characteristics—Women

AN OLD WOMAN

Visualize this example as being a time-honoured, motherly sort of woman, of the advanced age of sixty-five or more years. The normal cares of home and family life have caused a lack of virility, which is evidenced by a sallow, parched-looking skin, and a complete greyness masks an otherwise pleasing countenance. Large, though pale, freckles or "moth patches" are present on the hands and the sides of the neck—a sign of the advanced age due to a disturbance of skin pigmentation.

To portray this type, apply a first groundwork of No. $5\frac{1}{2}$ and complete the foundation with judicious touches of No. $3\frac{1}{2}$, then with Carmine 1 add a slight flush of colour in the region of the cheek-bones. The most conspicuous hollows will be those in the upper corners of the eyes, which descend to curve beneath the inner half of the lower lids; those under the cheek-bones, which taper and descend in the direction of the chin, the

FIG. 35. CHINESE WOMAN AND MAN

hollow of the neck extending from behind the ears down each side of the larynx to the collar-bone, and running along the line of the jaw to re-shape its youthful curve. Permanent wrinkles, consisting of those of the forehead, slightly arching; the two vertical lines between the eyebrows caused by frowning; the crow's feet, little lines radiating from the outer corners of the eyes and curving down on to the cheeks; the deep furrows that form around the nostrils and curve outward and down; the lines about the mouth and chin muscles, resulting from the actions of eating, talking, and laughing. To avoid a long repetition of details, however, I have illustrated them at Fig. 34. The four faces shown are intended to depict the gradual development of characteristics over a period of, say, forty years, with a view to laying final emphasis on the essential points that portray old age. In considering individual cases almost everything depends upon the natural state of the face to be worked upon; therefore, if the face is thin the shadow tones of the cheeks and neck may, with advantage, be omitted, and sharpness of features attained by the sole use of high-lights in the prominent bones. When this method is adopted, it is advisable to obviate a too pale appearance and to impart life to the skin by applying a few touches of dry rouge to the shadowed areas.

RACIAL EXAMPLES

"It takes all sorts to make a world!" One has only to look at an English crowd, with its endless diversity of types, to realize the truth of this saying. Single portraits of men and women can represent in a general way only the nation to which they belong, for no two individuals, not even brothers, are really alike. The mere cast of features, as seen in an unchanging attitude, has delicate characteristics which we appreciate when studying faces, but which often elude exact description and imitation. For the purpose of make-up, what must be looked for in such a national portrait is the general, well-marked, characteristics that belong to the whole race. With the purpose of directing attention to some of these well-marked peculiarities of the face in different races, groups of male and female faces are given—Figs. 31 and 33.

As a mark of race, the colour of the skin has, from ancient times, been reckoned the most distinctive of all, and it is, also, generally conceded that the colours of the skin, the hair, and the eyes are connected. In races with dark skin and black hair, the darkest eyes generally prevail, whilst a fair complexion is usually accompanied by the light tints of iris, especially blue. A fair Saxon with black eyes, or a negro with pale blue eyes, would be looked at with surprise. The natural hue of skin furthest from that of the negro is the complexion of the fair-white Teutonic people of Northern Europe, whose transparent skin, flaxen hair, and blue eyes can be seen in England, though not as often as in Scandinavia or North Germany. In such fair or blonde people the almost transparent skin has a pink tinge because the small blood-vessels show through it. In the dark-white nations of Southern Europe, such as Italians and Spaniards, the browner complexion to some extent hides this red, which among still darker people in other quarters of the world ceases to be discernible.

GERMANS AND DUTCH. Teutonics of Western Europe can be classed as medium-to-fair, with a predominance of fair types among the women.

In portraying young Germans men can use a foundation similar to that required for an English type of the same age, blended to retain rather more fairness of skin, with a corresponding tone of lips lightly made up with Carmine 1. Tint the eyes with blue. The eyebrows should be neither too heavy nor too dark. Naturally, light-coloured ones are best left untouched; dark ones can be lightened with chrome and relieved with touches of lake. The hair should be cropped close and brushed upwards to produce an erect, bristly effect. Should it be desirable to lighten it, a dusting of yellow ochre powder will achieve a blonde colour.

In characters of older men the foundation should be more florid, though still retaining clear fairness. A mixture of Nos. 3 and 5 as a base, with No. 8 subsequently applied, can be relied upon. Outline the eyes with brown, but omit colouring the eyelids. Although "Kaiser" moustaches seem to have fallen into disfavour with the Germans themselves, yet the popular stage conception of this type still remains, and can be used to advantage (Fig. 36, 1). Beards are common, the close-cropped, pointed type being favoured. They should, of course, be of a blonde colour to match the wig.

German women have an ivory fairness of skin. For these characters, and, in fact, any other blonde type, what may be described as a "peach and cream" tint of skin can be best obtained by using one of a good range of shades of grease paints, by a well-known maker, named "Star Girl," "Star Lady," and "Star Madam." These produce tones of warm yellow-pink, which, under modern lighting conditions, achieve a desirable natural transparency without undue paleness. When referring to the use of Nos. 1 to 3, in order to avoid paleness, on the one hand, or a too-pink appearance on the other, it is advisable to blend a little of the yellowish tone of No. 5 with such shades. This subdues the excessive pinkness of the older numbers, which is achieved in the newer shades without blending. The foundation for girls can be Star Lady or a mixture of equal parts of Nos. 1½ and 5, subsequently toned softly with No. 3½; Carmine 1 for cheeks and lips, and light blue eyelid colour. If the eyelashes are of medium colour, leave them without paint, but keep them free from powder. Lighten them, if too dark, with light-brown paint. This applies to the eyebrows, which are best lightened with chrome and carmine.

For middle-aged women use the same number as for girls, but blend darker, and shade with more No. 3½ and Carmine 2. The eyes should be a little darker than they are in youth, so use medium blue on the lids. The hair can be frizzy, dressed high and away from the eyes, and circled over the crown of the head with a band of ribbon or an ornament—(see Fig. 33, 3). Any attempt to colour dark eyebrows with light brown paint will give an undefined, lifeless result. To avoid this, first paint with chrome, then relieve the dullness, and re-create form by adding a few short, snappy lines of lake.

Dutch stage types are generally of the order made more emphatic by style of dress than any other means; women in their picturesque national costume, accompanied by Zuider-Zee fishermen or bargees. Girls are of a fair complexion, the hair being worn in one or two plaits. Women of the lower class are often tanned by exposure in the tulip fields.

Make-up for girls and women should be similar to that for Germans, a little extra No. 9 being added in the case of countrywomen. For the fresh, weather-beaten, colour of men, use a base of Nos. 5 and 13, toned up on prominent parts with No. 8 and a touch of Carmine 3. Though men, as a rule, are clean-shaven, characterization of older men may be assisted by the use of wig, full in the neck, and side-whiskers.

SCANDINAVIANS, AUSTRIANS, AND DANES. The north-east European group of peoples exhibit examples of the fairest of blonde types. Women of the upper social class are equivalent to the fairest and most beautiful Germans. There is frequently, however, evidence of the influence of a Slavonic element in the broad and rather flat nose, and a general angular cast of features, which fact may be turned to advantage as an aid in defining the geographical origin of a character.

Women should make-up on the same lines as for German types. Men can use the same foundation as for a fair German, but should obtain a bolder characterization by shading the ridge of the nose just above its tip, and placing high-lights on the wings of the nose, on the cheek-bones below the outer corners of the eyes, and at each side of the chin point to give a squareness there.

CELTIC includes Scotch Highlanders, Welsh, Irish, Manx, and Bretons. In the stage representation of any of this group, the dominant features of national characterization are usually costume and dialect. Straight parts should be made up the same as for English types, due regard being paid to any special requirements of an individual character. Comedy or burlesque parts may exaggerate any distinguishing national trait, almost to the extent of making a caricature, the art of which is to distort proportions and to exaggerate features in such a manner as to add a touch of satire or to strike a ludicrous note. To give humorous emphasis to outstanding peculiarities, one must exercise a good sense of humour, tempered with judgment as to where genuine drollery ends and the ridiculous begins.

A Comedy Scotsman. The typical stage Scot is usually a hardy Highlander, as sketched at Fig. 36, 3, of ruddy outdoor complexion, rugged features, a full head of sandy-red hair plus side-whiskers, and shaggy and low eyebrows projecting

FIG. 36. CONVENTIONAL NATIONAL TYPES

1. German Professor
2. Dutch Bargee
3. Scotch Highlander
4. Irish Caricature
5. Irish Colleen
6. French Artist
7. Spanish Toreador
8. Gipsy Dancer
9. Merchant Jew

over deep-set eyes. The mouth is firm and well-shaped, with a fullness of the lower lip.

The foundation may be of No. 3½, or blended in the usual way with Nos. 5 and 3 mixed as a base, No. 8 being used to obtain ruddiness. Add a touch of Carmine 3 to the cheeks, across the nose, and on the chin. Shadow the eyes to give a deeper inset, and outline them with reddish-brown. Tone in a few forehead wrinkles, two close frown lines, short nasal lines, and deep crow's feet extending to the temples. Appropriately high-light all shadow lines and prominent parts, then powder with a pale tan. A suitably coloured wig is required. The side-whiskers and eyebrows can be of crêpe-hair to correspond to the wig colour, which, however, may require to be blended from red and yellow crêpe-hair.

A Comedy Irishman. The capricious Irish peasant is a type that offers wide scope for quaint caricature. A suggestive example of burlesque is illustrated at Fig. 36, 4, the chief points being its irregular features—the tip-tilted nose, the wide, deep-cut, thin-lipped mouth, with a whimsical twist about the corners. The hair is unkempt and the face is over-run with a week's growth of beard. The general aspect conveys an expression of comical, vacant stupidity.

Before applying a foundation of Nos. 5 and 10, or, alternatively, No. 5 flattened with a touch of grey, and No. 8, the nose will require to be remodelled with nose-putty at the tip. With joining-paste or No. 3 grease paint block out the centre portion of the eyebrows, but leave the reshaping of them until after powdering. Place a deep shadow of grey or brown in the nose-corners of the eye sockets, and one on the ridge of the nose just above the false tip. Tone in a few irregular and scattered forehead wrinkles, which arch over the brows and dip towards the nose. Deepen the vertical indent in the centre of the upper lip; then, from the top of the indent, on each side draw a line that curves outward and around the wing of the nostril. To complete the effect of a prominent upper lip, slightly lighten the colour of the lip immediately beneath these lines. Paint the lips to appear thin and straight, and extend one corner of the mouth in a slanting upward direction; then, at the same side, deepen the nasal line to emphasize the whimsical tilt of the lip.

The unshaven effect can be obtained by shading the beard area with either dark grey or a sparse amount of black; but a more pronounced effect will result if, before powdering, chrome is applied in the area, with a subsequent dusting of chopped crêpe-hair over spirit gum, applied after powdering. If this latter method is done correctly, light and shade in the foundation will be retained to a much greater extent than with the former.

After powdering, the eyes should be made to appear narrow and round. To do this, outline them with fine, clear lines of dark brown, painted along the edge of each eyelid. These lines are not carried beyond the outer corners, but stopped abruptly at the point where they join. Then, from the same point, draw two short lines of lake—one inclining to the top eyelid, the other inclining down to the lower lid—forming an arrow-head pointing outward. Paint a small high-light at the centre of upper eyelids, and powder again about the eyes. Finally, the eyebrows should be painted arch-shaped, well spaced at the inner ends, and the highest point over the pupil of the eye.

An Irish Colleen. Irish women are difficult to classify as to complexion because of the diversity of types to be found in the Emerald Isle. As a general rule, however, the "Irish Colleen," famous for her beauty and charm, can be taken as the representative of national characterization. Possessing jet black, auburn, or blonde hair, she has a fair skin, her eyes are a soft blue fringed with thick black lashes, and she has black eyebrows of abundant growth. In this example all attempts at comedy effect should be avoided; the make-up conforms to straight lines with one or two special observations.

The foundation may be No. 2½, or, better still, a mixture of Nos. 1½ and 5, with the addition of No. 3½, the cheeks being heightened with Carmine 2. If the hair is auburn, the rouge colour can be inclined to an orange tint by adding a touch of chrome. For the lips, use Carmine 3 lightly applied, and shape them delicately full, forming little vertical dimples at the corners of the mouth. Flank these dimples on the outer side with a small high-light, and lighten the lower lip at each side of the centre. Eyelids should be coloured in the usual manner with medium blue, which is extended fairly well out beyond the corner, and the eyebrows shaded with lake, the whole application being powdered at this stage. Next, clean powder from the eyebrows and lashes, then with dark brown or black paint the eyebrows and edge the eyelids. Finally, intensify the eyelashes with water-black, or by loading them with melted heating-cosmetic.

PROGRESSING in the colour index, we come to dark-white races, which may be conveniently grouped and considered by taking typical examples.

FRENCH. In spite of the fact that the majority of French people really differ little from the English, it is usual when playing a French role to exercise a little stage licence by adopting a few well-marked features of peculiar national significance.

A French Woman. A fashionable Parisienne may be portrayed as elegant and original in dress, theatrical in manner, and exotic in details of grooming and ornamentation. Although she is more often dark-haired, her coiffure may be of an extravagant, artificial colour, unique in marcel design. The skin is rather pale, with a definitely olive tinge, and almost devoid of any bloom in the region of the cheeks. The eyes and lips are heavily made up.

Start the make-up with a foundation of Star Lady or Nos. 1½ and 5, toned with No. 3½ and a touch of chrome; No. 6½ and chrome will give a more olive tone. If the hair is dark, colour the top eyelids to correspond with dark brown, then apply a basis of lake for the eyebrows, but do not apply water-black until after powdering. Paint the lips with bright carmine, the upper one first, and get the correct outline for the lower one by pressing the lips together. After powdering, outline the eyes with water-black, and paint the eyebrows, which should begin directly above the inner corner, and continue in a carefully graduated line to the outer edge of the eye socket. Load the upper eyelashes with melted heating-cosmetic, but make no attempt to load the lower ones, as the line painted there is sufficient. Finally, freshen the lips with lipstick, a shade with an orange-red hue being particularly becoming to the brunette complexion, and with the hare's foot brighten up the complexion with light touches of dry rouge.

Of chief interest to women is a new and successful method of throwing light into the eyes, imparting to them a soft lustre and sparkle. Use Cream Eye-shadow, which is specially made for colouring the eyelids, in a variety of shades, all of which are flecked with either silver or gold. Thus, there is a shade of blue shot with silver, also a silver mauve and silver green—suitable for blonde types; for darker complexions silver brown and gold brown are more appropriate. To avoid the deadening effect of powder and to obtain the utmost lustre, it is advisable to apply these eyeshadows after the general make-up has been powdered off.

A Frenchman. For a typical young Frenchman the foundation should be similar to that for an Englishman with just a tinge of olive in it. Nos. 5 and 9 and a touch of No. 10 will meet the case, though a little carmine may be used on the cheeks just where the sun would tone them. Edge the eyelids with dark brown, and, if necessary, darken the eyebrows. A small dark moustache, with turned-up points, added solely, or in conjunction with a slight tuft of beard under the lower lip (as shown at Fig. 31, 3) is an aid to characterization. If the character is that of a student, an artist, or a similar type, the Imperial or Van Dyke beard will be appropriate, the hair, or wig, being worn rather long and brushed from the forehead straight back to the nape of the neck. (See Fig. 36, 6.)

When an elderly Frenchman has to be portrayed, a fuller beard of the Imperial or "fish-tail" shape should be adopted, and the colour of the skin blended to a fairly dark sallow tone with Nos. 5 and 10. The skin should appear much wrinkled, the eyes be deep-set, and the brow beetle-browed.

ITALIANS. In ascertaining the physiognomy of the true type of Italian, authority bids us look to the imperial busts and statues of ancient Romans. These depict a large, flat head, a low and wide forehead, a face broad and square, a nose thin and arched, divided from the forehead by a marked depression, and a prominent chin. Combined, these convey a nobility of expression. The type has changed but little, and is to be met with every day in the streets of Rome, principally among the burgesses or middle class.

Italians have a distinctly olive tone of skin, brown to black wavy or curling hair, and abundant dark eyebrows and lashes. A suitable foundation for women may be blended with Nos. 2 and 10, freshened about the cheeks and lower forehead with Carmine 2. Use the same carmine for the lips, giving them a full outline. The eyelids can be brown or dark blue, the upper eyelashes being enhanced by loading them with melted cosmetic, and the lower ones indicated by a line of brown. Paint the eyebrows with only a slight curve, rather low and close at the inner ends. Give the nose an arched appearance by placing a high-light on its bridge, and a shadow line of brown across the nose exactly where it joins the forehead. Finish with a cream tint of powder. Remember that the neck and hands should match the face in colour. Normally elaborate embroidered head-wraps and shawls are worn (*see* Fig. 37, 1).

For a young Italian man, the rather olive-tan skin colour is best produced by a blend of Nos. 6 and 10, with No. 9 added to prominent parts of the cheeks, forehead, and lips. The nose should be high-lighted from bridge to tip, and shadowed at its root near the forehead. Line the eyelids with dark brown, and paint the eyelashes and brows with black. The hair should be well-groomed, of glossy and sleek appearance. A moustache of the small toothbrush or fine curved type may be worn.

A Comedy Italian. Fig. 31, 6, shows a type of low-class, dusky Italian, sometimes seen in the streets of England grinding organs, roasting chestnuts, or vending ices. For the impersonation of this type, use Nos. 6 and 10 as a base, and blend No. 16 or No. 7 to obtain the dusky tinge. Shadow appropriately, with a mixture of No. 16 and lake to produce deep-set eyes, a pinched nose with a crooked tip, deep vertical nose lines, and a crease down the centre of each cheek, deep indents at the root of the nose and midway between the lower lip and chin. The forehead wrinkles and those about the eyes require to be numerous and heavy. High-light all shadows and wrinkle lines with No. 6, also the crooked tip and wings of the nose and the chin. Paint the beard area with a mixture of dark grey and blue, bringing it well on to the cheeks, and add a black, heavy moustache, with long curling ends. A wig of heavy, black, wavy hair is essential to complete the make-up.

SPANIARDS. The women of Spain are, notoriously, the chief representatives of brunette beauty. Their eyes, large and of a velvety liquid black, often flash evidence of the fiery temperament that is attributed to this people and give the countenance an expression of vivacity. The nose is delicate, with well-formed nostrils, arched ones being less common than among the Italians.

Use an olive foundation composed of Nos. 2 and 10, and for a rosy flush in the cheeks Carmine 2. Paint the lips to look well-shaped, full, and of warm tone. The velvety depth of eye colour is best produced by painting the upper eyelids with purple (a mixture of dark blue and carmine) or brown, and, after powdering, adding a touch of silver blue over purple or gold brown over brown to make them more luminous. Enlarge the eyes at their outer corners, and load the lashes with black; then define the inner corners with dots of red. Over-arch eyebrows of natural curve with black. The hair should be luxuriant, abundantly waved, and elaborately dressed. Students often adopt the artist's smock. Among the middle class the picturesque lace mantillas are a familiar form of headdress, and are accompanied by a richly embroidered shawl—refer to Fig. 33, 5.

Men have generally a sallow, dark olive tone of skin, with dark eyes of cold expression. Side-whiskers, short and straight or "boot-shaped," with either a shaven upper lip or a fine moustache curving down near the edge of the lip, are a typical fashion (Fig. 31, 5). Blend the foundation of Nos. 6 and 16 with a trace of dark blue in the shaven area, and a tone of No. 8 on the cheek bones. Colour the upper eyelids dark grey, and edge both upper and lower ones with fine lines of black.

A SPANISH TOREADOR. This glamorous *habitué* (Fig. 36, 7) of the bull-ring is conventionally handsome and debonair. When the gorgeous costume of this character is carefully considered, the make-up can be extremely effective. Use Nos. 6 and 7 heightened with No. 8; the forehead should be elevated, the nose arched, the chin roundly firm, the lips moderately thin and expressive, and the eyes dark and strong, with long lashes and arching brows. A toreador wig, the hair of which is long and bound in a tight knot at the back of the head, should be worn, also

FIG. 37. CONVENTIONAL NATIONAL TYPES

1. Italian
2. Portuguese
3. Gondolier
4. Tirolese
5. Bulgarian
6. Serbian
7. Cossack
8. Arab
9. Mexican

"boot-shaped" side-whiskers, otherwise the face is shaven.

The Portuguese are generally less handsome and dignified than their Spanish neighbours, the features of both men and women being less regular. The hair is usually dark and straight, the nose snub, the lips are thick, and the complexion is inclined to be swarthy. In general, the make-up may be similar to the Spanish examples.

BULGARIANS. The Bulgarians, or Bulgars, said to be of Tartar descent, are a healthy, sturdy, peasant people. Without any claims to smartness or good looks, they are clearly not of a true Slavonic type. The face is usually oval, the features are rugged, the skin is rough and the complexion swarthy. As a rule, they are dark but never red-haired, and the eyes are generally grey; the nose is flatly thick, and the jaw rather heavy. The artistic temperament of the women comes out more clearly in their costumes than in any other way. The costume consists of a dress elaborately embroidered in many colours upon the breast, sleeves, and skirt, with a handkerchief tied over the head, and frontals made of gold coins. Aprons of elaborate stripe and check designs are commonly worn. In the rose-producing districts around Philippopolis, famous for its otto of roses, the red and white blooms are a popular form of hair decoration. The men wear a thick, coloured, embroidered shirt, a cummerbund, and fairly tight, rough, white trousers, with blanket leggings, which, forming the sock, are kept in position by cross-gartering. In addition, they wear a jacket, embroidered on the front and sleeves, and a kolpak cap (see Fig. 37, 5).

AUSTRIAN, TIROLESE, AND BOHEMIANS. Comprised of a mixed stock, the Tirolese, having a predominance of Teuton character, and the Bohemians, inclining to the Czechs, have a great deal in common in their renown for folk-songs, folk-dances, and elaborately ornamented national costumes. In disposition they are more romantic and vivacious than the Bulgars. The Austrians have a medium-fair complexion with brownish skin. Men wear short, loose knickerbockers, with green or white stockings, an embroidered shirt, a short jacket, and a felt hat with a feather ornament at the back. A moustache or beard is seldom worn except by the aged. Women's dress varies, but everywhere it is dainty and remarkable for its variety of decorative embroidery. The brightly polished Russian boots, worn by the Bohemians, are a feature of their costume (see Fig. 37, 4).

For the make-up for these types women may use No. 6 with a dash of No. 10 rouged with dull carmine. The colour of the eyelids should be grey-blue, and that of the eyebrows and lashes brown. For the lips, not too bright, use No. 9 and a touch of carmine. Men should use a foundation of Nos. 4 and 10, with a trifle of No. 7 blended to give depth to receding parts and to produce the chief characteristics.

RUSSIANS. A conventional type of Russian is that of a Cossack (Fig. 37, 7). It is of a rather sallow brown complexion, and has broad high cheekbones, deep-set, half-closed eyes, and a flatly thick nose. The hair, eyebrows, moustache, and beard are usually heavy.

The foundation is of Nos. 4 and 10, toned up with No. 9. With No. 7 shadow the eyes, and extend the cheek shadows obliquely upwards towards the inner corners of the eyes to give prominence to the cheek-bones. High-light the wings of the nose and the cheek-bones with No. 6. Line the eyelids with dark grey, and to give increased length extend them beyond the outer corners. To give the mouth a hard expression, paint a thin line low on the upper lip and give a heavy squareness to the lower one.

For a more refined type, No. 4 or Nos. 5 and 8 provide a somewhat paler foundation, and the hair generally may be lighter in colour.

GREEKS. The stage representation of Greeks is generally confined to the classical types. The face is a fine oval; the forehead full and carried forward; the eyes are large, surmounted by classically curved and well-spaced brows; the lips and chin finely formed. The Grecian nose is a distinguishing feature; it is straight, with slight or no depression at the joint with the forehead—refer to Fig. 30, 1.

Women: Use No. 2 with a little No. 10 mixed; cheek colour No. 9, eyelids brown, cream, or pale tan powder. Men: Use Nos. 4 and 10; cheeks No. 8, eyelids brown, tan powder. In applying, blend the forehead a tone lighter. If nose-putty is not used to straighten the nose, place

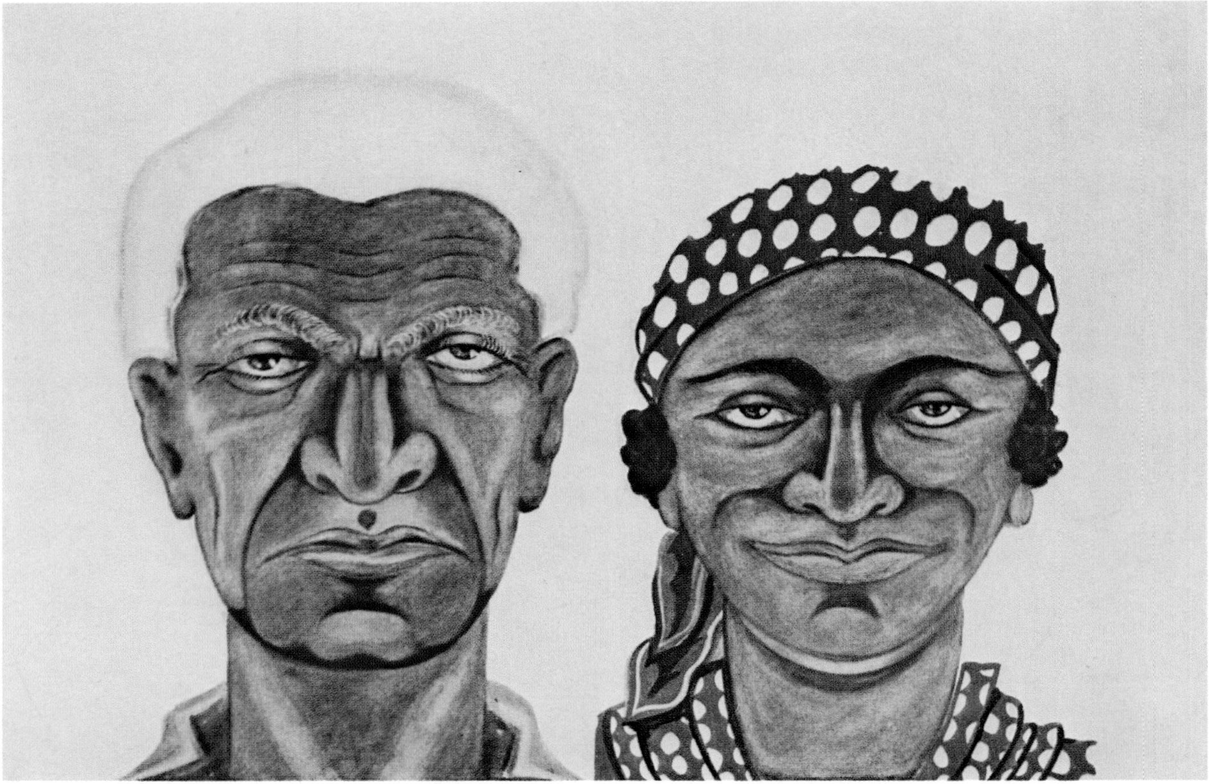

Fig. 38. American Negro Types

strong high-light at the junction of the nose with the forehead, flanked on each side by a right-angled shadow under the inner end of the eyebrow.

GIPSIES. A wandering race, probably of Hindu origin, varying little in type and international in character. They are nomadic, and are generally fortune-tellers, musicians, and dancers, or tinkers, rejoicing in the adopted picturesque name of "Romany." Of swarthy complexion, they are usually dark-skinned, dark-eyed, and possess jet black hair.

Use for the foundation Nos. 6 and 11, and No. 8 for toning the cheeks. Apply dark blue or grey for the shaven effect, or add a heavy, flowing moustache. Shade to produce a rugged appearance. Women should be made somewhat paler by adding No. 5 to the foundation, and Carmine to No. 8.

EGYPTIANS. Some uncertainty prevails as to the race to which the ancient Egyptians belonged, though authority conceives that existing monuments and mummies indicate that the noblemen were tall and slender, of a noble and dignified carriage, and that the women had great beauty. The shape of the face is inclined to squareness; the cheek-bones are prominent, the nose is aquiline, and the eyes, surmounted by nearly straight black brows, are large and dark.

The foundation for men should be a dark bronze, obtained by mixing Nos. 5 and 8 and darkened with No. 7. The nose carries a high-light of No. 6, wide at the bridge, and tapering towards the tip. Women can be made much lighter in tone, by using Nos. 6 and 7 with Carmine high on the cheek-bones. The curiously elongated eye seen on ancient Egyptian monuments depicts the custom of painting the eyes with kohl. This effect can be imitated by painting a black line along the edge of both the top and bottom eyelids, and, instead of joining them at the outer corner, extending them towards the temple. The eyebrows are then lengthened to correspond, as shown at Fig. 33, 7.

AMERICAN INDIANS. The American, so-called Red, Indian (Fig. 32) is a popular characterization, though often it is thoughtlessly made-up a fiery red colour. Of all the Red Indian peoples, the physically finest men are included among the Sioux tribe. The true colour is brown of a cinnamon tint; the cheek-bones are large and prominent under the eye, denoting an alert and watchful nature; the lower jaw is large and ponderous, cut off short in front; the nose is decidedly arched or aquiline, slightly flat at the tip, and the nasal cavities are of great size; the hair is long, lank, and black.

Unless a nose of nearly the right type is possessed, build it up with nose-putty. For the foundation first apply a blend of No. 9 and chrome (No. 15 is the same blend), then add enough No. 7 to obtain a coppery-brown colour. Make the cheek-bones prominent by creating a depression, running from below the inner corner of each eye and curving out beneath the bones, with a shadow of lake and brown. Then place a high-light on the bones, beneath the outer corners of the eyes. Outline the eyes with black, carrying the under lines well into the inner corners, and extend the blacked eyebrows well towards the nose. The lips are made to appear thin and compressed by colouring them just inside the mouth. Where exposed, the limbs should be stained with a wash made of a mixture of Armenian bole and burnt amber.

MONGOLIAN. The Chinese and Japanese show their connexion with the Mongoloid type in the familiar complexion and outline of features. The Chinese face is characterized by a forehead narrow in proportion to the width and projection of the cheek-bones. The nose is small and flattened, with a marked depression separating it from the forehead; the eyelids are not freely open, and are drawn obliquely up towards the temples, so that there is slight depression under the brow ridges, except near the nose; the eyebrows are flat and highly arched, and, like the coarse, long hair, are black—see Fig. 35. The skin is brownish-yellow. Before making up, it should be decided whether or not a pigtail wig is necessary. If a cap is worn and has not to be removed during the performance, a pigtail can be fastened inside the cap, in which case the hair about the temples should be painted-out to appear shaven. Otherwise, a blender type of wig, with attached pigtail, will be required. This should be adjusted before applying paint, and, in regard to the drag of the pigtail, secured with spirit gum. The foundation, to appear natural, ought not to be too yellow. Men should first produce a pale sallow-brown base of Nos. $5\frac{1}{2}$ and $3\frac{1}{2}$, and tone darker in shadowed areas with touches of No. 8. With foundation colour or wig paste, paint out the outer portions of the eyebrows. Then, with a dull blend of lake and light brown, narrow the forehead by shading the temples; flatten the nose by shading the ridge; hollow the cheeks with shadows beneath the cheek-bones; and paint a deep hollow, limited to the top inner corners, in the eye sockets. With No. 5, high-light the central part of the forehead to give roundness there; light up the cheek-bones under the outer corners of the eyes; broaden the nose, and give prominence to the chin with appropriate high-lights.

The characteristic Mongolian "almond eye" effect is obtained by an unusual method of lining. As may be observed at Fig. 35, a deep shadow line of lake and grey is drawn from the outer corner of each eye, extending the curve of the lower eyelid in an upward, slanting direction. The black lines marking the outline of the eyelids are then merged into this shadow, the junction being made just beyond the eye corner. A patch of high-light is then blended on the outer part of the upper eyelid, bordering on the upper side of the sloping shadow and up over the obliterated part of the eyebrow. Further to emphasize the effect, the eyebrows are painted on at an elevated angle. Instead of the usual red dot at the inner corners of the eyes, make short red lines with a downward inclination. Young Chinamen are usually smooth-faced; an elderly mandarin may have a scanty drooping moustache and a tuft of beard.

For a Chinese girl, use a foundation of No. 5, mixed with a little chrome, and No. 6. Add a touch of carmine to the centre of the cheeks, and paint the lips rather small with dark carmine. For making up the eyes, follow the directions given for men, lining the eyelids with black, instead of the usual method of painting or loading the lashes.

JAPANESE. Resulting from a mixture of Mongol and Malay, the Japanese male complexion is browner in hue than the Chinese. The nose is typically Mongolian, flat, and not too long, and the eyes are almond-shaped. Pigtails are less common than in China, and instead of hanging down the back, they are worn folded up and tied. The modern Japanese wear short-cropped hair, black and straight, growing rather low on the forehead—see Fig. 31, 9. The foundation colour is of Nos. $6\frac{1}{2}$ and 8, with little or no extra cheek colour. In other details follow the directions that apply to the Chinese.

The "Geisha" girl (Fig. 33, 8) is a distinctly theatrical type, and, consequently, may be made-up in a more exotic style than would be suitable for a native type. The foundation is of No. 5 with a small addition of chrome and No. 6 or No. $3\frac{1}{2}$. When applying, cover the lips and the natural eyebrows with this colour. The cheek-bones are made prominent by high-lights, and cheek rouge is placed directly under each eye. The lips are heavily painted with Carmine No. 2, but reduced to small dimensions of sharp outline. The upper lip has two points, slightly exaggerated in height, and the lower one is deep and narrow to give a puckered look. The "almond eye" effect is obtained by the method described for the Chinese and shown in colour at Fig. 35. In painting new eyebrows, start them rather low near the nose and make the slant upwards, parallel to the lines leading from the outer corners of the eyes. After powdering with Rachel, brighten with dry-rouge.

NEGRO TYPES. The negro type belongs to the woolly-haired group, and is dark-skinned, as typified by the African native. There is, however, a diversity of mixed types comprehended under the common term of negro—the North Carolina "negro," for instance, who has in his veins one-sixteenth or more of African blood. The Australians, with a skin of dark chocolate colour, may be taken as a special type of brown race. The negro, in spite of his name, is never really black, but varies from a dark chestnut to deep purplish-brown, with sometimes a yellowish tinge. The darkest hue never extends over the whole body, the palms and soles being a much lighter brown.

It is recorded that when a celebrated anthropologist saw the famous Kemble, made up with blackened face and wearing black gloves (to represent a negro), play Othello, he complained that the whole illusion was spoilt for him when the actor opened his hands.

The race most typical of Africa has a narrow skull, low forehead, wide and flattened nose, full and out-turned lips, and projecting jaws. The skin is black-brown, and the hair of the head woolly and black, but face-hair is scanty.

In make-up, the foundation colour should not be of a flat dark shade, but, instead, should be in the nature of a half-tone, which will give scope for light and shade effects. Such a tone may be obtained by a first application of No. 6½, followed by a larger amount of No. 11. The correct shape of nose may require to be produced with the aid of nose-putty. Shadows should consist of foundation darkened with black; high-lights of foundation should be lightened with No. 5. When applying Nos. 6½ and 11, blend the lower-centre region of the forehead, the cheek-bones, and upper eyelids a tone lighter than other parts, but leave the required margin of the lips entirely free of paint. Shadow the eye-sockets, connecting them with a line across the nose, and darken the ridge. Line the nostrils with black to enlarge them. Place high-lights at the sides of the nose; just above the nose between the eyebrows; and on the edges of the eyelids, excepting the outer corners. Paint the eyelashes heavily with black. Enlarge the lips with a thin coating of lake, and to make them appear protruding, add a high-light spot at the centre of each.

The powdering of a dark make-up presents a difficulty, for, if dark powder is used, all light and shade is obliterated, whilst, on the other hand, if a light tint is used a paleness results. In consequence, it is advisable to employ two shades of powder—a dark one, applied first and only over dark parts; the other should be blended to match the tone of the high-lights, and carefully applied only over the lightest parts.

In making-up for an aged negro, the foundation should be lighter, as age tends to fade the skin. The general characteristics of age require to be produced in light, shade, and wrinkles. Paint the wrinkles with black, using light grey for high-lights. If a wig of woolly white hair is to be worn, whiten the eyelashes and gum on eyebrows of white or grey crêpe-hair.

The popular "Kentucky nigger minstrels" are, of course, a burlesque type, and as such may be broadly exaggerated. The best blackening medium is "Negro Black," specially prepared not to rub off, but it will easily wash off with soap and water. To obtain the best results, the skin should be freshly washed free from natural grease and perspiration. Variously shaped spaces about the eyes and mouth may be left clear of black and filled in with wet white or grease paint.

MULATTOES, SAMBOES, AND OCTOROONS. The mulatto is half-caste, an offspring of parents one of whom is black and the other white. The widely used nickname "Sambo" is given to the offspring of a negro and a mulatto, probably because such are often bow-legged. The make-up for these types should be lighter in colour than for a pure negro, a suitable foundation being Nos. 6½ and 7. The features are of a less pronounced negro cast, but the hair remains black and frizzy.

A quadroon is quarter-blood, a cross between mulatto and white; whilst the octoroon, the child of a white parent and a quadroon, has one-eighth negro blood. The colour of these types is lighter than that of the mulatto. Use a foundation of Nos. 6 and 11, with No. 8 as colour for the cheeks. In general, other characteristics may be similar to dark European types.

When further information regarding racial types and national costume is required, reference should be made to a pictorial work such as *Races of Mankind* or *Peoples of All Nations*.

THEATRICAL MAKE-UP RECIPES

Cold Cream—

4 oz. Liquid paraffin
1¼ „ White beeswax
2 „ Rose-water
A small pinch of borax.

Warm the paraffin in a basin standing in a pan of hot water. Shred and melt the beeswax, add to the paraffin, and whisk the mixture while it is hot. Warm the rose-water in a bottle, dissolve the borax in it, then add drop by drop to the warm oil, stirring all the time. Pour the mixture into a jar or tin and allow to cool. This cold cream will keep fresh indefinitely, and is agreeable to use.

Liquid paraffin used without any preparation makes an efficient grease-paint remover.

Face Powder. Theatrical face powders are principally manufactured from vegetable starches: arrowroot, wheat, maize or cornflour, and rice, or mineral powders: zinc oxide, kaolin (white clay), talc (French chalk). So-called "violet powder" consists mainly of powdered orris-root and cornflour, sometimes with the addition of small amounts of zinc-oxide, boric acid, or talc.

Cornflour is fine and may be used alone, but is better mixed with an equal quantity of zinc oxide. A better powder of more transparent quality is obtained by blending

Kaolin . . .	35 parts
Cornflour . . .	35 „
Talc . . .	10 „
Zinc oxide . .	10 „
Light magnesium carbonate . .	10 „

Coloured Powder. White powder may be tinted by adding a powdered colour pigment. The best way thoroughly to blend them is to add the white to the colour, a little at a time, and to shake well after each addition, the exact quantity being judged by trial.

A pale cream or "Rachel" tint is obtained by the addition of yellow ochre; for a deeper cream add burnt sienna. For a flesh or "Natural" tint, a cream with a suggestion of pink is required; add a portion of white to a little of both yellow ochre and Armenian bole, then add together the mixtures. "Sun-tan" shade requires a blend of white, raw sienna, and yellow ochre.

Liquid Powder. (Wet white.) There are many variations of wet white. The following is easily made from simple materials—

2 oz.	Zinc oxide
1 „	Glycerine
½ „	White starch
6 „	Rose-water

Put the powders in a basin and with a spoon rub them until they are very fine, then add the glycerine by degrees, and mix to a thick, smooth paste. Pour the rose-water in gradually and mix thoroughly. The presence of starch is necessary to bind the ingredients and cause them to run smoothly and evenly over the skin. Glycerine helps the powders to mix, and it also has an emollient and soothing quality that allays irritation of the skin. This mixture results in a pure white liquid-powder, which may be given a flesh tint by adding a pinch of ochre or bole. A spot of colour from a tube of water paint will serve the same purpose.

Water Stain. To give the best results, colour washes for temporarily staining the skin require a special water base. This base contains—

Gum tragacanth . .	1 part
Glycerine . . .	4 parts
Distilled water . .	95 „

It is important that the base be prepared by rubbing the finely powdered gum with the glycerine in a mortar, then pouring in the water until a mucilage of uniform consistency results: otherwise the gum, which acts as a binding agent, will not dissolve.

Suitable colour pigment, in powder form, is then added to the base, about 20 parts of pigment being used for each 100 parts of mucilage.

Pigment	Colour
Vegetable black .	Black
Raw umber . .	Dark brown
Burnt umber . .	Reddish brown
Armenian bole .	Strong red
Raw sienna . .	Light brown
Burnt sienna . .	Yellowish red
Dark ochre . .	Brownish yellow
Yellow ochre . .	Dull yellow
Fuller's earth . .	Sallow cream
Zinc oxide . .	White

J. W. Debenham

A. H. SEXTON

MUSICAL PRODUCTIONS

DUMAYNE WARNE, Author (in Collaboration with Phil Forsyth) of "The House," "The Ultimate Revue," "Second Thoughts," etc.

INTRODUCTION

A. H. SEXTON

ABOUT one hundred years hence, when the history of our times comes to be written in better perspective, the decline and fall of the British Commercial Theatre will be recorded in its proper place and its causes analysed from the data unearthed by the antiquarian. In the course of his researches he will not fail to be struck by the collateral rise and growth of the Amateur *Stage Movement; and it may well be that definite and authoritative information will not be unacceptable to him. At all events it is the present purpose to contribute something to the general knowledge of the seeker after historical truth, and to confine treatment to the consideration of the purely operatic side of the Movement and of the assured place it has earned in the lives of the people.*

It can be stated at the outset that before 1890 *performances by amateurs of comic opera or musical comedy in fully-equipped theatres in place of small halls or schoolrooms were of rare occurrence, and that the operatic era can be dated from the last decade of the nineteenth century. It is therefore little more than* 50 *years of age.*

At that date the professional stage had begun to realize that there was a large and eager public for what may be termed musical drama, that is to say, stage plots, whether serious or comic, enlivened by dancing and by choral or solo musical numbers. The Savoy operas already ranked in a class of their own, and at the Gaiety comic opera gave place about 1896 *to musical comedy of a type not yet entirely forgotten. "Dorothy" belongs to the same period, with "Falka," "Pepita," and "The Old Guard," and elder brethren may recall their amazement that "Morocco Bound" managed to get past the Lord Chamberlain.*

At that time the theatre had no serious rival—other than the music hall—in the entertainment world of the general public, and lessees in the provinces had no difficulty in selecting from the touring companies attractions of sorts to please their patrons throughout the year.

It is, therefore, not to be wondered at that the entrance of the amateur into this privileged and hitherto exclusive territory of the professional thespian was regarded as unnecessary and impudent. It was alleged that an amateur operatic society, hiring and performing in a licensed theatre, thereby robbed a number of professionals of their rightful means of livelihood for that week. The allegation was never wholly true. Further, at the present time these societies provide a vast amount of money annually to theatre staffs that would otherwise be idle throughout the country.

Whether impudent or not, the intrusion has come to stay. The operatic society, with a full complement of fifty or sixty acting members, afforded an admirable, and indeed desirable, opportunity for the exercise by young enthusiasts of their latent abilities in acting, singing, and dancing, which the amateur dramatic company could not provide, and it may be seriously suggested that it was in no small measure due to the fact that the operatic movement came into existence at the peak period of activity on the professional stage that its foundations were so well and carefully laid. For it was no "stop-gap" innovation to fill empty theatres. Innovation it surely was, but in spite of the sneer that most of the earlier societies were founded upon a charitable basis and advertised their efforts as "In aid of local charities," the Movement would have had no chance of survival if the performances themselves had not been of sufficient artistic and technical merit to justify invitation for payment for admission to them. In this way and by this crucial test did the pioneer operatic societies claim their place and their right to add something to the history of the British Stage.

As he looks back upon what has been accomplished in little more than half a century, the future historian will note the permanent character of the allurement of operatic productions throughout those years, both to the amateur artists and the music-loving public. It has been unscathed by war, by the challenge of the saxophone, and the appeal of the cinema; and to-day it remains one of the most cherished amenities in the life of the community.

It will be noted, also, that with the decline, and in many towns the disappearance, of the theatre, or its conversion to a "picture house" the local operatic society is now the only remaining link with the "flesh-and-blood" theatre of the past, unless a dramatic society co-exists in the same town.

As to the causes, and how far the decline of the provincial theatre is due to the competition of the cinema and how far to taxation, trade depression, or the miserable inefficiency of the average touring company, analysis must be left to other hands. Not only have amateurs justified, and more than justified, their existence, but they have become through none of their own seeking the last hope of the British Stage, if it is to be saved at all from the commercialism that is strangling it.

Lamentations have been frequently heard that amateur operatic societies too often—and it may as well be admitted—waste their talents on works of little or no artistic merit, whereas they would be contributing something to the Art of the Theatre and covering themselves with glory by forsaking the beaten track and presenting original or unknown operas. There need be no disparagement of art or provocative comments upon the good intentions of such critics in reminding them that operatic societies are not educational organizations and have no funds for the purpose, and to suppose that they are is to imagine a vain thing. On the other hand, it would be unfair criticism to deride their prudent, if archaic, habit of keeping one eye on the box office.

One of the contributory causes of the eclipse of the theatre, which set in long before the cinema developed into its present "mass production of cheap emotion," was the stubborn policy of providing the public with what it used to want. Equally foolish would be a policy for amateurs to provide what the public ought to want in the minority opinion of irresponsible crusaders. As a distinguished critic has recently pointed out, the British public in the mass will have nothing to do with "uplift" in the theatre.

But to admit the truth of this statement is not to approve of, or even to condone, efforts wasted on the reproduction of works that have no artistic appeal whatever and are merely curious relics of a cruder and less cultured epoch. There is a wide range of operatic work of recognized merit, available for the amateur society, which lies between the inanities of the earlier musical comedies and the futilities of Broadway, N.Y.; and it is these works that provide the programmes of most societies and still delight the public.

Had it not been for a few far-seeing "wiseheads" getting together fifty years ago and forming the National Operatic and Dramatic Association, which has ever since fostered the amateur operatic movement, it is an undoubted fact that, as a nation, we should to-day be deprived of the privilege of witnessing many exellent productions that are "put on" by societies in an endeavour to keep alive the arts of music and acting by living artists.

CHOOSING THE PLAY

This section on "Musical Productions" is written for new or inexperienced societies which in the course of their careers will inevitably come up against problems that may cause them considerable trouble. It is not claimed that the solutions to these problems will be found here, but it is hoped to indicate where the management committees of societies may be able to find the solutions for themselves.

It is also hoped to indicate some of the difficulties that are known to arise from time to time in amateur musical productions and by the provision of warnings, to dispose of what might possibly become difficulties later, before they arise.

DUMAYNE WARNE

There are many efficiently run societies in Britain and their management is in the hands of committees who know from experience the many duties involved before a successful production can appear upon the stage. Their needs are well provided for in the more technical parts of this publication.

One of the first duties of a new society, is to select its musical play. Most societies rise phoenix-like from the ashes of some earlier organization or as the result of a split from some already established body. The result is that they start off with a fairly clear idea of the kind of play they want to do.

A society started from the survivors of a defunct group will, at any rate at the beginning, probably carry on the tradition of its predecessors. Similarly a society started as an offshoot of another, will either want to do the same type of show with a different cast (a common cause of the formation of new societies), or to do some other kind of show which the original group refused to undertake.

Even in an absolutely fresh venture it is almost certain that one or more of the promoters will have definite ideas about what should be attempted. In fact, the new society is likely to have been brought into existence by the determination of a small group of people to stage some particular show or type of show.

In all these cases then, and we are discussing the first show by a new society, the choice of work, or the kind of work, is not usually the main problem.

There are, however, several traps into which a new society may fall even when it has a clear idea of the play it wishes to produce. One is, that the piece may not be available for production by amateurs in the town in which it is to be presented at the required time. Right-owners have a habit of withdrawing the amateur rights of a play when a professional tour is to be sent out. Nothing is more annoying, and possibly expensive, than to start rehearsals of a work only to find that it cannot be presented after all. The correct course is to book the date with the right-owners before beginning rehearsals.

Many different details of a production must be dealt with more or less at the same time. Consequently while the business manager is making arrangements with the right-owners he must also insure that, having secured a licence to perform the play, rehearsal materials are also available. During the war the printing of scores or libretti was stopped and most of those in stock have by now been disposed of, consequently, if scores cannot be bought, it will be necessary to find out whether they can be hired from the National Operatic and Dramatic Association or borrowed in sufficient numbers from anybody willing to lend them.

Another thing to be borne in mind is the size of the theatre in which the performances are to take place. The auditorium must hold enough people to pay for the show at prices which the potential audience will be willing to pay. It must not be overlooked that this figure must include entertainment duty unless exemption can be obtained.

This leads, naturally enough, to the matter of costing. It is a huge subject that can only be touched on here. The procedure is to set down in a list the estimated cost (it is the business manager's duty to find this out) of each of the general heads of expenditure for the works under consideration, and then to see that a safe margin is allowed between the total and the probable receipts for the production. The word probable here should be regarded with the greatest possible realism. The usual headings of expenditure are—

Rent of theatre and wages
Royalty
Producer's fee
Scenery
Costumes
Properties (furniture, etc.)
Additional lighting, if necessary
Orchestra
Rehearsal rooms
Printing and stationery
Advertising
Miscellaneous

When the cost is much above the probable receipts nothing can be done, but in a border-line case a little deviation from the ordinary course, for example a (competent) amateur producer instead of a professional, may make a border-line choice into a probable.

Where an auditorium is too small to take enough money to pay for the production the possibility of playing twice nightly should be considered.

The size of the stage must also be taken into account. Although a small stage will mean a reduction in the number of members who can take part, this need not necessarily disqualify any particular play (unless it is essential that every member of the society should be employed) because a producer with imagination who is not afraid, can do wonders, especially if he cuts the book to simplify the *ensembles* as much as possible. An ingenious person is often able to suggest a crowd with remarkably few people, but of course nothing much in the way of chorus dancing can be attempted.

It must be emphasized, however, that cutting is a delicate operation. The danger is that in removing what seem to be non-essentials the spirit of the play may also disappear. In *Chu Chin Chow* for example if the innumerable effects which have nothing to do with the story are left out, the play is ruined. The plot by itself will not hold attention, so any alteration will have to be made in such a way as to suggest, with the available material, the oriental prodigality of the piece.

Too large a stage is much rarer and more easily cured. All that is usually necessary is to set the scenery nearer the footlights.

Summing up then, it seems that satisfactory answers must be obtained to the following questions before a decision is taken to attempt production of any particular work.

(*a*) Is the play available for amateurs at the required time and place?

(*b*) Is rehearsal material (scores and libretti) available?

(*c*) Can the cost of production be covered by the probable receipts, including sale of tickets and any other possible source of revenue, including members' and patrons' subscriptions, etc.?

(*d*) Is the stage large or small enough to enable the work to be staged satisfactorily taking into account the size of the scenery and the numbers of the company?

If all these points can be satisfactorily settled it seems as though, at any rate from the mechanical point of view, the new society should be able to embark on its chosen course with a fair prospect of success.

KINDS OF MUSICAL PLAYS

On the artistic side, presumably the new society will feel confident. The members are banded together to attack a particular show or type of show and it is to be assumed that they are confident of having the talent or they would not have made that selection. Their next difficulties begin either when they have done all the available works of the kind with which they started, or when the character of their membership changes and they must break fresh ground.

To attempt to group all musical plays into neat watertight compartments would be an impossible task, but there are rough divisions into which most of them fall. For the benefit of those who are faced with the position mentioned in the paragraph above they are set out here.

It must be understood that there is certain to be a number of exceptions; nevertheless if a committee can gauge roughly the strengths and weaknesses of their company they will know which group to tackle, and may thereby be saved a good deal of time in reading plays that it is absolutely useless for them to consider.

Gilbert and Sullivan apart, there are roughly five types of musical play, each having its own particular requirements that must be fulfilled before an adequate production of any one of them can be given.

SCENE FROM "CAVALLERIA RUSTICANA," WHICH ADMIRABLY ILLUSTRATES THE INTENSITY OF THIS KIND OF PRODUCTION

Photo by J. W. Debenham

They are—

1. Grand Opera.
2. Light Opera.
3. Romantic Musical Plays.
4. Musical Comedy.
5. Modern Musical Comedy and Revue.

Before discussing the salient features of difficulty of these five, a word must be said with regard to the term "adequate." What is regarded as adequate by one society is hopelessly amateurish and inept for another, and polished and remotely professional for a third. Possibly an adequate performance is one in which the degree of competence is such that the audience is enabled to forget that the actors are amateurs and to enjoy the production on its merits.

For the first of these types, *Grand Opera*, the chief requirement is a standard of singing such as is not likely to be found in any society except, of course, a singing school or some institution that brings together a large number of people who are talented at the art of singing in a way quite out of the ordinary.

It is necessary to be able to find singers, of both sexes with voices of outstanding range and quality, and musicians, trained in the more complicated branches of these arts, who are capable of singing or playing the difficult arrangements that the great composers include in their works.

There is a kind of intensity about Grand Opera which is absent from any other type of musical production. It is an intensity which, even in the lighter moments of the work, spreads over the whole thing and gives the audience a strange feeling of awe.

The singing qualification is not the only one that is required. Some people seem to think that in Grand Opera it is all that matters. This is not so. It is one of the most important things, but the most magnificent singing in the world can be wrecked by bad acting, and also by what, curiously enough, most opera singers are, on account of their art, likely to suffer from—a bad stage presence. The exactions of the singer's art are such that we have to accustom ourselves to see juvenile leads (of both sexes) of great bulk, and although we are able to overlook it at Covent Garden, where the ensemble is such that any *one* defect can be excused, this defect alone in a typically amateur production might have the effect of reducing an otherwise well-behaved audience to hysteria.

In the next section, *Light Opera*, are included those works such as *Merrie England*, *Tom Jones*, etc. These are, perhaps, the most suitable of all for a society to undertake which does not intend to begin with Gilbert and Sullivan, but which has some musical capabilities without any great experience of stagecraft. They are extremely musical, but at the same time they are not as difficult as, nor have they the intensity of, Grand Opera. They have good plots, but they do not require such strength and experience of straight acting as do those in the next section. In fact, if they can be adequately cast and mounted, and a competent producer found, a new society is more likely to give a satisfyingly pleasant reproduction of one of these works than of any other kind. In the process the members will learn something of stages and stagecraft that will be serviceable in subsequent productions.

The next type, *Romantic Musical Plays*, is probably the most exciting of all to play in. Although most of them have some fine music in them, they depend almost entirely for their success on the strength of the plot and the way in which the story is handled. From the point of view of the audience, there is no question of sitting and merely listening to music. They are intended to be gripped and carried away by the story. These plays have a kind of intensity, but it is quite different from that of Grand Opera. The difference is rather like that between tragedy and drama. An atmosphere of "bravura" pervades them, in fact they are thrilling rather than uplifting.

To secure this, it is essential that the stage presence of the leading characters should fit in exactly with the requirements of the book. The hero must be tall and handsome, with a manly baritone voice. The heroine must be beautiful with a soprano voice, either strong and determined or coy and wistful, as the case may be. The villain, of course, will look saturnine, and may talk his songs. For the chorus there are all sorts of excitements in the way of marching songs, drunken brawls, and genuine battles. *The Desert Song* and *The Vagabond King* are fair examples of this type.

Next comes the type which the new society that has some versatility of accomplishment beyond singing is best advised to attempt—*Musical Comedy*. It is most suitable for those whose singing ability is not perhaps of such a high standard as the ones who can successfully tackle Light Opera as a beginning, but in which there is a good deal of material ready for development in a dancing chorus.

It must not be assumed from the above that it is intended to belittle these plays or the societies that perform them—far from it—but the point is that they contain a much greater diversity of interest than any other type except Revue. Consequently a weakness (and there are bound to be *some* weaknesses in a performance by a new society, however brilliant the opening) is much less likely to affect the success of the show as a whole.

For example—a society that has a lady who can sing and act and dance a little could successfully cast her as "Prudence" in *The Quaker Girl*, whereas it could not attempt *The Vagabond King* unless the "Katharine" could look beautiful and sing and act outstandingly, although she might not be able to dance a step.

In plays of this type are to be found some numbers, which, together with their accompanying effects, have achieved a fame that will outlive all of us, e.g. "Tell me, pretty maiden," "She is the Belle of New York," and the "Totem Song" from *Rose Marie*.

It will have been gathered from the above that this class includes *The Quaker Girl*, *The Belle of New York*, *Miss Hook of Holland*, etc.

Societies that begin on this type will, almost certainly, proceed along either of two courses. They will either, after a time, during which the company will become experienced and develop their talents according to their own instincts, tend to the more musical type of production, ending up, finally, perhaps, with Grand Opera, or else they will go in the opposite direction and, passing through a course of Modern Musical Comedy, end up with Revue.

Which brings us naturally enough to the last two types of show.

It might be considered that each of these is sufficiently different to deserve a class to itself. They have, however, certain points in common that make it convenient to discuss them together for the purposes of this article. The first and foremost requirement (especially for *Revue*) is speed, and if they have any intensity, it is this. Neither type of show should be attempted by a society that is without members who have extensive stage experience, as the production is likely to become dull from lack of pace and pep if inexperienced amateurs are responsible for it. The fact is that the book of these works is often so thin that unless it is extremely well played, this will soon become apparent to the audience, with the inevitable result. After speed, the next thing is dancing; and that is why these shows are most suitable for societies which, as they have progressed, have developed their dancing rather than their singing. Not, of course, that the singing does not matter; but some weakness here can be overlooked, whereas a weakness in the dancing department cannot.

Apart from the solo dancers of one sort or another (Step, Kicking, etc.), it is necessary for these shows to have one or two teams of chorus girls, of any number between 6 and 16 each, according to the size of the society and of the stage, capable of looking smart and prepared to give up a lot of time to learning step-dancing, etc., and doing it together. This is not as a rule so difficult as it sounds, as once the girls get started they usually enjoy the work, and consequently they soon make progress.

It is much more difficult to find men. The principals are easily cast, but chorus men who have suitable clothes (of course they can be hired, and ordinarily one does not find 12 men with lounge suits all exactly alike) and who are prepared to go through the somewhat invertebrate contortions required of the male chorus in these plays, are difficult to secure. However, there are some societies that have not much of a male chorus and since what is in the book as chorus work for them can usually be cut drastically, this might prove to be an advantage in certain circumstances.

PHOTO OF THE FIRST ACT OF THE ROMANTIC MUSICAL PLAY "THE VAGABOND KING." EXCITING BUT NOT AWE-INSPIRING LIKE GRAND OPERA

Photo by J. W. Debenham

The chief difference between Modern Musical Comedy and Revue is that in Revue, since any part of it can be "starred" to order, more chance can be given to pure specialists such as singers, dancers, or actors, each of whom has only one talent, than is the case in a play with a plot. But all societies are warned against running away with the idea that Revue is easy—it is not. Because it is so nebulous in form it is likely to be nebulous in effect, unless it is put together with great discrimination and brilliantly played.

Remember, the worst concert party you have ever seen is a sort of Revue: can you guarantee that your show will be any better than that?

Summing up, it is clear that what you have to decide on is the main strength of your company, bearing in mind that strength means all-round strength and not that of your best performer, for it is a mistake to imagine that you can win success with one good turn in a weak show. It is much wiser to educate your company a bit; then when you are able to choose plays for your star, you will be able to back up him or her enough to make it worth while.

Having decided then on what is the strength, choose a play of the sort at which you are most likely to be able to give a performance of the highest general level, and then you are ready for the casting.

If there does not seem to be any special strength that should be utilized in particular, it is safer to choose either a Light Opera or a Musical Comedy and then to see what happens afterwards. You may find that after having done one or two of them, an enormous interest develops in the dancing, in which case you will know what plays to consider next; or you may find that nobody wants to dance, in which case you will be ready to attack Grand Opera when the time comes.

Remember, finally, that though it is a good thing to give your company something to do that may be a bit beyond them—otherwise they will never improve—it is the height of folly to start too ambitiously with something that is completely outside their powers. This might open the society's career with a failure, from the ill-effects of which, on both audience and members, it may never revive, and from which, after languishing for a few performances, it will most likely die.

THE TOTEM CHORUS, "ROSE MARIE"

A typical example of the sort of "effect numbers" to be found in productions of this type

Photo by J. W. Debenham

CHOOSING THE PRODUCER

The ordinary way of attacking the problem of whom to appoint as producer for an amateur operatic society is to decide first of all on how much can be afforded as salary and then to secure the best person available for the money. But this is not quite the right way.

Of course the question of expense will have to be settled, but it is not the first consideration.

The proper method is to decide on what kind of producer is required and then to decide what such a person would cost. It may be found that he will not cost anything. As in so many other matters, the easy way is to walk into the market and to buy the most expensive thing, on the principle that it will probably be the best. Probably it will. But will it be the best for you? An expensive instrument of any kind costs a lot of money, but, at the same time, it requires a great deal of skill to manipulate properly. It is probably equipped with all sorts of devices, the use of which is unnecessary for the purposes of a novice, even if he were technically equipped to handle them, which he is not.

A really first-class professional producer will certainly be expensive. It is, however, true that nothing is at all likely to go wrong while he is in charge. But the talent at the disposal of a new operatic society is almost certain to be such that the art of the first-class producer is considerably hampered. In fact, as he will have to spend most of his time in grounding the company in the rudiments of their hobby and will not have much leisure for polishing, he will not be able to use the skill for which his extra salary is paid.

Having decided, then, that the most expensive producer is not necessarily going to be the most suitable for your purpose, the next thing to decide is what kind of producer he *is* going to be.

Here you have to consider what kind of play you have chosen. In this connexion one should think of a producer as the man who projects a play upon the stage in a similar way to that used by a painter who projects his picture on to the canvas.

A real expert in stagecraft will, of course, get anything "over," especially if he has time to work it up. But a man with a more limited range may be less expensive and quite as suitable for your purpose if your play is one of his specialities. So, having decided that your play is to be a musical comedy or a light opera, etc., see that your prospective producer is known to have experience in the kind of play that you have chosen, or that you have some definite reason for employing him if he has not.

In the ordinary way, what the new amateur society wants is a man with a thorough knowledge of practical stagecraft. That is to say, of dialogue, movement, ensembles, music, and also of the mechanical departments, such as lighting and scenery. This sounds a tall order, but actually it is the stock-in-trade of hundreds of professional stage managers. One is not asking for a lot of high flown, "arty" production, but for practical common-sense knowledge of how to get a play over, with, perhaps, somewhat limited technical and mechanical appliances, together with the patience and understanding that are necessary to teach a company of beginners and to imbue them with the spirit that makes for successful productions. This spirit which, once developed, is of more value to a society than anything else, consists of, prosaically, such things as an appreciation of the value of speed, correct positioning, smiling, etc., and, aesthetically, of personal self-repression for the benefit and success of the show as a whole. In other words, team spirit.

We seem now to have established the fact that what a new society wants of a producer is someone who is sound rather than brilliant, patient with an inexpert company, and familiar with the work or the type of work that is to be attacked.

The next question that arises is where this person is to be found. The possibility that one of the people banded together to launch a new society may be competent to undertake the production should be considered. If so, he should be more than ever the best man for the purpose, for not only will he already be aware of the difficulties that face him, but, because he is interested in the formation of the society, he will be prepared patiently to overcome them and to shepherd the enthusiastic but incompetent company along the winding and difficult path that leads to acting.

There is one difficulty that must be considered in employing an amateur.

Some people find it difficult to submit to the imposition of discipline by one who has been a colleague, perhaps in another production, especially if there is a feeling that the producer is little, if any, more competent to do the job than the other experienced members.

And if enough members feel like this, the entire show, or even, eventually, the society may be wrecked. Production is a matter of discipline, and discipline is impossible if members of the company question the authority of the producer. But if they know him well enough they certainly will question it when he annoys them, as he is almost bound to do from time to time. A producer's fee is a small thing compared with the life of a society.

An amateur brought in from outside is in rather a different position from an ordinary member of a society who has been promoted. The fact that he is a guest and a stranger ensures him a degree of politeness and respect that may be denied a fellow member. His credentials will, in any case, be made the most of by the committee who invite him to work for the society, and even if they are not strictly accurate it will be difficult for any member to question them.

STAGECRAFT AND TEAM SPIRIT

So it seems that the mere fact of the appointment of a professional or an amateur as a producer is not likely, of itself, to make or mar the show. What is required is that the producer, whether amateur or professional, should be properly equipped to deal with the contemplated production, bearing in mind that a new society will lack experience in a number of matters that an old-established one will know quite well, and that he should be able to inculcate the beginnings of stagecraft and team spirit. This is the only possible way to give a new society a satisfactory send off.

A person must no more be appointed because he is a popular member of the society than a man of unknown suitability to whom a few pounds is paid because it sounds better to have a professional.

There is one other point that requires to be discussed before any definite arrangement is entered into with an individual. Assuming that a choice has been made of a likely person, it is necessary to examine the way in which he will work in order to see if his plans will fit in with the requirements of the members of the society. For example, if a professional producer is to be employed who is resident a long distance from the place of rehearsal, it may be necessary for him to stay in the town during the period of rehearsals. Since this would mean that he would be quite unable to accept any other work during the time, either the rehearsals would have to be compressed into as short a period as possible, compatible with an effective production, or the society would have to resign itself to the payment of a fee that would make it an economic proposition for him to stay in the town for a longer period.

For a society that is prepared to rehearse almost every night for a month, the music having already been taught to the company, the first of the above methods is suitable. But for a society the members of which can rehearse only, say, once a week, for a long period, something different must be devised.

A compromise that is sometimes adopted is to arrange for the producer to attend the place of rehearsal for a week, or perhaps a fortnight, several months before the production and then to leave it to the local staff to work up what he has outlined until his return a few weeks before the production.

EMPLOYING A PROFESSIONAL PRODUCER

Let us now assume that all the pros and cons have been weighed up, and a decision reached that there is no amateur available who is suitable to be entrusted with the production. So the committee are faced with the fact that they must employ a professional whether they like it or not, and if the society is really very new, it is possible that, even after having reached such a decision, they will not know what sort of fee the kind of man they want would expect to receive.

There will possibly be on the committee one or more members who can recommend a professional who is prepared to undertake the production.

This is quite natural, for any amateurs of experience (and there are bound to be some in the newest of new societies) will be certain to have had reason to become familiar with producers and to have earned the friendship of some of them. Although this may prove to be of the greatest advantage to a society, for finding a producer, unless somebody can recommend one, is a very difficult task, the matter of checking his credentials may cause some embarrassment when his sponsor is a member of the committee. But no producer should be engaged until his claims have been properly examined from the points of competence and cost.

The competence point of view is a particularly difficult one; practically the only tests that can be applied are such things as finding out, by means of writing to the secretary of the society, if his other productions have been successful; and by ascertaining if his previous employers are in the habit of re-engaging him.

With regard to the question of cost, there are certain things that may be borne in mind that define the position much more accurately. For example, if your man is a whole-time professional he expects to make a living wage while he is producing a play; perhaps a little over if he is to reserve anything for the periods of enforced idleness that members of the theatrical profession are unfortunately obliged to face. His living wage, therefore, will vary according to the amount of success that he has achieved in his career, ten pounds a week is not an unreasonable salary judging by present-day standards, but when an amateur society is faced with having to pay this for a period of two months, and perhaps a hotel bill as well, it will be seen that it may easily find that it has undertaken to expend much more than £100 on the producer alone.

The ordinary run of persons who produce amateur societies may not expect to be paid as much as £10 a week by any one society, and a difference of £2 or £3 here means a difference of £15 to £25 during a course of rehearsals lasting a couple of months. Supposing also that your man happens to live in the same town, or sufficiently nearby to get there with very little expense or wear and tear to the human frame, you will not be faced with his having to include a hotel bill in the charge for production; this might lop another £30 or £40 off the total. All this seems to point to the fact that a man may be secured, who is anything from competent to outstanding, for a fee that might reach £150 including expenses.

REHEARSALS

The period of stage rehearsals, variable, of course, is usually about two months. Singing, dancing, and reading rehearsals may have been going on for as long or longer than this beforehand, but in these the producer is not interested. He will expect to find the singing (he may prefer to find that the dialogue and dancing have not been tackled) ready for him, but he is not concerned as to how it is done, unless the circumstances are exceptional, such as the producer being engaged also as musical director.

It is usually a condition of the contract that a producer should hold himself at the uninterrupted disposal of the society by which he is engaged from the time that rehearsals begin. If, however, two societies that are situated sufficiently near to each other to share the services of a producer can do so without this militating against the success of one performance or the other, it is possible that they may thus be able to secure an entirely suitable person at a much lower cost to each of them than if either had to bear it separately.

This brings one to a consideration of how much the conducting of a single rehearsal is worth. For the benefit of those who have never had the opportunity, or the misfortune, to take a rehearsal of a musical production, it may be stated to be mentally and physically, even under favourable conditions, a most exhausting pursuit. The effort of driving the life and fire that burn within one into a body of amateurs is such as to leave the producer at the end of an evening, especially if he has had a good deal of imaginative or inventive work to do, in a condition that is not far from prostration.

It does not seem unreasonable that a competent producer should expect to get a guinea or more for an evening of his labours, although for a series he might be prepared to accept less. Supposing, then, that you have thirty rehearsals or so, your producer will cost you about thirty guineas. But if you have an appreciably smaller number, and he will accept less than a guinea each for a series, you might conceivably get down as low as twenty guineas.

The last point that has to be cleared up, supposing that all this time a committee have been considering what sort of man they should require without having any particular individual in mind, is where, when they have made up their minds, they are to find him.

An amateur can most easily be found by personal contact. It is possible that one might be secured by advertisement in the Agony column of the Press, but I have never heard of this method being adopted. Ordinarily he will be suggested by someone on the committee; more often still, he himself will be a member of it; in fact, he will probably be one of those primarily concerned with the organization.

METHODS OF APPROACH

There are, on the other hand, various means by which a professional producer may be obtained. The first of these is, again, personal contact and recommendation. The second is by hearsay and by inquiry of the secretaries of other societies. The advertisements of the theatrical papers may be searched to useful purpose, but care should be taken before engaging anyone who is discovered by this method to check qualifications and references. The last method, and perhaps the best, is to write to the director of such an organization as the National Operatic and Dramatic Association stating requirements and asking for suggestions. It is certain that anyone recommended by this body will be competent and trustworthy, and that his fee will be proportionate to his accomplishments.

AUDITIONS AND CASTING

The important thing to bear in mind when holding an audition is, as in most other tests, the end in view. This sounds ridiculous, but it is extraordinary how many committees vaguely hold an audition without in the least remembering that there are two entirely different kinds of audition, each of which requires to be conducted in an entirely different way, and each of which is designed to find out entirely different things.

The two kinds are briefly—

1. That held for the purpose of finding out if a person is suitable to become a member of the society.
2. That held for the purpose of ascertaining the suitability of a person, already a member of the society, for a particular part in a contemplated production.

The essential difference in the manner of conducting these is that, whereas in testing the suitability of candidates for admission to the society it is desirable that they should not be made nervous, in the case of one who is already a member, and who is being considered for a part in a production, this does not matter.

The candidate who applies for admission to a society may well be a little nervous at his first appearance, especially if his talents are, as yet, not well developed. But a little help and encouragement at this stage may bring into the society a member who, in a few years, may be most useful, whereas too much formality may cause a candidate to be rejected, only to be accepted later by the kinder and more intelligent committee of another society, for which he may become one of the star performers.

All candidates for admission to a society should be asked to complete a form of application, as it is of great advantage to the secretary for record purposes. Further, the manner in which the form is completed may reveal traits of character, personal details, etc., and lead to the acceptance or the rejection of an applicant without an audition. I give on page 548 a copy of the sort of form that will serve the purpose. This can, of course, be expanded or compressed as desired.

It does not much matter who constitutes the audition committee for testing newcomers to a society, provided that there is someone competent to examine them in all the branches that they offer—Appearance, Deportment, Diction, etc., and, in the case of operatic societies, Singing and Dancing.

It is best for the audition to take place in a fair-sized room, and for the committee (it is better to have three or four people rather than only one or two, but nothing useful is to be gained by having too many) to sit at one end of it, perhaps behind a table. The candidates should be kept outside the audition chamber, as it is nerve racking to have to perform at an audition with an audience (this applies to application for membership *only*). When the members of the committee are ready, the secretary, who acts as Master of Ceremonies throughout, will go out and, in as friendly a manner as possible, ask an applicant to step forward. He will then take in the candidate, and, as it were, introduce him to the chairman of the committee.

The chairman, who will previously have been provided by the secretary with the candidate's application form, should ask the candidate to get a book (which will have been placed at the other end of the room) and to read a passage from it. This will test two or three things at the same time, namely, appearance walking away and towards the table, the stance when stationary, the quality of the speaking voice, and if the candidate can read intelligently at sight. Of course, the candidate will read at a fair distance from the committee table.

Even in the case of applicants for the operatic chorus it is well to apply this test.

For the singing test, which should take place next, there must be a competent accompanist. A candidate cannot possibly show what he or she can do at an audition unless the music is properly played. If the candidate brings his own accompanist, the official accompanist should retire gracefully, and perhaps offer to turn over. The private pianist should be admitted to the room only when he or she is required. The degree of difficulty of the singing test will be governed by the number of members who are wanted. If more candidates present themselves than can be admitted to the society, the test may include sight-reading, etc. On the other hand, if there are more vacancies than candidates, the ability to sing in tune may suffice.

DANCING TEST

All is now ready for the dancing test. Lady candidates will have been warned by the secretary that they will be expected to demonstrate their skill at dancing, if they have stated that they are dancers, so they should be suitably dressed for stage dancing. (Girls have been known to arrive in long evening dresses.) For girls who wish to offer dancing but have not a solo to perform, it is well to have a competent person, such as an experienced member of the society, to teach all the candidates who are waiting their turn for audition a sequence of simple steps in the anteroom. This serves several useful purposes: (1) it keeps those who are waiting employed and prevents them from getting nervous; (2) it tests their neatness of movement; (3) it tests their faculty for learning quickly.

It will be found that some candidates pick up dances quickly but roughly; others slowly but much more neatly.

When all have done their speaking and singing tests, they should be asked to dance as a troupe before the committee.

When the instructress is sufficiently knowledgeable and absolutely fair, her opinion may be taken to settle the fate of the dancers. It is well for them to do their little dance before the committee, but if she knows her business she will quickly decide whether they have possibilities or not and can advise the committee accordingly about each candidate.

The disadvantage of this method is that the breathing of the singers may be slightly affected by their previous exertions, but in the case of candidates whose singing is only of the chorus standard this is not likely to matter much, and any who object can be taken inside before they begin to learn the dance. Alternatives are either to have the dancing audition on another day or to have it later in the evening.

Nothing is to be gained by having an elaborate system of marking at such an audition. All that is required is to discover whether candidates are good enough to become members of the society, or whether, in the opinion of the committee, they may, with encouragement, become good enough.

Whether or not latent talent is to be accepted is a matter for those who are responsible for the formation of a new society to decide when they see how many candidates offer themselves for audition, bearing in mind, if the number of applications is large, the desired membership of the new society. This may justify the use of a system of marking. The result should be communicated by each adjudicator in writing, so that it cannot be overheard, to the chairman of the committee, that the candidate is—

(1) Good enough.

(2) Will probably be good enough with further tuition and/or experience.

(3) Will never be good enough.

For the purpose of an audition of this kind this marking is adequate.

An analysis of the independent reports by the members of the audition committee will probably decide the fate of the candidates at once. Border-line cases will have to be decided by conference, the requirements of the society being the chief consideration, i.e. whether more members are required or not.

Applicants should be informed of the decision of the committee by letter and at the same time. This will avoid all sorts of unpleasantness.

AUDITIONS FOR PARTS

In the case of an audition that is held to determine the suitability of a person, already a member of the society, for a particular part in a contemplated production, the conditions should be entirely different.

In the first place, it is desirable that the audition should be held in the theatre or hall in which the performance is to take place. This is usually not impossible to arrange. Secondly, it is an advantage to have an audience (this should consist of members of the society), because the possible nervousness of candidates is not now of primary importance.

M. O. B. OPERATIC AND DRAMATIC SOCIETY

Application for Acting Membership

I desire to join the M.O.B.O. & D.S. I understand that I may be called upon to attend an audition.

Name ....

Please write clearly and state whether Mrs., Miss, or Mr.

Address .... Telephone ....

The candidate is requested to answer the following questions—

(1) Do you sing? ....

(2) If so, state the pitch of your voice..

(3) Do you dance?..

(4) If so, please state whether Ballet, Character, or Musical Comedy, etc.....................

(5) Have you any previous experience of the stage, either amateur or professional?...........

(6) If so, please say whether Operatic or Dramatic, Chorus or Principal, and give the names of any parts you have played, with the names of the plays and the company in which you played them ....
....
....
....
....

(7) Remarks. Please give here any information about yourself which might be of assistance to the Casting Committees and also say if there is any particular type of part for which you would especially like to be considered...
....
....
....

(If necessary, continue on back of form)

The selection committee should sit in the dress circle, or in some other suitably railed off part of the theatre, where they will be absolutely free from the influence of the remainder of the company (this is important). The others can occupy the stalls.

It is desirable for the producer to be present at this audition, whether he be allowed a say in the proceedings or not. His opinion is always of value in border-line cases. Some societies allow the producer to choose his own cast at the audition, but this raises a problem that almost insists on an article to itself. There are sometimes things to be taken into consideration that the producer, if he is an "outsider," cannot know.

Nevertheless, his reputation is affected by every production that he stages, and an inadequate performance by a member of the company may suggest to the audience that that person has not received sufficient attention at rehearsal, whereas the truth may be that the producer has almost made a silk purse out of a sow's ear. The audience who see only the result know nothing of what has gone into a performance.

The producer has a right to protect his reputation and in the final resort he must go back to the committee after giving their nominee a reasonable chance and ask for a change to be made. But this is not a happy position and should be avoided if possible.

There are other things to be thought of at these auditions. (1) Everybody applying or being asked to be tried for a part should have the same chances of seeing the book and the music; (2) if a scheme of marking candidates is adopted, every member of the committee that is responsible for choosing the cast should be agreed about the scale on which marks are to be distributed.

The allocation of marks at these auditions is most difficult. Different members have different opinions on what number of points out of so many a performance is worth. If a simple scheme is adopted, such as asking adjudicators to put candidates into a number of well-defined classes each of which has a name instead of a figure, much confusion is avoided. For example, if two adjudicators are asked to say in which of the following classes a candidate should be placed, they are much more likely to agree than if they are asked to give him a mark out of, say, 10.

(1) Excellent.
(2) Very good.
(3) Good.
(4) Very fair.
(5) Fair.

Apart from the question of artistic suitability, there are other things that casting committees have to consider in the casting of parts.

The policy of the society itself may be that the same principals shall not play the leading parts in consecutive shows. Of two candidates of equal suitability for a part, one may bring into the house much more money. With some societies this may not matter; with others it may. These and other points must be considered by casting committees before any announcements can be made.

The audition, which will have been conducted in much the same way as the first one, with the secretary as M.C., being over, the candidates will disperse, and the committee will adjourn to a suitable room for a round table discussion, a room in which all the pros and cons of each applicant's suitability or unsuitability for each part in the play can be talked over and a complete cast chosen.

Should one of the members of the committee be a candidate for a part, he or she should retire from the room when the part is under discussion. While it is desirable that members of the selection committee should not be candidates for parts, this restriction is not really practicable, as those who are no longer active in their interest may have lost touch with the needs and feelings of the moment, and those who are keenest may probably be the best performers. Nevertheless, any suspicion that members of the casting committee choose one another for the best parts should be avoided whenever possible.

When a complete cast has been selected, it should be typed and sent with a rehearsal list to each member. All the members should be informed at the same time, and the members of the committee themselves should do their best to overcome the evil that arises from "rumours" by observing a strict silence on all confidential matters.

In some societies the decisions of the casting committees have to be approved by a general committee. As the time between the two meetings is the danger period, it should be short.

Casting is a most difficult task. However well the work is done, some members are certain to be disappointed and dissatisfied. For this and other reasons members of the committee should be absolutely conscientious and fair, and particularly careful that the announcements of all their decisions are made in the proper form and through the proper channels. An amateur can bear a good deal more disappointment in the privacy of his house than he can in front of the members of the society. If, after having done their work conscientiously and made their announcements properly, the members of the casting committee receive a little more praise than blame they will have done very well, for praise of casting committees is rare indeed.

REHEARSALS AND REHEARSING

The rehearsals are one of the most important parts of any stage production, and not merely a necessary evil. For amateurs they should be as enjoyable a part of the show as the performance itself.

The chief difference between a professional rehearsal and an amateur one is that, whereas to the professional the rehearsal is work, and he must treat it as such or he will lose his job, to the amateur it is recreation, and when it ceases to be entertaining he can abandon it for something else. *Noblesse oblige*, of course, but the fact remains, and it accounts for a great deal of the difference in the manner in which they should be conducted.

There are two parties to every rehearsal—

(*a*) The Direction.
(*b*) The Company.

Successful rehearsals depend almost entirely upon how the two pull together. Pulling together in this case means the conscientious carrying out by the company of the reasonable requests of the producer, in the spirit in which it is required that they should be met.

The Direction consists not only of the Producer, although he is the chief, but also of the following, who may be said to be his staff—

1. The Musical Director.
2. The Accompanists, or the Band.
3. The Dancing Instructor, if the Producer does not arrange the dances.
4. The Stage Manager and his Assistants.
5. The Prompter.
6. The Property Master (usually one of the Assistant Stage Managers).
7. The Wardrobe Mistress.

The Company consists of the Principals and the Chorus.

These two parties are mutually interested that the production should be a good one, but whereas the company are also interested that the rehearsals should be instructive, entertaining, and enjoyable, the producer is only concerned with this in as much as it may help him to secure a successful production. The fact that the producer is also concerned with securing a fee is of no importance. Professional producers are a hard-working and conscientious race, and having once undertaken a production, they direct it "with all their skill and power."

As it affects the success of the production, the producer of amateur plays, knowing that the company wish the rehearsals to be, *inter alia*, amusing and enjoyable, will do his best to provide them with what they require.

But in making rehearsals attractive the producer is manifestly helping the show. One does not suggest that he should be a comedian, but his company will obviously learn quicker from him if he can contrive to be interesting rather than boring.

The chorus and some of the principals have another requirement, especially in view of the fact that they are seeking interest and amusement. This is known as the social side. Actually many societies owe their existence to the fact that they are social off-shoots of some other activity.

Catering for this is largely a matter of having a suitable rehearsal room. Many societies are not in a position to choose their rehearsal rooms to any great extent: they have to take what they can get or can afford.

The ideal rehearsal room really consists of a suite, containing one large room, with piano, for the chorus and numbers; another room (with piano, too, if possible) for the dialogue and principals' singing; and a third room for sitting out, as it were, in which the members who are not actually employed at the moment can read, sew, play cards, and chat to their friends. The rooms should be well ventilated and sufficiently lighted to make the reading of badly typed parts and of the musical score quite easy. There should also be adequate cloak-room accommodation for both sexes, with hot water and plenty of pegs for clothes, so that damp dancing dresses may dry (they will get very damp at a strenuous rehearsal), and the necessity for members having to carry bags to and from rehearsal be obviated.

The advantages of such a suite from the point of view of the company are—

1. They are not always being browbeaten and told to "hush."

2. The enthusiasts have somewhere to rehearse bits of dialogue, etc.

3. The studious have a place in which to learn their lines, read, knit, etc., when they are not wanted by the producer.

4. The sociable can talk to their friends without interrupting the producer.

Many committees will probably say "We could never afford a place like that." Probably not, but they could very likely adapt their present rehearsal rooms so that they might become much more like it. In any case such a place, properly used, could easily become, not an expense, but an asset. For example, a refreshment room could be started, which would probably produce sufficient profit materially to assist in paying for the room. Supervision would be necessary to see that this did not get out of hand. The fact that the rehearsal place was attractive would tend to lead people to the society for its social advantages. A larger membership would result, more tickets for the shows would be sold, and, in general, a feeling engendered that would carry the society from strength to strength.

A proper rehearsal room also copes with the next big requirement of the amateur actor at rehearsals. This is that he should not spend hours waiting about to go on the stage. It is easy to say that if a person is not keen enough to await his turn for rehearsal he should not be in the show, but we are dealing with the matter as it is, and not as it ought to be. Many societies are not strong enough to dispense with the services of all except the most enthusiastic. A rehearsal place that the company enjoy solves this difficulty.

If members are not provided for in this way, the producer himself must be more than ordinarily careful to do his best in the matter or he will be bothered greatly by absence from rehearsals.

PUNCTUALITY

One of the ways he can do this is by being punctual and by beginning at once, even if it is only with a small piece of dialogue, so that late comers feel themselves to be late when they do arrive, and will try to improve next time; otherwise a feeling establishes itself that rehearsals are not intended to begin until some time after they are called. Incidentally, most of the best work is done at the beginning of a rehearsal, while the members are fresh. One that starts sharp to time instead of half an hour late may well be an hour shorter and more useful.

Another thing the producer can do to make his company attend is to avoid having discussions in corners with the stage manager, the business manager, the wardrobe mistress, or anybody else, while the company wait about for the rehearsal to continue.

FREQUENCY OF REHEARSALS

If the producer has only one large room in which to work, he cannot employ the principals while the chorus dancing is being arranged, so he must call them on another evening.

A major difficulty occurs when only one or two rehearsals are held a week, and the production has to be staged within a limited time. In that case the producer simply must call everybody and try to organize it so that they all get some work to do without too much waiting about. His main difficulty will be the small-part principals. Their lot in an operatic production is a hard one as a rule. It often involves long periods of waiting, without, perhaps, much amusement to be got out of the parts when the time comes. Yet the way in which these small parts are played is of vital importance. The show with first-class principals can be wrecked by badly-played minor parts, and many a one in which the principals are weak can be quite a success if the little parts are efficiently played.

The obvious temptation for the small-part player is to feel that his contribution is so small that it does not matter if he is not present at one or two rehearsals, but the difficulty is that so many of them feel this on the same night that certain parts of a play may hardly get rehearsed at all because the proper people are never present.

It will not be disputed that in trying to provide this requirement for the company (that is, that they should not be kept waiting unnecessarily for their turn to rehearse) the producer is both being pleasant to the cast and assisting towards making the show a success.

The last big thing that the company expects of a producer at rehearsals is courtesy.

The amateur actor is not bound to suffer the whims of an ill-tempered or ill-mannered producer, and the one who attempted to behave rudely would soon find his company quickly thinning out. He would certainly never secure a re-engagement, even if he were not asked by the committee to retire before his first production actually took place. So the producer has to find other ways of getting his work done than by bullying the company. He must be sufficient of a psychologist to decide on the proper manner with which to handle each member of his cast, bearing in mind that, if they cannot immediately do as he wishes, he may neither browbeat them nor sack them.

CHANGES IN THE CAST

Circumstances will arise, however, in which the producer must insist on changes in the cast. Except on the rare occasions when he is solely responsible for the casting, the proper procedure is for him to apply in the proper quarter (probably to a committee) and firmly but politely insist on a change. casting committees are bound to make mistakes from time to time, usually because their conception of certain parts will differ from that of the producer. But since he is responsible for the success of the production, they must take steps to see that every possible assistance is given him to secure it, and accede to any reasonable request he may make.

The less friction there is over this and other matters that reflect on the comfort and contentment of the company, the more successful are the rehearsals likely to be. Successful rehearsals almost invariably mean a successful show. Unless something goes seriously wrong at the theatre, the well-drilled and well-contented company are almost certain to give a good performance. (The words "well-drilled and well-contented" do not refer to smug, self-satisfied, and incompetent companies.)

We have now considered what the company expect at rehearsals, and seen that in realizing their expectations the producer is almost certainly helping to ensure a successful production.

Now we must consider what the producer requires of the rehearsals so that a good show may result, apart from whether or not it is going to suit the company.

Firstly, he requires their concentration. Secondly, a competent staff of technical assistants, so that his scheme of rehearsals will go smoothly, culminating in a final rehearsal at which the show will be fitted neatly on to the stage.

REHEARSING TO PLAN

All producers work to a plan, and although it may vary in detail, the underlying principle is usually the same. Briefly the plan is to divide the rehearsal period into four sections—

(*a*) The teaching of the singing to the chorus and to the principals by the music director—the principals to learn their lines.

(*b*) Begins with the arrival of the producer, and consists of the working out of the movement and dancing by the principals and chorus.

(*c*) The joining up of the dialogue and musical numbers, and the work of principals and chorus.

(*d*) Final rehearsals for speeding up, continuity, timing, and rehearsals with the band.

The rehearsal period may last any time from six weeks upwards; two to three months is usual. The first section of this plan usually lasts a month or so; the second another month; the third section about a fortnight to three weeks, and the final one will be entered upon as soon as the show is sufficiently advanced, but not so early that there is any danger of the company going stale before the first night.

In order to carry through this scheme of rehearsals, the producer requires the loyalty of the company. Loyalty, among other things, means attendance at rehearsals.

Sometimes, however, absence will occur from unpreventable reasons, such as sickness, etc., and in a genuine case every effort will be made to keep open the actor's place until he recovers. It will devolve on him to acquaint those responsible with the probable duration of his period of absence. Sickness is a piece of bad luck, for which no blame can be attached to anybody. Cases, however, will occur where a member will absent himself for reasons the validity of which may not be so apparent to those in authority. It is easy to say that the person should be relieved of his part, but some companies would not be strong enough to act in this manner. They would not have enough reserves, or the show might be too near for the part to be got up in time by anyone else. In this case it is by no means easy to decide on the best procedure. Discipline must be maintained, but the show cannot be wrecked, so probably it is best for the committee to say nothing at the time, but to remember the matter when casting the next production, and to let the defaulter know quite plainly why he has not been given the part for which he thought himself so suitable.

THE PRODUCER'S STAFF

Assuming that all these matters can be satisfactorily settled, and that the company will attend rehearsals regularly and do their best, the producer has only one other thing to wish for, and that is an enthusiastic and competent staff of assistants; in fact, if they are enthusiastic, he may not mind if they are not extremely competent, as he can teach most of them what he requires them to do.

The number of these officials and of their duties is elastic. It depends on the size of the society and the size of the production. The following list is not intended to be hard and fast, but to serve only as a guide. In a big society the work of one department may be split up among several people, whereas in a small society the duties of several departments may be undertaken by one person.

The list of duties below is concerned chiefly with what is to be done during rehearsal. At the theatre, other and different work may have to be done.

The *Musical Director* must see that the company know the music, and he is also responsible for the control of the band. He begins his work before the producer makes his appearance.

The *Accompanists* are required to have the patience of Job. It is better to have two, as playing for a four-hour rehearsal is extremely monotonous, especially if one number is rehearsed a good deal. After spending months rehearsing with the company, they relinquish their positions at the approach of the performance in favour of the band, unless the music is orchestrated to include a piano, which is unusual.

The *Dancing Instructor* or *Instructress* arranges the dancing under the guidance of the producer.

The *Stage Manager* is the producer's right-hand man; in fact, he is sometimes confused with him. His duty is to see that the wishes of the producer with regard to rehearsals are carried out, and includes such things as calling rehearsals, taking rehearsals in the producer's absence, and (with his assistants) setting the stage for each scene to be rehearsed.

Nobody can produce a play with his head buried in a book. The *Prompter's* duty is to save the producer having to waste his time looking for a line that someone has forgotten.

Properties on the professional stage mean all the things that are not scenery or electrical equipment. To amateurs they mean the hundred and one odd things, not furniture or personal property, which have to be gathered together—special flowers, books, revolvers, inkwells, etc., are specimens. It is important that any extraordinary property should be provided at rehearsals as early in the proceedings as possible, in order that the actor who has to manipulate it during the performance may become accustomed to its use.

A *Wardrobe Mistress* should be appointed, whether the costumes are made by her or not. She is responsible for taking measurements, and for making sure that the company know how to wear the costumes if they are hired and that they are properly looked after. She must not send or call people away from rehearsals without the permission of the producer.

If all the duties of these officials are correctly carried out, and the company's keenness is kept up by an interesting producer, a performance that is of the highest level of which the company are capable is assured.

There is one other subject to which reference may be made, namely, visitors at rehearsals. That they sometimes act as valuable advertising agents is the single thing that can be said in their favour, but that is only sometimes, so that unless they are important it is better not to allow them. If they must be admitted, they should be unobtrusive, for any attention they draw to themselves is sure to distract the producer and the company, and so interfere with the rehearsal.

SINGING AND DANCING

This section is not a singing or dancing lesson, but a discussion on what is required of the singers and dancers in a musical performance, with a few notes on the difficulties when the available

talent is unequal to supplying the needs of the production in hand.

That the singers, principals and chorus, should learn their music properly and get it right into their voices by the time the stage rehearsals begin, goes without saying. But since an amateur society cannot (or should not) merely send for a professional to take a vacant place in their cast which cannot be easily filled by an ordinary member of the company, they are sometimes obliged to entrust a role to a member who is not entirely suitable. He may be competent from the point of view of acting or dancing, but his singing may not be of the required standard. Owing to shortage of available material, however, it may be necessary to risk the singing and hope to secure the success of the performance by virtue of his ability as an actor or a dancer.

In certain kinds of production this may not be difficult, while in the others it is quite impossible. In opera, for instance, the singing is all-important. There can be no such thing as faking the singing here. If there is an important part that cannot be competently played by a member of the company, a singer must be borrowed from outside, or the play changed. It is equally important in light opera, but the music of light opera is usually not so difficult as that of grand opera, and, although it needs to be as well sung, it is not as a rule so hard to find singers with the necessary qualifications to undertake the parts.

With romantic musical plays and ordinary musical comedies, a rather different level is reached. In grand opera there are no parts that can be played by anyone who has not been trained as a singer, whereas in the romances and comedies there are many songs that require to be talked rather than sung, especially by the comedians, although the leading parts require singing talent of a high order.

It is not a disadvantage to have good singers in modern musical comedies, but it is definitely not so important that the singing should be outstanding as that the comedians should be funny and that the dancers able to dance well.

In short, the importance of the singing declines as one passes from grand opera, in which it is everything, to modern musical comedy, in which it is only about a third of the production, the other two-thirds being the dancing and the comedy.

It should be emphasized, by the way, that everything stated in these notes is relative. A society does not wish to fall below its own standards. Rather should it try to improve; but what is good enough for the leading part in one society will be only of chorus standard in another. Every company likes to feel that it is quite the best that has ever been formed and certainly as near the professional level as can be imagined, but the fact must be faced that, in most cases, this feeling is by no means justified. Some companies are much nearer professional standards than others, but the worst are very bad indeed. It is only by taking the greatest pains to avoid anything slipshod in the way of casting of even the smallest parts that progress can be made.

Cases will arise, however, from time to time, perhaps as a result of sickness in close proximity to the date of the show, when even the strongest society may be obliged to fill up a part with an actor who would normally not be considered equal to it. Of course, in grand opera, there is little to be done. An opera is singing, and without singing there is no opera. This is perhaps the only case that justifies the paying of a professional to undertake the part, after careful search has been made (with the aid of the National Operatic and Dramatic Association) to see if there is not an amateur somewhere in the country who will step forward to fill the breach.

In certain other shows, however, something can be done to help in cases where the talents of the singers are not quite equal to what is required of them. For example, there is the device known as "talking" a song. Although this is far more difficult than it sounds, it is not impossible for any intelligent actor to do it adequately, and it is of especial value in comedian parts. But it cannot be done in genuine opera or in the real singing parts of any other production. If these cannot be sung properly the work should not be attempted.

Weakness in the chorus can be overcome by having other singers concealed in the wings to join in with them and thereby increase the volume. When this method is adopted, it is imperative that those on the stage should open their mouths wide and generally give the impression that they are working hard or the effect will be ridiculous. In modern musical comedies the standard of singing required by the chorus is, as a rule, not high. In fact, often a little enthusiastic shouting will serve the purpose. The musical director will, when teaching the singing originally, have stressed the importance of a good attack and lively delivery. Nowhere is it more important than in a chorus whose singing is not good.

On the subject of music there is another matter that needs to be dealt with, usually by the musical director, although it is one of the less artistic of his duties and one that can sometimes be handled by another official of the society. This is the engagement of the band. The nature of the task depends on the type of theatre in which the performances are to be given. In regular theatres, and in some cinemas, there will be a professional orchestra which may have to be taken over with the building. In such, care is required before attempting to supplant any of

the regular players or even to augment their numbers. Musicians have a Union which works unceasingly in their interests and what, to the layman, seems to be the most ordinary matter, may not conform with their views.

In a hall this is not so likely to arise, but whoever is responsible for engaging the band will find it worth while to have this at the back of his mind. A more likely difficulty at an ordinary hall is the absence of any proper orchestra pit and the resultant need to make special provision for the accomodation of the band. This again is a matter that the person responsible for the musical accompaniment to the show must ascertain early in the proceedings so that if any special arrangements (removal of front stalls etc.) are required, the necessary permission to do the work, and so on, may be secured.

One of the worst situations that can arise in any building is where the orchestra-pit is

right under the stage and some, or all, of the following occur.

(*a*) Neither the band nor the performers can hear one another.

(*b*) The musical director cannot see his band *and* the performers on the stage at the same time.

(*c*) The musical director can see the stage but the band cannot see him.

(*d*) The performers cannot see the musical director.

DANCING

The ordinary playgoer (to musical plays) likes to hear good singing in the theatre. Perhaps he knows a little of its technique, and although he will tolerate an efficient fake, if it helps the show, he knows it to be a fake. With regard to dancing, the situation is quite different. The ordinary playgoer knows nothing whatever about the technicalities of dancing, and, except for a curious enthusiasm that the company should be light on their feet, he does not know in the least how well or how badly they are dancing, provided that the result is effective.

Failure to appreciate this point results in a large number of amateur performances being less attractive than they otherwise might be. The performers waste their time learning a number of complicated dance steps, which the audience do not understand, do them badly, and the performance fails, because the audience do not realize how near they were to something out of the ordinary. They merely see that something has gone wrong.

From the dancing point of view, things that are difficult to do are not necessarily effective on the stage, while some of the simplest movements are absolutely astonishing in their effect. When the dances are arranged by the producer, this is not likely to go seriously wrong. He is concerned that the whole production should be as good as possible, so he will arrange movements which are within the powers of the company, but which, at the same time, have the desired effect on the audience.

When the dances are not arranged by the producer, but by a local dancing teacher, difficulties begin to arise. A dancing teacher, unless she happens to be experienced at this particular kind of work, tends rather to teach dance steps than stage movements, but many of the most effective stage movements are not dancing or dance steps at all; they are merely cleverly arranged walking about movements, in which a dancer, as such, has no interest.

The first essential for any stage dance arrangement, either for a principal or for the chorus, is that it should have movement. The most complicated dance step in the world, however beautifully executed, is of no value on the stage if it is too small to be seen. And this is where most ordinary teachers of dancing fail at stage arrangements. The business that they set for the chorus too often consists of a number of small dance steps which, although interesting in themselves, have, from the point of view of the audience, no value whatever.

From this it would appear that when a producer is in difficulties with regard to a suitable dance arrangement, he should make the company move about the stage as much as possible. Within the limits of common sense, this is so, and provided that the balance is observed between movement and restlessness, most plays can succeed on an incredibly small amount of actual dancing.

Should the company have any talent at all for dancing, the producer's task in arranging suitable dance numbers is much easier. But, unfortunately, dancing is a thing that few people, except those who specialize in it, trouble to do to any great extent. Even if they have been taught, they never practise, so that when they begin work on a production, the one or two who have had any experience are so completely out of training that they are no better than any of the others.

Almost everybody who sings does get a certain amount of practice, even if it is only by accident, as it were. People sing at parties, concerts, other shows, or at home for the love of it. But, except the specialists, nobody ever thinks of practising a few dance movements. For this reason every society is recommended to organize a weekly dance class. Usually it can be arranged on the most economical terms, over a long period, with a local dancing teacher. And it is no disadvantage that the company should know dancers' steps, provided that they are taught to use them in the proper manner on the stage.

Apart from the advantage of having a number of trained dancers always available, it is desirable that members of a company should be brought together as much as possible as this is one of the best ways of promoting the club spirit. Another point is that while the members are in the habit of going to a dancing class they will learn things which, although perhaps not of immediate value, may become more important on a change in the character of the productions usually presented by the society. For instance, the fascination of step or tap dancing may be explored. Tap-dancing, although not as essential in some of the older musical comedies as it is in the newer ones, may often be used with effect. There is no reason why a society should not start its own singing class too, if it is considered desirable, but a class for singing is not so necessary as one for dancing, for singers can practise by themselves, whereas troupe dancers cannot, even if they will.

On the subject of dancing, a word might be said as to the desirability of the chorus dancers wearing some kind of uniform at rehearsal. There is no need to have anything complex or in the least expensive, but from the point of view of helping the producer it is of great value that the chorus should be similarly attired. It is much easier to gauge the effect of a number when it is rehearsed by a company in uniform rather than in a variety of costumes.

For the men, grey flannel trousers and a sports shirt are all that are required. Girls will contrive to vary the simplest costume in such a way as to make it look different if they are allowed to do so. Difficulties may arise as to what some of the girls will wear and what they will not. Some refuse to appear unless they are enveloped in a gown that reaches almost to the floor; others are prepared to face with equanimity the idea of wearing a bathing costume. They might be allowed to vote for which of a few selected models they will wear, and having made up their minds, they should be urged to appear at rehearsal in the costume. There are one or two features about a rehearsal dress that are definitely desirable. The dresses should all be of the same colour, which should be one that will not vary much in shade. Black has a good deal to recommend it, as it does not fade, and it does not show the dirt. They should also not be so enveloping as to enable the wearer to seem to carry out a movement without in fact doing it at all. If skirts are worn, they should all be the same length above the knee. Two eminently practical rehearsal costumes are illustrated.

Finally, care should be taken that dancers are not allowed to stand about and to catch cold in thin dancing dresses after working strenuously at rehearsal.

DRESSING A MUSICAL PLAY

From the point of view of costumes, which, incidentally, by professionals are always known as wardrobe, almost all musical plays fall into two classes: (1) Costume, and (2) Straight, or modern dress. And whereas some societies provide all the clothes, whatever the nature of the play, others expect the members of the company to provide their own, unless the work in hand is a period or other piece, requiring garments that nobody could reasonably be expected to possess in the ordinary way.

This applies more especially to the principals. Costumes for the chorus will almost certainly have to be found by the management of the society. It cannot be expected that eight young men will all have lounge suits of exactly the same colour and cut. In fact, even their dress clothes may vary so much as to render them unsuitable for use on the stage. Grey flannel suits, which one would think should be serviceable, actually vary enormously in shade, and this is exaggerated by artificial lighting. The same sort of thing applies to the girls, although occasionally it is desirable that they should wear costumes of the same kind but different as to colour and detail. For example, in the opening scene in the musical comedy *The Girl Friend* the chorus girls first appear in travelling suits, and provided that these do not actually clash in colour or vary too widely in the texture of the material of which they are made, it is definitely preferable that they should not all be alike. Similarly, in *Derby Day*, provided that the race-goers suggest a sufficiently wide range in the social scale, they may wear almost anything; except the special characters—costers in "Pearlies," bookmakers, etc.

In short, apart from crowd scenes, of which both the above two are really examples, although there is singing and dancing work, the costumes for the chorus must be provided by the society.

There are two ways in which this may be done. Either they may be hired from a theatrical costumier, or they may be made by members of the society or by anyone else who can be persuaded to undertake the work. And for differing purposes each of these will be found more convenient from time to time, and occasionally it will be necessary to combine the two. For example, a party of ladies could not make eight lounge suits for the chorus men that would be as suitable from the point of view of price or appearance as those that could be hired from a firm of theatrical costumiers. But before the war, the ladies might very likely be able to make a number of chorus dresses for the dancing girls, of material that would look quite satisfactory from the auditorium, at much the same price as that at which they could be hired, and, owing to the fact that they would be made especially for the production, they might be more up to date and, therefore, more generally suitable than borrowed ones.

On the subject of the cost of hiring costumes, for the benefit of those who have no experience at all, it may be given as a rough rule of thumb that before the Second Great War this worked out at about half a guinea each provided that there was a reasonable number of them and that they had not to be sent an enormously long distance. For a small number it might have been almost double that figure. The present figure is about 7s. 6d.

It may be mentioned, in passing, that for operatic societies it is much more usual to hire costumes than to make them, chiefly on account of the numbers involved.

Whichever course is adopted, a wardrobe mistress should be appointed. If the costumes are hired, the duties, to a suitable person, will be quite light. Duties are always heavy when they fall to someone who is either unenthusiastic or unsuitable to carry them out, and the wardrobe mistress of an amateur operatic society is very much one of the silent workers, who must toil with little hope of praise, but with the certainty of having to endure a good deal of grumbling.

Among the duties of this member of the production staff for a performance in which the costumes are to be hired, are the following—

(*a*) To take the measurements of the company, enter them on the proper form, and send them to the costumiers. A wise course is to keep a loose-leaf book containing the measurement forms of all the active members of the society. New ones may be slipped into alphabetical order and old ones removed as desired, and, when a production takes place, the contractor's own form may be filled in with little trouble and without the necessity for remeasuring every member of the cast.

(*b*) To take charge of the costumes on their arrival at the theatre, and to see that they are handed out to the proper people.

(*c*) To check all the costumes delivered, and to communicate at once with the providers in the event of any omissions.

(*d*) To see that there are no glaring historical or other inaccuracies such as are likely to be observed by the audience, and therefore to distract their attention.

(*e*) To help the company into their clothes and generally to assist them to wear everything properly.

(*f*) Finally, at the end of the production, to supervise the packing and return of the costumes, so that there may be no argument afterwards with the owners that certain articles have not been sent back.

One other duty which falls to the wardrobe mistress in a show where the costumes are hired from a contractor, is to see that the company's treatment of the wardrobe is reasonably careful. Some members of societies treat clothes from the costumiers as though they are valueless rags. In fact, of course, the things that are supplied for some productions are valuable. But value or no value, they are the proprietor's stock in trade and not only does he expect to have them properly looked after, but also he must in self-protection take steps to see that they are not maltreated and enforce penalties against the offending society in the event of loss or damage. This, of course, is more than ever true while clothing material is scarce and replacement of a lost or damaged article is not only a matter of money.

The treatment that some amateurs mete out to costumes is past belief. Dresses have been known to be used as rags to clean off greasepaint. On one occasion, a chorus girl on finding that it was raining when she had to leave the theatre, changed her own dress for a beautiful period costume and went home in it. When such things occur, the costumier naturally expects redress.

Apart from cases of maltreatment, there is another way in which costumes are sometimes damaged in what appears at the time to be a legitimate manner, i.e. by inconsiderate treatment with scissors when the costume supplied is too large. The costume ought to fit, but, occasionally, it does not. The fault may lie with the supplier or with the society, but whoever is at fault, mutilation is unjustifiable. The whole matter is, of course, covered by contract which in the excitement of a dress rehearsal is apt to be forgotten.

It is here that the competent wardrobe-mistress can show her worth. Knowing how much a costume may be altered without violation of the contract she can effect allowable alterations without damaging the dress.

For productions in which the costumes are the property of those who are to wear them (or their friends), the duties of the wardrobe mistress are much lighter, but she should still be appointed, to help members in cases of difficulty and to carry out any other work which belongs to this department and which requires to be done.

MOUNTING THE PLAY

Before discussing the two different ways in which scenery may be provided for an operatic production, it is needful to decide, first of all, whether or not scenery should be used at all—in other words, whether or not the play can be effectively staged in curtains or in some other kind of formalized setting, such as screens.

Generally speaking, it is better to use ordinary painted scenery than any other kind for musical works. Perhaps this is because the situations that occur are so improbable. For example, in moments of physical danger or other emergency, the leading characters frequently burst into song instead of taking some quite obvious step to extricate themselves from the difficulty. This is so unlike real life that unless the settings look realistic the audience will not believe in the characters and will lose interest in them altogether.

In cases of grave difficulty curtains could probably be used by a skilful producer for some plays, but one cannot imagine many of the musical works with which one is acquainted being given in anything but the accepted scenery.

"Curtain settings," by the way, in this article mean the kind of curtains that are a makeshift for scenery, not the kind that are installed in theatres with stages of the most modern type, where the curtains are such as to make ordinary scenery completely unnecessary. On these stages settings can be devised that are far more elaborate than those possible with ordinary hired scenery. But even on these stages curtain settings would probably only be of use, to any great extent, in opera of the grander sort. This is probably because almost all other kinds of musical works include comedy, either light or low, and comedy requires certain external conditions, such as properties and environment, to help it to succeed. And honest-to-goodness comedy (with music) somehow does not seem to fit in with curtain settings, which are almost bound to be somewhat ethereal.

If a compromise is necessary, it should be remembered that the audience will accept, without demur, a convention, such as curtains, at the beginning of a play. If a change is made afterwards to ordinary scenery, they will probably not observe it, but will go home satisfied with the evening's entertainment. If the play begins in ordinary scenery and then changes to curtains, they are much more likely to notice the change, even if only subconsciously. They will have a vague feeling of incompleteness, which they will take home with them. What an audience feel about the end of a show is most likely what, in retrospect, they will remember of the performance.

It must not be imagined from the above that there is any prejudice against curtains or other formalized settings. In the production of revues, if these may be called musical works, curtains are invaluable, both for sketches and for other numbers. Unless the production is a particularly spectacular one, the audience see each scene for such a short time that they do not get tired of it, and making the necessary changes is greatly facilitated. For a little while, one strongly coloured property, such as a chair or a standard lamp, with suitable stage lighting, substituted for another equally strong property, will have the effect of making the stage look completely different.

Lest it should be imagined that curtain settings always mean plain black curtains set on the stage in the form of a box, it should be explained that doors, windows, fireplaces, and coloured backings are as much parts of curtain or screen settings as they are of canvas painted ones. The producer who has the misfortune to be faced with the necessity to stage, whether for a competition or not, any play, musical or otherwise, in plain curtains, is deserving of sympathy. The art of transforming a wall of a plain drab colour (one of the most useful for stage curtains) into a thing of beauty is merely a matter of having an adequate, not necessarily an elaborate, lighting outfit, and of knowing how to use it.

PAINTED SCENERY

It seems, then, that for the purpose in mind ordinary painted scenery will be more suitable than curtains or anything of the kind. The next thing is, as in the case of the costumes, to decide whether to make it at home or whether to hire it from one of the usual scenery stores. For ordinary musical productions given by amateur societies in the normal way there is no doubt at all that it is best to hire what is needed from one of the usual scenery contractors.

The following notes are included for the benefit of the society which finds, perhaps owing to some pecularity of the hall, that it is worth while to consider scene-building. The work is not to be undertaken lightly because like everything else, technical knowledge is required, (e.g. in building the sets for a sloping stage) and in these days serious difficulty will normally be experienced in obtaining the necessary timber, canvas, paint, and other materials.

But painted scenery is not the only kind that can be made at home; in fact it is, perhaps, the one kind that is best not made there. There are certain other ways of building sets that are worthy of consideration by amateurs who have to do so, although it is doubtful if either of these methods would secure the approval of the ordinary professional stage manager or scenic artist.

The first one is especially suitable for use in connexion with interior sets. It consists simply in pasting wall-paper on to canvas covered flats (the technical name for the big screens of which stage walls are built up) and back-cloths. This presupposes the possession of the necessary flats, etc. Since the walls of ordinary rooms are not covered with paper from floor to ceiling, it is necessary to paste other paper of suitable design into the appropriate places to suggest skirtings, dados, picture-rails, etc.

This kind of scenery looks surprisingly effective from the front, but it is useful in interiors only. Its most serious disadvantage is the difficulty of fire-proofing it properly. The laws with regard to fire-proofing scenery are most strict, and rightly so. The only variation that occurs is in the zeal with which it is insisted by local authorities that they should be carried out. In some theatres the weekly inspection of the scenery in use for the time being consists of actually exposing samples of the stock to a gas-flare or other highly inflammatory agent. The unpleasantness of a situation in which the whole of the scenery for a production has been condemned by the local fire authorities on the day of the dress rehearsal can easily be imagined. Yet it is quite within their powers to do this, and it is right that it should be so. For the cause of Art is no excuse for endangering the lives of the public; yet amateurs have been known to feel it unreasonable that they should not be allowed to jeopardize the existence of some hundreds of their fellow-beings in order to give a performance.

CANVAS SCENERY

Canvas scenery can easily be fire-proofed. There are certain complications with regard to the way in which the proofing matter affects the colour of the paint, but it is the scene builder's duty to be familiar with this and to do his work accordingly. Paper is quite another matter. A process is said to have been invented by means of which it may be fire-proofed for a short time, but what effect the preparation has on the colouring of the paper I cannot say. This aspect must be most carefully examined before any arrangement to use paper-covered scenery is made. The conditions under which the audience are admitted to the theatre have a considerable bearing on the amount of interest that the authorities take in the condition of the scenery.

Another disadvantage of using paper scenery is the ease with which it becomes torn and otherwise damaged. On the other hand, provided the canvas is not affected, it is easy to repair, and the whole thing may be covered with a different paper for a subsequent production.

The other way of making scenery at home before 1939 was to paste paper on to flats in the same way, but in this case the paper was supplied especially for the purpose by Samuel French, Ltd., of London. This firm made sheets of paper, double crown in size, printed, so that by pasting them on ordinary flats in the manner indicated above almost any scene could be built up. There was a sufficiently wide range of designs to make it possible, with a little ingenuity, to construct almost any scene, either exterior or interior.

They also supplied wood cut into suitable lengths and numbered so that flats could be made at home. These could be covered with a special linen, cheaper and lighter than ordinary canvas, to which the paper sheets could readily be fastened with paste.

Doors and windows were also available in various different designs.

The society which decides that the possession of scenery is desirable would be well advised to enquire of this firm.

Generally speaking, it is not much cheaper to make scenery by any method than to hire it. Pasting wall-paper on to flats is inexpensive, but the flats have to be procured and the necessary doors and windows fitted. The only advantage is that the society may be storing up for itself a stock that will much reduce the cost of future productions.

WALL-PAPERED SCENERY

It has been suggested that wall-papered scenery may be repapered from time to time; similarly, the other kind of paper scenery may be recovered, and the positions of the doors and windows changed in each production. Different curtains, hangings, carpets, furniture, and flowers will all help to disguise a set from time to time. But ultimately a society's audience will get tired of seeing the company in front of the same coloured background, and fresh expense will be necessary to provide new scenery.

It will be for the committee of a new society to decide, when they embark on their first production, what course they are to adopt, assuming, that is, that they are not pinned down to one kind of scenery or another by some extraneous circumstance. The following points will have to be borne in mind.

BASIC POINTS

Firstly, that nothing is to be gained by amassing a stock of scenery by a society which can expect to exist for a short time only, so that it can never secure a proper return on its investment.

Secondly, that a place must be found in which the scenery may be stored and not be damaged by moth or damp. If such a place can only be rented and not secured without payment, the aggregate of these payments over a protracted period, together with the initial outlay, must be considered.

That a place must be found in which the work may be carried out goes without saying. But also there must be some means of transporting the scenery to the theatre or hall at a cost which is commensurate with the economy that, it is hoped, will be effected by building the settings at home.

Great care should be taken, when the production is to be given in a hall which is not a regular theatre, that there will be no difficulty in getting the flats into the building. Theatres are provided with doors specially for this purpose; ordinary halls often are not. If the doors are unreasonably small and the difficulty cannot be overcome, the only possible solution, is to examine the possibilities of building and painting the scenery inside the hall.

When the committee have considered all these things, they may decide that it is not worth the trouble, in the circumstances, to make scenery, but that it will be preferable to hire it. The proper procedure, then, is for the business manager, or other official to whom the duty is allotted, to write to various scenery contractors stating the requirements and inviting estimates. The lowest will not necessarily be the most suitable. Sometimes it is necessary to send scene-plots (the technical name for plans of the stage and scenery) to the contractor before he can make an estimate. These are provided by the producer.

When the scenery is to be made at home, the scene-plots usually need not at first be as formal as when it is to be hired. When the producer can talk to the scenic artist and see the work as it is progressing, he can provide what is required from time to time. At first only dimensions and places of doors and windows are required. Later, further details become necessary. But when scenery has to be ordered by post from a distant town and sent by rail to the country, the plots must be most carefully drawn, or the building up of the scenery at the dress rehearsal (fitting up, as it is called) will be a long and wearying business—and in the end it may not be satisfactory.

It is most important that scene-plots sent to the contractor should include full dimensions. The depth of the stage and the width of the proscenium opening should be clearly shown, together with the distance that the backcloth is required to be from the footlights. All doors and windows must be accurately drawn, and if they are to open (the word "practical" written against them conveys the required meaning to the professional) it should be stated which way they must open, i.e. "off" or "on" the scene and "up" or "down" stage. Door-knobs, window catches, etc., must all be indicated or the contractors will be justified in leaving them out.

It is advisable for the producer, after he has sent the plots, to call at the store to examine the scenery that the contractors intend to send, with a view to checking the colours to ascertain if they will be suitable.

Some halls, other than regular theatres, have all sorts of curious regulations regarding stage scenery. Some will not allow stage-screws to be put into the floor or nails to be knocked into anything. Others will not allow the permanent borders to be touched. Few halls can fly scenery (that is, suspend it by ropes above the stage so that it may be lowered into position when required).

It is essential that all such peculiarities should be discovered and communicated to the providers of scenery, or tremendous difficulties will have to be overcome at the dress rehearsal.

For a big production the contractors will usually send a carpenter who is familiar with the scenes to superintend the getting in and fitting up of scenery. This saves a good deal of time and trouble, but, of course, it adds to the cost.

With regard to changing the scenery, it must be ascertained first of all that it is possible to make changes efficiently, and a suitable staff must be engaged for the purpose. In a professional theatre there will usually be an available staff quite competent to carry on after the carpenter from the scenic stores has left. In halls where there is no regular stage-staff the manager can usually secure the services of suitable people, or the work may be undertaken by amateurs, perhaps members of the society that is giving the performance. Scene shifting is just as much a part of stagecraft as anything else, and should be studied in the same way.

But societies are warned against what seems, until it is examined more closely, to be a reasonable economy; this is, in a professional theatre, to attempt to employ an amateur for work that a member of the stage-staff would ordinarily be engaged and paid to do.

Sometimes this is covered by a clause in the theatre's contract, but even if it is not it will not help in maintaining friendly relations between the society and the stage-staff, apart from the effect of any Trade Union regulations, for their members to be kept out of work.

PROPERTIES

Properties, to the professional, mean all the things that go on the stage, other than scenery or electrical equipment. Amateurs mostly think of them vaguely as the hundred and one odd things, other than furniture—that is, books, revolvers, inkwells, etc., which have to be gathered together before a show.

Actually, properties fall into four classes. These are—

1. *Furniture*
   This includes carpets.
2. *Small Properties*
   These are mostly for dressing the stage, but are not as large or cumbersome as furniture. Vases, clocks, etc.
3. *Personal Properties*
   Watches, walking-sticks, handkerchiefs, note-cases.
4. *Hand Properties*
   Lanterns, pens, tea-things, etc.

But it is not of great importance what they are called so long as nothing required for the production is forgotten.

The best way of ensuring that everything is remembered is to make someone definitely responsible for properties; in other words, to appoint a Property Master. He may be selected for each production, if more than one is given during the season, or elected annually, like any other official of the society.

His duties are, as the name suggests, to see that all the properties that are necessary for a production are secured, and that they are in working order when required for use. But this is only the final part of his labours. They begin early in the production, and culminate only with the appearance on the stage of, sometimes, dozens of small articles that have been culled, with an infinity of trouble, from many places.

His first act is to secure a list of what is wanted; in other words, a property list, or prop-plot, as it is usually called. This may be done in a variety of ways, and the one to be used in any particular case will depend on the nature of the production in hand. If the play is published, with a printed list of the properties required bound in the book, he is lucky. He is well advised to check it in any case, partly to see that nothing has been omitted, and partly to see that nothing has been included when the original production was given on a very large stage merely to fill up vacant space. But if a list is not supplied, one will have to be made. Sometimes the producer knows the play very well and can draw up a list from memory, or he may have a permanent one, which he is prepared to lend to the property master of any society for whom he is producing the particular play. If neither of these convenient situations arises, or if the play is original, it will be necessary to compile a list.

The proper person to do this depends on who is to arrange the settings. If the producer is responsible for the entire production, he can work out the property plot with the property master, but if the settings are to be arranged by a designer under the direction or with the approval of the producer, the property master will be obliged to work with both of them.

Having made a list of the articles, the next thing is to estimate the cost of acquiring them and to communicate it to the business manager or other responsible official. It will be understood that the order in which these operations takes place is capable of a good deal of variation. For instance, the whole of the estimating for the entire production may have been done when the play was chosen. In this case, the property master will have been allotted a sum, and he must keep within it. The point is that provision must be made in the estimates, whenever they are done and whoever does them, for the properties, so that the property master will be assured that any expenses he may incur will be refunded, even if at first he disburses the money from his own pocket, or, conversely, that he will be prevented from involving the society in unnecessary expense if he has a tendency in that direction.

The word properties in this connexion means not only the furniture, but also any of the other three classes of articles that will be left for the property master to secure. A certain number of these will require to be bought, as probably no one will have them to lend, and it may be impossible to hire them, but nothing is to be gained by amassing a large number of properties of any kind, as they are rarely of service a second time, and provision has to be made for their storage and repair.

FURNITURE

This is usually the largest and most expensive part of the property plot, so it may be convenient to consider it first.

It is definitely undesirable to buy furniture, even if the society can afford it. This is especially true in cases where there is stock scenery that must be used, with variations, over and over again. Different furniture, together with suitable curtains, cushions, etc., particularly if they are of marked design, can do more to change the appearance of a set than anything else, and the society that is saddled with a quantity of furniture which it is obliged to use time after time runs a risk of boring its audience at the sight of the stage before the company have been given a chance to open their mouths.

There are several ways in which furniture may be acquired, other than by buying it. One is to hire it from one of the firms that make hiring furniture to theatrical companies their business; and, although one hesitates to give a guess as to the cost of hiring furniture for a production without knowing the name of it, it may be mentioned that before the Second Great War a £5 bill would have been light, while £15 would have been heavy. These figures applied only when the theatre was near enough to the contractor's warehouse to enable him to deliver the goods in his own vans in the ordinary course of business. When they had to be sent by rail the cost rose proportionately. For this reason societies are recommended to secure their furniture from a nearby store whenever it is practicable to do so.

For ordinary modern scenes, furniture shops can sometimes be persuaded to lend the necessary material in exchange for a free advertisement in the programme, but they are not as a rule eager to do so, as the haste with which furniture has, perforce, to be handled in the course of scene-changing tends to damage it, and to render it subsequently unsaleable.

For this reason it is hardly fair to ask members of a society to lend their own furniture. On a stage, furniture is bound to suffer a degree of ill-treatment that is beyond ordinary wear and tear. Apart from the speed with which it has to be carried on and off, there is the risk of its being injured during the actual performance by dancers, etc. Again, the stage hands in a professional theatre are not accustomed to handling furniture in a way that will leave it suitable to take its place in the living rooms of an ordinary house. That to which they are accustomed has only to *look* suitable for the show; they have no interest in its before- or after-life. This is not to say that stage hands are necessarily clumsy: they are not, but their purpose is different.

The furniture hired from a theatrical furniture warehouse is suitably built, as a rule, to look effective without being too fragile, and provision is made in the price charged for its use to cover the cost of the rapid deterioration.

Wherever it is secured, the furniture is chosen by the producer or other person responsible for arranging the settings, and comes into the care of the property master either at the dress rehearsal or earlier, and he is responsible for it until it (all of it) is returned to the owners.

SMALL PROPERTIES

This section is the most interesting from the point of view of the property master, and in connexion with it he has a chance to show his ingenuity and powers of persuasion.

Furniture is so large that it is not an exciting subject. It is usually hired, and this merely means paying a visit to a warehouse and selecting it. But the small properties cover such a wide range of objects and are required for such a diversity of uses that an enthusiastic property master can provide himself with a good deal of entertainment in gathering them together. Some he will buy as cheaply as possible; others he will be able to borrow for nothing; the rest he may be able to make—in fact, some he will probably have to make, or to get made for him, as certain properties will look correct on the stage only if they are specially made. An example of this occurs in *Ten Minute Alibi* (although this is not a musical play), where the clock must be so constructed that it can be operated from inside, or it will not synchronize with the dialogue.

It will be readily understood that a keen property man who is deft with his hands can save his society a great deal of expense and uncertainty.

PERSONAL PROPERTIES

The property master should discuss with each member of the company the properties that each will bear on the stage, and arrange as to their provision, so that there will be no mistake as a result of each having left any matter to the other.

Sometimes a difficulty will arise when an actor or actress is called upon to provide a hand property, which, although sounding personal enough on the property plot, turns out to be an article that nobody in the ordinary way could be expected to possess or to be able to borrow. The property master (he is usually referred to as "Props") should go carefully through all hand props, as they are called, and make a note of all such things so that they may be provided for in the estimates, or he may find, when he is already as near the limit of his expenditure as he dare be, that he is suddenly faced with having to produce, and pay for, say, an enormous feather fan, the only reference to which in the book may be "Enter So-and-So with fan."

The responsibility in a case like this is shared by the actor. Everybody on accepting a part should immediately examine it from the point of view of hand props, and notify the property master of any articles concerning which there may be difficulty. The actor who can, when the question of providing an awkward property occurs, state confidently that he will arrange about it, is not only a friend to the property master, but also a most valuable unseen worker for the good of his society, always provided that he carries out his promise; if he does not, he is one of the greatest nuisances with which the Amateur Movement has to contend.

All actors should, on leaving their dressing rooms to go on the stage, make sure that they have all their personal props with them. The shorter the time between leaving the dressing room and going on the stage, the less risk there is that a property will be put down for a moment during a conversation in the Green Room, and be found to have disappeared when it is required, with subsequent recriminations and excitement.

If it can be done without causing inconvenience, it is worth while to slip on the stage before the curtain goes up to check that any property that one has to use during the action of the play (practical lantern, etc.) is there and in working order, though this is dangerous advice when a hurried change of scene is taking place, as it is obviously undesirable that the stage should be crowded with actors fussing with their properties. Their presence may, in fact, tend to cause the accident they are trying to avert.

HAND PROPS

This section includes all those things, other than personal props, which the actors take on the stage with them, or which they use when they are there. Revolvers, pens and ink, cups and saucers, and so on, are examples.

The chief feature about these is that, having been gathered together, they should be in position and ready for use when required; that is to say, tea-pots and wine bottles should be filled and revolvers loaded. With regard to this kind of prop, it is most important to see that it conforms with the requirements of the text of the play. For example, when an actor has to finish a glass of wine it should not be so full that he is faced with having either to contradict himself or to suffer physical discomfort that may affect his performance during the rest of the evening. Similarly, no player should be called upon to eat or drink anything which is unpalatable to him, or which may affect his digestion. For this reason cups and glasses that actors have to use on the stage should be hygienically safe. Sponge cake is one of the best imitation foods.

A word about revolvers. Always use the kind with solid barrels, if possible. The wad of a blank cartridge from a big pistol at a few yards range will kill, so, if it must be used, it should be issued by and returned to the property master each night, and he should keep it, and the necessary ammunition, under lock and key. When a revolver is to be fired on the stage, a double should always be kept in the prompt corner in case the one on the stage does not go off.

HANDLING THE PROPS

In a professional theatre there will probably be a property man attached to the staff. If so, the society will have to take him on along with the other hands. Then there will be little for the amateur to do. He may go about and see that all is well, and attend to any props that need special attention, but, ordinarily, when there is a professional, it is best not to interfere, as, once the latter knows what he has to do, he rarely makes a mistake; in fact, he is more likely to do so if he is supervised too much.

When the performance is given in a hall or theatre in which there is no regular stage staff, and the work is done by amateurs, the property master will have his hands full. Even in a simple play it is surprising how much there is to do, but in a complicated one it is always better to have sufficient assistants to relieve him of any responsibility for the manual part of the work, so that he may be free to superintend and generally to see that nothing is forgotten or goes wrong.

When a scene is being set the property men (it may be necessary to have two or three each side, apart from the scene-shifters) should get on as soon as possible so that there may be no delay in ringing up the curtain. All properties, such as letters, tea-trays, etc., which have to be brought on during the action of the play, should be placed ready in the wings. If there is room a small table or bench should be available at each side of the stage with the props laid out on it, and there should be a man in charge of each to hand the props to the actors. When there is not room for anything so elaborate as this, something must be improvised —the top of a skip in the wings makes a good substitute.

Properties should not be left about the stage unattended. When they arrive at the theatre they should all be checked and sorted out and put into order in the property room (it may be only an odd corner under the stage) to which only the property master and his assistants should have admission. Articles will then be taken to the stage or to the wings by the property men and returned by them as soon as possible. Properties handed to actors and retained by them until the fall of the curtain should be collected, or they may go astray.

Finally, the property master must arrive at the theatre sufficiently long before the curtain goes up on each performance to see that there is no panic at the last moment owing to something having disappeared during the night.

MAKE-UP FOR PRINCIPALS AND CHORUS

It has been observed that one of the first things for a new society to decide is its policy as to whether certain phases of its productions should be undertaken by its members, that is to say, by amateurs; or whether they should be entrusted only to professionals, and paid for. Among the factors that must be taken into consideration in arriving at a decision, are the available talent and the cost; and the proper order in which they should be considered depends entirely on the society. There are some societies that believe that a production is impossible unless it is professional, and that their members, in a professional setting, will be nearly, if not quite, up to professional standards. Others feel that the slight originality which is rendered possible by home-made settings, etc., is sufficiently acceptable to audiences to enable them to enjoy such productions as much as, or more than, those that are more stereotyped.

Whichever way the matter is regarded, the fact remains that there are amateur playwrights, composers, producers, scene-painters, costumiers, etc., and many societies are grateful to avail themselves of their services. When we reach the last thing to be considered before the dress rehearsal, namely, make-up, the fact still applies. Some amateur actors can make themselves up very well, and there are people who are prepared to give their services, as makers-up, to societies. But, except in a few cases, this is one of the things that committees are least inclined to entrust to members of the company.

This is all the more extraordinary when one remembers that making-up is just as much part of the technique and accomplishment of the competent actor, amateur or professional, as is efficient diction. Yet an amateur, who would be most insulted if his ability at singing or dancing were questioned, is quite unashamed to admit that he knows nothing about make-up. Perhaps some amateurs feel that it is beneath their dignity, and others that it is a dark mystery into which only the abnormal may probe.

Both groups are wrong. Make-up is a branch of stagecraft that everyone who is worth his salt, and who seeks to be a competent and well-equipped craftsman, should master, in the same way as he does his lines and his music.

Apart from the altruistic aspect, there is the financial side of the situation to be considered. A professional perruquier cannot be secured for much less than a guinea a night; with expenses it may be more. During a run of a week, with a *matinée*, ten pounds can be spent on his fee alone. For a big society that hands over hundreds of pounds to charity each year, this is trivial—simply an item of production expenditure for which allowance must be made. But for the small society that performs for two nights, with a dress rehearsal, in a local hall, with a turnover on the entire production of little more than £100 (most people would be amazed if they were informed of the number of such societies), three guineas for a perruquier is an appreciable percentage of the total. They might possibly secure the services of an amateur, in which case they would be lucky, as the number of competent ones is limited, and they are, of course, in great demand.

But how much better, in any case, that the company should be able to make themselves up properly, than that they should be obliged to rely on the kindness of a voluntary worker, or that their societies should be obliged to bear the expense of engaging a professional.

It is true that there is a great number of objections to allowing members of an amateur company to make-up, but the difficulties should be examined with a view to discovering if they cannot be overcome, thus helping societies that wish to be self-supporting, in this respect, to carry out their ideals.

DIFFICULTIES

The first difficulty is that most amateurs do not know how to make themselves up, and this is subdivided into two others, namely, that some people have no wish to make themselves up and so they will not bother to learn, and that others do not know where they can learn, even if they are willing to be taught.

With regard to the first of these groups, there is little to be said. For them a perruquier, either amateur or professional, must be found. Another member of the company who is competent and who has time to spare may be suggested. In time, it should be possible for a society to drop members who will not bother to learn how to make themselves up. (The hopelessly inept must be tolerated if they are otherwise valuable, but there are not many of these.) This disinterested attitude is temporary, and the few who cannot make themselves up, among a company of those who can, soon feel thoroughly ashamed of their incompetence, when they are obliged to go round from dressing-room to dressing-room seeking a friend who has leisure to make them up.

To deal with the second group is much more intricate, and its discussion is deferred.

Since we are concerned with musical productions, in which there is usually a chorus, the first difficulty to be overcome is that of ensuring that their make-ups shall all be in the same scale, as it were. When a professional perruquier is employed, it is simple, as he (or she) uses the same colours on each. But when they make themselves up, troubles, especially among the girls, begin at once. Almost all ladies realize that certain colourings suit their personalities and their appearance better than others, and, quite properly, in their private lives they take advantage of this fact to make themselves look as attractive as possible. The divergence of the colours they use, although hardly noticeable in everyday life, is much exaggerated by the glare of the artificial lights, especially as the make-up itself is required to be so much stronger for stage purposes.

Unless steps are taken to prevent it, this means that sixteen girls in a chorus-troupe are quite likely to appear on the stage in slightly different shades of make-up, which may vary between a deep sunburn colour and pale mauve. Although separately each would probably look extremely attractive, taken together under a strong artificial light, the effect would be most peculiar.

The cure is to give instructions beforehand to the chorus as to what colour the girls may use, and for the producer (or the stage-manager) to have authority, and the strength to use it, to order any offenders to make-up again if they appear at the inspection, which should take place each night before the rise of the curtain, in anything too markedly different from the others.

This *is* a difficulty, because however strict the supervision, ladies *will* make-up to suit what they consider best for their own complexions. But, provided that the actress is adroit, it is an advantage that she should be aware of the way in which she may best enhance her own attractions; the point is that she must do it in such a manner as to make it fit in with the rest of the scheme of make-up.

It must be remembered that the members of a professional chorus always make themselves up, and there is no reason why amateurs should not also learn to do so, especially when probably every member of it is a comparative expert in dry make-up in everyday life; grease make-ups are, after all, comparable with dry ones.

This difficulty only applies in cases where the chorus appear as a troupe. It does not arise when the chorus are required to appear all different, as in crowd scenes, although there may be reluctance on the part of some of the ladies to make themselves sufficiently repulsive in such scenes as Act I of *The Vagabond King.* This situation should also receive firm treatment.

TRADITIONAL MAKE-UPS

The foregoing remarks apply more especially to the chorus. The next difficulty occurs more often among the principals, although it sometimes affects the chorus. When the play is old and well-known, certain of the characters will have achieved the distinction of becoming like real people, who have an appearance and a personality that may not be changed. This sometimes occurs when a part has been created by an actor of outstanding personality who has made the character into himself. It is then necessary to reproduce the actor. The audience, in fact, know the character by sight, and for it to appear in a make-up that differed materially from the accepted or traditional would be like asking them to meet an old friend whose appearance had changed completely. This is, of course, especially true of the Savoy operas.

The professional perruquiers who make-up amateur companies know by heart all these characters and their proper appearance. Many of them, especially those whose families have been connected with the theatrical profession for generations, always have known them, from constant familiarity, so to speak. The amateur who is obliged to make himself up for one of these parts is in a difficulty unless he has had experience of it before. There are various methods, however, by means of which he can acquire information as to the correct make-up.

One method is to ask the producer, who is practically certain to know. Another is to acquire a copy of the issue of *Play Pictorial* that dealt with the original production, and to copy the make-up. A third is to discover and borrow, if possible, any photographs or drawings or any other particulars of the piece, and having obtained all the information that can be secured, the actor (or actress) should practise the make-up at home beforehand. Make-up should be rehearsed so that at the dress-rehearsal there is no rush to reach the stage because it has taken longer than was expected to secure the required effect.

ORIGINAL WORKS

In original works, where the actor is obliged to create the character, he will, of course, invent a make-up to suit the personality of the being that he has evolved in his mind. In this case he is by far the best person to apply the make-up, as no-one else knows how it should appear. The fact that the author or the producer may have definite ideas that they will communicate by means of drawings or demonstrations must not be overlooked.

At this point it is necessary to revert to the difficulty that arises out of the fact that members of amateur companies do not require suggestions as to copying traditional make-ups, but instruction in the elements of the art. The cost of tuition from an expert for each member of the company would be prohibitive. What then is to be done?

Firstly, books and articles on make-up may be bought, or borrowed, and read.

Secondly, lectures that the whole company can attend may be given. This is probably the better method, for not only do most people learn much more quickly from lectures (with demonstrations) than they do from books, but the cost of engaging a qualified instructor can be subdivided among a large number of members, instead of it being beyond the reach of the few who think of it.

CRITICISM

The usual criticism will be levelled at this scheme, that make-up is an art which is given to few. This is readily admitted, but although every person who appears on the amateur stage is not an artist, any amateur of average intelligence is capable of learning to put on a straight make-up in a short time, and with little trouble.

A short course of lectures is outlined below for the benefit of a committee who are anxious that the members of their society should learn to make themselves up.

The cost would depend on how deeply into the subject it is desired to go, but from the point of view of the chorus, it may be mentioned that it is not necessary to go very far. Further lectures could be held for the enthusiastic and promising, and they could pass on their knowledge either at leisure or in case of emergency.

The best way to secure a suitable lecturer is to apply to the National Operatic and Dramatic Association, the British Drama League, or to one of the good firms of wig-makers. When a candidate is suggested, his qualifications should be examined from the point of view of his ability to teach. His fee will, of course, vary according to the distinction he has acquired in his profession, but a guinea for an hour's lecture would be a very low figure. The amount, subdivided among all those attending, should be quite small per head if the number is reasonably large.

The amount of information to be imparted at each lecture would depend on the length of it and the number to be given, but a great deal can be done in as few as three lessons, if time is not wasted and a plan such as the following is adopted.

Lecture I

Demonstration of articles in use; grease-paints, liners, crêpe-hair, spirit-gum, etc.

Demonstration of straight make-up (juvenile) on a lady.

While the lecturer is making-up one member of the company, another will sit opposite and will carry out on her own face, unaided, the operations that the lecturer is performing on her colleague.

Comparison of results and correction.

Demonstration of method of removing make-up.

Lecture II

Test of a volunteer to make herself up, in front of the class.

Correction and comments.

Demonstration of straight juvenile make-up on a man.

Demonstration to be copied by another member as above.

Comparison and correction.

Removal of make-up.

Lecture III

Test of two volunteers, male and female.

Correction and comments.

Demonstration, on his own face, of the way in which grease-paint is used to convey increasing age.

All that can be shown here is the bare principle. Those who have aptitude will practise and progress, or perhaps attend further lectures. The others will require many lectures before they can make headway, and will get on best by inquiring of their colleagues.

It will be found that books on make-up become much more valuable after a short series of lectures, such as that outlined, has been attended. It is much easier to follow written instructions when one is familiar with the materials, and the manner of manipulating them, than when one is not.

With regard to members providing themselves with the necessary equipment, it should be said that, reduced to a minimum, little is required to effect a straight make-up. The temptation, on beginning to learn, is to buy a japanned box in three tiers, containing everything that can possibly be required. But this is quite unnecessary and in certain cases definitely undesirable (apart from the cost). The box is heavy and takes up a lot of space in the bag, whereas the essentials, wrapped in a towel, are light and occupy but little space.

The best procedure is to buy at first only the things that will actually be used—grease, grease-paints, liners (probably only about two sticks of each are absolutely indispensable) powder, puff, etc. These will cost little. As time goes on fresh materials can be acquired at a trifling cost as they are wanted, and after a short period it will be found that, unnoticed, an efficient but not unwieldy make-up outfit has been gathered together.

When all the members of the company are to be made up by one or more perruquiers, there is a point of simple mathematics over which new societies have been known to make mistakes, with consequent confusion and frayed tempers on first nights.

The time taken by an expert to deal with any straight make-up will vary, but most members will not require more than five minutes each. If a company has fifty performers (thirty-six chorus and fourteen principals) at five minutes for each, an hour and a half will be needed for one maker-up to deal with half of them. (There should be two for a chorus of thirty-six—a man for the men and a woman for the girls is usual.) As some principals require complicated character make-ups which take much longer, it is obvious that some members of the company must be in the theatre to be made-up at least two hours before the curtain goes up—if a scramble and "panic" at the last minute are to be avoided.

Someone must be responsible for seeing that some members of the company arrive at suitable times but there is no need for autocracy on the part of any official. The matter can usually be arranged amicably by the producer or the stage-manager, as some players prefer to be made-up in good time, while others may not be able to reach the theatre.

Finally, it should be remembered that few make-ups last the whole evening without occasional touching-up. A perruquier should be available to do any repowdering, etc., which may be required.

THE DRESS REHEARSAL

To the society with its own theatre, and which can, therefore, rehearse in conditions almost exactly similar to those in which the performances will be given, the dress rehearsal is not formidable. It is merely a final run-through to see that everything is absolutely in order before the opening night.

Unfortunately, there are not many such societies. Some are lucky enough to secure the use of the stage, without scenery or furniture, for the last few rehearsals; others, which make their own costumes, are able to try them out in their ordinary rehearsal room. But to most of them, unhappily, the dress rehearsal is the first and only time at which a number of the most important parts of the production are assembled. This fact, incidentally, accounts for a good deal of the roughness of many amateur performances, and, while it is much to be regretted, there seems to be no way of overcoming the difficulty.

The few that have their own theatre, or one that they can use as their own, are, almost without exception, dramatic, as distinct from operatic, societies. Their performances, as a rule, reach a high level. These notes, which are of no use to them, are intended for the consideration of an operatic society that has only one rehearsal on the stage, and the members of which have their one and only opportunity, at this rehearsal, to practise with the scenery, costumes, and properties.

A few words must be said at the beginning on the old saw: "A bad dress rehearsal means a good show," and vice versa. Of course, this is not really so, but it refers to a psychological truth of such importance that it cannot be passed over without explanation.

That a bad dress rehearsal is necessary to ensure a good opening performance is nonsense. What is necessary is that the dress rehearsal should be sufficiently disturbing to keep the company alert on the next evening, rather than that they should go home, after a comfortable and encouraging rehearsal, to return on the following night stale and over-confident, to give a flat and lifeless performance.

The effect of the audience on a production is great, and things *do* tend "to be all right on the night" owing to their influence—but only within reason. The tendency for things to go right is much fostered if the company are just a little anxious, rather than if they are over-confident.

Some producers, if they feel sure that their companies are capable of good performances, deliberately address them in a most discouraging manner at the fall of the curtain after a smooth dress rehearsal, with the object of keeping them alert for the morrow.

However, it is extremely improbable that the dress rehearsal will pass off so easily that everybody will be lulled into a false sense of security. It is much more likely to be so upsetting and disturbing that the company will go home overtired and depressed, and thus endanger the production for the opposite reason. Since any tendency to over-confidence can be cured by the producer, it is more important to consider how every possible precaution may be taken to prevent the dress rehearsal becoming depressing and exhausting.

The difficulties that are likely to arise are of two kinds: mechanical and mental, so to speak. Of these, the mechanical may have a serious effect on the mental.

To ordinary amateurs, the dress rehearsal is most stirring. Probably the majority of them penetrate behind the scenes in a theatre only occasionally. This experience itself becomes a matter of great interest. Then there is the thrill of dressing-up and making-up, to say nothing of the nervousness concerning their own particular part in the production. It is no wonder, then, that behind the curtain at the dress rehearsal there is a feeling of suppressed (sometimes not well suppressed) excitement, which may affect the most phlegmatic individual. There will be a certain number of temperamental members who will, for one reason or another, be ready to become obtrusive on slight pretext, and others who will have the unfortunate knack of irritating them unconsciously, or perhaps even consciously. Add to this the jealousies and petty conceits of all ordinary people, and it will be understood that the producer of an amateur operatic company has under his control a group of players in a highly emotional condition. This condition may express itself in rages, tears, etc., which will seriously impair the usefulness of the rehearsal unless considerable pains are taken to see that these emotions are not stirred up in the wrong way.

But the producer is too much occupied to have leisure for mothering the cast. He must rely on his staff to do this, and one of the most important qualifications for the producer's assistants is that they should be not only experienced in calming the excitable but also in realizing that trouble is brewing.

MECHANICAL DIFFICULTIES

Mechanical difficulties may affect the mental composure of the company. The reason is that the effect of a breakdown in the mechanical department, namely, scenery, lighting, etc., on a group of people in the mental condition that has been described may make them so lose control of themselves that they are quite incapable of rehearsing.

But with the society that has only one day to get everything ready for "The Night," it is extremely unlikely that all will be carried through without a hitch, more or less serious, taking place. Such a hitch will probably be beyond the power of the producer or his staff to avert, and he or they may be in no way responsible for what occurs.

It is necessary, therefore, to consider, firstly, how the danger of mechanical mishap may be minimized, and, secondly, how to keep the company in a good temper if anything should happen. Perhaps it will be better to discuss these points in the reverse order, and to decide, first, how to keep the company in a good temper, and then to examine the more technical matter of avoiding a mechanical breakdown.

The first thing is to be polite to the company. This is, of course, part of the stock-in-trade of a competent producer who hopes for a re-engagement. But he is not the only person with whom the cast come into contact during the last evening of rehearsal. There are the musical director, the stage manager and his assistants, the property master, the wardrobe mistress, and the makers-up. Any of these can, by an injudicious word or action, cause an upset that may lead to a number of frayed tempers. The amateur assistants to the producer in many societies seem to think it necessary to adopt a bullying manner while carrying out their duties. There appears to be no real necessity for this, and committees would be much better served by members who are less likely to cause unrest behind the scenes.

Another way to avoid putting too much strain on the patience of the company is to see that when there is a delay they are not kept unnecessarily on the stage, unable to go away, and yet doing nothing useful. If a long delay is obviously about to occur, it is better to tell the company to break, and to call them for a fixed time later on, in order to enable them to find entertainment for themselves in the meanwhile, rather than to expect them to stand about the stage, wondering why the rehearsal does not continue and afraid to go away lest they should miss their cues.

SEEING THE PERFORMANCE

During the dress rehearsal the company should be allowed to see as much of the performance as possible from the auditorium, partly because they are useful as an audience, and partly because, having seen the performance at the dress rehearsal, there is less excuse for them to loiter in the wings on the nights of the production.

Care should be taken to ensure that they do not become so absorbed in the play that they miss their cues. This common occurrence is most annoying, and if it happens often may have the effect of causing the producer to become irritable to the cast and to the call-boy.

Another thing necessary to keep the company contented and capable of doing their work properly, i.e. concentrating, during a long and tiring dress rehearsal, is that they should be adequately fed. This does not mean that it is essential to serve a five-course dinner on the stage during the evening. It means that a player who has arrived straight from his (or her) office cannot be expected to rehearse until midnight with nothing to eat or drink but half a sandwich and a little lukewarm coffee taken in the wings.

The periods during which scenery is being changed, or when something has gone wrong and a delay occurs, should be used to enable some section of the company, the technical staff or even the stage-crew, to break off and to secure refreshments. This course of action makes it easier for everyone concerned to get through a difficult dress rehearsal without loss of temper.

Its influence is, of course, also reflected in the performance the next day, because the company have gone home tired, but not exhausted, have probably slept well, and returned refreshed and eager.

Nowadays this would be a difficult task but arrangements can sometimes be made with the theatre or hall for the provision of refreshments for the cast. Failing this, a buffet can be organized by the society, which, if it is efficiently conducted, can easily be made a source of revenue.

In the unlikely event of it being impossible to arrange anything of the kind, members should be instructed to bring sandwiches, etc.

Nothing has yet been said about the main business of testing that all is ready for the production, but it must be remembered that we are primarily concerned with amateurs, and that it is probably better to pander to their frailties rather than to risk driving any player beyond the limits of endurance.

THE WORK AT THE THEATRE

Now to outline what has to be done at the theatre during the day of the dress rehearsal so that the performance on the following night may proceed smoothly. It should be borne in mind that it is assumed the society has the use of the theatre for the purpose on one day only.

Briefly, the scheme should be to arrange the scenery, properties, and lighting, and to unpack the costumes so that when the company arrives in the evening all that they have to do is to dress, make-up, and then go straight through the play. But, unfortunately, this is rarely practicable. Something invariably occurs, however careful the precautions which have been taken, which has the effect of upsetting the day's programme.

As examples of the sort of misadventures that cause delays may be mentioned—

(*a*) The scenery does not arrive at the expected time.

(*b*) The scenery requires so much alteration that several hours of carpentry are necessary before it can be set.

N.B. Little else can be done on the stage until the scenery has been set.

(*c*) The lighting demanded by the producer takes a long time to arrange, and cannot be started until after the scene has been fitted up.

THE STAGE PICTURE

Even if none of these eventualities takes place, or no accident, such as something suddenly breaking, occurs, the rehearsal may take a long time, as the dress rehearsal is the only chance that the producer has of fitting his production on to the stage. He will, of course, have in his mind a complete picture of how he wishes it to appear, but this is his only opportunity of making the necessary adjustments to carry into effect what he has in his mind.

If he is wise, he will have measured the size of the stage on which the play is to be presented, so that he will have been enabled to arrange all the movements in such a manner that they will fit. But there is another aspect of production that cannot very well be rehearsed beforehand. This is colour; and it is expressed in the costumes, scenery, make-up, and lighting.

Too much stress cannot be laid upon the importance of the visual effect of the production on the audience. The colourings will have been carefully worked out in advance, and the producer will have imagined the effect of his groupings in the production of a balanced picture. At the dress rehearsal he must be given the opportunity of fitting that picture into its frame.

Stage lighting has a big influence on the appearance of most fabrics. It alters them in various ways, the result being that a scheme which seemed to be quite satisfactory when the materials were in the show-room may be most unsuitable under the stage lights.

As the dress rehearsal is the producer's only chance of fitting his production to the stage and of making it look as he wants it to look, he will be tempted to interrupt and have adjustments made as he goes along. To my mind, this is a thing he should never do if he can possibly avoid it. Nothing is more vexatious to the company and more likely to upset them than to be interrupted during a scene which from their point of view seems to be going well.

It is difficult for a producer who sees something wrong and who wishes to have it put right straight away to refrain from interrupting, but to my mind he is rarely (if ever) justified in interrupting a dress rehearsal.

There are various things he can do to avoid such a difficulty arising. He may have a dress parade before each act to see that all dresses are in order before each performer comes on, and he may have a complete lighting rehearsal before beginning the run-through with the company.

If none of these is possible, his best course is to have beside him a shorthand writer to take down any comments or requirements that he may have to make; then at the end of the scene the players concerned, with the stage-manager and the chief electrician, should be summoned and the notes gone through. Incidentally, this method provides the producer with the opportunity of commenting on favourable points. After this review it may still be necessary to clear the stage and go back over some parts to make sure that all requirements have been fully understood.

One of the only cases in which I consider the producer is justified in interrupting a dress rehearsal is when the scene breaks down on its own account. Then he can begin "As we have stopped . . ." explain, and get the matter put right so that it does not cause irritation during the rest of the rehearsal.

The company should be made-up for the dress rehearsal as they would have to be for the performance. This is sometimes omitted by producers as being unnecessary, but it should be done, partly because some of the make-ups may be wrong, and partly because each member of the company should be familiar with the appearance of the others. Make-up is also affected by the lighting.

There is one other question to which reference must be made before leaving the subject of the dress rehearsal: whether or not an audience should be permitted. The policy of the society must decide it. Some societies treat the dress rehearsal just as a performance, and invite nurses from local hospitals, etc., to witness it. Others permit no one to enter the theatre who is not connected with the production. That an audience can be of assistance is undeniable. They tell the company how the performance is going, and give indications as to where it will be necessary to wait for laughs, and also where encores may be expected. Whatever course is decided upon, one thing is important—the producer must be allowed to stop the dress rehearsal, whether there is an audience or not, in order to make essential adjustments. Failing this, some other provision must be made to give him the opportunity to see that the production is in a condition which he considers to be satisfactory before it, and his reputation with it, are shown to the public.

When the dress rehearsal is over it is usual for the producer to pronounce a sort of valediction to the company before they leave the theatre. Nothing that he can say will have the effect of appreciably improving the production; therefore he is well advised to give the company as much encouragement as he can, as do the best generals before sending their men into battle.

THE AUDIENCE AND THE PLAY

After a course of training lasting, perhaps, several months, and culminating in a Dress Rehearsal that has been encouraging without being suspiciously effortless, it may be felt that nothing further is required to assure the success of the production.

But there is one other thing. This is an audience.

There is no such thing as a successful production without an audience, for an audience adds something to a play which the company themselves cannot add.

Since this is generally realized, it is the more extraordinary that certain amateur societies do not take greater care to ensure that nothing shall happen to the audience, when they arrive at the theatre, which may prejudice them against the performance, and so cause them to withhold their contribution, rather than to bring it eagerly and enthusiastically, to the evening's success.

There are several points that require attention. The audience will take them for granted when they are properly done and will take notice only if, by chance, one of them happens to be overlooked. These points are, for the most part, extremely small and, in the professional theatre, or in the big society that has been in existence for a long time and has therefore a regular machinery that comes into operation during the performances, they will receive attention automatically, as will every other phase of the production. Nevertheless, the omission to attend to one of these minor matters may have a deep effect on the spirit in which the audience receive the play, especially if the omission militates against their comfort.

In a professional theatre the business of showing the audience to their seats, and providing them with programmes, souvenirs, etc., is efficiently done by the paid staff. For amateur performances this is usually undertaken by members of the society, of either sex, according to the duty required. In some cases, those responsible for booking the theatre are obliged, by the contract, to engage the programme sellers, etc., ordinarily attached to the theatre. When this happens, there is nothing more to be said. With a modicum of supervision to see that they are, in fact, carrying out their duties, the permanent staff will do the work in their usual way with the minimum of trouble to everybody concerned.

When the entire arrangements for the "front of the house," as it is called, are in the hands of members of the society, there are several details to be borne in mind, the observance of which will make a great deal of difference to the comfort of the audience and which may, therefore, affect their attitude towards the performance.

The ordinary playgoer expects, on arriving at the theatre, to be able to dispose of his hat, if he is so minded, in comfort; then to proceed, without being jostled about, to his seat, which he expects to have found for him; and to be able to secure a programme without delay.

It is not, as a rule, difficult to find ladies and gentlemen who are willing to undertake the duties of stewards and programme-sellers at a performance given by an amateur operatic society; in fact, to many of them this is the next best thing to taking part in the production itself, for they are enabled to participate in it, to a certain extent, by undertaking this work.

Unfortunately, however, there *are* members who do not give their services entirely to help the society. Some do the work merely to see the play without being obliged to pay for a seat, and others so that they may have a good time. The intentions of the first of these groups are easily thwarted by passing a rule that no one can be a steward or programme seller who does not dispose of tickets of a certain value for the production. Then if they do their duties adequately, it does not matter if the front of the house staff enjoy themselves so long as they do not annoy the audience by so doing.

The difficulty is that a certain proportion of them do not carry out their duties adequately. Programme-sellers talk to their friends, so that some members of the audience are unable to secure programmes or else they have to wait, and sometimes they do not succeed in acquiring one until after the curtain has been raised, by which time they cannot read it owing to the darkness. Stewards are often careless when showing people to their seats. Nothing is more calculated to cause a member of the audience annoyance than to ask him to change his seat at a theatre, especially if the performance has started. Finally, both stewards and programme-sellers sometimes conspire to commit one of the greatest nuisances that an audience can well have to endure. This is whispering and laughing in the theatre during the performance. Their conversation is usually punctuated by constant openings and shuttings of the doors to the auditorium as parties of them pass to and fro, with the result that beams of light, which are a further distraction, are caused to fall across the seats.

One cannot be too overbearing with voluntary workers, but a few simple rules laid down at the beginning, with the clear understanding that they will be enforced, may have the effect of curbing the activities of some who, under the pretext of helping the society, are actually doing it an inestimable amount of harm.

RULES FOR STEWARDS AND PROGRAMME-SELLERS

Among suitable rules for programme-sellers are—

1. They should know exactly what they have to do: that is, whether they have to sell programmes *and* show members of the audience into their seats, or whether they have to sell programmes only.
2. They should know exactly where they are to sell the programmes: that is to say, whether they are to be responsible for a section of the auditorium, or whether they are to stand at the door and sell programmes to the audience as they enter. They should in any case be provided with some small change.
3. They must not talk in a manner that interferes with their duties or with the enjoyment of members of the audience, to anyone, whether personal friend or fellow member of the front of the house staff.

For the stewards the following are suitable—

1. They should know the exact position of each seat in the block for which they are responsible, and should be able to find it in the dark. They, also the programme-sellers, may be provided with electric torches, which they should use with discretion.
2. See rule 3 above.

The subject of dress, or uniform, is of interest. For the men evening dress is usual, and some kind of badge is an advantage, as it enables the audience to distinguish the officials in case of emergency. The ladies' dresses are much more difficult to settle. It is undesirable that they should be put to the expense of buying a uniform, but if they are allowed *carte blanche* difficulties are certain to occur. A suggestion is that all should be asked to wear black dresses and be permitted to adorn them with furs, flowers, and jewellery. A badge for ladies is also an advantage.

Properly and tactfully done, the stewarding and programme-selling can make an enormous difference to the comfort of the audience, and if they are comfortable there is no reason why, at any rate until the curtain goes up, they should not feel well disposed towards the production.

The form of the programme itself is an interesting subject. It can be a means of contact between the society and the audience; also a valuable advertising medium by which information about future productions, the members, and the history of the society and other matters may be circulated. Its format is a matter for each society to settle for itself, but personally it astonishes me that, although presumably it pays for itself, it is sometimes badly set out and printed.

THE NATIONAL ANTHEM

On the opening night of a production it is usual to begin with the National Anthem, and on subsequent performances to end with it.

This is often extremely badly played. There appears to be no reason why it should be so, and it seems to be bad policy, even if the audience have been placed comfortably in their seats, to begin the evening, especially at a musical entertainment, with an extremely indifferent rendering of an air with which everyone in the house is particularly well acquainted. It can produce only the most gloomy forebodings of what is to follow.

If the musicians who are to accompany the performance are not accustomed to playing together, they should rehearse the National Anthem in the same way as they do the rest of the music for the production.

PUNCTUALITY

Another minor way in which the audience may be prevented from developing a prejudice against a performance before the rise of the curtain is to see that the advertised time of beginning the play bears some relation to that at which it actually starts.

Some members of a theatre audience always arrive late. As they are, apparently, quite prepared to suffer the penalty of missing part of the performance there is no reason why the opening should be delayed for them. The fact that they inconvenience a few other people in reaching their seats is unimportant in comparison with the much greater number who are inconvenienced by the late start of the play. Waiting until the audience are in, before ringing-up, starts a vicious circle of the management waiting for the audience, and the audience not bothering to arrive in time because they know that the curtain will rise late.

It is legitimate to begin the overture within a minute or two of the advertised time of the beginning of the play, and except in special circumstances, such as a bad fog suddenly descending on the town, this is the only concession that should ever be made. A society's audience will soon learn that if a play is billed to start at a certain time, it will start at that time, or within a few minutes of it, and they will take steps to arrive suitably early. Besides being a kind of breach of faith, a late start suggests gross mismanagement behind the curtain.

Liaison should be maintained between the chief steward or house-manager and the stage-manager. These officials should be in touch with one another as the curtain is timed to go up, so that if delay is necessary each will know what to do.

The house-manager should be provided with a list of the times of the intervals so that his staff may be ready to open the doors, turn on the lights, etc., and the refreshment-room attendants be in their places when required.

APPLAUSE AND ENCORES

Most of what has been said up to this point has been directed to ensuring the comfort of the audience so that they may be encouraged to enjoy the performance. If all the measures that have been adopted are successful, and the production is of such a standard as to merit it, the audience will enjoy themselves and will indicate their pleasure by applause.

Applause is the audience's method of indicating their approval of a play or part of a play, and, if it is sufficiently enthusiastic and insistent, may be accepted as an expression of desire to see that particular part of the play repeated. In other words, encores should be given as the result of a demand for them. This is a point that seems to be seriously misunderstood by the managements of many amateur operatic societies, especially, curiously enough, by small societies with a marked paucity of talent.

Many societies seem to have not the remotest notion of what encores are for and when they should be given. One has seen cases where the company have repeated a number unasked, and sometimes unwanted, when the only reason for the repetition was that, in some former production, the number had been a success. But this is not a sufficient excuse. The spontaneous request of the audience should be the only reason for giving an encore. The fact that an actor has to sing a famous and popular song does not entitle him automatically to an encore. He must earn it by his ability and the strength of his personality, and if at the end of the song there is not a genuine demand for it the encore should not be given. The unwanted encore is one of the most obvious signs of amateur production and one that does more than anything else to earn for a society the name of being truly amateur.

This does not mean that encores should not be arranged. They should. But however carefully they have been worked out, they should never be given unless the audience ask for them. Persuading the audience to ask for them is one of the duties of the company, and they can carry it out only by means of their personalities, efficiency, and zeal.

Confusion exists in some cases as to who is responsible for deciding when an encore is desired by the audience. The proper person to decide is the stage-manager. If the producer is acting as stage-manager, then the decision rests with him. It should *not* be the musical director, because the musical director is not in a position to see that the company do not leave the stage as each particular item finishes, nor, probably, does he know if the play is running correctly to the time schedule.

PROPER PROCEDURE

The proper procedure is for the stage-manager, if he thinks an encore may be required, immediately to give an order that no one may leave the stage without his permission. At the same time, he should signal "stand by" to the musical director. When the applause is at its height he should signal to the musical director to proceed and send the company (or the soloist) on to the stage again. It is of vital importance that if an encore is given it should be taken up promptly.

However well an item is received, the players are strongly recommended to proceed as though they intended to go on with the play. Waiting on the stage in a perfunctory attitude for the applause to die down tends to have an adverse influence on the audience and is known as "asking for an encore."

While on the subject of encores and applause, it is worth while to discuss the presentation of floral and other tributes to the members of the company at the fall of the curtain on the final night of the production.

In the professional theatre, at the end of the run of a play, it is usual for some of the leading characters to receive flowers from their admirers. This does not seem to be any excuse for the ceremonies that take place after many amateur productions, however short the run. That it is pleasant for the leading characters to receive flowers cannot be denied, but in some cases the matter goes beyond the bounds of common sense. In some societies, when the final performance is over, and in full view of the audience, a procession of stewards, extending the entire length of the auditorium, pass from hand to hand flowers, chocolates, and other presents, to every member of the cast. This procedure may take any time up to an hour, and at the end of it the stage resembles a florist's or fruiterer's shop window, rather than a place of theatrical entertainment.

The inconvenience caused by such an arrangement has only to be indicated to be imagined. Apart from the doubt as to whether the audience are interested in the ceremony, there is the objection of certain members being obliged to buy expensive presents that they cannot afford, and the jealousies of principals who receive a few flowers, while popular members of the chorus are loaded with rich gifts.

Once the habit of giving presents in front of the curtain has been formed, it is difficult to break it without causing serious disappointment, but new societies are seriously advised to forbid such presentations until the end of the show and then to do it on the stage behind closed curtains. But even this practice should be prevented if possible. The only scheme to which there can be little or no objection is the placing of presents in one another's dressing-rooms by members of the cast.

As an amusing example of the kind of abuse to which presentations over the footlights may lead, the following case may be quoted. The leading man of a provincial operatic society, on the afternoon of the final performance of a play, bought himself a ready-made shirt and some socks in the town, and ordered them to be delivered to the theatre. In the evening, amid the rapturous applause of the audience, the parcel was solemnly handed to him on the stage by a steward.

There is one section of the audience to which, perhaps, special reference should be made. This section is composed of the representatives of the Press. It is not suggested that any attempt should be made to influence their opinions by lavishing hospitality upon them, but some societies go to the other extreme.

Newspaper reporters are human beings, just as much as are the members of the company. Therefore, they are more likely to think ill of a performance when they are cold and thirsty than when they are warm and comfortable. It is senseless to put a premium on the chance of their being unnecessarily severe on the production because they are uncomfortable, from the mere failure to attend to their welfare.

Proper consideration for its ambassadors is a sort of delicate compliment to the newspaper itself. *Two* tickets, by the way, should always be sent to any journal whose representative it is desired to invite, and they should always be addressed to the editor.

BEHIND THE SCENES

However efficiently and comfortably the rehearsals of a play have been conducted, it is possible completely to spoil the performances, from the point of view of pleasure in appearing in them, if certain simple rules with regard to behaviour behind the scenes are not observed by everybody connected with the production.

The company are not the only contributors to the success of a theatrical entertainment. The audience have also something to add, and one of the requirements of the cast is that they should bring the best out of them. The material comfort of the audience can help them to a certain extent to do their share. It devolves upon the company to assist them to do the rest. One of the best ways in which they can do this is to preserve harmony with them, and to preserve this harmony the company must bear good will to one another.

An atmosphere of irritability and unrest on the stage will communicate itself to the audience and spoil their reception of the piece. This will cause them to withhold their contribution to the success of the production, and so a vicious circle will be started that will end in the production being a failure.

As an example of this may be quoted an instance that occurred in a West End theatre, where the leading lady and gentleman had apparently fallen out with one another before the rise of the curtain. The play was a good one, and the leads went through their work with their usual skill and efficiency, but, unless the action required them to do so, they neither looked at one another nor smiled during the whole evening, and as the curtain came down on each scene they both lapsed into scowls. The play was popular and the audience were prepared to enjoy themselves, but on this occasion the coolness of their reception evoked comment.

Private differences of opinion among members of the company are occasionally inevitable, but players, while they are on the stage, should be sufficiently good-mannered to keep their tempers under control. But we are hardly concerned with minor quarrels of this kind. Our interest is that there shall be no wholesale disturbances which may affect the smooth running of the piece.

The danger of such disturbances, for example a fit of sulks among the chorus, may be minimized by the observance of a few simple rules such as are set out below. These rules are mostly a matter of common sense, but since they are often violated, it is desirable to state them.

Of course, all the good will in the world will not make a performance into a success if it is not adequately played, but the technicalities of producing are outside the scope of this article. Nevertheless a few hints are incorporated in each section, side by side with those on securing and preserving a proper mental atmosphere on the stage.

There is one piece of general advice that may be given to everybody connected with the production, no matter what his duties may be. This is: Be in good time. Punctuality is not enough. Performances by an amateur society are periods of excitement when needless anxieties are engendered and tempers quickly roused. Apart from the effects of lateness on the culprit, such as a feeling of flurry and a necessarily hurried make-up, there is the effect on the rest of the company. They may worry as to whether an accident has happened, and possibly make ill-judged comment when the delinquent makes his appearance. In the tense and electric atmosphere of the production, this may cause sufficient offence to begin a serious quarrel, the effect of which will probably make itself felt on the stage and perhaps even communicate itself to the audience.

So let everybody take to heart the advice, "Be in good time." In the notes that follow, for the use of each department of the production this has only once been repeated, but it should be understood to apply to everybody at all times.

THE PRODUCER

It is the duty of the Producer to make the company feel that he knows everything, at any rate about the production in hand, and therefore he should need no advice. But all producers are not perfect, and for the benefit of those who are beginning their careers in this field a word is offered for consideration.

The most important duty of the Producer during the actual performance is to keep his dignity, especially if he desires a re-engagement. Yet, in his eagerness to carry out his obligations faithfully, he may do his reputation a considerable amount of harm. Nothing is more calculated to undermine the authority of a Producer than to see him dirty and dishevelled, rushing wildly about the theatre, screaming all sorts of orders at everybody, and generally giving every evidence of complete loss of control.

Actually, the Producer's duties finish with the dress rehearsal, and the running of the piece devolves upon his assistants, that is to say the Stage Manager and his staff. But usually he prefers to be in the theatre while the performances take place, so that he may see that they are carried through as he intended that they should be. Then is his test. Unless he is prepared to trust his assistants implicitly, he is certain to interfere and so to upset the temper of some member of the staff.

In some societies this difficulty is overcome by appointing the Producer as Stage Manager also. There is no objection to this arrangement provided it is clearly understood that he is functioning in two capacities and that his duties as Stage Manager are not merely part of those that fall to him as Producer. Generally speaking, the Producer is the person who is most likely to know what is required to be done on the stage. To avoid his having to carry out some of the more undignified duties the office of Stage Manager exists, but if he can do them and still keep his dignity, so much the better.

THE STAGE MANAGER

Since the duties of the Stage Manager and the Producer are often carried out by the same person, it will be well to consider the duties of the Stage Manager next, as they are part of the same subject.

The Stage Manager is, or should be, absolutely "King of the Stage." A complete list of all that he *may* be called upon to do would fill a fair-sized book. During the actual performance he is responsible for seeing that the play begins and that it ends. He himself should not be required to do any manual work, as he is entirely responsible that nothing goes wrong while the curtain is up, or even while it is not up, and this entails his having to do so much supervising that he has no time for anything except to see that all are doing their work properly.

He requires endless tact and discretion, as he must soothe temperamental actresses kindly and rule hilarious choruses firmly. He is entirely responsible for deciding whether or not encores and curtain calls are to be given, but they should, in any case, have been rehearsed. Reprimanding latecomers and admonishing the noisy is also his work. The management of a society should do their utmost to support the authority of the Stage Manager in every possible manner. Even though his instructions are from a Committee or the Business Manager, he should appear to be responsible for the professional as well as for the amateur members of the stage staff, or he will not be able to control them.

The Stage Manager can assist in securing the artistic success of the production by suitable exhortations to the company from the wings on such subjects as speaking up, smiling, looking up, singing out, etc.

THE MUSICAL DIRECTOR

Ordinarily, the duties of the Musical Director would have been dealt with after those of the Producer, but as the Stage Manager and the Producer are sometimes the same person, their duties have been discussed together.

The best piece of advice that can be given to a Musical Director is that he should keep his head. If any of the principals or the chorus go seriously wrong during the singing, a Musical Director who has his wits about him may often save what would otherwise be an awkward situation.

He should be alert, so that he is ready with his orchestra as each band cue is reached, and he should have discussed with the Producer the subject of whether the introductions to the musical numbers are to be played during or after the preceding dialogue.

He must be sure that his musicians can play the National Anthem.

THE STAGE STAFF

The Prompter has a thankless task, for however well he, or she, does the work, the cast always grumble.

It is most important that the Prompter should not lose concentration for a single instant, for if he does a player will certainly select that moment to "dry up." The Prompter should attend as many rehearsals as possible, so that he may know whether a character has forgotten his lines or whether he is merely engaged in silent acting. Nothing is more aggravating than to receive a loud prompt in the middle of an artistic pause. If, however, a prompt is necessary, it should be given loudly enough to be heard by the player. It is better that the whole audience should hear rather than that the player should fail to pick up the prompt. Enough of the line should be given for him to recognize it. It is of no use merely to repeat the first two words over and over again.

The Prompter is responsible for telling the Call Boy to call the actors.

Some societies do not employ a Call Boy, as they feel that it is pampering the company too much to do so. But this is a bad policy, as most people make mistakes from time to time, and anything that can be done to obviate an uncomfortable stage wait should be carried out.

The Call Boy should be selected for his tact as much as for any other virtue, as a warning injudiciously worded may upset a player who is about to go on the stage, and ruin his performance. Nevertheless, if a Call Boy is present, he should call *everybody*, even though the person to be called is actually standing in the wings, for if a player expects to receive a warning he may stand there watching the play and fail to go on, unless he is reminded to do so. Conversely, he may be infuriated by what he considers to be interference by a busybody.

The Call Boy should ask the members of the cast, as he calls them, if they have their personal properties with them.

The other members of the Stage Staff include Assistant Stage Managers, Property Men, Electricians, and Scene-shifters. Without going into technicalities, for which there is no space, little advice of a general character can be given to them beyond that they should be conscientious, diligent, and sober.

THE COMPANY

It is now necessary to consider what is required of the Company to enable them to fit smoothly into the machinery that is to revolve about them.

The first duty of the Chorus is to arrive at the theatre in good time. This is chiefly to permit of the Makers-up being able to do their work properly. However quickly the Maker-up works, it will take him several minutes (longer, with a character part) to deal with each member of the cast. It is asking the impossible to expect him to be able to make-up a Chorus of forty members if most of them do not present themselves for attention until half an hour before the rise of the curtain. So the Chorus are enjoined to be early at the theatre, partly for their own satisfaction, that they may have a good and unhurried make-up, and partly for the advantage of the rest of the production.

The Chorus are required to observe a number of other rules, the task of enforcing which rests with the Stage Manager, and it is of inestimable assistance to him if these rules are carried out by the members of the Company without constant repetition and the reprimanding of individuals.

These rules are—

(*a*) The Company must not make a noise in their dressing-rooms that will penetrate into the auditorium.

(*b*) They should not leave their dressing-rooms until they are called.

(*c*) They must not make a noise in the wings.

(*d*) They must not peep through cracks in the scenery, nor bunch round doors that require to be opened during the action of the play.

Upon occasions performers on the stage have actually been unable to get off on account of the crowds in the wings.

(*e*) The Chorus must remember to await the Stage Manager's permission to leave the stage if there is any question of an encore. If the encore is given it must be taken up with alacrity.

The rules for the Principals are much the same as those for the Chorus. The chief addition is that they should refrain from being conceited. It is all very well, of course, to give advice in this way, and it is much more difficult to avoid feeling complacent when one is playing a good part well than when one is merely a member of the Chorus, and this is excusable. But it is inexcusable to be tiresome about it.

As they have lines to speak, the Principals will require to be prepared to cope with one or two unrehearsed effects, such as applause and laughter while they are on the stage. An intelligent appreciation of the proper way in which to receive applause may make a great difference to the readiness with which the audience give it.

MUSIC AND THE AMATEUR STAGE

EDWARD W. BETTS, Journalist and Dramatic Critic; Member of the Council and Executive Committee of the Critics' Circle

MANY amateurs think that music is best left out of an amateur society's activities. I do not agree with them. I am reminded of the experience of Sir Barry Jackson at the Birmingham Repertory Theatre. When he opened his famous theatre he decided that music was not necessary, except when it was definitely indicated as in *As You Like It* and *Twelfth Night*. A few months' experience showed him that a small orchestra was helpful in maintaining an "atmosphere" between the acts, and he has continued to include a few expert musicians as an integral part of his theatre organization.

The amateur stage can profit from this experience. It will be found that a small combination of instruments is of distinct value.

In the first place, amateur societies will, in many cases, have musical members who would be happily employed in an instrumental quintet. It should be easy to find a pianist, 'cellist, and three violinists—two first and one second—who would be capable of playing *entr'acte* music. The musical material available for such an ensemble is considerable, and every music publisher issues a list of compositions arranged for the instruments indicated.

The conductor can be additional to the quintet or he may be one of the instrumentalists. J. H. Squire is first cellist in the ensemble bearing his name, but I have known the pianist, or the first violinist, to "double" the position of leader.

One of the secrets of success in quintet playing is frequent and regular practice, and a fairly large repertoire is desirable, not so much for performance as to increase interest at practices.

When a quintet is formed, the first thing to do is for the members to meet to discuss the kind of plays the society will produce during the forthcoming season. Music should then be chosen with a view to suitability and appropriateness to the plays selected.

For a mystery thriller, or a heavy drama, compositions like the *Danse Macabre* of Saint-Saëns, the *Valse Triste* of Sibelius, and arrangements of the andante movement of Mendelssohn's Violin Concerto, the slow movement of Beethoven's *Pathétique* Sonata, and the Tchaikowsky *Chant sans Paroles* and *Chanson Triste* are indicated; while for a comedy or light piece there are numerous "possibles," such as Sullivan or Edward German selections, one or two of the Strauss waltzes—always popular—and any of the classical potpourri and more popular medleys, such as Herman Finck's *Melodious Melodies*.

It is a good idea to include some current musical favourites. Selections from Noel Coward and Ivor Novello successes are always sure hits, with *Bitter Sweet* and *Perchance to Dream* melodies leading in public favour. A selection from a contemporary musical play can also usefully be included in a programme, but the leader of the band should take care to ensure that there is plenty of variety in the music he provides for public performance. There is such a wealth of music available that every type of taste can be catered for.

If a larger orchestra can be recruited so much the better, but do not make the mistake of an amateur producer I know. He asked me for advice on starting an orchestra in connexion with a business house A.D.C., and I expounded to him on the lines of this article. A few weeks later when I met him and asked how the orchestra idea was developing he responded gloomily that he had to give it up. "I could not find any men in the office who could play the French horn or the bassoon," he said.

So when forming your orchestra do not try to outrival the London Philharmonic or the Hallé Orchestra. If you are fortunate enough to have more than five musical members you can add to your violins, or introduce a flute, a clarinet, or a trumpet, but to do this is to enter dangerous territory. Be quite sure of the proficiency of your trumpeter before inviting him to join your band!

From experience I strongly advise the young orchestra to stick to strings and a piano at the beginning. The musical results that can be achieved by a piano-string ensemble, if *real* practice is not grudged, are well worth while.

If there are more than three violins, one of the players can take the oboe part. In a small orchestra with which I was acquainted, the leader even introduced a mandolin to accommodate a more than usually proficient player of that instrument. But this is an example that must be followed with caution, although, in case you should be inclined to raise your eye-brows at the thought of the mandolin as a genuine member of the instrumental family, I may mention that Beethoven wrote a sonatina for a friend who was a mandolin enthusiast.

The main point to bear in mind when starting a small orchestra is that your playing members are joining together to have opportunities of making musical pleasure for themselves. The more this aspect is emphasized, the greater will be the musical enjoyment that will be disseminated when the ensemble plays before an audience.

No one should be encouraged to become a member of an orchestra unless he or she has a love of music for its own sake. I would put that desideratum even before technical skill. However, I will not be didactic, and will only suggest that every leader should use all his best endeavours, plus any amount of tact, to secure real music lovers to co-operate with him; and, having got them, to bring out all the best musical talent that they possess.

If it should happen that any of the embryo musicians require further coaching, or, it may be, would be all the better for having their music brushed up, there are expert teachers in all large centres, as well as facilities provided by local municipalities. The L.C.C. (County Hall, London, S.E.1) provides evening classes for all kinds of musical tuition, and particulars of local arrangements can easily be obtained by writing to the town clerk of your borough. Another useful means of securing an increase of musical knowledge is by joining one of the Workers' Educational Association's classes on "Musical Appreciation." (W.E.A., 38a, St. George's Drive, London, S.W.1. for all information.)

Although really outside the scope of this article, a brief reference to what is professionally called "canned music" can be made. There are situations where an orchestra, even a small one, is not practicable, and the incidental music will have to be provided by mechanical means. If you are lucky enough to have your performance in a hall "wired for sound," which means that you can use an electrical reproducer to play your gramophone records, there is nothing more to worry about; but if you are dependent on loud speaker extensions, take special care to see that all the speakers have a matched impedance, and, when playing records, exercise the utmost discretion in the use—or misuse—of volume controls. The bass should have special attention as nothing is worse then "woofiness" caused by the over-emphasis of the lower notes in the musical scale.

Music can generally be obtained through any local music shop, or in the case of difficulty a letter to the manager of the orchestra department at Messrs. Boosey & Hawkes, Ltd., would bring helpful information. If your performances are given before a paying audience, it may be necessary to pay a fee to the Performing Right Society, particulars of which are obtainable from Copyright House, 33, Margaret Street, London, W.1.

As the band parts are obtained they should be placed in the care of one of the members appointed as librarian.

Regular and consistent practice is essential, and it is a good plan to join the acting members in their last two rehearsals.

It is desirable to make out a programme, even for an ordinary practice. This adds variety and enjoyment to the pleasure of playing together. That is why I have emphasized the importance of obtaining a fairly large repertory of music right from the start. Include in your first batch of "parts" an arrangement of the National Anthem. Nothing spoils an otherwise good show quite so much as a hit-or-miss performance of "God Save the King."

Edward Dunn

MUSIC IN THE THEATRE

EDWARD DUNN, Hon. F.R.M.C.M., Director of Music and Entertainments to the Corporation of Durban, South Africa; former Director of Music to the Municipal Orchestra and Corporation of Bath

QUALIFYING the Musical Director's contribution to the presentation of a musical production, be it light opera or musical comedy, I am prompted to suggest that the most evident weakness is generally recognized in the mishandling of the instrumental forces (the orchestra). The root of many faults in the public performances of the show can be traced to the lack of cohesion in the orchestral setting. Unfortunately, many operatic societies, particularly those operating in country districts, are strictly limited in their choice of a candidate for the responsible position of Musical Director. Although the initial preparation of a production calls for knowledge of vocal technique, we often find that the dramatic issues are weakened by the undisciplined fusion of the combined forces of the company and orchestra.

Of two candidates for a musical directorship, I would vote for the applicant whose qualifications included the more extensive experience of instrumental music.

TECHNIQUE OF THE CONDUCTOR

Orchestral experience affords more facilities for diverse expression in characteristics of colour and rhythm resourcefulness than are exercised in choral technique. Hence, effective solo and chorus work, all too frequently, is ruined by inadequate control of the orchestra.

It is indeed gratifying to meet conductors of operatic societies who, primarily, are choral specialists, but who, nevertheless, are eager to open up their field of experience by development of their capabilities through mastery of the broad principles of orchestral management.

Because the efficient conducting of the orchestra offers the main obstacle to the peace of mind of the amateur operatic conductor, or, as so often happens, he follows the line of least resistance and leaves that department largely to look after itself, I propose to deal with the generalization of a practical technique which I trust will better qualify him in his command of this vastly interesting branch of his operations.

I will assume that the conductor is newly appointed and possesses a good working knowledge of general principles in choral administration, but claims little beyond a nodding acquaintance with orchestral work. Further, the situation will be surveyed in the light of the difficulties that are common to many operatic conductors throughout the country—the scarcity of consistently good combinations of instrumentalists to draw upon for the production.

Obviously and definitely, the first move towards a working knowledge of orchestral technique is to cultivate a closer association with those friends and acquaintances who are identified with the practical experience of orchestral playing.

There are few enthusiasts of orchestral instruments who fail to respond to a request to discuss the characteristics of their particular instruments. Add to their observations the invaluable information that is to be found in the many and inexpensive textbooks on instrumentation and scoring.

Without a ready appreciation of range, tone qualities, and transpositions, there are almost insurmountable difficulties and uncomfortable embarrassment awaiting the venturesome, but unequipped, conductor. Take advantage of any and every opportunity to attend occasional rehearsals of orchestral societies, and let the ear supplement the textbook information. In selecting players for an orchestra for a production use the utmost discrimination, placing first those players, when they are available, who have experience in vocal accompaniment. You will, of course, have your official accompanist to depend upon for safe and prompt entrances, but of the pianist's work I will write later. I have heard decisive and happy performances of musical productions with orchestras consisting of eight steady and reliable players, but more often is the efficient production of a society marred by an accompaniment of eighteen, many of whom are "passengers." The first step in the right direction is the choice of good string players. Spare no effort or cost to secure a capable leader. Next endeavour to secure the best available String Bass, Trumpet, and Percussion players. The cost of professional musicians on these stands is wise expenditure on the part of a progressive society. In the selection of the Wood Wind the choice is often narrowed down to the ranks of a local military band. In these circumstances will be found Wood Wind instrumentalists who possess only the old High Pitch instruments. This pitch is undesirable in production, from every point of view.

TUNING

Do not be misled into believing that High Pitch Wood Wind instruments can be tuned down to standard Low Pitch, although the difference is less than one semitone. To attempt such tuning-down is to endanger your own reputation as a *Musical* Conductor. In recruiting the Wood Wind department there should be particular discrimination, for two reasons, in the appointment of an Oboe player, if more than one is available. First, the tone of the Oboe is the most penetrating of this group; and, secondly, the technical construction of the instrument allows very little latitude over the tuning area. Consequently, if there is a perceptible difference in pitch between the Piano and Oboe, it will remain painfully evident to the audience throughout the performance, although a useful corrective can be adopted in having the piano tuned to the Oboe at the outset. The construction of Brass Instruments is such that the readjustment from High to Low Pitch can be accommodated without introducing any risks in the general intonation.

Reverting to consideration of the fundamental building-up of the personnel of the Orchestra, let us first concentrate on the String section.

Generally, there is a reasonable strength of string instrumentalists in those areas where operatic societies exist. If, however, the opportunities for orchestral practice in the district are almost negligible, then the enterprising operatic conductor will recognize, in the deficiency, another opening for his musical activities.

In musically limited districts co-operation with teachers of string instruments leads to a healthy feeding of the orchestra. The fact that the society's Pianist is usually employed in the Orchestra during the production materially aids the Conductor in making a conservative selection of reasonably dependable strings. Adoption of the following suggestions has produced a happy balance of strings: Three (or Four) First Violins, Two Second Violins, One Viola, One 'Cello, One Bass.

If there is a surfeit in any one department, then the surplus number should be restricted from playing during the Vocal Solos and quiet *melos* of the score. Often it is difficult to prevail on a good amateur violinist to take the responsibility of a Second Violin part. Many feel that to do so will reduce their status amongst their musical friends. It is, however, of great importance to the Conductor that the customary "after-beats" should be clearly and musically defined. It is unwise, musically, to utilize more than one String Bass, but it is imperative that such a player should be able to negotiate a solid and accurate, yet sensitive, foundation.

TRANSPOSITION

Another important point that should be considered, when appointing the personnel of the strings in particular, is the possibility of transposition having to be undertaken. In amateur societies an occasion often arises when a Stage Lead is allotted a responsible part on the score of histrionic qualifications rather than vocal virtues. Consequently, modifications in the compass of the vocal requirements are necessitated. These ultimately involve the members of the Orchestra in the hazardous pursuit of transposition. Vocal difficulties and their treatment will be dealt with later. If transpositions in any of the musical numbers are necessary, then lose no time in distributing the Band parts to the appointed members of the Orchestra; whenever possible, a series of independent rehearsals should be called in order that these, and major responsibilities similar to these, may be satisfactorily shouldered.

Even when there is no necessity for the transposition of a vocal number, it is sometimes desirable, for example, where a dance number has to be repeated several times, either for an encore or to exploit a good dance team, to play at least one repetition of the number in another key to avoid monotony.

Experience proves that a single team of Wood Wind players must suffice; even a single team is not always possible. As there is often a difficulty in securing a useful Viola player, I recommend the acquisition of a Second Clarinet. The part scored for Second Clarinet almost dominates the compass and covers many utility passages of the Viola.

Good Bassoon players are scarce. Important solo passages for this instrument can be allocated to the 'Cello or preferably to the muted Trombone. If it is impossible to secure a Clarinet for the orchestra, the muted Trumpet, within its limited compass, can be an effective susbtitute for indispensable solo material. Discourage the use of the Piccolo in any but full chorus numbers unless you are sure of the executive ability, and, more particularly, the upper register intonation of your Flautist.

In the Brass Section the usual complement consists of Two Trumpets and One Tenor Trombone; the addition of a Bass Trombone is inadvisable unless there is a full strength of Strings.

FRENCH HORNS

The Conductor who can incorporate one, or two, French Horns, is indeed lucky, for capable Horn players are difficult to find. Unless you are in possession of satisfying details of their qualifications and experience, move with caution and tact when the services of amateur French Horn players are placed at your disposal. No orchestra sounds complete without French Horns, but no orchestra can be quite so disturbing to the ears of an audience as one that includes an enthusiastic but inefficient French Horn player.

Although I am very conscious of the maudlin sentimentality of expression that has invaded the world of light music through the abuse of the Saxophone, nevertheless, I realize that there are many players of this instrument who can invest their tone production with a controlled embouchure; in effect, this technique means that a straight and pure unreedy tone can be cultivated without difficulty.

Having conducted experiments with the Saxophone as a substitute for the French Horn, I can offer every assurance that the results have more than justified the substitution.

SAXOPHONE TRANSPOSITION

Over a considerable compass of the Alto Saxophone it is at times difficult to detect the difference in tone from the tone of the French Horn. The occasions are rare in light opera and musical comedy when the range of the Horn descends below the compass of the Alto Saxophone, and only in isolated instances do we find the French Horn, in light musical fare, written for crooks other than the standard F crook. The F Horn sounds a Perfect Fifth lower than its notation—the E Flat Alto Saxophone sounds a Major Sixth lower than the notation; therefore the Saxophonist is called upon to negotiate one of the most simple of transpositions, namely, to read a tone above the notes written for the French Horn to reproduce the notes that would be sounded by the F Horn. Take, therefore, a bold stand and endeavour to prevail upon one, or two, competent Alto Saxophonists to undertake the Horn parts. They will enjoy the experience, and valuable colour will enrich the all-important harmonies of the accompaniment in your orchestra.

If this remedy is beyond the means at your disposal, then cue prominent Horn notes for the muted Trumpet or Trombone.

Passages that are difficult for the French Horn are comparatively easy on the Trumpet or Trombone.

Many arrangers now write composite parts incorporating Tympani, Side Drum, Bass Drum, Cymbals, and Effects for the convenience of a single Percussionist. If separate parts are issued, I advocate the writing of a composite part. Not every amateur drummer has the use of, or the ability to play, Tympani, and there is always the danger of a wrong substitution being made by means of the Side Drum for Tympani rolls. If definite solo rolls are scored for Tympani, they should be substituted with delicate applications on the Bass Drum. There are many opportunities in musical comedy for a resourceful Drummer to give point to knockabout comedy and dancing episodes. If such effects are desired by the Producer, then the amateur Drummer can pay greater attention to this useful work when he is freed from the anxiety of Tympani tuning.

Assuming that the official Pianist is included in the personnel of the Orchestra, I regard the following combination of instruments complete to meet the requirements of light opera and musical comedy—

> Four First Violins, Two Second Violins, One Viola, One (or Two) 'Cello, One String Bass, One Flute, One Oboe, Two Clarinets, One Bassoon, Two Horns (or Alto Saxophones), Two Trumpets, One Tenor Trombone, and One Percussionist.

Even where it is possible to recruit this full complement, the size of the hall or theatre must be a determining factor in the final selection.

To assist the Conductor in maintaining consistent balance with smaller combinations, I give an analysis of reduced Orchestras.

Diminishing, step by step, we reduce the ranks of the above full combination; at the same time, in each stage, we have a suitable, yet confined, distribution of parts.

The alphabetical indications suggest the order of reducing the ranks.

(A) Second Clarinet	(G) Second Trumpet
(B) Second Horn	(H) Second Violin
(C) Bassoon	(I) Flute
(D) First Horn	(J) Another First Violin
(E) First Violin	
(F) Oboe	(K) Tenor Trombone. Percussion

The Saxophone, when introduced in lieu of the French Horn, will prove to be effective in any combination, however small.

(The situation of the individual players in the pit of the Orchestra will be reviewed later.)

The skeleton ensemble left in the above plan would be—

> Two First Violins, One Second Violin, One Viola, One 'Cello, One Bass, Clarinet, Trumpet, Percussion, and Piano.

If limited resources make a further reduction necessary, I strongly recommend the introduction of a Mustel Organ to supply the needful tone colour of the Wood Wind and Horns. With the adoption of this valuable measure it will be necessary to embellish a duplicate score with the Wind cues as given in the score supplied with the band parts, the operations of the Organist being confined to the task of "filling-in" the missing Wind cues.

Lastly, there is the Official Pianist. After weeks of rehearsals with the company the Pianist has become habituated to ready command of the full harmonies under both hands, and the necessity for restraint is imperative. The Pianist should be seated immediately below the right-hand of the Conductor, and it behoves the Musical Director to indicate at which points certain lines in the notation should be omitted in the interests of the players of those instruments for which the passages have been scored.

I have attempted to meet, on broad lines, those difficulties that beset the newly-appointed Musical Director in a branch of his work in which the administration is invariably his prerogative. Having disposed of a line of action which I trust will, according to local conditions, assist in the initial stages of the orchestral policy, I will next deal with some of the major vocal problems common to operatic societies.

ACCOMMODATING THE VOCAL SETTING

I submitted suggestions to facilitate the administration of the instrumental forces to meet the general requirements of those operatic conductors who are not thoroughly familiar with orchestral routine.

In actual fact I may be wrong in estimating that the deciding issues of the majority of Selection Committees swing in favour of the conductor with the weight of choral experience as his staple qualification, but my ears and eyes have not deceived me into believing that the control of the orchestra, with many operatic conductors, is an inspiring undertaking.

Continuing with the broad survey of the technique that influences auditory impressions, I will proceed to landmarks which, to many of my readers, may be obvious conclusions; but on the principle of my first contribution, I will, in this case, present fundamental vocal theories for the conductor who is primarily an instrumental expressionist.

Let us recognize, at the outset, that the compelling urge behind the aspirations of those actively associated with dramatic societies is nurtured in the desire to clothe certain emotional experiences in spectacular robes. If the vehicle is the operatic society, there is the problem of whether or not the voice will creep through the audition to qualify for the chorus; I am, of course, dealing with the trunk, and not the specialized limbs, of the Society.

We must be prepared to meet the enthusiastic aspirants whose lack of musical knowledge and cool acquaintance with musical notation in no way dampens their ardour, providing there is some general evidence of a manageable voice. Whatever the degree of musical fitness of the rank and file, it must be clearly understood that the burning desire on the part of the musical director to ventilate the practice of vocal exercises at rehearsals must of necessity be ruled out. The producer has too much food for thought on the plate of each acting member to permit of any but the broadly essential musical condiments.

To reach a performance of commendable entertainment value the conductor will not only have to close one eye to certain musical ideals, but submit to being blindfolded on occasions. Frequently does this compromise apply in the case of certain principals, where the need for a competent player is imperative.

The set purpose at an audition for newcomers is obviously to look for voices of reasonably good quality, with a fair smattering of musicality, and a sense of pitch. Do not be critical of the songs submitted at the audition; where there is a lack of musicianship the candidate is not always judicious in the choice of song.

Allow for "nerves" and be on the alert for a sensitive response to the meaning of the song. Any lack of natural musicianship that can be traced at this initial stage may quite easily mark such a vocalist as fertile soil for an artistic bloom at a later date.

Do not adopt an academic examination standard in the sight-reading test; rather make for the satisfaction that the common intervals of unembellished notation can be safely interpreted by the candidate.

One most important point is: If you have accepted the musical directorship of an established Society, make a stipulation that you wish to hold private auditions for all acting members, whatever their individual records of membership. Any committee of vision will welcome and support this request, for the re-trials will often bring to light useful material to introduce a variation in the casting of a future production. At least once a year the musical director should give the sincerely ambitious members of the Society the opportunity of re-trials. Keep a concentrated record of your investigations; it will prove of value to the committee and producer.

As the full score has to be memorized after arduous spade work with the copies, music rehearsals cannot begin too early in advance of the production rehearsals.

The requirements of a heavy score invests responsibilities in Eight Sections of the Chorus: Sopranos (Two parts), Contraltos (Two parts), Tenors (Two parts), and Basses (Two parts).

In the early stages devote separate evenings to each section. An effort should be made to sustain an evening of full and active interest for everyone concerned. Therefore plan your work so that rehearsals concern everyone present.

For the all-important learning of the notations it is advisable to taboo the lyrics, and to work on the easiest mental process of la-la-ing the notes.

During this foundation work the Chorus, I suggest, should be allowed to remain seated; mental fatigue should be the only strain at this stage.

I do not recommend the planning of breath-marks until the sections are familiar with the notation; even then, no fixed rule can be established, for there are allowances, governed by stage movement and dancing steps, yet to be made.

INTERPRETATION

Before the sections are united for full chorus rehearsals, it will be self-evident that the conductor has made a thorough study of the score, analysing the musical setting in relation to the dramatic text.

I have previously mentioned the fact that the particular conditions of amateur light opera and musical comedy societies allow no margin of time for the application of serious vocal technique, but the closing of that door brings us to an opening the possibilities of which are not exploited sufficiently by a great many conductors, a technique that can elevate the prestige of a Society to envied realms of fine artistic achievement, namely, the Dynamics of Imagination.

The happy expression of music allied to action involves a two-fold musical direction.

(*a*) The acquisition of inspired harmony and balance for the peace-of-ear of our audiences.

(*b*) The conductor's physical definition, or bodily expression, showmanship if you will, which is essential for bringing our two units to a sympathetic point of contact.

IMAGINATIVE INSPIRATION

There should be no difficulty in convincing the members of your company that the artistic success of many celebrity artists is largely a matter of imaginative inspiration.

What of a voice of golden sonority, with a finely tempered and scientifically calculated technique—a thrill?—Yes!—but without the fire of a glowing imagination there are no epitaphs carved for posterity.

Maybe your own particular specialization is the Organ. It is with many amateur operatic conductors. If so, then I sincerely trust that your criterion of musical interpretation is not modelled on the traditional output for that instrument.

I venture to state that the shadows of banality that devitalize the musical presentations of some operatic societies can be tracked down to the square-cut definitions and Offertory austerity imparted to theatre music by those organist-conductors whose all-absorbing musical pursuit lies unswervingly in the flight from manual to manual.

The musical equipment that commands our admiration and awe in the exalted environment of the organ often lacks pliability in a wider area of emotionalism.

If we are to take the fullest advantage of the opportunity of making a refreshing musical experience for both company and audience we must be alive to the need for the condensing of technical ideals into small sugar-coated tabloids.

Shed the Cap and Gown and revered platitudes, and let the Freudian axiom, "From within, out, not from without, in," blaze the trail to a gratifying issue, in face of the mixed assortment of talent that is ours to mould and unify.

It is the complex of dramatic impulse that has inspired the congregation of our little army; consequently the pathway of successful leadership commanding the realms of imagination must be negotiated with bold steps.

Obviously you will attach the greatest musical importance to those numbers where stage movement is arrested during their delivery. In consequence, we must stress the necessity for sustaining the interest of the audience by the musicality of the interpretation. Quicken the spirit of adventure in your company by opening their field of vision beyond the limitations of the printed marks of expression.

PRINTED DIRECTIONS

If the interpretation of a great concert or stage artist teaches us to regard with suspicion many of the printed directions in classic composition, then we are more than justified in remodelling many of the oft-times careless indications in the printed score of a light musical production.

Warn your sections that they should be armed with blackleads for the full rehearsals; the time is short and the score too long to trust the mass memory with your subtleties of phrasing. It may even be desirable in some musical comedy numbers to add to the notation. On the other hand, for the purposes of emphasis, it is occasionally helpful at a climax to take out an isolated chord and substitute a jubilant "shout" effect, or a spoken phrase over the musical accompaniment may prove to be more colourful in shading the dramatic meaning.

It must be appreciated that, with trick effects, abysmal failure attends the experiment unless it is tackled with conviction and a downright attack. Before arriving at definite conclusions on the *tempo* of each number ascertain from the producer the approximate speed of those vocal numbers that incorporate movements.

In the standard light operas there is, more or less, a traditional interpretation, whereas musical comedy production offers the producer more latitude for adroit touches of individual ingenuity, and whilst we might have a formidable argument for the preservation of diction and enunciation, nevertheless, in this age of speed, we must be prepared to modify the construction of certain lyrical phrases, substituting a word here and there to meet what might appear to be an impossible singing *tempo*.

The common faults in a monotonous musical performance can usually be traced to the lack of rhythmical decision and phrasing curves.

In a company that cannot boast of any particular distinction in musical ensemble, there is only one excuse for an uninspiring vocal performance—the musical director.

I cannot believe that there is a society that would fail to respond to the enthusiasm of a conductor who had subjected each number to a searching analysis for the purpose of stamping the pregnant lyrical phrases with associative musical character.

What of the means to this end? Technically, the form and swing of the rhythm together with the rise and fall of the phrasing curve. Emotionally, the personal power to penetrate and illuminate the mass imagination.

A musical sentence has "a come-from and a go-to," and I maintain that the lay-mind will leap with you in framing this device, for it is a comprehensive theory that needs little argument to establish its objective as a common-sense medium to artistic expression in any agency of Art.

Rise and fall in phrasing, be it in tone quantities or the judicious application of rubato, is the mainspring of interpretation.

The high lights of musical attention, as previously mentioned, will be directed to those numbers that are not supported by stage action, to which we must add the big dramatic moments, the strongest of which usually ends the first act. Here, particularly, should the musical director act rather than conduct at this point of the rehearsal if the listeners at the actual production are to feel the thrill of the musical interpretation.

To make a big choral finale triumphant in the consummation of breadth, dignity, and power, so arrange the breath-marks that the four sections do not synchronize the intaking breath at the same points of the bar or phrase.

REHEARSALS (UNITED)

I suggest that the grouping of the Chorus should be varied at each full music rehearsal in order to accustom your sections to sing with confidence in almost any formation, thus anticipating the producer's distribution of players for tableaux.

The uniting of the sections calls for immediate consideration of the principles of interpretation, for remember that the score has yet to be memorized by the company.

Every conductor anticipates difficulty in realizing a bright attack in passages that exceed the normal singing range, but the demoralizing fear can be reduced if such numbers are at first rehearsed in a lower key. In the notation of full choral numbers we can frequently detect "packing" on the part of the composer, to keep the general body of tone active. A shrewd conductor will borrow voices from a section that is engaged on a "packing" line of notation to strengthen the vital melodic and harmonic pillars. Similarly, a unison passage for one section can be enriched and made more robust through the added strength of another section. Inverting this argument, the beauty of extreme *pianissimo* passages is enhanced by reducing the number of vocalists for the specified period.

Another interesting device that is well worth the preparation is the allocation of one choral number for a pre-arranged encore, when, on the repeat for encore, the melody line should be sung by its respective sections with the remainder of the chorus humming the harmonic background.

In concluding this section of tabloid hints for the direction of the Chorus, I must stress the importance of a watchful eye on the interpretative value of facial expression in singing. Spare no effort to emphasize the influence of registering the mood of the moment; it is a time-saver in arriving at an intimate and a sensitive interpretation of a dramatic peak.

PRINCIPALS

Principals: the operatic import of the word suggests a select company of solo vocalists whose preferment is attributed to distinctive qualities, not always musical, far removed from the rank and file. As my object here is to confront some of the major problems of the musical director I will confine the few observations to the treatment of conditions involving vocally unequipped principals.

Whilst the introduction of transposition leads to hazardous and uncertain pitfalls for negotiation by the orchestra, nevertheless such a measure must be admitted where the limited range of a principal makes the performance of a number in the original key unsafe. Occasionally this difficulty can be obviated through certain adjustments in the notation of the melody line of the original key, in order to narrow down the area within the compass of the voice under consideration.

One can rarely hope to find a competent exponent of a comedy character blessed with an unusually pleasing voice in musical numbers, and in these circumstances I unhesitatingly recommend that free licence should be given for the lyrics to be "pattered" over a light musical accompaniment, with the melody quietly played throughout the number by the first violins or a member of the wood-wind department.

After all, particularly in musical comedy, laughs are the all-important commodity to be circulated by a comedy character.

With the casting of a musical "part" to an unmusical but promising player, special private rehearsals should be undertaken well in advance of the full company rehearsals, to ease the natural anxiety of the Selection Committee in the justification of their particular decision.

Where the vocal qualities and sympathies of a team of principals are happily blended in quartet and trio numbers, the conductor should be on the alert for the opportunity of throwing into strong relief such musical character by reducing the thickness of the instrumental scoring.

Finally, in summing up the preparation of the vocal setting, I would urge the musical director, in his endeavour to make indelible the preconceived colouring and phrasing shapes, to appreciate the necessity for the company's timely assimilation before the producer takes over.

With the beginning of production rehearsals, retire from the scene of action for a while; the producer has a heavier programme of anxieties for all concerned. Not until the stage technique is almost subconscious with the players should the musical director attempt to draw the eyes of the company to his active direction.

However unimpeachable the progressive conductor's musical qualifications are, the golden achievement of an inspired musical performance is accomplished through the appeal to the heart more than to the head.

Colourful ideals are more spontaneously interpreted when they are graced and served with unflagging patience and sympathetic understanding for the complexities that the theory of music assumes to the lay mind.

COMBINING THE INSTRUMENTAL AND VOCAL UNITS

After weeks of absorption in the vocal requirements of the score, we go forward to meet the production, bristling with enthusiasm for the experience of marshalling and moulding our two armies into one unit, alert to the responsibility of intertwining the two mediums of musical expression, making of the whole an instrument unified in its balance and sympathetic in its interpretation of the unfoldment of a story.

The producer is now bringing the machinery of the stage—the science of colour and artifice in lighting, dressing, and setting of players in relation to his artistic conception of the libretto—to a point of consummation with the expression of the players.

If the Musical Director is experienced in the control of an orchestra, then we can reasonably anticipate a happy fusion with the stage sections from the greater resources of colour and reserves in tone quantities, available through the application of the orchestra.

Before submitting a few palliatives to meet certain contingencies in production, I must briefly review the case for the defence—the audience—on the general charge or criticism levelled by a few societies at the *efforts* of the orchestra.

Only fellow conductors of small-town societies could possibly appreciate the difficulties that beset the enthusiastic Musical Director when drawing together a body of instrumentalists for the production week.

There is usually sufficient strength of string players within easy distance of the majority of operatic societies. This strength, from a strictly musical point of view, lies more often in numbers than quality, but, in any case, there is recognition that technical demands are considerably less exacting than for the accommodation of pure orchestral workers. A small monetary grant is usually placed at the disposal of the Musical Director towards the expenses of the orchestra.

I cannot too strongly press for the engagement of a competent Leader, 2nd Violin, 'Cello, and Bass, even where such expenditure curtails the number of Wind players who are engaged.

Frankly, through my defence of the audience against evident orchestral embarrassments, I endeavour to sustain and strengthen the prestige of the Musical Director.

The following suggestions, I think, meet some of the major problems in the musical direction of orchestra and stage.

CONTINGENCIES (ORCHESTRAL)

The grouping of the instruments warrants first considerations. Broadly, I suggest the following plan—

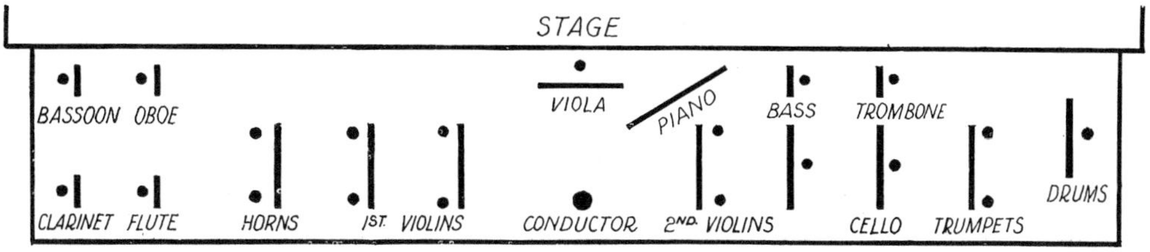

Out of the muddy criticism that is levelled at an obviously inefficient orchestra, nothing can prevent some of the mud sticking on the Conductor. I would, therefore, most strongly urge Gentlemen of the Baton to exercise the greatest care and tact in selecting the nucleus of their instrumental support.

At the outset concentrate on the choice of a small but reasonably efficient string section, with a competent drummer and corner men in the Wind department. Let a band of ten workers, good and true, be your ideal for a start.

It will be apparent that players of consistent and regular experience will easily surmount the technical requirements of the standard light opera score. In consequence, their attention can more readily be summoned for prompt entrances and the conductor's indications of tone quantities.

Sympathetic adjustment of tone quantity to the ears of the audience is not always an evident characteristic with pit orchestras, and few professional theatre orchestras can escape criticism on this score.

When the second public performance has passed the Musical Director, he should become more and more alert with each succeeding performance, tightening his grip on the attention of the orchestra for sensitive accompaniments. Orchestral players in light musical fare, on the whole, soon become dull in their sense of a keen response to the fine subtleties of phrasing in repeated performances of one work.

Give careful attention to the reading of the orchestra, having regard to the projection of the desk lamps. It is of the utmost importance that the Musical Director should have uninterrupted contact with the eyes of each instrumentalist. There can be no unified balance in the orchestral ensemble where the line of vision between player and conductor is broken.

It is imperative that the drummer should have a clear view of the stage, particularly in musical comedy when broad comedy and speciality dancing episodes call for percussion effects that are not indicated in the score. If you are fortunate in the acquisition of a full complement of sound players, it is advisable to limit the activities of the pianist.

Full string tone, supplemented by rich wind colour, is marred by the interception of pianoforte tone—except in the case of harp indications.

The value of the pianist in the orchestra cannot be over-estimated, for never can we be sure of vocal leads unwaveringly hitting every entrance at the exact time-spot. Many defects can be attributed to a false entrance: perhaps a bar too soon or too late, then the pianist steps in to support the vocalist during the accommodation of the orchestra to the unexpected emergency.

Keep a tight hand on the reserve power of tone quantity. I am conscious of the fact that this is not always an easy task, for amateur instrumentalists have often definite and decided views on the literal interpretation of *ff* marks. There are substantial arguments, all determined by the strength of the vocalists and the emotional import of stage situations, to support the revaluation of expression marks.

Except in powerful climaxes of big choral numbers, it is of primary importance that the Musical Director should be guided in the weight of instrumental tone by the strength of the vocalists' lyrics.

The audience—it should be remembered—have paid for the privilege of following, without strain, not only the main issues of the plot, but subsidiary innuendoes and inferences. No effort must be spared in impressing this all-important point on the minds of the orchestral players. Strangely enough, in the achievement of this object, it is possible that criticism will come from unexpected quarters—the acting members of the company.

If the accompaniment is measured in order to allow an easy hearing of the lyrics well back into the auditorium, it is probable that the vocalist of immature experience will complaint hat the instrumental background is too thinly textured and too difficult to define.

This presents a conjecture that the Musical Director should anticipate and predetermine on the eve of the production.

The company, in routine rehearsals, have been led through the notation by way of a piano immediately at hand, or better still, at ear. The rehearsal music, thus far, has been poured over the company to a point of saturation.

The dress rehearsal should bring further musical enlightenment to the company, and, if needs be, an understanding from the Musical Director of the appreciation of an intelligent presentation to the audience. In many productions I have seen operatic conductors working in a musical paradox that has achieved little in the direction of enhancing their musical presentation: vocalism brought to an excellent standard, through intensive application, but of little avail during the show period, because of the predominance of the orchestra.

The lyrics, at least in light opera, do mean something in the intellectual enjoyment of the audience, and it is the Musical Director's obligation to all concerned that the lyrics shall be received intelligibly.

Any criticism on the part of vocalists, on account of transparence to their ears, of the musical accompaniment, must be met with a request for keener aural awareness. In short, insist on the accompaniment functioning as an accompaniment, and not, as is so often heard, an inversion of the musical design.

The full weight of the orchestra can be exercised only in the overture, dance numbers, and dramatic climaxes, the latter according to the elasticity of the lyrics.

It is upon the Wind section that the conductor must impose the greatest restraint, for none but really expert Wind instrumentalists have sufficient control of the embouchure to sustain *pianissimo* passages for any length of time.

Do not hesitate to take out individual Wind instruments from phrases that, through incapacity, burden the orchestral balance; no great stretch of imagination is required to engineer such demands with kindly tact.

For a soloist with a voice of particularly light texture, I recommend, when the lay-out of the accompaniment permits, that the string bass and other strings marking the rhythm should substitute a *pizzicato* accompaniment in lieu of the specified *arco*; this variation, of course, must be applied in moderation. Where a dance number is repeated more than once, endeavour to relieve monotonous repetition by the introduction of different combinations of musical colour for each repeat.

Perhaps one of the greatest anxieties of the Conductor is to be found in the timing of a musical prelude to a vocal number during which there is dialogue. Usually only the cue immediately preceding the entrance of the voice is given. This is not a sufficient guide; consequently you arrive at the entrance too late, or, on the other hand, the cue is delivered before the musical vehicle arrives. Do not risk the penalties of giving the orchestra a confused beat by trying to follow the dialogue from the libretto; the precaution of writing the dialogue along the prelude bars should be taken.

CONTINGENCIES (VOCAL)

At the final action rehearsals, in which the Musical Director is called upon to officiate musically with the baton, I suggest that it is desirable for the conductor to be seated, so bringing the eyes of the company down in preparation for the show conditions.

The final preparation calls for a minimizing of gesticulation in arm movements, thus reducing the need for excessive movement in the theatre pit.

The grotesque sight of two arms silhouetted above the footlights, with every appearance to the audience of shadow boxing, is not an artistic adjunct to the stage picture. Allowances can reasonably be made for those numbers that are not associated with action.

I urge, in passing, the introduction of a simple device that I have found useful in calling the attention of vocalists to my direction, namely, a red signal light in the centre of the footlights operated by a switch on a loose lead from the conductor's music desk.

For the attainment of the best possible choral results arm the producer with a general musical summary and an indication of the strong and weak spots in the personnel of your chorus, inspiring the producer to render invaluable musical aid, through the consideration of blending strength with weakness, in planning sectional stage grouping.

A common difficulty with inexperienced principals is the pitching of a "lead-in" note. Comfortable provision is not always made in the score, but with slight alterations, or a simple addition, a remedy can always be effected, by the unostentatious sounding of the entrance note on the oboe, muted trumpet, or trombone.

Care should be taken in making judiciously delicate the fibre of those accompaniments that support a soloist of inadequate tone power. Where, as so often occurs in the instrumental scoring, an occasional phrase in the voice melody is doubled by one or more instruments, the non-carrying power of the voice dictates that we should curtail the doubling device in the orchestra, but in so doing, at least one of the instruments affected should be kept on the *qui vive* to pick up the solo melody if the conductor suspects that a deviation of pitch will become evident with the soloist.

Finally, keep a watchful ear on the attention of the company to the many-sided facets of the general interpretation at the third public performance.

At all costs it is necessary to avoid the little discrepancies that casually slip past with the accepted familiarity that oft-times is induced through repetition.

Just as the producer is ever on the alert to retouch situations, internal technique, and tableaux, so must the Musical Director be prepared to marshal the company for an aural review of apathetic indulgences.

CODA

Out of the many observations that have been made on the fundamentals of administration, I feel prompted to emphasize, over and above the many diverse aspects, the application of unremitting discipline in the adequate balance and control of the orchestra.

The members of the orchestra are not present to give an orchestral concert, but, for the purpose of argument, they must fall into line with the lighting and dressing plots in lending colour for the purpose of throwing into relief the vital issues of the dramatic presentation.

Usually it is possible to secure the band parts two or three weeks in advance of the production, and every effort should be made to mark in those variations in the interpretation of the work that are entirely the result of your personal expression.

Occasionally some of the numbers involve complex instructions. Leave nothing to the memory of your instrumentalists, insert typewritten sheets in every copy, and so dispose of confusion with its attendant calamities during a public performance.

A close knitted, lively, and smooth running performance is the ideal of every society. Consequently, I assert that the actual dosage of the production's ingredients should definitely be decided by the producer before the curtain rises on the initial performance; with the definite detailing of encores there should then be no deviation from the formula throughout the run of the work.

Where it is found necessary to interest the orchestra in some technical variation during the week of production, the requirements should be outlined in the retiring rooms of the orchestra, and not as a preface to the overture in view of the audience; the observant onlooker detects a note of unpreparedness when instructions are muttered from player to player, with attendant grimaces from a perturbed Musical Director.

The Musical Director may feel incensed to administer a corrective when the *tempo* of a number is being abused by the vocalists, by the obnoxious corrective of audibly tapping his baton on the music desk. Such reprehensible desires must be suppressed, although the motive can be couched in the terms of artistic defence. Forfeit your sense of duty to the composer and submit to the circumstances for the time being, in the interests of the reputation of your society.

Censure the delinquents after the performance, but certainly not during the show, for how many of your audience will be conscious of the error unless you advertise the fact to the entire auditorium through a stupid display of irritability?

Furthermore, it is a dangerous practice to endeavour to readjust the pulse by holding back or pressing forward the orchestra; this practice can quite easily rush the entire company headlong into a breakdown.

Of factors that are not directly influencing or influenced by the stage, I would urge that the members of the orchestra should be seated at least three minutes, for the purpose of tuning, etc., before the Conductor takes the rostrum.

I regret having to disturb the sensitive modesty of many sincere Conductors, but Conductors really must wear white gloves.

The National Anthem is revered to-day more than at any time in history. Do not insult the patriotic sentiments and common intelligence of any audience by allowing the members of the orchestra to decorate it with their individual ideas on harmony.